A Novel of Betrayal and Revenge

A Story of the CIA's Phoenix Program

A Novel by

Carl Douglass

Volume One of Two Volumes

PO Box 221974 Anchorage, Alaska 99522-1974

ISBN 1-888125-02-0

Library of Congress Catalog Card Number: 96-72473

Manufactured in the United States of America.

AUTHOR'S FOREWORD

I suggest the following to assist you in the reading of this book: The glossary, located in the Appendix beginning on page 956, will help in the easy recognition of unfamiliar terms and acronyms. The Vietnamese custom of naming is used throughout the book for the Southeast Asian characters. The surname is given first, followed by an extended family or traditional name and then the given name, the name that Occidentals place first. There is a cast of characters, found on page 14, to assist in keeping the individuals separate without having to review portions of the book already covered. Included in the Appendix, beginning on page 976, is a series of maps to help the reader visualize the subject area as the story unfolds. Also included in the Appendix, on pages 973 and 974, is list of the cost of the Viet Nam War showing the effect and scope of the CIA's Operation Phoenix.

"The very deep did rot: O Christ!

That ever this should be!

Yea, slimy things did crawl with legs

Upon the slimy sea."

Samuel Taylor Coleridge
Rime of the Ancient Mariner

Dedicated to all who were true to their ideals and to their countries in this conflict, who gave of themselves for the protection and preservation of the individuals with whom they served. To the people who manipulated and used the service of those dedicated and decent men and women for their own political, personal, or financial gain or who abandoned them in the end, fie on you.

The assistance of the following people who contributed to the book is gratefully acknowledged: Vera C. Nielson—critic, Glen I. Hicken and Glen Gabler—for their descriptions of military life, Robert Williams—for his military expertise regarding the Viet Nam conflict, Staffan CG Johnsson, MD and Towa M. Lindquist, RN—for help and translation of the Swedish sections, Ken Westfall—for his expertise on the computer, Chanintorn "Thim" Aksorntup Hicken—for her help with the Thai section, Sergeant John Moon for assistance on details of heroin smuggling, Karl and Leif Erik Nielson—for their assistance with Spanish translations and for editing, Edna Browne—for editing, Kim Yến Hathaway Gabler, Robert and Phi-Yến Nguyễn Hathaway—for their invaluable contributions concerning the color and language of Viet Nam, Ngyen Văn Thê and Lê Mỹ Liên—for Vietnamese translations and information, Mr. Nguyen Phong of the Danang Travel Service—for his patience in leading the author around Viet Nam and for his demonstration of many of the places described herein, Kristina N. Shimazaki and Richard Nielson—for the French translations, J. John Shimazaki—for details of Washington DC and for assistance with the maps. Without Evan Swensen and the staff of Publication Consultants of Anchorage, this book would not have been published. The author is grateful for their incomparable professionalism.

We shall not realize our objectives...unless we are willing to help free peoples to maintain their free institutions and their national integrity against aggressive movements that seek to impose upon them totalitarian regimes...It must be the policy of the United States to support free peoples who are resisting attempted subjugation by armed minorities or by outside pressures...We must assist free peoples to work out their own destinies in their own way.
President Harry S. Truman, Special Message to Congress Requesting Aid for Greece and Turkey, March 12, 1947.

Under present conditions any negotiated settlement would mean the eventual loss to communism not only of Indochina but of the whole of Southeast Asia. The loss of Indochina would be critical to the security of the US
National Security Council statement of American Policy, August, 1953

Recommended Courses of Action
A. The Special Committee wishes to reaffirm the following recommendations which are made in NCS 5405, the Special Committee Report concerning military operations in Indo-China, and the position paper of the Special Committee, concurred in by the Department of Defense, concerning US courses of action and policies with respect to the Geneva Conference:
1. It will be US policy to accept nothing short of a military victory in Indo-China...
Report by the Special Committee on the Threat of Communism, 1954

Table of Contents

CAST OF CHARACTERS

AMERICANS

Karl Oscar Isaacson	Swedish-American soldier, CIA contract agent: AKA Lars Magnusson, Anders Bergstrom, Remundo Mueller-Garza, and Steffan Johannson
Spencer Longren	Captain, US Army company commander, Fort Lewis, Washington
Cletus Washington Lee	Sergeant, US Army Drill Sergeant at Fort Lewis, Washington
Fort Lewis Boot Camp	Don Jose Miguel Sanchez deCastro; Stephen Solokowski; Yoshio Yamashita, recruits
CIA Training Agents, Camp Peary, Virginia	Charles Bancroft Tyler III; Sylvia Chin; Dr. Nguyen Colonel Travis Rice; Petrosian Ruben Smith; Mr. Danielson; MGSgt Colin McCluskey, USMC, ret.; Daniel Browning Pendergast; Armont Willetson Major, USA/SF; Nguyen Hai Truong
CIA Contract Agent trainees and subsequent agents	Lars Magnusson; Jon-Luc DuParrier; and Tring Van Dong
CIA Agents	Dustin Hauter (the 'Colonel'); Dieter Lutz, Polygraphist; Anderson Pelgrave, assistant to the 'Colonel;' Tandrosz Szabo, Psy-ops expert; Hugo Bartini, ROIC; Leo Conrad, Acting DCI; Wilmer Colding, DCI; Cleveland Howard,POIC and DDCI/0; Lane Duerk, Head of station, Saigon; Kent Ashworth, ROIC; Douglas N. Herter; Horace Steinweggen, Aide to Leo Conrad; Ms Parling, CIA attorney
Washington DC Police and court officials	Harold Beckwith Brandeis, Judge, Superior Court; Dwight D. Henry, Assistant District Attorney; Dimitri Staphanopolis, Public defender; Tom Bolten, DCPD sergeant, Lieutenant Dragich—DCPD; Homicide Detective Levy, DCPD Homicide; Ladies Man—Inmate central jail, pimp, and informant

Citizens of Zarahemla Utah	Olaf and Brigetta Isaacson; Doctor Nielsen; The Iversens; Sven and Margaret Hansen; Inga Haakensdatter; Andrew David Marshall Grant, Sr and Mrs. Grant; David Marshall Grant, Jr.; Hyrum, Lydia, and Gretchen Smith; Verna Hansen; Harvey Johnsen; Ivan Nelson; Coach Sigurd Swensen; Ben Jacobsen; Sheriff Bruce Hendricksen and Sandra, his wife
Apartment Army (US SOG irregulars in RVN)	Terry Brannigan, SEAL CPO; Mark Whitehead, SEAL CPO; Maxwell, PBR pilot; Jim Smith, Force Recon; Giles House-keeper, Sgt/Major SAS; Hank Weatherby, Mercenary; Duncan Hertel, Mercenary; Jaime Ortega-Gonzalga, Puerto Rican Policeman; Axel Hodges, USA/Airborne sniper; R.B. Lloyd,USA/Ranger; Greg Conklin, USA/SF, ret.
Other US military	Del Porterville, recuperating soldier; Vung Tau; LCDR McIntyre, RN/NC; Lt. Radcliffe, USNR/MC
Other Americans	Kareem El Farrukh, VVAW leader in Bangkok; Willie "Porkpie" Hardin Rogers, Texas oil billionaire and contributor to Iran-Contra causes

SOUTHEAST ASIANS

PRU Cadres	Y'Yool, (Montagnard) Deputy Inspector; Thau Thien, Provincial Police, RD/O and PRU/O; Nguyen Lui Tran, Number 2 PRUC, former VCI; Phan Duy Ky, former *Bui Doi*, and member of Binh; Xuyên Sergeant Le Duc Bach, former Kit Carson; Nguyen Van Dung, former VC sapper; Nguyen Tran Xuan, former Buddhist monk; Other members of the Thau Thien PRU: Duong Co Tho, Dang Thanh Hung, Dinh Van Luc, Hoang Quang Cong, Cong Bich Hai, Muoi Khuc Ba, Anh Xuan Oanh, Bach Duc Hieu, Tung Co Bon, Ky Van He, Tran Van Dong
LLDBs	Nguyen Cham, Nguyen Ly Hai, Nguyen Quan Giac, Nguyen Ba Ngoc
Citizens of Saigon	Hop Sing, Cholon tailor; Yu-en Chou Chen, Head of COSVN; Chen Chen Chen, Wife and assistant of Yu-en; Nguyen Ngoc Tram (Miss Nguyen), Secretary to Lane Duerk, CIA

Citizens of Hue'	Nguyen Cao Lai, Mandarin of Hue'; Lady Nguyen, his wife, and Nguyen Tri Lien, his daughter; Grand Master Nguyen, *Tay Son Vo Si* Sensai; Phan Pho Ngo, Coca Cola distributor and his daughter, Phan Doi Hang; Professor of History, University of Hue'
North Vietnamese	Nguyen Linh, NVA captain serving in Laos
Burmese	Captain Kyaing, UWA officer; Three legged Myo, Karen insurgent, Wa People soldier, heroin smuggler, Hmongs: Fang Pao Xe, Chang Chia Cher Chao Fa (Priest)
Montagnards	Y'Yool, H'Klois, Wife of Anders Bergstrom; The Shaman
Thais	Lan Chaphraphong, Wa People heroin smuggler and his wife, Thim

RUSSIANS

Russians	Crew of the freighter, Vladivostok; Captain, and third mate, Petr

SWEDES

Swedes	Doctors and nurses at the Karolinska Institute, Psychiatry Department

CHAPTER 1

General Taylor and other senior members of the United States
Mission in Saigon are outstanding men, and United States policy
with Vietnam is mainly right and well directed.
McGeorge Bundy, Special Assistant to President Lyndon B. Johnson
for National Security Affairs, Memorandum of February 7, 1965.

"**S**ergeant, yes Sergeant!" the slen-
der Hispanic recruit shouted in response to the DI's order and sprang
into the center of the circle of shave tail young men. He took up the
proffered pugil stick as if he were accustomed to using it.

Drill Instructor Cletus Washington Lee looked about momentarily
then barked at the largest man in the recruit platoon, "Isaacson! Git
yo'sef a stick."

"Sergeant, yes Sergeant!" the youthful but physically imposing Swedish-American boy responded, somewhat less crisply than Don Jose
Miguel Sanchez-de Castro had done. He looked dubiously at his diminutive prospective opponent, and moved with just noticeable reluctance.

Sergeant Lee glanced at an older soldier at his right for confirmation
of the man's wishes and received a slight affirmative nod. The DI
snapped his glance back to Isaacson and harshly inquired, "Y'all still
a vurgin, honkey? Got the first time chickens, boah?"

Isaacson shook his head by way of reply, shrugged his shoulders,
and squared off with Sanchez as ordered. Sergeant Lee lifted his
sinewy black arm above the powerfully muscled blond boy and the
wiry bronze Mexican Indian. His arm dropped, and less than a second
later the padded end of Miguel's weapon drove into Karl Isaacson's
midsection. Karl was surprised but unhurt; he appeared more disappointed than angry. Blows from Miguel's stick flapped in as fast as the
smaller boy could force his wrists and hands to move. Karl now stood
his ground and parried each thrust and flail with an athletic proficiency that belied his size, inexperience, and youth.

"Stop!" shouted the DI "What kinda patty cake ah y'all playin' at, Swede boy? Y'all suppos' to hit ya opponent, or didn't y'all unnerstan' that, white boah?"

Standing stiffly at attention, Isaacson said briskly, "I don't want to hurt him, sergeant, it doesn't seem fair...our sizes being so different."

"What'd y'all say sweet thang? Ah cain't heah yuh." The DI looked at the tall patrician man beside him who was wearing no insignia of rank but met only a diffident expression, as bland as a C-Rat cracker.

"Sergeant, yes Sergeant!" Isaacson shouted in proper recruit intensity. "I do understand, Sergeant! I was just concerned about Miguel, Sergeant!"

"Y'all try'n to do mah job, sonny? Ah worry about the platoon, y'all got enough just worryin' 'bout ya se'f. Stop that 'concerned' prissy talk and fight. Or would y'all like to go up against me, pinkie?" He goaded. His face was mock angry.

The sergeant and his companion were pleased with the steady unafraid gaze from the Scandinavian boy. "Sergeant, yes Sergeant" whatever you wish,...whatever," the boy said in a conversational voice. Karl's rugged Scandinavian face hardened, and he faced his cocky Hispanic opponent who was obviously enjoying the opportunity to see the big Anglo's courage questioned. Most of Karl's heat was directed at the DI now, although he tried not to show it.

"Go!" screamed Sergeant Lee, appearing really exasperated. His tone was less theatrical.

Contrary to the preliminary instructions enjoining against head blows on the first day of pugil stick training, Miguel threw two well aimed blows at Karl's head. The young Swede solidly stopped each blow and countered with a low sweep that buckled the Hispanic's knees and dropped him to the ground with an expression of consternation and grudging respect on his handsome brown face. Miguel sprang to his feet as if jerked by a puppeteer's stiff strings to give the lie to any doubt about his condition. He caught Karl with an oblique blow to the side of his head snapping the larger boy's body sideways.

"Y'all do somethin' rat fast o' Ah'll be a comin' in theyah aftah those sweet golden curls mahsef, yuh heah?" the black sergeant taunted from the edge of the circle. The other recruits sensed something more than a little pugil stick training was going on and distanced themselves from the fighters, from the DI, and his unofficial observer.

More blows were parried. Karl struck a stunning solar plexus hit on Miguel, and the Hispanic recruit sagged to the ground. Karl walked to the beaten opponent, and offered his hand to lift Miguel up to a standing position. The Mexican-American huffed for breath, took the larger recruit's hand, and allowed himself to be brought up to a near standing position. Just before he stood erect, the Hispanic boy coiled like a spring and avenged his machismo with a vicious kick into Karl's crotch. The blow was a fraction off center but stung severely and knocked Karl backward awkwardly; so, he fell squarely and comically on his butt.

The other recruits laughed nervously at first then derisively. "Get up, ya pansy." yelled the DI.

Karl Isaacson sprang to a crouch holding the pugil stick like a bayoneted rifle. The satisfied smile faded on Miguel's face; he sensed an ominous turn of events. Miguel held his own stick at one end and swung a desperate whole-strength blow at Karl's large blond head. The larger of the two recruits tensed in anticipation of the smaller Hispanic's well aimed blow and dropped to a squat with the agility of a gymnast. He aimed the blunt end of his weapon at the point where he calculated Miguel's chin would be when the padded end had reached full upward force. Miguel was off-balance from the exertion of his own blow that flew harmlessly over Karl's head and for that moment had lost sight of the other recruit and his stick. The blow from Karl's weapon landed with perfect accuracy and an audible crack like a bare stick striking a tree trunk. Miguel Sanchez-de Castro never heard the noise. He was unconscious before the sound vibrations could traverse either air or bone. The blow landed with such force that it lifted the small Hispanic off his feet and threw his limp body backward into the arms of the spectator recruits. Miguel did not even twitch.

A second later, Karl relaxed from his crouch, and backed away from his victim a little sadly as he visually took in the crumpled body, Then with an angry flash of his penetrating blue eyes, he locked onto the jet black irises of his real tormentor, the DI. There was an unspoken challenge, even a threat in those now hardened ice-blue eyes.

"Shut up!" barked Sergeant Lee at several of the recruits who were expressing their shock and concern. "Nevah seen nobody cold cocked befoah? Stop actin' lak little gulls."

The quiet middle-aged man beside Sergeant Lee tapped the black sergeant's shoulder with the backside of his fingertips slightly propelling him in the direction of the big angry Swedish-American recruit who was still holding the pugil stick in a position of wariness and attack. Sergeant Lee recognized reluctantly that the demonstration had not been completed to his taciturn companion's satisfaction. "Might's well get it ovah with," he thought. The honkey recruit had given him the evil eye; "tam ta brang him down," Lee determined.

"Alla you maggots has somethin' to learn 'bout fightin' if this man's ahmy is goin' to keep any of y'all alive," the drill sergeant said to the assembled platoon but without taking his dark eyes away from Karl Isaacson's blue ones. "Ya'll think this heah Scandahoovian is tough just 'cause he's big, don't ya? Well, we'll see 'bout that. C'meah honkey, let's us see what y'all ah made of."

The request was an order and nonnegotiable. A worried murmur ran through the platoon still discomfited by the inert body of Miguel Sanchez lying in the shade a few feet away from the main group. The recruit sent to fetch the medics had not yet returned. Karl had no expression of sympathy or concern now. His face reflected a single-ness of purpose—combat. He countenanced no distractions, an un-usual trait for a raw recruit, especially a teenager.

The sergeant donned a protective helmet deliberately and threw one to Karl as an aside. "The little whitey might just get hurt and cry to mommy if we don't use these pussified helmets. Y'all ladies ain't goin' to have all that much protection out in the jungles in Vi—et Na-am. Y'all bettah watch up real close, just might save youse sweet little tushes one day." His voice dripped with deprecating condescension.

Without formalities or warning, Sergeant Lee faked a blow to the right side of Karl's head, shifted, and threw a real shot to the left temple of the large white boy. Karl went down, mildly stunned. The sergeant pulled off his starched blouse and skivvy shirt with all markings of rank. His black skin, ebony in contrast to the stark white of the Scandinavian boy, glistened with a light sweat. The muscles of his angular body were hard and ropy beneath their dark covering. He had no detectable fat. It did not occur to him that the white kid would give up easily. He hoped not.

Karl moved to his feet shaking his cobwebby head maneuvering somewhat shakily. Sergeant Lee turned slightly to his rapt audience of raw recruits and let his lips curl in a self-confident malevolent smile. From outside the gloating man's peripheral vision, Karl's padded stick whooshed through the air with terrific force and too much speed to be seen or heard by the momentarily distracted DI. The practice weapon connected just below its intended target on Sergeant Lee's helmeted head and crunched into his covered ear and the lateral junction between his head and upper neck. He went down with an inadvertent small squeal of pain. As if it had never happened, the drill sergeant executed a kip gymnastic maneuver and was standing so fast that the inattentive would be hard put to be sure the DI had ever been on the ground. His cocksureness was gone. He cursed himself for having cried out. He stood to lose face in front of these maggots.

Sergeant Lee parried and thrusted, feinted and faked, but was unable to connect his desired educational blow. He was critical of his conditioning because he was now sweating profusely and puffing too noisily to maintain any semblance of the nonchalance with the troops. The boy was proving to better that he expected.

Karl shoved his pugil stick into his superior's ribs. The sergeant returned a hard blow to Karl's shoulder unbalancing the white boy enough to permit a pirouette turn and a low crunching blow against Private Isaacson's extended thigh. That strike hurt, and within seconds a golf ball sized hematoma was evident on the thigh.

Karl was beginning to tire as well, in part from the tenseness he had felt fighting Miguel and from hurting the smaller boy. Sweat stung his eyes. He blinked and caught a sickening blow on the vertex of his helmet which felt as if it had driven his head into his neck bones. He went down again. Sergeant Lee had forgotten the educational nature of the training session and now concentrated on winning, on reestablishing his position of dominance with the platoon, on destroying his white enemy, if the truth were known. He bore down with a lightening series of blows from the side and end of his pugil stick most of which connected with the exposed shoulders and ribs of the fallen recruit.

Private Isaacson became aware that he was in real danger; this was no longer a drill. The angry tough black sergeant threw a well-aimed kick at Karl's ribs, quite beyond the dictates of the training manual; but the private, now fully engaged and neither asking nor being willing to give any quarter, anticipated this illegitimate move, flipped over on his side, and drove his powerful arm into the black man's calf as it swept over the location where Karl's ribs would have been. Sergeant Lee was caught totally unaware by his novice opponent's deft move and toppled like a felled tree flat on his back. Cletus Lee fought to get air into his tortured lungs, and for the moment had no strength left to defend against Karl who sprang like a cat to his feet. Karl swept his pugil stick in a purposeful arc to catch the black man across his exposed neck in a killing blow. The young Swedish-American could already see the cartilages cracking in his red-tinged, combat focused mind's eye. In the primitive animal recesses of his brain, the sergeant was no longer a sergeant, no longer a man; he was just an enemy; and he was dead.

The blow never landed. With a speed of movement presumed impossible by the onlookers, the middle-aged officer who had been an immobile spectator up to now, caught the pad of the stick in the air with a perfectly accurate front kick before it could connect and sent the training tool awry. The officer then whirled out of his kick and crashed his full body force into Karl diverting the young blond from his vengeance. Now all three men sat on the ground looking at each other. The older Caucasian officer was obviously a man of authority, although he wore no rank markings. He spoke for the first time. "Enough," he said, laconically.

Drill Sergeant Lee met in a bare headquarters company room at 2000 hours that evening with the patrician soldier everyone referred to as 'Colonel,' the man from the pugil stick exercise, and with his two similarly unranked subordinates, and Captain Spencer Longren, the training company commander.

"Isaacson appears to be a good choice for the program. Thanks, Sergeant Lee, for your participation," said one of the Colonel's assistants. "Did you bring his folder?"

"Yes, suh," the precisely uniformed noncom answered. He was a little put off by the other man's lack of military designation, although the man acted every bit an officer. It was always safer to say, 'sir' and be wrong than to appear disrespectful when the stranger was in fact an officer type. "Spooks," he said to himself with the same disdain senior NCOs reserved for people who did not do the real work of soldiering—i.e. officers.

In the pause that followed, as the three men, dressed in plain green fatigues, began to peruse the private's 201 folder, Sergeant Lee began to fidget, feeling superfluous. The 'Colonel' turned to him and said, "Sergeant, it would be valuable for you to watch this man for another week or two before we complete our selections. Would you mind doing that and reporting only to me? This is a classified matter and is not to be discussed outside this circle of officers, understood?"

"Understood, suh," Sergeant Lee responded crisply. He watched for a sign that he was to sit or was to be dismissed.

"Have you anything else to give us? Anyone else who fits the profile we gave you Sergeant?"

"No, suh."

"Then don't let us detain you. We will get back to you when necessary. We will deal with Isaacson ourselves if we decide he is right for the program."

Sergeant Lee executed a fairly crisp about face, more than necessary under the sloppy military circumstances. "Spooks!" he thought as he left the nondescript government issue room.

Captain Longren handed one of the 'Colonel's' deputies two additional service jackets, both designated as 'lieutenant.' "These are the only two officers in the command that fit your specifications, Colonel. Neither one of them is in my company; so, I can't tell you much about them. Just for my curiosity, why Isaacson? I thought you only wanted officer types."

"You don't need to know, and it's better you don't, son, no offense intended," said the 'Colonel' blandly and finally.

"Of course, sir!" the captain responded crisply. "If that's all you require, I'll be off."

One of the deputies nodded affirmatively in brief acknowledgment. The 'Colonel' turned his full attention to Isaacson's service jacket. Captain Longren left the room muttering disdainfully under his breath, "Spooks!"

The 201 personnel service jacket on Private Karl Oscar Isaacson had been amplified into a fully fleshed-out dossier by discrete FBI and NSC investigations. The deputy began to read excerpts they had verified and considered pertinent to the other men in the sparsely furnished government issue office. From the cold facts and from between the lines of the file the men gleaned:

Karl was born in 1950 in the small Utah town of Zarahemla, a settlement of Scandinavians, mainly Danes, who came to that western state to pursue their new religion of Mormonism. The town's name came from their Book of Mormon, one of the faithful members' additional scriptures beyond the bible. Karl's parents were victims of a seemingly minor prejudice, having come from Sweden rather than from Denmark, where the majority and all of the better citizens of the town originated. The Isaacsons had two additional marks against them; they were poor, largely as a result of their own disregard for the elemental tenets of capitalism and the beehive work ethic cherished by the Mormon people; and they were inactive in the dominant church, by reason of general contrariness rather than any particularly deep-felt convictions or lack of them.

By nature, Karl's father was a thinker, more accurately, a dreamer, and not much of a worker—two traits which set him at odds with his straight-forward, devout, and conscientious neighbors. He also did the unthinkable in rural, one hundred percent teetotaling Mormon Sundial County—he drank to excess. Where a drink in a lifetime was a sin, Olaf Isaacson was an out and out alcoholic. The Isaacsons accentuated their differences with their more orthodox neighbors by having only one child in a community where 'multiply and replenish the earth' was taken to heart.

Karl's mother was a strong and effective woman, who agreed publicly with her husband's immoderate ideas, while privately deploring his intemperate lifestyle. She was arrogant in her own way, despite the family's socioeconomic straits, confident in the knowledge that she had married beneath her station and because her formal education exceeded that of any one of her robust and down to earth farmer's-wife neighbors. When Brigetta Isaacson's husband killed himself in an automobile wreck in the spring of 1960, obviously driving under the influence, and worse, while returning from a meeting of discontents in Salt Lake City, the town's people, usually the souls of generosity, were unwilling to provide anything more than the most proper aid from the Women's Relief Society, and that short-lived.

Karl was eleven years old when his father died in 1960. His mother, by necessity, and conspicuously lacking enthusiasm, started her career as an aspiring commercial baker. The boy learned to fight and did so every day at school and on the way home until he was fourteen when his size was so imposing, and his street record so convincing, he was largely left alone. Karl's school record was decidedly unimpressive, although occasional teachers told the investigators from the Special Education Fund for the Poor of Utah (whose home address was in Langley, Virginia), who bothered to inquire that spring in 1966, that the boy was a lot brighter than his grades indicated. If only he had applied himself when he did come to school, the most generous of his teachers suggested. His attendance record left considerable to be desired.

His mother fared poorly in the baking business due largely to her argumentative nature and her unwillingness to accept the concept that her customers were always right. She considered them seldom to be right, and all too often for her own good, let them know. She was a moody, rather asocial woman who saw to it that her neighbors, her only customers, understood in no uncertain terms that she could get along just fine without them, if they were going to be unjustly critical.

Brigetta Isaacson had always been a slender and attractive woman, proud of her figure and attentive to her carriage. After her husband, Olaf, died; and she began to work constantly, she became progressively thinner. Early on, she hid from her son and herself, her own gnawing fear about the lump in her breast and the need to do something until her abnormal weight loss was so noticeable that a chance meeting with the town's only physician caused him to question her bluntly. Her response was to tell the old busybody to mind his own business.

Brigetta continued to lose weight despite eating everything she could to maintain herself. She also became weaker and more easily fatigued. Her bakery business, that could ill afford any setbacks, began to suffer from Brigetta's growing ennui and physical weakness. The proud Swedish woman said nothing to her prying neighbors; but knowing that her son was becoming worried, she consented to see Doctor Nielsen, even if it was going to be a waste of money. She put it off as long as possible. By the time she did see the kindly old horse and buggy doctor, it was too long. Brigetta Isaacson was found to have sizable lumps in both of her breasts, and more than one in each. She demurred about having a biopsy; that cost money; and she had precious little money.

Despite her protestations, the biopsy was finally done at the urging of the doctor. The result was predictable: carcinoma of the breast with metastases. Brigetta went in secret to her closet and wept for the first time in her adult life. When she was again in control of her emotions, she returned to the doctor's antiquarian office. She refused to speak to Doctor Nielsen's sweet-tempered old secretary and insisted on seeing the doctor right then, no matter that he was with another patient. Brigetta whispered to Dr. Nielsen, "What's going to become of my boy?"

"You have plenty of time to settle your affairs, Brigetta," the doctor comforted before returning to his scheduled patient. It occurred to him that the ill-starred woman would get more help and sympathy from the towns-people, who were inclined to help those less unfortunate than themselves, if she would put out a little more honey and a little less vinegar.

The doctor was wrong about the prognosis. Brigetta Isaacson had inflammatory carcinoma of the breast. She was hospitalized in three weeks and dead in five. There was nothing anyone could do to impede the onslaught of that terrible scourge. Brigetta died friendless and a pauper in the Sundial County Hospital with only her boy, Karl, at her bedside. Karl was fourteen.

His mother was his last link to family, church, or government. The boy was moved out of the house he and his mother had rented when his minimal wage work at the sawmill proved to be inadequate to keep up with the rent, and was forced by court order to take up room and board in a foster home. His angry and combative nature militated against a foster family placement situation being easily successful, but he had no blood family anywhere; and the law mandated the placement. Orphanages went out with high-button shoes in family oriented Utah.

What amenities existed in the sparse quarters of his first foster home were from the kindness of the Mormon women's organization to which his mother had nominally belonged. The state and county provided the family a little money and adequate extra food unless the budget was tight; and, in that case, the Church had to fill in the gaps. Karl hated the home despite the well-intentioned foster parents' efforts, mainly because of the constant reminder that he did not control his life and because placement solidified his status as a lower class citizen, at least in his own mind. He muttered to himself that "you weren't nothing if you didn't even have a home," and he did not consider the foster family's house his home.

The Iversens did not much care for the county boy either. He was lazy and uncooperative. Their own sons got up at four o'clock to milk; what was so special about the Isaacson boy? He was huge and ate more than the rest of the family put together, it seemed to the disgruntled father of the family. In final reckoning he did not earn his considerable keep, and the Iversens returned him to the county authorities as a lost cause.

Karl was unhappy before he moved into the second family's house. Sven Hansen, his next foster father, was a no-nonsense burly farmer who was a blatant advocate of the homily, 'spare the rod, and spoil the child.' None of his children were spoiled, you can bet on that; and he was not about to let this notoriously bad apple escape the proper discipline. Karl was unhelpful and received a switch striping across his back as an admonition. The new boy took on the oldest Hansen son, age eighteen, when he referred to Karl as a 'square head,' and Karl made the mistake of leaving noticeable bruises on the older foster brother. For that he received a whipping with the antenna of a car radio that left fine scars on the skin of his young back.

Karl was surly about the physical 'chastisements' and for that caught a gnarled backhand across his insolent mouth. It hurt, and he bled a little. He remembered every aspect of that event and its predecessors in vivid detail. It was not in Karl's nature to forget slights or worse. When Karl scratched Sven's newly painted automobile with a four by eight beam he was carrying out to the barn they were repairing, the clumsy boy was tied arms outstretched to the posts of the corral gate and whipped with Sven's belt until enough blood showed in the stripes on Karl's back that Sven could view the punishment as approaching justice; and Sven's wife, Margaret, ever the soft hearted (Sven said, 'soft-headed'), begged him to stop. Karl made a special mental note not to forget even one pain or indignity of that beating. The fourteen year old did not cry, whimper, or speak to his foster father until an eventful day three and a half months later.

On Karl's fifteenth birthday, April 12, 1964, a Sunday, Margaret Hansen baked a Danish chocolate cake and carefully placed fifteen candles on top and spelled out "Happy Birthday" in party candies in the middle. Karl had behaved himself well, at least for him, the past three and a half months since the car scratching episode; and Margaret wanted to commemorate the positive conduct with something of a celebration. The big Swedish boy came into the kitchen from the north field at nine fifteen, dirty and very tired from a morning of irrigating. He was sweaty and hungry. Margaret smiled a greeting and took pleasure in the appreciation the big troublesome boy showed at her effort.

Sven entered in his Sunday suit, hair plastered down properly, shoes cleaned and polished, and looked at the dirty field hand in anger.

"What's the excuse for not being ready for Sacrament meeting this time? You knew from the beginning that one rule of the house was that we attend to our church activities. I am sick and tired of supporting a Jack. Get into your clothes, you ingrate. We'll all be late because of you," Sven said by way of greeting. Right was right, and it was time it was said. No accommodation made for the fact that it was doing Sven's irrigation turn that made Karl both dirty and late.

Karl did not move or protest the injustice.

"Move, you lazy whelp!"

Karl set his big legs and tightened his muscles. He clenched his teeth and glared hot daggers at the spruced up farmer edging toward him. It was a challenge, and no man worth his salt could back down from an insolent boy contradicting the fatherly authority in his own house. Sven took that to be a principle of the gospel.

Margaret feared the worst and tried to defuse the situation. She did not want to ruin another Sunday, especially the boy's birthday. Sometimes Sven could be a "little bit harsh," she thought to herself. She said with a pleading in her voice, "Couldn't we just have a piece of birthday cake? We can be a little late to meeting this once; please, Sven." The proposal sounded silly even to her; she knew Sven's rules about punctuality at meetings.

"I'll ask you not to butt into this, Sister Hansen." He called her by the formal church greeting whenever he saw the need to bring the woman up short; and this was clearly one of those times. "The boy needs discipline; and this is as good a time as any for him to learn respect for family, and well past time to honor the true religion and the Lord's commandments." Sven Hansen considered his authority as the head of the household to be a sacred obligation and to have been challenged by this upstart, undisciplined product of a home that had been lacking in the priesthood and the right teaching. Didn't the woman know anything? She spoiled the young ones with her unscriptural mollycoddling.

Margaret looked at her husband imploringly, then at the now openly defiant boy. "Here, Karl," she said, "Have a little piece of cake; we can talk about this over cake. Please, Sven." She was talking to the big boy but never took her eyes away from her husband. It was all she could think of to say to defuse the mounting tempers and tension.

"That beats all. Teach him discipline by giving him cake. That come from one of your library books, woman?" Sven growled. He hated it when she made him raise his voice. She knew it was necessary to reprove betimes with harshness, did she not?

"I won't be eating cake, Mrs. Hansen," Karl said more snappishly than intended. After all, he knew, she was only trying to be nice to him, the only one in that family who did. He started to back out of the kitchen.

"Come back here, young man!" Sven yelled. "We'll eat cake; we'll be late for church—the Lord will just have to understand—because after we finish the birthday-boy party, we're going out to the barn to have a chastisement that won't soon be forgotten. Now cut a slice for him. He's going to need his strength!" Sven was in a veritable fit of temper; there was no reasoning with him now, no mollifying the irate and wronged father. And after he had provided so generously for the ingrate orphan, and he was in the right.

Sven himself gouged off a slab of cake and slammed it down on a party plate. Margaret began to cry. Karl spoke to his foster-father for the first time in over a quarter of a year, "I will not eat that shit!" he snarled in a darkly threatening tone now caught up in a silly teenage rage matching Sven's.

Margaret clasped her hand over her mouth in disbelief. No one had ever used an obscenity in her home before, certainly not her husband even in the worst of his tempers. As best as she could remember, no one had ever uttered one in her hearing intentionally before that awful day. Brother Hansen recoiled as if he had been struck across the mouth. When he was able to recognize the right thing to do again, Sven stomped toward the filthy mouthed boy in blind rage and total menace. He swung a roast ham sized callused fist, reaching from the floor with a fully developed haymaker, prepared to see the rude boy's blond head separate from his lazy body. Karl knew the clumsy blow was coming before the man made his first movement. He had been watching the bellicose man's eyes.

The muscular boy stepped back enough to evade the killing blow and clenched his powerful big hand around the bulk of Sven's forearm as it followed the fist harmlessly by. He helped Sven fall face down into the chocolate cake scattering dishes, utensils, party favors, and the cake as if an

28

explosion had erupted in the center of the room. Karl said with the most unmistakable malice, "If you move from there, if you even look like you are going to move, I'll kill you. You will never touch me again!" His voice was unusually quiet, given the electricity crackling in the atmosphere. No one in the room had the slightest doubt about the boy's seriousness or capability to carry out his unequivocal threat.

That afternoon, after an extraordinary Sabbath Day convocation of the county juvenile matron, Bertha Thoralfssen, the wronged foster father, Sven Hansen, sheriff, Bruce Hendricksen, and Inga Haakensdatter, who agreed to take Karl in after some wheedling and cajoling by the other parties, Karl moved into the last home in the county that would take him. The stipend for foster parenting was increased as a one time incentive for this special circumstance. Karl was not privy to the discussion, and was a quiet and chastened teenager when the sheriff drove him to Mrs. Haakensdatter's and told him where the bear slept. Karl promised to shape up and not to disturb the bear again. Yes, he understood—his next stop would be reform school and—he would stay there until he was twenty-one.

His reputation was now the talk of the town. No detail was too small to escape the least informed or youngest citizen. Karl Isaacson was a pariah; and as such, was considered fair game for any and every taunt and incivility. Every day they encountered him, the town boys jeered and derided the teenager unmercifully despite dire punishments threatened in the Mormon ward (congregation) meetings because such behavior was unchristian and unLDS. It did no good. Every detail of his crimes against the Hansens was common knowledge in the rural community of Zarahemla, where real secrets were not only unheard of, but the pretense at keeping a secret was nothing but more grist for the gossip mill. Although he maintained a stoical exterior for the most part, Karl felt each barb personally and with a long memory. It was his long, detailed, and unforgiving memory that got him into the trouble leading to his enlistment in the army in the spring of 1966.

"I will go over the problems in detail that Private Isaacson had because they illustrate a lot about his character and reactions," said the 'Colonel's' deputy, still reading from his copious notes in Karl's dossier. The service jacket was now marked Secret, CT/SOG/RDC OFFICERS -Authorization Only. "This episode has the elements that make Private Isaacson an ideal candidate for a contract, and also suggests the note of caution The Company will have to have in managing him." The assistant used the formal dossier and filled in with his own insights:

Karl never viewed himself as an *untermenschen* or a member of the underclass in any sense despite his straitened circumstances. He remembered the intelligence and intellectual courage of his father when he stood up to the church, and the aristocratic bearing of his mother, even during her debilitating fight against cancer and poverty. He forgot, by stubborn self-protective effort, his father's intemperance and his mother's social ineptitude.

David Marshall Grant, at the age of eighteen, scion of the richest family in Zarahemla, was naturally the most eligible young bachelor in the city. He was one of the Sundial High's star basketball players in a state where there were only two recognized sports—basketball and football. He was the pride of the town and the Church, expected to fulfill a Mormon mission to some exciting and important place. He was a consummate actor, playing the role of most likely to succeed; and had, since childhood. He elected himself Karl Isaacson's lifelong nemesis.

When they had been children in Primary (the Mormon children's organization) David had tattled on Karl, so, to his lasting humiliation, he had had to have his mother fetch him from the classes more than once. David incited other children to taunt Karl with the standard, "square head" epithet, applied to Swedes, and "girlie hair," applied to the blond curls he knew Karl hated as being unmasculine. Karl got into fights to combat his tormentors and to defend the honor of his masculinity, thereby bringing down upon himself the wrath of the adult establishment of Zarahemla. Throughout their childhood and early teenage years, David was able to stand back and enjoy the largely self-inflicted consequences of Karl's reactions. He always seemed to be able to find Karl's sensitive spot, and an enduring enmity grew between the two boys. David took pleasure in recounting his large stock of Swedish jokes: "What is the smallest book in the world?" "The Who's Who of Sweden." "What's the second smallest book?" "The Book of Swedish War Heroes." "Hear about the farmer in Sundial Country who had the choice of buying two Swedes or two mules? He bought the mules because they're smarter." And David always seemed to be able to find a barb about Karl's mother, or about his orphan status: "Hey, you guys, hear about the Swedish kid that went to first grade? Teacher asked his name. 'Yon Yonson,' he said. Teacher asked him how old he was. 'Don't know,' little Yon said. Teacher asked the dummy when he was born. Yon said, 'I wasn't born; I yoost got a stepmutter.'"

Karl finally stopped going to church activities altogether after his fifteenth birthday, in part to avoid the constant unfavorable comparisons with the more popular older boy and to gain a modicum of respite from David's cruel tongue, as well as in defiance of custom and Sven Hansen.

Karl was more often than not referred to as the "Dumb Swede Squarehead" by his peers—an epithet comparable to "nigger" or "kike." He wore a mask of indifference but seethed inwardly. He knew it was counterproductive to fight back; he certainly was told that by his foster parents, teachers, and church leaders often enough; but it was hard for a teenager to absorb and not fight or to get revenge. He did fight when someone made reference to his father being a drunk; that was always too much.

The cumulative pain of the insults, like small cuts, and the loneliness of looking from the outside in, gave Karl a growing reserve of pain and anger. To be sure, David Grant was careful to make sure no adult heard the insults; lest he be thought guilty of a sin or worse, a character flaw. David was, by natural aptitude and social position, a born leader of the harassing boys, who came to know no greater pleasure than the discovery of some new small wound they could open on the big Swedish kid.

Karl got on well with his new foster mother, Inga Haakensdatter, a widow with four other children—to both of their surprises. She was pleasant enough, if not actually kind. She was just and treated Karl with no less and no more courtesy than her own children. She did not ask anything of him she was unwilling to do herself, and Karl in turn grew to respect the hard working and uncomplaining woman. Inga never raised her hand to the big boy, and he never gave her reason. He even became communicative in the months he sheltered under her roof. Inga was as sparing with her occasions for advice as she was with praise or criticism. She watched Karl struggle with his peers for weeks and finally counseled Karl to ignore the taunts, to stop fighting, and to try and make himself some peace by exercising more self-control; so, he could save himself some grief.

He was moderately successful for the year until he turned sixteen and was smitten with his first romance. Karl admired Gretchen Smith from afar during his freshman and sophomore years at Sundial Junior and Senior High. He screwed up his courage and overcame a lifetime of reticence with the town girls and asked the young lady to the 1966 Junior Prom, the Spring Fest. The dance was the last major social event of the school year and far and away the most important. Gretchen was a reasonably attractive girl but not one of the most popular set, certainly not one of the cheerleaders.

She was quiet and pleasant; and to Karl's surprise and relief, Gretchen accepted his invitation. Karl was totally inexperienced with the opposite sex, and he was hopelessly in love. She, on her part, was desperate for a date. With only two weeks left before the dance, it was apparent no one else was going to ask her. Her father had scared off all of the lower middle class boys who were at all likely to pursue her, and the more affluent set largely ignored the girl.

With a little effort, she might even be able to like Karl Isaacson, Gretchen reasoned, trying to convince herself. She knew his reputation for picking fights, and she knew her dad would "have a cow" when he found out with whom she was planning on going to the ball. That knowledge served to bring out the latent rebel in her and added some zest. She convinced herself that this was going to be fun.

Karl worked in the feedlot of the County Cooperative Stockyards, the most unpleasant but best paying job for a kid in the town, in order to get himself his first suit, a white shirt that fit, and his first proper black tie. Karl worked weekends for a month to be able to buy a reasonable corsage for his date. His enthusiasm was so engaging, and the change in his demeanor so apparent that his rather stolid foster mother taught him how to dance, at least the dance of her Norwegian heritage and generation. Karl had no way of knowing the Virginia Reel, the fox-trot, and the Viennese Waltz were not *de rigeur* with the current younger set, his contemporaries. He could not have anticipated David Grant's special plans for the dance involved him either.

David had his pick of the popular girls, as usual, although Verna Olafsen regarded the roguishly handsome young man as her steady. He would never have given a glance at one of the girls in the lesser-mortal set had he not gotten wind of Karl's great love. For a real coup against the despised Swede, David was willing to make some temporary sacrifices. He swallowed some of his well-honed social pride, picked times and places that were least obvious, and began to woo Gretchen Smith with a movie date, hamburgers and fries at the Avon Cafe, the former in-place for Zarahemla's teens. He confessed his sincerity when he let her know how sad he would be if she felt that she could not go to the Spring Fest with him.

"I know you already have a date, Gretchen, you told me that twice before at least. It is the biggest deal of the school year. Maybe you and me could even go steady if things work out. You understand how sincere I feel about you," David said without a trace of fraudulence or detectable hypocrisy in his voice or demeanor. There were only two days remaining before the night of the prom.

It took Gretchen about half a day to decide in favor of the biggest opportunity she would ever have. Her mother was aghast that she had ever even considered going to the most important dance of the year with that Swedish boy, what's his name? Bonnie Parkinson, her best friend, all but swooned when Gretchen told her that David Grant had invited her. No one in their right mind in Zarahemla or Sundial County would turn David down. By afternoon Gretchen was practicing writing 'Mrs. David Grant,' 'Mrs. Gretchen Grant,' and 'Gretchen S. Grant' just to see how they felt.

Her fantasies carried Gretchen through the difficulty of getting Central to plug in the number for the Haakensen home. Karl was not there; so the feckless and relieved girl left a telephone message with Andrew Haakensen, age eight. Andrew's writing skills were poor, and his attention span short when it came to phone messages. He gave up trying to copy down the message from the fast talking caller. He vowed to remember; he promised Gretchen he would remember to tell Karl. He wanted to remember. He forgot.

Two days later, on the afternoon of prom day, Karl spent an hour and a half bathing, putting on fu-fu, combing his hair meticulously and grumbling when the part would not stay in his unruly blond curls. He hated curly hair. Except today he couldn't hate anyone or anything. He was hardly aware of his surroundings as he floated about to get ready for his first date. It had been a long time since he had had a genuinely happy day, and Karl intended to enjoy this one without even the slightest sliver of discontent. The sturdy blond Swede assiduously scrubbed his shoes and his fingernails to remove any trace of the odoriferous stockyards. Karl had only one pair of shoes and even with three coats of boot black they were only passable. "Oh, well," he thought, "it will be dark anyhow."

His foster mother surreptitiously had her old Ford cleaned and put on her Sunday dress. She had become personally involved (at a distance) in the project of the date and saw it as one of the first breakthroughs to regular civilized behavior for the rowdy boy. Besides, it was so romantic. "You can use the car if you want, Karl. I will drive you and never say a word. You'll hardly know I'm there." Karl was touched by Inga's offer. He would never have dared to ask for such a privilege. He stammered his thanks, wishing he did not have to owe anyone, but the prospect of walking all the way into town and showing up dirty and sweaty at the love-of-his-life's door was too daunting to let him protest.

Inga drove the Ford to the Smith's modest two story brick home. Karl had not been able to learn to drive to get his license. The Smiths' old house was like two dozen others in the little town having multiple small second story bedroom windows to accommodate the extra wives during the bygone polygamy era. When Inga parked before the front walk, Karl said earnestly, "You don't have to come to the door with me, do you?"

Inga smiled affectionately at his innocence and shook her head. She wondered if the excited boy would collapse before he reached the stoop. He forgot Gretchen's corsage and had to rush back to the car. Inga anticipated him and held the small bunch of party flowers out the window on his side of the car without looking him in the eye. Karl was nervous and breathing briskly as he knocked firmly on the door.

When the door opened and Hyrum Smith, Gretchen's rather severe father, appeared, Karl was intensely mindful of etiquette, Mormon etiquette, even though he was more than rusty in his practice of the religion or its social amenities. "Good evening, Brother Smith," he said correctly and paused briefly. "I'm Karl Oscar Isaacson; and I've come to take your daughter, Gretchen, I mean, Sister Smith, to the prom."

Hyrum Smith smiled gently with benign amusement at the boy's overheated efforts at comity, but otherwise presented a face of complete bewilderment. "Come in, son," he managed to say properly but without warmth. Hyrum was not a warm man, and this boy's reputation as a Jack-Mormon and a brawler was not unknown to the man. He did not approve of the boy, but was polite enough not to let it show overmuch. He found the situation as uncomfortable as did Karl. "Better have you talk to the wife, . . . to Sister Smith."

Karl dispensed with his first cloud of faint uncertainty with the presumption that men were not supposed to know about these romantic things. He waited in the hallway while Gretchen's father went to fetch his wife. Lydia Smith paled as she saw the Swedish boy. First of all, she would never have let him into the front room, probably had heavens knows what on the bottom of those old shoes. Secondly, she realized in that instant that this young man was totally ignorant of her daughter's change of plans. She certainly hoped there would not be a scene. Swedes were hot tempered, none too thoughtful, and nowhere near as civil as the Danes. This was delicate.

"Well,. . . Karl, isn't it?" she started lamely. She knew she had to get to the plain facts. There was no easy way. Thank the Lord that Gretchen and that handsome Grant boy had already gone. Wouldn't that be a pretty scene if the second boy came to the door at the same time as the first?

"Yes, ma'am. I mean, yes, Sister Smith. Thank you." He felt dumb. There must have been something smarter he could have said. He knew she was just making polite talk trying to make him feel at ease. He did appreciate the gesture. He wished he didn't have to make such a big deal out of everything. She must think he was some sort of nincompoop. Mrs. Smith . . . Sister Smith, seemed nice but kind of nervous.

"Well…uh…Karl, there…there seems to be something of a mix-up. I don't know what happened. Didn't Gretchen let you know?"

Karl was confused, as much by Mrs. Smith's distress and unshared portent behind her difficulty in looking at him directly, as in what she was saying.

The portly middle-aged woman stood up straighter and smoothed her apron down over the well pressed homemade ankle length print skirt. She took a deeper breath and faced up to her responsibility. "I don't quite know how to tell you this, Brother Isaacson, but I'm sure you want the simple truth. Like the Savior says, we must let our 'nay be nay and our yea be yea,'" she prattled. The darkening look shuttering over the tall powerfully built boy's face caused her to take an inadvertent step behind her husband.

"Well," she persisted resolutely, "There's nothing to say but to say it. Gretchen went to the dance with that nice Grant boy. I'm sure you know him. Isn't he just a little older than you and Gretchen?" she made an effort to stop prattling.

Karl had resolved to display no emotion when he heard the bad news portended by Mrs. Smith's stammering. Instead, he reacted as if he had been struck a blow in his solar plexus. He grew pale, then flushed. He was afraid he was going to "pass out"—whatever that felt like. He sensed the real and imagined slights of fifteen years of benign and not so benign condescension culminating in Mrs. Smith's unintentionally insulting words. Tears stung his eyes making him angry with himself. "Oh, that's right...I just got the wrong night," he said unconvincingly in a futile effort to save face.

He was furious at himself for acting so silly and wanted to be anywhere else but in that doorway just then. "I'll be going now. Don't bother to tell Gretchen about my mistake. I'll see her in school."

Mrs. Smith felt acute embarrassment for the boy—he didn't seem like such a bad sort, after all—and was heartily relieved that there was not going to be a dreadful scene. Why didn't he just go?

As if the message were received telepathically, Karl turned on his heels and opened the front door to exit. He dropped the corsage without recognizing that he had done so; and said simply, "Good evening, then, Mr. and Mrs. Smith," as he walked on wooden legs out onto the porch.

Karl was almost unaware of his surroundings by the time he got back to the Haakensen's car and looked darkly into Inga's expectant eyes. Her look of confident anticipation tinged with amicable question turned to benevolent concern when she caught the expression of devastation on her charge's face. Karl stopped and collected himself before opening the automobile door. He started to get in but seemed to think better of it. He looked to be fumbling.

"What's wrong? What happened in there?" Inga asked her foster son quietly and gently, seeing the boy fighting to preserve his dignity.

"Oh, nothing, Ma'am," he lied. "I...I'm supposed to meet Gretchen...at the dance. There was some mix-up, I guess." She knew that under the facade of civility he was seething with anger. He had taken to calling her 'Inga' of late, and the 'ma'am' was a reversion to his original sense of alienation.

"Well, get in; and I'll take you right over. It's still early; don't worry, Karl. It's going to be okay." She could not keep the doubt out of her voice.

"Thanks, but I'd like to walk. I, uh…got too hot in this new suit. I think I need a little air."

"Are you okay, son?" the foster mother spoke in an uncharacteristically solicitous tone and recognized that she had never called him by a term of endearment before and did not think many had in this kid's short life. She felt most motherly toward him at that moment. He looked anything but 'okay.'

"I'm just fine, just fine, thank you," Karl lied in a soft voice. "I just need to walk, clear my head."

He managed a wan smile as he closed the car door and the conversation. He was polite but resolute. After a momentary pause, the once again stolid appearing Scandinavian matron drew away from the curb brushing away a tear she hoped he had not seen. Karl started walking the four city blocks to the high school unsure why he was headed there and especially unclear about what he intended to do when he got there.

In the four block walk his confused thoughts were at first kaleidoscopic with feelings of worthlessness, irritation that he must have made a mistake about the day or the time, then a sense of shame that anyone as low on the social ladder as him should have been so presumptuous, and thinking he was probably making things worse for himself by going to the school. Midway, he was anguished by the realization that he had been overtly rejected by the girl he had considered the nicest in the whole rotten town. What had he ever done to deserve that?

A block from the high school gym, where the dance was being held, he came to the jarring full comprehension that Gretchen had not even had the courtesy to let him know she was going with someone else and had left her mother to deal with the confrontation. "That stunk," he thought. That particular element of his anger was short-lived. He could not bring himself to remain angry with the beautiful girl of his mind's creation. As he started up the school sidewalk to enter the gym, his final rational thought was of David Grant. "That jerk did this on purpose, for the worst of reasons," he thought. "Why else would he ever have asked a girl he must consider a nobody to the biggest dance of the whole school year?" Anger and adrenaline were pumping through him taking the place of cognition as Karl walked into the aisle between the spectator benches in the gym.

He heard the strains of "Moonlight Serenade," the theme song of the prom, coming from Ellis Pride's band, The Pridefuls. They were the only band in the county and played for every city and church affair where a live band was called for and could be afforded. Tonight they were doing an especially creditable job, living up to their advertising slogan. In the big band era it had been 'Swing and sway with Sammy Kaye—for this band it was 'Slip and slide with Ellis Pride.' But Karl hardly noticed as he picked his way resolutely through the narrow entry way, crowded with boys too shy to dance, behaving with macho rudeness in the tradition of all inept boys and men.

Karl heard the raucous strains of the school's fight song altered with the irreverent lyrics preferred by the macho boys and detested by the faculty, girls, and mothers of the school now being sung as an irritant to the orthodox.

Fight, fight for old Sundial High,
You bring the whiskey; I'll bring the rye.
Send a sophomore out for gin;
Don't let a sober senior in.

Karl paid little attention to the familiar words he usually liked because of their manifest disrespect for the school, for the church and its temperance principles, and for authority in general.

"Hey, what's that smell? Could it be Swedish cow puckey?" a disorderly voice wafted out of the dimness beside the aisle as Karl passed.

Karl was almost oblivious to the disembodied voice and would have walked on by had it not been for the intrusion of a hand on his shoulder. Karl paused long enough to turn and see the leering face of one of David Grant's cronies, one of his little group of bold tormentors, brave enough only when he was in with David Grant's bunch. The insult registered then on Karl with the added stimulus of the touch, and the connection from the primitive part of his brain short-circuited the thought process into a direct focus on a physical response. With no warning, Karl fired a huge fist into the sternum of the other youth, erasing the smile from the leering face and dropping him backward on the hard floor gasping for breath. Scarcely breaking stride, the larger boy walked on straight into the crowd of dancers with a singleness of purpose—find David Grant. Rational thought was suspended; he had not formed a clear idea of what he was going to do when he found his nemesis; he had not thought that far ahead.

He was oblivious to the trail of chagrined and choleric followers from his encounter with the classmate who had suffered his passing wrath. Karl found David dancing mid-floor with Verna Hansen, his near-steady girl friend. He took in the forlorn Gretchen sitting dejectedly on the sidelines with the other wall flowers. Karl realized the unchivalrous insult David was doing to Gretchen and wound up his fury to an even higher pitch. There was no one to caution him, but he was beyond caution now, in any case. Without the slightest deviation, the large blond boy walked through the crowd toward David and Verna letting the dancers move out of his way or be run over. He dispensed with the preliminaries as soon as David became aware of his presence.

"Walk outside with me, Grant," he whispered with an animal hoarseness fearful that his voice would betray his emotional state. There was enough menace in his voice that he might just as well have shouted for the effect the feral communication had on David.

The older boy shrank away from Verna, his real date, leaving her between the primitive and mindless Norseman and himself. He whimpered, "Hey, what's the matter with you?" His face was a mask of innocence and wonder.

Silence and hot eyes riveted on David's eyes.

It was obviously too late in the day to pretend that what had taken place had not happened. David's quick mind raced to find something to defuse the escalating situation. He chose lamely. "Hey, Karl, can't you Swedes take a joke?" his quavering voice betrayed his fear, and he seemed all the more craven hiding behind his girl's skirt.

"Listen, rich boy,…you and me are goin' to finish this now. You want it in here in front of all your pretty friends, or do you want to be man enough to follow me outside?" Karl's eyes burned through the subdued light of the dance hall and into David's flicking eyes.

"I'm not about to have a fight over a silly mix-up about a date, not in my new suit. You know, you stupid Swede, the girl just didn't want to go with you. Can't you just get that through your thick head, no one wants you." He was feeling braver seeing the small crowd of his friends moving up behind Karl. "You don't belong, or hadn't you noticed?" David grew even braver as he slowly backpedaled and put distance between himself and the fury that faced him.

David's friends closed on Karl in a tightening phalanx. "Make it a fair fight!" shouted one of the football players who had figured out what was about to happen. He was from the wrong side of town and wouldn't feel too bad if the banker's boy got a little of what was coming to him. David thought that was not exactly what he needed right now—someone to stir the hotheaded Swede all the more.

Harvey Johnsen, the boy Karl had knocked down, was spoiling for revenge, but was not such a fool as to face the big stockyard worker and outcast alone. He said to his small crowd of excited friends, "Listen, if Karl starts anything that could hurt Verna, let's all take him at once. He can't take us all, okay?"

The brave warriors nodded assent and waited for the next move which had to come from Karl. David looked nothing less than pleading, but he was emboldened enough by the reinforcement from his friends to hiss, "Your dad was a drunk, and your mother was a chippy; everyone knows that. None of the Isaacsons is worth a pinch. Why don't you just get out of here and let the decent people alone?"

That was very much the wrong thing to say at precisely the wrong moment. David might just as well thrown a cup of gasoline on a small fire. Any inhibitions about violence that may have been lingering somewhere in Karl's subconscious evaporated in the heat generated by the inflammatory outburst.

"Move!" Karl snarled at Verna. She did so with alacrity and exposed her knight to the advancing Viking.

David was all but paralyzed. Karl's fists were clenched tight enough to blanch the skin as he cleared the five feet between himself and David in two strides. "Here or outside?" He malevolently queried. Karl left no room to negotiate, no opening for face saving, no offering of quarter.

David was so frightened that he could not speak. His lips quivered; his bowels felt loose, and his legs trembled. In the back of his mind he was furious with himself. He was looking like a coward in front of all of the guys. Verna was not ten feet away and taking it all in. He would never live this down, but he was too afraid to mount even a face-saving defense, not one on one. He could not think; so, he made the mistake of putting his hands in front of his face for protection and to blot out the vision of the Neanderthal coming at him.

Karl misinterpreted the movement of a childish defensive posture as the prelude to an attack. He cleared the few remaining feet between himself and David in less time than it takes to say it and hammered two ferocious blows into the older boy's handsome face. There was a satisfying crunch of nose bones and teeth and a splatter of exhaled blood passing out of the convoluted nasal passages before David crumpled, whining.

Three boys behind Karl moved on the cue of Karl's attack. The big Swede was entirely focused on the environment of the combat and ignored everyone in the hall except his attackers. It was as if he had eyes in the back of his head. He whirled about and awkwardly, but effectively, kicked at the first human part that came into his view. Harvey Johnson's right shin bone cracked, and he emitted an unearthly scream that galvanized every eye and ear in the gymnasium on the fight. The downed boy writhed in agony then fainted when he looked down at the jagged edge of leg bone sticking out of his pant leg. More than one girl looking on did the same.

Karl took a glancing fist blow to his cheek, blinked once, then drove his right fist into the chin of his next assailant knocking him off balance and dampening that boy's enthusiasm for continued combat. As that combatant paused, Karl had time to concentrate on David's third friend, Ivan Nelson, whose momentum propelled his whole body toward collision with Karl who was positioned in a tight leonine crouch. Before Ivan could bridge the last one foot gap between them, Karl drove his two fists like twin pile drivers into the oncoming face. The boy dropped like a puppet whose strings had been cut.

Ben Jacobsen, the boy who had been tough enough to hit Karl a second earlier, got up and came on again. Karl kicked him hard in the balls and dropped him to the floor in the fetal position. The boy mixed his copious vomitus with the blood patches on the hardwood gym surface and passed out.

By now, the football coach, burly Sigurd Swensen, had made it to the fight scene and enveloped the only fighter still standing. He caught Karl in a bear hug from behind attempting to pinion the boy's arms to his side. To his consternation, the boy anticipated the coach's momentum in a movement as natural as if he had been skillfully trained in *jui jutsu* and swept the coach aside in the direction of his own momentum. The coach fell unceremoniously into the pile of bodies accumulating on the floor. He slipped on a puddle of blood as he sought to right himself and to come at Karl again. Karl hunched his muscular shoulder and crashed into the off-balance coach. Coach Swensen tripped backward over Harvey Johnsen's mangled leg and landed like a felled tree on his own unprotected left elbow with a fully audible snap. The coach and Harvey both screamed unashamedly. No one else felt inclined to be the next authority to try and subdue Karl Isaacson.

With the scarcity of fresh opponents, the blood lust in Karl's focus began to calm down; and he became aware of the world once again. His right third knuckle stung where he had cut it on David's broken tooth. His cheek was throbbing and beginning to swell where Ben Jacobsen had connected. He was excited, but not the least remorseful. He was totally unafraid, even of the consequences of his actions, not that he was thinking clearly about potential repercussions yet. The tall powerful young man straightened up, glanced momentarily at Gretchen Smith with a withering look, and strode across the floor through the aisles between the benches, and out onto the school grounds without looking back. No one interfered with his march.

Sheriff Bruce Hendricksen was watching the Milton Berle Show on the tube, eating his second dish of Snelgrove's vanilla ice-cream, the best in the west and therefore in the US of A, when the call came in. "I knew it was too good to be true," he complained to his wife, Sandra. "Likely it's that stupid Alben Hancock tearin' up his cell again. Another fool Swede. I am gettin' bored with havin' to knock him up the side of his fool head," the sheriff muttered as he picked up the phone on its fourth annoying ring.

"Sheriff Hendricksen," he answered testily.

"Who started what riot?" he groaned seeing his quiet and pacific evening at home being trashed.

"How many did you say were hurt? The coach, too? You mean to tell me that Isaacson kid took them all on?"

40

"Where is he now?...the Isaacson kid, of course," the sheriff's tone was more irritable than he wanted it to be.

"I'll find him; and no, we don't need to call in the Highway Patrol. This is just one fool kid, not some Russian invasion. Just relax, Abe. I'll take care of it. You just stay in the office to handle the paperwork. It's goin' to hit the fan as soon as that Grant kid's dad gets wind of it.

"I'm on my way; calm down." The sheriff hung up the telephone.

Sandra put on her pained expression. "They don't pay you enough for this"—and said petulantly, "How long you goin' to be, Bruce? I'd sure like to get you for myself for a whole evening for a change."

The sheriff rolled his eyes gently and smiled a husbandly smile. "And what exactly did you have in mind?"

"Get your mind out of the gutter. I just wanted us to take in a little TV— 'Bonanza' and 'The Rifleman' are on tonight. Hurry back," she smiled affectionately, changing the implied subject.

"Maybe we can catch a little of 'I Love Loosely,' think about that," Hendricksen said as he departed.

Karl was walking resolutely toward Inga Haakensdatter's house, having no more concrete plans for the moment. Thoughts of the awful potential consequences of his volcanic outburst of anger were beginning to intrude into his returning ability to rationalize as he trudged along with the gravel crunching familiarly under his soles. The lights of the sheriff's car behind him awakened him to full reality. All fight, even the thought of fight, was gone out of him. This was the law, and Karl had a deep-set respect for the law. He stopped, turned, and faced Sheriff Hendricksen as the portly lawman approached.

"Had a big night at the dance, I hear, Karl," the sheriff said noncommittally and warily.

"I guess so, Sheriff," Karl returned.

"Care for a ride?"

"I guess so." Karl knew that he was in no position to refuse.

"I have to take you in, son. You know that."

"Yes, sir, I guess I do," Karl said. His fight was over for that night.

"You goin' to give me any trouble? Do I need the cuffs?"

"No, sir. I had enough trouble for one night."

"Good boy."

When Karl was sitting docilely in the juvenile cell, Sheriff Hendricksen told him, "I'll call Mrs. Haakensdatter and let her know so's she won't worry."

The three men in the cramped office at Fort Lewis took a breather at this point in the embellished narration. The second deputy, a litigation attorney before joining The Company, had researched the legal aftermath of Karl's venture into the social whirl. "I can summarize the rest of this in a few minutes; it's pretty clear what went on even though no one quite comes out and says it," communicated the assistant speaking for the first time that evening.

The 'Colonel' did not much enjoy excessive presentations, and he did not suffer fools patiently. "Good, get on with it. That will give us time to finish the review of the two lieutenants tonight and to get back to The Farm tomorrow," he asserted blandly but authoritatively.

The assistant continued his construct of the reported information:

Karl spent three days in jail, not formally charged with any crime, while the important people discussed, at times angrily, the crimes to be charged to the boy, and punishment to be meted to him. That a jury might be appointed for a judgment never crossed any of their minds.

Mrs. Haakensdatter suggested leniency, "Give the boy a chance to work off a fine but keep this off his record. It could ruin the lad to have a criminal record. He's not really a bad boy."

"Send the boy to the Point-of-the-Mountain (Utah State Penitentiary) until my boy grows new teeth," snarled David Grant, Sr.

"He's like a dog with the hyperphobia," opined David's aggrieved mother, crying. "Why can't they hang that scum up at the Point-of-the-Mountain like they used to!?"

Mr. Grant patted his wife's knee patronizingly.

"I think I have a better solution," said the sheriff after the discussion and ventilating. "I've got to tell you that nothing can be done without a formal charge and a trial unless we all agree to my idea. You should know that it is not going to be all that simple to get a jury to find him guilty. Things might not go the way you think."

A collection of angry and incredulous eyebrows raised in unison. "A little investigation shows that there was a lot of provocation in the past, even that night…Yes, I'm afraid so, Mrs. Grant," the sheriff said responding to the irate unspoken question on the woman's face.

"It would stretch the imagination for a jury to believe that one kid attacked four other kids and a big football coach. I know Sigurd Swensen, for one, would just as leave have nothing more to do with this little town problem," Sheriff Hendricksen continued, smiling a little at his recollection of his discussion with the chagrined big man.

"I take it you have a solution you think would be satisfactory, eh, Sheriff?" asked Mr. Grant, looking to reassert his influential role.

"I do. Karl Oscar Isaacson can be in the army and in boot camp inside a month from now, maybe within the week, if we get right on it."

"He's a little under age, isn't he?" asked the foster mother archly. "Just turned sixteen at last count."

"He is, but I think we can arrange for some exceptions to be made as long as he has no outright criminal charges against him," the sheriff said, and then paused to let the implications of his statement soak in. "You'll have to drop the charges. And to be frank about it, I'd rather there weren't a lot of idle questions about the arrangements or the paper work, if you get my drift," he added with a knowing smile just beginning to stretch his lips.

"Just so long as I never see that punk's face around here again," said David Grant, Sr.

"Seems to me that a little thrashing in the jail house before he goes would make this easier for me to take," said Mrs. Grant with unsatisfied vindictiveness.

Before Mrs. Haakensdatter could remonstrate, Sheriff Hendricksen appeased the Grants with the observation, "Your David will be off on his mission and out of harm's way before that Isaacson kid could get back here. I'm goin' to make it desirable that he don't want to come back." He closed the meeting with his usual, "I'll take care of it, then." The small town sheriff had never been known for being pleonastic. No questions asked and no lies given.

The CIA attorney leaned back in his government issue folding chair until it was comfortably balanced on its two back legs. "The rest is pretty common history,…has been since there were armies, I guess," he mused to the 'Colonel' and to his bored co-assistant.

"Sheriff Hendricksen, like the local gendarmerie everywhere, knows the drill. He persuaded the local draft board director, who is also the postmistress, that it was in the public interest to have Karl Isaacson's name rise rapidly to the top of the draft list. General Hershey would have been proud of the efficiency of his troop outback there in Podunk, Utah. Since the kid is, in fact, only sixteen, a few little alterations were added to his record. For instance, no one can find his birth certificate; and another for instance; his age happened to jump two years to eighteen on the enlistment documents. He's big enough. No one is going to squawk—not the kid—and certainly not anybody who matters in that burg."

"Anyone ask the kid what he wanted to do?" inquired the other assistant as an afterthought.

"What do you think?"

"Dumb question."

"I presume the good Sheriff gave him an offer he couldn't refuse," the assistant commented.

"Yep."

"We're good, but I'd like to have seen how a real pro handled one of his people," smiled the assistant with a jaded expression. He continued his descriptive rendition of the contents of the CIA dossier:

The 'scene' took place a day after the townspeople met and for the greatest effect the conversation was held in Karl's jail cell.

"Karl, this is a serious set of charges you are up against. You busted the coach's elbow and gave poor Harvey Johnsen a compound fracture of the leg bone. David lost his prettiest two teeth, got a busted nose, and has a LaForte III facial fracture," the sheriff said reading from the documents Doctor Nielsen had sent over. Neither he nor his listener knew what a 'LaForte III' was. "That is not to mention assorted bruises and abrasions and one case of very swollen nuts," he threw in for the sake of emphasis.

Karl was about to speak up in his own defense but thought better of it. He kept his eyes directed appropriately at the floor while The Law talked to him. There had been no discussion of lawyers or due process and such. Both knew the boy had no money for an attorney.

"Seems to me there's enough to put you away for quite some time," Sheriff Hendricksen said with a trifle more assurance than he felt. "You can imagine how a jury in this town is goin' to look at that one-man riot you conducted over at the school. Zarahemla isn't goin' to have much of a football team this year, neither. You listenin' to me, young man?"

"I am, sir, but I can't rightly think of much to say about it," Karl responded forlornly.

"Then don't say nothin.' Just listen and listen good. I got a idea that just might keep you outta jail and maybe even get you on your way to somethin' better than what you had goin' in this little burg. If you keep your nose clean, and I mean for the rest of your life, I might even be able to keep this outta your official record. What do you think?"

"I guess I'd do about anything, sheriff. What are you getting at?"

"This is the deal. You stay out of jail, and you enlist in the army first thing tomorra mornin.' I awreddy' got the papers signed by Edith Pinkston, you know, the draft board lady. You just sign up; don't never come back to Zarahemla; and the rest of it is forgot. I ever see you again, and I swear you will believe in the resurrection 'cause these here papers will reappear like magic!" the sheriff expounded, punctuating the air with exclamation points using the official investigation file for emphasis.

"Great choice," Karl sighed. "Jail or Viet Nam. What do I care, anyway. Even the army has got to be better than this place," the boy said morosely.

"Okay, here's what we do. We go first thing tomorrow to the Draft Office at the court building. Mrs. Haakensdatter will bring your things from her place, and you will be a soldier before noon and at boot camp by afternoon," the sheriff said with zest—glad at the amicability of the solution overall—more enthusiasm than that being displayed by the soon-to-be-recruit, Karl Oscar Isaacson.

Inga saw to it that the requisite birth certificate was misplaced in a timely manner, her part of the bargain. Karl signed a document that included such information as his age being eighteen with a statement that he swore all of the above was true. David Grant, Jr.'s name returned to the bottom of the draft list, and a phone call to the Salt Lake Armory confirmed Karl's place on the afternoon bus to boot camp at Fort Lewis, Washington. Everyone was happy. Almost everyone.

Karl had less than forty minutes to catch the Greyhound from Zarahemla to South Salt Lake and the National Guard Armory. Only Inga Haakensdatter and the Sheriff accompanied the young man to his departure. Karl was subdued, a little frightened; he had never been out of the town of his birth before. And he knew he was never coming back.

"Goodbye and the best of luck, Karl. Do remember that no matter what may happen, you will always have one friend. I will always be happy to help you if you need it,…son," Mrs. Haakensdatter told him sincerely. She was visibly working to spare the boy her emotions.

Sheriff Hendricksen said, "Now listen to me, boy. This is an opportunity no matter how you think of it now. Make the best of it—I really hope you will do well—but make no mistake. There is no place for you here. You are the army's now. Don't screw it up, and don't come back. Understand, boy?" The sheriff added as a final note for Karl to carry with him.

Karl nodded his understanding to the lawman and looking only at his foster mother, he said, "Goodbye, and thanks."

"Good old press gang," said The Company man. "Still works, after all these millennia. You have to admit it was a fine job of engineering the draft board."

"Anything in Isaacson's boot records?" asked the 'Colonel.'

"Not much. He's a good soldier. Kept his nose pretty clean so far."

"Give me the rundown, short version," ordered the older man.

CHAPTER 2

Wastefully, expensively, but nonetheless indisputably, we are winning the war in the South. Few of our programs—civil or military—are very efficient, but we are grinding the enemy down by sheer weight and mass. And the cumulative impact of all we have set in motion is beginning to tell.
Robert W. Komer, Special Assistant to President Lyndon B. Johnson, Feb. 28, 1967

Nguyen Lui Tran pedaled his bicycle through the sweltering Saigon streets annoyed at his sudden assignment. All of his assignments of late were sudden, it seemed to Tran. He would have loved to indulge his curiosity just once to know what message was so important that he had to make a conspicuous exit from his classroom again. "Surely," he fretted, "my absences were becoming suspicious." He knew better than to give in to that curiosity, however. The thought of the consequences of such a breach of security chilled the slender man who was now an established school teacher of Han Chinese and Vietnamese extraction, a trusted member of the establishment that shored up the Republic of Viet Nam, and a silent cadre of the Viet Cong Infrastructure. Tran cursed his pesky dilapidated bicycle as the rattling contraption wobbled over a small pot hole in the crowded street. The preoccupied bicyclist talked to himself in a muttering whisper as he passed the teeming occupants of the Cholon district, oblivious to their activities. He was as unaware of the grimy children, the shrill women with the singsong cadence of their Mandarin tongue, or of the men beckoning him to sample their capitalistic wares as he was of the silent ones monitoring his progress.

Tran was scrupulously careful about security. He followed the cadres' rules to the letter and added measures of his own. He prided himself on the fact that he invented a cover story for every courier trip he made, a different and plausible reason for him to be where he was when he was. The stories were believably simple; today he was delivering packets of expensive curry ingredients to a restaurant on the western outskirts of Cholon. He had gone to the trouble of collecting the small packets to carry with him on the days he used this device. He was wary and had excellent eyesight. He checked straight ahead, on both sides, and to the rear through his handlebar mirror without being conspicuous about it, always searching for the out of place figure or movement, the coincidence of seeing the same person twice, or for the telltale higher grade clothing of the Diem regime stooges. Tran doubled back, took the extra time to peddle up streets out of the way of his destinations, stopped in broth and tea shops, and watched for government tailers before finally satisfying himself and proceeding to the location where he was to deliver the precious envelope or package, absolutely unopened.

Tran did not even want to know the contents; he did not need to know, he had been told more times than he cared to remember. He was content in his success at avoiding even the very appearance of evil as his Catholic school teachers might have said. He was relieved on this sweltering day that he had once again completed his courier trek across the sprawling city without detection. He was also quite wrong about that.

To be even more certain that he had established the bona fides of his presence in the outskirts of the Chinese section of Saigon, Tran cycled by the Chang Loi cafe and paused inside long enough to maintain the fiction of his invented cover. He was another fifteen minutes down the dusty track that passed for a road into the backwash of Cholon, still in decidedly rural surroundings and felt comfortably alone when they moved in from the two side roads and out of the shanty by the main road to arrest him.

He was so baffled by the surprise of his capture, by the very idea that he might have been under suspicion, that he had an entirely genuine look of confused innocence as the muscular Vietnamese military police (White Mice, as the American invaders called them) kicked his bicycle away, hefted him like a child into the wire screened rear compartment of an olive drab unmarked US military troop truck, and punched his face and chest until he could do nothing more than double up into a ball of pain and curse his joss. He was not told who had abducted him or why. Neither of the abductors nor the driver spoke to him. The only word he heard from the snatches of conversation whispered by his captors that suggested the identity of the brutal and efficient policemen was the use of the acronymic, "VCS." As he was losing consciousness, Nguyen Lui Tran heard something about *"Chieu Hoi"* (Open Arms) and contemplated the reference to "open arms" as the darkness closed in.

Tran was hungry and sore when he aroused from his protective sleep sometime later, apparently quite a bit later. He had a heavy black hood over his face and could see nothing. He was aware of the passage of hours bumping along in the truck, now with other people, possibly even women. No one spoke. His arms were bound behind his back, and he felt his hands turning blue, then finally he could not feel them at all. While they rode in the truck, Tran's neck was forcibly tethered in an awkward forward flexed position by an abrasive rope around his neck tied to a cinch rope about his waist. The effect was like being forced to sit in a box too small for his body, but having to accommodate to the confines anyway. He was unbearably uncomfortable. Eventually, he had to urinate, and finally his bladder could hold no more. He cried out in Vietnamese for the privilege of going to the toilet. He begged in Mandarin for the truck to stop so he could relieve himself. He took a chance and called out in English now hoping that his captors might be Americans. The answer came in the form of a tooth rattling fist blow across his face. His nose cracked and spattered blood all over the inside of the black hood. His bladder found release.

Before the end of the interminable truck ride, Tran became aware of an increasing toilet stench gathering about him. His truck mates were obviously obliged to forego any fastidiousness as well. Tran was an educated man, careful of social amenities, exquisitely sensitive to nuances of speech or mannerism even alluding to reproduction or elimination. The man was shy at best. This was the worst—he was mortified, even through all the pain and positional discomfort.

Shortly after Tran presumed for the hundredth time that he could not bear another moment of the discomfort he was experiencing; and the fear of the unknown, with all its wild imaginings conjured up in his darkness, was about to overwhelm him, the truck stopped. Tran, acting the part of the vigilant cadre, tried to gain a clue as to his whereabouts. He tried to smell, but caught only the iron-dust smell of old blood coating his plugged nostrils and parched mouth and throat. He tried to hear but was aware only of shuffling feet and groans as his fellow prisoners and he were jostled off the truck. He could not have stood even if the rope tether had been loosened. His cramped muscles cried out for nothing more than to be left alone; even the thoughts of standing were painful.

Tran heard an occasional groan and the unmistakable blunt thud of a rifle butt connecting with some part of the thin anatomy of one of the other unseen fellow prisoners. It became apparent that several of them were being led, more accurately, driven, in a direction away from the small group around him. Not unexpectedly, Tran soon felt rough hands forcing him along, this time on a wooden path or dock. Hands grasped him painfully, at least four sets of hands, and lifted him about five feet into the air. When his feet touched down, it was on metal. He was jammed down into a tight container reeking of rotted garbage. The pushers forced him into a horrifyingly uncomfortable semi-crouch by pressing down on his bent neck, head, and upper back with a metal plate. To his horror, Tran realized that he was being forced into an old garbage collection bin. He would suffocate.

For the first time, the wiry Viet Cong panicked and tried to press his way back up out of the coffin like container. He was too hungry, tired, weak, and now, nauseated, to be effective; and the hands above him crimped the lid into place. Tran heard scuffling somewhere near him, outside his coffin, then heard a single muffled shot. He vomited on his chest, adding to the stench. The heat and atmosphere were infinitely oppressive; the reek was the worst thing he had ever experienced; but since he did not seem to be suffocating, there at least must be some air holes, he deduced. Tran lapsed into a sort of Zen-like trance, suspending thought. There was no room to struggle. What might lie in store for him next was too frightening to contemplate; so he simply suspended mental function.

Shortly, Tran's container was pulled and bumped over the planks of the loading dock and obviously lifted into the air. His bones were brutalized by a drop to the floor again. Tran heard the whump-whump-whump of a helicopter's rotors then felt the sickening feeling of momentary weightlessness as the helicopter apparently lifted straight up then careened to the side as it swept up and away from the landing. Try as he might, Tran could not completely purge his mind of the pain, of the tormenting position, and of the suffering sense of impending torture and death that lay in wait for him. He was crying silently when his kidnappers unceremoniously dumped him out of the coffin/garbage can.

The slender thirty year old Vietnamese was jerked to a standing position; but his legs failed him; and down he went to his raw knees. He was jerked and kicked to a standing position again and fell again. Finally on the third agonizing try there was enough blood in his knotted muscles to permit him to crouch. His neck rope was jerked forcibly, and Tran was propelled forward, still in utter darkness inside the opaque hood. He was now tied into a string of prisoners in similar condition to himself. First, he would fall, and the prisoner behind him would tromp over his bruised legs; then the prisoner in front of him would fall; and Tran would step on the thin legs under him, scraping and nearly falling himself.

After a wearying and bruising walk, he was untied from the prisoners in front and behind him and left standing by himself in the humid air and broiling sun. His face was raw from the bruises and abrasions and from the constant wetness beneath his opaque hood. Somehow, Tran did not faint.

He was prodded forward striking his forehead hard against what he surmised to be the crossbeam of a low door. His captor laughed at this sight joke as if it was an old and familiar routine. Tran crouched as much as he could bear and entered a relatively cool but fetid room with the aid of a harsh kick on his thin buttocks. The hood was lifted off, and although the room was shaded compared to the outside sun, it was blinding. The light was disorienting to Tran. He got a severe and nauseating headache before his eyes could adjust to the light, adding to his distress.

There were two brutish Vietnamese guards, one at each of Tran's arms. They wore impassive expressions, and neither spoke a word. Tran and the guards waited. After a frightening interval, an officer entered the low-ceilinged cell; and for the first time since his abduction, someone spoke to Tran. His voice was calm and non threatening. There was a chilling, flinty precision to the voice and to the careful choice of words enunciated in educated Vietnamese.

"Good afternoon, Mr. Nguyen. May I call you Tran?" he asked politely. Tran nodded. He felt in no position to insist on formalities.

"I take it you have Chinese ancestry, with the name of Lui. I too have Han people in my heritage." The extent of knowledge about himself possessed by the officer was disconcerting to Tran.

"Never mind where you are. Suffice it that you are in a government interrogation center. You will supply us with information, then you will be reeducated, become part of the *Chieu Hoi,* and will have the opportunity to redeem your past crimes against the people of Viet Nam and our republic."

Tran had had enough time to recuperate that he now glanced at the speaker with what the officer interpreted as a look of defiance.

The officer said, "Mark my words, cadre, you will do all of these things of your own free will. I have had you brought here to see the consequence of wrong thinking or behavior." He nodded to the two jailers indicating the direction of an opening to a tunnel on the far wall of the small dank room. The opening was covered with a pull down cot and mattress and only became apparent when the cot was brought to the floor as a primitive Murphy bed.

"I will be waiting here when your tour is over. Do not speak, Cadre. You will maintain silence until given specific instructions. In fact, you will do nothing while in this camp unless instructed," the Vietnamese officer stated matter-of-factly.

Tran was prodded and pushed around the bed and into the narrow passage way which was very dark, and its dirt walls were moist and moss lined. Tran and his jailers walked about thirty feet into a fairly capacious room lined circumferentially with two-man cells. The people, one could no longer tell for sure that they were men or women, were skeletons with vacant haunting starved eyes. All of them had awful festering sores, and few visible teeth; some had evidence of crude amputations; some were blind with oozing pits where their eyes had been. Several were missing a nose or both ears. None of them were able to stand. In several cells a gray-green gruel in a bowl sat untouched on the floor by the obviously starved prisoners. Some reached hands through the bamboo bars in supplication, moaning like the inhabitants of some outer reach of hell. There was an unbearable choking smell of rotten diarrhea and stale urine. Their tattered clothing and legs were coated with their excreta. There was also a worse stench, more subtle, but more troubling. It was the odor of a shroud; the people smelled as if they were dead.

Exhausted as he was, Tran, nevertheless, recoiled involuntarily as soon as his eyes fully adjusted to the darkness; and his mind comprehended the macabre scene. Comprehend was too strong a term, perhaps. He, at least, had some recognition of what he was seeing; and more importantly, that there was some sort of relevance to himself. The guards called the infernal chambers "cow cages." Any bravery he may have had or will to resist evaporated in that primeval dungeon. He wished only to leave the place; everything else he might endure had to be an improvement. He had no capacity to resist people who were capable of such things.

Satisfied that the lesson was indelibly imprinted, the two guards herded the tremulous Viet Cong, former Viet Cong, back through the narrow mossy earthen corridor, and into the wonderfully capacious antechamber room where the GVN officer was patiently waiting. It seemed to Tran that he had been in that hellish room holding the 'cow cages' for just short of eternity. In fact, it had been less than seven minutes.

Without preamble, the officer spoke crisply to Tran, "I trust you will cooperate in your education here and elsewhere. You are an educated man; I am impressed with what I have learned from our rather exhaustive dossier on you. I will only tell you this one time: we do not tolerate enemies of the Republic of Viet Nam. Do not even contemplate escape. We have eyes and ears everywhere. We can read your mind, even the most carefully hidden thoughts."

The man said it in such a straightforward manner; and Tran was in such a reduced mental state, that the hapless prisoner accepted the complete dichotomy of their power versus his without the slightest demurrer. He was indelibly and unforgettably impressed that this man and his assistants (located everywhere) could see into the core of his soul, and Tran erased all attempts at contrary thought from his mind and psyche. He was a complete convert from that point on, ruled by a gut level fear that he would never quite lose for the rest of his life no matter how safe he might seem to be.

The officer made a dismissive gesture, and Tran half walked and was half dragged back out into the afternoon's moist air and furnace-like sun. Tran was dizzy and felt faint. He chanced a look at the earthen building, roofed and sided with grass and low shrubs. He would not have believed that it was actually a building at all if he had not seen its horrors for himself. Or had he? His ability to concentrate was sapped by hypoglycemia and dehydration from his hunger and thirst, from the heat and exhaustion, and from the myriad of pains in his cramped body. His head was still tethered to his waist, and now the terrible and frightening hood was being replaced. All was darkness and evil smell and fear again.

The two guards rapidly turned the disoriented prisoner around and around where he stood; so that he staggered when the three of them set off in some unknown direction at a fast trot. Tran reckoned he had stumbled, staggered, and forced his legs to traverse about two kilometers, all the time fighting off his greatest dread, that of passing out. In that event these mind devouring monsters would do anything they wanted to him. For some reason that he could not fathom, he still wanted to live. He clung to that fleeting thought as he finally lost consciousness on the trail despite his efforts.

When Tran opened his eyes, it was light—morning, to be exact. He could not understand what had happened to him. He shook out the mental cobwebs trying to recall the awful nightmare he had experienced. Why did everything look so unfamiliar? When he finally woke up completely, a rush of adrenaline cleared his brain; and stark reality flooded back. He was no longer bound, but his muscles were so stiff and sore that he could not have run if he had known where to run. He was alone in a windowless cement cell free of any kind of furniture or decoration. At least it was fairly clean and dry. Tran was naked. His first formed thought was one of profound embarrassment that someone had stripped him of his befouled clothing. Then he realized that he had no face to save at this juncture.

Tran was starving; his stomach growled embarrassingly. The miserable man smiled wanly at himself for worrying about such trivia as little social niceties. Before he could think more fully about his predicament, the cell door opened; and a guard motioned him to pick up his putrid clothing from where it was crammed into a corner of the cell and to exit the enclosure. Nothing was said. Tran joined several other naked people who had been formed into a single file, all carrying their own bundles as he was. In the distance he could see a fire, and still further on he could make out a series of low cinder block red tiled buildings with men dressed in jungle tan uniforms doing calisthenics on the grassy yard in front of the presumed barrack buildings.

The guards, armed with American M-16s, marched Tran's group to the fire and gestured an order to throw their old clothing into the flames. Tran felt a minor loss of something of himself as he did so, something akin to the feeling he might have had at the funeral of a rather distant female relative. He felt nothing for the fact that there were several young women following his example, mindlessly, wordlessly, and shamelessly.

The group then marched to a set of cinder-brick shower stalls, obviously of American manufacture, including the plumbing, because they were better than he had ever experienced. The plumbing even worked, and the soap was soft and caressing to his abraded skin. He shampooed his hair vigorously to rid himself of the feeling of being dirty. Like most of his countrymen, Tran was an assiduously clean person, sometimes showering or at least washing off his sweat three and four times a day. After washing, Tran felt immeasurably better. He was handed a light khaki blouse, matching tan trousers, and military webbed belt with an unmarked shiny brass clasp. The guard placed well-made rubber sandals, the ubiquitous footwear of the common people of his country, on top of the delightfully clean, starched uniform. Lest he wake up and find himself back in the trash bin on the helicopter, Tran hurriedly threw on the clothing. Had that trash bin experience been real? His guard laughed briefly at Tran's enthusiasm.

The troupe then entered one of the barracks buildings; each person was handed a plate, a real ceramic plate, chopsticks, and a plastic tumbler. They marched along a row of bright clean steel warming trays and were served rice, chunks of fish in a savory Chinese broth, and a bar of pressed fruits and nuts if Tran could judge by the smell of the nondescript food item. Each inductee filed to a table where he or she sat in a chair western style. Cartons of milk, marked USDA, an almost unheard of luxury in a country where children averaged two or three glasses of milk a year, were located at even intervals along the long tables. The famished prisoners gobbled their food with their fingers and cupped hands, abandoning the chopsticks as woefully inefficient in their haste. The faint possibility that these devils might be feeding him poison flashed through every prisoner's mind for an instant during the gastronomic orgy, but no one slowed down or ate the less for the thought. As if reading the unspoken thoughts of the seated prisoners, other prisoners, evidently trustees, brought steaming bowls of extra rice and fish and set them on the tables with wooden ladles as if they were ladies and gentlemen. Tran was more convinced than ever that his abductors and jailers could read his thoughts, and he was glad of it. Still no one had spoken.

As abruptly as it began, the meal was over. The guards motioned the prisoners back into their single file line, and the line double-timed out of the mess hall and along a line in front of the barracks buildings to a separate, more finished stone building facing the end of the last barracks. A pole flying the yellow and red flag of the Republic of Viet Nam stood in the yard in front of the building. The walkway was lined with immaculately whitewashed stones of remarkably similar size and round shape. A small banyan tree across the walkway to the right of the flagpole was ringed with similar impeccable white stones. A small flower garden in the center of the building yard, the walkways, and the open area of the yard itself were pristinely free of trash; not even a cigarette butt marred the sterility of the place.

The prisoners were trotted along a side path and into an auxiliary entrance that led directly into a clean and Spartan classroom. A ramrod stiff South Vietnamese military officer, obviously the instructor, stood expectantly at the front of the classroom and impassively watched as the prisoners filed into their seats before small American school type desk seats. Six guards, silently menacing the classmates with their M-16s, occupied prearranged positions around the room. The only incongruity in the entire scene was the presence of a calm faced Caucasian man, questionably American, questionably European, sitting in the right corner of the front of the room as the prisoners faced him. He was dressed in tropical white linens with a subdued flowered tie. He was not sweating. The only non utilitarian decoration in the room was a new Republic of Viet Nam flag, its ends festooned with brilliant gold tassels.

The instructor began to speak with an efficiency of communication that was devoid of personality, clearly a memorized text. To Tran it sounded much like the cadre addressing a mandatory party meeting of the Viet Cong unit in which he had served an eon ago (yesterday). He had been in that unit as a secure member of the Viet Cong Infrastructure twenty-four hours ago, had been in just such a meeting less than a week ago; he was aware of a mental blur regarding time, dates, incidents, and allegiances. His LAF allegiance seemed historical.

The slim officer first detailed the rules of the training camp, then the agenda indicating that there was no time to waste; so, the full instructional program, and physical and mental development program would start that very day and would occupy every waking moment of the next sixteen weeks.

Tran had a passing thought, just passing, that no one had asked him whether or not he had other plans for the next four months. He felt it important, for reasons he could not clearly describe; and no one thought it necessary to communicate, to pay very close attention. He was impressed that completing the proposed course of study at this school successfully was more important than any other school certification he had yet earned. He was dead sure about that.

The officer's crisp voice intoned the rules, each one twice. He said, "Listen carefully; there will be no repetition of these regulations so generously provided for you criminals in your reeducation program, except in the weekly tests. I will explain the curriculum shortly. The regulations for the class are simple:

1. Do not speak unless spoken to until I tell you that this rule has been relaxed.

2. Do not converse with any other student at any time inside the classroom or out unless I tell you that rule has been relaxed.

3. When called upon, you will respond promptly, fully, and altogether truthfully. Even the smallest falsehood will be subject to punishment.

4. You will not lie, or cheat, or steal, and you will not tolerate those who do. Report any infractions you see immediately. We have eyes and ears everywhere, as many of you are already aware. Serious punishments await anyone known to harbor knowledge of an infraction. That will constitute evidence of return to your communist ways and will go hard with you.

5. Throughout your stay here, you are never to speak, not even one word with any guard. Any requests are to be made to the officer of the day, in writing, and at the end of the day.

6. You will arise at 0500, shower and dress before 0545, be present in the mess hall no later than 0600, and you will eat every meal. You will be present in exercise clothing on the parade ground at 0645. Sundays you will return to your rooms to review your studies and to read prescribed literature. On all other days you will complete your exercises by 0745, shower, dress in the uniforms provided, and will be present in the classroom by 0800. Punctuality is an absolute. You will move at the double whenever you are out of the classroom.

7. You will then participate in the classroom for four hours followed by thirty minutes of team athletic activity, then a fifteen minute lunch. You will then participate in the class-room for four hours followed by another period of team athletics and an evening meal. You will return from the meal for a final three hours of instruction followed by a final hour of exercise. You will study in your rooms for two additional hours then the lamps will be extinguished."

The GVN officer read each rule clearly and with precise enunciation twice before proceeding to the next regulation on his printed list. Each inductee/student/kidnappee listened intently as if his or her life depended on perfect memorization. Only later would they realize exactly how accurate that first impression would prove to be.

The officer continued, "There will be a mandatory twice daily period for self-disclosure. You will be required to convey with absolute accuracy and detail your every activity while a member of the Viet Cong Infrastructure—your former criminal life. There will be no hesitations when you are called upon. Remember, we already know all about those filthy communist activities from your dark past, and the self-disclosure sessions will serve only as an opportunity for you to confess your wrongdoing and to help you rid yourself of wrong thinking."

There was a pause while the still frightened and straining prisoners were allowed to contemplate the power of an organization that could know all about their deepest secrets, often activities hidden even from their families.

His voice intruded on Tran's thoughts once again, "Unfortunately many of you will fail and will be taken from here to be jailed for a term appropriate to your crimes. Sentences have already been imposed, but each you will have a chance to prove yourself to be free of the communist ideology and past and to be loyal citizens, soldiers in the war against the vicious communist enemy that would rob our citizens of their freedom and their lives."

Aware of some uncomfortable fidgeting in the hard chairs, the officer took two steps forward and commanded in the bark of a parade ground military order, "Stand beside your desks!"

Like automatons, every man and woman stood with remarkable speed if not with true alacrity. "Run in place! Faster!"

He watched until he could see chests beginning to strain and could hear heavy breathing, "Sit down!" He commanded.

They sat.

"Your daily schedule of classes will be presented next. The agenda is printed in our language, and also in French and English. You will be given notebooks that will be examined for neatness, accuracy, and thoroughness at intervals. Do not neglect them," he paused long enough to let the implicit threat dangle before them. "During your stay here you will become proficient in physical skills, the English language, the history of our glorious country, and will learn of the great contributions made by our president. You will learn the errors of the theory of international communism and the great value of our Vietnamese Personalist democracy."

Tran had a sense of *déjà vu* (already seen)—this lecture was even following the format of Viet Cong cadre meetings. The named enemies and friends were different—reversed; but so far, the approach was unmistakably similar. As a teacher, Tran was interested in the teaching method, and was automatically drawn into the format as a student owing to the familiarity of the effective approach. As at Cong meetings, he knew better than to let his mind wander. The consequences of inattention had been grim then, and everything indicated that he could expect similar implacability from the government officials. He forced his weary mind to concentrate. He had a mental glimpse of that frightful prison. He had to concentrate.

"You will learn English because you will be working with our great friends and advisors, the Americans. You will learn Vietnamese military skills," Here he glanced at the impassive American to his left. "You will learn the essentials of modern police work and communications from our esteemed advisors."

Did Tran detect a trace of sarcasm? The turgid adjectives seemed excessive, even by Vietnamese standards, but it was best he not judge, nor clutter his mind with irrelevant conclusions. He concentrated.

The Vietnamese officer studied his watch, did some brief mental calculations, then continued, "All stand."

All stood.

"You will follow your guards to the dispensary where you will be examined. You will then be interrogated briefly. Return to the class room no later than ten hundred hours. Dismissed!"

Not forgetting a detail of their instructions, every prisoner moved out of the classroom double time without being commanded further. Tran submitted to the medical examination with all its pokings and probings impassively, even the rectal finger. After four minutes, he was pronounced healthy, pulled his clothes on as rapidly as possible, and trotted at the double in the line of prisoners to a separate wooden building, one of four, behind the barracks buildings. The buildings were small, like sheds, and accommodated four persons, one chair and one small desk.

Tran was slightly out of breath when he trotted into the room and stood before the desk. The officer, whom he had seen first in the grass-roofed antechamber to hell, was seated stiffly in the only chair, black American ball point pen poised over an American yellow legal pad.

"Nguyen Lui Tran, is that correct?" asked the officer in mildly accented American English.

"Yes, sir," Tran answered, annoyed at himself for the slight quaver in his voice

"Are you familiar with the polygraph?" Tran had a blank look.

"Have you heard of The Lie Detector, prisoner Nguyen?" he queried directly into Tran's eyes. Tran felt those shark eyes bore into his soul.

"I think so, yes, sir," he said.

"Before you graduate and are allowed to return to honest and productive work for the defense of your nation, you will undergo a lie detector or polygraph test which will inform us if you are telling even the slightest lie. Today you will answer truthfully in order to prepare yourself to undergo that test; you cannot lie then. Do not do so now."

"Yes, sir," Tran volunteered, to fill the uncomfortable silence.

"First question. When did you first become a criminal in the Viet Cong organization, in the VCI?"

Small shafts of fear shot through Tran's brain. If he admitted that he was VCI, would he die right here, right now? If he hesitated or lied, would they really know? In less than a second, he made an irrevocable decision, hoping against hope that this was not just a deception to trick him into admitting membership in the government forbidden organization. It was a simple, albeit charged question; and Tran was a simple, straightforward man. He replied, "I was seven. That would be . . ."

"1943, Mr. Nguyen," interrupted the officer, impressing his standing subject with the uncanny accuracy of information about what Tran had considered heretofore as a very personal secret. "Am I not correct?"

"I believe that is the correct year, yes sir."

"I know it is correct. The CT computer says it is correct. It also tells me that you and your family collaborated with the Japanese against the French." The GVN officer made the statement as a fact, and it was true. Tran had heard a little about computers, enough to know that it was a Western, probably American, invention that worked wonders with mathematics and memory. He was chilled by the realization of his vulnerability to the device.

"At our session tomorrow you will submit a list of names and addresses or whereabouts of every cadre with whom you have worked, every cadre you know about, and every person you have reason to suspect is VCI. Today it will be enough for you to tell me the identity of your immediate superior."

Tran was being asked to betray the organization to which he had pledged fealty, for which his family had given so much, in which he had believed unswervingly, and that he had served unquestioningly since his country's enemies were the French, well before Dien Bien Phu. He had not been tortured, not really. His mind and body were intact. He could still serve his VC unit as a martyr. As he held this series of thoughts for one second, there intruded into his mind the feeling of the trash bin lid crushing down on his cramped body; there wafted into his olfactory imagination the odor of the fetid garbage as real as if he were still in the claustrophobic can; and for the next second, he could see those wretches in the hole in the ground cell, reaching their decaying arms out to him. He trembled visibly.

Tran looked at his feet in the new rubber tire sandals ubiquitous to the peasantry and foot soldiers of Viet Nam. Before the third second elapsed, he blurted, "Mr. Nguyen," intoning up on the first syllable by way of identification. "The postman in our district," he included quickly. "I live...I lived in Saigon, third district," he added unnecessarily.

"Correct," said the officer.

Tran knew that his interrogator knew. It was that computer. How could the poverty ridden Vietnamese communists fight an enemy with such weapons? Imagine, a machine that could read one's mind and could know all about a man's secrets! Tran had just become a traitor. He had crossed that line with virtually no hesitation. He was surprised with himself. He was ready, almost eager, to confide more of his secrets. His skin was clammy with fear, and he was not even sure of what.

"That will be all. I will see you tomorrow at the same time. Take this chit to your instructor in the classroom, and he will excuse you at the appropriate time." The interrogator closed a cover over the yellow writing pad upon which he had been busy writing notes. He stood, indicating that the interrogation was over.

Tran followed his guards out of the small building in a sort of depersonalized state. He had undergone a truly profound change, had betrayed his party and the cadres who trusted him; and the entire process had taken less than three minutes.

Tran's attention was shifted to a six by six meter clearing behind the three small buildings where he heard sounds of scuffling, and he thought he heard a muffled sob. Two guards each held a prisoner by the arms. One was an elder, a man in his seventies, by Tran's guess; and the other was a terrified girl, no more than twenty, if that. It was the girl who was struggling and sobbing and pleading. An officer walked from one of the other two small interrogation buildings and purposefully strode up to the girl. He grasped her slight arm, withdrew his American .45 caliber officer's handgun from the polished leather hip holster of his Sam Browne belt, extended his arm, holding the gun until it was fully outstretched with the opening of the barrel resting on the crying girl's head at a point just above and behind her right ear. He shifted his body so the gun pointed away from the guards holding her arms and without ceremony, fired once. The back of the pretty little head with its long black hair disappeared in a puff of bone fragments, gouts of blood and brain, and a patch of skin the size of a man's palm. The officer then walked to the elder and dispatched him in an altogether similar fashion with less reaction than if he had swatted an insect. Both people were dead but remained upright, held by the strong arms of the guards. Their bodies were whisked away as if they were felled tree limbs. Neither body touched the ground.

The efficiency with which the bodies were removed indicated to Tran that this was probably not the first time an uncooperative Viet Cong had been summarily accused, tried, convicted, sentenced, and the sentence carried out by these remarkably efficient people. Just before he bent over to vomit, Tran noticed ten or twelve other prisoners who stood looking at the clearing. Presumably, the point of the lesson was not lost on them either.

There were two empty seats in the classroom that day. The following day they were filled with two rather wan and frightened appearing new arrivals. The interrogators' excuse chits regularly summoned one prisoner or another from the classroom for brief absences. There were no more scuffles, gun shots, or even expressions of fear. The lessons were being absorbed with gratifying eagerness by their pupils, observed the guards and instructors to one another, including the occasional American civilian who made a temporary visit to their training center.

Tran adjusted to the routine, even coming to feel comfortable, as he toughened mentally and physically from the exhausting schedule. There was no time to ruminate for any length of time on his own history and life's direction before his kidnapping, or even to think of the events leading up to his recruitment. He was too tired most of time to care particularly. It was enough to remain alert in the classes, to perform the requisite number of push-ups, pull-ups, and rope climbs, and to run the grueling ten mile course through the jungle paths every day. It was all his mind could do to garner enough knowledge to pass the critical weekly tests. Each week one or two students failed to return to their seats.

When they were finally allowed to speak to one another in controlled areas of the parade yard after six weeks, the observation by some of the prisoner/students to the others was that the missing students had been seen dressed in black peasant pajamas trotting along behind guards, their hands bound behind their backs and their necks noosed into a severe forward flexion position. They left in the direction of the helipad. It was assumed that the failing students were on their way to some internment camp for recalcitrant VCI.

"I think they dump them in the ocean," said one fearfully.

"I have, myself, seen the places where they keep the prisoners, the comrades who have committed the worst crimes or who will not enter into the *Chieu Hoi* program as we have. They are called 'tiger cages,' fit only for holding wild beasts. When I was first here, I was assigned to drop food to the people. The cages were in pits in the ground with bars and an overhead walkway. The prisoners were most piteous—starved, beaten, some with mutilations, all with sores. They cry all the time, beg for mercy. If they get too loud, one of the guards drops a bucket of quicklime down on them.

"One day some American government people from their city called Washington came and argued with the camp commandant. They forced the commandant to take the American government people to see the cages. Those people became sick at what they saw. I was right there and saw these things with my own eyes. The round eyes shouted at the commandant, and he promised to get rid of the cages. When the Americans left, the commandant and his aides just laughed and said it was a big joke that the gullible Americans had not seen the 'cow cages.'"

From the talk, the men learned that the island on which they now lived, located 75 miles off the southeast coast of Camau Peninsula in the South China Sea, was fortified by the French in 1861 to be a prison for insurgents captured by their Chinese Nung and Filipino mercenaries and had served an infamous role for all succeeding ruling cliques because of its obscure location and its insulation from enemy attack. The mere mention of the name of the island, Poulo Condore, was enough to strike terror in the hearts of the populace of the three provinces around Saigon. Every family knew of someone who had been sent to the prison for one charge of antigovernment activity or another over the decades and had never been seen nor heard of again.

Such talk made Nguyen Lui Tran very uncomfortable. It brought back memories of what he had seen, for one thing; and it made him afraid that he would be arrested for sedition if he was thought to be part of such a conversation, for another. More than anything ever before in his life, he feared being locked away in one of those cow cages. He was dedicated to avoiding such a fate, and had no trouble admitting that fear ruled him.

The routine in the classroom included purposefully repetitious lectures on the history of Viet Nam and on the evils of communism that had led to the partition of the country. The students learned of the severe struggles and heroic successes of the Republic of Vietnam's present and past leaders. Explicitly, and implicitly they learned that their loyalty belonged to these people and to no one else, except, of course, to the American advisors who were such staunch allies and friends of the valiant Vietnamese people and their democratic and nationalist aspirations. The format was patterned transparently after the successful methods of the Viet Cong, but that soon became an irrelevant observation. What had started out for the prisoners to be abject fear and subjection was followed by wonderment and awe, and now was steadily evolving into real conversion. These cadres were becoming convinced South Vietnamese patriots; some, like Tran, who saw nothing of his old life to return to now, were zealots by the ninth week.

The political correction classes continued from start to finish, but they lost their harsh and chauvinistic edge shortly after the halfway point in the intensive indoctrination course. The sessions came to be more nostalgic, even romanticizing the virtues and heroes of their collective past. The former dissidents and fighters became patriots, at least they did for all appearances. The fact that they were better fed, cleaner, and even freer in some aspects than many of their former NLF comrades eased the transition. For Tran, the memory of the garbage bin and the hidden cells mounted a formidable mental barrier against thoughts of sedition, resistance, or escape. The final seven weeks of study, including their well planned physical conditioning, concentrated on specific techniques of silent jungle warfare, demolition, weapons of both sides, interrogation techniques, psychological warfare and propaganda, and police detention and transfer procedures.

These men and women, former criminal VCI or common criminals, were in training to be police officers in the Revolutionary Development counter terrorist program, specifically for the province to which they were assigned. The training which took them from rebellious saboteur and assassin to orthodox police zealot was the end result of a carefully planned, studied, altered, and improved program that utilized the best information and most successful practical techniques from the national police, the RVN military, American civilian advisors, American military (MACV), and not least, the Viet Cong.

The program was an ambitious consequence of American desire to control the information gathering and VCI interdiction aspects of the Indochina struggle against communism. The intelligence services of the US saw the long term picture as one of temporarily controlling all aspects of the counter terrorism program before handing the finished product over to the well indoctrinated and trained Vietnamese national authorities and the South Vietnamese Infrastructure. The murky guiding hand of the American Central Intelligence Agency was immediately behind or nearby every precept, action, and dollar; and the South Vietnamese Infrastructure did not seem to keep pace.

The former VCIs, now about to graduate as paramilitary police officers, the leadership cadres, were so zealous in their conversions they demanded of each other, even women, that an identifying tattoo be imprinted on each of their chests to help them to know their fellows; and, not incidentally, to discourage with finality, defections back to the Viet Cong. They selected a clear set of Vietnamese characters to be emblazoned on their chests, one word over each pectoral muscle. The English transliteration read, "Sat Cong" (Kill Cong)

During the last week of indoctrination of Tran's group of inductees, the American civilian advisor who visited the island periodically, smiled at his superior, Lane Duerk, back in Saigon when he reported the finesse of that touch. "The former VCI have come to accept the idea as having originated with their class, their people," he informed the Saigon chief of station.

"Adds to the plausibility of denial by The Company," said the superior, the Saigon CIA station chief. "The whole business looks like it belongs to the Viets; and the more it does, the more I like it. We will deny all knowledge of Con Son Island Prison except that it is one of GVN's. You will pass that on to the our people—we never heard of a 'tiger cage' or a 'cow cage.' The little brown men can take the credit, and they can answer to the folks from Geneva when they come around."

Tran passed all his tests including the polygraph; only 82% of the prisoner/students did. He was indelibly imprinted with the ferocious guiding sentiment of the program he had come to know by both its Vietnamese name, *Biet Kich* (commando team) and by the CIA American terms, The CT (counter terrorist) or SOG/RDC (Studies and Observation Group or Special Operations Group/Revolutionary Development Cadre). Tran was proud of the *Sat Cong* tattoo. He was well-trained by Vietnamese standards and ready for his assignment to Eye (I) Corps, Thau Thien Province, as a sergeant in the Provincial Reconnaissance Unit (PRU), the action arm of the Revolutionary Development program. He remembered his lessons about security learned first from the paranoid Viet Cong cadres, took to heart the lifesaving information he so studiously gleaned from his studies on Con Son Island, and could never forget the bonded imprint on his soul of the vision of the wraiths in the hidden cells, or his own recollection of the smell of the garbage bin.

CHAPTER 3

Only those who decide policy and military operations need have correct views…Only the government, the military chiefs, and their technical staffs need know the facts; among all others, blind confidence and blind obedience are what is most to be desired.
Bertrand Russell, Power, 1921

Karl Issacson's personnel file was detailed from the time he left his home town until the present—mid boot camp. He was a good soldier; more, he was a real achiever. The CIA assistant moved through the voluminous report as quickly as he could:

Karl took the lonely Greyhound bus from the small town of Zarahemla to the big city armory courtesy of the faceless friends and neighbors on the Selective Service Board of Sundial County. He was government issue from the time he took his seat on the Greyhound. The day was very hot; the bus had no air conditioning; and the windows did not open. When the bus pulled up to the shelter across the street from the armory, it passed through Karl's mind to stay aboard and keep on going despite the bake oven character of the interior of the bus. "Who would know or care?" he thought.

He did not, though. He got out and started across the street toward the dozens of other young men clustered in front of the main door, waiting for the time of their pre-induction physical examination appointments. There would be some three hundred of them that day. There was a good deal of grousing going on, even from the college boys who had deferments. Karl felt like asking them why they thought they had it so bad, but he kept to himself.

"You can get outta this," said one farm boy to another as the doors swung open at the appointed hour. "Just let them know that you are fag, a queer boy."

"I got a heart murmur," said another to no one in particular. "That makes you 4-F, don't it?"

Karl half hoped they'd find some obscure malady that would keep him out, as did about three-fourths of the rest of the young men shuffling about in the line. No one tried to get in at the head of the column. He did not want cancer or a heart attack or anything like that; maybe flat feet, or some obscure thing wrong with his eyes that only the doctor could see. Sometimes they did that, he knew.

He walked through the doors under the large brass letters, "Utah National Guard Armory" under which was a less permanent printed sign that read, "Armed Forces Induction Center." In the short entry hall, there were pictures of President Johnson on one wall and General Hershey on the other.

"Form up!" yelled the sergeant in charge of the exams. "Four rows!" The noise was terrific in the room, and the man had to keep yelling over and over. The inductees seemed to find it difficult to understand the simple commands to the mounting frustration of the sergeant.

Finally, the three hundred men were in some semblance of order. "Put your papers on the floor in front of you," the sergeant shouted when at last the room was quiet. The examinees seemed to be able to handle that. "Now, strip. Everything." There was a general rustle and fumbling. Many of the boys were rural and shy. Many had never had their clothing off in front of another person since infancy. The reticence was maddening to the sergeant who had a schedule to keep.

"Move it! Move it! Move it!" he yelled. There was somewhat more activity. Finally, there were three hundred plus naked men standing exposed. Some shyly held their hands in front of their private parts.

Doctors and corpsmen walked up and down the rows of men poking, probing, and shining lights into hidden recesses until any last vestiges of modesty were erased. The men ran in place to have their heart sounds emphasized and the light sweating of more than three hundred men added a faintly nauseating odor to the already stale air of the large room. Here and there a man would be told, and all of his fellows would hear, "Hypertensive," "Hernia," or "Heart murmur," or "Retardo." "Give him a 4-F and get him outta here."

The doctor who examined Karl's row, a short, pudgy, soft handed Slavic man, stood before Karl and looked up at his face a foot and a half higher than his own. "This is a big one. He's goin' ta like the army better'n eatin' hay and pullin' a plow like he's been used to doin.'"

The boy next to Karl was soft and round and of delicate temperament. He was fat with rolls of adipose skin on his chest and abdomen. The doctor made sure that everyone in the place heard him, "Look at those boobs. Make a good girl." The corpsmen and the men in the hot room had a good laugh at the mortified boy's expense.

The doctor checked the boy for hernias and undescended testes. The pudgy fellow's development was almost infantile, small genitalia and scanty pubic hair. "You some kind of queer-boy?" the doctor inquired in a Stentorian delivery of the question.

The boy looked over at Karl with stricken eyes. The only other time Karl had seen such a look was when a pig was being slaughtered. The boy glanced sheepishly back at the doctor. He suddenly unnerved everyone in the place by starting to scream and tear at his hair. The doctor and the corpsman retreated as if they had been struck. The boy then whirled about and ran for the door stark naked, displaying surprising strength and speed for all of his fat and effeminacy.

"Jeez!" said the doctor. "Latent homosexual psychotic break. I heard about that on psych, but would never have thought it would be so dramatic. Did you see that, Taylor?" The corpsman nodded his head. It was weird, sort of eerie. It took a while for everyone to calm down.

Karl took his turn in a small room alone with two corpsmen for the hearing test. He was still naked. "Can you see that eye chart on the wall?" The lead corpsman asked in his overwhelmingly bored voice. Karl was the one hundred ninety-second examinee that morning.

"Yes, sir," Karl said. He looked down the Snellen chart to find the lowest line of numbers and letters he could read.

One of the corpsmen laughed to the other and said, "Hearing okay; vision okay."

Just for the record, Karl read the last line perfectly for the corpsmen; the 20/15 visual acuity level.

The next man in was asked the same question, "Can you see that chart on the wall?"

"What wall?" came the reply.

"Very funny; Hearing okay, vision okay. Next."

Karl next spent fifteen minutes with one of the doctors, a draftee who obviously did not want to be there, taking down his unexciting medical history. He moved on to the shrink. "Do you masturbate? Do you like boys better than girls? Do you think about killing yourself? Do you like to kill little animals like cats and puppies? and a host of other perfectly silly questions so far as Karl could tell.

Karl's papers from the anonymous friends and neighbors of the draft board in Zarahemla, his questionnaire and medical history, and the document he signed committing him to enlist if he passed the induction physical were all placed in a sturdy brown manila folder, his 201 file. He and the national guardsmen who were unfortunate enough to have their unit called up for active duty, one hundred fifty of them, were instructed to dress and stand on the north side of the room. The 4-Fs and the college boys were sent home until the next time they were called in for a pre-induction physical.

The men with Karl were a sober lot. Their hopes of being found to have a disqualifying defect of some sort were dashed. They had all been told before coming to the armory for their exam that they should be prepared to leave for Fort Lewis, Washington that very day if they were found to be acceptable.

"Repeat after me," the sergeant ordered. "I solemnly swear."

"I solemnly swear," they chorused.

"I will defend the Constitution of the United States against all enemies."

The men repeated the sergeant's recitation, some of them stumbling over the multi-syllabic words.

"Foreign and domestic, and I will obey the orders of the officers and noncommissioned officers appointed over me."

They repeated the commitment, realizing that they were getting themselves in deep now.

"You girls are in the army now. You belong body and soul to Uncle Sam. You will do what you are told, when you are told—no more, no less. Go get on the bus," the sergeant barked. His voice had changed from that time long ago when they had been civilians.

The bus let the men off at the Fort Lewis Reception Center. An NCO yelled at them to form a single line, yelled at them not to talk, yelled at them to run double time into the building. They were taken into a large men's lavatory and ordered to empty their pockets on the shelf before them. "Listen up, maggots! Everything out on the table in front of you. Move it!"

Wallets, keys, pictures, pocket knives, crucifixes, coins—all on the shelves. "Dump them in the plastic bag in front of you! Move it!" The sergeant was shouting for some reason as if a spoken voice could not be heard in that cramped tiled room.

"Now all your jewelry, girls. All of it!" The NCO yelled.

Rings, watches, neck chains, religious images and medallions—all onto the shelf and into the plastic bag. They were removed of the last vestiges of themselves as civilians. The young men were cowed and silent.

They moved at the double with another contingent of men who were rushed out of another lavatory to the barber shop where there were ten stools and ten military barbers waiting, the oldest of which was nineteen. There were thirty-two men to a barber. Each man was required to have two dollars in hand to pay for his haircut. Each man was asked which of the four kinds of available haircut styles he desired and was allowed to make his choice. In ten minutes all three hundred nineteen new recruits sported identical GI haircuts and a few nicked scalps. The men were covered with their own hair and brushed off as fast as they could when they heard, "Follow me!" from the yelling noncom. He ran the men into the supply center where they were issued olive drab fatigue uniforms, skivvies, and tee shirts, socks and combat boots, a shoe shine kit, web belt, and a manual of rules and regulations.

They were hurried into their new clothes; Karl's were too small, but he struggled into them anyway; then, a commissioned officer read the puffing and sweating men the Articles of War, and the Rules of Engagement for the 'police action' in the Republic of Viet Nam.

At Headquarters Company each man was assigned a unit and given his army serial number. Karl was in Alpha Company, Fifth Battalion, Third Training Brigade. His serial number was RA-E-1990923.

Next they were herded into the dispensary, forming two lines. "Hold your tee shirt sleeves up," ordered an E-4 corpsman. "Hold your arms across your chest." The men then marched a gauntlet between four corpsmen and women who sloshed their arms with iodine and jabbed them with inoculation needles. Fourteen men fainted and were dragged off to recuperate.

From the moment Karl and the other inductees stepped foot on the US government property at Fort Lewis, he learned that all of them were the same. They all received the same whacks on the sides of their heads and were all treated as if they were deaf. They even had the same names, apparently. Either 'turd' or 'maggot.' After a series of brief interviews and aptitude tests with sergeants representing the various different army agencies, all but a handful of them were rated 'Military Occupational Specialty—745, Light Weapons Infantryman,' or, in army parlance, a 'leg.'

Fort Lewis is located in beautiful, forested country. The hills are deep evergreen, and it is often cold, wet, and drizzly. As his new 'home,' along with 110 other men in his company, Karl was assigned to an old WW II barracks, last used in the Korean 'Police Action.' There were fifty-five to a floor in double-bunks, two floors in the barracks. He was placed in a squad of ten men with whom he would spend the entire eight weeks of boot camp. There were four squads to a platoon; the platoon gave Karl his official army name.

"Seven Eighty Second," shouted Cletus Washington Lee, the absolute spit and polish, nasty tempered, drill instructor. "That is yoah name, boah. Never fo-get it. When ah axe yoah name, y'all tell me '7-8-2.' That cleah, turd?"

"Sir, yes sir!" shouted the new man, "7-8-2."

"Ah am only goin' ta tell y'all this one time, maggot. Y'all do not refer to enlisted men as 'sir.' Not evah. A sergeant is a man who works for a livin,' a man of respect. Y'all will address everah such NCO as 'sergeant,' nevah 'sir.' Am Ah making mahsef puhfectly cleah, Recruit 7-8-2? And put your hand down. Y'all do not salute sergeants, you hopeless enlisted swine."

"Yes sir, I mean Sergeant!"

"Drop down and give me fifty!"

The first night in Fort Lewis was a nervous and homesick one for a great many of the new men. They were learning to spit and curse, to put up a macho front. Most of them were Mormons used to saying their nightly prayers; but given the circumstances, that religious practice was suspended for the duration to avoid the accusation of being a sissy. It only took a few minutes in camp to ascertain that being different was a detriment, and the men strove not to stand out. The first night required a certain amount of learning to be wary.

The barracks, located on the north forty of Fort Lewis, was heated by a coal burning central stove. Wrap around metal piping served to heat the shower water for the men. When it was cold, as it was that first night, the stove was stoked up to red hot, and the water was heated until what flowed out was live steam. It came under such high pressure that the toilets flushed steam. The young inductees learned very quickly to reach a long arm in to turn on the shower, and to stand well away from the commode when flushing it.

On day one Karl learned how to brush his teeth, how to wash his behind, and how to wash out his clothes by hand. The clothes, even his socks and skivvies, were marked with his initials with an indelible pen, washed out in huge tubs and hung on a line with those of the rest of his platoon. Heaven help the maggot who lost his clothes. He was taught to roll his clothes up in a tight roll so that his initials showed, and to tie the roll up with string for placement in his duffel bag. Next came the critical lesson on shining boots, easily the most important task assigned to the new recruit, if the amount of emphasis placed on it by the DIs was any indicator. Karl had to be taught how to spit properly (the army way) to do the job right. No detail was left to chance.

Having mastered tooth brushing, spitting, and boot blacking, the recruits moved on to the next greatest skill for enlisted men to achieve—marching. They marched, seemingly endlessly, around the 'grinder,' the long cement parade promenade. They marched together for any and everything they needed to do, and everything they needed to do was always on the opposite end of the base from where they were at the moment. The shortest man in the company was selected to stand at the front of the column and to set the pace, i.e. the army marched only as fast as its slowest man.

If a recruit found it difficult to march in perfect unison with his fellows, or giggled, or in some other way demonstrated an adolescent level of emotional development or had unclean boots, he would be obliged to run circles around the platoon as it marched. More serious violations of good order merited both K-P and the running punishment. These included the unpardonable sins of not giving marching its due gravity. There were those who, instead of marching with the prescribed nine inch forward and back precise arm swing, were seen to swing both arms forward at the same time, or only to swing one arm, or to catch the heel of the man in front of them, or to do a quick step switch of right and left feet to throw off their marching companions.

Drill Instructor Cletus Washington Lee explained the simple and time honored rules of the military to his platoon in language a four year old could grasp. "If it moves paint it. If it doesn't move, sweep it up. If it's too big to sweep up, pick it up. If it's too big to pick up, paint it. Am Ah makin' masef cleah, gulls?"

"Sergeant, yes Sergeant!"

A slender Mexican-American named Don Jose Miguel Sanchez-de Castro leaned over to Karl and whispered, "I heard it goes, 'salute everything that moves, paint everything that doesn't, and never, never volunteer.' That keeps you out of real trouble."

Karl and the newly developed buddy in his squad, the wiry Mexican mestizo from Guadalajara and San Diego, earned the opportunity to circumnavigate their platoon for two days straight after demonstrating their adolescent retardation to, of all people, Captain Spencer Longran, the company commander. Karl and Miguel were assigned to cleanup duty in the motor pool. They listened to the banter and good humored prankishness of the regular enlisted men working in the garage and picked up on their unorthodox routines. The men, feeling secure in their anonymity, answered the telephone with such openings as, "Sherwood Forest, Robin Hood speakin'" or "Devil speakin,' who in hell do you want?" or simply, "Mabel's;" and Karl and Miguel adopted the role of humorists when they, too, picked up the phone when the regulars were busy.

It was Karl who actually answered the line when Captain Longran, a man of no humor, called to complain about the condition of his staff jeep when it had come back from the motor pool, having been kept there a day longer than promised.

The phone rang twice. Karl lifted the receiver, and in rapid, breathless voice rattled off, "This is the thirty-seven fiftieth motor vehicle squadron; you call; we haul. We got two byes, four byes, six byes, eight byes, ten byes, fork lifts, cleat tracks, trailers, tugs, jeeps, motorcycles, staff cars, pickup trucks, dump trucks, and 'dat big long job which go, 'Cshish Cschish, when you hit 'dem brakes. Whatta you need, boy?"

The frost came over the telephone wires. "Give me your name and unit number, private. Now!" Captain Longran was angry and meant to have this foolishness at the motor pool eradicated immediately and the man now conveying the unmilitary foolishness to be made into an example. Karl hung up, and found work in the bowels of the motor pool, well away from the phone desk.

When Captain Longran arrived and demanded that the master sergeant in operational charge of the garage produce the culprit, it took the man less than five minutes to produce two scapegoats. Knowing that it could not be one of his regular men; they were too professional for that; the master sergeant produced Karl and Miguel, the low men on the totem pole, mere boots. Neither man admitted anything. Both received the company punishment of running around the platoon for two days.

Karl learned what it was to be a 'grunt.' The lowliest of the military pecking order were so-called because they had to grunt with the weight of all of their gear. In boot camp, they had to carry it around at the double for the most part. Even his clothing was heavy and retained water from the Washington drizzle making it all the heavier. His combat boots were made of heavy leather and nylon; he had baggy trousers with multiple pockets; and whether it was hot or cold, the uniform shirt was long-sleeved and thick. He was obligated to wear a bullet protector flak vest jacket made of laminated layers of nylon and fiberglass. It added more than ten pounds to the ensemble. On his head he wore a 'steel-pot' helmet covered with canvas that was uncomfortable at best and, at worst, in the sun, baked his brains.

If he were lucky, he would carry a fourteen pound M-14 rifle; if not, he might be saddled with a twenty-three pound M-60, the light machine gun. He carried a pack filled with rope, collapsible shovel, a rubberized poncho, extra socks and underwear, GI food (to use the term loosely), a machete, flares, a rifle cleaning kit, and a few army issued personal hygiene items. He had to wear a standard web belt with two canteens full of water, grenades, a combat knife, ammunition pouches, and a first aid kit. Karl was a big strong boy, and he grunted under the weight and cursed the army like everybody else.

He determined that he did not want to be a grunt his whole military career. He quickly learned that if he did not excel, he would be relegated to a permanent 'leg' designation. He would be an 'Unlucky CS,' a ground pounder 1369. He endeavored to avoid that fate at all costs. He bought extra uniforms and boots that he kept stiffly pressed and mirror polished for inspections. He ran harder, climbed higher, and did more push-ups than anyone else in his squad. He made it a point to come to the attention of Sergeant Lee. Sometimes that was good, and there was no comment from the taciturn black man; and sometimes it was bad; and he got more K-P, latrine scrubbing detail, assignments to paint rocks or to line them up, and push-ups. Karl's biggest fault, as pointed out frequently by the DI, was that he looked his superior in the eye without blinking or looking away. "Ah look at y'all," Sergeant Lee said on those occasions. "Y'all look at me when Ah tell y'all, maggot. Got that?!"

"Sir, yes sir!" Karl replied in proper cadence and amplitude but without looking away, forgetting Sergeant Lee's antipathy to the word 'sir.'

And Sergeant Lee would always say, "Don't y'all 'suh' me. Ah am a workin' man, a sergeant. Ah y'all retarded? Why cain't ya remember such a simple thing?! It's simple! Them 'sirs' sits on theah cans all day. Y'all will treat me with the respect ah deserve. Call me 'sergeant.' Y'all heah me, maggot? Now get down and give me fifty!"

In some sort of unspoken communication, Karl learned that the DI liked him to stare him down and not to flinch or give up, despite all the shouted demands and punishments to the contrary. It seemed to Karl that his bunk was always sloppily made; and he had to remake it six times a day when the sergeant tore loose the covers, that his boots were always filthy even if he could have shaved in the mirror finish on their toes; and that his button holes or his cuffs were frayed and his blouse and trouser creases were limp. He did not protest at the abuse, day in and day out. Beneath the rigid and unfeeling exterior, Karl thought he caught an extra interest in himself by the DI. It got to be that Karl would think if Sergeant Lee missed an opportunity to whack his head or punch him in the arm or stomach, the sergeant did not love him anymore. Instead of hating the man, and wanting to punch him out, Karl worked at making himself the best soldier he could be, and thereby earning the drill sergeant's grudging respect. Every now and again, he thought he caught a glimpse of a slight thaw in Sergeant Lee's demeanor toward him.

He remained Recruit Maggot, or Recruit Turd, or simply 7-8-2 for all his efforts, just like everybody else. That was the one thing Karl liked about boot camp, about the army. Everybody was treated rottenly, but they all received the same despicable treatment. There were black, brown, white, and yellow men in his platoon; they were all abused alike. Black men were as good as white; Swedes would have been as bad as Danes if there had been any Danes. For the first time in his life, Karl felt himself to be on an even footing with all of the other men. Here, if he applied himself and merited it, he could expect to excel. Perhaps it was worth all of the grief.

The first physical test took place at the end of the first week of boot camp when it was felt that the morons, maggots, and turds had mastered personal hygiene and walking. They marched to the base pool, all 110 men in his company, and were issued swim suits. Karl's was too small and it outlined his parts which embarrassed him and drew good natured finger pointing and mock appreciative hoots from the guys in his squad.

"Line up at the deep end all you maggots!" yelled the base senior master sergeant. "This is the swim test. You will swim the length of the pool under supervision. If you cannot swim the length of this pool, you will take swim lessons in addition to your regular training schedule until you can swim the length of the pool. Is that understood?" The question was evidently rhetorical because the senior master sergeant did not look about nor wait for any questioners.

The DIs took up stations around the edges and ends of the pools. The battalion was lined up four abreast across the deep end and driven into the water at two second intervals. Men splashed, floundered, and fought the water. If a man could not make it and kept going under, the DIs fished him out with a bamboo pole, informed him that he was a turd, a maggot, and a moron and would have to take swimming lessons. Most of the men made it by main strength and awkwardness; a few were actually able to swim fairly smoothly through the water roiling with flailing disparate bodies; and Karl was able to move through quickly and with relative ease owing to his size and strength and that he had been able to learn to swim in the summer Red Cross program in Zarahemla.

The second test took place at the end of the second week of training. Karl and his platoon were given an hour's instruction in the function and use of gas masks and the deadly characteristics of military gas. The test consisted of being shut up in a room with masks attached to their belts, then unexpectedly, tear gas was released into the room. The recruits had to don their masks in time to save their eyes and respiratory tracts. A few, thereafter referred to as 'morons,' panicked and had to repeat the exercise several more times until they could do it. A couple of men freaked out and were unable to do it at all. They had not been standing up to the pressures of the physical and mental abuse to that point in time and were sent home. The rest of the men went around for days with red eyes and runny noses as the tear gas retained in their clothing leeched out and wafted upwards into their tender membranes.

The first four weeks of boot camp at Fort Lewis hardened Karl physically and mentally. He was homesick to start with, but soon recognized that he was more at home here than he had been in his foster homes or with the boys of his home town. He developed a grudging and unadmitted respect for the drill sergeant. Despite his harshness and unrelenting pressure, Cletus Lee was scrupulously fair. It took some time to realize it, but Karl recognized in the man someone genuinely concerned about the welfare of his charges and who took his responsibility to train men to survive in combat as a serious, personal, and professional obligation.

The routine included endless all night fire watches to make sure there were no fires from the old barracks boiler. The man on watch had to wear a special helmet and carry a baton for a night of endless marching through the barracks. Karl, like his platoon mates, pulled guard duty in the parking lots and the motor pool. The sergeants took malicious pleasure in throwing rocks, honking horns, and yelling to make it necessary for the man on guard to investigate; so, he could have no peace. Ten times a night, the guard would have to go through the challenges, "Halt. Who goes there? Friend or foe?"

"Friend," came the repetitious and obvious reply.

"Give me the password."

"You know who I am, you little maggot. Let me pass."

"Not without the password."

"Listen, maggot, how would you like to spend the week cleaning the latrines?" (Not rest room. There are no rest rooms in the army; Karl learned that on his first day when he was prevented from urinating because he did not know the proper nomenclature.)

If the fool recruit gave in and let the harassing DI pass, he went up on company charges. It took Karl only once to learn the lesson.

Their days were spent out on bivouac with three or four battalions force marching. The better performing men were rewarded by being placed in the front where they could walk and rest at times. The less capable were punished by having to stay in the rear and having to run all of the time. When the rear guard ran up to where the front men were resting, they were grilled about their names.

"Spell it, maggot." Recruit Maggot would spell his name.

"Spell it backward and be quick about it." Some Recruits Maggot could do that.

"Spell it phonetically." The few maggots who knew what 'phonetically' was and could spell their names in the weird way were subjected to another demand, "Spell it phonetically backward."

If somehow the recruit mastered all of that, he was required to repeat the entire process while doing push-ups. In the end of the exercise, all of the rear guard runners returned to their exhausting and ignominious drudgery of running while the front men got an occasional breather. It was a clear incentive to shape up. Karl figured that out the first day. He was in marathon runner shape by the time four weeks had passed. The cadres (sergeants) had no packs. Grunts (maggots and turds) carried full packs and sleeping bags.

At the bivouac site the Maggots and Turds set up camp with military precision and policed the area until it was free of the slightest hint of debris or disorder. Then the lead sergeant shouted, "Move it!" and they would transfer to another site and start all over again. This happened three and four times a night until the cadres got tired of it.

Mostly, they slept huddled in their ponchos against the drizzling rain. Karl learned to carry his poncho rolled on his web belt with blousing bands—the rubber bands used to 'blouse' out his pant leg bottoms—to save room in his pack, and so it would be readily available. They awakened as they had gone to sleep, wet, most days. In the morning, the men shaved, using cold water in their steel pots. Any man found to have remaining straggler face hairs or skin nicks would be 'put down'—forced to crawl through mud frequently with the DI's foot on the back of his steel pot to push his face into the slime. Then they ate with rain running into the imitation scrambled eggs or creamed chipped beef on toast (shit on a shingle) that was thrown onto their mess kits. Then they dipped their kits and cups in the large garbage cans filled with soap then into the water heated by an immersion heater to boiling to rinse.

> "Ain't no use in goin' home,
> Jody's got your girl an' gone.
> Sound-off, one-two."

They sang in cadence as they trotted along. "Up the hill, over the hill, airborne ranger . . ." and "She wore a yellow ribbon" were other fit marching songs for running in the fields or for running the ladders or in the leg withering sand pits.

The day started with reveille at 0500 (except on K-P days when it was 0400) and ended with taps at 2200 or 2400 every night. When they were not running in formation, they were being transported to such things as hygiene lectures in the company building—lectures and films on condoms, the evils of syphilis and gonorrhea, how to brush one's teeth, or to church on Sunday. Karl learned the necessity of going to church regularly. Failure to attend services resulted in automatic extra duty. They were transported in buses (really semitrailer trucks with long flat beds, open sides and tops that were fitted with rows of seats) known affectionately as 'cattle cars.' The heat and humanity were soporific. The men were so crammed in that they couldn't fall over; so, they took the rides as rare opportunities to catch some sleep.

When Karl and his squad and platoon were not running or shivering in the rain, or riding in the miserable cattle cars, they were at the firing range or cleaning their rifles. Each day the recruits picked up their M-14s from the armorer. In his unit, each man was assigned a weapon's card that corresponded to the rack site where the gun was stored. The card had the man's name and serial number, the weapon's nomenclature, and serial number. The card was presented to the armorer sergeant who made the recruit recite the weapon's serial number without looking at the card before handing out the gun. At the end of each firing session, the entire battalion lined up to clean their guns in the 55 gallon drums half full of solvent. Each man was required to take his gun apart piece by piece, immerse the receiver and barrel in the solvent, then wait in another line to get the cloths and brushes to clean the parts.

"Not good enough, Turd," Cletus Lee delighted in telling Karl about half of the days. "Do it again." That shot all his free time.

The rest of his free time, it seemed to Karl, was spent on K-P. His usual offense, like that of most of the better men in his platoon, was to fail on a detail. The most common offense for Karl came from the forgetfulness he suffered related to his chronic exhaustion. Combat boots came in two styles. The only difference between the styles was that one pair had white dots on the back of the boots and the other did not.

"White dots tomorrow," Sergeant Lee commanded late at night when the men could hardly see nor hear through their weariness.

Some days Karl appeared in boots without required white dots or slipped up altogether and stood in line with 'bad shoes'—he had been too tired to spit polish them the night before. Sergeant Lee never missed a dirty boot or missing dot or a chance to 'gig' Karl and his fellow maggots. K-P again.

Kitchen Penalty teams consisted of three individuals. There was an inside man who served the officers and cleaned and polished the floors and tables. The second man was on pots and pans. That was the worst of all jobs, and Karl did everything he could to stay on the good side of the cooks to avoid that assignment. The problem was that the recruit's boots got covered in grease and soaking wet. They still needed to be mirror polished the next day, and the extra work, beginning at 2200 when K-P chores ended, was a real drag. The third man was the outside man. He helped the cooks, worked in the back of the kitchen hauling garbage and cleaning up. He served the enlisteds (generally referred to as 'enlisted swine' ignoring the redundancy). His boots usually got muddy and required the same extra work after K-P hours. Occasionally, outside man would luck out and it would be a dry day.

And they stood in lines. Lines by company and platoon and squad. Karl stood in line to climb along the monkey bars (twice) before he could line up for chow, every meal. Then he stood, mess kit and cup in hand to receive food thrown into the kit. There were lines to stand at the long tables and eat when in the field, lines to get weapons, lines to get weapons cleaned, lines to return weapons, lines to get shots and physical exams.

"Get in line! Shut up maggot! Wait your turn turd!" Karl heard a hundred times a day. He would have had to stand in line, although informally, to get donuts at the ubiquitous donut shops dotting the Fort Lewis landscape over in officer country, were he ever to have been permitted to enter that hallowed land. The level of exercise exceeded the calories provided in the company messes, and donuts were the saving grace for officers. The best thing that could be said about the military was that none of the men went hungry.

Karl Oscar Isaacson did not know it, and would never have guessed from the abuse he received; but he came to the notice of his superiors through positive reports from his drill sergeant. From his officers, he was referred to Central Intelligence Agency recruiters looking for men with special aptitudes and who also lacked deep roots or strong family connections. The Company men investigated his background quietly, and Karl's name went to near the top of their list. They were looking for men who could work independently and covertly, men who lacked the slightest taint of suspicion of the zeal of their Americanism, and men who could do jobs from which lesser men might recoil. They were looking for Americans to control failing irregular warfare aspects of Revolutionary Development Programs in Viet Nam.

Sergeant Lee trotted along double time with his recruit platoon through the sylvan forest on a logging road cut through the Fort Lewis primitive area. He sang out the cadence with his men:

> Sound off…one, two
> Sound off…three, four
> Your lef' , your lef' ,…you got to go home on your lef,'
> Your lef,' your lef,'…your lef,' right, lef,' right.

He smiled at the bawdy lyrics made up long ago by a footsore soldier less than enamored by the glory of it all:

> Your pants are unbuttoned,
> Your shoes are untied,
> Your balls are swingin'
> From Left to Right
> Sound off…one, two,

Sound off…three, four
Sound off, one, two, three, four,
One! Two!—Three! Four!

The drill sergeant was rightfully pleased with himself. With the bunch of maggots he was given, he had done pretty well. They were already working as a team and even marched well enough to compete for the unit citation. He recognized the main incongruous note in the grouping; Private Sanchez, the brown shrimp, and Private Isaacson, the giant white ghost, insisted on being buddies and marching side by side. That made the skyline of the squad all wrong. Not that it really mattered much. The two of them were the quickest learners and had turned out to be the best soldiers. In this man's army the most likely to succeed were the most likely to survive, and Sergeant Lee's purpose in life was to keep as many of his maggots alive as possible for as long as possible.

There were four weeks of basic left for this platoon before he started all over again with a new bunch of rejects. At this point in the Viet Nam conflict, he was getting only those hapless souls that could not hack it in college. The spooks had told him to be ready to lose Isaacson. He was theirs when he finished basic. No one had discussed the boy's future with him, Sergeant Lee knew. Isaacson was government issue just like himself. He guessed the white boy did not need to know, at least not now.

The sergeant had a soldier's innate distrust for spooks. No one who went with them was ever seen again for one thing. They probably moved into the plush offices in DC and wined and dined at civilian's expense, but you never did know. Sergeant Lee worried a little about Isaacson being selected. He kind of liked the big kid even if he was a honkey.

"Hey, Isaacson! Fall in with me fah a minute befoah chow, okay?" the black sergeant called to the big blond.

"Sergeant, yes sergeant!" came the smart reply.

"Look, Isaacson, Ah wanna talk to y'all private-like about somethin' ah think y'all need to know," the sergeant said to the recruit when they had gotten away from the rest of the platoon.

Isaacson walked without speaking. He focused on his sergeant. The man had never before taken a moment to do anything but to order him around and to chew on his rear end; so, this had to be important.

"Isaacson…Ah ain't even s'posed to be talkin' wit'ch y'all 'bout this; so, don't let on Ah did, awright?"

"Yes, sergeant." Karl waited expectantly.

"Y'all 'member those guys that been hangin' around our platoon every now and again? No markin's on their fatigues?"

"Yeah."

"Never mind rat now who they ah, but they ah goin' ta axe y'all to sign up with their outfit, ah thank. Ah am suggestin' y'all play head's up ball when those cats talk. Mebbe they ah goin' to give y'all somethin' okay, mebbe not. Just y'all pay 'tention to what y'all ah gettin' yo'sef into when they come acourtin,' ya heah what ah'm sayin?' Ya have choices. This is still America even if it's the ahmey."

"I guess I do Sergeant Lee. I don't know what this's about, though. Who are they? How come they don't just get me a set of orders like the army does for everybody else?"

"Cause they ah not ahmy, least wise not this man's ahmy," the sergeant said with the emphasis he intended and as little evasion as he dared.

"What should I do, Sergeant?" Karl asked earnestly. The sergeant knew everything about the military, and Karl trusted the man completely even if Sergeant Lee had been harder on him than he had been on any of the other grunts in the platoon.

"Cain't ratly tell a man what he should do wit' his own 'fairs, son. Just leave me tell y'all a couple a thangs ah've learned in this man's ahmy in twenty-two years and three tours in Nam. Don't axe me no mo' questions 'bout it, 'kay?

"I'll try, Sarge," the private said halfheartedly.

"Let's y'all and me set heah," said the sergeant indicating a picnic bench beside the parade grounds.

"Ah don' usually talk a lot to recruits alone. Ah work on the unit, on savin' the unit and every man in it. But this is kinda differen.' Even tho' y'all ah a honkey oppressor," (here he smiled to indicate his lack of malice in the use of the racial epithet), "Ah thank y'all have some promise. And ah thank y'all ah goin' ta need some extra trainin' and learnin' to keep y'all alive in this hyah man's wah we got."

Karl moved as if to ask a question, but the ebony skinned senior noncom waved his hand in a slight gesture asking his listener to wait.

"Y'all got to stay alive, take care of numbah one. Ah thank y'all ah goin' to be in special ops and ah goin' ta be on ya own wheah it comes to takin' care of yo'ah little white behin.' Ah observe that there ah some old spooks and some bold spooks, but they ah verah few old bold spooks, if y'all catch ma drift. If y'all will let me, ah'll teach y'all everythin' ah know 'bout survivin' in Country. Ah do know somethin' 'bout fightin' and mo impotant, somethin' 'bout gettin' along in this man's ahmy—military," he amended. "Ah ain't no hero an y'all doan need to be one neithah if yuh ah goin' to get to be an old spook. Jist do yoah job, heah me, boy?"

Sergeant Lee paused to see if his message was sinking in and to let Karl acknowledge. "I'll do whatever you ask, Sarge," the recruit said simply. Karl was not much of a talker. When he said he would do something, it was a commitment. That was one of the things the black noncom liked about his honkey protégé.

"Y'all goin' ta wuk yo'ah tail off then fa y'all's own good. But when ah'm done wit'ch you, y'all'll be the best fightin' machine ah can make uv y'all. Don' get me wrong now, Ah'm still the same ol' hardass and ah'm still a racist. Y'all dint thank us Mississippi porch monkeys could be racists did ya? That's one of the big secrets the liberal college folks and gument people keep frum you white oppressors. Ah'll tell y'all tho,' I ain't no bigot. They'ah's a big difference between a racist and a bigot. Did y'all know that?" The sergeant was wound up in his explanation, and Private Isaacson thought it best to be quiet and listen. Sergeant Lee was not waiting for a reply.

"A racist recognizes the difference between different people, different races, like their size, their culture, their strengths and weaknesses witout makin' a judgment. He knows everybody's place. A bigot has his own mind made up before he gets any real info'mation; he has awreddy gotten a bunch of crap, mostly lies, from his daddy and momma and don' wan' ta heah anythin' mo'ah. Wus, he makes negative judgments 'bout people, lumpin' ev'ybody in a race all togethah and actin' agin' 'em fo' no good reason," the African-American continued in his soft Southern patois. "Ah have personally heard all of the insults and had to do that much mo' than the whites in this man's ahmy to get ahead. Ah do know what ah'm talkin' 'bout when ah calls you whites, 'oppressahs.'" His approach softened a little, "But y'all don' necessarily seem lak no oppressah to me. Y'all ah probly poorah than me. Tell me, Isaacson, did y'all evah even see a black man befo'ah y'all come inta the ahmy?"

"I confess I didn't, Sergeant Lee. The little town I grew up in had its little prejudices against the Swedes for reasons I'll never know. We all looked alike as far as I can see. I never even heard the word . . ."

"Niggah?"

"Yes, Sergeant. We just didn't have enough really different people in our town to have any real prejudice. The Mormons don't seem like the type to hate anyone just because they were black, anyhow. Even the stuff about Swedes was pretty tame now that I think back on it," Karl went on, now a little embarrassed about his long-windedness.

"Anyway," Lee continued, "what ahm gettin' at is that yo'ah collah don' mean nothin' ta me. Ah thank y'all ah wuth savin.' Wuk wit' me, yuh heah?"

The conversation had gotten a little deeper than Karl or Cletus Lee felt comfortable with. The message and the sentiment had been communicated, and it was enough. A certain limited bond now seemed to exist between the two dissimilar men. They did appear to have achieved an understanding. Karl was convinced of the need to follow his sergeant's advice taking it on faith without having a full knowledge of what underlay the unusual conversation. Karl maintained a sense of apprehension about the unknown as well as an air of anticipation heightened by Sergeant Lee's unusual one-on-one communication with him.

The three CIA operatives met one last time in their makeshift office in the headquarters building at Fort Lewis. They finished the review of the dossiers, and updated them since the preliminary onsite evaluations of their candidates. One of the lieutenants had sharply and even almost insultingly refused their offer of a contract. He wanted to be a regular army 'redleg' (artillery man— officer) and wanted nothing to do with the intelligence service. He had been proper but candid and barely polite. It was clear that the young man had only contempt for the 'shadow service,' his words—or more likely the phrase came from his father, the WW II vet. Lieutenant Cragin, the other candidate, had been intrigued from the start and accepted without demurrer. The three Company men had only to approach the enlisted man, Isaacson, to complete their work at Fort Lewis.

The reveille bugle called over the base sound system bringing groggy soldiers to their unsteady feet cursing and grumbling just as the call had been doing for hundreds of years. Some of the more morning alert types sang along with the clear notes of the bugler:

> I can't get 'em up,
> I can't get 'em up,
> I can't get 'em up in mornin!

The dirty sons of witches,
Won't put on their britches,
I can't get 'em up, I can't get 'em up,
I can't get 'em up in the mornin!

After the usual hurried breakfast, the platoon double-timed to the exercise field for calisthenics and close quarters combat training. Isaacson and Stephen Solokowski were first up. Karl was defending against Stephen's furious thrusts with the rubber bayonet affixed to his M 14. Stephen was big and strong but slow and stupid. Sergeant Lee had selected Karl's opponent on that morning for just those sterling qualities. The big polack seemed immune to pain, another useful trait. As the CIA 'Colonel' and his two assistants quietly joined the circle formed by the platoon, Karl parried a bayonet lunge by sweeping the gun aside with the flat of his fingers; then he upended Stephen by driving his padded elbow into the massive polack's chest. At the same time, Karl whipped his right leg behind the big man's legs neatly lifting him off his feet so he fell flat on his back, helpless. Karl finished with a simulated knife hand thrust to Stephen's exposed throat.

"Another daid sojer," laconically commented the DI to Solokowski who still lay on his back. "If y'all ah goin' to come back from the Nam anyway but in a body bag, y'all bettah look smartah 'an that."

"Lemme do it again, Sarge! I can kill him. He just tricked me again. I'll get him."

"Wilson, y'all be Solowkoski's dummy for a while. Start slow the first coupla tams then no mucy. Ain't no gooks goin' to go easy wit' y'all. Get on wit' it, y'heah?" barked the sergeant.

"We came to see Private Isaacson, Sergeant Lee. Would this time be all right?" asked the 'Colonel's' assistant courteously when the other men in the training platoon were out of earshot.

"Ah 'spose so, suh. It's as good a tam as any," the DI replied. "An what if it ain't?" he asked himself.

"Isaacson!" Sergeant Lee called. "Front and centah, boah! These heah gentamen need a word witch yuh. I 'spect to see y'all back by 1500 to go a round or two wit' me…that enough tam fo' you gentamen?"

"More than enough, Sergeant," said the assistant. "Would you come with us, Private?"

Even without insignia of office, Karl presumed that the men were officers. He recalled the enlisted man's pledge, 'Salute everything that moves; paint everything that doesn't.' He snapped a, "Yes, sir!"

Sergeant Lee and warned him to expect this interview. He wished that he looked more presentable. He and the platoon had been practicing hand-to-hand combat techniques most of the late morning, and his shirt was soaked with sweat. His hands, arms, and face were grimy from takedowns on the muddy ground.

When the men were seated around the gray utility table in the office with no adornments, it was the 'Colonel' who spoke first. "Private Isaacson, mind if I use your first name?"

"No sir."

"I'm sure you are wondering why we asked you to meet with us, Karl. I'll get right to it and explain, but first I'd like to ask you a few questions, if that's all right?"

"Okay, sir, no problem." Karl was unused to such civility.

"We prize honesty very highly, Karl. If you don't feel that you can answer our questions fully and forthrightly at any point, we can stop; and all of us can part and go on with our lives. But if we continue beyond a certain point, you will have to agree not to divulge what we say. In fact, I want you to agree right now to deny that this meeting ever took place. Can you do that, Karl?"

"I guess so. I really don't know what any of this is about."

"It'll be clear soon, at least what you need to know. Please be patient."

"Yes, sir." There was a great, deal of 'please' and 'thank you.' It made Karl suspicious.

"First, I want to get to know what you feel about our country, then I will ask you to answer some personal questions, real personal. All of this information will be strictly confidential. No one outside this room will ever know anything about what you tell us; and we are not going to write anything down, okay?"

"Okay. Yes, sir." Karl was a little edgy with the idea that these unsmiling men felt the need to proceed so carefully.

"Tell me how you feel about your country. Think about your answer."

Karl paused while Inga Haakensdatter's overzealous Americanism lecturing reregistered in his memory. He said, "America is the only true democracy in the world. We are the only ones who stick up for democracy and the rights of the little people. That's why we're in Nam. I don't know what else to say. We have a government of laws not just a rule for the big shots. We get to vote; we get to have the religion we want and can live anywhere we want. That's freedom, and nobody else has that kind of freedom. We need to fight to keep it. That's why I'm in the army…I can't think of anything else."

84

The three CIA men appeared to listen intently. The 'Colonel' asked his second question of the teenager, "Why do you think our country is fighting in Viet Nam? You see the news; a lot of people your age are protesting, think we shouldn't be there."

"They are aiding and abetting the enemy, sir!" Karl said brusquely indicating his firm conviction. He paused so as to avoid sounding too strident. "We are bringing democracy to Asia, at least to the Republic of Viet Nam. The North Vietnamese are communists trying to invade the South; we are protecting the poor Southerners so they can have their free elections and, and just live the way they want to. We are making it possible for them to be free like we are. It's like stamping out the Nazis in the Second World War."

"What are your feelings about the communists, Karl?"

"They are dictators, and they would spread that stuff, that tyrant stuff all over the world if it wasn't for the US," Karl said. "The commies are the worst tyrants, the worst mass murderers, the worst…it's the worst idea about government there has been. They want to make everybody the same, like slaves. We have to stop them no matter what the commie press says." Now he sounded like David Grant's father. He was a little embarrassed at his own vehemence.

"We feel the same way. Our organization is special. We fight the war against communism in special ways that the poor misinformed public can't know about. Think you would like to get into that kind of thing, Karl?" the attorney assistant spoke up for the first time.

"I think so. I'd have to know what you're talking about, though. I think the army is doing a pretty good job of kicking their butts, and I'm in the army all the way," Karl responded.

"That's commendable, son," said the second assistant. "Remember when the 'Colonel' said that we would have some personal questions?" Karl nodded. "Before we go on, we have to know whether we can trust you, whether you are a real patriot. When we are satisfied, then we can let you know what you need to know about our organization so you can make up your own mind about working with the real Americans."

The method of recruitment was the careful and practiced result of a long trial and error history of approaching members of the US military and was all the easier in approaching a boy as inexperienced and naive as this buck private from some cowboy town. He had not had the dubious opportunity of being 'contaminated at the pinko universities by the left-wing snobs' as the sitting Director of the CIA had characterized the spoiled students. The approach was comradely and gave the subject the opportunity to demonstrate shared beliefs with a sympathetic listener. The subject was allowed to talk and to be heard. This was becoming increasingly difficult in the country during the mid sixties with the patriotic young people's voices being drowned out by comsymps. Even President Johnson was finding it impossible to get his message across. The country was in real danger. The CIA officers were dedicated to their thankless task of protecting the misguided US public. They told themselves so with regularity.

"So," mused the youngest and most idealistic of the three officers. His specific contribution to the recruitment was about to begin.

"Karl, you remember the 'Colonel' told you how highly we prize honesty."

"Yes sir, I do."

"Have you ever heard of a polygraph test?"

"No, sir. What is that exactly?" Karl asked, aware that somehow the strange sounding test was going to have something to do with him.

"It's better known as a lie detector test. That ring a bell?"

"Yes, sir."

"You can leave now with no hard feelings and just forget that this meeting ever took place or you can stay and take the test. It is given to every CIA employee when they start to work and every now and again after that. That's one of the best ways to insure that all of our people are really who they say they are and are honest when they work with the nation's most crucial secrets," the specialist intoned looking at Karl's eyes all the while he was talking. He saw slight hesitation in those trusting blue eyes.

"I don't know. This is all new to me. Do I have to decide right now?" Karl asked.

"You do. You are either in or out. We can't go on or meet again without the assurances of a lie detector test. These questions and the polygraph are just the first steps in what we call the vetting process that determines whether you are a good enough American to be one of us. We need to be sure you can always be trusted. You can appreciate that need, right, Karl?"

Karl was flattered to be considered for such a significant position. Like all American kids, he had grown up with the romance of being a spy, of selflessly and secretly serving his country. It was a heady moment for him to contemplate a fantasy becoming reality. These were hard-core practical men. Karl was approaching a moment of truth about his future. He thought, "What can I lose? I'll give it a go? These guys are great...real Americans."

There was a small hiatus while Karl ran his thoughts through his mind and erased his doubts. This wasn't the army, and these guys were not Sergeant Lee, but this is what his DI had been preparing him for. He had listened carefully. Now he thought it over and made a fateful decision. "Okay, I'm in. I'll take the test."

"All right, Karl. Here's how it works. It's actually very simple. You must tell the truth. The machine is infallible. If you lie, we will know it. Tell the truth down to the slightest detail. Understand?"

"Yes, sir," the young man replied a little fearfully. His young and inexperienced mind recognized the gravity of the CIA officer's instructions, and he was concerned that the machine could interpret an answer of his as a lie just because he was nervous.

The officer affixed the electrodes to Karl's wrists and ankles, snugged into place an electronically activated sphyngomanometer, a pneumograph around his chest, and electrocardiograph leads. He busied himself with the connections at the machine's termini. When he was satisfied, he placed the machine to his side in a position that precluded Karl's visualization of the recording strip. It was unsettling to the boy.

"All right, now for the questions. Just answer 'yes' or 'no,' nothing more. Got that?"

"Yes."

Karl heard the machine turn on with a low hum and could hear the scratching hiss of the pens on the recording paper.

"Is your name Karl Oscar Isaacson?"

"It is."

"Remember, just yes or no, Karl. Don't be nervous."

"Sorry."

"Let's start again. Is your name Karl Oscar Isaacson?"

"Yes."

"Good. You are settling down."

"Are you originally from Utah?"

"Yes."

"Do you have more than one wife?" He chuckled a little as he asked the off-script question.

"No." Karl stressed his answer. He had heard the business about polygamy so many times that it was no longer amusing.

"Are you now or have you ever been a member of the communist party or one of its affiliates?"

"No."

"Are you in the United States Army?"

"Yes.'

"Do you like men and boys?"

"Yes." Karl answered quickly but was uneasy with the intent of the question, especially after those hygiene lectures.

"Are you a homophile?" the officer smiled a little as he anticipated Karl's answer.

"I don't know what that is, sorry."

"Are you a homosexual?"

"A queer?!" Karl replied with an air of suspicion that he was being insulted or made fun of. "No!" he snapped emphatically.

"Have you ever in any form had sex with another male."

"No!" This was getting bizarre to Karl's way of thinking.

"Have you ever had sexual relations with an animal?"

"What the crap!" Karl all but shouted. "Are you making fun of me? I never even heard of such a thing! Now ask me something decent."

The country boy was affronted, which amused the world-wise CIA officer. "Don't get jumpy," he smiled easily. "We have to have this stuff for the record. Just answer, and we can go on."

"Hell, no!" Karl almost never swore as a result of his limited Mormon upbringing, but he figured he was entitled.

"Is your background Swedish?"

"Yes."

"Do you speak Swedish fluently?"

"Yes."

"Do you have contact with members of the Swedish communist party?"

"No."

"Do you take money from any foreign power?"

"No."

"Are you eighteen years old?"

Long pause. "No."

"Are you sixteen years old?"

"Yes."

"Did you falsify your records in order to enter the Army?"

Thoughtful pause. "No."

The officer scrutinized the recording tape. There was a slight increase in the blood pressure and pulse rate but nothing clearly indicative of an intent to deceive.

"Well, then, did anyone else falsify your records with your agreement, Karl?"

"Yes, sir," Karl said quietly. He was getting anxious now. How did these guys know all this. He figured that he would be kicked out of the army now that they knew.

"Speak louder, son."

"Yes, they did, sir."

"Have you ever been convicted of a crime?"

"No."

"Are you a Christian?"

"Yes." He guessed he was.

"Do you use alcohol to excess or use illegal drugs?"

"No."

"Have you ever committed a crime that is not a part of your record with the army?"

Karl squirmed. He was convinced that he had not committed any crime in the fight with the boys that resulted in his being drafted. "No," He said. He was almost convinced.

The physiological parameters leaped on the paper making a telltale scratching noise that gave away Karl's answer as a lie even without the officer looking at the visual recording.

"Karl, have you ever been guilty of committing an act of violence against another person?"

"Well…yes."

"Are you in all respects a loyal American, Private Isaacson?"

"Yes, sir!" He was glad to be back on comfortable ground.

"That will be all for today. We will contact you soon if we wish to proceed. Remember that this meeting, this test, never took place."

"Yes, sir."

Karl returned to the bright sunshine of the Washington state afternoon a little surprised that it was still fully day. The time had seemed much longer in the dark little room where he had been interviewed. He could hear the characteristic cadence song of his platoon marching on the parade ground as they did every day. The entire platoon, including the DI, were off key but sang lustily to another of Sergeant Lee's dirty ditties.

> The Engineers, The engineers,
> We never sluff at trifles,
> We hang our balls on canyon walls,
> And shoot at them with ri-fles
> Hup, Hup, Hup, Hup

Karl fell in with the fast-marching unit. Sergeant Lee's platoons always fast-marched. It was a pain most of the time; but every soldier in the unit had to admit that they were tough, a lot tougher and better men than they had been a hundred years ago when they first saw the DI from hell. The sergeant dismissed the troops and kept back Karl and Yoshio Yamashita, the *Shito Ryu* blackbelt and only true volunteer in the platoon. Lee was serious about Karl's education, and Yosh was very obliging.

The US Army teaches very little of the martial arts to its boot camp trainees reasoning that in modern warfare hand-to-hand combat is obsolete so far as the great mass of men is concerned having been superseded by the technology and tactics of the advanced war machine. Sergeant Lee reasoned differently, in Karl's case at least, because he realized that the big Swedish boy would, in all likelihood, find it necessary to be self-reliant and would probably need the added protection of a serious unarmed combat skill.

The DI reasoned similarly about Karl's need to know about explosives, arms, and even enemy tactics. One thing Sergeant Cletus Lee did not do was to underestimate the VC or the NVA. He knew from grim experience that was a fatal mistake. He had taken Karl on as a special project teaching him every thing the boy could absorb. Karl was not the best marcher in the platoon; but he was becoming nearer to being a weapons expert, at least as much as Sergeant Lee could produce, and had proved to be a quick and apt student despite his lack of a high school diploma and the naivete born of his provincial education to date. The last two weeks had been as intensive as Karl could handle. Even the great reserves of youth had their limit, but Cletus Lee was proud of what had been accomplished in such a short time.

The karate lessons with Private Yamashita had been underway since the fourth week of boot camp because it was readily apparent even then that the two of them would have no other adequate competitors in the unit—Yosh because of his training and natural skill, and Karl because of his raw size, strength, and agility.

The sergeant was no slouch either. What he lacked in formal training, he had picked up on the streets of Jackson, Mississippi where he grew up, and in Viet Nam where he learned the next most important lessons of survival. He entered into a round robin tourney with his two recruits, learning and teaching. There was so much Karl had to learn to defend himself and so little time. As usual, the two younger men started the late afternoons first with a sparring match between the two of them. There was no time to teach katas which were Yosh's first love. "Karl has a special need to learn to fight. Ah'd appreciate if y'all would concentrate on that one thang," Cletus had asked Yosh when he first approached the Japanese-American recruit about the project to educate Karl.

Karl outweighed Yosh by nearly one hundred pounds and Cletus by more than forty, but had yet to win a match with either of the men. Yosh had yet to lose. The sinewy Japanese-American stood in his casual stance inviting a mistake by the usually overzealous Swede. Karl was well rested and had considerable nervous energy to work off after the tense session with the CIA paramilitary recruiters. He was ready and determined to avoid his previous mistakes; he was determined to win at least once. Yosh was so deceptively small that it still embarrassed Karl to fight him let alone to be beaten consistently.

Yosh flicked his annoying long fingers at Karl's eyes, and the big Swedish boy involuntarily blinked and bobbed his head back away from the visual threat. He took two rapid fire punches in the gut before he could recover from his moment of inattention. His Oriental opponent stood casually back in his original stance as if he had never moved. Karl was momentarily angry with himself for having been tricked. He had learned from both of his skilled opponents that anger was a tool for his opponent, and he was quick to control the rising emotion.

Karl made a lunging thrust at Yosh's solar plexus coming in at a low crouch. Yosh drove his fists down hard at the heavy fist to give a memorable painful block but passed only through air. Karl artfully hesitated at the last moment and fired his left fist at the Oriental's now exposed jaw. Yosh countered with a quick feint to his left away from the oncoming and unexpected facial blow and parry blocked the big arm. Karl had learned his last painful lesson from Yosh well. The two fakes were followed by his true intended attack. Yosh was off-balance leaning to the left and backward. Karl swept his right leg around Yosh's ankle and took the black belt Japanese completely off his center; so, he had to judo-fall on his back. Karl smiled at his little triumph even as Yosh tumbled neatly backward in a controlled roll that brought him to his feet facing Karl, now three feet away.

Karl felt rather that saw the double kick coming. It was too fast to think about; he had only to react with the training from Cletus about defending against this favorite and spectacular attack among Korean and Japanese martial artists. Karl instinctively knew that the first kick coming for his protected abdomen was a bluff and made only a perfunctory block. Yosh's legs scissored in the air with blurring speed sending the second frontal kick directly at Karl's forehead. Karl was crouched to defend against the first kick and was an easy target for the second well placed shot to his head. Except the foot never had a chance to find its mark.

With both of Yosh's feet off the ground, Karl left his feet planted firmly in place, leaned as far as balance would permit to the left and almost gently caught the Japanese boy's leg just at the Achilles tendon and lifted slightly upward. The lift combined with Yosh's own forward and upward momentum resulted in a neat and breath losing fall on his back from four feet in the air.

Cletus laughed out loud, and Karl grinned at his success. It was his night to win. He could beat the Oriental at his own game. Yosh had other ideas however. He chastised himself for his underestimation of his opponent making the classical oriental martial artist's mistake of presuming that the large and heavy-set Occidentals were also slow and clumsy and therefore no match for the superior craft of the Asians. He would not again be so careless. He cleared his mind of externals, focused on the one thing that counted right now, and assumed his fighting stance. Karl was aware of the change in his opponent and felt slightly intimidated by the determined demeanor of the clever smaller man.

It was well that he be alert because in the next few minutes Karl felt the lightening quick and precise but pulled punches landing on his shin, his exposed axilla, his nose, and choked briefly from the saber like fingers tapping his Adam's apple. Four well placed blows landed unanswered, and the smile of success faded on Karl's face. He blocked a round house kick and sent Yosh's leg spinning out of control and in a complete circle. He was not quick enough to realize that he had been suckered until the heel of that spinning foot completed its arc and landed a little more solidly than intended on Karl's occiput. Karl was dazed and fell forward to avoid the attack on the back of his head. Yosh was already back in position and drove his small granite hard fists into Karl's unprotected chin then into the side of his neck. Had they been seriously intended, either would have rendered Karl *hors d' combat* and vulnerable to whatever his opponent would have like to do next.

"Y'all ah a dead sojer, big boy!" Sergeant Lee cried out to stop the match. "It ain't goin' to be tonight that y'all carries home da trophy."

Ruefully, Karl had to admit defeat. He was also later defeated by Cletus after the black man and the Oriental recruit fought to a sweaty tie. Karl had learned some more this day—mainly that he had a lot more to learn.

The 'Colonel' and his two assistants met briefly for the final accounting of their evaluations of two men under consideration for the Counter Terrorism Program.

"Lieutenant Cleghorn is a shoo-in," said the 'Colonel.' About the only criticism I have is that he is too gung-ho. I have always been suspicious of red-hots. But that's just me. Any disagreement?"

The two assistants nodded their agreement.

"Now, Isaacson," said the attorney assistant scanning the handwritten data cards. He strikes me as being exactly what he appears to be— a straightforward middle-America simple believer. He just doesn't seem smart enough to be evasive. The boy believes the whole America Myth; he wouldn't know a homosexual until one bit him on the butt; and he is a fighter. I think all we have to do is make him our fighter."

"What do you expect from someone coming from Arizona?" said the younger assistant rhetorically with an Easterner's sneer.

"Utah," corrected the attorney.

"Whatever...Utah's all the more bovine. You ever hear of a traitor from Utah? Ever know a Mormon communist. I don't even think they produce any pacifists out there in those boonies, bless their little pointy heads," rejoined the older CIA assistant.

"Don't underestimate your friends is as good a rule as when the aphorism is applied to enemies," the 'Colonel' spoke for the first time. "First, I don't think Isaacson is as dumb as you make out. You are mistaking youthful ignorance and a woefully inadequate education for true intellectual deficit. His sergeant says he learns faster than any other kid in the platoon."

"I don't know that's saying much. The rest of them look like they are about a generation from swinging in trees," said the younger assistant.

"Now, now," chided the attorney, "Your Yale snobbery's showing."

"Secondly, you are overlooking the polygraph test details. The boy was not entirely ingenuous. You may recall that he was willing to lie to cover his butt," the 'Colonel' pointed out.

"Technically, it wasn't a lie, you know. He was answering something about his criminal record, as I recall. He was never formally charged with anything," responded the attorney.

"Spoken like an attorney,...but he certainly reacted like he'd lied," said the third agent.

"At one point in his answer I think he felt like he was going to be caught in a lie or interpreted as having lied and that is why he reacted on the polygraph hookups. My point is that he is young, just a kid, actually, and is not entirely above clumsily lying to protect himself," observed the 'Colonel.'

"Give him time," smiled the attorney. "He'll learn to lie as well as the average Company agent. You know, he needs to tell a little lie now and again for the kingdom's sake."

"And I don't think he is hiding anything about his past that matters. He can't be blackmailed. In sixteen years he hasn't had enough experience to matter. He's perfect," said the other assistant.

"They can fill his head at Langley with anything they want. He **is** perfect. Any reservations, Colonel?" asked the attorney-agent.

"Not really. I guess I have gotten old in this business. Nobody's perfect. Isaacson looks like the ideal choice; but you know, I somehow don't think we will have heard the last of Karl Isaacson when we send him off to The Farm. It's a premonition—just an insupportable feeling—and I'll leave that kind of judgmental method to metaphysics where it belongs."

"One last comment; we found this kid from our computer program partly because we prioritized men without families or strong attachments. The Company will be his only attachment, in effect, his family. That has to be a major plus," observed the second assistant.

"And that is the American way," observed the 'Colonel.' "I read a history of the Pony Express and was so impressed with how an advertisement for riders coincided with our present needs that I committed it to memory: 'Wanted—Young, skinny, wiry fellows not over eighteen. Must be expert riders, willing to risk death daily. Orphans preferred.'"

"Sounds like our kind of guy, all right," chuckled the assistant. "Who says there's anything new under the sun?"

"In or out?" questioned the lawyer who was anxious to get a steak and board the Company plane back to civilization.

"In," said the younger assistant ready to call it a night.

The 'Colonel' nodded his assent as did the attorney.

Karl's service folder gained another check in another box. If the boy himself agreed, the final mark would be placed, and the process would be complete at this end. The most junior of the three agents was elected, by an acclimation of two, to finalize the interview with Karl and to get the contract signed.

A day later Karl listened politely and thoroughly to the presentation by the CIA agent. After a lengthy exposition of the requirements of the service and the attendant rules but precious little about his own role in the Company, Karl began to ask questions that he had memorized as a list. "Where will I be trained? What will I learn to do, and where will I do it? What exactly is this Studies and Observations Group that I am supposed to work in?"

"You will be trained in the Company's own training camp. I can't tell you where that is for obvious security reasons. You will learn everything possible in four months about special operations weapons and tactics. The SOG/RDC/CT Program (He enunciated each letter separately, "SOG slash,. . .") is a special operation run by the United States government to identify and assist people who wish to throw off their communist oppressors and to undermine the infrastructure of worldwide communism," the agent said with a completely sober expression. Even to him it was apparent that he was laying it on a bit thick. It was also apparent to him that he had not really answered a single one of the boy's questions with useful information. He prepared himself for the hard questions.

Karl Isaacson looked into the agent's face with trusting eyes. He was young, needed to belong, wanted to do something important, and longed to be special after a youth of being in a near second-class citizen status. He said, "Okay, I'll do it. Count me in. Do you have the contract you told me about?"

"Right here. You understand that there is a difference between agents of the Company and contract agents. You have not had the full training to become an agent, but hopefully someday you will qualify and will get selected to go on—that requires a minimum of three years of continuous service. You will be under the orders of the agents."

Karl had hardly expected to be the chief upon starting his CIA career. His ambitions for the moment were limited to the need to master the proposed training. He would trust the Company to watch out for him just as he now placed his faith in the army. Karl signed the document after a cursory reading of the complex verbiage.

"Now what?" Karl asked.

"You are to be prepared to ship out with us when we give you the word. It will be soon, so keep your gear ready. You are forbidden to discuss our arrangement with anyone. Anyone!" The emphasis was not lost on the receptive boy. The last check mark went into Karl's dossier.

A week later, Karl heard the rumors that he was headed for OCS (Officer's Candidate School) passing through the squad. The recruits all hushed up when he came around and looked a little sheepish. He made an effort not to notice. He wondered where the rumor came from but said little. Miguel Sanchez and Yoshio Yamashita informed him that he could not be a hermit; tonight he had to go with them to the Enlisted Men's Club; someone was going to sneak in a stripper; and he had to go with the guys.

The entrance was dark when the three young privates sauntered into the entry way of the EM Club. Suddenly every light in the room burst on, streamers flew, and an out-of-tune chorus of half drunk enlisted men began to sing the privates' favorite song about officers.

> Oh! We'll cast-er-ate the captain,
> With a dirty piece of glass,
> Shove a rusty bayonet up...

> Competitors sang:
> I can come in any kind of weather
> That's because my bags are made of leather,
> I don't need no keys nor locks,
> I'll just slip it in your box,
> I'm your mail man!

Somebody dragged him into a corner and shouted over the din, "How's it feel to be an offsher?" Think you're hot stuff goin' to OCS?" "You goin' to 'member the rest of us grunts?" another drunken voice chimed in barely audible in the din from beery song.

> Hi, Ho Kafuzulum,
> Harlot of Jerusalem,
> Prostitute of ill repute,
> And daughter of the BaBa . . .

"Not for a minute," laughed Karl as he shouted over the youthful tumult and threw his massive arm around the black neck of Dixon Trambough who was laughing out of control. "More than booze there," Karl figured to himself as he smelled the peculiar sweet smoky breath.

> Kafuzulum was a wily witch,
> a brazen bitch,
> a no good whore,
> She causeth all the lips to twitch,
> Way down in old Jerusalem...

"Hey, honkey," came Sergeant Lee's unmistakable voice shouting in his ear. "Congratulations. Another white oppressah is 'bout to be born! No matter that a honkey is takin' the place of a deservin' bro.'"

Karl looked theatrically around the room to see if he could find the deserving brother then at the grinning DI quizzically, and somehow got across the question through the drunken cacophony, "Did you start this silly rumor?"

"With a little help. A little spook help."

Snatches of another choral group's efforts to compete with the first for lyrical shock and amplitude if not for harmony wafted from the farther room of the enlisted bar.

> Up and down Canal Street,
> Look in every door,
> Hey, Ser-geant, couldn't find a whore.
> When I finally found one,
> she was tall and slim,
> Hey, Ser-geant, couldn't get it in.

The DI's serious comment was a pretty good explanation for the odd activities that Karl had been involved in of late. His buddies accepted the OCS as the logical reason why Isaacson would be taking off shortly. It was also as good an excuse for a party as any, Karl guessed and smiled. Sergeant Lee looked the other way while the recruits surreptitiously sucked a drag on the joints someone had smuggled in for the party. He was heartened to see that neither Isaacson nor Yamashita touched the junk and silently wished that a bro' could be one of his successes. Maybe next group.

Not to be outdone nor to allow a vacuum of quiet to interfere with the festivities, the original set of army singers, the ones nearest Karl and anyone trying to talk to him, rang out another cheery blast of shouted song dwarfing the feeble efforts of their competitors.

> Bang away on LuLu, bang away all day,
> Who we goin' to bang on when LuLu goes away?
> City girls use Vaseline,
> Country girls use Lard,
> But LuLu uses axle grease,
> and rubs it extra hard.
> O, Oh bang away on LuLu.. . .

Karl's ears could bear no more; so, he moved out of the beer fumes, marijuana and tobacco fog, away from the inharmonious choral selections, and onto the EMC porch. His buddy, Miguel Sanchez, fought his way through the weekend revelers to get in a few words with the big young Swede, whom rumor control had suggested would soon be leaving the platoon.

"Hey, albino," the café au lait colored boy greeted his blond friend. "So, I hear you are too good for the rest of us grunts, *verdad*?" (True?)

"De veras, Miguel, eres muy intelligente!" (That's the truth, Miguel, you are very intelligent!) replied Karl in the best simple Spanish he could remember and with the most exaggerated accent. Miguel rolled his eyes.

Karl had been eager to learn a little of his friend's tongue and had proved to be a surprisingly apt pupil for a gringo, Miguel had told him grudgingly one time. Miguel had been quietly pleased that his friend was interested in his culture enough to dabble at learning the language. "Not many gringos would do that, and not many of the big dumb racists could learn the beautiful tongue, anyway," Miguel had observed to himself.

As the two boots trudged through the inky night back to their recruit barracks, Miguel told Karl that he wished him *"Salud, amor, y pesos y tiempo para disfrutarlos."* (Health, love, and money and time to enjoy them). He best expressed the sentiments of the platoon when he said, in a theatrically exaggerated Hispanic accent, "Jou, an offeecer?, I can no be-lieve eet!"

CHAPTER 4

It is important that the world become clear in mind, for example, that the operation run from Hanoi against South Viet Nam is as certain a form of aggression as the violation of the 38th parallel by the North Korean armies in June, 1950.

I am sometimes lectured that this or that government within the free world is not popular; they tell me that guerrilla warfare cannot be won unless the peoples are dissatisfied. These are, at best, half truths. The truth is that guerrilla warfare, mounted from external bases, with rights of sanctuary, is a terrible burden to carry for any government in a society making its way toward modernization. For instance, it takes somewhere between ten and twenty soldiers to control one guerrilla in an organized operation. Moreover, the guerrilla force has this advantage: Its task is merely to destroy, while the government must build and protect what it is building. A guerrilla war mounted from outside a transitional nation is a crude act of international vandalism. There will be no peace in the world if international community accepts the outcome of a guerrilla war, mounted from outside a nation, as tantamount to a free election.

Walt Rostow, Special Assistant to President Dwight D. Eisenhower for National Security Affairs, to the graduating class of the US Army Special Warfare School at Fort Bragg, June 28, 1961

At 0200, Friday, 1 June, 1966, two days before his formal graduation from army recruit training, Karl awakened from a deep and dreaming sleep to an insistent tap on his shoulder. In his sleep induced haze he started to protest, but a man's callused hand closed over his mouth to quiet him. Karl opened his eyes and focused on the stranger in the neat three piece suit standing silently over his bunk. The crewcut fit appearing man leaned to Karl's ear and very quietly whispered, "I'm from The Company. It's time to go. I'll get your stuff while you skin your lizard or squeeze off a loaf, whatever you need to do."

The meaning of the intrusion on his dreams registered on Karl; and he quickly alerted and then, within a few minutes, awakened fully. He stepped onto the cool highly polished linoleum floor in his skivvies and was mildly embarrassed by his full-bladder partial erection. The CIA officer was all business, took no notice of Karl except to ask, "This your duffel for the trip?"

"Yes, sir," Karl replied. "The one on top of my foot locker, the one with my name on it. That's all I have."

"All your personals in it?"

"Yes, sir."

The man's attention returned to Karl's olive drab colored duffel bag which he hoisted easily onto his shoulder. The agent was as alert as an insurance salesman at noon despite the very early hour. He looked for all the world like an insurance salesman except for his crewcut and his weathered hard face. "Do your personals and dress in civvies. I'll be outside in the car. Rear entrance," he said in his business man's tone.

Karl obediently trotted toward the latrine. His visitor strode up to him and tapped his arm. "No good-byes, no notes," he said with finality.

"I understand, sir," Karl responded and swiftly completed his preparations as the night visitor moved silently out the rear door of the barracks building.

Per instructions, Karl was allowed only one set of clothing for the transfer. Not knowing where he was going, Karl had set out his only suit, a threadbare, cheap cut, dark blue boy's outfit already an inch too short for his rapidly growing arms and legs. He put on his white shirt and clipped on the tie Inga had given him. He was ready in ten minutes. The boy briefly considered secretly saying goodbye to Miguel and Yoshio or leaving a note and counting on the prudence of his friends not to let anyone know he had communicated, but he rejected the idea as a bad start on his new assignment. He walked out of the barracks full of sleeping young men without looking back. He was in his stocking feet to avoid any noise. No one awakened.

At first, Karl could not see anyone nor a likely car as he exited the building. He sat on the steps and put on his old but highly polished black civilian shoes. When he looked up, a nondescript black Ford was waiting at the end of the sidewalk. He entered the front seat, and the officer drove off in the direction of the BOQ. When they arrived at the more attractive building, the officer parked in the umbra of a large maple, got out, and entered the building without an explanation to Karl. Karl waited in the dark.

In a little over fifteen minutes, the agent returned with a crisply military appearing young man dressed in casual civilian clothes, twill khaki slacks, oxblood wing tip brogues, and a rugby shirt. He sat in the back seat with Karl; and the agent drove out of the barracks area, through the primitive forested section of Fort Lewis, and to a base landing strip that was unknown to Karl. No one spoke during the ride. When he had stopped the Ford by a twin engine plane painted olive drab and devoid of all markings, the CIA agent said simply, "Gentlemen, get your bags out and loaded onto the plane. Have a good trip." He remained in his car.

Karl and the young man from the BOQ did as they were told, sharing a glance at each other, but in keeping with the paucity of communication thus far, did not talk to one another. Karl felt skittish; this was the first time in his sixteen years that he had been on an airplane; and he had a vague sense of dread of the unknown on that basis alone. The plane's interior was deceptively more commodious than its austere exterior would have promised. The seats were plush and comfortable, standard civilian airline first class seats. The two men were alone in the cabin section of the plane. They placed their bags in the overhead compartments and sat down. A few minutes later, a second insurance agent looking blond man entered the plane and stood before the two men in their seats. He could have been a clone for the first agent except for a prosthetic pincer hand protruding from his suit cuff. He spoke without greeting, "We will take off in a few minutes. There is no need for you to know our destination; so, don't speculate. It is okay to talk, but for reasons you will learn later, do not share personal information, even names. Do not discuss your understanding of your new assignments. I will not answer any questions. All that understood?"

Karl and the other man nodded their understanding, not ready to break the peculiar silence that had prevailed between them to that point. The agent handed each man a four month old magazine and took his seat behind them. Reading lights shone over each seat, but otherwise there were no cabin lights. There were no windows. The quiet of the interior was broken by the catching of the engines. The insulation of the cabin was as good as any civilian chartered plane, and the monotonous sound of the engines lulled Karl to sleep soon after takeoff.

The plane touched down awakening Karl, who was disoriented at first upon opening his eyes in the darkened unfamiliar surroundings. The agent stood before the two passengers again as the aircraft taxied, presumably toward a disembarkation point at the airport. Karl had no idea how long he had been asleep and could not speculate on where he might be. His watch showed 0412. The agent looked fully alert, relaxed, and businesslike as though he were about to announce the day's accounting assignments to the junior bookkeepers. "It is in your best interests and The Company's, which are the same thing, that you not know your present location nor your destination. Please put on these hoods. I put them on the seat beside you while you were asleep. You will be led down the stairway and to another conveyance. Don't worry. Have trust in the Company in this small thing. It'll help you to adjust to the new assignments. Please do not attempt to engage anyone in conversation from this point on until you receive further instructions. That is all."

With some trepidation but without hesitation both passengers donned their opaque hoods shutting out all light and muffling sounds from the outside. Karl's hood carried a scent of laundry soap and yet a faint unpleasant odor that was hard to place. A strong hand firmly took Karl's upper arm and indicated that he was to stand. He followed the hand in a disconcerting blackness through what was obviously the aircraft hatch and down the stairs to a tar macadam. Karl could not tell if dawn had begun to lighten the area yet. All he knew was that he was in total darkness being guided by the disembodied hand. There was no other communication.

The hand bade him stop, then directed Karl's right hand to a metal stair railing. The boy stepped carefully forward lifting his foot onto the metal first stair having correctly interpreted the tactile cues. He was led into the dark interior of a second, this time larger, aircraft, where his hood was removed. The friction of removal of the black cloth stirred up the odor again, this time clearly body odor; a special tang to the odor indicated the presence of sweaty fear from the previous wearer. In a few moments Karl was joined by his previous seat mate and then by two additional young, military looking, white men. The cabin hatch opening revealed only that the pitch black of night was reluctantly giving way to the predawn grayness of an apparently foggy or cloudy day. The hatch closed, and the men took their seats.

From the rear of the aircraft two men walked to the front where Karl and his companions were seated. Karl looked around to see four duffel bags piled in the rear corner, and that the men were the 'Colonel' and one of the two assistants who had been at Fort Lewis with the senior agent. The assistant was the man who had administered the lie detector test earlier at Fort Lewis.

The 'Colonel' addressed them, "Sorry about all the cloak and dagger business," he smiled. "Aspects of your new assignments are sensitive; and there is no need for others to know the nature of the work, the locations, or your identity. You are all going to be trained in a new craft, and the first lesson is simple and will be given now: Do not divulge information to anyone—anyone who does not have both authorization and the need to know. You will hear that admonition over and over again. Learn to keep secrets. If in doubt, shut up. Your safety, a mission's security, and the very lives of your associates may depend on your maintaining security on even details that seem completely innocuous to you. Keep the faith."

The assistant said, "Relax and enjoy the ride. It is going to be a long one. We have some breakfast in back; feel free to walk around, stretch out, and to talk to anyone, but keep the questions and answers to safe subjects. No personal information. Understood?"

It was indeed a long ride in the claustrophobic cabin whose windows had been covered over with opaque green-brown paint. Karl was soon surrounded by the monotonous drone of the plane's jet engines. The young Scandinavian-American joined a poker game being played for points since their wallets and identity cards had all been taken as they entered the first plane. The game was a desultory one that passed the time but lacked incentive or involvement . The magazines available were old hunting and fishing issues with absent front covers. Karl could not even tell when the magazines had been printed. It was more than six hours before they touched down.

Four humorless men dressed in olive-drab unpressed and unmarked fatigues walked into the cabin as soon as the craft came to a stop. "You will now be searched, then you will be allowed off the aircraft," a balding wiry middle-aged agent announced. "All stand."

All stood. Karl, like the others, was carefully patted down and then made to invert his pockets. A knife was retrieved from a leg scabbard on one of the men during the pat down. Nothing was said to him, but he was escorted off the plane first and went with one of the agents in a different direction than the remaining three men from the flight. Karl wondered briefly about what would happen to the man who had disobeyed one of the first and most emphasized orders for the transfer out of their military units. 'Take all your personal items but take no weapons of any kind. Do not take any military issue items with you.' Karl decided he had plenty to concern himself over for his own lookout without concerning himself about the other man's affairs. He did not need to know. He never saw the man again.

The men relinquished their remaining personal items, including dog tags and all items of personal ID, to the quartermaster for safekeeping when they were given a set of new fatigues, skivvies, and combat items. The military issue hardware had been carefully cleansed of identifying serial numbers, manufacturer's logos, or names or the appellation 'Made in the USA.' Karl received a helmet and bullet proof vest, a German Sig Sauer 9 mm handgun with an oversized 19 round clip, a Randall combat stiletto, an M-14 combat rifle, and a compact survival kit. The kit contained such useful items as a Gigli wire saw; flint and steel; four condoms sealed in their waterproof plastic packages; a bottle of Halazone tablets; a bottle of chloroquin tablets, a twelve meter length of piano wire on a spool; two small bars of hard, concentrated, medicated soap; two vials of tincture of iodine; a small set of sterile clamps, curved surgical sewing needles, 4-0 blue nylon sutures, folding scissors and a syringe of morphine. The kit was about the size of a woman's evening makeup kit and had empty spaces with Velcro straps for future items deemed to be of personal survival value.

There was a compact, very well constructed ruck sack lined with water resistant nylon. The pack had an assortment of various sized pockets made to accommodate the survival kit, two plastic canteens were provided, extra cartridges, and extra socks. The pack had a plethora of belt straps and closed with hardwood cylinder buttons and loops because Velcro was too noisy. The CIA had learned from the experience of soldiers in the field the value of tightly securing the contents of a kit bag against movement as the soldier walked. The sound of a man's equipment, especially of metal parts, in the jungle was all the enemy needed to home in on the soldier. The CIA had not shared its paramilitary designs with MACV.

Karl was fingerprinted, weighed and measured, photographed front and profile, and put through a very efficient and thorough physical and laboratory examination by four doctors and four nurses. He was inoculated for smallpox, cholera, yellow fever, and three unpronounceable tropical illnesses. He had x-rays of his chest, skull, spine, and a complete set of dental pictures. Both shoulders ached from injections.

Karl and his fellow travelers were assigned to comfortable dormitory rooms with the luxury of single occupancy and were told to rest. The training program was to start in earnest the following day at 0400. The young man stripped and lay naked on the twin bed in his room and was asleep almost instantly. His deep and dreamless sleep was disturbed three hours later by a quiet but insistent and persistent rapping on the door. Karl slowly came around to enough conscious-ness to recognize that someone was knocking, put on his skivvy shorts, then padded quietly across the polished wood floor to answer the annoying interruption.

"Get dressed and come with me," said the trim crewcut man at the door. He was dressed casually in Levis and a Yale University crew team sweat shirt.

Karl complied, dressing in the only clothing he had at this point. The fatigues, jungle boots, and underclothing all fit perfectly. Karl was impressed with the efficiency of that detail. He and the agent left the dormitory and walked briskly around the building, then along a forested path, and into a nondescript small slab-sided building located some one hundred yards further into the heavily wooded forest. The building and its location were not places that would attract attention. The agent told Karl to enter the front office of the building and to take a seat while the agent himself sat on a straight back chair on the narrow screened-in porch in front of the screen door. The only apparent difference between this building and a thousand others like it in the woodlands of America was the presence of latticed bars on the windows and doors. There were some inapparent differences as well that Karl did not notice at the time.

Karl had barely taken his seat when two agents entered the room from a side door from an adjoining, somewhat more elaborately furnished office. The room in which Karl was sitting had a single metal desk, a folding wood table slightly longer than a standard card table, and four metal folding chairs. The furniture was standard government issue; old, utilitarian, and had had no effort expended toward mainte-nance. The walls were now beige but were probably once white. They, like the exterior of the building, could do with a coat of paint.

Karl recognized one of the agents as the ubiquitous 'Colonel;' the other man was a stranger, but his age, demeanor, appearance of unchallengable fitness, and his efficiency of movement and sparsity of speech identified him as a senior agent. He did not have and did not need insignia of name or rank any more than did the 'Colonel.'

"Relax, Karl. You're part of The Company now. Sign this Official Secrets Act Agreement, and we can talk perfectly freely and hopefully can answer all of the questions you have—at least so far as you need to know. We have some information for you."

Karl examined the complex document as rapidly as he could so as not to prolong the awkward silence between him and his superiors.

The agreement spelled out the nature of his commitment: All information that came to him was to be considered classified and was to be conveyed only to proper authorities with a compartmentalized need to know. He was to avoid seeking additional information outside his personal professional need to know. While under contract with the CIA, he was never to publish in any form any information related to the agency, its work, or the activities in which he was engaged or of which he had knowledge. After termination of Karl's association with the Central Intelligence Agency, as spelled out in the contract, the contract agent could not publish any information even in the form of fictional writing without prior permission and censorship by the agency. The contract spelled out that the agreement was entered into during the time of war and violation of the terms, which were to be regarded as laws, could constitute acts of treason, and would be dealt with in the private agency judicial division. The stated penalties included long imprisonment, and even capital punishment.

Karl was sixteen years old and had no ambitions to be an author or a commentator. The term of the contract was one year with a mutual option to renew at that time. He signed the paper with no more than a hasty perusal.

Karl passed the document across the table and the 'Colonel' inserted it into a manila envelope. The other agent smiled at the boy and said simply, "Good."

The agent opened a manila envelope and withdrew several sheets of heavy bond paper. He placed a pair of half-glasses on the middle of his nose for reading and then looked over them at Karl. He said, "Karl, I am going to give you this packet of information to read for the next two or three days. I'd like you to bring it back when you have digested the information. You will find some ID cards and a passport inside. They are made out in the name you are to assume as your cover while you are here and are to be returned at the completion of your training. This is who you are now; forget that Isaacson fellow. I know this all seems rather melodramatic, but there is a serious purpose behind all of the cloak and dagger stuff, let me assure you."

Karl had a slightly quizzical look. The agent noted it and asked, "So, what's your question?"

Karl fidgeted, then asked innocently, "What's melodramatic?"

The two agents chuckled, looking amusedly at each other. "That just means 'overly dramatic, over acting,' a fancy word that the press likes to use about the way we do things."

Karl was embarrassed at his stupid question. He made a mental note to keep his mouth shut in the future. He also determined to get enough education so he would not have to be embarrassed again.

"You are to use the new identification exclusively from here on unless instructed differently and are not to reveal your own name and history to anyone else. That is to protect yourself and your family or friends or your fellow agents from exposure. We are not at all fond of exposure, as you will come to appreciate. For one thing, it is not good for health and longevity."

Karl nodded his understanding. "The training program is very rigorous. Most candidates fail, quite frankly. If you pass the course you will be a contract officer for the Central Intelligence Agency working under the auspices of Top Secret Operation Plan 34-A; your contract comes up for yearly review; and there is no appeal to civil service control. Like everyone else, you will be subject to a three year probationary period before being considered for 'agent' status, if you should be one of the limited number who survive this training period. You will find it more work than anything you have ever done. We are trying to cram as much into your head and to get you used to the realities of the enemies you face and the jungle terrain you will work in. We want you to be able to do a creditable job for the agency and for the country, but we want you to know how to survive. Believe me, you need to know the information in this brief period of training as a minimum. Pay attention."

"Yes, sir," Karl answered. He had no doubt about the gravity of the undertaking. His drill instructor had already convinced him of that.

The senior agent continued, "We don't use terms of rank in the agency except for certain obvious people like the DCI or ADCI. They are gods with whom you are not likely to fraternize. You won't have any badges, medals, insignias and neither will anyone else you work with. Not to worry; you will know who is in charge," he smiled confidently. "Don't be too surprised to see civilians engaged in military activities or vice versa. Viet Nam is not your usual kind of war. We don't fight in the usual kind of way. That's why your new activity is referred to as 'irregular warfare.' Get used to that."

"I guess I'll learn," Karl ventured unnecessarily in order not just to sit like a lump on his chair.

"I have full confidence in you, my boy," said the hard-faced agent noncommittally. "We don't pay any attention to precision marching or crisp saluting here. You are a big boy now and don't need to have someone to tell you to clean your room. Tidiness is not the prime interest of this training program. This is not boot camp; this is survival camp; we concentrate on the essentials."

Karl's face mirrored his enthusiasm for the real training to come as opposed to the large measure of chicken droppings back in boot camp.

"Not everyone is suited for our line of work. You will be worked and tested. If you fail, you will be back in the army ranks, and you will forget that this experience ever happened. The quickest—the most unforgiving way to find yourself out of the program is to fail your periodical polygraph vettings. After you are actively engaged in Company work, failing the lie detector may mean a Company trial and swift and sure justice—the least noxious result being dismissal. Any questions about the seriousness of that kind of justice?"

"None." Karl felt a little chilly.

"I will elaborate anyway. In the federal courts, the punishment for divulging CIA information is ten years in prison and/or a $10,000 fine. I am here to warn you that very few cases come to federal trial. We act as our own protectors; and we are our own judges, juries, and...executioners. You are going to hear the phrase 'The CIA neither confirms nor denies' used in the press frequently. That represents a lot of activity we handle ourselves. Don't worry about John Law—worry about me!

"Trust and loyalty are everything here. This is not the Boy Scouts. We don't go in for reverence, courtesy, friendliness, cheerfulness, or even cleanliness much. But we are big on trust and loyalty. You don't have to be too educated or even overly smart. Common morality may well be a drawback. The loyalty oath you just signed is a life and death thing. We have zero tolerance for traitors. There are no second chances. I know Company people that are queers, drug addicts, pedophiles, wife beaters, polygamists, card cheats, and murderers; but I don't know a single living traitor to the ranks of the Company." He paused to let Karl digest the import of his sermon.

The implicit and explicit threats were not lost on the boy. He let his calm and forthright expression be his answer. He was learning.

Karl was waiting on the front walk of his dormitory before 0400 the next morning with two dozen other young men. None of them had required a wakeup call. Karl observed in passing, without any particular concern, that there were no women and no blacks among the recruits. There were a few Orientals whom he guessed to be Vietnamese. The humid air was cool but not really cold. Some of the men were in workout shorts but most were in the fatigue outfit issued to each man on arrival. Karl was sleepy; this was an hour earlier than reveille had been at boot camp; and besides, he had stayed up late memorizing the information about his new identity.

He was now to be Lars Magnusson, a Swedish national, a representative of a wholesale shoe company. He had a dog-eared driver's license, passport, and a company card, a Swedish health service ID card, and a travel visa for the United States. His photograph was in place on the driver's license and passport. The papers looked to be genuine (they were), and Karl was impressed with the organization's efficiency and attention to detail. He was not sure how his new identity as shoe salesman was supposed to jibe with his presence in a combat training center. He reasoned that it was not his to know at this point. The first hints of light denoting false dawn were beginning to diminish the opacity of the predawn night.

"Form up, men," barked the man in charge, Master Gunnery Sergeant (Ret.) Colin McClusky, lately of the marine corps, looked askance at the ill-disciplined gaggle as he did every morning. Old habits were hard to forget. He would have liked to see men in impeccable uniforms at strict attention showing three chins. He would always feel more comfortable with the clarity of the marine command hierarchy, with his closely defined status as Gunny McClusky, and with the divine right as the gunny to abuse the trainees. This was not the marines (he lamented); this was the spooks. They had their own ways that were not the marines' ways. Still, this was a fairly cushy job; and the basic tenet of marine order that decreed that 'it rolls down hill' didn't seem to apply here, at least as overtly. While it annoyed him in his relationship to his underlings, that was, nonetheless a comforting thought for his own sense of security as he contemplated the beginning of another day in his unofficial post retirement job. He could still a draw good salary, eat well, take a siesta in the afternoon, and accept The Company's housing hospitality and perks while enjoying his marine pension.

The men formed up after a fashion in four irregular lines. McClusky rolled his eyes back in his head and growled, "Okay, move out."

He set off at a brisk trot for the football field sized exercise ground. There the men again formed four more or less even lines of twelve men each and a muscular Oriental stepped out to face the trainees. Without speaking, he dropped to the ground and started counting out push-ups on his extended fingertips, adding a hand clap each time he pushed all the way up to the extended arm position. Without being instructed, the trainees followed suit. The calisthenics instructor stopped at fifty; most of the trainees completed lesser numbers in a longer time. Lars Magnusson (the name change took some getting used to), felt more pain than tiredness. His fingers ached and finally would not support his heavy body; his arms felt strained but kept on cranking out standard push-ups until he had reached the requisite fifty. The last six were performed sans the leaping hand clap. Gunny McClusky kept up with the Oriental, Lars observed. He also kept up with the duck walk, the pull-ups, including the one hand ones, and the front and back rolling and flying judo falls that followed the Herculean push-up effort. Lars found that his body refused to do it all even though his mind told him to keep up. His muscles bulged, and his tee shirt was soaked. His lungs worked to take in enough of the humid, rapidly warming air.

"Time for the morning constitutional, lad…uh gentlemen!" barked the gunny's sergeant-voice. He set off running (not jogging) toward the narrow forest lane. Lars and the others groaned silently, picked themselves off the turf, and tried to keep up. The five mile round-trip run was uphill both ways, and Lars thought he would likely black out before the gunny stopped again in the expanse of the open exercise field. He was only lightly sweating, and scarcely drew a deep breath. The man was fifty if he was a day, Lars figured. This looked impossible. He thought the army people were tough. These guys were inhuman. The Oriental instructor appeared completely ready for some exercise. He might have just walked onto the field from his lawn chair if Lars did not know better.

Before breakfast at 0800, the instructors and trainees had completed a twenty-five foot rope climb, had carried a four foot long ten inch diameter wooden pole balanced on each shoulder over an obstacle course, had raced up and over a rope netting obstacle, had crawled on the triple over a timed course through gravel, weeds, and underbrush, had carried a two hundred pound sack of rice up a flight of stairs, and had done the three S's (Shave, shower, etc.) Lars Magnusson was one tired puppy when he joined his fellows in the breakfast line. He did not much note nor care that his clothes were scruffy. McClusky shook his head.

Breakfast consisted of a selection of reconstituted powdered scrambled eggs, white toast with real butter and whole milk, overcooked and rubbery Cream of Wheat, bacon, canned peaches, and creamed chipped beef on toast (the army served it on a shingle). There did not seem like any particular reason to make a choice; so, Lars ate as much of all of it as he could. The powdery eggs, soggy toast, and glutinous creamed chipped beef were wonderful. Lars sat by the Oriental instructor who appeared fresh and alert in his crisply laundered and starched fatigue pants, spit shined combat boots, and brightly laundered new tee shirt. The man ate his own breakfast selectively and inscrutably. He was disinclined to talk.

Karl tried to break the ice. He said, "Hello, sir, I'm Lars." He was pleased with himself that he had not forgotten and given in to his instinctual urge to say, "Karl Isaacson." Karl could not place the origin of the man, but thought better of his impulse to ask him where he came from. The man did not appear to be easily categorized as Chinese, Japanese, or even Vietnamese.

"Hello," the man answered surprisingly pleasantly. "I am called Truong." The instructor took pains to pronounce his strange sounding name very clearly, looking at Lars' face to see if it had registered.

"Truong," repeated Lars taking care to include the tonal inflections he heard.

Truong smiled, glad that the young Caucasian had tried, had even gotten his name nearly right since, unlike most of the other men in the training center, Truong was his real name. It was not often that the men made any particular effort to pronounce his name correctly. It was unusual for the white Americans to speak to him at all. Truong considered it a plus if their obvious faces did not register their open mistrust of his Orientalness. White people could not mask their feelings as people should, he had learned in Viet Nam and in his brief excursions outside the training compound.

Lars and Truong commented on bland subjects like the weather and the rigors of the training schedule. Truong signaled that breakfast was over and gestured to the exit. Lars bussed his tray and dishes and made for the door. The day's training schedule was posted inside and outside all public doors and in the several classrooms on the compound. From 0900 to noon, then from 1300 to 1600, the class of recruit/trainees was to attend a series of hour-long lectures. Today, the classes were: The United States Intelligence Services, Southeast Asian Setting, Overview of the History of Viet Nam, History of the Current Conflict in RVN, Basic Vietnamese Language, Basic Tradecraft in the Southeast Asian Theater. At 1630 the agenda read simply: 'Jungle Warfare Training, Exercise Field.'

Lars Magnusson followed the crowd and took his place in an

unoccupied, uncomfortable student chair desk combination. There were two prominent posters and a green chalk board in the utilitarian room. The poster nearest Lars read:

What you see here,
What you hear here,
What you do here,
Stays here,
When you leave here.

Lars had every reason to wish to comply with that set of commands. The second poster was printed in formal government script under the official seal of The Office of Civil Defense. It read:

In The Event of An Imminent Nuclear Attack

At the first sound of the air-raid siren—three loud blasts—leave your work area immediately, proceed to the underground shelter, and select a place facing away from the door. Remove all loose items from your immediate area; remove eyeglasses, watch, other jewelry, necktie, and belt. Sit in a tightly forward flexed position with head bent as far as possible. Tuck legs up to chest. Place arms crossed in front of legs and grasp toes. Then kiss your ass goodbye.

Lars chuckled, glad to find a little sense of humor in this otherwise completely no-nonsense compound.

The instructor entered the room which instantly quieted, turned his back on the students, and printed his name (Charles Bancroft Tyler III) on the large green chalkboard. His hair was gray; he was tall and thin; but to Lars, he appeared to be fit and had an aura of asceticism about him. Lars judged him to be between sixty-five and seventy. He was dressed in a stern professorial black three piece suit, heavily starched white broadcloth dress shirt, and a hand tied plaid bow tie. Lars presumed he was a diplomat of some sort, on temporary loan to the training center. Tyler III block printed the name of the class beneath his name.

THE UNITED STATES INTELLIGENCE SERVICES.

Tyler III told his students to take notes on pads provided but that all notes were to be returned to the security marshals at the end of training. He then launched into a didactic presentation of the current mission and status of the CIA (the funnel for six intelligence services) and its relationship to the brother security agencies (all with complete budgets and staffs of their own), the DIA, the NSC (with its budget hidden somewhere in the defense budget), the security arm of the Department of State, the NIS, and a myriad of smaller organizations. He chalked a carefully prepared command tree for the Agency with the offices and departments separated from each other on the flow chart and linked with a dizzying array of interconnecting arrows. The task was made easier because no names were included, a standard CIA custom. "The agency is listed in the Washington, DC telephone book, but by department extension number only," Tyler III said. "Any attempt to speak to an individual human being by name at the Langley office building will be rebuffed by the polite but unswervable operators."

Lars wrote feverishly and fought sleep produced by his own postprandial lassitude and Tyler's lecture style that was something like a librarian's rendering of the geodetic survey. The boy's head was throbbing before the hour was up. He learned about white research (the collection of public information), gray research (the collection of information by part-time agents and Americans abroad), and about magic (clandestine covert activity—"the only activity that need concern the assembled students," according to Tyler). The only incentive to learn, so far as Lars was concerned, came from Tyler III's parting statement, "You will be asked to reproduce this CIA organization chart, that serves to control more employees than are in the State Department, on your final examination. Don't be too cavalier about the dry stuff that bores you right after breakfast or lunch. Knowing this material may make the difference between making the grade or not."

Thus cheered, Lars and his classmates, pinched and slapped themselves into a semblance of alertness, and walked in a Zombie-file to the next door classroom.

"You look dreadful," chimed an enthusiastic young woman's voice from the back of the classroom after the men had all been seated just long enough to begin lapsing back into their torpor.

All eyes rotated to the source of the melodious voice. A diminutive Chinese woman, between fifteen and thirty-five, walked down the makeshift aisle with sprightly strides. "I am Sylvia Chin," she said with and engaging smile. "At least you can call me that; call me Sylvia. Nothing is as it seems to be around here."

"Good afternoon, Miss Chin," chorused a front row of somewhat older recruits with a good humored laugh. Lars guessed that these four or five men had spent some time in RVN. They sounded like the students in a Chinese grammar school greeting their favorite teacher.

Sylvia laughed with a bell-like sound reminiscent of a wind chime, melodious and attractive. She smiled and said, "Gentlemen, it is my job to wake you up and to teach you about the topography, geography, geology, flora, and fauna, of Southeast Asia, a most fascinating area, indeed. I see that my most challenging task will be to wake you up so you can absorb the delightful things I am going to teach you for the next four months.

"Jump up! We'll do some exercises!" She then perfectly executed a complicated *kung fu* kata, whirling, high kicking, and striking four imaginary opponents. She ceased movement and bowed crisply with her feet precisely on the spot where she had started, facing her students.

"Now you, I trust you know *wu xu*," she invited. She was pleasantly flushed, but her breathing was even and regular.

The men made a few shuffling movements and looked down at their feet embarrassed at their clumsy inability. She piped, "Hey, maybe another time we do the Four Swan kata. Right now, let's just jump up and down like jump rope." She showed them what she had in mind.

Now awake and free of mental cobwebs, Lars and his seat mates, pens poised over their official note pads, waited while Sylvia got her notes together. The small Chinese fireball then launched into a rapid fire, almost breathless, lecture on the magical region of Indochina.

"The Southeast Asian region is a sort of broken horseshoe of land around the South China Sea, made up of two peninsulas and scores of islands," Sylvia began with frequent reference to the large area maps and to the smaller country maps hanging on the classroom walls. "In the northwest we have the Indo-Chinese Peninsula—Viet Nam, Laos, and Cambodia—which extends off the mainland of Asia. Stretching down south from this peninsula is a long narrow body of land called the Malay Peninsula. In the south and east is the huge group of islands, the archipelago of Indonesia. The Philippine Islands lie to the northeast. Taken together, the islands and peninsulas occupy a land area comparable to one half the size of the continental United States.

"The Southeast Asian region is more than 4800 kilometers long from north to south and over 320 klicks wide. On the west is North Burma starting in the Himalayas through Laos, Viet Nam, Cambodia, Thailand, Malaysia, Singapore . . ." Sylvia's stick pointer traced the border on the maps. "The eastern border is the ocean. The region is very similar throughout in climate, terrain, flora, and fauna. The people have considerable similarities, being Asians, but also great diversities. In general, Southeast Asia consists of a huge mass of rugged and trackless mountains covered with deep, thick forests, rice growing river deltas, coastal plains, fertile inland hills and plateaus, and areas of vast swampy jungles. The borders are often formed by barrier mountains and large rivers.

"The countries share similar advantages and disadvantages, all being resources rich and technology poor third world nations. They are quite different from one another in their histories and in their forms of government and in their relationships to the outside world. Thailand is a stable country, relatively free of strife, has never been conquered, has a growing exporting economy, and is largely pro-Western and welcomes tourism and foreign business. Viet Nam, on the other hand, has a history of foreign domination met with fervid nationalist opposition. The nation is poor with an understandable mistrust of foreigners of any kind.

"Let me tell you a bit more about Viet Nam today, since it is obviously the country of most interest in the area. In the days to come we will learn several facets about the country so you can understand the nature of the people and the fight that is ongoing there. We have only a few more minutes today; so, I will bore you with some general details to let your brains rest before we get into the stuff you will need to memorize starting in our next class. That will be on Monday. I guess they told you there are no weekends here," she said with a wry smile.

"Anyhow, about Viet Nam itself. The country has about 330,000 square kilometers of area which is larger than all of Virginia, North and South Carolina together and is only a little smaller than are East and West Germany combined. The coastline of the country is very long, almost twice the length of England, owing to the S shape of the country's east border on the South China Sea. It goes for 3000 kilometers, uh, klicks, from north to south and is quite narrow especially in its midsection. At its widest point, which is in North Viet Nam, it is 600 kilometers wide, and at its narrowest point at the DMZ it is only 50 kilometers across from the coast to the Laotian border. Because of its long length and short width, the entire country is in one time zone—seven hours ahead of GMT.

"The Vietnamese tend to look on their country as a whole with the current division into North and South countries as unnatural and temporary. They call their country 'The Land of the Ascending

Dragon' after the old name for the Hanoi region. They have a poetic view of the country as being pictured as two large baskets of rice supported on a narrow bamboo handle. The baskets are North Viet Nam and the Mekong Delta, and the handle is the central portion of the whole country or the narrow northern portion of the Republic of Viet Nam or RVN as you military types would abbreviate it.

"The country, north plus south, lies between the Tropic of Cancer and the Equator, and is, therefore, generally tropical and constant in climate with a predictable dry and a rainy season. The country includes a cluttered collection of thousands of islands, archipelagos, found from the Gulf of Tonkin to the Gulf of Siam. That's the old name for Thailand, but in the sea, the old names persist. You can see here on the map that the coast of North Viet Nam presents a concave curve facing the huge Chinese island of Hainan in the middle of the Chinese Sea. Just for your information, many of the islands claimed by Viet Nam are in dispute with a number of other countries about their ownership. The controversy matters because their important fisheries and especially mineral resources in question.

"The great river of Viet Nam, of South Viet Nam, that is, is the Mekong. It is the seventh biggest river in the world. It starts in the mountains of Tibet and winds for 4200 kilometers down through Laos and Cambodia, and finally from the Cambodian border turns east to enter Viet Nam then passes out into the South China Sea at the Camau Peninsula in Viet Nam. The Mekong is known as the *Cuu Long Giang* or the Nine Dragon River because it breaks up into nine tributaries before flowing into the Sea. This is the great rice basket of the country. It is infested with communists."

Sylvia glanced at her wristwatch and stopped her narrative abruptly. "I have almost committed the unpardonable sin, going overtime. I will see you in two days time; and we will talk more about the country and its people, and its troubles. I will not be talking much about the war there; you get that from the Agency warriors. I am just a humble information technocrat," she said blandly but with a twinkle in her eyes that suggested that she was probably considerably more.

Lars was alert now but antsy. He was a doer, not a sitter, and needed some release. He jumped up and down, ran in place, and did some stretches before catching up with the rest of the trainees. The boy was completely revived from the exercise of the early morning, and he was at his peak. To his surprise, Lars was finding that he rather enjoyed the learning. Whereas high school, which he had never completed, was an irrelevant drag, he could see the importance of what he was being exposed to now. That justified some attention in his mind. Besides, he was absolutely dedicated to making it through the training program.

The last class before lunch, on what was to become the weekly day of didactics, was entitled modestly, "An Overview of Vietnamese History." Lars learned from his fellow trainees that the best stuff came on alternate days when they concentrated on pragmatics such as weapons, ballistics, tradecraft, jungle survival, hand to hand combat, and the like. Lars was doing more than putting up with the heavy book learning or passing the time until the 'best stuff;' he was beginning to take a real interest.

The men seated themselves in an entirely similar classroom to the one they had left. The teacher, correctly, professor, was waiting for them when they filed in and took their places. He was an elderly, thin, weathered Vietnamese. His long hair and beard were wispy flowing white, and his clothing was free of any taint of westernization. He wore a black silk robe over black silk pants which were cinched about his waist with a length of brown ribbon. The robe had red letters and ornate flowers embroidered on the lapels. He presented a professorial, albeit eastern, even wise figure that commanded attention, and the man spoke very quietly in old-fashioned French accented English.

"Good morning, gentlemen," he said as soon as the room had become completely free of noise. The men were hesitant even to cough in the presence of this august character.

"I am Doctor Nguyen, professor of history from the University of Hue'. My specialty is ancient Vietnamese history, and most of this class will therefore be about the people and events prior to the era that led up to the present unpleasantness in my country. My dress and habits are those of the mandarins who have provided culture and order to the Land of the Ascending Dragon for two thousand years. I appreciate your respect for the differences you see between me and your culture of some two hundred years making. I trust that you will carry with you a similar respect for the people of Viet Nam when you go there as guests of the republic. The land has not always known an American influence, I am sure you know. I wish for you to appreciate what Viet Nam has been and can yet be."

His voice was just above a whisper, and the men strained to listen. It was a very effective way to get their attention. Dr. Nguyen began his formal lecture with a preliminary statement of format. "Please do not ask questions during my lectures. It is considered most impolite in my country because it disturbs my train of thought and interferes with the flow of understanding between master and pupil. I am informed that things are different in America. I do not disparage the difference, but I do require the respect shown by the old ways.

"Today, I will give you but an outline of important dates and happenings in the long course of history of Viet Nam. In the days hereafter, we will learn more of each era.

"There is evidence of civilization in what is now Viet Nam having existed for four thousand years. That corresponds to the European preliterate ages and before. There were mountain highlanders living communally in Northern Viet Nam two or three thousand years BCE," the professor stated. He saw an unspoken question on Lars' face. "BCE refers to that period before the common era, meaning before the birth of the Christian deity, Jesus.

"The great events of history that determine the current thinking and character of the Vietnamese people can be dated to 111 BCE when the Chinese Han Dynasty conquered the people of the south, the Nam Viet, as they knew them, subjugating the people of what we now know as North Viet Nam. The Chinese ruled and spread their considerable influence for a thousand years during which time there was a perpetual migration of adventurers and populace southward. The farther south they went, the less they were within the reach and control of the thinning hold of the Chinese to the north. The Nam Viet developed their own customs and were influenced by other visitors and traders such as Siamese, Indians, Champas, Khmers, and perhaps Egyptians and Phoenicians. They fomented unrest with their Chinese overlords as often as possible thereby establishing an historical pattern of resistance to foreign dominance.

"The Han Dynasty ruled roughly from 200 BCE to 220 CE and was the first great Chinese power. They invaded and ruled most of China, Korea, and what was then Viet Nam and were succeeded by subsequent dynasties which were resisted by the Viets at every turn. The legendary Kingdom of the Nam Viets became the southern province of China and was known by them thereafter as Giao Chi. When the Han Dynasty collapsed in 220 CE, there was much chaos and unrest in China itself and several attempted revolts by the Vietnamese, some made famous in poetry, song, and legend. In time I hope to tell you some of these wonderful, historically based stories. Alas, today, we must simply outline.

"The ruling T'ang dynasty in China fell into disruption and the rule of the conquered kingdoms disintegrated. China itself broke into contending states in 907 CE and Viet Nam gained its independence in 938, after the battle of Bach Dang, becoming a united and independent country once again. The Land of the Ascending Dragon was an independent state for all but fifteen of the next 900 years. The seeds of the present conflict were sown as far back as those first years of the ill-fated Ngo Dynasty. Ngo was the Viet general at Bach Dang.

"Great families contended mightily for power; and the country divided into a myriad of more or less autonomous states, the boundaries and character of which were to change in a most confusing fashion over the decades and centuries. Recurrent conflicts took place with the Kingdom of Champa in Southern Viet Nam. The dominant influence of the Empire of China persisted, however. They viewed the country as a subordinate suzerainty and successfully demanded tributes up until the French influence began. It was not until 1802 that the Ly emperor, Gia Long, changed the name of the country to Viet Nam.

"My country fell prey to European colonization just as did most of the underdeveloped nations of that era. To our discredit, our ancestors invited the militant French priests in to assist them in their interminable internecine struggles in the early nineteenth century. The French laid siege to Da Nang, conquering it in 1858, leading to a gradual development of control until 1884 when my country once again formally lost its independence by being incorporated into the French Empire." Professor Nguyen paused for a moment as a dark cloud passed over his countenance. Lars was struggling with the multisyllabic vocabulary of the learned mandarin, and was feeling a little inadequate, or at least that his education thus far had been lacking.

"Once again my poor country became the scene of revolts and strife. The French stamped their influence on the whole land just as the Chinese had done before them; and the Vietnamese organized political, religious, and cultural resistance against the French just as they had done for the past two millennia against the Chinese. In 1930 the Vietnamese National Party staged the first organized armed uprising against the European hegemonists. As with previous nationalist revolts against foreign oppressors, this one was put down with such savagery that the nationalist party was virtually annihilated. The few survivors scattered, went into small underground cells, and disagreed politically. The most zealous and persistent of the groups eventually became the Viet Minh, the communists in the north and the nationalists in the south.

"In 1936 the Viet Minh succeeded in getting all of the disparate anti-French groups to set aside their differences temporarily to concentrate on the struggle to shake of French colonialism. The Second World War resulted in the temporary removal of the French from Viet Nam when they were replaced by the conquering Japanese. Although they were Orientals, superficially more acceptable to the Southeast Asians because of their appeal to racist divisions and the promise of future wealth and success with their vision of the Southeast Asian Co-Prosperity Sphere, the Japanese earned the undying enmity of the Vietnamese and all other peoples they subjugated. They were brutal murderers, slavers, rapists, and even less tolerant of the cultural heritage of the Vietnamese than the hated French.

"With the French out of the picture, the Viet Minh concentrated all their efforts on defeating the Japanese. The Japanese were finally ousted in 1945, and the Vietnamese once again became a unified and independent country. The French lacked adequate strength to return to rule Viet Nam; the Americans interfered with the French in any way they could; and the independence of the Viet Nam nation might well have persisted had the usual inability to cooperate not destroyed the nation from within.

"I am most sad to report that the victorious Viet Minh organization was successful only at making war and was a failure at creating peace, prosperity, or at making a nation. The divisions between great families present for more than a thousand years, the great political philosophical disagreements all contributed to the country's downfall again. The communist followers of Ho Chi Minh consolidated their strength in the north and drove the nationalists under Bao Dai and the Catholics south where their principal strength lay. The French took advantage of the debilitating divisiveness and rather easily regained their former dominance over my hapless and foolish land," Dr. Nguyen now spoke with an angrily quiet voice having a penetrating quality riveting attention on his words.

"Great repressions were visited upon the Vietnamese trying in vain to carry out the small daily activities of their lives. Dissidents were dealt with most severely until the contending factions in Viet Nam once again united in a part clandestine, and a part overt struggle to rid themselves of their conquerors. The Vietnamese were patient, planned well, and husbanded their resources until their forays against the French took a toll in what came to be known as the First Indochina War. The French called our great north to south highway, 'The Street

Without Joy,' because of the casualties they suffered. Finally, the Viet Minh pitted all their resources on one great gamble, one great battle. In the spring of 1954 they laid siege to the French garrison located in a small village on the border between Laos and the northern part of Viet Nam. Dien Bien Phu was more than 285 kilometers from the nearest French post. 60,000 Viet Minh attacked 16,000 Frenchmen. The British and Americans received appeals for help from the besieged French that they disregarded. On May 7, 1954, the city fell and with it a century of French dominance.

"There was a momentarily independent single Vietnamese nation with the abdication of the French. Once again what should have been a joyous victory and a great opportunity for the people of Viet Nam was ruined by the jealousies, political chauvinism, and avarice of the contending parties in the country. This resulted in another partition of the country. Above the 17th parallel, Ho Chi Minh and his communists established The Democratic Republic of Viet Nam, a country ruled by intimidation, murder, and extortionate tyranny. Eight hundred fifty to 900,000 refugees, mostly Roman Catholics, fled the tyrants and their forced collectivizations, theft of ancestral private holdings, anticapitalist pogroms, rapes, beatings, and murders and poured into the south.

"Below the 17th parallel the new Republic of Viet Nam was created after the Emperor Bao Dai abdicated in August, 1954 in the futile hope that in so doing he would ensure the independence of a united country. The divisions were so overwhelming that a Geneva Big Four Powers conference made formal the de facto two nation relationship between the contending Vietnamese factions and established a demilitarized zone at the narrow center of the country at the 17th parallel. Ngo Dinh Diem was appointed prime minister by Bao Dai to govern the entire undivided country, but Ho was appointed president by his increasingly powerful communists. The mandated free elections of 1956 never occurred; the partition became an established fact; and the seeds of the Second Indochina War took root. We Vietnamese are now engaged in an inevitable new chapter in the unrolling history of our wars.

"It will be the task of another instructor to help you to understand the current situation, of how the United States of America came to be involved. Let me just set the stage as it were by stating that President Diem inherited a country torn by sectional strife, inundated by displaced, panicked, and starving refugees. A multitude of agents, provocateurs from the communist regime, remained behind to undermine the southern state, and the government of South Viet Nam was further challenged by religious sects and a league of gangsters with their own armies and plans. No sooner had the partition been accomplished than Ho and his nefarious comrades began plotting the downfall of the southern neighbors. President Diem was assassinated, as I am sure you are well aware, in 1963. I will see you on other days to give you the details of the periods I have discussed. Until then, good day."

Professor Nguyen gathered his few teaching tools and walked out of the front of the classroom without looking back to acknowledge the class or to consider any questions. The trainees shortcutted across the quad to the mess hall. It was hungry work they had done that morning.

Lunch was hearty; self-constructed sandwiches of assorted lunch meats, cheeses, fresh sliced onions and tomatoes, and bowls of sliced fruit. Lars was thirsty and drank the root-beer with noisy relish to the near consternation of his nearest table mate. It was on that note that he first met the Frenchman. Lars' obvious enjoyment of the syrupy American drink was mirrored by an equal appearance of distaste from the dark curly haired man seated beside him. "Ow can you drink that vile stuff?" asked the man in thick French accent.

"Hey, it's my favorite," smiled Lars good naturedly.

"No Frenchman in the 'ole worl' lak that strange liquid, just give uus a little wine an' we are 'appy," the big clumsy appearing man opined with an equally friendly demeanor.

"I'm Lars," Karl lied, and wiped his hand before he extended it.

"I'm Jean-Luc," the Frenchman lied and took Lars' hand without bothering to wipe his own hand first.

Karl decided to try out his cover story and gave Jean-Luc or whatever his real name was the fable of his new name, his Swedish citizenship, his shoe salesman occupation and added the touch that he was there as a mercenary. The shoe company representative story could only be stretched so far, he reasoned. He found that he was getting fairly facile with lying.

Jean-Luc presented an open honest face, but his mouth was hard and thin lipped at rest, and he never smiled with his eyes. They were as expressionate as blank bottle caps. He cheerfully volunteered, "I am the bastard son of a French planter and a French heiress visiting the country, I am told. I 'ave no proper recollection of 'er, more's the pity. I was reared in Hue', schooled in the lyceum there, and did a couple of years at the Sorbonne. I don't like the commies; so, I volunteered for the best outfit fighting them, the CIA."

"Glad to make your acquaintance, Jean-Luc. I have a lot to learn about your country; I can see that."

"I will be most 'appy to assist you, *mon ami.*" There was a tinge of insincerity about the man that Lars discounted as being related to their cultural differences. Still, something bothered the boy about the older man.

Travis Rice Petrosian stood ramrod stiff at the front of the classroom as the trainees settled quickly into their places. No-nonsense seemed the order of the day. "I am your guide through the maze that is now the state of Vietnamese politics and the American relationship to the country. The present situation can only be understood by knowing enough history of the current conflict to develop an appreciation of the historical and limited place the United States occupies at this pivotal point in the struggle against world communism being played out in the narrow region of Southeast Asia."

The students shuffled their notebooks and prepared to write down the pearls that would have to be retrieved later to ensure their continuing place in the competitive program. Colonel Petrosian caught their collective attention, "No need to take notes, gentlemen. I will pass out a thorough outline. If you know the material in the handouts, you need not fear an examination. So, just settle back and pay attention."

There was an audible relaxation in the student ranks. "I am Travis Petrosian, Colonel of the United States Army, Special Forces. I earned my bones In Country with four years boonie service, four purple hearts, and recurrent dysentery. I am here in…uh, the academy training center getting over my latest purple heart, a little gun shot wound to the butt," the colonel said with a self-deprecating shrug.

"I have had enough time to pour over the newspapers and magazines and to collate my own experiences with the information services of the agency to come up with a reasonably credible overview of what has happened between 1954 and 1966. When I have presented that material to you, I am going to hazard the risk of telling you why we are over there. I, for one, would like to set the record straight so you don't get all of your point of view from the com-symp news media." Colonel Petrosian, USA/SF had an adamant delivery to match the stony crags of his resolute face. He was not, however, formal or stuffy. The soldiers in the group responded positively to this hardy character.

"Uncle Ho started the consolidation of his power in the north even before the Geneva Conference recognized the finality of the separation and the futility of pursuing the fiction that Viet Nam could be a

123

single and independent country. The United States assumed an attitude of paternalism toward what it regarded as a weak, dependent, and backwater country. This was an extension of our country's attitude toward Asians growing out of the Korean War. The Vietnamese, on their parts, never agreed to nor signed the accords. The agreements were no more than the machinations of foreign powers, some well meaning, but all rather ignorant of the realities and complexities of the world of the Vietnamese.

"Prime Minister Ngo Dinh Diem was appointed by the sitting emperor, a nice man who had been little more than a French puppet. Diem had the real power and exercised it with consummate wisdom. He arranged a workable political system—his Personalist Party—that was controlled by his own people, the Catholics, but that acknowledged the importance of the country's majority Buddhists. He resettled the refugees as rapidly as possible and was remarkably successful in helping them to assimilate. The Chinese were essentially relegated to Cholon, a district of Saigon. He had a number of challenges that he handled most successfully including the quashing of the military-religious societies, the Cao Dai and the Hao Hao and the gangster armies of the organized Binh Xuyên. Diem took over and improved the South Vietnamese military, suppressed the dissidents, and presented a much improved situation to the nation when he called for a national referendum in October, 1955.

"He won 98% of the popular vote and became the first president of South Viet Nam. Bao Dai stepped down, quite graciously, I might add. For all of his sycophantic and foppish ways, the man was a real Vietnamese patriot at heart. He stayed on as an advisor to the country, but chose to live in France.

"The United States became more or less directly involved in the Viet Nam situation in 1955 when we began to contribute financial aid to the country. We had financed 80% of the French war effort before that. Later in the year we sent the first military advisors to aid in the struggle for democracy. President Diem refused to permit the nationwide (north and south) elections required by the United Nations in 1956. The partition of the country was an accomplished fact by then anyway. You may not know, but the United States had never agreed with or signed the Final Agreement of the Geneva Convention, and was not at all disturbed by Diem's actions. The USSR and China were not keen on establishing a precedent of allowing popular elections in divided countries, and they didn't raise a fuss either.

"The US pursued and still pursues a worldwide policy of containment of communist expansion and ascribes to the domino theory of Mr. McGeorge Bundy that the fall of one Asian, especially Southeast Asian, country will result in the fall of its neighbor until the whole region will be under the communist yoke, and then they will be knocking at the doors of people in San Francisco. The pinko, Harry Truman, pardon my French, would not let MacArthur stop the Chicoms above Korea, but our current leaders have wisely determined that the commies will go no further than what they already have in Viet Nam. At least, we will see to it that South Viet Nam and its non-Communist neighbors will be able to live in a free society." Colonel Petrosian was wound up and felt his voice taking on too much of a preachy tone. He paused and collected himself, reminding himself of the task at hand.

"The US Military Assistance Advisory Group-Viet Nam (MAAG-V) was formed in late 1955 replacing MAAG and served as the organization to control the massive support our people sent to the free Vietnamese people. I'd like you to know, for the record, that the Congress was unanimous and the press was altogether supportive of the effort and were full of praise for Diem and his accomplishments. Probably the most definitive date we can choose for the beginning of the War in Viet Nam, the conflict the Southeast Asians know as the Second Indochina War, is 1959 with the aggression of Ho Chi Minh. He and his central committee decided in January to change from a political to a military war, and in May they started work on the enlargement of the Ho Chi Minh Trail. The first two Americans, noncombatants, advisors, innocents, were murdered by the Viet Cong in June. In December, we had no more than 800 military personnel in country, including adjunct people; and by the end of 1960, that number was only about 900.

"In May, 1961 Lyndon Johnson, the new vice-president, toured the country and recommended that we increase our action there. Diem requested US troops to train his armed forces a month later. By December we had 3200 troops in South Viet Nam and were considering a recommendation by Gen. Taylor to raise that number to 8000. MACV was formed in February, 1962 (Colonel Petrosian pronounced the initials of the acronym together as if one word in true brown shoe military fashion), and the president warned the communists that the US advisors would return fire if fired upon. We had some 11,000 US military people in country at year's end.

The Viet Cong waked everybody up in January, 1963 by decisively beating ARVN at the battle of Ap Bac. We appropriated a creditable 400 million dollars in American aid and upped the advisor numbers. That was a bad year for the Viets, a lot of political upheaval; but I'll get to that later in the course. It was a terrible year for the US, as you recall—President Kennedy was killed by that communist sniper Oswald, may his soul rot in hell." Travis took a deep breath.

"Two years ago, 1964, brought us into the conflict in a serious way. President Johnson ordered the removal of all US dependents; we started the search and destroy, clearing, and securing procedures; we cleared the junks off the coast of North Viet Nam; and the Maddox was attacked by communist patrol boats. Congress passed the Tonkin Gulf Resolution, and we sent in the Fifth Special Forces Group from Fort Bragg. We had 23-24,000 of our military people in country, and the ARVN nearly doubled its strength to half a million troops.

"The most up-to-date thing I can tell you militarily is that the Air Force started Operation Rolling Thunder a year ago this month to cut off the Ho Chi Minh trail and to carry the destruction right into North Viet Nam, and that is stopping them cold as of today. If you want my candid opinion, I think that is the best thing we have done since this stinking mess started. We're going to send significant combat units in any day now. The war will be over by year's end; you mark my words. Uncle Ho will be a lamb before New Year's. I just hope you can get over there before it wraps up—you'd hate to miss the whole show!"

After the trainees dragged themselves to the next door classroom, the 'Colonel' entered a side door and said, "Hello, Trav. How are you doing?"

"Dustin, didn't know you were back in The World. Welcome."

"Glad to be here. Caught part of your lecture. You were in fine form. Do you have an urge to fill in some of the blanks for these boys?"

"I'd kind of like to drop a hint about what organization sent Major Lucien Conein to North Viet Nam in '54 and '55 that just might have influenced the exodus of all those Catholics."

"Now, now, Trav. Mustn't be critical of the SMM. They did a lot of good work—like contaminating the oil supply and sabotage of bridges, Hanoi power plant, and the water facilities. For the record, 'Black Luigi'—you probably remember him as 'Lulu'—reported a disinformation campaign that resulted in the Viet Minh currency dropping to half its value in two days, and smuggled in eight and a half tons of supplies for the Haos with fourteen agent radios, 300 carbines, 90,000 rounds of ammunition, 50 pistols, 10,000 rounds of pistol ammunition, and 300 pounds of explosives. Not bad work."

"And some black work on the Catholics, you neglect to include."

"And I neglect to do so on purpose. Besides Special Forces has a few stones in its garden best left unturned, no?"

"I prefer the sanitized Company version of history better anyway," Colonel Petrosian mused and smiled. "Like Jehovah's Witnesses say, 'A little lie for the Kingdom's sake;' I guess that's why I'm here."

"Your back getting any better, Trav?"

"Some...not enough to let me run and play with the other kids."

"But, soon, no?"

"I don't really think so, Dustin. I am going to be a REMF for the duration, I'm afraid. If I don't get riffed, I will do some instructing, some pencil pushing, then have my twilight tour at Schofield or some other army resort if I can swing it. I still have four more for thirty. I hope they will give me that much. You never know, though."

"Nope. Especially with the bad press we've been starting to get. I'm afraid us old warriors will be unpopular at the end of this one. Now that you think of it, between wars we're like doctors when people are well; people don't like to think about us much less pay our bills."

"Um humh," Petrosian agreed. "Remember Kipling's lines -

It's Tommy this and Tommy that,
then let's chuck out the brute,
but 'e's the savior of the land,
when they begin to shoot."

"Too much truth in that for comfort," the 'Colonel' said quietly.

The two friends walked toward the classroom door to attend to their separate duties. Colonel Petrosian asked at parting, "If it's not out of line for me to ask, what's your rank now?" You've been the 'Colonel' since the middle of the great war when you were probably a captain."

"Well, I wouldn't want it spread afar, but I'm a GS 18 as of my return to The World this month."

"We-eell, congratulations, General Hauter. I'm proud of you. I have to think in terms of ranks like BG, I just can't keep those civil servant government numbers straight."

The trainees were beginning to show signs of mental fatigue. The intensity of the class material was more than most of them had bargained for; eight men had attended a university, and only a small handful had had the experience of getting a degree. The majority found the day wearisome even if interesting, and most of them had doubts about their abilities to cope with the extent of material that had to be learned. Lars was one of those.

The class on basic Vietnamese language was taught, surprisingly, by a tall, athletic, curly blond haired twenty-three year old who smiled at the wondering glances from the class. "I am Ruben Smith, gentlemen. I learned Vietnamese by living there. My father was in the diplomatic corps in the early fifties, and then he stayed on at the Saigon Bank when the French left in '54 and '55. I learned English at home and Vietnamese and French from the streets, the best place and at the best time of life—childhood. The Company thinks it is wise for you to learn some fundamental Vietnamese to be able to protect yourself and to be able to communicate enough to get the job done. There are no more than seven or eight Americans In Country right now that speak even passable Vietnamese. I think it is critical to your success that you make the effort to learn to understand and to speak more than the fundamentals, the sort of pidgin Vietnamese. You will not have respect from the natives until you do.

"Today, I will try to acquaint you with the language; and after today, we will gradually talk more and more. You will have to participate to learn the rudiments; you can't just sit there embarrassed to try. You will have to satisfy me that you have picked up enough to function In Country before I will certify you for having passed the class. You realize that you must pass every class to graduate from the training center." He paused to monitor the affect of his statements.

"This will be the only pure lecture class in the entire course. This is the only class you take every day. The trainee on the front row here is passing out the vocabulary words for tomorrow. Be prepared for at least that many new words every day. I have written them out in three forms. The first is the formal accented Arabic letter printing, called *quoc ngu*, the second is the phonetic pronunciation, and the third is the English equivalent. Don't worry too much right now about the written form; it is too complicated to deal with at the beginning. Remember, real Vietnamese is written in *Chu Nom,* in what are essentially Chinese characters modified by the individualistic Vietnamese for their own distinctive usage. For instance, the old Chinese ideogram for 'war' is represented by a roofed house containing two women. Also, don't worry too much about the spelling. There is no general agreement on the rendering of Vietnamese into English spellings. For example, you will frequently see such words as 'song' and 'son.' They are the same.

"English is a Romance language, a Roman or Latin origin language, that has similar roots, sounds, verb conjugations, and a familiar character with Spanish, Italian, French, Portuguese, German, and even the Scandinavian languages to some degree. Vietnamese is its own language with a heavy influence from Chinese. It will sound very different to your ears, entirely foreign at first. The language is a monosyllabic, multitonal one. That means that every sound or syllable is a separate word. Every syllable can be pronounced with any of six different tones in the dialect of North Viet Nam or five tones in the Southern dialect where you will function. It is worth remembering that if you hear an interrupted tone, you are hearing a North Vietnamese speaker. To be forewarned is to be forearmed, gentlemen," he emphasized.

"That is the hardest part about learning Vietnamese. If you had a word or phrase having just two syllables, it could have ten or even twelve meanings depending on how the speaker presented the tones. Listening to Vietnamese is like hearing oriental music; sounds going up and down, flowing or chopped, wavering or trilling, etc. The second hardest part about understanding this language is that they do not have absolute spellings of words. No official dictionary exists since there is no agreement on how to write words, especially place and person names. The easy thing about Vietnamese is that the grammar is simple, unlike English, French, or German. It is like Mandarin or Cantonese in that there are no articles—you don't say 'a thing' or 'the thing' just 'thing,' for example. No modifier endings are used on verbs or nouns; the Vietnamese just add another word in front of the verb or noun as a classifier. Verbs are not conjugated which will be a relief to those of you who have slaved over verb conjugations when you tried to learn one of the Romance languages.

"In every language it is as important to learn the cultural attributes underlying the language as it is to know the words of the language alone. Viet Nam is a formal, polite, even haughty country. There are very different forms of address depending on the age difference, family relationship, and sex between the person speaking and the person being addressed. Unlike us, the Vietnamese come from a culture thousands of years old that venerates older people and actually worships its ancestors. Old people are shown special respect. You address a female differently than you do a male.

"For now I will give you only one example of the difficulty of understanding." He wrote the word '*ma*' on the black board with no diacritical accent mark.

"*Má*," he said in high tone that then fell. "That is mother."

"*Ma*," he repeated with a high, flat tone. "That means ghost."

"*Mã*," the intonation was rising. "That means, a 'game."

"*Mả*," he said melodically; tone beginning low and rising. "A grave."

"*Mà*," the intonation was falling from a medium pitch. "That means, 'however.'"

"*Mạ*," he sang in a low flat tone with his rich baritone voice. "That describes a process of coating with silver."

Every head in the classroom shook in bewilderment. "I take it that is clear then?" Smith laughed at the confused faces. "I think this is going to be fun, no?"

"No," a few of the men muttered.

"Good. Now let's have you try…Let's count. That's always a good place to start." He wrote the cardinal numbers one to ten on the board and repeated each of them separately then the entire set several times, *ēMột, Hai, Ba, Bốn, Nắm, Sáu, Bảy, Tám, Chín, Mười.*"

"Any volunteers?"

Jean-Luc DuParrier's hand shot up. He stood and faced the class with a disdainful Frankish pose, "*Không, Một, Hai, Ba, Bồn, Nắm, Sáu, Bảy, Tám, Chín, Mười, Mười môt, Mười hai, Mười ba, Mười Bốn, Mười lắm, Mười sáu, Mười bảy, Mười tám, Mười chín, Hai Mười, . . .*"

"*Giỏi*" (good), Smith said with a hint of an edge in his voice. "Like a native speaker. I take it you have spent some time in Viet Nam."

DuParrier nodded, taking the statement as justified praise. He did not see or ignored the frowns of his classmates.

"For the rest of us, a few simple greetings to men."

He wrote '*Chảo ông*' on the board. "That is the greeting to a man of similar age when you first meet."

The next phrase was '*Chào Anh.*' "This is the most common greeting among men who know each other informally. It is in essence, 'hello, brother.' It is the greeting to a younger man."

Smith then chalked, '*Chào em.*' "This is the greeting to a younger brother, actually it is used for females as well."

"Divide into groups of two to practice," the teacher instructed.

Lars was seated next to Jean-Luc. The Frenchman turned to Lars as if they were longtime friends and said, "Ah *mon ami*, what an opportunity for you. We will be partners. I will teach you. This is a good day for you!"

The enthusiasm was guileless, and Lars took no umbrage at the presumptive braggadocio. "You are going to have a tough time. I haven't been able to understand a thing."

Jean-Luc gave a small Gallic shrug. "You will learn from me. Please repeat: *Chào Anh.*" His intonation and accent were flawless, not even French tinged.

Lars tried and failed, tried and failed. Jean-Luc had him repeat the phrase half a dozen times until Lars could hear the music. They did the same thing with the other phrases until Lars felt self-confident in his first brush with the ancient language. He was able to count well enough to twenty to be understood by a Vietnamese who was willing to make any kind of effort. Lars felt a boost to his self-esteem, and smiled his gratitude to his mentor.

"Better be careful not to let the others know that you are learning faster than they, that you have me for a tutor, my young friend. They will be jealous," the older of the two trainees said with a turn of his lips that Lars interpreted as being somewhere between a satisfied grin and a condescending smirk. And then class was over before Lars could realize how much his attention had been absorbed.

"Basic Tradecraft in the Asian Theater" was a class on acting and on lying or at least appearing to be something they were not for the most part. Lars was intrigued by the stories of unnamed Company heroes and legends whose exploits were described to illustrate the instructor's points.

Mr. Danielson, the only name he shared with the class, was dressed in tropical whites, a flowered silk tie, Panama braided leather huaraches, and had a matching handkerchief in his suit coat pocket. He was portly, plethoric, smoked an illegal Havana cigar while lecturing, and sweat profusely though the room was only a little over warm.

He emphasized the strict maintenance of one's cover story including the natural embellishments invented on the spot by the agent. He described the methods of surveillance, especially the 'figure of eight' doctrine of checking and rechecking, and detection of a tail. He told several stories to illustrate and to drive home the fundamental principle that there is 'no such thing as a coincidence.' Mr. Daniels said pointedly, "Have a high index of suspicion. No one is as they seem. You cannot believe anything you see or hear. Anything out of place or out of the ordinary, is bad. If you see a person twice in a day, he or she is an enemy. Today is the day to stop trusting anyone. That is not paranoia; that is just the reality of the world you have joined."

Mr. Danielson warmed to his subject punctuating the air with his cigar. He told of agents who lived because they recognized a subtle incongruity and of agents who died slow deaths because they chose to ignore the available signs. He captivated the audience of tired trainees and finished the class with a promise to teach them bit by bit over the next four months the lifesaving skills of espionage tradecraft as practiced by surviving old Asia hands.

"I nearly forgot, gentlemen. I need to give you the textbook. I require you to know this manual backward and forward. It comes under the heading of 'know your enemy.' Your tradecraft is being directed, at least largely so, at these clever little people." Danielson passed out a small yellow manual entitled, "The Viet Cong Infrastructure: Modus Operandi of The Selected Political Cadre".

When he and the others arrived at the exercise field at the end of the long day of sitting and listening, Lars was ready for the first set of instructions. He was given a set of black heavy silk pajamas and a pair of sturdy sandals made from a used tire and told to change into the costume in the nearby copse of trees. Lars noted the location of his clothes and returned as quickly as possible to get in the queue for the warm-up jungle run. The entire group set off behind Truong at a hard run from the middle of the mown grass of the exercise field and into the thickest part of the surrounding forest where they slowed to a trot.

Truong held up his hand to stop them, made a signal to divide up into groups of six, and put his finger to his lips in the universal signal for silence. In a matter of seconds, six totally camouflaged individuals emerged from the undergrowth, from the branches of trees, from invisible hatches in the ground, and sprayed the twenty-four trainees with red paint balls from air guns. The hits from the paint balls stung and raised violaceous lumps. The groups of six trainees were each the victims of an individual from the hidden world of the forest. Sylvia Chin ruthlessly destroyed Lars and his hapless squad. Lars and every other trainee, including the few with a tour or more in Viet Nam, were immeasurably impressed. There had been no hint of the presence of these adversaries. Surprise and chagrin were total.

"Now we will get down to the serious business of functioning in the bush," Truong said in a matter-of-fact voice. "Follow the agent who just humiliated you. Learn these lessons, or you will come back in a body bag."

Lars ran after Sylvia, who threaded her way noiselessly through the underbrush. The men behind her crashed and clattered over the dead fall and low hanging branches. After ten minutes of rapid movement, the panting entourage halted behind Sylvia's squared arm. "Did you hear yourselves, gentlemen? How many of you do you think would have passed through here undetected? You sounded like water buffaloes headed for water. Even your breathing was audible to an enemy. We will patiently learn two things today: the first lesson in moving quietly including the standard American military stealth hand signals and something about camouflage and concealment."

"Big man, walk ten meters into the forest and hide. I will do the same," she said indicating to Lars to break ranks. "The rest of you face south and don't turn around for a full minute. Then come and find the two of us."

The group turned obediently, fascinated by Sylvia's obvious skill and the challenge. The last head changed directions, and Sylvia melted into the tangled brush in complete and eerie silence. Lars picked his way through the bushes, leafy pathways, and snarling branches as carefully as possible but was painfully aware of the absurd amount of noise his big body was making. He hurried to get as obliquely far away from the five remaining trainees as possible within the limits of the prescribed ten meter distance. His breath came harshly from the tension and hurry to hide himself in the minute before the trainees were to fan out for their search.

The men crashed through the trees in a thirty degree angle arc from the point immediately behind them. Lars could hear them advancing upon him within seconds. He was discovered in fifteen seconds and felt inept and clumsy. He joined in the search for Sylvia. The men covered the thirty degree search arc to the ten meter limit together in frustration. Sylvia was not in the search zone. They expanded their search fifteen degrees on either side of their original arc covering the total sixty degrees in a few minutes without any sign of the Chinese girl. They were embarrassed and nonplused. Sylvia was offending their collective sense of machismo again.

They fanned out covering the remaining portions of the circle and despite the small circumference of the area could not find the agent. "She has gone farther away. I thought she only got ten meters like the blond guy," said one in angry puzzlement.

"She cheated," opined another of Lars' platoon-mates with conviction. "Maybe that's the lesson, here."

They looked at each other in bemused anger, embarrassment, and frustration lacking a leader or an organized plan until they realized that there were only five of them instead of the original six.

"What the . . .?" barked the most agitated of the men.

"Don't be a dip; she got one of us. I don't know how or when or where; but she did," a second said in admiration.

The men now felt challenged to the limits of their testosterone controlled psyches. They plunged into the surrounding undergrowth with enthusiastic noisy zeal. "Check back in...say. . three minutes, okay?" shouted the man who had deduced the implications of the short count of men.

When the men reconnoitered in the clearing, they had to laugh in consternation. There were only four of them. Lars said with determination, "She can hide with the best of them, but it will be a cold day before I let her sneak up on me. Let's get her and get this over with. This is getting humiliating."

Back into the bush. Lars watched the ground, the branches, the trees and strained his ears until he was attuned to every crackle and snap in the underbrush. He knew without seeing that the noise was from his three companions. He was only partly right. He edged around a large tree trunk keeping his back on the bark to allow a wide visual perimeter. The tree was just a few feet into the woods. He heard the noise that sounded like a soft twist of dry leaves. He stopped and listened intently for half a minute before deciding that it was only another sound coming from his cloddish fellow hunters.

He cautiously lifted his foot and watched where he would set it down to avoid making noise himself. As he did so, a small strong hand slapped over his mouth from around the tree trunk, and he turned back toward the direction of the hand too late to feel the prick of a small stab in the skin of his left costovertebral angle immediately over his kidney. "Shhh," she said. "You're dead, and you didn't get a chance to yell, okay?"

Lars gnashed his teeth and sat angrily down in the shadow of the big tree to nurse his bruised ego and his pricked skin. The skin break hurt far worse than its small size would have dictated because it was associated with the suffering of abashed manhood.

The three remaining men gathered in the clearing one more time now openly nervous. They had not found Sylvia and could not be sure that their missing companions had not been hurt. The anxiety of not knowing, of being fooled and shamed, was disconcerting and confusing. No one could come up with a plan and each of the three had to fight to damp down a mounting feeling of panic even though they knew it was all a training exercise—a game.

None of the three was ready for the fusillade of red paint balls that struck them from the cover of the nearby bushes. They could not have prepared themselves for the accompanying hysterical laughter from the high pitched woman's voice. It rippled with the most genuine amusement and satisfaction that it was ever the plight of a man to hear. Insult was heaped on scorn when the surrounding woods erupted with maniacal laughter from men releasing their pent-up frustrations. Sylvia emerged triumphantly from the brush, not two meters from the grassy edge of the little meadow; and shortly, her three victims joined the circle. The looks of mutual consternation were so ludicrous that they all fell to laughing uncontrollably. Tears ran down Lars' face.

Sylvia was still chuckling when she said, "I can't imagine why you are all laughing. You were just killed like the worst greenhorns on their first day in 'Nam. I guess the lesson is not lost on you gentlemen."

"I'm impressed," said one of the trainees who had spent a tour in the highlands of central Viet Nam. He spoke for the group.

"Okay, ready to get down to work then?"

The men nodded. They were sober now.

"Here's how to walk. Watch." Sylvia looked about in all directions; 360 degrees on the ground, in front, in back, and to each side of her, and above her head. She carefully selected her footfalls placing them in the spot with the least dry leaves; she stepped in a manner that had her pulling back slightly instead of pushing forward with the ball of her foot. "See how I twist my foot a little, then lift straight up, enough to clear twigs. Look at your feet and the ground near them. For one thing that kind of attention can alert you to the trip wire of a booby trap. Eternal vigilance is the price of success—I just made that up myself. Good, huh?" She smiled.

Sylvia tested fallen trees to see that they would not move before she stepped on them. She used the deadfall frequently. The effect was that she made no more noise than the wind in the leaves or the occasional forest creature. Having made her point about walking, she said, "Now, how to hide in the open."

She reached into the fanny pack she had carried all afternoon and extracted a fleecy camouflage jump suit with fine markings of a variety of earth tones. "The British proved this is the best kind of camouflage coloration as far back as World War I," she pointed out as she quickly donned the loose, soft suit. She pulled the hood over her head and said, "Stay here a sec. I'm not going far."

Sylvia stepped a few feet away into a thicker set of underbrush and squatted. She could not be seen. She moved again and stood in line with several gnarled tree trunks that held drooping small-leaved branches. Without actually moving behind the trees, she became very difficult to distinguish from the web of plant life. "See me well?" the diminutive Asian teacher asked.

"Um umh," the men muttered indicating their difficulty.

She showed them how to posture themselves, how to use the ambient foliage, how to insinuate themselves into obscure nooks and crannies to allow themselves to blend into the background. She taught them never to look eye to eye with a person searching for them. She told them this was an introduction—they would spend hours each day for four months perfecting the techniques of invisibility. Darkness was closing in.

"Time to quit! Follow me in for chow!" the exuberant girl called and took off at a swift jog along an ill kept path to the dining hall. After supper and a very brief review of his notes, Lars was asleep by 2100.

CHAPTER 5

To the compatriots of the country: Errors have been committed in the implementation of unity in the countryside...The Party and the Government have taken up seriously the subject of those lacks and errors and have determined a plan for their correction. ...Those who have been wrongly classified as landlords and rich peasants will be correctly reclassified. Those members of the Party, the cadres, and the population who have been the subject of an erroneous judgment will be reestablished in their rights and prerogatives and their honorable character will be recognized.
Ho Chi Minh, President of the Democratic Republic of Viet Nam, August 17, 1956

Tran's plane, an Air America C-46, from Saigon, put down at Phu Bai Airport in Hue' on the morning of the fifteenth of February, 1966. It was a cold, overhung day with frigid winds blowing in from the western mountains, the Truong Sons. He shivered, unused to the sensation of coolness having almost never been cold, and was sure he would not like the change of climate. He was decked out in his dress paramilitary police uniform complete with brass name plate and provincial insignia denoting his membership in the elite Provincial Reconnaissance Unit and was proud of his status as sergeant.

An American helicopter, a US Army CH-47a Chinook, stood by with its two three-bladed rotors whipping up the loose dust on the edge of the tarmac. The helicopter waiting to transfer the new PRU inductees and graduate enlistees to the Thau Thien Provincial Police compound located in a bush clearing 28 kilometers from the capital city. The chopper's markings were all provincial and national RVN with no indication of its American origin or involvement. Tran and the others ran to enter the helicopter shielding eyes and faces from the sting of swirling dust and trash. The Americans unaffectionately knew the Chinooks as the 'shit-hooks' because of all the debris they stirred up on the ground. The large chopper was powered with two Lycoming T-55 L-7 engines, each delivering 2,200 SHP. It was mounted with a 20 mm Vulcan cannon on its side, but the gun was seldom used because it caused so much vibration that it injured the airframe and decreased the useful life of the helicopter.

Seven men from Tran's *Chieu Hoi* training class on Con Son Island accompanied him, and they were joined by another group of seven in a thirty foot long by 7 foot six inch wide by six foot six inch tall cabin designed for thirty-three troops and a three ton payload. A second Chinook waited impatiently to take on an additional fourteen men.

The racket from the rotors and the induced dust storm chattering up from the beleaguered ground below them made speech, even shouting, impossible. The crew, three Caucasians who were presumably Americans, but were not identified by military insignias, indicated the simple needs of preparation for takeoff by aboriginal hand signs; and the two helicopters lifted off. They traveled at the maximum 150 mph cruising speed over the lush green carpet of jungle. It was only a matter of minutes before they touched down on a newly constructed, high quality helipad in the center of two rows of cinder block wall and banana thatch roof buildings. A huge red flag with a central yellow five pointed star of RVN hanging from a tall metal pole dominated the apex of the parade ground in front of a sturdy finished block house with a sanguine colored clay tile roof. The men with Tran escaped from the cacophony of sound and dust and waited by the base of the flag pole for directions from the men on the ground. The Chinooks lifted off and were gone. Tran brushed the worst of the dust off his new uniform and hefted his duffel bag onto his left shoulder leaving his right hand free to salute.

South Vietnamese paramilitary policemen provided the teachers, leaders, and security personnel of the compound. An occasional Caucasian came and left, but the operation was ostensibly Vietnamese. The one hundred twenty-five men in the PRU were divided into largely independent reconnaissance units of twenty-one men each. All of the units had an office liaison worker to handle communications, paper work, and to provide access to the American military machine's health care, computer works, and materiel requisition. The most pacified, most intelligent, most highly educated, with the least common criminal or VCI background, and especially the best connected men were assigned the rear-echelon positions. Tran would have qualified for one of those positions but for his NLF background.

There were no women in the PRUs in Thau Thien province, or in I Corps anywhere, for that matter, although a small number of women had entered the *Chieu Hoi* program (being more resistant to the blandishments of the GVN and less intimidated by fear than their male counterparts) and were rehabilitated into paramilitary PRUs closer to Saigon in III and IV Corps. I Corps was too close to the DMZ and was experiencing too many incursions to suit the Americans. They vetoed the placement of females in highly active combat regions for reasons indecipherable to the Vietnamese.

The early days in the new camp were spent in class learning the delicate arts of antipersonnel demolitions, simple and then complex South Vietnamese and American ciphers and codes, sapper techniques, map orientation, and close contact unarmed and non firearm combat.

The traditional and irregular martial arts were taught by *Tae Kwan Do* black belts from ROK ranger units and by mercenary civilian Japanese *Jui Jitsu* experts. There was nothing of a prison setting, no striped pajama uniforms, no guards over the PRUCs, no cells or window bars. The men were free to come and go as they pleased. For many of them it was their first freedom in many months. The only guards, concertina wire, and electrified fences were genuinely for their protection The message sent by these measures was one of trust, and the new PRUCs responded with enthusiasm. There were no deserters. The men were so intent on absorbing the advanced training and on becoming a closely functioning unit that they did not leave the compound during the first two months.

The cadres in Tran's unit of twenty-one men maintained a very vigorous self-imposed discipline of physical endurance training and learned the strange methods of the Americans from their tasteless dried foods to their wonderful weaponry. The Vietnamese learned the use of American M-14s and even M-16s but they were assigned antiquarian five kilogram M-1 Garands as personal weapons. Their free time, and there was a surprising amount of it after the regular early evening political indoctrination lectures, they spent in learning the lives and thoughts of their fellow PRU agents. Tran was especially attentive to the details of his fellow PRUC's lives.

Nguyen Van Dung had, perhaps, the most to contribute to his new unit. He was a well-trained, combat experienced and hardened NVA sapper. At least, he did his work for the NVA until he was swept up in the embrace of the *Chieu Hoi*. Dung was quite literally born to be a sapper. His father was a sergeant in the NLF Sapper Group at the DMZ, a highly disciplined 1500 man unit. There were four LAF/NVA regiments with 35 battalions in the south in addition to Sergeant Nguyen's unit. The boy had started to learn the techniques of infiltration, demolition, and mayhem at the age of eight from his exacting father along with the sons of the other enlisted men. His father was a thoroughgoing pragmatist who told Dung to remember that the quality memorialized in his given name, (*Dung* = courage), was not enough to ensure life and sometimes led boys and men to violate the trust of their family by engaging in foolhardy acts of bravery. Dung was to be wise and thoughtful if he was to live to maturity; with a mortality rate of seventy percent for sappers, the odds were against him; and they were fully impossible for heroes. When the elder N. Van (= male) Dung became a victim of one of his own devices, the son took his place in the sapper battalion. He was twelve.

As with most South Vietnamese fighting on the side of the NLF (VC) or the NVA, Dung lived with and fought for his family and his village. He had never been as far away south as the 95 kilometers to Hue', and had never even been to the borders of his home province of Quang Tri. Although he was now a regular in the North Vietnamese Army, he had never set foot north of the *Hien Luong* Bridge which spans the Song Ben Hai. The river is located almost exactly on the 17th parallel, the line dividing Viet Nam into two quarreling halves after 1954. The bridge was kept painted in vivid red on the north half and sun bright yellow on the south half. Five kilometers on either side of the Ben Hai River, so the Geneva Accords declared, was a no man's land to be claimed by neither side and to be kept free of intruders. This demilitarized zone (the DMZ) became a hellish web of concertina wire, man traps, buried ordnance, unexploded mines, and unspent artillery projectiles lying in tantalizing wait for the passerby to examine. The US Secretary of Defense had his military engineers erect a high and powerful fence ('infiltration barrier') on the south side, a massive and forbidding structure, that stretched for many kilometers and cost a billion dollars to construct, to guard, and to maintain. The barrier included the fence, wires, sensors, artillery, and combat troops. The North Vietnamese simply ignored it and walked around its ends.

The tiny village of Bo Ho Su and the five kilometer stretch of the DMZ were home to Dung; and from his first steps as a toddler, he learned to tread softly and carefully.

Historically, sappers were first described in the interminable middle-ages wars. They were the individuals that dug a narrow trench, or sap, to undermine a fortress wall and later to plant explosives. In keeping with that tradition, Dung had spent his active years tunneling, sliding his narrow body under the claws attached to concertina wire barriers, moving through the fields and dikes of rice paddies on his abdomen, snuggling into rock crevices or between logs as machine bullets wove a lethal ceiling over him, and planting the seeds of plastique that would grow lethal red and purple flowers of explosive destruction. He learned to lay mines, to string strands of grenades along the paths of GVN trucks, to operate command controlled demolitions, and how to become silent and invisible. He learned to be a world-class sprinter, hurdler, and cross-country runner.

Dung, like his father before him, found great favor with his superiors. He was promoted steadily to become the youngest sergeant in the history of his sapper group. That history went back to the time of discovery of gunpowder. His ancestors had used their skills against the hated Chinese conquerors before the despised long-nosed French colonialists, and long before the advent of the American running-dogs. Dung believed in his ancestors, his nuclear family, his village community, and in the cause of the National Liberation Front, in that order. He had no political feelings or aspirations; the communists had always controlled Bo Ho Su; and Dung was not one to question or to speak out. It was not the Vietnamese way.

Mid-morning in the late spring of 1964 when the twenty-one year old unmarried sapper was slithering through the elephant grass on a dangerous mission of destruction with his sapper group near the volcano Gio Linh, south of the Ben Hai River, an under strength unit of NVA infiltrated into his village. The overzealous political cadre determined that the village members would be given the opportunity to make still another sacrifice for the cause. He demanded that the headman present him a list of all boys over the age of twelve and all unmarried girls over the age of fifteen. The aging proud headman, was known by every inhabitant of the village as *bac* (uncle), a title of earned affection and respect. The headman was a Viet Minh hero renowned for his exploits in the struggle to rid the Land of the Ascending Dragon of the long-noses. He protested politely and apologetically; but when the young cadre insisted most impolitely, gave the list of adolescent names to the political officer.

The cadre gave an order that caused his men to murmur. He held a hurried and angry conference with the lieutenant nominally in charge of the company, and overruled the soldier. In the NVA, as in all communist armies, the political officer has the ultimate authority. The young NVA privates and corporals were silenced and dispatched to round up the children on the list. When it became evident that it was the intention of the NVA company to march away with the thirteen children, the eldest of whom was sixteen, the women began a keening wail of protest, of grief. Only the headman and Dung's mother dared lift their heads and to protest. Her daughter was only fifteen, knew nothing of soldiers and guns; she should not be taken. She was a child; they were all children. The headman said, *"Xin lỗi, đồng chí, nhửng ch ng nó không phải đi!"* (I am sorry, Comrade, but they must not go!)

Perhaps it was the fact that the headman had used a command phrase and tone that challenged the cadre in front of his men; perhaps it was his affront at any demurrer from the ungrateful and inconsequential villager, or perhaps he deemed it time to assert his authority to end any further question. Whatever the cause, the political commissar spit in the astonished face of the dignified village leader, then added the unthinkable and slapped the old gentleman as if he were a mere misbehaving woman. *"Bac!"* shrieked one of the frightened women in shock and fear. Dung's mother swept her arms out to herd the four nearest children toward the safety of the huts.

"Ngung!!!" (Stop) screamed the irate and flustered cadre. Dung's mother either did not hear or was insubordinate. Whatever the case, she did not stop. The cadre pointed at her and at the headman, barked a series of harsh commands to his men, and brought himself to stiff attention, his face contorted in anger. The men looked at each other with brief unhappy glances, then moved sharply to bring the disobedient woman and insolent old man before the political officer on their knees. The children who were to accompany the military unit were summarily marched out of the village while ten of the most hardened combat veterans remained behind to follow the next set of orders.

While her two youngest children looked on in fascinated horror, the cadre ordered two of the men to strip the foolish woman to the waist and to pin her supine on the ground. The officer walked deliberately up to the woman who was now lying passively on the ground, bent over her form, then in a lightening quick movement roughly seized her right breast by the tender nipple and pulled it as taut as he could elevating it from her thin chest wall. She cried out in involuntary pain, embarrassment since she was a modest woman, and in alarmed surprise. The brutal cadre then whipped a French flic knife through the air and amputated the soft appendage neatly at the level of the pectoral muscles. She fainted. The battle-hardened soldiers blanched and stepped back. The cadre nonchalantly threw the severed breast fragment to some dogs hiding under a nearby stack of bamboo poles. He calmly took out his service pistol and dispatched the meddlesome woman with a single bullet in the middle of her forehead. The two children, ages four and seven, stood mute. The four year old, the youngest daughter, never spoke again.

The political officer, using a conversational level of amplitude, then ordered two of the other NVA soldiers to bend the back of the horrified old man. They did. The cadre withdrew his regimental saber, jabbed it roughly into the middle of the old man's upper back, and when the headman involuntarily arched backward from the pain, swept the razor-like edge of the sword down across the nape of the man's neck with the force of a thunderclap. The dignified head, with a grimace of agony permanently etched on its wrinkled face, dropped into the red dust of the single village road. The body made two convulsive twitches before toppling on its side with twin fountains of blood geysering from the severed carotid arteries. Dung's little sister and brother were still staring vacantly at the distant horizon when the last of the soldiers left Bo Ho Su with the villager's children, and the terrified villagers straggled back in the gathering twilight.

Dung had been slightly wounded, and the wound had become infected which delayed his return from the lush volcanic mountainside with its emerald green terraced fields, reservoirs, and irrigation ditches looking benignly down on the Cham ruins. He and his fellow villagers and sappers zigzagged their way tortuously back home under the fire from the aggrieved ARVN garrison they had bombed. The fire was at first a furious fusillade, then a stuttering and desultory attempt, then no more than a few niggardly rounds. The ARVN men and their officers were no fools; they knew better than to chase their dangerous tormentors into the dank invisibility of the fields of sharp-edged elephant grass. Dung finally made his way across the secretly mapped path through the hazards of the DMZ. He was very tired, sore, hungry, and feverish by the time he slipped quietly into the village and bent down to enter the low doorway of his family's house.

It was late afternoon; the sun was sinking like a heavy red ball into the high bamboo spears to the west of the village's rice paddies. The inside of the main room of the neat little house was dark, and at first, Dung thought no one was there. His eyes adjusted to the light, and then

143

he saw his young brother sitting listlessly beside the form of the four year old girl. She was coiled into a fetal position. Dung feared that one of the buffalo had stepped on her and inquired if such were the case. "No," said the boy, his voice monotone and dead.

Dung looked at the thin child impassively, keeping his concern from his tired face. It would not do to betray his emotions. The boy began to speak, then it was as if he could not stop. He recounted the entire visit of the NVA company in exquisite detail, astonishing Dung with the clarity and intricacy of minutiae about the atrocities he recalled. Dung somehow managed to keep the shock from his expressionless face. The child gave his description with no more emotion than if he had been telling the story of the season's rice planting. Dung did what he could, then left to find his mother's body parts to bring them back to their proper resting place under the house with the ancestors.

The neighbors acknowledged Dung's presence as he walked through the village, but other than an occasional sympathetic nod of the head or a perfunctory wave, they did not communicate in any demonstrable way about the killings. After all, it was not their own family; and therefore they did not have to get too involved, thank the Lord Buddha.

Dung retrieved the remains from the hurriedly dug shallow grave and properly buried his mother under their house. He took the shivering boy with the dead soul and the silent girl, his brother and sister, and delivered them to old grandmother. Thereafter, he kept his own counsel. When, a year later, the *Chieu Hoi* leaflets told him of the safe opportunity to defect, he slipped away from the DMZ and changed his allegiances with less remorse than he changed his black pajama costume once each week. His performance in the debriefing sessions in Saigon and his patience in the detention camps accorded him favorable attention from the ARVN soldiers. His apparently genuine and unswerving animosity toward the VC and the NVA and everything they represented stood him in good stead, particularly with the CIA observers. Dung was a quiet but implacable foe of the communists despite a near total disinterest in their political theory; he had a *'Sat-Cong'* tattoo on his chest as soon as the Revolutionary Development leaders would permit it and was accepted as a completed *rallier* in no more than a few weeks of interrogation. He needed almost no military training.

Corporal Le Duc Bach was the ranking noncom in the PRU unit, since he was a Kit Carson scout with a long tenure with GVN forces.

He had assimilated into the PRU and into the SOG program with natural ease generated by his record of previous GVN service in irregular forces. His war had never been particularly personal, and he was a politically uninvolved highlander who had nothing more interesting or profitable to do. He did it for the money. It was dangerous work, he knew, but the pay was good, and he liked working with the American Special Forces soldiers. They were thoroughgoing professionals; they watched out for him just as they did for their own; and they possessed a passion for freedom from restraint that was completely unlike any other soldiers he had seen. He fit in perfectly, learned pidgin English, became facile with the remarkable weaponry of the Americans, and was welcome on their spectacular drunks whenever the green berets came out of the bush to terrorize one of their own military clubs.

Bach was amused at first that he should be accorded such honor and given such pay, especially after he learned that it would keep coming month in and month out for little more than guiding the Americans around the mountains he knew so well, and for the occasional killing. He knew how to avoid the VC and where their camps were. It was so easy that he was afraid the big white men would discover the fraud and kick him out. They never did and seemed genuinely to appreciate what he did for them. You could never tell with white men.

The French employed him for the same purpose before they left in 1954, but had been stingy and looked down on him as a lesser being. They treated him well for the most part, though, even despite his young age, and he did not dislike them. He had been fourteen when they left. He signed on as a ranger with the ARVN forces when they came through his mountain village four years later. He disliked them from the start. They treated him abominably because he was half Montagnard; they called him a *meo*. The word was hissed or spat rather than spoken. They refused to pay him some months and laughed when he protested. He retaliated by leading them away from the VC camps he was supposed to know about and to old abandoned ones that were unproductive so they would look bad to their superiors. Strangely, they did not seem to mind. Even the superior noncoms were not upset about his deceptions. He never saw an officer. Bach deserted and went to live with his cousins in a village further north until the loathsome Vietnamese left the area.

In 1963 the Americans came to the Montagnard villages and politely asked the people to move into defensible communities called Strategic Hamlets. The Americans had difficulty understanding the Montagnards' great resistance to moving since all of the land looked the same to them. They were making no appreciable progress and were beginning to look very frustrated until Bach took it upon himself to explain the source of their difficulty. Vietnamese revere their personal land above all else. The spirits of their ancestors dwell among the living people in the place where their bones are faithfully preserved. Most of the time that is in the house with the family. The ancestors are accorded reverence, and the land is hallowed for the family. It was a source of great grief when a family member was forced to leave the bosom of the family and relocate to another area. The members of the nuclear family would weep and lament for days on end mourning their loss and the fate of their loved one. When a family member died, there was no outward suggestion of grieving, why should there be? The loved one had only joined his ancestors in the joy of their companionship, and his or her spirit could linger to assist the remaining family. The bodily remains would rest with the bones of a dozen generations beneath the floor of the house.

The most terrible of calamities, the worst fate to befall people, was to be driven from their homes, to leave the bones of the ancestors untended. Death was altogether more preferable. It was unthinkable for an entire community to pick up and leave their collective ancestral spirits. That would forebode the most terrible joss. No, they would not be going. They would stay where they were and fight as need be, die as the fates willed. It was out of their hands.

"Is there anything we can do to help the people to be protected in this new program," the patient American with the green beret had queried of Bach.

Bach thought hard about it. He had never had to think of a change in the status quo before. It had never occurred to him that things might be really different. This was life. "How could you change life?"

After a decent interval, the special forces officer apologetically suggested a possible solution, "Could we use our soldiers and the families and move the bones of the ancestors with us to the new village?" he asked. Each family would, of course, ensure that their own ancestors were properly treated.

Bach thought about it again. It was a new idea, but not completely unheard of. There were stories of families who had had to leave an area because of a plague or a famine and had survived because they had had the foresight to take the ancestors with them. Evidently it could be done. He would consult the elders.

There was an interminable wrangling and bickering in the village. There was great excitement over the question. The issue was only decided when it was learned that the elders of two related villages were willing to proceed with the transfer if Bach's village would do likewise. The disinterments took more than a week with the old women standing about fretting and chattering their disapproval. The men were solemn and punctilious in their work. Finally, the village was moved and ensconced safely in their new Strategic Hamlet, and the big American soldiers could do their military work with the enthusiastic support of the village men. Everyone was happy, and Bach was rewarded by being given his job as a Kit Carson scout. The Special Forces lieutenant who hired him had told Bach that he must forswear his involvement with the VC and only work for the Americans. This situation was so much more advantageous that Bach agreed immediately. Bach was never sure how the Americans had known that he led the VC around the mountains, as well as them.

When participation in the new Special Observation Group was proposed to the half-breed Vietnamese-Montagnard in December of 1964, he readily agreed to lend his expertise. He was becoming a master at dealing with these foreigners. They offered him more money and full freedom to travel back home whenever he needed to. Who could ask for more? Bach was a happy recruit when he joined Tran and the others in the camp outside Hue'.

Phan Duy Ky was a *Bui Doi* (child of the dust) who had literally grown up in the streets. His original name, before he picked out the present one himself, had been Vo Ten—'nameless.' The baby was the Eurasian product of a careless liaison between a Frenchman, a carpenter, named Francois Malprene, and a high-born Catholic Vietnamese girl, Nguyen Thi Tuyet. 'Tuyet' means, snow; and she was named for the lovely whiteness of her skin, a rarity among Vietnamese. The girl was from Danang; and when the disgrace of the pregnancy was discovered, she had been sent to spend her confinement with a dowager aunt in Saigon. When the teenage girl was so foolish and indiscreet as to let slip the real paternity of her unborn infant, she was unceremoniously thrown into the street to fend for herself, whore that she was. Her father erased her name from the family records. She died of untreated murine typhus in a back alley of Cholon a month after delivering an oversized boy distinguished by an unVietnamese angularity to his face, and, worse, a long Frankish nose.

Other *Bui Doi* discovered the starving baby lying among the rags that covered his cold mother, then dead for two days. The little boy was still kicking at the rats who harried him, but he was losing the battle. When he was grown, Ky still bore the peculiar indenting scars from the rat bites on his infantile extremities. The children of the streets, amazed to discover a human being in worse straits than themselves, found an untapped wellspring of pity and worked gamely to keep the infant alive. Ky was made of good stuff. Despite all, the curdled milk, the rancid water, the odds and ends of vegetables and fruits, and the occasional germ-ridden scrap of meat the children could steal from the vendor carts or outrace the street dogs for, the little boy lived. He was smaller than he might have been with good nourishment, but developed a wiry strength and stamina that belied his circumstances. Children, and even adults, died about him on a regular basis. He contracted bacterial infections that should have killed or maimed him, but he lived.

Not long after he could walk, he was set upon by a starving dog and survived only because an elderly Chinese woman hated dogs and would not let the cur have its way; so, he lived. The boy carried the scars from the dog's fangs near the tear marks from the hungry rats. Like the other *Bui Doi*, he scratched a blue dot in the middle of his forehead denoting his out-caste status.

When he was five, he first became aware that he was different from other children. Even the *Bui Doi* had someone they could look down upon. He was despised by every other living person for his mixed parentage, for having one parent, a hated French person. It did not matter that he was poor, nor that he was probably a bastard, but no one, not even the children of the dust would leave the child of the French one alone. Ky was tormented and teased ceaselessly; it made him psychologically tough. He was set upon by the other children and robbed and beaten. He learned to fight. He was hungry, and there was no one to provide. He learned to steal.

When he was eleven, he was caught by a Chinese vegetable merchant as he was filling a canvas bag with old vegetables. The man struck the boy a vicious blow across his face breaking his nose leaving him with a permanently pugnacious, crooked face. When the man descended upon the boy again in righteous indignation, Ky slipped his knife from the string where it dangled protectively around his neck and buried it to the hilt in the Chinaman's left groin. Blood gushed from the severed femoral artery and splashed on the child. Ky ran out of the store, barely remembering to scoop up the bag with his vegetables.

The blood spattered on his face and his ragged shirt gave him away. He was caught by the Diem police; and without benefit of juvenile counselor, recitation of his rights (he had none), appeal to his parents, or even the rudest of trials, he was cast into Te Ban Prison where he met his first friends, the vicious adult and child criminals of Saigon. It was a hellhole where the law of the jungle prevailed—the many and the strong preyed on the few and the weak. At first he was raped and beaten. He fought back with fang and claw generating a grudging respect. The place made him mean. He lived. There he met his first semblance of a family, the Binh Xuyên. He was absorbed into the criminal organization, the Vietnamese equivalent of the Japanese Yakusa and the Italian Cosa Nostra but with a politically religious character. The eleven year old became a career criminal instead of engaging in mere sporadic street crime designed to keep body and soul together day to day.

Vo Ten was no name for an up and coming gang member. When he got out of the prison seven months later, the boy adopted for himself the name of one of the heroes slain by Diem's men during the purge of 1957. The other members were pleased with his choice of Phan Duy Ky. The novice gangster came under the control of a Fagan-like middle-aged Chinese called simply, *Bac,* (uncle) by the children who snatched and ran, picked pockets, filched salable wallets, handbags and radios, and carried packets to obscure places at night for him. He was better off than the hordes of children organized by the back-street mama-sans. *Bac* did not beat Ky much, and the protection of the gang ensured a fairly safe and steady diet, a place to sleep which, although cheap and poor by most standards, was not on the street itself; and with appropriate considerations a relative measure of security from harassment from the city police. Before the Diems and their harsh repression of the Binh Xuyên, they had been in near complete control of the Saigon police, and their tentacles still reached deeply into the constabulary.

With the advent of half-black Amerasian children among the *Bui Doi,* Ky's tormentors took less interest in his status. The Binh Xuyên had once been a criminal organization so potent that the new Diem regime had had to bow to their political power to the point that they were not only given free reign for their prostitution, gambling, and drug smuggling, but they ran the Saigon-Cholon police forces. After the purge, their political power had been forever crushed, and they were reduced to functioning as an ordinary well-organized, and successful syndicate of criminals. They still accounted for a heavy say in the day to day life of Saigon's back streets.

Ky graduated to minor extortion by the time he was fifteen, and to drug running by the time he was eighteen in 1964. His job was minor, almost menial. Ky acted as a lookout before the treacherous deals were consummated and as the final deliverer of the goods from the Laotian bandits to the Binh Xuyên. However, Ky was a bright boy, kept his eyes open and his mouth closed; and after a proper apprenticeship, began cultivating his own contacts from the Golden Triangle (The rich poppy growing region where Laos, Burma, and Thailand intersect). He brokered a few small deals on his own, became trusted (as much as was possible by the most suspicious men on earth), and began to lay aside a nest egg. He longed to be able to move up north, say to Thau Thien Province, to be closer to the Laotian source, to where the opium poppies grew, the opium paste underwent a few simple chemical processes to become diacetyl morphine (heroin); and the most lucrative, albeit the most hazardous, deals were made. Strangely, his second arrest became the answer to all his needs, an example of his good joss.

Ky was betrayed by one of his fellow Binh Xuyên members. It was almost as simple as that. It was not strictly for the heroin deal he was involved in when the police dragnet swept up him and the Laotians. It was because the men from the Golden Triangle were VC and Pathet Lao. Ky was, to his own way of thinking, nothing more than an unbiased Binh Xuyên businessman; and he could not have cared less about the political affiliation of his business partners. The deals were strictly in Piastres, and did not involve credit or political favors. There was no elaborate discussion on party doctrine. Ky was only dimly aware of the war with the communists; his main reaction to the conflict was positive since it brought in the *cố vên vĩ đai* (Derogatory Vietnamese term for Americans, one previously used for their Chinese conquerors, essentially overlords), especially the African variety, who couldn't get enough of his product; and his only other interest lay in the impediments to travel and transaction caused by the unpleasantries between people he cared nothing about. The all-knowing American computers, using surveillance data from a plethora of sources, including his latest partner in street crime, however, had unflinchingly identified Phan Duy Ky as an official clandestine member of the VCI.

Ky was arrested by the efficient CT officials and interned at Con Son

Island Prison where he learned about the rigors of the paramilitary life to his disgruntlement, and about the potential of assignment to the Provincial Reconnaissance Unit of Thau Thien Province to his enthusiastic approval. He was such a good student, appeared eager about the prospects of supporting the GVN against the VCI, and had convinced the powers that be that his actual involvement with the communists was minimal and peripheral. They made an unusual exception in his case, (besides the gift of survival) and allowed the eighteen year old the privilege of a brief return to Saigon to tidy up his affairs.

Ky ambushed the boy who had informed on him. He left the young man hanging from a hook in a Cholon duck market with both eyes cut out and both ears cut off, a message for other eyes and ears that might report their insights to the official establishment. He was not in the PRU camp more than a week before he had reestablished communication with his Golden Triangle contacts.

Tran Thuc Quyen, Ngo Van Khoa, Quoc Ngoc Ma, and Dao Khac Muoi all came to Hue' from the farthest point away in the Republic of Viet Nam. They had grown up in hamlets attached to the village of Phuoc My, near the city of Phuoc Long in An Xuyen Province, the southernmost of RVN's provinces. The village lay in the middle of the immense submerged plain, covered by swamps and entangled mangroves called the U Minh Forest (Forest of Assassins). The dense forest with its swampy undergrowth was permanent home to a dizzying variety of beetles, snakes (31, of which 29 are poisonous), leeches the size of a bird's egg, monster mosquitoes, and Viet Cong.

By day the GVN forces alternately cajoled and threatened the villagers, conscripted the boys into ARVN, and established their people in the village administrative positions. The Americans made a few incursions on search and destroy missions and denuded vast reaches of the irreplaceable forest with their death rain, the defoliants dropped from planes. The night belonged to the Viet Cong.

The four boys served their families and communities by working in the cajeput tree forests. The cajeput trees possess special oily resins that are prized by Orientals. They only flourish in brackish water in a true tropical climate. Each day the four teenagers, along with several dozen more from other hamlets, trudged into the trees, and spent an easy day working their buffaloes dragging the heavy wet logs. These four boys stood out from their peers because their families were wealthy enough to have more than one of the beasts, the other being reserved for the critical work in the rice paddies. As day laborers, the boys could expect to earn nearly 50 Pee (Piastres, about 50 cents) a day. A buffalo, on the other hand, was consistently worth about 70 pee because the beast could do more work, a sensible arrangement. Since the peasant farm families were chronically in debt to the owners of the land they worked, the extra money meant that they could enjoy the little extras that made life enjoyable, like an extra pajama shirt for the men, another cotton dress for the women each year, and an occasional chicken.

At night, the hamlet chiefs, appointed by the GVN, left for the fortified village protected by ARVN soldiers. Neither the administration officials nor the security soldiers ever ventured out into the inky tropical blackness, and none of them ever even considered sleeping in the hamlets. That would have been tantamount to suicide. The inhabitants of the hamlets were on their own from the last rays of the day's sun until the full sunlight of the following day.

While their parents gathered in one hooch or another to discuss community needs, the problems of debt—even in a good year no one's budget was ever so good as to square the family with the landowners—and the current spate of illness running through their community, the teenage boys gathered outside in small cliques to gossip about the day's events and about girls. The girls stayed in their hooches where they belonged. No one talked about the country, its leaders, of history, of the Americans, or of the war. No one in the village could afford a newspaper or a radio; so, they knew little of these externals. It was on these nights that the Viet Cong cadres came.

The cadres stepped from the moist blackness of the forest night and either seduced the boys into venturing into the trees with them or influenced them to do so at gun point. Actual force was almost never necessary; the boys were bored and curious; the VC were in near total control of the province as they were in more than half of the rural villages of the country; and they were seldom as violent, arbitrary, or avaricious as their GVN counterparts. True, they required taxes of the people, but less than half the demands of the GVN people. The cadres led the boys deep into the dense mangrove jungles, selecting relatively dry areas, then lectured at length on the corrupt practices of the government, the immorality of the landowners who wreaked suffering and oppression on the backs of the peasants, and on the wickedness of the foreign running dogs, the *cố vên vĩ đai,* who, like the French before them, were virtual slavers. The lectures were repeated four or five times over a two to three month period.

The tired boys would be released before morning to return to their work. Quyen, Khoa, Ma, and Muoi were all very impressed by the lectures. Although they themselves had not been witness to the oppression by the GVN administrators and landlords nor to the unspeakable atrocities committed by the *cố vấn vĩ đai*, it would have been impolite to speak out in argument. What the cadres said must be so since they were such educated and dedicated people. The boys did not see with any clarity what it all had to do with them, however.

The festival of Thanh Minh honoring the dead takes place during the third lunar month (in April on the twelve month standard calendar) and is an important opportunity to refurbish the family's bonding by ancestral worship. In 1964, the hamlet's graves were swept, and gifts of fire crackers, paper streamers, money, food, and especially flowers were offered to enhance the afterlife of the ancestors. It had been a good wet year and the rice harvest was abundant; so, the community feasted on large wild tortoises and *te te*, the spiced meat of an elongated lizard-like forest creature. There was an abundance of fresh fruit and vegetables, *nouc cham* (a dipping sauce made of fermented fish paste mixed with chilies, lime juice, brown sugar, garlic, and ginger) and *cha' gio* (spring rolls); and for dessert, they satiated themselves on sweetened bean curd and the village's special sweet soup made of coconut milk, lychee fruit, bananas, and pineapple.

That night, after the festivities, and the women, who had prepared all of the food and decorations, now cleaned up, the four boys stepped into the edge of the hamlet clearing to rest from their gorging. There they met four heavily armed and apparently angry Viet Cong cadres.

The four black pajama clad soldiers made clear their displeasure with the feasting when people were starving under the yoke of foreign oppressors. It was to be more than that. This night they were not in the mood for lecturing; they leveled their rifles at the four young villagers and herded them into the forest at a forced march taking them far to the south and into a cleverly secluded military camp situated on a tree-shrouded hillside. Quyen, Khoa, Ma, and Muoi never saw their village again, but they later learned that the cadres had killed a village woman by decapitation before they had left. The VC stabbed a note to the unfortunate woman's chest that read in blood-red Vietnamese *chữ nôm* ideographic letters, the single thought, *"CHỈ-ĐIỂM VIÊN"* (INFORMER). The four naive peasants were now VC, like it or not.

The life was not particularly hard; it was mostly boring. The daily schedule consisted of eight hours of political and Marxian economic lectures broken up at midday by one and one-half hours of physical exercise, mostly nondirected to military functions, and then an hour of social life. This social life was nothing like free time, and was not discretionary. The men learned to sing the heroic revolutionary songs, to recite revolutionary poems, and watched revolutionary puppet shows with a message. The final hour of each day was spent in discussions, actually round table turns at confessions of past capitalist sins.

They were patiently and repeatedly told to abandon their belief in Buddha which was an opiate to numb the minds of the people. Attempts to purge a belief in Christ, as required by the manual, were soon abandoned because none of the boys had ever heard of Jesus. The young men were not given guns and did not participate in any military activities. After six months of indoctrination, their journeyman apprenticeships were completed; and the four boys were split into two groups to accompany two seasoned recruiters. The four man recruiting teams left the camp for three or four days at a time.

Disenchantment came in two ways to the four boys who managed to stay together through all of their activities with the VC. Once they were considered reliable, they were given more weighty assignments. Quyen and Khoa and their senior cadres slipped into a village at night. The older VC dragged a pair of young women out of their hooches and bound and gagged them in the center of the village. While the older men held AK-47s at the ready, the younger VC were directed to awaken the rest of the inhabitants and to assemble them in the field in front of their hooches. The seasoned cadres then harangued and threatened the cowed villagers for over an hour by the light of a few torches. They announced that an NLF military tribunal had examined undeniable documents that the two trussed up women before them had informed on the VC recruiters and had been the cause of the death of one of their comrades. Sentence had been imposed and would be carried out forthwith.

Quyen was ordered to hold the first woman by the hair with both hands, and Khoa held her by her bound wrists. The larger of the two seasoned cadres then produced a scimitar, swung it over he exposed neck of the girl, and neatly separated her head from her body. Quyen vomited, and his weakness was met with an icy stare of denunciation. The second girl fainted at the sight and was blissfully unconscious when the second man decapitated her. Unfortunately, two strokes were required.

Ma and Muoi were obliged to stand by and witness the execution of an entire family of landowners in another obscure village. The father, mother, grandmother, three small children, and a cousin were forced to kneel while the cadres methodically dispatched each of them with a single bullet in the back of the head. For emphasis, the children were killed first as the parents were made to watch. There was some question about how it had been determined that the hapless family were landowners. The boys learned the lesson, once again, that it was not their place to question orders.

Each of the four young men from Phouc My village fell afoul the NLF hierarchy by their responses to criticism in the weekly sessions designed to purge wrong thinking. The VC had a remarkably democratic military structure in that any and every enlisted man was not only free to criticize the leaders and his officers, but was positively required to do so. That was not so hard once the naturally reticent country boys became accustomed to the routine. What was difficult was that they in turn had to be subjected to public criticism which did not sit well. They were evidently not well enough imbued with the comradely spirit since they not only became angry at the criticisms they considered to be unfair and displayed that anger in an unseemly fashion, but they appeared to side with each other against the leadership and the rest of the men in their proper pursuit of the party's correct programs. The four boys were sent to the NLF reeducation center in the forest near Tay Ninh.

The regimen there was mind numbing. Hour after hour of shouted lectures, confessions that went well into the night and left no subject inviolable. Did they participate in the bourgeois practice of masturbation? Did they revere their family's ancestors more than they respected the NLF state? Did they harbor a fantasy belief in the old God, Buddha? Had they had dealings with the GVN? "Tell us about your family's collaboration with the nationalist forces." "Confess." "Confess." "Confess." Endlessly.

When they found a *Chieu Hoi* cartoon leaflet in the forest, the four boys saw it as their salvation. When the first opportunity presented itself, they slipped away into the night and gave themselves up to the GVN officers.

Initially, life was not much better in the Saigon Open Arms Center. They were beaten some and insulted regularly. They had to listen to endless dull lectures that sounded much like the VC ones—full of history and economics and about people they had never heard about. What made the difference was that they were given 20 pee a day each for nothing, and were exposed to the extravagant riches of the government regime for the first time. The military machines were mind-boggling. There was no way this power could be stopped by the VC in the forest. They were told how the government was effecting land reform, reducing the power of the landlords, would win the war, and that the people would all be affluent if they would but support the GVN. Finally, the physical abuse and insults stopped, and the young men were promised jobs. They were only too willing to be part of the PRU program and to move to Thau Thien Province.

Duong Co Tho and Nguyen Lui Tran were the only two men in the PRU with educations beyond grammar school. They were among the fifteen who were fully literate. Most of the PRUCs, like most of their countrymen, were literate for simple pragmatic communications. Tran and Tho had spent two years at school in Paris, Tran at the Sorbonne, and Tho at the Jesuit University. They came from relatively affluent and educated families who had prospered under the French, and who had eventually joined in the fight with the Viet Minh against the oppressive colonial regime. Tho's family had done so openly and had suffered terrible repressions. The French had done away with his father by roping him up with eight other partisans and dropping them off a bridge into the Sai Gon River. The French referred to this activity with the jocular term, 'crab netting.' As a result, when the hated French eventually left, Tho and his sixteen siblings were in favor with the incoming Catholic Diem regime and remained ardent supporters of each successive South Vietnamese junta and dictator. Tho's reward was to be granted enlistment into the relatively safe PRU which rescued him from the draft into the ARVN.

Tran was born a Viet Cong from a family of Viet Minh who bore that secret up until the day Tran was arrested in Cholon. He was born in Saigon, was educated in the Jesuit Lycee by French Priests, and became an accomplished student of French, English, mathematics, and history. From the time he could obey clandestine instructions, he performed small tasks for the underground Viet Minh and, later, National Liberation Front causes along with the rest of his family, even the other children. His covert life became so much a part of him that he had no difficulty in living an habitual lie in his dealings with the colonialists.

Tran's family leaned hard to the political left, and were part of the subterranean forces loyal to Ho Chi Minh when the division of Viet Nam occurred. They would have preferred to exit the Republic with the rest of the Viet Minh when the Geneva Accords demanded their expulsion, but the party deemed them to be more valuable in place. They were not suspected by the GVN and served as loyal soldiers, as part of the VCI (Viet Cong Infrastructure) without ever firing a shot in anger.

Tran progressed in the NLF (VCI) apparatus until he became an important courier for the cause as a result of his unassailable cover position in the University of Saigon as an English teacher. He did not ask questions of his superiors in the cadre apparatus, was scrupulously and fearfully honest, and was rewarded with ever more sensitive and important missions. Although he did not know it at the time of his arrest, he was delivering Uncle Ho's directive to the Saigon area commanders to launch into the new phase of the struggle. No longer were they to stand back and watch their numbers be decimated by the cruel regime of usurpers; they were to start the program of systematic executions of selected government and police targets. Tran was also unaware that he had been betrayed by his cousin who was given the position of Assistant Postal Director for the greater Saigon and Cholon region as a reward, a most lucrative post indeed. The alternative of life in Te Ban or even Con Son Island prison for the cousin when he was apprehended had been too terrible to contemplate. Betrayal, even of family, and a switch of sides was common enough to be the norm in the Saigon of the '60s.

On the day of Tran's capture, five of his siblings, his father, and a perfectly innocent uncle were detained. The activities of due process, the South Vietnamese variety, were the very model of efficiency. The Nguyen family members were apprehended, incarcerated, tried, and summarily executed. The process was completed in six working days; it was a matter of speculation about how Tran would react. He had never been told.

The bulk of the PRU members came to the organization from more prosaic backgrounds. They were a soldiers, ARVN, some *Chieu Hoi,* like Tran, many of them were from modest landowning families with at least some stake in the survival of the Republic of Viet Nam, or more accurately, in the persistence of the present regime. The majority of them were criminals on conditional release to the PRU. To their credit, many of the men were among the better soldiers in their respective units, although they were not the best. The most promising, brave, and intelligent ARVN soldiers were either seconded for more training in the Vietnamese Rangers, or if they came from any one of the three most northern provinces of RVN (Quang tri, Thau Thien, and Quang Nam), they were placed in the elite Hue' garrison corps led by one of the most able and least corrupt generals in the entire South, Major General Truong Cao Hai.

The example of one of the regular soldiers will suffice to illustrate. Dang Thanh Hung was the eleventh of twenty children of a Catholic family that settled in Hue' after fleeing the communist regime of North Viet Nam along with 860,000 other people during the dark period following the fall of the French. In the north, being Catholic, they were automatically suspect. Being landowners made them frank targets, and they had known that their days were numbered. They had been ardently anti-French and had fought valiantly with the Viet Minh to expel the foreigners. When the French departed, Hung's family celebrated a great success with their village compatriots. The great success shortly became the family's worst nightmare. Acting on Ho's directive to cleanse the country of the last vestiges of enslaving capitalism, the cadres found a double reason to target the Dangs. They were religionists with allegiance to the foreign ecclesiastics, and they were landowners of record.

The campaign of cleansing was pursued with a zeal that exceeded Ho's vision. Starting at Hanoi and working south, the returning Viet Minh and the in-place cadres began the systematic public murder campaign of some 50,000 people before it was called to a halt by the dismayed and saddened Ho. The zealots quickly dispatched every single landowner uninformed enough or foolish enough to remain on his or her land. There were not enough to make a good showing; so, the junior cadres became inventive. They found and exterminated persons whose families were known to have owned land in the past; then, they expanded to round up the people who were accused of siding with the actual landowners in past disputes; then, they took it upon themselves to eradicate the remaining reactionary elements such as those who had been privileged to learn to read, who wore glasses, or who could speak a foreign language.

In an extraordinary gesture, Chairman Ho not only announced that the killings would stop, but he acknowledged that the program was improper, and he formally apologized to the nation.

By the time of Ho's extraordinary public confession and apology, it was too late. There was a panic in the countryside. Whole villages, whole Catholic parishes with their priests, packed what belongings they could on their backs and formed up with the swell of refugees streaming south, taking with them a legacy of bitterness and hatred for communism and for anyone and everything connected with it. The general mood of alarm gave way to terror and panic as the countryside was electrified with reports of the slaughter of innocents, rumors of wholesale massacres of entire villages, of the violation of nuns, and the castration of priests, and finally of the partially substantiated rumors of bridges and churches being bombed and of hit and run sneak attacks by mysterious marauders.

The latter fears had an altogether real basis and were the work of a handful of American Central Intelligence Agents and their hirees under OPLAN 34A. These Americans and South Vietnamese were dispatched to the troubled northern portion of the country to ensure that panic grew out of the alarm over the ongoing murder campaign and to accomplish the long-term goal of the United States of America that Viet Nam would never unite into a single independent nation under a communist flag. The majority of South Vietnamese commandos of OPLAN 34A were killed in action or abandoned by the CIA to their fates. Those who were captured languished in prison, some for decades. Their families were paid the princely sum of $100 a month by the US and RVN governments until it was decided that such payments would be an implicit admission that the forces of democracy had been involved in spy type activities. The solution was to terminate payments and to abandon the families as they had abandoned their faithful men.

Hung's family were among the relatively lucky refugees. They had supportive extended family well established in Hue'. They were able to find work in the Diem administration's apparatus in Thau Thien Province. The large family was poor but industrious with all of the children above the age of eight having a job. There was no provision for education beyond rudimentary literacy, and no need. There was work enough available without the requirement for educational credentials. In time and with meticulous husbanding of resources, Hung's family was once again able to purchase a little land. The Buddhists' large land holding claims were deemed not to be in the best interest of the country by the Diem regime, and when land reform laws came to be carried out, a disproportionate amount of acreage changed hands from landowners to peasants at the expense of the Buddhist owners. The laws did not seem to impinge as harshly on the minority Catholics, and Hung's family was able to acquire a few extra parcels of property during the period before the fiction of land reform was abandoned altogether.

There was land enough for the first four sons to support their wives and eventual families, but not enough for the rest of the eight brothers. There was, of course, no thought given to providing a share to the girls. The next three sons in line of seniority by birth were rewarded by being granted placement in the generous government's infrastructure of minor functionaries and exemption from the universal draft in return for certain 'considerations.' There were no more 'considerations' left in the family coffers when the final five sons came of age. The best that could be provided was placement in a police rather than a military unit after initial training when Hung and his brothers were called up.

Hung spent his first week in the army filling out forms and in receiving his uniforms and boots. He was sent to the Quang Trung Army training center near Saigon where all of the other conscripts spent their first four months of military life. It was a boring, tedious, but safe and calm life spent in performing menial labor tasks. He and his platoon cleared underbrush and strung concertina wire around the perimeter of the training center, scrubbed floors, whitewashed barracks, polished boots, and cleaned officer's vehicles. A minimum of time was spent in learning military skills such as marching, military judo, gang firing, running, crawling, saluting, and about military protocol. He did not fire a gun enough to become proficient, and the weapon he was assigned was heavy and cumbersome and often malfunctioned. He did not learn the use of mines, grenades, or jungle warfare techniques. There was only a modicum of political indoctrination.

Hung was paid 3300 Pee per month including a 1300 Pee allotment for family allowance even though, technically, Hung did not have a family to support. He received a single raise of 100 Pee a month in his four years in the army. Hung's unit made a large number of forays into the countryside against the enemy. The company never fired a single shot at an enemy; they never saw a VC. The nearly unspoken motto of the unit was to have 'No risk, no victory, no contact.'

When Hung asked what his main purpose was in the army, a senior NCO told him bluntly, "To save your life. In my platoon, you and the others will learn how to save your life. There is an old Chinese proverb: 'There are thirty-six ways of saving your life, but the best of all is to run away.'"

The ARVN soldiers of Hung's acquaintance were generally very polite with the villagers they encountered. Not caring to sleep in discomfort on the ground, they often requested permission to stay in the villager's houses. At times they paid for the privilege. At times they stole from the villagers who were as powerless against the GVN coming in the day as they were against the VC who ruled the night.

When he completed his first year of soldiering, Hung was given his permanent assignment. He was sent back to Hue' where he joined the Province Police Unit. He lived at home with his family. When the Americans made their request for policemen to man the PRUs, Hung and several of his friends were assigned. There had been no consideration of volunteering. Hung had learned better than to volunteer.

From the various ARVN and police units in the province came the partially trained, more or less loyal and anticommunist men to man the remaining PRU positions. Besides Duong Co Tho, Tran came to know, or at least to have more than a nodding acquaintanceship with Dang Thanh Hung, Dinh Van Luc, Hoang Quang Cong, Cong Bich Hai, Muoi Khuc Ba, Anh Xuan Oanh, Bach Duc Hieu, Tung Co Bon, Ky Van He, Tran Van Dong, and Nguyen Tran Xuan.

There were two remarkable things about the men Tran bothered to know reasonably well out of all the PRUCs in the compound. For the most part, they were not common criminals as were the rest, and the only other somewhat remarkable thing about the assemblage was in their names; in a country where fifty percent of the people have the family name of Nguyen, there were only three men (Tran included) with that appellation. The remaining names were the common ones making up eighty-five percent of the surnames in Viet Nam.

The only clearly unusual name on the roster was of a man yet to be seen. He was a decidedly unusual man, as well. Y'Yool had risen to be Deputy Chief Inspector of Provincial Police and was now to be the commander of the PRU compound and its one hundred twenty-five men. Y'Yool occupied his significant police post for the most unusual of reasons in the Republic of Viet Nam—he merited the position. There was every reason why he should not have been given a command post. Y'Yool did not come from a prominent family. He had no political connections; he was the wrong religion—not even a Buddhist; he did not take or dispense graft; and worst of all he was a Bahnar Montagnard, a despised minority that the arrogant Vietnamese called *meo,* a word that meant something like savage and implied bodily filth and odor, social primitivism, and religious ignorance. Y'Yool was a very unusual man.

CHAPTER 6

Assist Free Vietnam to develop a strong, stable and constitutional government to enable Free Vietnam to assert an increasingly attractive contrast to conditions in the present communist zone.

Work toward the weakening of the communists in the North and South Vietnam in order to bring about the eventual peaceful reunification of a free and independent Vietnam under anticommunist leadership.

Support the position of the Government of Free Vietnam that all-Vietnam elections may take place only after it is satisfied genuinely free elections can be held throughout both zones of Vietnam.
National Security Council statement of American goals, 1956

T he routine of day two at The Farm started for Lars Magnusson like day one except the workout was harder and longer. Lars noted that the ranks were a man or two short after yesterday. No comment was made about the absences. The instruction for the day started in an open front shed with the men standing in separated groups around six tables laden with a variety of weaponry, most of which was of origins obscure to Lars. "Listen up, everyone. Stay with the group around your table and through the day we will shift tables until we have covered the lot. This is a familiarization day; the next four months we'll make certified experts of you in all these devices." The speaker was Gunny McClusky who had, by some miracle, transformed himself into a clean shaven, spit and polish, senior marine noncom in contradistinction to the sweaty and bedraggled trainees despite having participated in the same grueling four hour morning workout.

Not one for wasting words, the gunny turned his full attention to the three men at his table of weapons, one of whom was Lars, and began without further introductory comment, "There is not a single American-made weapon on this table and not a single American military standard issue item here. Forget what you have learned in your

162

military training so far and concentrate on the enemy's weapons for now." He picked up an AK-47.

"Tell me what you know about this piece." He put the question directly to Lars who was unprepared for being the center of attention.

"I, uh, well, let's see," Lars stammered, a little flustered.

Gunny's face was unpleasant.

"It's the communist's rifle, like our M-14…It's an automatic."

Gunny McClusky was not a patient man. He looked at the three men facing him. "The AK-47 or Avtomat Kalashnikova, 1947 model, or Kalashnikov Assault rifle, was invented by a Soviet gunsmith named Mikhail Timofeyevich Kalashnikov or at least copied and improved from a World War II German model. The weapon weighs 4.8 kilograms fully loaded, and is 87 centimeters long without its extended bayonet. It has a thirty round detachable magazine that fires standard M-43 ammunition—that's 7.62 by 39 millimeter—intermediate powered cartridges. It is a gas operated, blow back system, rotating bolt gun with a muzzle velocity of 715 meters per second, and it has an effective range of 300 meters on full automatic, 400 meters on semiautomatic setting, and perhaps a little more on single shot setting. On automatic it fires a cyclic rate of 600 rounds per minute and 40 rounds per minute on semiautomatic. The weapon is essentially an elongated machine pistol that fires from the open breech position to avoid cook-off. The standard model has a simple, sturdy wooden stock, but there is a collapsible folding metal stock model available."

"Question?" McClusky responded to the uplifted hand.

"What's cookoff?" the man on Lars' right queried.

"Premature cartridge ignition due to heat. Deadly problem for the shooter that was solved after World War I and never really improved upon. Anything else?" None of the men proffered further questions.

"In order to be useful submachine guns must be portable, use ammunition that is small and light enough to be carried in quantity, essentially pistol ammunition, and must have a recoil minimal enough to permit fire from the shoulder, the hip, or from the prone position.

"There is a reason why this masterpiece is the most popular light arm in the world. It is produced in the greatest quantities of any infantry gun and is used in more than thirty-five countries because it is cheap, light, durable, reliable, and most importantly, continues to function with lethal accuracy under the most adverse conditions. It has a straight-line stock to maintain accuracy during rapid fire or in bursts. For the purposes you new 'Christians In Action' have, there is an added advantage. The bolt action is quiet; if you are careful about it, you can work the mechanisms virtually silently. And it can easily be fitted with a hush puppy (burst suppressor-silencer). Any idiot can learn to use the weapon with a minimum of training. It is easy and quick to dissemble and clean, easy to maintain, easy to strap to one's body, and takes up little space because it is slender. By the end of this day everyone of you will be able to load and fire the weapon on all three settings, disassemble, clean, and reassemble in the light in thirty seconds and in the dark in a minute. You will learn the few trouble-shooting tricks necessary, and you will accept this as your weapon of choice. When you get In Country, steal one."

Each man was given a Kalashnikov to heft, aim, and explore. Gunny McClusky patiently demonstrated the disassembly technique taking care to lay out the component parts in an orderly sequence born of long habit of handling complex weapons. He pointed out and described the function of the barrel, receiver, breechblock, safety catch, firing mechanism, magazine housing, return springs, the longitudinal slot for the cocking handle, and the extractor. He made sure they understood the purpose of every groove, slot, and protuberance so they would achieve a correct replacement and fit every time they handled the piece.

Every trainee was capable of executing similar weapon handling techniques with American guns; so, the educational process went simply and efficiently. In less than an hour every man could load and unload, disassemble, clean, and assemble the submachine gun with practiced facility in a blindfold. Gunny was pleased but took his usual pains not to let the men know it. It went against the grain of the old marine.

"We'll have plenty of time to fire these beauties tomorrow. We've got a lot to cover, and you'll shoot your shoulders sore starting tomorrow. Now, let's take apart the next greatest weapon, compliments of our communist comrades in arms." He presented the B-40.

"This is a standard issue, shoulder fired rocket launcher. Like all other communist light weapons it has the great advantages of simplicity and durability. It is not as handy as our M-79 because the missiles are harder to come by. I'll have to vote for our M-79 grenade launcher as weapon of choice between the two." He demonstrated the salient characteristics of the communist weapon and placed it beside the American one comparing and contrasting the two, and thoroughly demonstrating the care and usage of each until his charges were completely comfortable with both sides' weapons.

"It's worth appropriating one of these along the way, but I

164

wouldn't go to great lengths to try and keep one. Just take yourself a new one when you need to." McClusky gave a meaningful glance to the young combatants.

"Anyone got any questions about the Kalashnikov or B-40 before we take a look at grenades and mines? That will take us up to lunch." He glanced about peremptorily and continued. "This is an RDG-5 Warsaw pact fragmentation hand grenade. Weight: 310 grams, Length: 114 millimeters, Diameter: 56 millimeters—a nice handful, Blast charge: 110 grams, Fuse delay: 3 or 4 seconds, Effective radius: 25 meters. It has the old Soviet UZRG percussion fuse and a substantial HE charge. The charge is snuggled compactly into a serrated fragmentation liner.

"Again, its main advantages are simplicity, light weight, reliability, usefulness at close range, and compactness. It can be thrown farther than American grenades, and more can be carried by the individual. These are worth appropriating from a body count person when you get a chance. You will like to have a couple of bandoleers of them out in Indian country."

Indicating a dark cylinder about the size and shape of a soup can with a long protuberance on top to which was attached a large ring and a downward pointing metal lever, he said, "I'll mention in passing this other bit of Soviet and now VC ordnance. This is an RG-42. It is bigger—400 grams, longer—127 mm, and has a little bigger HE charge—118 grams. It has only a 20 meter frag radius. I don't like its clumsy shape, the lever that sticks out further than the 5, the weight, or the lessened effective distance. You are better off with the American grenades even with their excessive kill radius. Leave these guys on the Cong. Not worth the bother to expropriate."

Lars picked the last remaining grenade, a smaller model, more similar to the American made explosives. "F-1," said the gunny. "Good to have a pocketful of these crackers in a pinch." He then described the smaller weight, smaller but still considerable charge, and effective killing distance. "It's the same size as the Polish rifle grenade, a good and reliable weapon."

The gunnery sergeant took another two hours to familiarize his three trainees with the advantages, disadvantages, usage, and maintenance of the final table top full of deadly small eastern bloc arms. He described with loving affection the 9 mm PM or Makarov, the Soviet special pistol closely akin to the German Walther PP series, the 9 mm APS or Stechkin with its twenty round magazine and 200 yard effective range. He liked the attachable wooden holster stock and adjustable back sight for longer range shots. He had models of the 7.62 mm PK general purpose machine gun, the 762 mm RPK light machine gun (not much larger than an infantry rifle of either side) and the 7.62 SVD sniper rifle better known as the Dragunov. He showed them in detail the workings of a much used older German Walther P 38, and PPK, a Heckler and Koch with an 18 round magazine, and several older type hand guns including the Browning Modele 1900 made by the Fabrique National of Belgium, the Luger P'08 of Germany, the Colt 1911 A1 from the US, all of which were known still to be in use in Viet Nam.

"Right after lunch, I'll show you something of the possible older weapons that you might encounter in country but are not in common enough use to spend a lot of time on them. I've got older assault rifles like the German paratroop gun FG 42, the Sturmgewhehr 44, CETME Model C Spanish rifle, and a Type 56 Chinese knock-off of the Soviet Degtyarev RPD. Don't be too surprised to see the occasional Chinese weapon, especially Simonov 7.62 mm SKS carbines, or even the occasional Chink himself in their light khaki uniforms. They are not supposed to be there—mostly in Laos, but then neither are we." He smiled conspiratorially with his students, and they broke for lunch.

Jean-Luc DuParrier sought out Lars and made it a point to sit with the younger man. He regaled Lars with Viet Nam lore, quoting from Graham Greene's book, "The Quiet American", to punctuate his descriptions. He was conspiratorial whenever he talked, looking about for eavesdroppers, and whispering intently when he had something particularly gossipy to say about the CIA and its checkered past in Viet Nam. "You know, Greene described the CIA chief of station to perfection, but of course without naming Ed Lansdale by name. The man was well-meaning but a dupe of the Diems," Jean-Luc told him with an enthusiasm that bordered on smirking.

Lars was flattered by the attention, not altogether sure what had brought it on. He felt that he was gaining a friendship, perhaps for the first time in his life. His recollections of Zarahemla, Utah, scarcely a quarter of a year ago, but a lifetime in the past were devoid of anyone he could consider with more fondness than acquaintanceship. He found himself looking forward to the next opportunity to talk to the worldly and urbane Frenchman.

At 1300 sharp Daniel Browning Pendergast began his presentation on United States military small arms and did not stop until 1500 on the dot. He was a small, bespectacled, balding, middle-aged soft appearing intellectual with an encyclopedic knowledge and memory about armaments. He spoke without notes.

"Our Vietnamese allies use the M-1 Garand rifle, 30 caliber M-7s, and Browning automatics of Second World War vintage primarily," he said without false modesty (he was one of **The** Brownings). "Some of the more elite ARVN outfits are supplied with our more up-to-date M-14s."

He laid out an M-14 with surprising dexterity and in perfect orderliness, rivaling the performance of his burly predecessor, Master Gunnery Sergeant McClusky, earlier in the day. He looked up from his completed dissection and again lectured, "Just in passing. You are going to have to deal with M-1s and M-2s. The 2 is just a lighter version of the standard Garand rifle; all of the Ms are gas operated submachine guns. The 1 and 2 have eight round magazines, fairly impractical for modern warfare, especially in the jungle. They fire a bullet entirely comparable to the hunting rifle 30.06. They are too heavy for use in the jungle particularly for small Asians. The M-14 is a fine improvement on the old World War II infantry issue but also does have the flaw of being too heavy. For now I am going to demonstrate the 14, but we will spend the bulk of our time learning a new gun, the ArmaLite, or M-16A 1. First, the M-14."

Pendergast moved rapidly and perfunctorily through his demonstration of the standard issue infantry weapon knowing that all of the men were completely familiar with the weapon. "We have here a gas-operated 20 round magazine utilizing .308 inch ammunition. That is 7.62 by 51 mm." When he was satisfied that each man at his table could satisfactorily dissemble, assemble, and knew the function of every part and aspect of the M-14, he turned their attention to the newer gun in the armamentarium, the M-16.1A "There were a few in use," he explained, "more experimentally on trial than anything, because of disturbing reports of failure, and jamming in adverse conditions.

"The main body of this new rifle is made of aluminum alloy, and the stock is plastic. Both materials are light, durable, rustproof, and resistant to corrosives. The main advantage is the rapidity of fire and power. It possesses a twenty or a thirty round magazine—both models are being considered—and can fire 700 to 950 rounds per minute. The ammunition is small, compact, easily portable .223 inch or 5.56 by 45 mm. It is two pounds lighter, and 5 inches shorter than the M-14 and yet has the same effective range of 500 yards. In metric terms those numbers are 0.9 kilograms, 12.7 centimeters, and 457 meters. The rapid fire power, the light weight of the gun, and its ammunition make this potentially the finest infantry rifle in history. Let's take a look at its insides."

The men handled the new gun enthusiastically and failed to take notice of Pendergast's use of the descriptor, 'potentially,' in reference to the M-16 and were veritable mechanical experts in its use within three-quarters of an hour. Pendergast took note of the men's uncritical enthusiasm and repeated his caution, "Don't forget the tendency to jam in wet and muddy conditions. A number of small arms experts feel that the rifle is somewhat flawed due to its hasty mass production resulting in jamming and stoppage. You will love the gun on the shooting range here, but it requires excessive field care and cleaning—deucedly inconvenient in actual hurry-up unclean battle conditions. I second the suggestion made to you earlier in the day by Master Gunnery Sergeant McClusky to have an AK-47 Kalashnikov in reserve until the bugs get worked out of this one. Incidentally, this is not a Browning product. It was invented by Eugene M. Stoner and is made primarily by the ArmaLite company—you will hear the weapon referred to commonly as the Stoner or ArmaLite, I might add. Or as the Colt Commando for the shortened barrel version," he said with a tone somewhere between defensiveness and disdain in his voice.

Pendergast next presented another familiar weapon, what appeared to be a modified shotgun, the M-79 grenade launcher. He broke open the breech and inserted a 40 mm grenade cartilage, closed the breech, and sighted away from his students. He removed the grenade, dismantled the weapon and briefly but thoroughly described the function and idiosyncrasies of the simple parts. His only evaluative comment was, "Fine weapon, best in the world."

After 1500, the men had a short break; Jean-Luc managed to find Lars for a bit of gossip while they waited for the section of lectures on mechanical man-traps and mines. "Do you know where you are, Lars, *mon ami?*" He queried as an ice breaker.

Lars had been too busy to think much about it. "Somewhere in the US, or maybe even Mexico judging from terrain and trees," he ventured.

"But precisely, *mon ami*, this is in the United State of Virginia. We are at the place quaintly known as 'The Farm.' It is located northeast of the city of Williamsburg on the west bank of the York River off Route 5. We are close to Allmondsville and Croaker. It is a big secret of the CIA, but to no one else. But surely you knew that," Jean-Luc said smugly, relishing his air of having superior sources.

"How do you know that, Jean-Luc? I was blindfolded when I was brought here. I didn't have a clue. We could have been in Asia for all I know. Weren't you prevented from seeing the place until you were brought right into the compound?"

"Ah, indeed, I was, *mon ami*, but I have my sources. Matches under my nails could not force me to divulge them," the Frenchman said with mock seriousness. "You will just have to trust me, my brother spy." He was grinning guilelessly.

'The Farm,' as it was affectionately known by insiders, was Camp Peary, Virginia. It was a twenty-five square mile section of wilderness that served as a huge training site for CIA agents, infiltrators, covert operators, and for special ops military units as diverse as SEALS, Army Rangers and Special Forces, PRU leader trainees, and the Delta Force. It was located just northeast of Williamsburg, Virginia running between the highway and the York River. Its existence, location, and purpose was an intensely held secret by the CIA and the organizations that have made use of its unique training environment and instructors. Its location was openly discussed by locals and pointed out to tourists. About the only persons unfamiliar with its location were those totally devoid of curiosity, newly arrived, nonpolitical, nonmilitary immigrants, and liberals who accepted the fiction of a benign US foreign policy.

Lars shook his head good-naturedly, and the two young men walked to the lecture hall for the course on booby-traps; the 'I-Love-Boobies' class, as it was affectionately known. Lars' mind was overfilled and yearning for a rest. He had thought the brain work required in high school in Zarahemla, Utah was tough. He had no idea then what tough was. He had been "just a kid", he mused as he walked.

The Special Forces man, complete with green beret, detailed to teach the traps and explosives introduction lecture had designated one the classrooms as his sole possession for the duration. He kept a gallery of gruesome photographs, chilling diagrams, and a museum of artfully designed miniature scale models that worked in vividly instructive accuracy. He introduced himself, "Major Armont Willetsen, USA/SF," and started his lecture on close combat traps as matter-of-factly as if he were describing the production of cardboard boxes.

"This is known as a Panji or Pungi stake or Pungi stick. It is a primitive device, to be sure, but has been used in warfare since the dawn of time and has proved its usefulness time and again. The simplest use is to place a spike, sharp edge up in the middle of a jungle path to pierce the victim's foot. This fellow and several of its mates can be placed in a hole, deceptively covered, for a victim to fall upon or can be fixed to a device held under tension and linked to a trip wire to impale a victim who has the misfortune to trip the triggering device.

"In the present theater of conflict they are usually made of bamboo spikes. That material has the great advantage of being very hard and of forming naturally sharp edges when cut. A definite improvement in the use of these weapons came in Viet Nam when the clever little people placed dung, usually the excreta of diarrheic men, on the points to cause an infected wound. Think for a moment of the value of a simple wounding as opposed to killing. Not only does that render the victim *hors de combat*, but his platoon mates are then obliged to carry him about. The NVA and VC are much more scrupulous about caring for their wounded than are the ARVN; so, wounding a few of them may be more beneficial to the cause of right and truth than simply swelling the body count.

"While we will have plenty of time to practice our creativity in making these devices in the field in the days to come, I do believe you will benefit from a study of these diagrams and miniatures." He pointed at the tables with their charming models.

"Please note these fundamentals," Willetsen said as he drew diagrams of various devices in multiple colors of chalk on the board. He showed them pungi pits covered with branches and leaves, covered with a platform balanced on a pole that served as a bidirectional trap door, and an ingenious Venus flytrap. This contraption consisted of a crude pit with downward curving and interlaced metal spikes imbedded in a wooden support just below the innocuous appearing ground surface. In this variation the victim's leg became instantly ensnared and every attempt he or she made to extract the leg only shredded it further.

"Sort of like a demonic Chinese finger trap," he observed in an aside. He accurately drew a more sophisticated version in which a solid wooden frame was used to hold razor-sharp, barbed steel spikes. "The spikes are thin and flexible enough to give with the pressure of the victim's leg, but not small enough to break off. The hapless victim is held in place until his fellow soldiers release him, a time-consuming process, which then requires care of the wounded soldier, or he waits alone until the unfriendlies return, quaking in abject fear at their expected reception."

Willetsen described in detail the manufacture from materials found in the ambient setting of a variety of 'descending' traps. He showed how a spiked log could be hidden in a tree above the trail supported only by an improvised flimsy holding device attached to a trip wire or vine. Tripping the wire would cause the heavy barbed log to crash down the trail sweeping into the victim. Another simple device was a log or heavy board loaded with downward pointing spikes that dropped on the victims head immediately after his foot brushed the taut trip wire.

The men learned the principles of construction of mechanical traps. Major Willetsen accurately drew a board device mounted over a shallow pit. When the victim stepped on the leaf covered board, he automatically caused the other end to lever up into his chest or face filling him with a square foot of nails or spikes. He showed them how to set up an arrow connected to a heavy rubber band stretched tightly and set to be released by encountering a trip wire.

Willetsen gave each man his own multi-dose vial of a curariform drug to be used on the tips of his arrows or spikes when he began his work for the American way in the Republic of Viet Nam. He talked rapidly and was very thorough. Lars took copious notes, drew crude diagrams, and found his brain crying out for rest.

"Now, we have to return to the more mundane art of using pre-manufactured booby traps, especially explosive ones. The most obvious booby trap, or man-trap, is the mechanical antipersonnel trap set by our forefathers to snare poachers or trespassers. They are lighter and less apt to spring on the trap-setter than a bear trap and work by clamping the man's ankle with a set of jaws with serrated teeth or with mean little barbs. They are chained to the ground or a tree. The disadvantages are obvious; they are heavy and cumbersome to lug about and are noisy to set up. They are only practical when you have the full advantage of control of an area and wish to ensnare an unwanted intruder. Your government has thoughtfully supplied you with an assortment of these fine weapons that will be available In Country on request through proper channels, wouldn't you know?"

Willetsen and an assistant hoisted several boxes onto the table in front of where he stood lecturing. They removed and set out a variety of antipersonnel mines. "Land mines are a nuisance, but are quite a part of the scene for you in RVN. You must have a thorough working knowledge of these weapons to inflict the proper amount of damage on your enemies and to protect yourself from them as well. They can be set off by tripping a wire, applying or releasing pressure on a specifically designed pressure plate, causing vibration, or even by shedding light.

"First we have the US M-14 mine. It is a small antipersonnel devices that kills by blast concussion, rather than by shrapnel. It is a plastic casing that is buried in a shallow hole after removing a safety clip, like this," he demonstrated with a neutered model. "The step of a man's foot on the pressure plate sets it off. Most small animals are too light to trip it." He showed the men the component pressure-plate, Belleville spring, striker, main charge, and detonator. He brought out a rectangular shaped Claymore mine and spent a similar period of instruction on that weapon. He pointed out that it could be rigged to be pressure sensitive and that it propelled its projectiles in a fan pattern to a 50 meter range like a shotgun blast. The Claymore served as an excellent perimeter defense weapon, the CIA instructor told them. "But," he said, "be fairly warned that the VC have stolen Claymores aplenty and use them with equal facility to protect their positions. You don't want to be caught by second hand 'friendly fire.'" He smiled at his little attempt at humor.

Willetsen showed them a VC/NVA mine produced in a local village as most of their devices were. It was round and was filled with pieces of steel connecting rods.

"These homemade babies are lethal to several hundred yards. That is why an American soldier is guaranteed a Congressional Medal of Honor if he falls on one of these or a grenade. He saves a whole platoon.

"The Claymores and other types of mines are either command detonated or controlled traps that can be set off in a variety of ways by a distant observer such as by pulling wire or cord, by radio control, etcetera. Your people in Viet Nam will have to teach you the use of such devices as are available to The Company agents when you have the leisure to learn and the availability of devices. The subject is too sophisticated to dwell on today. Just know they exist."

He pointed out devices containing clockworks. "These, of course, are time bombs. We will spend some time on these because of the element of creativity and ingenuity involved, and you can come up with your own weapons from a few simple materials available in most civilized countries—and in much of Viet Nam, I should say. Now, what we must have are a few fundamental components. There must be the clockworks, a combustible fuse or some sort of chemical clock, such as acid that will eat through a connection, permitting either the making or breaking of the vital circuit, and the explosive. Gather round, and we will learn some of the fascinating art of bomb making. Quite simple, really."

By the end of the day, Lars and the others could make simple time bombs, knew the principles of making traps from jungle materials, and were familiar with and respectful of mines. He had learned, or at least had heard a presentation of how to detect the presence of trip-wires and the telltale evidences of hidden mines. In the end, it boiled down to a phrase put by Major Willetsen, "Eternal vigilance." Lars swore to himself that he would not get lazy and dead in Viet Nam.

After supper and a chance for a short rest, the men gathered on the exercise field and were divided into groups of four, including an instructor. The exercise was to be hand to hand combat, martial arts in the true sense of the term. The last half of each evening and frequently well into the darkness of the rural Virginia landscape, the men learned the intricacies of ambushing, tracking, camouflaging, hiding, and coping with the demons of the night. This was the pattern for the rest of the four months at the CIA paramilitary training center.

It was on the fourth day at The Farm, after a training session in unarmed hand-to-hand combat, that Lars Magnusson met the real Frenchman, Jean-Luc DuParrier, and grew up.

CHAPTER 7

I should lay it down that the existence of secret agents should not be tolerated as tending to augment the evil against which they are used...But in the sphere of political and revolutionary action, relying on violence, the professional spy has every facility to fabricate the facts themselves, and will spread the double evil of emulation in one direction, and of panic, hasty legislation, unreflecting hate, in the other. However, this is an imperfect world . . .
Joseph Conrad, The Secret Agent

The Frenchman delighted in his skill in Savate, French hand and foot fighting; and he was especially ready that day to demonstrate his skill against the Asian. He supposed that it was only sensible to have them in the service, but Jean-Luc resented the idea that they were ostensibly accepted on a footing equal to his own. By his own observation and experience, the little Vietnamese were at best lazy; and if not outright cowardly, then they were notably reticent to engage an enemy. Even if these Americans did not, he resented the Viets for letting the whites do all their fighting and dying. Likely as not, this little man they called, Dong, was unskilled in the sophistication of serious martial arts; certainly the training ARVN soldiers received was third class, again a studied opinion based on experience. The two young men were selected for the demonstration of hand to hand combat techniques on the fourth day of their CIA paramilitary training course. Jean-Luc looked forward to an opportunity to demonstrate his prowess; and, he reasoned, this would be his chance for some needed practice to keep him from getting rusty.

The instructor was an unlikely looking fighter. He was about thirty, lean, and Ivy League looking, not a street thug, or a mystical Oriental, or a seasoned soldier in appearance. Jean-Luc figured it would be a real feather for him to instruct the instructor as well, but one thing at a time.

"All of you possess a certain skill in close quarters combat or you

174

would not be here," the boyish instructor began. "Some of you are quite skilled, I am informed," he continued; and Jean-Luc detected a brief eye contact from the agency instructor that the Frenchman accepted modestly as his due. He looked down.

"When we have gotten well into this course, I am confident that each of you will be convinced that you have more to learn. I hope to convince you in the next few days that your very lives and those of your subordinates depend on your full attention, so that you will spend your four months here in productive learning. We will cover fighting and killing with bare hands, with certain small weapons you can carry concealed on your person, and with implements you can easily improvise as the occasion demands. From the outset expunge any thoughts or feelings you may harbor that fighting is a sport, or that there is any such thing as clean fighting or fair play. Those notions are for boxing or judo; this is not boxing or judo. The only rule in a knife fight is that there are no rules. This is systematic dirty fighting free of any and all dicta. This class, above all the rest you take here, will determine whether you remain in the class and with the Agency. If past classes are indicative, fifty percent of you will quit voluntarily and return to wherever you came from before this course is completed. With this and the other rigors expected of you men in the class, no more than thirty percent those of you who started will leave here with a Company assignment.

"That's encouraging," whispered Lars' sotto voce. The instructor looked at him and smiled boyishly.

"Do we have a volunteer?" He smiled more broadly. Lars looked away and shook his head in negative nods. The young Frenchman looked so earnest in his desire to participate that Ivy League pointed at him and said, "C'mon, something makes me think you are a willing volunteer." Jean-Luc walked slowly over to the center of the clear area. Ivy League gestured to Tring Van Dong to join the Frenchman.

"Now, this is a body contact activity. When I tell you to go, I expect you to protect yourself. I don't want anybody killed or maimed; so, for the time being, I guess there are some rules," Ivy League said looking toward Dong and Jean-Luc. Then he said to the rest of the men, "When these young gladiators have gotten their feisty feelings out, I will start to teach you some useful techniques."

"Stand here, and when I say go, let's see how you boys handle yourselves. The rest of you will get your chance."

The instructor saw that both men were set; then, he raised his hand to drop it for the official start. His mouth began to open to say the word, and the muscles in his arm tightened preparatory to dropping it. Before a sound or a movement occurred, however, Jean-Luc's leg whirled and his heel caught the unsuspecting and unprepared Vietnamese painfully on his right flank. Dong reflexively bent forward and shied back fast enough that the strike was a sting rather than a rib breaker. Jean-Luc laughed at his cleverness and exclaimed smugly, "Savate!"

Dong did not know nor care about whatever 'Savate' was. He was not about to be caught unaware again. He blocked the punch that headed for his chin with his doubled left fist and swept the fist back again to catch Jean-Luc a thudding blow on the point of his own chin. Lucky punch or not, Jean-Luc was now more respectful. The men circled each other probing for openings; each missed a kick and a punch. Jean-Luc slipped a stiff fingered hand into Dong's ribs causing a substantial bruise. Dong was able to bring his knee into Jean-Luc's exposed lateral thigh causing the Frenchman to gasp and to limp noticeably. Jean-Luc backed away almost as if he were going to turn and run. Dong moved in on him, sensing the chance to put his opponent down. Jean-Luc began falling forward toward the turf, and Dong jumped forward to bring both of his small strong fists down on the falling back. Instead, he met a hard direct back kick centered at his navel. The surprise and the blow knocked out all his wind, and now his fight was for breath. Jean-Luc bore in for the kill.

He threw a spinning back kick at Dong's temple. Dong did an instantaneous squat and the foot sailed harmlessly off his head. He gasped for breath, felt faint, and wanted more than anything to lie down and catch his breath. They could continue after that, he reasoned, knowing instinctively that his thought was irrational. Jean-Luc continued to bore in striking Dong a hard but unimportant blow on the slight Vietnamese man's exposed arm. Respirations were coming a little easier. Jean-Luc connected with the point of his foot into Dong's inner thigh, and Dong nearly went down. He spun away and regained his balance in time to counter a front kick to his head. By now his breath had returned; so, he did not think he would die; and Dong parried Jean-Luc's foot sharply upward and completely upended him. Dong was fully recovered by the time Jean-Luc was back on his feet and in position.

"Okay, that's enough!" the instructor yelled. "We'll give everyone a chance in a minute." Dong backed up and lowered his guard. He looked at his instructor waiting for the rest of the instructions.

As he turned slightly away, Jean-Luc sneaked in one last blow, a nasty and full force fist against Dong's cheek bone that opened a small cut. Dong staggered backward and sagged into Lars' arms; he was pale and looked sick. It was several minutes before he rallied.

"I said, enough. Now, stop!" Ivy League emphasized. He looked at Dong with no sympathy but shared with Lars a brief look of disapproval.

Dong shook the cobwebs out of his head and stepped away from Jean-Luc never taking his eyes off the Frenchman. He looked at the man with distrust and disrespect. Jean-Luc ignored him; he was not worthy of notice, nothing but a Vietnamese.

"There was a lesson in that demonstration. Anyone care to describe it for me?" asked the instructor tartly.

"Play heads-up ball," ventured one observer.

"That's a pretty good summary, I'd say. I might have also said, 'Never trust anyone.'" Ivy League concluded and looked pointedly at the impenitent Frenchman.

"Today we will start with face to face encounters. What you will learn here in the next sixteen weeks is how to protect yourself, how to fight. I have no definitive style to teach, but I have taken from the major disciplines the best I could find. In the short period of training we have, it is up to me to impart as much of that information as you can assimilate and use. You will find elements of Korean *Tae Kwan Do*, Japanese *Jui Jitsu*, Indonesian *Silat Lincah* and *Silat Sendeng*, Chinese *Kenpo* and *Kung Fu*, and Vietnamese *Tay Son Vo Si*. I have a few tricks of my own you might find enlightening. What I have to teach will never take the place of modern weapons; but, mark my words well, you will save your life one day with what you learn and suffer here. We will work until you can outnumber three opponents. Now pair up," the instructor ordered.

Jean-Luc sought out Lars that evening at supper and sat with him. He asked if Lars had seen his demonstration that morning. Lars said nothing. Jean-Luc overlooked the discourtesy. "If you would like, I will teach you some things about the Savate one day," he offered

Lars knew there was nothing to gain by being overly sensitive to the treatment of the Vietnamese man. He replied in a pragmatic vein, "Good, I'd like to learn any of it. That Savate stuff. Isn't it just another kind of karate'?"

"Oh *oui!* but more. This is the French foot fighting, and we are the best in the world," he declared ex cathedra.

Jean-Luc was wearing a bit thin on Lars' nerves, and he found an excuse to keep away from the man for the rest of the evening while the recruits once again played serious hide-and-seek in the heavy forest. Lars did not see his French classmate for the rest of the evening. He went to his room early to get some well-earned rest; he would dispense with studying that night.

His door was unlocked, and Lars was sure he had locked it when he had exited at four that morning. He did not think overly much about it, but his antennae went up. He listened harder and did not enter the room in his usual tired and unwatchful manner. He felt the hair on his arms stand up as he heard a faint but unmistakable rustling noise inside. The room was dark.

Lars eased the door open a peek at first then for a full view. The light from the hallway illuminated the left half of the dormitory room, and the rustling noise stopped. Lars knew that there was no element of surprise now. He called into the room, "Who's in there?" He did not step into the room. There was no answer, and no other sound.

Lars had a very fleeting thought to turn away and to leave and perhaps to inform the security people. He damped down the thought with another—he would handle this himself. He did not want to draw any special attention to himself, especially as a whiner. He quickly took off his fatigue shirt and rolled it into a cylinder. He placed his hat on the end of the stiffly rolled shirt. He announced, "I'm coming in, and there'd better be an explanation for you being in my room!"

He did not step in; but rather, immediately extended the shirt and hat into the room. His paranoia was rewarded. From the dark side of the room a knife whirred through the air and slashed the shirt where Lars' arm might have been. Lars dived into the room in a tight fast roll. Less than a full second had expired since he had started to speak. He was on his feet in a fraction more time.

The explosive action coupled with the failure to maim his opponent threw the knifer off-balance. He pushed himself off the wall with one hand and tried to locate his opponent in the blur of movement. He was too late. A big shoe came up from the floor and cracked his arm just above the elbow. The jade-handled knife flew out of his hand and the extremity rapidly lost all feeling and became useless. The intruder hurled himself on Lars, but the keyed-up Swede was already turning away very quickly. The knifer fell off balance on his outstretched but useless right arm and landed gracelessly on his face.

He was as quick as Lars, and both men sprang to their feet in silence. The silence was deadly; it was no drill; and the man who walked out of that semi-dark room would not have to be asked if he had won or lost. Lars looked full into the face of his intruder and attacker in the half light of the room and recognized him instantly.

The attacker kicked out with first one, then another expert strike of his wiry muscled legs. He found both kicks blocked by fists the size of cantaloupes attached to arms like fir tree branches. His opponent was a giant, and in the small room there was no room for the intruder to maneuver. Lars, the young giant, was fast and relentless. Lars bore down on the smaller man and sent two telling blows into the small bones of the man's face. Lars felt a satisfying crack and heard the wheezing spatter of blood fly out of the crushed nose. One of the intruder's cheek bones fractured with the second blow.

The intruder fell backward and landed on his back on the flat of the knife. The weapon did him no harm. He rolled quickly to one side, picked up the knife with his functioning left hand, then rolled on the other side. He saw the white face coming at him and lashed out in a last desperate attempt to save himself. The tip of the razor-like blade cut a shallow line from Lars' mid-cheek to his ear. The cut was deep enough to result in a quick flash of blood, but not enough to expose the fat or to transect the tiny filaments of the facial nerve. Lars heaved himself back out of immediate harm's way. The supine man struggled to his feet as rapidly as possible using his legs and functional left arm. Despite a blur of pain and the blood from his nose spattering into his eyes and interfering with his vision, he was able to move very quickly and effectively.

Not quickly enough. As he suspended himself momentarily in an awkward three point stance, Lars' foot drove through the dimly lit air and caught the intruder full force in his already damaged and tender face. The intruder was unconscious before he hit the floor.

Lars switched on the light and confirmed his original recognition of the identity of the intruder. Jean-Luc DuParrier's face was scarcely recognizable, but it was him, all right. Lars looked toward his chest of drawers, still opened, and immediately saw his passports lying on the floor. He rudely dragged DuParrier's limp form to the bathroom and laid him over the rim of the bathtub. Lars took a moment and removed the unconscious man's shoelaces and tightly bound his thumbs together behind him just as Cletus Lee had taught him. He then fetched a glass, ran the tub faucet until it was good and cold; then he doused Jean-Luc with glassful after glassful until the limp Frenchman revived.

Lars waited until he thought Jean-Luc was conscious enough to understand and to talk. Then he snarled, "Tell me what you were after and why. Give me any crap, and I will kick your teeth down your throat!" He twisted the mangled nose to emphasize his unwillingness to tolerate a delay or a wrong answer.

Jean-Luc cried out and moaned in pain; he coughed a gout of blood that had collected in the back of his throat. Lars backhanded him across his face that was already ablaze with pain. Jean-Luc hurried to talk.

"I had to find out about you. I had to know what you were about."

"Why, what do you care?"

"I don' know. I have always protected myself wit' the information. It was stupid, *mon ami;* but I meant no harm."

The explanation seemed dubious, weak; but Lars guessed it was in character. Another one of Jean-Luc's self-vaunted 'sources.' Still, he looked at the vanquished Frenchman with earned distrust and loathing. He felt no inclination to be generous with this spying rat.

"I overreacted. I was afeared that I would be reported. It was instinct to go at you wit' the knife. I felt I could not bear the shame of being caught as an...'ow do you say?. . burglar?"

Jean-Luc looked as if he would say more. Lars' anger got the best of him, and he just told the Frenchman, "Shut-up. Just shut-up. You might have killed me. You're crazy. I really think that's what it is. Keep away from me for the rest of my life!" Lars was so excited that he was afraid he was losing control. He was shaking with the letdown from the tremendous adrenaline rush that had now subsided. He felt almost as if he would cry. It was hard to think. The last thing he wanted was to do was to get involved with the base security; he was leery of cops in any form, even if he seemed to be completely in the right; but now there was no other choice.

The dormitory rooms did not have telephones; so, Lars would have to leave DuParrier in his room to contact the security people. Unable to come up with anything else, he took out the shoelaces on his dress shoes, took off the Frenchman's shoes and tied his great toes together with circulation strangling tight knots. He then jammed a broom handle through the crook in Jean-Luc's elbows and retied the man's thumbs in front of him effectively pinioning his upper extremities. It was temporary, but Lars hoped the binding would keep the Frenchman secured long enough.

"Don't try to get away, Frenchman. I will get to you and make your face look like hamburger. Get me?"

Jean-Luc nodded in resignation.

When Lars returned with the security guard, they found DuParrier still on the floor where Lars had left him with his strictured thumbs and large toes. He had managed to work free of the broom handle.

"*Monsieur*," the battered man whispered through swollen lips, "Please to cut these strings. My fingers and toes are dying."

The security guard clamped handcuffs on DuParrier's wrists before he cut the shoelace bindings. His sergeant and a second guard, both burly and serious men, rushed into the room to help.

The sergeant barked at Lars who looked the better able to talk of the two despite the cut on his cheek. The bleeding had stopped quickly in the heat of battle, the clotting time diminished by the physiological mechanisms of fight and flight. "What is going on here? What happened?"

Lars told him in quick and unembroidered detail.

The sergeant of the guard then turned to DuParrier who, by now, was standing with the support of the two guards. "That about right?"

DuParrier gave an assenting shrug, no longer able even to make excuses. He was had, and he knew it. He also knew the consequences. He could envision the scene with the training camp directors even as he stood there in shame and in abject pain. His only hope would be to wheedle himself out of a brig sentence.

The sergeant clapped the subdued Frenchman in the camp brig, a very secure building completely free of windows or other frivolous amenities. The cell was a fully barred cage on all sides, barely enough for a man to stand in. He would be able to touch all four sides from the center point with his outstretched arms, hands doubled back to expose the palms. The toilet, using the term loosely, was an inspiration from the Paris streets, a hole in the floor with a slight indentation to permit drainage. The floor was cement. There was neither bed nor sink. An alert guard sat facing the cell with a 12 gauge riot gun loaded with number 2 shot across his knees. The pump action had chambered a round. The guard did not talk. The sergeant did not think it necessary to disturb the officers at that time of night; so, he put off his report to the camp commandant until morning. He gave no thought to the possible need for medical assistance for DuParrier's mangled face.

The camp doc sewed Lars' face and was proud of the extra care he expended to do a nice plastic job. "Eventually, you'll hardly notice the scar, son. I really think it'll be okay," he reassured the big recruit.

The guards took a thorough statement and had rousted a secretary to record it in shorthand. Lars was thrifty with his descriptors and details and described the essentials in a succinct and matter-of-fact manner that was appreciated by the security men. That meant they would be able to get off shift on time. No use wasting any of their time. Lars signed the typed 2820 CIA incident statement when it was ready, and the guards sent him back to his room.

When he returned, the room was already scrubbed; and his passports were lying neatly on the top of the chest of drawers along with a wicked looking jade-handled knife with a double edged blade that did not belong to him. The guards had thoughtfully called out the cleaning people, and they had been most efficient. Lars speculated that it may not be such a rare occurrence to have to clean some blood from a room in this camp considering the quality of some of the recruits. He hid away the passports in a more secure nook and put the knife away with his few personal effects. It took him an hour to settle down; fortunately his face hardly hurt at all owing to the doctor's liberal use of local anesthetic. He slept well until it was time to start the following morning's exercises at 0400.

Lars was no more tired than usual but had a few extra bruises when the noon whistle sounded. He carried his tray toward his usual table but was intercepted before he sat down by one of the agents he had seen at the 'Colonel's' office his first day. The agent quietly said, "Please come with me. The 'Colonel' would like a word with you about last night. Bring your tray." His face betrayed no malice or anger. Lars was a little jumpy but otherwise not too worried.

The two men sat in the 'Colonel's' office. Lars ate his lunch at the agent's insistence. Presently, Dustin Hauter, the 'Colonel,' walked in and took his seat behind his desk. "Finished?" he asked perfunctorily. Lars decided that he was.

"Tell me simply and quickly. When you are done, we will give you the chance to repeat your story with a polygraph. Make it good the first time so you won't have to explain any lies." His voice was business-like, neither angry nor friendly.

Lars told his story again, then repeated it with the polygraph leads on. The 'Colonel' looked at his watch and said, "Tell them where you were. You won't miss much of the history of the current conflict class. Oh, and I needn't remind you that they don't need to know anything else about this meeting. I'll get back to you."

It was mid-afternoon before Jean-Luc was able to be interrogated. His jaws were wired closed making clear speech hard to come by. It was a strain for Jean-Luc and his listeners.

"Let's come right to the point, DuParrier. You were in another recruit's room uninvited last night. I want to know why. When he caught you, you attacked him with a knife. That essentially the facts Mister?"

"But, *Monsieur*, permit me to tell you the actual events. Perhaps you will understand."

"Do go ahead, DuParrier. Make it good."

"This is what 'appen.' The young one invited me to his room after the night maneuvers. 'e 'ad apparently mistaken my friendliness for something else. You know?"

"No."

Must I be so crude as to spell it out?" Jean-Luc questioned plaintively.

"This is getting good. I, for one, would definitely like to have it spelled out completely," snapped the impatient CIA man.

DuParrier looked embarrassed. He even blushed. I do not know why the young one would ever think of me as that kind, one who likes boys. But he made it clear to me that he would like me to be with him. You know…in the way a man is with the woman."

Hauter was exasperated. "Oh, for…give me a break. I'm supposed to believe that kid is queer. I would as soon think the DIC or Hoover was a fruit."

"But, *Monsieur,* I can only defend my actions, my attack on that ground. Why else would such a man as I become so upset? My honor, my very man'ood was attacked. I could not think. I have not suggested that I was physically attacked by him, that I had to defend myself. I lost control, any real man would, no?"

"What makes me think this smells like the Copenhagen fish market?"

"You think that I lie?" Jean-Luc had a genuinely hurt expression.

'That's the general gist of it. You seem to have broken the code."

"Then give me…'ow you say, the lie detector test. Make the boy take the test as well. You will see. I am guilty of having a bad temper when my honor is questioned, but of nothing else. I am ready to suffer the punishment for that, but I am no thief or 'omo," the earnest Frenchman said ingenuously.

"This sounds like a crock to me: but, okay, we will give you that much benefit of the doubt."

Jean-Luc looked relieved.

"Get Dieter. I want DuParrier vetted right now. Let's get it settled."

Dieter Lutz strapped the electrodes, sphygmomanometer cuff, pneumograph, and EKG leads in place and proceeded through the monotonous routine of yes-no about the mundanities of DuParrier's past. That established, Lutz came quickly to the point of the vetting.

"Are you a homosexual?"

"*Mai non!*"

"Have you ever participated in homosexual activity?"

"No, *mon ami!*"

"Confine yourself to 'yes and no,' please. And give your answers in English."

"Yes, sir.'

"We will continue. Were you invited to the dormitory room of Lars Magnusson last night?"

"I was." He looked at Dieter and quickly added, "yes."

"Did Magnusson suggest that you have homosexual relations with him?"

"Yes." There was no hesitation.

"Did you attack him as a result?"

"Yes."

"Did you enter Magnusson's room to steal?"

"No.'

"Did you attack him with a knife to cover your criminal acts?"

"No."

"Are you telling the whole truth and nothing but the truth about the events of last night?"

"Yes, *absolutamen!*"

"That is all of the questions. The 'Colonel' asks that you return to your room and consider yourself under house arrest until he completes his investigation."

The results of the polygraph were in Hauter's hands within an hour. Lutz formally wrote in his report that the subject gave no indication of lying; there had been no suggestion of an increase in blood pressure, pulse rate, respirations, or change in the EKG tracing at any question or answer.

Hauter met with his two deputies. He said, "I repeat; if that kid from Utah is a homo, then I am. This DuParrier is the coolest liar and the best actor I have seen. One more thing; he is completely devoid of compassion for his fellow beings and is of a racist French colonialist mentality by every report from his instructors. You have seen the one from Shephard Howell. He would just as soon kill a Vietnamese as look at him. He is a real Nazi."

"There could be another explanation. He could just be a fiery Frenchman with an overworked machismo. His polygraph says so," said Anderson Pelgrave, the more Yalie of the two assistants.

"I've been around for a while. That one is a psychopath. The polygraph is useless with him. What's your verdict? What do you want to do?" Hauter directed the question to both assistants facing him.

"Off with his head," responded Tandrosz Szabo dourly. He had a narrow, even cruel, Slavic face with low set hairline, black unflinching eyes, and a mouth perpetually set in an expression that could pass for a wry cynicism or even a sneer, but never as a smile. He did not make jokes. Pelgrave gave a nod of resigned agreement.

"Out he goes, then?" Hauter pushed. "Can't come up with another suggestion, eh?"

The two men squirmed a little under the 'Colonel's' inquisitive gaze. They both recognized his tack having been in this Socratic tutorial situation before. It was more economical to wait until they were presented with the correct solution from their leader.

Hauter smiled at the understanding of the dynamic with his assistants. He did not pursue the Socratic method further. "DuParrier seems like the ideal psy-war operative to me," he said. "He will need tight control; but he is disposed to be very, shall we say, task oriented and does not let little things like the milk of human kindness or egalitarianism get in the way."

Szabo was well ahead of his boss.

"So, Tandrosz, can't you see this fine upstanding citizen working as your psy-ops assistant? Not everyone is suited, don't you agree?"

"We all serve where we best can," responded the Slavic subordinate, slightly defensively.

"Indeed. If you agree, you can take over the training of DuParrier from today forth. He seems smart enough to grasp the concepts and won't be hampered by an overactive conscience. He shows every aptitude for pursuing a mission to its successful conclusion and is able to obey orders. To a degree. I think you could control the man, don't you, Tandrosz?"

"I am aware of him, and of his idiosyncrasies. He has potential."

"He should fit into your special little group quite nicely. He has some of your sterling qualities, don't you agree?" Hauter taunted none too gently.

Szabo did not rise to the bait. He had a new man. He had to agree; DuParrier was psychopath enough to serve the needs of his operation. It would not be necessary for the Frenchman to remain in the standard training program any longer. Szabo would have to convince DuParrier that he would need to apply himself and his hidden talents to realize his full potential by the fall deadline Hauter, the 'Colonel,' had set.

Lars went through the mechanics of the day and arrived at his dorm room, showered, and sat down to study the class notes on Vietnamese culture, language, and geography until he was disturbed by an insistent single rap on his door. He admitted the 'Colonel.'

The officer spared the preliminaries. "You passed the polygraph. The incident can be forgotten. I will take care of the Frenchman. Don't get any big ideas about revenge."

"I don't want to have that one around so I have to worry about my back. He'd better not cross my path, but I won't go out of my way to get at him, if you insist," Lars responded reasonably.

"He has been reassigned. Let it drop. You may see him in a future duty assignment; I'd suggest you give him a wide berth."

"Yes, sir," Lars said doubtfully. He gave more than a passing thought to that future assignment alluded to by the 'Colonel.' It was a dubious prospect that he might have to deal with the Frenchman again.

Szabo's face was coldly expressionless masking the pleasure he felt. He had obtained a near perfect assistant and had the man securely in his thrall. Jean-Luc DuParrier was intelligent, perceptive, a reasonably skillful actor, an undetectable liar, completely devoid of the impedimenta of sentiment for his fellow beings, and best of all, would owe his very existence to Tandrosz Szabo. Tandrosz had DuParrier's criminal record from the first precinct in Hue' before him for review. The Frenchman had been granted a conditional pardon at the behest of the CIA operative dispatched by Szabo in order for him to serve the needs of the PRU.

A signature on a preprinted card would set in motion a very efficient series of steps that would end with DuParrier spending the rest of his life in the Thau Thien Provincial Prison with thousands of irredeemable ethnic Vietnamese criminals. The cockles of DuParrier's heart would be gladdened at the prospect of devoting himself to the cause of truth, justice, democracy, the American Way, the Central Intelligence Agency and to Tandrosz Szabo personally, (In reverse order of priority.) Szabo mused.

"Uh, um humh," DuParrier coughed tentatively to bring the CIA agent back to the scene.

Szabo spoke for the first time, "So, *Monsieur* DuParrier, you have jumped from the fire into the kettle of fish. Do you know how it is that you were given the opportunity to leave that unpleasant place in Hue'?"

"The Agency contracted with me to work for it against the VC."

"That is only partly correct. What you may not realize is that it was my choice, and my signature that resurrected you."

"A thousand thanks," DuParrier said in full sincerity.

"Not necessary. Again, do you have a clear idea of how it is that you came to be sitting in this office talking so pleasantly with me instead of dangling your legs over the cot in The Farm's brig…or worse?" Szabo paused more for effect than in wait for the answer. His purpose was more to convey a rhetorical comment than it was interrogatory.

"I suspect that your hand was behind it, Sir. Am I correct?"

"You have once again justified my faith in your perceptiveness, *mon ami*. You don't object to being considered *mon ami*, do you?" Szabo was enjoying this.

"*Mais non, mon capitaine*. It is a privilege." He had a pretty clear sense of where this was going.

"Then I need not explain the simple bureaucracy that would be invoked by my signature to rectify any error in the conditional pardon process. Perhaps it would be different if you were a citizen," he let the rest of his intention dangle. Szabo had posed the statements as declaratives, but DuParrier clearly perceived the underlying question of commitment.

"I will be in your debt and at your service, for always, *mon capitaine*," he committed.

"Splendid! Splendid! You and I shall have a most productive relationship. On your part you will be freed of the odious responsibilities of beating about in the bush with a bunch of gooks even for training. Your services will be sought only after the element of danger is past. The work is clean, efficient; and if I do say so with a touch of immodesty, it is very well studied out by yours truly. You and I will form the finest psy-ops team in the service.

"You will not find time to marry, to pursue the leisure activities of the crass soldiers you will associate with from time to time, or to form relationships, of course. You will dedicate your life to your important work; that is to say, to me." Szabo smiled with malignity. His eyes, as always, did not contribute to the expression.

Jean-Luc knew there would either come an eventual reprieve from the involuntary servitude just described, or he would find a way to profit from the relationship. For now, any option that kept him out of that pestilential South Vietnamese prison was acceptable. "When do I begin to learn your craft?" the Frenchman asked with an appropriately downcast glance by way of signaling his readiness to bind himself to his benefactor.

"Now," declared Szabo. It was most satisfying to harvest the fruits of one's diligence.

———————— ●◆ ⬥ ◆● ————————

Lars spent the nearly four remaining months in training for irregular warfare by learning the principles of long-range reconnaissance, sophisticated tracking, camouflaging, combat swimming, sniper shooting, hand to hand and small arms combat, parachuting, and by becoming an expert survivalist. He felt he had a workable knowledge of the Vietnamese geography and climate, the culture, the people and their thinking, the enemies of democracy in Viet Nam, the melodic principle Vietnamese language, and of American, Soviet, and Chinese small arms.

The young man had hardened physically and mentally in the period of preparation. Lars regularly ran five to ten miles twice a day on uneven terrain, did 200 push-ups and sit-ups, pulled himself up for 25 two hand and 15 one-hand pull-ups, climbed ropes, passed the obstacle course in minimum time once each day, and once a week crawled through brambles and mud, up a tangled incline, and emerged from a day-long exercise of escape and evasion. Despite his size and coloration, the young Swede had no peers in his ability to avoid detection. He was honed to a sharp edge, and more grinding would impair his sharpness or the temper of his metal. He was one of eleven left of the original twenty-four trainees.

"Gentlemen, your training period is nearing its completion. You have all successfully passed the written examinations. Tomorrow you will hand in all of your notes and the new identity papers you were given on your first or second day here and will have the rest of the day off. At 0400 day after tomorrow, you will be taken to a testing place for your final examination. Those who succeed will then participate in a real mission. You will be informed of the location and part you will play in the mission in due course as you need to know," announced Anderson Pelgrave, the Yalie-looking agent.

There was something of a rush the following morning to hand in papers. In the confusion, Lars ended up still holding his new passports and supporting cover papers in his hand after depositing several other documents. He considered returning to the officers and trying again to get credit for handing in the required documents; but when he did, he found their attentions directed to other inquiring recruits on the opposite side of the table. On impulse as much as anything, he marked an 'X' at each location on the Agency form indicating return of the cited document, pocketed his expertly crafted CIA forgeries, and departed to spend a completely relaxed day alone. He had not been alone for more than twenty or thirty minutes during a single day for the entire three and a half months of training with the exception of the weekly evasion testing day. That did not count in Lars' reckoning since he spent every one of those days in tension and discomfort. He reveled in the mid-June sun in rural Virginia.

The early morning rousting, the clandestine plane ride, the behooding as he passed through an airport, all brought back unpleasant memories. This time the air was cloyingly damp; his shirt was soaked with his sweat and humidity of the tropics before he and four other recruits and three agents disembarked the cramped quarters of the plane's passenger compartment. He was unaware of what country he was in, but it certainly was not the United States. He was standing on a small bare knoll at the end of the rude jungle landing strip looking at a dense forest studded with occasional palm trees. The vista was a sea of green rolling over gentle hills. In the far distance was a swatch of deep blue that Lars surmised was the ocean. Since it was west of where he was standing, it had to be the Pacific.

"The first man will be let off here. Big fella, what's your name?" the Yalie, Anderson Pelgrave, was looking directly at Lars.

"Lars Magnusson, sir," he replied dutifully.

"I have here all the equipment you will need for this campout. Your objective is to be in the Cantina Flores on the beach of Santa Felipe five days from now. You will have no more than eight days. If you are not there by then, we will leave the country presuming the worst about you. It is altogether impossible to conduct any kind of search in this stuff. You are on your own. As the crow flies, it is about fifty miles due southwest of here, compass reading 188 degrees to be exact. For your information, you are in Costa Rica. Needless to say, it would not be considered particularly good form to discuss your reason for being a guest in this lovely country."

Pelgrave handed Lars a weather-beaten passport with his picture on it made out in the name of Remundo Mueller-Garza, occupation, field geologist, a large knife with a serrated spine, a compass, and a canteen. Lars smiled at the paucity of equipment.

The Yalie agent commented, "When I had my survival test, I only got a compass and a knife; consider yourself privileged."

He and the other men finished their stretches, drank a couple of

Cokes; then, turned and departed in the Agency plane. When they were out of sight, Lars sighted on his compass, picked out a small cropping of bare rock sticking up out of the green velvet cover of the rain forest at about 188 degrees and began trudging toward it, trying to keep the elusive landmark in view most of the time. He checked his equipment. McClusky had let drop the nature of the final test; so, Lars had secreted a length of string into one of his pant leg pockets. Otherwise he was left with the items he was given.

When Lars strode into the Cantina Flores, he was clean, having rinsed off in the Rio Verde on the outskirts of the Central American beach village; but he sported a scraggly six day growth of beard (about what a grown man would produce in two), a tattered shirt, makeshift shorts crafted from his fatigues to accommodate the steam oven jungle atmosphere, hardening scabs on both knees, a long scratch on his left shoulder, and a nine-foot long snake blithely coiled around his muscular torso. He laughed and teased the crowd of grubby children who followed him into the main plaza of the village by making sudden movements of himself and the snake at them producing delighted squeals every time. Although he looked a little the worse for wear and was five pounds lighter than when he started, he was fit, and appeared to be having an altogether fine stroll back from the woods. Lars had passed that first week in October somewhere in the rain forest with the giant beetles and spiders and snakes. He had lived on roots and small animals he trapped with his contraband string.

Lars sold the friendly reptile to a local entrepreneur on the steps of the run down bar, and walked into the smoky gloom with just enough profit to buy a round of beers for the house. Lars was the second of the CIA contract officer candidates to get to the Cantina Flores. By the tenth day, when the CIA group departed Costa Rica as planned, three of the four trainees had returned.

The three Company agents in charge of the final test exercise shared a few anxious looks but did not comment. Loss of the trainee would put a smudge on their records, they presumed. For the three trainees it might have augured poorly for the future; but had these men been particularly future oriented or upwardly mobile, they likely would not have been under CIA contract and in the plane heading north to Managua, Nicaragua. Had they been worriers by nature, they might well have allowed concern for their own safety to determine their choice in the upcoming mission. All seven men, agents and recruits alike, recognized the pragmatic reality: it was impossible to launch any kind of search for the missing contract agent let alone to marshal the forces necessary to find him. The man had to be considered expendable. They all knew that about themselves. Nonetheless, Lars felt very uncomfortable about the missing man.

The plane touched down on a remote airstrip outside the capital city of Nicaragua at midday. The seven men joined another group of six recruits, now full-fledged contract agents, and three Company agents. Hugo Bartini, the senior agent, had a cold beer passed to each man. He spoke while standing by a blackboard like a school teacher delivering an introductory algebra lesson, "Presently, we are two klicks north of Managua. Our objective is a hacienda in the hills five klicks southeast of the city." He illustrated with a rough chalk map of the Managua area.

"Our information—reliable sources—tells us that there are fourteen security men working in shifts around the perimeter of the yard and in the house. There are roving patrols passing along the two concentric ring roads around the property and along the entrance road." Bartini erased the chalk drawing of the first map then hurriedly chalked a diagram of the hacienda.

"What we have in mind is to drop in four standard teams at the four corners of the rancho in the dead of night; each team will proceed in close to the following points," Here, he X'd in marks at the edge of his chalk drawing's house yard. "Rendezvous by radio at 0500.

"Our executive approach will then be conducted at 0510 on the dot. Each squad will take out the guard or guards they locate outside, then the two squads on the northeast side of the house will rotate to secure the outside perimeter. The southwest squads will enter the hacienda proper from the front and back entrances. Here is a drawing of the interior, floor by floor." He passed out Xerox copies of a to-scale layout. "The guards are a lazy bunch and may well be asleep, we are told. Don't bet on it, though. Our inside informants were beaners, and you never know.

"The best intel we can get says the inside guards are young, not very well trained, and probably poorly disciplined. They are relatively new to party ranks and are likely to be there for the good life rather than for any great conviction of their contribution to the upcoming proletariat revolution. Take them out quietly if at all possible, because the family are hard core Marxist soldiers from way back and should not be underestimated. Best to get them sleeping if there is any way you can. We have it on good authority—that is from one of our own people— that all of the Guzmans will be in the house, and they will have a party high kahuna as a guest. He will be the icing. Even the children are dedicated communists and every living being in the place has to go."

"Go?" asked one of the older agents, his face tanned nut brown. "Does that mean 'go' as in 'out of the house'? or does that mean 'go' as in 'termination'?"

"Let me put it this way, Rikers," Bartini said. "If you want to take a prisoner for some ungodly reason, you get to lead him back to the road and then walk back here with him. You'll be alone in this humanitarian activity."

"Check," Rikers said in understanding. The rest of the company gave short nods of understanding as well.

Bartini then explained the back up system that would engage the remaining Company agents and contract agents. The executive group was to consist of one agent with two new contractors in each of the four sets. Of the remaining four contractors, two were assigned to guard the entrance to the estate along with an experienced agent; and the last two were to drive a Sanchez Dairy truck, impressed into Company possession for the occasion, into the compound on call from the agents on site for cleanup. One of the experienced agents would accompany them. The remaining agents would pilot and copilot the Sea Wolf helicopters and provide security at the base airstrip.

The men went through a series of drills on a mock-up of the grounds and hacienda buildings for the rest of the afternoon. After the evening meal, Bartini handed out the assignments, one to each man. "Every assignment is critical to the operation. For you recruits, doing a good job will finish your course at The Farm. You will have performed a great service for the security of our country; but as you can well imagine, there won't be any parades or medals. If you are unlucky enough to catch one here, we will ship you back to your families as a casualty in a training exercise at Fort Bragg or somewhere. If you are inept enough to get caught, you will keep your mouth shut; and we will think, 'poor schmuck,' and keep on truckin.' Everyone is expendable here. It is up to you not to get expended. We won't have heard about you if you get left behind."

Lars was assigned to one of the two squads that would hit the house interior. He was unbearably excited and unable to sleep. This was to be his first chance for action, his first opportunity to strike a small blow against the worldwide communist menace. He was proud of his people, The Company, and pleased with himself. He walked with a little swagger around the airstrip until it was time to leave. He was keyed up and hyperalert as the Sea Wolf helicopters lifted the executive teams away.

Lars parachuted into the dense and pitch-black forest landing less than ten meters from his nearest teammate and no more than thirty yards from either of the other man in his team. The three men donned night vision goggles turning the blackness into a phosphorescent and eerie greenness. Lars was always impressed with how well the goggles let him see, and it took only a matter of seconds to adjust to the strange world the goggles afforded. The field of vision was narrow and required Lars to move his head frequently to see around him. He felt a little top heavy in them, but the enhanced visibility made the minor inconveniences well worth it. The men rolled their chutes up into tight bundles and secured them with the straps brought for the purpose. The plan called for removal of every piece of equipment or telltale sign. Lars, the youngest man, was assigned to carry the cumbersome bundle of parachute paraphernalia through the dense bush.

Even though the three men moved slowly and very cautiously, they were at their assigned perimeter location with an hour to spare. They kept just back from the well-manicured lawn in the cover of the trees until the 0500 radio rendezvous hour. From their vantage point the team could see the first hints of light opening over the spacious grounds and the clockwork punctuality of the guards who circled the grounds at ten minute intervals. The CIA teams' locations remained swathed in blackness.

The team agent, Leo Conrad, sidled up to Lars and whispered in faint but very clearly enunciated tones, "Not enough cover to take the guard man on man. Use the crossbow. He's your responsibility." It was not a matter for discussion; it was his first real combat order. Lars was neither a worrier nor a moralist. This was a communist, an enemy to be dealt with, a target, nothing more; he told himself. But he was shaking and his teeth chattered in his closed dry mouth so loudly that he was sure his teammates could hear them. He was afraid he would humiliate himself, wet his pants or something.

Lars was good with the silent killing weapon and handling it was automatic, even in the inky darkness, as a result of his intensive training. This was his chance to see if he had the right stuff in him for real action. The increasing ambient light of the lawn area made objects stand out in stark relief against the green light background through his goggles. He could see well through the crossbow scope. At 0510 the guard was not there. The world remained silent. Lars began to sweat.

He was sure he would not be able to do it if he had much more time to think about it. He could not yet bring himself to call his act, the act he was trembling over, a killing. It was still just 'it.'

At 0511, a minute late, the strutting guard walked around the house and passed directly in front of Lars and his team. For some unfathomable reason he chose that moment and that spot to take a leak. He walked to the edge of the lawn so as not to contaminate the richly cared for grass, opened his fly, and let out a satisfying exhalation of relief. Lars felt an insistent tug on his pant leg. He looked through the scope, saw the crosshairs centered two centimeters to the left of the midline of the chest at the estimated level of the fourth rib. As he gently squeezed off the trigger, the last thing he saw was the man's pathetic white penis standing out starkly from his dark pants. The mechanism band of the crossbow released with a dull twang, and the guard disappeared from view.

"Move!" hissed the agent from the grayness beside him. Lars came out of his torpor. His training took over, and he crept out of the bushes on the double streaking toward the relative safety of the walls of the house. He almost stepped on the inert body of the guard who had fallen face forward into the ornate hedge at the yard's periphery. A shaft the size of a pencil protruded from near the midline of his back. Conrad led the two contractors stealthily along the wall to the rear edge of the house. They might as well have strolled with nonchalance. In the middle of the back lawn the rear northeast team was silently carrying a dead guard toward the thicket.

Leo Conrad waited until the lawn was quiet again. It was too light out to wear the night vision apparatus now and besides the goggles interfered with side vision. The three men hurriedly removed the devices. Conrad murmured into his radio speaker then held the device hard against his ear to muffle any of the sound of reply. He signaled with a thumbs-up sign that everyone was in place and the situation was clear.

He pointed to Lars' companion contractor and indicated the rear entrance of the house. The man slid up to the latch of the French doors, found it locked as expected, and took out a thin, high quality steel bar about the shape of a metal file but with a gentle curve at one end. He placed one hand on the latch and eased the curved end of the metal bar into the opening between the two halves of the French doors. He pried for less than a second, then the door sprung open with no more than a faint click of the lock mechanism as the male end disengaged from the female end.

The three-man team was inside the house in under a second. The elapsed time from first application of the bar to the latch until they were safely inside was slightly more than three seconds. Conrad smiled to himself in the dim light. Things were going well. He chanced another radio transmission and learned that the front door had taken a little longer, and had been noisier. The first floor guard had presumed that one of the outside guards, lazy brute, needed to come in for some coffee or to take a leak, and had opened the door for the team. He was dead.

The hacienda was a well-preserved remnant of Nicaragua's colonial heritage. The outside walls were of regularly whitewashed stucco with a symmetry of form that extended to twin pillared porticos, front and back. Inside there were matching stairways leading to the second floor, and a single stairway at the rear of the second floor leading to the third. The floors and stairs were carpeted with thin tightly hand-woven Pakistani runners narrow enough to expose the Honduran mahogany parquet floors on each side. Leo gestured to the front hall team; they were in agreement; and both teams surreptitiously crept up the stairs. Each team of three men carried a crossbow, one M-16, three combat knives, and three baffle suppressor equipped Austrian Heckler & Koch HK4 sidearms, one for each man. Leo Conrad went first, then Lars, then Carl Albright who fixed his attention back down the stairs the team had just climbed.

The second floor hallway was empty and silent until the front team appeared. There was no more noise than if the six men had been shadows as they slipped through the darkness on crepe soled shoes. The hallway was wood paneled with bedroom doors spaced at intervals along both sides. Leo Conrad entered the first bed room on the right at the same time the agent from the front entered the first bed room on his right. Lars crept forward in the semidarkness aware of the thundering of his own heart. He worried irrationally that he would not be able to hear over the racket his physiology was making. A 'splut' sound came from the bedroom Conrad had entered. Lars diverted his attention transitorily toward the sound and missed the opening of the third door on his left. He turned in time to look directly into the sleepy eyes of the *pater familias*; both he and Comrade Guzman were momentarily stunned and unbelieving. The difference between the two men was that father Guzman was half-asleep, up only because he had a full bladder; and he was unarmed, depending on his body guards. Lars was intensely awake, hyperalert, effectively armed, and purposeful. Without even a momentary pause for thought or concern about the sanctity of a life, Lars brought his silenced handgun up with both hands, adopted a habitual forward spread leg stance and fired two 9 mm parabellum rounds into the side of Paulo Guzman's exposed chest. The sounds were about the same intensity as dropping a large book on a carpeted floor. The entry sites were less than two centimeters apart. Guzman pitched forward with a look of surprise frozen forever on his face and was one with the angels before his body crumpled noisily to the floor.

Two more silenced H&K reports were heard in the bedrooms at the front and at the back of the long hallway. The eerie pantomime-like silence of the action was abruptly ended by a horrified scream of a child in the front bedroom, followed by a 'splut' and then a chaotic cacophony of screams, bedroom doors slamming, rapid book drop noise discharges from the sound suppressed weapons, then a single muffled sob, and then silence again. Every Company team member reappeared in the hallway; Conrad counted noses; and the second senior agent gave the high sign with his thumb signaling completion of the twenty second operation.

Lars had not flinched at killing two men in less than half an hour. His performance was so ingrained by training that he had behaved in a combat reflex. He had not been prepared for the aftermath, however. No amount of training prepared a man for what was to come. He looked with a measure of sadness, but without remorse at the man he had killed. The man was a communist enemy of his country and deserved to die. Still, he had been so defenseless. Lars shook it off and went to complete the cleanup with his team. He walked into the first bedroom and almost fainted at the sight. A girl of about seven and two girls, twins, of thirteen or fourteen lay dead in their beds. The smaller girl had a neat little hole in the center of her forehead and a pillow befouled with blood, tufts of hair, and patches of bone and grape sized irregular lumps of gray fatty stuff. The two older girls could have been asleep except for the small holes in their chests. Their bed linens were clean; their nighties were full of expensive lace, silk tassels, and small satin bows. They would sleep forever.

The other two men were wrapping the bodies in their bed linens taking care to remove all traces of the gore that underlay the little one. Lars was horrified at himself and completely surprised when he vomited all over the child's bed clothes as he stood transfixed over the activity taking place on the little girl's bed.

Conrad looked at the big blond youth with a mixture of amusement and doubt. Lars backed out of the room and into the hall. Company men dragged more bodies wrapped in their bed clothes from the bedrooms. There was a total of eight. Lars was fainting pale when he came into the hallway, but his color improved when he did not have to look directly at the night's work.

"You'll get used to it, Lars," said Conrad without condescension.

Lars checked out the eyes and expressions of the other men. They were not interested in him; either they were too busy with the physical labor that had fallen to their responsibility; or, in the case of the recruits, they had some queasiness of their own to deal with. He pitched in to help carry the bundles down the front stairs and onto the porch. There were six additional corpses waiting the arrival of the family in the hastily improvised open-air mortuary. The agents outside had dispatched the underzealous hacienda guards with a quiet efficiency that was mindful of the neighbors' need for rest. They had summoned the Sanchez Dairy van by radio and that innocuous looking trade vehicle was pulling into the circular driveway at the same time as the first bodies from upstairs were placed on the porch.

By 0700 the van with its stacked grisly cargo had left for the airstrip base, and the teams had loaded into Sea Wolf helicopters. A neatly typed note was left prominently on an inlaid wood Serrento table in the entrance hall. It read:

> The Sandinista People's movement allows no room for traitors to the cause of justice for the campesinos. Let all who read this Party document and know of this family's involvement take heed. We shall overcome the imperialist oppressors, whatever measures are required.
> Hipolito Suarez, Commissar, Managua 2nd District

The men had time to turn in their weapons, to breakfast, and to change into old work clothes before the Sanchez Dairy truck returned to their base outside Managua. Thoughtfully, the agents who remained behind had dug a four foot deep trench with a back hoe along side a seldom used foot path leading into the jungle. They had stacked bags of powdered quicklime at intervals along the trench. When the truck arrived, the bodies were carried to the site of the preparations; and the bodies were laid neatly in the trenches, and covered with the quick lime. Then the trenches were filled with water covering the corpses by two feet. Dirt was then graded in over the trenches and mounded a foot over the graves to allow for inevitable sinkage. The jungle would begin to grow over the fresh dirt in a week and would have full cover in a month. In a year, there would be no trace, even if someone were to dig there on purpose.

Lars and his fellow contract agents were returned to The Farm in Virginia, again blindfolded, for their last day in the compound, October 22nd. They found their former dormitory rooms occupied by new recruits and their belongings neatly stored in a separate building where they were to spend the night sleeping on futons, apparently as a reward for their job well done.

The 'Colonel,' Dustin Hauter, briefed them one last time. "You have had a taste of action. There is more to come starting tomorrow. You will be transferred to another training base in another country for some final jungle survival instruction. We have found that some of our people were getting into trouble in country because of their failure to understand the necessities of life in the Southeast Asian bush. We are determined to improve on their training. Be ready at 0400 for departure.

"I have one more comment. It's about Company policy concerning capture and interrogation—I mean if, for some strange twist of happenstance, you are captured. The CIA does not demand that you be heroes. Give your cover story as effectively as you can, but no one expects you to have to submit to torture. You can stall, lie, and send your captors on goose chases. You are hereby given permission to give your name, to describe as much of your mission as you need to get them to lay off, to list your physical assets, and let go some of the indigenous operatives if you have to, and in general, to get yourself off as easy as you can. It goes without saying that we won't know who you are if you get caught; you are expendable; and we won't come after you."

Lars repacked his things, noting that his original personal items from Fort Lewis were missing. He had managed to squirrel away the three passports and sets of identification papers he had acquired for whatever good they might do in some remote future situation. He could, at will, be Karl Isaacson of Zarahemla, Utah, USA, Lars Magnusson of Stockholm, Sweden, or even Remundo Mueller-Garza of Managua, Nicaragua. He would be glad to be quit of The Farm and, hopefully, of his nightmares about the hacienda in Nicaragua. He was ready for the next chapter in his rapidly unfolding life.

———————◆•●•◆———————

Leo Conrad sat patiently in the outer office of the chief executive officer of the Union Fruit and Produce Company in downtown

Managua. He was neatly attired in a cream colored tropical linen suit, a stiffly starched white shirt with French cuffs and Vietnamese carved jade cuff links, and a paisley tie and matching pocket handkerchief. He wore brilliantly shined two-tone Mexican oxfords. He had just showered and appeared fresh. Conrad carried an expensive leather brief case. His neat short cropped blond hair suggested that he could be a businessman from the German community in Paraguay, an expatriate American, or perhaps a man from the Canadian distribution complex in Ottawa. It was hard to tell, but somehow he fit in.

Conrad was not kept waiting long. He was escorted into the CEO's inner office by its lone occupant, a distinguished Spanish gentleman in his early sixties. The man was imperially slim, richly dressed and manicured. He was, by all appearances, an aristocratic European. He wore a thin-line scrupulously edged mustache. The CEO was busy, and Conrad was not one to waste the busy man's time with idle pleasantries. He opened the brief case and presented the other man a folder of photographs of the home of the owner of the Fruits of South America, SA, Paulo Guzman. There was a particularly clear picture of a number of bodies laid out together on the front porch.

"Usted tiene una hacienda nueva, Señor Presidente. La familia Guzman está desgraciadamente ausente. Permanentemente. Pienso que desde ahora no habrá competencia con la compañia Frutas de SA"

(You have a new hacienda (ranch), Mr. President. The family Guzman is unfortunately absent. Permanently. You will have no competition from now on with the Fruits of South America Company, I think.)

"Bueno. Señor Horstmann, usted puede informar a sus líderes que una porción generosa de mi hacienda está lista para el entrenamiento de nuestros amigos mutuales, La Guardia Nacional de Somoza. Siempre a sus órdenes."

(Good. And, you may inform your leaders that a generous portion of my hacienda is ready for the training of our mutual friends, the Somozan National Guardsmen. I am always at your service.)

"Ah, mil gracias, Presidente. Nuestros negocios éstan terminado. Buenos dias."

(Ah, a thousand thanks, President. Our deal has been completed. Good day.)

Conrad and the Union Fruit and Produce Company executive shook hands and smiled in the mutual satisfaction of having done good business.

CHAPTER 8

SECRET: In camera session, Senate Intelligence Oversight Committee,
Testimony of Wilmer A. Colding, Jr., Agent in Charge, Viet Nam, Central Intelligence Agency
   11 June, 1966
   0935
Subject: Revolutionary Development— Counter Terrorist Program in Republic of Viet Nam.

Chairman, Sen. Tittlebaum: Thank you for appearing on such short notice, Mr. Colding.

Mr. Colding: My pleasure, sir.

Sen. Tittlebaum: If it is all right with you, we will begin the questions from my left, the majority members, and continue through to my right until our esteemed colleagues, the minority members, have had an opportunity to question you.

Mr. Colding: Fine with me.

Sen. Fineton: Let me extend the appreciation of this committee, and I am sure I can speak for the entire Senate in so doing.

Mr. Colding: Thank you, Senator. I consider it no less than part of my duties.

Sen. Fineton: Let's get down to cases then. Please state your name, governmental title, and responsibility, and relationship to the Revolutionary Development program in question before us today—for the record, if you would.

Mr. Colding: Wilmer Axel Colding, Jr., Central Intelligence Agency Director of Operations, Republic of Viet Nam. The Revolutionary Development program is directly under my auspices.

Sen. Tittlebaum: Let's have some coffee, gentlemen...and lady. Then please sir, would you describe the program and its goals.

Short break in the testimony.

Sen. Fineton: You were about to share with us the goals and activities of the Revolutionary Development Program in Viet Nam at the break.

Mr. Colding: My pleasure, Senator. The RD program falls under the general CT program of the Agency for all of Southeast Asia. We run the program under the ongoing operations of the SOG.

Sen. Fineton: For those of us unused to military acronyms, would you spell out the abbreviations?

Mr. Colding: Of course, sir. The CT program is the overall Counter Terrorist initiative for Southeast Asia and as you may deduce, is primarily directed at the communist threat. In Viet Nam, our energies are directed toward the NLF, that's the National Liberation Front, also known as the LAF, the Liberation Armed Forces or VC—Viet Cong, as the in place South Vietnamese communists are popularly known. The RD or Revolutionary Development program is a new action organization under the SOG which is a wholly American run para-military unit, the Studies and Observation Group. The CT program has been in place in one form or another since we entered the scene as long ago as 1954. The difference at this point in time is a matter of pragmatic decision based on our intelligence regarding the relative success of the GVN, that's the Government of Viet Nam, in dealing with the VC threat in the countryside.

Sen. Fineton: What is that success, in all candor, Mr. Colding?

Mr. Colding: Limited Senator, in part because of lack of organization and leadership, in part because of a lack of funding and facilities, and sadly, in part due to corruption and waste in the system. You are well aware of the Strategic Hamlet program with its objective of placing the people of a district together in a secure and defensible location to permit them to carry out the programs of the South Vietnamese government. We now have to admit that the program is unworkable, and it is time for the US to take over the concept if it is to work; that is, if we are indeed to win the hearts and minds of the people.

The people of Viet Nam are superstitious, and disinclined to change. They have steadfastly resisted relocation to the Strategic Hamlets because that would require uprooting themselves and their families from the bones and spirits of their ancestors, as they believe. The Diem and subsequent enlightened administrations have tried everything possible, even force, to dissuade the people from their age-old superstitions, but to no avail. Also, in a number of cases, the people who did move, found themselves in poorly arable locations, unable to make an independent living by their primitive agricultural methods. In some unusual instances, they found that unscrupulous individuals, acting under the cloak of the government's aegis, had simply misappropriated their ancestral lands for their own use. In short, the rural people of Viet Nam do not trust their government and will not consent to or cooperate with any relocation program. The Strategic Hamlet idea, however well intentioned, is dead.

A new and more pragmatic attitude has replaced the older concepts. The real problem is the terror program by the VC that causes the people to cooperate with them out of fear, and to fail to develop their own country along the democratic lines of the GVN administrators. The answer is Counter Terrorism, and the method is Revolutionary Development. We are training and financing native RD Operations chiefs and Cadres to live and work in the villages and hamlets and to report VC activity to a central information network. GVN people, including ARVN units can effect interdiction of the communists where they live. This will convince the countryside people of the efficacy of their own government and will instill in them a pride of membership, of ownership, if you will. Our own SOGs will serve as advisors for the RD/Os and RDCs to help them to remove the VC threat.

Sen. Fineton: By remove, do you mean a military action?

Mr. Colding: No, sir. This is an information gathering police program at its outset, followed by police procedure arrests with an American style due process legal system. The RD program, and all American programs under our sponsorship and leadership are noncombat, nonmilitary in character. We want the South Vietnamese citizens to witness their government in action under a democratic system based on the rule of law. The Provincial Field Police will be absorbed into the program with a better training regimen, a better administrated organization, and with more and better facilities including computers.

Sen. Fineton: I can only compliment you and the Agency on the fine work. It is about time that we took over and shaped up the running of the Viet Nam government, and this is a good start. We will expect a report of your successes in future interviews. I have no further questions, Mr. Chairman.

Chairman, Sen. Tittlebaum: It is nearing the mid-morning break. Let's adjourn for, say, twenty minutes, then Senator Clyde can resume the questions.

Session adjourned until 1110.

CHAPTER 9

These conclusions are as follows:
1. The battle against communism must be joined in Southeast Asia with the strength and determination to achieve success there, or the United States, inevitably, must surrender the Pacific and take up our defenses on our own shores. Asian communism is compromised and contained by the maintenance of free nations on the subcontinent. Without this inhibitory influence, the island outposts—Philippines, Japan, Taiwan—have no security and the vast Pacific becomes a Red Sea . . .
2. There is no alternative to United States leadership in Southeast Asia. Leadership in individual countries—or in the regional leadership and cooperation so appealing to Asians—rests on the knowledge and faith in United States power, will, and understanding.
Vice-President Lyndon B. Johnson, Report to President John F. Kennedy on his visit to Asian countries, May 23, 1961

Deputy Inspector of the Thau Thien Provincial Police, Y'Yool, returned from the Long-Range Reconnaissance School (RDC section) at Vung Tau to join the Provincial Reconnaissance Unit at their compound after they had been in training for seven weeks. He brought with him a policeman's knowledge of procedure, a nationalist's zeal for his own country and people, and an unswerving dedication that one day foreigners would not be necessary. He was grateful to the Americans because their stated goals were temporary and because he knew his country lacked the facilities and training to accomplish the task at hand—the eradication of the threat from the tyrannical and murderous communists. Given his nationalism, it was somewhat anachronistic that the Bahnar Montagnard would have given such wholehearted support to a program that was in virtually all respects an American one.

When Deputy Chief Inspector Y'Yool strode purposely into the building housing the third PRU, Tran and the other Provincial

Reconnaissance cadres reflexively snapped to attention. The man's very carriage and demeanor inspired such respect and fear. "It is not necessary to salute, *các ông* (gentlemen). We will be informal here. We will respect one another, and our leaders, but we will not need to have outward displays," the new leader said, his military bearing apparent but understated in his straightforward fatigue uniform.

"I have our first Revolutionary Development assignments, a list of VCI and their locations. Let us become acquainted for a week then we will make arrests." Y'Yool continued, "Could we assemble in the building. I would like to discuss formal arrest procedures."

Y'Yool wasted no time in introducing himself to the entire PRU, presenting the arrest and detention procedures under the Provincial charter, the Revolutionary Development Program, and the US Articles of Engagement, and their relationship to the CIA, the Province Chief—POIC—(CIA), and the district police authorities. The relationship with ARVN was simple; it was nil. They were to have no contact. Y'Yool spent the remainder of the week in an exhaustive training review with the men who were impressed that here was a leader who was not only capable, but willing to engage in their work. He was as good as the best at every phase.

The Deputy Chief Inspector divided the one hundred twenty-five member PRU into separate three man teams selected in part from the men's natural preferences and in part from an objective knowledge of the needs of the individual teams and the PRU as a whole.

Y'Yool discussed the information he had on the persons who were to be arrested, taking care to allow each RDC team to know about only those persons assigned to their responsibility, and they were to report only to him at each step. "Secrecy will protect you," he pointed out to the entire PRU group when they assembled for their final briefing the night before they were to make their first surprise raids and started to ask a stream of operational questions. "No one can inform the other VCI of their danger, and no one can expose you to the communists since no one will know your whereabouts or plans except the three men in the group, and me. It goes without saying that you owe absolute loyalty to your team, to the Revolutionary Development Program directors, and to your brother cadres in the PRU, who work directly along side you. He spoke in a softer tone than the usual Vietnamese dialect spoken in the South, because he had learned the language from the six tonal North dialect speakers, and due to the influence of his Bahnar native language.

The concept of loyalty to the team had been taught in exhaustive repetitiveness for as long as the PRUCs had been training as the action arm of the RD Program. It was a harking back to the old concept of a close-knit community and acknowledged that the majority of Vietnamese were not ready for the concept of loyalty to the nation as a whole. Nationhood had always been a somewhat foreign concept to the Vietnamese who saw their world as revolving around their own village. They had had a saying since before written Vietnamese history: "*Lệnh vua Thau lệ làng.*" (The authority of the emperor stops at the village gates.) (Set down by Bhep Vua Khua La Lang)

It was 0300 and still as black outside as the men's pajamas when the three man units began to leave for their first assignments. Each set of men had been given one target, a single VCI individual targeted by the informants contributing to the computer information network. The name, physical description, habits, place of residence, workplace, friends, family, and associates of each target was given in detail. A plan of action including a map, rendezvous sites, and modes of transportation were fully detailed. The men were impressed with the thoroughness of the information and planning and were jittery with anticipation to get going. Sea Wolf helicopters fluttered in and lifted the teams to their separate locations.

Y'Yool had selected Ngyuen Lui Tran to go with him because he wanted to select a number two man for the one hundred twenty-five member PRU, and Tran appeared to have the natural leadership ability. Y'Yool wanted to see up close Tran's function under the stress of a real mission. Nguyen Tran Xuan was the third man in their small unit. The Deputy Inspector did not know the former ARVN sergeant as well as he did some of the others since Xuan had been granted family leave for a portion of the brief and hectic first week of Y'Yool's tenure. Xuan was fit and willing, seemed cool under pressure, and Y'Yool was satisfied with his selection.

The three men were dropped at the outskirts of Hue' where they were picked up by a Vietnamese policeman in a US Army jeep. The officer drove them to *Tho Moc Pho* (Street of the Carpenters) and let them out. "Pass along the street in twenty minutes to pick us up. Repeat the drive every thirty minutes after that until you find us. No lights."

The policeman saluted crisply and left, following the instructions of his superiors not to engage in unnecessary conversation and above all else not to ask tactical questions. The less he knew, the better. That was all right with him. He was perfectly willing to shy well away from any of the operations of men dressed in black pajamas. He was put at ease, because he was acquainted with the Deputy Inspector, who was obviously in charge.

The three PRU cadres kept their silence and stood rigidly still for five minutes in the shadows of the trees lining the street. "*So mười sáu, bảy mười* (number sixteen seventy)" whispered Y'Yool telling the other two men the house in question. He signaled with his hands and the three men sprinted from shadow to shadow, pausing to check that they had now been detected, until they were standing in the overhanging branches of a weeping willow tree introduced long ago by the original French colonial owner. Y'Yool hooked his finger toward Tran to have him go around to the back entrance. He and Xuan pried open the front door with no difficulty and let their eyes accommodate to the objects in the dark hallway before moving. The policeman knew his quarry slept in the first room to the right in the single story old house.

Tran glided silently along the thin rug of the hall floor and stopped on the rear side of the bedroom door. He waited until Y'Yool and Xuan padded up to the other side of the door. They could better feel than see each other, it was so dark. The senses of all three men were keen. They waited until the sounds of their own breathing calmed. Y'Yool whispered to Xuan to watch the hall and motioned to Tran to follow him. He very slowly turned the doorknob. It was old but well oiled reflecting the good care the old home had received by the carpenter and his family. The door gave without a sound, and the two men slipped silently inside.

According to the computer information, Nguyen Chi Le slept separately from his aged wife Thi Giua. There was no second wife. There were seven children living at home, most of them late teenagers or young adults who occupied the remaining three bedrooms along the hall. Mr. Nguyen snored. The noise was disconcerting except that it was so loud that the two intruders realized that it masked almost any noise they might make. He was peacefully dreaming.

Tran held with both hands a three inch wide strip of adhesive tape torn six inches long. On Y'Yool's signal, he swiftly pressed the tape over the dreaming man's mouth. The man gave a startled and completely muffled yelp, and his eyes popped open. Y'Yool slapped a similar strip of tape over the old man's eyes, then both PRU agents grasped a frail arm and pinioned the man's thin frame to the bed. There was a frightened ruffling of the bed clothes, then stillness. Y'Yool held the point of a knife at Mr. Nguyen's throat and whispered calmly,

"*Sủ im lăng!* (silence), *cộng-sản* (communist). Đền (Come);" and he and Tran jerked the petrified man from his bed.

The old man obeyed like a robot and made no protest. He feared for his family, and hoped that his full cooperation would contribute to their safety. The three-man PRU team trotted their prize down the hall, out the front door, and into the cover of the hanging branches of the weeping willow. Xuan had heard the jeep pass while the other two agents had been in the man's bedroom; so they settled in for a twenty-five minute wait. The prisoner squatted in shivering silence despite the heat of the night. After what seemed an eternity, the jeep made its way down *Tho Moc Pho*; and, as it slowly crept past number 1670, Xuan was dispatched to stop the vehicle. Tran and Y'Yool half dragged, half trotted their captive into the street and then him into the back of the jeep. It was still pitch dark, and the soft rumble of the well-tuned engine and the wheels on the gravel road were the only sounds in the night. No one in the household, nor in the neighborhood, heard them. Nguyen Chi Le was treated politely by his captors and handed over to the Province Chief's staff at the camp as soon as the Sea Wolf chopper landed. The prisoner was transported away to a location unspecified to the PRUCs. The family had absolutely no idea what happened to their husband and father.

Four teams of three men each had gone out that first night as a test of the method, and twelve different teams the following night and the two nights after that. All missions were conducted in the city of Hue' and had been selected for their ease as first ventures. All arrests had gone textbook perfectly with the exception of one man who had awakened and had been stabbed to death (by Ngo Van Khoa), and there had been two incidents of theft associated with the arrests (by Phan Duy Ky and Tran Van Dong). Y'Yool was satisfied with the performance of all of the three man teams otherwise. The LAF in Hue' was decimated with the sudden disappearance of many of their best people.

The CIA Province chief (POIC), or Revolutionary Development Cadre Operations chief (RDC/0), as he was more properly known, Cleveland Howard, had no complaints at all, especially with the killing. Khoa had taken the Cong body along, leaving no trace of the violence in the man's home. The Cong would be listed in that week's body count in Saigon during the 5 o'clock Follies; and so far as the POIC was concerned, no discussion was required. Y'Yool gave a short congratulations to all of the units, then called Ky and Dong separately into his small office.

Each man was kept standing unlike the unmilitary informality that prevailed other times and elsewhere in Y'Yool's PRU. Then, the men were admitted into the PRU/O section chief's office separately. The interviews were carried out in an identical fashion. After a moment of quietly looking at the man, the Deputy Inspector surprised him with the flash of a toothy grin. He knew that expression, coming as a surprise, never failed to unnerve the person being interrogated. Perhaps, he thought for his own amusement, it was just that none of them ever expected a smile in that tense situation. Or perhaps it was because his front four teeth, top and bottom, had been filed to sharp symmetrical points, and all of his teeth were painted shiny black with high gloss lacquer. Y'Yool's face was very dark brown, his hairline low; and his eyes were black and piercing. The effect was riveting, especially for superstitious country boys who had visions and nightmares that looked uncomfortably like the grinning spirit before them.

When he was sure he had the man's attention, Y'Yool said very simply, "*Kẻ trộm.* (Thief)" He said it quietly and matter-of-factly. He did not elaborate, or even seem to be accusing. The affect on Ky and Dong was for them to believe in Y'Yool's omniscience since they had been sure their thefts had gone unnoticed. The scene was played out twice in exactly the same way with the same results with each man.

The thief started to speak, and Y'Yool silenced him with a slight hand gesture. They were not to speak until the Inspector invited them to do so, the gesture communicated. "You have been, are now, and will always be a thief. I cannot change that. However, you will not again steal anything, not the slightest or most insignificant thing, from anyone we arrest or even from the village where we arrest a VC. Is that understood?"

"Yes, sir," was the short reply. It was evident that Y'Yool did not wish further dialogue.

"I will not interfere with your criminal activities outside our work as long as it does not reflect on the PRU or interfere with its work. If you are caught, I will not help you. I will not know you, and you will be left to the kind mercies of whoever catches you. Is that understood?"

"Yes, sir," each man had answered.

"You will go with Tran, Nguyen Lui Tran, at night within one week and return that to its rightful place which was stolen. You will not be discovered." It was an order.

There was a look of predictable consternation on the man's face. Y'Yool smiled his nightmare smile and pierced him with his black eyes. "Yes, sir," both Dong and Ky had dutifully said. It was not spoken of again.

The following day, Y'Yool called in Tran, now officially his number two, and had him shuffle the assignments of the three man teams. That evening, the commander called another briefing and gestured to a second sheaf of papers indicating that each of the papers represented a person, more accurately, a Viet Cong Suspect.

He spoke to the men after they had settled into their chairs. "Tonight, we will have another exercise. This time all of the targets will be from the countryside. We have reassigned each of you into a different three man team for this mission; the objective is the same. You are to arrest the individual assigned to you and bring him or her back. We will draw up plans for nine groups, and I will not go with you this time. I will be coordinator. We will meet again tomorrow night for a debriefing."

Tran passed out nine sheets of paper, one to each three man unit. Y'Yool sat thoughtfully during the pause. He spoke again. "We will go over this again and again. Let me remind you that you represent our republic, our government, and that you are part of the plan to build the confidence in our people in their own country. Treat the people with respect. Do not steal their things, Do not harm innocent people. Do not molest the women. If you cause me and the PRU and the RDC/O to lose face, we will have you shipped to Con Son Island. Do not forget, even one time."

Tran shivered inwardly at the mention of the frightful prison island and had a short, unwanted flash of memory of the wretches in the dugout cells. He was not likely to go astray.

Lars Magnusson and Truong were flown together to Washington D.C. at the end of the week. The two men had been blindfolded before leaving The Farm, but no effort was made to keep secret their destination. They deplaned at Andrews AFB, given enough money for a decent hotel and for food and sundries, and were ordered to be back at Andrews the following evening by 1800. They were dressed casually in slacks and rugby shirts and civilian loafers, and noticed a large number of very military appearing men dressed similarly on the base and in the city. The Pentagon had standing orders to all military personnel to keep a low profile, to avoid the appearance that the nation's capitol was a city embroiled in military activity. Hippies and other vociferous dissenters were in conspicuous evidence as well.

"What's the best hotel in the city?" Lars asked the cabby as soon as he and Truong settled in the back seat. They had caught the cab immediately in front of the base, taking their turn with a long line of young men in civilian casual dress waiting for a long line of taxicabs.

"The Shoreham, Sarge," the corpulent black cabdriver said making the usual presumption regarding the conspicuously inconspicuous young man.

Lars was feeling frisky, feeling his first freedom in months. "Okay with you?" he looked at Truong. The Asian man smiled and nodded. He would let Lars do the talking.

Lars said to the driver, who was anxious to get a move on, "The Shoreham, it is." He was feeling rich, having more money in his pocket than he had ever had at any one time before.

Each man carried a small leather overnight bag, civilian, not military. They checked into one double room; they did not have enough to splurge on separate rooms. There was no interest evinced by a Swedish national traveling with a Vietnamese citizen in the most sophisticated hotel in one of the most cosmopolitan cities in the world. Lars liked that. He noticed everything, having never been in a large city before. One thing he noticed (from a luggage tag) was that his friend and former instructor's name was Nguyen Hai Truong. Lars wondered briefly how the Vietnamese could tell each other apart; they all seemed to be named Nguyen.

Truong was as ingenuous as Lars. He had never been in a large American or European city. He was born in the central highlands of Viet Nam, and Danang was the largest city he had ever visited. He was more at home in the forests of his own country, and was frankly daunted by the stretches of asphalt, the marble buildings, and the incomprehensible variety. The two men hurried about the city by cab and bus to see a supermarket for Truong and as much of the mall, the monuments, and the Smithsonian as either of their minds and feet could handle. They were deliciously exhausted by eveningfall. The two men overate in the splendid hotel dining room, and each fell on his bed and napped peacefully for three hours.

"Lars! Wake up! We can't sleep through the night and miss the city!" Truong exclaimed.

Lars was disoriented, but came around enough to grumble, "Something the matter? Some reason to wake up?" He sounded drunk. Truong laughed, something he rarely did.

Lars staggered to the bathroom and showered which revived him. "Let's go to a nightclub, Lars," Truong said. He was feeling adventuresome and irrepressible now.

A cursory check of the newspaper and a quick call to the concierge did not yield a promising nightclub. "Maybe a movie," suggested Lars disappointedly. Truong had never seen a movie and thought that would be interesting, but he preferred to "be with the people of the most powerful city in the world," he said.

A bellhop overheard the two young men and suggested, "They've got a show at the Last Condor, kind of a burlyque, ya know. Decent drinks that don't cost ya an arm and a leg, neither. Want me to get you a cab?"

"Why not?" Lars and Truong said with a shrug.

The Last Condor was an midscale nightclub not that far from the mall that was big enough to have a small stage and two bars. Truong and Lars were early; it was only nine o'clock; and there were plenty of empty tables. The two men selected one near the stage. The first show was scheduled to begin at nine-thirty. The waiter asked for their drink orders, after eyeing Lars suspiciously; he did not look twenty-one. "Before I take your orders, gentlemen, could I see your IDs. Just routine, but we get a lot of young servicemen. The laws are strict here in DC"

Truong showed the man his passport. He was in the clear, born in 1930. The waiter laughed and shrugged his shoulders, "Rules are rules."

Lars showed his Swedish driver's license that indicated that he was twenty-two. The waiter was still doubtful; but the guy had proper ID; what could you say?

"So, okay, what'll you men have? We get pretty busy when the show starts; so, we have to serve the same drinks each time; can't get a variety, you understand."

Truong ordered a beer. "What kind?" asked the waiter. Truong had drunk Bud with the marines in Danang at the base; so, he said, "Bud," and that satisfied the waiter who appeared anxious to get to his next table.

Lars was not sure what to do. His Mormon upbringing nagged at him even though he had not been much of a practitioner of the teetotaler religion. He was also unsure of his own capacity. He had never had a drink of alcohol before and did not want to make a fool of himself. If he ordered a Coke, everyone around would think he was a titty. If he drank booze, he would probably puke.

"Hey, c'mon gimme a break. I gotta get to some of the other tables," pleaded the waiter. He was friendly, trying not to push too hard, but this was getting ridiculous.

"Okay, bring me a Coors," Lars decided. At least he remembered seeing that brand where he grew up.

"Buddy, this is Washington DC, not Denver. How 'bout I put you down for three Buds like your friend, okay?"

"That's all right," said Lars relieved to get it over with.

The waiter turned away muttering and rolling his eyes. Six beers, two glasses, and a pitcher of ice came to their table just before the show started. Truong downed his first one with gusto. Lars tried to drain his bottle as Truong had done, but the stuff was bitterly nasty. He could not force anymore down after the first mouthful. Lars could not, for the life of him, figure out how people could think they liked that stuff. He would get a Coke someplace before they went back to the hotel.

A beautiful girl of indeterminate heritage and exotic look emerged from the center of the suddenly lit stage seeming to float out of a fog (from a recessed tub of dry ice). She was young, had a beautiful figure, and a fresh face. She was dressed in a filmy material that seemed to lie on her curves just suggesting what lay beneath, but did not really show anything. There was soft music playing in the background. At first, Lars could barely hear the strains of the pulsating melody. He was entranced by the lithe young woman's graceful ballet movements.

She whirled and pirouetted around the stage streaming ribbons of the gossamer cloth behind her as she turned and dipped. Colored lights followed her faithfully; the affect on Lars was captivating. She was the most beautiful girl he had ever seen, and she seemed to be looking right at him. As she passed his and Truong's table, a filmy sash floated off her dress. Somewhere a bawdy man's voice hooted. Lars was embarrassed for the graceful girl. He felt like yelling at the guy to shut up. He kept quiet.

The handsome Nordic youth sat so spellbound staring at her that the dancer became aware of him despite the crowd of catcalling and rowdy patrons all around him. She had to laugh at the innocence that radiated from his square jawed face. She figured he was being shipped out to Viet Nam and thought she would do something a little special for the boy. As she danced by him in her whirling jazzy ballet, she paused each time to let another wisp of her costume flutter down to him. He was not so backward and dumb that he could not figure it out; this was an intentional striptease; and the realization of that fact caused the Swedish boy to blush. He was excited, intoxicated, by her. Her belly became bare; her breasts were revealed except for a filmy bit of gauze that artfully displayed her lovely charms but hid the little treasures beneath. Lars was aroused. He was feeling conspicuous. A drunken voice at the next table offended Lars by shouting an obscenity followed by a lewd whistle.

The performer stood with her back to Lars and Truong then sank to her knees facing away from the inexperienced young men. Then, in a remarkable gymnastic feat, she bent over backward until her eyes met Lars.' He could see all of her breasts. His heart was pounding, and he was flustered. She smiled an angelic smile at him, for him alone; and he felt very self-conscious. Then, as quickly as she had come; she was gone. He was disappointed when she performed her acrobatics for another man on the opposite side of the stage.

The lights began to dim; the music was getting louder, faster, and more throbbing. Lars did not know it, but Revel's "Bolero", being played on the hi-fi behind the curtain, had been having the same affect on men for generations. The music approached the climax. Lars was panting. The girl dropped everything except for a slim G-string and two small beribboned tassels magically adhering to her areolae. Some jerk yelled, "Take it off! Take it all off!;" and the overenthusiastic crowd of men took up the call as a chant. Lars was angry. It spoiled the effect. He knew she was a nice girl and would not like them shouting that kind of stuff.

Lars had never seen a naked girl before. She was not quite naked, it was true; but it was almost as though she was finishing undressing only for him. He resented the invasion of hers and his privacy. "Let's see the muff!" screamed the slurred, drunken voice at the next table. Lars was so angry that he could not look at the guy. The thundering climax of the music coincided with the girl suddenly facing away from the crowd of cheering men and discarding her G-string. The lights went out on the stage, and the music stopped abruptly. Lars felt drained, exhilarated, stirred, disappointed, thrilled, and angry all at once. And it was over. He shielded his eyes as the house lights went up.

Lars turned to look at the creep sitting at the next table. He was still shouting and catcalling. He stood up and did an impromptu bump and grind. "Hey, baby, come on out and give us a little; how about it?"

"Why don't you shut up?" blurted Lars, his face showing his arousal and anger. He was flushed. Truong put his hand on the Swede's arm to get him to be quiet.

"What was that, boy?" the athletic shorthaired young man said, still standing. He made sure Lars saw the academy ring on his right ring finger. The other three men at his table could have been his clones.

Responding to Truong's silent, unspoken advice, Lars controlled himself and replied only with a small dismissive gesture.

The drunk, obviously an officer, lurched toward Truong and Lars' table. He had been attracted to the pair of men by Lars' remark, but his attention was now absorbed with Truong. "Hey, they let anybody in here," he said. Lars formed a quizzical expression and looked at Truong in mild puzzlement.

"Neighborhood's sure going down, isn't that a fact, gentlemen?" he said looking back at his clones. They were all strapping young men. Their testosterone levels were as elevated as Lars.' "Bad enough we have to fight their war for 'em, now we gotta drink with 'em."

There was no longer a questioning look on Lars' face. It had changed to frank anger. His testosterone rush was changing from his libido to his aggressive center. He made a move to get up, but Truong gave a furious shake of his head. Lars sat back but never took his eyes off the annoying bigot from the nearby table.

Two waiters hurried over to the tables sensing trouble. "Hey, guys, let's have a good time, eh? How about a drink on the house? What'll it be?"

Lars just shook his head and watched. The neighbor progressed a couple of more steps and was no more than an arm's length from Lars. "Hey, gook. How'd they let you in here with the people, huh?" he said leaning pointedly toward Truong's face.

"Shut up," hissed Lars, barely audible, but unmistakable.

"Hey, slope lover. You know who you're talkin' to?" The inebriate presented his academy ring elaborately so the two men at the table could have no misgivings about the importance of their lecturer. He was an officer. With a capital O.

"Can't you talk, slant? Cat got your tongue? or don't they teach you gooks how to speak?"

Lars stood up.

"Maybe you don't know an officer when you see one, boy. Take your seat in the presence of your betters." He was looking imperiously at Lars.

Lars tensed his muscles and by habit sunk into a loose karate' stance.

"Why don' you just go back where you came from, gook? Go back and hide in your hootch." The officer brought his full height up against Lars.' They could smell each other's breath.

Lars doubled his fists and clenched his jaw. The officer advanced a half step causing Lars to lean back slightly on his heels. The three other officers pushed back their chairs and stood up. The waiters tried to step between the three men still by the table and their friend and Lars. Truong stood up, small and insignificant looking against the tall fit Americans. One of the waiters made an obvious hand signal to the bouncer. The bar crowd became very quiet.

"You have insulted my friend," Lars said into the officer's face. The man brought the flats of his hands up to push Lars away from him.

Before the hands came to rest, less than a half second interval, Lars said in a malevolent growl, "No one ever puts their hands on me."

A derisive sneer started to form on the aggressive officer's face notwithstanding the fact that Lars stood half a head taller and probably outweighed the other young man by thirty pounds. The sneer never had a chance to finish its course across the man's lips. Lars brought the top of his head crashing down like a cannonball squarely on the officer's fragile nose. The man shrieked and went limp. The surprise and terrible pain completely undid him. Lars brought a knotted fist with all the evening's pent-up fury rocketing from the floor to the man's chin snapping his head back. He slumped into a heap at Lars's feet, blood running freely from his ruined nose. He did not stir again.

"Take him!" yelled one of the three West Point clones, and chairs and table fell aside as the three men struggled to move past their impediments and to get at Lars.

"I'll get the gook," the smaller of the three yelled and took a step around the overturned chair, looking down at the furniture to avoid tripping. He never saw the spinning back kick from the huge blond man that caught him on the side of the head. He was propelled back across the table, breaking off one of its legs with his shoulder. He did not notice the pain. He did not move.

Truong vaulted his and Lars's table and put both of his feet into the chest of one of the two remaining gladiators. The man fell back but caught himself and was able to get into a protective karate' stance before Truong could deliver another offensive attack. The athletic young officer faced Truong as if it were a contest; he relished the sport; and it showed on his face. In deference to the sporting match underway, he ignored Lars who now was standing close by him, facing the final remaining out-of-uniform soldier in the direction opposite to that faced by Truong's opponent. Lars readied his leg for a frontal kick and Truong's opponent prepared to deflect the expected attack by the Vietnamese.

Without looking in the man's direction, Lars jammed his foot full force down on the exposed fibular head of Truong's opponent's leg. There was a gratifying crack as the bone snapped and the lateral collateral ligaments of the knee gave way. The exclaim of alarm, pain, and protest at the foul was even more satisfying. The man was falling in the direction of his useless leg, his attention occupied by the agony in the knee, when Truong brought his shoe sole hard up into the man's face. The face became a mosaic of crumpled bone, blood spewing from the mashed nose, broken teeth, and flattened maxilla. Truong did not need to attack again. He did need to turn his attention to the brute of a bouncer moving through the crowded nightspot crowd with a singleness of purpose.

Lars took a glancing blow on his right shoulder, the price for having diverted long enough to maim Truong's quarry. He swung his left fist across his body in a classic frontal block that moved the straight-ahead vector of force of the officer attacking him to a leftward direction, brought the man's head down, and allowed Lars time and space to use his free right elbow as a weapon. The strong arm and shoulder drove the elbow into the man's right eye. The officer saw stars then blackness from the concussion to the sensitive globe. He was disoriented from the sudden deceleration of the frontal lobes of his brain. While the now lone standing opponent shook his head to reorient, Truong caught him twice in his right kidney with steely little fists and once behind his right ear. Lars kicked the man in the shins, then in the apex between his thighs, then in the solar plexus, all with one leg, all without returning his foot to the floor, and all in less than a second. The cumulative affect was too much. The recent military academy graduate crashed into chairs and tables looking for a place to be safely unconscious. He was successful in coming to rest beneath the table of a "Newsweek Magazine" reporter named Derek Dancek and his lady companion. It was turning out to be a very exciting evening for the gentleman and his married lady friend, their first illicit rendezvous.

Truong almost casually bent forward and then drove his slim left leg hard backward and full into the midsection of the onrushing bouncer. A whoosh of air escaped from the big man's lungs. He moaned and stopped for breath which was something of a logistical mistake because Lars and Truong turned the full malignancy of their combined attentions on the unfortunate guardian of the peace at the Lost Condor. A rapid-fire series of fist, elbow, knee, and foot blows descended, ascended and rained in upon the bouncer. He succumbed.

There was pandemonium. Women screamed; men yelled; and the place began to clear as if someone in the crowd had yelled, "Fire!" The exiting patrons met inrushing DC police who knew only that they had been called to a bar disturbance that was taking on the proportions of a small riot. They clubbed the occasional patron with their truncheons, stepped on fallen victims, and charged full force into the room.

Truong slipped unobtrusively into the fleeing crowd, but Lars was so big and conspicuous that he could do nothing more self-serving than to stand over the four unconscious military officers and wait on the mercies of the gendermarie.

The telephone rang in the bedroom in Hauter's house in McClean, Virginia. It was ten forty-five, and the senior CIA officer thought, "it had better be important," as he left his shower, still partly damp and shivering from the evaporating water. "Yes?" he asked brusquely.

"Duty officer, sir, McMurtry," came the crisp voice of the agent at the other end of the line. "A man who says he is one of yours—told me he's Vietnamese, name of...Truong." There was a faint rustle of papers at McMurtry's end.

"Ummmh, and what did he want?" Hauter asked, knowing it was not going to be trivial if Truong was trying to contact him.

"Wouldn't say. Just gave me a telephone number. Have a pencil and paper, sir?" McMurtry asked and paused.

"Okay."

McMurtry read off the numerals. "Thank you. McMurtry, is it?"

"Yes, sir."

"I'll take it from here." Hauter put down the receiver.

Truong was sitting quietly in his room in the Hotel Acknell in the heart of the black section of the city. He had taken the different room to preserve his status at the Shoreham Hotel, then called the duty officer at Langley. He hated having to call and now sat dreading the return.

He startled slightly when the overly loud bell on the phone sounded. "Hello," he said.

"Truong?"

"Yes, sir."

"You know who this is?"

"Yes, sir."

"I presume there is an important reason for calling me?" Hauter inquired flatly.

"Lars Magnusson is in the DC jail. He had a fight in a nightclub tonight. I think the cops and the officers he fought with are planning a lot of publicity as well as, how do you say? throwing the books at him."

"Who'd he fight with? How is he? He kill anybody?"

"Some off duty army officers; he is well; they are not; but no one was killed."

"You have any more information?"

"We have a room at the Shoreham, under Nguyen and Magnusson. I have the name of the police officer in charge, Tom Bolten. B-O-L-T-E-N. And there was a Newsweek Magazine writer sitting right next to us who seemed real interested."

"Get that one's name?"

"Derek Dancek. D-E-R-E-K, last name, D-A-N-C-E-K."

"Good work. Might I ask how you got that guy's name?" Hauter was smiling at the phone.

"He gave it to me. He interviewed everybody," Truong told Hauter.

Hauter paused a moment to think. Then he said simply, "Truong, just go back to the Shoreham. Pack both your's and Magnusson's bags, and wait in your room. I will ring three times, otherwise don't answer the phone, all right?"

"Okay, sir." The line went dead.

Sergeant Tom Bolten had arranged for the four men who had been rendered out of action in the bar fight to be taken to Walter Reed emergency room, and had just seen to the last of the paper work on the John Doe, who evidently had single-handedly staged his own riot at the Lost Condor, when his captain called him. Bolten groaned; he was already half an hour over the close of shift. It had been a long night.

"Bolten?" Capt. Anderson said.

"Uh, huh." Bolten replied laconically, not inclined to be helpful.

"I understand you got a guy, maybe a John Doe, in tonight from a bar fight. Hear he cleaned the clocks of some hot shot Army officers."

"Uh huh," Bolten replied, still lacking in enthusiasm.

"You got a name, Sergeant? I mean for the John Doe?"

"He isn't talkin' cap'n. I can't get a thing out of him except he told me the four guys insulted his friend and jumped him. I have had a lot of helpful suggestions from the army brass tonight, things like puttin' the guy's head on a pike, transferrin' him to the base for a gentle interrogation by their stockade friendlies. Nice stuff like that."

"This is your lucky day, Bolten. You get to forget about him. Period. Orders from the High Kahuna. This one has something to do with national security, the usual line of crap; but anyways, he's out. Cancel the prints and anything else you got going on him and give him a ride to the Shoreham Hotel. Any problem with that?"

"Of course not, Captain. We let chain-saw murderers and King Kongs like this go all the time. Never mind the stack of sheets from all the witnesses, and the four poor...fellows up at Walter Reed." He was careful with his language. Captain Anderson was a born-again and hated bad language. The thick sarcasm was as brave as Bolten felt for the moment.

"Everything goes. This incident never happened. Can I count on you to take care of that?"

"Oh, yes sir!" Bolten exclaimed with theatrical enthusiasm.

Captain Anderson waited for a moment trying to decide whether or not to call his subordinate on the uncalled for sarcasm and finally figured that he had what he was after; so, he hung up.

Derek Dancek received a new assignment in Portugal. The "Newsweek" editor was apologetic that the notice was so short, but Derek would understand, he knew. Maybe there would be a little something in it for Derek if he handled this story the way the editor knew he could. And, yes, it would be necessary to drop everything else.

Editors of three Washington DC newspapers quietly indicated that the story was not worth running. Only Edmunds of the *Post* quibbled and had to be promised an exclusive item from Langley at the soonest opportunity.

Lars Magnusson and Nguyen Hai Truong boarded a United Airlines 747 with tickets to Manila at midnight that night. The tickets were waiting at the counter at Dulles Airport. Neither man needed to check any luggage. The telephone caller had been explicit; they were to be on that flight that night, no fail. They would be met in Manila. Neither Lars nor Truong talked much at the Shoreham, in the cab on the way to Dulles, or on the flight. Truong did say, "I am grateful that you would risk yourself for me."

"You can take care of yourself. I just got mad," Lars said brushing off the whole incident.

"Perhaps. But those men were American officers. They insulted my race and my country. I will not forget that you made a fight with them about such things."

"It was nothing, Truong. We're friends," Lars said, discomfited with the intimacy.

"That is true. That is very true. And I will not forget."

Lars let it drop.

A week after Y'Yool's arrival at the compound, only three PRU teams went out. The computer list supplied by the office of Cleve Howard, the RDC/O, had no more VCI listings within the major cities in the province, and now the teams would have to snatch their quarries from insecure hamlets in the boonies, a decidedly more risky set of circumstances. Tran took Nguyen Tran Xuan and Bach Duc Hieu; the Kit Carson, Le Duc Bach, took Tung Co Bon and Cong Bich Hai; and Y'Yool selected Nguyen Van Dung, the *Chieu Hoi* rallier and former VC sapper, to see if he was really as anti-VC as he professed, and Dinh Van Luc, who seemed weak and insipid—a man to keep off the missions if his first impressions were true.

Y'Yool decided on a whim, more than for any well thought out reason, to leave Duong Co Tho in charge of the remainder of the cadres in the PRU for the three days while they were gone. He seemed the most intelligent, or at least, the best educated of the men. Y'Yool was generally slightly prejudiced against educated men, but he was interested to see if the man could live up to his potential and be a leader, or if he would be a good administration officer. Nguyen Lui Tran had already proved himself in the Deputy Chief Inspector's mind.

Tran's team of three sweated in place from 2200 until 0200 when it was darkest. Y'Yool's information had told them that the area around the hamlet of Tra Anh, near Tra Ve village was highly insecure and controlled completely at night by the NLF. They were to expect patrols and booby traps. Their informer had sketched a map through the mine fields around the village; they would have to depend on that flimsy bit of information. They were to arrest the headman's cousin, a ranking *Dich-Van* (Moral Intervention) team leader. He was known to terrorize the region, shanghaiing locals into the VC ranks, and was a particularly effective propagandist with the use of a skinning knife on the bodies of recalcitrant GVN supporters left as mute testimony to the populace. His capture had been a priority for Cleve Howard since the RD program had gotten underway. This was the first real break for the Company in its long and patient efforts. A VCI woman captured in the first night's raids by one of the PRU teams had broken under persuasion. It was unusual to be able to break down a woman. Howard had not felt it to be necessarily within his purview to inquire of the ARVN officer in charge the details of that persuasion.

Her information had been good; it corroborated the observations of the GVN man in Tra Ve. The VCI courier had supplied the last necessary piece—exactly where the DV would be staying on one specific night.

Tran had memorized the map but still had to check it from time to time in the inky blackness of the jungle night. He was nervous about flashing his penlight to review the map but did so with such care under his pajama top that almost no light escaped. Not even his team members had seen his light. Anything was better than getting off track and into a pungi stake trap or an antipersonnel mine. Their progress was agonizingly slow; they were crawling most of the way, a full klick and a half. They found and sidestepped or dismantled half a dozen booby traps. It was approaching 0430 when they finally positioned themselves behind the right house. The captured VCI had been very explicit. The DV would be sleeping with his concubine in the third thatched roof hut from the left as they faced the open horseshoe of the hamlet's grouping of its fourteen homes.

Although the three men were tired and nervous from the long careful approach, it had been easy, completely uneventful. The girl's information was exactly correct thus far, which gave the three man team every expectation of achieving an easy and undetected success. They had not encountered a guard or even a dog. It was a poor village, and the luxury of having a loose dog was not possible in a village where a family could only expect to eat meat once or twice a month.

Tran whispered to Hieu to circle to the front of the house and to lie in the ditch with his weapon ready to defend the other two if the snatch went wrong. Tran took Xuan with him, and together they crawled silently into the hut. The house was a typical rural Vietnamese peasant dwelling, basically an umbrella of well-woven Nipa palm thatch standing on a single hardwood pole. The family's meager belongings were neatly lined along the periphery of the mat that constituted the floor. There were three straw mattresses lying toward the back, and a hammock hanging behind the house.

Xuan sidled up to one of the mattresses as quiet as a snake, and Tran crept between the other two. Tran very slowly rose to a squat and strained his eyes in the darkness to see the sleeping man on the mattress. He strained his ears to hear the deep breathing of sleep trying to decide which mattress held the DV they had come to capture. He squatted there for nearly five minutes. There was not a sound except his own breathing. He finally determined that he could see no one. He took out his Randall combat stiletto and held it ready. Then he passed his hand over the mattress. Empty. He turned slowly and silently and passed his other hand quickly across the second mattress. Empty. Tran then stepped across the empty mattress startling Xuan and felt the third bed. It too was empty. Tran cursed softly and whispered, "Let's get out of here. There's no one around."

Xuan whispered back, "Want to try one of the other houses?"

Tran had thought that option over even before he had given the order to leave. He replied, "No. It wouldn't do any good. We have no idea which house to try. We'll just get ourselves into a fire fight. Let's just get out of here."

They fetched Hieu from his hiding place in the ditch. He asked no questions. He knew they had to pick up their chopper ride by 0600, or they would be left. Hieu was not at all enthusiastic about that alternative. Besides, this was no different than the ARVN missions he had been on. He was glad they had not made contact. It seemed to him that this was the way wars should be fought.

Le Duc Bach and his team had been dropped by Tou Rout village near the mountains. The headman was described in the computer printout as a double agent—GVN's man by day, and a loyal VCI by night supplying infiltrators coming down the Annamite Cordillera with guides, food, and information about ARVN units in the vicinity. Cleve Howard knew the man personally, and it galled him to talk to the hypocritical little sycophant about protecting his village from the VC and NVA squads passing south and expropriating his village's food and boys all the while knowing that the man was laughing behind his back.

The road into Tou Rout was large, smooth, and the underbrush had been cleared for more than fifty meters on either side. Bach decided to take the easiest route right up the middle of the road until they were within one hundred meters of the village itself. He kept a very wary eye open for any signs of guards along the road or in the bush well to the sides of the road. He reasoned correctly that it was so dark that the guards would have as much trouble seeing him as he would seeing them. When they closed in on the village, Bach, Bon, and Hai slipped off the road and crept into the underbrush. They were all headed toward the center house in the village, the largest, and the only one fully enclosed, as befitted the headman. Bach split them all up, and they kept about twenty-five meters away from each other.

Ten meters from the back of the headman's house, Bach sighted the first sentry. It would be impossible to proceed without eliminating the guard. Although it would leave a trace of their having been there, it could not be helped. Bach slid to a standing position lining himself up with the trees and began to move in the direction of the sentry. He took a full five minutes to cover the scant ten meters. The guard was sitting in a half-doze staring at the back of the house instead of out into the jungle where he might have anticipated the more likely sources of danger. It was a fatal mistake. Bach cut his throat before the sentry realized that anyone had come near him. There was a gurgling death rattle, then complete silence again.

Bach sensed Bon in the brush and startled his teammate so badly that Bon defecated in his pants. Bach ignored the odoriferous *faux pas* and gestured to the humiliated PRU agent to circle around the house moving clockwise while he, Bach, would go counter clockwise. Hai crept up to Bon, the smell had given him away. Bon had Hai come with him. They met Bach by the front entry way; there was no door. Bach made Bon stay outside and guard the entrance and against any late night strollers or wandering VC. He and Hai slipped into the two room hut. There was a faint glow of embers from the supper fire in the front room. There were no people in that room. The two men crept silently into the second room and heard the soft snoring of a contented man coming from their right.

Both of the intruders walked to the bed and took up positions on either side of the mattress. They could see three other beds, all occupied. The corpulent headman was sleeping on his right side. Bach took out a short sap made of curved lead shaped like a very fat shoe horn that was encased in thick black leather. He pointed to Hai to watch the others, then Bach whipped the sap against the mastoid process behind the headman's left ear. The headman did not stir. A woman nearby gave a sharp groan and turned over at the sound, but never awakened. It was her good fortune because Hai had his M-1 pointed half a meter from the point directly between her eyes.

Now, the two men had a problem. They were going to have to carry the unconscious headman out of the house, out of the village, and up the road or through the jungle without arousing a disturbance. He was fat; they were small. Bach cursed his joss.

He and Hai hefted the man onto Hai's shoulder in the fireman's carry. Hai was the stronger of the two; and besides, he was less familiar with real combat should they be found out. They struggled out of the house, Hai grunting with the effort. They had succeeded in getting out without causing a disturbance. Bon moved directly along the trail that ran in front of the houses of the village. He deduced immediately and correctly that they could not haul their inert captive through the tangled dark bush without making a noise or becoming completely thwarted by the density of undergrowth. Bach brought up the rear. It was slow going; the team had to slow down for Hai and his burden.

The three men stopped just beyond the village and moved a few meters off the road to transfer the headman from Hai's shoulder to Bon's. All remained quiet in the village. The PRU team stepped back to the edge of the road and began to make the best time they could toward their point of rendezvous with their pickup helicopter a full three klicks away. Hai was still sweating from his exertions, and Bon was grunting and straining with the fat man on his shoulder. His energy was rapidly depleting. They had struggled along for about thirty-five meters when they heard the first sounds from the village.

A woman's voice called out in anger and fear. "Truc!" she shouted, calling the headman's name. It was presumably his wife.

Shortly after her cry, there was a padding of running bare feet, then the distinct metallic click of cocking rifles, then the jumbled male voices of villagers now alert to the fact that their headman was missing.

Bach, Hai, and Bon, with the kidnapped headman, turned and ran into the bush. The fifty meters of clear space contained very uneven ground, and Bon stumbled and dropped his heavy bundle. The headman groaned in his stupor, but did not move. Bon and Hai grabbed his arms and legs and struggled the rest of the way into the dense forest. Bach moved more slowly and cautiously behind the other men, covering their escape. They could hear people running about in the village and out into the bush, shining flashlights with heedless disregard for their own safety from the unseen enemy. Three black pajama clad figures raced out onto the road carrying AK-47s and shining lights down the gravel road and off into the bush along the sides of it.

Bach knew he could ignore the three men and hide there in the bush almost indefinitely, but his problem was to get himself, his men, and their captive back to the LZ. He settled on the only plan he could think of for the moment; it had to be a quick one. He whispered breathlessly to the other two men, "Head for the landing zone. Go along the edge of the trees. I'll take care of the three Charlies, then maybe we can move along the road. If you hear a bunch of noise, keep near the trees and forget about me; just get back to the chopper."

He slipped across the open area along the road taking care to stay behind the three running men. They were looking ahead and to either side and were ignoring their rear. Bach presumed correctly that they did not perceive a threat from behind and that they thought their headman was being taken along the road. It was easier to run there at least, and as good a place as any to search. Real danger lurked in the forest; there was no point of going in there.

The three black clad figures were moving rapidly and noisily down the road. Bach had almost no cover but decided his only chance was to ambush them one by one without having to use his gun. He set out to do that in a methodical fashion. He overtook the rearmost man and stabbed the surprised villager in the back, the knife entering just to the left of the fifth rib. The man died without knowing what had happened to him. It was only painful for a fraction of a second. Bach lowered him quietly to the ground. He encountered his first trouble as he did so. The knife was wedged deeply into the side of a rib after having ripped a hole in the heart. Bach was having great difficulty extracting it.

One of the remaining two villagers became aware that he could no longer hear his compatriot's footfalls behind him. He pondered that idea for a few more steps then stopped to listen. He could only hear the man in front of him. He turned to see where his friend was. It was still very dark, but the villager could see enough to tell that there was a dark figure at the side of the road some fifteen meters behind him. The figure was crouching. A dark object as big as a man was on the road. It took a few moments for the scene to register fully. He was looking at two men, one of them stretched out full length with the other straddling him. He shouted to the man in front of him, *"Ngừng lại!"* (stop!)

The villager dropped to a crouch and fired two shots in the general direction of the crouching figure, making no attempt to hit him since for all he knew it could be his friend from the village who had subdued the intruder. If it was the attacker crouching there, he expected his shots to frighten him. He learned the error of considering those assumptions when a single well-aimed round struck him full in the center of his breast bone. The sternum shattered; the left ventricle of the man's heart stopped the rest of the force of the bullet; and he fell dead with half a curse at his stupidity on his lips. Bach rolled off the road and scratched himself up thoroughly getting out of sight temporarily. He had to abandon his knife.

The forward villager was not as disciplined in LAF policy as his friend, and took no thought of conserving precious ammunition. Seeing the unfortunate man behind him fall, he clicked his Kalashnikov to full automatic and began rattling a spray of 7.62 mm bullets erratically down the road and to both sides. None of the slugs touched near Bach, but he prudently kept his head down until there was a pause in the barrage. He then leaned up on his elbow, took careful aim, and when the next flurry of muzzle flashes flared, he fired a single round at the flash. In the distance he heard a sharp scream; then the firing stopped.

Bach zigzagged up the road as fast as he could run, diving off to the side of the gravel track at intervals. He paused for less than a second to kick the second corpse of the three and to satisfy himself that there was no further danger from that quarter. He came upon the last man who was on his knees clutching at his throat as gouts of blood erupted from the side of his neck. His mouth was moving, but no sounds came out. Bach reached for his knife to put the poor man out of his misery, realized that the knife was missing, and kicked the wounded man as hard as he could in his exposed temple. There was a sickening crunch as the thin temporal bone shattered. The villager dropped back like a stone, a froth of blood bubbling and hissing out of his ruined throat. In a couple of seconds, the stertorous breathing stopped.

The villagers were now fully aware of the location of the brief firefight. They shouted and fired a few desultory rounds up the road; but prudence ruled; and they kept to cover near the village. There was nothing they could do for men foolish enough to venture out alone. They were needed to protect the village against imminent attack. One of the younger, more committed, Viet Cong men organized a defense, positioning the villagers and their guns at strategic locations to repel the expected invasion. From the sound of the firing, they deduced that there was a sizable squad coming at them.

Bach ran as quickly as he could for the tree line. He trotted back in the direction Hai and Bon were coming and intercepted them about one hundred meters behind where he had killed the Cong with his knife. He was completely breathless when he overran the position where the two PRU men were hiding. He was lucky they did not shoot him and ask questions later. He was having pretty good joss that night.

When he caught his breath and his heart stopped thundering, Bach told his teammates in short chopped sentences what had transpired. "Let's get out of here while we have a chance. I didn't see any other Charlies coming out after us right now, but it won't be long."

Hai and Bon did not need any encouragement. The headman had awakened with a ferocious sick headache, but he was able to walk. The three men made him run instead by convincing him that it was better to feel bad for a while than to see his head roll in the jungle. The hapless double agent administrator was nothing of an exerciser. His breath rattled and his chest heaved with exertion. Whenever he showed signs of slowing, Hai jabbed him a prick with his stiletto to keep him focused. He did not collapse until the four men were lying at the edge of the LZ.

The UH-1D helicopter dropped out of the sky with a gratifying thump of its rotors into the center of the open landing zone at the exact moment agreed upon in the Y'Yool's planning session. The chopper crew had been instructed to wait no more than ten minutes in the landing zone before leaving. If they did not pick up troops, they were to repeat the rendezvous two more times at thirty minute intervals then to wait two hours and make one final pass. The crewmen's prayers for a cold LZ (no fire action) were answered. The PRU's prayers that the evacuation helicopter would be on time were answered. The prayers of the double-agent headman went unheeded.

Y'Yool and his chosen team, Nguyen Van Dung and Dinh Van Luc crawled through brambles and through patches of elephant grass for more than three hours to get into position. It was 0310 when they were finally ready to move into the house. Their mission was to bring out or kill two brothers who intermittently stayed in and terrorized the tiny hamlet of Kon Ba on the Trung river between Tou Rout and Pe Ker. These two targeted young men made no pretense of following Ho's dicta regarding good treatment of the people of the countryside that would enable them as Viet Cong to slip along like fish in a pond, mingling with all the other fish. They had learned early the heady realization of what the use of naked force could get them; and according to the sources used to guide Y'Yool and his men, they killed and tortured villagers for the purposes of both intimidation and for the thrill of it. Cleve Howard had learned from a number of sources that the people of the countryside, although ostensibly committed to the Viet Cong, would welcome the removal of these two troublemakers.

Y'Yool mapped out a simple plan, and the men moved in among the hamlet's buildings. The two LAF cadres were known always to sleep in different houses, and always to be heavily armed. They were also known to be very light sleepers. The PRU team was silent and exquisitely vigilant taking care where they placed each foot pad as they moved in the shadows of the hamlet. Most of the houses were surrounded by twenty foot high stands of bamboo that effectively isolated each hut from its neighbors. Y'Yool dispatched Dung and Luc to get one of the brothers in the house described by the informants, and he crept into the second house after the other brother.

No sooner had he passed into the cool darkness of the house, than he was attacked by three men. It could not have been because of any noise he had made; he was certain of that; but the team must have been detected earlier in the night, outside the hamlet. He was in a silent fight for his life. He felt the searing slash of a knife blade sliding across the tender skin of his belly. He tensed the muscles and retracted them. The burning pain was severe, but he did not feel that his belly cavity had been violated. He brought his own large bladed knife up and drove it deep into the solar plexus of his nearest attacker. The man who had slashed him swept his arm back for another, deeper pass. Y'Yool caught the glint of the steel in the moonlight and instinctively threw up a parrying left forearm to catch the man's returning hand. He brought his right foot down in an oblique stamping motion scraping the sole of his shoe viciously down the knife-wielding assailant's bare shin. The man squawked and diverted his attention for a brief moment. The pause was fatal. Y'Yool swung his right hand with its knife across his chest and caught the assailant in the throat making an oblique slash from the lower right to the upper left cutting cleanly through both sternocleidomastoid muscles, carotid arteries, jugular veins, and the trachea as it traversed.

The third man had Y'Yool around the throat with a wiry thin but powerful forearm. Y'Yool could feel the man tensing himself, and the Deputy Chief Inspector could all but feel the knife stabbing him in his vulnerable back. He made a lightening quick feint to his own right side, then dropped to a tight squat held fast to the encircling arm and threw the man behind him over his left shoulder. The point of the man's knife jabbed into Y'Yool's shirt and made a deep nick in the middle of the eighth rib before the attacker landed fully outstretched on his back. With the wind knocked out of him, the man was helpless. He could not even cry out. He could only wait for the end and hope it would not be too painful. The end was very swift. The Montagnard hilted his knife in the middle of the man's chest. The VC grunted and writhed briefly then expired without another sound.

Y'Yool made a quick finger inspection of his abdominal wound, decided it was superficial and was happy to realize that it was not very painful. His heart was pounding. The adrenaline was coursing through his veins so that he could see in the dark; his blood clotted almost instantly; and his muscles were all two steps more highly toned. He looked about and quickly recognized that there was no one else in the house. Just then he heard the awful racket of M-1, A-K 47, and a .45 caliber hand gun firing at once followed by three grenades. He dropped to the floor grinding dirt into his open laceration and started crawling like a startled snake for the door.

Luc ran past the door where Y'Yool was lying and never looked back. Bullets stitched a line up the trail behind him but miraculously did not catch the fleeing man. The light of the firefight sporadically illuminated the center of the cluster of houses enough to show Dung jumping and running from cover to cover, firing as he went. He was running in the opposite direction of Y'Yool. It appeared calculated; that Dung was drawing the fire of the VC away from his teammate. Y'Yool made his way outside and into the bamboo thicket. He moved through it until he was behind the two men he could see firing at Dung.

Y'Yool held the M-14 he had appropriated for himself at waist height and opened fire on full automatic. The two VC jumped and jerked convulsively like poorly controlled puppets, reacting to the surprise, pain, and finally to the disruption to their nervous systems that came from being riddled with two dozen 7.62 X .51 mm slugs each. Behind him, Y'Yool heard a combination of fire from the deep bark of the M1 carbine (lighter than the standard Garand rifle) that he had found for Luc since the man was not very strong and then the characteristic higher pitched chatter of several AK-47s. Soon only the Kalashnikovs were firing. That sounded ominous to the Deputy Chief Inspector. Ahead of him, he could hear a furious firefight. Dung was obviously in trouble. Y'Yool ran zigzag in the direction of the fire.

A bullet grazed his left shoulder. It felt like someone had struck him with a ball-peen hammer. Y'Yool whirled instinctively and fired at the muzzle flares coming from his left. The flares stopped. He ran some more and almost collided with a terrified man in black pajamas. Blood was flowing down the side of the man's head, but he was still capable of running a world class sprint. That ended when Y'Yool skidded to a stop and dropped to a crouch. He opened fire within a meter of the astonished foe who pitched forward dead spraying blood and bits of bone on Y'Yool. The man fell into Y'Yool causing him to stagger backward two steps. The deputy inspector tasted blood.

Again the chatter of an AK-47 rang out somewhere to his right. He dropped to the ground and again whirled his M-14 around to return the fire at the muzzle flares. Nothing happened. His rifle was empty. He did not have time to reload; a line of bullets traced a deadly path right toward his chest. He could see death coming five meters away. A single foreign sounding shot cracked in front of him, and the Kalashnikov firing abruptly stopped. Y'Yool felt almost faint. He rolled off the trail and into the heavy bushes. There was an eerie silence. There were not even any animal sounds in the usually noisy jungle of the night.

"Inspector, Inspector!" came a harsh whisper from somewhere in the gloom. Y'Yool recognized Dung's voice.

Before he could answer, the voice sounded again, now from a different direction. "Inspector, you still there?"

"Yes," Y'Yool said as loudly as he dared. "I'll meet you back at the entry point...two minutes."

The Deputy Chief Inspector was lying hidden in the overgrowth alongside the trail when Dung padded noiselessly by. "Dung!" he hissed. Dung stopped and dropped automatically off the trail.

"You all right, Inspector?"

"Yes, let's get out of here."

"What about Luc?"

"I haven't heard anything from him for twenty minutes."

"Think they got him?"

"Either that or he ran away. I don't think we can find him in this stuff. Let's get out of here, what do you think?"

"All right. We can hole up in the forest and come after him when it starts to get light."

"Like American movie heroes," thought Y'Yool, but kept that idea to himself.

The two men joined up and ran as fast as their limited vision would permit. They did not stop until they considered themselves safe in the middle of the largest section of chin-high elephant grass. Y'Yool's left shoulder and his abdomen were beginning to throb and he was aware of a hundred little additional hurts once they stopped for rest. The two men got an emergency bandage on Y'Yool's raw wounds and the two of them sagged back in exhaustion. There was no more noise from Kon Ba village.

At the first light of false dawn, the two men picked their way back down the trail in the direction of the firefight Y'Yool had heard behind him. A second trail, coming in from the south, veered off into the jungle from the village. A short distance along that trail and in the dense stand of trees they found four dead men, all in black pajamas. One of them was Dinh Van Luc. The two survivors could do nothing more for their comrade there; so they rapidly retreated back down the trail and on to the LZ carrying his body.

* * *

Douglas N. Herter met Lars and Truong at their gate in the Manila International Airport as soon as their United Airlines 747 touched down. Lars recognized the sweating, out of shape, plump man in black horn-rim government issue glasses as the CIA attorney who had accompanied the 'Colonel' and the thin, unsmiling, unsettling man at Lars's first interviews back in late spring of 1966 at Fort Lewis. He was surprised at the man's openness on this occasion; Herter introduced himself immediately after coming up to Lars and Truong. As soon as it was discrete, he presented his Central Intelligence Agency credentials, as if the other two men might have mistaken him for the Manila Welcome Wagon.

They were thirteen hours out of sync with DC time and neither Lars nor Truong had rested much on the long flight. The effect was to make them dazed and off-balance. Lars expected a reprimand or at least a lecture from Herter about his conduct in DC. Instead, Herter kept to banalities, "Hottest summer in Philippine history, and that's going some, I'd say. I guess you heard that Lane Duerk is the new station chief in Saigon. I presume Colding will get the job for all of Southeast Asia. I guess you haven't any better idea about who is going to get the Viet Nam spot—I mean, be the head honcho?"

Lars thought he might mention to Herter that no one thought to share Company gossip with him, but said instead, "How about the 'Colonel'"?

"Good thought. Be a jump for me. I would swing along on his coattails, I presume. You never know what'll happen in the club, though."

Truong was bored. He was the ultimate pragmatist and had an almost religious lack of interest in things that did not concern him. He was quiet, and sat looking inscrutable and oriental all the way to the Pacific Breezes Hotel. He was glad to be away from Herter; brass made him nervous, whether Vietnamese or American. He was most comfortable in the forest doing what he did best, and was getting antsy to get back to real work.

Herter handed Lars a package and turned to go. Lars gave an embarrassed little cough to get the senior man's attention and said apologetically, "Uh, sir, we left DC so fast that we don't even have clothes, and we don't have enough money to pay a hotel bill or to eat for even one day. Can you give us an idea what to do?"

It was Herter's turn to look apologetic. He answered without hesitation, "My oversight. Stupid of me. I think it best for you to handle your transactions with cash, don't you? Here's something to tide you over. I'd reckon on you being here for a few days, a week at most. I've got enough on me to get you through today. I'll have an envelope delivered to the hotel desk tonight. That be okay?"

"Sure. We didn't want to bother you, but we're kind of strapped."

"Indeed. That package I gave you has some instructions, I understand, although I am not privy to the details. The 'Colonel' did ask me to convey a further small bit of information to you, Lars, Truong. I think you are already apprised of your assignments, pickup arrangements, and that sort of thing, aren't you?"

"Yes, sir," Truong answered. He had orders to be in Saigon on the twenty-fourth of October. Everything he needed to do his work was already there in his room at Revolutionary Development headquarters in the terminal building at Tan Son Nhut, the seventh air force base.

"Perhaps you wouldn't mind if I had a few words alone with Lars here, then," Herter looked meanfully at Truong. Truong nodded his understanding and left for his hotel room.

"Now then, Magnusson. You are to buy three or four tropical suits, shirts, ties, and shoes—get them custom made by one of the tailors around Subic Bay; they're excellent; and they're cheap. Buy a commercial ticket to Saigon; you'll probably have to go to Bangkok first. Be there on the twenty-ninth and go over to the Saigon First Precinct Police headquarters. You'll meet Lane Duerk in the Saigon Revolutionary Development Liaison Office in the First Precinct station. Just get a cyclo and tell the man where you want to go; those guys know every nook and cranny of Saigon. Don't feel that you need to explain to anyone the nature of your business in the city. There are thousands of nonmilitary, European looking, and non American types there. You can just be part of the crowd. Any questions?"

"I guess not," Lars replied. "And thanks for the money."

The Company had sprung for separate rooms for him and Truong. The two men agreed to meet for dinner in the hotel restaurant six hours later, and both of them settled in for a much needed respite from the hectic pace and multiple changes of the last three days and to shake off the pervasive lethargy of jet lag. When he was alone, the young Scandinavian first opened the package Herter had given him. He found a brief handwritten but unsigned note, presumably from the 'Colonel.' It read: "Due to the fuss in DC you are not all that popular. Lay low and keep out of trouble. Learn the new cover story and keep only the new documents. Burn any old ones. This is who you are going to be all the time you are In Country."

In fact, Hauter had been lucky to get Lars out of the country; army types were after his head. The light colonel Hauter had talked to presumed that Lars was one of Hauter's spooks, and his people in Nam would be on the lookout for one Lars Magnusson; the 'Colonel' could bank on that. A hasty change of identities was in order. The new set of documents had already been prepared and would have been given to Lars by Herter as they were had it not been for the altercation in the Lost Condor. As it was, the only change was in the name; and that had been simple enough for Herter to do.

The documents were genuine; proper paper, official photographs, letters of introduction from the International Inspection and Monitoring Commission of the Red Cross with offices in Stockholm, rental agreement for the apartment in Hue' leased to the commission, and an official pass document from the Republic of Viet Nam, Department of Defense, signed by General Khanh himself, permitting free travel to all zones and free access to any and all officers and men of the Armed Forces of the Republic of Viet Nam to accomplish the monitoring program's aims. The pass was dated, 25 November, 1962 and had the imprint of the Diem administration affixed. The passport was Swedish and identified him as one Anders Bergstrom, born 7 July, 1948 in Malmo where he still maintained his permanent address. The passport and accompanying Vietnamese visa were stamped with multiple entrance and exit markings from 1962 to the present. The package contained two Red Cross arm bands and a heavy enameled steel badge to be worn on the front of his suit, presumably.

Lars was getting used to the spook game of changing identities, and practiced using and signing the new name until he was comfortable with it. He and Truong shopped for the new clothes as ordered, bought some second hand leather luggage, and took a jeepney tour of Luzon from Manila and Quezon City to Laoag on the coast of the South China Sea where they lolled on the beach and swam in the warm and balmy waters.

They asked the driver they hired by the day to take them someplace authentically Philippine. They drove out of Manila in the late morning to escape the worst of the traffic. Their route took them past Smoky Mountain—the horrendous pile of trash at the Manila garbage dump. It was a shock to Lars to see people picking over trash in the smoking rubble. It was more of a shock to learn that 60,000 people lived there all the time. Lars (he still had to use that name while dealing with Truong) had only imagined that he had seen poverty before in rural Utah. He was beginning to get a sense of world-perspective reality.

"I know best place in the PI," the smiling driver told them. He filled them in on everything from local gossip and the results of the last typhoon, to his myopic world view. He was embarrassingly pro-

American and repeatedly told and retold his father's story of serving with the Americans in the Second World War as a scout. "We are going to Villa Escudero. You will love it there. Lotsa great Philippine (he pronounced it 'pilipine') food and animals. Nice place. You will like, you bet."

Remembering their request for authenticity, the driver pulled over at a large rice warehouse where hundreds of enthusiastic Filipinos were headed. "Cockfights. Big time!" the driver said. Inside there was a frenzy of activity. Money changed hands as fast and heavy as in the New York Stock Exchange. The Christo, the man who held the money as an intermediary for a small percentage, collected pesos as fast as he could handle them. Both hands bulged with currency. "Bet on the black one," the drive insisted.

"Why the black one?" asked Lars.

"I gotta hunch. Feel lucky. Bet, and you see." The driver was wholly absorbed and completely convinced about his fortunes.

The black rooster put up a very game fight but lost. Lars was out a few hundred pesos. The losing rooster was battered and dragged one wing. Its owner wrung its neck.

Lars and Truong were booked for two days in Villa Escudero in San Pablo City in the Laguna district south of Metro Manila. The jeepney parked; the two men paid in advance for their rooms and food and climbed aboard a carabao cart and were taken to their rooms. Everything about the old plantation that had been converted into a resort was authentic. Bamboo walled, palm roofed houses served as rooms. The food was excellent and plentiful. Lars sat down to his opening course—Philippine jumping salad. He had not had chopped fresh green vegetables for some time and looked forward to the pleasure of the salad. He poured the oil then the vinegar provided as the dressing. All of a sudden the salad began to move, literally to jump. Lars fished around in the greens and found the source—dozens of small shrimplike creatures, still alive, that moved about when the vinegar irritated them. He passed on the salad. It violated one of his fundamental rules in eating—leave live things alone.

The atmosphere was enervating and completely restful. When he was not eating with his legs dangling in the knee-deep water at the foot of Labasin Falls, he was either sleeping or lying about on a raft on the pond. It was a fine temporary escape.

Truong took a night flight out on the twenty-seventh, and Lars

234

picked up his new suits on the twenty-eighth. Using his old documents as Lars Magnusson, flew on Filipinas Orient Airways over the Gulf of Siam to Don Muang Airport in Bangkok-Thon Buri early in the morning of the twenty-ninth. He was in Thailand only long enough to clear customs, to change identities, and to see the view from the airport. He changed airlines, this time flying on Thai Airways International under his new identity of Anders Bergstrom, and arrived at Tan Son Nhut Airport in Saigon at 1305, 29 October, 1966.

Cleve Howard mulled over Y'Yool's report with a jaundiced eye. The native Deputy Chief Inspector's teams had performed so well the previous week that Howard had been the object of a spot of faint praise from Lane Duerk in Saigon. Those crumbs of positivity were hard come by, and Howard knew he needed a bigger pile of them if his career was going to go up and out of Thau Thien Province any time soon. Duerk had been the Saigon station chief for two years, and must be in line for a promotion. In all modesty, Cleve Howard could see himself in Duerk's chair, the youngest agent ever to head the Saigon office. Now this distressing report from Y'Yool.

As soon as he could debrief his PRUCs and piece together the events of the week of countryside hunting, Y'Yool had sent his report to Howard in the RD office in Hue'. The Inspector detailed the abortive raids and the ambush at Kon Ba. He described the fight in detail including the known and presumed VC dead and the death of his own man, Dinh Van Luc. He reckoned there had been ten VC killed with an actual body count of eight, not counting Luc. There were several suspiciously failed team missions. Y'Yool came right to the point in his report. There had been too many coincidences, too much luck' for the VC. That might have been explained as just his bad joss; but the Kon Ba hamlet reception for himself, Dung, and Luc was a well planned ambush. The uncomfortable thought that there might be a VC infiltrator in his PRU was made part of the report.

Howard thought on the problem of how to make a silk purse out of this sow's ear. He decided to let the facts speak for themselves—the actual body count came to eleven, counting Luc as a VC. The prevailing tendency at the Saigon follies was to count every dead Vietnamese who was not actually in ARVN as a VC, and Howard was only following the unspoken policy. Duerk cabled back a terse: "Good couple of days' work. Too bad about missing the brothers Grim."

Y'Yool had presumed that he had kept each of his operations fully

235

separate from the others and therefore as secure as they could possibly be, but he could not shake the fact that there was no good alternative explanation for the coincidental failure and ambush. He reviewed his own procedures since he was the only man who knew about all of the separate operations. He had given instructions to each three man PRU team separately and in a secure place. He had not revealed the exact targets or locations until the team boarded their respective helicopters on the morning of the actual raids. There had been no discernible pattern in the selection of the targets. He had kept all of the computer information, target data, and his own mission operational plans out of sight in his office. That led him quickly to the conclusion that the most likely suspect as an informer had to be either Dinh Van Luc, who was dead, or Nguyen Van Dung, who had shared his night in the jungle.

The answer seemed obvious. Then, Y'Yool felt a surge of adrenaline. It was a sudden guilty realization that he had been a culpable fool. Some one or more of the PRUCs must have been in his office unknown to him and had seen those plans. He had been a naive trusting fool, and that foolishness had resulted in failure and worse. The Deputy Chief Inspector slapped his forehead with the flat of his hand with a resounding smack; he did not have a safe; and he had not even worried enough to put the papers in a securely locked desk or closet. He broke into a sweat as his mind ground down on the recognition of his unprofessional performance and on the fact that he had broken with his own habit and better counsel and had confessed his suspicions openly to the American, Howard, in his report. He was a fool and a compound one.

Y'Yool's forehead knitted in tense and angry lines as he strove to think through the fog of his own emotional response. He concluded that there were one hundred twenty-five suspects, every member of the PRU, not just Dung, who had fought valiantly alongside him; and he could not count on nor confide in anyone. His mind cleared with that sobering thought; he was not the guilty one, obviously; and Luc was dead; that left one hundred twenty-three suspects. "Just one hundred twenty-three," he sighed to himself. Y'Yool set his mind to the task of setting a trap for his suspected traitor.

CHAPTER 10

We have fully recognized France's sovereign position and we do not wish to have it appear that we are in any way endeavoring to undermine that position.

At the same time we cannot shut our eyes to the fact that there are two sides to this problem and that our reports indicate both a lack of French understanding of the other side and the continued existence of the dangerously outmoded colonial outlook and method in areas.

On the other hand we do not lose sight of the fact that Ho Chi Minh has direct communist connections and it should be obvious that we are not interested in seeing colonial empire administrations supplanted by the philosophy and political organization directed and controlled by the Kremlin.

Frankly, we have no solution of the problem to suggest.
George C. Marshall, Secretary of State. Cablegram to French Embassy in Paris, 1949.

Thai Airways International flight 1232 made a smooth landing on the shimmering runway at Tan Son Nhut International Airport in Saigon and promptly disembarked 312 passengers. Wet heat of the July afternoon came at them as if from the mouth of an unseen blast furnace. The hot wet air was oppressive especially after the comfort of the air-conditioned interior of the 747. The lovely Thai stewardesses had served the passengers as if they were house guests; and Anders Bergstrom, Swedish Delegate of the International Red Cross, was understandably reluctant to get out. He followed the largely civilian group of passengers across the tarmac and into the huge main terminal building as fast as they all could move. The passengers were mostly well-to-do Vietnamese who spoke French to each other, with a few nondescript Occidentals like himself whom he took to be American and European civil servants and diplomats or businessmen, and a smattering of clannish Chinese.

237

Anders had to smile at the courtesy he was afforded at each step of the check-through and customs process. The diplomatic seal on his luggage, granted by his International Red Cross posting, spared him the boring and time-consuming search of his baggage. The practiced eyes of the officials ranked the passengers, and Anders was moved to a place near the head of the line. He thought that he could get to like this VIP treatment.

He changed his American dollars, at 100 pee to the dollar, and his Philippine pesos into Vietnamese Piastres at the currency exchange; and twenty minutes after the plane had come to a full stop at its terminal gate, Anders was standing on the sidewalk in front of the entrance to the main terminal. He looked back at the huge building feeling that despite its well-maintained interior and facade, the edifice maintained a perverted temporary look—the special characteristic of government buildings that gave them permanence despite the original plan calling for a short life.

Tan Son Nhut Air Base was located just on the outskirts of Saigon and was home for the South Vietnamese Air Force, the US Second Air Division, and the Seventh Air Force. It was also the location of the MACV headquarters, the massive 'Pentagon East.'

Young boys and girls selling everything from homemade popsicles, packages of gum, and C Rations, to assorted services crowded around the newcomer. "You come 100 Pee Alley, get pleny 'boom-boom.' Cost American dollar. One dollar for you, marine."

Cyclo pedalists swarmed Anders until he selected one to get out of the roiling sea of aggressive humanity as much as anything. He had been carefully schooled to ask the price before getting on one of the human-powered conveyances, and he haggled briefly with the pedicab puller. They agreed amiably on a price of 35 pee; the taxi man grinning to himself for having overcharged the westerner by at least five pee; and Anders wondering that the man could work for such a pittance. The skinny Vietnamese pulled the pedicab out onto the wide thoroughfare of Duong Cach Mang Avenue and on toward the city center.

Anders was a completely inexperienced traveler. His stay in Nicaragua could not be counted, and the week in the Philippines had given him only a small taste of the great world beyond his home back in Utah. He was unprepared for the density of human activity—Saigon has the densest population on earth. The main thoroughfares were jammed with cyclos, bicycles, pedestrians, motor scooters, old DeSoto and Packard cabs, jeeps, an occasional old Chevrolet or Ford passenger car, military trucks of all types, and squealing children darting in and out of traffic daring vehicles to try and hit them.

The streets smelled of sewage, human sweat and armpits, strong French cheese, frying fish, rotting fruit, fresh popcorn, garlic, incense, and petrol fumes. If he closed off individual sounds, Anders heard an amalgam of the loud hum of motors from trucks, mopeds, and cars, the whir of bicycle pedals, the padding of thousands of moving feet, the melody of the national language being spoken and shouted everywhere, *dan day* (three-stringed lute) music drifting from behind shuttered windows, the slow beat march music of flutes, guitars, finger cymbals and *sinh tiens* (rattles) as a parade of saffron robed bonzes paraded with solemnity along a side street. This background hum was added to by the quacking of ducks being herded across busy roads against the protests of irate travelers, by chickens hanging upside down in open crates on the back of bicycles, and by pigs being led reluctantly by ropes in the hands of children.

He had the luxury of watching the tapestry of life in the most densely populated city on the planet—double that of Tokyo—being woven much as it had been done for more than a millennium, since the time when the city was Prey Kor, major city of the Cambodian royal state. He had time to see old women and children making baskets and brooms in open door markets, limes being hawked by street vendors, languid old men enjoying bamboo pipes of opium in sidewalk smoke shops, and riders carrying baguettes on the back racks of their bicycles. There were small knots of elderly expatriate Frenchmen in black berets, part of the 15,000 who chose to remain behind, playing *boules* in parks, and animated old Vietnamese women gossiping in French and French accented Vietnamese. A man and woman were washing their toddler in a bucket at the side of the street. People everywhere greeted each other in the traditional way by pressing their palms together in front of their chests and making quick bows. The color and energy of the city included the ubiquitous conical straw hats on black pajamad workers, the wisp thin graceful girls flowing along in Ao Dais—the traditional white silk trousers and colorful long blouses—and people drinking or washing from old French and American helmets, 'steel pots.'

There were chronically dilapidated French colonial neoclassical residences, country-type thatched roof huts serving as both dwellings and sidewalk shops, well cared-for Catholic churches, colorful and ornate pagodas, and houses with upswept Chinese roofs. Mercantile life was being carried on in single product shops, some with walls and roofs of rusting corrugated sheet metal with an uncountable number of different wares, and in cooperative cottage industries.

There were restaurants featuring Vietnamese, French, American, Chinese, Indian, and Thai meals, and movable vendor carts selling beer, American sandwiches on French baguettes, fresh fish, cooked and uncooked, *cha' gio* (small aromatic rolls of minced pork or crab meat, chopped fragrant mushrooms, and vegetables wrapped in thin rice paper and deep fried fresh and crisp, then rolled in a lettuce leaf, then dipped in *nuoc cham.*). Small stalls featured piles of fresh fruits, frozen drinks and popsicles made from the fresh juice of mangoes, papayas, pineapples, and various sizes and shapes of green and yellow bananas, durian fruit, and lichees.

Anders thought he was hotter, sweatier, and tireder than his cyclo driver by the time he passed the Thong ông Nhât (Palace of the President of South Viet Nam) at 7 Le Duan Boulevard and stopped in front of the American Embassy building on the corner of Le Duan Boulevard and Mac Dinh Chi Street. The building was nothing less than a fortified cement cube that had once been a French bank. Anders stepped out of the cab, looked into the bland and smiling face of the cab puller who had barely broken a sweat, and felt that 35 pee was not enough for all that work; so, he gave the man 40. The man's expression never changed. He said, "*Ông quá tử tế đối với tôi*" (You are very kind to me.) and trotted off without looking back. In good form Anders replied, "*Không có chi*," (Nothing) but the man was out of earshot and unable to share Ander's pleasure at his little linguistic success. The cyclo puller was thinking that this was undoubtedly a newcomer since he had overpaid, and could not be an American because they were such pinchpees.

Anders was still unsure where the First Precinct Police Headquarters was located and asked a well-dressed businessman. "Behind the 'Bunker,'" the man directed in French accented perfect English, pointing first to the embassy, then hooking his finger to indicate the building behind it. The American Embassy was so nicknamed because, first of all, it was a true bunker; and second of all, it was the headquarters of the American ambassador, Elsworth Bunker. Anders lugged his suitcases into the lobby of the police building noting the wrought iron grillwork on all of the windows and doors similar to that he had seen on all of the other buildings in the central metro area. The only other people in the lobby were a woman in a Ha Dong silk Ao Dai and a man in a black tunic and turban who were seeking renewal of their national identification papers.

Anders approached the desk sergeant. The wary officer gave Anders close scrutiny then good directions to Lane Duerk's Revolutionary Development National Headquarters Office. Anders walked up the single flight of stairs, turned into the appropriately marked office, and presented himself to the well-tailored Vietnamese lady secretary in the outer office. She was dressed in western attire and had a short hair style similar to that Anders had seen frequently in Washington, DC.

The benign sign over the door, and the crisp, small, nonmilitary office, seemed out of place for the head of station for the CIA. The CAS (Saigon Office of the CIA) was at Tan Son Nhut—Anders had seen it as he passed through. The official Saigon CIA station occupied the top three floors of the Chancery Building. It was a little strange to have the real office somewhere else. It was one of those things you just had to know, Anders decided.

"I am Anders Bergstrom, of the Swedish Red Cross," Anders said, comfortable with the fiction of his cover by now after nearly three days of practice with it. "I believe I am expected."

She looked at her appointment book. "Yes, Mr. Bergstrom. To see Mr. Duerk. I have no time listed, but I believe the chief wanted to see you as soon as you got here. Take a seat, if you would. I will see when he will be free." She was not young, but otherwise was of an indeterminate age that makes mature Vietnamese women interesting.

Anders sat and waited. In fifteen minutes the secretary stepped out of Duerk's office and gestured to the Swedish gentleman to come in. "Ah, Bergstrom," said the tall, rangy figure from the inner sanctum of his office. "We've been expecting you. How good to see you."

"Thank you, sir. I'm glad to be here. Real glad to be out of the cyclo. I'm Anders Bergstrom of the International Red Cross Monitoring Commission checking compliance with the Geneva Conventions," Anders said for the benefit of the lingering secretary.

"You have already met Miss Nguyen, I presume," Duerk said nodding in the direction of his secretary.

"Not formally," Anders said. "I am pleased to make your acquaintance," he said to her.

Miss Nguyen lowered her head in a small bow of acknowledgment.

Anders fidgeted impatiently waiting for the opportunity to talk to the station chief alone. As if reading his thoughts, the senior agent said, "I have no secrets from Miss N., Anders. She is fully vetted, works for The Company. You can speak freely here. Let's all sit down."

They took seats on a comfortable velvet upholstered French sofa and overstuffed chintz chair. "I take it you are to be assigned to one of the PRUs as section ops officer, that right?" Duerk asked, getting right down to business.

"That's what I understand, sir. I learned about Thau Thien Province and understood I was going there."

"Up in Eye Corps. Gets rather hairy up there at times, close to the border of Laos. From the look of you, I'd guess you can handle yourself. You seem kind of young, though. Had any experience leading men, natives, that sort of thing?"

"Not really. We did a lot of training and had a lot of classes about Viet Nam, general stuff. We had some training in PRU leadership techniques at The Farm. I have to confess that I'm still not so sure I know exactly what I'm supposed to do when I get to Hue'. "

"You're not alone, son. We're going through a learning curve ourselves, and one of the things we've learned is that the men who arrive here fresh from The World need some seasoning to be able to do their jobs decently and to avoid getting themselves hurt. Even the military vets and the stateside policemen have a good deal to learn before they can be effective in our program. It's different than what any of us are used to, and the stakes are high. We need to do a better job with our intelligence gathering and apprehensions if we are going to get this little country stabilized."

"I'm kind of in the dark about how this affects me. I'm here to do my job, but I guess I will need some help from you," Anders agreed, glad to hear that he did not have to be completely in the dark about his assignment and what it entailed.

"I want to spend some time with you about this. I guarantee that you will be up to snuff when you walk into the PRU compound, but you'll need to have some time with men who are already up and running. You'll learn a lot. Guaranteed. I'll give you the details of what I have in mind. Unfortunately, I have to go up into Stieng homeland north beyond the Middle Be River and quell a little rebellion. Seems one of the chiefs has decided the National Liberation Front has the most to offer even after being lavished with the kindness and materiel of the generous American people."

He then said in a sententious tone, "I am to be the cruel regicide, the Pyrrhus of Viet Nam,

> With blood of fathers, mothers, daughters, sons,
> Bak'd and impasted with the parching streets,

That lend a tyrannous and damned light
To their vile murders: roasted in wrath and fire,
And thus o'er-sized with coagulate gore,
With eyes like carbuncles, the hellish Pyrrhus
Old grandsire Priam seeks...

"Should take less than a week. Miss N. will get you settled; then, when I get back, we can get you off to your first assignment. Okay with you?" asked Duerk with an expression that indicated that it did not much matter if it was not okay.

"All right," Anders replied. He had not understood the classical reference, but felt it prudent to say nothing. His inclination had been to say, "Huh?" but he knew that would not sit well. He was in no hurry to stop being a tourist; so, Mr. Duerk could spend all the time he wanted being 'hellish' up-country.

"Come with me, please, Mr. Bergstrom," directed Miss Nguyen. They left the station chief and walked to the outer office.

"Mr. Duerk likes Shakespeare. You'll get used to it," she commented.

"I'd better get settled in somewhere. I don't know anything about the city. Any suggestions?" Anders asked Miss Nguyen.

"It is not a worry. I have taken care of your quarters. You will stay at the BOQ on Le Loi Avenue."

"But I'm not an officer," Anders remonstrated feeling awkward.

"You are not even an American, remember, Mr. Bergstrom?" Miss Nguyen replied with a touch of amused smugness. "Nevertheless, we have certain perquisites in the city; and you are registered at the Rex Hotel for the duration of your stay."

Anders was not sure what 'perquisites' were, and he was not about to ask. Whatever they were, he was glad to be on a team that had some. "Can you help me get a taxi to haul all my stuff to the BOQ then, Miss N?"

Miss Nguyen fixed Anders with an unsmiling gaze. First she assessed his face to measure his intent to insult or demean her. Caucasians had such revealing faces. Seeing no affront in the young man's guileless face, Miss Nguyen answered, "I will help you by use of the station automobile. My name is Nguyen Ngoc Tram. For your information that means 'precious hat pin.' Gentlemen refer to ladies in Viet Nam with formality. I prefer Miss Nguyen, never 'Miss N.'"

Anders blushed, "Sorry," he said with a youthful downturn of his expressive blue eyes.

"No offense taken. Let us get ourselves over to The Rex."

On the way to the BOQ, Miss Nguyen maneuvered the heavy Packard expertly through the tangle of pedestrian and vehicular traffic threading her way along the maze of narrow streets chatting amiably all the way. She told Anders that she would have no work with Mr. Duerk gone for the week; and if he wished her to do so, she would be happy to give him an insider's tour of the city.

"Sounds great to me. I...this is the first time for me to be in Saigon, and I don't know my way around at all." Her indulgent smiled conveyed the unspoken message that she was not entirely surprised to learn of his inexperience. She was much too polite to say so, however, which he appreciated.

He smiled boyishly at her and said, "I really haven't traveled much at all...I guess it shows, huh?" His ingenuous face had a look of innocence she had seldom seen on a foreigner, much less a CIA agent; and she warmed to him.

"Please permit me to show you the real Saigon, the Vietnamese Saigon and Gia Dinh."

"Great!" he said with genuine enthusiasm.

"We must start early in the morning if we are to see the real city, not just the colonialists' or the Americans' city. Say 0630?"

"Fine with me. I'll be waiting out front here. And thanks."

"Perhaps tonight you can take in the five o'clock follies at JUSPAO for a diversion. Everyone who comes here ought to do it at least once."

"I don't know what any of that is," Anders said bemused.

"Oh, I'm sorry," Miss Nguyen said. "I get so used to all these American abbreviations and joke names that I forget what they really are and that not everybody knows the colloquialisms of Saigon yet. JUSPAO is Joint US Public Affairs Office. At five o'clock every day, the military command gives the official body counts and recounts the action of the day before. The newspaper people call it the 'War Du Jour' because every day they select the action in some one region to tell about. It's also called 'the follies' because there is so little accuracy to the figures they give out that it is regarded as silly. The real war the correspondents see bears no resemblance to the one the brass describes in the follies. But you might as well take in one session just for the fun of it," Miss Nguyen told Anders. She did not seem particularly amused by the foibles she was describing.

The computer printouts from Cleve Howard and the logistical plans to capture the VCI identified were now kept in different places at different times, and Y'Yool took special pains to prevent any one of the cadres in the PRU from having any unsupervised access to them. He very carefully crafted his hunt and capture and hunt and kill plans so as to include a different mix of men on the three man teams for separate forays. He devised a cold-blooded plan to allow the VC infiltrator to incriminate himself, targeting certain teams and individuals by finagling an accidental viewing of the plans by one of the members, and watching to see which plan went awry, which team failed because the quarry had been forewarned or an ambush awaited his PRUCs. It was cold blooded because some of his good men would be likely to be killed without being warned about the potential of a traitor in their midst. That, regrettably, could not be helped.

The Deputy Chief Inspector called each man on the team under investigation in for an individual briefing. One of them was left alone in the room with the plans folder evident on Y'Yool's desk while he contrived to speak separately with the other two. The process was a painstaking one of considering human combinations and permutations with confusing and frustrating results. Most of the missions were successful, even easy; but at times the PRU cadres found they had been sent to the wrong hamlet, or to the wrong house in the hamlet, or that their quarry was not there when they struck, or they ran into unexpected VC interference. Y'Yool had to sort out the plausible from the very improbable sets of events, then to begin to relate those events to a narrowing set of PRU agents on the suspect list. It was frustrating and time consuming, but the commander was beginning to have a strong suspicion of one of the men.

Y'Yool had first investigated Nguyen Lui Tran, then Corporal Le Duc Bach, the Kit Carson, then Nguyen Van Dung, the former NVA sapper. He was very cautious at first, then blatantly exposed his plans, and then finally exposed himself to attack by each of these men on separate raids. There was never a hitch in any of the missions with those three. A fourth man removed himself from the suspect list in Y'Yool's mind very early on by saving the commander's life.

Phan Duy Ky, whom Y'Yool always thought of as the criminal (with good reason), his Number Two man, Nguyen Lui Tran, and the operations commander, Y'Yool, himself were on a team together two weeks after the ill-fated mission where Y'Yool had been shot and Duc had been killed. Y'Yool's left arm was still stiff and sore, and with too much exercise, occasionally bled a little. He was barely able to pull his own weight on that new mission.

Y'Yool had made sure to have Ky see the plans beforehand and to let him think he was unobserved while he read them. Ky had taken the bait fully and had read the complete contents of the folder. He had looked a little sheepish when the Deputy Chief Inspector returned, but a westerner would never have noticed the subtle facial signs of guiltiness. Y'Yool watched his back and made sure he knew exactly where Ky was at all times when they moved deeply into the bush.

When the night was its deepest black, the three men set off crawling the last two hundred meters to the targeted hamlet staying parallel to each other and about ten meters apart. The effort of crawling brought on great pain in Y'Yool's only partially mended shoulder, and he began to stiffen up. Try as he might to remain attentive to the dangers of the night and the forest, he found himself drawn into a self-centered absorption with the pain that diverted him. He concentrated so hard on simply drawing himself forward that he did not keep the piece of elephant grass he held in his mouth to detect trip wires well enough to the front. Consequently, he missed the wire when it did cross his path and ran the top of his helmet straight into the taut trigger device.

Before he could react, he heard a log swooping out of a tree above. He rolled quickly to his side to present a smaller target and thereby missed having his head crushed by the heavy hardwood stump. The log thudded with a nerve jarring crunch into his good right shoulder and knocked the Montagnard three feet to the left leaving him gasping for breath. Y'Yool thought his arm, his good arm, was broken. The pain matched that of the throbbing in his left shoulder. The two upper limbs were in such muscle spasm that they functioned as if in semi-paralysis.

The commander knew the noise of the crashing log was likely to bring undesirable attention to his location; and with all his handicaps, Y'Yool hurried as fast as he could to crawl out of the exposed situation. He was sure that there would be no more booby traps in close proximity; so, he moved very rapidly in the dark forest mostly on his hands and knees. He reasoned that the greatest danger lay in being close to where the log had crashed into him. In his acute mind's eye he could see the VC closing in on him. In his headlong, awkward crawling rush he did not see the signs of the second trap twenty meters directly in front of him. He should have because the trap was unfinished and the debris of construction was all around him.

Y'Yool grunted with surprise as the leaves covering the ground under his hands suddenly gave way somersaulting the wiry Montagnard soldier policeman into a four foot deep pit. It was fortunate that the pungi stakes had not yet been installed in all their upright viciousness, but unfortunate in that the ground in the hole was full of spaded rocks and broken root stumps. He landed flat on his back and lay there in stunned pain and confusion. His senses were still keen enough to hear the rubber-tire sandaled foot falls of the men who ran up to his open earthen crypt. He fought to shake the cobwebs out of his brain, but with only marginal success. He somehow could not force his weary and pain-ridden arms to react. It would be so pleasant to rest for just a moment, to let the blackness in that was so crowding the edges of his vision and his consciousness. It would be so fatal, he knew.

He was still lying on his back, essentially helpless, when he saw the outline of the conical hat move over him. It was too dark to make out any more of a man than that. Y'Yool struggled to remember if either Tran or Ky had worn a conical hat. He tried desperately to remember why that mattered. Did it matter?

There was noise, scuffling, sliding of feet on the damp ground, a shriek, then more cries of pain, the thud of weapons being dropped, then the heavy gasping weight of a man falling, doubled up, directly onto Y'Yool's exposed belly and testicles. Y'Yool gasped and fought for air. His head reeled. Then the noise stopped, and it was silent again there in the forest. He waited for death.

The weight of the man's body was slowly lifted off his own. Then strong hands grabbed the front of his black pajama shirt, and he was being lifted up. "Can you stand?" the vaguely familiar voice asked.

"Yes," Y'Yool said and promptly crumpled back down into the uncompleted pungi stake hole.

"You've got to help me. I can't lift you all the way out of this hole by myself," came the voice again. Now, where had he heard that voice before? Y'Yool thought it would be helpful to close his eyes and think about it for a while.

The man with the voice slapped the drowsing commander with a stinging slap. Y'Yool's eyes snapped open and for a few moments he was fully conscious and alert. He saw Phan Duy Ky standing over him, assaulting him. He forced his knees to stiffen. It occurred to the commander to strike back, but somehow that seemed wrong. Instead he lifted one foot after another onto roots and rocks as Ky half dragged him to the ground surface again. The momentary alertness lapsed again when he felt the flat ground out of the gnarly interior of the hole in the trail. The *Bui Doi* slapped the Montagnard smartly on his exposed cheeks twice again, pleading, "*Dới đi! Dới đi! Dới đi!*

247

(Move!, Move! Move!) They'll be here in a minute. There'll be more cong here any second. Hurry!"

In a nightmare of pain, confusion, and rush, the two men struggled their way deeper into the undergrowth toward where Tran was supposed to be. Ky gave the prearranged signal; Tran responded; and shortly, the three men rendezvoused somewhere in the blackness.

When Y'Yool came around and was fit to move, he asked Ky, "How many were there?"

"Four, "Ky answered.

"I would have been dead."

"Yes."

"I will not forget, Ky. I owe you a life. My ancestors thank you."

Ky grinned in the dark. "Deputy Chief Inspector, I never thought I could save a policeman, but then I was never part of a team before. I think of you, of Tran and the PRU as my family and only friends. It was no more than what either one of you would have done for me, đóng-chí (comrade), no?"

"That is true,...bạn thân (dear friend),. . . anh (brother)," the Montagnard of the frightening smile said. Ky knew he meant it. Y'Yool was neither a sentimental nor a demonstrative man. When they left the deep undergrowth and walked over the beaten down grasses of the LZ to the waiting helicopter four hours later, the three men picked their way along unabashedly holding hands. Y'Yool had a short list of four of the PRUCs upon whom he could rely. Now, he had only somewhat over a hundred-twenty more to test.

It took months of patience to narrow down the list and to check and recheck his suspicions. The effort had been lightened when Y'Yool finally decided that he could fully trust Tran, Ky, Dung, and Bach; and he could take them into his confidence. The list eventually narrowed down to six possibles, of whom three were probables. The five men could not narrow the field further. They settled on Dang Thanh Hung, Cong Bich Hai, Anh Xuan Oanh, Nguyen Tran Xuan, Tran Thuc Quyen, and Ngo Van Khoa as the possibles based both on past associations with the VC that the five investigators could ferret out in seemingly casual conversations, and on present associations with suspiciously failed missions.

Y'Yool, with his policeman's suspicious mind underlined Quyen, and Khoa as the most likely culprits because of their frank VC backgrounds and Oanh as the third most likely suspect because of his having been on one failed capture mission and on another where the party was discovered and his two teammates had had to extract themselves from heavy fire while Oanh had come out completely unscathed. Ky, Bach, Dung, and Tran were skeptical of the choice of Quyen and Khoa; they did not seem smart enough; and there was no good evidence that they had actually taken the bait and looked at the plans.

By mid-September the PRU was posting impressive reports to Cleve Howard and onto Saigon, but Y'Yool seemed to be no closer to exposing his VCI spy than he had been a month or two before. It was frustrating and frightening. Then in a seven day period, the list tightened down to only three serious suspects.

Quyen, Khoa, and Tran had gone on a highly successful remote hunt and kill foray and had notched six actual VC kills in an ambush despite both Quyen and Khoa being shown the detailed plans in advance as if it were a routine for them to know their commander's mind. What Quyen and Khoa did not know was that Bach had separately followed the three man team and had watched their actions. The five investigators took the two men from the Mekong Delta off their list.

The effort to entrap or expose two of the remaining three suspects, Xuan and Hai, involved Ky. The *Bui Doi* took the two suspects on a three day mission to ambush and hopefully to capture the province executive secretary of the LAF (as the VC preferred to be termed to highlight the mixed communist and nationalist makeup of the insurgency forces). This was not the first time that a mission had been mounted to capture this individual. The hope was that her entire cell would collapse if she was taken. However, on this mission headed by Ky, the secretary never showed when or where the computer data said she could be anticipated with certainty; and Ky found Hai stabbed to death in the bush. Xuan's name shot to one of the top two positions on the list of Y'Yool's suspects.

Oanh secured a tie for first on the list after going out on a mission led by Dung. The third man on the team was Bach Duc Hieu. Hieu had previously proved himself to be entirely lackluster but above reproach in a series of routine and successful arrests and kills even though he had full foreknowledge of the plans for the missions. He was not a suspect. Bach had been the secret fourth man on two of those missions of Hieu's and cleared him emphatically.

Oanh, on the other hand, had been seen by Tran talking to an unidentified man one afternoon when most of the PRUCs had been idling around the camp waiting for another batch of computer arrest or death warrants to come in. It had been at some distance, and Tran was not altogether sure whether or not the other man had been a stranger. Tran reported what he had seen to Y'Yool who designed a trap for Oanh.

The following night Bach, Oanh, and Hieu, at the RD/O, Y'Yool's, order, secreted themselves along a well-traveled jungle pathway to wait for a local warlord, a Chinese, described by the computer information available as a mercenary, more accurately, a pirate, willing to lead his motley band of smugglers and cutthroats to a variety of clandestine operations for either side, always opting for the highest bidder. The LAF had been the highest bidder for sometime, evidently. The bandit became marked as permanently unreliable, and a termination order was given.

Sometime in the night of the carefully planned ambush, the three PRU cadres were themselves the victims of an apparent counter ambush. It seemed clear that the warlord had received advance knowledge, and his jungle-wise cohorts had been able to get within yards of Bach and his two men. In the chaos that occurred during the ensuing firefight, Hieu received a bad sucking chest wound, Bach took one round in his right buttock that was humiliating and painful but nonthreatening, and another one that furrowed him a new and permanent part for his hair. Somehow the Kalashnikov bullet skimmed along the galea aponeurotica of Bach's scalp without penetrating his skull. The two halves of the scalp sagged apart in what would have been a comical appearance if it had not been for all of that blood. Tran was the secret backup and poured fire into the rear of the warlord's counter ambushers. He saved the lives of all three men on the PRU team. Oanh was not hurt; he was the only one on the south side of the trail and away from the hostile action at his own insistence—something about shooting better from that vantage point. Oanh looked shocked, like he had seen a forest *phi* (spirit), when Tran joined the other three.

Bach was convinced beyond reasoning that Oanh was their man, their mole. He argued vociferously against the man on the basis of the old Company dictum that there was no such thing as a coincidence. By identical reasoning and with equal passion and certainty, Dung knew that Xuan was the guilty VCI. When Y'Yool complained that he was on the horns of a dilemma, Tran suggested the old Viet Minh solution—"kill them both."

"That is efficient, and maybe we'll come to that. But let me point out that we are soldiers in the struggle to make our country one ruled by laws, not by efficient whims. Besides, we have lost three dead and one out of action for the rest of the war in our unit. We need every good man. Maybe one of these two is a good man.

"The five of us need to bait a trap for Xuan and for Oanh that will force them into the open on a mission. Then we need to kill the traitor," Bach said, gritting his teeth against the pain as he shifted in his seat. He looked like a cartoon character with his elaborately parted hair.

"Maybe we will find both of them are VC," said Dung. "We may yet kill them both."

Y'Yool solved the dilemma for himself by baiting the snare with details of a planned raid on the two brothers who were still terrorizing the Trung River hamlets around Tou Rout, Kon Ba, and Pe Ker. He deliberately showed his two selected team members, Oanh and Xuan, one at a time, the plans before saddling up for the trip to the river valleys. The other four investigator cadres protested to their operations officer at the unnecessary risk at taking both top suspects as teammates on the same mission. Y'Yool agreed readily to having Dung and Tran both as secret protective backups.

The Deputy Inspector felt relatively safe with the details of his latest entrapment plan because he already knew that one of the two men was innocent, a loyal team member. He preferred to bring in a *fiat accompli* by keeping his discovery from all of the other men until he had solved the mystery and had dealt with the traitor in his own way. It would cast his authority in concrete. He knew his nemesis because he had seen the man creep off into the bush on the periphery of the compound one night and hand several papers over to three men in black pajamas who had materialized out of the night, and who vanished into their world of darkness as ephemerally as they had come. Y'Yool was ready to spring his trap, using himself as bait, knowing that he only had to fear one of his colleagues.

Anders could tell by the smooth deep rumbling sound of the engine that Miss Nguyen's Packard was a more powerful and better kept machine than it appeared on the outside. The sun was just beginning to show itself as she stopped curbside in front of the Rex to pick him up.

"Hello, Mr. Bergstrom. Please get in," Miss Nguyen said and indicated the back seat. She was as carefully polite and as correctly dressed as the evening before, this time in a ba'ba suit.

"Thank you. This is a nice time of day, not so hot," he said.

She looked both directions up over the steering wheel and pulled out from number 141 onto Nguyen Hue' street which was already beginning to fill up with pedestrians, bicycles, and vehicles. "It is my favorite time of day here," She agreed. "Shortly I will show you one of the reasons why I love my city."

Anders settled back into the plush gray velvet seats that had obviously been reupholstered, and very professionally. The throbbing panorama once again unfolded for the young man as Miss Nguyen moved along the streets, honking occasionally at particular bottle-necks of people or animals. It was not nearly as busy as when he had come in by trishaw yesterday, but it was still easily the busiest city he had been in. Washington DC was the only big US city he had spent time in, and it could not hold a candle to the intensity of Saigon.

Miss Nguyen passed the railway station and pulled to a stop on Dien Bien Phu Street behind a smoky DeSoto bus. "Please indulge me a moment," she said and looked a little embarrassed. She walked swiftly into a small grocery store and shortly returned holding a handful of tickets.

"National lottery," she said almost apologetically. "My only vice." She smiled with a careful self-deprecating smile that showed her perfect teeth for the first time. She was an attractive woman.

"We are on our way to the Ben Thanh Market district; but first, I want you to see one of the reasons I love Saigon." She turned 180° directly into the horde of people and vehicles going both directions against her. She kept a completely placid expression as if she did not see the oncoming traffic. Anders took a short breath and winced. No one honked or even seemed to pay attention. The young American relaxed with difficulty.

They drove swiftly to the *Ben Chuong Duong* (Belgian Dock) Wharf road and followed the *Rach Ben Nghe* (Chinese) Channel a short distance until Miss Nguyen pulled to a stop in a small riverside park just beyond where the *Rach Ben Nghe* and the main branch of the Saigon River joined. She pointed east toward the rising sun and got out of the car. Anders followed suit. He adjusted his eyes until he could see what she saw.

On the embankment of the Saigon River, hundreds of people, young and old, peasants and businessmen, men and women were moving in what appeared to be a graceful and sensuous slow-motion dance without music. Each person moved to a rhythm all his or her own. To Anders the dance movements were reminiscent of karate' katas; only these katas were performed in a deliberate exaggerated and reduced velocity motion and with consummate grace. Even elderly women had let down their hair that now flowed out silvery in the light early morning breeze. The figures of the dancers were held in vivid relief by the golden orb of the sun and the backdrop of the deep green beltway beyond the river at their backs.

They were clothed in a brilliant variety of colors; men in black suits and white shirts, menial workers in black or gray pajamas, city clerical workers in brightly patterned dresses, and students and other young women in lovely Ao Dais with a collage of blouse colors sinuously moving atop the ubiquitous flowing white ankle length trousers. It was a scene of serenity, grace, and beauty in motion allowing a brief rejuvenating respite from knowledge of the war just beyond the tableaux.

"*Tai chi chuan*," Miss Nguyen said softly. "You will see these exercises everywhere in Viet Nam if you will take the time to look at the people in the morning."

"Thank you," said Anders. It was enough of a comment. Words seemed inadequate and even excessive at the moment. Miss Nguyen climbed back into the driver's seat, and Anders again got into the rear.

They turned left onto D.L. Ham Nghi street that took them to its junction with Le Loi and Tran Hung Dao Boulevards where the Ben Thanh Market stood. Anders could tell they were approaching the market because the density of humanity and the amplitude of the din increased in a crescendo that reached its zenith at the market itself. There was a veritable sea of humanity moving slowly in a whirl of directions. Anders could not see the ground; and without effort, could not distinguish individual persons in the blur of color and movement.

The market itself covered more than ten thousand square meters and was filled to overflowing with an extraordinary variety of people and things. There were products from all countries in Southeast Asia, France, America, and Taiwan. Dried ducks hung in serried rows in butcher shops; live piglets grunted and squealed from their wooden cage boxes; pots of *nouc mam* (pungent fermented fish sauce) sat beside plates of vegetables, fish, and Chinese spring rolls; and children moved through the throngs hawking platters of food, cigarettes, and liquors.

There was a heady mixture of aromas: *nouc mam,* that the American GIs called 'armpit juice' in describing its smell; spices; fresh and dried sea food, including fresh and salt water fish and salted crustaceans; the yeasty aroma coming from an opened keg of Indonesian Tiger beer; the delectable variety of food stall odors wafting from the rear of the market; and the inescapable tang of old body odors.

Vivid colors stood out everywhere—the bright green of the thorny looking smelly durian fruit, the soft watermelon green of jack fruit, the yellow of tree-ripened bananas and of cherry-sized longan fruit, the cherry red of fresh lichees, and everywhere the red and yellow of the republic flag.

The chatter and laughter of haggling voices, the calls of merchants to their help, and the shouted gossip trying to be heard over the background din combined with the mercantile sights and smells to constitute an assault on the senses. Ben Thanh Market was a cornucopia that spilled out onto the sidewalks on all sides and into the surrounding streets making traffic move with glacial celerity.

"Had breakfast, Mr. Bergstrom?" shouted Miss Nguyen over the tumult trying to make herself heard.

Anders shook his head, "no" signaling both his answer and his inability to compete with the din. He realized for the first time that morning that he had worked up a terrific appetite. She gestured for him to follow her to the food stalls. There was almost nothing Anders recognized as food as he knew it. He was expected to choose from stalls exhibiting food as varied as fried locusts and rice beetles, eel soup, snails in garlic and pepper sauce, bean thread soup, fertilized duck eggs with embryos inside complete with feathers, *nouc cham*, (*nouc mam* plus extras including chilies, lime juice, and sugar), barbecued fish cakes, steaming bowls of sticky white rice, and *pho* (hot egg noodle soup spiced with cilantro in which chunks of pork floated). He decided on a simple rule—it had to be recognizable to be eaten. He selected a bowl of *pho*, some fried bananas, and a plate of slices of a variety of fresh mangoes, papayas, and pineapples.

He shared a pot of aromatic tea with Miss Nguyen, having chosen that over a dizzying variety of other beverages—juices of whose origins he was unsure, Asian beers, and Black Snake wine. The wine was homemade and stored in gallon jugs. The dark coils of the serpent could be seen plainly through the turbid whitish fluid. The food was wonderful and did not seem at all strange. He felt his courage enhancing; so he finished with a platter of fried sweet potatoes, piping hot doughnuts and sweetened bean curd. He was having a very good time and had entirely forgotten his purpose for being in the exciting country.

Miss Nguyen next took Anders to the Thieves Market on Huynh Thuc Kang and Ton That Dan Streets. There was the same bustle and cacophony, but the tiny stores were different. Here they were crammed with recognizable American goods: radios, typewriters, portable TVs, C Rations, helmets, costume jewelry, American brand beer and cigarettes, fans, office chairs and filing cabinets, and canned milk and fruits. Anders easily connected the market's name with the source of the goods. It was not news to him when Miss Nguyen pointed out the obvious, "All stolen from American PX," and many with the 'PX' marking still clearly visible. He nodded darkly, somehow offended by the implication.

"This is nothing, my friend. This is just the glimpse of the corruption of American money on the Viet Nam economy and its people. That money has turned this into a nation of thieves, and the American government makes an actual effort to be both blind and deaf about it," said Miss Nguyen with energy. "It makes me mad. So mad that I'll take you to see the real corruption. You haven't seen anything yet!"

They walked to a stall that openly sold US uniforms—from helmets to boots—at very reasonable prices. Miss Nguyen spoke quietly to the proprietrix, a toothless, saggy women of about sixty. They discussed in hushed tones for three or four minutes, then the woman called for a boy. "Take them to the big store," she said and went back to the pressing business of getting a US NCO a properly fitting uniform. He had not been able to find one in the PX.

As the boy led Miss Nguyen and Anders around a maze of narrow closed in streets, Anders asked Mr. Duerk's secretary what it was she had said to the old crone that resulted in the guided tour. "I just told her that we needed to buy some weapons and ammunition. I had to convince her that we had the money. That's all," Miss Nguyen answered.

They passed the food and liquor black market store by the Redemptorist Church and were finally taken to a faceless warehouse and led to the second floor. The boy who had acted as their guide waited, hand outstretched, until Miss Nguyen covered the palm with Piastres. The young CIA contract agent and Mr. Duerk's secretary were shortly standing in a large room where racks of neatly stacked weapons and munitions lined the walls. A pleasant young man, dressed in a crisp cream colored linen suit, who acted for all the world like a shoe salesman showing his wares, took the pair around. There were bins of standard issue grenades and N-26 fragmentation grenades, gun racks and unopened crates of M-14s and M-16s, most still in their creosote coating. The submachine guns were listed at 8000 P; 105 mm mortars went for 40,000 P; and light machine guns were listed at 25,000 P.

There were long racks on which were hanging full uniforms, fatigue and dress, for all American services and in all available sizes, all neatly segregated and labeled. The best part was the easy payment arrangements. The customer could pay with Piastres, dollars, even MPCs, and personal checks. The enterprising young salesman assured them that the company had its ways to process MPCs, which were expressly for use by GIs to avoid black marketeering, and more ominously that they had their ways of finding bad check passers. The payment plan was the simplest: 100% down and no troublesome monthly payments.

"If you are in the market, we can get you a very fine jeep," the oily salesman volunteered. "Our people can cut it in half for you if you need to transport it," he offered helpfully.

Anders was incredulous and had to make an effort not to let it show in his young expressive face. Miss Nguyen had to stifle a sneer. She presumed he had seen enough and; when the disappointed salesman was out of earshot, said, "I'm told that the PX is a $300,000,000 a year enterprise and $75,000,000 of that goes into the black market to make rich Vietnamese crooks even richer. It's a sort of bribe; you Americans are 'guests of the Republic,' you know. I've had enough of this. It just makes me mad. Let's see some religious buildings and monuments, then we can siesta before the races in Cholon this afternoon. We can get the taste of this out of our mouths. Would that suit you, Mr. Bergstrom?"

"Sure, I want to see it all. We've only got a few days."

Miss Nguyen first took him three blocks away to the Mariamman Hindu Temple on Truong Dinh Street, then on an exhausting drive-by tour of Buddhist temples and pagodas. They stopped to look at the oldest pagoda in the city, the Gia Lam in the Tah Binh district. Anders looked at the curiously carved wooden pillars in the main building covered with peeling gilt designs. Miss Nguyen told him, "Those markings are *nom* inscriptions, the old writing. The monks wrote constantly on clay tablets when they lived here. The red tablets lined on the tables are biographies of the great bonzes who worked in this place. We passed their portraits on the way in."

The Vietnamese woman and the tall blond young man spent an hour in the small but elegant *Ngoc Hoa* (Emperor of Jade) Pagoda on Mai Thi Luu Street. The edifice was brilliantly colorful, unlike any house of worship Anders had ever seen or imagined. Strong incense and the smoke from hundreds of candles created a delicious smelling haze that gave a quiet and mysterious atmosphere for viewing the large and strange array of wooden Buddhist and Taoist statues. One of the most ornate and largest of the statues was of the Emperor, himself, robed in his ceremonial royal attire. Anders was a little taken aback by the most striking statue in the Pagoda, that of the mother of Buddhas with three heads and a host of arms. Anders counted fifteen. Miss Nguyen told him there were eighteen.

They drove down Nguyen Trai Street to see the well-kept and

beautifully decorated Thien Hau Temple named for the goddess who protects sailors, and the Ha Chuong Pagoda with its statue of the Chinese god of happiness, and the altar for sterile women. On Dong Du street they passed the Mosque, and on the main square they drove around the remarkable red and white brick Cathedral of the Notre Dame with the statue of the Virgin Mary looking beatifically down Tu Do Street (the Rue Catinat when the French held sway in the capital city). The Cathedral looked out on the main square of Saigon with the statues of Monsignor Pigneau de Behaine and of Prince Canh, the son of Emperor Gia Long, looking back on the church.

"This is *Nha Tho Duc Ba*, the Catholic Notre Dam Cathedral, built between 1880 and 1900," Miss Nguyen told Anders. "It sat on a hill, and its spires were so tall that for people coming up the Saigon River it used to be the first thing they saw in the city. Are you Catholic, Mr. Bergstrom?" She asked.

"No ma'am," Anders told her.

"I hope you don't take offense at such a personal question."

"Of course not." He rather enjoyed the familiarity.

"You'll find that we Vietnamese are very curious. We think nothing of asking someone we just met all about themselves—how old they are, how they make their living, what is their religion, how many wives or children they have. We are very courteous, and we do not find such questions discourteous. I have found that some Europeans and Americans find such questions rude. Do you, Mr. Bergstrom?"

"No, just friendly."

"Very good. I think you will get along well here."

Soon afterward, Miss Nguyen could see that Mr. Bergstrom was getting sleepy and probably a little bored. "He is probably like any other man, gets tired shopping or sightseeing after a short time, unlike women who can do either or both all day," she thought. "I will take you back to the Rex for a nap then we can go to Hippodrome for the races when it cools down in the afternoon. Would that be acceptable to you, Mr. Bergstrom?" She asked.

"I'm game. Thanks for showing me around. I came from horse country," he said and vaguely regretted the suggested revelation of his origins that probably did not sound Swedish. She did not seem to take notice. Anders knew that she was privy to all his secrets anyway.

The afternoon seemed every bit as hot and oppressively humid to Anders as had the late morning. He marveled at Miss Nguyen's completely dry and fresh appearance. It seemed impertinent to him even to consider that she could sweat. There certainly was no sign that she did. His shirt was soaked and yellow stains were forming in the armpits despite a second shower of the day following his nap, and it was not yet four in the afternoon.

She drove the big Packard across the Van Kiep Street bridge and on into the teeming Cholon (Big Market) center. Unlike Saigon proper, the architecture was simple, colorless; and the skyline monotonous with low buildings. The only reprieve for the dullness was the frequent salting of pagodas and churches. The city was made for commerce and bustled with frenetic activity. The districts and streets were filled with small shops and family factories.

The district and street names bore evidence of the history of commerce in the Chinese sector. The districts or congregations, as they were called fifty and a hundred years before, were divided into guilds of manufacture and family tong associations. Specific pagodas served as the association and community centers and often represented the region of China from which the various groupings of people had originated—Cantonese, Hakkanese, Fukienese, etc.—and the special areas of commerce in which they specialized The streets were so designated. Miss Nguyen pointed out the Vietnamese signs for *Hung Pho, Tran Tuong Cong Pho, Hai Pho, Gai Pho, Lo Xu Pho, and Ma Pho* (respectively; Slaughterhouse, Cabinetmakers, Bootmakers, Hemp makers, Coffin makers, and Makers of Votive Paper (Paper to burn for the dead) streets). She also pointed out that there was great wealth behind the seemingly small conglomerations of businesses.

The effect of these semi-independent sectors and their streets was to create a lasting maze of narrow byways with poorly built houses and businesses that frequently went up in the fires that swept recurrently through Cholon. Originally, the *pho* were impenetrable at night because they were separated from every other *pho* by walls or by removable partitions. The march of modernization had removed those impediments to travel a hundred years ago, but not the attitudes that erected them, and mistrust and secrecy were hallmarks of the society in the Great Market.

The races were only shadows of the grandeur of the past and of the great tracks of England and France after which they were patterned. The exclusivity of the European gentlemanly sport had passed the way of the ornate and magnificently maintained race courses when the French left. Now Anders rubbed shoulders with the great mix of mankind that is Saigon. He placed his small bets at a window manned by a Cantonese Chinese in a line with Khmer dock workers, minor GVN clerks, taxi dancers from the country who were forced by poverty and war into the city, high-rolling Vietnamese and Chinese businessmen, diplomats and their staffs from half a dozen countries, laborers, housemaids, concubines, pharmacists, and even a resident sorcerer whom Miss Nguyen assumed had come down from the highlands.

Anders lost every bet, a total of 200 pee, because he insisted on maintaining his independence from the placid and self-assured Vietnamese woman who won every bet she placed, a total of 700 pee.

When they left the racecourse, Miss Nguyen asked Anders, "Our evening will require a black tie. Did you bring yours?"

"I have a dark blue one with stripes; will that be okay?"

Miss Nguyen looked at his face to see if he was joking with her. She had not met a European so naive, so inexperienced; and she was unsure what would be the polite way to inform the young man, to instruct him. Despite her efforts, a smile forced the corners of her mouth up; and it was only with difficulty that she could stifle an insistent laugh. "No, Mr. Bergstrom," she said gently with a small cough that masked her laugh, she hoped. "That is not quite what I had in mind."

"Sorry," Anders said, sensitive to the amusement in her face. "I have tropical whites and the shirts and ties to go with them. Nothing dark except the one blue tie."

"I beg your pardon. What I meant to ask is if you had a tuxedo. I must go to a small party at the Chez San Jacques and formal dress is required. I will need an escort and would be pleased if you could go with me."

"I don't have a tuxedo. That's the last thing I thought I'd need in Viet Nam. Think we could borrow one?"

Miss Nguyen laughed as the image of him trying to get into one of her countryman friend's tuxedos. She caught herself and smiled at him. "Mr. Bergstrom, you are so big; it will be difficult; but we can try. I will have to exercise my brain."

She was lost in quiet concentration on their way back to Nguyen Hue' Boulevard in the center of the city. By the time she stopped at the curb in front of the Rex Hotel entrance, she said with a smile of success, "Mr. Duerk has an old suit that he wore when he was overweight. I have a tailor friend who owes me a favor. We can do it by reception time I am sure."

"Are you sure, are you really sure that Mr. Duerk won't care?" Anders queried doubtfully.

"Quite sure, Mr. Bergstrom. I can handle it."

Anders just bet she could. Miss Nguyen was a very capable woman.

He was glad she was on his side. He waited impatiently in his BOQ room as instructed. An hour passed, then another thirty minutes. He was startled by a knock on his door. A bellman delivered a handsome tuxedo with all of the accessories. Anders tipped him 5 pee. The pants were too short and the coat was very tight but manageable. The shirt barely did fit around his chest, but he could not button the collar stay. His arms would not fit the sleeves, not even close. He was dismayed.

In ten or fifteen minutes the same bellman arrived with a message for him to call Miss Nguyen and gave the number. There was no telephone in his room nor on his floor; so, he slipped on casual clothes and used the lobby phone.

"Hello. Mr. Bergstrom?" Miss Nguyen answered.

"Hello, Miss Nguyen. It's me. I got the tuxedo, thanks."

"Does it fit, I hope."

"Some of it does," he said cautiously to avoid hurting her feelings since she had tried so hard.

"Not big enough, eh?" She surmised. "I'll pick you up, and we will go to the tailor's on the way to Chez San Jacques. If it is fixable, he can fix it. If not, we will have to subdue a waiter, I guess," she laughed. He like the music of her unguarded laughter.

They drove quickly to *Pho Tho May* (Street of the Tailors) near the Chinese Channel. Traffic was scanty at that hour. Sing Hop looked with elaborate dismay at the immense European and then at the too-small tuxedo and shirt. "Quite impossible, Miss Nguyen," he clucked, muttering more to himself than to her.

Mr. Hop lengthened the trouser legs again, this time to the limits of the cloth available, increased the waist size, and moved the collar button to the very edge of the cloth. The shirt sleeves were impossible; so, in desperation, he finally cut them off, taking care to preserve the stitch lines so they could be reattached later. He fretted and fussed and sweated making little singsong mutterings in Mandarin as he labored. He was quick and worked without wasted movement. When he finished, he presented the suit to Miss Nguyen with a stern look, his arms folded resolutely across his chest. He was not about to permit any criticism given the very trying circumstances. He hated to have a piece of his work look so…well, comical.

Anders was able to fit into the outfit, barely. He thought he looked great. Miss Nguyen appraised him coolly and pronounced the work acceptable. She overpaid Mr. Hop, which melted his defenses; and he smiled and bowed, grinned and kowtowed, glad to be of service.

Despite the lateness of the hour, Miss Nguyen did not hurry toward the Chez San Jacques. She obeyed the routing of the White Mice (Saigon Police) directing traffic and avoided bottlenecks. She was very observant, using her rear and side-view mirrors as much as she did the windshield. It seemed paranoid, but Anders adopted the habit as well. He was sure no one was following them, and he did not see anyone even suspicious let alone worrisome.

The only really out of place thing he did see was a group of whooping and obviously drunk Americans who looked like frat brothers going to a costume ball. They were dressed in brilliant powder-blue jump suits that looked for all the world like air-force flight suits but for the outlandish bright color and the ragtag collection of patches, badges, rank insignias, and what looked like bottle caps attached to the suits.

"What is that?" Anders asked incredulously. Viet Nam was a strange place, and it seemed that the American presence there was the strangest aspect of it.

"Oh, ignore those silly boys. They are just pilots blowing off steam. They are wearing what they call their 'party suits.' They get the Cholon tailors to make the most absurd ones they can. They have no dignity." Miss Nguyen fretted with a tone of intolerance Anders had not heard her use previously.

She was more tolerant of a 'cowboy' on his motor scooter who cut them off in a mad dash to evade an irate American in a jeep. The long-haired young Vietnamese boy had driven alongside the jeep, reached over the edge of the open vehicle, and, using a curved metal strip of his own device, reached in and snatched the driver's watch from his wrist. Anders took the reciprocal approach to Miss Nguyen's in his forming his opinion about the two incidents, but kept his thoughts to himself.

Chez San Jacques was an unpretentious three story fading colonial French building in the center of old Rue De Gualle. The neighborhood and the street had been fashionable and upscale in the early 50s before the decline of the French hold on Indochina. Now, the area had gone somewhat to seed; the handsome elms lining the avenue were unkempt; and the building itself needed paint and some minor external repairs to keep it from looking frankly down-at-the-heel. To the uninitiated, it was identified only by a small brass plaque over the doorbell.

Miss Nguyen was admitted on sight. She introduced Anders to the powerfully built doorman who was obviously carrying a large pistol under the coat of his tuxedo. The tuxedo looked even more incongruous on the man than Anders' did on him. She said, "Tho, permit me to present Mr. Anders Bergstrom. He is the Swedish monitoring delegate of the International Red Cross Commission."

Tho nodded after giving Anders the once over. He did not speak. He moved aside to let the couple enter. The room was dimly lit, smoky, and hummed with soft voices and sounds of roulette wheels and the bouncing plastic ball. When his eyes fully adjusted to the ambient light, Anders saw that the room was a well equipped casino with several tables manned by professional croupiers. He recognized the roulette wheels having seen them in a book somewhere. The craps table had the familiar dice, otherwise it and the rest of the tables were all new to him.

He was hesitant to ask questions fearing he would look like a bumpkin. He felt distinctly out of place in the opulent surroundings, too much like a hayseed among the handsomely dressed and obviously very affluent men and women taking their pleasure at the tables. There were several tables with a culturally mixed group of men and women playing poker. Miss Nguyen nodded and smiled politely and familiarly with several of the players as they passed. At one of the poker tables, she paused and waited to catch the attention of a man who, at the moment, was telling a joke to the largely American appearing group at the table. "War," he was saying, "is a by-product of the arts of peace. The most menacing political condition is a period of international amity." He accepted the chuckles of his table mates and shifted his glance to Miss Nguyen.

"Ambrose Bierce," she said smiling at him, correctly identifying the author of his witticism. The lean crewcut man looked like most of the other CIA agents Anders had seen, as if he had just strolled across the street to the Chez San Jacques from Yale University.

The Yale transplant laughed out loud. "You've heard my best stuff too many times, Miss Nguyen. Glad to see you anyway."

She smiled a small victory smile. Then, remembering Anders, she said, looking directly at the Yale alumnus, "Excuse me. Gentlemen, please allow me to introduce my escort. This is Mr. Anders Bergstrom, the Swedish monitor of the Geneva conventions from the International Red Cross. Mr. Bergstrom, may I present Mr. Cleveland Howard, Revolutionary Development Chief for the National Security Forces for Thau Thien Province."

She nodded at each of the men at the table, a mixed career group who nodded perfunctorily back. Anders nodded to each man, then shook Cleve Howard's hand. "Pleased to meet you," he said.

"We did not mean to disturb you, gentlemen. Please go on with your game," Miss Nguyen said and drew Anders away with her.

The couple sauntered to a very quiet table. The language being spoken, more accurately, whispered, was French. Anders saw more money on the table than he had ever seen in one place at one time before in his life. He made a few quick calculations at the dollars, francs, Piastres, and MPCs on the green felt cover of the handsome mahogany table with wire billiard ball catchers and came up with a figure that could have supported his entire family back in Zarahemla, Utah for more than a year without scrimping. He must have had his mouth open because Miss Nguyen jabbed his arm with her elbow.

"That is Chemin de Fer," she explained in a whisper. "It is an old French game. The word means 'railroad' although I have no idea why. The older game from which this one comes is the Italian Baccarat which means 'zero.' That does make sense because the picture cards and the tens have a value of zero. It is really quite a simple card game, essentially between two players; watch."

After the callman, standing in the center with the dealer, indicated, in French, that the cards were to be dealt, the dealer passed out two coups (hands) of cards from the shoe, holding multiple decks, to one player, a rotund Chinese woman dressed in a magnificent silk tunic over a long black skirt. He similarly dealt himself, as banker, two hands. The two active players then faded (placed their bets) on the appropriately marked spaces, 'player' or 'banker,' as appropriate, on the green felt table cover, about $2000 each. Then the remaining, presently inactive, players, and several people standing by placed huge side bets on either the 'player' hand or the 'banker' hand. The dealer signaled an end to the betting; and he and the Chinese woman examined their cards. She overturned neither of the hands she had been dealt, and said in a clipped voice, "*Passe.*"

The dealer's cards added up to a score of eight, a *la petite*; that he displayed, face up, to the crowd. The woman had a hand with five and one with seven. She grimaced in defeat and passed the stack of Piastres in front of her to the dealer. His swift eyes tallied the sidebets, and stacks of money shifted back and forth with the deft movements of a long thin paddle. The five percent house commission was quickly reckoned and collected. The dealer directed his attention to the next player seated at the table who became the next 'banker.' There was no talking.

Miss Nguyen whispered, "The winner is the hand that is closest to but does not exceed a count of nine on two or three cards."

Anders nodded with only politeness. It was of no great interest to him. That game was richer than his blood would ever be able to tolerate. He and Miss Nguyen made their way to a table of Chinese men and women. On the way, he sampled the delicious canapés from the silver tray of a passing waiter. Two men and two women were seated at the table playing *ma chiao* (mah-jongg). The game, like its predecessor, dominoes, was invented in China, and is played with 144 tiles, rectangles of hardwood faced with ivory imposed with both Chinese characters and Arabic numerals, that, at the moment, were being drawn and discarded with an almost laughable intensity. Unlike the Chemin de Fer table, there was a great deal of high-spirited, animated discussion. Miss Nguyen explained, with an amused smile, that there are no fully agreed upon rules since there are as many forms of the game as there are provinces in China. "The best comparison I can make is that it is something like rummy," she said.

She obviously knew all of the Chinese people seated at the table. She was pleasant and businesslike but careful and not as openly friendly as at the other tables when she introduced the man who was the apparent spokesman. "Mr. Chen, may I please introduce Mr. Anders Bergstrom of the International Red Cross? He is a Swedish national. Mr. Bergstrom, this is chairman Yu-en Chou Chen. He is head of COSVN (she said it as if the initials were one word) of *Quan-Doi Giai-phong*, the Liberation Armed Forces of South Viet Nam."

Mr. Chen smiled broadly and openly, quite apparently pleased to be recognized. "And this is my good wife, Chen. That is her given as well as her family name. In fact, he chuckled at an old family joke, her name is Chen Chen Chen. We call her 'Triple Chen' in the family."

Anders did not have time to react. He realized suddenly that he had just been introduced to the leader of the Viet Cong for South Viet Nam. He was glad for those long boring lectures at The Farm where he had picked up a smattering of knowledge about the NLF or LAF, the Viet Minh, and the NVA. He said stiffly, "Pleased to meet you, Mr. Chan."

"It is 'Chen,' Mr. Bergstrom," the small bespectacled and inconspicuous Chinese man corrected gently.

"Forgive me, sir," apologized Anders with a more marked Swedish accent to his English than usual for some reason.

Mr. Chen made a dismissive gesture. "What brings you to our humble country, Mr. Bergman?" He glanced away to arrange his tiles, cognizant of his responsibility to the other players since he had been selected by chance as East.

Anders smiled. "Bergstrom," he corrected, equally gently.

"Ah, tit for tat," Mr. Chen said with a fetching grin. In the ongoing game, the bamboos, characters, circles, winds, dragons, flowers, and seasons were displayed, shuffled, shifted, and dismayed over as the two men talked. Anders admired the man's powers of concentration; he, himself, had enough to do to keep up his end of the conversation.

"I am the delegate from the International Red Cross Commission on Maintenance of the Rules of the Geneva Convention for the conflict here," he answered. Then he corrected himself modestly, "One of the delegates, I should say. I am the agreed arbitrator since I am from a neutral country."

"Indeed. Perhaps my office can be of service to you, letters of safe passage, introductions, and the like. Please feel free to come by my office. I will alert the staff," Mr. Chen offered graciously. "I am being a bit pompous. I have only one secretary in the office at any one time; budget you know," he modestly added.

Anders accepted the calling card proffered by the chairman and thanked him for his offer. "I will be happy to take you up on your offer," he said. "I will only be in the Gia Dinh-Saigon area for a short time; but I will be returning often, I am sure. Then perhaps we can meet again when I return."

"I will look forward to your visit, Mr. Bergstrom."

The players were now tallying their scores, arguing over their kongs, robbed kongs, woos, pungs of dragons or prevailing winds, bouquets of flowers, chows, terminals, and walls. It was all very good natured; and, to Anders, the game was totally indecipherable.

As soon after leaving the Viet Cong table as possible, Anders flooded Miss Nguyen with questions. "What on earth are those people doing at a party with the leaders of South Viet Nam and the US military? How come you know them? Isn't it a risk for me, for my cover, to have the head honcho of the VC meet me face to face? Why didn't someone arrest the guy, or shoot him, or something?"

Miss Nguyen put up her hand in self-defense against the rapid-fire barrage. "First of all, everyone in the military and in the intelligence community knows him and regards Mr. Chen as a mere figurehead. He is so obvious and public that he could not possibly be the real leader or the VC or even the VCI. The real leadership is supposed to be their central committee located in their war zone C somewhere near the

Cambodian border. I am in the minority. I think Mr. Chen should be under constant surveillance, and that our side should make the greatest effort to put one of our people in his organization. I am a mere woman, and so outvoted," she shrugged. "As for your cover, Mr. Bergstrom, every agency in the country on both sides knows you are here and suspects you as being an agent for the other side. It seemed like a good idea for you to be introduced as the Red Cross delegate in wide-open society. Who knows? People just might believe you. It was Mr. Duerk's idea.

"Secondly, there is a sort of truce, an understanding about the Saigon-Gia Dinh area. For each side it is useful to have a special zone as military neutral ground. You will notice that there is no heavy fighting here, no artillery exchanges, just the occasional 'incident' usually minor bombings, that sort of thing. Our side accepts the fiction that COSVN is a benign organization of nationalists, both communist and non-Communist, that is working for the peaceful reunification of the two Vietnams. The Americans are opposed to reunification, but are seen to be willing to accept a differing point of view. On the communists' part, their 'convincing explanations,' as they call their propaganda, spread the word that it is useful to preserve the most important city and the biggest port in the south for the purposes of rebuilding after the communists win and take over. It works pretty well, most of the time."

Anders shook his head. He had a lot to learn about the labyrinthine politics and military arrangements and programs in this country despite the efforts to educate him back on The Farm. Having accomplished their purpose of allowing Anders to make his public debut as the Red Cross monitor, there was no real reason to remain in the rich atmosphere. Anders and Miss Nguyen passed a table where four elderly Europeans, evidently French, were playing *Quatre Cent Vingt-et-un* with a flourish of the dice reminiscent to them of the elegance of the lost days of their colonial power. To Anders they just looked old.

CHAPTER 11

Anders' education was to be increased the following day by Miss Nguyen. She told him to wear casual clothes. They were going to travel to an outlying district. This particular outing was not Mr. Duerk's idea, she assured him. "I would rather you didn't say too much about where we are going and what you see there. It is supposed to be a big secret, but I think a great many people are aware of what is going on," she confided in a conspiratorial tone.

They motored northwest in the direction of Tay Ninh Province and the Cambodian border. The farther they got from Saigon, the more intense the military traffic became. On two occasions they were stopped by ARVN roadblock units, and their papers inspected. All along the way they saw bomb craters pockmarking the landscape. Miss Nguyen stopped in the small town of Cu Chi at the tiny Kim Khoi Hotel, thirty-two kilometers from the center of Saigon. The town was located on a terrace of land above the Delta flood plains. There, in the lobby, they met a Vietnamese man dressed in ARVN enlisted uniform with identifying unit patches but no rank insignias. He joined them for the trip to the outskirts of town avoiding the huge American military base. They stopped a short distance from the barbed wire perimeter of the base, and their guide stepped out holding up his hand cautioning the other two to remain in the car.

"Get out and come with me," he said in heavily Vietnamese accented English after looking over the terrain.

The three walked a distance of forty or fifty meters away from the base fence. "What do you see?" he asked Anders.

Anders saw a flat grassy bramble dotted countryside with the occasional low tree, nothing of interest, nothing man made. "Not a whole lot," he said wondering what they were doing there.

Miss Nguyen was impassive. Anders figured she knew what was going on.

"Look again. More closely," said the guide.

"Still nothing," said Anders after a careful scrutiny. He was feeling ill at ease, not being in on the secret.

"Look to your left, about ten meters ahead. Still see nothing?"

The ground was a little more even there but was covered with the same vegetation. Then his eye caught a straight line, a subtle anomaly in the otherwise completely natural landscape. He squinted at the line. It took on the appearance of something lifted up above the ground by a few millimeters. He was seeing a slit in the earth with the black of a hole beneath.

"That's a trapdoor, I'd bet!" he exclaimed, relieved that he was in the know at last, at least partially.

The three walked directly up to the anomaly, and Anders confirmed that it was a trapdoor, the cleverest job of concealment he could have imagined. Gingerly, the ARVN guide inserted the barrel of his M-14 into the opening and pried open the hatch cover a few more inches. "Careful," he said.

"Doesn't look like anyone's been here for a long time," Anders observed.

"I'm more concerned about cobras than people right now," the guide said and very deliberately raised the cover standing at full arm's length using his weapon as a pry bar, a sort of extension of his arms.

The trap door was opened enough to allow them to peer inside. It was dark, but Anders could see for ten meters or so as the round tunnel made an oblique penetration of the earth in the general direction of the base fence. Unlike the mine shafts Anders had seen in the hills of his native Utah, there was no timber, cement, or steel support shoring the tunnel walls.

Miss Nguyen selected that moment to lecture Anders. "These tunnels are not used now. The Viet Minh used them in their struggle against the French. They can be kilometers long, strong enough to withstand artillery or a tank driving on them. The Viet Minh and later the Cong maintained hospitals, supply depots, arms caches, quarters, offices, and even schools in these tunnels. They called this area the 'Land of fire and iron.' Sometimes the Cong come back. Only they know the real extent of these tunnels."

"How'd they make them. I mean, this opening is right by the base," Anders said grudgingly impressed with the accomplishment.

"All by hand. They carried the dirt they dug and spread it over several kilometers of land so it couldn't be detected. They packed the earth of the tunnels by hand. They didn't have cement or wood to hold up the sides; so, if there was a cave-in . . ." Anders could imagine suffocating in the dust. "No one has any real idea of what sacrifices these people made."

Anders bent down and scraped at the dirt with his hand, then with a small stone he found. It was like digging through rock. In his mind's eye, he could envision the enormous and time-consuming effort. As they returned to Cu Chi and then to the relative safety of Saigon, Anders thought to himself over and over again, "Who can beat people who are willing to do that?" The answer was a chilling one for the American.

———————————————————————

The Chinook helicopter took the three man Thau Thien PRU team to a large LZ that was still known to be serviceable. It had bee carved out of the bush on a hillside several years ago by the US Army Corps of Engineers. The other two men serving as backups for Y'Yool, Tran and Dung, had been dropped in the day before, unbeknownst to Oanh or Xuan, the insurgency suspects. The night was humid and was growing cold. It was mid-November, and weather was becoming unpredictable, rainy, windy, and intermittently chilly in the higher elevations. Y'Yool led his two visible and ostensible teammates up to the ridge above the LZ and followed the contour of the gentle hills until they came to a well-traveled foot trail. Here they descended for a kilometer coming near to the edge of a man-made clearing where a cluster of four simple farm buildings stood.

Y'Yool silently indicated a position for each man to take; so, they could create an effective field of fire in front and on two sides of the main hut at a distance of between sixty and seventy meters. Each man was ensconced in the underbrush just inside the edge of the trees and was wearing elaborate camouflage clothing and full face paint. Oanh and Xuan were emplaced on either side of the clearing with their M-14s, and Y'Yool faced directly into the front door of the hut where the two, so-called, "Brothers Grim" were presumed to be staying the night. He cradled a Dragunov 7.62 SVD Soviet sniper rifle in his arms and intermittently moved the rifle carefully into position and sighted through the scope at what he presumed was the door of the hut.

Cleve Howard had come back from Danang on one of his appropriations soirées with the remarkable rifle in hand. There had been a considerable stink with the marine Lieutenant Colonel, and even with the full bird, over the PRU getting the fine weapon the marine squad had taken off a sniper who had sorely harassed them for weeks. MACV headquarters had finally cast the deciding vote. PRUs had first choice on the special weapons; besides what were the marines going to do with a long-range gun that was essentially a hunting rifle? Cleve had had the PSO-1 370 mm 4 power optical telescope removed and replaced with a Zeiss 2-10 variable power telescope coated with light gathering phosphors. The weapon was accurate and effective to within sixteen centimeters at 1000 meters, to within ten cm. at 800 meters, and its 'point-blank' range was 400 meters. 'Point blank' is the distance at which a gun is accurate to within four inches of the center of the anatomical kill-zone of an animal on all fours facing in profile. The kill-zone is located below and behind the axilla, an eight inch square. Cleve had had the barrel and metal works dulled and the original glossy black plastic coated with a dull nubby covering. Y'Yool, himself, had lovingly created the camouflage encasing for the instrument.

He could not possibly miss at this range, and with this vantage point. He frequently fondled his second and more important weapon, lying within easy reach of his right hand—a shortened barrel, over and under, pump action 12 gauge combat shotgun. That was for the traitor who would come for him in the night or during the firefight that would commence when the first VC brother stepped out of the hut for his morning ablutions. A razor-sharp Bowie knife with deeply serrated notches cut into the back of the blade was ensheathed in a quick-draw scabbard attached to the side of his left thigh. The no-slip haft was moist with sweat from the frequent handling it got to verify its exact position chosen for instantaneous use.

Tran and Dung, the secret watchers, crawled into position behind and as near as possible to the locations Y'Yool had described where he had situated Oanh and Xuan, the suspects. It was dark, and the area unfamiliar enough, that neither backup man could be at all sure he was close enough to be a worthwhile help if or when the traitor decided to move on Y'Yool. The deputy chief inspector and his secret watchers were all convinced the attack on Y'Yool would happen before sunrise.

Y'Yool did not allow himself the slightest diversion or lapse of attention. He heard an occasional something go bump in the night which heightened his vigilance all the more. He shivered involuntarily from the cold and anxiety. He figured he was ready for whatever might come.

———————————◆━◆━◆◆————————

Lane Duerk was in his Saigon office Tuesday morning. Miss Nguyen left Anders a message through the reception desk at the Rex that the boss was back and wished to see him that morning.

"How did your trip up north go?" Anders asked after Duerk motioned him to take a seat. Although the station chief was enjoying a mug of steaming coffee, none was offered to Anders.

"No problem. Now, about you. Did the ever efficient Miss Nguyen take proper care of you?"

"Yes, sir."

"Then let's get down to business," Duerk continued abruptly, his patience with what he considered to be inanities already at an end. "There are a few people I want you to meet today, and some instruction; then we will make ready for a little trip. That suit you?"

"It does."

Duerk leaned to push a button under his desk. Miss Nguyen entered the office quietly and smiled an ever so slight a smile at Anders and nodded formally to Mr. Duerk. "We'll need the armored vehicle," he said.

She handed him a folder of dispatches and the latest local messages, collected his coffee cup, and retreated. Duerk did not open the folder. "It'll keep," he said, and rose, indicating to Anders to follow him. The CIA chief was wearing a shoulder holster with a Heckler and Koch VP-70 9 mm pistol with an 18 round clip. He pulled a regular officer issue Colt A1 .45 from a desk drawer and slipped it into a belt holster, adjusted the fit, then asked Anders, "You have a handgun on you?"

"No sir. I was instructed not to at this point. Didn't fit the cover."

"Good enough for now, let's go."

The two men descended to the street level lobby of the police station. Duerk walked nonchalantly across the shining tile floor until they reached the heavy metal door with its outer grillwork. He had the ARVN door guard open the door for him, then carefully looked out of the doorway by leaning over the line of closure of the door but without stepping out. When he was comfortable with the view, he stepped quickly out, then just as quickly stepped back in and waited for a moment. Satisfied, he motioned Anders forward; and they walked swiftly the six paces to the waiting armored personnel vehicle and climbed in without further ceremony.

Their driver took them across the Van Kiep Street bridge over the Ben Nghe Channel that looked more like a series of canals because of the highly regulated traffic. They sped through the crowded streets of Cholon scattering the Hoa (Vietnamese of Chinese extraction) pedestrians and vehicles, moved down Nguyen Trai to a small cafe' on Do Ngoc Street a short distance from the A Chau Hotel, and stopped abruptly. The driver got out, looked carefully about, then opened the door on Duerk's side. The senior man took his own quick look around before stepping out and abruptly walked the twenty steps into the dark cafe'. Taking this action as a cue, Anders duplicated his superior's careful and brisk exit from the armored car.

It took a moment for his eyes to adjust to the semidarkness. At first Anders could not locate Duerk. He saw no Occidentals in the establishment. He walked slowly back into the depths of the restaurant along the single aisle between two rows of French cafe' tables and curved cane-back chairs. There were two booths on each side at the very rear of the cafe'. Lane Duerk was sitting impassively in the more forward of the two booths on the right. Anders sat facing him.

"Sit on the same side as me, facing the door," Duerk ordered. Anders complied and switched places.

"Hungry?" Duerk asked.

"Yes sir, starved. What do they have?"

"Just about everything. We eat here often and do a little business. They like the money; and we have plenty of that, what with Uncle Sugar being our generous benefactor; so, we are given some perquisites. All that security stuff I do is only so much posturing, I realize. It is nothing of a secret where we take lunch, I'm sure. We are quite safe here—the 'understanding' with Yu-en Chou Chen and his COSVN people and all. Miss Nguyen tells me you have met the head honcho of the Victor Charlies himself."

"Yes, sir. Seemed strange."

"Sort of like 'marrying the Devil's daughter and having the old folks to dinner,' as some one once said," responded Duerk. Anders gave him an appreciative nod.

"You like the local food?"

"So far."

It's a good idea to start a steady diet of it now, so your guts can get used to it. Takes a while. Where you'll be, they won't have hamburgers and fries. A lot of American military types turn up their noses at Vietnamese food, but I thrive on it. Can't say I'm particularly fond of pigeon heads, blood pudding and hundred year old eggs; but I manage with the rest."

They perused the menu, and, remembering the bottomless purse that fed them, ordered a very hearty breakfast. Anders ate *com* (rice) cakes with eggs in the middle, a slab of watermelon, and a bowl of steaming *pho* (hot soup of egg noodles and beef spiced with cilantro). Duerk ate a well-done steak, two eggs mixed with snails in garlic sauce, a stack of toasted bread and marmalade, and a bowl of sticky *com* with *nouc mam*. As they were finishing, a Vietnamese man wearing a business suit approached them, looking carefully behind him from time to time to be sure he was not followed. Duerk motioned him to join them.

"Coffee? *Cha*?," Duerk asked, slipping into the Chinese usage for tea.

"Nothing thank you very much, Mr. Duerk," said the man, who appeared nervous and furtive.

No introductions were given. Anders and the Vietnamese man nodded at one another to acknowledge each other's presence for the sake of politeness. The man reached into his suit coat pocket, an unannounced movement that caused Anders to flinch slightly. He cautioned himself to stay still. The man produced an envelope and handed it to Duerk, who pocketed it. The CIA agent in turn handed an envelope to the Vietnamese businessman who quickly slipped it inside his suit jacket and stood up to go with only a small nod of recognition.

"You can count it, if you want," Duerk offered.

The man's fingers went to the opening of the envelope almost reflexively, but he stopped himself and took a step away. "Not necessary," he said. "We are gentlemen."

Before he could take a second step, a dull metallic clunk noise came from the door. From his vantage point, Anders could see a *Honda ong* (motorcycle) and its rider flashing past. He and Duerk, by some sort of soldierly telepathy, flashed the briefest of glances at each other and ducked under the table. The blast shattered out the entire front wall of the cafe'—door, windows, security grillwork, and all. The sound was deafening, and a choking cloud of plaster dust and cordite smoke billowed back through the room.

Their Vietnamese guest lay face down on the cafe' floor. Anders took one step out from his seat, grasped the back of the man's suit coat with one hand, and hoisted him like a bag of laundry and shoved him under the booth. When it seemed that there were not going to be any more explosions, Anders and Lane Duerk slipped out of their seats, pulled the Vietnamese out from under the table, and turned him over. He had a few bleeding spots from tiny shards of glass in his face and hands, but was more frightened than hurt. He had been playing possum. "They know about me," he whined.

"Could be a coincidence," observed Duerk. "Could just as well have been this place's turn, or maybe they were after me. Did you consider that possibility?"

"They know about me. I'm finished. That's the last information I can get for you. I am going to get a transfer," he said in a bleating voice and began to hurry away. Duerk made as if to speak, but it was too late. The man was gone and beyond hearing, and he had a very determined look on his face. "He was not likely to be a hero and meet Lane Duerk from the United States CIA again," thought Anders.

"Do I get to know what just went on?" asked Anders figuring he was entitled to something after just having been almost blown to pieces. He was feeling very shaky inside.

"He is somebody in the GVN Ministry of Defense. This is a list and description of the whereabouts and habits of several VCI working in his department; some thirty percent of the people in his ministry are sympathizers or card carrying members of the infrastructure. He was an excellent source for our RD computer. I don't believe in coincidences any more than he does. They were after him all right. I will have to trash my day and make arrangements to help him before the opposition completes their job.

"Let's get out of here before we have to explain ourselves to a lot of local gendarmerie," the station chief said, already moving for the open front of what used to be a cafe'. Anders could make out at least six dead people, those who had been sitting nearest the front. There were some extra body parts on the floor and on one table that he could not readily associate with any of the bodies on the floor.

The armored vehicle was already waiting for them when the two men reached the pavement that was now badly scarred. At the point where the entrance had been, there was a three foot deep ragtag trench. Duerk and Anders were out of the wrecked building and into their car before the klaxon sounding police cars and ambulances rounded the corner. Their driver made a sharp 'U' turn in the street and headed away from the A Chau Hotel and the direction from which the sirens were coming. The military and emergency vehicles did not pay any attention to them.

"You should have learned a little something about tradecraft today, Anders," commented the unshakable CIA agent once the two of them were settled into the speeding vehicle. He was the most unflappable man Anders had ever seen. They might have been leaving the movies for all the excitement that showed on the senior agent's face.

"I am not sure what," answered Anders.

"Did you notice where I sit, where you will always see me sitting?"

"Toward the back, in a booth." Anders thought a brief moment then drew the conclusions, "So you can see anyone coming toward you without being seen yourself; and so the hand grenade, or whatever, will take out the whole front half of a restaurant before it gets to you. I already knew better than to believe in coincidences."

"Good boy. Slip that into your memory bank. Other people's bodies make a good buffer. Live careful every second you are in this treacherous country, and maybe you'll live."

The trip back to Saigon proper was even more rapid than the earlier trip in had been despite an increase in the ambient traffic. Pedestrians and vehicles had no choice but to get out of the way of their heavy vehicle. "To the Rex," Duerk ordered the driver.

"I'll let you off back at the BOQ. We can get together again tonight. Why don't you make your way to the 'Continental Shelf' at about 1900. We'll have a good dinner then get back to the office to start getting you ready for your move tomorrow." The 'Continental Shelf,' so-called, was the verandah of the Continental Palace Hotel where guests drank and dined in wicker chairs and learned everything worth knowing in Saigon. It was so-named, the newspapermen in the city said, because one was likely to find so many odd fish there.

"Can you give me a few directions?" Anders asked.

"Do you have a map of the city?" Duerk countered.

"Yes." Anders produced it, and Duerk pointed at the map as he talked

"Okay, you are staying at the Ben Thanh—that's the old name for the Rex—which is now the BOQ. It's here at 141 Nguyen Hue' Boulevard. The Continental is on Tu Do Street—number 132 to 134. If you need to ask anyone, tell them Rue Catinat; that's the name everybody knows. The hotel is on the north side of the square. If we have time, maybe we can get over to Maxime's after dinner. You can see the real old Saigon. See you at seven o'clock."

The first man came out of the farm hut while it was still quite dark. Y'Yool raised his starlight scope, a six inch diameter, eighteen inch long dull gray tube with a single rubber eye piece. He squeezed the trigger on the underside of the device to bring on the shadowy green image made possible by the enhancement of available light from intensification of starlight. Under the best of conditions—standing in the open on a clear moon and starlit night—he could have expected to see the shadowy outline of his man even in the dark. However, in the jungle, with its canopy of foliage blocking out the stars, the device proved useless. Y'Yool could just make out the shadowy carriage of a muscular, well-fed man, but nothing of his features. He was most likely a soldier; Y'Yool was sure he was one of the two brothers he sought. He put down the scope and picked up the sniper rifle.

His dilemma was whether to pick this one off with his sniper rifle and chance losing the rest of his quarries when they spooked from the shot or to wait to get them all. If he fired now, he could hope that the other two men on his team would respond with a raking crossfire and turn the sleeping cabin into a sieve.

His adrenaline was up, and he made the decision in an instant. He put the crosshairs on the man's face, took a breath in, then slowly squeezed the trigger as he slowly exhaled. His gun barked, and the man's head exploded like a melon full of black ink as seen through the phosphors of his rifle sight scope. The body never twitched.

A second man, obviously not an experienced soldier, made the mistake of giving in to a sudden flash of curiosity upon hearing the report of Y'Yool's rifle. He stuck his head out of the door of the hooch for a peek. M-16 fire from two directions scythed through the communist soldier's neck nearly decapitating him. Y'Yool blinked away the bright blips of light from the gun flashes intensified a thousand times in the night scope and tried to adjust his vision; so, he could find any other VC who might turn up or out.

There was a sound of running feet going out and away from the rear of the hooch, then sporadic bursts of chattering AK-47 fire coming roughly toward the woods from where the VC thought their enemies had been firing. Their muzzle flashes served only to draw more fire onto themselves. One of the muzzles was extinguished in the first burst of return M-16 fire; but the other VC gun fired and moved, fired and moved, causing a deafening outpouring of return fire from the frustrated PRUCs.

At the onset of automatic weapons fire, Tran and Dung started forward toward the direction from which they judged that their own men were positioned. Tran was headed toward Oanh, his designated responsibility. Dung set out to interdict Xuan should he prove to be the traitor to the PRU he was suspected of being. The desperate hope of both Tran and Dung was to get to the right place at the right time to prevent the assassination of the Deputy Chief Inspector during the confusion of the firefight. It was all but impossible to see. They were on the forest floor where it was shady by day, but no glint of moon or star light could penetrate the canopy of overhanging trees at this time of night. The two backup men inched ahead moving their arms in protective motions like children playing 'blind-man's buff.'

The night became momentarily quiet, eerily silent, after the racket of gunfire. The forest animals had sought their holes and were waiting for the excitement to go away. Then there was another chatter from the Kalashnikov followed by a prolonged response from an M-16, then silence again. This time the silence held.

Both Tran and Dung were frustrated in their attempts to intercept their selected quarries during the thirty minute period of waiting silence. The only sounds either of the backup men could hear were the rattle of their own excited breaths, their pounding hearts, and the soft rustle of the vegetation of the jungle floor as they inched forward. Tran finally sighted his man, Oanh, when he had moved up to the very edge of the clearing where the farm buildings were standing. It was now predawn and just light enough to make out the activities in which Anh Xuan Oanh was engaged through the settling smoke and haze from the firefight. The PRU cadre was dutifully harvesting the ears from the fallen VC enemy. Tran slipped back into the darkness and pointed himself in the direction where he reckoned Y'Yool had positioned himself.

Dung did not see his man, Xuan, that night. Nguyen Tran Xuan had been busy, Dung discovered. He found cartridge brass scattered all over the area where Xuan was placed during the night. It was too dark to locate him now; and if he made noise, Dung knew he would either be killed as a presumed Viet Cong, or he would give away his presence and alert the traitor to the fact that he was suspected and being hunted. Dung turned and began crawling toward where Y'Yool had told the watchers he would be hiding.

Dung got to the Deputy Chief Inspector's position first, before Tran. He presumed it was Y'Yool's hiding place as he approached the heaped up branches; then absolutely sure.

Y'Yool was dead. His body was pinned to the tree trunk behind which he had been hiding in the silence and darkness. A long bayonet that had been sharpened on both edges and thinned down to a narrow blade like a skinning knife had entered the back of Y'Yool's neck, passed through the skin, ligamentum nuchae, the cervical spinal column, transected the spinal cord, and had exited through the midline having opened the esophagus, trachea, and the right carotid artery. The point of the blade was fixed in three inches of wood of the dead trunk. The sniper rifle, and shot gun were missing. The man's ears had been amputated.

Anders Bergstrom left his trishaw at the Cathedral and walked the last kilometer down the narrow Tu Do Street through the old French Colonial heart of Saigon to the Saigon River absorbing the sense and culture of the city. He retraced his steps to where the Municipal Theater faced across to the hotel about half way back then crossed and entered the main lobby of the Continental Hotel. The handsome building with its colonial facade, built in 1880 and host to dignitaries of the world, now needed a new coat of paint.

He submitted to a brief body search in the foyer. This time he was carrying a weapon, his .45. He need not have concerned himself about his cover. It was altogether commonplace for gentlemen to carry firearms to attend social functions in Saigon, and the ARVN military policeman was polite and professional as he shelved Anders' gun until after his engagement. A marine lieutenant entering the ornate lobby behind Anders protested loudly that "no gook was going to relieve me of my sidearm," as he was confronted. The man's speech was slightly slurred, and he adopted a belligerent stance. A marine M-P stepped from his discrete sentry post behind a column and walked authoritatively up to the marine junior officer.

"You will need to hand over your weapon, sir; or you will not be permitted in tonight. We have been having heightened concern over VC terrorist attacks. MACV and ARVN have jointly agreed to disarm all comers to the crowded hotels, sir. I will have your weapon."

Anders watched the mini-drama unfold, waiting to see if the officer would prevail just because officers are officers.

"Give me your name, boy," the lieutenant ordered and for dramatic emphasis took out a pen and small olive drab case containing note paper.

The 'boy' the lieutenant was addressing happened to be a 240 pound, six foot two inch tall, lean, mean ebony black-skinned combat veteran who had elected to serve his third tour In Country with the military police corps because he had had his craw full of abuse and fool orders from the kids fresh out of Quantico. 'Boy' was not his favorite form of address, either.

"Sir, Sergeant Alphonse NMN Brady, sir!" he snapped crisply in unmistakably well enunciated syllables..

"Brady, step ashide," the lieutenant slurred. "And we will forget this sorry matter ever happened. I will not have to report your insubordinate tone and behavior, and you will not have to march around out there with the other boonie-rats after tonight. Am I making myshelf clear, perfickky clear?"

"Clear, sir. And if you want to enter this establishment you will give me your piece, or you will have to go through me. Is there anything about my orders you would like to have clarified further, sir?"

Anders walked past *Le Perroquet* (The Parrot) nightclub and cabaret in the hotel lobby then proceeded up the red carpeted stairs to the rooftop overhanging enclosed porch bar and dining area known to generations of European and American visitors to the capital city as The Continental Shelf. Anders was pretty sure that Alphonse, no-middle-name, Brady would handle the situation in the lobby without the need for a kibitzer.

Lane Duerk saw the big Scandinavian man from across the room and silently hailed him with a wave. Anders strode over to the table and took his seat. He, like Duerk, was dressed in a linen tropical white suit, white pinpoint Oxford cotton shirt, and paisley tie. Anders' suit was mildly rumpled; he found it impossible to keep the linen from wrinkling; but Duerk's entire ensemble was flawless.

"Nice outfit," Mr. Duerk said and laughed. "Your mother must know how to dress you."

"You have pretty good taste, too, Mr. Duerk," responded Anders. He had to smile as well at the idea that he appeared to be aping his superior.

"You okay after our little reception party this morning?"

"Yeah. How about our Vietnamese friend?"

"He'll be all right. He wasn't hurt, just scared out of his wits. His worst problem was explaining to his clothes cleaner about that stain in the back of his trousers."

"Don't blame him. I was a little shaky myself."

"You'll get used to it. You seemed pretty cool under fire, Anders. I like that. Don't get too cool, though. I've been here for six years, and I don't let down my guard for a minute. Believe me, that is why I am still able to be here."

"I'm learning. The main thing I've learned so far is not to trust any situation. I don't know what to think about the people."

"That's a good way to think; keep it in mind. Be suspicious of every living soul you run into here, and you will be right most of the time."

The tuxedoed waiter delivered two bottled waters and the menu which was in French with no English or Vietnamese. "Wine before dinner, gentlemen?" he asked in French accented English.

"Anders?" deferred Duerk with a nod.

"No thanks. I really don't know much about wine. I'll pass."

"Something light for me…How is the Chardonney?" Duerk asked the waiter.

"We have a good '62 and a better '56. I understand the sun and rain were considered perfect that year."

"Then, by all means, let me have the '56. It's a celebration. Just a half carafe, though, please."

After the waiter returned and poured a touch of wine in Duerk's goblet; and the CIA chief went through the perfunctory cork smelling, swirling, sniffing, and sipping routine. Anders commented, "Mr. Duerk, how do you learn all that stuff about wine? I don't think I could tell the difference between the best wine and Nehi grape soda."

"You want to know a secret? Its nothing but theater. I have been doing the whole routine for years; and I have never smelled vinegar, seen nasty dregs, or tasted a spoiled batch. One year is the same as another to me. I think the waiter gives you that crap about one year being better than another for no other reason than to sell the more expensive bottle. They must get a commission or something."

"But there are real wine experts, no?"

"The whole wine business is snob theater from start to finish. I read one time that in Bordeaux a winery was discovered to have mixed cheap wine and bottled punch concentrate with its most expensive brand, best year and all that, and peddled the stuff all over the world. Made a bundle. No one, no one anywhere in the world, recognized the difference, just went on sniffing and swirling, until some whistle blower from the winery let out the secret. Wine tasting is another example of 'the Emperor's New Clothes' in my book. I like the stuff anyway."

Anders looked over the menu. The only thing he recognized that night was 'American Spam.' The rest of the fare was written in French with no apology to strict English speakers. Anders let the Saigon Chief of Station order for them both.

The two men enjoyed a sumptuous French meal almost without talking. Duerk told Anders it was one of his little rules for the enjoyment of life not to clutter the important business of eating with the unimportant business of business. Anders had just started his tortoise and sherry soup when he heard the loud voice of the marine lieutenant who had made it up to the dining room. On the marine's arm was an attractive Vietnamese woman.

"I want real food. No Froggie food, and nothing made with armpit sauce, get me, Garcon?" He pronounced the French title with a glottal-stop 'c' and sniffed the air dramatically when he referred to *nouc mam*.. "The only thing Vietnamese I wanna see is this little piece here." He pointed a thumb at his impassive companion.

Lane Duerk did not seem to notice, so Anders ignored the boorish American officer. He had *Purée Crécy* and *Anguille au vin blanc et paprika* at Duerk's insistence, *Salade' brésilienne* because he knew from Miss Nguyen how wonderful the fresh pineapple of Viet Nam was that time of year. His entrée was *Bouillabaisse à la marseillaise.* Duerk laughed at the younger man when he was obviously not full after such a repast.

"Takes a lot to fill up your hollow leg, Anders," he smiled. "I like a man with an honest appetite. Better eat up tonight, gets pretty lean out there In Country sometimes.

"I'll bet. Anyhow, this stuff is great. I'm ready for dessert."

"I'm full. I can't even eat all of my beef. Want to finish it for me?"

Anders could not see any problem with that himself. He searched Duerk's face for a fraction to be sure it would not be taken as hickish if he did, then gladly accepted and finished the *Filet mignon* with the remaining garnishes before he sighed back in his chair.

The marine officer was even drunker after a bottle of wine he consumed without sharing with his date. He was louder. "This stuff tastes like sour binger, uh, vinegar," he was saying as he brandished the bottle of French wine overhead. "How come you slopes don' have any good stuff, California wine, instead of just all of thish Frenchie horse pish?"

Duerk ignored the man. Anders tried to, but was only partially successful. Duerk waited until Anders had finished his *Mousse de bananes* before resuming conversation. "Anders. It's time for you to get to work. Starting tomorrow anyway. I want you to meet some of the most effective fighting people in all of Indochina, spend a while with them, and learn how to do a good job for The Company, and how to stay alive. Especially how to stay alive. You are no good to us dead; so, I want you to learn from the best. We have a big job to do here. We have a computer full of VC and VCI that need to be dealt with, and we are heading up a police type system to take care of them. MACV will never be able to do it. They can't figure it out. They march around in the rice paddies, burn villages and jungles; and two days after they leave, the Cong come back out of their holes; and country life goes right back to the way it started. They concern themselves with territory, and we try to deal with the people. We are going to make the difference. Get rid of those hard core bandits you never see so the GVN can function. That's where you come in. We'll get you in charge of one of the PRU action units as soon as we can. You will be part of the real change here. Make this place a fit place for Americans to work

281

in. For the Viets, too, of course. Are you ready to go tomorrow?"

Before Anders could answer, there was a stir at the marine lieutenant's table that distracted him. The waiter was leaning awkwardly over the table, the marine officer's hand clutching the front of the man's starched shirt. He was saying, "I can do anuthing I want withs thish little piece, see?" He reached into the front of the woman's dress and waggled his hand around vigorously enough that everyone in the restaurant could see what he was doing, could see his control of his companion, could see his disdain for all things Vietnamese, and could see that he was hurting the woman. She tried to appear detached from the scene, but her eyes were blinking in humiliation and physical hurt.

"Please, sir. Please do not continue that activity here. Madam Nhu's morality laws are still in force. We cannot permit public displays of affection," the waiter said as quietly and delicately as possible.

"I'll do whatever I want. Ungrateful pukes anyway. We come and fight your war for you, and can't even have a little fun. Thatch what this little country lass ish for. Lotch of fun." He gave her a particularly hard pinch to punctuate his argument.

The girl gave a little outcry. He withdrew his hand from her dress front and gave her a nasty contemptuous look. Even some of the Vietnamese tables were beginning to murmur and look frankly at the noisily insulting scene in contradistinction to their usually rigidly maintained politeness. Anders tensed his muscles, and his eyes narrowed. Duerk placed a hand on the young man's forearm. When Anders looked at his superior, Duerk gave a little negative nod. Anders complied, but did not like it.

The Vietnamese woman had managed to extract herself from her lieutenant's grasp and gaze long enough to slip away in the direction of the powder room. She walked with more dignity than could have been mustered by most persons under the circumstances. Her exit seemed to calm the marine down, and he sat noisily slurping from her soup bowl.

"Now, where were we?" asked Duerk, his voice even and calm. "I remember. I was just about to tell you about our trip to Can Tho tomorrow. Any idea where that is?"

"No, sir."

"In the Mekong. It's sort of the capital of Cochinchina, the Mekong Delta. The navy runs it. We have some good friends there. I think you will like them. Worst bunch of reprobates you ever saw—our kind of people," he laughed slightly in amusement, more at himself than anything. "I guess we had better tuck you in. I still have a couple of details to work out. Why don't you plan to meet me at Tan Son Nhut at ten bells tomorrow. Dress casual, civvie, all right? Bring all of your stuff, even your metal. I'll take care of security."

Anders preceded Duerk as they made their way between the dining tables to leave the Continental Shelf. Anders made it a point to glare down at his boisterous countryman. The lieutenant was busy with his plate of lamb and did not notice. Anders was nearly out to the foyer when he turned to see Lane Duerk lurch awkwardly as he walked by the marine lieutenant's table. The maladroit move, uncharacteristic for the usually agile CIA agent, resulted in the tablecloth getting entangled in Duerk's folder of papers. As he swerved forward and to the side to avoid bumping the table and upsetting the dishes, the accidental entrapment of the table covering had the opposite result. A pile of dishes, greasy with unfinished lamb and sugary with glazed vegetables, and a half-empty glass of deep maroon Bordeaux tumbled in succession down the marine officer's crisp blouse and slid sloppily into the lap of his starch creased dress pants leaving a trail of grease patches and indelible purple stains.

Mr. Duerk apologized profusely, abjectly, and insisted on taking care of the cleaning bill. He would not hear a "no." He showed his good faith by proffering a neatly printed calling card that read: Procter C. Layne, INDOCHINESE IMPORTS AND EXPORTS, 22 Rue Napoleon, Vientiane, Royalty of Laos.

The half-drunk besmirched marine was somewhat mollified by the solicitude, and Lane slipped away leaving the American military officer alone at his shambled table. A party of Vietnamese businessmen and their wives seated next to the American's table made pantomime silent hand clapping gestures, and a pair of Chinese mandarins sitting near the foyer bowed respectfully as the CIA officer passed.

CHAPTER 12

Oanh and Xuan were airlifted out of the LZ near the Trung River by the same Chinook that had ferried them in and returned to the PRU compound that same morning. They each had a necklace of human ears as bounty trophies. Their stalkers, Dung and Tran, came later carrying Y'Yool's body laboriously through the undergrowth, sweating and straining, to the same LZ where they were removed by a slick (Huey, or UH-1D Bell helicopter) sent out from Hue', rather than the compound, to avoid any knowledge on the part of the other PRUCs that the two of them had been involved in the mission.

Xuan reported finding the body of his leader to the helicopter crew; so, they could pass the information to RD headquarters. He informed them that the situation had been too dicey to be able to bring back the body. It was likely to remain too dangerous for days or weeks he reported. Cleve Howard, although cognizant of the truth, publicly announced the decision to leave Y'Yool's remains where they were rather than risk further loss of life in the attempt to recover them. For Xuan, Oanh and the rest of the PRU cadres, the matter was closed.

Nguyen Lui Tran, Nguyen Van Dung, Le Duc Bach, and Phan Duy Ky, along with Mr. Howard, were the only ones to attend the funeral and internment. The time and place of the burial were kept a secret. There were no verbal expressions of grief, no teeth grinding, no lamentations. Vietnamese seldom do that, knowing that the deceased now abides in a better place; so, why carry on as do the Westerners? The only recognition of Y'Yool's passing was the wearing of white head bands with his name hand painted on them, the color and method of honoring the dead. The gravesite and position of miniature house had been determined by an astrologer on the CIA staff in accordance with Feng-Shui, the Chinese characters for with and water, the forces of nature. The astrologer was able to assure harmony of these forces at the tomb site. The need for secrecy prevented the four men from placing their departed leader's belongings in a miniature house above his gravesite. In three days, before his widow could receive them, the personal belongings and weapons of Y'Yool were missing anyway.

When all public interest in Y'Yool had passed, and he was forgotten by the majority as one more casualty of war, the four—Tran, Dung, Ky, and Bach—met during a rest period on a day of training to discuss their options. Cleve Howard, making no effort to disguise his distaste for work in the field, had reluctantly assigned himself to direct the activities of the PRU until a suitable replacement for Y'Yool could be found. He had taken up temporary residence in the fortified block-house. The four Vietnamese men discussed telling all they knew to Howard, or simply staging an ambush and killing Oanh and Xuan, both or either one, or ignoring the matter and seeing to it that none of them was ever assigned with either of the suspects. The Vietnamese way would have been to let it go. There were VC everywhere, infiltrating into the fabric of Vietnamese life like unseen termites, nibbling away at the core of the society and government. Why stir themselves over the VC among their unit? Why not look the other way?

Bach and Tran were for doing just that. They were discouraged with what they now perceived was another failure by the government.

"Kill them both. I have said that before. I said it to Inspector Y'Yool. It is simple, and it takes care of the problem. That would be the Binh Xuyên way," was Ky's recommendation.

Dung was more thoughtful. "We all are here because we believed that the government, at least with the American CIA leading, can make a difference. Eventually we can hope to be left alone to do what we and our families want, and we all thought at one time that the Revolutionary Development program was the way. Speaking only for myself, it was good to believe in something bigger than myself or just my family. Once I believed in the communists, and they murdered my innocent mother.

"Later, I believed the GVN had the answers. Now I am not any more sure of the this government than I was of the one in the north, but I do believe in one thing that I didn't before. I believe in our PRU. Not every man in it, of course. But I believe in the unit. I believe in us four, if nothing else. I will be loyal to you; and I believe you will do the same for me. That is something, a start.

"If we turn away; if we do nothing like the rest of the people in the countryside, we will be like pigs waiting for the slaughter. The communists will come; and they will tell us how to live, if they let us live at all. My family knows people murdered by the hundreds south of Hanoi when Uncle Ho's '*những kẻ giải phóng*,' ('liberators') and he fairly spat the word, "took over. I want to fight. The PRU is the best way I have seen, and I want to belong. If there are traitors in our unit, they have to go; or we can't fight the enemy. If we just murder those two men, then we are no better than the North Vietnamese communist murderers."

"What if they are both guilty?" Ky asked archly, still convinced of the value of his uncomplicated plan.

"They can't be. There was too much activity against the VC during the firefight for both of them to be sneaking around in the bush to murder Y'Yool."

"And I saw Oanh in the clearing as soon as the firing stopped. At least he could not have gotten with Xuan to kill Y'Yool. I am pretty sure Xuan did it. I think Oanh was not involved, but I do not know either of those ideas for certain," interrupted Tran.

"Let's give the team, the unit, a chance. I say let's tell Chief Howard what we know, and let him decide. He is lazy, like most Americans, but he is smart. He knows how to get things done," Ky said.

"All right with me," said Bach, who did not like prolonged discussions. He liked the idea of shifting the responsibility.

"I guess I agree, as long as the four of us stay together. I will not go out with anyone else," acquiesced Tran.

"Unless it is to set a trap for the one (or the two) who killed Y'Yool. I'll go along. After all this is our own little democracy," said Ky sarcastically.

That night the four Vietnamese men surreptitiously made their way to Cleve Howard's room in the most secure of the compound buildings. Howard had commandeered two rooms for himself and had furnished them with a comfortable antique and entirely incongruous mahogany bed left over from the French occupation, an overstuffed chair that did not have holes in the upholstery, a hot plate, a table, and two twenties vintage floor lamps. He even had a new brown all-purpose carpet that had once covered the floor of a marine colonel's office. All of the accouterment had wound up in Howard's possession in this outpost in the jungle by way of one judicious barter transaction or another. Cleve Howard was a world-class scrounger who believed in his comforts.

Tran tapped lightly on the Province Chief's bedroom door. The four men had easily gotten by the sentries. They made a mental note to discuss that fact when they got the opportunity. There was no answer. Tran whispered Howard's name harshly. No answer. They could not make any more noise without attracting unwanted attention. They were staying in the open too long, the four men realized. Tran tried the door and unsurprisingly, found it locked.

He stepped back to have a whispered consultation with his three coconspirators when the door suddenly flew open. There, protruding from the darkness into the semi-light of the hallway, was the dull-blue barrel of a duckbill shotgun that throws 4-0 buckshot over a wide horizontal spread. It was leveled belly-button high at Tran. An arc of three or four degrees in either direction was all that was required to include all the rest of the nighttime visitors.

Instead of pulling the sensitive trigger, Howard communicated by whispering out of the darkness of his room, "Speak."

Tran seemed to have been elected spokesman for the contingent. He quickly damped down his initial surprise and feeling of panic at seeing the barrel of the weapon and whispered back, "It is I, Nguyen Tran. I come with Nguyen Dung, Corporal Bach, and Phan Ky. We come in respect."

Hearing the names of the men that Y'Yool had described in his report as his most trusted, Howard relaxed a little. "What do you want? It's 0300. There's nobody out at this time of night but burglars and bad women. Which are you?"

The four Vietnamese did not understand the American's attempt at humor, did not understand that it was humor. "We must talk with you. We have information that is important, and we cannot let others in the PRU know we have talked to you."

Howard stepped quietly to the side of the doorway, set himself with his weapon at the ready, and said, "Come on in then. Don't make me nervous, or my finger might twitch, if you get my meaning."

The four men walked warily inside. Howard flashed on the room light and swiftly closed the door behind them. He had slipped on a pair of nearly opaque sunglasses he had bested from an airman in a swap, and was protected from the glare of the brilliant light from the naked bulb in the center of the room. The four Vietnamese men were dazzled and could not see momentarily.

"Hands on the top of your heads, fingers intertwined. You know the drill," ordered the senior CIA agent.

The four men complied. Howard expertly patted each of them down making Tran glad that he had insisted that they bring no weapons along that night. Satisfied that his nocturnal visitors were bare beneath their black pajama uniforms, he said simply, "Sit."

They sat.

"What's this about, gentlemen?" Howard asked, his voice calm and relaxed unlike his hands on the shotgun.

"We mean you no harm. We are not a danger to you. Please put down the gun. It will be hard to communicate with a 12 gauge aimed at us," requested Tran, still the spokesman.

"Try," said Howard.

Tran shrugged, then launched into a detailed presentation of the history of the activities of the PRU since its inception, and gave a lucid account of their suspicions about a traitor among them. He named Nguyen Tran Xuan as the most likely culprit.

Howard heard him out, and listened while the other three men made their contributions. "Why is this the first time I ever heard about anything like this?" He queried pointedly getting to the heart of the matter for him. "Deputy Chief Inspector Y'Yool never said a thing about a VC infiltrator in any of his reports. Why should I believe you more than a man whom I knew and for whom I had the utmost respect?" That was not quite a true statement, Howard knew, remembering a brief report from Y'Yool, but it seemed more profitable to find out everything these men knew without tipping his hand.

It was a good question, and one the men had anticipated. They had suspected that Y'Yool either did not trust the Americans or their Vietnamese help in the Province headquarters in Hue' or that he was ambitious and wanted to present a fiat accompli having dealt with the traitor to his own credit. Both were consistent with the Vietnamese way. Dung nudged Tran.

"We discussed this problem many times with the Inspector. He did not want to cast suspicion on any one unjustly until he had proof. He was a policeman, a man of evidence. When he was killed, he was trying to catch the traitor with red on his hands."

The expression was apt if not exactly in the usual form, and Tran's answer had the ring of truth. There seemed to be no particular reason to come to him in the dead of night otherwise; and it was too elaborate of a plot to get rid of a rival or competitor even for Vietnamese, he reasoned. He relaxed his aim on the shotgun. Nothing happened.

"I'll think on it," he said.

With ten minutes to spare, Anders walked briskly through the main Seventh Air Force terminal building and to the VIP entrance that faced Hotel Three, the helicopter landing pads—six in number. The rear of the pads was a high chain-link fence topped with three rows of razor wire. American airmen patrolled the perimeter constantly, and the VC just as regularly cut the wires at night if only as a reminder of their omnipresence. VIPs landed and took off from the cement squares; lesser lights were relegated to the grass strip cleared between the squares and the fence. Anders wondered which he was going to be that day.

He shoved his military duffel bag and his civilian two-suit bag up to the gate desk. The duffel was beat up and heavy, mostly from the artillery he packed. Anders had accumulated a Colt .45 and six clips of ammunition he obtained in Nicaragua; a 9 mm Walther P-38 with extra clips, and two boxes of shells, an M-14 rifle, and the all purpose survival kit given him at The Farm in Virginia; a Randall stiletto knife, a special forces Bowie knife purchased in an army-navy surplus store in the Philippines, and a jade handled double edged knife taken from the defeated Jean-Luc DuParrier.

The attendant was a strong appearing staff-sergeant, an unattractive thirty-two to thirty-five year old short-cropped brunette woman. "Ticket?" She asked brusquely and correctly.

He had no ticket. "I'm supposed to meet someone here."

"Sorry, no tickee, no laundly," she said in her best effort at a friendly but definitive reply.

"I'm supposed to fly out with Lane Duerk this morning."

"Oh," she said with a quick perusal of her manifest. "Take a seat. I'm sure Mr. Duerk will be here shortly. The STOL crew called in about ten minutes ago. They should be ready when you are." There was a decidedly new note of respect at the mention of Duerk's name.

Anders sat on one of the vinyl covered and thinly padded straight back benches resting his feet on his duffel bag. He was dressed in a loud printed Hawaiian shirt and faded blue jeans with no belt. He wore black, high top tennis shoes that one of the salesmen in the army-navy store had suggested as change off shoes for the jungle. He was not a reader; so, Anders had nothing to occupy his mind. He sat and twiddled his thumbs.

He had killed no more than five minutes before Lane Duerk and two other men dressed in civilian clothes hurried into the waiting area. One of the other men was weighted down with two heavy duffel bags. The second, a short haired man of about thirty, could have been a military officer except for the sloppy denim shirt and old corduroys and penny loafers he was wearing. The beast of burden, with the two duffel bags, had a tattoo of a bikini-clad cupie doll on each muscular upper arm; so, there was no question of him being an officer. He wore a sweaty, but clean Tee shirt, and a pair of camouflage pants. His lace-up plain toe brown shoes were scuffed and grease stained but still looked incriminatingly old-style military. He was forty or so and had a well-maintained beer belly that tended to fit the description as well.

"Ah, good. Anders, this is our pilot Andy," said Duerk when he had ushered the two men to where Anders was now standing to greet them.

"Andy, I'm Anders."

Andy nodded.

"This is Chester," Duerk indicated the puffing beer-bellied man.

"Chester," Anders said and inclined his head in a nod in response to the tired man who just nodded at him. Not a talkative group.

"I presume you have met Bull," Duerk said giving a wry smile in the direction of the air force sergeant terminal attendant.

"Um hum," replied Anders. "My kinda girl."

"I think that's her usual line, but you are welcome to try your luck," Duerk laughed.

"I'll pass."

"I guess we are ready to head out," said Mr. Duerk. Andy waved for the other men to follow, and Anders and Chester trotted along behind bearing all the bags.

The STOL (Arava Short Takeoff and Landing) plane was standing ready on one of the large cement squares, its engines idling. When the men and their gear were aboard, Duerk told Anders that The Company liked to use the versatile quick little planes with their civilian pilots throughout Indochina. The two crew members looked very much military to Anders, but he did not bother to comment.

"Big bag you have there," the CIA station chief said. "What kind of weaponry are you toting?"

Anders told him.

"I can do you one better. I'll trade you that old timey M-14 for a shiny new M-16."

"Fine with me. Great!"

This ArmaLite is the best combat small arms weapon on the planet. I used to think the Kalashnikov was the best, but everything I hear says this new miracle of American know-how beats the Ruskie model hands-down."

Anders made the substitution of the guns.

"You didn't mention a shotgun, right?" Duerk asked.

"Right. I don't have one," Anders answered.

"Okay. This is your lucky day, just like your birthday. I just happen to have an unaltered 12 gauge combat shotgun that everyone seems to shorten for some unknown reason." He produced the new gun and several boxes of 2-0 buckshot ammunition from the duffel bag Chester had carried onto the plane.

Anders had to remove and repack everything into his duffel bag. Some underwear and tee shirts wouldn't fit back in. Anders got around that by putting the .45 in his trousers waist and two clips of shells in his pocket. With superhuman effort he was able to squeeze the top clips close enough to each other to get the duffel bag closed.

The noise in the plane cabin was too great to carry on any kind of a conversation or for good hearing health. Both passengers inserted earplugs for the rest of the flight to Can Tho, a *thi xa,* or autonomous municipality, sitting at the junction of a tributary and the main Song Hau branch of the Mekong between Phong Dinh and Vinh Long Provinces. It was located eighty kilometers inland from the South China Sea and 169 kilometers southwest of Saigon.

The scene rolling out below the plane was one of rich green sameness cut at intervals by brown rivers and meandering interlacing channels. The Mekong River that produced and sustains the Delta is one of the world's greatest, between 3800 and 4500 kilometers long stretching from the foothills of the Himalayas of Tibet down through China, Burma, Laos, Cambodia, and with a final hook into southern Viet Nam, ends in the South China Sea near Viet Nam's tip, the Camau peninsula, where the U Minh and Nam Cahn Forests are located. In the Mekong Delta, the river is called the *Cuu Long Giang* or Nine Dragons River which reflects its nine tributaries. The major branches, from north to south are named the Mekong, the Bassac, the Co Chien, the Ham Luong, and the My Tho. The silt carried by the great river has laid down nine million acres of farm land, and the river continues to produce an increase in the land mass of Viet Nam of some 250 feet each year.

The 26,000 square mile Delta is Viet Nam's rice basket and could have been one of the world's greatest rice producing areas were it not for the interruptions to farming and trade that have accompanied two thousand years of continual war. It was the United States military's IV Corps zone of tactical operations. The area was once part of the Khmer Kingdom and was the most recent area in the country to have been conquered by the warlike and colonizing Vietnamese and to be ruled by the Nguyen Lords. It was the most varied in population, the least governable, and the most dangerous, even without an active war.

Swamps (like the large Rung Rat Swamp delta of the Saigon and Dong Nai Rivers—the area from which the LAF sappers operated with impunity), great flat plains (like the massive Plain of Reeds in the north), ever changing tributaries, inlets, and even islands, and fringes of impenetrable tangled forests (like the foreboding U Minh Forest in the south) provided ample places to hide for those who wished to carry on life away from the scrutiny of society. Such reticent people included politically ambitious groups like the Viet Cong who, out of sight, controlled about eighty-five percent of the land and the people, peculiar insular clans and religious communities, individualists and adventurers, and American deserters. The city of Con Phung was a haven for American deserters of which there were more than a few.

The STOL dropped down over the river that was in the process of changing from its milky-brown summer character to the clear waters of winter. It landed at the 9th Infantry Division landing strip. Anders, Lane Duerk, Andy, and Chester stepped out of the plane into the palpable humidity and steam-room heat of Can Tho and the Delta. It was ninety-two degrees and one hundred percent humidity; Anders looked up to see if it was about to rain.

"It's like this the whole rainy season. There is no summer, just rainy season. Then there's the hot-dry season, no winter either. Great place," commented Duerk with the first rivulets of sweat beginning to trickle off his forehead and into his eyes and down his nose in the early November morning.

"It's hard to imagine doing anything. I don't feel like moving. I guess you get used to it," said Anders as they stepped around to collect their baggage.

"Nah. You never get used to it. You always feel like you're melting. You just do what you have to do. Don't expect too much in the way of activity from the locals, though. It's only 'mad dogs and English-men who go out in the noonday sun.'"

Andy, the pilot, set out six boxes marked, "Rice—Gift of the Generous American People". "You guys mind helping me and Chester carry these over to the truck?" He asked.

"Sure," said Anders. He bent to lift one of the boxes, expecting it to weigh about twenty-five pounds at the most, based on the box label. He was glad the truck was nearby because it weighed more than eighty pounds, as near as he could tell. Heaviest rice he had ever seen.

Duerk walked briskly over to the truck and drove it to the STOL and the three sweating men. "If the mountain won't come to Mohammed;

then, Mohammed will come to the mountain," he said with a smile as he alighted, having cut their labors by a factor of ten.

The men hefted the duffel bags and the six boxes of rice into the cargo section of the dull-finish, olive-drab colored, but otherwise unmarked and thoroughly beat-up and rusted pickup, covered them with a greasy tarp, and Duerk and Anders climbed into the cab, Duerk in the driver's seat. "Until next time, gentlemen," the CIA agent said to the crew of the STOL. Andy and Chester headed for the terminal office and a couple of cool ones before turning around and heading back to the comforts of Saigon.

Duerk drove through the congested streets and made his way toward the HQ/USN building. Anders asked, "What kind of rice is that? Weighs a ton."

"Well, Anders. There's two kinds of rice. Soft rice and hard rice. You eat the soft variety; they grow the soft variety here by the ton; so, there's not much need for us to bring any of that kind in—like hauling coal to Newcastle. There is always a shortage of the hard variety; and Uncle Sugar supplies our friends with all they need. This particular shipment of hard rice that you and I are privileged to deliver and share includes some WP rounds, Claymores, 40 mm cartridges for M-79s, F-1s, and PE." He was speaking of White Phosphorous or Willie Pete, antipersonnel smoke rounds; Claymore antipersonnel land mines that are detonated by command or are pressure sensitive with a lethal range of 50 meters; break-open shotgun weapons that fire grenades; standard issue Warsaw Pack hand grenades, favored because of their small size; and plastic explosive—explosives made by adding waxes, oil or plasticizers to highly explosive chemicals to give the material the useful quality of being moldable by hand.

Anders understood.

They pulled up to the HQ building and parked in the space reserved for officers. Duerk beckoned a young marine PFC, otherwise unoccupied except with a weekend pass to go into town and make an effort to catch one of the incurable varieties of gonorrhea. He ordered him to stand guard over their cargo of hard rice; then the CIA chief spoke briefly to one of the marine sentries at the gate who made a short phone call. Duerk and Anders were admitted with stiff salutes from the marines despite their very casual civilian attire.

Anders followed Duerk to a sheet-steel reinforced door marked, Task Force 116, which they entered without knocking. The attractive woman first class petty officer, serving as secretary and aide to the commanding officer, looked at the inappropriately dressed interlopers then stood abruptly and demanded, "Who do you think you are? Didn't your mother teach you to knock?" Getting no reply in the half second space for answering, she continued, "No one sees Captain Jessup without an appointment. You don't have an appointment. Call the main desk. Please close the door quietly on the way out."

"No need to be uncivil, dear," Duerk said with an intentionally benign smile. "Ask the man:

> What would he do
> Had he the motive and the cue for passion
> That I have? He would drown the stage in tears
> And cleave the general ear with horrid speech,
> Make mad the guilty and appall the free,
> Confound the ignorant, and amaze indeed
> The very faculties of eyes and ears."

"What?!" the petty officer exclaimed in confused exasperation.

"Peace." He held up his hand in a conciliatory gesture. "I'll write it out for you; you can give it to Fearless Leader, and all will be made aright." He quickly scrawled out his arcane message on a piece of scrap paper he took from her desk, signed it, "Your servant, Hamlet," and gave it to the perplexed enlisted woman.

Anders lifted his eyebrows and shrugged his shoulders in response to her unspoken question to him. PO1 McIntire gave up and took the message to her boss. She had only been in the office for two weeks, two weeks too long, and was sure she would never understand the goings on in the place. In a few moments she returned with a written message; this one even less legible than Duerk's.

> . . . Modest wisdom plucks me
> From over-credulous haste: but God above
> Deal between thee and me! for even now
> I put myself to thy direction,. . .
> -Your friend, Macbeth.

The door to the inner office opened about a minute later, and an arm reached out to beckon them to enter. PO McIntire shook her head and got back to things she understood, like the Riverine fueling schedule invoices.

"You know, it would be nice if you people from the dark forces could make regular appointments like real folks. I really wonder how inimitable it would be to our national security if you let my secretary in on the secret of your arrival time," Captain Jessup said extending his large hand. He was smiling, obviously fond of his visitor.

"Cap'n Jessup, this is Anders Bergstrom. He is going to be the guest of some people of your acquaintance for a while."

"One of your Ton Ton Macoutes, I presume," bantered Jessup dryly.

"Anders is the representative of the International Red Cross monitoring compliance with the Geneva Conventions. You will need to be on your toes while he is among you, Captain. To be forewarned is to be forearmed," Duerk said with a completely flat expression.

Captain Jessup laughed. "Lane, you're as full of it as a Christmas goose. He's going to work with Terry and the Pirates?"

"The same."

"Glad to have you aboard, son. You'll be with the nicest bunch of irregulars as ever cut a throat and scuttled a ship," Captain Jessup said and reached out to shake the large Scandinavian boy's hand. "You look like you can handle yourself. Remember to keep your head down out there."

"Thanks, sir. You are not the first one to suggest that this isn't a completely healthy place. I'll learn from your people."

"That's the attitude!"

"Now, say goodbye to the nice man, Anders. He's busy moving the papers around on his desk, and we mustn't keep him from his work," Agent Duerk said as he began to back toward the office door. "We're off."

"Good hunting, boys," the captain said in parting. Duerk and Anders smiled pleasantly and gave a 'ta-ta' wave to PO1 McIntire as they crossed her office to leave. She ignored them.

The Company men drove The Company truck and The Company cargo back in the direction of the airport to a section of the city known as *Phong nho Ke Trom* (Den of Thieves), and also known to be one hundred percent Viet Cong. It was nearly 1300 when they picked their way down a series of alleys to stop in the side yard of an especially run down gin-mill on *Bai Pho* Street (Street of Playing Cards, referring to the not so far distant past era of gambling dens), the trip being lengthened by a couple of false passes. Enlisted American marines and seamen flocking to the brothels, massage parlors, tattoo shops, fortune tellers, cheap liquor stores, and opium dens paid scant heed to the danger to which they were subjecting themselves in the core of enemy territory. They did know enough to give the section a wide berth as soon as the sun started to set. Any uneasy truce in the interest of business was canceled every day at dusk.

Duerk pulled off his shirt and substituted a faded yellow tee shirt with a logo and the company name, Pacific Architects and Engineers, on it, some of the letters now obscured with paint and grease. He produced another one for Anders, equally dirty and smelly. He had miscalculated the young man's size, and Ander's muscles bulged out of the sleeves, and the trail of hair leading from below to his navel was exposed. Anders wrinkled his nose and held his breath when he slipped the noisome garment over his head. The two men walked into the bar.

An elderly Vietnamese man dressed in a black pajama top and a pair of US Navy dungarees sidled up to the pair of Americans, placed the palms of his hands together, bowed obsequiously, and said with a smile marred by broken, rotting, missing teeth, "cố vấn vĩ đai.," (The derisive term for Americans formerly reserved for Chinese overlords) presuming that the round-eyed foreigners would not understand.

Duerk said nothing and did not even pause as he strode purposefully toward a set of rickety stairs leading up into the dark. His only gesture of recognition was to give the old man the finger. Anders kept a close watch on the disreputable looking men slouching around the bar staring at Duerk and him. The very much out of place blond young man was alert for any sign that offense had been taken at Duerk's obscene gesture. There was none. The men were all armed, scarred, and cruel and hard looking. There was not the least glimmer of friendliness anywhere, but no one moved, so, Anders followed his leader obediently up the stairs.

The raucous sound of instrumental American rock and roll music (to use the term loosely) came from behind the closed door at the head of the unlit stairs. Mr. Duerk knocked four times very hard so as to be heard over the noise of the ghetto blaster inside. The door flew open, and two disheveled Occidental men with long dirty hair and beards, one in a chartreuse peacenik shirt, and the other in a Pacific Architects and Engineers logo tee shirt, Hawaiian shorts, sandals, and submachine guns aimed chest level appeared. The red haired man holding the Swedish K SMG recognized Duerk, lowered his weapon, and indicated to his companion holding the grease gun to do the same.

"Been expecting you poltergeist representatives of the dark side of war all morning," the red haired man said, extending his hand to shake Duerk's. He pulled the agent the rest of the way up the stairs and into the hazy room.

Anders followed close on Duerk's heels feeling more wary about this new bunch of thugs than he had been about the Vietnamese variety of cutthroats in the bar below. No one got up from his chair to greet the two newcomers. None of the ten or so men gathered in the spacious room, with its air obscured with caustic tobacco smoke, gave any indication they recognized Duerk's officer status.

"This is Terry Brannigan, USN, SEAL Team One, out of Coronado, California, Anders. He is the commander," announced Duerk by way of introduction. Terry shook Ander's hand with a hearty callused grip. He bore a heavy indented facial scar from his left ear to his chin bearing roughly the same course as the one on Ander's right cheek, but much more evident and menacing in appearance. His smile was genuine and toothsome.

Anders relaxed with the warmth of the smile and shook the proffered hand firmly. "Anders Bergstrom," he said to Terry and looked around the room. The other men nodded their greetings.

"This is your new home for a couple or three months, Anders, here in the care and protection of Terry and the Pirates, as they are affectionately known by their peers. The name is not just cute; they are the meanest there are," said Duerk to his subordinate.

"Welcome to our humble home, Anders. We pay triple the legal rent allowed by rent control laws for this dump. Let me show you the place and introduce you around," Terry said. He first led Anders to the other SEAL, Mark Whitehead, from Minnesota.

"This is Mark. Mark this is Anders."

Both men nodded and smiled in greeting.

"The three of us will be a team while you're here. I take it from Lane that you're here to learn special-ops. I know you've had a lot of experience murdering old men riding buffalo and kids in black pajamas, with the grunts or the airbornes or whatever, but this is different. We'll teach you from the ground up. You do what we tell you, no crap about it. That okay with you?" Mark asked, his face now serious.

"Sure. That's why I'm here."

"We depend on each other absolutely. You learn what we know because it works, and we survive. You have to be the kind of guy we can hunt tigers in the dark with. Lane thinks you are, or you wouldn't be here, right, Agent Duerk?"

"That's about it," Duerk said. "Do you need any more money from the Pacific Architects and Engineers?"

"Nope. We can continue to cope for the time being."

"I have enjoyed our little chat, Terry; but it isn't good to stay overlong in my line of work. I'll buzz off. Give me a progress report from time to time. You can tell Miss Nguyen anything you want if I'm not there. You know how to reach me."

"Thanks, Mr. Duerk. I guess I'll be hearing from you," Anders said, and the senior agent and the younger contract agent shook hands as the older man took his leave.

All ten men and Anders trekked out to the truck and hauled up the boxes and Anders' duffel bag and suit bag by the rear fire escape. Duerk drove the truck out of the cluttered yard and down the narrow alley without a backward look.

"That one can look you in the eye and pick your pocket at the same time," one of the men said admiringly.

"And he can shake your hand, pat your back, smile sweetly in your eyes, and pee in your boot top all at the same time. They all can. It would do you well to remember that about Company people," said Terry. "They don't know about friends."

Anders was introduced to each man and learned his origin and specialty: Army special forces in his second tour; marine commando (Force Recon.), retired and in his second career; two regular army rangers; a Puerto Rican policeman; an expatriate San Franciscan who was vague about his recent career as a merc; an airborne sniper who had not been made to feel welcome in his army unit; and an SAS (Special Air Service, Great Britain) Sergeant-major who took his assignment to be the watchman over his American cousins. The men were happy with the hard rice Anders and Duerk had brought. They neatly stacked the cases behind false wall paneling and started their supper of strictly Vietnamese food.

After they finished their shrimp, beans, and rice soaked in a *nouc cham* that included hot chilies and fresh lime juice, well scrubbed and peeled squash and carrots, and sesame cakes, they sat back to sip cold *ba ba ba* (333, the national beer). Anders passed up the alcohol and had a huge glass of near frozen mixed tropical juices purchased fresh from the same vendor every day. The refrigerator in the apartment had two settings, too hot and too cold. The latter had been selected.

Terry explained the general rules, then told Anders that they (Mark, Terry, and Anders) would be heading out tomorrow morning at 0200 on a mission. "There are no officers here. We are all good soldiers, but we are all sick of putting up with officers. We do have discipline, the kind that counts. So…the rules: No fu-fu." A questioning look on

Anders' face. "No cologne or perfume. No smoking, no tobacco in the field. No drugs including Mary Jane or Delta Dust...ever. If you have a problem with that, this is the time to let us all know. We all left our regular units in part because of the putzes there that went around stoned and could not be trusted. Here, we count on each other, in the field and on the streets, in the day with our own types and in the dark with the Indians. Do your drinking back here. If you have a drinking problem, we'd rather you moved back to the regulars of your own volition." Terry paused pointedly so Anders could reply.

"No drugs. I don't drink."

"I don't know if I can trust somebody who doesn't drink," said one of the rangers. The men laughed. Nobody in the large apartment was in any danger of being considered too mushy because he did not have one vice or another; and personal preferences were tolerated with wide latitude, even Anders' extreme choice.

"Secrets. This thing we do is secret. Where we live is secret. We don't talk or write about our secrets. Gremlins read our mail. This is Charley's bar down stairs. We don't have friends outside this special-ops unit, even CIA friends." Terry looked pointedly at Anders who nodded firmly in agreement.

"I am going to tell you one of my private thoughts. I think some of what we do might be construed as being war crimes by the pinko press and the bleeding heart liberals back in The World, and by the long hairs who pass through here on official visits from time to time. I think it is best to keep our own counsel, and keep everything we see and do in the family. That's what I think."

"Same at home, yanks," interjected the SAS commando. "Don't none of us need to write our memoirs in the future. Take my word for that bit of wisdom."

"I am the daily ops controller since we are nominally under the supervision of the River Patrol Force, number 116. We all had our In Country training at Vung Tau, except you. We are all confident with that extra polish, and we've proved it out in the bush with our three man units. We don't know about you, man. We just have to wait and see. For you, Anders, that just means you do what I tell you and keep back and down until I think you are ready. Can you live with that?"

"I can, but I'll be ready for action as soon as you give me the chance."

"Fine, but there are no heroes here. Do as you are told."

"Okay, boss."

"We wear flak jackets whenever and for as long as we are in the field, day and night, and don't leave them off until it cools down. It never cools down. We never leave a man behind, no matter what, dead or alive. One promise we make each other is that if we buy the farm, at least we don't have to let the VC have a party with the remains.

"If we have a bitch with one of the other guys, we are up front about it and handle it back at the ranch, not out in the bulrushes where we can't afford to have our attentions diverted. If differences can't be ironed out, then one or the other of the disputants has to go. That'll be determined by vote; and there is no appeal to officers. I even have Captain Jessup's word on that. Our little slice of democracy stays here with us.

"The second best thing about this line of work, besides all of the freedom, is that we get all the toys we need. You know the old adage; 'he who dies with the most toys wins.' We are definitely the winners at this point. We have enough ammunition cached around to mount World War Three. We have grease guns, Stens, BARs, Swedish Ks, the latest M-16s, sniper rifles, two big steamer trunks full of Cong ordinance, a shed full of grenades, rockets, LAWs, and just about anything you will ever need. You can have your choice of weapons. We travel heavy."

———————————•◆━◆•———————————

Cleve Howard thought on the problem; the potential but unproved problem bedeviling his PRU teams. Indeed, Y'Yool, his operations officer, was dead, no getting around that; but he could have been killed by the VC just as easily as by a traitor in the PRU. On the other hand, there was no reason to disbelieve the four men who had approached him in the middle of the night and scared him gray headed. There was no evidence to incriminate either of the two suspects beyond the suspicions of the living cadres and any knowledge that Y'Yool might have taken with him to his ancestors. Howard even went so far as to review the reports of all of the missions of the PRC to date and found nothing that convincingly revealed a possible *agent provocateur*, the *corpus delicti* of a crime, or a clear pattern of deceit. Aside from Y'Yool's hint of suspicion expressed in one terse report, there was not much to go on. He did not think it was necessary to study all of Y'Yool's background notes; it was sufficient to draw his conclusions from the succinct formal reports the Inspector had so faithfully dispatched.

The truth of it was that Howard did not particularly want to deal with this problem on any long term basis, certainly not to the point that he might have to stay in the field himself. It was not in him to order the summary execution of two of his men, at least one of whom could be innocent. He thought on it and solved the dilemma to his own satisfaction.

To the assembled four accusers two days later, Cleve Howard announced his decision. "I agree with you men that we have the makings of a situation that could be dangerous and that must be dealt with. I have heard more hints of suspicion about the man, Nguyen Tran Xuan, than about Oanh; so, I will deal with Xuan earliest and most carefully. I am going back to Hue' to the Revolutionary Development headquarters and will take Xuan with me. I am expecting experts from America sometime in the next couple of weeks. One of them can do a lie detector test on Xuan. Later, if necessary, we will get Oanh down in the capital as well. In the meantime, Oanh stays here in the bush under the scrutiny of you four men.

"I am placing you, Mr. Nguyen, in temporary charge of the PRU's daily operations until a replacement for Deputy Inspector Y'Yool can be assigned. I expect you to monitor Oanh's activities and report them to me in detail each week, in addition to your other reporting duties. I will arrange for a clerk to come and assist with the necessary paperwork because I like to receive a good set of reports as do my superiors in Saigon and Washington. This is quite a feather in your cap, Nguyen; see that you make the best of it."

The idiomatic reference to feathers was lost on the Vietnamese, but otherwise, they understood the meaning of Cleve Howard's communication. He was dumping the problem on them for the most part, and sidestepping the rest. They had no harsh thoughts since it was the way a Vietnamese would have handled the problem and seemed like a matter of course to them. They, too, would do what they had to do.

"And one more thing. My very thorough review of the records indicate that you men have not only been doing more than your share of the mission work, but there is reason for concern about your continued ability to work efficiently. As of today, you are to be placed on family home leave for a month. I will find someone to direct training activities on base while you are gone, and when you return, we will resume our police duties. That is all," Howard announced. He handed each Vietnamese cadre an official set of leave papers, then made a display of delving into his overwhelming pile of paperwork so as to signal the conclusion of the meeting and to forestall questions on the part of the men.

If Xuan's suspicions were aroused by his transfer, he hid them well in a mask of practiced oriental inscrutability. Howard could not detect anything in the man's face, demeanor, or behavior that betrayed any anxiety or deviousness. Oanh, on the other hand, was alerted to the excessive concerns and solicitousness of his four PRU comrades the first day. Tran made the tactical mistake of assigning Oanh, who was entirely devoid of even the slightest clerical skill, to the compound office.

Oanh came to Tran, who now was obviously in charge; and in a most uncharacteristic fashion for a Vietnamese, especially a shy and retiring one such as Oanh, broached the subject of the suspicions openly.

He bowed, palms of hands together in front of his chest, and said, "Leader Tran, I am most concerned about myself. I fear that I have lost favor with my superiors, and I am unaware of the cause. I am willing to confess publicly any wrongdoings or errors and will change as you direct. I, however, do not know the nature of my shortcomings. Please to advise." He kept his head deferentially bowed and his eyes fixed down.

Tran was totally unused to anyone treating him like a mandarin, like the person in charge. He was uncomfortable with the mantle. "I am not at liberty to discuss the information because it comes from our superiors," Tran fibbed as a beginning gambit.

"How can I improve if I do not know?"

"I will have your performance observed, cadre Oanh. If correction is necessary, I will inform you."

Oanh was not quite ready to concede in his quest. "Has my performance on the mission where our leader, Y'Yool, was killed been called to question?"

Tran was uncomfortable. "As with all of us," he answered. Oanh was of medium intelligence but free of cunning. He did catch the 'us' in Tran's reply, and confirmed his previous concerns that there had been others in the dark forest that night.

"I wish to volunteer for the most dangerous of assignments. I will go with you or with anyone to demonstrate my worth. And my loyalty," he added.

Tran was about to say that that would not be necessary, but Oanh had more to say. He was determined to clear the cloud that he now knew hung over him. "I served Y'Yool well. I did not betray him if it is that of which I am suspected." His usually undemonstrative eyes now burned with intensity although, with effort, he maintained the dignity of his face. "I did not kill him."

Tran was fairly sure the man spoke the truth because of his own observations of the other suspect, Xuan. He told Oanh, "Do not worry. Do your work. Answer questions honestly when they come to you. If you are innocent, it will be apparent. When the Americans bring their computer, they will know. It is not possible to escape their machines that know what we cannot hide."

Anh Xuan Oanh accepted the statement of his new leader, Nguyen Tran, for whom he had developed respect. He had a lifetime of functioning with demonstrable loyalty to respected leaders. Oanh had never been out of Thau Thien Province, a characteristic that made him a statistical representative of the majority of the men in the PRU. His father and mother were peasants who lived in the foothills of the Annamite Cordillera not far from the Laotian border. Their hamlet was securely in the GVN camp by choice, since every person in his hamlet (Soc Ba), third in size of six attached to the main agricultural and defensive center, and in the primary village (Ho A Soc) was a Catholic. They were all ardent Ngo family supporters both before and after the assassination of their revered leader, Ngo Diem, and his brother, Ngo Nhu, in 1963.

A strong, presumed secret, five-man cell of Ngo Dinh Nhu's *Can-Lao (Can-Lao Nhan-Vi Cach-Manh-Dang),* or Revolutionary Personalist Worker's Party, used Oanh's hamlet as a secret headquarters to help exert totalitarian control over Thau Thien Provincial politics. That the cell operated in his hamlet was well-known to Oanh and his family; but they never spoke of it, except when it became necessary on those rarest of occasions when the family was affected. The purpose of the *Can-Lao* in Thau Thien, including its capital city of Hue', was the same as in the rest of South Viet Nam—preserve, protect, and enlarge the advantage and dominance of the Ngo family and its nurturing Catholic religion.

Oanh learned loyalty to those aims as he learned and accepted the political catechism. He learned from his humble and obedient parents that they owed their land, their protected privilege of working their fields in peace, and all elements of good fortune to the Catholic culture in which they flourished. They had followed the Virgin Mary when she had been driven out of their predominately Catholic section of the Red River Valley of *Bac Bo* (the North of Viet Nam); and they would follow her until they died; and their children and their children's children were secure in their allegiance and would carry on the faith.

The Anh family had worried about their ability to pay the ever escalating taxes, but reasoned that they paid less than people in other villages who contributed to the Viet Cong as well as to the GVN. They

303

did not chafe or complain, and did not permit their children to speak the slightest disrespect for the government started by the Ngos since, rightfully in their view, the Catholics played such a predominate role in it. The parents had wondered about their ability to grow their rice and to till their cabbage and squash fields when the ARVN conscripted three of their sons, all of the ones over seventeen. They did not complain, knowing that all things happen for the best. They taught their fourth son, Oanh, that simple and tranquilizing philosophy to carry him through the vicissitudes of conflict when it came his turn to go.

Oanh had proved to be bright, more so than his docile and retiring character would have suggested. He did so well at soldiering that he was rewarded with an assignment to the Revolutionary Development Program, with the implication that he would be safe from combat. His placement in the Thau Thien Provincial Reconnaissance Unit with its active engagement in hostilities on a small scale had given the lie to that implicitly promised reward, but Oanh had not lost faith. Things were still for the best. He knew that.

Oanh had earned a reputation as a steady, careful, and even effective soldier in the PRU; and he patiently carried out his assigned duties, not concerning himself overmuch about the right and wrong of things or over the apparent interminability of the conflict. He respected and even liked his leaders and gave them, in large measure, the same loyalty he reserved for his family, the *Can Laos*, the Catholic Church, and the nation (in descending hierarchical order).

Anh Xuan Oanh was, therefore, understandably deeply surprised, and chagrined to depths of his spirit, when he became aware of the unjust suspicions that had been cast upon him. He felt more than a personal slight; the family and The Church that he represented stood to be sullied by these undeserved, and to Oanh, thoroughly vague, allegations whatever their substance might be. That was why he was willing to brave the lion in his lair and to speak openly with his PRU leader, Tran. Having done so, he was confident that all would turn out for the best; but recognized that he had a duty and need to be patient.

The cardinal difference between Anh Xuan Oanh, and his fellow suspect, Nguyen Tran Xuan, was not in the intensity of their loyalties, nor in their inalterable religious faith, nor had it to do with one being a democrat and the other a communist. Such was not the case; both were anticommunist nationalists. The difference lay in the spiritual, doctrinal, and political diametric opposition of their two religions. Xuan was a Buddhist. Where Oanh tended to be a passively accepting, unquestioning stalwart of the Roman Catholic faith, implicitly French in its introduction and therefore foreign; Xuan was a true and committed Buddhist zealot, fervidly jealous of the intensely Vietnamese character of the faith with which he was imbued. He was a priest, although no one in the Revolutionary Development Program was aware.

Xuan was born and had lived his entire live in Hue' until he left for the ARVN military training center in Quang Trung in 1963 at the age of twenty. He had no recollection of his parents, presumably peasants, and thought of the matrons of the orphanage, and later the priests of his pagoda, as his family. Buddhists traditionally have found the very concept of an orphanage repulsive, and worse, foreign; but the degradation of society and the dislocations of the family occasioned by decade upon decade of continual war produced an inescapable need, even for a people as dedicated to the perpetuation of family as are the Buddhists. When his parents were killed in a flood, there were no other nuclear or extended family members in Hue' or Thau Thien Province. No other family could be expected to take in Xuan, and it fell to the responsibility of the orphanage attached to the Giac Mu Pagoda to care for the child.

Buddhists do not permit adoptions. Young Xuan was cuddled, loved, nourished, and nurtured by women whose ideal in life was to emulate the compassionate Buddhist protectress of children, Quang An. Legend tells that An sacrificed her own life to beg in the mean streets for an abandoned baby, and the women of the orphanage felt they could do no less. As a young boy, Xuan's haircut marked him on sight as a child of the orphanage—long bangs in front extending almost to his eyebrows and cut precisely straight across and shaved head behind the bangs that started a quarter of the way back on his head. There was no stigma to being a ward of the orphanage, nor was there any sympathy evinced or responsibility felt for the lad by any outsiders. The environs of the orphanage and its pagoda became his world; and the gentle and loving women of the orphanage, and the priests serving the pagoda, became his parents, brothers, sisters, uncles, and aunts; all that was important to the vulnerable and developing child.

Before he entered puberty, Xuan entered the long path of the Mahayana priesthood and wore the gray and brown robes of the priests from the age of eight until he passed his third step examinations at age twenty to be awarded the privilege of adding the title, *Thich* (Venerable), to his name. Mahayana or the Greater Vehicle, differs from the more prevalent, more southern Hinayana or Lesser Vehicle, branch of Buddhism. Adherents to Hinayana or Theravada, as some call it, wear the commonly seen saffron robes, go about in bare feet, beg for food, and eschew any concern for the things of the earth. They stress individual salvation.

Priests of the Greater Vehicle, the common branch in Hue', wear yellow robes only on dress occasions; and while they solicit contributions, they do not beg for food. They stress the need to help others as well as themselves to achieve Nirvana. They are definitely more progressive, and are very political in their opinions and involvements. It is not unusual to see a priest driving a car, and a man of the Fifth level or even the Fourth, may have a chauffeur driven classical Mercedes. Although both branches subscribe to a celibate, simple, and hungry pattern of life, actual observance among the Mahayana appears to allow a considerable measure of personal preference. It is a bit disconcerting to see an overweight priest of the Greater Vehicle eating from his candy bowl; but it would be a considerable error to doubt the intensity of their commitments; Xuan's dedicated life serving as a paradigm.

At the age of eight, Xuan was given the novice robe that fastens along the side and was morally bound by the five cardinal Buddhist regulations that the boy had to memorize by rote until he mumbled them in his sleep:

Do not kill
Do not steal
Do not have sexual relations with women
Do no lie
Do not drink alcoholic beverages.

Within two years, the earnest boy had proved his proficiency with the first four basic books of Buddhism—books of prayers, Buddhist rules and regulations, proper manners, and doctrine—presented in the classical Chinese—by passing a rigorous examination. It was unusual for one so young to do so. A special small robe that buttoned down the front had to be made for one so small. Having mastered the requirements to achieve level two, Xuan was bound by an additional set of Buddhist regulations:

Do not use cosmetics
Do not attend worldly entertainments (movies and theater)
Do not sleep on a comfortable bed or large mat

Do not eat other than during proper hours
Do not possess precious things

Nguyen Tran Xuan changed from a scampering and mischievous boy into a sober priest in a few years by adherence to a grueling discipline and schedule. He came to believe the deepest tenets of Buddhism—that existence is suffering and that passions are the origin of suffering. He was content to spend the rest of his life in the shade of the Beneficent Buddha.

Xuan's day, like that of all of the other novices and junior monks, began at 0400 with a sudden awakening and getting out of bed. No luxuriating. Xuan and his contemporaries took their turn beating the great bell of the Giac Mu Pagoda 108 times until 0500, the exhortation to prayer that sounds 365 days a year to remind Buddhists of the 108 intrinsic illusions. The young monks alternated between the morning bell beating and that of the evening (between 1930 and 2030). The juniors and seniors congregated between 0500 and 0600 for collective prayer chanting, then the juniors spent the hour between 0600 and 0700 learning how correctly to perform the host of religious duties to which they were bound.

Because their order was a progressive one, the hours between 0700 and 1130 were passed in performing social welfare missions and catching up on household chores. Between 1130 and noon, the monks of the pagoda again collected for prayers. From 1200 to 1400 there was lunch, one of two daily meals. Lunch had a very simple variety of options—some days there was rice and vegetables, sometimes rice with vegetable oil, and other times rice with soy. The real variety in the diet came with the soy which could be prepared fried, boiled, pickled, fashioned like a pork chop, or minced and served as a patty, much like the western hamburger. There were always rice cakes and milk. Both branches of Buddhism are vegetarians; and in all of his life in the pagoda, Xuan never tasted fish, poultry, red meat, or eggs. After being satiated, as much as a man could be on their plain fare, the monks were permitted to take a siesta if there were still time.

Xuan and his fellow junior monks spent the next two and a half hours, until 1630, in Buddhist studies the first four days of the week and in gardening the following three. Free time was provided from 1630 to 1800. They were free to read their Buddhist texts, to memorize the lists of regulations, to pray, and to meditate; they were not free to leave the temple. Those whose turn it was then beat 108 strokes on the bell for a little less than an hour, and again all went to common prayers that were completed by regulation at 2030. This gave the monks two hours to study their Buddhist lessons or to conjugate French verbs. All monks had to be in bed and lights out at 2230 except those authorized to study for examinations.

Xuan's head was shaved twice a month. Xuan was a serious, austere, and thoroughly dedicated young man by the time he presented himself in 1963, at the minimum age of twenty, to pass his examinations on the twelve books of Buddhist studies, to be accorded the status of level three and to obtain the title of *Thich*. He needed to be committed, because, he was then put under obligation to obey, with strict application, 240 additional regulations. Nor had the young man neglected his secular education. He graduated from high school, was well into his third year of college studies, and had begun the ponderous twenty year minimum apprenticeship that would move him to level four with its additional fifty-eight regulations when the time of troubles for the Buddhist community reached its zenith, and irrevocably involved Xuan in a new destiny.

1963 was a tumultuous year in Viet Nam from the very start. On the first of January, the armed forces of South Viet Nam with vastly superior forces, arms, and equipment suffered its first major defeat in the battle of Ap Bac against the relatively homespun LAF. The warp and woof of Vietnamese society seemed to be coming apart. There was a 60% tax delinquency rate; senior ARVN commanders spent their time planning and unplanning plots and counter plots to unseat Ngo Dinh Diem, Madame Nhu, and her husband Ngo Dinh Nhu, the president's brother; ARVN lost more and more weapons to their enemies (nearly 28,000 between 1962 and 1964); students rioted. There was widespread discontent among the population at large, and particularly among the majority Buddhists against Mme Nhu and her 'Women's Solidarity League' morality laws that outlawed all French first names, forbade divorce, abortion, contraception, nightclub and even private home dancing, singing sentimental and 'twist' songs, spiritism and occultism, and the sale of cigarettes by children. By the most optimistic estimates, from a government that never did a census, less than 50% of the people of the countryside were under the control of GVN. The NLF claimed 80% of country people swore their allegiance to the insurgency.

The Buddhists were involved; at least, the Mahayannas were. The South Vietnamese Catholics constituted about 10% of the population; and even discounting those who were Buddhists in name only, the

Buddhists made up 70—80% of the population. Yet, this massive group of people was scarcely included in government at all, and they seethed. In the Delta, the Hoa-Hao Buddhists (*Phat Giao Hoa Hao,* or Purified Buddhism), many of whom had never surrendered to Diem's forces, constituted a small but dedicated religious-military army that now aligned itself with the Viet Cong. They cooperated with the Binh-Xuyên in Saigon who were lusting for the opportunity to regain a measure of their former glory. The Buddhist *Vien Hoa Dao* (Saigon Institute for the Implementation of the Dharma) became an insistent political voice and *Thich* Tri Quang was becoming a political force in the capital city. Matters deteriorated drastically on May, 8, and events of that day led directly to *Thich* Xuan adopting a new course that would lead him to violate every rule and regulation to which he had committed except the proscriptions against the use of alcohol and having intercourse with women.

The professors of the relatively new University of Hue' (established in 1957) were, for the most part, Buddhist, and were activist anticommunists and pro-nationalists who deeply resented the preferential treatment accorded the minority Catholics. They despised Diem, and finally despaired of hope for their country under his Personalist regime. The professors and their students formed a political party called The People's Revolutionary Party and proposed civilian rule. On May 3, in spite of the Diem ban on Buddhist activities, the bonzes of Chua Tu Dam Pagoda prominently flew banners celebrating the 2527th anniversary of the Buddha's birth. On May 8, 1963 the Buddhists staged a minor counter demonstration to protest a progovernment rally held by the Diem government two days earlier to celebrate the ordination of Diem's brother, Monsignor Thuc, former bishop of Vinh Long, as the new Archbishop of Hue'.

The professors, students, and bonzes had the temerity, once again, to fly a Buddhist flag in defiance of a new government edict banning religious banners. The Buddhist banner flew in the midst of a cloud of Vatican banners, that somehow had escaped the scrutiny of the edict. Diem's soldiers struck down the Buddhist banner; 20,000 Buddhists staged a peaceful protest; government troops threw two hand grenades near the crowd; the crowd became excited then unruly. Finally, the troops fired indiscriminately into the unarmed crowd leaving nine people dead. A fire of political radicalism was ignited in the Giac Mu Pagoda, and *Thich* Nguyen Tran Xuan was caught up in it.

Government troops raided Buddhist pagodas from Hue' to Saigon desecrating sacred ground and relics and infuriating even the more passive Buddhists. In August, a large statue of Buddha was destroyed by GVN troops. From north to south the Buddhists were in open defiance of the government, and the ouster of Diem became a religious cry. In the depths of Giac Mu Pagoda, a solemn discussion was held about what would be the role of their temple in the struggle against the barbarians and their foreign religion. Finally it was decided that sixty-six year old *Thich* Dao Ngoc Lan would accept the honor of demonstrating to the world the great outrage suffered by the innocent Buddhist community of Viet Nam. They devised a plan whereby the American supporters of the corrupt governmental regime in their own country, not just the 11,000 advisors in Viet Nam, would have cause to take notice. *Thich* Xuan begged to be able to join with *Thich* Lan in his great path but was refused the honor by a unanimous vote of the other bonzes because he was too young. He was permitted to join those who would assist, but he was not to be The One.

Four bonzes, including *Thich* Xuan and *Thich* Lan traveled in the Pagoda's fifty's vintage Austin to the heart of Saigon. Discretely, they informed a member of the foreign press corps that a photo opportunity was about to take place.

Thich Lan, dressed in his finest formal yellow robe, seated himself in the lotus position in front of a prominent government building, and waited quietly, fingering his chain of 54 hallyoak beads, until a small crowd gathered. *Thich* Xuan was the first of the bonzes to see the camera crew, and he nudged the others. When that crew was setup, drinking coffee, chatting, and waiting to see what would happen, the three accompanying priests swiftly extracted jars of gasoline they had been carrying beneath their gray and brown robes, opened the lids, and doused their brother priest with the flammable stuff. Because of his intense desire to be a participant, *Thich* Xuan was given the privilege of applying the match. *Thich* Lan was immolated in a burst of consuming flame, and, with a serene facial expression and immobile body coming from his deep satori (cosmic awareness), was caught for the newspapers and posterity on the foreigners' film. His suicide ignited a political firestorm and burned the soul of a dedicated political radical into *Thich* Xuan. When she was informed of the fiery immolation by reporters, Madame Nhu was quoted as referring to the monks having put on a "barbecue show."

From May to August of that stormy year, there were a series of monk suicides and bloody retaliations that seared the consciences of the world. At the instruction of his senior bonzes, Xuan let his hair grow, ceased to pursue his Buddhist studies, and began taking lessons in the martial arts and in the use of weaponry. Finally, after a stint with the coconspirator Hoa Hao monks in the Delta, when he was considered to be ready, he volunteered to join ARVN pretending that he was a Catholic, all with the express permission and encouragement of the bonzes of Giac Mu Pagoda, and all in great secret.

With a studied policy of avoiding assistance to the present administration, the United States backed away from its protégé. On the first of November a military coup toppled Diem and Nhu who were placed in an armored personnel carrier and later in the day assassinated by their own troops. No one came to their aid, not even Dinh's much vaunted Can Lao. Coincidentally, on the same day, the US Army's "Stars and Stripes" newspaper in Saigon carried the inch high headlines, "VIET VICTORY NEAR." Cinc Pac Admiral Harry D. Felt announced from his vantage point in Washington DC that the South Vietnamese should achieve victory in three years. On the twenty-second of the same month, John F. Kennedy was assassinated in the United States; and his vice-president, Lyndon B. Johnson, assumed the presidency of that country vowing to prosecute the war with all out vigor.

In Hue', the flames of revolt reached Catholic Monsignor Thuc. While archbishop, he was known as the 'viceroy' because of his control of the provincial administration. Persons desiring even such mundane privileges as the right to make charcoal from logs had to secure permission from the archbishop's office—for a fee. The people hated and ridiculed him. He became infamous for his sexual promiscuities and was referred to as 'the father of the pelvic thrust and sexual movement.'

When Thuc recognized the intensity of the feeling against the regime of which he was an integral part, the Catholic leader took refuge in the American Consulate. With the solemn assurances of his safety from his friends, the Americans, and that he would receive a fair trial, Monsignor Thuc was delivered into the hands of The People's Revolutionary Party. It is more than a coincidence that he was executed by firing squad two days after the anniversary of the May massacre in Hue'. He was forced to face a pagoda when he was shot at Chi-Hoa prison. Two black ravens flew overhead—a sign; and Nguyen Tran Xuan watched the proceedings with a strong measure of satisfaction.

CHAPTER 13

Anders found it hard to sleep and kept looking at his watch. He was anxious about the upcoming morning's mission and was also afraid he might sleep through the alarm. He did not want to get off to a bad start with these guys who were obviously very experienced combat veterans. Anders had not disabused them of the notion that he had seen his share as well, and was uneasy about being found out in his inexperience, and especially for his youth. He looked at the luminous dial of his watch and saw 0100, then 0130. He tried to keep his eyes closed. Sleep would not come until 0145, then he dropped off into a dreaming semi-coma. He jerked awake at 0155, angry that he had had to fall asleep right then instead of for the rest of the night.

He scrambled into his clothes more hurriedly than was necessary, he realized, when he looked around and saw that Terry and Mark were just rubbing the sleep out of their eyes and had not yet put a foot on the floor. He kept telling himself to calm down, but the reminder did not help much. It was his first real combat mission, and he guessed he could be forgiven a case of the jitters.

In ten minutes, all three men were ready to go. Dressing into their work-worn civilian clothes, including tennis shoes, was quick work, not like getting into full battle gear. Anders felt nearly naked with nothing but his two hand guns.

"Do you have gear for me in the apartment?" He asked Terry.

"On the boat. We packed up yesterday, even put in some C Rats." He grimaced at the thought.

Mark grabbed the keys to the pickup, and the three men left their building. No one was in the downstairs bar, and the street was dark and quiet. They drove to the docks where the LSTs were moored and parked the pickup in the yard workers' lot instead of using one of the naval personnel lots. They looked about, saw no one, and moved to their PBR. The River Patrol Force had experimented with and rejected air-cushioned vehicles that were able to move at high velocity over even shallow marshy areas, but the vehicles were too noisy for the kind of work done by the River Patrol and especially by the SOGs. Besides, they were too mechanically sophisticated to be kept functional in the Brown-Water War. Chief Maxwell, the real navy man, was already aboard trying to make the vessel shipshape and complaining about the river-rats and their mess.

"Chief, this is Anders, a new guy. Just got here from Saigon," Terry said as they slipped onto the steel deck.

"Maxwell," said the CPO, and extended his hand that was greasy from his preparations.

Anders shook the burly man's hand, met the rest of the four man boat crew, and settled in with the others. Terry outlined their mission. "The LLDBs operating above Ngoc Tran have seen a mobile VC camp moving around the tributary banks for a week now. Yesterday they got a fix on the gook position and figure they will be bedded down for at least a day. We're on an S&D to take them out. They are probably the same gooks that have been planting the mines in the river and who ambushed one of our patrols a week ago. They are priority.

"Our driver," nodding in CPO Maxwell's direction, "and his crew stay with the PBR full time and provide security. We will go in overland, then we have to swim across to Charley's side to light them up. You an okay swimmer, Anders?" Mark asked.

"Yeah," replied Anders.

"We can take turns sleeping for about fifteen minutes each. We'll be in position to leave the boat in a little over an hour. Mark, I'll go first, Anders second, and you third. That way we'll always have one of our men on watch with the crew. As soon as we leave the Can Tho docks we are in Indian country. The real thing starts now, Anders," warned Terry. He interlocked his fingers behind his head, and was asleep.

The chief, Mark, and Anders put on their flak jackets and steel pot helmets, and watched the low tree-lined banks whiz by. PBRs were fiber glass boats about thirty feet long, equipped with radar and radios, and were armed with a twin-mount 50 caliber fully automatic machine gun in front, a 30 caliber machine gun mounted on the aft deck rail, a rapid fire 40 mm grenade launcher, and a rifle fired 81 mm mortar, also astern. The crew members themselves were armed with their own M-16s and .45 automatics.

They were moving quietly through the turbid brownish water at 25 knots. Anders could not sleep when his turn came, but was glad for the chance to get his head down and to close his eyes. As they raced the miles farther away from Can Tho and safety, Anders could not help but feel more and more antsy with each additional mile.

All too soon for Anders, the chief cut the engines to half speed, and Terry whispered, "About two klicks more. We're going to move at half-speed for another three-quarters of a klick then we coast into a little creek off to our side. The enemy is supposed to be on the starboard bank about 200 feet into the bulrushes. No noise now, not the least little bit. We'll use hand signals from here on out."

The PBR glided noiselessly into the small offshoot channel with its prow pointed forward for a fast getaway if the need arose, as it often did. The information from the LLDBs was right on so far. By gestures, the men got their IBS inflated and loaded with gear. Each man had an M-16, a daisy chain of grenades, his flak jacket, a starlight scope, and a hand gun in the raft as well as an M-79 with its supply of grenades for the three of them. Terry's M-16 had been modified into an M-203 by the addition of a black tube on the underside of the barrel so he could fire grenades from his own rifle. Anders wrestled his way into the large black Navy swim fins. Everybody seemed to underestimate his size. The men quickly applied green, black, and brown cammo face paint; and Anders pulled on a rubber skull cap to cover his almost luminescent blond hair that caught every ray of light from the quarter moon. After a last minute check by Terry, the three men slipped noiselessly over the side and into the cool, turbid, slow moving current along side the IBS (Inflatable Boat, Small).

It felt good to be moving, to be in the cool water and out of the cloying heat and humidity of the Delta jungle night air. Anders side-stroked with his arms in the water rescue position and moved the heavy fins effectively through the murky water. Each man held onto the loaded gray IBS with his uppermost arm and guided it upstream. When Terry guesstimated they had gone about a klick and were therefore within a half or three-quarters of a klick from the point where they expected to find their quarry, he had the men make an obtuse angle aimed for the opposite bank. He intended to cache their IBS within a quarter of a klick from the point; so, they would not have far to go to find the camp; and they would not have far to run if things got hairy later.

Near the bank, the overhanging vegetation protruded out over the river like a lean-to roof creating a pitch-black water lane in which to travel. Although they were now gliding along almost blind, Anders felt relieved. He would take his chances against some stump in the water rather than from a sentry's spying them on shore. Terry caught a root and halted their progress. He pulled himself to the bank but could not get through the tangle; so, they made their way upstream another twenty meters or so. There they found a narrow clearing, obviously man-made; and Anders could guess by whom. He felt an involuntary shiver at the realization of where they were.

They backed up a few meters and tied the inflatable rubber craft fore and aft beneath the gnarled roots of a ghostly black tree, well camouflaged from prying eyes. Anders only hoped he would be able to find it when the time came. Terry led the way, first squeezing as much water from his clothes as he could to cut down any sloshing noise. The other two men did the same. After a moment to get their bearings, they started up the path. Anders' senses were working at 150% capacity; he had never been so awake. His lack of sleep earlier in the evening was forgotten. He relished the heavy claustrophobic feel of the flak jacket and the heft and weight of his friend, the M-16. Mark had shown him how to secure the grenades around his chest and waist so they would not rattle. The men had brought nothing with them to eat or drink except some Halazone tablets and a condom to fetch and hold some water.

Every ten meters or so, Terry paused to listen; and hearing nothing, walked slowly forward. The only other thing moving that Anders could detect was a yellow-billed black-footed magpie eating worms. Fifty meters in, the men left the trail, keeping no more than six meters apart with Anders in the middle. He knew they were doing it to protect him, and it was a little embarrassing. Nevertheless, he was glad for any modicum of extra security however small or illusory, and swallowed his manly pride without difficulty. He thought affectionately of Inga Haakensdatter's friendly kitchen and wished he was there. He wished he was anywhere but where he was. He shook out the intruding thoughts and worked at focusing his mind on the task at hand. He was sure that daydreaming was an non-salutary pastime right then.

After a very slow and cautious fifty meter walk through the entangling brush, taking care to place each step precisely to avoid the slightest noise, and sometimes finding the growth so thick that it was impassable, Terry had the men get down and crawl. Anders figured they must be within a hundred meters of where the VC camp was supposed to be. They came to the edge of a small clearing after a bruising and skin scraping crawl of only twenty-five meters; so much for Anders' ability to figure distances on a map. They were twenty to twenty-five meters to the left of the main trail and were looking at a cluster of three tents set as far into the dense brush at the edge of the clearing as possible. Anders could make out one sentry making his rounds among the tents. No one else was about, so far as any of the American irregulars could tell. The only real problem then was to determine if this was the only camp.

Terry pointed strongly at Anders then at the ground. "Stay here," he was saying. He pointed right for Mark and left for himself. Each man nodded his understanding, and they separated into the sylvan ink pot of the night. Anders did not like being alone, and he did not like having to sit there. He thought of Inga's cozy house again, scolded himself, and scrunched down as far as he could.

Terry returned in ten minutes. It seemed more like an hour and a half. He held up two fingers and pointed in a curved fashion toward the right. Anders guessed that he meant that there were two more tents a short distance away, but he could just as well have meant two more men. The fuzziness of that datum contributed to Anders' already keen insecurity. The sentry walked slowly their way. His body language spoke of tiredness and boredom, of a need to be in his hooch. Terry pointed at the man, then at himself; then he drew his index finger in a cutthroat gesture across the front of his neck.

Coupling action to his communications skills, the SEAL slipped silently and blackly onto the wet grass and let the VC sentry come to him. He had to have ice-water for blood, Anders thought. Terry let the man walk right past him; so, the sentry was walking away from his predator. Terry stood up in a move that a cat would have envied, threw his powerful left forearm around the man's throat, and reared back with such force that the cong's feet left the ground. He never had a chance to cry out at the intrusion of the huge Bowie knife that entered his right costovertebral angle and split his kidney and renal artery. The pain from the stab wound was so sudden and intense that it was impossible to make a sound. Terry gently settled the corpse on the grass, and crept back to Anders.

He pointed at his watch, indicating the three, then the nine on the luminous dial, indicating 0345. It was then 0340. He made a shooting gesture and pointed at the tents. They waited an interminable five minutes until the specified time, then Terry followed the second hand around to the nine. When it got there, he unclipped two grenades in rapid succession and tossed them with deadly accuracy at the tents.

Not having been fully forewarned, Anders was a little behind and fumbled for a moment to get his grenades off their clutch belt. He was accurate in hitting the third tent much to his surprise, given the suddenness of the move into action. There followed in very short order a series of grenade explosions from area of the second encampment from Mark Whitehead, the other SEAL, Anders presumed. There was a distant clatter of AK-47 fire followed by the sharp staccato of an M-16 then silence.

Ten seconds elapsed before Terry waved the 'follow-me' signal and began running in a zigzag hunched fashion toward the smoldering tents. Anders tore after him not wanting to be left in the dark forest, and worse, to be lost from the men to whom he had given over the full trust for his safety and life. He was frightened and glad for the exhilaration of the run. He zigzagged twice as frequently as Terry and consequently arrived well behind the sprinting SEAL. Terry probed the remains of each tent with a short burst from his ArmaLite, six rounds at each pause. Nothing stirred. Anders was puffing slightly, but Terry was breathing easily. After so treating each of the tents, Terry returned and probed the debris for bodies. Here and there he found what remained of a person, not all of whom were male. When he found a head, he cut off an ear and quickly dropped it into a small pouch he carried on his belt. He paused after removing the first ear long enough for Anders to catch the drift and to do his job of cutting off the other ear. Anders had to stuff his ear collection (six examples) into his front pocket.

"Let's head for the trail and pick up Mark. Time to get out of here!" he whispered directly into Anders' ear, cupping both palms around the pinna to dampen carriage of any sound. Anders nodded, understanding.

They met Mark on the main trail, a distance of seventy-five meters, in about three minutes. Mark was half-pushing, half-lifting a battered naked man in front of him as he approached double-time toward Terry and Anders' position. The man, more accurately, the boy, was battered and burned, the right side of his face unrecognizable. His left arm hung limply at his side, shredded at mid-biceps. He did not make a sound, but the expression of terror on what was left of his face spoke volumes. Anders did not think he could tell the ages of Vietnamese people with any accuracy, but this one looked to be not a day over fourteen. The flow of adrenaline was such that he felt no more pity for the unfortunate boy than did his two more experienced team mates.

"Thought we could use a booby-trap tester going down the main trail," Mark said, taking a few extra gulps of the thick night air to catch his breath. He had a necklace of six human ears on a long boot string encircling his neck.

"Good plan, Sam," Terry told him.

"Has to be faster than crawling back through the brambles."

"And with all the racket you made, there's no telling what else might be crawling around out there."

"Me!? Who ran around wasting government property on bonfires?"

Anders hoped the camaraderie would soon end, and they could get their skinny behinds out of the place. He expected to see half the North Vietnamese Army descend on the area any minute. To his relief, Terry finally announced, "Lets get the flock outta here."

Mark trotted along as point-man pushing the terrorized VC as far in front of his own body as he could and still keep the boy under control. The descent to the river bank took less than ten minutes thanks to the relative freedom from brushy impediments along the well-cleared trail and to the velocity of travel they were afforded by having a 'volunteer' booby-trap sweeper pushing along in front of their little parade. The diminutive Vietnamese country boy, come Viet Cong terrorist, was whimpering softly in an agony of pain and near-psychotic fear by the time the four of them reached the end of the rude trail. There was still no sight or sound of pursuers, and they had encountered no traps. That must have encouraged their captive a little, Anders thought. Mark kept his vice grip hands on the skinny arms of their captive while Terry looked out onto the river.

"Nothing," the team leader said in a harsh whisper. He was speaking a little louder now that he sensed a decrease in the imminence of danger.

Anders suddenly developed a sobering thought once he could allay his own fears enough to collect himself. How were they going to get back to the PBR with their dingy, all their gear, and a prisoner? Any sympathy he might have been feeling for the injured Viet Cong evaporated into a sense that this enemy posed a passive threat to him an his team. "How do we get him back to the boat?" he whispered to the two SEALS.

Mark looked at Anders for a moment, then said with what Anders was sure was more than a tinge of sarcasm, "You can tie up his arms and legs, and give him the cross-chest boy scout lifesaving carry across that current. He won't fit in our inner tube, and I am not up to it."

Anders looked to Terry, who just shrugged.

"So what do we do?" Anders asked with more of a plaintive quaver in his voice than he wanted which made him angry with himself. He was growing afraid that he knew the answer already and knew he had asked a silly question.

"Anders, you and Mark get the gear into the boat; and I will take care of the problem," said Terry without any indication of condescension in his voice. There was a tinge of world-weariness.

Anders chose not to think more about it. It was not up to him. He and Mark took a minute or so to stow the gear which brought on another spate of criticism from the SEAL. Anders had taped two ammo clips together to feed into his 'black magic' ArmaLite, the way he had been shown by one of the combat experienced students back at the Farm. Mark profanely told Anders that he was guaranteeing that his M-16 would jam that way. They had to take time to untape and to clean off the clips. "Look, there's nothing wrong with the M-16. It doesn't jam unless you mistreat it. If you use clean clips, it's the best gun ever made. I'd of thought you would know that by now." It was all Anders' psyche needed right then.

He and Mark swam with the rubber dingy along the bank to where Terry was now standing alone at the trailhead. He slipped silently into the water beside them. There had been no other sounds. Anders did not feel the need further to expose his ignorance and greenness by asking about the fate of the enemy.

The current was with them, and enemy response was not. The three irregulars were back on board the PBR in a matter of a few minutes. Chief Maxwell guided the boat back into the main current headed toward Can Tho (home); Terry Brannigan took first watch, and Anders and Mark rearranged and stowed the gear.

"Good easy first trip, Anders. Glad you could get your feet wet on your first trip without a lot of Indian trouble," said Mark when they leaned back against the unpadded metal bulkhead to rest.

"It went well; I'm glad. I'll be more help once I get onto things better," Anders said.

"You did okay, kid. Nobody expects you to know everything all at once. You seem to be made of the right stuff; you'll be all right."

Later, when Terry switched off with Mark at watch, and settled in beside Anders, the big Scandinavian said to the SEAL, "Sorry about acting like a kid about that VC terrorist. I just didn't know what goes on. You know I don't have a lot of experience. Thanks for educating me."

"Look, Anders, it's good to care. Don't lose that quality entirely or this place will make you into a monster or drive you crazy, one or the

other. You'll go crazy if you care too much, you know. We just do
what we have to do. There are a different set of rules in the newsroom
in Saigon and back in The World."

"So I'm learning. I was scared. I hate to admit it, but I was scared out
there. Do you ever get scared?"

"Sure. Sometimes more than others. I don't even think about being
a short-timer; that makes me scared out in Indian country like the
prospect of going back home will jinx me or something. As I said, I
just concentrate on doing what I have to do. I don't have to like it."

The three men were back at their apartment over the Viet Cong bar
in time for breakfast—an All-American spread of waffles, steak and
eggs, orange juice made from concentrate, and two pounds of bacon.
Anders found his appetite was not quite as good as that of the rest of
the men that morning.

During the stagnant days spent in idleness around the RD headquarters in Hue', Xuan had time to recall his brief tour of duty with ARVN.
Mostly he had stayed in the barracks with the other officers and men
who demonstrated a steadfast reluctance to take to the field, particularly at night. On rare occasions, when they were shaken loose from
the security of their protective compound, the South Vietnamese
soldiers had walked noisily through the jungle clanging their canteens
to ensure that any VC in the area were well aware of the presence of
their GVN patrol and could clear out. He never heard a shot fired in
anger. He did furnish accurate reports to the VCI courier operating on
the ARVN base and thereby contributed to the demise or capture of
a number of his fellow soldiers.

He had repeatedly made his desire for action known to his superiors
(those in the VC, who cared, not those in the ARVN command, who
would have thought that he had taken leave of his senses). His wish
had been granted, and he had been instructed to apply for the position
of RDC back in his native Thau Thien Province. Since it meant a
closer involvement with the Americans, and the potential of facing
danger, there was little competition when he volunteered. The prevailing attitude with the South Vietnamese soldiers and officers alike
was that this was the Americans' war; and if they wanted to go out and
betray their families by dying, let them do it. Having Xuan volunteer,
had taken some of the pressure off the others to make a showing. Xuan
had studiously tried to appear average among the Revolutionary
Development Cadres at the PRU compound to prevent any attention

being drawn to himself. He was eminently successful in his betrayals, and his VC overseers considered the earnest young man a most valuable asset.

Cleve Howard casually mentioned, one day, to the assembled men at the headquarters nestled inside the fortified MACV compound, "A team of information experts all the way from the United States of America will honor us with a demonstration of their ability to learn the truth from men, even those who wish to hide it from them. I think you will find it very interesting."

Xuan found the idea interesting and could not help but wonder whether or not that apparently chance bit of information had special relevance to himself. The team of three men mentioned by Leader Howard arrived by C-46 a day later, unannounced, and were brought to the compound from the airport in a covered troop carrier in the middle of the night. Xuan learned of their arrival the following morning not by any formal announcement, but from the mouse-like little cleaning woman who attended to his wing of the building. She learned of the arrival of the trio from the gardener, who was informed by his contact over the wall. It was felt that Xuan had a need to know this information, even though the significance of the visit was not yet altogether clear.

The three newcomers were bedded down for the night in the VIP section of the RD headquarters, under heavy security. When he was informed of this, Xuan felt a vague uneasiness although he could not have articulated a reason why exactly.

At a gentlemanly hour, Cleve Howard slipped into the new men's quarters, having dispatched all nonsecurity personnel out for a morning of needful exercise. "Gentlemen, I have heard a great deal about you and your abilities. You could not have been available at a more opportune time. It seems that we have a suspected VCI in our very midst despite our constant vigilance. We would be delighted to have you demonstrate the betrayal without the betrayer being the wiser. We would like to deal with him in our own way and time."

That was agreeable to the visitors. Heretofore, they had been plying their psy-ops trade in the distinctly unpleasant environs of the Delta, and were glad to be in Hue' where it was cooler and to be among a better class of people with whom they would work. Dieter Lutz, the polygraphist, was new to Howard. "You must be Lutz," Cleve said and took the man's hand in a comradely grip.

"The one and only," smiled the German-American, who still carried a detectable accent.

"Welcome home, Tandrosz, and you too, Jean-Luc. How nice to have you back in the Imperial Province," Howard said with a broad welcoming smile. He had thought he would never see that sadistic criminal, DuParrier, again and groaned inwardly, very inwardly. He always felt, when he came into the presence of the hawkfaced Tandrosz Szabo with his nefarious reputation, that he should be wearing a garland of garlic and be holding a large crucifix in front of him. His smile radiated warmth on them both.

"Glad for the opportunity. It will take us a day to set up, preferably not here in the MACV compound, of course; then, we can begin our investigations for you." Tandrosz said benignly. DuParrier smiled at some private source of amusement.

"Anything we can do to facilitate matters, let us know. We will be more than glad to help," said Howard officiously. He was glad for small favors, at least the coven would be ensconced away from his bailiwick. He always felt as if he had to scrub his hands whenever he ran into DuParrier.

"We have some field work, I understand. Some recalcitrant individuals detained by the PRUs, I believe you told me. Should we begin our work with them, or do you want to do the vetting on your own people first?" asked Szabo.

"The vetting, if you please," replied Howard. "The urgency to take care of suspicions is more pressing. The others aren't going anywhere."

"It might help loosen them up if you made an announcement that every one, but everyone, on the staff is going to be examined. That includes the guards, the maids, the gardeners, and any hangers-on. Let them know the polygraph is infallible, it will ferret out their innermost deceits," said Dieter Lutz with his usual enthusiasm for his craft, half believing his own propaganda. Szabo and DuParrier smiled their enigmatic smiles. "It never hurts to let them sweat a little, we've found," Lutz added.

That afternoon, Mr. Howard assembled the entire staff of the Revolutionary Development Center; menial help, cadres, and all. "I have an announcement, ladies and gentlemen," he indicated, coming directly to the point of their having been brought together. He gave them Lutz's message, and canceled all leaves and off-duty privileges which brought groans of minor disapproval from the marine guards and drivers, but only inexpressionate faces from the Vietnamese.

Howard's secretary called Xuan into the RD office at 1630 and gave him a printed agenda of the scheduled appointments. Every person in the headquarters, even Agent Howard himself, had a scheduled time neatly typed in. Xuan was not on tap for two days. The process appeared to be a most routine one, like a yearly spring inventory. "Nothing to be alarmed about," the secretary reassured him. He must have betrayed a concern on his face. He was embarrassed at his failure to maintain perfect outward control as he had been taught at his home in the Giac Mu Pagoda.

The knowledge that a lie detecting machine was to be used, gave Xuan a sense of an evil portent, a foreign evil. He could not shake the conscious idea that his clandestine activities in opposition to the PRU would be a target of discovery even in the depths of his mind where he hid the memory protectively. He, nevertheless, had supreme confidence that Sidhartha Guatama, whose guiding light reposed in the great statues of the Beneficent Buddha he so revered, would protect him and insulate his mind against the intervention of the foreign device. He drew strength from his Buddhist Thien, the philosophy that gave a dedicated man the power to master himself. Xuan found an unused storage room in a seldom frequented corridor and locked himself in. He took no food or drink, no vessel to hold his evacuations, no pillow for his head or padding for sleep into the room for his seclusion. He would not need any of those things. In the next forty-eight hours, Nguyen Tran Xuan would gain and maintain such control over his material body that he would not require sustenance, would not make eliminations, and then he would gain complete serene control over his mind.

At the thirty-sixth hour, Xuan was burdened by the fullness of his bladder, by the dryness of his tongue, and by the gnawing pain in his stomach. He concentrated on the Thirty-six books. He recited the chants in Chinese, then as an exercise, repeated them, all of them, in Vietnamese. He would have done so in French, but by the thirty-ninth hour he had conquered the flesh. The last element of the trance induced by his transcendental meditation was to overcome the core phenomena; most bonzes took many years to achieve this level of mastery. He willed himself to go deeper into his communion with the Buddha until finally all was light. He sat in the lotus position with unseeing eyes; his blood pressure declining; his pulse rate slowing; and his breathing becoming scarcely perceptible. He was in full control. Sovereignty over self was so complete no outside forces could penetrate. Torture could not affect his body; the foreign devils could not touch his mind. His secret was safe.

CHAPTER 14

Our hatred knows no bounds, and the war shall be to the death.
Simon Bolívar

I'm tellin' you, that kid is not up to it, Terry," said Mark Whitehead, referring to Anders Bergstrom, the new man. They were driving back from the Task Force 116 docks to their apartment two days after their successful eradication of the Viet Cong encampment. "He's too soft, too young, and too inexperienced. How old would you guess he is? Eighteen? Less?"

"I'm not sure how old he is, Mark. He's big and tough; but I'll grant you, he's young. I suspect Lane told a little white lie about how much combat the boy has seen. But I don't exactly see what he did that was so wrong," Chief Brannigan said.

"He didn't do anything. That's it. And he hasn't got a clue. Take that little VC murderer back as a POW, gimme a break. That kid hasn't got the nerves for it. He makes me nervous. I don't trust him to watch my back, not by a long-shot."

"He's only been here three days. Give him a chance. Let's get him on a couple of other river runs and see if we can tone him up. He's got a lot to learn, maybe even some growing up to do; let's see if he can do it."

"Two trips. No more. Deal?" asked Mark.

"Okay. If he can't cut it then, I'll give Lane a call, and get him back to spookland," agreed Terry.

At the apartment, Anders was aware of a coolness from Mark. Terry and the others seemed okay. He did not say anything—that would have made those men think that he was sensitive guy. He kept mostly to himself until Terry got done planning missions with the other team members, then came to over to where Anders was sitting by himself.

"Anything the matter, Anders?"

"Nope."

"Okay, come over to the table so we can get our next trip into this water wonderland all set up. Look at the funny papers with me."

Anders joined Terry and Mark at the table where a military map of the region just south of Can Tho was spread. There was a pile of aerial photos and a small stack of reports on the table's edge. Terry said, "Listen up. Tomorrow we are going to head into Vinh Tuong country. The office has beaucoup (pronounced 'boo coo,' by the American SEAL) reports of infiltrators coming up from the U Minh forest, hitting the GVN posts, and getting back into the jungle along the tributaries with all the help they could ever need from the people. We are going to go down there and rattle our sabers a little, show them the Americans aren't going to sit on their dimes while Charlie does his thing all over the place."

"Just what are we going to do, Jefe?" asked Mark. He liked things the short and simple way. "Tell me the plan; show me the comics; and let's get to bed. Your mornings start too early for a night person like me."

"I just wanted you to know that this was a crucial mission in the cause of liberty, justice, and the American way. But if you want it just operational without the greater meaning . . ." He had a wry smile.

"Yeah, 'just operational,'" said Mark

Anders smiled at the two friends' banter. He wondered how long it would take before they really accepted him. For now, he listened while Terry laid out a detailed plan for an ambush operation. It was based on four consecutive nightly sightings of a small flotilla of boats passing a point alongside a marshy tributary tucked down in high elephant grass where a unit of LLDBs led by an American green beret had been maintaining an observation post. All three SOGs in the Apartment Army were encouraged by the presence of the American's input in the report. Not prejudice, really, just good to know that one of your own guys was giving you the straight skinny.

0200 again. This time Anders was sound asleep, and was disoriented and humiliated when Mark roughly shook him out of his deep slumber. Mark was fully dressed and ready to go. He did not look exactly pleased at Anders' state of readiness. While Anders hurried into his clothing, Mark said to Terry in a quiet offside, "Second trip, and already this kid's sleeping in. Any reason he can't get up with the rest of us?"

"Get off his case for a minute," Terry whispered, afraid Anders would hear. If something needed to be said, he was the man to say it. He did not want the boy to start out a mission insecure; that would not help.

Mark headed for the truck. Anders was ready in three minutes. He looked clear-eyed and hot to trot. Terry liked the kid's eagerness. He wished Mark could cut him some slack, but he trusted Mark's judgment and would watch Anders very carefully today. He did not want a screw-up out there with him either. This was not Sunday school, he did not have to remind himself.

The PBR could only take the three men as far as Nang Trun where they were picked up by two armed jeeps provided for the rest of the trip by the Ninth Infantry's Armored Division. The road was dusty and riding in the second jeep was made miserable by the dust pluming from behind the speeding forward vehicle. Anders and a driver, Corporal Lansing, could scarcely talk—opening their mouths allowed the dust to coat their throats. They moved at top speed over the pot-holed road to limit the potential of an ambush. Anders had no idea how the drivers knew where to go, let alone how to get there. He relaxed as best he could with his face turned away for the front until the disorientation of that view of things began to make him nauseated.

Anders heaved a great sigh of relief when the two jeeps finally stopped, allowing the dust to settle. He spat dust and rubbed it away from his eyes as best he could. It was heaven to get out. They were parked on the bank of a small canal in the middle of nowhere in an opaque ebony-black night. "This is the end of the joyride, compliments of the Ninth Infantry, sailor," said Corporal Lansing. "Back to the Brown-Water War you go."

For Anders, the Brown-Water War would be a blessed relief after that ride. He gratefully washed his begrimed face in the muddy canal before entering the LSSC that had been docked at the river bank earlier that night by four of their apartment mates. The four extra men now provided temporary security, wished the three actives good hunting, and drove back to Can Tho with the jeeps.

Terry briefly consulted his map with a penlight, extinguished it, and told Mark to start the Ford 427 engines of the LSSC. It started with a low rumble, catching on the first ignition, "Will miracles never cease?" commented Mark.

The armaments of the Light SEAL Support Craft were a comfort— two .50 caliber medium machine guns, a direct fire 60 mm mortar, and a mini-gun designed to fire up to 3000 rounds a minute. Some SEALs called this weapon the dragon gun because of the fire it seemed to exhale when on full automatic firing mode.

"The motor made a lot of racket," observed Anders to himself. That did not seem too good, but who was he to question the planners? The shallow draft boat fairly flew along the water under the thrust of the powerful engines, and the men made excellent time. They hugged first one bank then the other to confuse the cong, but Anders thought it was more inclined to disorient him than them. "This is it," said Terry after another quick perusal of his map and reduced the speed by half and the noise by three-quarters. "Maybe another klick before we go backpacking."

He cut the big engines entirely and the three men oared their way another 200 meters before beaching the craft on a sand bar near the east bank. "How deep do you think it is here?" Terry asked Mark as they sat in the darkness on the tiny sand island.

"About four feet, I'd guess. Won't know until we try."

"Anders, how 'bout you walking over toward the bank while we get the gear out?" requested Terry. "I'd like to know how deep it is before we carry our shooting irons. Wouldn't do to drop them in the drink."

"They'd likely catch the diabolical dribble-drabble or tsetse-itis from the filthy stuff," joked Mark.

"Sure," said Anders and slipped quietly into the fairly brisk flow of the brown water. The mud on the edges of the sandbar sucked his feet up to his knees, and he had to work hard to move forward. He got onto firmer ground and walked across without difficulty but found the water to be more like five feet than four feet deep. He returned and reported. The three men made two trips each to cart all of their military gear from the LSSC to the bank.

"We pack it all. We need all the artillery and ammo we can get for the ambush. It's going to be a long hot day, I reckon, so take a couple of condoms for water, don't forget your C-rats, the halogen tabs, and a P-38 . We ready?" Terry instructed.

Anders and Mark indicated they were set, and the three men trudged out. They stopped once after 50 meters and again after 150 to check the map. "I think we're going right, but it is so dark, I can't be sure, Terry said.

"That's real encouraging, fearless leader. I like the thoughts of wandering around lost in tiger country quite a lot, don't you Anders? Isn't that your idea of a good time?" asked Mark. His voice was calm and in good humor, just the traditional gripe and banter of the grunt.

"I haven't been able to see anything since we got off the LSSC," said Anders. "So why be different now. We could have been lost the whole night for all I know."

"Enough crap, you guys, lets hit it again," ordered the LPO.

Each man was carrying well over a hundred pounds of gear which made the prospect of 'hitting it' uninviting, but they did as they were told. Anders was sweating heavily, but was feeling okay, not nearly as apprehensive for some reason as he had the first night.

Terry nearly stepped over a five foot embankment and into the main tributary feeding myriads of little swampy canals like the one they had boated on when he came to it in the dark. "Oops," he said. "We're here."

"Where's here?"

"On the main channel. The Charlies come up here and perform malicious mischief every night according to our Special Forces guy. They figure they own this area and can't even imagine anyone messin' with 'em so far down into their own territory. They can get to a mangrove swamp and one of their camps in an hour or so, according to the intel. There's supposed by a big, sharp curve somewhere along here. That's the ambush site."

"Any idea which way?"

"Anybody's guess. Anders, you go left; and Mark, you go right for no more than 100 meters, then come back here. We'll see if we can find that very helpful curve."

"I guess even a blind hog can find an acorn; but it's so dark, even with the starlight scopes, I don't think we are going to be able to find a thing," said Mark.

"Takeoff. Here's your scopes." He handed each man one of the overrated aids to night vision. Anders turned to go. "Hey, I forgot, Anders; take off your shoes and go barefoot. Understand why?"

"Yeah, I guess so. It'll look like native tracks. Except my feet are size thirteen. Ever see a Vietnamese with a size thirteen?"

"They'll just think there's giants stalking the moors; take off," Terry had to chuckle.

Anders did as he was instructed, took off his black tennis shoes and started down stream. Mark was on his way upstream. The elephant grass was stunted and thick, probably due to being under water so much of the time. Nowhere in the Mekong Delta is a patch of ground more than ten feet above sea level, and floods ebb in at intervals submerging vast areas for a time then flow back to the sea leaving alluvial silt deposits to alter the terrain until the next cycle. The foot-high grass blades cut little nicks in his ankles and into the sides of his feet, making him sore, but the mud was soothing. Anders wondered what he must look like, caked with the stinking mud created by the dust from the road and his own sweat, and now an inch of gooey muck reaching almost to his ankles. There was a musty, fetid odor all about.

When he had walked what he estimated to be 100 meters and found no change in the fairly straight channel, he turned and retraced his steps. Mark had done the same thing in the other direction. Terry told them to try again, this time to go 200 meters.

At 200 meters, perhaps a little more, the channel made an abrupt turn toward the north, almost ninety degrees. Anders had found the site. He was glad he could be the one to make this contribution, albeit a small one. He trotted back to where Terry was sitting.

"It's my way," he said. "A little more than 200 meters, I'd guess."

Terry checked the luminous dial of his watch—0400. It would be light soon. They would have to get a move on if they were going to get set up before first light. He was impatient for Mark to return. Finally the other SEAL padded into the rendezvous point panting and sweating.

"Any luck?" he asked.

"Yeah, Anders found the spot. Let's saddle up and shag. It's about 200 meters his way," said Terry already putting his gear back on.

"Oh, goodie, another mud hike with a pack. Better check for leeches pretty soon, Anders. I found one by feel on my back, probably have more that I can't tell about yet," said Mark.

That cheered Anders up. The very thought of some primeval creature sucking his blood, made him feel crawly. "I don't feel anything, pain or anything," he said.

"They don't hurt. Tricky little vampires. Suck you pale before you know what's happening," Mark told him.

Anders was really feeling uncomfortable now. He became aware of a thousand little skin sensations and in his mind's eye saw the blood-gorged slugs from hell beginning to cover him. He blinked twice to rid himself of the apparition, quickly put on his gear, and forced himself to move along through the sticky slime underfoot as fast as his legs would carry him. His size thirteen bare foot prints were etched three inches into the mud. He had to smile when he thought of a 120 pound, four foot eight VC seeing those prints and estimating what the 400 pound, seven foot tall monster that made them looked like. He paid no attention to the nicking shards of grass flicking little sores on his lower extremities.

At the bend in the waterway, Terry reconnoitered, found a place with some cover, and whispered to his companions, "Check this out. Okay with you?"

Both Anders and Mark thought it was as good as any. Since this was likely to be a place from which they would have to fight, it was prudently democratic to have a vote, and was satisfying that they were unanimous in the choice. The first ethereal light of predawn, diffused by the heavy moisture in the air, was beginning to appear. They had to hurry to get dug in and camouflaged before someone came by and saw or heard them.

"Why don't you boogie over to the opposite side, Anders; so, we can get them in a crossfire?"

"Okay."

Anders did as he was told but was uncomfortable with being on the opposite side of the river, with being separated from the two combat experts—with being alone.

Terry and Mark dug their holes about 20 meters apart, so they would not be clustered if the enemy threw grenades or fired ship's mortars at them; and so, they could create their own narrow oblique crossing field of fire. It was fast digging by the bank of the waterway. The mud was soft and gave way easily, but the edges of their foxholes tended to sag as the holes got deeper which was frustrating. Terry crossed over the river quickly and checked Anders' hole. "Deeper," he said. "About two feet deeper."

"Didn't that sound like boot camp?" Anders thought.

"You are so big, you will need more room. You will love every inch you dig now when a firefight starts. Nothing better than being able to get your head down."

That was inescapable logic. Anders dug three feet deeper. If a little was good, a lot was better. He could sit or kneel on the bottom of his hole and have his entire head below the top. That should be enough. It was getting lighter, definitely now.

The payoff for the heavy lugging came now. Mark set up the M-60 machine gun, and Terry put the M-79 grenade launcher in place. Anders sat hunched in his foxhole with an M-16, his own shotgun, and a small mountain of hand grenades, CS tear gas, and smoke grenades. The three Americans were ready and quiet as dawn came rapidly up over the hill-free marsh. The only noise was the racket of a million buzzing insects. Flies covered every square inch of skin not occupied by a mosquito. The mosquitoes were the size of dragon flies. It was a real strain not to start slapping himself and to run screaming like a banshee into the water, but Anders thought better of that idea and endured.

When it was light enough, he discovered the leeches. He felt spooked. There was eight or ten of them he could see, and they were so engorged that they were beginning to fall off of their own accord.

Mark and Terry had told him that nothing he had learned in training (like putting salt or kerosene on them, or setting a match to them, or covering them with paper or plastic) really worked to get them off; so, he might as well be patient. The creepy things made him shudder and cringe anyway.

Anders heard a distant sound, or thought he did. He strained his ears. Then he was sure he heard it. It was a voice. Then he could hear the definite cough and rattle of a tiny outboard motor coming nearer to his position from the direction of the distant mangrove swamps. Unless this was someone delivering the mail, he knew he was about to encounter the enemy.

A rubber dingy, a US rubber dingy, with a US made Mercury trolling motor rounded the bend in the river. Seated in the boat were four men, all dressed in black pajamas and conical straw hats. They looked to him like peasants going about their business; so, Anders held his fire.

From the opposite bank the M-79 coughed out a grenade that landed two meters behind the dingy. As if in slow motion, the four men in black turned to look at the explosion; then, galvanized into lifesaving action, propelled themselves into the murky river just as the second grenade hit their craft dead center on outboard motor. The dingy blew into pieces the size of salad plates; the motor was vaporized. A head, an arm, and a disconnected torso erupted up into the geyser of dingy rubber, river mud, and patches of black cloth. Miraculously two men scrambled, weapons in hand, toward Anders' side of the river. The first man whirled about as soon as he had footing and scattered lines of 7.62 mm bullets erratically along the mud flats on the far bank in search of his tormentors. Anders raised up and fired one true shot that passed through the Viet Cong's chest to the left and just below the second rib. The communist soldier died with a surprised look on his face and pitched forward into the ooze at the water's edge.

The second enemy soldier crouched in the shallow water and turned his automatic weapon in Anders' direction, orienting protectively toward the sound of Anders' M-16. Anders kept his head well below the ground-level line of his hole, cringing as lethal missiles whizzed and whined over its opening. The cong whirled and fired at Terry and Mark, who similarly ducked into their holes The Vietnamese must have presumed that he had killed his first adversary; because after the first fusillade and no response, he ignored Anders' position. Still crouched in the water, he pulled the pin from a grenade and tossed it at Mark's location, missing by about four feet, but sending a drenching cascade of water into Mark's hole and soaking him. The second grenade explosion landed a meter and a half above the opening of Mark's hole, blowing a plume of swamp-smelling mud on the dripping man. "Why me?" muttered Mark to himself. "Why doesn't he spread the wealth?"

Anders peeked over the edge of his hole in time to see the lone enemy getting set to pull the pin on a third grenade. He was as agile and quick as a professional baseball player, and Anders and Mark were certain it would be, three strikes and you are out! When the next grenade was thrown now that he had had an unopposed opportunity to test the range and trajectory. Terry peeped out and received a short burst of Kalashnikov assault rifle fire in his direction for his effort. Anders could see the thumb about to snap the grenade pin free. He felt momentarily paralyzed. If he raised up to get a shot, he would expose himself. He was afraid that being shot would hurt terribly. If he stayed down, the communist soldier would surely kill Mark, and probably pick off the other American at his leisure, then turn on him. The man in the black pajamas and conical hat seemed nine feet tall and superhuman to Anders.

Anders stood up like a stalk of corn and, in the slow motion rendering of the moment when a man faces death, watched the Vietnamese turn and look in his direction raising his AK-47 with one hand as he did. Anders fired first, a single well-aimed shot fired as a hunter would coolly shoot a charging lion. The bullet struck the Cong in the biceps of his left arm which did not impede the round in the slightest. It passed through the intercostal muscles of the left sixth and seventh ribs and transected the ascending aorta before imbedding itself in the rock solid vertebral body. In fast motion, the body of the Viet Cong man involuted on itself, and he folded forward into the water and disappeared from sight. It is a Hollywood fantasy that victims of gunshots are blown backward or to the side by the blast. The sudden collapse of muscle function in death favors the extensors, no matter from what direction the bullet impacts nor the caliber of the missile; the flexors give way first, and the body pitches forward consistently.

Like the groundhog, 'Punxatawny Phil,' Terry popped his head up to see what the weather was like, why it had suddenly gotten so quiet. Mark, too, looked over the edge of his foxhole like some sort of chocolate statue. The two SEALS saw Anders standing chest and shoulders out of his hole on the opposite bank; a very reassuring sight.

The dead Viet Cong, the first man out of the water, lay where he had fallen. There was so sign of the second man. Anders drew his finger across his throat as a message. Mark threw his right arm in the air, thumb up. He was glad to be alive and credited Anders. Terry reached up and pulled on his ear, a recommendation for further action on Anders' part.

No other boats were in sight. The only noise was the infernal burring of the insects. Anders took up his M-16, lighter by two bullets, and leaped out of his hole. He dashed to the dead man lying in the mud in the prone position, grabbed him by his long straight black hair, and indelicately whacked off both ears with his Bowie knife. He stuffed the trophies in his belt pouch (He was learning) and kicked around in the water where the second man had gone down. The body was lying in three feet of eddying water. Anders repeated his ghoulish task, including a stab wound in each side of the chest to deflate the lungs, and dropped the man back into his watery grave. He started back for his hole.

He caught the motion of Terry's arm waving at him. Terry was pointing back at the man still lying on the mud. It dawned on him what the senior man meant, and was embarrassed that it had not occurred to him automatically in the situation. He returned to the corpse, caught it by the pajama top cloth collar and dragged the body up and over the channel bank and dumped it in a shallow furrow out of sight. He returned to his hole and to the misery of waiting with the hordes of bugs. At least the leeches seemed to have had their fill, and had dropped off. Other than the deep tracks in the mud of the stream bank, there was no sign that a skirmish had taken place at the river bend. Anders ruminated over the fact that he had just taken a man's life; two men's lives. He felt vaguely ill and upset over it. He felt immoral even though he knew it was in the line of duty. It seemed wrong, nonetheless, however irrational the thought was; and he felt guilty.

About thirty-minutes later, with the sun presenting itself over the horizon, the unmistakable sound of a large boat came from the opposite direction from which the first boat had come. Anders figured that this one was returning to its berth somewhere in the tangle of the mangrove forest after a night's villainy. The throaty rumble of the engine bespoke a large vessel, and Anders made himself small in his safe little hole and waited, hardly daring to breath hard for fear he would be detected.

The boat had a large throbbing engine. It looked like a river tug boat bristling with armament. There were .30 and .50 caliber machine guns, ship's mortars, and stationary grenade launchers affixed to the gunwales. A dozen alert LAF soldiers lined the catwalks and the fore and aft decks with unslung AK-47s cradled in their arms ready for battle until they could once again slip into the oblivion of their uncontested swamp territory. Anders saw that much in the tiny peep out of his hole that he permitted himself. He was not about to stick anything of his up again, and his only other hope was that the two SEALS lurking on the opposite bank would follow his example and leave this target alone.

In what struck Anders as a calculated act of sheer contrariness, Terry fired two grenades from the M-79 in rapid succession as soon as the armed boat was directly in front of his position. The after deck erupted in flames and sent showers of red-hot metal shards in all directions. The forward progress of the boat was unaltered; its engines and hull were undamaged. The screams of wounded and dying men were immediately joined by the heavy chatter of Mark's M-60. Men began to fall forward onto the narrow deck and into the water like so many tenpins. Other men had the presence of mind to try and open fire at their as yet unseen enemy somewhere on or along the bank. The return fire was erratic and well wide of the mark.

Terry tossed two hand grenades and missed, only churning up twin plumes of river water. He opened fire with his M-16 on full automatic and heard the satisfying chatter of the bullets puncturing the thin bulkhead of the boat and saw two men fall in the line of his fire. The still functional boat guns, in some perversely inappropriate logic, centered all of their malevolent attention on Anders, and turned to fire a murderous barrage from mixed weaponry in his direction in a rapidly shrinking target circle. The ammunition made splotting sounds in the mud around the top of his hole causing little splatters of mud to coat his clothing.

When the firing seemed to diminish, Anders took a nanosecond squirrel-like peek out of his hole. What he saw made him duck his head in terror. Half a dozen determined and heavily armed black-pajamed men were leaping over the side of the boat and into the water on his side. "Why my side?" Anders thought desperately.

Their exit from the starboard side of the craft drew fire from Terry and Mark with the result that one man slipped under the surface of the brown river and did not join his companions who were able to get to the relative safety of Anders' side of the river. Two men went above, and three went below the hole where Fort Bergstrom was located. The boat was now dead in the water and partially blocked the view of Terry and Mark for Anders' hole and of the enemy soldiers.

The Viet Cong took advantage of the relative lull, and dug themselves into shallow ditches that served primarily to let them lie low enough that they were no longer such easy targets. There seemed to be only the five survivors, but they all appeared to be intact and armed; and they were all in close proximity to Anders.

Occasionally a shot would be fired, but no one had a target, and soon the battlefield became quiet—the Vietnamese version of a Mexican standoff. In the cramped dirt box with the insects tormenting him and the sun roasting him as effectively as if he were in a metal Dutch oven, Anders had time to think. That was the worst thing that could have happened to him at that point. The more he thought, the less he was able to control his thoughts. The longer the standoff lasted, the more fearful the young man became until he could not keep his terrors at bay with even the most strenuous of mental efforts.

Anders bobbed his head up for a frightened look, like a rabbit looking out of his burrow when he hears the noise of a predator. He saw black forms lying in low furrows of mud. He was sure he could see them crawling inexorably toward him. He panicked. In his haste to get down into a cowering position of momentary safety in his hole, Anders' foot slipped out from under him on the slippery mud and he fell face forward into the wall of his hole. His forehead grazed a severed root that opened a three inch long jagged and fairly deep gash a little below the hairline. Anders sank into his hole in a misery of hurt and an agony of real and imagined fears. Blood poured over his eyes obscuring his vision

The Swedish boy huddled for what seemed like a long time; then to the horror of both his realities and his imaginations, he could hear real voices, getting closer. They were speaking Vietnamese, murmuring like a hypnotic Lorelei to Anders' overcharged psyche. Despite all his training; despite every pragmatic impulse to the contrary; despite the demands of his conscious mind, the Scandinavian boy became nearly catatonic. He scrunched down as far as he could and waited for death. He was powerless, held by an unyielding and overpowering but internal force. He started to whimper softly.

Anders heard, or thought he could hear, the slush, slush, slush of men crawling toward his burrow. He drove the thought out of his mind. A short volley of M-16 fire from the opposite bank was followed by an AK-47 response from the grim specters on Anders' side; then it was quiet again., except for the squirming slush, shush, slush noises.

Anders' mind took a trip away from that hellish place. He might have been unconscious; certainly, he had nothing but the dimmest awareness of his surroundings. That Death in black clothes was creeping up on him no longer mattered. The bemused teenager had a faraway look in his eyes, unbuttoned his fly, extracted his limp penis; and he began to masturbate absentmindedly. The momentary and infantile sensual pleasure served to remove him and to insulate him even further from the grimness of reality and from any capacity to defend himself against real and imminent danger. He had given up.

Death's head popped over the edge of the embankment of Anders' hole and took a very quick look inside. Anders was totally unaware now, absorbed as he was in the transporting value of his neurotic self-indulgence. The Viet Cong could hardly believe what he had seen. Since no one fired at him, he at first presumed the round-eye was dead. When he saw his enemy, the man he had tortured himself with fear over, lying in the fetal position in a mud hole playing with himself, it confused him at first. He took another quick peek to confirm the impression of his first glance. Indeed, his enemy was lying in the filthy hollow doing the one man sex play. This time the Viet Cong saw the bleeding gash on Anders' forehead and decided that the man had been shot in the head and was no longer in possession of his mental faculties. He smiled at the irony of the situation, then chuckled at the absurdity of it. He was laughing out loud when he kneeled on the edge of the hole, pointed his Kalashnikov rifle, took aim, and died from a series of M-16 rounds coming from across the river that ran from his xyphosternum to the middle of his forehead.

The cong dropped his weapon, barrel down, into the pit where Anders lay incapacitated by his demons. The sharp edge of the sight hit the edge of his exposed ankle causing a sudden jolt of acute and surprising pain. This was followed by the crunching impact of the Viet Cong soldier's body rolling into the trench directly and suffocatingly on top of him. Blood gouted out of one of the jagged holes in the man's neck and coated Anders face and ran thickly into his slack-jawed mouth. The pain, the crush of the body, and especially the nauseating salty iron taste of the jellied blood jarred the inexperienced and fear-crazed Scandinavian back to something near full possession of his senses.

Anders clawed desperately for his knife and came up with his

Randall combat stiletto from his clutch belt. He had no way of knowing that the man was dead. A primordial self-protective impulse drove him to stab the body several times in vicious succession. Anders grunted in disgust and heaved the thin man's body off his own. There was not enough room in that hole for two bodies, and the force of Anders lifting the dead man, elevated the inert body well above the ground line. The movement drew fire from both M-16s and AK-47s. Anders' head was now clear. He held his rifle like a soldier now. He would have to fight to live. His mind sought a plan now that it was free of its deadening torpor.

Anders heard a shuffling and sloshing of the mud somewhere near his hole. He could not wait any longer. He knew that he had wasted precious time. He pulled the pins from two grenades, counted quickly to two, then threw them in opposite directions out of his hole. The two explosions were deafening and raised a mushroom of mud that rained down on him. A rubber sandal plopped into the hole followed by a severed foot.

Anders leaped fully to his feet and began firing blindly in a rapid spinning 360° arc until he could make out targets and lowered his aim. He saw men raise their weapons and die. He saw a surreal landscape of dismembered bodies from his grenades, and the threat of pain and death from two moving black forms as he whirled about taking in the kaleidoscope of vision. He briefly concentrated on the one moving form and peppered it with M-16 bullets. He did not stop to see his enemy fall, but whirled in the direction of his last assailant. The muzzle of the Kalashnikov had been pointing directly at him and in his mind's eye Anders could actually see the trigger being squeezed. The image changed suddenly when a hail of bullets caused the black-pajamed body to twitch and convulse in a death dance. The enemy crumpled forward like a rag doll whose stuffing had been removed suddenly by a giant vacuum.

"The cav is on its way," whooped Mark. He and Terry were in the middle of the river treading water and firing their M-16s like crazed water acrobats. Anders suddenly became conscious of his ridiculous position. He quickly reinserted himself and flipped closed his fly. He turned away from the two floundering SEALS and buttoned himself praying fervently that the other two men had not seen him. He did not care whether there were more enemies around him waiting to kill him. He was determined that if he had to die, it would not be with his silly penis hanging out for all to see.

Nothing stirred from the Viet Congs' positions if one could dignify those hastily scrabbled furrows in the mud with the term. There were five dead men; at least five. Where the two grenades had exploded, there were an assortment of body parts that did not readily conform to a finished puzzle.

When the two SEALS got to him, Terry said, "Well, I think we've had enough of Delta life for one day. Let's clean up and get out of here, *tout de suite;* what do you guys say?"

"Okay with me, boss," said Mark who was busy searching for weapons to keep them from falling back into VC hands.

"You don't have to coax me, neither," said Anders who was beginning to tremble involuntarily now that the adrenaline charge was receding. He clasped the stock of his M-16 until he was white-knuckled to avoid his fellow irregulars seeing his childish display of nerves and fear.

"Hey, man, you're shot up bad. That's a pretty grungy graze on your forehead. You okay?" Terry inquired of Anders having begun to focus in on the matters of next importance now that the frenzy of the firefight excitement was subsiding, and he could think in an orderly fashion again.

"Geez, what a *mensch*!" exclaimed Mark. "Shot in the head, comes to, throws off the body of his attacker, jumps up and mows down the whole company of Viet Cong! You're a genuine 24 karat hero, buddy. Shake on it!" 'Hero' was Mark's greatest compliment.

Anders laughed brittlely, embarrassed. The humiliating truth of his condition in the foxhole welled up in his mind, and he felt like a complete phony. He had a boyish desire to confess it all, to have a cleansing catharsis. Mark had taken three giant steps to stand directly in front of Anders. He grabbed the teenagers hand and shook it almost violently.

"Let me look at that bullet track," he said solicitously.

"I don't think it's too bad," Anders said. That was about as much as he was going to say about his adventures in the hole, he guessed. It would not do anybody any good to know the details. He said a silent prayer of thanks that the Lord had spared him the humiliation he had feared. He resolved to try and forget about it. Confession was for Catholics, he decided, and not for him, after a moment of sober thought about his fleeting idea of telling all.

Terry joined Mark in looking at Anders' forehead injury. The CPO took a wad of field dressing and poured some clean water from one of his condom water containers onto it. He gently washed off the gore, and gave a small grin of relief. "I think you're gonna live. Lucky they just shot you in the head. Could have been someplace serious."

The three men laughed harder than the bit of gallows humor was worth, but the inappropriate mirth had a healing affect they all needed. Back to the business at hand, the three efficiently stacked the enemy weapons in a pile; and, standing at a safe distance, threw grenades at the pile until the combat equipment was blown into useless bits of steel pipe, springs, and wood splinters. It required four throws. "No professional ball careers for us," Mark opined which again tickled their funny bones, and once more they laughed semi-hysterically.

They harvested the bounty ears and stabbed the dead cong in their lungs to let them sink under the muddy waters of the tributary watching the last bubbles floating to the surface and chuckling at the popping bubbles for some inexplicable reason.

Finally, they got their cognitive functions back together, collected their own equipment, and backtracked in the humidity and cauldron heat of the Delta afternoon toward their LSSC perched on the sand bar and on to civilization (the Can Tho variety at least). There was no further question of Ander's reliability on the combat team after his performance that day, except perhaps, in his own mind.

CHAPTER 15

You and your like are trying to make a war with the help of people who just aren't interested.

They don't want communism.

They want enough rice, I said. They don't want to be shot at. They want one day to be much the same as another. They don't want our white skins around telling them what they want.

If Indo-China goes . . .

I know the record. Siam goes. Malay goes. Indonesia goes. What does 'go' mean? If I believed in your God and another life, I'd bet my future harp against your golden crown that in five hundred years there may be no New York or London, but they'll be growing paddy in these fields, they'll be carrying their produce to market on long poles wearing their pointed hats.

. . . They'll be forced to believe what they are told, they won't be allowed to think for themselves.

Thought's a luxury. Do you think the peasant sits and thinks of God and Democracy when he gets inside his mud hut at night?
Graham Greene, The Quiet American

Dieter Lutz looked at the Vietnamese man Cleveland Howard had alerted him about. The man seemed strange, maybe high on something. He walked and talked fairly sensibly but slowly and deliberately. A peculiar one.

"Sit down, please, and relax," the CIA polygraphist directed.

Xuan took a seat as instructed and submitted to the application of the unfamiliar electrodes and pastes dispassionately knowing nothing could harm him. He recognized the sphygmomanometer cuff, and regarded it with indifference as well.

"Answer yes or no. Answer all questions. That clear?" bade Lutz.

"It is clear," came the hollow answer.

Dieter threw Xuan a critical look, now almost sure he was on something. It would probably invalidate the test, but Lutz decided to go along with it for a while at least.

"Okay, first question. Is your name Anh Tran Xuan?"

Xuan nodded his head, "Yes."

"You have to say it so I can hear."

"Yes." The inky scratches on the jerkily moving paper indicated no emotional response, no indication of a lie as the pen squirmed and wiggled under the influence of the parameters being monitored.

"Are you a policeman with the Thau Thien Provincial RD unit?"

"Yes." Smooth tracing.

"Are you a PRU cadre?"

"Yes."

"Do you use drugs?"

"No." No agitation in the recording.

"Are you under the influence of drugs or alcohol now?"

"No." Still smooth. Lutz raised one eyebrow briefly.

Lutz included a long string of unimportant questions to relax the subject and threw in an occasional test question to see if Xuan was going to lie on small issues which would give the lie detector technician an idea of his responses to the more critical ones. He asked if Xuan had masturbated, had had intercourse with women, or if he was a homosexual. To all of these Xuan had answered, "No," and to Lutz's surprise, the recording sheet had continued to indicate that he was being truthful.

"This is indeed a peculiar fellow," the CIA agent thought to himself.

"Are you part of the VCI?"

"Are you a traitor to your Provincial Reconnaissance Unit?"

"Have you ever given secrets to the Viet Cong?"

"Have you ever betrayed your unit or any of the men you work with?"

"Have you killed or caused to be killed any person in the government of Viet Nam?"

"Did you kill Deputy Inspector Y'Yool?"

"No, no, no, no, no, no," came the crisp answers. It still seemed to Lutz that he was dealing with a man who was not fully with him, that something was wrong with the man. He could not identify what that peculiarity was exactly, however.

"That will be all. You may go."

Xuan smiled a mystical smile and left. He knew the Westerners would never be able to match the *Thien* power of control over their minds that his people, at least the Buddhists, had. He knew without a doubt that he had dominated in the test; and the round-eye believed him completely. It was all quite easy, really.

Something big was shaping up. Terry was gone for most of a week in mid-November and would only say that everyone was going to be involved when it happened. Since there was nothing else to do for the lax week, Mark asked Anders if he wanted to look around the city with him.

"Not much to see, but anything is better than this dump," he said as he surveyed the untidy men's apartment in the sleazy building, on the rundown street, in the poor-class section of the third world country.

"Amazing how the river changes," said Anders as they crossed the Song Hau. The previously chocolate brown water was now translucent. In another month it would be crystal clear.

"Happens every year," Mark told him.

They were going to stop in town, then drive north to the Don Tam (United Hearts and Minds) camp built by the navy thirteen klicks from My Tho. The commissary was reputed to be the best in the Delta. The My Tho River, northernmost branch of the nine tentacles of the *Cuu Long Giang* (Mekong), was supposed to be worth looking at this time of year. Mark had friends at the marine barracks he had not seen for months; and besides, it was something to do.

The drive into the heart of town took them past the Can Tho Central Market spread out along Hai Ba Trung and Nam Ky Khoi Nghia streets displaying mangoes, bananas, pineapples, sugar cane, coconuts, mounds of rice, and a wretched smelling fruit the natives called durian that tasted good despite its awful odor. There were bins containing leaves of tobacco, soybeans, sesame seeds, melons, pumpkins, tangerines, corn, and potatoes. Other markets inside the complex had fish; some still alive in tanks, having been shipped directly from fresh fish farms in the northern delta; crustaceans; live ducks and chickens; wiener piglets, and ill-tempered ducks ready for dinner once the purchaser killed and dressed his or her guaranteed fresh meal. That was the only guarantee of freedom from spoilage in a tropical city where the only refrigerators were in the hands of the foreign occupying army and navy.

The waterways were beyond congestion; boats with up pointed prows having eyes painted on them to help to see their way, sampans, barges, log pirogues, boats of plaited bamboo, and dinghies were bumper-to-bumper. Fishermen lay in the bottom of their sampans taking in the sun. Girls in black, and wearing checkered neckerchiefs, balanced lazily over oars. Crowds of traders lined the sides of a scull ferry. It was possible, at points, to walk across the stalled marine traffic to greet friends or to make a purchases and to keep dry feet.

Despite a meager existence rife with delays and manifold inconveniences, the Delta people were complacent and polite. Harsh words were unusual, and fights almost unheard of in daily commerce. A war raged around and outside them, but they ignored it to pursue a life hallowed by two millennia during which little had changed in their way of doing things. Watching them always suggested that when this invader and the next and the next after that had come and gone, you would be able to look out on the river and see men and women in conical hats and black pajamas selling ducks and rice to one another as they had done in prehistory. Should a nuclear holocaust consume the industrialized world, few of these people would know and even fewer care. Their simple thatched houses would still be there, and the main concern of the day would be how to get their produce to market.

Can Tho was the largest, most modern, busiest, and in its business district, the cleanest city in the Delta. It was the only city in Cochinchina to be able to boast of having a university. Actually, the university was not yet formally established; and the buildings were still under construction, thanks to American help; but classes were underway, some even in the open. On that particular day, Mark took Anders to watch the end of a canoe race in which the university competed with canoes from several southern villages. The canoes were huge, 25 to 30 meters long, with as many as fifty rowers; brilliantly painted; and could only move with the permission of an accompanying gong. There was no way that one canoe could tell its own gong beat from any other, Anders was sure.

For lunch the two men went to Mark's favorite place to eat when he was not obliged to consume the styrofoam-like C Rations out in the field or inventing culinary masterpieces in the apartment. The Hoang Cung Hotel on Phan Dinh Phung Street had good food, was willing to accept the American and European construction crews in their grimy clothes, and made allowances for their lack of civilized manners and even accepted American military men. One could not be in a hurry. This was a Vietnamese restaurant; and the very concept of fast-food would not be understood, and if understood, rejected. The food and the talk were important. It was good for the digestion and for the health to savor the sounds and smells of the restaurant before one enjoyed the food. Two hours was a reasonable allotment of time for a civilized meal.

There was a large menu, too many choices for Anders; so, Mark suggested they share a combination platter of local delicacies. The platter included elephant ear fish, shrimp, turtle, cuttlefish, snake, and because it was a festival and race day, huge frogs. Mark washed his meal down with huge draughts of Indonesian Tiger Beer; Anders stuck with pineapple juice.

My Tho, on the left bank of the Tien Giang, or upper river, was disappointing, just another sleepy Delta village even though it had a population of seventy or eighty thousand and was the provincial capital. It was located seventy kilometers south of Saigon. There was a definite suggestion of a Chinese influence since the city was established in the late seventeenth century by Taiwanese refugees. The town and the region were justifiably famous in Viet Nam for lush green orchards of coconuts, mangoes, citrus fruits, bananas, and longans and for orchids. The Bao Dinh Channel was teeming with Vietnamese marine mercantile activity. Despite the temporary intrusion of the American military, the panorama of Vietnamese life daily unfolded in its traditional way.

In the outlying villages people paddled, for society and commerce, from house to house in little boats on the complex network of small waterways; here and there a husband plowed while his wife transplanted the rice plants. Fishermen with eyes fierce and red from exposure, cast nets into the river while their wives sat patiently by their small homes mending the secondary nets. At more than one house a drowsy woman cooled her small brown children with a bamboo fan. Gentle wind fluttered the golden heads of rice. Mushroom shaped hay stacks stood patiently in the fields. The sounds were those of a tranquil existence. Wooden bells called the water buffaloes back to the stables; and at times, Anders and Mark could hear the rustle of stork wings over the rice fields. Young girls with the color of their lips enhanced with areca and betel nut juice waved to the two young Americans as they passed.

Their traditional society, apart from the war that was not really any of their affair, was as placid as the landscape and the unchangeable tableaux presented to Anders and Mark. These people lived in a community where elders were respected, both the living and the dead. It was a shame to talk back to one's parents much less to disobey them. People hid ill feelings toward their fellowmen behind pacific faces to avoid troublesome speaking out, arguing, or contentions. They did not participate in body contact sports for the same reason.

The huge navy base did not really interest Anders, and the close proximity to officers soured the visit for Mark. He had allowed his enthusiasm for seeing a different area and his desire to check in with his old marine buddies, who were out on bivouac, to overshadow his good judgment, and to bring him back into contact with the brass hats he so studiously avoided most days.

The bulk of their day was spent on Phung Island, four kilometers from My Tho by ferry. The island was the sometimes home of Ong Dao Dua, the Coconut Prophet. He was a curious character who founded the Tinh Do Cu Si religion that flourished only on that island. The prophet and his followers practiced a synthesis of worship of Buddha, Jesus Christ, and his mother, the Virgin Mary. The charismatic prophet had gotten his title by meditating under a flag pole for three or four years eating nothing but coconuts. Much of the prophet's adult life, including the year of Anders' and Mark's visit, had been spent in South Vietnamese prisons for his antigovernment activities. He and his followers had the temerity to preach peace and to advocate peaceful means of reunifying the divided Viet Nams.

The followers were friendly, made only limited and polite requests for donations, and were happy to show the two off-duty soldiers around the open-air sanctuary where the prophet addressed his worshipful followers on those occasions when he was out of prison. The sanctuary was supported by columns on which were carved brightly colored circling and entwining dragons. There was a multitiered tower in the sanctuary with a huge metal globe as its roof that did not seem to serve any apparent purpose, but Anders and Mark found it interesting, nevertheless.

There was one distinct and salutary outcome for Anders in the otherwise sleepy day off from duty. He learned about Mark Whitehead; and the two young men grew to be friends. Anders became aware that he had missed having a friendship thus far in his seventeen years.

Before joining the navy, Mark had led a prosaic life—the All-American mid-western boy next door. He was twenty-two years old in late 1966, when Anders met him, and had lived the first eighteen of those years in the city of his birth, near Minneapolis. Mark's father was a pharmacist who chafed away his life working in the Rexall Drug Store owned by an old man who was singularly parsimonious with both money and approbation. Mark watched his father wither away in the community where he and his parents and his parents' parents had lived; and Mark determined, when he was still a child, that he would not live and turn gray in that somnambular town. From the inverse of his father's example, he decided to have a life of adventure; he determined to become a hero.

Mrs. Whitehead, Mark's domineering mother, taught school—K through 8—in the three room school house built for the city of Morrow's Lake, northern Minnesota, in 1916 when the population was 946. It still served the town adequately during Mark's school years from 1950 to 1958 when the population had grown to 1128.

Mrs. Morrow was one of three teachers, all women. The issue of appointing one of the teachers to be the principal was so loaded with emotion and controversy that it had been tabled ten years previously and never broached again; the three teachers did just fine without a titular leader. Each of them regarded themselves as the *de facto* nabob, and each maintained a semi-regal dignity about her place in the school and in the town. From his mother's unspoken example, Mark decided that Morrow's Lake was too ordinary a place for one such as he; and the lure of foreign places came to possess the boy.

Mark delivered the Minneapolis Star Tribune every day, had a job cleaning the tailings at the Morrow's Lake and Eddy Mountain Saw and Planing Mill when he was eleven. He worked the soda fountain in the Rexall from the time he was twelve until he quit high school at the Manitoba County Union High School after the eleventh grade in 1965 to enlist in the navy—the Viet Nam conflict was just beginning to be noticed by the American public. He was bored to death with existence in the mid-west including the distinct four seasons, the prim white clapboard churches, the plain vanilla homespun virtues of the populace, the fact that no one locked their house doors; and there had never been a burglary in the history of the village. There was not a single ethnic person with whom they could have a minority problem. Every person in the county was a white, Anglo-Saxon fourth generation or more Protestant of one or another of the seven denominations represented by the well kept chapels. Before he would sign the enlistment papers, the twenty-one year old demanded and received one concession: he would be assigned to San Diego, California.

His fellow recruits thought Mark a little crazy. He was the only boot who actually liked boot camp. He was the best of the best in everything he did, everything the platoon did. He studied naval history, naval tactics, gunnery, and passed his high-school equivalency test (GED) to be a high school graduate on his own time. He was offered OCS when his boot training was completed; but, to everyone's surprise, Mark declined the offer. It was not only that he disliked officers, regimentation, and military order so much as it was that he had found his place. He wanted to be a SEAL; so, he could realize his lifelong overt desire for adventure (and his covert urge for heroism).

Mark applied for the basic underwater demolition/SEAL (BUD/S) course immediately after basic. The first day in training, after filling out the forms, he was told to put on a bathing suit and to "follow me" by the most unfriendly man he had thus far met in the military, which was going some. The PO led him on the run, which was not unusual after the boot camp experience, across the Coronado beach to join thirty other men. It was a cold, drizzly January day, and the other men were attempting to stand in formation in the rough surf. The fifty degree ocean water was chest high. Mark thought the shock of entering that cold water would stop his heart. Shortly, the effect of the progressive hypothermia, made that initial shock seem like the best part of the exercise.

As the men stood on the unsure footing of the sand and braced themselves against the efforts of the unrelenting surf to sweep them out of alignment, they were subject to the carping criticisms of two officers, who kept dry on the beach, and four petty officers who occasionally got their feet wet.

"Fifty percent of you will drop out. That's a fact. It might as well be today, tadpoles. Save yourself a lot of grief. Give it up now, go back to the fleet; and no one will fault you for it," harangued the petty officer in charge of morale destruction.

The tadpoles were turning blue and numb from the cold. Through each man's mind passed his options: 1: kill the officer 2: kill the petty officers 3: huddle up against the other guys to share warmth or 10: quit. Items one and two, however tempting, would only lead to more grief; each tadpole recognized that from his brief exposure to the UCMJ in boot camp. Items four through ten meant ignominy; and for Mark Whitehead, certain failure in his lifelong goal to be a hero. That goal had crystallized into a specific— he intended to win the Congressional Medal of Honor, an award more experienced men referred to as "the Medal of Horror." The tadpoles instinctively chose option three and moved closer to each other to try and eke a little sustenance from their fellow sufferers. Once the officers and noncoms saw that the twin objects of the exercise, the test of mettle to weed out the quitters and the formation of embryonic unit solidarity, had been achieved, they ordered the men out of the water before anyone died of exposure.

Two men did not accompany the training unit to the stores building to pick up their gear for the course after that introductory trial. On the wall of the storehouse was tacked a sign that read: "Defeat is worse than death; you have to live with defeat." Mark figured that if he could stand this first test, he could endure the rest of what they were going to dish out.

Phase I of frogman training was basic hell, as opposed to Hell Week proper that was refined hell. Phase I was designed more to weed out the unfit than anything else. Physical training and conditioning was the title. Everyday, five days a week, Mark and his unit ran everywhere they went. More often than not they carried logs as they ran. The exercise of carrying around trees was not as mindless as Mark first thought. There were men of all sizes in the unit, and a way had to be found to permit the short ones and the very tall ones to help, because without them, the unit could not move its trees from one unnecessary place to the next inane location without the participation of every man. Unit integrity was the lesson, and it was learned in a thousand painful and memorable ways.

Phase I was a ritual of hardship, mental stress, and change. Every day started with running to breakfast and eating in the standing up stance and as fast as possible, doing calisthenics and PT as a unit, running, and swimming. They ran even though they were tired, nearly exhausted, and even though it was raining; or the tourists laughed at their antics. They swam though the water was chilly, and they were tired. They appeared at breakfast with shined boots every morning or they did more individual calisthenics and running, or the whole unit was punished for the laxness of the individual. The tadpoles began to enforce their own unit cooperation; they had to for survival. After a particularly grueling run or freezing swim, there would be another helmet liner or two left on the ground by a man who was sick of being called a tadpole or a banana (soft on the outside, soft on the inside) and being subjected to the physical and mental abuse. No more of an announcement was necessary than to leave the helmet liner on the exercise field. Mark gritted his teeth and kept his helmet and its liner.

He got smarter. It did not take a genius to know you cannot shine a pair of water soaked, salt stained boots. He got a second pair and kept one of his sets shined all of the time. He learned to soak the impossible pair in fresh water, let it dry out, and then to shine it. He bought stacks of clean white tee shirts; so, he would never have the misery of finding out too late that all of his shirts needed laundering; and to pay and pay for that awful breach.

Phase I ended with Hell Week, as if the preceding hell had not been enough. The purpose of the dawn to dark harassment and punishment was for more than the sadistic pleasure of the trainers, although it would take time and contemplation for Mark to come to an understanding of that. Each man was subjected to his limit of unfair criticism of his physical stature and prowess, his lack of ability, the cut of his jib. Slower, weaker men were left behind to run longer and harder. When they complained or appeared ready to die, they were assigned more. Once they were told that their experience could be likened to the motto of the French Foreign Legion—"March or

Die." All of the men were doused with cold water if they looked as if they might be drying out, pushed again into the mud if they looked as if their previous layer of dirt might be flaking off, and convinced by every act and order, large and small, from the officers and noncoms, that their lives did not belong to them. Each half day, they learned that they were expendable. Five more men dropped out.

But the remaining men learned to overcome. They learned not to quit. They were told over and over again that every second of suffering in training prepared them for the real test—survival in combat. Mark thought of it as preparation to be tough enough to get that blue ribbon he coveted; so, he endured.

After running and swimming, and crawling in the mud, Mark and the other men in his six man boat crew ran around carrying their 250 pound twelve foot long IBS (Inflatable Boat, Small). When they were tired from doing that, they had log PT—hoisting a short heavy telephone pole from shoulder to shoulder until they bled and became callused. When he was not doing a drill, Mark cleaned the M1 rifle he was issued on his first day of BUD/S training. He had to swim with it and drag it through the mud with him; so, he had to clean it. He did not have to fire it, just clean it. When they were so tired that they started to fall asleep, one of the sadists would devise still another drill. They had to pound each other awake to get through the drill to keep from bringing more dumping on the heads of the unit. If a man did get caught sleeping, he was tossed into the ocean and forced to return to the classroom and sit soaked during the lesson. Then, while the other men rested or ate, the offender had to mop the classroom floor he had fouled.

The punishment for being off guard, or for being slow, or for having a rumpled shirt, or for having a salt stain on one's boots was to be forced to run into the waters of the bay then to have to do the day's run in wet boots and soaked pants. If one was really bad, such as being caught cheating and circumventing the required PT assignment, he was forced to dangle his legs in the shallow water and let the grains of sand collect so that his skin would be 'sandblasted' when he made the run. Bloody blisters on the feet were painful, but not as bad as that sand scraping the privates. Mark got still smarter—he bought silk underwear—a secret he kept from his unit mates - which helped a little.

During Hell Week, the sixth week of the training course, Mark learned to put up with being herded into the water by trainers firing blanks at him, to crawl under barbed wire while explosions were set off near him setting his ears to ringing and his nerves to jangling, to eat mud in the mud flats of Coronado Cays, to jump in and out of a swimming pool while bystanders laughed at the mindless activity, and to endure without responding to endless insults. He learned to work intimately and quickly with the men in his unit while under duress; to be one with them. They schemed and lied and cheated and stole to get around anything they could to make life a trifle easier. They were punished together when they were caught. There was no other stigma to cheating; it was expected, pragmatic.

The final tests required a mile ocean swim, often done while asleep, or nearly so; drown proofing by lying face down in water with hands tied behind; and when that fiendish test was completed, to do it all over again with legs tied together as well.

Hell Week- Phase II—passed. So did diving phase (III) with its two mile swims, four mile runs, faster obstacle course times. The O course consisted of twenty one obstacles that progressively tested everything a man had— agility, endurance, balance, and will. The worst segment, the one that Mark failed time after time and brought upon himself punishment after punishment was the pole jumping course. He had to jump from one pole set upright in the ground, pole to pole in a series, some short, some high and some far apart. The last pole, when the man had exceeded his endurance, required a ten foot jump to the ground. Mark either smashed his shins on a pole or missed and fell on his chest or got the order of poles mixed up and had to restart the whole miserable stupid process time and time again. Each day an officer taunted him unmercifully, cast aspersions on his manhood, and derided him in front of the men. Mark finally jumped off a pole and headed for the lieutenant with blood in his eye.

"That's not the way," yelled one of his mates. "They'll lock you up for the rest of your life. Don't do it!!!" Another man in his unit tackled Mark before he could get himself into trouble. Then they acted as a unit and all went after the officer in his clean pressed uniform. The officer thought it best to absent himself from the remaining two days of that particular week.

The lesson—the one about dealing with officers—was given to the entire boat squad the following day. Seven men to pay for the mistake of the one. The overriding purpose of the patently unfair punishment was the achievement of unit integrity; so the men were told. They were led out into waist deep freezing water where the NCO hatchet man commanded, "Squat. Weapons over your head! Keep in formation!" He watched the men as their thigh and leg muscles knotted up, and they began to sway with the strain.

Hour after hour it went on—the trainees determined not to quit. The NCO, comfortable in the folding chair he had brought along for just such eventualities, was just as determined to break them down. As he nibbled on a candy bar or chug-a-lugged a Coke, the sadist called out invitingly, "You can quit anytime. Just leave your helmet liner on the ground, and it's all over. Back to the fleet, soft bed, warm food, cushy work, never see me again." The last enticement was truly tempting, but they all held on.

"I feel bad for you bananas," the petty officer announced after an eon passed and all of the men were cramped and insensate in their legs. "I'm not such a bad guy," he said. That made Mark sure that the worst was yet to come. "You little tadpoles can get up now, and we'll do a rest exercise."

It was easier said than done. The tadpoles tried to make their frozen legs unlock, but there was great resistance. "Move it! Move it! Move it!" the petty officer yelled, his minuscule patience span already exhausted. The tadpoles struggled. "Hurry it up, girls!"

They were back on land. "Down for push-ups!" the petty officer yelled. Some rest exercise. They all assumed the position.

"Not that way," the PO groaned. "I told you that this was to be a rest exercise," and he accented the word 'rest.'

The trainees looked at their tormentor dubiously, not understanding. "I will demonstrate for you cretins," the PO said disdainfully. He assumed the prone position then lifted up, so he was balanced on the tips of his toes and on his elbows on the cement sidewalk bordering the O course. He spent about half a minute in that position. "Now you," he ordered rubbing the points of his elbows.

Mark and his six boat squad mates adopted the position. It was terrible. Their elbows felt like they were going to disintegrate. Their legs quivered from the strain. Their backs were ready to break. "Now enjoy your rest, ladies; it's the last one for a while," taunted their petty officer.

After an hour of this and the men were looking as if they would collapse, the NCO smiled down at them and asked, "Wanna quit?" When no one took the bait, he gave a new order, "Right elbows only, girls. Be quick about it. Anyone in the squad can't do it and we'll have another session in the water to help you concentrate."

Right elbow for a while. Left elbow for a while. Mark was one bag of pain parts. When the men began to totter and to fail in that static position, the PO ordered them to crawl. On their elbows. The pain was searing. The tadpoles grimaced in distress. The petty officer then walked across their backs, and the exercise was over.

In addition to all the pain, Mark did considerable formal learning. He became deadly proficient with Swedish Ks and M-3 grease guns, and spent quality time with experts learning to ambush, plan combat missions, reconnaissance patrols, and amphibious raids. On a more mundane level he and his remaining SEAL candidates did hydrographic surveys and were indoctrinated in the mission of the United States irregular forces.

The last phase of BUD/S was the 'S' portion—SEAL training—work with scuba systems, sounding harbor depths with lead lines, compass directed underwater swims, demolition training, patrol and small unit tactics, and running navigation and orienteering courses.

During the final phase Mark and his unit lived on San Clemente Island, seventy-five miles off the California coast. Here they did the longest ocean swim yet, five miles against the swift current with dolphins for companions. It was a little unnerving at first, seeing those dorsal fins gliding through the water. All of the swimming now was with sidestroke to lessen fatigue and to cut down swimmer noise.

Mark somehow steeled his will, ignored his body's outcries, and suspended his sense of fairness and justice to get through the insults and petty demands on San Clemente Island. He learned a little about being in combat and laying demolitions on beaches and in the water. Mostly he learned to endure insulting Mickey Mouse drills—digging trenches and covering them back up again, running with a pallet on his shoulders, and being made to sing by the lieutenant he had attempted to murder after the pole jumping exercise. Mark notched up one more reason to hate officers and vowed again and again not to quit.

Mark passed the tests and completed the eighteen week BUD/S course and was recommended on to SBI (SEAL Basic Indoctrination) with a thirty day leave. He allowed himself to be a hero in the local bars and with the California blondes. This was the payoff for him, and he reveled in his status.

Throughout the navy enlisted, SEALS were considered the elite corps. The teams were formed in 1962 at the order of President John F. Kennedy who was something of a lover of heroes, like Mark Whitehead. SEALS first saw action in Viet Nam in 1965, most of which was in irregular warfare. Their uniforms were the sharpest looking; they got all the best military toys and the town girls; and they seemed to get away with murder in bars and with military regulations. Besides the envy, there was a little fear of these wild men, the self-professed man killers.

By numbers alone, they were an elite corps—150 in Seal Team Two in Little Creek, Virginia, and 150 in Seal Team One in Coronado, California. They kept to themselves, haughty and malign, when they chanced to interact with their nominally fellow service members. They drank too much, partied too much, brawled too much; and Mark Whitehead had to be one. Mark knew he was half way there and chafed to get it over with and to get that trident— he wanted that insignia as much as any Jason ever wanted a golden fleece.

The hardened and still gung-ho mid-westerner entered SBI and immediately put on fatigues to begin learning about the small military. He was intensively trained in small arms, small unit tactics, SEAL Team One ambush methods that preferred setting up a static ambush site and letting the enemy come to the unit, covert land warfare, special SEAL weapons, and more sophisticated map and compass work. The instructors were humorless, but no longer sadistic, not even drill officers as had been the case in BUD/S. There was more accent on the classroom, on tactics and head work, more responsibility and accent on individual initiative.

When Mark and his fellow SEAL candidates put on their camouflage fatigues and took to the field, it was more intense, more professional. They learned about traveling light and fast, about booby traps—how to make them, and how to recognize and avoid them—and how to see the enemy before being seen. In general they learned how to be in control of hostile action.

SEAL teams were divided into seven man units with every man a specialist and every man able to do all seven jobs. Mark Whitehead never lost his unspoken ambition to get The Medal; so, he opted for the position of point man in his unit because he was told there was more action in that spot and more chance to reap glory. He paid less attention to the caveat that the glory came at the greater risk of death and maiming. Mark Whitehead was a typical young man in that regard; he had no visions of mortality, saw no flaws in his invincibility.

The units learned to walk in the jungle, one or two abreast, depending on conditions. They were drilled in the truism that it was fatal to pursue an enemy into his own ambush. They did E&E (Escape and Evasion) drills until they could think with hair trigger speed. When they moved on land, Mark was at point. He was responsible, by the imaginary clock, for fields of fire from ten o'clock to two o'clock, and no others. The next men in line were responsible for fields from two to four or eight to ten, depending on the side, right or left, where they marched. The man bringing up the rear was to cover from four o'clock to eight o'clock which required him to swivel his head frequently and to make sudden turns to try and detect an ambusher coming from behind. All of this orderliness had been learned the hard way over years of combat. Without restricting the direction in which a man was to fire, soldiers and SEALS had died by being shot in the back by men in their own units. Every man was expected to be able to shoot as well from his left shoulder as his right.

The SEAL trainees learned to maintain a safe distance from each other so that the red hot spent shell casings would not impact the neighbor unit member as he concentrated on his own field of fire. It was most disconcerting to have a scorching brass bullet jacket fly into one's shirt front at a time when it was all one could do to defend his own direction of responsibility.

The training took on a new intensity and significance since all field firing was with live rounds now.

On the water and under the water, Mark learned the most sophisticated designs of demolitions and grew as accustomed to the small boats they used as he was with his own car. The primary mode of transportation was the STAB (SEAL Tactical Assault Boat), a sleek fiberglass crew boat propelled by twin Mercury 110 horse outboard motors and sporting .50 caliber tripod mounted machine guns, M-60s, and 90 mm shoulder fired recoilless rifles. For more surreptitious incursions the preferred craft was the smaller LSSC.

There was still PT. Mark thought he might be going a little crazy when, one day, he realized he actually liked physical training. It was like a minor drug addiction that gave him withdrawal symptoms when he laid off on weekends. The SEALS were expressly ordered to take it easy on weekends and specifically not to do their daily PT. To fulfill their craving for action and to yet obey the SEAL law, the men developed an interest in hide and seek that bordered on an obsession, at least among the unmarried men. Mark found himself relishing the long weekday runs in his hot steel helmet, kapok flak jacket, and carrying a full pack, vaulting logs and dodging tree branches. He was a true believer. The sign in the SEAL gym read, "The more you sweat in training, the less you bleed in combat." He believed that. He was a SEAL in mind and body, a non quitter, a 'can-do' guy; and he had fixed in his mind a scene wherein the president put a blue ribboned medal around his neck.

Near the end of the long training, Mark felt like an expert; he was an expert. He could dismantle, reconstruct, and use in the field weapons ranging from the best Wham-O Sling Shot to a complex Hechler and Koch or a LAW or an AK-47. He, like most of his friends, came to prefer the Kalashnikov for its reliability. He could swim with it, drag it in the mud, drop it off a building, subject it to dirt and rust; and every time he had to use it; the gun fired. Mark could blow a hole in a complex concertina wire barrier with bangalore torpedoes, destroy a bridge or a building with rigged satchel charges, lay limpet mines on the hulls of ships, and do all sorts of diabolical things with dynamite, nitroglycerine, and plastique. He was an able parachutist, martial artist, combat swimmer, navigator, survivalist, and commando cadre. He felt more than ready to try his hand in actual combat where the medals were being given out.

The CPO in direct charge of his training made a comment from the classics concerning the young man when he graduated from SEAL school that: "The millstone of God grinds slowly but exceedingly fine.

It grinds some men down, and others it polishes. PO 3 Mark White-head is one who came out polished."

The day finally came—Mark Whitehead was given his black beret and his trident—the gold uniform insignia that the wags called a 'Budweiser.' He was thrilled to wear the striking black trousers bloused out over his expensive new brilliantly shined boots. He was one of them! He no longer wore underwear. SEALS do not wear underwear. Like most SEAL lessons Mark learned, he came upon that bit of tradition the hard way. He went into a downtown San Diego bar shortly after getting his 'Budweiser' and found a group of fellow SEALs sitting around getting drunk. One of them took notice of Mark's fine new uniform; and several of the men checked him out to see if he were wearing underwear, despite his vocal and physical protests. He was, and an entire squad jumped him and tore his skivvies off him and ruined his uniform. The barkeep rolled his eyes and kept cleaning the glassware; SEALs were too good of customers to call the cops on them.

Mark was given the option of attending any of a dozen post training schools—ranger school in Florida, Arctic survival, advanced weapons schools, and language courses. He refused them all. He wanted to go to Viet Nam. He was afraid, based on the glowingly optimistic reports in the press that year, 1965, that the whole thing would be over before he could get there if he did not grab the brass ring as it came by him now. He was assigned to a squad headed by CPO Terry Brannigan where he learned to work with a functioning unit. They reconnoitered beaches, mapped sub-surf terrain, worked with pre-PRU trainees at Camp Machen in the Cuymaca Mountains outside San Diego, scared motorcycle gangs, and enthralled women until they got their orders for a six month tour in My Tho, Republic of Viet Nam.

The man from BUPERS came to their unit headquarters and explained about additional death benefits and supplemental insurance and how to have their pay checks directly deposited into checking accounts. His visit underscored what every officer and noncom had told Mark and the other men from the time they started in BUD/S training so many weeks before—they were expendable.

Properly inoculated, identified, and indoctrinated, Mark, Terry, and their unit boarded a C-118 and headed for South Viet Nam, four days away. The seating arrangements were sparse and scarce. Their greasy web strap hammocks served as both seat and bed. They were cramped in with packed gear and boats that were secured by cargo netting in the center of the aircraft bay. Their lavatory was a single chem toilet at the front and a hole in the floor for urinating in the rear. They ate C-rations. Mark was truly happy to see My Tho when the plane finally touched down in the RVN.

A State Department, all business, all serious, welcomer met them on the tarmac. State considered the military to be criminally negligent in doing its duty to inform the incoming American soldiers about proper attitude and deportment while they were guests in the country. The Yale graduate embassy deputy assistant undersecretary (They were all Yale graduates who found their places in the Department via the Yale pipeline) could not have stressed that fact more frequently—they were guests of the Republic of Viet Nam, and were to behave themselves as such. The State Department Yalie did not even deign to answer questions that suggested that the Vietnamese ought to be treating the GIs with the preferential courtesy since, after all, the Americans were coming in to fight their war for them.

Mark chafed under the scrutiny of officers around My Tho, and their regimented way of conducting operations. Later, after his and Terry's SEAL team were relocated to the Task Force 116 headquarters in Can Tho, both men literally jumped at the chance to move out of their regular SEAL unit and into the irregular SOG outfit when they were offered the opportunity. The two friends trained together at the Vung Tau long range reconnaissance school, then moved into the Apartment Army with the rest of the degenerate looking mavericks that earned the appellation, 'Terry's pirates,' and took on the cover of working as construction men for Pacific Architects and Engineers. Their tours were extended by six months, then another six months, unlike regular half year SEAL tours.

Anders and Mark left the sultry sun of the Can Tho afternoon to enter the fetid darkness of the downstairs bar of their apartment building after parking their truck in the sidelot. It was Mark's turn to cook, and Anders' turn to wash up. Having nothing better to do, Ander's pitched in to help defeather and to clean the chickens.

Mark said, "We're gonna have my best recipe—Vietnamese Chicken. Know how to make Crispy Vietnamese Chicken?"

"When I made frozen dinners, everybody thought I threw away the best part when I pulled off the tin foil," said Anders truthfully.

"Well, okay then. I'll teach you how to make Crispy Vietnamese Chicken…First you have to napalm a chicken farm…," Mark smiled mischievously.

Anders laughed. "This is beginning to sound like work," he said.

"We could go out and get Chinese, I suppose. There's a place in town that has great food but there is one drawback."

"What's that?" Anders asked suspiciously.

"It's a gay restaurant."

"A Chinese gay restaurant?" Anders' was appropriately incredulous.

"Yeah, it's called Sum Yung Gai? You heard of it?"

They laughed and made an edible mixture of strips of chicken dipped in rice flour, then deep-fried in oil, Chinese peppers, pineapple chunks, durian fruit, onions, and squash. They had rambuton, a small spiny inch long red covered fruit with translucent meat, similar to lichee, for dessert.

"That stuff smells bad," said Anders as he cleaned up the peelings. He determined that the smell came from the durian. He wondered if it had been rotten and if he would be sick. Had not tasted bad, though.

"You know what they say about that stuff—"smells like hell, tastes like Helen," Mark replied to Anders' comment and upturned nose.

"I gotta tell you my next best recipe—the one for making marinated macaw," Mark said. Anders looked at him suspiciously. "Yeah, it's delicious. And you thought macaws were just for good looks."

"So go on," Anders said. "I'm dying to learn how to make a meal out of a parrot."

"Since you insist," Mark said, wearing his mischievous little smile again. "First you stick the bird in boiling water so you can pluck his feathers. Then, tie it spread eagle to a little two by four board and put him in a mixture of good brandy and plum wine to marinate for two days. You take out the bird and set the marinade aside and save it. The bird, still on its board, goes into another soak, this time a mixture of good bourbon—doesn't matter what brand—and peach schnapps for another two days. Then you remove the bird, save the marinade aside, and put the bird in the oven at 450° for four hours. Occasionally bast it with beer. When the time is almost up, pour the marinade you've been saving over the macaw and let it simmer for another fifteen or so minutes."

Anders was listening expectantly. "And?" he asked.

"Then it's time to serve," said Mark. "You carefully take out the pan of liquid and the macaw, take it off the board, throw away the macaw, eat the board, and drink the liquid." He threw back his head and laughed uproariously at his own joke. Anders was in a great mood, and joined him.

After dinner, two men washed the dishes; two men dried them and stowed them away; and four men threw darts at the photograph of Hanoi Jane sitting on a North Vietnamese-Soviet antiaircraft artillery piece. Most of the rest lolled around reading *Playboy* and other pornography or catching up on last month's technical journals.

After dinner and cleanups, Terry gathered all of the men in the apartment to learn of their part in Operation First-Punch that was to disrupt the command structure of the Viet Cong prior to a major

Army-Navy-ARVN penetration of the U Minh Forest called Operation Foreplay. It was the first time all of the SOG irregulars would unite in a single mission; and that, in itself, had to denote a very determined effort to restore control of the Delta to the GVN. Besides VC villages and military bases, farms that supplied the nutritional needs of a guerrilla army, and a labyrinthine hideaway, there were reported by US and GVN intelligence to be as many as twenty-five American and SVN POW camps, a capper incentive to every SOG in the apartment and every member of the US armed forces who got wind of the impending operation via the rumor mill.

Dieter Lutz met in Cleveland Howard's office at the Revolutionary Development Headquarters in the MACV compound in Hue' to report the findings of the polygraph tests and the vetting procedures for Howard's staff. In addition to Lutz, Cleve Howard, Tandrosz Szabo, and Jean-Luc DuParrier were in attendance.

"First of all, a lot of the locals . . .," Lutz started.

"He means 'Gooks,' interjected DuParrier.

"Try and contain your racism for the moment," chided Szabo.

DuParrier nodded with a sullen look.

"As I was saying, the Vietnamese on your staff are a bit hard to characterize. First of all, many of them are poor candidates for the polygraph because they were so frightened of the apparatus that their parameters were practically off the recording sheet before I even asked a question. Others could not answer the questions with a 'yes' or 'no' no matter how many times I gave the instructions. They start out looking and acting like they understand English and are well-indoctrinated civil servants, but after a while . . ."

"The Chinese have a popular old saying that fits the whole bunch of them," said Jean-Luc. "*Lu fen dn, biaomiam guang.*" That is best translated as "Shiny on the outside—just like donkey droppings."

Lutz continued as if DuParrier had not interrupted, "All in all, they came across okay. However, I did find three subjects who were clearly lying about matters material to your security and work, Cleve. With a little extra investigation by my zealous colleagues, it is clear that two of them are frank Viet Cong. We suggest 'putting them to the question' as our hero, Tomás de Torquemada, would have advised; so, we can cleanse their souls. The third one is your Nguyen Tran Xuan. He was interesting."

"I'm interested," agreed Howard.

"He lied," Lutz said, flatly. "He was outwardly cool, calm, and altogether forthright; and he lied...about everything material to his being your traitor. I couldn't quite put my finger on it, but I think he was trying to beat the polygraph by using drugs or some kind of self-hypnosis. He seemed to be sedated, almost like he was in a trance or something. It didn't matter; every time I asked a question about the murders or his involvement with the LAF, his pulse, BP, and the rest shot up. He's your man. I figured you would want to deal with him in your own way; so, I let him think he did just fine. He has not had a visit from our 'persuaders.' I'll leave that up to you."

Jean-Luc DuParrier spoke up before Cleve Howard could reply and before the look from Szabo could shush him. "My father told me that the French had a way of dealing with Xuan's kind. When they captured one of the little yellow rodents, they slowly cut one arm off, took a photograph, then beheaded them and took another picture. Then they sent the two photographs to the family like postcards."

"The idea has merit, DuParrier," Howard said, half serious. "I wish we could be as open about this sort of thing as the froggies."

"Whatever you decide, it's in your hands, now, Cleve," repeated Lutz with finality.

The RDC/O said, "You did the right thing, Dieter. Now I have to figure out what is the right thing for me to do. If I keep him here for any length of time, he will know he is a prime suspect and will probably boogie off into the bushes with the black pajama boys. If I send him back up to the booney camp, he'll go right on disrupting our progress and killing our people. If I summarily execute him, I will lose the propaganda value of having him caught flagrante delicto in front of his heathen peers. I want them to have the best object lesson possible. I also want it to be apparent to the rabble up there that the Americans and their information networks are infallible, and that it is us who will deal with any traitors to our RD and SOG programs. We want these primitives to develop a childlike bonding to their team, and Xuan may provide a valuable negative symbol for them," Howard said, sort of thinking out loud.

"That requires that you take care of the catching and the punishing since you are not only the head honcho of this American program, but right now you are the only American in sight," observed Szabo. Howard did not like that idea and had come up with a better one as he and Szabo exchanged comments.

"I find myself in the traditional position, unfortunately the position that America has been thrust into. As Kipling said:

'Take up the White Man's burden,
And reap his old reward:
The blame of those ye better,
The hate of those ye guard.'

"I need to keep a distance—you know, the officer and the enlisted, no fraternization, the Bawana, the High Kahuna, that sort of thing. But Lane Duerk told me he will have an American here within the month to run the PRU as operations officer out there. The new guy can take care of the Xuan problem with proper advance warning. Lane said he is a pistol and can handle a little in-the-field unpleasantness. The best thing about this new guy is that he is just a contract agent, expendable; even if he buys the farm, we haven't lost a real Company man," Howard said with a facial expression that was working to suppress a smirk.

"We'll leave that one up to you, Cleve," said Szabo. "Do you want us to handle the other two VC in your clan? One of them is a woman, an older one at that. You squeamish?"

"I'd say we need the information they can provide. I don't want to know the details of how you get the data, just give me useful stuff for our computer," said Howard. DuParrier positively brightened at this green light for his work, and even Szabo came as close to a smile as the fixed lines of his taciturn face would allow.

In two days time there was a sheath of notes, full of incriminatory evidence about the local Viet Cong Infrastructure including names, whereabouts, unit positions, habits, and foibles to be entered into the central computer. There had been some awkward noise coming from the PIC the first day, but by that night, the casual eavesdropper would have concluded that an entirely civilized interchange was taking place between interrogator and subject. Without comment, Xuan was sent back to his PRU team in the central provincial wild country. Howard did go to the effort of taking Tran, Dung, Ky, and Bach, the operatives who had alerted him to Xuan's nefarious activities, into his confidence, and swore them not only to silence, but to cooperation with the plan to wait for the new American replacement for the departed Y'Yool to arrive on site.

The four PRU men scheduled a month of training exercises for the cadres, and assigned themselves each a three week family leave. They had no intention of participating in a mission that could put themselves or their fellow PRUs into mortal danger from the traitor during the last month of 1966 while they awaited for the vaunted American to come.

CHAPTER 16

8 December, 1966 found Anders and his ten fellow SOG and apartment companions engaged in their portion of the last few weeks of organized chaos accompanying a major military campaign. They were at the Can Tho USN docks working along side the American and ARVN soldiers and sailors loading the field camp equipment, food, armaments, and ammunition on the LSTs (Landing Ships, Tank) and PBRs; the ammo belts, barrels of defoliants, and canisters of Napalm onto the planes. Their own set of three PBRs had been ready for two days, stocked for a three week long range reconnaissance mission. Operation Clean-sweep was to commence on 1 January, 1967, after the infiltrator-assassin-hunter-killer squads had softened the underbelly and command structure of the entrenched enemy in the far south of the country in the U Minh forest in their own Operation Foreplay. That operation had to be completed before the end of the year. Lane Duerk had sent an enthusiastic bombast (fittingly, the word derives from the old French *bombace*, 'cotton padding') that had detailed the pivotal role of the SOGs and had ended, not unexpectedly, with the Shakespearean exhortation, "Cry havoc, and let slip the dogs of war."

Anders sweated from his exertions on the docks and took note of the seemingly endless supply of barrels marked by different colored bands being loaded into Air Force C-123 flying boxcars marked with the motto, We Prevent Forests. "What is that stuff?" he asked Mark and Terry.

"They're called by the name of the colored band on the barrel so dummies like us don't get confused with big words. So we have Agent Orange, Agent Blue, and Agent White. Up until last year, we also had purple and pink. They are all defoliants, herbicides. The airdales spray the forests and kill the trees and plants where Charlie hides; pretty effective. We wouldn't stand a chance without this great stuff," the two SEALS told him.

The barrels of Agent Orange were marked with their chemical

name, if one were inclined to be that inquisitive. The barrels held a notation that they contained 2,3,7,8, tetra-chlori-benzo-para-dioxin (TCDD) or Dioxin, for short. In addition to use in Operation Clean-sweep, Dioxin was sprayed on Viet Nam from 1962 to 1970 under the aegis of Operation Ranch-hand (so named because the flying boxcars with their land clearing chemicals were known as Ranch-hands). More than 53,000 dekaliters (140,000 gallons) of Purple, 47,000 dekaliters (120,000 gallons) of Pink, and 7.2 million dekaliters (19 million gallons) of Orange, Blue, and White were sprayed until the program ended in 1971—374 pounds of pure Dioxin.

The chemical agents killed trees by stripping the foliage, but the poisonous vapors seeped deeply into the soil and polluted the water table. Millions of hectares of ancient forest were destroyed, and the poison lingered to thwart natural and governmental efforts at reforestation. The people in the sprayed areas, including military and civilian personnel, Vietnamese and American, developed disease related to exposure to the toxins. The women miscarried and had stillbirths. Newborns of the people soaked in the American poisons were delivered with congenital mutations and deformities. Large numbers of American and ARVN lives were spared by exposing their enemies and removing the covering foliage that hid the Liberation Armed Forces and People's Army of Viet Nam. (VC and NVA).

The SOGs had detailed plans for kidnapping VC district officials, key couriers, and tax collectors; and for taking out the deserter-traitor American soldiers. These Americans were known to be assisting the VC by calling in air strikes on ARVN and MACV forces and to be providing information concerning the whereabouts of specific units or marked individuals. The SOG plans included logistics for disrupting communist communication and supply lines, headquarters and command structures, and for sowing fear and discontent among the citizens and supporters of the insurgents. Anders and his fellow military irregulars from the SOG outfits were boated to the U Minh Forest under cover of darkness to implement the plans.

Some units entered from the coast off the end of the Camau peninsula, the southernmost tip of Viet Nam; and others, including Anders, Mark, and Terry, were taken by PBR to the northern edges of the dense forest and turned loose for their missions of havoc. Each unit of three American irregulars had a Vietnamese guide, either a Kit Carson Scout or an LLDB. The SOGs held their Vietnamese in a high level of esteem and respect because of their pragmatic knowledge of the land and its people, and because of their courage and military skill. These men (and sometimes women) had been actively engaged in continuous combat for years; in some instances, decades.

The four men in Anders' team made a rude and well camouflaged base camp in the swampy flood plain facing the mangrove forest and waited until the darkest part of the night of 8-9 December before entering the primeval quietude of the jungle. They ate dry cold C rations tasting reasonably decent to Anders, an idiosyncrasy of his. They had no fire, and they whispered. Every effort was expended to prevent the clanking of metal. When they slipped into the periphery trees along an ill-marked trail known to their Kit Carson, each man was carrying everything he would use to sustain life for three weeks. They had opted to pack less food in favor of more ammunition, counting on their training and abilities to live off the land and to steal. Each man carried a syringe full of morphine on a thong around his neck.

For two nights they moved deeper into the forest that Anders would have presumed to be impenetrable had he not actually seen their guide locate a passable trail, and had he not actually walked through it. The men were all barefoot, carrying their shoes tied to their waists. They secreted themselves in cave-like enclosures formed from the tangled mangrove and banyan tree roots by day and traveled only after dark. It was hot and humid in the forest as opposed to the blistering relatively dry heat of the swamp plain adjacent to the forest proper. All four men grumbled with the discomfort, but were willing to wear their sleeveless flak jackets. They drew the line at wearing their helmets. The steel pots were like the inside of a Dutch oven; the effect was akin to having one's head baked.

Even in the day, there was no more than a half light because of the dense umbrella of upper level foliage. There were leeches, centimeter long red ants, battalions of huge and nightmarish beetles, and other formidable insects to haunt their reveries. The men doused their clothing and skin with the 'bug juice' they carried in the four ounce plastic bottles kept under their helmet straps. They drank the brackish swamp water liberally laced with Halazone tablets at the rate of a mandatory three-quarter dekaliters (two gallons) a day because of their extreme loss of body water in perspiration. The four men rarely urinated. They marched and crawled through the underbrush again at 2200 on the third day; their objective was no more than a klick away.

The Kit Carson stopped the Americans and took off his fatigue shirt to cover the potential exposure as he pointed animatedly at different places on his map by the feeble illumination of a penlight. He showed them that they were shortly to come upon a hamlet located on a low hill above a narrow stream. Even without the added communication, the Americans could tell they were not far from a village because there was a characteristic nauseous putrid smell in the air. From experience, the three men knew they were smelling *nouc mam* in its early preparation stage, a certain sign that they were within two hundred meters of the habitations by the almost gaseous intensity of the aroma. Downwind on a good day some hint of *nouc mam* could be picked up two klicks away.

The process of making the favored fish sauce of Viet Nam is one that Americans are better off not knowing about if they are to enjoy the pungent final product. First, a layer of ungutted raw fish is spread over an open area. Salt is then liberally applied to the layer of fish. Additional layers of fish and salt, about ten to fifteen in all, are heaped on and allowed to putrefy for three or four weeks in the broiling sun until an oily black liquid runs off the sides. That piquant effluent is collected in bowls and served over rice, often with pieces of fish or vegetables added. "Yum!" rasped Mark Whitehead with exaggerated gastronomic enthusiasm when he perceived the smell.

A man-sized corrugated aluminum pipe extended from the edge of the hamlet atop the rise down to the stream and served as the town's sewage and garbage dump. The pipe was large enough to allow a large man to crawl or even to walk in a crouched position from the stream unseen to the hamlet. The headman of the hamlet was also known to be the deputy chief of the regional VC unit, a very significant target in and of himself; but more importantly, he should know where the commander of the unit would be, and where his headquarters, complete with plans and logistical data, was located. It was a first priority mission to take this man out and critical to bring him out alive.

The three Americans drew lots to see who would be first up the pestilential sewage pipe and to take out the perimeter guard or guards. Anders drew the short straw and shuddered secretly. He was shivering with fright. In order to prevent the other three men from seeing his cowardice, the sixteen year old moved quickly and without any attempt at discussion to the mouth of the pipe. The stench emanating from the conduit overwhelmed Anders' previous nausea from the *nouc mam* odor. He felt as if he had been miniaturized to about the size of a spider and was standing in the hole of an outdoor privy. The smell of human excrement and fetid wet garbage was that strong. He paused for a few minutes to fight down his desire to vomit or to turn tail.

Anders started into the corrugated metal tunnel in a squatting, duck-walking position, but soon found the exercise painful and exhausting. Against everything he held sacred, he gave in and got down on his hands and knees and crawled. He went as far as he could with his fingers fully outstretched to keep the putrid mud on the floor of the pipe off the rest of his hands; but it was impossible; and he finally resigned himself and slogged his way along, up to his wrists in gooey excrement. He was sure he would be too sick and worthless to be able to do his job when he finally got to the top. No matter what was up there, it had to be better than this, and he hurried along as best he could, given the difficulties.

Anders was so attuned to danger that he could have heard a fire ant pee on a cotton ball. He heard a very faint slithering, rustling sound there in the pipe with him. At first he denied its existence; then, he could not escape the fact that there was something or someone else in there with him. It did not take much of a mental effort to conclude that no other person was crazy enough to make himself go into the horrifically rank cylinder. He had to conclude that it was a rat, and the specter of meeting a woodchuck sized rodent in that claustrophobic space was a daunting one. Anders was moving along silently and could not have attracted attention; certainly not enough to lure some other idiot into that witch's cauldron. While he feared meeting a reception committee when he emerged, he did not feel any apprehension that he was about to bump heads with some villager in his pestilent tunnel. Still, he could hear the squishy sound of the mud being moved somewhere above him in the tunnel. It did not seem that far away now, either. The darkness in the cavernous hollow was absolutely impenetrable.

Whatever it was, the thing in the dark was all but upon him. He was trembling with fear and loathing. He felt helpless, powerless against it. He could never out crawl it, could not make noise, and in all probability was defenseless against a creature that could see or smell him in the sticky darkness. The slithery squishing sound came so close he thought the denizen of the sewer pipe was about to touch his face. He decided to remain frozen. To protect his face he laid out fully prone with his hands in front of his face in the muck to keep it from going up his nostrils or into his eyes. Anders' worst fantasies were fulfilled in a matter of seconds after he flattened himself against the floor and one of the side walls of the tunnel.

He had the incomparable horror of feeling a thick, long snake, probably eight feet long, slither down his helplessly exposed body. He could detect the reptile lying the complete length of his own body. The scent of fear that oozed out of his pores was nearly as bad as that of the excrement and the offal around him. Although he was not generally given to conjuring up the worst case scenario in a given situation, Anders was as sure as he could be that the only snake of that great length and weight that was at all likely to be lurking around a sewage pipe was a king cobra. More young people die in Viet Nam from cobra bites than from any natural cause. Anders waited for the quick pain of the fanged bite and prepared himself for the agony of suffocation and muscle cramping he knew would come.

American soldiers, and rural Indochinese civilians alike, have a consummate dread of having to defecate at night. Cobras, as well as scorpions, tarantellas, and black widows are drawn to latrine holes and wait with a fiendish desire to bite the poor unsuspecting man seeking relief from the ubiquitous gut cramping diarrhea that afflicts everyone in the bush. The bite occurs with inordinate frequency on the genitals or exposed buttocks adding indignity to the horrific pain and real risk of death. In secure areas, the latrines are steel barrels set in the earth and set afire before every elimination. The problem with that is the vermin are attracted to the warmed hole, and the second man in line is in more danger than the first. The option of lighting a fire in that oppressive tunnel was not available.

With inexorable and exquisite slowness the snake crept down Anders' full length. Anders could count the ripple of each encircling reptilian muscle. He wanted to whimper, but dared not to make the slightest sound or movement. Then the creature was gone, gone to wherever such denizens of the dark disappear to after they destroy the soul of a man they have encountered in a Cimmerian tunnel.

Feeling drained and old, and thinking foolishly that he had just defecated in his pants, Anders pulled his filth ridden body along until he thought he could detect the wonderfully refreshing aroma of raw *nouc mam* coming from the freedom of the tunnel opening. He could not have enjoyed a perfume more than that smell of fermenting putrefying salted fish. Anders put his head out of the opening for a quick peak. He need not have exercised any significant caution to avoid being seen. The night was so dark, a naked eye could not have made him out. He realized he had more to fear from the demon's breath odor that permeated the air wherever he moved. He wearily drew himself out of the tunnel pipe and onto the grassy flat in front of the nearest thatched roof hooch.

He lay there in the gloom contemplating his situation until he heard the soft pad, pad, pad of bare feet approaching him. He eased himself to the side of the pipe on the side opposite of that from which the footfalls came. He was well lubricated so the slide to the new position was easy and silent. He could be glad for small favors.

A young man dressed all in black came to the opening of the pipe and stood there urinating into its opening. The warm hissing sound and smell of the man's urine added to the delights of the evening. He held an AK-47 loosely in his left hand as he attempted to flip away the universal last-drop-that-goes-into-the-pants from his limp organ. He was so industrious at it that Anders had a moment of humorous recall of his old DI, Cletus Lee, getting on one of the recruits for being overzealous in his hygiene, "Mo' than fo' flips o' dat thing, an' y'all ah aplayin' wid it," Sergeant Lee had announced.

The man turned to continue the sleepy drudgery of ambulatory guard duty about the periphery of his secure little hamlet where nothing had ever happened in the history of its existence—except tonight. Anders drove the marine Bowie knife into the non vigilant young VC's back adjacent to one of the mid-thoracic vertebral bodies on the left neatly transecting the descending aorta. The internal eruption of blood snuffed out the man's life before he could react to the pain or sound a cry of alarm. It took a second for Anders to realize what he had just done. He had killed a man standing less than an inch from him. Anders felt sicker at that moment than he had done when he was in the hellhole of that sewer pipe. He was not one to think deeply about the meaning of his actions, but his sudden mental response was one of deep, almost frightening remorse. The logic of his situation, there alone in the night on a military mission escaped him for the moment.

Reality intruded, rapidly, fortunately for Anders. He dragged the dead soldier's body over near the sewage pipe, cut off the ears and dropped them into the convenient little pouch on his belt, then reconnoitered as best he could in the inky darkness. Anders slowly, and as near silently as possible, made his way the better part of 360° around the small hamlet keeping to the edge of the forest, walking just inside the treeline. He figured there were six houses, and was about to conclude that he had taken out the only guard, when he nearly walked directly into the second sentry.

His sense of smell saved him. The guard was violating the most cardinal rule of survival in the dense and hostile forest. He was smoking! The acrid odor of some ersatz brand of far eastern cigarettes wafted Anders' way as the first cue that he was approaching a person. Attracted by the odor, Anders stood stalk still and waited. In the dark, the guard must have turned in Anders' direction because the glowing tip of the smoke lit up the man's position clearly. Even his face could be seen; he and Anders were that close. Anders took care not to look the other man in the eyes—he thanked Sylvia Chin back at The Farm for her grueling lessons on silent movement and camouflage in the forest. The guard could not smell Anders despite the tremendous odor he was emitting because his sense of smell was irretrievably impaired by his tobacco habit.

The American agent waited what seemed to be about three minutes, almost holding his breath, and hoping that his own putrid body odor would not give him away. The glowing cigarette tip slowly turned away. Anders took several very careful steps in the darkness that brought him within striking distance of the smoking sentry. He slipped his razor-sharp Bowie knife from its scabbard on his belt and held it tightly by the handle, blade aimed at his own chest. The young Swede did not breathe. He edged closer to his target making baby steps. He was finally sure of his position directly behind the man. Anders swept his large powerful arm out and around the guard's unprotected throat, caught the man's chin and in a fraction of a second had elevated the chin up and away from the vulnerable throat and inclined it toward the left. At the same instant he swung his right hand, blade in line with the anterior neck of his pinioned victim, and drew it hard across the middle of the man's throat.

The guard was speechless with the shock of being grabbed from behind. The Viet Cong's mind screamed that the man who held him must be three feet taller and have arms like tree trunks. The sentry remained speechless with sudden and persisting paralytic fright for three tenths of a second. That was his last thought on earth. The scalpel sharp blade was wielded with far more force than necessary due to the giant's excitement. It sliced through the exposed skin as if it was cutting feta cheese; then in less time than it takes to tell, the knife had severed the left sternocleidomastoid muscle, external and internal jugular veins, the common carotid artery, and passed obliquely upward through the larynx cutting off any last possibility of a vocalization. The final cut severed the lower part of the right internal carotid artery. The only sound was a bubbling as the escaping air from the severed trachea in the Viet Cong's antepenultimate breath encountered the life's blood of the man who was exsanguinating through his neck. Anders gently and silently lowered his victim to the ground taking every care to avoid the slightest noise. Thus far there had been none.

Satisfied now that there were no more sentries, and that no one in the huts was suffering from insomnia or weak kidneys, Anders removed the trophy ears, then stepped out onto the grass and moved swiftly back to the sewage pipe. He felt around on the ground and found a small pebble then through it down the hillside at the spot he presumed his teammates were hiding in the darkness. It was a prearranged signal, and the response was almost immediate.

He scarcely heard the barefoot steps as the three men rushed up the incline. Anders gently cleared his throat to let them know where he was. The four men went into a huddle.

"Two sentries, both dead. I don't think anyone else was disturbed," whispered Anders, his voice betraying his excitement. He had a minor quaver that suggested his dismay at what he had just done, but Anders struggled to control it.

Terry said, "Our man is supposed to be in the second house to the right from the imaginary line extending from the pipe. Mark, you and Ngoc get him. Alive. Don't forget; we have to have him alive. Anders, you provide security against anyone coming into the hamlet along any of the tracks. Do what you have to do, but be quiet about it if you possibly can. I'll provide security just outside the hooch. Oh, there's supposed to be two wives and a little girl in there with him. The source said our man sleeps on the far right by himself, the child is in the middle, and the two wives sleep together on a futon on the far left. There is a center fire pit; watch out and don't fall into it. That would make a big racket. Any questions?"

"No questions," Mark rasped. "Except what is that horrible smell? I didn't know anything that bad could come from a human being. What went on up here?" He had laughter in his whisper.

"Very funny," rejoined Anders, embarrassed.

"Nuff talk. Go do it," ordered Terry.

Anders moved into the middle of the grassy plot in front of the buildings whose silhouettes he could barely make out in the gloom and squatted down. His M-16 was cradled in his arms in readiness. Anders set the lever to full automatic.

The three others were gone five minutes. Anders heard their group footfalls before he could see them. Finally they were beside him half pushing, half dragging a portly Vietnamese, naked except for a ragged Tee shirt. He was making small gurgling sounds, probably suppressing an involuntary welling of sobs. He smelled of cabbage and *nouc mam.* Mark slapped a three inch strip of gray duct tape across the headman's mouth, and Ngoc, the Kit Carson, expertly bound the man's hands. Terry prodded his fat back with his combat stiletto making the man move along smartly. It was a real team effort. Terry attached a grenade booby trap to the hooch's door latch with a wire so that the first person to depress the latch would trip the grenade.

Ngoc led the little procession out of the village. Anders presumed that the nimble little ranger could see in the dark like a cat because they ran through the dense forest along a trail Anders could not see at all. He was glad to be bringing up the rear. Ngoc stopped abruptly so that Anders ran into Terry's back almost causing a mid forest fall like dominoes. They waited a few minutes, apparently while Ngoc got his bearings. Anders was glad to know the man was not perfect. The group then set out on a run for a distance of 100 meters. The SOGs had come about two klicks from the hamlet. They were standing in front of a well-built, log walled, thatched roof house. Ngoc slipped up to the door, carefully looked in through the door, then entered and did a quick search.

"Is okay, is okay," the Kit Carson assured his companions, and the three Americans followed him inside, shoving their Vietnamese prisoner in front of them. The headman, who was known to be the deputy commander of the NLF region, sat very uncomfortably on the bare floor, bound with his wrists taped to his ankles and his mouth taped shut. His breath came in shallow noisy blusters through his congested nose. The other men did not notice the man's discomfort, but Anders was concerned, sympathetic. He thought he would be regarded as soft, or weak livered if he spoke up on the man's behalf; and he did not need that; so, he held his piece. The men took turns on watch, two at a time. Anders' turn, with Ngoc, brought them to the beginning of dawn.

Shortly before full light, Ngoc stepped beside Anders and bade him look carefully out the window. Anders' attention was immediately and fully aroused by the sight of two Vietnamese men in tiger-stripe camouflage uniforms carrying M-16s walking purposefully to the building, taking no precautions about the building's potential occupants.

"*Của tôi,*" (Mine), said Ngoc.

"You were expecting them?" asked Anders, surprised. He guessed that it was one of those things he had not needed to know.

"Part of plan. Best part," answered the Kit Carson.

The two men were shown into the room where the prisoner was being held and spoke quietly with Ngoc in Vietnamese. Terry and Mark heard the slight noises from the speech, and both men were suddenly fully awake. The prisoner, who had not slept for a minute the entire night, now had an alertness in his eyes akin to panic, bordering on hysteria.

"Let's get what we came for," said Terry to Ngoc before he had even made introductions.

"Okay. These RVN Rangers," Ngoc said gesturing and bowing toward his countrymen. "These American SEALS," he said and nodded in the direction of the three Americans. The rangers nodded respectfully.

Mark walked to the Viet Cong who had fallen to his side and was crying. He grabbed the man by the hair of his head and jerked him to the crouched position again. The two RVN rangers stepped to the man, one on each side, and spoke to him harshly in their common language. The man's eyes showed abject terror, but he shook his head, "No."

Suddenly both rangers began punching the helpless captive with rapid fire strikes all over his face and ears. Just as suddenly they stopped. Again one of them spoke harshly to the enemy deputy commander. He was resting on his fat buttocks in an imbalanced position. Again, he shook his head, "No."

The two Vietnamese soldiers then began to kick the villager systematically up his legs and thighs, up his back and in the exposed part of his chest. They were accurate and controlled. The headman slumped onto his side struggling to get his breath. His nose was broken, and his face was turning purple. Anders said firmly, "He can't breathe. We'd better take off the tape or we won't have a prisoner to get information from."

"Leave it to them. It's their war; it's their job," ordered Terry.

"These guys are only giving back something of what their people suffer from the communists. They are the most vicious monsters you can imagine. Don't waste your sympathies," said Mark.

Anders shrugged and watched. It was not his show, obviously. He quietly vowed to himself that he would find another way when it finally was his show. For now it was just watch and learn. He knew he had to toughen up.

When it seemed that the man's heart would give out, or that he was about to die immediately from suffocation, one of the rangers reached to the man's face and brutally ripped off the duct tape taking with it tufts of beard and a few patches of skin. The prisoner greedily drank in the air, struggling to capture as much with each gasp as possible. The rangers asked him where the headquarters of the NLF for that region was located. When there was no answer, the questioner kicked the captive a ferocious blow to his ribs that made the man cry out in sudden pain.

The ranger promised the Viet Cong that he would be allowed to live, even that he and his family would be relocated to a safe place if he would do only one thing—lead the party to the site of the headquarters. The headman procrastinated a moment, evidently thinking over his response. Finally, he said, "*Không,*" (No) and cringed.

A hail of blows descended again, the longest volley yet. The skin on the man's face was broken; he spat teeth; his eyes were already swelling shut. Terry held up his hand for the rangers to stop. They did, and looked to the SEAL for whatever it was he might have in mind.

Terry said, "He's no good to us dead. He can't lead us anywhere if he can't see. This doesn't seem to be getting us too far. Let's get on with the convincing part of your interrogation. We don't have lots of time."

The rangers grinned their agreement. One of them sat the prisoner upright then tore off his blood spattered Tee shirt. He reached into a small black tool box he had carried into the hut and took out a pair of pliers and a set of wire cutters. He politely addressed the headman. "Now you will tell us what we need to know. If you do not, you will suffer. Your family will not recognize you. Speak now."

The terrorized victim showed every indication of wanting to speak. He gave his torturers an imploring look as if to say, "I am only a soldier; you cannot expect me to betray my comrades." What he actually said was, "*Làm ổn! Làm ổn!*" (Please, Please).

That was an inadequate response. The man with the tools swiftly picked up the pliers and clamped the jaws on the captive's left nipple causing him to scream in sudden agonizing pain. The ranger gave the pliers a wrenching revolving twist and pulled away the nipple leaving a bleeding hole in the chest. "*Nói!*" (Speak)! the ARVN ranger shouted in the man's ear.

The Viet Cong officer blubbered incoherently. The pliers were snapped onto the man's battered nose and a ferocious jerk applied that almost lifted the tethered man to his feet. When the pliers broke loose, there was a segment of the nose hanging in the jaws of the instrument. Blood was spattering everywhere.

The GVN soldiers were sweating from their exertions. They paused to rest. It was long enough for the communist prisoner to compose himself, and long enough for him to think over what was really important in his life. He said through battered lips and with a hiss of air through missing teeth, "I will lead you. You must promise to take me and my wives to the safe place. You must promise!"

With a display of comradeship, courtesy, and concern, the more senior of the two rangers leaned over the pounded and bruised POW and said solicitously, "But of course we promise." When you help our people, the government of Viet Nam, you will be welcomed into *Chiêu Hồi*, into *Phong Trào Chieu Tap Khang Chiêu Tập Kháng Chiến Nam Dủổng*. You will have an opportunity to show your repentance and to confess your crimes. Then you will be reeducated to serve our glorious country." He smiled graciously.

"Cám ổn ông! Cám ổn ông! đồng-chí!" (Thank you! Thank you, comrade!) cried the repentant communist fervidly. Vietnamese seldom say 'thank you' as a matter of custom, and the expression is formal, meaningful when they do. The POW meant every syllable. He saw that these men were giving him his life. He began to pour out verbal paragraphs and pages of information, things he had not been asked. He spoke earnestly and rapidly so as to avoid leaving out even the smallest detail, including volumes of information about which no one had specifically inquired. He communicated faster than anyone could comprehend or write down. He was a true convert. It was an inspiration to see.

After an hour of most productive, almost cathartic, intelligence gathering, the SEALS figured they had obtained all they needed, and were beginning to get antsy about staying around the hut much longer. Ngoc felt the same way and was beginning to fidget and to pace, taking frequent looks out the small window and the open door.

"Okay," Terry said to Ngoc when a lull in the monologue occurred finally. "Let him know that he will be going with us to the headquarters. He will be treated fairly if he is not lying. The demon *phis* of the forest will come for him if he is. The two rangers need to get this information back to command. We are going to need a heap more bodies when we hit the HQ. They can radio us at 2300 tonight so we can coordinate our rendezvous. Got that?"

"Yes," Ngoc said. Anders admired the little man's thrift of asseveration. Ngoc spoke rapidly and with hand gestures to the other two Vietnamese, handed them the sheath of notes compiled from the POW's communications; and they were off into the forest without a verbal reply.

Mark had one more question for the now fully and volubly cooperative convert, "I want to know when and where the tax collectors come through here. I want to know exactly."

Mark got his answer through the medium of Ngoc's interpretation. They let their informer rest for a short while, then untied his ankles. For comfort and convenience's sake, the Americans retied the headman's wrists in front of him. They left him completely naked because that way he was very unlikely to try to escape. Vietnamese react in a most peculiar way to nakedness. They are so polite, reserved, and modest that being naked has an almost paralyzing effect. For most adult Vietnamese, it would be unthinkable to run off into the forest without clothing. The loss of face upon encountering a countryman would be too much too bear. The former Viet Cong cadre was shaky when he first stood up and was still in misery from his wounds. He was only able to travel slowly.

Ngoc took them to a secluded forest glen surrounded by giant trees laced with caves from the massive roots and deadfall. They were on the edge of the Gan Hao River near the center of the immense submerged flood plain overgrown with rain forest. The men took refuge from the sweltering heat and burning sun deep in the hollows. Before they sat down, all of the men, even the prisoner, scoured the enclosures for venomous snakes, leeches, and insects, successfully sweeping out no small number. There was no evidence that anyone had been in this area, and they had seen no people and no houses through the entire cajeput forest through which they had passed. The men settled in, intending to use this site as their home camp for the three weeks they expected to stay in the U Minh forest.

Each of the Americans and the GVN scout began to shed his equipment. Anders watched bemused as the Kit Carson removed his belongings. They amounted to a walking camp trailer's collection. First, he set down his M-16 and the combat shotgun that hung down his back on a thong. Then came the bandoleers of ammunition and grenades, an air force K-bar knife, a foldable machete, a set of Chinese throwing knives arranged on his belt in small quick draw individual scabbards, a regulation Colt .45 1911-A1 handgun, and a Randall stiletto in an ankle scabbard. He was wearing heavy olive drab uncamouflaged fatigues that he only removed to wash, and that was not frequent. He liked them, he said, because they let out his body heat in the daytime, protected against elephant grass cuts and thorns, and kept the bugs off at night. He kept extra socks wrapped around his ankles and soaked in insect repellent. He demonstrated that his skin was free of bites, and there were no sores from leeches. He swore by bug juice to get leeches off even though he ridiculed it as a protector from mosquitoes. Anders learned something from that. Ngoc, like the rest of the long-range reconnaissance team members, did not wear underwear. "They just rot and make your skin hurt," he said.

Ngoc removed his fatigue shirt and revealed his personal medical kit wrapped around his chest and held in place with ace bandages. He meticulously inventoried the kit's contents: amps of morphine, small white tablets and a few one-a-week large orange malaria pills, scalpel blades, suture, scissors, and needles, bottles of tetracycline and ampicillin for infections, cortisone and neosporin salves, sterile dressings, five milligram dextro-amphetamine tablets and caffeine tablets to keep him alert on long marches and watches when vigilance was critical. The four pockets in the fatigue shirt held all his personal needs: aspirin and salt pills, toothpaste, small bars of hard soap, condoms, a miniature picture booklet of Buddhist prayers and a wooden statue of the Lord Buddha, a Catholic cross, a collapsible gun cleaning kit with a supply of cotton patches, a P-38, a small pair of needle-nosed pliers, a wrinkled photograph of an attractive Vietnamese woman and two small children, and a well-protected picture of a beautiful young woman with flowing long black hair standing beside the entrance to a Saigon bar smiling radiantly. There was no money.

Next came his trousers. The pockets held a country store of necessary items. The pockets were filled with packets of hard candy and the small bars of chocolate from SP packs that Americans refused to eat because of its rocklike consistency and terrible chalky, muddy taste. He had small bags of dried fruit, rice, chewing gum, chewing tobacco, and experimental LURP packages.

The acronym came from the men for whom the food (LURP) was intended, the recon units—long range reconnaissance patrols (LRRPs). The military was experimenting with the use of freeze dried very long lasting foods, an idea that came from backpacking supply companies. The foods were ultra-light, and were packaged in quiet plastic wrappings. They required only water for reconstitution, and in a tight situation, could be eaten unheated. Cooked over a sterno stove, or over a small can of lighted C-4 plastic explosive, they were nutritious and were fairly decent tasting albeit bland. Old hands like Terry and Mark rejected them out of hand because they just didn't seem right, not like the time-honored C rations (which they, like every other GI in history, detested). Terry described LURPS as 'woodpulp' and 'woodchips' (referring to the bits of meat and vegetables that often failed to absorb water fully), or, less affectionately, as 'Styrofoam peanuts.' When they had to be eaten dry, LURPS were just 'rocks.'

The three Americans shared a small laugh at the arsenal, haberdashery, and convenience store their respected Vietnamese counterpart carried. They knew they relied overmuch on the supply bases and helicopters of the American military machine, and would not do as well, stranded in Indian country for any extended period of time, as would the sturdy, self-reliant Vietnamese tracker and fighting machine. Ngoc had been engaged in continual warfare, in uniform, for twenty-two of his thirty-six years. He had been conscripted by Hoa Hao forces at the age of twelve, went into the regular GVN forces (ARVN) when he was fourteen, where he remained continually except for a two year hiatus between his seventeenth and nineteenth years when the nation was briefly between foreign invaders. He had married and fathered two daughters whom he saw for three weeks out of each year. He provided well for his small family since he had no need for money himself. Except for the three weeks of family leave each year, he had not lived in a house in his adult life.

The four men and their prisoner enjoyed the luxury of eating the last of their C-rations cooked over burning C-4. The Viet Cong's corpulent body required considerable fuel, and he had had nothing to eat since the previous night. He had trouble chewing with his broken teeth, and the foreigner's food was strange and tasteless. They ate it; so, it must not be poison; and even if it had no more nourishment than he suspected from the taste, at least it helped to fill the void in his gut. They were strange people; they did not even have rice. He lay down to rest and to pass the time before they had to set off again in the dark.

At dusk, Ngoc asked for a volunteer to help him hunt for food for their meals for the next several days. Anders spoke first, and the two SEALs were only too glad to grant him the opportunity. They made a religion out of getting as much rest as they could on these outings.

Ngoc made not the slightest sound as he and Anders set out on their hunt. Since he would not dream of firing a gun, he did not even take one with them. He carried a length of rope, his machete, and a knife. Anders had his Bowie knife. They walked to the edge of a swamp, then Ngoc signaled for Anders to move into the trees at the edge of the animal trail. The two men then waited patiently for almost an hour. Their patience was rewarded by the sound of slithering feet sliding along the trail toward the water's edge.

Ngoc put his finger to his lips in the universal signal for silence. He opened the loop he had made in the length of string and held it like a miniature lariat. The animal made surprisingly loud slurping sounds, soon sounding satiated and secure. Ngoc stepped out of the treeline hiding place taking care to disturb nothing, hardly bending the grass. He inched his way until he was standing directly over his quarry. He waited until the drinking sounds stopped, then seeing the animal lift its head slightly, dropped the noose around its thick neck and jerked strongly upward, lifting the reptile off its front feet. The Kit Carson then held the string with its gesticulating victim in his strong left hand, slipped his K-bar knife out from his teeth where he had been holding it, and plunged the blade into the beast's chest. The struggling ended with two convulsive jerks. Ngoc gave a short low whistle, and Anders joined him.

"Te te," he said, evidently naming the strange animal that looked like an elongated lizard, a cross between a lizard and a snake. Anders had never seen anything like it. He did not experience any pangs of hunger at the sight. Ngoc, on the other hand, smacked his lips in appreciative anticipation.

On the return trip to their camp, they crossed into a dense stand of cajeput trees for twenty or so meters before Ngoc had them stop. He listened very intently for a moment then smiled broadly and pointed to their left. "There," he said.

Anders wondered 'there' what?, but followed obediently. A bee landed on his exposed forearm, then another and another. Soon there was an intense buzzing; the two men were in a veritable cloud of bees. "Walk slow, and brother bees will not sting you," Ngoc said as he walked along completely oblivious to the presence of the stinging insects. He was wrong, Anders did get stung. He was not happy 'there.'

"Ah, ha!" exulted Ngoc in an excited whisper.

Anders was almost afraid to find out what 'Ah, ha' portended. It had something to do with bees, and Anders was strongly against agitating the creatures. Ngoc handed the dead reptile to Anders, squatted down and took two deep breaths. He then sprang up into the air and came down with a wild bee hive. Anders looked on incredulously at the crazy little man. "Now what do we do?" he asked in an anguished whisper.

Ngoc gave him a look that spoke volumes about his opinion of Anders' powers of reasoning and said, as his legs began to pump into a world class sprint, "Get out!" It was enough said.

A fury of bees surrounded the two men as they leaped downed trees and raced across small open areas. The reptile banged along on its string getting into the way of Anders' legs as he tried to outdistance the angry insects. Ngoc and the beehive disappeared into the water of the marsh. The stinging bees gave ample prompting to the young American to imitate his Vietnamese instructor, and Anders hit the water and ducked under as fast as he could. He thought he could still hear the furiously buzzing hymenopteran insects above him, and he held his breath until he thought his lungs would pop before coming back up.

"Is better now. They are gone, the brother bees," said Ngoc happily.

Anders was even happier. He still had the reptile on the string, and now he could see what Ngoc had accomplished with his daring-do. He was pulling the soggy structure of the hive away from the center core which was made of a ball of firm honey and rich, proteinaceous royal jelly. They carried their treasures home and set them aside for tomorrow's feasting. Terry and Mark were apparently familiar with the te te, and seemed pleased with Ngoc and Anders' night's work.

It was midnight, the time their prisoner had told them the tax collector made his rounds. They trussed the VCI leader up very securely. He prayed to the Lord Buddha to deliver his enemies from harm so they would come back to him so he would not have to lie there and starve. The four men set off into the night to the spot that the deputy commander of the VC had indicated his tax collector and courier would pass that night. It was a forced march in the darkness, but the men were backtracking toward the village and knew the way. The distance was not far enough to be particularly dangerous, and they were not going to have to come very close to the village that they presumed would be on hyperalert after the abduction of their headman.

They were to expect the tax collector any time after 0100, and the Americans and the Vietnamese scout were in position well in advance of that time. They arranged the ambush so that the courier would pass one of them (Ngoc), be taken out by two of them setup one on either side of the trail (Anders and Mark), and with one of them further along the trail to act as a fail-safe (Terry). They had only been in place for twenty minutes when the VCI cadre came down the trail laden with a large backpack and an AK-47. He was concentrating more on his burden than his weapon, since he had been carrying the same pack for three years full of money collected from the hamlets all along the serpentine trail through the dense forest without incident. The NLF owned the U Minh Forest, the Forest of Assassins.

The NLF justified their taxes that were an added burden on the impoverished populace because they lived alongside and at the same socioeconomic level with their taxed subjects. They did not try to justify the fact that they often took the uttermost farthing from hungry peasants who had gone through an extortionate tax visit from the rapacious GVN representatives during that same day. The hierarchy of the NLF turned a deaf ear to any pleas for relief from the villagers and to the onsite cadre who might think to plead their case. He was responsible for collection of taxes for the war effort and was, in part, responsible for the control of the populace. That control was to be accomplished by any means necessary including terror, torture, and murder. The Viet Cong ruthlessly exploited the miserable status of the peasants, caught in the pincers between two warring factions.

The VC monitored the inhabitants, their families, and their movements. If they stepped out of line, such as being unable to pay their taxes to the NLF, cadres came by and confiscated their GVN identity cards rendering them incapable of carrying on their everyday lives and commerce. When the GVN or American forces gave the hapless villager an even worse time, the villagers had little choice but to ally themselves with the VC. They were forced to give up their hard earned money, money that needed to go to pay the past due rent on the land where they lived as tenant farmers. The GVN men and the people from the American Revolutionary Development program sided with the landlords against the tenants in payment disputes. The small-plot farmers were forced to feed the VC cadres. They became unwilling VCI, acting as couriers and mules for fear of terrible reprisals, even public beheading. Many were forced to give all the information they could garner regarding their own sons who had been conscripted into ARVN.

It was, therefore, not hard to understand why Terry and his pirates had no compunctions about interdicting the tax collectors with maximum prejudice.

Ngoc let the black clad man pass. Fifteen meters ahead, the VCI walked between two American commandos, completely unbeknownst to him. Mark sprung from his hiding place among the low bushes and tackled the tax collector, plunging his stiletto into the man's chest. The man's arms and legs flailed in a parody of struggle, but he was already dead. It took his nervous system a second to send that message to every part of the body. Mark gave the bird-chirp signal agreed upon; and within seconds, the other three men were at his side.

Terry stripped off the courier's back pack and examined its contents. Ngoc rifled the man's pockets. Mark divested the dead enemy of his ears, and for good measure, quite expertly cut out the man's eyes, producing the globes suspended on a two centimeter long stalks of the optic nerves. The pack contained a substantial stack of Piastres, about 40,000 P. ($400); the pockets had nothing of value—a few coins, a pocket knife made in Thailand, and a matchbook advertising a bar in Camau, the largest town in Anh Xuyen Province, the farthest south in South Viet Nam, and an official VC certification of his status as a tax collector. Terry pocketed the money, and Mark slipped his trophies into his belt bag. The four men dragged the corpse well off into the underbrush.

"10,000 P. each, a big 400 bucks total. Hardly worth the effort," said Mark.

"We can put it in the apartment party fund," soothed Terry.

"Then let's do it again. The gook said we would find two more collectors bringing their ill-gotten gains in from the swamp farms and hamlets on their way to the major collection point in Camau town. They should meet up about here," Mark said, now pointing to a pair of map coordinates illuminated with his penlight.

The map had been amazingly accurate thus far. The information contained in it had been painstakingly tortured out of captured VC, and had cost more than one ARVN ranger's life in the survey. The maps were divided into square klick boxes and had numbered gridlines that intersected, allowing the user to plot an objective point using the six figure coordinates to an accuracy of close to one hundred meters. For Operation Clean-sweep, there were helpful notations about terrain, presence of swamps, approximate locations of hamlets, all of which were considered to be under VC control, outlines of streams and rivers, and assiduously accurate trail markings.

"We have been lucky tonight; and I must say, efficient. We still have time to hit the Y here," Terry pointed to a prominent trail sign on the map. "And maybe get another courier."

"Maybe even two," said Mark with malevolent enthusiasm. "I'm feeling lucky tonight." Mark felt lucky most nights.

The irregulars set off at a trot along the well-marked and well-traveled trail. In areas it was a meter and a half wide. Each man worried about the potential for booby traps; but, like Mark said, they were feeling lucky. Nonetheless, they kept very wary eyes open. There were no incidents.

They were at the Y in an hour, and their ambush was set up in another thirty minutes. They had no way of knowing whether the tax collectors had already passed that way or not. They would just have to hide and wait in the rich moist darkness of the rain forest.

It did not appear that luck was not going to be with them any more this night. But, around 0300 the men finally heard the sound of rubber sandals padding along the trail. "At least something was about to happen," Anders thought. It was spooky out in the bushes doing nothing. Besides, his legs were cramped.

Mark jumped out and leaped on the man on the path. He drove his stiletto in an upsweep from his knees aimed at the man's solar plexus. He connected instead with a grenade belt that deflected the stiletto blade innocuously away from any human parts. The VC shouted, *"Xin giúp! Xin giúp! Người ngoại quốc! Người Mỹ!"* (Help! Help! Foreigner! American!), and was about to shout again when he lost his voice from a slash of the dagger. It took Mark two more thrusts to stop the remaining signs of life. The shout carried like a cannon shot in the stillness of the jungle night. Anders saw a second silhouette stop at the sound of his comrade's voice, strain to listen, then make an abrupt about face and begin to streak back along the trail from where he had come. Anders was the only one who saw the other VCI. The young American jumped from his hiding place, swearing at his stiff legs while trying to get them to go full speed. Anders was big and well fed and well-conditioned. The small VC was relatively weak, unathletic, poorly fed, and in poor aerobic condition. It was a race against death, and the predator was the predestined winner.

The Cong dodged and swerved, zigzagged in an out of the bushes, and made for the trees before the large blond man leaped full-bodied onto the enemy's back sending him crashing face first into the rough ground. The enemy cadre struggled and twisted so ferociously that he was able to wrench himself free from his larger opponent. He attempted another dash for the trees. Once in the trees, Anders knew he would not be able to find the man; and once on the loose would be able to inform his comrades that the Americans were in their area thereby not only endangering the three of them (four, counting Ngoc), but probably wrecking the chance of a surprise attack on the regional headquarters. Anders made a sudden decision, one he knew was fraught with consequence. He pulled out his .45, skidded to a stop, adopted a spread-legged stance, aimed with both hands for his one shot, held his breath, and while exhaling, squeezed the trigger. The noise was like a bomb; it probably carried for two klicks. The bullet snapped the Cong's spine and blew a hole in his heart eight centimeters in diameter.

Anders moved like he had been propelled from a mortar tube. He was on the man's body in a pair of seconds. He ripped off the back satchel, paused long enough to cut off the man's ears, and made the mistake of turning the body over. His intent must have been to locate a weapon, or a piece of useful information, or perhaps even a trophy. Whatever the reason was, he forgot it as soon as he discovered that he had just killed an enemy by shooting the soldier in the back; and the soldier was a woman, a girl, really. She could not have been as old as sixteen. Anders felt a wave of nausea, remorse, fear, dread of retribution from a just god, shame, and a sense of cowardice flood over him all at once. Big soldier! He had just made a heroic kill—a little girl. A girl with long flowing black hair whose breasts were just budding out, whose family would be worrying about her by morning and would be hysterical by noon. He had just committed a murder. A feeling of torpor settled on him.

The sound of hurried footsteps coming from the Y in the trail toward him brought him back to reality. He leveled his Stoner (M-16) at the sound. Out of the gloom he began to make out the figure; it was too large to be a Vietnamese. Anders ran out from the edge of the trees and intersected with Mark. Mark took a couple of breaths and asked, "I presume that was your shot, no?"

"Yeah."

"Every gook for two square klicks heard it. We have to get our tails outta here. Let's boogie."

That was fine with Anders; and he took a couple of running steps before Mark, in an afterthought, remembered, "Did you pick up your man's weapon? We're in it up to our lower lips. We just might need to use a Kalashnikov."

"I'll get it." Anders spun around and sprinted back to the girl's body and snatched up her AK-47. He also picked up her satchel. He shuddered a little at having to touch the body that was already beginning to cool, at least in his imagination. He and Mark joined Terry and Ngoc at the Y and tallied weapons. They were now heavier by two AK-47s and several boxes of ammo.

"Not that this is an appropriate moment or anything," said Terry as the men prepared to take off for their camp. "But, I thought you might like to know that we hit the jackpot. My courier alone had two million Piastres on him. Anders' had something like a million. They both had some packs of dope, but I think we can leave that stuff with the bodies."

"Whew," whistled Mark softly. He was the mathematician among them and had figured that the take per man would be more than $7,500. Not a bad night's work. "I've got a suggestion. A quickie. Take the dope and throw it out into the swamp someplace. Maybe the commies will blame this little encounter on a robbery. Might even sew some seeds of discontent in the ranks. Whadda you think?"

"Smart," said Terry. "I don't care what they said about you in SEAL training. We'll do it. Now, lets get on our ponies and get out of here." The men started back down the trail from where they had come earlier that night. They moved at a hard lope despite their load of weaponry.

Terry tossed the two bricks of heroin well out into the bush and had a moment of pause about so casually throwing away close to half a million bucks. They settled down to a steady eight kilometer per hour trot and appeared to be home free as they moved off the trail at the point where they had ambushed the first tax collector (the 40,000 P. man). They stayed off the trail leading in the direction of their camp but paralleled it, moving as swiftly as they could and still maintain near silence. Two hundred meters from the ambush site, Ngoc signaled for them to stop.

He motioned toward the trail and in the direction from where they had just come. Within seconds a platoon of well-armed VC came trotting down the trail, obviously very vigilant, and not on any casual night patrol. They sent scouts into the forest at intervals; it took no great act of deduction to know that the Cong were hunting them. It would only be a matter of time, and not much of that, before the hunters would be on them.

One of the VC hunters trotted right into the middle of the four SOG men, who had quickly taken cover, and could not be seen. Ngoc dispatched him with a garrote. "We can't just hide," whispered Mark to Terry. "The locals will be ahead of us in a few minutes, and we won't know where. They will be able to set an ambush. We have to get there fustest with the mostest."

"Which means we are going to have to run our little hearts out. Let's have Ngoc trot down the trail behind them as backup. We can not, repeat, can not have any survivors. We are dead, eventually, if we do. Mark, do you and Anders remember the first swamp pond just after the descent into our little valley?" asked Terry.

The two men nodded quickly. "Okay, you guys split and get on the other side of the trail and beat the gooks to the trees just on the edge of the swamp. I'll take this side. If we are fast enough, we can catch them in a cross fire. If not, see you in hell," said Terry. "Oh, and use tracer rounds; so, we can know where we are. I would feel real bad if we took casualties from ArmaLite rounds. Kalashnikov wounds would be bad enough."

The four men took off for their assigned areas at an all-out, lung bursting run. They had to expect to make a little noise; and occasionally, a single Kalashnikov round ricocheted near where they had last been. The Viet Cong were most reluctant to waste ammunition; and, unlike their American enemies, seldom fired their weapons on automatic. Terry found his spot and was in place well in head of the Viet Cong patrol that had slowed down to probe the forest along the way, after hearing suspicious noises in the bush. This same caution allowed Anders and Mark to stagger into the trees near the leading edge of the swamp pond opposite where they presumed Terry would be set up. Hearing no noises of combat, they were sure they were ahead of their prey, rather than wasting their energies setting up an ambush after the quarry had passed by. They were also sure that anyone within two hundred meters could hear their explosive gasps for breath as they insinuated them into as hidden and as secure a position as they could find.

Ngoc's problem was to keep from running into the back of one of his enemies. When he started to make time, and determined that the Cong patrol was once again moving out quickly, he learned that he had been over anxious. He was saved from detection only because the man he had almost run over had his attention directed, by order of his superiors, up the trail, not back from whence he had come. It became almost laughable because the calls were so close. But Ngoc was not a man to laugh.

Contrary to good military order in jungle warfare, the platoon-sized group of seasoned Viet Cong, led by an experienced NVA officer in his bright green uniform, and one of the omnipresent political cadres, marched single file in close proximity to one another along the open trail. Apparently, they felt secure in the darkness because they made too much noise, loading and cocking their weapons, clanking their canteens, and whispering loudly to one another at times. The officer concluded that they were on a wild goose chase and that instead of flailing around in the night after boogey-man Americans, who had always been too cowardly to come into the U Minh Forest, he should be giving a demonstration on party and NVA discipline. He should be back in the headquarters village holding public interrogations to catch the traitorous murdering intolerable thief or thieves in their own ranks. That was what he should be doing.

The NVA officer was wrong, dead wrong. His last thought on the earth was about the slackness in discipline that had brought him out on a sticky hot night to waste his time and the people's resources. The officer was cut down by a line of small but lethal 5.56 mm bullets from Terry's M-16 that traced across the middle of his chest. He did not live to see eight of his best men drop within two seconds of his own wounding. Then Anders and Mark opened up on full automatic, firing M-16s until the 30 cartridge ammunition clips were emptied. The two Americans set down their hot-barreled ArmaLites and rapidly resumed firing with their captured Kalashnikovs until those magazines were also empty. Fourteen of the enemy had dropped to the earth, dead or dying, in a three second firestorm of lead and ruby red tracers. Seven of the Vietnamese communists had been able to get off a few ill-aimed shots co-mingled with green and white tracers before racing headlong back up the trail toward safety.

Ngoc lay along side the trail and heard the running feet headed his way as soon as the briefly cacophonous firefight had ended. None of the Cong had dared to depart from the known security of the trail in favor of the demons that lay hidden in the tangled forest in the awful night. All seven were rushing headlong, having thrown aside all caution and discipline, some even their rifles, for the moment. Their rigid standards of training would take hold in a few minutes, and they would regroup. In the meantime, however, it was critical that they get out of the deadly crossfire; so, there would be some of them left to regroup.

Ngoc laid down a killing fire from terrifyingly close range. Bodies fell within feet of him. He had taken out four of the remaining seven VC in his first barrage. It was probable that at least one of the remaining three escapees was wounded. Mark and Anders charged the trail and met Terry coming in from the opposite side. They knew Ngoc was fully engaged. "Anders, come with me! Mark clean up here!" Terry shouted. He was already running toward the sound of the guns.

Mark administered a *coup de grace* to each soldier on the trail. It took fourteen shots in as many occiputs to finish the job that had started three minutes earlier. Four men had been alive (to varying degrees), some moaning and pleading for help. Terry and Anders raced up the trail firing on the run, joining the red tracer bullets from their weapons with those of Ngoc. The tracers served to keep the converging fire from pointing at the friendlies. There was a conspicuous absence of return fire with green and white tracers. Ngoc popped out onto the trail, and shouted, "Hey, don't shoot me, misters! It's only Ngoc!"

"You heathen…you okay?" Terry shouted back.

"Hokay!" came the quick and simple response.

"Let's get a count. I made twenty-one before the firefight started."

"I think mebbe one he got away. Shine you light right here, Mebbe find blood trail!"

Anders knelt down close to the trail and flashed his light quickly on the dirt. There was trail of magenta spots, that were rapidly changing to black, leading to the left into the grass and toward the swampy tangled trees. "We have to get him," said Mark who had joined the others. "Careful, now. He has nothing to lose, and he is not dead until you have his ears."

The four men fanned out, keeping low and zigzagging through the grass and low bushes. They kept in touch and gave regular signals of their relative positions by squeezing their clickers (metal children's' toys that make an insect-like clicking sound when their metal tab is bent). Anders' heart was pounding noisily and rapidly in his chest. His adrenaline was charging through his arteries; so that, his pupils practically filled his irises; and his every sense was tuned into the surrounding danger. He stooped to flash his penlight at random moments to look for the blood trail. He had a one-fourth chance of being the one to find it and to follow it to its logical and deadly conclusion. With any luck, he would only have to be a spectator.

Anders heard a very slight shuffling sound, then nothing. He dropped prone on the moist grassy ground and waited. Nothing. He took a very quick chance, extended his arm full-length and oblique to the direction in which he was lying, and flashed his light. In that instant he saw a distinct trail of bent-over tufts of grass and the undeniable small glops of blood that were beginning to coalesce into a continuous line. The brief illumination from his flashlight produced a muzzle flash from his right. Anders felt the sear of the bullet as it made a through and through passage in his right forearm, the one holding the penlight, a small fraction of a second before he heard the high clattering sound of the AK-47 being fired once. He rolled instinctively to his left and heard three more rounds thud into the ground where his chest and balls had been. He felt the latter target intuitively. It is the natural and principal worry of all men in combat.

Do not let anyone let you think that a rifle shot happens so fast that it does not hurt. Anders was aware of the sudden thump on his arm as if he had been struck by a ball-peen hammer. This was followed by the most atrocious jolt of pain the young man had ever experienced or imagined. It felt like a glowing poker had been slowly pushed through his muscles. Then the pain subsided to a feeling like the arm was being held down on a lighted stove top. The only thing more riveting of his attention than the arm was the overwhelming and instinctive conviction that he had to get out of there or die.

"Hey, Anders. You okay?" came Mark's voice from somewhere in the blackness. Anders knew his teammate would understood if he was discourteous enough to stifle a reply.

Anders rolled over three more times, as quietly as he could. He had a pretty good idea of where his wounded assailant was lying. Anders doubted that the man could move very far or very fast. He began inching his way on his belly toward his memory of where the muzzle flash had come. He heard a gasping sound then a gurgling suppressed cough, the sound of a man strangling on his own blood in order not to give his position away. Anders laid down his M-16 and took out his .45 and cocked it. He slid forward noiselessly on the slick wet grass. Then he could see the struggling form lying outstretched on his back broadside to him. Apparently the communist detected Anders at the same time because Anders saw the man's rifle swing slowly and waveringly in his general direction.

Anders' right arm was less than useless. Not only would it not work, but it kept sending attention-getting shocks of pain. Anders concentrated for all he was worth, holding the .45 in front of him with his usually unreliable left hand. The two men were six meters from each other, their presence recognized only in dim silhouette. Anders saw the end of his enemy's gun coming around slowly so that in a few seconds it would zero in on his head, and Anders knew that the pain of that would be perfectly horrible. He squeezed the .45's trigger twice. The wounded Cong let out an unnerving, "Aaag–aaaagh!!!" after the first pistol crack, and a final hissing sigh, "Hss,aah!" after the second. He was out of his misery.

The young American rolled to the side after firing and waited. There was no more movement and no more sound of wetly labored breathing. Anders crept closer, his handgun tensely ready. He slipped in a pool of blood that had spread around the dead man like a dark aura. Anders was beyond caring. Added to the stench of the tunnel mud that still permeated his hair and clothing, he now included the smell of bloody death. Anders perfunctorily felt the enemy's neck for the carotid pulse. There was none. The man and the world were finally still.

Anders felt sick and was unable to muster the energy to help his teammates to drag the earless corpses off the trail far enough that they would not be immediately incriminating—in case everyone in the woods was deaf and did not know about the firefight already. He took one of his ace bandages and wound it tightly around the throbbing forearm. That made it feel much better, to Ander's surprise and pleasure. He began to feel less nauseated, weak, and syncopal.

"You able to walk out of here?" asked Terry in a tone that indicated that a real man would be able to jog and to leap small buildings in a single bound by now.

"Uh huh," affirmed Anders with as much enthusiasm as he could muster. It sounded less than halfhearted anyway.

"Good man," said Mark. "Takes more than a little slope bullet to stop a red-blooded American." Anders had certainly proved that he was red-blooded, he thought, looking desolately at the soaked elastic bandage on his aching arm.

"I understand the gooks smear *caca* on their shells to infect the guys they wound," Mark continued, talking rapidly due to his continued excitement. His adrenaline had not yet cleared.

"Hey, Mark," hushed Terry.

"Oops. I was just trying to cheer him up," Mark laughed sheepishly.

"Did a nice job of it, too," said Terry. He added to Anders, "Don't pay any attention to Mark; he just has a sick sense of humor."

Anders' niggling fears were not much mollified by the interchange. He was feeling much better, though. He took his share of the papers and weapons collected from the dead, and trotted along with the other three boogey-men back to their secret lair before first light.

CHAPTER 17

Ky would have preferred to take his three weeks of family leave during the warm months; it was cold in the mountains in the end of December. It was the first time he could ever remember being cold. But he was not really inclined to complain. The three week break was a fine surprise, an affirmation that he was trusted, and a great opportunity to consolidate his business affairs and to cement his business relationships. After all, he reasoned, the war could not last forever; and the unquenchable craving of the Americans for his product and services would only be profitable as long as they were in occupation. Ky was not a political person; he did not care, particularly, that Americans occupied his nation and prosecuted their war in his countryside. There was plenty of room; and they did not interfere with business. On the contrary, they were his best customers.

As soon as he learned that his presence would not be required in the compound, nor for any PRU activities, he sent word to his Burmese partners that he was available for a business venture. He had been in frequent contact with them via couriers ever since he had landed in the compound and had made small deliveries of the plastic wrapped bricks of powder whenever he could. He was scrupulously honest with those people, never held back a P. from the sales. He was an assiduous accountant, smart and quick. These traits, as well as his enviable position as one of the American's Revolutionary Development Program cadres, endeared him to the pirates, gun runners, and drug dealers who lived in Laos for convenience but moved freely throughout Indochina, Burma, Thailand, and China ignoring borders, tax collectors, human rights, common decency, and laws.

The North Vietnamese government, the NVA, and the NLF did not interfere with the profitable traffic fanning out from the Golden Triangle. It served their war-effort purposes to move the soul destroying powders into the willing hands and veins of their American enemies, and they found the smugglers to be strict in their obedience to the reasonable requests from the communist tax collectors. The marketing system worked so well that the couriers and smugglers were given written safe-conduct passages for the entire region, issued in the name of the Pathet Lao. This enlightened program extended even to members of the American CIA who, for unknown purposes of their own, participated in the handsomely profitable system. Ky was the proud possessor of such a document.

When Tran set off by military airlift to visit his family in Saigon, and Dung slipped back toward the 17th parallel to find, and hopefully, to help, his younger siblings; and Bach returned to the highlands to visit his family, his clan, and his ancestors' bones, Phan Duy Ky took an extended hike for business purposes. The Viet members of the cross-border system included some of his old contacts from the Binh Xuyên, and he was welcomed heartily as soon as he entered their safe village. The village was safe because the Americans and their protégé allies, the ARVN, had no interest in the obscure community (The Company had suggested that there were better places to hunt), and because the Viet Cong used the locale as a place of respite and as a center for the collection of their essential taxes. They, too, were happy to welcome Ky since the VC were confident that his presence would soon mean an increase in their coffers.

"I bring greetings from your old *ba* in the city," said the eldest of the three smugglers seated in the house with Ky. "He informs us that you were a good boy; and Nguyen, who unfortunately met with an accident, trusted you with deliveries in Gia Dinh. We are happy to have you with us. You will be able to move some product for us, no?"

"I will. I will be traveling in the province from time to time and can take packages to various places. I will be able to go into Hue' frequently and will carry large bags that will not be inspected. I am a policeman now, you know," said Ky and smiled.

The man with the dirty black patch on his left eye and the ridged scar running onto his forehead and down his cheek giving him the fearsome look of a classical pirate, that, indeed, he was, added, "We go to great effort to bring the white powder in from over the border. We have great expenses. Sometimes we even lose a man, even a man from the family. Because of the foreigners, we have a very profitable business even with those costs. We reward our people well. We do not forgive those who steal from us. We will search forever for anyone, however unimportant in the organization, who informs on us; so, the greedy government people can take what we have worked so hard to produce."

"I agree with that policy. I will be happy to help you protect that which is yours. It is in my interest to do so. I wish to become a rich business man like you, once I have proved myself. This war cannot last forever, then who knows how such as we can make a decent living?" replied Ky.

The decent living to which Ky referred involved a very complex economic system starting with the prosperous farmers of the Golden Triangle: that area of Laos, Burma, and Thailand, blessed with the perfect mixture of alkaline soil, sun, water, temperature, altitude, isolation, and freedom from government interference, that so favored the growth of *Papaver somniferium*, the opium poppy. Tens of thousands of industrious workers planted, watered, and cultivated the poppies, incised the fruits and collected the milky juice of the unripe seed capsules, air dried the juice into a brownish mass of gum. Others further dried and watched over the gum until it became the transportable lumps, cakes, or bricks, or the final powdered product. Still others extracted the purified opium alkaloids (morphine, codeine, papaverine, and noscapine), made semisynthetic narcotic analgesics and hypnotics (e.g. heroin) in their sophisticated plants. Some worked to transport the raw materials out of the jungles, to collect the product at distribution and manufacturing centers, and to distribute the powder to wholesalers for cutting and diluting. The final links in the business chain provided the end-product to street-corner sellers and their addicted buyers. The most important of all of these products was the semisynthetic $C21H23N03$, Diacetyl morphine—heroin, four to eight times more potent than the legitimate narcotic, morphine. In its purest form, China White Number Four, the powder was valued at two to three thousand dollars an ounce, one hundred to one hundred fifty thousand dollars a kilogram in Asian markets—wholesale.

The industry had a significant reawakening with the advent of the Americans in Viet Nam. The traffic between China, India, and Burma slowed to a trickle after 1917 when those countries agreed to pursue its interdiction with full vigor. The faithful addicts of China and Indochina found it more difficult even to get the raw opium they needed for their bamboo pipes. The presence of the American soldiers, after 1945 and especially after 1965, with their overwhelming craving for heroin and marijuana and their close proximity to the Golden Triangle greatly simplified the supply, demand, and transport problems making the risk/profit ratios once again worth the effort for the enterprising people of this clandestine industry. The yearly worldwide legitimate medicinal needs for opium products, some 750 tons, over and above the synthetic and semisynthetic products, were supplied by the major legal opium producing and exporting countries, India and Turkey. That left the Golden Triangle to cater to the world's other needs for opium alkaloids—the value of which was known to be many times that of the medicinal uses.

A financial arrangement was struck between the four men in the house; then, they set out for the mountains to teach Ky the trail and the pickup and drop-off places. For three weeks Ky and the men walked along the mountain trails and boated along rivers meeting cooperative Montagnards and Hmongs. Ky learned which villages were accommodating and which ones would betray them. He was given the location of small arms caches left for emergencies, and became acquainted with the villagers and farmers in northern Thailand and southeastern Burma, who grew the poppies and started the process of making the gum balls that were refined into the white powder that men would kill and die for. Ky met the key workers across Laos and North Viet Nam (PL, PMS, and Hmong), who operated because the NVA and communist Pathet Lao government permitted them to do so.

"You will recognize that nothing has been hidden from you because you are to be a partner in our enterprise. That knowledge puts you in a very strong position to make your fortune and to help us with our work. I would like to show you the price of betraying us and giving others that knowledge," the pirate told Ky on the last day he was to be in the triangle. Ky had to get back to the PRU compound in two or three days. He had four kilo bricks in his rucksack.

Ky followed obediently, although he felt disinclined, preparing himself so he would not be shocked by anything. It was well that he did. He was taken to the center of a hamlet dependent on the village where he had been staying as a base of operations while he and the other men toured the primitive mountainous territory.

In the center of the open field located in front of the houses stood a pair of poles secured in the ground and kept separated and in position by a crossbeam lashed to the top of the two uprights. A pair of stout ropes were tied to the cross beam about six feet apart. Suspended on the ropes was a man, a Montagnard, from his long hair and from the blackened and filed teeth showing through the autumn leaf dry half-open lips. On the ends of the ropes were attached pig hooks, heavy, rusted, and stained, dull pointed pieces of curved iron used to hang hogs for butchering. The hooks had been driven through the skin and pectoralis muscles of the man's upper chest, and he had been hung from the cross beam. To prevent him from wriggling himself off the hooks by tearing them out of his flesh, his ankles had been lashed to the poles keeping him spread-eagled in the roasting sun. A wooden stake had been driven through the fleshy space in front of his Achilles tendons, and the ropes secured to the slivery pieces of wood. So his hands would not be used to tear at the hooks, they had been hacked off with a crude ax.

Ravens were perched on the man's head and shoulders and had already pecked out his eyes and were clawing with their talons at the festering blood and eschars around the infected sites where the hooks held the chest. The man's genitalia had been turned to charcoal, and his thorax was studded with scorched holes. Ky wondered how long it had taken for him to die, how long he had been dead, and how long he would be left to hang there as an object lesson. The only thing causing the hardened Binh Xuyên criminal, and more recently appointed official provincial policeman, to flinch was when he saw the corpse wince and withdraw from a particularly savage clawing by one of the ravens. Ky knew that the man still had more to pay.

None of his new partners in the heroin trade felt the need to say anything more regarding the graphic lesson provided for their novice man. Ky joined them for a night's convivial drinking before they were to set out in the morning across the pass through the Truong Son Mountains (Annamite Cordillera), and back into the Thau Thien Province of the Republic of Viet Nam. The businessmen feasted on *cồm chiên bọ hung lớn* (huge fried rice beetles) brought up from the lowlands and enjoyed *con dế mèn* or when cooked, *con dế chiên* (fried crickets), *con nhện* (tarantella), and *con khỉ* (monkey) roasted on a spit. They became pleasantly drunk on potent vinegary palm wine provided by the Montagnards. The four partners set off in broad daylight the next morning taking little in the way of security precautions along the trail for which they had a long-standing proprietary disposition. Phan Duy Ky had no illusions that he could ever extract himself from the brotherhood of smugglers, not that he would have wanted to. The previous day's lesson was indelible.

———————————— ◆ ◆ ◆ ◆ ◆ ————————————

Mark's mental motor ran too fast, and he was too restless to lie about in the cave of roots listening to the whining of the captive and the Ngoc's high-pitched tuneless humming. After the fourth full day of crouching and cringing in seclusion waiting for the dragnet searching for them to lose enthusiasm, he was sure things were back to normalcy in the Viet Cong controlled jungle. He importuned Terry, Ngoc, and Anders, "We can get another headman, hit a site deeper in the forest. It'll be a piece of cake. Let's go out tonight; I've got a plan. We can find another tax collector; you've gotta admit that was a nonproblem the first go around."

Finally Terry wearied of the repetition, although he did not change his perception of the risks, and said to Mark, "okay, okay. If you are so hot to go out and get your head blown off or to be roasted on a spit, do it. I can't authorize more than one of us, and that means you only, to go out. The priority of this entire mission is to hit the district commander's HQ with all of our guys. The rest of them will be here in two days. That gives you tonight and tomorrow night only."

"Check, boss," said Mark with a devil-may-care smile that made his arguments seem so plausible.

"Two things, Mark. And I'm serious. I wanna know exactly where you're going and some idea of how long you are gonna be. Second, is just the usual advice or, in this case, request; no heroics, okay? I don't want to have to write one of those letters. Understand?"

"Check, boss. You know me, old Mark P. Whitehead. Prudence is my middle name."

Terry rolled his eyes. "So, what do you have in your adventurous mini-mind, Prudence?"

"I am gonna return something. It's just a little trick I picked up from our cong friends. I'm gonna give them the old sees-all-hears-all-knows-all treatment."

"Where?"

"This guy's village," Mark said indicating the captive.

"How? I mean, how are you gonna tack them up without making enough noise to bring the whole camp down on you?"

"Already thought about that. Thought about it before we even came. I brought pushpins. I'll just tack them up nice and quiet-like and slip betimes away into the primeval forest. No one will be the wiser until morning," said Mark, his face revealing his boyish pleasure at recounting his cleverness.

Terry rolled his eyes back into his head.

Anders said, "Look, I'll go with him. Give him some backup at least. Is that okay?"

"It's not okay. No. I can't let that happen. We have to be here for sure to hit that HQ," said Terry emphatically. He was annoyed that he might have to argue with the younger man as well as his perpetually troublesome fellow SEAL with his overactive boyish zeal.

"But," started Anders. Terry gave him a look.

"I'll be all right, guys. This is just a lark. No big deal. Nobody is gonna see me on my walk in the park."

Terry's look assured no more argument although every man except Mark knew Mark's plan was crazy, too much risk for too little gain. Mark put on his flak jacket and a suitable armamentarium. He made sure he was covered, even to the point of putting on camouflage gloves. He had Anders apply camouflage face paint. He wore the expression of a teenager going out on one of his first dates when he slipped away into the dark.

It was a little over three hours before he returned, sweating from the heat of the night and from what the rest of the men presumed was a run of some distance.

"Well?" asked Terry.

"Piece of cake. Nobody saw me. When they wake up in the morning and take a stroll past their granary, they'll know the eyes of the government can see everywhere and the ears can hear even in their homes. Make 'em nervous, at least."

The following night Mark's limited patience ran out again. "I'm ready to take down another tax collector. 'To interdict the Viet Cong Infrastructure economic supply-line and thereby abbreviate the conflict by preventing the accumulation of necessary tactical materiel,'" Mark said in the pompous and obfuscatory jargon of the military command.

"Just relax a couple of days; be patient," Terry said to the other SEAL.

Mark persisted, "It might be half a week before the rest of your pirates arrive on the scene. Let's take advantage of the time. Create a little havoc for Lane Duerk and the American Way."

"Do you even know where to find another courier?" Terry asked, beginning to wear down. "No way are you going to go back to any of the same attack sites where we've been. You have to agree to that or nothing doing."

"No suh, massa," Mark mocked, bowing and shuffling in his best Stepin Fetchit routine. "I have located some fine print on our map that tells me that there is another route a bit farther south."

Terry thought he knew every detail of the map and sounded a little put out when he replied, "You sure? Show me."

Mark showed him.

"That's at least a two day round trip if you move in the day and not just at night," Terry complained expressing a legitimate concern.

"We can scurry right along, do the bidding of our wise leaders by relieving the VCI of the ill-gotten gains extorted from the good people of the countryside, and be back here in two days, three tops. We should have four full days before we meet up with the rest of the Dead-End Kids and go after the big game."

"Oh, all right. Who's 'we'?"

"Best to have three. But like the Sea-bees say, 'Can do' with two."

"Think two."

"So, do I hear the sound of volunteering?" Mark said looking innocently at Anders for a moment then shifting his glance to Ngoc.

"Well, I'm hot to trot," said Anders with theatrical enthusiasm. "I could use the activity. I will be more than a little crazy if I stay cooped up in here for another two days."

"Settled," said Mark. Terry accepted his defeat with grace and laughed at his overzealous SEAL partner and the ardent CIA agent.

"Don't get yourselves killed. I'll bring you up on company charges if you do. I am too tired to haul your dead carcasses out of this tropical paradise."

They left at 2200 when it was fully dark. The two young men were in excellent condition and made good time through the night. Fearing that the trails would all be booby trapped in honor of their last appearance, Mark and Anders kept off the beaten tracks and well into the forest paralleling the trails. They slept through the morning when the activity of the local people was at its height and moved again during siesta. They were at the planned ambush site by midnight after a strenuous push through the day.

"I have the crossbow," Anders reminded Mark. "Think we can do this real quiet? Like no convincing display of the awesome firepower of the righteous?"

"Like Indians?" Mark said and pantomimed a skulking red skin using two fingers to represent feathers.

"Yeah, like that," answered Anders. "Let me ask you a question. What do you really think of all of this? I mean, is the war effort really as much of a joke to you as you make out?"

Mark thought a minute. "I guess I do think it's a kind of big joke. I think the big chiefs—the WOMS—in Washington in their marble buildings and the military brass sitting in their restored mansions in Saigon have got it all wrong. They think they are going to make these dinks want democracy. None of those little people care for sour owl puckey. Not one in ten could tell you the name of the president of the country, or even the official name of the country. They don't want America's democracy or America. They just want to be left alone. They'd like to go out during the day with no one shooting at them. That's the joke of it—the idea that those men in starched white shirts and ties in big, clean, sweet smelling America know what is best for little Nguyen with his water buffalo. That our morality means something here.

"Terry told me once a thing Aristotle said, 'Little boys throw rocks at frogs in jest, but the frogs die in earnest.' It's no joke what goes on in the field, in the rice paddies and jungles. Good guys die. Even decent slopes are being killed for nothing. I only believe in one thing: that's in our guys, just the guys in our apartment. We do our job and do it well, just like the marine grunts, and the airbornes, and the brown water navy boys, and the airman, and all the rest. That's all anyone can ask. It's enough to believe in, and that part of it is no joke."

It was the longest speech Anders had ever heard Mark give—Mark who always seemed to make light of the seriousness of their involvement in the conflict, who always seemed to have a joke and seemed to think of the fighting and killing as some kind of fun. Anders sat quietly in his hideout of tall grasses and bushes to contemplate what Mark had said as the two men waited patiently for the tax courier.

Their patience was rewarded at nearly 0415. Two men came along the dusty trail, both wary and alert to every sound. One of them was small and carried only an AK-47; the other was a large man who had an American M-79, and an American .45, as well as his Kalashnikov. Evidently, news of the previous attacks on tax collectors had reached throughout the forest, and no one was taking any chances. Mark had not used the crossbow before; and while he agreed with its use, he relegated that weapon to Anders who had had experience. He guessed that Anders had had some decent training after all. Mark trained the sights of his M-16 on the rearmost of the two men, giving Anders first shot with the silent weapon at the man in front.

"Don't fire unless you have to. Give me a chance to get them both first," Anders whispered directly into Mark's ear.

Mark gave an unenthusiastic thumbs-up.

Anders let the men get directly across from where he and Mark were hiding before taking full aim. It was dark, only the light of the stars and half-moon illuminated the targets. He fired. Nothing happened. There was no sound of the arrow, certainly no indication that it had hit either of the men. The tax collectors kept walking warily along. Marked nudged Anders, prompting him. They could not afford to have the tax collectors get out of range. Anders concentrated and fired again.

The Viet Cong in front dropped over dead in front of the well-armed soldier behind him. It was eerily silent, so quiet that it was as if an invisible stroke from God had felled the man. His partner was much more nonplused by the sudden soundless death of his comrade than he would have been if a mortar had taken him out. That he could have understood. For a moment he stood in consternation looking down at his comrade. Then he whispered loudly for the man to get up. He must have thought that was silly of him; in a second he would realize that the man was dead, somehow killed by an unseen enemy.

As the second target made his thorax inviting by pausing, Anders was able to insert a new arrow shaft and to let it fly. This time all of the men heard the thunk of the arrow as it stuck the VCs unprotected chest and collapsed his lung. He was stunned but able to cry out. He sagged to his knees clawing at the terrible thing sticking out of him. He began to cry out, but he found the struggle to get breath all he could do as his hemithorax cavity with the collapsed lung began to fill rapidly with blood. He was still very much alive when Mark sped out of the brush and up the trail toward him. The cong courier was not fast enough to get his AK-47 up for a shot, but he had a knife in his hand before Mark was upon him. Anders was on the run toward the pair, two seconds behind Mark.

The game fighting Viet Cong slashed the air with his knife in his right hand keeping Mark momentarily at bay. The man held on to the painful stump of the arrow with his left. Anders did not see the knife as he hurtled up onto the dodging and parrying men. The Viet Cong swept his blade at Anders and opened a sizable gash across the front of the large blond man's right thigh. His momentum carried Anders on into the fighting man knocking him over. Mark jumped in grabbing the still dangerous knife wielding arm of the dying man. Anders punched the cong's face with all the force of his strong young body and of the momentum of his hurtling body. Mark held the wrist with both hands in a death-grip. Anders whipped his Randall stiletto from its leg scabbard and plunged it into the depression in the enemy's throat where the two clavicles met. There was a final very brief furious thrashing of all four limbs and a devilish gurgling from the man's open throat. The stiletto blade had broken in half. The Viet Cong was finally still.

"You okay?" Anders asked Mark, panting from his exertions.

"Um hum," Mark replied. Then he saw the blood soaked pant leg on his partner.

"What's that?"

It registered on Anders for the first time that he had been wounded. Even his right forearm started to hurt where the bullet had passed through it days before. "I think he cut me," panted Anders.

"That looks like another Purple Heart to me. Let me see it." Mark opened the slashed area of Ander's fatigue pants further and did not like the looks of the deep cut. "Man, you are clumsy. Accident prone. First your head, then your arm, now your leg. You gotta be more careful. For one thing, you might die of lead poisoning next time. Whatta my gonna do with you?"

"For starters, how 'bout wrapping this cut."

"Yeah, good plan." Mark took off some gauze pads and expertly wrapped the wound tightly with two ace elastic bandages. He used Anders'—did not want to waste his own.

"Can you walk?"

"Sure. It'll hurt, but I'm a spook; and spooks are tough."

Anders could walk without too much difficulty, but it did hurt. The two men dragged the bodies as far off the trail as they could, threw away their weapons and rifled the tax collection ruck sack. There was no contraband such as heroin, but there was a neat stack of Vietnamese Piastres and even some nearly newly minted American twenty dollar bills, neatly banded. Mark hurriedly counted a total of twenty-two thousand American, including the Piastres at the going exchange rate.

"Nice haul," he said. "Worth the aggravation."

"Especially if the aggravation happens to the other guy."

"Well, that's a true statement. All in all, I've kind of enjoyed it. Other than for that little mishap, how did you like the play, Mrs. Lincoln?" Mark joked. Anders could do nothing but shake his head and laugh.

The two Americans were back in their cave in thirty hours after a forced march through the dense jungle. It was exhausting, but Mark wanted to get Anders' wound worked on before it got infected. Terry shook his head in pleased disbelief at the handsome addition to their stock of money and in displeasure at the wound. He set about to inject it with lidocaine local anesthetic then scrubbed it with soap until it was bleeding freely, then stuffed an iodine soaked cloth into the gash. When the bleeding subsided, Terry expertly sewed it up. It looked clean. For good measure, Terry checked out the injured right arm which was entirely free from swelling or other signs of infection. It was only mildly tender. The simple through and through entrance and exit wounds were ragged but otherwise as healthy as could be expected under their present conditions. It was still throbbing and painful, but his fingers worked all right; so, there did not seem much to worry about. Ander's two week old head wound had become a livid fresh scar, but was not a problem.

Terry said, "I think we should divide up the tax collectors' donation to the apartmental cause; so, we can have as much of it as possible if one of us buys the farm out there."

Ngoc protested momentarily saying he had no use for the money. Terry sensibly pointed out, "Maybe you don't need anything out in the bush, but think of your family—think what they can do with this money we took away from our enemy's use."

Ngoc thought about his family and accepted his share with no further statement of demurrer. Each of the four men now held on his person the comfort of over $15,000 in American and Vietnamese cash. That much money would keep Ngoc's family in style for two years or would allow them to buy land, to become one of those terrible capitalists the VC were always complaining about.

———————————•◆•━◆━•◆•———————————

During his three week family leave Dung did not find his siblings, his younger brother and sister. His ability to search was limited because he could not make inquiries nor let his presence known in Bo Ho Su where he was regarded as a traitor, and the children and their grandmother were no longer in the adjacent hamlet. He returned to the PRU base after two weeks and tried to enjoy sitting around.

Bach treated his Montagnard family to a trunk full of brightly colored bolts of cloth, new knives made of good steel, two radios (of dubious value because there was no electricity) which were the most popular items in his gift pack, bottles of buttons, sequins, and multicolored and various sized beads, and, most significantly, to a great feast of hard to come by meat and fruits. He returned to the PRU compound with his status as a man of significance fully established in his village.

Tran was shocked and grieved when he learned of the deaths of his family at the hands of the South Vietnamese government. The fact that they had been given due process of the law did not mollify Tran nor erase the resentment he felt at the six day course from arrest to execution of his loved ones, nor did it alleviate the deep affront he felt at not even having been informed of their deaths. He did not know where they were buried, or even if they were buried. That added uncertainty and fear for the future of himself and all his generations to his already grievous pain. It occurred to Tran to seek out his old VCI comrades, but he realized it was too late for that. His 'Sat Cong' tattoo alone would make such a visit foolhardy, and the memory of the terrors of Con Son Island Prison was enough to erase such foolish thoughts from his confused brain. The only family he now had were the men of the PRU. He was thoroughly disillusioned in the government of Viet Nam, in the Viet Cong, and in humanity outside the three men in his own PRU team upon whom he counted. Tran was back at the compound in less than a week.

Ky came in on the last day of 1966. He seemed to be a little the worse for the wear but to be brimming with enthusiasm. He, quite evidently, had had a fine time on his family leave. Tran and Dung envied Bach and Ky.

All four men looked on in disbelief when they saw Xuan and Oanh moving about the compound as freely as they. Cleve Howard himself informed them that the lie detector and the computer had cleared Oanh, but that Xuan had been established to be a VC traitor. Howard enlisted the four men to observe Xuan, but to do nothing more than that until the new American operational chief arrived in the first of the new year, 1967, that would officially be the year of the sheep after the lunar new year. They were very watchful.

The remaining eight men, Terry's other pirates, and their four Vietnamese rangers straggled in to join Terry, Mark, Anders, Ngoc, and their captive by the tenth day of Operation Foreplay in the U Minh Forest, reconstituting the whole Apartment Army, as the Force Recon commando, Jim Smith, had originally characterized them. Jim was something of a joiner; in addition to being a member of the marines and the Apartment Army, he was a charter member of the Jim Smith Society of America. The only requirement for membership, besides the nominal dues, was that your name be 'Jim Smith.' By 1966, the society boasted of having 12,000 members, thirteen of whom were women.

The sixteen men spent the major part of the next three days drawing up, haggling about, and revising their plan of attack on the District Chief's compound. Ngoc, Anders, and another of the Vietnamese rangers made a midnight reconnoitering of the area; and their information was used to set up the final approach and plan. The compound was deceptively benign in appearance, a collection of thatched roof huts with families, the occasional skinny dog and potbellied pig, and no obvious evidence of armaments or prominent security arrangements as might be expected for a major regional center of an army. The men and women who served their country (different from the ones who served the government of South Viet Nam) in the capacity of running the resistance and liberation struggle were content to appear innocuous, to live in simple surroundings with their power bases scattered in small segments throughout their sector of the forest. They lived in strict accordance with President Ho's admonition: 'The army and the people are like fish and water...The soldiers must not steal even a needle or a bit of thread belonging to the people.'

More practiced eyes, like those of the SOG irregulars and the Vietnamese rangers, could locate telltale evidences of serious security measures in the village marking it as an important center. There was an armory in what passed as a rice storage building. Machine gun nests were insinuated between closely proximate buildings, behind large bushes, and piles of rock. The village trash pile, maintained in careful visual disarray, held three mortar emplacements, each tube pointing in a different direction. There were well concealed hatch covers that lead into dark tunnels. That was as much as the American and Vietnamese commandos dared learn. The villagers maintained patrols of fully alert and very well armed sentries.

Terry's plan called for four groups of three-man teams to situate themselves at the four corners of the village and to have the heaviest firepower possible, all the M-79 grenade launchers (each with its 15.24 centimeter flip-top adjustable sight removed to prevent catching on the snarling branches of the forest bushes), M-60 machine guns, and the two M-72 LAWs brought in by the SAS Sergeant-major, Giles Housekeeper, and the army special forces associate with the pirates, Duncan Hertel. One man was assigned (by drawing of lots) to guard the captured village headman. Mark was furious at having drawn the short straw and protested vehemently and ineffectively.

A set of three of the men was assigned to enter the village proper, to find, and either to kill, or if possible, to kidnap the VC section chief. Terry reserved the right to head that unit. By another lottery, the other two men were chosen. The lots fell to Hank Weatherby, the expatriate San Francisco mercenary and to Nguyen Quan Giac, the Vietnamese ranger who had led Jim Smith and Jaime Ortega-Gonzalga, the Puerto Rican policeman, into the U Minh. Anders was not allowed to draw a straw because of his wounds.

Two days before the intended attack, Axel Hodges, the airborne sniper, Bonly Lonly Lloyd, the active duty army ranger, and Giac, the LLDB were sent out to sew discord in the communist ranks by disturbing a village south and west of the HQ camp. Lloyd got his name the army way. He was christened with initials instead of Christian names; so, when he joined the army, he was listed on official documents as B (only) L (only) Lloyd. In no time he became Bonly Lonly Lloyd.

The three commandos moved into the tiny targeted community in the night and kidnapped the elderly first wife of the headman and a pregnant teenaged girl. The two women were mercifully knocked on the head and rendered unconscious; then, they were decapitated. The unborn infant was cut from his mother's womb. The fetus was far enough advanced to be able to determine its sex. The heads of the two women were impaled on the two gate posts of the entrance to the village. The women's bodies were suspended upside down by their ankles, an intended insult; and notes in Vietnamese were pinned to their naked breasts. The notes read, "*CHỈ-DIẾM VIÊN*" (INFORMER) on the older woman and "*KẺ PHẢN-BỘI*" (TRAITOR) on the younger woman, the victim of the rude Caesarean section. The fetus was hung from a branch. His sign read, "*TRÁI CÂY HU THỐI*" (ROTTEN FRUIT). The murders, mutilations, and 'progressive information' signs, as the NLF euphemistically called their propaganda, were typical of Viet Cong retaliations; and the villagers would readily blame the VC for the atrocities. The anguish would be all the worse since the women were innocent—willing providers for the NLF.

On the night before the main attack, while the other teams were moving into place, Ngoc, Nguyen Cham, and Nguyen Ly Hai, with Greg Conklin, the retired special forces master sergeant, and Giles Housekeeper as unseen backups, terrorized a village. They chose a very small hamlet, one having only three dwellings. Presumably, the occupants were all interrelated.

The North Vietnamese military-political apparatus uses three specialized formal units of enforcement—The *Trinh Sæt* (TS), military intelligence apparatus consisting of units composed of one sergeant and three NCOs in uniform, The Đ*ich Vên* (DV) or the specialists of 'moral intervention' as the armed propaganda psychological warfare units were euphemistically known, and the *Công-An* (CA). The DV and CA units employed every tool from friendly persuasion to public torture, kidnapping, and murder to convey their messages.

Posing as DRVN *Cong-an* (Civilian secret police), the three Vietnamese impostors rousted the entire hamlet from their beds and lined them up in front of the headman's house. Cham, the best actor of the group, harangued the sleepy and frightened people for nearly an hour, accusing them of collaboration with the corrupt GVN oppressors and of betrayal of the righteous cause of the people. From a long rice-paper list of crimes Cham read in terrifying slow magisterial tones. It was an indictment and death sentence in one. The paper had been prepared in the apartment before the men left Can Tho. Experience with VC tactics, and capturing similar documents from villages they had passed in the course of their nighttime missions had enabled the pirates to prepare a thoroughly believable warrant with the linguistic and calligraphic help of a secretary from the Task 116 office.

When Cham finished his communistic condemnation of the hamlet, he announced that the headman must suffer for the crimes of the rest of the villagers and would serve as an example for other would-be betrayers of the people. Cham stepped aside, and Ngoc and Hai dragged the petrified old man to the center of the line. There was muffled weeping from the other family members, even the men. The headman was made to kneel, then he was decapitated with a scimitar that had been taken as a trophy on an earlier foray by the Apartment Army. The indictment document was laid on the blood covered thorax of the headless corpse, and the scimitar was stabbed through it so the blade remained standing in the dead man as a deep lesson and as evidence of VC culpability should proof be required by disbelieving villagers from neighboring hamlets. The terrorized villagers were convinced by the lesson they had witnessed; they indeed feared the Viet Cong cadres all the more, almost as much as they feared and mistrusted the representatives of the RVN who pillaged their homes and raped their women by day.

All sixteen SOG commandos moved surreptitiously into their positions around the village that the compliant captive had previously identified, and the three man team had reconnoitered. Every man was as heavily armed as he could carry, and all of them were wearing either the heavy fiberglass flak jackets or the lighter bulletproof breast plate they called a 'chicken plate.' It was 24 December, 1966, as planned.

Only Mark complained about his assignment. He looked at the captive with unremitting malice, and the helpless man cringed and shivered.

Terry Brannigan, Hank Weatherby, and Nguyen Quan Giac crawled into the village with painstaking slowness, inching their way over and around trip wires and by feeling for buried Claymores with their outstretched finger tips or by inserting slender metal probes at a thirty degree angle into the earth near the suspected mines. They spent fifteen difficult minutes cutting their way laboriously through the bramble of concertina wire artfully laid just inside the treeline bordering the clearing. The three men made their way on their bellies all the way to the house identified as that of the headman and as the regional VC headquarters. The headman was presumed to be one of the senior advisors to and functionaries of COSVN—one of the leaders of the 8,000 person organization. Brannigan, Weatherby, and Nguyen were in place by 0300 and had successfully escaped detection by any of the two man guard patrols.

Terry signaled for Giac to follow him into the front door and for Hank Weatherby to cover them at the rear entrance. The pirate captain and the slender brown ranger slid without sound into the main family room of the house. They found the building to be an impressive armory. Stacks of Kalashnikov assault rifles, SKS knock-off copies, M-7s, M-14s, B-40 NVA grenade launchers and several score of their 88 mm projectiles, neatly arranged two pound hard yellow bricks of NVA plastic explosive, and piles of village-made hand grenades filled one-half of the living quarters.

There were baskets of grenade parts and a table with partially assembled hand explosives. The grenades had wooden handles that had holes bored down the center. Sheet metal strips were rolled around a collection of C-4 and an assortment of nails, metal fragments, shards of broken glass, mainly from GI Coke bottles, and small hard kernels of human feces. Lying on the table were fuses, C-4, black powder, pre-cut metal strips, and hard cylinders of wax. This was home to the chief, his arsenal, and the principal munitions factory for a third of the U Minh Forest. The plan to kidnap the VC officer now seemed inadequate. Terry made a mental note to have his pirates drop a few grenades on the house as a gesture of parting once they had the headman on his way back to a Riverine Patrol base for interrogation by G-2.

He and Giac moved cautiously through the building and into the sleeping quarters. It was very dark in that room. Terry could make out Hank's silhouetted form in the blackness at the opposite edge of the bedroom. He had come in through the side door, leaving it open to afford a little more light. By passing alongside the futons, Terry and Giac could make out the forms of an older man sleeping in his underwear flanked by two younger men fully dressed in black pajamas. They presumed they were looking at the chief and his two aides-de-camp or bodyguards. There were two woman, one probably older, and one, a young woman lying with her limbs askew on her mat in perfect innocent repose. Three children were tangled together on one large mat, their arms around each other in familial security.

Terry signaled Hank and by hand gestures assigned him the task of killing one of the guards and had Giac take out the other. He put his finger to his lips, an unnecessarily obvious gesture. Terry, himself, moved directly over the snoring headman. He stuck the edge of a six inch strip of duct tape to his left forearm and unsheathed his marine Bowie knife.

Terry whispered in the dark, "One, two, three." The two men beside Terry clamped vice-like grips over their sleeping victims' mouths and simultaneously plunged their stilettos into the VCs' chests aiming to the left of the sternum at where they judged the 4-5 intercostal space to be. Terry slapped the strip of duct tape over the regional commander's mouth and jammed his knife blade hard enough against the man's throat to draw blood. There were a few convulsive sounds of a death struggle on either side of the senior man, but no outcry. The VC District Commander saw the futility of struggle immediately and stared up at the face of death above him in the dim light.

The two women stirred, and one sat up on her futon. Giac harshly ordered her to keep her mouth shut, or he and the Americans would kill her husband. If she sounded the alarm in less than half an hour, he and his men would no alternative but to kill him. She promised to be quiet, begged for her spouse's life, and settled back onto the futon cringing. Terry cut off the man's underwear briefs, so that he was naked; and he and the others hurriedly slipped out the side door and onto the grass of the open area of the village. Giac left a simple grenade booby trap with its trip wire stretched across the open front door, four inches off the floor.

Hank walked around the corner of the commander's house and in the thick mantel of darkness ran abruptly into one man of a two sentry patrol knocking both he and the sentry to the ground. The surprise was too great for the VC man on the ground, and he died from Hank's knife before he could sound any alarm. The second man jumped on Hank's back and started to pummel the American. He did not have his knife out; and at such close range, his Kalashnikov was useless. Terry piled on seeking to determine in the darkness which body was the VC and which was Hank's. Size made the determination. Terry stabbed the smaller body repeatedly. The VC man called out for help in his last extremity. It was not immediately apparent if he had been heard.

Terry, Hank, Giac, and the naked headman began to sprint across the open field toward the location of the American fighting position nearest the main trail. When they reached the coils of antipersonnel wire, they were well away from any opening and had to slow down to snip through the tangled strands. From the headman's house they and everyone else for a square klick heard the screaming voice of the woman who had promised to be quiet yelling, *"Gooks! Gooks! Bon Gooks đã bắt người sĩ quan chỉ huy! Hãy gan dạ lên và tì ông ta! Mọi người hãy vững lên!"* (Gooks! Gooks! The gooks got the commander! Be men and find him! Everyone up!) (The pejorative term, 'gook,' was used by Vietnamese to denigrate their American enemies, probably before the Americans did the reciprocal.)

Hell broke loose from its sleeping tethers. The front door grenade booby trap went off. Two score fighting men and women burst out of the huts, some half-naked, but all wielding AK-47s. They were well-disciplined and held their fire until one of them detected the tell-tail snapping recoil of a released wire at the village periphery. A fiery barrage of automatic weapons fire converged on the opening hole in the village's defenses.

Giac dropped from a line of bullets that marched up his back. Hank went flat on the ground trying to make himself one with the earth. Terry had just completed the last wire cut and was pulling the reluctant captive head man through the opening when the firing erupted. Sensing his chance, the captive jerked back to retreat toward his own men figuring that Terry had all he could handle to get himself out of there. It was a mistake on his part. Terry turned in an instant and shot the kidnapped man once in the middle of his bare chest with his service .45. Hank crawled over the dead man's body, and he and Terry made a beeline for their own defensive position. Ruby red tracers were now pouring out of the Americans' improvised bunker co-mingling in the night air with the communist white and green tracers. The sound was deafening, and now the sky was intermittently as light as early dawn from all the firing.

The three other American positions now opened fire with everything they had and the surprised village cong fighters were caught in a winnowing crossfire. They began dropping in twos and threes until they dived for whatever cover they could find. Terry and Hank dived into the improvised defense position kicking the original occupants in their chests and extremities as they landed awkwardly. The two newcomers were soon firing furiously as well.

Stray bullets ricocheted all around Mark and the prisoner who had betrayed his regional commander. The solitary SEAL dared not return fire for fear of giving away his position. Mark contemplated his situation and his situation and found it unacceptable. He needed to be with his fellow pirates. He shot the captive in the back of the head as the headman cowered in among the branches of the bush where he and Mark had been hiding. Then Mark tore through the underbrush for where the American's were carrying on the majority of their fire fight, yelling about baseball at the top of his lungs so his own men would hesitate before shooting him.

Anders' position, directly opposite that now occupied by Terry and Mark, was jolted by a 61 (mortar) round that struck just in front of the pile of protective logs. Wood splinters blew everywhere and pelted the men behind the barrier like a brief cloud burst that rained slivers. Everyone felt the sting of dozens of the small barbs, but otherwise no one was injured. There was a gaping hole in their defenses, and their position would have to be abandoned.

Anders and Ngoc went left, and Bonly Lonly Lloyd and Nguyen Cham crawled over the remaining right wall taking opposite routes to join up with the far position where they knew Terry was in charge. Confusion was on their side; it was impossible to see a target in the dark or to differentiate the noises of a moving man from the general cacophony.

Terry frantically radioed on his hook (handset radio), "Mayday! Mayday!" he screamed and gave his call sign.

"We read," came back the terse reply. The reception was excellent.

Terry gave the precise map coordinates, repeated them, then shouted, "Boo-coo Victor Charlies. We got a Number ten here; make that a ten thousand. Need an air strike pronto!"

"Roger, bro," came the calm, jovial, and jivey reply from the black radioman at the other end. "Cobras (AG-1H Assault Helicopters) and a 'Spooky' (AC-47 fixed wing fighter armed with 7.62 mm Gatling machine guns capable of firing 2000 rounds a minute, hence the other nickname—'Puff the Magic Dragon') on the way, maybe in fifteen. What's your Zulu?"

"Two Kool-aids, few minor wounded."

"Hang on bro. The cavalry is on its way! Out."

"Out."

Cham was caught in the withering crossfire descending in his direction as he made his way to the defensive position and was killed by a stray bullet to the head, either from the cong or maybe even from friendly fire. Anders took a painful, but nonserious hit through and through the muscles of his lateral abdomen. He scarcely noticed the injury in his relief upon diving into the now crowded American stronghold. All of the men were now collected there except for Cham and Jaime Ortega-Gonzalga who had been slow in getting out of his group's bunker when a 61 shell struck it. He died instantly while trying to get over the wall of deadfall.

There were now thirteen men in the defensive position. It was too crowded, and Terry was nervous that they were an unprofessionally concentrated target. On the other hand, they had such firepower among them that they could defend themselves for an extended period against any assault the Charlies could muster. Concentrated fire began to pour in from behind and around them in the forest. The remaining Americans and LLDBs returned the shots which were blind from both camps except for the tracers. No one was hit. Terry radioed again to make sure the Cobras did not blow them up.

"Spread out, get as separate as you can," Terry directed.

A pair of enemies darted out of the trees not ten meters from where Mark was sitting, and he killed them both. That drew a hellish fire down on his position. His muzzle flashes and tracers had been vectored in on. The situation was grim, but neither side could get at the other effectively for the time being. It had been five minutes since Terry first called, although it seemed like five days. Anders took a few minutes to make a pad bandage and to tape it over his bleeding side wound. He was scared that his guts had been hit, but did not say anything. He hoped that his fears were unwarranted since he seemed to feel all right.

The firing died down to an occasional shot from either side; as they say in the cowboy movies, "it was too quiet." The characteristic report of a B-40 changed that. There was no immediate explosion since the distance between the launcher and target was so short. The small grenade fell almost exactly in the middle of the assembled Apartment Army. Every man crouching around the improvised defenses could see the small deadly ball lying there deceptively still, ticking off the four seconds until it exploded. For the first half second, time was suspended, and no one did anything. The imminence of death crossed the mind of every man, but as if in the slow motion paresis of a nightmare, they all froze in place.

Something snapped in Mark Whitehead's brain, and without thinking or deciding, he sprang athletically from his crouch and landed belly first on the explosive devise. It lay under Mark's flak jacket for a another quarter of a second then blew up under the SEAL. The protective jacket took most of the force so none of the shrapnel or concussion force affected the other soldiers. Mark's chest caved in and turned to a pulpy red froth without any semblance left of any of his organs. His abdomen shattered and spread out the contents over a ten foot radius. Terry was the first to return to reality from the surrealistically horrible suspended animation of the wait. He screamed in an agony of his soul.

After that, it was quiet. The Americans sat in stunned silence, occasionally gasping a sob-like breath. Their Vietnamese compatriots clicked their tongues on the roofs of their mouths. Anders was the first to speak, "Listen! Hear that! They're moving in on us." There was no time for mourning. All of the men could hear the rustling of the brush as the unseen visitors of death crept toward them from all sides.

Terry could not function. He sat dumbly beside Mark's remains with his hand on the scorched olive-drab fatigue shirt. Giles Housekeeper rose to the occasion. He snapped a series of clipped orders, "You, Anders, take the hook. We need to get out of here ASAP. Everybody. Synchronize time—I have 0442. Keep down for exactly one minute then let's have a 'mad-minute' then get your heads down again. That clear?"

"Roger," came the obedient responses. It was a more secure feeling to have someone in charge. The crackling of the branches and the slithering sounds of the approaching enemy was enough to strike terror in the best of men. They were hopelessly outnumbered.

"Now!!" yelled the SAS Sergeant-major.

Every man leaned instantly over the protective barricade and began to fire his weapon until it was empty taking no pains to aim. They inserted new clips or picked up a second weapon or threw grenades for the full extent of the 'mad minute;' then as suddenly as the *Sturm und Drang* hellfire had started, it was over. A stygian gloom settled with a cordite smoke cloud obscuring the laager and the field of fire.

Anders radioed, "Situation ten thousand. Hotel Alpha critical!"

The radio barked back, "Low bridge; cobras and a dragon on the way!"

Two assault helicopters swept in and made a pass without firing but dropped illumination flares that changed the scene from midnight to midday in an instant.

"Give us a purple smoke flare! Next pass we'll have fried Chuck!" came the radio message. Hank scrambled to fire the identifying flare.

The first cobra returned and dropped Willie Peter (White Phosphorous) incendiaries and canisters of CS (tear gas) on the center of the village green. Shortly, an acrid choking and blinding smoke filled the area. The second cobra fired two rockets almost simultaneously. The first blew up the village latrine building, and the second hit the arsenal-munitions plant that served as home for the regional VC commander and his family. A horrendous roar erupted from what seemed to be the bowels of the earth and a giant ball of flame belched into the night sky. The Americans and LLDBs hugged the ground as pieces of metal, wood, earth, and flesh blew 250 meters into the U Minh Forest in all directions. Then 'Puff the Magic Dragon' roared in low breathing death fire to anything else moving in the village center. The first cobra flew over again with its .50 caliber machine guns blazing tracks of yellow-hot lead over everything that could possibly move in the burning rubble. After the third pass, nothing moved.

The radio crackled again. "That's all the bloods can do for you honkeys down there," the lead cav pilot shouted. "You better Hotel Alpha now!"

"Get out! Move out!" screamed Sergeant-Major Housekeeper. No one could hear after the blast, and no one could see through the dense encompassing smoke. None of them could breath from the awful irritation of the tear gas. They were tempted to shed their chicken plates and flak jackets because of the skin irritation from the enveloping toxic fumes, but the Sergeant-Major vetoed that suggestion. Somehow they figured it out, and all of them followed Sergeant-Major Housekeeper toward the trail. Occasionally they encountered gunfire from straggler Charlies in the woods, but they moved so rapidly and fired so convincingly that no one was injured.

Anders realized after a few meters that he did not know where Terry was. He had not seen the SEAL get out of the defensive position with the rest of the men. He turned to go back and bumped into Ngoc. "We have to get Terry!" he yelled even though it was now relatively quiet. "He never came out!"

Ngoc was not a believer in heroics, but the first rule of fighting with other men was to get every living fighter to safety if at all possible. The second was to bring out the dead. In the present confusion and terror, they would be doing well to obey only the first rule. Back in the center of the defensive laager, Terry was trying futilely to hoist Mark's shattered form onto his shoulder in order to carry his remains back to base. The body was so disarticulated that Terry could not get it on his shoulder or into his arms. He was crying in bitter frustration and impotent anger.

Anders ran back and hurdled the barrier in a single bound. He came up to his leader's side. "Terry, we have to go. The rest of the VCs will be on us any second. We have to get outta here!" Anders yelled at the CPO SEAL.

"No. Never without Mark!" Terry yelled back even though he and Anders were half an arm's length from each other.

There was no time for discussion. Anders felt despair. He did not know what to do. The horns of his dilemma had him abandoning Terry on the one horn or staying and trying to help the SEAL get his buddy's body out and being killed by the rapidly advancing remaining VC on the other. Anders vacillated.

Ngoc saw problems and solutions in much more concrete terms. He slapped Terry brutally first on the right then on the left cheeks almost knocking the larger man off his feet. The light seemed to turn back on in Terry's eyes. "Aaaagh! he groaned in realization. "Let's go then. I'll never be able to forgive myself."

"There will be no one to forgive if we don't get out of here, my American friend," said Ngoc soothingly but unpatronizingly. The two Americans started to make their way out of the rubble strewn position; Ngoc stooped to retrieve Mark's portion of the money expropriated from the VC tax collectors; and the three men faded into the darkness running to catch up to their comrades in arms.

The cobra helicopters radioed that the Operation Foreplay force would be evacuated from an LZ one klick from their present location at 0520 sharp. The map was clear and easy, and the group of weary men was assembled and waiting by 0500. They could hear the frustration of the communist soldiers as they hunted around in the still black night for their attackers. There was an occasional rifle shot by an excited pursuer; but the cong were off the correct trail by a klick and a half; and the sounds of their search were getting farther away.

The men hid in the tall grass adjacent to the designated landing zone. Terry said to Anders, "I'm putting Mark in for the Congressional Medal of Honor. He is certain to get it—the one guaranteed way is to fall on a grenade to save your platoon. It doesn't really seem like much, but I know it is the one thing Mark would have wanted more than anything else if he had to die out in this green hell."

"Great. Maybe someone can go back in and get him out tomorrow. If they come back here in force in the daylight, maybe they can mop that place up and get Mark back to The World for a decent burial. You got to think that way, Terry."

"You're right. Did you know that I am a super short timer? My DEROS is less than a week. I've had it. This one is enough for me. I'll go see Mark's family in person. It's the least I can do," Terry said. He indicated that he did not want to talk any more and settled into a Zen-like reverie.

Anders lay quietly in the grass waiting for the wonderfully welcome sound of the helicopter rotors. He had had enough himself. After a few minutes of quiet, he heard Terry softly singing "Rodger Young," a ballad by Frank Loesser, from another war:

> *Oh, they've got no time for glory in the infantry.*
> *Oh, they've got no use for praises loudly sung.*
> *But in the heart of every soldier in all the infantry . . .*

The SEAL CPO's face was a mask of pain. He had mentally removed himself from the rest of the men.

> *. . . Shines the name Rodger Young.*
> *Fought and died for the men he marched among . . .*

Terry pressed his forefingers tightly against the bridge of his nose.

> *. . . Caught in ambush till this one of twenty riflemen,*
> *Volunteered, volunteered, to meet his doom . . .*

He shook his head disconsolately.

> *. . . It was he who drew the fire of the enemy,*
> *That a company of men might live to fight,*

Then his voice quietly trailed off.

> *. . . Fought and died for the men he marched among . . .*

CHAPTER 18

In effect, we will find ourselves mired down in combat in the jungle in a military effort that we cannot win and from which we will have extreme difficulty extracting ourselves.
John A. McCone, Director of Central Intelligence Agency, internal memorandum to National Security Council, April 2, 1965

The tropical sun was hot and enervating, and the slight breeze blowing in off the sea at Bai Sau (back beach), the longest and most beautiful of the four Vung Tau beaches, made for an afternoon of languid relaxation and solitary sensual pleasure. Anders lay half asleep with a cloth shielding his eyes from the brilliant sun overhead and reflecting off the white sands of the beach. His body felt good after nearly two weeks of rest and healing. His right arm and abdominal gunshot wounds and his thigh slash injury had required minor operative debridement under general anesthetic, and it was only in the past two or three days that Anders was able to feel that he was free of the affect of the powerful anesthetic chemicals. The marine surgeons had insisted that he needed an exploration of his abdomen because the missile had passed dangerously close to the lining of the abdominal cavity. He had told them that he felt fine, just needed to get rid of the small nagging infection in the wounds. When they insisted that it was the service rule to explore every suspicious body cavity wound on any marine, he told them he was not in the service and that he would take his chances.

Now, twelve days later, it was satisfying to have been proved right even over doctors and officers. He was fit, having healed all his injuries and having followed a self-imposed exercise regimen running along the coastal sands; and he was ready to get back into action. Lane Duerk was supposed to come to Vung Tau that afternoon with his new orders; he was restless and wanted to get out of the military resort and back into the boonies. His nap was interrupted by a mildly effeminate

414

man's voice with an unmistakable Texas accent speaking almost directly into his ear.

"Y'all sleepin'?"

Maybe if he ignored the guy, he would go away.

"Hey, y'all asleep or what?"

"What?" Anders asked, annoyed.

"That's what I thought," came the excessively cheerful voice.

Anders shook his head. Had he missed a sentence in the conversation?

"Hey, Ah'm Del Porterville outta Farmer's Branch," the disembodied voice announced making Branch a two syllable word. "Ah been seen' y'all around fer a while. Looks like y'all been shot up pretty good. Those million dollah wounds lak mine?" he asked, ingenuously, persisting with conversation.

Anders gave up and removed the cloth from his eyes and turned over enough to face his tormentor. The voice belonged to a plump sunburned young man sporting a three day growth of beard, longer than marine regulation hair, and a right knee swathed in bandages. "Anders Bergstrom, pleased to meet you," said Anders noncommittally.

"Ah am the shortest of the short timers. Already had my PCOD, am takin' mah last few doses of 'no-sweat' pills (Tetracycline—considered by G-Is to afford them 'no-sweat' over gonorrhea and syphilis, a false and wishful thinking notion); and ah am on the downhill coast run. FIGMO. Got this great little injury that will send me back to The World tomorrow on a 'Freedom Bird.' Already got all mah papers. Ah wasn't suppos' to git shot up; ah was just lucky. Ah ain't nothin' but a cook, a REMF, and proud of it. Put in fer the slot jist ta keep frum gettin sent home in a body bag. Worst part of the war fer me was livin' with eight other REMFs in a two bedroom (eight by eight) house that cost 16,000 P. That's triple the rent control ceilin.' And the privy kept overflowin' so's the sewage got stuck between the floor boards. Miserable!

"Ah did have me a concubine, though. Best thang about Vi-et Nam. Cost me 7000 Pees a month—best money Ah evah spent. Said Ah wuz nicah than huh Vi-et Nam fellas. Funny thing, she nevah could git mah name raht.

"Then some gook dropped a mortar right in our cook tent. Kilt the sergeant and one of the tame Vi-ets. I jist got this million dollah knee wound, a purple heart, and a ticket home."

"That's great; I mean, that's tough. I'm sorry about the knee," said Anders for politeness sake, not quite certain whether to commiserate or congratulate. It was a measure of the weirdness of Nam that two men could be discussing the blessing of having a mortar wound and permanent damage.

"No need to be sorry. It gets me outta this pesthole four months early. Ah kin walk okay, jist won't be able to run the hunnert under ten flat," he laughed. "As if ah evah could. Ah'm a lovah and a eatah, not a fightah or a runnah. Anyways do y'all git a ticket outta heah with all those purple hearts ah kin see?"

"Fraid not. I go back into Indian country any day now."

"Y'all oughta put in—ya nevah know, ya know."

Anders was getting bored with the conversation. It was a definite relief that Lane Duerk chose that moment to walk across the sand and to interrupt the medical conference. The CIA station chief looked clean, dry, and out of place, as usual in his tropical linen suit, starched shirt, and tie. The only concession he had made to the sweltering heat was to wear his tie loosened.

"Sorry to interrupt, gentleman. Please excuse me, but I need to have a word with the suntanner here," Duerk told the short-timer marine and waited until Anders left the other man to the joys of the sun and sea breezes.

"You all right?" Lane asked Anders as soon as they were out of ear shot of the homeward bound marine cook.

"I feel great!"

"Ready to start earning your keep? It is downright embarrassing to see one of our own with a rich man's tan."

"I'm ready. What do you have in mind?"

"Anders, there is a real shortage of our people in this country. I have an important job for you up in Eye Corps. I want you to go up and run one of Cleve Howard's PRUs. Think you're up to that?"

"I guess so," Anders said. He was not at all sure what the job entailed, but it sounded like he would be some sort of boss; and at sixteen, that was a heady prospect.

"This is a real step up, Anders. It'll do your career a world of good if you look good in this. This little war is accelerating very nicely, and you and I are in exactly the right place at exactly the right time to capitalize. Don't screw this up."

"I'll do my best. Is somebody going to tell me how to be in charge of a PRU, somebody like you; or do I just go up there and figure it out for myself?" Anders asked, comfortable enough with his boss to take a familiar tone.

"Yes, I'll brief you about the general set of things." Cleve will give you the specifics about the local situation. Over iced Cokes Anders learned from Duerk about the history of the attempts to interdict the VCI and the failure of the Vietnamese to accomplish either that goal or the related one of winning the hearts and minds of the people. He learned the prevailing attitude among the CIA people that it was now time for the Americans to assume control, something Lane had advocated from the first time the SOGs were introduced and started to work with the spiritless locals. "The new year, 1967, is going to see a definite change," Lane insisted, "a tight ship run by the professionals of The Company.

"I know you have more than a nodding acquaintanceship with the PRU concept, Anders," Duerk said. "Provincial Reconnaissance Units are police units, mercenaries, actually, that use individuals from the local province and communities to enforce VCI interdiction. The fact of the matter is that many of the PRU cadres are out and out scum, pardoned criminals, mostly. The key is that the leadership is entirely Company. That's where you come in, Anders. You will be the high kahuna for your unit, answerable only to Cleve Howard, Rex Dragerton, and me. Cleve is the Provincial RDC/O, and Rex, down in Danang, is the Regional RDC/O. Big deal for a young man like you, but The Company is a great place to make your career if you have the balls and the smarts and are a team player. Your unit is in the back country of Thau Thien Province. Cleve will fill you in on operational details."

"All right, when do I leave?"

"Tomorrow. Catch a hop out to Tan Son Nhut and fly from there on Air America to Hue'. Wear tropical whites—look Red Crossy, okay?"

"Will do. I guess I get whatever else I need besides what's in my duffel when I get there."

"We have the best stuff in the world up there in Eye Corps. You'll have your pick. Some good men, too, I understand. So, do good for the team and the country; I'll see you from time to time. I'll have to be getting back. My Huey ride will be agitating. Good luck!" He was already on his way out of the officer's quarters bar.

"Thanks," Anders called after his boss perfunctorily. Duerk was beyond hearing; and Station Chief, Saigon's mind was on to other matters already.

Anders was getting used to having minimal contact with other people in his organization. The only other visitor who came to see him during his two weeks in the R&R center at Vung Tau had been Terry Brannigan. The SEAL CPO touched base with Anders the day before he was to leave Viet Nam.

"Just wanted to tie up my loose ends, Anders," he said. "I wanted to be sure you were okay."

"I'm okay. How about you?"

"I'm all right. I was just about the only one to come out of that last scrape unscathed. You took several good licks. I'm glad none of them were too serious. I'll be glad to be quit of this place, to get back to a real life. Even killing people gets old after while, don't you think?"

Anders nodded. That the question had been asked of him, even facetiously, seemed to confirm Anders' position in the company of the old boys of combat. He liked the designation. "You all right...you know,...about Mark?"

"Pretty much. I hate it that he had to die. It took all the heart out of me. I have never dreaded anything in my whole life as much as having to tell his folks face to face. I think when I do that, though, my war'll finally be over."

"I guess so, Terry. Good luck. I don't envy you that job. Keep in touch, okay?

"Yeah. Oh, I almost forgot. Two things, in fact. Here's your share of the take from the VC tax collectors. Ngoc kept it, took Mark's part off him; so, we could divide it up." He handed Anders a bulky envelope when he was sure no one was watching. "And I thought you'd like to know that they've put Mark up for the Medal. Falling on a grenade for your outfit is just about a sure thing."

"He deserves it," Anders said with feeling. "I wouldn't be here now if he hadn't. I don't think I could ever do it. I won't forget Terry Whitehead—ever."

"Me neither. Listen, buddy, I gotta go. Keep your head down."

Mark Whitehead became one of 116 members of the River Patrol Force to receive the Congressional Medal of Honor.

Anders wandered back to his BOQ room and showered, then started putting his stuff together for the return to duty. He had reveled in the peace and quiet and in the beauty of Vung Tau, but his psyche had developed a craving for action that made him nervous and edgy as soon as he was well and was just passing time. He would miss the navy nurses, the swaying palms, and white beaches. Vung Tau, the Bay of Boats, called Cap Saint Jacques in French colonial days, was located 125 or so kilometers southeast of Saigon and was at the farthest extension of the Annamite Cordillera. The city of Vung Tau was the fifth largest in Viet Nam at 40,000. The area served as the long range reconnaissance training center and the R&R center for American troops and the Riverine Warfare Command Center; so, it was protected by an army of security troops. Anders had been free to roam around the four beaches—Bai Trouc, Bai Dau, Bai Dua, and Bai Sau—Front, Mulberry, Pineapple, and Back beaches, respectively. The beaches were spread out at the feet of Nui Lon and Nui Nho—big and little mountains.

During the first week he had exhausted his interest in the limited tourist attractions—the light house, the view from the coast road, the huge Catholic statue of Christ, the one hundred Buddhist pagodas, especially the Chua Hon Ba Pagoda on the island off the east coast from back beach, and the Dinh Than Thang Tam Pagoda with its ancient statue of Buddha. The second week, he had gotten himself a nearly all over tan and bleached his already blond hair white in the tropical sun. He had drunk fruit punch and eaten popsicles until he could forget the taste of the Vietnamese food and brackish water that always tasted like latex that he had gotten used to in the field. He knew that if he stayed any longer in that paradise he would have to take up reading, and he was not ready for that.

Anders went by helicopter from the Bien Hoa airport to Saigon—34 kilometers. Bien Hoa base compound was the site of the first American casualties in the war in South Viet Nam—July 8, 1959, when two US servicemen were killed by a terrorist bomb. The big Swedish-American boy now walked through Tan Son Nhut and past the Pentagon East (MACV headquarters) with the unconscious swagger of the battle hardened veteran that was somewhat out of place in his white tropical linen suit with the Red Cross arm band. Anders was accorded deference and priority seating, and found the trip to the ancient imperial city scenic and comfortable—gentlemanly, not at all like the transportation on the military end.

He was met upon arrival in the main Hue' airport by a Vietnamese in olive drab fatigues. The man was familiar, but Anders wondered if he were only slipping into the tired excuse of 'they-all-look-alike-to-me.'

"Greetings, Mr. Bergstrom. I am honored to present myself. Tring Van Dong, by name. I will be driving you to the compound to see Mr. Howard, the Province Revolutionary Development chief.

"Thank you Mr. Tring. I take it we have common business interests."

"We do. If you permit a familiarity, I remember you from school."

"The Farm?"

"As it is so quaintly called. You are a large person with such white hair that I would not forget you. At the training center, you were an associate of Jean-Luc DuParrier, were you not?"

"Until I learned better." There was a darkness in the blue eyes that Dong noted and appreciated. His own association with the Frenchman had been brief and bitter.

"I, myself, have cause to remember the man with less than affection," Dong said as a way of identifying with Anders' sentiment.

"Ah, yes, I remember you now. You were the one that DuParrier clobbered when you were not looking. Typical. I learned from him and you though. Never turn your back on a friend or an enemy. Good rule."

Tring piloted the jeep over the poorly kept streets at a high rate of speed that caused Anders to conclude that his driver was out to enjoy his first driving experience. He hoped it would not be his last. Anders was also led to conclude that Tring was hard of hearing. He carried a portable battery radio and played AFN at ear splitting intensity. There was an uninterrupted series of rock and roll and soul music pieces that drowned out talk.

When they stopped inside the high walled compound, Tring asked Anders, "Do you like the Chicken Man?"

"Yeah, he's pretty funny. I like how he always says, 'Goo-ood Mo-orning Vie-et Na-am!,' but I try not to be up early enough to hear him most mornings."

"We have to walk through a maze to get to Mr. Howard's office. I will lead you. The boys will guard your things in the jeep. I think, Mr. Howard wants you to go right up to your assignment today. Later, perhaps you and I can meet in the city for an evening of entertainment."

"I'd like that once I get so I have some idea about my new job."

"Oh, I suspect that it is the same as mine. I will be going over by the border to be the operations head of a PRU unit there. I leave tomorrow."

There were two very large black marine noncoms guarding the entrance to Cleve Howard's office. They carried .45s and Uzis, and did not appear to be the type that were there for show.

Tring presented his pass, and said, "The RD chief is expecting us. This is Mr. Anders from the Swedish Red Cross."

The senior of the two guards checked the pass against a printed schedule and gestured with his thumb at the closed door without speaking. Tring knocked.

"Enter!" came a Caucasian voice. The two men opened the steel reinforced door and walked in.

Cleve Howard was sitting in his swivel desk chair with an attractive, well-dressed young Vietnamese woman on his lap. He was fondling her breasts. Neither of them displayed the least hint of embarrassment.

Cleve smiled a toothy grin which said that he and his visitors were old friends The woman excused herself.

Cleve smiled conspiratorially at the other two men when the woman had left. "Do you know what electric train sets and women's breasts have in common?"

Dong did not understand that this was a joke. Anders said, "I give up, what?"

"They were both originally intended for use by children, but it's the fathers who play with them the most." He laughed heartily at his own joke.

Anders and Dong laughed politely.

"I am Anders Bergstrom. I believe you are expecting me. Lane Duerk sent me."

"I'm Cleve Howard. I'm the HNIC here. Glad to have you on board. You two have already gotten acquainted, I see. Good. You will both be heading up PRU units, so you are brothers under the skin, so's to speak."

The two men nodded at each other and to the chief.

"I'd like to tell you how it goes here. First of all, we have some very fancy intelligence gathering apparati—computers, polygraphs, and the like. We can supply you with a regular list of VCSs and the information and fire power you need to detain them. It is your job to bring them in or to terminate them depending on the particular set of instructions I give you. It is not your job to judge whether or not they should be captured, nor to speculate on the outcome of your work. And it is not up to you to interrogate them. We have experts for that. In fact, just this week, we had the Hungarian and the Frenchman here for just that purpose. Any questions?"

Tring and Anders shook their heads, "no."

"Well then, let's get you loaded up and off to work. We will get together at times to parlay, report, and party. For now, we have to make a good showing for Mr. Secretary McNamara and his bean counters."

Anders followed Dong through the heavy door. As it was about to close, Howard called to him, "Oh, Bergstrom, one more thing. Could you come back for a minute?" Dong went on, and Anders turned back.

"Yes, sir?" Anders asked.

"There is something else we need to discuss. Something I did not think Dong needed to know. I want you to keep your lip zipped about what I am going to tell you, okay?"

"Yes sir." Anders replied.

The Province RDC/O then told the young new PRU leader in full detail everything he knew about the traitor, Nguyen Tran Xuan, and about the four men in the PRU that seemed to be most useful and reliable—Tran, Ky, Dung, and Bach. Howard, and most Americans, regularly used the men's given names, written or spoken last in Vietnamese custom, rather than their family names because he found it easier than trying to keep track of the many Nguyens, Les, Dos, Dinhs, or Hoangs that made up the majority of family names in the Southeast Asian country.

Anders left the city on a slick having not really seen the imperial capital from the ground. From the air it was an exotic, apparently tranquil place with ancient appearing buildings nestled around the gently undulating curves of the Perfume River. In twenty minutes he was in the PRU compound dragging his gear out of the helicopter, and remembering to keep his head down.

The main RD office had evidently radioed ahead because there was a formation of soldiers standing at attention when he moved away from the dust storm created by the whirling rotors. The Huey lifted up and was away in minutes. Anders was unused to being the recognized leader, and was unsure how to act at first. He wanted to make sure that he did not appear to be nonplused; but he did not want to come across as some sort of strutting martinet, either. He would never be able to maintain much of a facade; so, he decided to be himself, reserved and generally self-confident.

Anders walked over to where the formation was standing and spoke to the man who was apparently in charge. Nguyen Lui Tran was apprehensive. He had never seen a man as large as Anders Bergstrom; and although he had seen the light colored hair of some of the Americans, he was unprepared for the near whiteness of the young Swede's crop of wind blown hair. Anders disarmed Tran with a wide smile.

"Hi, I'm the new PRU operations leader, Anders Bergstrom."

"Please call me Tran, sir," the thin Vietnamese said allowing a faint smile on his own face.

"Please call me Anders, not sir," the newcomer said. He extended his hand in the Occidental custom of shaking hands. Tran accepted it. He had been ready to salute but was glad to know that the new leader was not going to elicit respect based on the forms of military courtesy. The man evidently expected to gain that respect, if at all, on merit. Tran liked that as a beginning.

"Would you like to meet the men?" Tran asked deferentially.

"Yes. First, I'd like to take a look at them as a group then get together with you to go over their 201s before meeting them one on one, okay?"

"Fine. Anders, this is Nguyen Van Dung." Anders nodded and walked slowly past being given the full name of all the men as he passed. "Tran Thuc Quyen . . ., Duong Co Tho, he is our admin. man . . ., Bach Duc Hieu . . ., Corporal Le Duc Bach . . ., Tung Co Bon . . .—120 men.

When they had completed the brief introductions, Anders asked Tran to dismiss the men.

"Could we get something to eat? I haven't had anything all day," he asked the Vietnamese PRUC who had obviously been assigned the role of second in command and had been number one for some time while the action unit had been waiting for Anders to arrive.

"We have only Vietnamese food, si...Anders," Tran told him.

"Good, I am in Viet Nam. We eat what the Vietnamese eat. I am used to it. I like it—even *nouc mam.*" The two men laughed.

After they had eaten, Tran got out the personnel files that were now kept under chain lock, and the two of them started to go through the folders one by one reading Y'Yool's old notes and the official documents in each dossier. Tran filled in a description of the men and their capabilities and weaknesses. Anders was impressed with his number two's canny evaluations and insights and his phenomenal memory. He did not waste words nor emotions. Tran left Xuan's folder until last.

"So, this is the special folder. I presume there isn't much in the 201 about his extracurricular activities," Anders commented before they opened the folder. Tran had been careful to say nothing being uncertain how much the new leader had been told.

"I am sorry, Anders, I do not know the word 'extracurlier,'" Tran said before committing himself.

Anders laughed. He remembered being in the position of having to ask people the meaning of some big word. It felt rather good to be on the other end for a change. "'Extracurricular.' Means things done out of school, away from the regular duties."

"Ah, yes, good word. Are you aware of something 'extracurricular' about Xuan's activities?" Tran asked, still unsure how much to say.

"I have heard something," Anders parried. They were verbally fencing, and Anders had to decide whether to confide in Tran or to go it alone. Cleve Howard had told him that he could trust Tran all the way, and he had developed the same feeling on his own over the course of their long working afternoon.

"Look, Tran. Everybody has to take chances, has to trust somebody. I am going to ask you to trust me, and I will be straight with you. I was told that there is a VC traitor in this PRU. The best anyone can tell is that it is this Xuan guy. He is responsible for the deaths of several good people, and he has to go. Do you know about that, and do you know anything I should know? I would kind of like to go on living, maybe even get back to The World someday. That is not very likely if I can't trust my own guys. How about it?" Anders blurted.

Tran spoke calmly and directly. He, too, felt the need to trust and to confide in someone having lost the capacity to trust in any system or organization. "I know for certain that there is a traitor. I and three others worked for long months with Y'Yool, your predecessor, to find out who the traitor was. We narrowed it down to two men, and Mr. Howard narrowed it to Xuan. I am sure that Xuan suspects that we know about him, but I am also sure that he thinks that he is still getting away with his criminal activity. That makes him all the more dangerous. He will try to kill you, and eventually those who are close to you or who seem to be leaders.

"Who can I trust out there?" Anders eyes moved toward the bush.

"As you said, you have to be able to trust someone. The men you can trust here are not altogether those you might choose in the safety of your rich country. They might well not be nice or proper men, may even be criminals. Here, all that counts is whether one man can depend on the other for survival. That is the real meaning of the war for men like us. The men I trust are: Nguyen Van Dung—he was the NVA sapper, for your information, Le Duc Bach—he is a Kit Carson and might have worked for the VC at one time, and Phan Duy Ky—he was a Binh Xuyên, a criminal; and I presume he still is. I have entrusted my life to these three, and they have not failed me.

"I am asking you to trust me," Anders said simply, knowing that he needed someone to watch his back.

"That must be earned," Tran answered directly. "You are the senior officer here; Mr. Howard is the Provincial Chief. I am obliged to obey you, and I will. Trust will come more slowly. A man must be very careful in these times."

"Thank you for your honesty, Tran. I will work to earn your respect and for now would ask for your help in getting the unit into readiness."

"What about Xuan?" Tran was obviously less interested in getting the job done than he was in achieving safety in his own ranks.

"What do you suggest?" Anders asked deferentially of the Vietnamese cadre, the older man.

"Ky, Dung, Bach, and I have devised a plan." Anders listened intently and agreed with the proposal.

Anders spent the following week running the cadres through strenuous PT until he was satisfied that they were fit. He reviewed their weapons familiarity and ability to work together in three and four man units and was confident that they had made good choices in their pairings. Xuan stood out by not having a definite group with which to work; so, Anders personally asked him to join Tran and himself on the next mission.

By the dictates of Tran's plan, Xuan was not to know that Bach, Dung, and Ky were going to be a shadow unit following Anders and his two personally chosen associates. Anders also made it known that all operations would be on a black basis; no group would know the mission of any other group with compartmentalization being absolute. He did not elaborate the one exception; there would be complete sharing of information among Tran and his trusted comrades and Anders. No one else in the PRU was to know his own assignment in advance of the time of departure for the mission.

Xuan took his selection to the leader's team not only to be vindication of any suspicion he may have been under, but as an affirmation of the high quality of his soldiering and the gullibility of the Americans. He was comfortable in the knowledge that he had been able to foil the overly vaunted lie detector of the American running dogs, and began to a plan of his own. The ugly big blond man's ears would be trophies that would do much to cement his standing in the LAF.

The only advance warning the PRU units involved had was that they were to have their weapons and supplies of LURPS ready for a five day mission beginning at 0200 the following morning. They were informed after the smoking lamp had been lit, and Anders posted conspicuous sentries to guard against any man being able to leave the compound to inform the enemy. Seven separate, fairly long range, missions were planned, based on Cleve Howard's instructions. There were to be two abductions, two single man assassinations (or 'interdictions with malice,' to use Howard's euphemism. He did not like to use direct terms even in verbal orders, and never wrote anything incriminating on paper), a family to be 'interdicted' with the same 'malice' and one S&D of two northern Thau Thien villages with authorization to engage any VC suspects. It was presumed that every man, woman, and child in those villages was either frank VC or VCI, or was an indoctrinated sympathizer for mission purposes, according to Mr. Howard's directive. Two separate three man PRUs were assigned to that operation.

Anders, Tran and Xuan were to abduct the niece of the headman of a small hamlet in the hilly region within two klicks of the Laotian border. The computer had her identified as a major courier and private secretary of the COSVN vice commander for the province. So far as anyone knew, her uncle was an untainted GVN supporter. Anders wondered briefly about the validity of the condemnatory evidence and the sources of the evidence that would shortly alter this girl's life so completely. He was too unsophisticated to ponder the abstractions of due process of law, but had a passing concern for the concept of the rights of individuals. He dispensed with his vague anxieties over such imponderables with the reassuring idea that it was all in the interest of the war effort whose ultimate goal was the establishment of democracy for the Vietnamese people. He had been indoctrinated into the principle that the ends of the CIA justified the means, and he believed it. It was considered crucial that the girl be captured alive to take advantage of the tremendous fund of intelligence she supposedly could divulge—with persuasion.

Ky, Bach, and Dung left a day earlier than the rest of the PRUs, ostensibly for a more distant assignment. That gave them time to be in place before Anders, Tran, and Xuan came on the scene so as to keep Xuan from detecting them. Anders and his two official Vietnamese PRUC team members sleepily boarded their Huey at 0200. Although it lacked belly guns, their 'slick' helicopter had been transformed into a highly mobile attack and defensive center. Rocket packs had been installed on the sides, unlike their other compound Huey with its twin side mounted XM-40 30 mm cannons, and their present conveyance had added a nose mounted M-5 40 mm grenade launcher capable of firing 220 rpm. The aircraft's 1400 SHP Avco Lycoming engine cruised to the LZ at its 127 mph best speed. It could keep up that speed for 318 miles.

Anders and his PRUCs inhaled the engine fumes and dust churned up by the rotors on the way into the initial LZ, ten klicks from the targeted village. The operational plan devised by Anders, Tran, Ky, Bach, and Dung called for a two day slow and careful approach to the collection of hamlets with the planned arrival in the immediate vicinity of the village early enough to permit sight reconnaissance in the gathering dusk. What Xuan was not to know was that he would have three professional shadows as he made his way through the forest, four, counting Tran.

At the LZ, Anders unfolded the map and went over the topographical details at some length. The three men, Anders, Xuan, and Tran, selected their own routes to the village that would bring them to three opposite positions by 1900 the following night. Xuan was given the most southerly approach, and Anders took the center. Tran listened with rapt attention, giving the impression that it was the first time he had seen the map or heard the operational details, the same as Xuan. His personal map had additional details from the one Xuan carried, however; such as where the three back up PRUs would be waiting. The conspirators in the plan against Xuan had devised a system of signals using the Montagnard reed whistle that mimicked the call of one of the ubiquitous jungle birds so well that only a longtime forest dweller could tell that it was artifactual.

Anders elaborated the ostensible kidnapping plan, "All right. At the village, Tran will move to the front of the girl's family hooch at 0100; Xuan will go to the rear at 0130; and if all is clear, each of you will give one click on your cricket. I will return the click and move into the front making sure that we don't have company. We will all be barefoot, and we will leave our rifles at our waiting positions. Silence is the key here. Xuan will give one more click, and Tran and I will give one then move in if everything stays clear. Xuan watches our rear while we get the girl. We all meet at point two." Anders indicated the marked area on the field map, a point lying on the edge of the village's northernmost rice paddy.

All three men compulsively tested their clickers, nothing more than children's toy metal noisemakers—crickets. They shook hands, rechecked their gear, and saluted each other before melting into the early morning gloom of the canopied forest. The heat was already stifling, and the sun would be hours before making its appearance. The sweat of the day was already trickling down his back, and the day had yet to begin, Anders observed. He also observed Xuan's route of entry into the jungle out of anxiety more than practicality. All three men were swallowed up into the path of their own devising and were as obscure to each other as if they had been on different planets. Anders knew that he could have been within feet of the man he distrusted without detecting him. For that matter, he was not totally certain of his safety from either of his companions yet.

All that night and the following day into the early evening was spent picking his way through ten kilometers of dense brushy forest as silently and unobtrusively as possible. Anders thanked Sylvia Chin back at 'The Farm' once again for her patience in teaching big lummoxes like himself how to be effectively stealthy and to blend in with the undergrowth. Anders visually encountered individuals and small clusters of people at streamlets doing their early morning ablutions or preparing breakfast or moving their potbellied pigs into the woods nearby their hamlets. He skirted widely around each sign of activity or indication of habitation and moved steadily, although in what was a circuitous and convoluted pattern toward the targeted village.

Anders was in final planned position by 1600, able to hear the conversational voices of the villagers from his vantage point. He spent his time slowly building a matting of brush over his hiding place that would make it impossible, even in daylight, for anyone to discover unless they walked right over him and had the curiosity to look deep into the tangle of vines and branches. He felt reasonably secure from the VC patrols and from the people in the villages, but knew that both Tran and Xuan had exact map designations of his position down to a few meters. His main concern for defense and security was to protect himself against his fellow cadres.

Tran had told him about Y'Yool's fate, the assassination of a man whose life was attuned to the dangers of the forest in wartime and who was specifically on guard from an attack from his rear from one of his own men. If Anders had been a young man given to worrisome ruminations, he might have been seriously daunted by the fact that his predecessor had been silently murdered by an unseen traitor despite all those precautions. Instead, Anders set about to make his own preparations to defend himself and left off thinking about the jeopardy of his position. He did not make the mistake of underestimating his enemy, however.

Tran had been given the longest and the physically most difficult route to the village, but the one least populated. Despite the irregular terrain cluttered with deadfall and a score of small streams to ford, he was in position before either Anders or Xuan. Contrary to the plan disclosed to Xuan, Tran had taken up a hiding place between Anders position and that projected for Xuan, so he could be a last line of defense for Anders if indeed Xuan decided to take the bait and attack the PRU leader, and if he eluded his three stalkers.

Xuan was good. He was small and agile, strong and quick. He moved through the leaf and root carpeted forest swiftly and in almost a straight line toward his designated waiting site. He was slowed by having to hide and wait for the passage of small VC patrols along the well-worn paths through the jungle, upon which they felt so secure that their women went about their endless round of chores—gathering sticks, nipa branches, and water, or carrying produce to one or another of the neighboring villages without security guards.

Xuan had been warned that the area was well populated, but at times it seemed ridiculous. He felt impatient, but he knew that he must control himself if he were to be able to carry out his main plan, that of killing the new PRU leader, the big white-headed American. Xuan knew that he would not be able to continue in the PRU after the death of a second commander on a patrol of which he was a part; so, he had decided to join his VC comrades after the killing of the oppressor of his people.

Xuan found the place established as his hiding spot by 1915; it was still light with sunbeams filtering through the latticework of the surrounding overhead vegetation. Instead of reconnoitering around the village as the American's naive little plan decreed, Xuan stripped down to his black pajamas and took only a crossbow and K bar knife as his weapons. He made a pile of branches in the very rough form of a man hunched over looking at the village and fitted his discarded flak jacket and helmet on the rude dummy, arranging and rearranging the shape until it was reasonably convincing from a distance in the gloom of dusk.

He suspected that he had been followed on the patrol when he had killed Y'Yool, and he was taking no chances on premature discovery this time. He had seen no sign of anyone on his tail as he had made his way through the tangle of vegetation, but he was determined to be fully careful until his personal mission was complete. The new American leader seemed to be nothing but a boy, a very large one, but a boy. Xuan doubted that Anders would be a worthy opponent out there in Xuan's element, the bush; but he was aware of the folly of underestimating his enemies when he was this close to success. His greatest advantage, he knew, was that God was on his side.

What Xuan did not know was that he had been within sight of one or the other of two of the best jungle trackers in Viet Nam since he left the landing zone. The third, Bach, was ensconced in a well chosen tree, hidden by the enveloping branches and protected by his elaborate camouflage clothing and face paint, with an unobstructed view of the locale where he knew that Xuan would choose to make his hiding place. Bach had been selected for his particular task because it was accepted that he was the most patient and could endure the long wait in the uncomfortable tree perch.

He had been in position for three hours when Xuan appeared on the scene. Bach did not come down out of his tree until Xuan left his own hiding place that held the dummy he had made. There were still several hours to go before the rendezvous at the VC hooch that had been agreed upon by Anders, Tran, and Xuan. It took Bach the better part of half an hour to rub life back into his cramped legs before he could walk and crawl effectively.

Ky and Dung were impressed with Xuan's stealth and silence as their quarry made his way with infinite patience in the direction where they knew the American leader was supposed to be lying in wait for the night's planned operation. The two watchers had found each other and had kept in sight of Xuan and of each other all during the serpentine approach to the blond man's location. Xuan no longer watched behind himself, evidently content that there were no followers or watchers or that he had eluded them if there were. He was proceeding with full confidence that this night's work would be a repeat of his previous triumph. Bach was able to keep his position and movement secret from all of the others even though Ky and Dung had to know that he was somewhere near them.

Anders tied the thin strand of piano wire he had been given in his kit on the first day he had arrived at The Farm for training to his left great toe and painstakingly threaded it circumferentially around the perimeter of his hiding place in a six meter radius circle about twenty centimeters above the ground. He positioned three combat knives within reach of one of his outstretched hands and practiced finding them over and over with his eyes closed. He secured the scabbard of still a fourth knife to his chest and practiced quick draw maneuvers until he was confident that he could have his knife ready in a fraction of a second after hearing a wrong sound or feeling a telltale tug on his toe. His service .45 was ready in its quick-draw holster in case he had to use it in desperation, but he was determined to maintain silence for the ostensible main mission despite the added danger to himself. Had the aim of ferreting out and trapping the traitor been the only consideration and the remainder of the plan nothing more than a sham, Anders would have laid out a string of Claymores along his perimeter to eliminate his nemesis.

There was no twilight. Darkness descended like a black curtain as soon as the sun disappeared below the horizon of the trees. It was pitch black within thirty minutes of seeing the last rays of the sun filtering through the overhang. The oppressive dank smell of the rotting vegetation cloistered in on Anders as he hugged the earth. Sleep was impossible; his tension and the extant danger were too great. He was convinced that an attack would come tonight. He had provided too fetching an opportunity for Xuan, or for Tran, for that matter, to pass up, if indeed he was the advertised traitor, for Anders to be able to close his tired eyes. His life depended on an extreme and unrelenting vigilance, and Anders knew it. A man as well trained and more experienced than himself had been in the same position before and had been the victim of the quarry of his own trap. Anders was resolved not to make the same mistake.

Xuan slithered on his belly toward the spot where the American had to be hiding. He listened intensely, sniffed the air for the body stink of the white man. Those people had a smell that they could not get rid of no matter how long they lived in his country. Most of them could be tracked by simply trailing the scent of the perfume they wore like women. This one was smarter, it appeared; but his body odor would still be pungent enough to permit detection, Xuan was confident.

Ky and Dung teamed up and followed Xuan's trail through the blackness by feeling the overturned decaying vegetation of the jungle floor where it was pressed down by Xuan's crawling body. They knew they were within ten or fifteen meters of the hiding position set out in the pre-planning session with their young leader. The two of them were only a few meters from actual contact with Xuan. They moved centimeter by centimeter to keep absolute silence. Still Xuan did not suspect. Bach had decided to circle the others and to come up in front of Anders' position between him and the hooches of the nearby hamlet. He wanted to be there in case Xuan became tricky, or in case some VC unluckily chose that particular spot to relief himself that night.

The tension was palpable. Anders strained to hold his breath. His exhalations sounded like the rush of a wind turbine to him. He waited in the blackness.

The background noise of the forest was quite prominent—chirping cicadas, squawking birds, the tripping of tiny animal feet along dry branches. Xuan had accustomed himself to the background sounds long enough to be able to suppress their perception into a kind of soft buzzing white noise. He strained himself to hear the unusual sound—metal clinking, the shifting of a large body on soft earth, a cough or snuffle, or deep breathing. The Americans, indeed all people except his Buddhist monk companions and himself, were incapable of controlling their vital functions enough to make their breathing shallow and silent over an extended period. Xuan laughed inwardly as he recalled his success in controlling his heart rate, blood pressure, and breathing to defeat the American lie detector machine. His own breathing was now at its shallowest and quietest.

Xuan heard a deep breath immediately to his right. To a less attuned ear, the faint sound would have been swallowed up in the surrounding forest noises, but Xuan knew his quarry was near and shifted the angle of inclination of his crawl toward the direction of the sound. He heard it again. He placed his K-bar knife between his teeth. He could not be more than a few meters from Anders.

Anders cursed himself for holding his breath. When he ran out of air, he had taken a deep breath, no, two. They had sounded to him like the firing of a cannon in the stillness. Nothing happened, and he smiled at his own paranoia. Xuan was not superhuman, and the breathing, in reality, had been little stronger or noisier than normal. A man had to breathe. Anders settled down to wait for the attack that probably was not going to come. He was more aware of the strong smell emanating from his armpits now than he was of his breathing. He lifted his arms to let out some of the vapors. He was not fit for human companionship at present, he smiled briefly to himself.

Xuan thought he caught the faint waft of a human scent. It came from the same direction as the sound, or he would not have noticed the change. It still could have been the smell of the dank earth. He continued to inch his way toward the spot where he presumed that Anders lay hidden. A faint glow of light came from the dying fires of the village caused the trees and bushes to stand out as dull silhouettes. Xuan realized that he was looking at an unnaturally rounded shape against that faint lighted background, one that would not have been apparent in full light, but one which had the appearance of contrivance rather than the haphazard tangle created by nature. He was now sure he was moving in the right direction toward Anders. He knew he would have to move faster because the 0100 deadline for moving to the village was rapidly approaching.

Dung and Ky were aware of an abrupt right turn to the trail they were following. They both thought that Xuan had seen or heard something, and their own senses were heightened to the maximum.

Bach was close enough to Anders' hiding place to be able to touch it. He was certain he was right because he had felt several freshly broken ends of branches.

Anders felt the slight tug of the wire loop on his great toe. At first it was so slight that he surmised that he had caused the sensation by his own movement. But then came the very hard tug. Xuan or Tran or whoever was out there must have laid down full length on the wire. A loose branch rustled, not unlike the sound of a tree squirrel scurrying along it might have made, but coincidences did not happen in this sort of situation, Anders knew instinctively. He silently withdrew his knife and strained his eyes against the darkness. The trouble with his wire was that it encircled him, and he could not tell from the tug the direction from which the pull had initiated. He would have to revise his wiring arrangement in the future—if there was a future.

Xuan heard the rustle of the twig caused by his movement. He was briefly caught on something and cursed his bad luck and carelessness. He ceased all motion and took in air by osmosis.

The two followers, Dung and Ky, were close enough that they also heard the sound and paused. Bach heard nothing although he was no more than ten meters away from Xuan and the two other PRUCs. The tension of waiting hung in the air. Anders felt the sword of Damocles hanging by its thread over his vulnerable head.

Xuan moved again, inching his hand slowly and delicately about to detect impediments. He knew he was at Anders' hidey-hole. The moment of truth was close. He listened with all his energy for telltale breathing and was rewarded by hearing a distinct short inhalation. He could tell that the big man was holding his breath. Xuan felt an internal alarm sound. Anders must be waiting for him, must be aware. He had come too far and was too committed now for there to be any other explanation for his presence in this vicinity. If caught, he would have no excuse. He had to act. He had to find the branchless opening Anders had made; so, he could enter and exit his hiding place quietly.

Anders felt a release of tension on his toe. His enemy had moved, apparently back away from the perimeter. He thought he could hear breathing, but that had to be his imagination. He was hyperalert, his pupils huge in the darkness, his skin covered with goose pimples, and his heart racing. He squeezed the handle of his knife as if it were struggling to get away. He sweated.

Xuan reasoned the American boy was right handed and would build the entrance on the right as he was now facing. He shifted his weight and edged back and to the right, getting off whatever was caught on his leg and felt the edge of the pile of brush. His hand found the empty space he was looking for. He drew himself toward the opening like a snake.

Ky felt a branch being moved into the trail. He heard a soft crunch of the wet leaves as Xuan hurried his pace of crawling. He reached back and pulled Dung's hair as a signal that they had to move more rapidly. He sensed with every fiber that the moment of action was irretrievably close at hand.

Anders crouched like a cat ready to spring, his body in a tight coil, his knife pointed blade upward, his hand gripping it for immediate action.

Xuan hoisted himself into a squat, poised on the balls of his feet, ready to pounce. He needed only to hear another breath to spring into his attack.

Ky and Dung painstakingly brought themselves out of their prone positions and into a combative crouch suppressing their groans as their joints protested.

Bach instinctively felt rather than perceiving with his senses the electricity of imminent combat in the air. He extended his right arm at the place he had last sensed that Xuan was lying, the point of his knife was aimed at the imaginary center of his enemy's chest.

For a few breathless seconds there was complete stillness and silence in the humid jungle. Even the insects seemed to have an awareness of the scintillating drama. Xuan made his decision. Anders had to be lying stretched out full length just inside the opening. He could not be more than a meter away, maybe half a meter. Xuan silently called on the Great Buddha to guide his hand, gripped the handle of his K-bar, and plunged it with all his might low to the ground at where he imagined the American's chest to be.

Anders heard the sudden swish of the air as the knife hand penetrated his sanctuary. The attack was well below where he lay crouched. The extended attacking arm disturbed the nearby piled tree limbs causing an unmistakable rattling clatter of the branches that activated all five men involved in the drama unfolding so precipitously in the inky blackness.

Xuan instantly knew he had missed and withdrew his arm for another strike. He was crouched at the opening and started his arm in a deadly upward arc into the soft interior.

Ky and Dung sprang out of their crouched positions at Xuan's rear, knives hurtling toward the unmistakable sound of their enemy's attack.

Bach moved forward toward the sounds, no longer caring that he made noise by upsetting the branches.

Xuan's second knife thrust grazed Anders' left calf causing a sudden sear of hot pain that he ignored. His hyperacute kinesthetic sense gave him an outline of his attacker's body, and he brought his left arm sweeping up to contact the thinner man's arm. It was wiry and hard and was moving at full force and speed. Anders' wrist struck Xuan's forearm and instantly adjusted to clasp the wrist like a great clamp. Xuan twisted violently.

Anders heard the branches part over his head and felt a pair of hands brush quickly but tentatively around his head and across his shoulders like a blind person establishing identity. He drove the knife hand of his opponent onto the ground. There were a series of three simultaneous grunting thuds, followed by three short coughs of effort and an undeniable gurgle of death agony from one man's throat. The attacker's arm went limp and the knife fluttered from his grip. The entire attack and counter attack was over in less than five seconds. The sound generated carried no more than fifteen meters, well short of the village and its sentries.

Anders became aware of the smarting along the shallow cut on his leg. Bach whispered hoarsely, "Anders, you okay?"

"Yes," he replied. "Who's here?"

"Half the town," laughed Ky.

"Tran, Ky, and Bach," whispered Tran more seriously. He had made his way up to the gathering point of the combatants just as Xuan had committed himself.

"What about Xuan?"

"Dead. Everyone of us stabbed him at least once."

There was a pause. "Thanks," Anders said in a quiet low voice. "I won't forget." His body was drenched in sweat, and he was trembling slightly in the aftermath of the tension and the attack.

"We won't let you," said Ky.

"Let's drag the body in here and go after the girl. Everybody okay?"

"Yessir, boss, the sooner the better," said Ky. The men swiftly moved the body into the enclosure, and Anders crawled out.

"You be backup, Bach. Tran, you come to the front with me and Ky, go in the back. The girl is the oldest of the children and will be sleeping alone. I don't know in which bed. I think we will be able to see in the light from the fire. Tran, you hold the duct tape. I'll grab her. Ky, you watch for surprise visitors. Use your knife if possible. Get back here before we head back to the second LZ. You need to know where it is in case we get separated."

The men gathered their faces near the ground as Anders flashed his penlight to show the men LZ—2. "Got it?" he asked in a low whisper.

"Yes, boss," came the chorus of whispered replies from the other men. Anders liked the tacit acceptance of himself as the leader. Perhaps they thought he merited it. He was determined to convince them by how he handled the rest of the night.

"Let's go," Anders directed.

They were in position in ten minutes. Unbeknownst to the three PRUCs standing at the doorway of the hooch, a hamlet sentry was making his rounds, circling behind the houses. He was about ten meters from Bach when Ky took him out with a crossbow. Ky heard the hiss of the steel dart as it flew through the air and then the thud as it punched the man in the chest. The only other sound was a short moaning gasp and the crumpling fall to the ground. Ky ran over and administered a probably unnecessary *coup de grace* with his knife.

Ky slipped back into the shadows and reloaded his crossbow. He then insinuated himself through the rear entrance, and Anders and Tran entered through the front. Bach stayed outside to provide security. There were no doors. The soft glow of the campfire coals in front of the entrance and from the cook fire in the center of the single room hut cast a faint orange glow around the room. It was enough to make out the sleepers. The night was hot, and the only person with a cover was the older woman sleeping beside her snoring husband. Two sets of children slept on futons on the floor in the corners. There were three children on one of the mats and two on the other. An older girl lay calmly sleeping on her back close to her parents. She was pretty, slight, and unnervingly vulnerable lying there on the futon, her shimmering black hair pooling around her dainty head. She was bare above the waist; her midriff was tiny and concave. Her breasts were small, those of a little girl.

Anders pointed at the young woman. Tran softly padded over to her mat and poised himself above her head, tape extended and ready for immediate application. He checked with Ky whose knife was unsheathed. He had moved nearer the parents' bed. Anders held up three fingers. The other men nodded their understanding.

Anders held up his fingers for the count. At three, Tran slapped the tape in place and Anders threw his huge body over the diminutive girl completely pinioning her arms and legs and obscuring her from view. She awakened instantly with terror in her wide eyes. She mouthed inaudible screams and tried in vain to flail her arms and legs. Anders held her until she was still. Tran snapped a sharp blow on the bridge of her nose to silence her attempts at screaming. She recognized the hopelessness of her situation and went limp. It was very quiet in the room. The only sound was the soft snoring of the older man and woman.

Ky took the tape from Tran and threw a band around her ankles. Anders turned her over, abdomen down; Tran twisted her small arms behind her back; and Ky applied tape to her wrists. Anders slung her over his shoulder like a half sack of grain ignoring her grunting efforts to breath. They slipped out the rear entrance with their prize.

Fewer than three minutes had elapsed since they had entered the small nipa hut. They were trotting along the main village trail and well out of range of the collection of hamlets in another twenty minutes. The men stopped, and Anders removed the ankle tapes. Tran told her that she had to run along with them and not make noise or she would be killed. A venomous mix of terror and hatred blazed from her black eyes, but she nodded her compliance. It was still fully dark.

They made good time, keeping to the main trails with Bach running along ahead and Dung bringing up the rear to catch sight of any patrols or stragglers or pursuers until it was time to veer off trail to head across the jungle to their LZ-2. It was four klicks away by the time they decided to hole up in the underbrush for the day. It was now too light to travel safely. All around them came the sounds of people rousing to the chores of the day. Animals brayed, oinked, chirped, barked, and squawked. Women cursed their lazy husbands. Children protested the morning. Day had begun. It was shortly after nine when the sounds of a commotion came from the direction of the village from which they had abducted the girl. Three shots were fired in rapid succession, and Anders and his PRUs could see small patrols of black pajama clad VCs scurrying along the trails impotently trying to find a sign of the kidnapping party.

It was miserably hot lying there in the dirt under the spreading branches and broad leaves of the overhanging trees. They ate a few packages of LURPS, wet from the nearby stream, but uncooked. The taste was bland and uninviting without seasonings, but the worst thing about the stuff was its consistency. The water had only partially softened the plasticfoam-like vegetables and pasta, and the meat chunks were like pieces of balsa wood. The effect was a huge disappointment for the tired men.

"What do you have?" Bach asked Ky.

"Wet sawdust," Ky answered without a trace of humor. "What is that treat you have, my friend?" Ky asked Bach in return.

"Ah, these are meats, I am told," he said flipping over the wood chip like morsels. "Sawdust with rocks."

The girl would not eat the insipid stuff. She was convinced that her captors were trying to poison her. Her only consoling thought was that she had not been molested. She had been told that Americans were great and voracious rapists and that her virginity would be torn from her when she first encountered the foreign devils. Instead, the huge white headed American had covered the nakedness of her chest with his own shirt, and no one had touched her with anything but gentleness to move her in the desired direction of travel or to get her to eat. It could have been worse, she mused. And it still might be.

The five men were all free of significant injury, no real casualties for the operation thus far, unless one was inclined to count Xuan. Anders had the scratch on his left leg, and Bach had run through a thorny patch of bamboo shoots and had been punctured numerous times with the sharp pricking sticks. The small wounds, about three millimeters across were already beginning to fester. From experience, Bach knew they would become pus filled sores requiring vigorous scrubbing with antiseptic soap for several days and would heal with scars that were small black holes that looked as if he had been punched with an oversized tattoo needle. It was no worse than a nuisance however.

With three hours to go to pickup time at the landing zone, Anders got the men and their captive in motion. They were at the edge of the rice paddies just as the sun went down, and each of them knew this was likely to be the most dangerous portion of their mission because they had to cross the open fields while there was still a little light. They ran the risk of stepping on mines, and the only safety they could hope for was the small signs printed on hand cranked presses reading: "*Tử Địa*" (Death Area) and "*Mìn*" (Mines) that were sometimes erected by the VC to warn themselves and the farmers working in the areas they controlled of the location of a mine. The signs were written in Vietnamese in the naive presumption that because the Americans were too stupid to read Vietnamese, they would be unaware of the significance of the signs.

The PRU men chose to cross the rice fields along the dikes on the supposition that the mines would be in the wet paddies and that the farmers would have been taught to walk on the dikes. Bach was point man and found two small skull and cross bone warning signs. "*Dừng lại! Dừng lại!*" (Stop! Stop!) Bach said and held up his arm. At his direction the group all stepped gingerly over the area of the signs.

They made it across the open area without being sighted. There was an hour to go before pick up. Anders had them hunker down in the tall elephant grass at the edge of the low mound that was to serve as their LZ. He radioed by clicking the button three times, waiting and repeating the series two more times. This was the prearranged signal over the preset frequency.

With twenty minutes to go, a voice crackled over the radio set, "PRU, Your savior incoming, ETA twenty or less. How many? What's your Zulu? Over."

Anders dared a reply, Six. Zulu: no WIA, no KIA. One POW. Over."

"Copy. Out."

The welcome whumping sound of the heavily armed UHI Huey came and with it the knowledge that the next few minutes were the most likely time to die of the entire mission because of the attractive noise and because of the necessity to halt long enough to load the helicopter.

The Huey hovered four feet above the ground with the whup, whup, whup of its rotor arms kicking up a blinding dust. There were no military markings per se, but the front of the fuselage was emblazoned with the motto "We Live to Kill Charlie" that left little doubt as to the helicopter's origin or sympathies. Anders took one last look at the area then shouted at Bach to, "GO!"

Bach lit out like a brown streak for the open doors of the helicopter. The first burst of automatic weapons fire came just as he clambered aboard. Dust spots kicked up several feet from the entry hatch. The two door gunners inside the chopper opened up with their swivel mounted M-60 machine guns and sprayed the area from which the enemy fire had come. The gunners fired 600 bullets a minute each. The two helicopter crewmen were sitting on their steel helmets to protect the parts of their anatomy all soldiers consider most precious in case of a stray bullet came through the thin metal floor of their slick. They knew in their well trained minds that the helmets would not stop the enemies' bullets, but it was nonetheless psychologically heartening to have that extra steel in that critical location. It was not unlike the VC practice of clenching a metal Buddha ornament between their teeth while in combat.

Anders and his men on the ground fired a few three round bursts of controlled fire in the same general direction as the M-60s. Their controlled short bursts marked them as professionals. The scanty intermittent fire from the communist side underscored their paucity of ammunition.

"GO!" Anders ordered Ky, and the athletic young man ran a fast zigzag to board the plane. There was no shooting.

"GO!" Anders shouted at Dung, and the third man struck out for the helicopter. This time, fire converged at the runner from three or four different locations. The Huey's 60 opened up on full automatic and swept the grasses in two concentric arcs resulting in a satisfying pair of screams of pain from one location. Anders and Tran fired three round bursts at the sites where they thought they had seen firing. Bach and Dung fired their M-16s out of their side of the Huey to add to the cover fire and general confusion.

"Come! Come! Come!" screamed the pilot. "Ten seconds more and I'm outta here! Hotel Alpha!" he yelled.

His copilot was radioing in to report the hot LZ; he described it as a "ten thousand."

The girl chose that hectic moment to make her break. She bolted toward the forest. Anders tripped her and slugged her sharply on the jaw knocking her out cold. He swept the light body onto his shoulder and set out at a run for the chopper. "Cover me, Tran!" he yelled as he went.

Tran kneeled and fired several sets of controlled bursts at the semicircle of brush behind and to both sides of him. Receiving no return fire, he, too, broke into a crouching, zigzag run for the Huey stopping intermittently to turn and fire, holding his M-16 on semiautomatic in one hand. Anders was ahead of Tran. He threw the girl into the open hatch and pulled himself in. Everyone on board opened up a cover fusillade that was met by a determined but ill-aimed rattle of AK-47 fire and a few mortar rounds fired by black pajamad men who were resolutely keeping their heads down.

The fire from the Huey was intense enough to cause the VC to lay low, and their shooting stayed well wide of the mark. The pilot lifted off while Tran was only half way in. The other men pulled him the rest of the way on board. The 60 gunner sprayed the area peripheral to the hot LZ as the craft lifted off, veered to starboard, and got out of there. The impact of a few light arms rounds zinged off the metal skin of the helicopter. Tran murmured a soft prayer over the Buddha that hung around his neck. The only casualty was the unconscious co Viet Cong, and she would be all right in a short time. On the whole it had been a good couple of days' work. Anders felt a deep relief at the knowledge that the traitor in his outfit was with the angels or in the underworld.

Cleve Howard's reply to Anders' report was a laconic, "Well done." He sent a new set of orders complete with the operational dossiers on the targeted VCI—enough for three missions involving the entire complement of PRUs in the compound. There was to be a definite increase in S&D and capture activity stemming from an increasingly efficient nationwide intelligence gathering capacity.

Two more missions were executed smoothly. There was one casualty among the PRU; one man was shot in the foot, probably by friendly fire during an S&D. The wounded man earned a six week furlough. Anders received an invitation to spend Tet with Cleve and the office staff; so the young PRUC/O turned the reins over to Tran for a week— for one full mission for all the PRU crews—and left for Hue'.

CHAPTER 19

Anders flew into the Imperial City on a twin engine propeller cargo plane. The pilot took him east to the edge of the South China Sea then down over the Hoang Son Mountains and across the Annam Gate and showed him the source of the Song Gianh River. The plane circled the Imperial City to give Anders an unparalleled view of the seat of ancient kings and the current capital of Thau Thien Province.

Hue' was a river city of about 140,000 people, third largest in South Viet Nam, although the census methods in that era left something to be desired. The city was located 10 kilometers west (inland) of the South China Sea coast and 100 kilometers south of the DMZ. The communist controlled Mekong Valley of Laos lay only 200 kilometers from the coast. Vietnamese Highway 1, originally the Highway of the Mandarins; but later, after the French suffered untold losses defending the highway, it came to be best remembered as the "Street Without Joy," passed through the city.

The Huong Giang, River of Perfume, separated the city roughly in half. On the northern bank was the Citadel, the seat of power of the Nguyen emperors. It was a three square kilometer section surrounded by high thick walls (600 meters on a side, 5 meters high) built in the early 1800s. Around the walls formerly lay a large moat (15 meters wide) filled with dark blue water. There were hollow rooted lotus plants all along the banks of the moat which were densely covered with a heavy green treeline. The Citadel had lush gardens, attractive and exotic palaces that were colored red, gold, blue, and purple. The imperial buildings were noted for their intricate stonework. Much of the splendor of the Imperial City (*Hoang Tranh*) lay in ruins from old battles when Anders first flew over it in late January, 1967.

On the south side of the Huong Giang lay the more modern city with its decade old university, the university library, the French style Provincial Capitol building, the country club, the Cercle Sportif with

442

its well manicured wide green lawns stretching along the river, the Hue' City Hospital at number 16 Le Loi Street, a triangular shaped residential district; and in capitulation to the current war, there was the USN boat ramp directly across from the Citadel and the MACV compound. In preservation of the city's history the outskirts of the south side contained seven imperial tombs, the most splendid being the Minh Man, Tu Duc, and Khai Dinh.

After alighting from the cargo plane, Anders took a pedicab to the Province Chief's office in the MACV compound. The ride took him down dark tree lined avenues, past pagodas with gonging Buddhist bells, lotus ponds, and houses with a delicate French architecture. The residential district was a peninsula, bordered by the river on the north and by the Phu Cam Canal on the south. On the south side of the river, university students dominated the scene. It was possible to forget the very existence of a war while passing through this open and airy city of arts and scholars, its calm and rational core of normalcy, undisturbed by distant guns or by the menace of the North Vietnamese state only 100 kilometers north past the Song Ben Hai River where it was spanned by the Cau Hien Luong (bridge).

Anders paid his driver 5 P and entered the MACV compound. His papers were checked by the marine guard; and after a call to Howard's office, Anders was admitted with a pass. The compound was well fortified and impressive. There were several two and three story buildings and a well maintained old hotel. The Revolutionary Development building was three blocks from the MACV building.

Cleve Howard was absorbed in a jovial chat with several of his office staff and two marine lieutenants as Anders walked into his office.

"Come in, come in," Cleve bade, beckoning the young man to come and join the group. "Let me introduce Lieutenants Staffroy and Bennett of the American Marine Corps. Gentleman, this is Anders Bergstrom, the delegate of the International Red Cross. He is Swedish, if I recall correctly." Howard made no attempt to introduce the Vietnamese in the group.

"Gentlemen," Anders said and offered his hand.

The marine officers shook his hand. Since both of them were well aware of Cleve Howard's roll with the CIA, and since there was a certain roughness and a controlled aura of aggressiveness about the newcomer, they were not altogether convinced of Anders' Red Cross bone fides; but they greeted him as if they accepted him fully at face value. Anders extended his hand to the Vietnamese secretary and to

443

the two male assistants as well, somewhat to their surprise. After a brief informal chat, more on gossip about the American expatriate community in Hue' than on military matters or concerns of state, the officers excused themselves. The staff people returned to their desks, and Mr. Howard led Anders into his inner office.

Anders took on a serious face and started to speak when Cleve Howard interrupted him. "I'm sure you want to talk over some business, but this is Asia; and we should discuss weighty matters only after an adequate preparation with libations, a bath, and a night on the town. It's Tet, time for us to honor the ancestors and to party hearty. We'll get to your assignment in due time. Incidentally, you have been doing a bang-up job with your action unit. Your performance has not gone unnoticed. That's why we have an important and sensitive mission for you. I'll tell you all about it after a couple of days of relaxation. Out here in the hinterlands, you don't want to take things too seriously, or move too swiftly. It's important to get into the proper frame of mind before contemplating great actions."

"All right, I'm game," Anders said.

"First we'll need to get you some more appropriate clothes. You are altogether too formal for this gay and frivolous holiday. I know just the place to get some casual attire."

"Cleve took Anders to a Thieves Market on Tran Thuc Nhan Street where he bought some Levis, Hush Puppies, and a Philippine Barong shirt that was his size. A label on the collar read "Custom made for G. Terrell, LCPL USMC". At Cleve's suggestion, Anders chose to believe that the shirt had been sold by the lance corporal to finance an evening of fun and entertainment. Cleve helped Anders get a room with an excellent view of the river at the Huong Giang Hotel at 52 Le Loi Street despite the clerk's insistence that the hotel was full. Anders was impressed not only with Mr. Howard's ability to function so successfully in this alien environment, but by his evident zest for life there. He was obviously enjoying the war.

Anders commented on that fact, and Cleve replied "I just bloomed where I was planted." Anders thought he could learn something about the good life from this guy.

The educational process started with their immersion into the festivities of Tet. The city had come alive in the past twenty-four hours, although the plans and preparations had been underway for at least the past two weeks for this most important of all Vietnamese holidays. Tet Nguyen Dan is the Vietnamese celebration of the

Chinese lunar new year. The exact solar calendar date varies from year to year but it occurs in late January or early February on the day of the full moon between the winter solstice and the spring equinox. Each year is named for an auspicious animal in a repetitive series of twelve. 1967 was the year of the sheep; the year before was the year of the horse, and 1968 would be the year of the monkey. The festivities last seven days, preceded by a week long flower festival. Hue' was still resplendent with fresh blooms. It was the most beautiful and vibrant city Anders had ever seen.

Every drab little corner was festooned with a kumquat tree, or a bouquet of flowers, or a small colorful ancestral shrine. This was the Eve of Tet, a spontaneous outburst of exuberance and an intense celebration of commitment to family. Fireworks exploded at lake-side—enough firecrackers to make Anders twitch a little; they were too close in time, space, and sound to his recent exposure to Kalashnikov fire for full comfort. Fireworks of all descriptions were being sold in shops and by vendors throughout the city. Joss sticks were available in bales. Regular business, bowing to the inevitable, had ground to a virtual halt two weeks ago. Shops that had existed to sell clothing or electronics, or vegetables now operated twenty-four hours a day to make the favorite lotus seed candy or bean curd cakes or to dispense colored paper, or to provide noise makers—clackers—not unlike those the PRUs used in the field to signal one another.

The street vended food was enticing for its aromas, variety, and quality; but Cleve told Anders to hold off; he had something special in mind. We've been invited to dinner in the best place in town. "You'll need to spiff up, wear your best suit and tie, spit polish your shoes, the whole bit. I'll pick you up at 1900 and surprise you," Howard told Anders as he let him off at the Perfume River Hotel to get a shower and a nap before the start of Tet Eve's formal activities.

The week prior to Tet, Vietnamese perform the first and most important ceremony of the year. It is necessary for each family to send its own household Hearth God up to heaven to make its yearly report to the Jade Emperor. In order to ensure a good report and therefore the benevolence of the Jade Emperor for the upcoming year, it is necessary to please the Hearth God so it can depart with a happy report. The whole family joins in to clean the entire house from top to bottom, inside and outside. The octagonal mirrors located in strategic places to reflect away bad spirits are polished until they sparkle and gleam. Walls are scrubbed and white washed; rugs are taken up and cleaned;

and most important of all, the family altar is meticulously cared for. The graves of the ancestors are scrupulously swept, washed, and painted if necessary. The *Cay Neu* (New Year's Pole), with its attached clay bells, is set up in the yard or in the house. Lime powdered bow and arrow replicas are mounted in strategic places to frighten away the evil spirits. The people, especially the older ones, don their traditional conical hats and chew betel nuts, something they may not do otherwise all year long.

On Tet Eve, every effort is expended to ingratiate the ancestors and to make them feel at home with the family. *Tất niên*, the ceremonial dinner in honor of departed ancestors is prepared with the finest New Year's foods. The family, nuclear and extended, gathers for one great feast and wishes each other *"Mừng Tuổi đầu năm"*—traditional New Year wish for longevity. A guest is greatly honored to be invited to these exclusive and festive family occasions.

Through Cleve Howard and his position as the American civilian Province Chief, Anders Bergstrom was invited to join one of the foremost families in all of Hue', that of the resident Mandarin. It was a singular honor, and Cleve took pains to make sure that Anders knew that, and was cognizant of and respectful to the ancient Chinese and Vietnamese traditions he was about to share. Anders felt out of place and cowed as he and the Province Chief pressed the buzzer on the Judas Gate at the entrance to the estate. The main gate was red lacquered for luck and encrusted with gold chu nom letters. Across the yard the house, with its ornamental crimson roof with upswept eaves, beckoned.

A liveried servant walked slowly out to the small side gate and welcomed the two men in. The driveway was lit with Chinese New Year's paper lanterns that cast a softening golden light on the surrounding trees and flowers. The servant opened the great bronze doors; and there a second servant, this one, an older and more elaborately costumed Han Chinese, took the invitation card from Cleve, and from it, announced the arrival of the guests. Cleve had been thoughtful enough to hand write in Anders' name.

An elegant and exotic oriental woman aged sixty years or so, whose origins could have been Chinese or Vietnamese with a little Indian or Malay insinuated into the mix, flowed across the gleaming marble floor to greet them. "She is the number one wife," Cleve whispered to Anders as the handsome woman approached them.

"Good evening, Mr. Howard. How nice of you to grace our humble home. I have not had the pleasure of meeting your companion," she said bowing. Anders extended his hand, but the woman did not take note of it, and he embarrassedly let it fall. She was the most delicate adult human being he had ever seen. Her skin was creamy and flawless, so translucent that her delicate veins could be seen through the thin skin. Her make up was so precise and symmetrical that she seemed more like an animated porcelain doll than a person. She was dressed in an exquisite blood-red silk dress embroidered with fine gold thread—the traditional colors of fun and happiness. It had a demure mandarin neck and long sleeves. Her slender long fingers held long curved vermilion lacquered nails and rings on every finger, some of which blazed with the fire of diamonds and stars of sapphires.

"Permit me to introduce my associate, Lady Nguyen. This is Anders Bergstrom of Sweden, the International Red Cross delegate to the Geneva Convention Commission of Viet Nam. We are most honored to be guests in your lovely home on such an important occasion." He bowed, and Anders followed suit.

Lady Nguyen bowed from the waist, holding her hands close to her chest, palms together, fine fingers pointed at the carved teak ceiling. Anders bowed again in a fashion similar to that of the hostess, but lower, as Cleve had instructed. Her perfect face smiled a perfect smile of greeting and formal welcome. The woman was the quintessence of formality, but conveyed a real warmth and invitation to join her family, all with a look. She seated the two men on a brocade divan and announced, "The Mandarin will join you presently. Please excuse me while I give last minute instructions to the servants." She backed out of the room so smoothly that it was hard to believe she walked on feet like the rest of mortals.

"I forgot to mention, one does not touch these people. We are not of their station," Cleve whispered to Anders rolling his eyes back very briefly. "Listen," he said with a pointed movement of his eyes, indicating conversational and laughing voices coming from a distant room.

Anders could hear the sounds of children, women, and occasionally, of men in animated communication. Although he could not understand a word spoken, knowing that it was Mandarin, Anders could sense the familial conviviality. It was as if he and Cleve had been invited to a different party.

"The family," Cleve answered Anders' inquiring look. "We outsiders get to meet them in due time. We are less important than family, and this is a small symbol of that, being kept separate from them until the dinner hour." He was sitting very stiffly on the divan, feet squarely planted close to each other on the floor and hands folded carefully in his lap. Anders copied him and took the moment to look about. The ceiling of the ornate room was supported by decorated red lacquered pillars. The floors, walls, ceiling was of teak—the floor polished to a mirror finish and the walls and ceiling intricately carved panels. There were ornamental lacquer-ware screens, chicken and duck eggshell paintings, photographs of ancestors with incense, and small offerings of oranges and bananas in front of them. There was an ancestral shrine covered with gold name inscription.

Presently, the sliding panel door reopened, and a girl walked into their sitting room. The bright lights of the kitchen shone behind her haloing her in lamplight. The red silk embossed wall coverings of the hallway imparted a sensuous glow around her backlit figure. She was the most beautiful creature Anders had ever seen. He stopped breathing for a moment as if that bodily function would disturb the wonderful kharma that accompanied the lovely young woman. He guessed her age at sixteen; she could have been twenty. Her faultless skin was white and soft, and she required no makeup. She had waist length gleaming black hair that glistened with highlights and softly framed her jewellike face. She had high cheekbones, almost Eurasian, slightly almond eyes that missed nothing, a faint pink glow to her cheeks, and naturally soft warm rosy lips, fuller than the usual Vietnamese girl's. She was dainty, tiny, but appeared to have a full measure of confidence that gave her an appearance of strength. The most unusual feature about the girl was her ample bosom, modestly covered by a fine brightly patterned Ao Dai in Picassoan blue, orange, red, yellow, and green flowers. The upper garment was slit up the sides to reveal supple slender lower limbs clad in gleaming patterned white on white full trousers. She wore silk evening slippers inlaid with fine gold and silver chains in a paisley pattern. The men stood as she approached their seat.

"Good evening, gentlemen," the lovely creature said. "I am Nguyen Thi Liên, youngest daughter of the Mandarin and Lady Nguyen."

Anders was completely tongue-tied. At least he had the presence of mind to bow in response to her graceful gesture. Cleve responded for both of them, "Good evening, Miss Nguyen. Thank you for welcoming us into your home. I am Cleve Howard of the American government, and this is Anders Bergstrom of the Swedish Red Cross."

"It is our humble family that is honored. Would you like to come and meet the rest of the family now?" Liên requested. She led the way into the spacious family room where a large collection of very well dressed, very proper oriental people were sitting about on floor cushions. There was not a single person dressed in western clothing, and no one rose to greet them.

Liên moved the two men about the room introducing them to everyone—brothers, sisters, aunts, uncles, in-laws, cousins, and children in flawless, only slightly Oxford accented English. They met eldest males first, then the rest of the family ranked by age first and sex second. Children were introduced by given (last name) only except the boys who were all called *van* (male) in hopes of producing more male heirs in the future, as well as by their personal name. The children were at first subdued then began to squirm and to giggle as do children all around the world. No one touched the Occidental men. Anders and Cleve were invited to sit on a cushion and to bask in the family's festive mood, but no attempt was made to engage them in conversation or to depart from the use of Mandarin and Vietnamese as the only languages. Cleve knew that most of them spoke French as he did, and many of them could hold their own in English.

Around the periphery of the room were Ming porcelain stools and vases in the shape of elephants holding potted palms. The walls held elegant Chinese calligraphy scroll paintings. Jade figurines sat in wall niches.

Anders could not take his eyes off the beautiful daughter of the Mandarin, although he made a conscious effort not to appear to be staring. During a lull, when no one was paying any attention to the two Westerners, Cleve said, "Her name means 'Female,' that's the 'Thi.' It is very common for girls to have that as a middle name in hopes of enhancing fertility and the womanly virtues. Her given name, 'Liên' means 'Lotus' designating purity and beauty. Hue' is the lotus city."

The two men were seated separately, each among the younger members of the family. Anders was disappointed to be placed well away from Liên. The family ranking was apparent in how close the individual was seated to the Mandarin at the head of the table. He had not as yet made his entrance, and did not do so until every member of the family and the two guests were in their places. There was one empty place at the table symbolic of the missing ancestor.

The table was bare except for a large centerpiece of fresh cut tropical flowers. It was made of Chinese teak and was inlaid with a mother of pearl avian design. The chairs were of matching material and design. There was an antique hand knotted Chinese rug on the cherrywood parquet floor. The family major domo, dressed all in black silk including a small pillbox hat, stepped into the room; the room hushed by preordained signal. "The Mandarin," he announced in a Stentorian voice. The loudness of the announcement was so out of character with the subdued tones of conversation up to now that Anders was startled and had to stifle a laugh.

The Mandarin of Hue', wearing his black-winged Ming dynasty bonnet, walked purposefully into the room on cue. Everyone stood and bowed their heads in respect. It seemed the most natural thing in the world to Anders. "Please be seated," the Mandarin requested in his rich quiet voice. He spoke English for the benefit of his guests, then made the same request in Vietnamese; and the assembled guests took their seats. The Mandarin looked over his pince nez glasses in an encompassing scrutiny then raised his right hand in a quick little gesture directed at the major domo who was standing six paces behind the authoritarian elder of the family and a little to his right. The major domo did an about face, that would have done a marine drill team proud, and slightly opened the door to the kitchen.

Instantly, six servants dressed in gleamingly and stiffly starched white pants, coats and tall baker's hats marched into the room, laid down finely woven bamboo place mats, polished hardwood chop-sticks, and lace damask napkins at each setting and began to serve the appetizers—shrimp toast and small dishes of melon seeds and pine nuts. The Mandarin rose to speak as the guests sampled the simple dishes. He was very small, and very old. He was dressed in a burgundy colored silk brocade coat and black trousers. The coat was embroidered in black with dragons and his family crest. He had a wispy goatee and a long but scanty white mustache. His face was lined with years and cares, and he looked yellowed and tired; but his eyes were alert, intelligent, and captivating. For all his age and wrinkles, his aura of self-possession and control, gave him the appearance of a strong man, despite his diminutive size.

"I most flattered that you have chosen to honor our family by joining together as we commemorate our mutual ancestors, the foundation of our family. This is the most important day of our year, and it is well that we can meet as a family to acknowledge it. I am sure that the old ones are aware of our concern for them. I am equally certain that our Hearth God will bear a good report to Jade Emperor on our behalf." He smiled down at his family.

The assembled family and the two guests inclined their heads to show their accord. "Brother Xuan, Sister Lydia, Uncle Ko, Aunt Ling,

I greet you and commend you and your families. I thank you for gracing our poor home." The named guests smiled shyly.

"Let us drink a toast to the family," The Mandarin suggested and raised his glass of white wine, the only concession to the western world in evidence that evening. All toasted the success and long life of the old ones and of the living family. "To the family!" the assemblage chorused as one.

"Our honored guests, Mr. Howard and Mr. Bergstrom, welcome," the old man said looking down at the two men benevolently. Cleve saluted The Mandarin by inclining his wine glass in the old man's direction. Taking his cue, Anders did the same. The Mandarin smiled his thin lips, smoothed his trousers, and sat down. He raised his right hand, and the servants gathered the appetizer plates and exited the room.

The major domo reentered, bowed, and snapped his fingers. Six more servants, these dressed in fine gray cotton uniforms, brought in hand bowls of celestial soup—scallions in peanut oil and soy sauce, spiced with cloves. Like everyone else, Anders gripped his bowl with two hands and sipped it. There were no spoons. He did not feel comfortable making the same slurping sounds the family made to show their enjoyment, nor did he smack his lips to indicate that he was done. The servants removed the lacquer bowls.

Next came Five Flower Pork and Pork with Bitter Melon, Hand Pressed Duck, Drunken Chicken, and Red Simmered Fish with Snow-Peas as successive entrees. The family was encouraged to rest and to talk as the servants removed all of the dishes and washed and oiled the table until it gleamed.

They replaced the mats with fine cloth ones and brought in ivory chop sticks with intricate carvings on the hafts. This was for the *pièce de résistance*, Peking Duck, served with steaming cups of aromatic tea. The ducks had been personally selected by the chief cook, inflated with air, then roasted to make the skin crispy. Anders had never tasted formal and haute cuisine Chinese food. It was wonderful. He said so several times and was rewarded with a genuine smile of shared appreciation from the men seated near him. The major domo grinned with pleasure at one of the young Occidental's exclamations. Cleve Howard obviously relished the food as well but was more restrained, as befitted his important status.

Dessert was Almond Float and *Hung Pien* (Chrysanthemum tea sweetened with rock sugar). The table was cleared again and tiny porcelain glasses of amber colored *Shaoshing* (yellow wine) were distributed for a series of toasts to the family and for the new year. The delicate vessels were decorated with a reverse swastika design for good luck. The Mandarin seemed a bit sleepy now. He made a pronouncement that the Year of the Sheep would be an auspicious one, and an announcement that it was time for him to retire. All stood as he left on the arm of Lady Nguyen and the major domo.

The men retired to the smoking room, and the women went to the silk room. Strains of five tone Vietnamese music played by the girls of the family on three stringed Chinese lutes, on *kin* flutes, and *dan thap luc*, sixteen stringed zithers, came from the far room where the women were congregated.

Servants brought in bamboo pipes for the men who reclined on cushions. Cleve tapped Anders' arm insistently and gave him a hard negative nod. Anders watched. The pipes were two feet long, made of straight bamboo with brass or ivory at the ends. Two-thirds of the way down the shaft of the pipe was the bowl, darkened and polished by the long history and frequent kneading of the gum ball of opium on its convex surface. The servants, this time, all women, placed a needle into the small cavity of the bowl and released the opium then reversed the bowl to heat it over a small flame. The beads of opium bubbled and popped quietly as the men inhaled the pungent thick smoke. Conversation waned as the men of the family became tranquil and sleepy. As the hour approached midnight, most of them were sound asleep from several pipes, some able to inhale a whole pipe in one breath; and the room was fragrant and dreamy with the narcotic smoke.

Guests began to say their good-byes, and Lady Nguyen showed the elderly guests to the door while the other two wives escorted the middle-aged family members. Liên stood quietly by Anders and Cleve Howard. When Cleve decided it was the proper time to leave, shortly before midnight, he purposely caught Liên's eye, and the young woman led the two men to the great bronze doors. Anders attempted to make eye contact with the lithe girl, but she would have none of it. She kept her eyes demurely and resolutely down whenever he looked at her. As they walked out of the Judas Gate and into the cacophonous street, Anders was thoroughly sated gastronomically and a thoroughly confused and infatuated young man. Cleve took notice and laughed to himself.

At the stroke of midnight, they were standing on the busy festive street a short distance from The Mandarin's palatial home waiting for a *xy clo*. Cleve looked carefully at his watch as the second hand approached midnight on the dot. "Listen," he said and smiled.

In a matter of seconds the air around them exploded with the noise of ten thousand drums beating and a hundred thousand fireworks bursting to bring in the Year of the Sheep. It was deafening and joyous, French Mardi Gras, Hindu Deevali, and American Fourth of July all put together. The city erupted into a great party ushering in seven days of colorful, fragrant, boisterous, and noisy activities.

Their *xy clo* dropped the two men off at the Perfume River Hotel. Cleve asked to come in and chat a while with Anders. "Lets sit in the lounge," Cleve directed. The lounge was comfortable with padded easy chairs covered with fine old leather. There were two vats filled with ice water and bottles of beer—this was a country in which refrigeration was exceedingly scarce. The labels of all the beer bottles had been soaked off and floated in the water. There was no reliable way of telling one brew from another

The barman asked, "A brandy and soda? Some cognac?" The men shook their heads.

"333? Tiger? A highball?"

"A vermouth cassis for me," Cleve ordered.

"Nothing for me," Anders said.

"Perhaps hot lotus tea?" the barman persisted, trying to be of service.

"No thank you. I've had enough to eat and drink tonight," Anders said.

When the man left to fetch Cleve's cassis, Cleve inclined his head toward the younger man and assumed a fatherly expression. "I was pleased to see that you did not partake of the demon opium, Anders. Nothing will get you in more trouble faster than that stuff. Robs a man of his spirit, takes away his edge. The Company looks askance at those who use it. Not a good idea to go native too much, for that matter. But I must say that you will need to develop a taste for booze just to be friendly with the right people. Everything in moderation, of course. Can't be Puritanical or like the Mormons out here. Gives you a 'stuck-up' reputation, if you get my drift. Alcohol is the lubricant of social interaction in The Company. Good to keep that in mind."

Anders just nodded. It didn't seem like a matter of any moment to him.

As he sipped his drink, Cleve rambled about Company gossip, the direction the RD program was heading, and about the joys of living in Asia so long as you had the right situation. "Anders," he said, "It's a matter of playing along with your own kind of people, doing your part, don't you see?"

Anders nodded. He was not sure he did see, but he nodded anyway.

"To get down to cases, there is a very important assignment for you. Comes right from Saigon. The best intel has it that Phan Pho Ngo, a well known businessman here, is secretly and heart and soul working as a VCI, right up there in COSVN." Anders gave no sign of disbelief and was not inclined to comment; so, Cleve went on. "We need to take him in as an example, even the high kahunas are not immune from prosecution if they play footsie with the cong or Uncle Ho. This man is heavily guarded, and will be hard to nab, but we want him. We want you to do the job. Here are the particulars." He extracted an envelope from the inside pocket of his jacket. He placed his hand on Anders' indicating that there was plenty of time to peruse the documents later.

"We have outlined a plan. Needs to look like the VC did it. We will need your best men. It goes without saying that you have to be personally low profile. This could be quite a feather in your cap, career-wise, Anders. Bear that in mind. I expect big things from you."

"I'll give it my best shot, Anders said." Something about the assignment sounded a little hokey to him, but it was not his place to reason why, he supposed.

"I like your attitude—a team player. I suppose you will be wanting to get back to your unit tomorrow then?" It was more a directive than a question. It was also the signal that the visit was over. Cleve Howard reached out and shook Anders' hand and strode out of the hotel to catch a taxicab back to the MACV compound.

CHAPTER 20

During a single week near the end of January, 1967, Inga Haakensdatter of Zarahemla, Utah received a series of telegrams and letters. The first telegram read:

> 19 January 1967
> Dear Mrs. Haakensdatter:
> We regret to inform you that your ward, Karl Oscar Isaacson, PFC/USA was killed while serving his country in the Republic of Viet Nam 16 December, 1966. Stop. He was the victim of an automobile accident. Stop. Further information will be forwarded by his commanding officer. Stop. Your president and a grateful nation extend condolences for your loss. Stop.
> Signed: Lyndon B. Johnson, President
>   Clark Clifford, Secretary of Defense

The shock of that devastating telegram, similar to those that eventually crossed the doorsteps of nearly 58,000 Americans, had not had time to wear off when the letter came:

> 24 January 1967
> My dear Mrs. Haakensdatter:
>   Please accept my profound sympathies for the passing of your ward, Karl Oscar Isaacson, PFC/USA. He was a good soldier and a fine young man who contributed his best to the war effort. You can be proud of the service he rendered. On the morning of 16 December this past year, PFC Isaacson was killed in a collision of two military vehicles in the capital city of Saigon. If it could be of any consolation to you, your ward died instantly and without suffering. Most unfor-

tunately, there was a fire following the collision, and PFC Isaacson was badly burned. His remains will be returned to you in a sealed coffin as required by US law. He will be sorely missed. His officers and the men of his unit sorely regret the passing of PFC Isaacson, and a grateful nation acknowledges your sacrifice.
Sincerely,
Ronald F. Patricio, CAPT/USA

Two days later, Mrs. Haakensdatter received a second telegram (the second telegram of her life). It read simply:

26 January 1967
Inga Haakensdatter:
Pursuant with the wishes of Karl Oscar Isaacson, PFC/USA, deceased, you have been named the sole beneficiary of his Armed Forces Life Insurance policy. Please find enclosed a US government check in the amount of $10,000 (ten thousand dollars). We would appreciate it if you would take the time to fill out the simple attached form acknowledging receipt of this document and the payment. Thank you.
-No signature

On the same day a notation was filed in BUPERS in the 201 file for Karl Oscar Isaacson with the order that his file be sealed:

Karl Oscar Isaacson, PFC/USA was reported AWOL from his temporary assignment as a cook on USS Martin Fontaine on 12 August, 1966 at 1430 Zulu. He was awaiting assignment to a combat unit in RVN when he jumped ship. SP officers were summoned to investigate an alleged homicide at a bar called The Mabuhay Location on or about 2300 on 16 December, 1966. The SP officers found a body that was subsequently positively identified by USA dental records to be that of PFC Isaacson. He was buried in the Manila public cemetery. The ship's Master at Arms, Hartley Conrad, CPO/USN reported that PFC Isaacson was a troublemaker and a misfit and had been disciplined repeatedly for public drunkenness and fighting. A fitness report was being prepared with the recommendation that the above named enlisted man be presented before a Captain's Mast and hearing board to consider discharge from the service on other than honorable grounds at the time of his going AWOL.

In the Manila public cemetery records there is a line that reads: Plot 1432, Section 18, Site 4: Karl Oscar Isaacson, B:4/13/50, D: 12/16/66. There is no headstone at that location.

Mrs. Haakensdatter knew nothing of the BUPERS document nor of the Manila cemeterial records. She banked the $10,000, purchased a small grave marker, and buried Karl Isaacson in his sealed regulation US Army 20 gauge silver-gray steel casket that the Greggs (Graves Registration Personnel) delivered to her. He was placed in her family burial plot in the Zarahemla cemetery. The cost of the burial plot and funeral was $327.00. Mrs. Haakensdatter put the flag that had draped the casket neatly away in the small box of Karl's things. She was the only person, other than the mortician, who was also a Mormon bishop, to attend the brief graveside service held for the boy. She was the only one who mourned him.

CHAPTER 21

Viet Nam is a land of great extremes, so vastly different...that we never really learn to adjust. The mountains and jungles are hostile, the rice fields unending—and all the time the fierce sun and wet heat force all growth to its limits and overexcite our nerves and emotions. The land teems with so much life that death doesn't seem to matter. Animals kill animals, men kill animals, and men kill one another too—its all part of a brutalizing process. Violence is commonplace, an everyday occurrence; and our senses become permanently drunk with all this pulsating vitality...It's a land that fires the senses, not the intellect. That's why we don't learn anything. It's a land so elemental that sooner or later the brute climbs out of every man. Nobody's immune...all your restraint and self-discipline can dissolve here.
Anthony Grey, Saigon, 1983

It was a fine, dry, quiet first of February, first day of Tet when Anders left the Huong Giang Hotel. He stretched his limbs, yawned, and became aware, for the first time that morning, of his hunger pangs. He sought out a small cafe and took some baguettes and cold cuts and a cup of beef broth out to a table facing Le Loi Street to watch life start up in Hue'. The revelries of the Eve of Tet were over; and the first day of Tet was, as usual, going to be quiet. It was a day for families to eat picnics in the cemetery and to have simple meals at home. It was a cleanup day after the high spirits of the night before.

Anders found himself thinking of Nguyen Thi Liên, the Mandarin's daughter, who was as delicate as her name. Cleve had thought it silly that he should even consider a courtship with such a girl, whether out of his own white versus yellow prejudice or because the daughter of a Mandarin would not look beneath herself at one such as Anders Bergstrom. He let his mind drift.

The day was slowly getting into motion. Here and there an occasional person was warming up with Tai Chi exercises. A pig merchant was carefully laying out the parts of a hog on his sidewalk table while his son carted away the entrails of the animal on his *xy clo*. The blood and water used to wash it away were still collected in eddying puddles around the man's stall. The ubiquitous rice merchants were now awake and could be heard calling out to passers by. Two shaven head bonzes in their gray-brown robes were walking slowly by with their empty rice bowls in one hand. Thus far, they were finding no givers. A wheel of a cart load of squealing and lamenting piglets was stuck in the crack between the board walk and the open sewer trench running alongside it. Carts overloaded with chickens, ducks, GI surplus, vegetables and fruits, and used clothing began to make their way out into the market day traffic.

A few children were still lighting firecrackers to ward off evil spirits and were lingering near the stalls of fireworks dealers hoping to be able to snatch up one of the displayed explosives. When he finished his small meal, Anders walked up the street browsing at the stalls selling everything from bicycle parts, to condoms, to American cigarettes stolen from the PX by trusted workers, to bottled water. Anders bought a bottle of nongaseous Evian water and a few left over New Year's cookies and ate them with chips of dried mandarin peelings and licorice root. The street was virtually lined with kumquat trees which symbolize the coming of money into the family in the new year and were further beautified by the numerous collections of apricot flowers, peach blossoms, and artificial flowers of all descriptions. The twenty-four hour flower markets were beginning to pick up business after the early morning lull.

Anders caught a pedicab back to the airport and haggled with the scrawny puller over the already ridiculously low fare. It just seemed like the thing to do. Everyone was in a good mood that day. He was sleepy from the heavy humidity in the air and from the heat, and when he got back to his bunk at the PRU compound, he took a siesta. He went to sleep dreaming of Liên.

The following morning, Anders did his PT longer and harder than usual to make up for the days of indulgence in Hue'. He started early to avoid the heat and was already puffing and sweaty when he had the other PRUCs assemble for the group PT. They were all in exceptional condition—lean and quick, with excellent stamina, and did not complain when Anders pushed them. They knew he had already done considerable exercise that morning and admired him for leading from the front even in physical training instead of from behind or worse, from the comfort of his quarters or office as did most of their former Vietnamese officers.

After the PT, Anders made the men grumble good naturedly by ordering them to field strip and clean every weapon on the compound and by assigning teams to inventory every asset and to scrub down every building and bunk. He spent the rest of the morning going over the dossier on his next quarry, Phan Pho Ngo.

The information on Ngo was considerably more complete and detailed than had been the case on previous targets among the VCI. There were newspaper clippings, synopses of surveillance team reports, a compendium of evidence against the man, and even a legal brief justifying the detention of the prominent merchant which Anders thought extraordinary enough to wonder why.

Phan Pho Ngo, the reports indicated, was a fifty-six year old ethnic Vietnamese with a ten generation genealogy in the country. He was the first son of a wealthy banker whose bank had been in Hanoi prior to 1954 and whose assets had been appropriated when the Communist government wrested power. His family was Christian—Presbyterian—but they had been forced to flee with the Catholics when Ho Chi Min's forces began their socio-politico-religious-ethnic cleansing program. The father was a broken man both in spirit and in health by the time the family finally settled permanently in Hue'. Ngo, the eldest son, became responsible for his mother, six sisters, and his brother, the youngest of the Phan family.

Ngo possessed only a good education. He parlayed that asset into a successful business career by getting himself hired and promoted through the ranks of the Coca Cola bottling and distributing company until he was named the principle distributor for all of the Republic of Viet Nam in 1962. His chief success had been to accumulate the lion's share of the bottled nonalcoholic beverage market from the nearest competitor, Pepsi Cola. That difference had to date amounted to tens of millions of dollars for the company, prestige and a handsome home, wife, and living for himself.

Ngo was not always wholly temperate in his speech nor entirely circumspect in his political associations. He had not bought into the Diem Personalist Democracy and had the temerity to say so in open forum. After Diem's death, and despite his wife's pleadings, Ngo had opted to align himself with several different nationalist but non GVN political parties over the years. He had become a champion of sorts to the disenfranchised non-Communists.

On the dark side, there were well documented reports of associations, or at least meetings, with several individuals known to be VCI or sympathizers with the insurgency. Ngo made no apparent effort to be clandestine about these meetings, and had made it simple for RVN secret police and later for RDCs to produce incriminating photographs of these meetings. Ngo visited the COSVN office and had been a guest at more than one dinner and more than one social event hosted by Yu-en Chou Chen, COSVN chairman, and his wife, 'Triple Chen.'

Anders had a flash of *déjà vu* when he saw the Chens' names. He recalled the brief meeting he and Lane Duerk's secretary, Miss Nguyen, had had with the COSVN chairman and his wife in the swank gambling establishment in Saigon. When he examined Ngo's photograph more carefully, he was sure that he recognized the face as one of the men who had been seated around the LAF leader's table that night. Anders firmed up a personal antipathy for Phan over and above the incriminating evidence he was perusing.

Finally, there were a series of letters from prominent business associates, certified as loyal to GVN, attesting to their personal knowledge of activities of Phan that were antithetical to the current government of South Viet Nam; and one frankly linked him to pro-LAF activities. That one stated without reservation that Phan Pho Ngo was a part of the Viet Cong Infrastructure.

There followed a minutely detailed chronology of Phan's very orderly and predictable activities. He was a man who lived by careful habit, a family man, who routinely joined his wife and four children for a family gathering at 1800 hours precisely. He also routinely left home and hearth at 2000 hours and returned at 2200. In that hiatus, he was seen to enter the home of one Yen Thi Hanh, an exceedingly attractive widow, who lived beyond the means provided by her secretarial position in the defense ministry. She was known to have family in the Democratic Republic of Viet Nam. The unnamed source whose affidavit had stated flatly that Phan was a VCI asset asserted that the clandestine meetings between Phan and the VC occurred during those evening *tête à têtes* at Mrs. Yen's apartment.

A personal secretary of the bottling company executive had made a photocopy of her employer's itinerary for the coming month, a document that presented in detail the meeting times, travel arrangements, and lodging accommodations. To the photocopy was attached the handwritten notation: "Informant completely reliable—active CIO agent. Confirmed CAS".

461

Ngo had two bodyguards, one known to be a GVN informant; and the other was suspected to have VC leanings. Both, however, were unquestionably loyal to the personal safety of their employer; and one or the other or both was constantly at the Coca Cola executive's side, even when he was at home. The divided and shared loyalties of the bodyguards were unspoken evidence of the enigmatic social web that was Viet Nam during the era of the second Indochinese war. Anders' problem was to devise a plan to capture the executive alive, to do so without exposing his unit's identity, and to leave disinformation that would allow even the most critical to draw the conclusion that Phan Pho Ngo was another victim of VC terrorism.

Anders summoned Tran, Bach, Dung, and Ky after evening rice for a late night planning meeting. By midnight they had sketched the broad outlines of an ambitious plan that would involve three sets of his PRU cadres—nine men total. Anders would not be able to be present physically during the execution of the plan. It would seem out of place for a six foot three inch tall blond Viet Cong to be kidnapping the Coca Cola distributor.

Anders sent off a shopping list to Cleve Howard in Hue' that included ARVN uniforms and passes, VC pajamas, rubber tire sandals, leaflets, 'Traitor to the NLF' notes, captured homemade grenades, and nine AK-47s with ammunition. The needed equipment was sent to the compound two days later in sturdy wooden crates clearly marked "CARE—Gift of the generous American People."

The young PRU operations chief held a final briefing with the action team before they left the compound the following night stressing the critical need to take the target alive. He spent a sleepless night visualizing the team landing in the LZ, and setting up their ambush in the dark forest beside national highway one, in the Deo Hai Van (Cloudy Pass) near the summit of Bach Ma (White Horse Mountain). On the other side of the pass lay Danang (formerly Cau Han), the provincial capital and US Marine base, the place where the first 3500 marines landed in South Viet Nam March 8, 1965. It was Mr. Phan's destination. He was scheduled to meet with his distributors in the bar of the Danang Hotel on Dong Da Street. Anders was determined that the man would not be in attendance.

Tran was the designated leader in the field. He had reconnoitered the pass by day and by night for the past forty-eight hours and had selected a nearly ideal site for his men to stage the ambush. His lot was made easier by wearing the ARVN uniforms and by showing his authentic documents to the ARVN and to the US Marine roadblocks. Cleve Howard had made his contribution by informing the GVN authorities and the Lieutenant Colonel of the US Marines of the exact time of his operation; so, the marines could conveniently absent themselves for a couple of hours. There was such heavy routine GVN traffic that the PRU cadres had not encountered VC anywhere along the main highway, even at night.

Tran had his men set up a classical crossfire ambush well out of sight of the road, and positioned two trucks one hundred meters apart, one above and one below the ambush point. Both were to feign a breakdown when the hour came for Mr. Phan's Coca Cola truck and the jeep bearing his guards to pass Tran and his men and to drop into the waiting net.

The clouds hung low over the mountainous roadway obscuring vision for anything more than fifty meters in any direction. The PRUCs, sweating in the oppressive heat and humidity in the brushy inclines adjacent to the highway, were virtually invisible to vehicles passing them. Bach was the lookout. He was situated half a klick north on the highway itself in a buffalo drawn cart plodding slowly and patiently up the incline. He had stopped every few meters so as to avoid being too close to the ambush site and kept moving just enough to maintain the fiction of a farmer moving a load of dung to his fields on the warmer and less humid south side of the pass.

The Coca Cola truck was late by an hour. The cadres' nerves were frayed by the dreadful heat and infesting insects that tormented them mercilessly as well as by the frustrating wait. They began to doubt the information that had put them in that position. They grumbled to themselves; but they did not move; and they made no noise despite their discomfort.

At 1315 Bach visually picked the gaudily decorated soft drink truck from the meager flow of traffic; and when he was certain, he gave the signal to Tran—four rapid sequence depressions of his radio transmitter button repeated twice at fifteen second intervals. The PRUCs alerted to Tran's terse radio message, "Subject in sight".

The ambush trucks started their engines while still pretending to be at work under the opened engine hoods. The Coca Cola truck and its accompanying security jeep passed the first truck. The driver and Mr. Phan saw nothing amiss. The security guards were relaxed. Ahead a truck approached from the gloom of the overhanging cloud. It evidently blew a tire because it suddenly lurched and swerved in front of them. It stopped obliquely across Highway 1, and a puff of smoke belched from beneath the hood signaling serious engine trouble. The Coca Cola truck was twenty-five meters from the distressed truck and slowed to a crawl seeking a way around the other vehicle. The two body guards aroused from their torpor and began to look for trouble. They found none.

Two men alighted from the stricken truck and were gesticulating and cursing at their inanimate vehicle. Downhill, a second truck unobtrusively positioned itself across the roadway. One of the guards saw that activity through the mist, and for the first time, became concerned.

Before he could chamber a round, the crackle of Kalashnikov automatic fire assaulted his ears, stunning him momentarily with surprise and terror. "VC!" he yelled.

The guard flipped the ivory Buddha hanging on the thong about his neck up between his teeth, chambered the round and set his weapon on automatic in less time than it takes to say it. A single perfectly placed round struck him directly in the nasion, dead center in his low forehead. He did not have time to get off a shot in return.

The second guard, the driver of the jeep, wrenched the wheel hard to the right and accelerated to bring himself alongside the Coke truck that was now disabled by 7.62 mm bullets that riddled every tire. He jammed on the brakes of the jeep and stood up to rake the roadside with automatic fire from his M-14. He was too late. He felt the searing agony of a line of bullets as they tapped holes up his right leg, the lateral portion of his abdomen, and twice across his right arm causing him to drop his weapon and to pitch in a clumsy somersault over the jeep door and onto the dusty street. The guard was glad to be alive, terrified, and in excruciatingly severe pain. Every one of the seventy two entrance wounds had erupted into a maddening burning and stinging anguish. He feigned death hoping his ruse would keep him alive.

The Coke truck driver leapt from his stopped vehicle and raised his own M-14 to fire at the black pajamad VCs he now saw pouring from the underbrush. He was too slow by half. His gun fired, but into the sky because he was blown to pieces by so many AK-47 rounds that for a moment his lifeless body flailed uselessly in a standing position, a sort of macabre *pas de mort*, before he crumpled.

Phan Pho Ngo sat transfixed in his passenger seat in the Coca Cola truck. It was the first time the combat in Viet Nam had touched him close-up. He was spellbound by the noise, the smell of cordite, the visions of the dances of death performed by men he knew well and trusted. He screamed, but no sound came out. He soiled himself.

Ky ran up to the guard jeep and satisfied himself that one of the guards remained alive and helpless. He made sure that the wounded man could see his black pajamas and rubber tire sandals as he sliced off the dead guard's ears and nailed one of the "Death to Traitors" signs onto the corpse's forehead. In his rush Ky accidentally on purpose dropped a small bundle of LAF propaganda leaflets, also within sight of the wounded guard.

Tran put an unnecessary *coup de grace* bullet into the back of the Coke truck driver's head then opened the truck passenger door and dragged the terrified civilian out onto the road. He said, "You are the prisoner of the people. You will pay dearly for your crimes of exploiting the masses for the benefit of the round-eyed criminals." Ngo fainted and had to be dragged into the PRU truck.

The PRUCs left the scene as it was, dropping two communist assault rifles for good measure as they departed. It never occurred to them that they might have been overdoing the disinformation theatrics. They merely wanted to be certain that no one, including the security guard, had cause to entertain the wrong notion as to the perpetrators of this particular outrage.

They were at the landing zone with time to spare, and in eighty minutes touched down in the exercise yard of the PRU compound and unloaded their black hooded captive. Tran gave Anders the laconic report: "No casualties (he did not count the nonPRUCs); VCI detainee unharmed and in custody; evidence in place."

"Well done," Anders congratulated the teams equally tersely. He was not used to giving effusive praise, and they were not used to receiving any at all. On balance, it seemed like good pay for their efforts.

Mr. Phan was led under his own power into the main blockhouse, still blindfolded, and tied to a chair under guard. No one spoke in his presence. He asked questions at each stage of his captivity; but after receiving no answers, he became silent. He shivered and shuddered beneath his hood and against his bindings, but was so thoroughly cowed that he made no attempt to escape or even to test the efficacy of his strictures.

In his office Anders radioed Cleve Howard at RD headquarters on the secure frequency. "Have parcel. Await instructions," was his transmission.

"Accompany same to this location," came back the reply.

Anders had the hapless man taken back to the Huey, and he and Dung clambered aboard beside the kidnappee. In twenty minutes they were in the MACV compound on the heliport site. They accompanied their prisoner into the holding room in the rear of the RD HQ along with two vicious looking, all-business, Chinese Nungs, mercenary employees of The Company.

Cleve Howard gave him a thumbs up signal as his 'attaboy' for the successful mission, and Anders was happy for that much. The Company gave out plaudits uncommonly, medals rarely and privately, and official commendations to contract agents never.

Mr. Howard gestured to his Nungs and to Dung to remain with the prisoner and took Anders with him out of earshot of the frightened captive. The two men took seats in the Province Chief-RDC/O's office before Cleve Howard began to speak. "Anders, this is a real check mark in our plus columns. I expect this little traitor to be a gold mine of information. The company computer will get another injection of the fuel it thrives on from our new VCS."

"Sounds good to me," Anders commented, not really knowing what was expected of him. He thought for a moment, then asked, "What if he doesn't talk, just accepts his fate and goes to prison?"

Howard looked at the boy to see if he was really as naive as his question suggested. Satisfying himself that the young contract agent was truly guileless, he said, "This is 1967, Anders. If he is reluctant, there are ways, nothing crude like torture, of course, but nonetheless highly effective. In fact, we have three men coming in tonight for the very purpose of draining our Mr. Phan of everything he knows. They are quite expert. I want you to be present when he is interrogated."

Anders nodded. He felt uneasy about the invitation; but it was part of the job, he guessed. He had been comfortable up to now just doing the field work, thinking of it as basically military in character, and had been content to avoid thinking about the aftermath of his missions. Only combatants got hurt when he and his PRU cadres did their work; the hands-off rules after he delivered his prisoners had suited him fine. What he did not see, he did not need to suspect because Anders Bergstrom was not an inquisitive fellow by nature. His attitude was something like what he reasoned a high altitude bomber must feel. As long as he did not see it, he was not causing much harm. Anders accepted the drink from Cleve, and settled back to wait for the next act in the unfolding small drama. Mr. Howard left the young Swede to his own thoughts and went out to pursue one of the many tasks that had befallen him that day.

After two hours Anders felt the pangs of hunger, and it occurred to him that Dung might be hungry as well. He scouted around the RD building until he found a small kitchen where an elderly Chinese mama-san was making stir-fry. Anders watched her as she liberally dropped in quantities of small brown chilies. He spoke in Vietnamese, but she ignored him. The noises he made did not sound like words to her Mandarin-language ears; besides, she was busy. By gestures he indicated a desire for some of the aromatic mixture of vegetables, fried rice, and chunks of savory meat. By return gesture she had the young round eye pick up an extra bowl and chop sticks and to follow her. He remembered to get one for Dung.

As he had presumed, the bow legged old lady limped her way to the secure concrete room where the two Nung mercs and Dung were guarding their prize. Anders knocked on the heavy steel door, and a peep hole opened. The men inside unbolted and opened the door and admitted the elderly Chinese lady and the large blond man. The Nungs were pointing British Mark II Sten guns at his chest. He set down his bowls and chopsticks, stretched out his arms full length, and splayed his fingers. He made a 360° turn, looked at the men with the submachine guns, and waited until they smiled and nodded. They were shortly all one big happy family, including the old lady, putting away the ragingly hot Chinese food. No one thought for a moment that Mr. Phan might want something to eat.

There was a change of guards at dusk. Anders and Dung scrounged around to find a couple of cots and caught a nap. After about an hour Cleve Howard awakened Anders with a gentle shake of his shoulder. The Province Chief was standing with his arm outstretched as far as he could possibly reach and was pushing with the tip ends of his fingers. Anders found that precaution amusing and laughed; Mr. Howard had no idea why. "Our visitors are here. I thought you might like to meet them."

"Do you want me to wake Dung?" Anders asked.

"Not necessary," Mr. Howard replied.

"Give me a minute," Anders requested. He had diarrhea from the chilies, and that would not wait.

Feeling better, the young Swede followed his boss out of the HQ building and across to a small cubical cement block building that had the appearance of a bunker or an air-raid shelter. There were Nung guards at the only entrance and one along each external wall. Evidently, it was as undesirable to have unwanted persons entering as it was to have selected persons leaving uninvited. Anders was glad he was on the right team at the moment and shivered a little at the thought of the imagined fate of prisoners, those on the wrong team.

He followed Mr. Howard into the single room building. In the middle of the room was a table, something like a doctor's examining table but with unusually tall and sturdy legs. Mr. Phan Pho Ngo was strapped to the table by leather restraints that had been applied to his neck, both wrists and ankles, and around his midsection. At the moment he was unconscious.

A steel instrument table stood at right angles to the examining table and held an assortment of stainless steel surgical tools and electrical wires, alligator clamps, and long needles. A second table held a very modern Navy gray machine with a console that contained a confusing array of knobs, buttons, and dials, and two small oscilloscopes that were presenting straight lines of light at that time. Electrode connectors were plugged into the appropriate ports on the console and the attached wires dangled off the side of the machine. Each electrode wire held a long needle. Close scrutiny would have revealed traces of blood on the needles.

There were three men standing facing Mr. Phan with their backs to Cleve Howard and Anders Bergstrom as the two RD men entered the blockhouse. Anders felt a prickle of vague recognition as he looked at the back of one of the men. He had a premonition, and a feeling of unrealness, of anger, and of fear; and he did not know why exactly. He sought to fix his recollection, to understand why the man's back looked familiar, and what had prompted his internal alarm button to go off.

The internal alarm had flashed for two reasons. The three men turned to greet Anders, the PRU/O, and Cleve Howard, the POIC. This allowed Anders his first glimpse of the battered unconscious body of Mr. Phan and his first distasteful contact with the reality of what his own work was about, the reality he had heretofore been able to deny with plausibility. The second reason for his apprehension was that he recognized two of the men, one of whom, he had expected and hoped never to see again.

"Greetings, *mon ami*," said the Frenchman extending his hand in a gesture of warm cordiality. For Anders to see Jean-Luc DuParrier in this remote outpost was nothing less than astounding. He felt exactly as if he had been stuck a sharp blow to his solar plexus.

When Anders did not respond, DuParrier spoke again and waved his hand in the young Swedish-American's direction, "I suppose you did not expect to see your old friend and training partner in this place, this PIC. Let me assure you that I am the custodian, not the internee." His face was beaming with good fellowship.

Anders pretended he did not see the extended hand. He could not bring himself to shake that hand after the episode at Camp Peary and especially after seeing the condition of the helpless VCS on the surgical table. It was as if the proffered hand were dirty, and some of that dirt would rub off. Anders recovered his composure quickly enough to keep the absence of response to the social amenities subliminal to all but Jean-Luc and himself. Jean-Luc continued to smile with his entire expressive face except for his eyes.

"Greetings, Jean-Luc. It has been a long time. And Mr. Lutz, isn't it?" He recognized the polygraphist who had vetted him a year ago.

"The same," Dieter Lutz said and nodded perfunctorily. It was his version of an enthusiastic greeting.

"This is Tandrosz Szabo, the senior psy-ops agent for The Company in Indochina, Anders," Mr. Howard said to introduce the two men. "Anders is Company; he's our asset in charge of the mid province PRU and doing a fine job out there for us."

"Anders," Szabo nodded in acknowledgment.

"Mr. Szabo," Anders nodded in turn. It was not a warm group.

"No news from this one," Szabo said matter-of-factly to Cleve Howard. He inclined his head toward the prostrate man on the table. "Either he is innocent and knows nothing, or he is made of very stern stuff. Any more drugs or Jean-Luc's electrical persuasion, and this VCS will join his ancestors."

"He's not innocent. We have too much on him. Maybe he needs a helicopter ride," replied Howard.

"Not worth much alone, let me assure you, chief. It's either the NIC or bring along someone special to the suspect," Jean-Luc volunteered.

The NIC—National Interrogation Center—in Saigon was the most effective place in the country and, perhaps, on the planet, for extracting information. It maintained a combination torture room and mortuary in room P-40 at the Saigon Zoological Gardens and was the last stop in the series before transfer to Poulo Condore—Con Son Island Prison—and final internment for survivors. Tran could have told Anders much about the latter location.

"Probably right," agreed Howard. "I'll arrange for 'someone special.'"

Anders was fairly mystified, but kept quiet. He felt a mounting desire to distance himself from the suggested activities, even from knowledge of them; but he was growing progressively doubtful that he would be able to do so.

Back in the RD/O office, Cleve Howard asked, "Anything I need to know about what's between you and DuParrier? I take it you two know each other." Anders was impressed at how little escaped his observant boss.

"We know each other. We trained together at The Farm...That's it." Anders answered somewhat abruptly.

The RDC/O looked at the young paramilitarist for a moment with careful scrutiny. "If it affects our work, I need to know."

Anders shook his head.

"All right, then—to business. You are going to provide the 'special person' I promised the three Tontons Macoutes in there."

"Me!?" Anders exclaimed. His face betrayed his thorough bemusement and displeasure.

"You and yours. Don't look so pershimmered. It's really quite simple. You are going to pick up Phan's teenaged daughter; she's VCI, too, so far as we can determine. Her presence should make the old man more tractable, don't you think?"

Anders did not really know what 'tractable' meant, but in context it was quite clear. The father would be more easily extorted into betraying his comrades with a close-up potential threat to his daughter. Anders sincerely wished that this cup could pass from him, but he did not say so.

He shrugged, like the teenager he still was, and said obediently and quietly, "How do we accomplish that?"

"I'm the *Jefe*, the RDC operations chief; you're the action man. You come up with the plan. But, it has to be tomorrow."

"Tomorrow!?" Anders was incredulous.

Cleve laughed. "It's not all that tough. She's a school girl—at school every day. Piece of cake to find her. Here's a couple of photographs of the girl." He handed a manila envelope to Anders.

"She takes the same route home every day and always at the same time. I just happen to have a copy of the route complete with times. The organization, of which you are a probationary member, does meticulous work, no?"

Anders quickly perused the material in the envelope. "Yes," he answered, impressed again.

"And while we're at it, let me suggest to you that The Outfit is not crazy about its employees telling it that they 'can't.' Try and remember that in the future. Oh, there's one more thing."

Anders was afraid there might be. "Shoot," he said, warily.

"She rides home under guard in an armored vehicle. She is daddy's pride and joy."

Anders raised both his eyebrows and frowned. Cleve Howard smiled malevolently and said, "So, best be on your way. You have your work cut out for you. No mistakes, Anders; I want the little *tovarich* intact." His face held a dismissive expression. Anders left. He did not shake his head until after he was out of the room.

An hour later, he had Tran, Bach, and Ky with himself and Dung. It had been no difficulty to helicopter them down to Hue'. The Huey pilot at the compound was bored. The pilot was gung ho, liked flying and action, and got little of either when Anders was gone; so, despite the hour, he was ready to go as soon as Tran got the message at the compound.

To clear their minds and to get out of the RD building and the MACV compound, Anders took his friends to dinner at the Song Huong Floating Restaurant on the Perfume River between the Huong Giang Hotel and the old Clemenceau Bridge. There, the five men worked out a plan of sorts in the next hour, assembled and checked their weapons, and caught some needed sleep before the following day brought on its expected spate of action.

The four Vietnamese PRUCs clandestinely observed the routine at the Phan house. It seemed quite casual despite the fact that the head of the household had only recently been kidnapped, and the family and retainers and guards must have been aware of that. Tran assumed that the household did not consider the possibility of lightening strikings twice. The guards brought the armored vehicle to the front of the house and waited until the girl trotted out, smiling, and waving goodbye to her mother. The guards did not have weapons on their persons, presumably having left their arms in the front. The girl jumped into the rear of the vehicle, and the guards closed and locked the doors. They climbed up front and drove straight to the *Ecole pour Jeunes Filles* along the route that the CIA operatives had mapped for Anders and his PRUCs. There was no additional security at the school.

Counting on the accuracy of the timetable of the family's activities provided by Cleve Howard, Anders and his men passed the day in idle pursuits until about an hour before they expected the Phan guards to bring the family's armored vehicle to the front of the house in order to fetch the girl from her all girl's school. Their routine was to dust off or wash the car every day before leaving to bring the girl home. Anders arranged to stroll up the opposite side of the street with a Vietnamese girl, one of Howard's people, letting the neighbors assume she was his concubine, while the other four PRUCs separately converged on the vehicle on the same side of the street as the Phan home.

Ky shambled up to one of the guards, pretending intoxication, and extended his hand as if begging. Tran sidled up to the opposite side of the van-like vehicle, out of the direct line of vision of the two guards. Dung and Bach walked nonchalantly from the opposite direction holding hands. Ky engaged one of the guards in conversation; the guard kept refusing to give a handout; and Ky kept insisting.

Anders slowed his pace directly across the street from the Phan house and the growing activity around the vehicle. Dung suddenly threw a vicious punch into the left kidney of one of the two guards who crumpled with a groan. The guard who had been talking to Ky diverted his attention toward his fallen companion. Ky caught the man neatly on the back of his neck with a sword hand blow, and the guard toppled to the ground unconscious.

Anders left the girl with whom he had been walking and walked briskly to the scene. He cautioned himself not to run. Bach extracted the keys from the unconscious guard and opened the rear doors. The five men dragged the two guards quickly into the armored vehicle and laid them out on the steel floor. There were two comfortable chairs bolted to the floor and to the walls inside the van, and Anders and Tran took them. Dung stood in the corner with a combat shotgun trained on the two men on the floor. Ky drove, and Bach sat on the passenger side with his face averted to avoid startling the schoolgirl.

The armored van was sitting in its prescribed location when the girl skipped out of the school yard and waved a cheery goodbye to her school mates. The PRUCs were glad she came to them, because it would have been almost impossible to pick her out of the crowd of uniformed, black haired girls, and would undoubtedly have entailed considerably more ruckus to have to go after her.

The two Phan family guards were fully alert, if a little queasy. Tran explained to them what they would need to do if they were to live. Simply put, they were to get the girl into her usual place in the van without attracting the crowd's attention. The menace of the short barreled shotgun in each of their mouths was adequate inducement.

The girl was mildly curious that neither of the guards got out to greet her as usual. She was relieved when they stepped out of the rear of the van and led her to the doors. She had not counted the added men, nor had she thought anything about the significance of their presence. She was rendered mute with consternation when she first saw the shotgun and the .45 cal handguns bristling out of the interior of her heretofore safe haven of transportation. Anders kept his .45 trained on the guards, and Tran and Dung swooped the girl into the back. Tran banged on the side of the van-like vehicle to signal the driver, and Ky jumped out and closed the rear doors on the girl, her *hors de combat* guards, and her captors. The vehicle sped away.

As prearranged, Ky drove to the eastern outskirts of town, about two klicks from the nearest habitation, and released the guards. The two guards were thoroughly vanquished, but essentially unharmed. Along the way, they had been subjected to a litany of communist doctrine and had been invited to join in the insurgency struggle against the usurpers and their round-eyed running dogs. Frequent references had been made to their *Đồng-chí ngưởi Nga* (Russian comrade).

The girl wept uncontrollably. She had evidently not heard about the inscrutability of the Orient. She was terrified; so frightened that she could not speak. The most alarming thing about the whole horrifying affair was to be in the presence of the *trang ngưởi khổng-lồ* (white giant) with his ugly cruel face and nightmarish *tóc trắng* (white hair). She had never seen a man so huge, so spectral. In her fog of anguish and confusion, she thought of him as a *con ma* (ghost). In all her fourteen years of life it was her first time to be in the same room with a foreigner, a man of a different race. He might as well have come from Mars; he was so strange and alien. The giant white ghost remained enigmatically silent throughout.

Cleve Howard was unusually complimentary. "Thumbs up, Anders. You and your *ralliers* have done well. I trust that there was no undue unpleasantness at the girl's home or at the *Ecole pour Jeuves Filles?*"

"None. Her two guards are on a hike from the outskirts of town. We didn't hurt them overmuch, and they can spread the tale that the girl was taken by VC."

"Nice touch."

The Nungs guarded the girl who was petrified by their cruel visages. She scarcely moved throughout the afternoon. At full dusk, the Nungs delivered the completely compliant girl to the PIC, the forbidding block house situated separately on the MACV compound. Cleve ordered Anders to accompany the girl and her guards. This time Tran went with Anders. The three Company psy-ops inquisitors, the Tontons Macoutes bogeymen, were waiting inside. The girl's father was sitting in a straight backed cane chair in one corner of the austere room with three Nungs poised over him. It hardly seemed necessary. The middle-aged man appeared old, tired, dull—the picture of docility.

Mr. Phan aroused to a level of frantic alertness when he saw his daughter. Her Nung guards kept the schoolgirl ten meters from her father at a hand gesture from Tandrosz Szabo. Jean-Luc DuParrier stood by with an expectant smile that included only his lower face. His opaque eyes watched the prisoner intently, like those of a circling shark. Dieter Lutz was seated by his polygraph equipment looking detached.

Szabo addressed Mr. Phan in quiet slow and enunciated Vietnamese. He was surprisingly fluent and articulate in the language. "Mr. Phan. Our patience has reached an end. In five minutes you will produce for us a list of names, dates, ranks, and activities of your *chiến-hữus* (comrades-in-arms) with the LAF, or I will be obliged to place your tender daughter under the able questioning of my assistant." Jean-Luc made a self-conscious little bow in the direction of the Coca Cola executive. He looked at the girl with predatory eyes.

Mr. Phan pleaded and wept. He repeated over and over that he knew nothing. He had nothing to do with the VC. He was not a VCI or even a VC sympathizer. He was a loyal subject of the Saigon regime. His pleadings fell on deaf ears. Szabo gave a sharp head nod, and the two Nung guards hoisted the girl to the examination table. She was as limp as a cloth doll, totally unresisting. Her father knelt on the floor in supplication and begged Szabo for mercy on his firstborn daughter. The Nungs looked down at the man with undisguised loathing; the man was humiliating himself for a nothing, a female-slave person.

Anders inadvertently took two steps backward in an involuntary effort to distance himself from the satanic scene. It was Cleve Howard who reacted most decisively. He said, "Tandrosz, may I see you for a moment?"

Szabo walked to the RDC/O's side and looked at him. Howard spoke very softly, almost whispering, "This does not seem to be getting us anywhere. We do not have time to waste on this interrogation. I would like to suggest the definitive abbreviation to this activity. Why don't you just take them for a moonlight tour over the South China Sea? The girl and her father have both seen us. The VC pretense is hardly viable anymore."

"I can get the girl to tell us everything she knows or ever knew," DuParrier said, unable to make even a pretense that he was not eavesdropping. "The father will break when I do. I know he will." There was an urgency, a yearning quality to his voice.

Szabo shot Jean-Luc a look that made him instantly quiet. "I am inclined to agree with you, Cleve. Besides, it is the RDC/O's jurisdiction and call. Do you want to come along?" The senior interrogator asked Howard.

"Not me. I have things to do. I am sure you will handle it altogether appropriately." The two men shared a look. "But I do want my man here to go along. He is still going through the learning curve, in case you hadn't noticed. It would be good for him to get involved all the way, don't you think?"

Anders heard every word and his heart sank. He hoped the evil looking Slavic agent would think the helicopter too crowded or something. He knew it was wishful thinking, and Szabo confirmed his worst presumption when he said, "Time the boy was in like the rest. Help him to be a team player."

In forty-five minutes they were in a helicopter over the South China sea traveling at about three thousand feet. The moonlight shimmered and sparkled on the calm surface of the water casting beautiful but eerie shadows from the silhouettes of the archipelago of islands. There was a single US Navy destroyer making its way toward Danang and a few sampans sitting at anchor, the lamplights and cooking fires on their afterdecks creating dots of light on the surface of the black water.

Anders, Tran, and one Nung sat on the fold down seats on one side of the helicopter's cabin; and DuParrier, Phan Pho Ngo, Szabo, and a second Nung were crowded into the seats on the opposite side. The softly whimpering girl lay in the fetal position on the greasy steel deck of the chopper. The Nungs were each armed with a .45 and a cruel looking curved two-edged dagger. There were no signs of resistance, and none of the occupants talked until they were well out to sea. There was only the steady loud rattle of the craft's engine and rotors to interrupt the silence of that starless night.

Szabo spoke into his microphone. "Circle," he said. Anders felt the helicopter begin to make a wide banking clockwise circle.

Szabo turned to Mr. Phan. "*Kẻ phản-bôi*" (traitor), he shouted over the din of the machine. "You have one chance to repent and to make yourself clean. Do it now. If you don't, you alone are responsible for your daughter's fate."

Mr. Phan begged, cajoled, pleaded, and cried in a stream of nearly unintelligible Vietnamese. Anders was quite facile with the language, but the man was going too fast for him, and more than half of what he said was lost in the rumble of the engines and steady whumping of the rotors. It was obvious that nothing the man was saying was responsive to the question Szabo had so threateningly posed. Szabo turned to DuParrier and jerked his thumb in the direction of the cabin door.

DuParrier shouted in the ear of the Nung guard seated next to him. The Chinese man roughly grabbed the diminutive girl by her blouse front and the belt of her blue pleated school uniform skirt. He easily lifted her off the vibrating floor and duck walked to the open door with the terrified girl. *"Khô-ô-ông!"* (No-o-o-o!) screamed the girl's father when the full realization of what those monsters had in mind hit him. *"Tôi không biết gì hết! Không biết gì hết! Tôi van xin ông!"* (I know nothing! Nothing! I beg you!) he pleaded.

Anders believed the man, but knew he could not interfere. Tran sat transfixed by the scene. Somewhere in his core boiled up the memory of his passage in the garbage can on the way to Con Son Island many months ago. He felt paralyzed.

Anders was sure it was only a tactic. Surely, the VCI would relent and let this nightmare be over.

"Tell me!" menaced Szabo. "Five seconds!" was all he added. He looked straight into the stricken father's eyes and began to lift the fingers of his right hand methodically.

Phan watched the number of fingers increase in horrified fascination. He was as if he were struck dumb. He dropped his face into the palms of his hands, and his body shuddered with his sobs. Szabo jerked the captive man's head up when the five seconds had elapsed. He nodded to the Nung.

The Chinese mercenary sneered at the girl then made a sign of crossing two fingers in front of her as a mortal insult. Then he made a sudden violent jerking motion and pitched the hapless little girl into the black void. Her decrescendo screaming trailed off into the night. Anders thought he would faint. Of all the things he had ever heard or imagined, this was the worst. He was sure that he would awaken and discover that it had all been a bad dream. He had to concentrate not to urinate in his pants. He looked at DuParrier, who returned his glance and smiled a frozen grin—Anders knew he had looked into the face of evil incarnate. He could not hold the gaze. Tran just stared, his mask-like face devoid of expression or emotion. He was gripping the edge of his seat with knuckles blanched from the strain.

Anders had heard and ignored rumors that the CIA backed system had condoned the torture and killing of old people, women, and even children, sometimes for mere sadism, sometimes for petty revenge. This reality he had just witnessed made even the worst of what he had heard about have a deep ring of truth.

Szabo turned to Mr. Phan. He was going to shout, "Now you know we mean business! I will have the information I need!" but one look at the man made him keep his silence. First, Mr. Phan's right arm and leg became flaccid and dangled like wet spaghetti at his side. The left side of his face became slack. He burbled unintelligibly, emitting a nearly inaudible syllable salad. Then he slumped to his right. Phan Pho Ngo, the Coca Cola bottler and distributor for South Viet Nam, was dead. When his daughter flew out of the helicopter door, his blood pressure had shot off the manometer; a blood vessel deep in the putamen of his brain burst from the strain and blew the left side of his cerebrum to pieces.

Szabo swore under his breath. The Nung guards and DuParrier looked cheated. Tran's face relaxed, and Anders felt a peculiar sag of relief. He could only think that this was the best way out for the man. The picture of the girl falling out of the helicopter door, her arms and legs akimbo and the gale force wind blowing her skirt obscenely over her immature legs was a wrenching one. The look on her father's face at the moment she fell and then the man's brain dying would stay with the impressionable boy forever.

DuParrier gestured angrily at the two Nungs. They took hold of Phan's limp body and pitched it unceremoniously out over the South China Sea. There would be no evidence of their night's work. Szabo spoke into his headset microphone. "Home," was his only message. No one attempted to talk on the way back to the MACV compound.

At the RD/HQ Tran was excused and left to find his cot for the night. DuParrier found an opportunity to be alone with Anders. Anders glared at the unwanted company, but Jean-Luc had something to say. "Now you know what your part of this war is about, no, *mon ami*? Someday the slopes will know who is in control. Until then, you had best keep your mouth shut about our wet work if you don't want to get yourself tried as some kind of war criminal; *comprendre, mon ami*?" Jean-Luc took perverse pleasure in the delivery of the implied threat. Anders started to react; but knew it was futile; so, he said nothing.

Jean-Luc could not resist twisting the knife in a little deeper. "You are thinking that at least those two might have been VC, traitors to their country; and that they at least deserved capital punishment. How much you have to learn. How naive you are. Ask your boss who turned Phan in to the NPIASS. It is time to grow up, *enfant. C'est la guerre!*" He tightened his thin lips into a reptilian smile and gave Anders a gloating look. The young Swede's body tensed like a snake coiled to strike. Jean-Luc backed off laughing.

Cleve Howard came from his briefing with Tandrosz Szabo. He did not seem particularly upset. His face wore an incongruously contented expression. He met Anders and handed him a bundle of manila folder dossiers and an envelope that Anders assumed contained his orders for the upcoming weeks.

"Too bad we didn't get more info for the computer. I am beginning to wonder if old Phan might not have been as ignorant of the VC as he said he was. Oh, well, can't get 'em all right." Anders was shocked by the cavalier attitude expressed by his commander. Though he tried to appear inexpressive, his youthful and expressionate face gave him away.

"Didn't relish the experience, eh, Anders?"

"Not particularly."

"I'll be straight with you; I guess you do need to know. Things turned out just as planned. This was a snatch and snuff from the beginning. The powers-that-be, including the Regional Director, sent me orders that this one had to be handled with maximum prejudice."

Anders hated the Company euphemisms. Why could the prissy agent not just say 'killed,' or 'murdered?' He was having trouble controlling his temper, and his angry curiosity got the better of his presumption that he was treading on dangerous ground when he asked, "Tell me one thing, Mr. Howard."

"Cleve."

"Yes, sir…Cleve. Please, there is something I'd really like to know."

"Um hmmh. Who turned Mr. Phan into the NPIASS?"

There was a very slight pause before Cleve Howard smiled and answered, "Oh, I thought you knew. I thought that item was part of the dossier from the computer printout. It was the Pepsi Cola head honcho."

Anders was disgusted, angry. He felt that he and his men had been used, a sort of betrayal. He knew he had lost his innocence. There was nothing he could do about it now. He supposed Jean-Luc was right, *'C'est la guerre.'*

Howard's face became hard. He did not like the expression on Anders' face. It was not the look of a team player. "Let me tell you a little parable, boy. It will help you to understand all of this. Something you might want to think about.

"This is an old Nguyen era story. Seems there was a young peasant hurrying home along a mountain road in the middle of a cold season night. It was icy and freezing. He saw a small bird lying along the side of the road nearly frozen. Its little feet were sticking up in the air, and it was all but dead. The young man was soft hearted. He bent over and picked up the little creature and put it inside his coat to warm it up. The bird began to revive, which made our peasant happy; but he knew that he could not continue to provide the bird's much needed warmth out there in the cold. He pondered what to do.

"Just when he began to despair for a plan, he happened to walk past a steaming pie left by one of the buffalo herd on its way to pasture. He stuck the little bird up to its beak in the warm mess and left happy that he was instrumental in saving a helpless creature's life.

"The little bird revived completely and was so overjoyed at being both alive and warm that it began to sing at the top of its little lungs. The sound attracted the attention of a fox who was hunting nearby. The fox ran over and ate the little bird. End of story."

Anders looked at Mr. Howard completely nonplused.

"Ah, I see that an explanation is in order. You see, Anders, this story has a moral, in fact three of them. You might want to bear them in mind.

"First, it's not always your enemies who put you into it. Second, it's not always your friends who get you out. And third, if you're in it up to your beak, it's best not to open your mouth."

CHAPTER 22

When the enemy is away from home for a long time and produces no victories and families learn of their dead, then the enemy population home becomes dissatisfied and considers it a mandate from heaven that the armies be recalled. Time is always in our favor. Our climate, mountains, and jungles discourage the enemy; but for us, they offer both sanctuary and a place from which to attack.
Vietnamese Marshall Tran Hung Dao, AD 1280.

Anders Bergstrom dreamed of an angelic white haired woman about whom there was a bright golden luminescence. She was dressed in milky, misty flowing garments and was ephemerally beautiful. In his dream he sat on his bed, and she came to him. Although neither the elegant apparition nor Anders spoke to one another, there was a fundamental communication between them. The basic message that Anders came away with when he awakened was that all was well; he would find good fortune in his endeavors in the near future. It was a pervasive feeling he could not shake—not that he wanted to do so—and it stayed with him throughout the following day. To have such a pleasant and reassuring dream was incongruous with his recent terrible and destructive experiences in Hue'. He had had trouble getting to sleep that night and had expected fitfulness at best or nightmares at worst.

As a result of the unusual dream, Anders was relieved of the vague sense of self-loathing he had been left with from the hellish night on the helicopter out over the South China Sea. The effect was so singular that he decided to ask Tran what he thought about it.

After explaining the dream in detail to his Vietnamese friend, Anders asked Tran if he thought it had some meaning. He remembered his childhood with the Mormons; they had dreams, very significant ones, he recalled.

480

Tran smiled brightly with a look of full comprehension. "I know your dream very well, my friend. It is one that many of our people have. It is a deep part of us and comes from our most ancient stories. I will tell you the story, but first let me tell you that the dream means that whatever it is that you have planned, whatever mission you embark upon, will be a great success. It is the very best of all possible omens. It is very good joss. People will want to be near you just to get some of that joss."

"Let's hear the story," Anders requested; his curiosity was fully piqued. He was unsure how it could be that he should have had such a uniquely Vietnamese dream. He presumed that this was evidence that he had really gone native. That did not seem bad to him.

"The dream comes from the story of the origins of Viet Nam and the Viet people," said Tran. "It happened in the mists of time, even before time was. The great Dragon Lord of Lac left his own country far to the north to explore the lands situated by the Great Salt Water that no one could see across. In his explorations he saw the many wonders of the world. The most curious and the most wonderful thing of all was a woman, the Fairy Princess named Au Co. She had the fairest of skin and was crowned with dazzling white hair. She was a great beauty and had many wonderful virtues. The Dragon Lord was captivated by the woman and set out to court her. He was finally successful, and they were married.

"Au Co had the special virtue of making men happy. Whenever she smiled upon a man, rich or poor, great or small, the enterprise upon which that man was embarked invariably proved to be successful." Tran smiled pointedly at Anders. "She was much loved by the people and by her husband. The couple was most happy together.

"Then, Au Co gave birth to one hundred eggs that hatched after only a week's gestation to produce one hundred stalwart and handsome sons. For reasons that no one understands, the Dragon Lord was not happy at this curious event and told Au Co that they must separate. When they did, fifty of the fine sons went with the father, and fifty stayed with the mother. The father and his sons traveled to the Kingdom of the Great Waters, and Au Co took her sons to the mountains of *Bac Bo*. Those brothers founded the beautiful land of Nam Viet, which name was later changed to Viet Nam by the Chinese overlords. The descendants of those people, my people, still call themselves *Tiên Rồng, Con Rồng, cháu Tiên*, (*Tien Rong*, the Children of Dragons and Fairies). Both characteristics bring very good

481

joss. A dream of the Fairy Queen, Au Co, is the very best of omens as you can plainly see."

"How about bad dreams?" Anders asked, skeptical, but listening.

"Like all peoples, we Vietnamese have unhappinesses that bring on bad dreams. But the important bad dream, the bad joss dream, occurs in a mysterious way and at unexpected times, like the wonderful dream of Au Co. If you see a dark faced, hairy, and frightening monster, dressed in black, who may have a cane, coming to you in your sleep, it is well not to ignore the warning." Tran was completely serious as he explained. "You are destined to have a great failure in your next endeavor, even a catastrophe. He is one of the underworld *phi* who act as wicked forest spirits. The Vietnamese soldier will not go out to fight if the evil phi visits him or his companions. Some think you can ward off such bad joss and bad happenings by doing nothing, by staying home and stopping all activities. I am not so sure."

"I'll settle for my dream of Au Co, and leave the monster dream and the warning to the future. There is enough to do for today, I'll let tomorrow take care of itself," Anders said.

The endeavor of that day for Anders and Tran was to interdict the pay couriers coming over into northern and western South Viet Nam from the Ho Chi Minh (or Truong Song) Trail in Laos. They had extensive reports of VCI activity in support of the insurgency coming from across the border, and hence untouchable until it was inside the RVN borders. The reports told of regular sightings of VC paymasters and tax collectors making their rounds in broad daylight near the border on the west. Anders decided that today would be as good as any to try and interfere with the money supply to the South Vietnamese insurgents. Tran thought, on the basis of Anders' dream, that it was the best of all possible times for such an enterprise.

Anders and his four regular PRUC cohorts spent two days planning a number of kidnappings, assassinations, and intimidations for the other sets of PRUCs—the customary work of their organization. The five men in Anders' team worked out their own particular mission in detail. The plan was an ambitious one, a long range reconnaissance from the western border back to Hue', almost on the sea coast. They would be out for a week to ten days, and mapped out the VC safe areas with care to give them something productive to do all along the way. The risk of moving across country without prearranged support was not lost on them, but they planned for very rapid hit-and-run attacks. It was time, all of them thought, that the VC became a little less complacent and secure in what they considered their own territory.

Anders had the men pack LURPS as the only food they would carry because of their very light weight and easy storage. They planned to live off the land mostly, but also to buy provisions from the villagers along the way. Tran was made the banker and carried bundles of MPCs, greenbacks, and Piastres to pay the villagers. Anders knew that Terry Brannigan had insisted that his pirates pay for everything they got from a village, and Anders had seen the value of that simple practice. The pirates had been able to move about fairly safely in areas that were only partly pacified because the Vietnamese considered them to be traders as well as soldiers, and did not go out of their way to turn them in to the omnipresent VC. The PRUCs agreed with the practice. In fact it was the first time the villagers encountered either an ARVN or an American soldier that did not just take what he needed and let the public relations effect be negative.

Tran, Bach, Dung, and Ky privately agreed that this young American giant had brains as well as bigness. Tran told the others about the girl, Mr. Phan's daughter, calling Anders the 'con ma da trắng khổng-lồ, (white giant ghost) and soon it became an affectionate descriptor for their leader. The men were beginning to relax and to trust him. For one thing, he recognized that he was young and did not know everything. That valuable quality was altogether lacking in the ARVN officers with whom they had dealt, and the contrast was a welcome one.

Each of the five men carried a combat shotgun, an AK-47, and two chest bandoleers of thirty cartridge clips, a large marine K-bar knife, a colt .45; and they carried a 60 cal machine gun, and an M-79 grenade launcher and the appropriate ammunition, and two radio sets distributed equitably among them. They portioned out bricks of C-4, fuses, and igniters; so, that every man had a near equal burden. Each man had his own night vision visor, and Anders carried an extra starlight scope. Ky was in charge of the Halazone tablets, antimalarials, penicillin and sulfa, bug juice, condoms for water, and the hard rock candy. The latter fell to Ky because he was the only one who did not care for sweets and could be trusted.

Anders commandeered French camouflage uniforms from a stockpile that had been kept at MACV headquarters for some inexplicable reason. They all wore rubber tire sole sandals and took extra ones along. Each man took one extra shirt and extra long pants; none of them took underwear.

The Chinook dropped them off at a US Special Forces base barely inside the Vietnamese border. They were not received with any comrade-in-arms warmth by the green berets or their Montagnard mercenaries and were given to understand that it would better all the way around if they left the fire-base with all due haste and alacrity. Anders felt himself lucky to receive updated maps and some general directions from the reluctant Lieutenant Colonel in charge. It appeared abundantly clear that the spook and his gooks were all considered *persona non grata* and to be interloping on the special forces' territory. Anders considered the territoriality to be stupid but left that thought unspoken.

He and his Vietnamese cadres made a smokeless camp eight klicks from the firebase and deemed themselves well rid of the need to trouble the snobbish special forces.

"With them for friends, we don't need any enemies," Anders groused to Tran.

"It's not as bad as all that. Staying out here makes a man short tempered and protective of his own unit. We have all learned that the only men we can count on and that we can protect are those in our own unit. You learned that in Hue' last week; the rest of us have known it all along. Don't expect too much from the green berets; they are just acting like us," Tran told his young officer.

Their maps showed a trail in 'Indian country' as the Lieutenant Colonel had described the area. That trail led to a series of fortified VC villages with which the Special Forces and their *PMS* mercenaries maintained an uneasy weapons-bristling truce. In part, the special forces officers were worried that the irregulars would upset that unstable balance. There was a most enticing reason for the PRUCs to go where no one wanted them to go despite all the danger and the Americans' misgivings. The westernmost of the villages was the gathering point for the paymaster couriers to receive their instructions and their money pouches from the VC tax collectors and to spread out to the fan of safe VC villages whose fighters depended on the regular infusion of funds to keep functioning. The NVA/NLF money was the mainstay of the fragile war footing economy in the entire region because the war had so disrupted the traditional agrarian cycles. On the first full moon of each month, with unswerving regularity, Anders and his men were told by the computer documents from Saigon, the main bankroll was brought into the village.

Security was known to be extreme in the principle village and on the trails departing for the east and south. However, the VC were so certain of their own security on the approach into the village that they relied almost entirely on stealth, on looking every bit the same as all of the other peasants. The army were the 'fish and the country people the water' as chairman Mao and Uncle Ho had said. The NLF troops generally got on well with the people because they shared the commoners' hardships and did not exact taxes when the people were poor and starving, for all their harshness as rulers. They stood out in contrast to the ARVN forces who helped the old landlords collect back rent and to abuse the poor people. Anders and his men planned to find an ambush site somewhere along the incoming trail and to wait there long enough to determine the location of the money wagon then to take it.

The moon was two days from reaching fullness. The mountain road into the village was well maintained, and the bush at the sides of the road had been defoliated for many kilometers with stolen American chemicals. There was no reasonable place for the PRUCs to hide. The only saving grace about the approach into the hub village was that traffic was thin. The single option available to the PRU team was to place themselves on the road and to blend in. The only other applicable rule, one upon which all of the PRUCs agreed, was to improvise.

Tran walked the road from very near the Laotian border as rapidly as he could to try and identify the man, men, or vehicle transporting the funds. The others stationed themselves at intervals with Anders and his large size and blond hair keeping out of sight in the fringe of trees and scrub brush beyond the edge of the defoliated road border. Tran had begun to despair of finding the couriers, even in full daylight. He had walked more than fifteen kilometers on an assortment of roads and trails before he saw a suspicious wagon. He was only a short distance from Bach when he did, and Ky was only a half a klick or so farther on.

Tran ambled up to where Bach was standing and set his bundle of sticks down to urinate. To Bach he said, "I think it is here. I mean right here. I have seen nothing else that seems likely. What I have seen is a wagon of rice sacks being pulled by two buffaloes. There are two men in the seat, both young and fit looking, and I think the rice sacks are riding well up in the bed of the wagon. I think there is another layer of goods in the bed, and it is probably heavy. The two young men do not look at all like farm boys, and the wagon looks fairly new."

"See any weapons?"

"No, but I couldn't look too closely, or they would take notice of me."

"So you really think these are the ones, then?"

"As near as I can tell."

"If you are wrong, we end up killing a couple of innocent farm boys, and making enough noise to alert our enemies in the vicinity. Do you feel that sure, Tran?" Bach asked.

"I have given it much thought; and, yes, I believe the wagon is VC and has enemy materiel, maybe gold or silver bullion or maybe weapons. I think it is worth a try."

"All right. Should we wait and get Ky?"

"No time." He gave a slight head gesture in the direction of the road. The wagon was passing them and was no more than twenty meters away. Tran replaced his pants, picked up his bundle, and trudged purposefully back onto the dusty road moving in behind the wagon.

Bach crossed the road and began to walk swiftly along until he had passed the slow moving wagon. He was carrying four large bamboo poles and his AK-47 inserted in the middle of the bundle. Their positions gave the two PRU men a short range crossing field of fire. They were close enough to each other to have to be concerned about the other man's friendly fire. Tran gave a prearranged sharp nod of his head and suddenly dropped his bundle of sticks.

Bach let the four bamboo poles he was carrying clatter to the ground. He and Tran commenced firing three round bursts at the drivers of the cart. The surprise was complete, and the man on the right fell forward off the cart striking his head on one of the buffalo's muscular hind quarters before falling under the heavy wooden wheels of the wagon. Despite an aimed fusillade by enemies firing from two directions, the second man, the one seated on the left, was unscathed. He leaped from his perch with speed and agility, and demonstrated his combatant status by carrying an assault rifle along with him. It had been lying at his feet in the wagon.

He was a sprinter, and made it ten meters across the defoliated clearing leading to the jungle in the near distance before finally catching a round in his left shoulder. He dropped to the ground and began to fire back at his tormentors. Tran and Bach ran to the wagon and took cover behind it. The two buffaloes snorted and shuffled their feet but otherwise took little notice of the human crisis unfolding behind them.

As he had been trained, the VC frantically hollowed out a shallow depression in the dirt and flattened himself prone in it. His shoulder was very painful, but the joint was intact, and with terrible effort he was able to use it to steady his Kalashnikov to fire at his tormentors.

Ky began to run as fast as his legs would go and as hard as his breath could sustain in the direction of the submachine gun fire. He began firing at the VC well before he was in any reasonable range just to provide a diversionary focus for the communist soldier.

The VC was not diverted. He had been selected for his critical assignment by popular vote of his fellows in his platoon because of his excellent soldierly qualities, not the least of which was his coolness under fire. He waited and watched for an opening.

Neither Bach nor Tran could see the VC soldier in his shallow depression in the ground, and their firing was ill aimed as a result. Bach became frustrated and jumped to the space between the rear ends of the dark, dirt encrusted beasts of burden and the sturdy wagon. He fired two short and hurried bursts at the spot where he presumed the VC was lying. Bach was too slow; the enemy saw him, having expected such a move, and fired one well-placed shot. The bullet struck Bach obliquely in the right side of his chest.

Corporal Bach felt a sudden sear of pain in his chest as it he had been pushed with a hot poker. Then he felt a sudden profound shortness of breath and pain all around the right side of his chest. He felt groggy and knew that he was going to lose consciousness. As his last waking effort, Bach threw himself backward toward the safety of the heavy wagon wheels.

Tran sprayed the area with a full magazine of AK-47 rounds with his rifle on full automatic aiming at the place from which he guessed the damaging shot had come. Ky zigzagged in the direction of the VC's hiding place as fast as he could go but took time, at erratically chosen intervals, to keep low and to hit the ground. The VC raised up and fired two bursts at Ky; one bullet passed superficially through Ky's left buttock, deep enough to make a track through the muscle proper, but not causing any serious damage.

The wound stung severely, but with a gingerly testing, Ky was reassured that he could move everything, and there did not seem to be much bleeding. Getting shot made him angry. It also made him smarter. He did not like the thought of getting hit again. He rolled several times to his left which brought him within easy crawling distance of the road side ditch. He slithered into it thereby providing himself with a better defensive position than the VC who was on the gently sloped incline leading away from the road way.

Tran saw Ky go down and was frantic with worry. He rained lead over the VC's position. When he paused to insert a new ammunition clip, the feisty VC rose up slightly to return Tran's fire. For the first time, and only for a second, he made himself a target. From his vantage point, Ky aimed and fired one burst of three rounds, then hesitated after hearing a satisfying outcry of pain from the VC. The man must have been hit seriously because he now sagged down onto his elbow rather than dropping to his abdomen.

That proved to be a fatal pause. Ky had another chance and used it to his full advantage. He put three 7.62 mm slugs into the Vietnamese communist's chest, and the skirmish was over.

Tran was attending to Bach when Ky limped up to the wagon. "Any more?" Ky asked, out of breath.

"Only one; he's by the wagon."

Ky checked. The man was dead. "What now?" he asked Tran.

Bach spoke up, coughing blood flecked sputum, "Don't worry about me. I think this isn't too bad. I'm short of breath, but I think I can make it on my own power."

Ky snorted.

Tran said quietly. "Not possible. We can use the wagon."

Ky said, "I didn't think about the wagon. Think that's were the goods are?"

"That's why we started all of this. Would you check it please?"

Ky ran back to the wagon, glad to have something physical to do. He rummaged among the bags of rice until he found solid wood boxes with locks on them forming the base of the wagon load. The Vietnamese markings indicated ammunition in some of the boxes, and others contained treasure—small gold bars stamped with the old *chu nom* letters 'DRV' and the encircled numbers, 99.9. Ky was entranced.

He returned to Tran and helped his friend carry Bach to the cart. They hurriedly opened a hiding place in the middle of the rice sacks where Bach could lie without being seen, at least by the casual observer.

"Let's hide the bodies. I'm sure no one heard the shots or else we would have company by now. If the bodies can stay out of anybody's attention for a couple of days, we will have a better chance," Tran said.

Ky nodded at that bit of understatement.

The bodies of the two killed VCs were half dragged, half carried into the edge of the heavy underbrush by the two sweating, cursing, worried men. Tran and Ky mounted the seats on the wagon just before a farmer and his family walked into view around the bend from the south. Coincidentally, a Chinese military troop truck approached from the north carrying more than a dozen deep green uniformed NVA soldiers.

The troop truck arrogantly swept past the peasants in the buffalo cart and by the farm family raising a choking cloud of tan dust. The brief dense dust storm obscured the PRUC's wagon from the family of onlookers, and caused their attention to be drawn away from the wagon's unusual position in the middle of the road. Tran and Ky greeted the family as they passed each other. The family was not interested in another slow and unquarrelsome wagon of rice.

Tran and Ky found Dung and signaled him to follow at a distance until they came to the landmark that indicated the near proximity of Anders' hiding place. The men stopped and clambered down from the wagon and did a theatrical bit of stretching. Anders crept out of the nearby woods and trotted up to the other men. Dung joined the group as soon as they and their wagon were alone on the road.

Anders' first concern was the gray complexion and bloody shirt front of Bach. "How bad is it, Bach?" He asked excitedly.

"Chest," the wounded man wheezed, trying to conserve his breath. "Not too bad, though. I don't seem to be getting any worse."

Anders hurriedly opened Bach's pajama shirt, took one of his own bandages and wiped off the surface blood. There was a hole in the right upper chest wall the size of a pencil eraser. Occasionally with a particularly heavy breath a few blood tinged bubbles appeared. Bach seemed able to breath, but was dyspneic.

"Anders, we have to go. We can't be seen here like this!" Tran said urgently. Anders stepped back down off the wagon.

"Ky, you drive it. Tran, you and Dung walk on ahead. I'll get in the trees. We have to get past their main village. Once we are a klick or two down the road from the village; stop, so we can decide what to do," Anders ordered. It was late afternoon, and the men were still fully exposed in the light of day. That was their greatest source of concern.

It was dusk when the rendezvous took place. None of them had encountered even passing interest from the villagers let alone direct opposition. Anders had circled the busy little crossroads community keeping to the heavy forest. There were so many people coming in and out of the woods that he had to walk as 'silently as wind across grass,' as Sylvia Chin had taught him. At other points, the dense rain forest gave way to a weald causing him either to have to make a wide detour or to sprint across the open rolling woodland hoping against hope that he would not be seen. All of that took time, and he was the last of the PRUCs to present himself at the rendezvous.

Bach did not seem any worse for the three hour jarring cart ride. "I am holding up, Anders. You do not have to be worried about me," he said as soon as Anders' concerned face gazed down at his. The color of Bach's skin seemed less cyanotic, but perhaps it was the rapidly fading light.

Anders said, "Most important, we have to get Bach out of here and to a hospital. I think his chances are better if we are not all together. Also, we seem to have quite a prize here—the Cong will be frantic when they find out it's gone." He gestured with a hitchhiker's thumb over his shoulder at the burdened cart. "Come up with an idea."

Ky did. His wounded buttock had now knotted into spasms, and he knew he would not be fit to walk long distances for several days. "I'll take Bach and the gold back to the compound. The chopper can get him to Danang, and I can take the gold to a place I know where we can make a reasonable black market trade." It must have occurred to one of the men that, by rights, they should see to it that the booty was given to their RDC/O chief in Hue'; but, if it did, that man did not speak up.

Anders wrestled with his own thoughts, and it showed on his face. Ky sensed Anders' turmoil, "You can trust me, boss. You," and here he swept his hand about to indicate all present, "are my family, my only friends. I do not betray my friends," Ky entreated.

"No one distrusts you, Ky," Anders insisted, a little too late to be entirely convincing.

"Besides, this PRU stuff is too much fun to miss out on by going it on my own." Ky smiled broadly as he said it.

Anders looked at Tran and Dung. He turned back to Bach. "That okay with you?" he asked the injured man.

"I trust the gangster," Bach replied simply and conclusively. "Besides, his injury would slow us down."

The men packed Ky's and Bach's weapons in strategic hiding places on the wagon, gave them a supply of water and LURPS, and gave the two travelers a parting nonmilitary salute.

"Now what?" asked Dung.

"Mischief," answered Anders. He drew the remaining two men up into a cluster of bushes that hid them from view of the road and together the three of them determined their own and the next village's positions. "I figure we have no more than a two hour walk to the town. We can hang out in the bush until it is late and dark enough, then we can go in and make a kidnapping. If we are right, and this is Vung Bo, then we have the VCI accountant for the region right here. Our computer description is complete right down to the house he lives in.

His two sons serve as couriers, a nice little family of traitors." There was agreement on the general plan; the details could be worked out while they passed the time waiting for a late enough hour.

Tran reconnoitered the village circumferentially and spotted six guards. Like most good VC villages, the security was unobtrusive. The six guards sauntered in and out through the village's dusty paths as if purposeless or benignly social. Their weapons were concealed in bags carried over their shoulders. Tran could discern at least two mountain mortar emplacements in pig sties, and a Kalashnikov PK tripod mounted medium machine gun lurking in a rice storage hut. They were serious people there.

Tran suggested that all three of them make their way separately and by their own devices to the hootch where the VCI family was known to be quartered and to meet each other there. They could then simply enter the hootch and kill the VCI accountant and his two sons, get out separately, and again, on their own, get to a point two klicks down the main road. Anders and Dung agreed. It was three hours before they needed to set out on the night's mission which left the men time for quiet reflection and occasional whispered conversations.

Tran was stretched alongside Anders. He said, "Do you know what Vietnamese fear the most?"

Anders answered, "The Dragon Lord?"

"No."

"Snakes?"

"Um ummh. Vampires."

"Really? I didn't know that old story had even been told here."

"Oh yes. Not your European version, but old stories, really old stories of blood suckers that roam around in the forests at night. That is one of the reasons why you almost never see peasants in the forest after dark. Mothers scare their children with vampire tales to keep them from wandering off."

"Hmmh," mused Anders. An idea was germinating. A fiendish, diabolical inspiration.

"That gives me an idea," he said to Tran.

"That sounds bad," Tran said.

"It is. For now, let's just modify our plan a little. I want to knock our VCIs out and keep them alive for a while. Pass that on to Dung."

"Do we get to know what you have in mind?"

"Sure," Anders said without completing his implied sentence.

There was a pause. Both men could have laughed if it would not have been so unsafe. "When?" Tran finally asked to break the pregnant silence.

"Soon," Anders said, still noncommittally. Tran shook his head in the darkness.

At the appointed hour (0230—"O dark thirty," as Anders put it), each of the three PRUCs began a laborious crawl out of the forest, across the grass, dust paths, and through the alleyways between hooches toward the known VCIs' house. There were long pauses to outwait sentries, or to duck away from a man relieving himself near where the PRUC was hiding, breath held and weapon with a chambered round. It was 0310 by the time all three men had made their presence known to the each other around the hootch.

They coordinated their entrance; and one by one the men slithered into the house, quieter than the breathing of the sleepers inside. All three of them were now wearing their night vision glasses and had adjusted to the green light and head heaviness that accompanies the use of the night vision devises. By habit, each of them moved his head to and fro frequently to compensate for the limitations of peripheral, especially side, vision. There were three persons sleeping, two teen-agers and a middle-aged man. None of the sleepers stirred as the night stalkers entered their sleeping chamber.

Each PRUC took one of the victims as his responsibility; Anders stood in the center towering over the older man. He held up three fingers, then counted silently, one...two...three. As one, each of the PRUCs slapped a lead filled leather sap hard against the side of his victim's sleeping head. Then each pasted a strip of wide duct tape over the mouth of the man beneath him. Only Anders' man stirred requiring another blow from the sap. It had been very quietly done; the noise had not carried outside the walls of the well ventilated hooch. Less than three seconds had elapsed from the time Anders had reached his count of three. A circlet of tape was wrapped around the unconscious VCIs' ankles and wrists, trussing them adequately for the short time Anders had in mind.

Dung took a quick look outside the house then went all around it to see if anyone had ventured about while the PRUCs had been at work inside. He was gone a full five minutes and reported that all was clear and quiet when he returned. The PRU cadres loaded their unconscious bundles over their shoulders, squatted low, and duck-walked out of the low door, Anders in front. He stepped to the right outside the door; Tran stepped to the left, and Dung exited and led their cautious way up the gentle grassy incline out of the village and onto the well-trodden, secondary trail out of the community.

The men walked nearly a klick into the inky blackness carrying their prisoners. The traverse was made possible only by their night vision apparati. Anders signaled a halt. "I think this is far enough," he whispered, his voice slightly raspy from the exertion.

The three PRUCs gratefully dumped their captives ungently onto the ground which roused each of the VCI partially. As the captive men lay groaning on the ground, Anders verbally outlined the last step of his plan to his teammates.

As the first step, the powerful Swedish-American stepped behind the small VCI men, one at a time, lifted the man up to a semi-sitting position and cupped the man's chin in one hand and the base of his skull in the other. He lifted the man's head up as hard as he could, then sharply twisted counterclockwise pushing the chin down and the opposite occiput up. The resounding snapping noise was followed by an instant painless death as the first and second vertebrae separated, fractured, then sheared apart narrowing the intraspinal space drastically and physiologically transecting the cervico-medullary junction of the nervous system.

Next, the two Vietnamese PRUCs stripped the bodies naked and strung the three up from tree limbs, head down. Then, using the sharpest pointed knife they had, two punctures were made into the engorged jugular veins, and the still fluid blood flowed freely and darkly into a rich pool at the base of the tree. Anders had his men strip the legs and abdomen down to milk as much of the blood out as possible.

Using the men's abandoned clothing, the PRUCs cleaned the telltale blood off their pale bodies. A small sump of fetid water nearby served the purpose well. It was 0440. The village would be stirring in an hour.

Once again Anders and the two Vietnamese paramilitaries hoisted the blood drained and blanched corpses onto their shoulders and trotted as fast as they could back into the vicinity of Vung Bo, the sleeping village. Finally, they hung the bodies by their wrists so that they were high enough, outstretched enough, and near enough to the main trail to command immediate and complete attention.

Anders agreed to a change in plans proposed by Dung. They would wait on the side of the village opposite to where the bodies were hung long enough to see the reaction of the townspeople. Then, as planned, they would take the easterly trail, instead of the main trail, and would see what additional disruption they could create now that they had cried havoc and loosed the dogs of war.

Dawn eased into the village gently with the light coming in overhead from the mountain tops before the sun made its first appearance. Sunlight dappled through the trees gradually bringing the light and heat of the morning to the just arousing people. A woman was singing:

> *Nhà anh chín aun mưới trâu,*
> *Có thêm ao cá bắc cầu rửa chân*
> *Cầu này là cầu ái ân.*
> *Mội trăm con gài rửa chân cầu này.*

> (I have nine hayricks and ten buffaloes.
> I also have a fish pond where there is a plank
> bridge for people to wash their feet.
> This bridge is the bridge of love,
> Where a thousand girls have washed their feet.)

Children began to herd their families' potbellied pigs into the nearby forest to graze. Vibrations of the 108 morning pagoda gongs reverberated through the village. Women began to cajole their lazy husbands to get up and to go out to the green carpets of the rice fields that were now undulating in the slight breeze. Half-asleep men cursed the perfidy of their buffaloes and jerked the nose loops unnecessarily, causing the powerful beasts to wince and stamp their feet. Ducks quacked; roosters crowed; and boys and girls began to yell friendly insults at each other across the dust now rising between the close order rows of nipa huts.

Suddenly all of that stopped. From the edge of the forest of slender areca and coconut trees on the west, along the secondary trail, came the high keening wail of a woman in terror. All else, even the animals, became silent; and the village was momentarily transfixed in soundless suspended animation. The sentries reacted first. Three of them raced across the village in the direction of the screaming woman and away from where the PRUCs had hidden themselves. The sentries began to shout, a lamenting, rather than any call to action; and with that, the population of the village departed en masse to where the source of such dismay was located.

Through their binoculars, Tran could read the expression being formed on a dozen lips of the townspeople, "*Ma hút máu!*" and "*Ma cà-rồng!*" (Vampire!). The chatter soon died down to an eerie frightened silence. The villagers stood looking at the three pale bodies suspended from the trees not daring to speak.

No one noticed the three intruders as they quietly departed in the opposite direction. It was light enough that they kept off the busy trails for the rest of the day. They were too heavily armed to allow even the Vietnamese PRUCs to be seen. Travel was slow and circuitous through hot, humid, bug infested, fecund forest and swamps, and through brambly thick undergrowth. Most of the time they were following the contours of the hills and canyons through densely forested terrain that slowed the men and exhausted them. Their weapons were heavy and became burdensome. Their clutch belts and grenade bandoleers chafed their skin raw under their sweat soaked clothing. Their feet were becoming blistered from the ill fitting tire soled sandals they had made for the mission. They drank several gallons of water each, out of necessity, which caused even further delays owing to the need to search for the critical liquid.

Anders had his men force march for sixteen hours until they were in the proximity of the next major village before he let them have a real rest and food. They ate their LURPS dry and gagged them down with stale water. All three of them were too weary to talk; so they insinuated themselves into the cover of surrounding bushes. Anders made them take out their camouflage paint sticks and reapply the protective colors before they slept. Anders was the last to give in to the overwhelming weariness. He made sure that he could not see his men in their hiding places before he curled himself around the base of a tree and pulled a clump of bushes over himself.

Night was rapidly closing in on the men when they finally began to come out of their exhaustion induced stupors. Anders had been up for about twenty minutes studying the maps. He was fairly certain they were north and west of Hue' by fifty or maybe even sixty klicks at this point. His ultimate route of escape was to follow the main road from the west down into the Imperial City, but his plan was to stir up things in the series of VC controlled villages where he and his men now found themselves, as much as a diversion as a principle part of the mission. He then planned to wheel to the south until they intersected with the main road. He hoped that the enemy would concentrate his search in the vicinity of the villages that he and the PRUCs were planning to hit and to mistake the fact that he and the PRUCs were headed out by another route.

The plan worked well because it was uncomplicated and not particularly ambitious—the KISS principle ("Keep It Simple, Stupid"—another Sylvia Chin-ism). That night, the three men stealthily killed four well-armed, but careless sentries guarding two hamlets of the village of Co Bi. They cut off the ears, and at Anders' suggestion, the eyes as well. Then they tacked the gruesome trophies to the walls of various village common buildings—the message being simple enough—"the eyes and ears of your enemies are ever upon you." That was the kind of message that struck fear into the very heart of the people and increased their suffering several fold. The local VC command became increasingly frantic to find the perpetrators and to eliminate their successes at frightening the locals who had heretofore been so easily dominated and cooperative with the LAF.

It was clear by the second day after the vampire incident that there would be no more easy coups. Recon of the villages they passed, day or night, revealed intense security, full alert level. The PRUCs kept to the jungle almost all of the time, and they were frustrated at being rendered ineffectual. They left the string of villages to the north and east unscathed and turned south toward the Bo Giang. Anders now planned to follow the river east toward Hue' and to break off to arrive back at the PRU compound. At their present rate of progress, the men would be back to safety in under two days.

Anders was convinced that he was right in his presumption that the LAF, now his pursuers, would chase him toward the north and east and would neglect the more southern route. That was evidenced to the young man by the relaxed atmosphere he and his men saw in the villages they came to scrutinize after wheeling to their right. The two Vietnamese men with him now traveled the busy country roads openly carrying rolls and lengths of textiles draped over their shoulders and over their upper limbs like Mexican serapés to cover their weaponry. The weather was hot and sultry; and the long walk became boring, even stultifying in its monotony; and the two men relaxed their vigilance despite all their warnings to themselves and from Anders who was struggling along through the deep forest. It was difficult to fight off drowsiness shambling along on the roadway.

For Anders the going was tougher by necessity—it would not do for a six foot four inch, 225 pound white haired giant of a man to present himself among the small brown people—and he had no opportunity to relax. His problem was to be able to see and not be seen and to walk quietly and quickly—a difficult and attention demanding occupation.

It was easy to be lulled into a sense of security, to maintain a self-defined feeling of being invisible, as Tran and Dung trudged miles in the open without passersby taking notice and after leaving all signs of hostility. It was especially easy to do so in the heat and humidity and monotony. It was also a great folly, but Tran, Dung, and even Anders, to a some degree, were all less vigilant.

The lesson came shortly after the PRUCs made a right angle turn and began to walk along the north bank of the Bo Giang. Tran and Dung were hungry for a simple rice ball, some fish, and a little fruit after a steady diet of water soaked but uncooked freeze-dried food. Under best conditions of preparation, the substance advertised to be food was tasteless, and eating it cold and soggy made the Vietnamese question the sanity of the Americans who made and dispensed the plastic stuff. They longed for some real food. Tran and Dung were emboldened by the complete lack of signs of the LAF in the villages. After some argument, it was agreed to allow the two Vietnamese men to venture into the next village to satisfy their overweening hunger. Anders, by agreement and prudent necessity, kept to the shadows.

In retrospect, it was apparent that the PRUCs had not only not been invisible, as they had supposed; but they had undoubtedly been under VC surveillance all along. They had underestimated their foes. On its surface the town seemed quiet and not unfriendly. Tran and Dung walked along the dusty entry road past ponds laden with floating duckweed. There was a small open walled school where children sat obediently studying from their *Quoc Van Giao Khoas* (National Language Texts). Drying nets swayed in the easy breeze. Here and there an old man sat mending a fishing net. A cuckoo sang its cooing song.

No sooner had Tran and Dung stopped at the rice seller's stall than they became aware that they were being watched. They were strangers and expected to be held in suspicion; but this was different. It was patterned, organized scrutiny. Both men felt the prickling sensation of the hairs raising on the backs of their necks. They were cognizant of being followed and scrutinized; and the townspeople in general were playing at insouciance, an unnatural response to the presence of outsiders. To test that presumption, Tran a made sudden about face and was rewarded with seeing two athletic looking young men suddenly change course and become particularly interested in the activities of an old crone working a weaving loom.

Tran nudged Dung who, in his turn, made a head gesture to indicate that they should begin a retreat. They fingered the triggers of their

497

shotguns beneath the drapes over their shoulders. The eyes on them were now more than suspicious; they were unequivocally hostile. The nonchalance of the ordinary people around them was disappearing. Men began to press in toward the two PRUCs who were now walking watchfully back the way they had come in along the single village road. As they walked, Tran and Dung swiveled their heads constantly to detect the first overtly hostile action. The tension was transmitted throughout the town. The villagers were beginning to thin out from in front of the two strangers.

Four hard faced men now stood in the path. The villagers melted into the side paths and booths. The men facing Tran and Dung wore black pajamas; and if that were not sufficient announcement of their allegiance, the AK-47s the men held in the crooks of their arms were nakedly convincing.

Tran's senses had been on high alert, and now adrenaline rushed through him to put his reflexes on a hair trigger. His mind raced and his eyes looked for an escape route. The fact that he and Dung were still standing indicated to him that the VC preferred to take the two of them as prisoners more than they wanted them dead. Tran presumed, correctly as it turned out, that the leadership had ordered their capture, and the Viet Cong were nothing if not supremely disciplined to obey orders to the letter and the minute. Tran counted on that characteristic in his enemies to grant him a moment of hesitation by them when he acted.

Anders had drilled the PRU constantly on the need to react immediately, better to kill an innocent than to flinch and become the victim. It was also a new concept harped on by Anders that they change old thought patterns and become innovative. They had come to know that such thinking was often a prerequisite to success in a small unit living off the land under spec-op conditions. The ability to think innovatively meant the opportunity to act first. The communist penchant for concrete thinking and eye-blindered obedience was a flaw to be capitalized upon for a fraction of a second's advantage, Tran now hoped with every fiber.

The Kalashnikovs started to elevate. The VCs' eyes locked onto those of Tran and Dung. The decision to surrender or to fight had to come in the next fraction of a second. There was no real option of surrender, of course. Tran and Dung knew all too well the fate of men who fell into VC hands when they were presumed to have valuable information. Dung settled the question. He flipped his shot gun up at umbilical level under the serapé like sheet of textile he was carrying and fired through it. There was no need to aim. They were that close.

A look of consternation flashed over the face of the cong second from the left as Tran and Dung faced them. The dismayed look was transitory and changed to horror for a brief additional portion of a second as his eyes dropped to the ragged hole in his chest and the spreading ring of blood around the irregular opening. He was sagging to the ground before any of his comrades could react. The VC were at a double disadvantage: they wanted to capture the traitors-to-the-will-of-the-people alive, and they could not fire their assault rifles without inflicting random casualties among the gawking villagers, many of whom were relatives. The disadvantages became slight hesitations. Another of them dropped from a blast from the muzzle of Tran's hidden twelve gauge.

The remaining two cong opened fire, one parsimonious round at a time, another ingrained action from their frugal training. Ammunition was precious and not to be wasted, they had been ceaselessly drilled. It cost them everything. Both PRUCs dropped to one knee and fired their shotguns again wounding one of their assailants. Dung took a slug through and through his left triceps narrowly missing the spiral nerve and the artery hugging his humerus.

The shotgun blast wounded VC fell to the ground and continued to fire erratically from an awkward semi-prone position. He succeeded in killing an old woman and an eleven year old boy as the two PRUCs rolled to the ground and out of harm's way on opposite sides of the village road. The other, unwounded, communist soldier had recovered his full composure and was now aiming and firing two round bursts, but he could not hit the writhing and erratic targets. Tran and Dung fired occasionally to keep their adversary off balance as they punched their way behind the food and clothing laden market stalls.

The clatter of the full-blown fire fight attracted the attention of a dozen or more VC soldiers who had been secreted behind the sparse bits of cover offered by the village. They now sprinted toward the village's mercantile street. Several of them had AK-47s, but most had long barreled M1s or even more cumbersome old British .303 Lee-Enfield rifles. The .303s were accurate for distance shooting and their mechanisms were easy and fast to operate. However, they were heavy and unwieldy, being a full 113.3 centimeters long and could not be brought into effective action in this suddenly changing situation in time.

Tran went left, and Dung went right. Dung rolled through an odoriferous pile of durian fruit and into a latrine trench dug behind a canvas backed stall. The fruit vendor slapped his hands over his face in dismay at the destruction of his livelihood, then hit the ground in self-protection. Dung spat and cursed but did not let any fastidiousness he might have had about the pungent odors slowing him down. Tran's path of escape resulted in a cacophonous release of chickens, pigs, ducks and the shouting of frightened and offended people; all of whom were scattering helter skelter. The scene was one of sudden and pure pandemonium.

The VC reinforcements streaked into the town's center smashing stands and upsetting displays to locate the GVN enemies of the people and to add to the general bedlam. They were careful about firing, however, since every person they could see was one of their sympathizers. Uncle Ho and Chairman Mao had both stressed the critical need to avoid unnecessary injury to the people as well as eschewing theft and acts of injustice among those upon whom they depended. They held their fire and gradually became systematic hunters. From the centrifugal pattern of dispersal of the townsmen the cong became fairly sure of the general location of the two GVN killers. They knew it was only a matter of time before they had the capitalist lackey soldiers trapped. In a now coordinated pincer they began to close in on Tran and Dung.

Every hunter had a full magazine, a round in the chamber, and the action of his weapon was off safety. A straining finger twitched over the trigger. It would only be a matter of seconds before one of them sighted the enemy. All thoughts of taking prisoners had now evaporated in the heat of the conflict.

A great reversal of fortune then occurred in the form of Anders Bergstrom. The wild-eyed, white haired giant tore out of the fringe of trees lining the approach into the village and ran full tilt into the market roadway. The encircling VC, so lost in concentration on the last tense seconds before closing the jaws of their pincer and flushing their helpless quarries, were unaware of the huge man's approach until he was terrifyingly close. An obedient VC from the village populace, a little boy, yelled a warning, calling out the soon to become universal label for Anders, "*Coi chừng!*!! (Look out!!!) *con ma da trắng khổng-lồ*!!!" (White Giant Ghost!!!) The communist fighters reacted very quickly, but not fast enough to dodge a spray of lead pouring out from Ander's M-60 machine gun that was spewing death at 600 bullets a minute..

When he heard the boy shout, Anders planted himself in the middle of the road heedless of the need for protective cover. His powerful young legs were locked in an adamant crouch. He stitched lethal lines of bullets through living VC targets, flimsy market stalls, and hapless townspeople. The firing was like a hailstorm of hot fatal projectiles. The VC attackers were scythed down where they stood. Eight of them were dead before they could answer Anders' fire. And by the time the others could react, he was gone from their sights.

"Tran! Dung! Jump! Follow me outta here!" the blond fighter yelled over and over again as he crashed and zigzagged through the line of market stalls knocking anything down that got in his way, like a maddened buffalo. He ran toward where he had seen the VC coterie heading.

The two PRUCs were galvanized into action and streaked from opposite sides of the market street toward Anders' voice. Even though Anders was crouched in an intermittent fighting-firing attitude, his men could see him immediately and almost constantly. The three men met up and began to back-pedal toward the forest and safety along the river bank. They laid down sporadic withering cover fire as they retreated from the regrouping VC.

The LAF (VC) soldiers had gained a healthy respect for their enemies' firepower and were keeping their heads down for the time being—enough for the PRUCs to exit the town's periphery. Thirteen LAF fighters had been killed outright; three more were seriously wounded, and eight noncombatant civilians, including old ones, a pregnant woman, and two children had been slaughtered in the brief deadly exchange.

The three PRUCs were running headlong through the spindly trees of the forest. The trees were so close together that the men had to swerve and dodge like broken field runners in the American game of football. The covering textiles Tran and Dung had been carrying had long since been shed, and their gun butts clattered against the trees like the sound of a bull elk fleeing through trees and striking its antlers. There were no shots coming their way; so, Anders, Tran, and Dung concentrated fully on putting distance between them and their pursuers and only rarely paused to look back.

Anders' body was pouring sweat, and his lungs felt like they were about to burst. The toll on his stamina of running with the heavy machine gun as well as his personal weapons was beginning to wear him down despite his superb physical conditioning and the adrenaline surge from excitement and fear that goaded him. He kept on, ignoring the outcries of his tortured lungs. He lost his rubber sandals in the rush through the tangled underbrush but continued to run in spite of the bruising and small lacerations accumulating on his lightly callused feet.

Dung was running on pure adrenaline and courage. At times he was unaware of his surroundings. His left arm was becoming swollen; and when he gave thought to it, the limb was very painful. A steady debilitating trickle of venous blood slid down his arm from the bullet's exit wound. The pain was agonizing if he tried to use it. Despite the bullet having missed the radial nerve, the artery, and the humerus itself, the limb was now all but useless.

Tran was so charged by fear and the stimulation of the fight and flight that he was scarcely aware that his breath was beginning to come in short, labored gasps. He was too old for this. All three men were beginning to stumble and to crash into trees. They all felt as if they were going to pass out. Dung finally did, and that brought the unit's temerarious flight to a halt.

They rolled into a section of thick brush behind a large boulder. Their chests were heaving as they fought to drink air into thirsting lungs. Tran was able to rise first and to look back from where they had come in such a headlong rush. No sign of their hunters. Anders ministered to Dung's wound, wrapping it with a clean set of gauze pads and an elastic bandage. He gave his friend an injection of morphine.

After a few minutes, when they had caught up on their air hunger enough to talk, Anders said, "Look, I know its tough, but we have to keep going. We can't hole up yet. They'll be on us in no time." He was mildly surprised that he was speaking Vietnamese without first mentally translating from English and without forethought.

"I don't think I can. I am as weak as a newborn piglet," Dung sighed. His eyes were glassy, and he was pasty with cold sweat.

"You can," Tran said with finality. "We can help, but you have to get up and go on. Anders is right. Our only chance is to take advantage of the distance we can put between us and them right now. We can't stay here."

"I am so tired, Dung panted. "Just leave me. I can hold them off while you get away. At least, the two of you can make it," he said more pleadingly than heroically.

"No one gets left behind. And we have to go now," Anders ordered, his voice set with finality. There was to be no more discussion, his tone announced. Tran looked at the young American with new-found respect. The young man was becoming a real leader.

Dung groaned. But the wiry Vietnamese was made of very good

metal and somewhere deep inside himself found a hidden reserve of strength. He struggled to his feet slowly, fighting nausea and syncope.

They were all standing. With Anders' urging, they all began to walk, slowly and unsteadily at first. Anders' feet were like ground meat, and each step was as if he were fire walking. He concentrated his will power to go one step at a time. Tran helped Dung. Anders carried Dung's weapons.

In the far distance the three men could hear the sporadic sounds of men's shouted voices, but by night fall they had not seen any of the enemy. The PRUCs were out of food and water and had jettisoned most of their weapons as their exhaustion demanded. Each man had kept a Kalashnikov assault rifle, six refill clips, and a knife. Tran kept the M-79 and two bandoleers of grenades. Anders could not bear to give up the M-60 MMG (medium machine gun) despite its 23 pound weight. They did the best they could to make a defensive position; and in spite of shaking with exhaustion and pain, dug themselves shallow fox holes. None of them was in condition to take first watch; so, they settled in for a short but deep sleep, taking the security risk.

Anders awakened at midnight temporarily disoriented. He shook the fuzziness from his head, and was able to keep watch most of the rest of the night. Tran took second watch until dawn, and the two of them let Dung sleep.

In the early hours of the morning, the men took stock of their situation. They still had enough defensive firepower, but their food and water situation was bad and on the brink of getting desperate. Their tremendous physical output of the previous day had taken its logical toll and had left them weak and dizzy from lack of adequate rest and from hunger. Thirst, though, was the most serious and immediate problem. They could not be sure how far they were from the river, nor how many people they might encounter trying to get to its banks. They knew that they would not live another day in the parboiling heat and with physical effort required of them if they did not get something to drink. Although it was no more than twenty or thirty klicks to their compound and everything they needed to sustain themselves, the PRUCs would have to raid a VC village to get the needed supplies to go on even that distance.

Anders had money and would have been happy to purchase their needs, but he knew that he was in hostile country. All GVN pretenses of having pacified the country side were hollow propaganda. Rural Thau Thien Province belonged to the communist insurgency. Even in the unlikely chance that they could stumble into a friendly or at least neutral mercantile minded town, he would never be able to trust the people long enough to count on getting in and out without being betrayed to another VC squad. No, they would have to take what they needed. Their present situation did not leave room for 'winning the hearts and minds of the people,' as the Saigon REMFs were wont to say from their comfortable desks. Since the three men's strength was ebbing with every passing hour, they would have to act very soon. Like it or not, the raid they were going to have to stage would need to commence in broad daylight with one of their number seriously compromised.

Anders wrapped his feet with strips of canvas cloth torn from his extra pair of pants. The added support and protection made a world of difference. He carried the 60. Dung's left arm was now tightly strapped to his thorax. He was assigned a fully loaded AK-47 and would be placed at the exit point from the village they selected to raid. Tran was hungry and sore; but for practical purposes, was intact—the best of the three. He would do the talking and would lead the raid.

The three weary paramilitary soldiers hobbled and crawled through virgin forest grumbling at the brambles and dead fall but feeling more secure in their relative obscurity. They encountered no signs of booby traps. They had been chastened by their recent experience. All of them knew that the arrogant carelessness that had allowed them to walk on the open roads thinking they were invisible could not be repeated if they were to survive this day. The mistake had nearly been fatal and could never be repeated. Even the good joss coming from Anders' dream of Au Co could only be invoked so far.

A Novel of Betrayal and Revenge

Last Phoenix

A Story of the CIA's Phoenix Program

A Novel by

Carl Douglass

Volume Two of Two Volumes

PO Box 221974 Anchorage, Alaska 99522-1974

ISBN 1-888125-02-0

Library of Congress Catalog Card Number: 96-72473

Copyright 1997 by Carl Douglass
—First Edition—

Manufactured in the United States of America.

Synopsis of Volume One

K arl Isaacson of Zarahemla, Utah fit the requirements perfectly: young, tough, innocent, patriotic, impressionable; and, best of all, a man without relatives or human ties. He earned pariah status in the small town where he was born and reared before his enlistment in the army was engineered by the town sheriff and the draft board. The CIA wanted him for its paramilitary force in Viet Nam, and convinced him and his boot camp drill sergeant that he would best serve his country in a shadow world capacity. The "Colonel," who controlled the lives of his CIA recruits like a master puppeteer, recognized in Karl his best potential—he could be made into a remorseless killer.

Karl learned to be a Provincial Reconnaissance Unit Cadre/Officer (PRUC/O) in the supersecret Central Intelligence Agency training camp in Virginia. In four months, the boy became a man; the innocent learned the facts of survival and lost his innocence; the ingenuous adolescent learned duplicity, along with brutality, the leitmotiv of the rest of his life; the affable lad gained a mortal enemy; and the nation gained what it needed most at the time—a dedicated, proficient, methodical, state sponsored killer. The formal training took four months.

Karl learned from diminutive Sylvia Lee to be an invisible and deadly silent forest assassin. He learned the rudiments of Vietnamese language from blond, urbane, Ruben Smith. He became a weapons expert under rough tutelage of Gunny McCluskey who preferred Russian AK-47s to anything American made. Karl learned the best method of procurement of needed ordnance: kill the enemy owner and take what he wanted. He learned the first rule of hand to hand combat from an Ivy League gentlemen: there are no rules. Karl was befriended by Jean-Luc DuParrier, a Frenchmen released from a Vietnamese prison to join the PRUs. That friendship ended in a brutal and deadly knife fight and an even deadlier lifelong enmity.

Karl's final test, before becoming a full-fledged CIA contract agent, was to participate in the contract murder of a family with wrong political connections in Nicaragua. Hard training changed Karl into an indoctrinated, muscular, reflexively proficient cadre and a formidable opponent, free of any vestiges of his boyhood aspirations or illusions. He gained a new name when he entered the training center—Lars Magnussen—and still another when he arrived in Saigon—Anders Bergstrom, compliments of the CIA. The "Colonel" wrought a change that was near perfect.

On the other side of the world, Viet Cong Cadre Nguyen Lui Tran, ostensibly a university professor in Saigon, delivered a message from COSVN to unknown recipients. On the way back home, through the great market, Cholon, he was abducted by unknown and unnecessarily brutal captors. He endured a hellish transportation to an infamous Paulo Condore prison on the feared Con Son Island where things became rapidly worse. He saw men and women who had once been dissidents or opponents of the South Vietnamese regime locked in unimaginably cruel "cow" and worse "tiger" cages who had become shambling living dead. He saw summary executions of recalcitrant Viet Cong Infrastructure Cadres like his former self. Nguyen Lui Tran leaned quickly and indelibly from the visual lessons he was presented. In minutes he stopped being a dedicated VC courier and saboteur and became a zealot policeman for the established government of South Viet Nam, complete with a tattoo, that, emblazoned on his chest, was the stirring motto of his PRU comrades: *Sat Cong* (Kill Cong!).

He was assigned to a PRU camp in Thau Thien Province outside the old imperial capital of Hue. There he was joined by other recently certified policemen. Among these were Phan Duy Ky, a member since childhood of the murderous criminal organization, Binh Xuyen; Nguyen Tran Xuan, a Buddhist monk sworn to poverty, chastity, vegetarianism, and nonviolence who became a deep cover VC mole who preyed on his PRUC comrades; Nguyen Van Dung, a former VC sapper who converted to the opposite side when an NVA lieutenant brutally murdered Dung's mother in front of his young siblings; Corporal Le Duc Bach, a Kit Carson scout who worked variously for the French Legionnaires, American Special Forces, ARVN rangers, and the Viet Cong as time and circumstance required; and an unlikely assortment of criminals, former communists, and unlucky government soldiers.

The chief of this unit of assassin/policemen was the most unusual man of all, Y'Yool, a Bahnar Montagnard. The unusual quality of the man lay not in the fact that he was a member of a despised minority who rose to the position of deputy inspector of police on his merit, nor because he had lacquer blackened teeth filed to sharp points. It was that he was nearly unique in South Viet Nam—an honest official and a true patriot.

Karl Isaacson, now Anders Bergstrom, arrived in teeming Saigon and met Lane Duerk, the enigmatic Saigon Chief of Station for the CIA. Duerck recognized Bergstrom's chief flaws, his youth and inexperience, and assigned him to fight in the Mekong Delta with a ragtag group of irregulars known unaffectionately to regular army, navy, marines, and South Vietnamese military as Terry and His Pirates. Anders went on hunter/killer patrols and entered the life of daily terror, self and friend preservation, and assassination of enemies. He bonded with Terry Brannigan and Mark Whitehead, navy SEALS, and experts in Brown Water Naval irregular warfare. He plotted and fought with them, learned their lessons of how to stay alive and how to kill, and sorrowed when one mission resulted in Mark becoming the posthumous recipient of the Congressional Medal of Honor, more commonly known among the irregulars as the Medal of Horrors.

When Y'Yool, leader of the Thau Thien Provincial Reconnaissance Unit, was murdered by treacherous Nguyen Tran Xuan, Anders Bergstrom was given the dubious honor of succeeding the noble Montagnard. Cleve Howard, Hue Province Chief for the CIA, and Anders' direct superior, knew Xuan was the treacherous murderer but failed to have him removed, leaving that to the unsuspecting Anders. Anders was aided by Nguyen Tran, Bach, Ky, and Dung in setting a trap that exposed Xuan unequivocally as traitor and to summary execution by his fellow PRUCs.

Anders and the PRUCs became inseparable confidants, trusted and battle tested companions, coconspirators in a drug smuggling operation moving China White Heroin from the Golden Triangle to South East Asian markets; and together they became thoroughly disillusioned with the aims and methods of their CIA superiors when they participated in the kidnapping and murder of an innocent merchant whose death was purchased by a competitor with access to the nefarious Phoenix apparatus as the CIA version of Murder, Inc. had now become known. When Anders asked questions, he was told a chilling parable whose moral centered on the value of being a team player and the fate of those who chose to speak of the unspeakable things they knew.

The volume nears its end with handsome young Anders Bergstrom, in his cover role as a Swedish Red Cross official monitoring the adherence to the Geneva Accords by both sides of the bloody Viet Nam conflict, meeting the lovely daughter of the Mandarin of Hue, Nguyen Tri Lien. The young American CIA contract agent was given the rare privilege of attending Tet (New Year's) dinner with the Mandarin's family and left the venerable old aristocrat's home thoroughly infatuated with the beautiful and unapproachable daughter, Lien (Lotus). The volume ends with Anders and his PRUC comrades on an ill-conceived mission; hunted, wounded, and in deadly peril of imminent death, or worse—capture.

CHAPTER 23

The village Anders and his men chose was quiet. Most of the men were transplanting rice in the paddies on the outskirts. A small gang worked together to repair a sagging dike. Mama-sans gathered sticks for fuel and tended clusters of naked laughing children. Young girls sat in the shade of their open walled homes making baskets and doing laundry. There were no young men.

Anders crept to a vantage point on a low rise where he could visualize most of the center of the village and set up the M-60 on a tripod and placed his AK-47 close beside him. He made himself invisible in the underbrush and waited.

Tran and Dung walked purposefully straight into the heart of the village, all of their armamentarium in full view. They made no attempt at pretense of being noncombatants, but neither did they act with menace nor give evidence of their allegiances. Their ragtag out of uniform appearance was vague enough to raise doubts as to their origins and alliances. Most villagers presumed them to be stragglers from any of a number of mercenary squads roaming the hinterlands mostly intent on banditry. The mercenaries were allied to one warlord or another and were the full equivalent of pirates. The villagers quietly and fearfully eyed the newcomers with ingrained and well warranted suspicion.

Tran asked for the headman. "Not here," he was told.

"Next man," he then requested.

"Not here," he learned. He tapped the semiautomatic dangling free from his shoulder.

There was a look of complete ignorance, passivity, and regret at their inability to be of service to the esteemed visitors on the faces of the town's people. The benign faces were belied by occasional eyes that could not suppress smoldering hostility.

Comity and patience were not working. Tran and Dung knew that every minute they remained exposed increased the danger they faced from their pursuers. Tran turned and walked to the first hooch on his left.

He picked up long sausage like tubes of rice wrapped in linen and slung them over his shoulders and around his midsection. He ignored the outcries of the protesting owner. Next, he scooped up several handfuls of dried fish, found a burlap bag that was less filthy than the rest in the pile, and dropped in the fish. He handed the bag to Dung who tied it to his clutch belt. Dung added a handful of fertilized eggs to his own sack. The mama-san was shrieking her protests and invectives incoherently.

Tran pulled out a handful of Piastre notes and set them on a meal barrel. The woman of the house stopped crying and carrying on almost immediately after seeing the money. Almost as suddenly, other women scattered to their own homes and came back with food stuffs in hand, ready to trade. War, pestilence, tribulations, and fear aside, Vietnamese peasants since time immemorial have been pragmatists. A chance to trade is a chance to persist in an uncertain world. The women gathered around haggling happily with Tran and Dung over the price of chilies, dried lizard, cooked chicken, and the like. The two Vietnamese PRUCs overpaid and walked south out of the town overweighted with a feast.

Anders watched a squad of VC cadres as they silently crept in between his position and the village hooches, swiftly and efficiently setting up their ambush. There were at least twenty of them. If the people in the village were aware of the incoming LAF fighters, none of them betrayed the slightest indication. Tran and Dung were too busy fending off the determined sellers to be fully observant of any unusual activity beyond their immediate vicinity.

As soon as four VC men in black pajamas and conical straw hats had been set at each end of the village, the LAF commander, in full view of Anders, who remained silent and almost holding his breath to avoid being discovered, gave a series of hand signals that started her men creeping down to the center of the town. Anders was faced with a decision, not so much what to do as when to do it. He had a nearly free field of fire but was only one man. He knew that his adversaries would go to ground immediately after he fired the first shot and would turn on him. He also knew that he could not afford to have himself or his men pinned down for any kind of protracted fight. Survival for his small unit demanded mobility and access to food and water. Survival of himself, Tran, and Dung was all Anders could care about right then. It never occurred to him that he might abandon his men to their fates and to save himself unscathed, a possibility that existed if he kept quiet.

Anders determined where the greatest concentration of VC were, kept a mind's eye view of those men, then swiveled his M-60 toward the group of four men now blockading Tran and Dung's southern escape route and commenced firing. The four VC selected as first targets did not have a chance. They were cut down like a mower through alfalfa. Anders arced the muzzle of the gun back to the largest concentration of VC who were already starting to scramble for protection and began a methodical traverse of fire up and across the consolidation of men. Many of those men screamed and toppled from the unseen hail of machine gun rounds. The rest went to ground as best they could. Anders then released the 60's trigger and switched to his AK-47 and began firing short controlled three round bursts into the men directly below him. Some of them were killed while in the act of turning toward his hiding place to begin shooting at his location. Others were still stunned by the rain of unexpected death on their fellows across the way and hesitated long enough to die from bullets in their backs. The wounded screamed; smoke and the smell of cordite permeated the moist morning air; and everywhere people scrambled to get out of harm's way as best they could.

Tran and Dung ran due south down the village's main road. Had Anders not neutralized the four men waiting for them at the exit point, the Vietnamese PRUCs would not have made it twenty meters. As it was, trails of dust clouds kicked up by submachine gun fire skittered after them, missing them only because of their rapid pace zigzag retreat.

Anders swept up his weapons and rolled south with them, keeping his head less than two feet above ground. In a matter of seconds his former hiding place was inundated with grenades fired from a captured M-79 and a heavy concentration of submachine gun fire. He would have measured no more than two inches square in the largest dimension of any remaining piece had he tarried even a few seconds more. His ears were ringing from the horrendous noise, and he had been tattooed with stinging pellets of dirt and pebbles kicked up by the grenade blasts.

Brave LAF fighters charged Anders' emplacement. Anders was now oblique to that spot of real estate and had an excellent view and field of fire. He opened up with the M-60 again and the charging men toppled like felled trees littering the hillside with fresh corpses and writhing wounded. Anders again raked the lower approaches to the village with his MMG until he ran out of ammunition. He quickly and briefly rose to a kneeling position, wrapped the red hot barrel in his shirt and swung it hard over his head. The vulnerable junction point between the stock and the barrel snapped in half as the powerfully muscled young man smashed the gun against a hillside boulder rendering it irreparable. He left the two pieces where they fell.

Kalashnikov 7.62 bullets were seeking him out and drawing closer by the second. It was time posthumous to leave. Anders dived for cover behind a clump of bushes then made an exhausting mad dash up the hill instead of down as his enemies had been expecting. That move gave him a moment of reprieve but sapped precious energy; and Anders had little left, even with his youthful reserves.

Tran and Dung were out of the village and had struck off into the forest on opposite sides of the road in a banana peeling coordinated move. They ran, stopped, fired, dove for cover, rolled, crouched, and ran some more until they were the better part of a klick south of town and could no longer detect evidence of followers and could no longer keep up the pace.

Anders was taking all the heat. Enraged at the deaths of her men and smarting with the humiliation of having her own carefully planned ambush itself be ambushed, the VC commander, a thirty year old school teacher, ordered a full attack on the *con ma da trắng khổng-lồ* as Anders was now universally being called after the previous village firefight. She was determined to avenge her men and to restore her lost face among the survivors. She also had a gut wrenching fear of having to explain this current fiasco to her own commander and to the NVA officers whom she knew by personal observation to be a completely unforgiving lot.

Anders' chest was heaving. He was drenched with sweat having wrung the last vestiges of available water from his parched system to do so. His oxygen starved muscles were beginning to cramp. He was afraid he would black out and shuddered inwardly at the thought of what lay in store for him if he was taken alive. He did not much care for the other alternative either. His mind was racing because he knew they were on their way for him.

Anders Bergstrom, PRU operations commander, had no one to turn to for help. He did not have a radio, and no one would have come had he been able to call. Officially, he did not exist, had no legal warrant, belonged to no documented unit; he was expendable; and he was on his own. It was an extremely lonely feeling just then. He tried to conjure up a vision of Au Co, but the press of danger intruded.

Anders forced his quivering legs to take him around the contour of the low hill, crouching low which further sapped his ebbing strength and cramped his quadriceps muscles. The small surviving squad of

VC crested the hill and overran his last position. They howled in frustration when they found him gone. He could hear the woman commander's shrill soprano above those of her men. They were heedless of noise and were running like outraged maniacs, crashing over bushes and rocks in an unbridled bloodlust after their nemesis.

Anders had two slim advantages over his pursuers. He knew where they were, and their noise kept him fully aware of their general location. They did not know where he was and were running in chaotic unmilitary disarray with an uncharacteristic failing of discipline. Anders' disadvantages lay in being both outnumbered and in uncomfortably close proximity to his tormentors and in his steady physical weakening. If he ran, he would be seen. If he stayed in his inadequate hiding place, he would be found, and soon. His strength was beginning to fail noticeably now. He knew he was approaching a state of heat exhaustion there under the broiling sun in the heavy humid air. Sweat ran down his body in grimy rivulets. He was becoming seriously dehydrated, and he knew it. His muscles were cramping sporadically, and he was nauseated. He tried not to think about it.

Anders' agonizing over what to do was very short lived. A screaming cong ran right over him. The young Vietnamese zealot was so intent on his run that he did not see the large Caucasian until he literally fell over Anders. Anders rolled onto the thin boy with his knife already unsheathed. The boy was the same age as Anders but weighed about half as much as the Occidental youth. Anders was tired, and his muscles trembled. The VC was remarkably strong despite the wiry slimness of his young body. He writhed and struggled ferociously. He tried to bite Anders' arm. He kicked his legs like pistons in high gear.

Angers ignored the boy's pounding left fist and used both of his own large arms to break the VC's right wrist. Then he used the advantage gained thereby to cut his enemy's throat.

For a few seconds Anders was actually unconscious. He fell over his victim and covered his own chest with the boy's gushing blood. Fortunately for him, the fight had been carried on in near silence and out of the line of sight of the other communist soldiers. He awakened quickly, feeling wretched, only dimly aware of his surroundings. It took him seconds to clear his addled brain. The primeval core of his nervous system cried out to him to move, to act, to react. His conscious brain murmured for him to rest, to collect himself. He heard the approach of more angry men.

Anders' body protested, and he had to shake himself to force full alertness. The meaning of the sounds finally intruded fully. He came to a crouch behind his protective bush in time to see a VC rushing his position with a fixed bayonet. Anders had time to step to the side, to dodge the blade, and to bring his hand down hard on the gun barrel deflecting it away harmlessly. He drove the heel of his hand full force from a down to up direction into the nose of the still rapidly oncoming soldier. The man's head snapped back like a hatch door hinge. Two knife sharp shards of bone from the man's disintegrated nose sliced through the protective dura under the frontal lobes of the man's brain and severed both anterior cerebral arteries. The concussive force of the blow rendered the VC soldier instantly unconscious, and the brain hemorrhage killed him seconds later. He did not have time to feel pain.

Anders rolled away, adjusted his remaining weapons, and bolted straight down hill. He was able to run for a full twenty seconds before he was discovered, and the bullets began to crackle behind him. The lead missiles crisscrossed harmlessly through the dust clouds he kicked up as he plunged down the hillside and into the ramshackle and disrupted village.

The withering fire behind him began to be frighteningly accurate only after Anders had crashed his way into the labyrinth of buildings and was lost to his pursuers' vision. There were only four of them left now, and they had their own problems trying to run and shoot at the same time.

Anders ran like a National Football League fullback bobbing and weaving around obstacles and running over any luckless person who got in his way. His flight through the village was a reprise of Dung and Tran's violent passage. To the villagers he was like a charging buffalo, and no one made the slightest attempt to interfere with him. A wounded VC rose to fire at the hurtling blur and received a grenade in his lap for his trouble. That worked so well that Anders began flipping off grenades right and left indiscriminately wreaking terrible destruction on the flimsy dwellings and unfortunate village dwellers as he ran.

At a distance in the forest Tran told Dung to stay put and to cover him and Anders when they made it back, then he sped away, turning back toward the sound of the resumption of firing in the village. He met Anders about two hundred fifty meters outside the southern border of the village. The young white man was staggering, barely able to keep his feet. He appeared to be all in and would have been helpless had the

VC been able to converge on him. On their parts, the VC believed themselves to be up against a superhuman and had become inordinately cautious. Moreover, they did not know where the white giant ghost's criminal comrades were and had to fear an ambush.

When Anders saw his friend coming, he sagged to the ground unable to do more. Tran ran up to the boy and took his head in his lap. Tran gently poured a little water from his condom water vesicle into the boy's feverish lips. The water was warm and fetid, but it was the best Anders had ever drunk. It worked a little magic. Anders tried to gulp more, but Tran insisted that he take it easy. They had enough safe time, Tran thought, to let Anders take in a full liter and to begin to revive. Tran had gotten a complete refill in the village and had drunk all he could handle. While he and Dung had been holed up waiting for Anders, they had both been able to eat some food, real food, not the plastic foam and pebbles the Americans had provided.

Tran helped his operations chief to stand on wobbly legs, no mean task given the differential in their sizes. Together, they began to negotiate their way back toward Dung. Tran stopped every few minutes to look back and to get some more water into his friend. After fifteen minutes of this erratic stop-and-start movement, Anders was able to handle a little of the cold cooked rice Tran had purchased. Despite the anxious circumstances, Anders was beginning to grow stronger.

The first LAF soldier appeared between the trees about one hundred meters behind them. Tran was sure he had seen the man without being seen himself. The PRUCs hit the ground.

Anders said, "We have to get out of here, or we have to kill him before the rest of them catch up. He's the tracker."

Tran nodded. "Easier said than done," he thought.

"We'll trap him," Anders said. "Let's get farther away; so, we have some time to make a pungi trap.

"Let's get going then," Tran said after first looking back to see that the man was no longer in sight.

The two PRUCs crawled, duckwalked, and scuttled away to the south as fast as they could. They found a small, obviously heavily used, VC trail where the dirt was soft enough to allow them to dig rapidly and began to work furiously, excavating with their combat knives. There was no time for an elaborate trap, and they could not afford the noise of an explosive device.

When the pit was about half a meter deep, the two men swept the collected mound of dirt into the brush at the side of the trail. They cut down eight shafts of bamboo from the huge poles that draped gracefully over the trail and hurriedly split and sharpened one end of each into a knife-like point. They then jammed the sharpened stakes, blunt end first, into the soft earth of their pit and packed dirt around their bases as firmly as they could. Finally, they spread leafy branches and large leafed succulents across the opening and smoothed dirt over the top. The final result was something less than perfect, but was quite acceptable given the rushed circumstances. Even an experienced tracker would have to look carefully to detect the disturbance of the ground surface.

The two men left a few tell tale traces of their passage over the trail trying not to be too obvious. Then they secreted themselves out of sight on either side of the trail. Anders was content to have the little rest afforded by the wait to spring their ambush. He longed to eat some of the fish and to urinate, but he knew the tracker would catch the smells in a second. He could not even release his bladder in his pants for that reason. He waited patiently while bugs crawled up his pant legs and over his bare chest. He was coated with his former victim's blood and the insects were drawn to the appetizing proteinaceous stuff. Anders felt and resisted a near frantic need to scratch and to squirm.

The LAF patrol scout, the best tracker in the area, trotted effortlessly and soundlessly down the trail smiling to himself at the carelessness of the GVN criminals and their big round-eyed advisor. In the first place, all the effort to disguise the big man's tracks, even to the point that it was evident that he had wrapped his feet with cloth, were useless especially to an experienced man hunter like himself. No Vietnamese in history had ever had feet that large, bare, rag wrapped, or rubber sandaled not withstanding. No Vietnamese, even one carrying a heavy load, ever indented a trail surface that deeply. He was on the right track, and it was gratifyingly easy. The capitalists and their lackeys were no match for the dedicated Liberation Army cadre, the tracker smiled smugly to himself. He could tell that his quarries were getting tired. They were walking more slowly, and their stride lengths were diminishing. He would find them when they stopped to rest and would bring his platoon back to ambush the traitors to the people.

While he was thus engrossed in his soliloquy and in lauding his own superior cleverness, the tracker kept a trained eye for any sign of the enemy lurking in the underbrush to ambush himself. He even took care to look up into the trees and bamboo stalks to make sure no one was lurking there. While thus engaged, he put his right foot through the flimsy cover of the pungi pit roof. His full weight drove down onto one of the knife edge points and the stake passed all the way through his foot from sole to dorsum. His momentum carried him forward, and he felt onto his left knee. That knee was impaled with a second stake, neatly entering the joint through the hyperflexed heavy patellar ligament. He emitted an involuntary shriek of mingled agony and terror. The pain was so horrific that he quickly began to lose consciousness. The shock was so abrupt and intense that he could not give thought to firing his M-1.

The tracker did not have time to upbraid himself for being so careless or to recognize that he had been bested in the deadliest game there is. He could only function on a subconscious level, and that level told him he was about to die. He was certain that he was imminently going to meet his ancestors.

And he was right. Anders and Tran both leaped from their hiding places and tackled the agonized and helpless VC cadre. They plunged their knives into the acutely invalided man's black pajama clad chest time after time. The only reason he did not fall over entirely was because he was fixed on the stakes in his lower extremities, and the PRUCs were holding him up to keep stabbing him. He was long dead well before they let him fall.

Anders caught his breath. "Tran," he gasped, "Take care of the hole. I'll get rid of him." There was a sucking sound as Anders extracted the lifeless foot and knee with difficulty from the impaling pungi stakes. Gouts of blood splashed over his chest and back as Anders hefted the inert body onto his shoulder.

After dumping the corpse far enough into the forest to prevent it from being discovered immediately and removing the man's sandals, Anders returned to help Tran finish the repairs on the trail.

"You look ghastly," Tran said to Anders.

"Thank you very much, sir. I wouldn't brag much myself if I were you," Anders responded. He was fitting the dead man's sandals onto his own feet as they talked. The VC would not be needing them any longer.

Their remarks, fired at each other in spontaneous staccato Vietnamese, seemed outlandishly out of place and funny to the two exhausted men for some giddy reason, and they began to giggle then to laugh like a pair of maniacs. For a few minutes it was a scene to rival a meeting of demonic serial killers over some fire pit in hell.

Anders got control of himself first. "We have to get going. It wouldn't be very nice for our friends in the black outfits to find us like this."

The prissy way he said it once again started Tran in to a fit of the giggles. Anders shook his head in serious rebuke and began to laugh despite himself. Still wiping tears from their eyes, the two embarrassed warriors began to walk away from the site of their trap toward Dung's hiding place. They were holding hands, a natural act of both great camaraderie and security.

Anders had time to muse as they walked. He observed to himself that he had been positively revolted the first time he had seen a man killed, and again when that family was slaughtered in Nicaragua. He had cringed inwardly with a personal horror when he had killed his first man in combat and then up close. He had developed a shell of toughness so that after a dozen or so killings he was able to accept them as the fortunes of war. It was kill or be killed; and thus far, he had been the killer. Anders had a moment of serious questioning introspection as he trotted along behind Tran because the realization came to him that he had now come to the point that he liked killing. He got an emotional charge out of the act that was more than self preservation or simply doing his duty. And perhaps the worst comprehension he had about himself was that he no longer cared.

While they were gone, Dung had scouted around and had found a good place for the three of them to hole up. He knew they could not keep moving; they were all done in. Maybe it was time to set up and fight if that was what was required. Anders could hardly hobble on his raw feet. Dung, himself, knew that his own left arm was useless and that he was none too functional generally. The shoulder and upper arm throbbed incessantly, and they were out of morphine.

Dung found his friends, and the three men joined up in a copse of trees and finished the last of the wonderfully flavorful salted fish eaten cold and dry, and some the cold cooked rice. They all took long draughts of water and sagged back to accept the waves of weariness and lassitude that washed over them. Precarious as they knew their position to be, none of them had the strength to mount a formal watch.

After his comrades discovered the tracker's body, the VC posse was not about to venture deeper into the forest after dark. A standoff of sorts was reached, neither side knowing quite where the other was, the degree of battle weariness and wariness, nor what their adversary was up to. They were the poetical 'ignorant armies that clash by night,' except they were all too done in to do it that night.

At 0300, after sleeping a dangerous six hours, Anders awakened to the sounds of an undisturbed jungle night. He stirred about quietly and looked all around their immediate area. Nothing moved out there. He gently shook his men by their shoulders and held his index fingers to his lips. "I think they are camped for the night. I also think we ought to get outta here; what do you say?" He whispered his question to each of his comrades.

Tran said, "You hope they have camped, don't you mean?"

"Sure, I guess that's right. Still, what do you think about us getting out of here?"

Tran and Dung communicated with each other by eye contact in the moonlit semidarkness. Anders' suggestion seemed the lesser of evils. They both nodded affirmatively despite their overwhelming weariness.

"Okay, let's get out of here. Nothing ventured, nothing gained," Anders said. That must have been something his mother used to say, he thought. It sounded peculiar in Vietnamese. Odd what came to mind right now.

The three men trotted on weary stiff legs, Anders on his sore feet, through the remaining hours of the night. To keep their bearings, and to avoid any further contact with VC, they bypassed Hong Thuy village and made their way to the bank of the Bo Giang and followed it due east. After three hours steady march, they could recognize landmarks they knew to be in the vicinity of their compound. They had escaped the Viet Cong dragnet. Now if they could only get into their own safe territory without being shot by friendly fire.

CHAPTER 24

I can conceive of no greater tragedy than for the United States to become involved in an all-out war in Indochina.
President Dwight D. Eisenhower, Press Conference, February 10, 1954

Fontor a full week, the three sore men convalesced at their home compound. Anders went over plans for the other three man units in the PRU and helped in the refinements of the kidnappings, arrests, snatch and snuff operations, or frank village attacks. He had to impose disciplinary actions on some of the teams. That should not have come as too great of a surprise to Anders since the majority of his men were in the PRU after having been given conditional releases from jail. In general, the PRUCs were probationer thieves, murderers, rapists, and assaulters. The circumstance for which Anders had to lay down the law occurred the day before Anders, Dung, and Tran returned from their long range reconnaissance.

The Company had established a bounty as an incentive. For each weapon and for each set of ears, the probationers were paid a reward. Several men in Anders' PRU became overzealous, raided a South Vietnamese military armory, and made off with large quantities of weapons. When they brought the arms back to the compound and naively requested their reward from Anders, he found it necessary instead to lock them in the compound brig for three days to impress on them the wrongfulness of such enterprises. He did not make it into a huge crime, and they did not get overly affronted by having to be punished.

A marine colonel wrote an official complaint to Cleve Howard that was forwarded on to Anders complaining that Anders' PRUCs had been seen to cut out and eat portions of the liver of their VC victims. It was the colonel's contention that even the CIA should draw the line somewhere, and cannibalism seemed like an appropriate place. What the colonel did not understand, and Anders did, was that his men were only finalizing their action of killing the hated communist. It was their belief that by taking the bite out of the dead person's liver, the victim would not go to Buddhist heaven intact and would, therefore, be forever unhappy. The young PRU/O thought the ritualistic action was not really any different from the dismembering and green face painting performed from time to time by SEALS on their victims. Anders round-filed the complaint and never heard more about the matter.

A few of the teams needed their backsides kicked for laziness. They had become overly involved in an old Vietnamese game called *Cò Túong* and were engaging in tournaments put on by US Marines in the pacified villages. This took them away from their assigned missions, and caused some dissension among the ranks because it was unfair for some to play while the others worked and took the risks. The most unpopular thing Anders did as PRU/O was to issue an order banning any participation by PRU cadres in the well intentioned tournaments.

The PRU compound was a busy, well fortified, small base; and Anders Bergstrom had real, if not recorded, authority well beyond that which his age or rank would have indicated. He discussed the missions of mayhem, terror, and disinformation while keeping his swollen feet therapeutically elevated above the level of his heart and never once had a moment of moral pause. Whenever he had a period of introspection about his professional activities, Anders tended to compare himself favorably with the torturers Szabo and DuParrier. That was one place where the seventeen year old commander of men drew the line.

The only time Anders brought his feet to the dependent position was to soak them in Epsom salts. He was out of action for the time being, and did not feel all that bad about the enforced relaxation. Dung's arm required only some regular cleaning and fresh bandages, and he was able to be up and about the camp. He seemed to prosper from the exercise; so, they did not bother to get him to a medic or to Danang to a doctor. Tran required only food, drink, and rest.

By the end of the second week after the three of them had returned home, Anders began to get progressively anxious about the whereabouts of Ky and Bach. The PRU had not heard from or about the two cadres since Ky had volunteered to take Bach and the treasure wagon to safety.

"What do you think?" Anders asked his two remaining squad members after mulling over the concern about the man he had trusted.

"Ky has his own way and his own resources," Bach answered. "He is loyal to us, no matter what else he does, though."

"You really believe that?"

"I do. He has always shown me that."

"I do, too," added Tran.

Anders shrugged. He remained dubious, but decided to exercise all his powers of self control and patience and to wait. The wait stretched out another two weeks, and by then all three men in the unit were starting to have doubts. Anders' ability and willingness to give Ky the benefit of the doubt was stretched as thin as his young psyche could endure. He and his men were fit and chafing to return to action, and they did not want to go without their full team complement. PT was an inadequate substitute, and they all knew that the assignments were piling up.

On 1 March the whumping of an OH-6 Cayuse observation helicopter's rotors caught the attention of the compound. No incoming flights were scheduled; so, this had to be something unusual. In Anders' experience unusual tended to mean bad. He was at the edge of the landing pad when the olive drab, unnumbered loach (abbreviation for light observation craft) settled down. The rotors continued to throb as the side doors opened. Ky and Bach stepped out, bowed their heads to duck under the rotors, and scurried away from the whirring arms of the helicopter.

"Hey, boss!" Ky said as soon as the aircraft lifted off, and they could make themselves heard.

"All right, Ky," Anders demanded with an ear to ear grin of relief, "how about telling us all about your little vacation."

Ky laughed. He carried an infectious ambiance of good humor about him as usual. He was in great spirits, "Well, boss, Bach should tell the story. His was the most important part. I just did a little business and patched up my sore backside."

Anders, Tran, and Dung all raised their eyebrows theatrically. Anders shook his head good naturedly since Ky's ebullient mood had captivated them all. "Okay, so Bach, tell us about it."

Bach appeared tired and rather wan. He was in a good mood, but was obviously physically subdued. "Not much to tell," he began. Bach had always been a bare-bones detail person. "Ky drove the wagon over every bump from the border to Danang. We were stopped three or four times; and once Ky had to kill a couple of cong; but generally, it was pretty easy. I had a slug in my chest, and the lung was collapsed. Ky took me to the marine hospital at China Beach. They put in a tube to blow my lung back up. After I could be up and around, they kicked me out. That's it."

Ky said, "I called Mr. Howard, the RDC/O chief; and he got Bach into the hospital. Being the RDC/O makes you important."

"And what were you doing during those three weeks while brother Bach was in the hospital?" Anders asked Ky.

"Playing by the beach, the one the G-I's call shit beach." (So-called because the VC regularly used it at night as their lavatory and covered the remains with an inch or two of sand, usually not enough to do the job.)

"And?"

"Business." Ky was obviously going to drag this out as long as he could. He was enjoying himself.

"What kind of 'business'?" asked Tran urgingly.

"Big," Ky replied, poker faced.

"Ky!" All three impatient men rejoined in a mock menacing unison.

Ky laughed. He was having a good time, but figured he had reached the limits of his friends' patiences. The others glared at him to let him know that they may well be his friends, but murder had not been ruled out. He held up both hands in a gesture of submission. "All right, the whole story. I left the wagon and the stuff in it just the way it was all the way to the coast. Only after I got rid of Bach, I checked through the whole bottom without the rice bags. Lots of happiness there. I took the wagon back up to Hue' since I couldn't think of any better way; and besides, I guess I looked the part of a farmer. I have some business acquaintances…uh, associates, with offices along the Perfume River; so, I took the wagon there.

"They were very pleased. I was able to negotiate a good exchange and gained much face with those businessmen. That will bring good relations for the future."

"How much?" Anders and Tran asked, unable to contain themselves.

"Patience, brothers," Ky entreated them. "My associates gave me a quantity of Piastres to cover the gold and bank notes that were boxed in the wagon. I banked the cash in the National Bank of Hue' with another associate who has the courtesy not to ask too many questions about cash transactions. He receives a consideration, of course."

"Of course."

"Now…how much!?" The anticipation was too stressful.

"I had the funds changed to American green back dollars at a good exchange rate—113 to 1." He paused for effect. It was exasperating. Ky kept a stolid flat expression. "4,000,000 P., 35,300 US greenbacks."

The three PRUCs who had been listening intently dropped their jaws. Anders smiled at the fact that they did. He had seen the phrase in books and assumed it to be only a literary expression. They all recovered enough to give an appreciative whistle. Ky laughed with childish glee at the prolonged trap he had sprung. He was pleased with himself that he had drawn out the surprise to the very end.

"Are you serious?" asked Anders.

"Absolutely," answered Ky.

"Under what name?" asked Tran.

"Each of the five of us separately," Ky told him.

Bach paused a moment. "Do you think we ought to give it to the RDC/O chief?" He looked quite serious.

The returning looks from his PRU brothers was answer enough. "I was just wondering," he yielded defensively.

All four men laughed and repeated the magic figures. "Four million P., $36,000—$7500 each" until their joy was complete, and they had convinced themselves of the reality of the windfall.

"Did I not tell you that the dream of the Au Co was very good joss, Anders?" Tran asked the Swede.

"I am a believer," Anders said. He was entirely serious.

Anders transferred all of the money he had been hoarding from his CIA pay and from his share of the take garnered from the Riverine War in the Delta with Terry and his pirates. His expenses had been virtually nil during his entire time in Viet Nam. He was excited with the total. He now had an official bank credit of $72,000—"not bad for a seventeen year old from the sticks," he thought. $20,000 had come from money he had saved from drafts from the Revolutionary Development treasury provided by the CIA. He made multiple $10,000 requests over his time as the PRU/O because that amount was given without any serious questions being asked or paper work.

It was past time to get back to work. The most pressing demand was for his PRU to round up a string of VCI couriers working from Danang to the DMZ and from Hue' to Hong Thuy. A VCS was persuaded by Tandrosz Szabo and Jean-Luc DuParrier to supply the names and functions of the first couriers in the system, and one of Cleve Howard's prior *ralliers* was able to fill in additional names. The ARVN post in the Imperial City knew of three more men in three other towns, and the PRU was now in possession of information implicating an entire clandestine ring. Anders' PRUCs were linked to an ARVN and US marine operation to eradicate the espionage network. The PRUCs were to start inland (from the west) and to work toward Hue', and the

ARVN and marine contingent would work north up from Danang. The orders allowed for capture and detention as the preferable option, simple detention and termination, or general search and destroy methods depending on the commander's field decision. The latter category had had to be included to gain the cooperation of the marines.

Anders deployed all but two of his teams. The mustered teams moved for the first time as a paramilitary unit for a single operation in well coordinated surgically clean strikes, taking six prisoners in four days without a single casualty on either side. Anders wondered briefly about the genuineness of the alleged complicity of some of their detainees, but he had learned better than to ask unnecessary questions and dutifully helicoptered each of the VCSs back to Cleve Howard for disposition. His one hundred fourteen man action team did not encounter trouble until they came to Kanh Dinh village, fifteen kilometers from the city limits of Hue'.

It was late morning on a typical hot, dry day. The PRUCs had very stealthily infiltrated the dense woods around the large busy village and planned to try and move into the center across the rice paddies singly or in pairs to avoid attracting attention. They encircled the town in order to snare their man even if he became alerted to their presence and no matter which direction he fled. Their quarry was reputedly the person who arranged the couriers' schedules and was thus the linchpin of the entire operation. The orders to Anders, and to all the units involved in the operation, were to capture or to eliminate this particular VCI at all costs.

Anders designated fifty of his men to remain in position around the village. After a two hour period of preliminary searching and probing for sentries and trip wires and having dealt with several of each, Anders signaled that it was time to proceed. He watched as the first set of his PRUCs started to cross the paddies and the second small group set out to walk casually along the main road into town. No one paid any attention to them as far as Anders could tell because there was so much activity in the center of the village. It took the young PRU/O several minutes to determine that there was too much activity, and that the activity was unusual.

He strained to see what was going on through his field binoculars. The distance was too great for good detail, but Anders could discern that there were far too many people clustered in the center, and a disproportionate number of them were armed. As he moved into the rice paddy in front of him and grew closer to the far side of the marshy farmland, his binoculars yielded more detail. The armed men were in ARVN uniform—a platoon of ARVN infantry. He had not gone twenty meters before he realized fully that the units coming up from the south had beaten his PRUCs to this village; it belonged to them. Anders regarded the region of Thau Thien province north and west of Hue' as his turf, not by any official decree, but by dint of the effort that he and his men had put in to the past pacification effort; and it rankled him a little.

He was not about to be left out altogether. He gave the hand signals and marched across the calf deep water of the paddy. Tran led a group from the east, and Ky came from the north with his men. Each of the squad leaders took the risks of stepping on a concealed antipersonnel mine and their men locked into echelon behind their leader. Anders' philosophy of leadership, which came from the SEAL Terry Brannigan, was to lead from the front; and that entailed taking risks. All sixty-four PRUCs made it into the village without mishap.

By the time the PRUCs had collected near the center of activity in the town, the situation appeared to be well in hand. An ARVN corporal trained an XM-148 grenade launcher at the village common building. Anders could see a powerfully built master gunnery sergeant Force Recon marine conferring with a senior ARVN NCO while the ARVN infantry men were herding the townspeople toward an open field on the north, beyond the houses. There were no officers present which was not particularly unusual. ARVN officers usually led from the rear unlike the situation in the NVA or VC platoons, and that ARVN style usually consisted of keeping as far to the rear as possible, most commonly from their city offices. The single US marine noncom was an active advisor for the ARVN platoon.

All eyes turned toward Anders and his men. The muzzles of one hundred fifty guns turned automatically in their direction as well. Anders held up his right hand in a gesture of peace and kept his hands away from his weapons. His men followed his lead.

"And, you, little man so spic and span, where were you when it hit the fan?" asked the gruff marine as soon as Anders was close enough to talk. "Where did you come from?"

"Hue' PRU," Anders answered, keeping the communication as vague as possible.

"Nothin' better to do? We have the situation under marine control here." The Recon marine neglected to acknowledge the ARVN presence.

"I see that," Anders said. "We will just pass on through. This is the last village on our schedule."

"You do that, sonny," the marine said. It was more like an order. His ARVN counterpart smiled. He loved to see Americans put down.

Anders was not fond of being called sonny, and it was not at all clear to him what was going on. Tran, Bach, Ky, and Dung were now at his side. They had sensed the vibrations of tension between their leader and the marine.

Outwardly, Anders remained cool and did not betray his umbrage at the implied insult in the use of the diminutive to address him. However, he was not ready to leave quite yet. "What's going on?" He asked matter-of-factly.

The marine stood up to Anders' face and breathed malignantly, "None of your business, sonny." He was carrying an M-75 that added to his personal air of invincibility. (An M-75 is an automatic grenade launcher capable of firing 200 rpm.)

Instead of reacting the way his testosterone demanded, Anders turned away and asked the same question of the ARVN NCO. The man was surprised to hear the young white man speaking his language fluently. It was of no consequence to him to have the buttinsky American and his Vietnamese lackeys know what was going on. It was just war, and he was just doing his job. "The cong we came to get is gone; the people tell us. We do not believe them," the Vietnamese sergeant answered. The US marine snapped off an implied order to his ARVN counterpart to shush him. The Vietnamese soldier did not take well to being shushed in front of his men, especially by a foreigner.

"We are going to persuade them," he continued. He gave a pair of desultory hand signals, and his men swept up three villagers and started to beat them furiously with truncheons. Their screams shortly filled the square.

"Satisfied? Now beat it," snapped the marine used to having men jump when he said froggie.

"I don't think so," Anders said. "Not yet." Had the man put it another way, perhaps Anders would have given some consideration to the prudence of doing what he had been told. The marine's tone did not inspire cooperation in the young Swede, and he stayed put.

The marine was not used to being disobeyed. But a real clash with some of his own people, to use the term loosely, even some wet behind the ears would-be CIA bogeyman and his PRU scumbags was not worth the sweat.

"Suit yourself, spook," he said and returned to his professional duties. Anders did not like what he was seeing—the 'professional duties' as they were unfolding there in the little village common area. However, it would be unprofessional of him to interfere, he figured; so, he and his PRUCs contented themselves to do no more than to follow along as the center of activity moved toward the open field.

Evidently the pace of progress was not fast enough to suit the ARVN NCO. He appeared exasperated at his men and the villagers. He walked up to the Recon marine gunny and spoke privately. The marine nodded an okay, and the ARVN soldier shouted crisp orders to his men. At first they appeared reluctant to move. The orders were, "Round them up and stand them in the middle of the field."

When the marine abruptly turned on the ARVNs and started to raise his M-16, they suddenly got over their deafness or moral qualms and quickly force marched the frightened villagers into a tight clutch.

The NCO barked a second order, and his men moved into a close order circle around the periphery of the clutch of villagers, placing themselves about fifteen meters from the people, who now appeared nearly paralyzed with fright. The ARVN platoon brought their M-14s up to the crooks of their arms.

Tran edged closer to Anders. "You know what they're going to do." It was a simple declarative, not a question; and it conveyed a world of shared meaning. "Do we want to be here when it happens?"

"Why not?" Anders asked stubbornly. He, too, was sure what was about to unfold.

"Everybody here is going to get dirty, and somebody is going to remember," Tran insisted.

He had a point. Anders thought hard on what he was seeing and about the ramifications. A revelation came to him as he watched the ARVN rifles slowly raise. The marine and the ARVN NCO looked on with business faces. "This bit of work had to be done, and it was time to get on with it," their countenances said.

Anders had a painful flash of memory. In his mind's eye, a girl clutched desperately for the uprights of an open helicopter door. He saw himself frozen to his seat unable or unwilling to help her and to stop an atrocity, and he disliked himself in that instant. Anders had a conscience despite all that he had seen and done, and it manifested itself inconveniently there on the village green. He made an almost reflex decision, one that he would have cause to review at his leisure many times over in the future. Right now, however, he did not have the privilege of retrospection or even careful introspection. He acted from his gut.

"Tran," he ordered loudly, "Move all of the men around the villagers. He was speaking in Vietnamese, and the ARVN soldiers turned as if one man to look at the source of the diversion.

"All of us?"

"Every man. Now."

It was a measure of the bond between Tran and Anders that he would obey. The decision was a life and death one, and it was a moment when impending death could be averted and avoided. Tran walked in front of the ARVN NCO and the Force Recon marine oblivious to their challengingly disapproving glares. He softly told each of the PRUCs standing outside the ARVN infantrymen to walk to the inside of the ring of men and to place themselves between the Vietnamese villagers and the firing squad arrayed before them. When Tran had spoken to the last PRU cadre, Anders stepped forward and walked over to stand half a meter from the nearest villager who cowered, expecting the worst, before the giant of a young man.

The marine started to react, but it was too late. Before he could do anything more than sputter, every PRU cadre had walked forward and had placed himself in harm's way to shield the mass of villagers.

"What do you think you are doin', fool?" The marine shouted and rattled off a list of innovative expletives and invectives directed at Anders.

Anders chose to keep quiet and to let his actions speak for themselves. After a moment, he turned to the villagers and ordered them once in Vietnamese to sit down instead of standing there. On their part, they were only dimly aware of the intense scenario being played out before them in which they were the pawns. Most of them were numb with terror.

The ARVN NCO was visibly furious. He ordered his men to take aim. "*Sửa soạn để bắn!*" (Prepare to shoot!) he barked. One hundred fifty rifles came to as many shoulders and took aim.

The marine yelled another string of profanities that would have enshrined him in the manly language hall of fame, then ended with a pertinent and sensible question directed at the blond interloper, "Do you want to die? Do you want all of your men to die? Because all of these Charlies are going to die."

The ARVN NCO asked an even more pragmatic question from his perspective, "American. Are you going to fight us? We are going to shoot these people and you if necessary. Do you think you can stop us?" They were words borne of more bravado than he actually felt and certainly exceeded the tenor of courage felt by his men.

Anders knew that events had proceeded beyond the point where any kind of protracted dialogue or debate could take place. He also knew that he was closer to death than he had ever been. He was facing into the countenance of the Grim Reaper, and it was a soul searing experience.

"Move out of there now, or we will shoot you where you stand," the marine demanded. His face was nearly purple with rage. The veins stood out prominently on his face and neck. He cursed Anders' heritage, his sexual inclinations, his religion, his CIA association, and a number of his body parts. Anders seemed unaffected.

Anders was beyond being frightened by something a man said. He was still looking at the Grim Reaper and felt a small shudder of a chill tingle down his back despite the intense noonday sun as the ARVN soldiers chambered a round as ordered. The moment of truth was no more than a second away, and now it was a matter of who would blink first. Events moved in slow motion clarity.

It was Anders who acted first. He gave his men an order. "Lay down your weapons," he commanded. By some miracle of control that, by now, was on a nearly spiritual level, every Provincial Reconnaissance Unit Cadre set his rifle on the grass and steeled himself for his last moment. Most of them clenched their small wood or ivory icons between their teeth. They appeared almost calm.

The ARVN commander was ready to say the word, "*Bán!*" (Fire!) and the command was already forming on his lips as he looked at the marine for a final confirmation. The American soldier had the flame of murder burning in his eyes. His mind was running rapid-fire over the options with the speed of a computer. He would have to kill and bury every single person, villager, and PRUC, and even then he knew that he could never rely on the silence of the ARVN infantrymen. He was, above all, a soldier; and in this moment, he recognized that the irregular warfare business had gotten out of hand, way out of hand. He, himself, had begun to have concerns about the possibility of criminal prosecution for what some of the liberals might have regarded as atrocities in some of the actions in which he had been involved even before this fateful confrontation. This situation was one that could never; and he meant never, be known. And he knew that he could not guarantee that without killing an entire platoon of Marvin ARVNs. That was the truth of it, and that was impossible.

If he let these villagers and their misguided miscreant protectors go, he would lose big face with the little brown men he advised. But then, he could always whip them into submission another day, and he could never get the dead men back. He hesitated and the ARVN commander saw that hesitation. The ARVN NCO did not make his command to fire audible.

The infantrymen looked on with dark fascination at the mental interplay between their commander, their foreign advisor, and the white giant. Anders and his brother PRUCs stared at the Sword of Damocles, steeled themselves for death, and made their peace with their several gods. The hesitation hung over the obscure village on that otherwise historically immaterial day as if the universe were holding its breath.

The Force Recon gunnery sergeant blinked first. He never allowed the hatred of his eyes to leave Anders; but he cursed mightily and gave the order, "Let's get outta here. Call them down." He directed his last sentence to Anders. "And you, you pansy, you have not seen the last of me. Not by a long shot. You and your *Chieu Hois*—they're nothin' but VCs gettin' fattened up or medically treated by us before they sneak back to their commie regiments. You better look behind you as long as you live and worry about me and them both."

The ARVN NCO reluctantly complied and gave the command to stand down. On their parts, the common ARVN foot soldiers heaved an unabashed collective sigh of relief. There was not a man among them who felt the slightest justification in the killing of all of those defenseless civilians. They would be glad to be quit of the place.

One of them whispered to the man standing next to him, "Do you know who that round eye is?"

The other man shook his head.

"I think he is the one the cong call *con ma da trắng khổng-lồ.*" Both men ventured glances in more than a little awe at the large white haired man.

In five minutes the ARVN platoon was gone from sight. Anders and his men stood like human statues rooted to the ground for another five minutes. Several of them stroked their Buddha neck charms and murmured their thanks. Some pinched their bodies to convince themselves that they were still alive. It was difficult to believe it was over. Although it had seemed hours long, the confrontation, in its entirety had lasted less than fifteen minutes.

Anders broke the spell. "We can move out, too. There is nothing more for us to do here. Tran, you and Bach get the men going. Ky and I will cover the rear."

That bit of routine security turned out to be altogether superfluous. There was not a man, woman, or child in that gathering of the damned and reprieved that could have done the least offensive act. As it turned out, it was the wrong village, and no important VC or VCI had ever spent time in the town. The PRU was in no danger from VC in the general vicinity, since they were concentrated more north. Anders decided that his PRU had done its work for that day.

In his sleep, back in the security of his compound bed, Anders had a vivid dream that night. Once again, Au Co came into his room, beautiful and gleaming white with shimmering and scintillating blond tresses. She sat beside Anders on his bed. As before, the apparition said nothing; but Anders felt a deep warm sense of peace. He felt safe and secure there in his dream. He knew that Au Co, if indeed that was who his visitor was, approved.

CHAPTER 25

In the councils of government, we must guard against the acquisition of unwarranted influence, whether sought or unsought, by the military industrial complex.
President Dwight D. Eisenhower

Anders sent his report to the RDC/O chief the following day detailing the mission, but he left out all references to the confrontation in the village. He reported only that they had not been able to find the last, and unfortunately, most critical, of their quarries, and neither had the ARVN unit had any better success.

It was nearly a week before he received a reply, a laconic, "Report to RD HQ this day. Full debriefing required." That did not sound promising, but Anders was not prone to paranoia; so, he chose not to worry much in advance. He changed into his Red Cross Panama suit, took only his .45 in a shoulder holster, and boarded the compound's slick for Hue'.

Sans preliminaries, Cleve Howard said, as Anders entered the RD office, "Would you tell me, please, whatever possessed you to interfere with an operation run by the United States marines and the Army of the Republic of Viet Nam?"

"I, uh . . ." Anders attempted. Howard was not finished, and he peremptorily interrupted the younger man.

"As I understand it, there are some two hundred twenty-five Vietnamese communist insurgents, avowed enemies of the lawful government of this country, in which we are guests, who still carry on their activities on behalf of the Evil Empire to the North because of your overactive sensitivities. Please explain that to me."

"They were no more VC than . . ."

"How would you know? Were you in charge there? Did you do the interrogations, or even take time to find out the results of those debriefings carried on by the men who were in charge? Do you

534

suppose yourself to be somehow omniscient so that you have more access to better information than all the people who input into our national computer?"

Anders could only guess at the meaning of omniscient. "I didn't. There was no . . ."

"I have half a mind to cashier you altogether. Your gutless, thought-less action was an abuse of what little authority you have and has resulted in a serious deterioration in relations between ourselves and our own military people and with our hosts in this country. I person-ally cultivated the working relationships and will have the devil's own time regaining their trust and help." The RDC/O chief was livid. "I spent a most uncomfortable afternoon explaining away your blunder. About the only defense I could muster was that you are so young.

"That is also the only reason I am going to cut you any slack at all. And it is only going to be this one time. That excuse won't cut it another time. I am only going to warn you this once, boychik. If you screw up again, I will cut off your contract, and you will be left out there wherever you are. Forget any silly idea about going back to East Podunk, or wherever it is you came from in The World. You are officially a deserter and will just get yourself a bunk in the can as soon as you step off the plane. I will see to it that it happens. No sir, boychik, you signed on with The Company for better or for worse. You don't get to quit like this is some grocery bagger job.

"Tell you what I'm going to do. I will write this up for your official record, and I will place you on temporary suspension of duty and pay for a month, but I will stop short of seeing to it that your contract is terminated this one time. Willfully work at counterpurpose to me or to The Company, which is the same thing, again; and you will be out. Capiche?"

Anders 'capiched.' He indicated the same by a brief nod of his head. He was too angry and chagrined to dare to speak; besides, it would not do any good.

"You are not to have contact with your cadres for a month, understand?"

"Yes, sir." Anders had no intention of obeying, but he kept that bit of insubordination to himself.

"Now get out of my sight."

Anders turned and left. Apparently there was nothing more to be said; and even if there were, he was not going to be allowed to say it. His first thought was to get a little money out of the National Bank of Hue'. Mr. Howard probably thought he was going to semi-starve during the month without wages. That was the only small plus in the scenario.

535

He did not have an immediate answer to the question of what he was going to do with himself for a month in Hue'. He was standing on Le Loi street in front of the MACV compound feeling more than a little lost. He turned and walked along the bank of the River of Perfumes until he came to the university district. The area was full of university students, and he felt distinctly out of place. Anders walked among the laughing and joking young people who were flirting, courting, picnicking, debating weighty ideas, and generally taking themselves seriously as university students are wont to do. Here and there a student hurried to class packing a heavy bag of books and looking concerned about his or her status. Nothing about any of them or their cloistered world suggested that a war was in progress on the very outskirts of their own city. Nothing about their eager young faces betrayed any knowledge that actions as dreadful as Anders had witnessed as a routine were a part of their world. Their innocence seemed at once hopeful and sadly naive to the young and disillusioned Swede.

Then he saw her. The girl walked along not with, but surrounded by, her companions. The other girls chattered and gossiped among themselves, pausing and turning every now and again to Nguyen Thi Liên for approbation. She was taller than her companions and that gave her a regal quality, a height from which she dispensed her graces without condescension. She was more beautiful than her classmates, with fairer skin, glossier, longer, blacker hair; and they, like Anders, were drawn to her, in hopes that some of her popularity or attractiveness would somehow be transmitted to them. It was obvious that her peers enjoyed the simple pleasure of being within her aura.

Liên was wearing an Ao Dai, not unlike the other young university students around her. But to Anders the garment on her was the embodiment of grace and modesty. Even he recognized that his assessment was something less than objective; but he did not realize how smitten he was by the girl on this, only the second time he had seen her. He found himself following her in violation of his sense of common courtesy and without a clear reason even for himself as to why he was doing so. Liên walked along with her classmates to the edge of the university campus where she waved goodbye to them. She passed the cafes and small shops filled with students, most a little older than Anders but who appeared so much younger and more innocent. She browsed in a bookstore, bought flowers at a flower sellers, then began a resolute walk into the residential avenues. Liên was unattended by guards and appeared to be completely at ease.

Anders quickened his pace behind her drawing close enough finally to call out. It took all of his courage to do so. "Miss Nguyen," he called.

Surprised by his voice, she turned. Liên was even more surprised to see the greeting, in Vietnamese, had come from a large Caucasian man.

"*Bonjour, Monsieur*," she said when he drew up to her. "*Je suis étonnée que vous vous souvenez de moi, Monsieur*," (I am surprised that you remember me, sir) she said smiling up at him with self assurance.

"Pardon me, Miss Nguyen, but I do not speak French," Anders said in well accented and toned Vietnamese. "May we use Vietnamese?"

"Of course," she said switching back to her native language. "Or we may use English, if you prefer."

He thought it best to preserve his cover and indeed was embarrassed to admit, "My English is not as good as yours. Maybe we could speak Swedish." He smiled at her.

Liên laughed. "You have me there. I guess it will have to be Vietnamese." She paused and looked at him expectantly. After all, it had been him who approached her. He remembered his only other romantic foray—that unpleasant boyhood memory seemed like something from the dim past, that long ago time when he had lived in The World. Anders was altogether unskilled in matters romantic or even in the ordinary social refinements, and he was acutely aware of his shortcomings as he looked at the sophisticated young woman's face. He knew that he was in the presence of the Mandarin's daughter, the very definition of social refinement.

"Miss Nguyen, may I walk you home?" It sounded so adolescent.

"Why?" she asked. There was neither guile nor coquetry in her expression.

He felt stymied by her honest and direct response. He did not have a good answer. The truth was simply because he wanted to be in her company, but he knew instinctively that he could not say anything that banal. "I...uh . . ." he was determined not to stammer, but there he was doing it anyway. He drew in a breath. "It isn't safe. There is a war going on. You shouldn't be alone. I can give you some protection," he declared.

"Hue' is safe," Liên stated flatly. "I walk here everyday from home to school and back. So do all my friends. All the fighting is in the south, and the government has the situation under control." She said it with such certainty. Anders felt he was in no position to dissuade her of her naiveté. His knowledge of the spec-ops war being fought with such murderous ferocity made him feel old, or dirty, or secretive, or something.

"Besides, how could you protect me? Don't you work for the

American civilian relocation program or something? Something not military?" She asked. He scrutinized her to see if she was mocking him.

"No . . ., yes," he said. She gave him a quizzical look.

"No, I'm not American," he lied, "I'm Swedish; and yes, I'm not in the military; so, it's yes and no, or I mean, no and yes. I mean, I'm with the Red Cross." Anders had begun to sweat as he botched his way through the convoluted explanation. This was not going well, and he would not have blamed her for simply walking off in confusion.

One part of him wanted to defend his masculinity and to assure her that he was a competent protector. He could not do that, and Anders knew instinctively that she was not the girl to be impressed by the crudity of his covert paramilitary life. The other part of him wanted to convince the girl that he was a sophisticated official of an international organization, a peaceful executive type. He was definitely not enough of a thespian to carry off that charade. He was feeling more and more like an awkward boy, and his face easily betrayed him.

"So," he responded like a boy, "Whatever. Miss Nguyen, I would just like to walk with you." Simple as that.

She looked at the earnest young foreigner with sympathy and wished that she had something else to tell him. She said, not unkindly, but with complete candor, "No." Simple as that.

Anders was thoroughly deflated.

"Is it...because you don't like how I look, that I am not as educated as you? Is it because I am a man of a different race? It doesn't matter to me. Is it just me?"

"It is not you, Mister...I'm sorry. I remember meeting you at Tet Eve dinner, but I can't remember your name. Caucasian names are so hard to remember.

"Anders, Anders Bergstrom." That she could not even remember his name did not help improve his downcast mood.

"I owe you an explanation, I suppose. It is not permitted for me to be alone with a young man, any young man. It is not permitted for the daughter of the Mandarin to be involved with a foreigner—a person of a different race even with a proper chaperone. When the time comes, my father will arrange my marriage. The choice is not mine."

It seemed outlandish, cruelly foreign to the ardent young suitor, and his inexperience would not allow him to accept the explanation as the last word. He was smitten and not in a state to be objective.

"How can I get to talk to you?" He asked, almost pleadingly.

As straitened as the limits imposed on her conduct might have been,

Liên was not devoid of susceptibility to the boyish side of a man, one who was ardently pressing his efforts to woo her. She offered, "If you were a student in university, we could meet as classmates," she said and smiled at him. He leaped for the crumb causing her to add, "but not romantically. You must not forget that."

There was hope. "Then I will be a University of Hue' student," he declared emphatically.

A shadow crossed her face. "I am afraid it is not that simple. There are many forms to complete. I do not know of any foreigners attending the university. Maybe there is a rule against it."

From the sound of that, there seemed to be less hope. Anders looked crestfallen. In reaction, Liên came up with an idea, "My father, the Mandarin, is a regent of the university. I know he could help. He can get you in if anybody can."

"Let's go see him," Anders blurted impetuously. He turned as if to start up the street at that moment.

"You can't just go and see the Mandarin of Hue', Mr. Bergstrom. He is a very important and very busy man. It takes weeks to get an appointment to see him at his office."

"I don't have weeks. Please."

"What can I do? I am nothing but a lowly girl." She said it without suggestion of humor or rancor. It was simply a declaration of how things were for the elegant young lady in her culture.

"But you are his daughter. He would do it for you." He remembered the old man's obvious affection for his daughter displayed at the Tet Eve party. He knew he was right. "I know he would do anything you asked." He grinned broadly at her, satisfied that he had countered her every excuse. In his mind's eye he could already envision the meeting with the venerable institution of a man.

"I suppose there is some truth in that," she conceded. "In some matters," she corrected herself. She did not want the young foreigner to get his hopes up too high. In the last analysis matters of courtship and marriage were based on cultural rules cut in stone. "I must go home now. We must not be seen spending time alone. Please. People will talk."

"All right. Send me a message, please. I will be in the Huong Giang Hotel." He smiled. "If I don't hear from you by tomorrow, I will come knocking on the door of your house and ask you father for your hand in marriage," Anders said facetiously.

Liên looked shocked. She was unaccustomed to people making jokes about serious matters. It was not done. She put her hand in front

539

of her mouth and tittered nervously. "You mustn't." She was not sure whether to be angry or to laugh. After looking at the young man's mock-serious face, she laughed. It was a delicate, musical sound.

"I will do what I can. please do not do anything silly. Promise." She warmed his soul with an imploring smile.

"Cross my heart and hope to die," he said and made a cross gesture over his left breast with his index finger. She looked at him in bewilderment. He had to forego the explanation, suddenly remembering that it was an old American idiomatic expression that, by rights, he should not be familiar with.

A gentle tapping on his room door awakened Anders the following morning. He went to open it trying to shake the sleep out of his eyes and head. There was a folded message on Perfume River Hotel stationery laying just inside his door: "Appointment confirmed: Ten AM today. Office of the *Tap Hien Vien*, Mandarin of Hue' ." I iên was as good as her word.

The *Tap Hien Vien* was the Counsel of Wisemen, who, at one time, advised the Emperor regarding the ethics and practices of Confucius (Latinized form of Kung Fu-Tzu) and his student, Menscius—the principles upon which all Chinese based governments functioned. The Counsel was above the law, and its chairman, The Mandarin, served, in effect, as the supreme court. The Counsel was second only to the lofty *Do Sat Vien*, the Board of Censures, a body of civil mandarins who supervised the practical running of the government and alone could make criticisms of the Emperor. With the abdication of Bao Dai, the emperorship, the Board, and the Counsel became superfluous and archaic.

However, the Confucianism upon which the Chinese emperorship and the system of governance by mandarins was based had a profound effect on Viet Nam; and the Mandarin of Hue', in whose being reposed the essence of obedience to the established order, still occupied a position of considerable influence as a result.

The concepts of diligence, economy, integrity, and righteousness, those pillars of the establishment, were imported with 2000 years of Chinese influence and indelibly etched on the psyche of Viet Nam by 1000 years of occupation and rule. Politically, Confucianism perpetuated the social and moral order and stability of the state, and made static all class and economic statuses. Change was anathema to Confucianism, and The Mandarin stood as a bastion against societal transformation even though his governmental power was a thing of the past. More than anything else, the old Nguyen noble stood for all the moral codes that the Vietnamese deeply held to be right. He represented the inculcate desire of Vietnamese toward obedience on the levels that mattered, generation after generation, irrespective of the winds of political and military change or philosophical or religious shifts; obedience of emperor to country, of minister to emperor, mandarin to minister, citizen to mandarin, son to father, younger brother to elder, wife to husband, and student to teacher. For doing so with unfailing fealty, for demonstrating the exemplary conduct that should meet the moral demands of rank and office, The Mandarin of Hue' was revered.

Anders had dared to hope for a visit from the girl herself. He was disappointed but had to admit that getting the appointment at all was more than he should have expected. There was no address given. It was presumed that everyone knew the location of such an important building. Anders went to the lobby to find out the address and the route to get there and his request was greeted with the deferential condescension reserved for tourists.

He had time to get his suit pressed at one of the steam shops and presented himself to the Mandarin's male secretary in the Imperial Administration Building on Bach Dang Street facing the Dong Ba Canal, near the Dieu De National Pagoda north of the Imperial City. The building itself was a step back in time to a more tranquil and stylized age. Around it were gathered the pastel, stucco walled, balconied French Colonial era business and government buildings. The Mandarin's building, as it was generally known, was an anachronism among those post-modern period structures.

It was the smallest building within sight and possessed old-style upswept roof eaves, shining black tile peaked roof, and brightly painted all-wood walls with ornamentation of vivid reds, pinks, and yellows built as a similitude of the ancient khans' imperial tents. The Mandarin had insisted on assiduous maintenance; and therefore, it looked as if it were new, albeit circa the second century BCE in comparison with the genteel decay of the French buildings that had languished since shortly before Dien Bien Phu. The Mandarin's building was very Chinese in a country that professed to eschew everything Chinese even more than it vitiated all things French. It was an anachronism.

And so was the Mandarin. In a Buddhist world, he was a Confucian. In a world of tropical linen modern suits or tiger stripe fatigue uniforms, he wore the traditional attire of the tenth century courtier. He was dressed in a floor length skirted caftan-like black silk smock embroidered with brilliantly colored dragons, the symbol of strength, goodness, and good luck. He wore a pillbox black silk hat.

The man himself was diminutive, wizened, and wore a wisp of a chin beard that could have been a patch of duck down feathers. His skin was waxen yellow and wrinkled into deep dry furrows that gave him the look of a permanently etched configuration map. His facial expression, resulting from the deep creases of his skin, appeared inscrutable, neither smiling nor frowning. His fingernails were fully two centimeters long and sharpened to rapier points. They shone with several laminae of clear hard lacquer. The nails were the second thing about the Mandarin that captured Anders' attention when he was ushered into the man's presence at precisely ten o'clock by a silent servant padding along on slippered feet. Anders had removed his own shoes upon entering the building in the common habit of Asia. He walked quietly across the luxurious old hand knotted Chinese carpets of the man's office as he had done previously over the parquet floors of his home.

What captured Anders' attention immediately and most strongly were the deep black piercing eyes of the ageless Mandarin behind his pince nez glasses. Any suggestion of bodily frailty was in contrast to the intelligence and focus of those riveting almond eyes. The man sat on a small raised dais behind an ornate carved Vietnamese hardwood desk given to him by the office of the last emperor of Viet Nam, Bao Dai. When he first took his prestigious place in the administration of the city and province in 1917, it was the year before the State Literacy Examinations and the institution of the Mandarins were done away with by the French. The eminently dignified old man looked out over the mirror finish of the desk and down toward Anders Bergstrom. The young Swedish boy felt the man's eyes penetrating his thoughts.

The Mandarin scarcely moved, sitting almost mannequin-like in his stiff-backed carved wood chair, but his eyes took in everything. Irrespective of his mode of dress, the appointments of the handsome room in which he sat, or the officially only ceremonial character of his office, the Mandarin of Hue' was a most impressive individual. He beckoned the awkward youth forward with a cane thin finger.

"Please come closer. My hearing is not as it once was," the Mandarin said in a rich deep voice that belied the infirmities of his advanced age. He spoke heavily accented but clear English.

"Would you prefer Vietnamese?" Anders asked.

The Mandarin smiled. At least Anders thought the change in his paper thin lips was a smile. There was even a brief display of yellowed teeth.

"Please indulge me. I do not often get the opportunity to practice my limited skills in the language of Viet Nam's current occupiers. Now what is this that my daughter tells me about your desire to matriculate at the University of Hue'?"

"My work will keep me here for several years, it appears. I would like to get a college degree. I am sure the university is a fine one. Liên told me I would need your help to get in," Anders responded.

"Indeed that and more." The Mandarin was thoughtful for a moment, then he cut to the chase, "Is that all there is to it?" He looked quietly but without blinking directly into Anders' eyes, into the inner reaches where lying would be futile and self-defeating.

"No. Not all. Sir, I wish to see your daughter, and she told me I could only do that at the university."

"That corresponds to Lien's conversation with me," her father said. Anders was glad that he had been straightforward. "I have two further questions, and the decision to exert influence on your behalf will be determined by the quality of your responses."

"All right," Anders said. He was beginning to feel at ease. The powerful personality of The Mandarin had relieved Anders of any need to practice deceit. It was a refreshing experience after his short life with The Company. It did not occur to Anders that the Mandarin might yet wish to intrude into the area of his work.

"First and most important, what are your intentions toward my daughter, my Liên?"

"I would like to see her. I mean, I would like…well, I don't know how you would say it. I want to be her boy friend."

"Her suitor? Her beau?" Under other circumstances, the archaic usages might have been amusing.

"Yes."

"I will return to that question. But first, what are your educational goals, or did you only wish to enter the university as a pretext for keeping company with Liên?"

"Well, sir, I want you to know that my intentions are honorable," He bowed slightly. "I think she is a very pretty woman and a good one. I might hope to marry her one day if she would have me."

"I was asking about educational desires," prodded The Mandarin gently.

"Oh, yes, that's right," Anders corrected himself and was a little embarrassed "Until now, I hadn't given it much thought, but I would like to have a college degree. Since I met Liên, I want to be somebody."

"That is laudable. I believe you are sincere. On that basis, I will help you. But . . ."

Anders held his breath.

"There is a condition. You must swear to me now and forever that you will not pursue my daughter romantically." Anders' face fell. He looked as if he could break into tears.

"I realize that I am making a very difficult demand of you. I have studied something about your western culture. The concept of romantic love, of 'falling in love' and that two young people can 'conquer all obstacles' is deeply ingrained in your culture. You take great pride and tout to all the world your opinion about freedom, as you define it.

"You must understand that Liên comes from an entirely different culture. Here, face and family are far more important than abstractions about choice and individual aspiration. Liên will marry a suitable Vietnamese, a young man of my choosing. To do less would cause her to lose face and her family to bear a measure of disgrace. To act willfully and to follow a foolish whim and to marry a foreigner would be shameful. She would not have a place in the family.

"I will be very candid with you, young man. Your culture permits behaviors that are unacceptable to our people. I must have your absolute assurance that you will not attempt to inveigle my innocent girl into giving her heart to you. She is a virgin, and her very life depends on her remaining chaste. Chastity is sacred in old Vietnamese families. If Liên were to be touched in that way, or were even to be suspected to have been, she would be cast out of the family and out of society. It is very possible that her brothers, who protect her and the family, would find it necessary to erase such a great humiliation from the honorable state of our family. She is only a female, after all.

"Do you understand, young man?"

Anders was blushing deeply. He felt guilty although he had done nothing improper. The venerable old wizard had wriggled the beam from his eyes into Anders' secret thoughts, into the area he had not admitted even to himself.

"Yes," Anders replied with an involuntary air of chagrin.

"Will you give me your promise, make a covenant with me? I believe you are a man of honor, a man of your word; or I would not have agreed even to meet you."

What else could he do or say, "I promise," Anders said dejectedly, but without equivocation.

"Good. I will help you with your application. Also, you have my permission to associate with my daughter as her friend and as the friend of my family without need for deception. You will always be in the company of others. Now, tell me of your education thus far."

Anders had not thought of the educational requirements up to this point. In truth, he had not thought about the mundanities of actually attending school, studying, taking tests, and the like. He felt himself come squarely up against reality with the Mandarin's question. He felt like apologizing for wasting the leader's time and abandoning the whole idea as he thought of his dropout status. It would be easier to avoid Liên, the university, and even Hue' in the future. He could almost see the Mandarin's reaction before he rushed out the miserable facts. "I didn't finish high school; I didn't graduate." He hung his head.

If he were troubled by Anders' admission, it did not show in his craggy old face. "Are you literate?" The Mandarin inquired. He considered the possibility in his own mind that this young man's hopes may be well beyond his real capacity.

"Can I read and write? Sure. I have a lot to learn, but I am not stupid. I can read okay, and I have had to learn a lot by reading."

"It is not a matter of your intelligence; it is a matter of your preparation and also of certification. The thought occurs to me that there may be a way. You realize, of course, that the university will not let you enter without the lower school diploma. The Americans have the simplest method. Many of the their young soldiers did not finish lower school before joining the military, I am told. The army gives them a course of education, then they can obtain a certificate called the GED for General Educational Development, a high school equivalency diploma.

"You will have to have that type of degree in hand; then we can proceed. That is your responsibility."

"I understand."

"When you have that GED in your possession, come back and see Mr. Ngu for an appointment." The Mandarin had reached a conclusion. He glanced at the heavy door. Anders got the hint.

It would be easy enough to arrange for the GED course through the marines, Anders knew. He figured, as he stood on the street, that he would be able to complete the correspondence course in time to start at the university in the fall. All in all, the meeting had been a considerable success, if you did not count it having totally destroyed the young man's romantic dreams.

For the present he had a month to kill; and he decided he might as well be a tourist. Nothing to do, no responsibilities. He had even been forbidden to contact his PRUCs; so, he had no liability for the unit's assignments and projects. It was a feeling more of having been cut adrift than of freedom or vacation.

The first thing Anders did on his first day of unrequested leave was to go back to the airport and to arrange for a message to be sent to Tran at the compound telling him about his suspension—in direct violation of his instructions not to communicate with the PRU cadres. He let Tran know that he would be staying at the Huong Giang Hotel. Anders decided that obeying orders was not necessarily his best personal quality. Then he hired a taxi driver for three days so he could see the city.

Hue' was an airy vibrant place, the third largest metropolis in South Viet Nam with a compact population of nearly 140,000. It was located twelve kilometers west of the South China Sea coast and the Truong Son Mountain range, 80 kilometers from the Laotian border, 200 kilometers from the Laotian Mekong Valley, and 100 kilometers from the DMZ in the north. In the antiquity of Buddhist myth, the city was the lotus flower (*lien*) growing from the mud.

During the second century, BCE, it was an important city, the command town of the Han Chinese army and bore its most ancient name, Tay Quyen. Four hundred years later, it was Kêiu Sou and was the principle town of local war lords. It became an unimportant frontier outpost of the Champa Empire in the second century, CE, called Kandapurpura. After sporadic raiding and fighting by North Vietnamese between 900 and 1400 CE, Hue' came to be the most important city of the Nguyen Lords. Between 1558 and 1636, it was elevated to the status of capital of the autonomous Nguyen dynasty and entered into its brief golden age with a short lived period of opulent prosperity. Elegant stone-walled houses on the order of sculptured Chinese mansions were built and furnished with silken cushions and window dressings and ornamented with delicate dynastic vases and bronze dishes. Furniture was made of the most precious Southeast Asian hardwoods. The smell of perfumes, incense, and sandalwood permeated the air breathed by the rich.

In keeping with the turbulent history of the region, there followed two hundred more years of inconclusive fighting culminating in the Trinh family wresting control from the Nguyens in 1775. In 1795 the ferocious Tay Son Rebellion took place and reinstated the Nguyen family, and the city became the national capital of a united north and south Viet Nam. It became the ancestral home of the great Southern Nobles. Under one of those descendant emperors, Gia Long, the ancestral altars were moved to the city; the French were invited in and directed the building of fortresses to surround the important city; and its name was changed to Hue'.

The French Protectorate government built a modern colonial city on the side of the river (east and south) of the old city opposite the Imperial Palace. Long years of fighting destroyed most of the old imperial city so that even the location of many of the grand buildings was open to speculation by the time Anders made his grand tour.

Anders' guide and taxi driver pointed out the quadratic plan off the districts with the citadel at the center. North (up river) on the west was the residential quarter, originally built for the important people of the city in the traditional arrangement transmitted from the Chinese. The Pagoda of the Heavenly Mistress was the signal landmark of that quarter.

Directly north of that was rural countryside; down river and to the east was the commercial area with its broad streets, and even further south was the Chinese sector with its traditional narrow hectic streets bustling with trade. South, on the far side of the Huong Giang, was the new city built by the French where the MACV compound, the hospital, the university, the post office, and the National School were located. During the First Indochinese war, the French influence waned, and the buildings deteriorated. After the fall of the French at the culminating siege of Dien Bien Phu in 1954, little improvement or maintenance of the once handsome buildings took place. The modern city developed a look of seedy sophistication and vitality, a seasoned and corrupted urbanity. It was frayed at the cuffs, and its necktie had gravy spots, but Hue' was still the heart of Viet Nam. For that reason the city was left alone by both the South Vietnamese and their American allies and by the LAF and the NVA. Anders was able to see and to enjoy the city in peace and security.

Anders and his driver spent the hotter midday hours in the Vy Da District across from the citadel walking among the students, artists, side walk poets, and scholars. They joined the exuberant students in an open air cafe as they ate flavored rice and fish and desserted on beignets powdered with sugar. They drank steaming tea and listened to the American Armed Forces Network presentation of the gripping drama, The "Shadow," who knew what evil lurked in the hearts of men. The students were as absorbed by the melodramatic radio theater as they might have been by an Ibsen, Pierre Corneille, or a Jean Genet production. The AFN switched to an hour long offering of soul music that bewildered Anders and the older cafe patrons and enthralled the western experience hungry students.

Contrapuntal to the modernity of the cafe and in immediate juxta-position to it was an astrologer's booth, harking back to the traditional and enduring Vietnamese concerns. The belief in uncontrollable fates, veritable Gods of Joss, occupied a place in the hierarchy of Vietnamese customary faiths just below family fealty. No real Viet-namese could go a day without some revelation of the fortunes of the future. Every commercial street and every village had a shaman, swindler, and seer with ancient and wise demeanor to provide the critical information and to lighten the truth seeker's purse.

At the booth by the students' cafe sat an archetypal withered Chinese sage. Before him on the pavement were set out the whole panoply of his predictor's profession—tarot cards, collected small bones and oddly shaped stones, a crystal ball kept hooded to protect its secrets, a bowl of washed sand, and a re-inked phrenology skull. Behind him on black flannel curtains hung Zodiac astrological charts, Confucian, Tao, and Vietnamese poetic quotations dominated by the omnipresent red lettered exhortative wisdom of The Tale of Kieu. The day's horoscopes hung on the drapes artfully veiled with gauzy cloth to tantalize the onlookers.

Anders and his guide paid to have their horoscopes read, 4 P each— a bargain. In the background they could hear the discordant strains of American Rock and Roll music grating on the ears and sensibilities of the carefully reared listeners. Blatant sexual and scatological references in the lyrics of the throbbing and blaring music coming over the AFN impacted people who would have regarded the public mention of pregnancy or public displays of affection as irremediably coarse. The students, like their counterparts the world over, yearning to shake off their culturally imposed restraints, embraced the decadent western music.

The ancient Chinese Sage (in fact an elderly out-or-work Catholic church sexton) intoned indisputable pearls of detail regarding the most mundane activities of Anders and his driver's upcoming day. For his part, the driver gave his undivided and wholly ingenuous attention. Anders enjoyed the show and began to think he might be developing a taste for the music coming out of the cafe's radio.

In the late afternoon they crossed the Trang Tien bridge and wove their way through the Central Market at the northeastern corner of the outer walls of the Citadel and then along Tran Hung Dao Street marveling at the splendid crumbling Imperial City. The Citadel was three enclosed cities within a city, concentrically arranged. From outside to inside were the *Kinh Thanh*, the Capital City; *Hoang Thanh*, the Imperial City; and innermost *Tu Cam Thang*, the Forbidden Purple City. Easterly were civil buildings and the men's pavilions and westerly were the military buildings and women's pavilions. Ten gates admitted entry into the Citadel.

The four square kilometer area *Kinh Thanh* was enclosed by walls seven meters high and twenty meters wide, originally built as earth works in 1804. Fifteen years afterward, they were renovated to brick with a series of twenty-four bastions and four observation posts, most of which were in a state of advanced disrepair when Anders walked beside them. The outer walls were ringed by forty meter wide moats and a circular canal. The banks of the water works had heavy foliage including a carpeting of lotus plants with a few crimson buds in blossom.

Anders entered the seat of the old imperial government through the central bastion—the *Ky Dai* or King's Knight. The French called it the Flag Post. The tower was three stories high and held a flag pole that extended another thirty-seven meters. It was completed in 1809. At the base of the tower sat the nine cannons, the *Cuu Vi Than Cong* or spirits of the Nguyen nobles. They also represented the changing seasons and the primal elements—earth, wood, metal, fire, and water. The guide was reverential as he and Anders passed the cannons.

The remnants of the official Nguyen houses and offices, military headquarters and religious departments were there. Where once there had been all the elements of a bustling town within the walls complete with broad walks, ponds, municipal buildings, houses, gardens, ponds, and surrounding verdant green rice paddies, there was now little more than a rubble strewn pasture. Anders' guide was a humble adherent to the *ancien regimé* and had been a self-appointed guide through the ruins all of his life as had his father and his father's father. He knew little of the world outside Hue', not even the name of the current leaders of his country. He would have been at a loss to explain the conflict ranging just outside in the province and knew nothing at all about the western world. But the man possessed an encyclopedic knowledge of Hue' and the Citadel and minutiae about the history of the region from the very beginning down to the abdication of the last emperor, Bao Dai, in 1945. So far as he was concerned nothing of consequence had occurred since. Time had all but stood still for him. The old driver and sage was eighty-one years of age.

The old man walked with an increased spring in his step when they entered the *Hoang Thanh*, also known as the *Dai Noi*, or Great Palace. He remembered back to the time when the complex was home to palaces, elegant pavilions, and was the seat of civil and religions ceremonial affairs and the original site of official audiences with the civil mandarins. He could remember when Lien's father, the last Mandarin, had been forced by the long-nosed, bad-smelling French to move to his present official location outside the Citadel and across the canal. He would have been hard put to remember anything that had happened in the city the previous day or even what he had for breakfast that morning.

The original glazed tile roofs of the buildings were visible for a considerable distance, yellow for the buildings of the great ones, and green or plain for the lesser ones. The Imperial Enclosure had its own wall five meters high and 600 meters on each side. It had its own moat, fifteen meters wide, that was now dry and strewn with weeds. Anders and the enthusiastic guide entered on the north through the *Cua Hoa Binh*, Gate of Peace. There was a gate in each wall: the *Cua Hien Nhian*, Gate of Humanity, on the east, *Cua Chuong Due*, Gate of Virtue, on the west, and *Ngo Mon*, Meridien Gate, on the south facing the River of Perfumes. That gate's name had reference to the emperor whose symbol was the sun that focused on the gate most brightly at noon. The splendor of the Imperial City was a matter of history, but Anders could almost visualize it through the fervent old man's recollections.

The two men walked past the Gold Water Pond with its three bridges, the *San Dai Trieu Nghi*, Esplanade of Great Welcome, so important to the court mandarins, civil and military. They faced the *Dien Thai Hoa*, the Palace of Supreme Harmony, once brilliantly red and gold painted wood, now faded and chipped. Here the emperors presided from their Throne Room. Anders respected his old guide's reverential homage to the emperors' and dignitaries' funereal tablets as they passed through the *Mieu*, the Temple of the Generations.

Anders, himself, was more impressed with the nine huge bronze urns, called *Cuu Dinh*, which symbolized the nine Nguyen nobles as did the nine cannons he had admired at the base of the flag tower. The urns were handsomely decorated with the Nguyen symbol of stability and with a flowing panoply of the sun, moon, stars, trees, rivers, animals, mountains, and soft scenes from nature conveying the eternal harmony between the Emperor, his people, the earth, and the universe. The urns weighed two tons each. Because he was young,

Anders had difficulty calling to mind the splendor of yesteryear, but he could not help but be touched by the homage paid by the elderly man in this, to him, nearly holy place. It had to do with the soul of Viet Nam; even Anders as a foreigner and no more than a boy, could begin to appreciate that significance of the place in which he now stood.

They walked on and approached the inner city, the once sacred abode of divine right emperors. There, the imperial family shared magnificent buildings and lived in unabashed opulence and incomparable luxury surrounded by the most sumptuous wearing apparel, earthly treasures, and bodily adornments. *Tu Cam Thanh*, the Forbidden or Purple City, a faithful replica of the one in Beijing, was the place where only the imperial family and its retainers could tread. For anyone else entrance was barred on pain of execution. The royal palace, that was the Purple City, once occupied three hundred meters on each side of a square and was surrounded by a three meter high wall perforated by eleven gates. The palace was actually more than sixty buildings in twenty courtyards with their own individual walls, walks, and galleries arranged rather haphazardly. The buildings, though decrepit when Anders saw them, stood as mute testimony to the grandeur of the united Viet Nam. Anders' guide kept his silence as they meandered through the once sacrosanct quarters and grounds. There was still evidence of reverence for the lost era— old women walked about scattering magnolia petals around the floors of the Khiem Lang audience court and on the remaining stone statues.

Anders was surprised at how tired he had become when the guide finally stopped his ancient wheezing Peugeot taxi at the front entrance of the Huong Giang. The old taxi driver seemed energized by their visit to the repository of the ancestors of the Viet Nam state. He was disappointed when Anders begged off from a predawn visit to the Imperial Tombs the following day to see the sun rise over them. The two men compromised on a seven AM start.

Tran accepted the message from Anders and the defacto command of the PRU. He was quietly happy for a prolonged rest from field duty and planned to let the paper work and orders pile up. Ky was more pleased than Tran and quickly made plans of his own to spend the period of respite profitably, emphasizing the profitably in his mind. A return visit to the Golden Triangle was overdue, and a full month would grant him enough time to do real business. When he went to see Tran, he had to work to contain his enthusiasm knowing it would not do to appear to be in a vacation mode. It strained his imagination to come up with a plausible excuse for the need to be absent. He hit on a novel idea, quite original in his experience. He decided that he would tell Tran the truth. Some of it, anyway. Enough to convince the man. He also planned to include his comrade-in-arms into his business affairs to ensure his success and security. He hoped to inveigle the stuffy Saigon native into performing part of the real work as well, if possible, and into accepting direct payment.

He reckoned that Tran's involvement would be ensured if the man accepted money; and it would make his, Ky's, own lot less burdensome by taking away one more tier of deviousness and duplicity he had to remember and to contend with. With Tran working with him, it would not be particularly difficult to involve the other four members of his team, even the round eye.

Ky made his pitch in the context of a casual conversation with Tran the following day. Tran was sitting at Anders' desk.

"What do you plan to do with the unit for the month, oh, exalted one?" he queried with a jocular smile.

"Nothing," Tran responded.

"Sounds good to me," Ky said. "We might get a little soft and loose, don't you think?" he posited.

"Oh we'll do PT, keep tough. But Anders wants us to keep our heads down for the month, keep out of trouble. He thinks it will throw the VC off, and I think we need the rest. How about you?"

That was the opening he had been seeking. "Well, since you ask, my friend, I'd like to put an idea before you. I have a need to do some serious business elsewhere. Over west." He nodded his head in the appropriate direction. He paused to see Tran's response. There was nothing of note.

Ky drew in a breath between his teeth and exhaled his next paragraph. "I need to be gone for the month without a lot of records showing my absence. I have some business associates outside this country who are willing to pay well for some services I can do for them. I would be willing to share some of the profits with you and the others."

Tran's eyebrows arched a little. He knew about Ky's involvement in the heroin trade, but what caused his reaction was the suggestion that he be included as well.

"We are in a perfect position for this business, Tran. Think about it. We can plan all our own missions without anyone telling us when or how. We can come and go without raising questions from anyone who matters. We have access to planes and trucks and to guarded mail. We can get money from the Americans' bottomless money bag. The American CIA covers our strange activities with all its secrecy, and it has come to me more than once that the CIA itself is deeply involved in the traffic. We are good soldiers, a strong loyal unit, and do not have to trust any outsiders. We're perfect," he exaggerated.

Tran was thoughtful. Ky took that as a positive sign. "What business? Drugs?" Tran asked as if he were unaware.

"Heroin, the best China White. I can't tell you the details about the Golden Triangle end except to say that there are two armies that control growing and manufacture, and protect their runners, me. Those people are touchy, very, very careful people. But we can control our end. I'd like to get set up; so, we can eventually buy from them and sell for what we can get. That is something I hope to arrange this trip."

"How does that involve me, us?" Tran queried cautiously.

"Money and time," Ky said flatly.

"For services?"

"Yes, like protection when I take a delivery. There are bandits all over the roads and hills, and . . ."

"And?"

"And I would like to take money with me and to try to make a buy this trip."

"And you don't have enough on your own."

"Not enough to make such a long and dangerous trip worthwhile. I would just go and be the errand boy again without it."

Tran digested all of that for a long time. Ky had to sit patiently. He knew he had said enough. If he appeared to be pleading or to be overselling his position, he would spook Tran and queer the deal.

"How much money?" Tran finally asked. Ky knew he had his teammate hooked.

"You mean for me to take over to the Golden Triangle?"

"That and how much do we stand to make for our risks?" Tran asked pragmatically. He was responding like a businessman. Ky's spirits started to soar.

"I figure that we can start with a hundred thousand dollars worth. We should be able to come up with that much between us. The demand is so high for that stuff now that the Americans are here that we ought to be able to make upward of a million dollars just on one trip!" Ky was unable to control his rising ebullience. Tran was responding, too.

The prospect of having enough money to be independent, secure from the vagaries of Asian politics, endless war, and of being rooted to one poor place while others controlled him was eminently tantalizing to Tran. He had never allowed himself the luxury of fantasizing about financial well-being before. He had always been a rule obeyer, even if the rules he obeyed were not always in exact concert with the nation's laws. At least his actions had always been honorable in his own sight. He felt a degree of pride in knowing that none of his activities had been for personal gain. And the thought wriggled its way into his thinking that his so-called honor had brought precious little benefit for him, and maybe it was time for him to look out for himself. It was too late for his family.

Another thought worked its dark way into his reverie. He had not knowingly injured an innocent person, certainly never for his own profit. What about this drug business? People got hurt; he had to admit to himself; and he could not get around the knowledge that he was contemplating being a part of the traffic. Use of the poisons was, nevertheless, a personal choice, he rationalized; and he would only be one to reap the profits. If not him, then certainly someone else.

Opium had been around for centuries doing its harm, always by the choice of the user, so long that it was accepted as an integral part of traditional Asian life. Heroin was moving toward the western world in vast quantities, literally by the ton. The users knew what they were doing, east or west; no one forced them; it was a matter of their free agency. They did not have a disease that required them to use addictive substances; they simply enjoyed the effects of the substances. Doubts nibbled at his complacency, but he was able to relegate them to his underactive Asiatic superego.

Tran turned to speak. He had been very thoughtful, obviously weighing an important decision. Ky thought that alone was an encouraging sign for him. He felt hopeful as he watched Tran's mouth begin to open. He all but held his breath.

"I will talk to the others today. Everyone has to be in or no one. Except you. The unit is more important than the money. I made that decision a long time ago, Ky," Tran finally said.

Bach and Dung were less convinced when Tran put it to them. Ky was able to persuade the two of them that their role in the massive drug trade would be as middle men. They would neither produce the product nor induce the habit in the users. Their expertise would be to move the merchandise through an uncertain and often dangerous transport route. Ky was less convincing when it came to the matter of personal finances—the backing required to fund the first purchase. They argued with Ky and at times with Tran about the risks. Finally, Tran offered a compromise. He acknowledged the appropriateness of their concerns for the safety of one man carrying so much money through such hostile country. It was his idea that one of the other PRUCs should accompany Ky. Ky was leery of how his partners at the western end would react to a second man, but finally was forced to agree to the condition. A coin toss determined that Bach would go with Ky.

Tran dreaded broaching the issue with Anders; but Tran was accepted as the number two in the unit; and the lines of communication usually went from the Tran to the American PRU/O. No one could really tell what went on in the minds of the Occidentals, and that increased the difficulty. Anders was very young and might react with a young man's idealism. For all Tran knew, Anders might be a quiet Christian zealot of some sort and could react with great righteous indignation. However, he had not protested when they had kept the VC money and gold for themselves. How much of a hypocrite and purist could he be? The others had decided that Anders was more like a world-wise Vietnamese than an adherent to that strange Judeo-Christian ethic, that seemed to change with the winds and the seasons. "He is a soldier who does not flinch at killing—that is a violation of that Christian way, isn't it?" Tran reasoned as he got his courage up to talk to Anders.

These troubling thoughts mulled about in his mind as he arranged for the Huey pilot to take him into Hue'. At 1800 he was waiting in the lobby of the Huong Giang Hotel when Anders walked in after his day long tour of the Citadel and the Imperial City.

"Uh, oh," Anders said to himself, and then aloud, "This must be pretty important," to Tran when the two men saw each other in the lobby.

"I think it is, Anders. Can we talk here?" Tran asked. He was keeping enough distance between himself and his Caucasian PRU chief that others people in the lobby would not notice that they were conversing.

"No, better in my room—212. Wait five then come on up." Anders was already walking away.

Tran tapped lightly on the door to Anders' room in the prescribed five minutes, and Anders let him in. "Okay, what is it?" Anders asked without preamble. Tran was still not used to the American directness. A Vietnamese would have chatted about a dozen different unrelated and unimportant topics before getting to the consequential issue. The more significant the communication, the longer the interval of polite patter.

"It's about Ky, about an idea he has," Tran launched right in. Anders gave a little sigh of relief that he did not have to listen to some bad news about his men. He let Tran tell the whole story, give all the pro and con arguments, and wrestle with the moral question without interrupting.

Only after Tran signaled that he had said it all did Anders take his turn. "I don't like it personally. People in police work shouldn't be involved; people shouldn't use that junk. People shouldn't make money from it." Tran let him ramble. It was very reminiscent of his own conscience's wrestling match. Anders was musing out loud; something he had to do to get it out of his system; and it was his usual way of working out problems with Tran.

Tran briefly interrupted, "In a perfect world, it wouldn't happen. We would have plenty of money and safety. People wouldn't be poor, and armies wouldn't tromp all over them . . ." Tran let his sentence trail.

"But it's not a perfect world. That's what you're getting at, right?" asked Anders.

Tran nodded. He was willing to wait for Anders to take the logic all the way through.

Anders continued his out loud musing, "I've thought about money a lot. My folks never had any, and we were treated like dirt. People like us never had a chance against the rich people. We just clean up after them. Then I saw how the poor people, the really poor people in the Philippines and here live, always under someone's heel.

"I have also put a lot of thought into our situation. I have more than a sneaking hunch that the blame for this dirty little war is going to fall on guys like us who don't get to see the whole picture or to make the big decisions. One of the Company guys warned me that we might be charged as war criminals like Hitler's people even though we were just obeying orders. My dad always said that it always runs down hill, and the little guys are always at the bottom of the hill waiting for it to fall on them.

"When they shanghaied me into the army, I made up my mind that I was not going to end up like my dad or any of the other poor fools at the bottom. I also swore that I would get even. The difference is money. Without it you get crapped on. With it you have a chance. This war can't last forever. I suppose I'll have to go back to the World someday, and I am not going to go there without money. A lot of it.

"I guess that means I'm in." When he came right down to it, Tran guessed that Anders had put it just about as accurately as it could be stated for any of the men. Right or wrong, dangerous or not, he and his friends were about to step over the line; and tomorrow morning they would be international drug smugglers. Also, in the end analysis, Tran was not too upset by the notion.

Perhaps Anders was too tired to ruminate about it; or more to the point, he believed that he was basically accurate in his description of how the world worked and that he must take his share, and then some, by his own force; or someone else would eat his lunch before he got the chance. And he would be down there at the bottom where his father had spent his life. Or perhaps he had seen and done too much at a young age to visualize himself going back to some little job, a wife and kids, and being a church deacon. There was too much blood on his hands for him to be accepted in ordinary society again; he knew that much instinctively. He might as well make the best of what the fates had determined. Whatever was the case, Anders did not let it interfere with his deep and dreamless sleep.

CHAPTER 26

Ky and Bach flew out of the compound on the PRU helicopter before dawn the next morning. They were laden with weapons, concealed money, and enough food for emergencies. They expected to be in the Golden Triangle in a week if Ky could make all his contacts.

———————————◦◆◦———————————

Anders' alarm was the radio, Armed Forces Network. The broadcast began at six o'clock exactly, as it did every morning, with the Chicken Man's long drawn out "Goo-o-od mo-o-orning Vi-et Na-am!" followed by a selection of currently popular American rock and roll music that sounded to Anders like monkeys banging on pots and pans with spoons. At least it was too loud to let him stay in bed. Anders struggled to get up and forced himself to wake up enough to face a shower, a shave, his clothing, and the day.

The old man taxi driver, guide, and Hue' historian extraordinaire was waiting in front of the hotel in his puffing Peugeot when Anders stepped out into the sunshine at five of seven. He had sheltered the perverse hope that the guide would be late.

"Get in, get in, young sir!" the old man's cheery, crackly voice called. He was leaning across the tattered front seat and straining his wiry old body to hold open the passenger side door for Anders. It was too early to be voluble and much too early to hurry.

The Peugeot motored along dark tree-lined streets coming alive with the movements, sounds, and smells of another day. Anders took in the sensual pleasures of the sight of the lotus ponds, the sound of gonging Buddhist bells, and the smell of spring flowers. They passed the MACV compound, blatant symbol of the American war machine, the Provincial Capitol building, a potent reminder of the French Colonial era, the Cercle Sportif with is verandahs and its furnishings that were new and elegant in the 1930s, and the decade old University of Hue'.

The elderly guide filled in the travel time with a patter about himself and his every day life, about his multitudinous family, and with gossip that might have brought a smile to Bao Dai and his intimates but which was too archaic, pedantic, and exclusive to be of any interest to the young American whose limited education and concerns were centered elsewhere. They drove south and west to the line of mausoleums holding the remains of seven of the thirteen Nguyen emperors from Gia Long to the site reserved for Bao Dai "who was still alive, but not still an emperor," bemoaned the guide. The tombs were placed from farthest away to nearest the Citadel in order of earliest to latest emperor. The Valley of the Nguyens was selected to shelter the bones of the ancestors of the Vietnamese state and represented a break with the old tradition of burying even the greatest leaders in their home villages; so, their bones could be in common ground with their ancestors.

After a bone jarring ride, Anders and the elderly driver parked on *Bach Son*, White Mountain, sixteen kilometers from the King's Knight tower and looked back over Hue' as morning warmed and lightened the city. The tomb of Nguyen Anh, or Gia Long, as he preferred, was perched on the top of the mountain in a pine forest, and even Anders with his limited imagination could envision the splendor of the building and its grounds as it had been when it was completed in 1820. The dilapidation of the buildings and the overgrowth of the forest infringing on the once manicured grounds did not detract from the natural beauty of the location.

As the two men alighted from the older Vietnamese driver's antiquarian vehicle and prepared to walk to the tomb, a black pajamed young man, carrying an AK-47 at the ready, materialized from nowhere, startling the preoccupied tourists. Anders made a reflex move for his concealed weapon. The old driver put his hand quickly on Anders' forearm as a caution. "VC tax collector," the old man whispered. Anders remained tense.

The young VC approached them warily, but amicably. "Tourists?" He asked in the harsh dialect of the north.

"Yes, Comrade Collector. I am but the humble driver. The tourist is from Sweden . . . with the Red Cross."

"100 P.," the young man said blandly.

The old driver attempted to haggle but was stopped abruptly. "No bargain. This is the people's tax. Tourists . . . all tourists must pay to see the treasures of Viet Nam."

The old driver protested that he was not a tourist, but a worker. It was to no avail. Anders forked over the 200 piastres, and the young VC melted back in to the adjacent forest. Anders shook his head in disbelief—a tax collecting shadow government operating with complete impunity within ten miles of the capital city of a South Vietnamese province swarming with US and GVN military personnel. It was a matter of course to the old Vietnamese driver. He motioned Anders to follow him into the mausoleum compound.

The buildings had long since been desecrated by uncaring peasants who drove their domestic animals over the areas that had once been luxurious gardens and had pillaged the structures themselves until only shells remained. "Do you wish to know of our illustrious ancestor, young sir?" asked the earnest guide. Anders could not say "no."

"Our Nguyen First Lord was a man known in his early life as Thang Chung and also as Nguyen Anh or Nguyen Rhuoc Anh. Only this young man survive the Tay Son Rebellion and so was made king and general of the loyal army in the year 1780. He invited the French to give aid, and signed a treaty with them in 1787, but the long nose governor refused to honor that alliance and would not come to brave Nguyen Anh's aid. So, the king turned to his friend, the hero, Monseigneur Pigneau de Behain, a French missionary, who helped bring in French volunteers despite the governor. The king changed his name to Gia Long and gained control of the whole of Viet Nam and founded the great Nguyen dynasty in 1802. He united the country, created a central government, and made Hue' his capital. He was a great man, a man of strength of the loins who had thirty-one children—thirteen of them were sons." The old man's eyes glistened with pride and nostalgia as his mind's eye beheld the grandeur that was now lost in antiquity.

Gia Long's tomb consisted of several buildings: *Minh Thanh*, the Temple of Radiant Perfection, on White Mountain; the mausoleum itself stood on *Chanh Trung*, the Center Hill; and the Pavilion of the Stele was on *Thanh Son*, the Blue Mountain. Anders walked rather reverentially behind his enraptured guide as they picked their way through the ruined funereal courtyard, along the Triumphant Way lined with the remains of once handsome and meaningful statues, and down the short walls of the six tiered terrace. The guide read the inscription in the Pavilion placed there by Ming Mang, Gia Long's fourth son, as an honor to his father and to one of his wives and a sister.

Emperor Ming Mang's tomb was next on the itinerary and had to be reached by boat. The two men found a boatman back at their starting place, the Perfume River Hotel, directly across from the mausoleum. The funereal center was located at the confluence of the Ta Trach and Huu Trach branches of the Huong Giang. As the boatman poled over to the mausoleum, Anders' guide told him about the second emperor. "Nguyen Phuoc Dam, who took the name, Ming Mang, was the fourth of Gia Long's sons and was against the long noses and all Europeans and Christians." The guide could not disguise his antipathy toward foreigners and their ideas, Anders being the notable exception, Anders supposed. "He published the anti-Christian edicts in 1825 and made his people proud of all things Vietnamese. He was the one who built the Imperial city. He, like his great father, was a man of strong loins. He had one hundred forty-two children including seventy-eight sons. His death was greatly mourned." The guide looked mournful.

The funereal site lay nearly fourteen kilometers upriver from the Citadel. The multiple buildings were the grandest of the tombs, the work of anonymous craftsmen; and the actual burial site, was situated on a mound, the whole area modeled after the Ming Dynasty tombs in Beijing, China. The buildings were completed in 1843 at the zenith of the Nguyen Dynasty. Anders and the old man entered via the *Dai Hong Mon* (Grand Red Gate) and wandered about admiring the Pavilions, bridges, porticos, covered buildings, funerary tablets, temples, the *Trung Ming Ho* (Lake of Pure Light), and the *Tan Nguyet Tri* (the Lake of the New Moon). It was the best time of year to visit the tomb site because the two lakes were resplendent with a covering of crimson colored lotus flowers on large floating lotus pads.

The tomb itself was approached by Anders and his guide via a path named the Triumphant Way. The mound on which the mausoleum sat was surrounded by statues of elephants, military mandarins, and stylized bronze lions that guarded the emperor's last resting place. Anders found the site of the palace in miniature to be a place of tranquillity, a place he liked to linger, there in the Thau Thien morning.

"He died after he fell off his horse," the gnarled old guide said, breaking their quiet contemplations. "Such an insignificant end for one of the truly great ones."

Anders found himself in complete agreement and also found his thoughts tinged with sadness for the country at the loss of Ming Mang. He reconciled his own Mormon upbringing and American citizenship against the emperor's anti-Christian, anti-foreigner attitudes and policies and decided that Ming Mang acted appropriately and realized that he, Anders, now felt much the same way. He was surprised at the degree to which he had gone native.

The next tomb in the line going back toward the Citadel, now ten kilometers from the King's Knight, was that of Nguyen Hoang Thi, the eldest son of Ming Mang, a man who was even more rabidly hostile to all things foreign than was his father. He destroyed every foreign object that came into his presence. "He made jokes about the French and their tantrums. He was a great emperor, a conqueror," explained the enthusiastic guide. The old man regaled Anders with anecdotes about the emperor's triumphs in battle against the Khmers, his insults to the French, and his cruelties to the accursed Christians. Anders found himself regarding Nguyen Hoang Thi as a hero. His own George Washington, Abraham Lincoln, and Dwight D. Eisenhower, were fading from the front of his consciousness. Nguyen Hoang Thi's mausoleum housed the remains of a man who died of a stroke brought on by news that "the long-noses were bombing the Vietnamese coastline," his guide told Anders. "How sad," he added, "because it was only a rumor."

Nine kilometers upriver from the King's Knight, the two men stopped at the tomb of Nguyen Phuoc Hoang Nhan or the Tu Duc. They were hungry, and the old man pulled out a baguette for each of them, some excellent French summer sausage from which he cut thick man-type slices, and a ball of jasmine rice flavored with *nouc mam* and tightly compacted. A peddler came by, and Anders bought some longans and grapefruit for which the area was renowned. They drank Evian water and stretched out on the rock slabs laid down by the emperor's workmen over a century ago.

"Nhan was the youngest son of Nguyen Hoang Thi. He reigned for thirty-six years, the longest of any of the Nguyen emperors. He had one hundred four wives, more concubines than that and yet he died leaving no heirs," the old man told Anders as they soaked up the sun. "It was the fault of the long-noses. He lost the force of his balls from catching their smallpox disease!" His old face wrinkled in ire and hostility at the very thought of the great loss.

"How come the oldest son wasn't made the emperor? I thought that was how those guys did it in those days?" Anders asked. His arm was crooked over his eyes to shield them from the intense sunrays. His skin was so darkly tanned that he was past getting a sunburn.

"Ah, yes. Most unfortunate. The elder brother was one Hong Bao. He lost his birthright because he led a revolt in 1848. Nguyen Phuoc

Hoang Nhan became a hero, led the counterrevolt and had his brother and all his family killed to save the country. The accursed Christians were behind it all; and so, the new emperor, now called Tu Duc, rightfully set out to stamp them out."

"I guess he didn't do that too well, judging from all the Catholics and their churches I see around the country," Anders observed.

"Almost right, young sir," the guide agreed. "However, the reason he was not successful was beyond his control. The long noses and the ones called the Spanish (he pronounced it Spain-ish) took the chastisement of their co-religionists as an excuse to invade our country. They occupied South Viet Nam and called the area they controlled by the force of their devil's weapons a colony, saying it belonged to them. They gained control of North and Central Viet Nam also, may their souls be separated from those of their ancestors forever," he spat. His expectoration was thick and red—the product of a big chew of betel nut, areca leaves, and lime juice

After a nap, Anders and the old historian-guide walked around the *Xung Khiem* (the Pavilion of the Emperor's Boats), on Kheim Lake where Tu Duc had come to fish and to write poetry. They ascended the staircase and walked into the main building. Inside the cool dark building, there were remnants of the original luxurious furniture, vases, and assorted other antiques. They browsed about the interior of the Luong Kheim Mausoleum, once a second royal home, where there were still votive objects and urns present for the worship of the emperor and his wife. "I think he is not buried here," the old guide said in a conspiratorial low voice. "The Montagnards who did the work were executed after it was finished so no one could live to tell where the actual burial site was located." The two men left the mausoleum and admired the twin rows of man and animal statues leading to the stele engraved with stone etchings of the emperor's hand writing.

Anders was taken to the Duc Duc Pavilion and pagoda erected to the memory of the hapless successor to Tu Duc. The young nephew (adopted by Tu Duc) had led an improper life, failing roundly to observe any of the Buddhist laws or rituals. He was obese, at times indulging in orgies of gluttony with fifty course meals, and given to debauchery in defiance of the laws of self-control and abstinence. Only three days after ascending to the throne in July, 1883, the Counsel of Regents sentenced the young man to starve to death. In a week he was dead. He was interned near Tu Duc.

The next small mausoleum on Anders' tour that day was that of Heip

Hoa, Tu Duc's brother, who was crowned in the summer of 1883. He offended the same powerful regents and was assassinated

After hearing about these violent policies and ends, Anders asked his guide if that was the way everybody lived then, and was surprised by the terse answer from the old fellow, "And now," was all he would say. Anders had to admit that his scanty knowledge of American history suggested that his own people were not much gentler.

The guide continued, "The nation fell into bickering. The Hue' Court Counsel controlled the weak next emperor, a mere boy of fifteen. The infighting in the court left them all weak, unable to prevent the Chinese pirates from raiding successfully whenever and wherever they wanted. The long-noses took that weakness as an excuse to become the policemen for the entire state. They made all of Viet Nam into one of their protectorates by June 1884. The young emperor was poisoned by one of the regents, it is said. It was the beginning of the end for the proud nation of Viet Nam. The beginning of the end for the Nguyen Emperors' dynasty."

Anders had to shake his head. It sounded altogether like what he had learned about the English or the European monarchical histories. People in power were alike all over the world, he decided. The Vietnamese were no better and no worse than the rest.

"Ham Nghi, the next emperor in line, did not have a better life," mused the old driver as he drove the wheezing vintage Peugeot toward Chau Chu village where the tomb of Khai Dinh, or Buu Dao was located. "He was another nephew of Tu Duc," the old man said of Ham Nghi, "who was only placed on the throne because the Frenchmens wanted him there. The long-noses then divided up and completely conquered our country after that. They did not conquer our spirits, though!" he said defiantly, again showing his young chauvinistic spirit breaking free of the tethers of his old body.

"Then still another of Tu Duc's nephews was coronated in 1885— Dong Khanh. The country was ruled by a long-nose governor general. He was like the French President. They lumped together Viet Nam, Cambodia, and Laos into something they called Indochina and tried to rule it all like one country. The foreigners did not understand the people of these countries. They did not know that we were very patient, and one day would see them all gone! Poor Dong Khanh, he died of malaria in 1889 and was buried near Tu Duc. The country gave up all of its rights as a sovereign nation, and its economy and social life came to be firmly under the control of the French. The next emperor, Thai, was deported and had to live out much of the rest of his life in Cap St. Jacques—Vung Tau—and on Reunion Island off the coast of Africa. He returned after the Second World War to live for a few years and to die in Viet Nam. He was also buried in the Tu Duc mausoleum grounds near his father Duc Duc." By this point in the tour, Anders shared his guide's antipathy toward the French.

The old guide said, "Duy Tan, who was the son of Than Thai, was made the next emperor in 1907. He was eight years old at the time of his ascension. In 1916 he became a hero to the Vietnamese people by plotting to overthrow the long-noses. They deposed and deported him to their Reunion Isle. But in 1945, the president of the long-noses, De Gualle, asked him to return as emperor to replace Bao Dai who had abdicated to the Viet Minh. They were fighting the invaders, the ugly ones, the Japanese. He would have come back and restored the dynasty to its great glory, but that was not to be. The airplane carrying him from the long-nose island crashed, and he was killed. As yet there is no proper burial place for this hero of our nation." The old man finished his monologue as he pulled in and stopped at the tomb of Khai Dinh.

The tomb for Khai Dinh or Buu Dao was located on the right band of the River of Perfumes and was a tall one, as high as that of Ming Mang. It was in Chau Chu village, ten kilometers from the King's Knight.

The guide started up his narrative as he and Anders walked about the grounds, "This one was the son of Dong Khang and became emperor in 1916. He was thirty-one. He, too, put up a struggle against the accursed Frenchmens. He knew them close up because he had lived in their country and knew what terrible people they are. When he tried to make Viet Nam a modern country, but a Vietnamese kind of country, the long-noses stopped him. He died in 1925. Let us look at his funny burial place," said the guide smiling at the prospects of showing the garish structure to another client who had become used to seeing the handsome traditional architecture of the foregoing tombs.

"Okay," said Anders. He was tired, tired of looking at old buildings; but he did not say more, fearing to offend the genial old man who was such a fountain of knowledge about the land Anders had come more and more to think of as his adopted home.

The tomb was built in a completely out-of-place flamboyant 1920s European pop art style somewhere between a European castle and an ersatz cathedral, not unlike that of John Gaude, the Barcelona architect, whose work inspired the term 'gaudy.' There was nothing about it that fostered tranquillity as did Ming Mang's or Tu Duc's resting places. It was very prominently located atop a hill and was enclosed by a cement wall on which were studded porcelain tiles, colored glass, and small colored stones. The grandiose mausoleum was fronted by a courtyard located at the top of a long stone dragon staircase on whose sides were a pair of matching pavilions.

At the top of the those stairs, the two visitors had to rest. The old man had to admit finally that stairs were his undoing, and would his young friend mind if they gave his old legs a chance to get the blood flowing again? The courtyard in which they sat was lined with statues of elephants, horses, and civil and military mandarins giving it a busy, almost alive appearance. The old man caught his breath.

Another set of stairs led to another Triumphant Way, so popular with the architects of the Nguyen tombs over the centuries. In the center of the Way was a pagoda stele that was built by the last emperor, Bao Dai, and inscribed with a complimentary message in Chinese lettering in honor of his father. After another rest and another drink of water, the guide made himself go on. The two of them climbed the stairs to the Triumphant Way, crossed it, and climbed still another set of stairs to the main mausoleum building. They rested one more time before going in. Anders was becoming concerned about his companion.

A peculiar cement portico, built to look like a tent flap or a French awning, stood over the center piece of the entire funereal architectural collection. The walls were decorated with tens of thousands of inlaid ceramic and glass fragments depicting animals, flowers, and trees. The floor was paved with colored tiles, and the ceiling was decorated with a huge mural painting of a dragon in the clouds. "The artists painted the entire picture holding their brushes with their feet," the guide told Anders. He and his guide looked with measured awe at the handsome and dignified bronze statue of Khai Dinh sitting on his throne. His remains lay buried beneath the statue. "I knew this one," the guide said politely. "He tried his best to bring back our proper Nguyen dynasty government and to restore Viet Nam to the way it should be." He bowed his head in traditional courtly respect.

"I think we should call it a day," said Anders when they had descended the series of steps and retraced their route back to the old car. The elderly taxi driver and historical guide looked to be overly tired.

"Yes, sadly, young man," said the old guide, almost apologetically. "Our day is done. You must return one day to see the last tomb, that of Vinh Thuy when it is completed."

"Vinh Thuy?"

"Better known as Bao Dai."

"But he is still alive, right?"

"True, but his tomb has been planned so that when he dies, he can rest in this valley of the Nguyen kings. No matter what he says, he is still the emperor of Viet Nam. Even he knows it in his heart," the guide suggested, "because he keeps the imperial seal with him all the while he lives the life of a playboy—are you familiar with that term?—in France." Anders nodded his understanding.

Bao Dai was born in 1914, the only son of the sitting emperor, and originally named Vinh Thuy. At the age of twelve, in 1926, he was crowned as his father's successor. He traveled to and studied in France on several journeys over the course of a number of years. He was returned to Viet Nam by the French to assume titular power only, but failed to cooperate. In fact, he refused to share any control of his country with the French nor they with him; so, he spent most of his time trying to maintain a fragile peace and to hold on to the last vestiges of dignity left the former dynasty. However, when the Viet Minh gained full control of the North from the French usurpers, Bao Dai formally abdicated in 1945, handing over the imperial seal to the Viet Minh. Ho Chi Minh appointed him a Supreme Counselor.

Shortly thereafter, Bao Dai could not stomach the autarchy of the communists any better than he could tolerate control by the French interlopers; so he publicly severed relations with the Viet Minh and their government and went into exile in Hong Kong. He was briefly reinstated as emperor by the French in the vain hope that his presence could at least establish stability and at most, in the long run, reestablish the union of the north and south. His return failed in both aims—the polarization of Viet Nam on political, religious, philosophical, and even family bases was so great that no amount of diplomatic machination could halt the crystallization of the division. The French were defeated and driven out at the siege of Dien Bien Phu; the Geneva Conference codified the differences that could not be resolved; and inevitable open conflict, the Second Indochinese War, resulted. All of this Bao Dai watched from the safety of his exile in France, the old guide informed his young charge.

Anders got something important out of his two days with the venerable old guide. He became vitally interested in an academic subject for the first time. He determined that he would understand the history of Viet Nam and, as a derivative, the American involvement in the Second Indochinese War when he started his school career at the

University of Hue' in the fall. It seemed that he had been In Country for years, for most of his life, even though it was more like a single year. More and more, he had come to think of Viet Nam as his country, if not quite his home yet; and he wanted very much to know what he could about it. He harbored a small hope that, by doing so, he might be able to make some small contribution to peace in that assailed land. That, he knew, was a peculiar and grandiose ambition for a young man whose sole assigned purpose was to prosecute the American involvement in the dirty little war by kidnapping, killing, and undermining the nationalists in the country, and was a heady aspiration for one lacking a high school education, recognized rank, or even unequivocal individual identity. But he was young; and like the young everywhere, billeted idealistic notions of his own significance somewhere in the back of his psyche despite all of that.

Ky and Bach scrambled off the Huey and onto the grassy landing zone in less than an hour from the time of takeoff from their PRU compound. They were within walking distance of National Highway 9 and within hailing distance of the city of Khe Sanh and the border of Laos. At first, the area was silent and empty; so, the two men slipped into the fringe trees at the edge of the grassy meadow where they had landed and settled in to wait for their guides. They did not wait long; in twenty minutes Ky and Bach had the unpleasant sensation that they were being watched. They turned to look into the forest and saw three submachine guns leveled at their chests.

They were being circumspectly eyed by three Kachins from Burma who had been waiting all night and were prepared to take them across the border and on to Burma if they proved to be the right people. The reputation of the Kachins as cannibals made it highly desirable to be the right people. The Kachin soldiers were a taciturn trio who spoke very little. They waited, stone faced, until Ky gave them the agreed upon pass word for their safe conduct—"General Wu."

The Kachins nodded, lowered their guns, and beckoned for the two Vietnamese to follow them. The five men trotted through a narrow copse of trees until they came to a heavy Chinese produce truck parked on an obscure logging road connected to a main feeder to Highway 9. Ky and Bach laid their weapons and gear on the floor of the truck bed, and the Kachins rearranged the boxes of vegetables and fruits to hide them. A narrow space was left to accommodate the two Vietnamese, and they got in the back. The Kachins sat in the cab and wound their way over the dusty roads through the majestic purple mountains near Khe Sanh until they reached the border.

The truck waited at the border crossing point outside Khe Sanh for about an hour. The Vietnamese side required a careful scrutiny of all relevant papers and a modest bribe; and the Royal Laotian agents on the other side were less punctilious about matters of form, and more exacting about the gratuity. The five men were in the Kingdom of a Million Elephants and a White Parasol before the breakfast hour. Newspaper reporters covering the war there referred to Lao as "The Land of a Million Irrelevants."

Their next stop was at Seno where National Highway 13 intersected with Highway 9 and headed north. They dutifully stopped at the roadblock, paid the required baksheesh, a few hundred kip, and got out to stretch. The Kachins were secure enough that they now let the two Vietnamese men out to stretch and to get something to eat. There were rice vendors abounding in the busy town, and that was the only thing available to eat.

The importance of rice to the Laotians cannot be overestimated. There are thirty thousand kinds of rice in the northern Southeast Asian and nearby Chinese region. The Laotian word for breakfast, literally translated, is 'the rice that is eaten in the morning;' the word for dinner is 'the rice that is eaten in the day;' and the word for supper is 'the rice that is eaten at night.' It is the custom in weddings in Laos for the bride and groom to stand before the assembled family and to be served their own separate bowls of rice. Then, as the final symbol of their union, the couple mixes the rice from each of their own bowls into a single new one; and they eat from the common bowl.

Bach and Tran ate their fill from the bowls and with the chopsticks provided by the vendor they had chosen. The greasy little man wiped off the utensils and the eating bowl on his apron in preparation for the next customer. As they walked around and stretched their legs, the PRUCs saw many NVA soldiers and officers going about their duties in a land that was obviously theirs, or at least entirely under their grasp. The other military presence, and that in full abundance, was the Pathet Lao with soldiers in bulbous floppy hats on their heads and confident expressions on their faces. Of the Royal Laotian Armed Forces, there was not the slightest suggestion despite the Royal Laotian Government being the titular authority in the country.

The clothing stalls held a rich supply of foreign and domestic goods: *song kaboi*, Thai cowboy pants for young men; Vietnamese Ao Dais for young women; and American camouflage military clothing, still in the plastic wrappers marked PX. The only language spoken was Lao, the mother tongue of the ethnic, Buddhist Laotians, the Lao Lum—people of the low valleys. These people were contemptuous of the other sixty-seven ethnic groups.

When the five men began to clamber aboard the sturdy old truck, the Kachins divided up their places with one of them driving up front with Ky, and the other two sitting in the bed of the truck with the boxes of fruits and vegetables with Bach. Ky and Bach had been scrupulous in avoiding any impropriety that might have offended their hosts and had not touched any of the produce. The two Kachins smiled at that and offered the Vietnamese men as much as they could eat. In a further gesture of camaraderie, the fierce looking Burmese hill tribesmen shared their home-brewed hearts of palm wine that was old and thick, and tasted like varnish. They also shared gossip and useful trafficking information. All indications of suspicion and distrust vanished, and the pleasant and amicable natural instincts of the Kachins toward those deemed to be friends took over. The word Kachin means 'dancing friend and companion,' and the three Burmese men lived up to that description.

"Don't ca!e or the Lao Lum," observed the man driving the truck to Ky. "Too important, they think. Not treat the mountain people right. We of the UWSA, the people of Pang Hsang, know the Lao Theung, the Lao of the mountain sides, and the Lao Soung, the Lao of the mountain tops, and the Mien (Yao or Hmong) as friends. We help them, and they help us. It is well for you to meet them and to learn their routes. Could save your skin one day."

It was the dry season, two months past the monsoons. The truck rumbled for four days over the rutted highway, here and there swerving around a bomb crater, passing stubbly brown rice fields, recently harvested and awaiting the next planting. Occasionally they sighted an individual house or a small village, all on stilts with rooms open to such breezes as might occur. Under the houses were the necessities of family life—fish traps, live chickens, pigs, and the occasional cow, large earthen urns of fish paste, and firewood. Each home had its own jar of fermenting salted bamboo shoots used for the popular national dish, sour bamboo soup. Adjacent to many homes was a bomb crater fish pond. The people went about their agrarian existence oblivious to the international turmoil swirling just outside the range of their hearing.

570

Along the road they saw Viet Cong in black pajamas, NVA in their green uniforms, the occasional Chinese Red Army platoon in light khaki, flocks of ducks, pigs, and goats being herded to market, and women bearing the traditional burdens of fuel kindling, banana fronds, and cut reeds for house construction and repair, and urns of brackish water. Timber trucks bearing loads of rosewood, teak and sandalwood rumbled by going south in the direction of the capital, Vientiane.

Their first problem occurred just north of kilometer 50, not far from Vangviang, along highway 13. It was dusk. The source of the problem was not from the Laotians or the NVA, nor even from the frequent small bands of bandits, but from a thunderous raid by American bombers. All traffic scurried off the road as the already execrable path was bombed into a crater pocked dust track. The PRUCs and their Kachin hosts were unscathed—good joss—but had to delay their progress while some semblance of normalcy returned. Along the road they saw scores of civilians working their way back onto the road; many families keening their anguish over a child or a favored auntie that had absorbed the deadly pellets from one or another of the thousands of half fist-sized American bomblets (CBU-24s that contain 600 golf ball-sized bombs (bombies to the Lao), each of which holds 300 steel pellets) scattered by the unseeing monsters in the sky. The Kachins and the Vietnamese shrugged, "Too bad," they thought, "glad it wasn't me." They could not stop to give aid; after all, these were not their family, nor even their friends. The begrimed, dazed, and frightened innocents lifted clenched fists in anger and defiance at the now disappeared Americans.

At Ban Xanghai the Kachins turned abruptly west toward Louangphrabang, the second largest city in Laos, and once the royal capital, close to the Thai border. They stopped after dark in the highland outskirts of the city and spent the night in the moist heat of the truck. The following morning all five men bathed in the Xeng River with hundreds of local people, men and women, sharing the cool water with no suggestion of false modesty. An occasional small boat rowed by a lithe young girl, her glistening black hair extending below her waist, poled by. Small herds of brown cattle and black buffalo came down to the river to drink. The river banks were steep, planted in vegetables and marijuana, and here and there studded with a dud bomb sticking out of the muddy bank. No one touched the potentially lethal objects.

The women had spread homemade banana thatch mats to accommodate *phak nam*, a type of watercress, they harvested to be eaten as a popular leafy vegetable or dried as an herb. In other areas along the river, men, women, and children were digging bucketfuls of black sand for gold. They sifted the sand through leaky wooden pans, added silvery globs of mercury, and squeezed the mixture in cotton clothes the size of handkerchiefs. The mercury attached itself onto tiny flecks of gold. Merchants from the city were already at the river bank haggling with the peasant dredge miners to buy their products—compact dry balls, the size of a lichee nut. The Kachins explained to Ky and Bach that the merchants would now take the sandy balls back to town and blowtorch them to evaporate the mercury and leave the gold separated and nearly pure. Each peasant could earn a day's keep from his or her efforts thereby maintaining the hand to mouth existence in yet another way in that poor country.

The real purpose of the visit to the river was soon evident to the Vietnamese visitors. The three Kachins homed in on a thriving cluster of thatched sheds where oil drums could be seen sitting on top of hot beds of coals. "*Lau lao!*" (rice liquor) said the Kachins grinning in anticipation over what was evidently one of the better things in life.

The five men bought a tin can mugful each at the exorbitant price of fifty kip, half a day's wages for an employed peasant laborer. It was well distilled, smooth, and warm, but chokingly strong, approaching 200 proof. All five of them were mellow and full of conviviality when they weaved the truck into Louangphrabang later that morning. Bach was beginning to think that he could learn to like this drug-trafficking life. Ky knew he could.

In the market they saw for the first time the colorful Hmong people. Turbaned women who had come down from their mountain villages openly bartered their season's yield of opium and brilliantly patterned textiles they made on their family looms for cooking pots, soap, bacon, and salt. Many of the men carried stud roosters in compact woven bamboo cylinders for rental by the city dwellers who could not seem to produce the fine fighting stock so prized in the mountains. Every adult they saw, except the Buddhist bonzes, was armed to the teeth. A theater in the center of town advertised Bulgarian and Chinese movies with a local actor-translator taking all of the speaking parts in both movies.

There were money changers, Thai farmers hawking their produce, Viets and Thais selling western fashions, vitamins, and ginseng, small processions of nuns and monks walking to the beat of small wooden drums called Buddha's ears, and ubiquitous soldiery. There were no cars.

No one interfered with the five men, now bosom friends; their fraternal association oiled by the ethanolic lubricant, nor questioned their right to be a part of the mélange of humanity milling about the narrow streets. They drove past and admired the monasteries, Wat Xieng Thong, Wat Aphay, and Wat Vixun, built by the Khmer kings, all ancient and in a state of venerable decay. The men took a turn past the former royal palace, now virtually empty, but still decorated in gorgeous gold and brocade. They ate a brunch in one of the better restaurants, a soup with chicken, noodles, vegetables served with rice cakes and sticky dyed tapioca. The five visitors responded to the fine food and congenial surroundings in the same manner as the Laotians in the restaurant did. They placed their hands together and bowed to the proprietor and the cook and to the other patrons and bowed to show their unfeigned *maun* (enjoyment).

That evening, just before the border gates closed, the men crossed the Thai border from Ban Houayxay (after making friends with the border guards on both sides by humbly giving them gifts), passing over the Mekong River. They were in the Golden Triangle—the rich growing region where Laos, Thailand, and Burma join. They encountered no roadblocks until they entered Burma, a short distance to the north before the town of Mong Hsat. Here, the Kachins spoke directly to the border guards and presented a document to them. After a short wait in the Burmese customs building, the Kachins saw what they had been waiting for. A troop transport truck bearing the insignia of the United Wa State Army. A wiry intense platoon sergeant strode purposefully in and glanced rapidly around the room. Seeing the three Kachins and the two Vietnamese, he walked directly to them.

A grin opened his face showing yellow and decayed teeth in a broad, dentist's-nightmare grin. "Cousin!" he exclaimed, and clasped the youngest of the three Kachins in a bone breaking embrace. The two men clapped each other on the back, then the sergeant gave each man a Burmese cheroot, a gap-toothed smile, and gestured for them to follow him out to his truck. They left a generous tip in kyat, the Burmese currency, that the money changers had been happy to provide for a grossly inflated black-market commission, with the customs workers who responded with gracious and friendly bows.

The roads were much better in that section of eastern Burma than they had been in war ravaged Laos and neglected rural northern

Thailand. The young cousin followed behind in the troop truck. The two truck caravan passed west almost to the Salween River and made good time. They traveled north for over six hours at high speeds, approaching one hundred twenty kilometers an hour at times. The roads had been improved considerably over the past decade to accommodate the important teak wood logging trade.

Burma supplied nearly eighty percent of the world's teak, exporting upwards of eighty million dollars worth yearly. The heavy slash-and-burn deforestation logging methods left whole hillsides ugly, barren, and eroded. One of the Kachins told the Vietnamese guests that the harvest was nearly 500,000 tons a year of the strong yellow-brown wood, and that the forests were disappearing at the rate of between 200-250,000 acres annually, and were nearly half gone in 1967. They would be wiped out in twenty years, he estimated. It was not difficult to believe that. The troop truck was uncomfortable with only fold down canvas seats, but even then it was a better ride than the bed of the vegetable truck had provided.

The region was sparsely populated owing to the inability of the national government to gain control over the warring Kachins, Karens, and drug lords sufficient to ensure safe settlement. Over a third of the country was in control of one rebel organization or another. Only about ten percent of the Texas sized nation's twenty-four million people lived in the mountainous rural region.

Burma was a land of forests, valleys, and villages. The small cities, really overgrown villages, were clean from the Water Festival associated with the recent Buddhist New Year celebration where everyone doused every other one with water from hoses, buckets, water cannons, and an assortment of pumps. To honor their dead ancestors and the Lord Buddha the streets had been swept free of debris, and the ubiquitous pagodas gleamed like small suns from their new coverings of tissue paper thin gold leaf, applied each year at that time to give solemn thanks to Him for the bounties of the harvest. It had been a good rice, tea, grapefruit, and opium poppy production year, and the pagodas were especially resplendent.

The small cities were full of 1940 vintage automobiles and trucks, giving Ky and Bach the sense of having been caught in a time warp that put them back into the World War II era. Most of the buildings were moldering and falling into a ramshackle state—only the sturdy brick British colonial buildings appeared to have weathered the long storm of neglect.

Attractive girls carrying large trays of lemons and limes gracefully moved along the crowded streets, their faces covered with yellow patches of Thanaka, a powdered bark paste thought to prevent skin deterioration from the blazing tropical sun. Children wore the yellow paste in painted stripes giving them a festive mask-like look, as if it were national chipmunk day. Men walked, worked, and idled in patterned long tube like skirts called longyi, the traditional dress of both men and women in Burma. They smoked cheroots made of tobacco, ground bark, and corn husks that sparked and fumed, obscuring their faces.

The two trucks, after slowing down for a hairpin turn, were stopped at an impromptu roadblock thrown up on a winding mountain road. Kachin insurgents surrounded the trucks and demanded to see the driver's pass. An older man curtly demanded to know if they supported General U Ne Win and grinned a toothless smile when he was satisfied that the Wa State Kachins and the two Vietnamese were sympathizers with the old man's own cause. He offered to take them to see the shrine set up for U Aung San, the hero of Burma's independence, in his village. "Aung San was a great man," the old warrior declared. "He beat both the British and the Japanese. Our people in the frontier areas trusted him; and after he died, we never trusted anyone else from the government." The Wa State Kachin soldiers convinced the old man of their undying affirmation of Aung San's greatness, and that seemed to satisfy him.

When Ky and Bach's driver presented his clearance from the Wa State, the younger Kachins became friendly and even accommodating. The insurgents shared their lunches of yellow watermelon, garlic and chili spiced peanuts, and fished *jaggery*, a sticky candy, from boiling pots. They helped the two trucks to an allotment of their own black market cache of scarce gasoline and permitted them to purchase enough to fill their tanks at only double the fair market price in the cities. For the safety and success of their trip, the mother of one of the Kachin separatists approached Ky, Bach, and the Kachin guides. She was a famous local spirit medium, known throughout the Kachin State and even across the Shan Plateau, to have great influence with the powerful, and often malevolent netherworld spirits called *nats*. In honor of the visitors she presented offerings of rum and rice wine to keep the spirits, whom she knew by name, in good humor.

"The Brother Nats of Ke-hsi met particularly terrible ends at the hands of that living demon Ne Win," she growled and spat to punctuate her distaste, "and so they are always in a bad mood as they travel these hills. If you will wait here with us for the time of four days, we will honor these two Nats with a *nat pwe* (Nat Festival) and hopefully induce them to be protector Nats instead of causing so much trouble. What do you say?"

The Kachin drivers knew exactly what to say. "Old mother, we regret that we must be on our way. We have important business for the United Wa State Army, but we would be honored if you would accept this small contribution to your *nat pwe* so you can buy more good rum to appease the unfortunate brothers. Perhaps you can convey to them our respect."

The old lady clucked her regret, but showed that she understood by humbly and gratefully accepting the handful of khat notes proffered by the Wa State Kachin soldiers. The stop had been profitable for the travelers as well since they left with full gasoline tanks and with the firm knowledge that they need have no qualms about the mood of the local Nats.

The scenic journey took them past rivers thronged with graceful sampans piled to an unwieldy height with loads of bamboo, vegetables, teak, and large clay urns. The hillsides were dotted with circular hamlets where traditional communal living in a classless society still held sway. They encountered tough and turbaned hill Shans, short wiry tattooed Karen National Liberation Army soldiers wearing garlands of grenades, and patient villagers maintaining the languid pace of life so characteristic of historic Burma. The locals, now expert home builders after millennia of practice at the same skills, were at work constructing houses of leaves, straw, and giant bamboo with thatched roofs, woven mats and wall panels, open to the cooling mountain breezes. Pony carts, bicycles, trucks, and ox drawn wagons shared the roadway amicably. Pigs, chickens, goats, and cattle were audiences for the wallowing of water buffalo in ponds green with slimy algae. The travelers' eyes were treated to a verdant green landscape with tall straight teak trees, pyinkado and padauk hardwoods, and giant bamboo stalks dotted here and there with the pink or white blossoms of wild acacias and splashes of orange where domesticated opium poppies bloomed in a patch beside a rural home.

CHAPTER 27

The exercise of morality and the exercise of statecraft are
separate crafts.
Chanakua, advisor to Mauvyan Kings of India about 500 BC

After several hours of an
hematuria producing Burmese mountain road drive, the two trucks
made an abrupt left turn into a roadway that led through an unhar-
vested dense hardwood forest. There were guards every twenty
meters armed with ArmaLites and new appearing Kalashnikovs. At
intervals there were bunkers with swivel mounted large machine
guns, and on side roads there were tanks. Ky and Bach surmised
correctly that they were entering the Pang Hsang headquarters compound of the UWS.

Security was tight, and the soldiers were rigidly disciplined and
correct. Though he passed into the compound several times a day, the
Kachin sergeant had to display his papers and orders, and every man
went through a strip and body cavity search before being allowed to
enter the compound's triple ring concertina wire protected interior.
Ky and Bach were tired and covered with red dust from the compound's
single road. The Kachins took them to a small but well-appointed
BOQ where they were given a room to share.

"You are to rest tonight. Business tomorrow," the young UWS
sergeant told them. Otherwise no one spoke to the two Vietnamese.
The UWS were all business, and their business was the growing of
opium poppies, the extraction of the crude gum, and the delivery of
their product to the SUN people for processing in their refineries along
the Burma-Thai border. Nothing else mattered around that compound.

The 15,000-35,000 person army of the UWS, or the Wa People, as
they preferred to be known, controlled most of the poppy production
in Burma, and throughout the Golden Triangle—a horseshoe shaped

forested highland area east of the Salween River roughly the size of the American state of Nevada—and were, therefore, the largest single suppliers of opium in the world. Opium was Burma's most important product; and its growth, processing, and transport was a mainstay of the common people of the country as well as a source of enormous riches and power for its military-minded elite. The security of having such an army was neither pretentious nor extravagant. The Wa People and their enterprises had to contend with the large military forces of the national government under General U Ne Win, the Revolutionary Burma Communist party, the small armies of the multitudinous ethnic groups, and roving bands of freelance bandits.

Until 1962, Burma was the world's largest exporter of rice, shipping two million tons annually. But after the socialists, under General U Ne Win, seized power in that year, closed all borders, nationalized all industry, imprisoned all intellectuals and U Nu government executives, halted all developmental activities of the World Bank, forced all Indians and Chinese (the only indigenous Burmese businessmen) to flee the country, and drove out all foreign business—her economy failed.

The rice export fell to 170,000 tons; and civil warring among the seventy fractious ethnic groups made anything but opium production unprofitable for the majority of the peasantry. More than one-third of the gross national product became accounted for by smuggling, a natural response to the needs of the impoverished populace. To people whose average annual income did not exceed $179, the niceties of how one made a living were relegated to a low place on the list of concerns. The Burmese became rice importers and sophisticated drug refiners, transporters, marketers, and exporters.

The SUN, or Shan People as they preferred, maintained a 20,000 man army and concentrated their activities on the running and protection of refineries that turn out heroin by the ton. Together with the UWS, they owned and controlled more than 75% of all of the heroin produced in the area, and they were the largest supplier (70%) of the insatiable American market. They were responsible for 50% of the entire world's supply. The Shan People jealously guarded that status. Their $4-10 billion yearly trade afforded them ample profit to maintain a more than adequate security establishment and to deter any government that might foolishly try to rein them in. It also allowed them to participate in the hugely profitable and perfectly legitimate business of mining rubies and sapphires, the only other product worthy of mention in Burma.

"We welcome you, Phan Duy Ky. Our Wa People in Viet Nam have spoken highly of you," started the officer as soon as the two Vietnamese were seated for a working breakfast with the Burmese drug officials.

"Thank you," replied Ky decorously.

"We do not know your companion. We are uncomfortable with people we do not know, Ky. May I call you Ky?"

"Yes, sir. I prefer that my friends call me Ky."

"You may call me Captain Kyaing." The officer's face was blandly friendly, but his eyes were not. They were sculptured in an eternally suspicious squint. He spoke in clipped English, their only common language, since the Vietnamese were not versed in any of the more than a hundred indigenous Burmese languages or even more numerous subdialects. His accent was upper crust, Harrow or Eton, reflecting a holdover from the British colonial era when English was the official language and his own English public school undergraduate education. "Please introduce your companion."

"This is Le Duc Bach. He is a member of the Provincial Reconnaissance Unit of the American CIA and Vietnamese police."

"As are you."

"Yes."

"Your Binh Xuyên people vouched for you in the beginning; and you, yourself, have proved that you can be trusted; or you would not be here. We must have reason to develop such a trust in your friend."

"I can vouch for him. Sergeant Bach has been at my side in many battles and has proved himself to be an honorable and trusted friend."

"He knows much about our business having driven here without being prevented in any way from seeing and hearing. The council has decided to permit this irregularity and to make an exception in your case on the basis of your past performance. I will state only once that we are a family here, and we live for one another. We do not tolerate betrayers or thieves which are one and the same. There is no place on earth far enough away or obscure enough to hide such a person. I believe you know that, Ky. I will say no more on the subject."

Ky indeed remembered his object lesson—the man hanging between two poles in the mountaineers' village with birds pecking out his eyes while he was yet alive. He shivered. That response seemed to satisfy Captain Kyaing. He turned to Bach, and for the first time spoke to him rather than about him in the third person.

"Sergeant Bach, is it?"

Bach nodded deferentially.

"You will become part of our family, as Ky has done. You will profit handsomely. You will contribute importantly to the family of the Wa People. We will adopt you as one of our own. You must understand the significance which we attach to family loyalty. You must not ever give us reason to suspect you. As the Christians say, 'you must avoid even the appearance of evil.'" The man's eyes spoke volumes about cruelty and vendetta.

Bach bowed again. "I will earn your trust." Captain Kyaing appeared to like that succinct response.

Captain Kyaing continued. "There is a saying among our people that you might take to heart, Ky and Bach. 'I and my father stand against my brother and his family. My father, my brothers, and I stand against my uncle and his sons. My family, my uncles, and my cousins stand against the clan. My family and my clan can stand against the world.' We view the world as being divided up into 'us and them.' Because you have come here and have seen our enterprise, you can only be in the clan, or dead. Ky will be responsible for you, and you for him. Never allow yourselves to forget that nor to underestimate the Wa People."

"We would not betray the family," Ky said calmly and as matter-of-factly as he could but emphatically. "We look forward to a long and fruitful relationship. And we wish to include others of our police unit whom we can trust. Their names are Nguyen Lui Tran, Nguyen Van Dung, and a round eye named Anders Bergstrom. I have written them down for you. That way, you will know we remain family even as we include others whom we require for help."

"It will be necessary for me to meet them one day, and the council will have to approve them," stated the Burmese captain flatly. "Who knows, perhaps this Wa family can be of service to them. Remember that as well as you do the fate of traitors. We, too, look forward to a long and profitable relationship. If you have finished your morning meal, perhaps we can get down to the details of our business."

Ky produced the Vietnamese currency amounting to nearly $100,000 American dollars. Bach had been reluctant to have the money displayed until the deal was done, and the two bricks of pure white heroin were in hand. Ky had overruled him, saying that the act of placing all of their money on the table in such a totally unreserved fashion would be an indication of their unrestricted trust and allegiance. Bach kept his qualms to himself.

"Ah, a fine investment. Because you are family, we will give you two kilos for the price that only one would bring in Bangkok or Hue'.

We expect you to meet your expenses with the profits you will earn. Please note that this is China White, Heroin Number Four, not Black Tar. We will have the product loaded on one of our trucks, and you can leave for your homeland tomorrow under the protection of our Kachin brothers. Of course, you are free to inspect the bricks any time you wish." Ky took note of the fact that the captain had not deigned to count the currency before placing it in a large manila envelope.

Ky wisely followed the captain's example and said, "That will not be necessary, Captain Kyaing, my brother." The captain acknowledged the mutual gesture of trust with the barest wisp of a thin lipped smile.

That afternoon, the Kachin sergeant and the three men who had brought them from Viet Nam to Pang Hsang came to sit with Ky and Bach in the shade of a large parasol to watch a game of Chinlon. The men playing the game expertly kept the woven bamboo ball in the air without using their hands. A steward brought the visitors a delicious mixed rice, fish, chicken, and vegetable dish with a base of a *ngapi* sauce—a pungent, fermented and pickled fish paste—and bottles of chilled Tiger beer.

"I regret to tell you, my brothers, that two changes will occur on your return journey. First of all, different ones of our Kachin brothers will have to accompany you. Captain Kyaing's orders. Second, you will have to return by a different route through Laos. It is not safe to follow the national highways of Laos carrying the product. You will have to pass over the mountains with our brothers, the Hmongs and the Montagnards of your own country. It will cause you considerable delay, most regrettable; but it cannot be helped," the most senior of the affable Kachins told Ky and Bach.

The men spent the better part of the next hour enjoying their food and pouring their attentions over an excellent map. It was necessary for them to commit the map to memory since, for security reasons, the map could not be allowed to accompany them.

That night the compound held a Kachin sacrificial celebration, part animist, part Buddhist, and all Burmese. The traditions antedated the Kachins' involvement with Christianity. The men and women danced, sang, and played fast paced raucous music as they engaged in an orgy of monetary donations to the *bhikkus* (Theravada monk) who had been invited in for the traditional alms-giving ceremony. The happy contributors gladly parted with their treasures of carved wood, lacquer work, gold and silver artifacts, and pocketfuls of khat notes to the *bhikkus* despite their nominal adherence to Christianity. They danced themselves into exhaustion around a bonfire of old copies of "The Working People's Daily", the national government's official newspaper, in a festive gesture of defiance.

The Kachins were adoptees into the Wa People's army and joined them for the most fundamental of reasons—the pay was better than they could have dreamed possible in any other line of work, and they had been starving before entering into service as soldiers of the drug lords. There were estimated to be between 600,000 and one million Kachins and their close relatives, the Chins. The men who drove Ky and Bach to the headquarters and protected them through two countries were a combination of Christian and animist by religious preference which set them apart from the eighty-five percent of the rest of the country who were Theravada Buddhists. They came from very close knit families and supported each other absolutely. They were fiercely loyal employees once they pledged their allegiance to a leader or an organization; and with the familial good treatment they received from the Wa People, they were dedicated to the protection of their benefactors. They enjoyed a reputation of being the best and the most ferocious mountain and forest fighters in all history. In the Second World War, the Japanese army quaked at the prospects of engaging the indefatigable Kachin men in furtive guerrilla combat—men who decapitated their prisoners of war and feasted on their flesh. Given the chance, the Kachin's preferred method of killing was by slow roasting.

As strong as was their affection for and loyalty to the Wa People, they held the national government in an equally intense animus. They had nearly starved when, in the early 1960s General Ne Win, the Thakin, had overnight destroyed the value of the nation's currency and impoverished millions of previously prosperous citizens, including the Kachin hill people. Ne Win had capitalized on a national fascination with astrology and destroyed confidence in the currency by printing all notes with serial numbers that contained nines or multiples or additives of nine, the most unlucky number in the whole zodiac, thus rendering the money useless. The vicious efforts to put down the Kachin people and to stamp out their language and customs earned the dictator undying enmity. The Kachins' basic tenet of social intercourse with other peoples became an adherence to the age old principle of 'the enemy of my enemy is my friend.' The SUN and UWS drug lords were among the most virulent of General Ne Win's enemies.

Ky and Bach were glad to have the Kachins on their side. They were not overworried by the prospects of their return journey. The Burmese are mellow people, and the departure was delayed until nearly noon the next day. The stewards had to be sure that the guests had breakfasted; the captain insisted on giving them enough Burmese kyats and Laotian kips to see them through without embarrassment; and the compound sentries returned their weapons, insisting that they make a full inventory before accepting repossession.

Ky, Bach, and the contingent (four) of Kachins who accompanied them were delayed in their crossing over to Ban Houayxay in Laos by a brief firefight between government troops and a unit of the Karen National Liberation Army. The Burmese Army had made an incursion just to show the colors and to keep the Karens off their ease; but for the Wa People and their Vietnamese guests, it was all very civilized. The army set up a road block and halted all traffic until the skirmish was over, ostensibly to prevent civilian casualties, but more likely to prevent reinforcements to the hard pressed Karens. Whatever the reasoning, they only lost a day, and a few thousand more kyats to the Burmese Army major before they were allowed to proceed on their way, unmolested.

After transferring the customary border tribute, first in kyat, then in kip, the six men made good time back through Louangphrabang. It was late morning, and it appeared that all 50,000 inhabitants of the little city had chosen to clog the streets that day. A convoy of trucks hauling multicolored coffee beans bore the logo of an East German coffee brokerage. The trucks had snarled traffic so thoroughly that the Kachins decided to stop at a roadside stand for something to eat while the trucks cleared out. They bought a bag of frogs grilled to a crisp, a huge barbecued chicken, and four slices of Spam.

The six men ate lustily and observed the passage of Southeast Asian life while the parade passed inexorably slowly by a pair of water buffalo sleeping in the middle of the street. The animals were surrounded by a clutch of Buddhist monks holding out their begging bowls. A group of Hmong girls, decked out in their finest black clothing blazing with intricately applied brilliant embroidery and wearing kilos of silver and semiprecious jewelry around their necks and wrists, sold jewelry and embroidered fabrics, for which they were justifiably famous, to passersby who had to slow down at the bottleneck anyway. From somewhere, wafted the music of a *khene*, the traditional bamboo wind instrument.

At noon the drug smugglers passed through Ban Xanghai and started down National Highway 13. By mid afternoon they were on the Xiangkhoang Province Road traveling due east into the Plain of Jars. Although it was not late, the Kachin in charge pulled the truck to the side of a small house and announced, "We stop here."

"Why so early?" asked Ky. He was becoming anxious to get back to the relative safety of his home in the PRU compound and to turn the bricks of white powder they carried into a fortune.

"Friends," said the Kachin in his usual laconic fashion. "Too dangerous on the plains after dark."

Ky knew better than to argue with the men who traversed this route safely many times a year. He knew there was a reason for each stop and each transferal of bribe money. He did not have to like it all particularly, though. He and Bach had no real option other than to be patient. They sat on the verandah of the little house and watched the red orb of the sun sink into the Mekong in the distance and listened to the myriad frogs croaking in the drainage ditches. A middle-aged, toothless man and his teenaged wives, three of them, served the men a portion of their monotonous diet of rice, soup broth, and fermented fish. Because they were guests, the six men were treated to a baguette sprinkled with fish sauce and a shot glass full of Mekkong Whiskey.

The man sent his wives out to draw more water. One of them, dressed in white for mourning, retired to her room. The husband explained that her baby had died that morning of a febrile illness. The six men smiled at the bereaved father, and he smiled back in proper etiquette. They all acknowledged with their pleasant expressions that the baby had been taken by kind angels to a better place and would be greeting the ancestors. More than 100 infants out of every 1000 born in Laos die, and the people could not afford lengthy mourning periods nor elaborate funereal ceremonies even if they were inclined to expressions of great sadness at the transitions. "What has come about has come about," observed the husband expressing the stoicism of Southeast Asia.

The man of the house gratefully accepted the kip owed him and bowed humbly when the lead Kachin gave him extra for the small feast that would be held in honor of the departed child. He was tired from his daily grind of carrying water, pounding rice husks, and hoeing the grudging soil. It was dark, and he went to bed. The six guests chatted together for three hours after the evening meal until it was nine o'clock, then found a futon on the relative coolness of the verandah and went to sleep themselves.

The husband and his wives and twenty-two children eked out an existence on their small farm and by renting out their two buffaloes to neighbors. He supplemented the money coming into the family's coffers by providing a safe house, one of an extensive series of such homes away from home, stretching across the Golden Triangle and down to Bangkok on the south, to Hanoi on the north and east, and along the Annam Cordillera south and then east to Hue' and on down the coast or through the highlands to Saigon. The system was elaborate, under the most rigid security, and highly profitable. Low valley farmers, hill country Hmongs, Black Thais, and Montagnards were loathe to betray the source of their families' survival. The routes then went by sea to Europe and New York where the costs went up in multiples, and the profits went up logarithmically.

"Pay attention to these places," the Kachin instructed Ky and Bach. "You can depend on the people. You must never forget to pay them, and you must always treat these persons with decency and respect. They are our lifeline, and for that they deserve to be paid as businessmen."

The next day they proceeded into the Plain of Jars. As they entered the edge of the archeologically fascinating plain, they met an itinerant herb and root doctor and stopped to ask him if there were any problems ahead. "A mother bomb exploded forty kilometers west of the village of Viangxai," he told them, "and the bombis killed twelve children from a school class. The people have blood in their eyes. They are seeking any Americans or Vietnamese who help the murderers. Be most grateful today that you are not on the wrong side." The Kachins thanked the doctor, and the two Vietnamese made themselves as obscure as possible.

CBUs (Cluster Bomb Units) were dropped by the hundreds of thousands on the low valleys of Laos, across the Plain of Jars, and on the Pathet Lao headquarters in the limestone caves of Viangxai. Even those that did not decimate villages, farms, roads, and animals outright, lingered unexploded to beleaguer hapless villagers, all too often children, whose curiosity about the tiny bomblets spewed out from the mother bombs cost them limbs, sight, or lives. In this particular instance, a full CBU had lain dormant until a village truck bearing the town's entire grammar school student body had run over it. The CBU is a giant pea pod of the devil, a canister full of bomblets (bombi to the Laotians), each of which holds about 250 small steel pellets. The truck and the children had absorbed the entire blast turning them all into unrecognizable shreds.

The Kachins drove with caution trying to attract as little attention as possible, but their route necessarily took them in the direction of Viangxhai on their way to Barthelemy Pass and the border with Viet Nam. The cut off to the pass was in the middle of the plain, and with any luck, the inevitable road blocks would not be set up this far west, the Kachins hoped.

Their hopes were in vain. They were stopped before the main cutoff to Viangxai by a mob of sullen Lao Lum, the angry revengeful villagers. They were armed with AK-47s and grenade launchers indicating that the American's bombs had, at least, been appropriately directed at Pathet Lao or their supporters. All six strangers were required to alight from the truck and to show their papers. The headman of the Kachins did all of the talking, and greased their way with liberal applications of kip from his seemingly inexhaustible baksheesh supply. "VC," he answered in response to the obvious query about Ky and Bach. The villagers, some of whom recognized the drug traffickers from previous runs, were mollified, and allowed the truck to pass. The usually unflappable Kachins were lightly sweating when they could afford that luxury some kilometers further along.

The *Plaine des Jarres* (Plain of Jars, or PDJ) was a fascinating place and had been for more than two millennia. The flat landscape was liberally dotted with various sized sandstone urns of unknown purpose, some twenty-five feet around and seven or eight feet high. The speculation by foreign archeologists was that they represented funerary containers or grain storage urns, but the Laotians believed them to be receptacles for the potent rice wine made when the ancestral mountain-dwelling giants walked the earth. In recent years the flat valley had become pockmarked with bomb craters.

The truck stopped at another safe house in the foot hills before the Barthelemy Pass. The men feasted on deer, wild pig, and python and drank themselves mellow on rice wine provided by the Black Thai family who took them in. A considerable stack of bahts traded hands in order to transfer all of the Vietnamese men's boxed bricks of heroin and their armamentarium onto an elephant drawn wagon. The Kachins had been instructed to go no further in the direction of the DRV, but had made provision for Ky and Bach to do so.

The cost for use of an elephant, while somewhat greater for the drug traffickers than for locals, was related to the considerable expense of catching, raising, and training the lumbering behemoths. It regularly took ten to fifteen men a month away from their village to catch a pair, or even one little one, and to escape the rage of the mother elephant.

The cost at times included the loss of a father, son, or brother who was stamped to death by an infuriated elephant matriarch. The families considered the investment a reasonable value since a well trained grown elephant that could drag teak logs two at a time out of the forest was worth a small fortune.

As they ascended the sometimes gravel washboard two lane, occasionally paved and potholed one lane, and always dusty road, up the Barthelemy Pass, the Vietnamese and the Black Thai family encountered no vehicles. The road was impassable for motorized traffic. Nor did they did encounter any military interference. The Pathet Lao (Lao Country) and VC soldiers they met were polite, even helpful. After all, these mountain dwellers could be depended upon to pay their taxes regularly and without complaint, and were known to be scrupulously neutral in the secret CIA-Pathet Lao war, which was all the communists required of them.

Ky and Bach watched small groups of sickened villagers as they trudged out of the forests and toward such medical help as they could find in the villages of the plain. They were vomiting from contact with the defoliants dropped from the American tanker planes to uncover the communists' hiding places. For the villagers, however, the effect was the destruction of their livelihood, the stands of noble trees, and the poisoning of their families. Many of the trees the men were looking at were second growth bamboo, scrub, and wild bananas. The United States dropped 200,000 gallons of defoliants on Laos, a country the size of Oregon with a per capita income of $156, in 1966 alone, as they prosecuted their secret war to halt the domino effect of the spread of communism through Asia.

The borderland terrain was inhospitable jungle covered mountains, some of them 1500 meters high. The border was illusory; there were no guards or customs agents; and there was no sign indicating when the crossing was made. The DRV exercised such de facto suzerainty over northern Laos that there was considered to be no need for such formalities. The Black Thai family unloaded their elephant cart of the PRUCs belongings onto a patch of tall coarse *tranh* grass, bade the two men a safe journey, and turned back the way they had come.

A small band of over-armed Hmongs came trotting out of the jungle undergrowth as soon as the Black Thais were out of sight. Ky was uncertain whether he was in the presence of bandits, VC, GVN pacified villagers, or a gang in the nominal employ of the Wa People. He decided to listen and learn.

The Hmongs pointed black powder flint lock long rifles, British Enfield .303s, captured Japanese infantry rifles, World War II Sten guns, M1s, and a prohibition era tommy gun at the two thoroughly docile Vietnamese policemen-drug runners before they spoke.

"Papers," demanded the headman.

Ky and Bach handed over their UWS safe-passage certificates hoping against hope that they had chosen the correct documentation. They could have produced their credentials as part of the police force of the Republic of Viet Nam, but gut instinct told them that would be the wrong thing to do. They knew that, by chance, they could be in the company of VC dominated hill tribesmen, and worse, of zealots in the cause of purity and protection of the people, who would take great, and probably fatal exception to their small cargo of illicit drugs.

The Hmong headman spread his lips in what was intended to be a grin, Ky and Bach decided. He flashed his handsome set of filed and red lacquered teeth in a smile reminiscent of the one owned by their former commander, Deputy Inspector Y'Yool. Soon the men were all bowing, clapping each other on the back, and shaking hands in friendly gestures covering a trio of disparate ethnic customs. In a matter of moments it was clear that they had no common language.

No matter. The Hmong had been expecting the drug smugglers and their precious cargo, and knew that they would be handsomely rewarded by rendering aid. The Wa People had informed them in advance of the coming of the two men. They had been waiting, secreted in their jungle hiding places, for two days.

At the Hmong village, several of the women and older men spoke French, and the two South Vietnamese nationals were able to converse freely with the generous villagers in that language held over from a former foreign occupation.

"*Nous vous remercions de votre hospitalité,*" (We thank you for your hospitality.) said Ky.

"*Vous êres les amis de nus amis, le peuple Wa." Ils sont respectueux et ils nous payeur correctement. Vous pouvez nous faire confiance.*" (You are the friends of our friends, the Wa People. They are respectful and pay us fairly. We can be trusted.) was the stock reply to almost any line of inquiry or to any request.

Ky and Bach were fed the best the people had. The townspeople sat together in common at meal times in the communal long house. The PRUCs were given the staple, dry rice, and a large assortment of vegetables, wild game trapped or killed with crossbows, roasted monkey, and a marinated rat. Because they were honored guests they were given the village delicacy, lizard salad, and were initiated into the tribe by being offered the true test of a man's strength.

Both men were placed on three-legged stools in the front of the long house. The dye vats were even moved aside for the occasion. They were presented with a sandstone crock filled with rice water and an assortment of fruit juices all fermented and aged to a murky brown color and a gritty, pulpy consistency. A bamboo straw had been inserted to the dregs of the mixture. To a village-wide chanting and with the help of two bare-breasted girls each, Ky and Bach were expected to suck the contents of the crock dry. Not only was it a feat of alcohol consumption seldom rivaled in other cultures, it was a test of sucking power that required every ounce of strength of the two PRUCs' cheek, tongue, and pharyngeal muscles.

Neither man was able to remain conscious enough to enjoy the soaring tribal music nor the sensuous dance put on by the liquor mellowed Hmongs. They slept until the following noon amidst the peace and tranquillity of the villagers into whose bosom they had been accepted. The two PRUCs enjoyed the same monumental hangovers experienced by every Hmong in the village over the age of ten when they did wake up. Everyone laughed at everyone else's pained expression and head holding until their own pain caused them to squint their eyes and to sit with a cool compress on their foreheads. The village was a town of cool compresses and low moanings. Ky and Bach felt like they were fully in the family and were glad for the security that guaranteed for the present and for the future. They were convinced that neither of them was man enough for more rites of passage in the other villages where they would be welcomed.

Now, all travel was by night through forest pathways obscure to all but the Hmongs. Ky and Bach considered themselves to be in good physical condition, but their chests heaved and their legs trembled as they trotted behind the apparently indefatigable mountain people, about a fourth of whom were women. The stringy people tirelessly carried Ky and Bach's armaments and bricks of heroin up hills, across gullies, and through tangles of underbrush that seemed impenetrable at times. They moved at a jogging pace at its slowest and ran at race speed in areas of high concentration of southward marching NVA. They steered clear of branches of the Ho Chi Minh trail because of the high likelihood of encountering hostiles. At times they were in Laos, at others in the DRV. They passed Ban Karai', CO Ta Roun, and eventually the 17th parallel, the DMZ, marking the 1954 demarcation of Viet Nam into its two unnatural halves. There was nothing to indicate that transition there on the cool tree filled mountain sides.

The serpentine path they followed was difficult at best to remember, especially in the dark. At times they ran through clouds with visibility reduced to feet by the soupy moisture in the air. Ky and Bach worked diligently to maintain a sense of distance and place to be able to retrace their steps when the need arose, but knew that their task was nearly hopeless. At each Hmong village, they picked up new guides, men and women with special knowledge of the terrain and the continually changing trails.

The people were supremely careful. They seemed to hear the heartbeats of soldiers in the mountains. They all wore tiger stripe fatigues and were bare above the waist, men and women. The Hmongs went out loaded down with their own weapons, ammunition, emergency medical supplies, and an assortment of demolition equipment and explosives. They moved silently through the terrain, even in the dark, with their gear fastened to their bodies so there would be no rattling, shifting, or clinking of metal upon metal. The point man, always one of the village elders and a man with great forest experience, did not cut down underbrush with a noisy machete. Instead, he parted it to look before they ran on leaving the last man or woman in the line to replace the twigs and branches to their original position.

They were loyal to the Wa State Drug runners who paid them fairly and treated them as business equals and to the United States Army Green Berets with whom they worked as friends and fighting comrades. The people who guided Ky and Bach detested the NVA, VC, and ARVN equally and for the same reasons—each governmental group, from no matter which side, came with honey on their tongues, promises and presents; they abused their laws, took away their young men, disrespected their women, and then often withheld their hard-earned pay and treated them with hauteur and disdain.

At each friendly village, they were given a meaningful amulet or small, distinctive totem with which to identify themselves on future forays through the village's vicinity. Without the identifying physical certificate of passage, an interloper would be killed by the invisibles of the forest. The game was made all the more difficult because other Hmongs, Montagnards, and Meos pledged their allegiances to the communist side and received a bounty for the capture or killing of a Green Beret or an incautious ARVN unit. It was with a great measure of relief on Ky and Bach's part when the last set of guides stopped short of a well-traveled, but rustic jungle thoroughfare.

The road was controlled by the GVN, at least during the daylight hours; and therefore, the Hmongs considered it off-limits. They accepted the last payment from the two Vietnamese men with happy file-toothed smiles and hand signs of friendship, then melted back into the green gloom of the rain forest. In less than an hour, an old French military truck rumbled to a stop near a small Buddhist funereal shrine, a miniature house, constructed at the roadside for some dearly departed family member in the not too distant past. Ky and Bach watched cautiously until the driver hopped out and beckoned to them. They were hidden in the tall bushes at the side of the road and could not have been seen by the driver; but, nevertheless, he knew they were there. Bach turned to Ky and said, with admiration, "The Wa People think of everything, don't they?"

Ky nodded his agreement.

The driver was a genial young man of indeterminate ancestry who was dressed in faded denims, American gym shoes, and a Philippine Barong—the picture of the small rural capitalist. He chattered about local gossip, about what he knew about the war, and about the great opportunities there were for business nowadays. Ky stole a look behind the seat of the truck cab and caught a glimpse of black clothing and of the muzzle of a Kalashnikov. Evidently the young capitalist hedged his bets at night.

The young man was an excellent driver and steered the vintage vehicle over a road that became at times a daunting track and always at breakneck speed. Bach could not look, and Ky was white knuckled but felt obliged to hold up his end of the erratic conversation. After a bone jarring day, the old French truck was drawn up into a dust cloud producing halt at the undesignated road leading into the PRU compound.

Anders used his sightseeing time to become thoroughly familiar with the avenues, buildings, and out of the way alleys and side streets of Hue'. He absorbed much of the culture made possible, in part, by his facility with the language. He worked hard into the night on his GED studies, and his hunger for knowledge spurred him to move at a rate triple the usual pace. He was covering a high school grade level every two weeks and wanting more. At the University Library he requested books on Vietnamese history and was given a moving account of the Tay Son Rebellion to start with.

When he discussed the book with Nguyen Thi Liên, she told him of a fascinating offshoot of the Rebellion—the development of classical Vietnamese martial arts.

"I am pleased to see that you are earnest in your studies, Master Bergstrom," Liên had said, gently mocking her suitor's serious demeanor. Let me tell you something practical that came out of the Rebellion. She told him of the fomenters of the rebellion, Nguyen Hue' and Nguyen Lu and their book of rules for training and practice of a martial art meant to be uniquely Vietnamese that they called *Tây Sỏn Vỏ Sĩ.*

"My father is great friends with the old grand master of Hue' in the art, Master Nguyen Van," added Liên.

Anders was feeling logy and out of shape from the period of indolence ordered by his Company RDC/O chief. He longed for the physical training of boot camp or his self-imposed regimen of PT at the PRUC compound. His ears perked up when he heard about the martial arts form.

"Could I be a student of Master Nguyen?" He asked the attractive girl.

"Impossible," she stated evenly. 'Impossible' seemed to be one of her watchwords when referring to activities open to foreigners in the closed ranks of upper echelon Vietnamese society.

"Why?" Anders asked ingenuously.

"Master Nguyen takes only the most promising students, and you appear large and ungraceful," Liên told him, candidly. "And he only takes pure Vietnamese." That was that so far as she was concerned.

"Could your father help?"

"Yes."

"Would he?'

"He is too busy for such trivia, Mr. Bergstrom. You should find one of the students' studios and practice there."

There was that determined look again. Liên remembered the look from the time a couple of weeks previously when the young round eye had desired to matriculate in the Vietnamese university and would not hear 'no' and had finally persuaded her to arrange an audience with her father, The Mandarin. This time she would not disturb her father with another request for a favor. She secretly feared that her father kept a careful list of all the favors she had obtained from him and that the repository of gifts and preferences was finite. She did not want to waste any of her potential on this mere foreigner.

Anders sweet talked her, and even Liên was susceptible to a little honey. He presented cogent arguments, and she was receptive. He cajoled, pleaded, and even begged; and she gave in. Then he laughed, and she was delighted with this white bear of a man's funny ways. He was not so bad, after all, she thought, even for a foreigner. Of course she took pains not to let him know that.

The Mandarin granted an audience easily. He seemed eager to know of Anders' progress in completing the requirements for admission to the University of Hue'. When the young man showed him what he had accomplished in the short time since their last meeting, the old man was genuinely impressed and pleased to have mildly misjudged the boy's capabilities and the degree of his earnestness. The request for an introduction to his old friend, Master Nguyen, whom he called Van, unlike any of the old master's other acquaintances, was some-what thorny. Master Nguyen, he knew, was xenophobic, and avoided all contact with foreigners. He demanded the same of his students— they were expected to keep their art pure and all Vietnamese. The Mandarin told Anders only that he would arrange for an introduction, but would not use his influence for more than that—he certainly would not exert any pressure.

"Thank you, sir," said Anders with real gratitude and humility. He knew he was being allowed a small entering wedge with which to have a glimpse into the very standoffish Vietnamese high society. He determined not to foul up his chance.

The Mandarin's major domo himself drove Anders to the appointment with Nguyen Van whose home and studio were located up a winding forest road above the Tu Duc mausoleum. No less a companion would have been accepted.

Anders was introduced into the master's study by a servant who gave Anders' name and Red Cross affiliation status out in English. The use of the foreign tongue was designed to place him at a disadvantage, Anders construed. He, himself, spoke only Vietnamese and took every care to use the most educated and precise words and intonations of which he was capable. He knew he was making small progress in his presentation of himself and his desire to learn *Tây Sơn Võ Sĩ* from the old master, when, upon occasion almost unconsciously, the old man corrected a word or a phrase as Anders gave his monologue. Anders seemed inspired, and knew that he was speaking Vietnamese the best he had ever done.

The old master explained how, regrettably, he could not teach the ennobling art to a *người ngoại quốc* (foreigner). Despite his elaborate politeness ingrained over a lifetime, the old man fairly hissed the word.

"I respect your decision, Master," but I would like to ask that you make an exception in my case. I believe that I can prove myself worthy of your efforts," Anders said quietly making every effort to avoid a pleading tone. He would not make the request again

The master recognized that the young man was not one to give up easily, but he was a foreigner and would not be able to endure the rigors of the *Tây Sơn Võ Sĩ* discipline. The master knew that much for certain about foreigners. They were too weak, given to their pleasures, and lacked endurance. Perhaps he could please The Mandarin and get the odoriferous Occidental away from his studio all the more quickly and permanently by taking him in and subjecting him to the hell that all novices had to endure before coming out into the light of instruction in the true art. Master Nguyen's countenance darkened briefly as he recalled his own hard days at the hands of his eminent master. He made the decision to accept the white haired boy and to remove the foreigner's desire to learn the sacred skills and mental aptitude of The Art as quickly as could be done, that very day if possible. Occidentals were the weakest of the weak; seeing the coming and the going of the long noses had convinced Master Nguyen of that. This one was, what...a Swedish? Had they any history?

There was a long thoughtful and inscrutable pause as Master Nguyen pondered his decision. To the young man's credit, he did not speak as would most of the boorish westerners. Master Nguyen made his decision and stated it as unkindly as he could. He considered his comment only an accurate depiction of reality. "I have decided to change my mind. Because The Mandarin made the request, and for no other reason, I will accept you into my dojo for novice training. You will fail because you lack the will and the endurance. You must promise not to bother me again once you fail, not to plead to have the way made easier."

Anders nodded his agreement to the condition without betraying his soaring emotions in his face.

"You will begin this very day under the direction of one of my white belts. He will be your master and you, his slave. I will be watching. And, there is one more thing. You will eat only wholesome Vietnamese food, not decadent French or western food; and you will bathe twice daily. I cannot have your offensive breath odor and body smell contaminating my dojo. Until that smell is gone, you will do your work separate from the others. Do you agree?"

"I agree; and, thank you," Anders said. He had to stifle a grin at the old Asian's prejudices. It was an almost novel experience to be the subject of discrimination instead of being in the group that held the prejudices. He could not help but remember his treatment at the hands of the Danish boys back in the home of his childhood. The incipient grin disappeared as that memory clouded through his consciousness.

"Can you pay? This is not a charitable institution," The master said rather harshly.

"I can," Anders replied simply and directly.

"Enough idle talk, then," Master Nguyen finished. "Go to the anteroom of the studio and ask for Duc. Tell him you want a broom and directions of where to sweep. He will teach you how." There was a faint trace of malign amusement and insult in the sharp old eyes.

Anders, broom in hand, set about to learn *Tây Sơn Võ Sĩ*.

During the month he spent in Hue' having an enforced vacation, learning to sweep, to clean, and to sit on his haunches for hours at a time and to do stretch exercises until he thought his muscles would rip, Anders also mastered his GED correspondence program to the eleventh grade level; and his eighteenth birthday came and went. There was no one to celebrate it with him, to give him a present, or to so much as acknowledge the occasion. Anders treated himself to a Parisian French dinner, all rich sauces and winey creams, and otherwise gave it little thought.

He returned to the PRU compound three days after Ky and Bach got back from their working tour of Burma, Laos, and North Viet Nam. Ky had spent two of those days in Hue' doing business. The result of that business was that the bricks of heroin had been delivered to the hands of the next set of couriers who would see it delivered into the hands of New Yorkers; the money given in exchange had been banked to the National Bank of Hue' account and then transferred to a numbered account in the Union Bank of Switzerland. The contract with the bank required it to distribute up to one-fifth of the account total to any one of the named owners after they enumerated the code sequence. Ky reported the account total to his four confederates at their first meeting when all of them were together at the compound— slightly over one million US dollars.

CHAPTER 28

The United States is so dominated by its technology and its wealth that it has lost touch with people. The United States believes it can spread democracy and maneuver politics by technology and money only. This may well be a fatal error in the life of our nation.
William J. Lederer, Our Own Worst Enemy

Between the middle of April and the end of June, 1967, Anders' one hundred twenty-two member PRU produced a steady and reliable number of VCSs for the provincial and regional interrogation centers—averaging twenty-three per week—and a consistent number for the body count of VC that could be reported in the weekly Saigon five o'clock follies—averaging fourteen. The numbers were the important thing to McNamara and his Ford 'whiz kids' and their DOD computer. The requirement was for a recording of quantifiable results of bombing and on-the-scene actual body counts. That the providers of the numbers were none too scrupulous about the evidence indicating that their accumulated numbers in fact, represented VCI, was not a matter of bureaucratic concern to the DOD, the provincial or regional CIA officials, or the National Registry. Nor was it a reason for hand wringing on the part of the members of Anders' field units or himself. He had become inured to the implications of his activities, accepting as his only criterion of success, the approbation or lack of it from his RDC/O chief, Cleve Howard. Without recognizing a clearcut date of demarcation from his conscience, Anders Bergstrom had became a Company man. His contract was renewed without reservation.

At the end of April, Ky made a second business trip to Burma, this time with Dung, in order to insure that all of his Vietnamese PRU associates would eventually be recognized by the Wa People and their Hmong and Montagnard confederates. Ky took pains to make sure that Anders would be identified as a friend and coconspirator at each stop and with every individual along the way by showing them a good quality photograph of the white man. It was out of the question to attempt to smuggle Anders along the actual drug transport route. A six foot four inch, two hundred fifty-plus pound cornsilk haired Caucasian would stand out like a Martian in Laos, Thailand, and Burma, just as he did in Viet Nam. It was planned to have a set of two of the PRUCs make the business trip once every other month, anticipating a profit of at least three-quarters of a million dollars each time, barring an increase in business expenses.

June was an auspicious month. Anders completed his GED requirements; so, it was only a matter of a month to six weeks before he would have his high school equivalency diploma and would be able to complete the matriculation process for entering the University of Hue'. Toward the last week in the month, Master Nguyen Van had relented his stance about Anders' participation in the *Tây Sơn Võ Sĩ* martial arts training at his studio, and had allowed the foreigner to advance from broom, paint brush, and garden scythe to floor calisthenics with the children.

Anders saw Liên once a week, now finding her easily at a prearranged time and meeting place beside the university book store. That she was there each week counted as a moderate success to the still ardent young suitor. The routine was broken at the end of the month by a radio call from Cleve Howard, himself.

"Get me the RD/O" Howard ordered the radioman on duty.

"He is in PT, sir."

"I'll wait. Hurry it up."

Howard did not wait patiently. The radioman hurried out to the running course the PRUCs had made and after a frustratingly long effort to locate Anders, finally intercepted the sweat drenched leader as he jogged by.

"RD/O chief on the hook, Anders," he said.

"What's he want?" puffed Anders.

"He didn't say. But it's important enough for him to wait. I think it's important enough for you to hurry, if you ask my opinion."

Anders felt like saying that he hadn't asked, but knew that his PRUC only had his best interests in mind; so, he did hurry to the radio shack. He was out of breath when he picked up the receiver and spoke into the scrambler mike.

"Bergstrom here," he was able to say as he caught his breath.

"Howard. I need to have you and your number two at the RDC HQ tomorrow morning even if you have to cancel an assignment or two."

"What's up?" Anders did not really expect to be told over the radio, but his curiosity was piqued; so, he asked anyway.

"Some new arrangements for you and your guys. We'll be heading for Saigon. Lane Duerk has the straight skinny. Can't say more now, okay?"

He sounded calm and friendly. Anders' first presumption that he had somehow run afoul of one of The Company's many unwritten rules seemed less worrisome now. "Okay, see you tomorrow," he answered.

"Civilian dress. We'll go Air America or CASI. No obvious weapons. See you by ten sharp. Out."

"Ten-four," Anders ended.

Before noon on the last day of June, Anders, Tran, Cleve Howard, and Kent Ashworth, the new RD/O regional chief stationed in Danang, were sitting in Lane Duerk's office in the Saigon First Precinct Police Building sipping coffee and eating finger sandwiches served by Miss Nguyen. Anders' old acquaintance from the CIA training center, Tring Van Dong, Duerk, now the SVN chief, and Rex Dragerton, the new Saigon Chief of Station, who had been promoted out of Danang, were also in attendance. Tring and Anders swapped stories about their exploits in the boonies of Thau Thien province until the formal meeting started.

While Miss Nguyen busied herself setting up several printed organizational hierarchical charts, Duerk said, "Time to get down to the issue at hand," suggesting that the ten minutes of chitchat over refreshments had been excessive. "A new wind blows, and I am supposed to bring you up to date." He had the attention of every man.

"No more Revolutionary Development. We will now work out of a civilian organization,…what's it called, exactly, Miss Nguyen?"

"CORDS—Civil Operations and Revolutionary Development Support, Mr. Duerk." Miss Nguyen said in her usual crisply efficient, mildly annoying manner.

"Cumbersome name, but it is a good idea. This outfit, which we will run, of course, was established in May to coordinate all US military and civilian pacification programs in the whole country. The action arm will still be the PRUs which we run exclusively. The powers that be have finally realized that our little yellow friends can't be trusted to run their country in a reasonable fashion and have now formally turned the whole responsibility for VC detection, control, and pacification over to us in a once and for all efficient outfit. The new program will be called Phoenix. It's counterpart with the Viets is named after their favorite bird, *Phung Hoang*—a reference that is a bit off, but at least it's a mythical bird. His reference related to the fact that the *Phung Hoang* is classically regarded as a significant symbol of peace and is represented as holding a flute touting virtue, grace, harmony, and tranquillity. Duerk pointed to the picture of the new program's symbol being displayed by Miss Nguyen. It was a colorful and formidable looking bird standing on ashes and holding a ribboned scroll in its sharp beak.

Cleve Howard let a small indication of his doubts creep out in the form of a slight negative nod of his head. Duerk caught the sub rosa gesture.

"Be not the first by whom the new is tried, nor yet the last to lay the old aside," Duerk said with a look one would expect from a professor to his hidebound departmental associate.

"Very appropriate," Howard agreed. "Shakespeare had a quip for every situation."

"True, except that was Alexander Pope, "An Essay on Criticism.""

"I stand corrected."

"Public school education showing," smiled Duerk, taking pleasure in his small feat of oneupmansship.

The moment of conviviality passed. "The organization will be pretty much the same as in the old RD units. The *Biet Kich* will report to a Provincial Officer in Charge—that's you, Howard; and he will report to the Regional Officer in Charge—that's you, Ashworth; who will report to me, like before. The *Biet Kich* in the PRUs will be the main action arm. The military will report any and all VCSs to us—that's new, and they don't like it. Tough titty. We are in on the ground floor of the CT program; and they have had to agree to cooperate; so, we can get the job done. Orders right down from McNamara and Westmoreland. All anti-VCI functions are ours, and they will all be coordinated by the mainframe computer in Saigon linked to the DOD machine in DC.

"Furthermore, the mandarins in Washington and here in Saigon have finally realized that we cannot defeat the communist insurgency in any of the Southeast Asian countries, what with the domino effect, without thoroughly undermining their infrastructure. Therefore, the counterterror program will have three areas of focus. First, with a Herculean effort of investigation, we will identify and track every party secretary, finance and supply unit, information service, social welfare provider and unit, and proselytizing section. Second, we will launch a psychological warfare program and a hearts-and-hands-to-the-people program on a national level with rewards such as were used so successfully in the running dogs war in Malaya and with informational leaflets on a grand scale. Third, we will employ small counterterror teams on a scale never before imagined until we bring real fear, danger, insecurity, and death to the communists and their functionaries even in the areas of the cities and the countryside where they now feel secure. As never before we will fight fire with fire; we will employ their own Viet Cong methods against them. This does not go beyond this room, but the methods will include everything from psy-ops, to intimidation, to physical persuasion, to literal counterterror. That is where units like Van Dong's and Bergstrom's and his man's, here, come in."

"You mean we've reached the point that was described after Hitler was killed and Berlin was in smoking ruins. Only Martin Bormann was left. He was asked how he would carry on. His reply was that he 'would build the Fourth Reich just like Hitler did the Third, except this time there would be no more Mr. Nice Guy,'" joked Cleve Howard, goading his boss with his barb of humor.

"I think you've got the picture, even though I take umbrage at the choice of comparison in the analogy. I like to think that we are acting in the best Judeo-Christian tradition, as in Proverbs—'The wicked flee when no man pursueth; but the righteous are bold as a lion.' It's past time for us to take off the gloves and to stop letting the com-symp press tell us how to run the war."

"You've got my vote, Herr Kapitan," Howard said, a bit too quickly and without being able to resist another little goad.

"I think we are a long way from the goals and *weltanschaung* of the Nazis, my friend." There was enough stress on the 'friend' to alert Cleve that he had pushed his little humorist's edge too close to the core. He desisted.

Duerk, with Miss Nguyen's assistance, spent the rest of the afternoon detailing the methods of reporting, the complex hierarchy, the technology available for data storage and retrieval, and the help that would be provided the teams in the field. Anders and Cleve Howard took particular interest in the communication that money would be freely available to accomplish their purposes.

"The countryside up in Thau Thien is Bergstrom's and Tring Van Dong's. The cities will be targeted by separate teams. Some of you may remember Sylvia Chin from The Farm. She is going to head up the teams in Hue' and Danang cities proper. We are going to bring in another onetime Farm instructor, Nguyen Hai Truong for Saigon. I mention these two just to indicate the quality of the individuals who are going to be involved."

Anders perked up his attention at the mention of the two outstanding instructors whom he remembered with admiration. "The program had to be good," he thought.

"We'll have Tandrosz Szabo and his lieutenant ranging throughout the provinces heading up the psy-ops. They are setting up their own units even as this meeting goes on."

Anders again heightened his attention at the mention of the two men he despised. "The program would probably be effective," he mused, but he was much less sure how good it would be.

"Now, what I am going to say next is top secret. Any breach of security on this subject will be dealt with maximum prejudice. Everybody capiche?" All heads nodded their understanding.

Satisfied with the rapt and respectful attention he was now receiving, Duerk went on. "We are going to run over-the-fence programs into Laos, Cambodia, the DMZ, and North Viet Nam. We'll go after them where they live and breed, but we'll do it so the mandarins and the movers and the shakers have plausible deniability. You will not be captured; you will not be induced to spill your guts. We never heard of you if they get their claws into you. We're going to hurt them. Don't you get hurt."

The men were suitably silent. From the beginning, the United States had denied any incursions into the other Southeast Asian countries, despite the near all-out war being waged in Laos. More bomb tonnage was being laid down in that pitiful little country than had been dropped in World War Two, and yet the bulk of Americans were unaware of the fighting there. The focus of the world's attention was on South Viet Nam, and the WOMs and the directors of Phoenix wanted it to remain there.

"Phoenix is going to be the union of all the police, military, and paramilitary intelligence gathering programs and insurgency interdiction in the whole region; and it is going to be under direct and continuous United States control. We are going to eliminate duplication and conflict among the contributing agencies. The Company and the President have had enough with all the career creating bureaucrats. We are going to get down to the business of coring out the heart of the Viet Cong organization. Hopefully, this will leave MACV and ARVN the military theaters and battles against armies without having to worry all the time about the knife sneaking in to their underbellies. I am confident that Phoenix will do just that. The character and the quality of this war has changed; it is bigger and more complex, and Phoenix is a concomitant change for the better."

Lane Duerk, the South Viet Nam CIA chief of station, had never appeared so enthusiastic; and his fervor was infectious. He had been juggling the ineffectual conflicting aims and enterprises of Census Grievance, Revolutionary Development, independent Counterterror Teams, Provincial Reconnaissance Units, Military intelligence organizations of MACV and ARVN, PICCs (Provincial Intelligence Coordination Committees—on the books, but as yet not in effect), Regional and Popular Forces, the Field Police, Public Safety, *Chieu Hoi*, AID (Agency for International Development—State Department), and MSS (Military Security Service—ARVN). He had kowtowed to the martinets of the American military and the peacocks of the Saigon government for years. He was glad, at last, to have the chance to rein them all in and to begin to have a coordinated and effective program. He felt like the big brute about to go into the bar and toss all the bar bullies out while his more frail partner stayed outside to count the victims of his righteous wrath.

After supper, Tandrosz Szabo and Jean-Luc DuParrier came into the office lecture room. "These are the psy-ops experts assigned to the whole theater," introduced Duerk, "in case any of you are unfamiliar. You will be seeing a lot of them."

"How could I be so lucky?" groused Anders to himself. Tring Van Dong endured the introduction with clenched teeth. DuParrier avoided looking at either of the two PRU operational chiefs during the evening.

"We will detail how the local penetration process takes place, how we get effective recruitment to give us the information for the computer that you will find so useful. You will have to become active in the recruitment process," lectured Szabo. That was a new facet of Anders' duties. He was not at all sure he was going to like that duty. Szabo then related the experience hallowed methods used by his people to gain the necessary intelligence. Recruitment required any and everything from recruitment in place of active VC to become double agents, to bribes, to sexual entrapment, to extortion, to drugs, to threats of exposure to the VC in their villages, to pandering to the uneducated villagers' superstitions—the Tonton Macoutes methods.

In his turn DuParrier enumerated the ways of using the Asians' love of family against them; tricking relatives into betraying the whereabouts of VCSs, taking innocents hostage, and using all of the recruitment devices against the relatives; so, they would betray their insurgency family members. He illustrated with actual case histories as examples. He presented leaflets and brochures that were to be airdropped or tacked on trees. It sounded to Nguyen Lui Tran every bit the same as the NLF methods.

Szabo presented a lecture and discussion on the newest and most useful drugs, and DuParrier finished the evening with a rendering of the methods of physical intimidation and playing on superstitions. It was a thorough and clinical education in the refined inhumanities of man to man condensed into one short session, but the two psy-ops men expected the lessons to be learned and to be put into practice as soon as their students returned to the field. Cleve Howard, Kent Ashworth, Rex Dragerton, and Lane Duerk maintained poker faces; but Anders, Tran, and Van Dong betrayed a little of the squeamishness of their novice status in terms of psy-ops.

"The old police method is to investigate, arrest, convict, and send to prison," Szabo explained. "The intelligence method—and this is an intelligence operative program—is to investigate, capture, and to turn in place if at all possible and by any means. This is not Sunday school, and this is not US liberal due process. Maybe sometime down the line we will be able to afford such time-consuming luxuries; but, meanwhile, there's a war on."

Lane Duerk added a note about the scope of their enterprise at this juncture. "The GVN intelligence people estimate that, across the board, all of their country's governmental and military units are twenty percent infiltrated by VCI; and even they admit it is a conservative estimate. We think the number is much higher. There are, at least, seventy thousand full and part time sympathizers who contribute to the LAF cause over and above the eight thousand full time formal employees of COSVN. Of South Vietnam's fifteen to eighteen thousand villages and hamlets, no more than a very few hundred can be considered to be secure and pacified enough to hold real elections. We are going to change their minds, and we are going to do it in a serious way. This year we will spend seventy-five million dollars on the VCI interdiction program, and that is only the start."

Anders knew from first hand experience that much of the money spent was wasted on corruption and diversion. He had seen the men who had become rich by cynically misappropriating the funds, including, he suspected, Cleve Howard. As a result of that cynical observation, the great expense described did not impress him particularly. Considering that each PRUC (exclusive of the few Americans directly involved) was paid the equivalent of ten dollars a month, considerable portions of the available funds would continue to be diverted to corruption at every conceivable level—even his own, he had to admit, thinking of the extra $10,000 he banked in his personal account from time to time. Since they were CIA assets acting outside any codified law and were, for the large part, beyond any formal monetary accounting system, the PRUCs would continue to make their own use of the available funds. Anders had been around long enough to have become a thoroughgoing skeptic, and he was only eighteen years old. Also, he was not altogether on the side of the angels himself, he acknowledged with self-revelatory candor.

When Anders and Tran stepped out onto Tu Do Street in the wee hours of the morning after the meeting, a cowboy on his Honda X was idling away the night listening to a ghetto blaster he had exchanged with a black American soldier for some of the forgetting powder and a night of boom-boom. The radio was playing a song popular in Saigon that year, a lullaby by Mien Duc Thang.

"Sleep tight my child…When you grow up, you will sell your country to become a mandarin."

The glitter of the bars on Tu Do Street beckoned them into establishments such as the Shack, The Capitol, and Fifth Avenue indicative of the American adoption of the decadence of old French colonial role.

They were approached by a woman selling Coca Cola and beer. They shook their heads, "No." They knew better. There was very real danger in succumbing to the temptation to slake one's thirst from vended beverages. Drinks had become potent and frequent weapons—VCI laced the fluids with broken glass and poison or acid. Women who succeeded in killing an American or ARVN soldier were awarded a banner inscribed: *"Nư Anh Hùng Giết Mỹ"* (American Killer Heroine). Long time success warranted receiving a special medal with attached red and yellow silk.

Similarly, the two men avoided children. Anders had an American's natural affinity for children he learned to control. The LAF, knowing that Americans were lonely and missed children, used them mercilessly in their terrorist campaigns. Small children ran alongside troop trucks waving and laughing at the American soldiers and accepting their gifts of chocolate then tossing a live grenade into the truck. Shoeshine kits rigged with bombs blew up outside GI bars. Children themselves were fitted with explosives attached to their bodies and turned into unwitting living bombs. Anders and Tran knew, that for every inhumanity they committed against an adult foe, the VC countered with an indiscriminate bombing of innocents in a crowded market or movie theater, or a school full of children. The two men could sympathize with GIs who had to shoot children and then to suffer the hypocritical epithets from the Vietnamese and their own countrymen calling them 'baby killers.' In Viet Nam, the US soldiers heard the chants of "Hey, hey, how many babies did you kill today?"

So, Anders and Tran were careful, to the point of paranoia. That was how they stayed alive. They watched each other's backs, always alert. They could never be sure that the cowboy sidling up to them on his *Honda x* was not about to pull out a pistol, or that the woman with the infant was not ready to pull a grenade from her blouse or from her baby's diaper.

Anders and his PRU went back to work steadily increasing their results throughout the summer. They developed an effective and functional network of VC turncoats still in place in their villages who made the PRU's tasks relatively easy. When the dossiers came in along with orders to capture, to turn, to snatch and snuff, or merely to intimidate, Anders had already obtained enough information the orders could be executed with deadly speed and efficiency. The body and capture counts began to climb, and Anders' stature increased.

Cleve Howard invited Anders to the new CORDS building on the MACV compound in Hue' where Howard's new offices were now located. The request came at the time Anders was going through the admissions and orientation process at the University, and at a time when his karate' master was beginning to ease up on the nonsense routine and to teach the capable young man in earnest; so, Anders had little spare time during his trips to the city.

"Thought you might like to see this, if you haven't already," Howard said. He was in a good mood. He handed Anders a rice paper leaflet that had obviously been torn from a tack someplace.

Anders' reading of modern *quoc ngu* Latinized Vietnamese was barely rudimentary, and this document was in old *chu nom* symbols. He could only gaze at it perplexed. Miss Le, Howard's secretary, glanced at him; and Anders responded, presuming it was an offer of help. He passed the note to her.

"I will read it verbatim"—she did so in Vietnamese: 'Wanted dead or alive. 100,000 P. reward for capture or undeniable proof of death of the cruel capitalist tool of death-and-destruction of the peace loving and innocent people of the villages of north and east Thau Thien province, the Caucasian man known not by name but by the ugly title he has earned: *con ma da trắng khổng-lồ*.'"

"It appears that you have gained something of a reputation. I take it that you understand what they are calling you," Cleve said to Anders with amusement.

"White giant ghost. I've heard it before."

"There are thousands just like this being spread all over the province this week. You have made an impression. I just wanted to tell you that represents a job well done. I might also mention that you need to have eyes in the back of your head. A hundred thousand P. is a lot of money to some of these poor folks, and they might be tempted to take a chance they would not have before," Howard said. He was being sincere.

"I'll be careful," Anders replied unnecessarily.

The first wanted poster Anders actually saw for himself was tacked to a tree in the vicinity of a village where he and his own team of PRUCs had gone by night to capture a known VCI senior accountant. This poster had upped the reward to 200,000 P. and included details (all false) of the predations, rapes, and torturings attributed to the 'white giant ghost.' There was even a cartoon depiction of the ghost, a fearsome scraggly haired demonic creature.

The PRUCs were given a raise to twenty dollars a month (2000 Piastres) soon after the inception of Phoenix. When they all saw the poster with Anders' likeness, they felt it was time to celebrate. The men arranged to have a supply of Tiger Beer and 333 flown into the compound and from somewhere, not investigated too closely, they commandeered T-bones, Russet potatoes, and six New York Deli cheese cakes topped with cherries. While they were still in a postprandial mellow mood, one of the men, Ky Van He, announced the arrival of the featured entertainment of the evening. Anders groaned inwardly expecting a bevy of prostitutes and a major break in security. The location of their compound could not be compromised, and he became fidgety over how he should handle the sticky situation. He could not let the women go back to the city knowing the location.

A white Air America helicopter fluttered down onto the cement square landing pad. Its rotor blades kicked up enough dust that Anders could not tell in the gloom who or what got out. There were three individuals was all he could ascertain for sure. He advanced to the pad to meet the visitors. The helicopter pilot came along as well. Anders recognized Cleve Howard as one of the passengers, and was duly astonished. He was accompanied by two elderly men carrying what looked like tool boxes. Their heads were shrouded in black hoods. Cleve and the pilot lead them haltingly across the uneven ground.

"Well, greetings, chief," Cleve said jovially. "How come we didn't get an invite to the party?"

"I, uh, never thought…never imagined that you . . ."

"Might like a party?" Howard finished Anders' sentence for him. "I love parties. Make up excuses to have parties. I used to have unbirthday parties when I was a kid because I couldn't wait the whole year." If he hadn't known better, Anders would have thought that his boss was drunk.

"Well, c'mon in. We've got plenty of great leftovers. Bring your friends—the more the merrier," Anders said with a laugh.

"Oh, yesh," Cleve said. He was drunk, Anders realized. That was pretty funny. "Theesh are my two ole buddiesh frum Hue'. " He pronounced it 'Huey.'

Anders had a couple of the PRUCs lead the poor, somewhat frightened, and thoroughly disoriented men accompanying the POIC into the block house where the steaks had been served and allowed them to remove the hoods inside the building. "Hey, who are these guys?" Anders finally asked Mr. Howard who was enjoying his private joke immensely.

"Speshialishts," he slurred. The man was thoroughly, silly drunk. Anders found it difficult to reconcile the image of his powerful CIA executive agent boss with this jocular inebriate.

The entire PRU had gathered in the hot room. They had already consumed enough beer to make them all a step beyond mellow. They waited with impatient anticipation to learn why the two strangers had been brought to the camp. Finally, Cleve Howard obliged.

"Open your chases," he commanded the two men. The cases contained needles, small vials of dyes, and electrical plug in boxes with long extension cords. Shortly, the cords were plugged into the room's electrical outlets.

"Tattoo artists," the commandos murmured among themselves. The tattoo artists spread out vivid drawings of a flagrantly colored exotic bird that looked like a cross between a peacock and an eagle. The bird's sharp beak held a scroll.

"The blacklist," Anders whispered to Tran as he pointed at the scroll..

"Ah right, great white ghosht leader," Cleve Howard said to Anders with a mischievous leer. "You firsht."

Anders demurred. He did not want a tattoo. He thought they made a man look low class, and besides his old Mormon religious background frowned on the practice since it defiled the body regarded as a temple. However, the men would have none of it. "C'mon, Anders," some of them called. "Do it, oh white giant ghost," Ky and Bach said. All of the men were laughing and demanding.

Much as he did not want to do it he figured he could let the men put a small picture somewhere it did not show, and by so doing demonstrate that he was a good sport. "Okay, but just a little one. Here on my chest." He took off his shirt. "One like Tran and the rest of you have." He referred to the '*Sat Cong*' lettering over the men's pectorals.

The tattoo artist had him lie down supine. In cooing Vietnamese, the man bade Anders relax and above all else not to move. "Will hurt little bit," the man said.

It hurt more than that, but soon Anders was the proud possessor of the *chu nom* letters that spelled out 'Kill Cong' on his chest. The two tattooists were experts, very quick and precise, and soon had decorated the chests of every man in the camp with the same eternal message. Every man except Cleve Howard, who, even drunk, could not be cajoled into participating in the body markings.

The tattoo artists then set to work on volunteers to decorate their posterior right shoulders, arms, and backs with the elaborate Phoenix bird tattoo, running the electric needles over ready skin expertly, quickly dabbing the small drops of blood and working swiftly and flawlessly. The artistic work was very attractive and distinctive. Howard told Anders that the PRUCs all over the RVN were being tattooed that week, and that it was being done as a way to unite the men as a group. Anders took his turn sometime in the middle of the night as Howard slumbered noisily on a bench. Anders was of half a mind to order a tattoo to be placed on the unconscious POIC, but knew he would regret such a decision ever afterward and restrained his enthusiasm.

Anders' tattoo was very large owing to his size, his exalted rank (so far as the tattoists were concerned) and to the ardor of the artist. It covered most of the right side of the large back and powerful shoulder and triceps. When Anders extended or abducted his arm, the wing of the bird would unfold. It was very impressive. The decoration barely fit under his shirt.

The University of Hue' freshman class for 1967 was filled with the best and the brightest the region had to offer, and the young men and women came almost exclusively from the most affluent families. Anders Bergstrom was the exception in nearly every sense. He was large, foreign, Caucasian, came from a poor family and background; he was obligated to work (as a paramilitarist) and therefore to miss considerable class time and all extracurricular activities. His fellow students were small, Vietnamese to the core, Asian in appearance and in thinking, enjoyed gentle upbringings in families from the upper levels of society, and had come to school not only to learn didactic material, but to cement social connections through their participation in sports, arts, drama, and the many campus clubs. They disdained everything military, and their influential fathers frantically pulled strings to keep them out of military conscription.

Anders had in common with the best of his classmates a very fine mind, and bested them in his determination to succeed, to make up for the time he had lost educationally thus far. At first, he was an object of curiosity—it was not lost on his classmates that he was the first foreign student in the history of the university. Soon the press of studies and their exhausting round of social involvements caused interest in him to subside. He did well in all of his classes, and his classmates' curiosity gave way to a low-grade grudging respect.

The schedule Anders was obliged to keep was a dizzying and exhausting one, and only his youth and gritty determination allowed him to carry it off. He did as little as possible with the PRU, delegating as many of the missions to the leadership of Tran, Bach, Ky, and Dung as he could. Nevertheless, Anders found himself missing days of class, making excuses to professors, and struggling to makeup class work and examinations.

Tây Sổn Vổ Sĩ is a brutally physical body contact activity as well as a refined art. Most days Anders woke up stiff, sore, and bruised. Every evening, he spent three hours diligently proving himself in the dojo of Master Nguyen. The *Tây Sổn Vổ Sĩ* sensai and other novices in the martial arts studio, like Anders' university classmates, began to accept him for his merit and to overlook his inordinate size, his body odor, and his foreignness. Anders explained quite honestly to his *sensai*, as he had done to his professors, that there would be periods when he would be absent, but that his heart was into the art; and he begged his master's indulgence. The young foreigner showed such great promise and genuineness that Master Nguyen allowed him enough latitude that he could continue with his group.

His friendship with Liên had grown firm and deep and had changed in character. He was in love with the girl, but knew within himself and without further reminder from Liên or her family that there could be no courting nor thoughts of marriage—ever. He would have to be content to worship at a social distance. She laughed at his aching walk and sighed over his many bruises, but accepted all of that as the foibles of young manhood. She gradually came to look upon the huge foreigner like a brother. He was so vulnerable and needy. She observed his poor attendance record and made it her personal project to tutor the truant through his lapses. He adored her for her kindnesses and assistances as much as he marveled at her great beauty and impeccable character. He kept his feelings to himself except that he was protective of the fragile young woman to the point that it amused her and her sycophantic friends and sometimes proved annoying.

Anders was enrolled in the same classes as every other freshman student—the curriculum in the first two core years was mandatory and was designed to provide a common base to the well-educated future leaders of the republic. He took Vietnamese writing and literature; it was presumed that every student was a native or at least fluent Vietnamese speaker. He was obliged to take French and had to suffer the ignominy of being the only beginner in the freshman class. French was taught faithfully in Vietnamese high schools despite the antipathy toward the French military and bureaucracy and the domineering nation's eventual defeat and evacuation from Viet Nam. Anders doggedly took extra classes in oral French, determined to make up for his prior inadequacies and endured the snickers of his more fluent classmates with equanimity.

The most important class for all students was the history of Viet Nam, a class that stressed the glories of the culture, the sufferings of the people at the hands of foreign interlopers and would-be conquerors, and the military triumphs of the determined Viets. It was a class in which Anders excelled because of his fascination with the world of learning about Asia and the people with whom he dwelled. He was intrigued to know what made these determined, contradictory, multi-faceted people tick.

His other life, that of a commando, was incongruous with his role as a student. He was dirty; and he smelled; he was as wary as a jungle cat out there. He ate what was available, sometimes using his M-16 muzzle flash guard to twist and cut the stiff wire holding the C-Rat cases together, and at others sharing plain rice or a lizard with his cadres.

At times, alone in the bush, he would ambush and kill an unsuspecting VCI on an obscure trail and bring back the man's ears as proof positive of his deed. At other times, he was linked up with marines or army rangers who always saw the military objective in addition to the specific irregular ops mission. He had to learn not to be disturbed or at least not to express his distaste when the soldiers leaned out of their Sea Wolf helicopter to shoot at peasants in their conical mollusk hats sitting on the backs of water buffaloes or at fishermen in their sampans. They shot at some people because they ran at the approach of the American military machinery and at others because they froze in position, depending on the rules of engagement in the areas where the soldiers had first been introduced to the horrors of the Viet Nam war. It was only with difficulty that Anders learned to compartmentalize his life. Part of the difficulty lay in the fact that there was no one to whom he could tell his experiences or with whom he could express his feelings.

With Liên he experienced peace, even gentleness. He became such a familiar figure near her that he was accepted into her home almost as a part of the extended family. The Mandarin was pleased that the boy had kept his word not to pursue his daughter, and her mother liked the fact that the huge and powerfully built young man was so overtly protective of the delicate flower of the family.

Liên tutored Anders on his French verb conjugations—*aimer: aime, aimes, aimous, aimez,* and *aiment. Finir: finis, finis, finit, finissons, finissez,* and *finissent.* She showed him how to pucker his lips and to press his tongue to his gums and to begin to master the nasal vowels, the diphthongs, and all of the unique pronunciation that was critical to learning to speak French usefully. They drilled the endless declensions and the vocabulary lists with flashcards by rote and in practice with Liên collapsing in laughter at Anders' fractured enunciations. He accepted it all good-naturedly because it came from her.

Because he could not ever have her romantic love, Anders unconsciously courted Liên's mind. He did everything he could to prove his intellectual capacity to her, to improve himself in her eyes. She grew to respect and to admire his efforts and eventually his integrity and accomplishments. Despite the fact that he was a foreigner, she came to like him. He was more like a brother to her than her brothers, all of whom were old enough to be her uncles. Liên and Anders settled into a comfortable platonic relationship as much a brother-sister connection as was possible between these two dissimilar young people.

Vietnamese literature came alive for Anders when Liên talked to him of the classics of her country. The tale of the Dragon Lord of Lac and of the fairy princess Au Co was all the more vivid for her telling it. He could also appreciate the story, told in a stylized play, and explained in detail by Liên, of the Trung sisters, Princesses Trun Trac, the older, and Trung Nhi, the younger. As they watched the play, Liên whispered her explanations. "The older sister's husband was brutally executed by the intolerable Chinese occupation army. The sisters, in their bereavement and righteous indignation, rallied the people in 39 AD., raised troops into an army, and drove out the hated Chinese. Trung was proclaimed queen and reigned fairly and peacefully for three years. In 43 AD. the Chinese reinvaded and conquered the land of the Viets once again. Seeing that the situation was beyond hope, the Trung sisters committed suicide by throwing themselves into the river. It was all very sad and very heroic." The Vietnamese were not an easy people to subjugate, Anders learned, and it was only 600 years later that the Chinese were able to change the country's name to Annam—The Pacified South.

Had he heard the "Tale of Kim Van Kieu", written by Nguyen Du in the eighteenth century, in a Sunday school class in his home town, Anders would have dismissed it as melodramatic and hypermoralistic. When Liên expanded on the university professor's didactic presentation of the classical Vietnamese story, Anders was touched by its content and its insight into the way Vietnamese people thought and reacted and how they felt they should behave. "Kieu was a maiden of great innocence who lived in piety with her principle affection being reserved for her family. When the girl's family was unjustly accused and threatened with being sent to debtor's prison, Kieu abandoned her fiancee and sold herself into prostitution to help them. For fifteen years the girl kept herself pure in her mind and soul as she suffered misfortunes and endured great indignities. Finally she visited the gravesite of a famous singer who lived a highly generous life and received spiritual peace. In the end Kieu was able to be reunited with her grateful family and to take up where she left off with her lost love."

Liên's eyes glistened with welling tears as she recounted the story. "The last verse of Kieu gives us an inspiration to be able to endure," she said to Anders. "'Deep inside us there lies the root of good. The heart means more than all talents on earth.' I have learned from Kieu not to question Buddha's directions. What will be, will be. We must retain our essential goodness no matter what happens around us. Don't you agree, Anders, my brother?"

Anders wanted to agree but knew it was too late for him. He had lost that essential 'root of good' and would never find it again. Whereas, he once considered himself to have a 'mandate of heaven' as the Confucians put it, he was no longer even sure of that.

By the first of December, Anders was proficient enough to pass his first examination in *Tây Sởn Vỏ Sĩ*, the first American, and almost the only foreigner ever to do so. He had mastered the forms, the katas that catalogued the weaponless defenses, and could use his hands and his feet as weapons in a dozen different ways that were becoming habitual and almost instinctual with the endlessly repetitive practice. He was now a student like all the rest in terms of acceptance by the *sensai* and the senior tutors. To his fellow students, he was giant who was learning their art at a threatening rate.

Like all students, Anders made a great many mistakes, noted unfailingly by the sharp-eyed *sensai* and the senior instructors, for whom even the slightest deviation from the correct path to perfection in the hallowed art was cause for repetitive instruction and practice. Master Nguyen's favorite quotation when Anders made another in a series of mistakes was from Kung Fu Tzu, "*Khi ngưới bặn cung bắn hụt trung tâm điểm, ông ta quay lại và tìm hiểu xem lý do nào đã gây ra sửử thất bại của chịnh mình.*" (When the archer misses the center of the target, he turns around and seeks the cause of his failure within himself.) Many was the night that Anders stayed late to seek and root out such failures.

When school closed for the holiday vacation period, Anders was selected for special honors in his history class, a singular experience for the young man who had never before in his life received an accolade. To obtain the honor he had had to master written modern Vietnamese—*quoc ngu*, the common language based on the Portuguese alphabet devised by Alexander de Rhodes, a seventeenth century Roman Catholic Jesuit missionary. Anders had brought himself, with Liên and her father's unselfish contributions, up to date on ancient Vietnamese history until he could contend with the native Vietnamese in his class during discussions. He wrote a paper on the lasting effects of foreign influence prior to the advent of the French.

In so doing, Anders became a fledgling scholar of Viet Nam and developed a lasting and genuine interest. He took pleasure in pouring over the best translations and railed at himself because he could not comprehend the *chu nho* Chinese ideograms or the *chu nom* Vietnamese renderings so vital to the reader of the old tomes.

Nonetheless, Anders grasped the root themes of the long, convoluted history and developed a sympathy for the Vietnamese' deep antipathy toward foreign influence born out of their chastening experience with recurrent domination from the outside. As he immersed himself in the literature and thinking, his attitudes about 'us and them' gradually leaned toward himself being aligned with the Vietnamese and against 'them,' the outsiders, thereby placing himself, at least his mind, in a schizophrenic position.

Anders gained more from the Mandarin's personal insights on his country's history than he got from the university. "Permit me to share with you . . ." , the old man would often begin . . ."the first battle of Dien Bien Phu, the one that took place in 1758. At that time the foreign overlords were the cruel Laotians who invaded *Bac Bo* nearly at will over the centuries. To intimidate the good people of Dien Bien Phu these terrible people drowned one hundred forty of their children and left their small bones to bleach on the river bank. Then they marched the people of the village to see the remains of their little ones and to be afraid. The people of Hanoi longed for a way to drive out the invaders and finally selected a great general named Hoang Cong Chat. General Hoang lacked a great army and had little in the way of supplies; but he was very determined, and he was clever.

"The general used his men to gather a large herd of goats secretly and to hide them in the hills above where the main encampment of the Laotians was located. In the night he had lighted candles tied to each of the goats' horns and then herded the animals with their flickering little lights down a mountain pass taking no care to avoid detection by the murderous Lao people. The enemy saw the great number of glimmering little lights and presumed that a huge reinforcement army had been gathered from Hanoi and was at that moment descending the hillside to overwhelm them. The Laotians fled in a panic leaving their belongings, and they never returned."

There was a lull in the PRU activity in late December owing to the CIA agents' desire to celebrate Christmas holidays. They gave a year end bonus of an extra month's pay to the contract agents and to the PRUCs, and lightened their work load. The largely Buddhist contractors were happy to have still another holiday to enjoy and made no distinction that it was a Christian one. Anders used the time to cram for his history final.

He memorized dates—the first Viet kingdom, i.e. south of the

Yangze, was recorded to have existed from 500 to 330 BC. and the first people who could be considered Vietnamese came down from there and settled in the Red River Delta of *Bac Bo* sometime between 300 and 200 BC. In 207 BC. these people stopped warring each other and united as the Kingdom of Nam Viet and controlled the area of Northern Viet Nam down to the plains below Hue'. In 111 BC. the Han Chinese conquered the southerners and started the era of domination marked by periodic unrest, including the brief resurgence in 39 AD. of the Vietnamese state under the Trung sisters, but persisted until 938 AD. In that year General Ngo Quyen led a successful revolt and for the next 900 years, Viet Nam was an independent state (except for one twenty year period of reoccupation).

Liên drilled him on the dates until he knew them almost in his sleep. He was amused that he had nowhere near the facility with the dates of significance in his native America as he did in his adopted Viet Nam. The Mandarin had taken such a liking to Anders that he too joined in the drilling. It became a family project to see the pleasant young foreigner through his difficult first year at the university.

Medieval Vietnamese history was in the Mandarin's area of scholarly expertise; and he guided the young man through the convolutions of the Great Viet State, established in 968, the conflicts of the Dinh dynasty with the Champa Kingdom to the south, the establishment of the Ly dynasty in 980 and their defenses against the aggressions of the Kingdom of Kampuchea. They named their country Dai-Viet and started the 700 year march to the south that culminated in the Viets establishing firm control from the Chinese border to the tip of the Indochinese peninsula by 1780.

The Lys were succeeded by the Trans in 1225 who repelled three Mongol invasions in their 175 year reign. The Chinese reinvaded and again took control in 1407 and made Viet Nam a southern province of China under the harsh Ming Dynasty. The country was divided north from south for 150 years ending in the late 1770s when the Nguyen family reunited the country and established their dynasty. The Tay Son Rebellion of 1778, led by three brothers, resulted in an unrelated Nguyen, Hue', naming himself emperor of a once again reunited Viet Nam.

In 1802 Nguyen Hue' was replaced by Nguyen Anh, who called himself Gia Long, after further bloody struggling. The Ching dynasty of China recognized the new Emperor and his country the following year after Gia Long agreed to a negotiated biannual tribute payment. Gia Long's great mistake was in accepting the help of the avaricious

French in his struggles thereby granting them an entering wedge and setting the stage for the First Indochinese War, another in the endless series of struggles characterizing the existence of Viet Nam from its inception to the present day.

Anders was more than content to leave the modern era, the French Colonial years and beyond, to the winter quarter of 1968. With the Nguyens help he took top honors in the Viet Nam history class by scoring an unprecedented one hundred percent on the final examination and by his paper on the pre-French era domination by foreign powers and their lasting influence. Ordinary Vietnamese steadfastly denied such influence, jealously holding to the uniqueness of their country's customs. Anders' paper caused enough of a stir to warrant a favorable article in the student newspaper about his level of scholarship. The Mandarin now introduced Anders as his protégé and took personal pride in the young man's accomplishments.

The war was never far from Anders' mind, no matter what else he did. Despite any questions he had about his own or his country's involvement, he remained dedicated to his purpose, which was, in his mind, to contribute to the defeat of the Viet Cong. When he was at work, he gave his whole attention; and he did so with a sense of personal mission. First of all, he felt an almost religious devotion to his group, the PRU. Secondly, he felt an obligation to his employers, the CIA and the United States; and lastly, he hated and despised the Viet Cong enemy. A newspaper article confirmed that sense of outraged loathing. The headline article described an atrocity perpetrated that month, December, 1967, by the VC. They burned the 256 villagers of the Montagnard village of Dak Son to death with flame throwers and razed their village to the ground. Anders was incensed and rededicated himself. His fervor did not, however, prevent him from taking the time to pursue his studies, to practice his martial art, or to cultivate the Mandarin's family.

Anders was invited by the senior members of the family to join them in the celebrations for their ancestors in the upcoming Tet celebration, a singular honor. Even Cleve Howard considered it a dramatically positive addition to Anders' cover story. Anders looked forward to Tet 1968 with more relish than he had ever done for a holiday or a celebration before. He felt more as if he were the member of a family than he had ever done.

CHAPTER 29

SECRET: In camera session, Senate Intelligence Oversight Committee.
Testimony of Wilmer A. Colding, Jr., Chief, Far Eastern Division, Central Intelligence Agency
   14 July, 1967
   1000
Subject: Phoenix Program, South Viet Nam

Chairman, Sen. Tittlebaum: Thank you for appearing, Director Colding.

Mr. Colding: My pleasure, Senator.

Sen. Tittlebaum: I don't think we are up to speed enough to ask the right questions at this point. May we begin with a statement from you followed by questions from my distinguished colleagues? For those of you who may not know, the subject before us is a new program instituted by the agency called Phoenix.

Mr. Colding: The President, Joint Chiefs, MACV command, and the Central Intelligence Agency have, for some time, become aware that we were failing to prosecute one aspect of the conflict in South Viet Nam adequately. That aspect is the infiltration of every facet of administrative life in the country by communists. We refer to the infiltrating insurgents as Viet Cong Infrastructure, VCI, for short. I am sure you realize the political delicacy of what I am about to say. However, it is now beyond question to state that the South Vietnamese are incapable of dealing with the problem. Their military lacks the means or the expertise to deal with the VCI. They have their hands full prosecuting the conventional war.
   A number of programs have been instituted to counteract the problem of infiltration, aiding and abetting the communist enemy, and singly, and in aggregate, they have failed. In part this is because there are two many programs, in part because they have conflicting aims; and in greatest part the failure is a result of the woeful inadequacy of the government of South Viet Nam to deal with it. They

617

simply lack the fortitude to pursue this aspect of the war, and equally importantly, they lack a police function nationwide, or even an effective police function in most major cities or anywhere in the countryside.

Sen. Fineton: Sorry to interrupt; but given that fact, why is it our responsibility to run their police force? I'm beginning to wonder what we are doing there at all if the Vietnamese aren't interested enough to save themselves from a communist takeover.

Sen. Tittlebaum: Please, let's not interrupt the director. But allow me to answer succinctly. We are the world's policemen against the insidious and violent growth of communism. We have seen the loss of North Korea, North Viet Nam, China, and McGeorge Bundy's aptly described domino effect is well underway. It is up to us to stem the red tide, even if the immediately threatened country lacks the vision to see the danger.

Sen. Fineton: I suppose.

Mr. Colding: In concert with GVN and ARVN we, and by that I mean the CIA, are to assume full control of the 'Hearts and Hands' and 'Pacification' programs. Phoenix will replace Revolutionary Development, Strategic Hamlets, Field Police, Open Arms, CT, and military intelligence functions relating to nonmilitary activities. In short, we will take over police activities in South Viet Nam and bring these criminals; they are not soldiers; to swift and sure justice. We are in the process of establishing a data base that will allow us to identify, track, and to arrest the criminals and to provide a documentary base for prosecution. If our efforts are to succeed in Viet Nam, then the United States, as a matter of practicality, will be obliged to assume police duties. Phoenix is that agency. We will establish the American justice system in that undeveloped country, and we will institute and maintain the due process of law.

Sen. Tittlebaum: How is the Phoenix program to be funded?

Mr. Colding: I believe, sir, that the funds will come from Agriculture and Defense without designation. Phoenix is Top Secret and will remain so, including its funding and administration.

Sen. Tittlebaum: The floor is open to questions from the committee.

Sen. Clyde: As I understand it, this is an entirely new program?

Mr. Colding: That is substantially correct.

Sen. Clyde: And it is a nonmilitary, police activity only?

Mr. Colding: Yes, sir.

Sen. Clyde: Will this require more Americans to be involved, more draftees, in effect, another escalation of the war? We already have demonstrations on our city streets against expansion of this conflict.

Mr. Colding: Aside from a few more senior police officials from the United States to supervise subordinates, there will be no escalation. The Field Police and Provincial Reconnaissance Units, both composed of fine Vietnamese police officers, will be absorbed into the Phoenix program. They will need some retraining, but will be ready in a matter of few months.

Sen. Clyde: That's all I have.

Sen. Tittlebaum: Sen. McMurtry?

Sen. McMurtry: Did I get this right? This is not a military activity, and the Phoenix program is not intended to increase the VC body count?

Mr. Colding: You are right. We have MACV and ARVN forces to conduct the military side of things—the body count, if you will. Phoenix is strictly a police action, not an executive one. Phoenix is not in the business of killing or fighting pitched battles with a military opponent. Phoenix is the Vietnamese counterpart of the FBI charged with the responsibility to identify, investigate, accumulate evidence, and to arrest perpetrators. The fate of the criminals arrested will be in the hands of the Vietnamese court system; but we will, by these sophisticated police methods effectively cut off the head of the snake.

Sen. McMurtry: I appreciate that. I, for one, would not wish to give my vote to sanction a secret police outfit, an organization above the democratic law of the land. I certainly would not be a party to supporting a program of clandestine terror or murder. I hope the agency will bear that in mind. The American people will not stand for that. I fail to see the need for such secrecy if the organization's heart is so pure and its hands so clean. Are you entirely sure that this is not another Diem type state terrorism organization?

Mr. Colding: Of course not, Senator. It pains me that you should feel the need to mention such a thing. Our hands are indeed clean.

Sen. Tittlebaum: Ladies and Gentlemen, Mr. Colding, it's time for a coffee break. We'll adjourn for half an hour then we can resume with the Senator from Pennsylvania, Mr. Apton, and his questions.

Session adjourned until 1130.

"Two main conclusions that developed from this testimony are these...First, the South Vietnamese lacked commitment in this war; that we need to win the war; it just does not exist. Second, if our economic program in South Viet Nam is ever going to succeed, it is only going to succeed because we completely Americanize it from beginning to end...And the ranking administration spokesman in this area acknowledges very candidly that the South Vietnamese commitment to the war effort is so inadequate that the annual United States two hundred million commodity import program in Viet Nam is actually a political ransom paid to powerful South Vietnamese commercial interests...It is a ransom; it is a ransom we must pay to prop up a house of cards in Viet Nam...It seems to me that if we want to continue to have the support of the all powerful commercial interests in Viet Nam to the war and their commitment to the stability of the government we have got to be willing to pay ransom...It comes from the pockets of the American citizens...What a sorry state of affairs...We will invest this year a quarter of our national budget, some thirty billion dollars. Why?...To create a military shield, a temporary military shield. The South Vietnamese economy is growing fat on US financed war economy...So, as things stand presently, the other war is not being won, and with these conditions it cannot be won.

"There is now clear evidence that the South Vietnamese are not pulling their share of the load in the war there. They are pulling less and less of their share of the load each day...The stakes are too high. This is their war. They have to fight it...We have an unmanageable mess...Perhaps we are crossing the line in terms of Americanizing this entire operation in Viet Nam, and we can never come back."

Statement of Congressman Reigle, quoting testimony of a Mr. Poats, head of the US economic program for Viet Nam, The Congressional Record, 90th Congress, first session, Vol. 113: Number 147, Washington, DC, Tuesday, September 19, 1967

CHAPTER 30

As time went on and the communist threat became real and dangerous, American involvement grew and took on increasingly moralistic and self-righteous overtones. It took on the quality of a crusade. But somehow, perhaps very soon in its inception but apparently too late to change, the leaders took a wrong turning. The captains and foot soldiers did what was expected of them, but they were lost. One wonders whether Gibbon's comment on the medieval crusades may not apply to our own: 'The lives and labor of millions...would have been more profitably employed in the improvement of their native country.'

Chester L. Cooper, The Lost Crusade—America in Vietnam

Anders Bergstrom, formerly of Zarahemla, Utah, USA, welcomed the approach of Tet, 1968, in Thau Thien Province, RVN, with as much excitement as he had ever had for Christmas and Santa Claus during his childhood in The World. If anything, his enthusiasm exceeded that of the populace of Hue'; but Anders scarcely noted the muting of excitement and preparation for the lunar new year in the city. For the first time in his recollection, he was enfolded in an important family celebration, and he reveled unabashedly in the activities of the large nuclear and extended Nguyen family of The Mandarin. He was accepted as a fixture in the family's preparations, even accorded the singular honor of eating at the family table. When guests from outside the family came to call, Anders was seated in the inner room with the closest relatives. The Mandarin and his family gave Anders a sense of belonging that he had heretofore lacked.

Anders received an embossed zodiac card from Mme Nguyen giving his horoscope for the year. She said that the family regarded him as having been born, to them at least, in *Nhâm Thân*, that Can+Chi Year of the Monkey. The card read:

*Bạn dược sinh ra dưới mội dâu hiệu thậnh công nhất.
Ban lá môt người tư tin và thông minh, mạnh mẽ và
cương quyết. Ban luôn phấn đấu để trở nên hoàn hảo.
Ban hòa hợp với tuổi con Rồng vá con Chuột và tuối
tối ky với bạn là con Cọp.*

(You are born under a most successful sign. You are
persuasive and intelligent, forceful and determined.
You strive to excel. You are compatible with the
Dragon and the Rat and your opposite is the Tiger.)

He stored the memento away in the same safe hiding place where he
kept his extra passports (Karl Oscar Isaacson, Lars Magnusson, and
Remundo Mueller-Garza) and his mad money—the cash in American
dollars, Vietnamese Piastres, Laotian kip, Thai baht, and Burmese
kyat—funds to permit an escape if ever that were to prove necessary.

The entire family, The Mandarin and Mme Nguyen, and servants
included, worked several days well into the night to make the family's
lotus seed candy. Anders was completely unfamiliar and inexperienced with any kind of cooking or candy making and made a terrible
sticky mess around his work area causing Liên to point out his
ineptitude to everyone in the family. The mess became a family joke
and was memorialized in an affectionate photograph of Anders and
Liên holding mangled paper flowers by the stickiness of their forearms. That photograph was also placed in the hiding place with his
passports and his mad money.

The Mandarin consented to pose in full costume with each member
of the family individually and honored Anders by asking him to join
with the patriarch for his own picture. That memento joined the other
in Anders' small collection of personal treasures. Even the old and
honored grandparents joined the entire large family for a formal
portrait. They were dressed in their cherished and nostalgic velvet
turbans, brocade silk and satin robes; she in embroidered slippers, and
he in velvet royal shoes.

The air in the Mandarin's home was filled with the scent of incense
and moistened sandal wood. Mme Nguyen had hired a group of
traditional string players and singers. They filled the air with muted
strains of kit flutes, three and four stringed lutes, dual string and steel
string violins, and castanets. There was an deep sense of warmth, and
culture, and belonging.

The family and Anders collected or made fireworks and joss sticks, set out the required Kumquat trees in teak boxes around the house and on the street, and kept the peach blossom and cut flower decorations fresh throughout the house and gardens. Anders even joined the giggling children to make paper *Phung Hoang* birds, lanterns, and dragons. The family preparations assumed greater importance to everyone of them because the week long flower festival in the city, preceding the actual three day Tet Nguyen Dan festivities, seemed lackluster compared to other years. In fact, the people of Hue' seemed less active, less involved, and in every way less visible than in years past. Anders and the family wrote that observation off to their having seen the festival too many times in the past and to their own overly high expectations for the festival.

Cleve Howard took a different point of view of the same observations. He had Anders and Tring Van Dong come to the new CORDS building in the MACV compound early in the afternoon of Tet Eve— January 31, for a briefing. In the headquarters office, Anders saw Sylvia Chin and Nguyen Hai Truong again for the first time since he had come to Viet Nam.

"Hello, again, giant," effused Sylvia in her usual bantering voice.

"Hello, yourself, Miss Chin. I'm glad to see you. They told us you were going to be here in Hue'. I'm glad to know you are still on our side," Anders said, returning her smile.

"You're just glad that you don't have to play hide and seek with me anymore."

"For sure," he said both smiling and smarting at the memory of The Farm wilderness experience.

"You know Truong, don't you, Anders?" Cleve asked gesturing to the handsome Vietnamese who had been standing by quietly.

"Certainly do. Great to see you again. Keeping out of trouble in bars lately?"

Truong extended his hand. "You should talk," he said joining the bantering tone. Anders and Truong shook hands warmly. Their facial expressions conveyed their genuine pleasure at the renewal of their old friendship.

"And this is Tring Van Dong, our other RD/O. I guess we just call him a PRU/O now, something like that. They change programs so often, I have given up on proper titles," Mr. Howard said. The contract officer shook hands with the two Company agents and with Anders.

"The main reason I wanted to have you come in this afternoon is to get you together in one place. We will all be working as something of a team and will share information, reports, and the like. I'd suggest that you four get to know each other better, work out some codes and radio frequencies; that sort of thing. I have more than a hunch that we are going to be needing one another as time goes on."

That seemed to foreshadow a revelation. Everyone waited expectantly.

Howard went on, "That's right," he said, reading their faces, "I think something's up. So does General Ngo. Maybe you've noticed how little activity there is for Tet. The people seem to be going through the motions, but aren't really into the season. They aren't as excited as in years past. Am I imagining things?"

"I don't think so, chief," Tring Van Dong offered. "Out in the countryside where my PRU is working, we see more people than usual. I think fewer of them are coming in to Hue' for Tet."

"I don't think there are nearly as many people in Hue' this year. The Year of the Monkey should be a big one, and it is not shaping up that way. I spent most of my childhood Tets here; this is the least exciting one I've ever seen," said Truong.

"Anders?" asked Cleve.

Anders shrugged, "I haven't noticed anything much out of the ordinary. But then, this is only my second Tet. I'm having a good time."

"Don't have too good of a time. I think something is going on, and it bothers me not to know what. I just want to insert a note of caution. Don't get lulled. For one thing, I think there has been an increase in guerrilla activity in the past month or so despite the increased activity with Phoenix. Did you all read about the massacre at Dak Son?"

Every head shook to indicate they had. Their faces took on a harder edge.

"Anyhow, keep your eyes and ears open. Let us know here if you pick up anything. It's Tet Eve tonight. I don't expect anything to happen until after the three day Mardi Gras, but with the VC you never can tell. General Ngo is pretty skittish, too. He has put the garrison on one hundred percent alert. He wants all of us to come over to the Citadel to his HQ for a flag raising ceremony tonight to bring in the Year of the Monkey in style, okay?"

The three men and Miss Chin nodded dutifully even though they all had had other plans. Anders was the most disappointed because he was going to be at The Mandarin's family dinner. He knew firsthand what great food was going to be served. He had looked forward to sitting by Liên. He shrugged and accepted the call to duty as overriding, but he was not that pleased about it. He tried not to show his lack of enthusiasm in his face.

"Spruce up in your formal best—my request," continued Cleve Howard after he had obtained the assent of his troops. "And bring your weapons—General Ngo's request—just to be on the safe side. He has no combat troops, only garrison and administrative people. He feels like his butt is hanging out and wants any firepower he can get. It's probably nothing. Maybe the brigadier and I have just become a pair of old ladies, but indulge us anyway."

It was a pain, but Anders picked up an M-203 (an M-16 modified to hold a 40 mm grenade launcher barrel attached to the front hand grip guard under the main barrel) and a .45 hand gun with plenty of spare ammunition magazines from the master sergeant in charge of the CORDS armory. The marine gave him the usual hassle about seeing to it that everything came back in good order and that he be able to account for every round fired. Anders had to sign two forms in four places, as usual, and was in a mildly foul mood by the time he had found a place to stow the weaponry until the night's activities in the Citadel started.

Liên dispelled the gray vapors of his negative mood by bestowing a smile and her arm to lead Anders into the family's meeting room for the annual Nguyen tradition of honoring the ancestors. They always started promptly at three o'clock in the afternoon and heard the timeworn but still fresh and exciting stories of The Mandarin's and Mme Nguyen's illustrious ancestors until seven o'clock, after which they went together to dinner. It was also a tradition for one of The Mandarin's children to recount the life of the patriarch of the family. It would smack of self-aggrandizement for either the old man himself or for one of his wives to tell of his distinguished life. This year, for the first time, Liên, the youngest, had the duty and honor. She was a little nervous.

After two hours of great stories told in an entertaining way by the old father and mother to an appreciative audience, The Mandarin signaled a break and the servants brought in refreshing draughts of chilled Vietnamese plum wine and slices of fresh French brie. In a few minutes it was Liên's turn.

"Father was not always The Mandarin," she began. The grandchildren and cousins looked perplexed. They could not imagine a time when he had not occupied his lofty post.

"No, he was once a boy. A very special boy. In those times, long ago, the emperor's court selected the very best boys to take places in the court, in the government, and in the military. They appointed civil and military mandarins from among the most talented and quick young men

625

in the whole country. Once they were selected, these men served the emperor and the people for their whole lives and were given great honor.

"Young Nguyen Cao Lai was a good student, the best in his school. He was also known to be one of the town's best boys. So, when the great State Literary Examinations were announced, Lai was recommended by the director of his school." Simply hearing The Mandarin's given name of Lai out loud caused a minor flutter among the family who could only regard the venerable old man in a formal way. Anders was fascinated by the insight into the high society of Viet Nam and willed Liên to hurry along with her rendition.

"It was 1917, the next to the last year the test was given, although Lai did not know that at the time. The test was first given in the year 1075 of our common era," she avoided use of the term 'AD.' because of The Mandarin's preference to avoid all things Christian or otherwise foreign on this great holiday.

"The only real change in the classical Confucian style test over the years was that the French required the addition of questions on modern Colonial administration, and the test was given in both the Vietnamese and French languages. There were a series of tests, actually, designed to find the best of the best and to elevate them to important places in the administration. The tests required great feats of memory about Chinese philosophy, Chinese and Vietnamese literature, and demonstrations of the greatest skill in *chu nho* writing. It was required of those taking the tests to recite passages and to prove points based on the *ngu kinh* and the *tutho*—the five ancient and four classical books, on the works of Kung Fu Tzu, and on the *suky* histories of Viet Nam."

Anders could only remember something about 'Confucius say...' jokes, and marveled that The Mandarin had been able to learn and to discuss all of that seriously.

"You know that passing any of the five stages of the examinations guaranteed an honorable place for a boy. Those who passed the lowest level examination, the *Khao Khoa,* in their county did not have to go into the military service, do forced labor, or pay taxes, but they were not given a position nor a title. The *Hach Thi* was given in the province only once every two years.

"Three years," came The Mandarin's quiet correcting voice. Liên blushed scarlet.

"Thank you Father. I have not done my work well enough, I'm sorry." He dismissed her concerns with a charitable paternal nod of his head. She was doing very well being only a girl.

She went on, "The *Hach Thi* served to qualify those who passed it for the *Huong Thi*, the regional examination, which also was held only once in three years. Depending on how well they scored, the young men were given titles and ranks in the mandarinate. Many thousands took the test; about a hundred or maybe as many as three hundred became *tu tai*. Lai, our Father, scored so high that he was awarded *cuu nhan* level and qualified to take the *Hoi Thi* Capital examination. He was only one of eleven who did so. His parents were overjoyed at the success of their eldest son.

"The *Hoi Thi* was also held every three years. Father passed with a high score and was allowed to take the highest test, the *Dinh Thi* Palace examination. The emperor himself made up this examination and chose the final successful candidates." There was a polite but audible oohing from the young people listening raptly to Liên.

"Father Lai was taken to the Imperial Palace," more oohing.

"Each of these, the highest examinations, were held in the Imperial Scholar's Quarters and to guard against the sin of cheating, the Minister of Rituals assigned monitors to watch over the men as they worked. The men taking the tests were not allowed to bring anything to the examination center except their personal clothing. They were provided with a small tent and a floor mat to sit on, paper, pens and brushes, and a one man writing desk. In each examination period lasting twelve hours, there were five subjects that required a lifetime to master. The young men wrote on the *Van Chuong, Van Sach* and *Van Luan,* the *Bai Tho, Bai Phu,* and *Doi Lien.*"

There was a pause in Liên's narrative while her elder brother Nguyen Bai Lon quickly whispered to Anders the nature of the five areas of testing. The *Van Chuong* were the literary periods which required identification and explanation of meaning; the *Van Sach* and *Van Luan* were responses to interrogatories regarding political events at any time frame in Vietnamese history. *Bai Tho* was a composition in verse in the traditional style, an original work. *Bai Phu* required the candidate to write, in poetic style, a descriptive commentary on some important Vietnamese geographical feature, event, or person. *Doi Lien*—the matched inscriptions—was a composition written in the difficult method of parallel verse. Anders listened and nodded, trying not to draw too much attention to himself or to detract from Liên's carefully practiced presentation.

"Then Father and the other candidates wrote papers on court practices, training for imperial service, tributes to the mandarins, principles and practices of taxation, military conscription and service and the like.

"In 1917, Lai was the only man who passed the test. He did so well that he was given the highest title, that of *Tien Si*." To Anders Liên said, "Doctor."

Anders smiled his thanks. Except for such archaic and esoteric terms he was pleased to see that he was now keeping up with the presentation in Vietnamese quite well.

"Even those who failed were awarded tutorships with the great nobles or became teachers, or even became lower ranked officials. Our ancestor, still living, became the Emperor's Mandarin, the most important civil post in the country. He was awarded his degree and his position at a state banquet given by the emperor himself. He received his cap and gown and this blue parasol." Liên delicately presented the beautiful and honored family heirloom to the view of her audience. The treasured parasol was only brought out once a year on Tet Eve for the family to see. No one else was granted such a privilege. Anders felt humbled at the privilege he was accorded and bowed his head in suitable deference.

"The young Mandarin was given a horse in the imperial garden and rode through the streets of the imperial city in his cap and gown in a grand parade for all to see and admire. He was only the 2031st chosen in the years from 1057 CE to 1918. It was a great day for our family. The ancestors were very proud." It was The Mandarin's turn to bow his head in acknowledgment of having been able to bring honor to those Great Ones.

"Our Mandarin's name was inscribed in Van Mieu at the Temple of Literature then he was given a feast in his honor by the mandarins of all Hue', our Father's home city. His parents and his betrothed, our honored mother, were invited, and their hearts almost burst from pride at the honor their son had brought to the family." Mme Nguyen was crying softly with joy at the remembrance as she did each year at the Tet Eve retelling.

Then The Mandarin surprised them all by asking for their attention. "I wish to pay homage to this woman, my dear wife," he announced. It was a most uncommon thing to call formal attention to the woman of the house in family gatherings. "I would like to compare her to the eternal woman described by our great nineteenth century poet, Tran Te Xuong.

Quanh năm suốt tháng xuôi giòng nửớc

Tần tảo nuôi chồng lẫn năm con
Thui thủi mội mình trên sa mạc
Bương hã thuyền nan bắt kịp dòng

All the year round, she is trading along the river bank
To support her poet husband and her five children.
Either walking lonely on desert lanes
Or hurrying up to catch the ferryboat.

Mme. Nguyen averted her eyes from those of her husband. Her emotions were too intense at that moment to bear his glance. They were glistening. Anders was touched by the muted display of familial pride and the obvious deep affection the old man and woman shared.

At seven that evening, the prescribed hour, Liên concluded her delivery of the annual tribute to The Mandarin, and the members of the family responded with careful applause. They stood in respect for the old patriarch and for the family. Anders took a few mildly critical glances when he clapped overly loudly. Mme Nguyen left to greet the evening's guests, and the remainder of the assembled family made their way into the family's private dining room to reminisce and to sample hors d'oeuvres.

"Good bye, Liên," Anders said, in French, as usual, as he put on his suit jacket. He had warned her earlier that he would have to leave before dinner.

"It is sad that you cannot be with the family for this important dinner, brother," she said shyly in the same language. "But I understand the necessity to show yourself at the Citadel's celebration and to represent your Red Cross superiors. I have already given your regrets to Mother and Father. They understand as well. You are invited to come with us tomorrow for the cleaning and decorating of the ancestor's graves."

"I will be there. I plan to bring flowers. Is that proper?"

"Very much so. Even if you were not so accepted by the family, it would be well to show your respect to the ones departed. Until tomorrow," she extended her tiny hand toward his large one. It was the first time he had shaken her hand; in Viet Nam it was rare for males and females to shake hands.

As they shook hands, Anders caught sight of Master Nguyen Van, his karate' instructor being ushered into the guests' waiting antechamber. He left Liên and bowed low to the grand old man of Hue' martial arts.

629

"*Thầy Nguyễn,*" (Master Nguyen) he said softly, "*Tôi rất lấy làm hân hạnh được gập ông vào dịp quan trọng này.*" (I am honored to see you on this important occasion.)

"*À, người học trò Việt Nam tóc trắng của tôi,*" (Ah, my white haired Vietnamese student,) the older man replied with a wry smile. He was known still to advertise that his dojo remained pure Vietnamese. His unspoken affection for the Caucasian boy, and Anders' respect for the *sensai* and for things Vietnamese were so apparent and genuine, that no one felt inclined to dispute the accuracy of the claim. "*Tôi cũng hài lòng được thấy anh. tôi để ý thấy anh duy trì được sậu yêu chuộng của gia đình vị quan Đại Thần. Điều đó thì tốt. Tôi sợ rắng anh sẽ quá ham mề buổi tối hôm nay và sẽ bị nhọc sữc vào ngào mai,*" (I, too, am pleased to see you. I take note that you maintain your good standing with the family of The Mandarin. That is good. I fear that you will overindulge this night and will be a drudge of a student tomorrow.) he said; his eyes contained a laugh.

"*Tôi sẽ có mật ở đó sớm và sẵn sàng thách thửc những đối thủ của tôi,*" (I will be there early and ready to challenge my betters.) Anders said with emphasis but humility.

"*Hãy tử tế và đừng có làm ồn ào. Đai óc già nua của tôi không còn tinh thần chịu đựng hay những giờ giấc trễ nải mà tôi đã có lẩn làm. Tôi nghi ngớ rắng Vị Quan Đại Thần sẽ nhử tôi dính líu vào cả hai điầu này.*" (Be kind and do not make noise then. My old head does not tolerate spirits or late hours as well as it once did. I suspect The Mandarin will tempt me to indulge in both.) They both smiled, and Anders bade him good night.

It was cool, unseasonably so. Anders shivered in his tropical white suit. The monsoon season was still in the heavy misted air. Anders took a pedicab first to pick up his weapons, then to the Citadel, nodded perfunctorily to the yellow RVN flag with its three red stripes unfurled on the Flag Tower, and entered the Imperial City. He walked briskly to the northern portion of the walled enclosure where he met Tring Van Dong, Sylvia Lee, Cleve Howard, and Nguyen Hai Truong as they were all converging on the grassy patch where the flag ceremony was about to begin. They were greeted personally by their host, Brigadier General Ngo Quang Truong, commander of the ARVN First Division. As he shook hands with each of them, he eyed their weapons appreciatively.

"Thank you for coming. I regret that it is not a more pleasant evening. Perhaps I can tempt you with something to drink." The guests all nodded and accepted, even Anders who did not wish to offend or explain his heretofore staunchly maintained teetotaler status.

The ceremony and the polite interchanges afterward were pleasant enough and correct, but uneasy. The general had canceled all leaves, and Anders could not remember seeing ARVN soldiers at such a state of readiness. The ARVN First Division was one of the most respected in its country's armed forces, and the general was one of the few commanders accorded respect by the American military out of his sight. Around midnight, the conversations waned, and the general announced that he had work to do. He had an adjutant show the guests to quarters emphasizing once again his feeling that precautionary measures seemed prudent.

Anders was very tired. The excitement of the family activity following upon his months of pursuing a very hectic schedule were catching up with him. He retired to the incommodious military cot, and heedless of the discomfort occasioned by having too much body and too little cot, went fast asleep, too deep for remembered dreams.

At precisely 0340 in the dark and drizzly morning of 31 January, the sky over the Citadel and the city of Hue' was rent with a cacophony of rocket and mortar fire coming from the surrounding forested mountains. The Viet Cong and North Vietnamese Army had launched the Tet Offensive of 1968 upon Hue' and at dozens of selected sites all over South Viet Nam. The offensive had been planned for weeks, and the infiltrators had brought in artillery pieces, small arms, and ammunition in small hidden lots with great patience. Communist soldiers had surreptitiously infiltrated into the city along with holiday festival traffic. Once in the city, they shucked their disguises and donned their military uniforms. The main early barrage was directed at the MACV compound on the south side of the River of Perfumes.

A steady thump of B-40 rocket propelled grenades cascaded against the concrete defense walls of the US military enclosure. Satchel charges, mortars, and small arms joined in the barrage. The VC and NVA were attacking the MACV compound in a ground assault. Shortly, a similar artillery attack was launched on the Citadel. Anders and the other CIA operatives were up, armed, ready at the first sound of the rockets and mountain howitzers. At that point, the ground attack did not include the ARVN forces in the Citadel; so, there was nothing to shoot at. The CIA agents kept their heads down in the best defensive positions they could find. Brigadier General Ngo and his men did the same. The situation was chaotic; no one knew precisely what was going on.

Across the river, from MACV, the hastily mustered Americans began to return fire. They opened up with a fierce fusillade of M-16s, grenades, and M-79 grenade launchers. The misty cold air was choked with the acrid smell of cordite. Canisters of CS tear gas exploded sporadically making visibility very limited. The American return fire was so intense that the ground attack was called off, and the communists barricaded themselves into nearby buildings to keep up withering fire on the American defensive position.

The Mandarin's family had made preparations for an attack, and they and the Tet Eve guests who stayed over fled quickly into a concrete bunker basement to wait out the fire storm. Less affluent citizens of Hue' quavered behind closed doors. The least fortunate died in the onslaught, and the only living persons who could be seen on the streets were grieving relatives covering the bodies with white shrouds of mourning and squatting by the corpses wailing in grief and fear.

Brigadier General Truong and his meager garrison forces and the few foreigners and CIA operatives trapped with him became responsible for the defense of the Citadel and the north side of the river. There was precious little they could do; so, Ngo elected to do nothing. Anders and the other fighters were frustrated but could not fault the general for his inactivity.

The miserable weather became worse, offering further aid to the attackers. The temperature dropped to fifty degrees, and a strong monsoon downpour drenched the town. Heavy ground fog hid the movements of the two attacking regiments (7500 NVA and VC in eight battalions) as they overran the city. The invaders started a campaign of slaughter of Hue' civilians in a prearranged manhunt, killing defenseless citizens named on extermination lists.

A huge Viet Cong flag was mounted over the Imperial Palace from 0800 on the first morning of the offensive. Anders and his people, and the ARVN soldiers fired sporadically at small incursions; but the bulk of the battle was taking place elsewhere out of their sight. The brilliant red, blue, and gold NLF pennant fluttered over the palace day after day to taunt the men and women trapped inside the limited protective walls of the Citadel.

Frantic radio messages brought marines from Danang, at first in limited and uncoordinated groups, and later in the day, in organized units. They were transported in limited numbers by helicopter at first, and then their units were able to enter the city across the Au Cuu Bridge over the Phu Cam Canal and across the Nguyen Hoang Bridge that the NVA engineers had not had time to destroy. They did not even have a map of the city until a grunt obtained one from a battered Shell gasoline service station. By nightfall of the first night of fighting, the marines were methodically and painfully locked in door to door combat in the early efforts to dislodge the determined communists. In the dark and secret, the murders proceeded. It was a scene from Dante's Inferno.

The fighting continued at full intensity into the next day. The silver bridge (Nguyen Hoang) was blown making communication and traffic from the north side to the south side very difficult and hazardous and gave the communists a much needed boost. From day two as many ARVN forces as possible were infiltrated, fought, forced, or sneaked their way into the Citadel to reinforce the beleaguered First Division. Finally, a reasonable fighting force was assembled under Ngo's control including two companies of the first regiment, fourth battalion, members of the second and third regiments and the third division, Vietnamese marines, and the first ranger group. There were substantial components of Task Force A and the twenty-first and thirty-ninth battalions. Ngo would not squander his forces against the overwhelming numbers and firepower arrayed against him, and was roundly criticized by the US Marines for not breaking through and establishing a second, pincer, front against the enemy. Anders, Sylvia, Dong, and Truong chafed at having to stay put and being only able to fire occasionally and ineffectively. Cleve Howard kept his head down and reminded his people that it was not their responsibility to mount a war. They were policemen.

The NVA troops were constantly being reinforced by fresh soldiers rushed unimpeded down the myriad paths of the Ho Chi Minh Trail and from the villages and farms throughout Quang Tri, Thau Thien, and Quang Nam provinces. They pulled out all the stops and committed all of their assets, hidden and open. The hit squads continued their daily work of murder along with the commitment to the hot battle raging from building to building, street to street, and neighborhood to neighborhood. Every time the ARVN forces attempted to move out of the Citadel, they were driven back. Anders thought they were not trying very hard; but then, he realized he was not in possession of all of the facts coming in to General Ngo.

The weather was atrocious and continued to work in the NVA and

VC's favor. Visibility was minimal; and the marines, who had to do it alone, could not advance more than a few blocks in a morning, sometimes no more than a few feet. The orders to the ARVN troops were to stay put and to keep their casualties to a minimum. They complied until they were backed up into a small section of the northwest corner of the Citadel. Anders was becoming angry and frustrated. He was all for breaking out and making an attack, or sending out snipers and ambushers, anything except sitting there.

By February ninth, the tenth day of fighting, Brigadier General Ngo swallowed his pride and requested assistance from the US Marines who were, themselves, locked in a deadly struggle for survival, let alone advancement. Nevertheless, on February 12, they came. The five CIA people gave vent to cheering as they saw the marines sailing in force up the river to the Bao Vinh Quay north of the Citadel where they disembarked. The marines advanced on the northeast wall of the old Citadel fighting furiously as they went. When they entered the narrow streets in front of the wall, the Citadel tower, house windows, doors, sheds, and ditches erupted into a hell storm of gun, rocket, and grenade fire. The marines could do nothing but duck into the protection of civilian homes. They drove out the terrified citizens and helped themselves to the few belongings that had not been taken by the wave of communist soldiers who holed up in the homes before being driven out by the marines.

Anders emitted a groan audible over the firefight. He spoke for the entire garrison in so doing. He vowed that he would not go down cringing in some little hole there in the reduced area he and his cohorts controlled. He gritted his teeth and swore that he would fight and die doing so rather than hiding and waiting just because a soldier whom he, by now, did not respect, had given orders. This was not the time, however. An attempt to leave at this point was suicide. If he were not killed by the VC or NVA, he would be brought down by friendly fire. He would have to sit there frozen in the cold rain for a while longer. He and his friends had had little to eat and less sleep, and the exposure and deprivation were beginning to take their tolls.

The fighting around the Citadel continued unabated for a full four days. Navy cruisers fired heavy artillery that made a noise like a freight train coming in; and they and the 106 mm recoilless rifles fired by the marines on the scene slowly pounded the tower, most of the Imperial City, the Citadel, and the emperors' tombs into varying degrees of rubble. Irreplaceable architectural treasures already badly damaged in the First Indochina War were destroyed. Finally, the communists retreated.

In the relative quiet that prevailed after the main battle subsided, Cleve Howard, now fully armed and appearing fit and ready, called all of the CIA people together.

"We have work to do. It won't do anybody a bit of good if we all buy it here. Dead heroes are worthless, and I don't propose we hang around and fight to the last man for some piece of glory attached to the Battle of Hue'. Tonight, we are going to skedaddle. I've been studying the areas for escape routes, and I have a detailed set of sites where I think we can get out safely, if there is any such thing any more. Besides, my butt is frozen off; and I'm hungry. Here," he said and showed them the map he had drawn during his hours of evident inactivity.

That night all five of them deserted. They each took a different route but arranged in advance to place at least one Asian appearing agent with a Caucasian to minimize the likelihood of being killed by friendly fire at least. It was pitch black, freezing; and the rain was pouring down. It was the best possible time to go, and they all left in separate pairs around 0230.

Anders and Sylvia went out together. He wore an old olive drab skivvy shirt over his head to tone down the reflections from his golden hair. She moved with less ostentation than a shadow. Along the way, shrouded in darkness, they happened on bodies of dead soldiers, but what disturbed them to their cores was the discovery of unarmed civilians lying face down in ditches with their thin arms bound behind their backs. They had been shot in the back of the head. In one hellhole of a concrete drainage channel they found dozens of corpses of civilians who had been burned alive. They had been dead for several days.

The two of them and the remaining members of Cleve Howard's group made their way safely to the MACV compound and, after an elongated discussion necessitated because they had no idea what the password of the day was, were admitted under the muzzles of a hundred M-16s. Everybody was dead tired and dead serious.

The counterattack started after the battle of the Citadel was over. It took a month of hunting, fear, surprises, and killing to drive out the last of the PAVN and VC forces from the city and surrounding country-side. Five thousand of them were killed in the battle. When it was all over, 216 Americans were dead, 1,364 were seriously wounded, 384 ARVN regulars had been killed and 1,830 seriously wounded, and 6,000 civilians were dead. In the investigations during the aftermath of the offensive, it was determined that at least 3,000 defenseless civilians had been murdered over and above those who had perished in the crossfire. In one mass grave there were 1,200 bodies. The murder victims included RVN government workers, priests, intellectuals, and nonVietnamese. In one group, there were 400 individuals whose only crime was that they were Catholics. They were taken from their church sanctuary and marched around the countryside being murdered in small groups; so, the bodies could be hidden. There were men, women, and children; age and sex were no protection. Some of the victims were killed simply because they had been witnesses to the atrocities. Fifty percent of the venerable old city of the Nguyen Lords was destroyed leaving 116,000 homeless.

With these planned, prearranged killings, and sporadic uncalled for atrocities, that included groups of terrified civilians who had surrendered to the invaders, Hue' lost its innocence, its security, its treasured old buildings, and its belief that it was exempt from the war. In the days that followed, there was a climate of bitterness, hatred, and fear that was almost palpable. And the people who feared the most were the Viet Cong and the NVA stragglers hiding in the hills and their helpers in the villages and on the farms. The Sword of Damocles teetered over them, and they were deeply aware of their well-deserved danger.

Lane Duerk was patched through to Cleve Howard as soon as communications could be restored.

"You have the list of suspects. Nobody who helped these monsters gets away because of some timidity on our parts, got that? There has to be retribution. 'Cry havoc and let slip the dogs of war,' brother," he ordered succinctly and meant every word and drop of vehemence.

And there was retribution. From its vaunted blacklist the Phoenix program cranked out scores of names of VCI, and the PRUs all over South Viet Nam went after them with a coldhearted vengeance. Anders spared no one he suspected as he rolled through the names and places supplied him. For a month, he and his men participated in a near demonic program of retaliation. Phoenix accounted for twenty thousand killings of VCI and VCSs in the next two and a half years. The US counterattack was the personification of brutality on the remnants of the VC not already cut to pieces in their desperate and militarily unsuccessful Tet offensive. 1968 was a year that would live in infamy and would result in the virtual destruction of COSVN fighters in any kind of useful force. By 1969, nearly the entire war was conducted by the regular NVA. The communist forces lost, during the Tet Offensive and its aftermath, 40,000 KIA, 5,000 disabled, and 3,000 captured. Thousands of supporters of the NVA/VC cause paid the ultimate price for the temerity of that offensive. The military cost and defeat might well have spelled the end for the communist insurgency.

Ordinary activities of Hue' closed down for months while stunned citizens wearily tried to clean up and to rebuild their shattered city and lives. Sewage, water, electrical, garbage, and police services were nonexistent for a time. The doors of the university and its library were closed. The cafes no longer blared jazz music. There were no prolonged circuitous intellectual discussions. The students conversed in hushed tones about their ultimate exposure to reality. There were no more illusions. War had come to Hue'; no place was safe, or sane, or had promise for the future. A profound depression settled over the old city.

Anders and his PRUCs were peripherally involved in one of the major military campaigns of the post Tet offensive period. The Apache Snow campaign was scheduled for early May. The Phoenix program information detailed the whereabouts and activities of a large number of VCI and the units they served in the region of the A Shau Valley. It was the PRU's assignment to help neutralize that support before the main campaign got underway.

The A Shau Valley was located in southwestern Thau Thien Province on the Rao Loa River very near the Laotian border and the Ho Chi Minh Trail. The area was rough and untamed, largely uncharted. It consisted of remote rugged forested mountains and was sparsely inhabited. Because of its strategic location near a major infiltration point, the US special forces had organized the locals into a CIDG six years previously. Their camp was overrun in March 1966 by regular NVA and was abandoned to the enemy who established it as a major base. Several operations had been mounted to dislodge the PAVN forces during 1968 and early in 1969; but none of them constituted a major effort; and none of them were successful.

Apache Snow was a major campaign mounted for both strategic and psychological reasons. It was long and well planned and involved a significant commitment by the US 101st Airborne, 1st Infantry Division, 9th Marine Regiment and the ARVN 3rd Regiment.

The POIC ordered his lieutenants to a meeting and outlined their assignment in Apache Snow during the second week in April. "Interesting development," he told them. "Turns out the most dangerous force out there is a bunch of girls." The agents looked askance at one another.

"It's true. The intel we picked up as well as what comes in from the marines is that there is a full platoon, maybe more, of guerrillas who are tough, effective, mobile, very well supplied, and all female out there in the Ngu Hanh Son range. The Congettes have been disrupting marine patrols, blowing up arms caches and ammo dumps, and sabotaging vehicles and artillery pieces for three years. They are good, very, very good. But we are better, and we are going to get them. Here's the plan we worked out with the marines. You might guess that they were none too happy to admit that they were stymied by a gang of women."

Howard outlined a plan of infiltration of three and four man scouting teams into defined areas where the female platoon was known to operate. The women's *modus operandi* was to work as a unit, and as soon as they were located, the rest of the PRUCs would be flown in to take them in force. They were to have the best communications, armaments, and helicopters for quick hard strike capability. They had three weeks to eliminate the threat.

"Now, here's the kicker. Since we are fighting a band of Vietnamese Amazons, I decided it was only fair to put Sylvia Chin in direct charge of our operation. Okay with you, Sylvia?"

"You betcha, boss," came her exuberant reply without any hesitation. "Only one thing,"

"What's that? Howard asked. She was smiling mischievously.

"I don't get any surgery to assume the role," she laughed. Howard did too, appreciating her oblique reference to the mythological race of women warriors who cut off their right breasts (hence the appellation, a-maz on) to prevent any interference with their ability to loose their arrows. Anders and the others, with their less classical educations, were bemused.

The PRU groups fanned out into the rugged terrain west of Danang the following week. It was tough country. Ngu Hanh means 'the five elements—metal, wood, water, fire, and earth.' The PRU cadres felt themselves reduced to the elemental in those rugged hills and forests. With the intensity of the search, however, it was only three days before the location of the VC platoon was discovered. Phoenix proved its worth by feeding the field units information about a VCI orders courier who had been making an unusually large number of excursions into the forest in the last several weeks. She was followed to a camp that betrayed the femaleness of its occupants by the amount of clean laundry hanging on stringers laced through the trees.

In the dead of night on 26 April two hundred thirteen provincial reconnaissance cadres assembled five klicks from the VC encampment. They were briefed and taken to positions in a wide circle around the area. Then they moved in. Point men probed for booby traps. The first ones were found and dismantled at fully one klick from the camp. One man stepped on a trip wire connected to a bouncing betty antipersonnel mine set up in a thick bamboo tube just off the trail, panicked, and lifted his foot suddenly. The spring loaded mine flew up to crotch height and exploded mangling everything from umbilicus to knees. He was not killed outright, and had to be evacuated. Luckily for the plan, the explosion occurred far enough away from the camp to be out of earshot.

The attackers inched their way to the cong camp encountering dozens of traps, pungi and explosive. No one else was hurt. The women maintained excellent security with small squads of three sentries making regular and surprise inspections around the periphery of the camp but failed to see the expert sappers and woodsmen-soldiers moving in on them.

Great stealth was not the order of the day for the PRUs after they were in sight of the women's camp. Once they were in place, they planned to attack in force. Sylvia gave a three click signal over her radio. The PRUCs on the east opened a hellish fire that caused startled shrieks and pandemonium inside the camp. Willy Pete flares lit the camp and its periphery like noonday. The women raced to their protective bunkers and were cut to ribbons as they fled. Some died standing and firing their Kalashnikovs. A contingent tried to retreat into the forest in the opposite direction from which the enemy fire was coming. They ran directly into the PRUCs waiting there for just that eventuality, and every woman was killed. There were no casualties among the GVN and American paramilitary troops.

When only sporadic defense fire came from what was left of the VC compound, Sylvia radioed a cease fire. She had been ordered by the POIC and ROIC to take prisoners if possible. It was presumed that the women could provide links to other units throughout the region and could help locate the strength of the opposition before the commencement of Operation Apache Snow. Sylvia waited until complete darkness had once again descended. Only the fires in the strafed hooches provided any light.

Sylvia gave a two click signal, and every other PRU cadre advanced. They were not over confident. The reputation of the VC unit they were facing was too formidable to be careless. One man died when he tripped a wire and exploded a line of Claymores. He was directly over one and never knew what happened to him. The other mines in the string extended up a trail that fortunately was unoccupied at that point in time. When the men indicated that they were well within the middle of the encampment, Sylvia signaled for more white phosphorus flares to be fired, and again, the compound took on a surreal white brightness.

One skirmish line opened up with small arms fire and a few grenades, but none of the PRUCs took any serious hits. Three men sustained minor shrapnel injuries, but the firing of the women gave away their position and the PRUCs laid down a debilitating cross fire over the heads of the enemy fighters. Tran, Anders, Bach, Dung, Truong, and six other men who had drawn the short straws before the mission was started crawled forward. When they were within range they put on gas masks and tossed canisters of CS gas into the depression where the women were lying prone to save themselves from the nearly homogeneous criss cross of M-16 bullets and tracers.

Sylvia heard the frantic coughing and gasping coming from the obscuring cloud within and over the last defense area of the VC. She called a halt to the firing. She shouted "Surrender now!" in Vietnamese. The women must have been astounded to hear the incongruous woman's voice coming at them from the smoke. They knew it was futile. They were unable to fight, even to talk. The women knew, because they had been told, that torture and rape awaited them, so the officers and NCOs began to shoot the others.

Sylvia recognized instantly what was happening and screamed to Anders and Truong, "Get in there! Save some of them!"

The two leaders and the other nine men moved as a unit heedless of their own safety. Anders leaped across the flimsy defense barrier with his .45 in his outstretched hand. He fired twice killing two ranking VC and saving their intended victims. The other men followed his lead a second later and dispatched three others. There were four women left alive, one of them was mortally wounded, her head being cradled in the lap of a dazed sixteen year old girl who was too shocked and battered to react. One of the women screamed in terror, *"con ma da trắng khổng-lồ!"* when she saw the huge white haired man coming toward her; and then she mercifully fainted. The others hung their heads and waited for the inevitable.

The terror felt by the women was not groundless. They were

watching two PRUCs cutting out a segment of one of their dead comrade's liver and eating it with gusto.

The PRUCs served as backup units during the Apache Snow campaign proper and saw only sporadic action over the two weeks of the attack. On May 10 they watched from a distant hill as the battle for Ap Bia Mountain unfolded in all its ferocity. The mountain earned the grisly descriptive title of 'Hamburger Hill' in the battle that ensued. At first, the seventh and ninth battalions of the 29th NVA Regiment repulsed assault after assault and caused terrible losses among US and ARVN forces. On 14 May they drove back an attack by the US 3rd Battalion, 187th Infantry. The slaughter continued until 20 May when the 101st Airborne, a battalion of infantry, and the 3rd ARVN Infantry Regiment reinforced the beleaguered attackers, and the NVA fled into Laos.

Apache Snow was a qualified success for the GVN and US forces. They were exhausted and had taken awful casualties to regain their tenuous foothold on the Laotian border. In less than a week, 245 Americans perished. They had pushed the NVA out and had reoccupied the base. In a matter of months, however, the NVA were back in control of the base and the region.

Anders did not see the inside of a university classroom or a martial arts dojo before the middle of June. Even then, the only purpose for going was to make plans for the coming fall. No one had the spirit to conduct or to attend classes then.

The young Swede turned nineteen while on a snatch and snuff mission, and had better things to concern himself with than to take notice of his own birthday. Now, he killed with a passion. Every black pajamad man or woman he shot or stabbed or strangled up close was nothing more than an accounting, an eye for an eye, stripe for stripe, life for life. If he lived to be a hundred, Anders would never forget the helpless, bound, burned, and charred victims of the Viet Cong and People's Army of Viet Nam atrocities in Hue' and Dak Lop. He became in fact the *con ma da trắng khổng-lồ*, the avenger who brought the nightmare of death in the night to the murderers. The reward posters for him now promised a million Piastres, dead or alive.

CHAPTER 31

US Aims:
  a) To protect US reputation as a counter-subversion guarantor
  b) To avoid domino effect especially in Southeast Asia
  c) To keep South Vietnamese territory from red hands
  d) To emerge from crisis without unacceptable taint from methods

John T. McNaughton, Assistant Secretary of Defense for International Security Affairs, to Secretary of Defense, Robert McNamara, April 16, 1964

Anders became obsessed. He poured over the military and newspaper accounts of the numbers of nonmilitary individuals assassinated by the LAF—fifty to sixty thousand government workers murdered was one grim statistic. He was sure that the most inflated of the claims were underestimated. He became driven to do his part to even the score. He became more rash, planned less scrupulously, and sometimes seemed careless to Tran, Ky, Bach, and Dung. They began to be uneasy about going out with him. He goaded them on, canceled all business trips to Burma, and by July, was requiring that all three man units be out in the field on at least two missions a week. His personal body count was rising steadily, and he was making a definite contribution to the numbers report passed out at the Saigon five o'clock follies.

Finally Tran cautioned his younger commander and friend, "Anders, we all have to take a rest. We need to regroup. We need to make better plans, or we will get in trouble. The VC won't be on the run forever. The reward for you is a million and a half now, two if you are captured alive. They are just waiting for you to make a mistake."

Anders was not so far removed from rationality that he could not heed a warning, and he respected Tran's judgment implicitly. He did not want to slow down or quit, but he realized that he needed to compromise. "You're probably right. I have one more capture to make. The POIC sent me a no-fail order to bring in Wu Fat Lee, the war lord who used to be listed as a GVN and Company asset. Apparently he has gone over or is doubled, or something. Whatever it is; he has got Howard completely dedicated to breaking him. I know where he stays, or at least where he'll be one day next week. After I get him, we'll close down for a while. Maybe even get ourselves a hop down to Vung Tau for a week or so. You four can lay low and rest until then. I'll get a couple of the other guys to go out with me. I want your promise that you'll keep the unit from getting into trouble while I'm out, deal?"

Tran was skeptical, very skeptical. He did not want to agree. He wanted to break off the frenetic paramilitary campaign then and there and to get themselves together before they started again. He could see that Anders had clenched his jaw in a determined set and would not compromise further. Perhaps it was his youth. He gave a sigh and said, "All right, Anders; but no more after that. Is this Chinaman going to be tough to bring in? Do you know if he has an army, or what?"

"Not supposed to be too bad, Howard told me. He has a bunch of men like all the other bandits roaming out there in Indian country, but the plan is not to fight him. I plan to snatch him in a night ambush. The Phoenix reports say he will only have two or three of his thugs with him. At worst, we'll have to take them out. It would be a pretty good catch—give us some points with the high kahunas, you have to admit."

Tran had to admit it, all right. Except, he just didn't care about points. Staying alive himself, and keeping his young hothead leader alive as a bonus was all he really cared about at this point. "Okay, I'll help anyway I can. Keep your head down."

It was the first time in two years that Anders had gone on a mission without at least one of his four brother cadres. He had faith in every member of his PRU, but he still harbored nagging doubts as he and his two teammates for the mission began setting up their ambush. Cleve Howard's intel reports had pinpointed the exact route warlord Lee would take that Tuesday night. His favorite niece was getting married in the town less than a mile from his mountain side headquarters. In his concrete reinforced fortress bunker Lee was nearly invulnerable. Howard had tried to get him once before when the two men had had a falling out, and had failed, to his lasting embarrassment. Lee had seemed magnanimous afterward, and had repledged his fealty to the GVN and CIA side. Howard had always been suspicious, and Lee had never stopped being wary of the POIC's intentions.

The plan to take the Chinese bandit was foolproof, Howard told Anders. The quarry would have to walk single-file toward home down the jungle trail. He would not dare to flash a light; and so, he would be very limited in his defenses in the dark. Anders and his crew were to have night vision goggles which would give them the necessary edge. And Anders would have the advantage of surprise. The plan was simple and unfair to the target, exactly the way Anders liked it.

The night was steaming hot. The temperature had not dropped ten degrees from the 120° of the day. Anders was in a clasping position around a tree, his feet braced on low set branches. He had attached branches to various sites on his gear for camouflage. Sweat dropped from his face, neck, and chest and ran in rivulets down the rest of his body. Droplets fell regularly from his extremities onto the broad leaves of the tree. He had been waiting two hours for the war lord to pass his way. It was approaching midnight.

Anders' legs were cramped, and his arms were aching from the strain of maintaining his position without making a sound. Bugs crawled freely over his torso and face causing a crawly tickling sensation that the young man would never get used to. Because he was in a position where he could not tend to it, his nose itched furiously. At 0030 he heard the first footfall on the path below. The walker was still fifty meters away, Anders estimated. He slipped the uncomfortable night vision goggles into place and allowed his eyes to adjust to the heightened light reception as the man approached. Men.

There were three of them, Anders could tell, now that he could see better. They were heedlessly incautious. Although all three carried weapons, none of them were at the ready. This would be easy. Anders exhaled in relief. As soon as the last man passed his position, he slid painfully down the rough bark of his tree and onto the soft dirt at its base. He had made no sound. His two PRU teammates similarly appeared out of the gloom. They had been stationed at ten yard intervals from Anders with the Swede in the middle of the two Vietnamese.

According to plan, the first PRUC, the man in front of the advance of the three men on the trail, stepped out into sight and brandished his M-16 at the three men. They turned as if to run and met the muzzle of the second PRUC ready to fire at can't-miss range. Anders brought up the rear after first checking to make sure that there was no one else following.

The three capturees were surprisingly docile and cooperative. They laid down their arms as soon as they were ordered to do so and made no demurrer at the command to lie face down on the moist dirt of the pathway with their hands on their occiputs, fingers interlocked. It did not occur to Anders so much that this was too easy, but he had a gut feeling that there was something wrong with the picture he surveyed.

In two seconds he knew what was amiss. All three of the men they had subdued were thin, young, humbly dressed Vietnamese. They were after a fat Chinaman who never ventured out in public without his silk brocade shirt and vest. The man he sought could come by any minute, and they would have given their ambush away for nobodies. It dawned on him that he and his men had been so intent on binding their prisoners' wrists, that none of them had bothered to provide security. He had not looked back down the trail for several minutes. He had a rush of adrenaline. This was the kind of carelessness Tran had worried about; this was how cocksureness could cost everything. He spun around to make a belated visual check.

What he saw was his worst nightmare. Three hard faced, cruel eyed men were standing less than five meters from where the PRUCs were busily trussing up their inconsequential prizes. One of the new men was a fat Chinese. The two Vietnamese with him, dressed in black pajamas, held Hechler and Koch MP 5 automatics directed torso level at the three PRUCs caught with their figurative pants down. The Chinaman calmly pointed a new appearing Remington 870R (riot) combat shotgun in their direction. He was smiling. Anders was caught so unawares that his first thought was that these men had better weapons than he and his men. How could that be?

Anders thought of himself as reasonably brave but certainly no hero. He froze in place, afraid to move even a finger. Dang Thanh Hung was braver or less prudent. He hurtled himself to his right, raising the barrel of his M-16 as he did. Both H&Ks shifted to their left and fired at once nearly cutting Hung in half. Anders' second teammate, Hoang Quang Cong, was a good deal more prudent. He saw his friend's fate and flung both arms skyward dropping his rifle without a qualm. The movement attracted the shooters and they wheeled to their right. Their automatics spat out a short staccato stream of death at the rate of 600 rounds a minute. In two seconds of such fire, Cong, like Hung, was dead. Anders had not moved. He had another pair of absurd thoughts under the circumstances—first, that he was lucky; they had missed him, and second, that these were wasteful VC. One bullet would have been all that was required, and ordinary cadres would not have used more. He felt his bowels loosen.

The fat Chinaman shouted for his men to halt. He said he wanted to keep the white one. They obeyed tensely. Anders could all but feel the bullets waiting for him.

The Chinaman gestured with his shotgun and told Anders to drop his weapon without using words. He had no idea that the white man knew Vietnamese. In French he said, *"Les mains sur la tête! A genoux!"* (Hands on head. Kneel!)

Anders understood, but elected not to react, somehow thinking that it would go better for him in the long run if none of his captors knew that he could understand their talk. The Chinaman made his intentions clear by further gestures with his gun. Anders knelt in the dirt and put his hands on his head. The three hyper-vigilant captors approached. The Chinaman stopped a meter from Anders and kept his gun directed at the white man's face. The two Vietnamese, presumably VC, guards circled their captive and warily forced his arms down behind him and applied steel handcuffs. One of them prodded Anders with the business end of his gun until he understood to sit with his legs outstretched. The second VC slapped a pair of leg irons over his ankles snapping them too tight making Anders squirm in pain. A twenty centimeter chain attached one leg ring to the other.

The VC toppled Anders to his side and looked up at the Chinese war lord. The fat man gave the slightest affirmative nod. The two guards began to kick Anders mercilessly all over his arms, legs and back. Anders could do nothing more than to cover his face, groin, and belly partially by doubling up into a tight fetal position. The kicking was professionally done. All of the blows hurt, but none of them struck a vital spot. The cumulative effect was to weaken and to cow their victim. Both effects were extant after a few minutes of such treatment.

Not wanting to have to carry the huge Caucasian, the Chinaman barked his order, *"Ngừng lại!"* (Stop!) The rain of blows ended instantaneously. Anders recognized that he was under the power of a very disciplined set of men. That chastened him all the more. He could not expect any foolish mistakes.

His battered body was forced to stand by a series of directed probings by gun points. His legs were wobbly. The bodies of his two teammates were kicked out of the way like so much trash, and Anders was forced to hop and trot up the trail between the two guards. The war lord's compound was located half way up a steep hill and was built over a labyrinth of limestone caves. The small protruding face of the building belied the extent of the stone rooms and tunnels lying behind it. A direct artillery attack on that evident external portion of the structure would do little real damage to the important sections of the large internal fortress. It was an agony for Anders' injured muscles and shackled ankles to climb up the serpentine trail leading to the entryway, and his pain was augmented at frequent intervals by a kick or a jab from a gun butt. A noose had been thrown around his neck, and he was jerked along like a balky animal. The path and the entryway was crawling with guards. The security force had to number in the dozens, Anders reasoned.

He was clubbed into unconsciousness the minute they crossed the threshold. When he awakened, Anders was alone in semidarkness, completely disoriented as to place and time. He was first aware of the throbbing in his head, then of aching bruises that were now evident in purplish swollen blotches all over his body. The last thing he realized as he regained full consciousness was that he was tied to a heavy wooden frame. The four by four beams were in the form of a double 'T' with cross bars top and bottom. He had been tied down with both arms and both legs fully outstretched, to the point of near tearing strain, to the cross bars while they lay on the floor. Then, the double crucifix had been raised to the upright position. Anders was naked and completely helpless. He had no idea of how long he had been suspended there, but long enough that his hands and feet were numb and cold despite the oppressive damp heat of the room.

Anders did a quick assessment of himself. He could move his head and neck, albeit painfully. With effort he could contract most of his muscle groups, except that he could not move his fingers or toes. He attributed that to the overly tight bindings. He could see some of the bruises, but was unaware of any serious injuries. He concentrated on his genitalia and was gratified to be able to detect sensation in them. It was too much to expect movement; they had shriveled up to self protective unresponsive smallness. He was glad to be alive at this point and wondered to himself, "why?"

After the passage of some time, how much Anders could not judge with any certainty, the answer to his question was given. The Chinese war lord, two of his goons (a different pair from those who had helped him up the trail), and a small, middle-aged Chinese woman came into the dank chamber where Anders hung in suspended expectation. A generator motor somewhere outside the room started up, and shortly thereafter bright lights flashed on in the dungeon-like room hurting Anders' eyes. The Vietnamese guards laughed at his discomfort.

The Chinese woman served as the interpreter conveying the war lord's questions and comments in broken English. The others in the room spoke freely to one another in Vietnamese presuming that Anders was ignorant of that language. Anders almost wished that he were ignorant because most of what the men said to one another was deprecatory of him and threatening. The woman stood on tiptoe and shoved reward poster in Anders' face. It was one of the 'white giant ghost' ones. At least part of the reason he was still alive and in captivity lay in the reward offered—2.5 million P.—for bringing the "cruel anti-people ghost" in to any COSVN officer. The specter of what lay behind that offer was what chilled Anders' bone marrow.

"You are worth much to us alive, young man," translated the woman. Her accent was so thick that Anders managed better from the Vietnamese communications of the fat man. "And we plan to keep you that way. However, the poster does not make any demands on your condition otherwise." Anders blanched.

"I promise to limit the worst things if you will be cooperative and supply us with a little information. I want to know the exact location of your PRU compound, the codes, radio frequencies, and passwords that enable you and your criminals to operate against the peace-loving people of Viet Nam and against businessmen such as myself." After the demand was translated, the Chinese leader gave Anders an expectant look. Anders shook his head.

"I was afraid that would be your response. You realize that you will never be free again and that you will not leave captivity alive. You can only determine the duration and intensity of suffering that you will have to endure. If you give up your friends, I will turn your remains over to the proper military authorities unmarked." Even with his mind clouded by discomfort, Anders knew that the man was right about one thing; he would die whether or not he betrayed his friends. He was also sure that the Chinaman's promises were barren of truth. He would just have to tough it out and hope to goad his captors into enough anger to kill him outright. Bad as this option was, Anders dreaded falling into the hands of the Viet Cong even more. He shook his head again.

The Chinaman shook his head in resignation as if he had tried to reason with a recalcitrant child and now would have to apply the strap despite his humanist nature. He stepped back and allowed the two Vietnamese thugs to move between Anders and himself. He nodded, and the two men flicked out short stiff braided leather quirts. The war lord gave one last, almost imploring, look into Anders' eyes; and seeing no bending of the white man's will to his own, nodded again to his men.

The whips snapped and striped across Anders in a blurred fury. He wanted to cry out for them to stop for just a moment, so he could catch up. The stinging, tearing blows came with frightening rapidity. Anders steeled himself not to cry out. The burning pain from the last blow had not subsided before the next one landed. The men were sweating. When the pace began to slow because their arm and shoulder girdle stamina was being exceeded, their leader took pity on them and signaled for a stop. The flaying ended as abruptly as it had started.

"Have you changed your mind, young man?" asked the war lord through his interpreter. Anders managed to shake his head, no.

The whipping recommenced. Again the blows ended abruptly when the Chinaman gave the order. He arched his eyebrows in an unspoken question posed to Anders. The Swede again managed a negative shake of the head. The war lord said, "That will be enough for now. Think about it. You and you alone can make this easier on yourself. I respect your bravery and your loyalty to your people, but tomorrow you will see that it is not bravery but foolishness to keep silent. Until then," he made an oddly graceful about face considering his ponderous size, almost an effeminate motion, and exited the room with the woman.

One of the thugs sloshed a bucket of brine over Anders' naked striped integument and laughed mirthlessly when Anders writhed with the torment of the stinging salt water on his torn skin. Anders was unconscious when the two men walked out.

Hours passed, hours of misery from the hundreds of sore welts on his skin and from his muscles aching from their overstretched and awkward position. The room remained hot. He was thirsty and hungry. He had no way of judging time and was alone with his thoughts and imaginings that were almost as bad as the physical punishment he had endured up to now. He could not know it, but the time was eleven in the morning before his tormentors returned. The Chinaman appeared well rested and satiated from his ample breakfast. Two different men accompanied him this time. They were older and had less expressionate faces. Both of them had eyes with no more feeling or life than beer caps. They carried identical small black cases.

The Chinese woman carried a large bowl of steaming rice in which were a generous number of pieces of fish and chopped vegetables. The aroma was wonderful, haunting. She also brought in a pitcher of water and allowed Anders to get a good look before setting it down on a small table beside the Chinaman.

"Have you had enough time to think over your choices, son?" His voice was soft, friendly, comforting in its native Vietnamese. The woman tried to match its solicitous character as she translated, but fell short as she searched for the correct vocabulary.

Anders made no reply.

"I have a proposition for you, young man." He smiled. She smiled. The thugs smiled. "Give me the information I seek, and I will permit you to eat your fill then deliver you this very day to the law loving people's government without the slightest further unpleasantness. What do you say?"

Anders waited for the full translation. As it was being given, he could hear the thugs speaking of 'cuts,' 'long pain,' and 'vengeance' in the background. Their facial expressions did not match their threatening conversation. The woman completed her circuitous efforts at communicating the gist of her leader's proposal.

Anders said, "No."

"I have lost patience." She translated and included pantomimic threatening gestures. "You will regret this decision. My assistants are very persuasive, as you shall see." She grinned toothlessly as she gave the description.

Anders, by a great effort of will, remained impassive. He watched as the two older men opened their cases and brought out a pair of stainless steel scalpels each and set them neatly on the table.

"How regrettable," said the war lord, his face a mask of cruelty now. His reference was not to Anders' decision or to the knives, but to the loss of perfectly good food that he was now pouring out onto the filth of the dungeon floor. From what he had heard in the darkness, Anders knew that the rats would make quick work of the leavings as soon as they had the chance.

"Perhaps you have heard of the old Chinese custom of the Death of Thousand Cuts?" Anders gave no indication of even having heard the man or his translator. "No? Well, my boy, you are about to become an expert." The great humor of his own clever witticism caused the Chinaman to laugh until his adipose jowls shook. Suddenly, his expression returned to stone, and he executed another pirouette of an about face and strode out of the sweating stone room.

The two middle-aged technicians remained behind. They wore identical dispassionate expressions. Each picked up one of his knives and approached Anders from the left and the right. He tried to writhe, to make some escapist movement; but he was fixed like a bug pinned to a corkboard. The first cut was six centimeters long and happened so quickly that it took Anders half a second to realize that his skin had been opened. The first sear of epicritical pain gave way to a prolonged burning. The injury had been inflicted just below his right clavicle and above his 'Sat' tattoo. The second cut was placed on the opposite side above the 'cong' tattoo; they were mirror images. The well-practiced torturers took professional pride in the precision of their cuts. Besides their learned and practiced sense of artistry and symmetry—each incision was the same length and depth and location side to side—the cuts were calculated to hurt and to frighten, but not to result in excessive bleeding or enough pain to cause unconsciousness. The cuts were never deep enough to transect a vital structure, body cavity wall, or major artery.

They were methodical; each incision was inflicted after an interval that allowed the recipient to appreciate the full measure of the cut before. They worked on Anders like machines creating rows of cuts down both the lateral sides of his chest to his pelvis, then down a second, more medial, row. Anders was in a welter of agony unlike anything he had ever imagined let alone known. The terrible quick pain of each laceration added its pain to an accretion of misery created by the aggregate of all the others. He could not pass out. His greatest effort was to avoid crying out. He was determined not to give the Chinaman or his lackeys the satisfaction.

The men must have belonged to the torturers' union. They took breaks every two hours and ate snacks and drank small bottles of tea. At 1700 sharp they stopped, wiped off their knives, packed their little black cases and left. Anders was again alone. He gave way to whimpering. His once handsomely sculpted torso was now ragged and dripped blood in irregular runs and tributaries down his chest and abdomen and along his lower limbs. Sleep was unthinkable. His mouth tasted black. For the third time that day, he let go his bowels and bladder to join the rest of the offal on the floor. And then the rats came.

The next day was like the first. "Would he betray his friends?"

"No."

Regrets that pain had to be inflicted; "it is all so unnecessary." The grinning translator, the thirst and hunger. Then the two methodical little men and their knives. This day they put in their hours cutting down his back. Some perverse sense of esthetics kept the man on Anders' right from cutting into the Phoenix tattoo. He was able to find plenty of other skin to open, however. By quitting time, there was one difference. Anders was no longer aware of pain. He could hear screaming from somewhere. When the two men left his cell, the noise continued, and he realized for the first time that it came from him.

The morning of the third day was different. Anders was barely conscious, but aware enough of his surroundings to sense that a greater passage of time had occurred. It was not like his union cutters to be late. Maybe they had taken pity and had left him to die. On the first day he had been very afraid to die. Now, he was afraid that he would not, and that he would live on in terrible agony waiting for the next pain and the next and the next. He feared that his mind would let go; and he would betray his friends; and all he had suffered would be for naught.

At 0930 or a little later, Anders heard sounds for the first time. Expecting to hear the heavy door swing open and the sound of his tormentors' voices, he tensed himself. Instead, the racket of automatic small arms fire came from above him. The chatter of the rifle fire was punctuated at times by the explosion of grenades and mortars. He could hear the characteristic low throated whump from a mountain howitzer. Parts of the building were crashing down someplace, he deduced from still other loud noises. Men's voices, rifle fire, hand guns, and running feet all came closer to his dungeon. Anders trembled, semistuporous, in the cloying darkness. He awaited the inevitable.

Finally the door flew open. Only on this occasion it was blown down. Five men charged into the dully lit room yelling in Vietnamese. They were saying, "Kill them! kill the big one!" Anders squinted his eyes shut. He did not want to see the men taking aim at him. So this was the way he would die—live by the sword and die by the sword.

He was unconscious, dreaming. That had to be what was happening. Because what he heard was the voice of Nguyen Lui Tran. It was as clear as if his friend were in the room beside him. That part of the dream was pleasant, but he could feel the pains of his kicked, whipped, and cut body. Wasn't that strange?

Tran and Bach called three additional PRUCs and together they hoisted the double crucifix frame out of the post holes in the floor. It was very heavy and unwieldy with Anders' heavy frame on it. He was dimly aware of the straining men lowering him to the ground. It was hard to understand what all of this could mean. He awakened when the men cut the ropes binding his blanched and mottled hands and feet because the sudden resurgence of blood rushing into the arterioles and capillaries of his digits was shockingly painful. He recognized Tran, Bach, Ky, and Dung. It had not been a dream, but he still wrestled to comprehend what was going on.

Tran lifted up his head and poured a small draught of warm water into Anders' parched throat. At first, he choked and coughed himself blue. Then the lubricant effect of the water enabled his withered throat mucosa to accept the flow of more life-giving fluid. He gulped greedily until Tran had to make him stop.

"Hurry up!" urged Ky. "There'll be more of the bandits anytime. We've got to get out of here. Now!" he emphasized.

Anders was placed on a litter. His bloody back annealed itself to the canvas of the litter upon which he was being borne. The litter bearers were running as best they could jouncing Anders' pain wracked frame until he could not stifle a cry. Still, he had enough of his faculties to know he was being rescued. They stopped to rest. They stopped again to have a short furious firefight. One of his litter bearers—he learned later that it was Cong Bich Hai, a diminutive, hard worker who never complained—was shot through the head.

He was loaded on a chopper landing on the steel floor with a head rattling thump. The bodies of Hung, Cong, and Hai, and a fourth man, Tung Co Bon, were laid about him. It was a miniature charnel house with him in the center. The helicopter lifted off in a roar of its engines and whine of its rotor blades mingled with a deafening fusillade of machine gun fire from the open doors and the ping and kathunk of bullets coming from below striking the undercarriage and struts of the aircraft.

The helicopter stopped briefly at what Tran told Anders later was the PRU compound to remove the bodies. They could not be officially identified nor accounted for. The men who cared buried their comrades in unmarked but remembered graves. There was another lift off, this time sans gun fire. Anders was unconscious when they wafted into Danang marine base and when he was admitted to the casualty room of the 95th Evacuation Hospital, China Beach.

CHAPTER 32

Apportionment of American Aims in South Viet Nam:
    70%—To avoid a humiliating US defeat (to our reputation as
    a guarantor)
    20%—To keep South Viet Nam (and then adjacent) territory
    from Chinese hands
    10%—To permit the people of South Viet Nam to enjoy a
    better, freer way of life
    Also—To emerge from crisis without unacceptable taint
    from methods used
    NOT—To 'help a friend,' although it would be hard to stay if
    asked out.
*Report of John T. McNaughton, Assistant Secretary of Defense for
International Security Affairs, to Secretary of Defense, Robert
McNamara, March 24, 1964*

T he supervising nurse, LCDR/RN/ NC McIntyre, protested to the ER doc, Lieutenant Radcliffe, USNR/ MC when he sent up the orders to admit the young man, "I can't accept the word of some Vietnamese that this guy is eligible to be admitted in this facility. The gook himself says our man is not even an American. He swears that the patient is not military, and as near as I can tell, he's right. No records on an Anders Bergstrom. We're full. My nurses are wiped out."

"And he has to come in, Lieutenant Commander McIntyre, nurse corps, regular navy. This is like the old joke where the guy comes to the ER with an ax sticking out of the middle of his forehead, and the battle-ax nurse says, 'Do you have an appointment?' What're we going to do with him?" asked the doctor. He stressed her rank just to nettle her. She was brown shoe navy, and he was a draftee. He didn't have to follow the military rules.

"I don't appreciate the characterization. And you will take full responsibility, Lieutenant Radcliffe, Medical Corps, USNR," she retorted, enunciating the 'R' with explicit disdain. The draftee reservists were such a pain. This one was a hippie, completely undisciplined.

"If it will make you feel better, I will personally call to this CORDS place. The guy who brought him in gave me the number."

"It will make me feel better," she said caustically. It was hopeless. He didn't have the foggiest idea how to use the marine communication system. He wouldn't do it; she knew that. Or, worse, he would screw it up. She grabbed the piece of scratch paper containing the number, and he laughed.

He assumed a theatrical hangdog expression. She smiled in spite of herself. "I owe you another favor," he said.

"Right," she said sarcastically. It was a pain working with the reservists, but most of them were pretty decent doctors even if they were screw-ups militarily.

Radcliffe had spent the afternoon and evening with the corpsmen trying to clean up the wounds. There was not much else he could do. Even if everybody in the place sat down to sew up all of those cuts, it would be the wrong thing to do. They would just get infected. The guy was awake when they scrubbed them out. He didn't complain or fight the nurses and corps wave who helped; he was one tough hombre Dr. Radcliffe decided. He had been polite and grateful. Radcliffe could not send the patient back out there—he had been tortured systematically. Jeez, what a terrible place this was.

Anders had the advantage of youth and of being in superb physical condition. His cuts healed quickly although some of them required that the wounds be debrided in the Hubbard tank every day for a couple of weeks. He had no allergies, and Doctor Radcliffe gave him megadoses of Pen and Strep IM to prevent septicemia. Anders was cleared for admission by MACV headquarters in Hue' within an hour of Lieutenant Commander McIntyre's call to the CORDS number. She learned in no uncertain terms that all she or anyone else needed to know was his name. "Spooks," she had muttered. He seemed like a decent kid, though. She shuddered to think what he had seen and what had been done to him.

Tran came to see him once a week and repeated to Anders, "I told you so," every time. Anders could not get too upset with his friend because he knew that Tran had saved him; and, more than incidentally, he was right.

Anders had to get the story from the other cadres. Tran was too modest. Ky, Bach, and Dung gave him enough pieces that he could figure out in some chronological order what had happened after the failed ambush. Tran had reckoned on a twenty-four hour mission, and became antsy when Anders and his two mission mates failed to return in thirty. He knew Anders' entire plan down to the mapped location of the ambush. He rallied the other three of Anders' brothers, and they broke all speed records in getting to the spot. It did not take them long to discover Hung's and Hai's bodies. The bandits were so secure in their territory that they were in no hurry to get rid of incriminating evidence. It was easy to follow Anders' big tracks up the trail. They saw the guards before they were seen themselves, and returned to the PRU compound for reinforcements.

Tran called Cleve Howard from the PRU compound.

"That's tough," the POIC had said when he learned of the capture of his operations officer. Whatever his sympathies may have been, he told Tran that his arms were tied on this one. "We can't go in after him. He doesn't exist, and we don't exist."

"So we abandon him?" Tran had asked politely.

"Who?" Howard had countered.

There was a long pause. Howard relented a little. "Now if somebody were to fraudulently requisition a chopper or two and had some unauthorized firepower, how could I help it?"

Tran had shaken his head at the transmitter. He said only, "Poor what's his name."

The POIC said, "Ten-four."

Three helicopters landed on the compound's pad after Tran made a couple of calls. He told the crew chiefs at MACV that he couldn't explain, but one of their own needed help. Now. All one hundred twenty-four PRUCs volunteered when asked, and they suited up like high tech cavalry. There was enough fire power to take on an NVA regiment.

They landed six commandos, including all four of Anders' closest friends, by night. Those men crept from guard post to guard post silently killing the security men. The three Cobra assault helicopters swooped in just after first light and poured rockets and high concentration machine gun fire on the remaining positions and on the fort itself wiping out the outside defenders to the last man. The inside personnel were largely individually oriented pirates, and very few of them regarded their current employer worth dying for. Their line of defense buckled with the heat of the all out attack by the PRU who came at the fortress in force.

Tran, Bach, Ky, and Dung blew down the main front door with

LAW rockets and entered with a hail of gunfire from their automatics that scattered those remaining few members of the Chinaman's security guard. Any of the guards who made even a halfhearted attempt to fight were cut to pieces. Most of them were craven cur who fled into the escape tunnels and out into the tangle of the jungle. They were headed for the next mercenary job.

The Chinaman and his two personal bodyguards held out to the last. The fat man was still firing when Tran and Ky blew down the door to Anders' dungeon. One of the torturers had obliged as to its location in exchange for his miserable life. Bach had killed him anyway. As soon as they saw Anders and the full brunt of his condition hit them, the four went back out and helped in the mopping up process. Ky estimated that the war lord had a thousand bullet holes in his body when the firing ceased. He was scarcely recognizable as having been a human being.

Anders said, "What can I say but thanks? I owe you, and I won't forget."

Tran reminded him that he could say that he would not be stupid again. The five men now had a bond of blood that would out last armies, secret services, countries, and time.

Anders was present at roll call for the start of his second year at the University of Hue'. The institution's buildings were much the worse for wear after the apocalyptic Battle of Hue, and the students and faculty were changed forever. They were sober and chary now. They had survived a cataclysmic introduction into the realities of their country. Youthful enthusiasm won out, and the talented and intelligent students and superb faculty were able to carry on. The professors did not relent a whit on the severity of their academic discipline. Anders was buoyed up by this piece of normalcy.

Most of the day to day operations of Anders' PRU were being handled by Tran during the period of Anders' convalescence. Anders had spent three weeks at Vung Tau letting the sun's rays heal his open wounds, then the rest of the summer at the compound or in Hue' regaining his strength and his stamina. By the first week in September when the university reopened, Anders was altogether fit. However, Cleve Howard had decided that his contract officer needed more recuperation, and ordered Anders to take off another month with pay.

Anders had used the summer months to handle the Hue' end of him and his friends' special business. They were now back to making monthly runs. The distance the PRUCs now had to cover had been halved. The Laotian hill people had formed loose alliances with the

Wa People of Burma to move the heroin. At intervals the people of the two large opium producing countries (Laos was third after Burma and Thailand) warred with each other and made the traffic as difficult as possible. Better business sense prevailed in 1969 and now, fortuitously for Tran, Ky, Bach, Dung, and Anders, they could pick up their bricks of the narcotic at the Laotian border and transport it in less than ten days, sometimes less than five, to their own compound. Business remained brisk, and profits were such that all five men had rich Swiss bank accounts.

The bulk of Anders' time after the end of August was spent in learning the Vietnamese point of view. In time, Anders came to appreciate fully why the South Vietnamese resisted full participation in the ongoing war that was so ostensibly for their own benefit. To understand that, Anders had to see the scope of history through Vietnamese eyes.

He had two excellent teachers—The Mandarin and his professor of history at the University of Hue', Phan Doi Hang—men of a similar age, background, outlook, and dedication to their country.

The senior professor declared, "Throughout Vietnamese history has run the current of familial conflict in the quest for power that has pitted north against south. Ideologies have always occupied a lesser position. Despite a multiplicity of foreign interventions, the Vietnamese themselves have always looked at the struggle for power, control, and even union of the two main segments of the country as an internal struggle, a Vietnamese problem. The majority of the opponents on both sides of any issue in the country and of all wars have wished to be left free of foreign help for either side. When they succumbed to the temptation to include foreign help for their side, they always came to rue the day they did.

"Their attitude, in the final analysis, was and is, that this is the struggle of Viet Nam. It was not a question of the power of the Chinese or the need for their cultural contributions or the Europeanizing influence of the French any more than it was a matter of the need for the communism of Ho Chi Minh or the democracy of the United States of America. All of the foreigners and their dogmas were unwanted; and the Vietnamese, in large part, believed they could out wait any current intervention so they could get on with their own business," lectured the professor on the first day of Anders' sophomore year. The remainder of the three quarter course was to provide the information to the students to convince them that the professor's statement was true. In so doing, the teacher's intent was to make his students of varied backgrounds and beliefs united in one singular aspect—they would be Vietnamese to the core.

On many evenings The Mandarin would underscore the professor's lessons by providing examples, stories that enlivened the sweep of history as the professor collated and transmitted it. Anders soaked up the knowledge, including the Vietnamese world view, with an uncritical mind—it was his first introduction to the excitement of scholarship—and he adopted the Vietnamese bias as his own.

Professor Phan calculated the modern era of Vietnamese pain and history to have begun in 1857 with the first military incursion by the French. "Trade flourished throughout a colonial era that extended from the 1400s to the early nineteenth century and included increasing contact with China, India, Portugal, The Netherlands, England, and France. Increasingly the competing colonial powers took control of the countries of the Asian hemisphere, and France made a calculated decision to establish its own empire in Southeast Asia. They sought a pretext.

"As many of the colonialists had done, the French had used as their entering wedge, the missionaries then the priests of their Christian religion. The Vietnamese recognized the threat these foreigners posed—they would change the people's philosophy to that of an alien set of beliefs, and they would usher in an unstoppable progress of foreign methods, peoples, attitudes, and controls. The nationalists threatened and at times harmed the priests and their followers. They drove them out and banned their practices. Emperor Gia Long made the fatal mistake of inviting in the French military to help him in his struggles with the Chinese only to find out that he had traded one bad and unwanted master for another. That left a French military force in place.

"When the French perceived a threat to their religious people, they used that threat as a pretext to begin conquest. The date of the modern era, bringing with it the antecedents of the present conflict, was September 1857 when the French navy laid siege to Danang. They conquered that first city in 1858, then took Saigon in 1861. The emperor in Hue' formally accepted the French as the colonial power in 1862. In 1867 the foreigners gained full control of the Mekong Delta and in 1883, the Red River Delta in the north. They did away with the name Viet Nam and adopted the attitude that the three principle areas were semi-automatous French protectorates under the general heading of French Indochina. *Bac Bo* (North) became Tonkin;

Trung Bo (Center) became Annam; and *Nam Bo* (South) became Cochinchina. In their arrogance they had chosen a most insulting name in their selection of Annam. The Chinese ideographic character representing Annam is a contented or pacified woman under a roof. Nam, of course, means south. The United States became involved, entangled is a better term, in 1945 with their President Truman's decision to resist but to preserve the French colonial aspirations."

Anders did not spend all of his time in learned pursuits. He helped at CORDS headquarters with the mountains of governmental paperwork three afternoons a week and was amused at the copious on-paper activities of CORDS that shrouded its more serious and less public endeavors. He kept his amusement to himself. It was during that first month of his attendance in his sophomore classes and participating in the mind numbing rear echelon drudgery that Anders made his most important contribution to the special business that occupied his friends' attentions.

He established a relationship with the marine colonel in charge of the Danang Quartermaster General's storehouse. He met the officer at an all-service social given by MACV to welcome the new commanding general at Danang. Through chance comments by Cleve Howard, Anders learned of the quartermaster's great latitude in dealing with the logistics of supplies coming and going at the port and through the country. Anders acted as Howard's emissary on several occasions to obtain needed, but not necessarily authorized, armaments—hard rice. Some money changed hands.

The colonel knew Anders' real function, basically. He also knew that some of the CIA people were making a lucrative career out of their sojourn in Indochina. The colonel even suspected, as did many others, that the US Central Intelligence Agency was, itself, directly involved in the heroin traffic. He accepted the CIA payment graciously and hinted broadly about his own straitened economic circumstances and even more broadly at his willingness to improve them. Anders cultivated him and probed about the man's possible trepidations about the drug trade. The colonel came across as an amoral pragmatist. "I don't use the stuff, and I don't advocate it. But there are always going to be sorry buggers who do, and rich buggers who make a profit from the trade. It might as well be me as the next guy," he had concluded.

The result of such conversations was an arrangement for the colonel to ship in bags of acetic anhydride, the chemical used to convert opium to heroin, in military cargo holds that were as untouchable as the diplomatic pouch. The bags were discretely labeled and handled. The chemical was transported in flour sacks marked with the large lettered logo, C.A.R.E., and accompanied by a statement "Gift of the Generous American People." In the course of their business arrangement, the generous American people shipped in thousands of pounds of the valuable chemical which was then transported by US Army trucks over GVN highways without VC attack and transshipped across the borders of Viet Nam, Laos, and Burma without Pathet Lao, police, or customs agent impediment. A considerable amount of money changed hands; large profits were realized; and a triumph of international relations of sorts resulted when a common language and purpose (money) was involved. Other pipelines started with Saigon businessmen and funneled American arms to VC and PL enemies with faces-turned-the-other-way understanding by American diplomats and ranking soldiers. It was a very peculiar time.

The marine colonel left Viet Nam in 1970 a modestly wealthy man, retired from the service, and entered the employment of the Wa People of Burma in New York City, where he continued to prosper; and he did not pay taxes on his increase. Anders and his PRUCs were minor middlemen in the transactional process, but were paid a fair return commensurate with their contributions. Everyone concerned learned an increased respect for capitalism as a result.

In long talks in the Mandarin's study, the venerable old institution of a man told Anders, "The love-hate relationship between the Vietnamese and the French colored every aspect of the history of Viet Nam from the siege of Danang in 1857 to well beyond the siege of Dien Bien Phu." The Mandarin felt very strongly about the foreigners, but maintained a fund of knowledge wide and deep enough to allow him to be objective. He went on, "The French, like the Chinese before them, found the Vietnamese difficult to control, much to their ongoing distress. The old Chinese proverb, 'Once you ride a tiger, you may find it difficult to dismount.' applied. In 1885, the twelve year old emperor, Ham Nghi, mounted an insurrection. He was exiled in 1888 for his efforts." Anders vaguely remembered his old tour guide's rendition of the youthful king's futile attempt.

"After 1887 the French had so consolidated their position that they regarded Indochina, including Cambodia, as a French possession, French soil. Their influence was everywhere and in everything. They abolished the State Literary Examination." The old man's countenance darkened. "And many of the young people began to lose their Vietnamese ways. They no longer respected the Chinese or Vietnamese type education and turned to French schools in this country; and the most ambitious and affluent of them were educated in France herself. Those foolish young people absorbed western ideas, rejected our Confucian tradition of order and obedience and proved to be a two-edged sword for their new masters, the French. They learned to be radicals and revolutionaries from the French themselves."

"And is that the origin of communism in Asia?" Anders asked.

"Of radicalism and nationalism first. And, yes, the struggle produced communists. The rapid and seemingly overwhelming progress of western ideas and practices was met with resistance. The nationalists and those who respected the Asian ways cheered when the Japanese defeated the Russian navy in 1905. Many of them in China and Viet Nam turned to or at least admired the Marxist revolution and the communist philosophy and saw it as a way to stem the tide of western civilization in this hemisphere."

"Like Uncle Ho, true?"

"Nguyên Ai-Quôc, alias Ho Chi Minh, was certainly one of the early and most dedicated. He is yet a man not to be underestimated. The leaders of South Viet Nam do not make that mistake; but the Americans, like the French and the Japanese before them are ignorant and do not respect him. That is a great flaw."

From the university professor, Anders learned the details of the long and painful resistance by the Vietnamese to their French Colonial overlords. In balance, it became evident to the young student that both sides suffered greatly. The French called National Highway One, 'the Street of No Joy,' in commemoration of the sufferings of their armies over the years. Ho Chi Minh never tired of recounting his imprisonment at the hands of the harsh French regime.

"Because of the anti-western feeling, and the great desire on the part of a wide majority of Vietnamese to shake off the yoke of the foreigners, secret societies of nationalists of all sorts of persuasions were begun in the late 1920s and early 1930s, much like the radicals and anarchists of Europe and the Triads in China. The feelings were most intense in and around Hanoi. In 1930 an uprising at the town of Yen Bay, north of Hanoi, was savagely put down by the colonialists and the nationalist movement was decimated, nearly destroyed. The survivors had to go deep underground. The communists were the most dedicated and best organized; and they forced their way into the positions of leadership," the professor told the class of young Vietnamese and one Swedish-American.

"Was that the start of the Viet Minh?" Anders asked at one point in the lecture.

"No, young man, that came later," he was told.

"But I thought that it was the Viet Minh who beat the French."

"Only in part. The Japanese occupation of our country broke the hold of the French forever. The Viet Minh just completed the process. It was a costly and well intentioned process, don't get me wrong. The contribution of the many different factions that made up the Viet Minh should not be minimized.

"Bao Dai appeared to be a compromise. The young emperor was educated in France and returned home in 1932 at the request of one group of nationalists. The French allowed him to ascend to the throne, but cynically prevented him from exercising any power. Those who wished for peaceful means of regaining rightful Vietnamese power were discouraged and were finally silenced by the more radical elements of the French opposition.

"France fell to the Germans in 1940 and lost its hold on Indochina. Many embraced the coming of the Japanese as deliverers. They did wrest real control from the French colonialists, but allowed them to remain in place with the appearance of having authority. The French became paper tigers. French troops stayed in their garrisons, for the large part, while the Japanese military consolidated its control throughout Southeast Asia. However, the Japanese soon proved to be terrible and cruel tyrants, much worse than the French. The Viet Minh joined western forces to undermine and to fight them.

"To counteract the support being given to the west, the Japanese granted independence to Viet Nam in 1944 in return for a fraternal relationship. Bao Dai, acting as emperor, proclaimed that Viet Nam was once more an independent and unified nation. He was unacceptable to the northerners who were strongly under communist influence; and finally, in 1945, the emperor abdicated to Ho Chi Minh who claimed the presidency of a new republic with the approval of the vast majority of the people of Viet Nam."

"Did he not know Ho was a communist?" One of the students asked.

"He chose to ignore the fact. Bao Dai would see only the nationalist character of the Viet Minh and of the new republic and believed that the western allies gave their full support to Ho. He even consented to stay on as a counselor to the president. The Democratic Republic of

Viet Nam was proclaimed, and the communist domination of its government was kept secret. Many have viewed the division of our country into north and south sections as unnatural, and Ho's actions to unite the two segments as heroic. However, the great differences between the two areas were not solved by the proclamation; they are quite obviously still potent today; and I will predict that they will still be important causes of division among our people long after the Americans and their war are gone."

In October, Anders resumed his place in the PRU. The passion he had felt after the Battle of Hue' subsided at least to the point he was no longer careless. He smarted from his freshly healed scars. They were a constant reminder of his lapse. He was a different man than the one who allowed himself to be captured. He was older than his years and more sober, quieter. Anders Bergstrom had come face to face with death and respected the experience. He had had little that could be described as a childhood, and with the wrenching experience at the hands of the conscienceless Chinaman, he had lost all vestiges of his adolescence. Although he still appeared to be young; on the inside he felt old.

His loyalties were confused. He had once had a simple world view—the Americans were good; the Mormons were right; the Buddhists and Catholics were misguided; and the communists were the empire of evil. He had known where he fit. Now, he had seen too much and had done too much to maintain his innocence. He knew too many secrets for one so young. The picture of America Inga Haakensdatter had painted for his young mind was blurred. He could hate and want the destruction of the Vietnamese communists for their atrocities, but what could he do about the headlines in the Hue' newspaper that day in November—"Mai Ly Massacre: American lieutenant, William Calley, leads slaughter of whole village." Phoenix did things to people that were unspeakable and had contrived them to appear to be the work of the Viet Cong with the argument that the ends justified the means. He knew that first hand, and his own hands were not clean. Anders was no longer so sure—about anything.

The struggle against the French that ultimately resulted in the First Indochinese War would remain a subject for the first quarter of study in the new year. Anders' biography of Ho Chi Minh won him plaudits; and that, and his good examination scores, kept him near the top of his class. The Mandarin, as usual very well informed, gave a party in Anders' honor.

"*Frère Anders*," (Brother Anders,) Liên said quietly at a point in the evening when they chanced to have a moment alone. "*J'ai quelque chose à vous dire. Pourriez-vous aller à la bibliothèque de mon père et m'y attendre? C'est important.*" (I have something to say to you. Would you please go to Father's library and wait for me. It is important.)

Anders had little will to resist Liên. He left the gathering directly and entered The Mandarin's sanctum. It was a wonderful room, peaceful, sedate, calming. It was the room where The Mandarin conducted his most serious interviews and made his most significant decisions. It was a rich and beautiful place, a room of prodigious learning. There were Philippine mahogany bookshelves from wall to wall and floor to twelve foot ceiling. At the six foot level there was a cat walk to permit access to the higher situated volumes. There were few pieces of furniture—a handsome reading desk and matching chair from Singapore, both inlaid with mother of pearl in an intricate design depicting the first battle of Dien Bien Phu, matching Louis XIV chairs with petit point seat and back covers with a picture of the Louvre and the Versailles that faced the reading table. These were chairs for supplicants or family members who met The Mandarin in a formal audience. Aside from three 1930s art deco floor lamps, the only other piece of furniture was a deep green leather overstuffed chair and matching ottoman. A ten by twelve foot hand knotted silk rug lay on the mahogany floor. The rug was ancient and had been a gift from Bao Dai himself. The rug was made by children and had taken three years to fashion the six hundred knots per square inch treasure and at a cost of blindness for several of the children.

The striking feature of the room was not the elegant old rug or the exquisite furniture. It was the books. There were leather bound classical volumes of the *ngu kinh*, the *Complete Works of Shakespeare*, the *Bible*, the *Koran*, the *Talmud*, and the *Kama Sutra*. Hard bound books from several nations' best works and in their languages were arranged as to subject. There was no dust; The Mandarin's staff had emphatic instructions to maintain the room in immaculate condition. Most of the volumes bore evidence of having been opened and read, and many of them were dog-eared from use.

The Nguyen Mandarin was a most learned man; evidence of his erudition stood on the book shelves like awards. There were works in French by Moliere, Rousseau, Montaigne, and Montesquieu. Copies of German works as varied as *Das Kapital, Mein Kampf,* and *The Psychopathology of Everyday Life*" sat by Machiavelli's, *The Prince* and Darwin's, *Origin of the Species*. In a walk around the room, Anders could locate *Prometheus Bound, Oedipus Rex, A Doll's House, The Meditations of Marcus Aurelius* and *The Critique of Pure Reason*. The room was the quintessence of culture, sagacity, and sophistication. Anders knew it to be the haven of decency and uprightness as well.

Liên softly entered the room and came over to Anders who was sitting in the overstuffed chair thumbing through a copy of *Moll Flanders*. He put it down with mild embarrassment.

"*Comment allez-vous ce soir, mon frère?*" (How are you tonight, my brother?) Liên began rather timidly. She was speaking French as had become the custom between the young man and woman.

"*Je vais très bien,*" (I am very well.) Anders said. He felt as if he were waiting for the other shoe to drop.

"*Je voulais vous féliciter de votre succès à l'université,*" (I wanted to congratulate you on your success at university.) she continued. It was unlike the girl to be anything but direct, a quality of hers that he admired; so, he had a growing feeling that she had something troubling to say. He waited until she could work it out.

"*Merci,*" (Thank you.) he said and smiled. Her return smile was somewhat forced.

"*Je suis contente que vous puissiez être avec la famille ce soir. Çà fait quelque temps que vous n'avez pas été chez nous.*" (I am pleased that you could be with the family tonight. It has been some time since you were here with us.) It had been two weeks.

"*Comme d'habitude, çà me fait plaisir d'être ici.*" (I am glad to be here, as usual.) He did not know anything else to say. He could see her tension mounting and wanted to help, but felt instinctively that it was best to give her the room she needed.

"*Anders, mon ami et mon frère,*" (Anders, my friend and brother,) she blurted, now speaking rapidly to get out her message without further uncomfortable hesitation or to risk interruption. "*Mon père m'a choisi un mari. Nous devons nous marier dans six mois. Ma mère et moi nous irons à Saigon pour rencontrer le jeune homme et sa famille pendant la fête du Têt. Nous serons connaissance à ce moment là parce que nous serous correctement chaperonnés. Je suis désolée. Vous saviez que c'était inévitable. Continuez à être mon ami s'l vous plaît.*" (My father has chosen a husband for me. We are to be married in six months time. I and my mother will travel to Saigon to meet the young man and his family during Tet. We are to become acquainted at that time when there can be proper chaperonage. I'm sorry. You knew this was inevitable. Please still be my friend.) the message rushed out to its completion.

Anders was dumb struck. He could not keep the anguish he felt from showing in his face. He would have been less injured if someone had struck him with a poleax. He had known from the very beginning that this day would come. It was no less depressing to him that he had anticipated it. He had tried to sublimate his passion for the lovely girl, but it had lain smoldering beneath the surface from the time he first met her at the Tet Eve, 1967, family dinner. His mind reeled, and he fought to gain control of himself. He was terrified that he would break down in front of her, an unforgivable loss of face for each of them. He clenched his jaw muscles and squeezed his eyes so tightly shut that they hurt. Only a glistening of tears betrayed him. He stemmed the tide of sobs that racked him inwardly.

Her engagement and marriage would be scrupulously respected; Anders swore that as an oath to himself just as he had covenanted with her father, The Mandarin, as a condition of obtaining the old man's patronage. The love would not go away, marriage to another man or not. He would have to be content to be her brother and to keep his other feelings to himself. All of this raced through his mind before he felt he could speak without humiliating himself.

"*C'est m'étonne*, Liên. *Il me semble si subit, si inattendu.*" (I am surprised, Liên. It seems so sudden, so unexpected.) He should not have said that; his emotions were too close to the surface. He had to pause to keep the quaver from his voice. "*Félicitations. Il est l'homme le plus chanceux du monde.*" (Congratulations. He is the luckiest man in the world.) Anders could not bear to look at the Vietnamese beauty, the lotus flower. He turned his head away. Hers was lowered, and she watched the silk rug intently. Then she softly sang the old Vietnamese song of sorrowing lovers"

> *Phải chi ngoài biển có cầu,*
> *Anh ra aến aó giải sầu cho em.*
> (If there were a bridge on the sea,
> I would go there to allay your sorrow.)

Nothing more was said. There was nothing to be gained by prolonging their mutual pain. After a few moments Liên padded softly from the room leaving Anders alone and feeling bereft. She hung a small pendant from the outside door latch of the library, a signal to everyone in the family not to disturb the occupant.

Anders felt all of the pain from all of his wounds—the cuts on his chest and back that were still purplish, the old bullet scars on his arm and flank, the lacerations on his face. None of them compared to the clenching he felt in his chest. His face was contorted with anguish, a torment that exceeded any of the slights or injustices he had suffered in his childhood or the fears of his early experiences in combat. He opened his shirt and looked down at the ugliness of his chest. He felt unacceptable. He felt very much alone.

The Mandarin ignored the sign on the door latch and slipped inside. He saw the boy's suffering and left again giving him the privacy a man needed at such a moment. Anders did not notice. In his Confucian wisdom, The Mandarin recognized that this experience was as necessary for the young man's character to develop his inner core of strength as it was for young women to subdue their passionate natures in order to preserve their virginity. It had been a difficult step for him to take for the best interests of his daughter and the family, and the old man emitted a small sigh of resignation.

CHAPTER 33

No one really knows how many of the 20,000 'Viet-Cong' killed last year were only innocent, or at least persuadable villagers...
Report of Senior White House Aide, Michael V. Forrestal to President John F. Kennedy, February ll, 1963

Keep asking me no matter how long, On the war in Vietnam, I sing this song: I ain't got no quarrel with the Viet Cong.
Muhammad Ali (formerly Cassius Clay) On the Draft—February, 1966

Anders spent a lackluster Tet of 1970 with the members of his unit at the compound. They did not even bother to fly into Hue'. For the other men it seemed like an invitation to be caught in the middle of a fight, and to Anders it was pointless. The city had become expensive—the Piastre was now devalued to 160 to the dollar on the black market. The Mandarin's house was closed up for the celebration because the entire family went to stay with relatives in Saigon. Anders did PT until he nearly dropped from exhaustion each day. It helped him not to think of the budding courtship taking place in the capital city.

Phoenix shifted its focus progressively toward the Cambodian and Laotian borders, determined to interdict the assistance being given the PAVN forces that streamed down the Ho Chi Minh trail and into the south. The militarily disastrous Tet Offensive of 1968 had rendered the VC, per se, a virtual nonentity. The VCI networks, on the contrary, continued to function with the same near impunity. Phoenix amassed volumes of information on The Infrastructure and prosecuted that data to its fullest. At the end of 1969 they were only 466 short of their projected goal of neutralizing 20,000 LAF agents. Some of those numbers were inflated, and among the actual victims were individuals who were completely innocent. They were ensnared by over enthusiastic PRUs for no other reason than to satisfy the insatiable appetite of Phoenix for numbers to forward to the Saigon five o'clock follies and on to the secretary of defense.

Some of the people listed were nothing more than defenseless victims of corrupt GVN officials running extortion rackets, and others were betrayed by acquaintances for revenge or profit as was the soft beverage distributor by his competitor whom Anders had watched being pushed out of a helicopter over the South China Sea. But, nevertheless, the figures were impressive. Phoenix was set up to interdict a political system that relied on secret police, midnight arrests, torture, arbitrary trials, and a dubious right to kill. Very shortly Phoenix had become all that it ostensibly opposed in the name of a life and death struggle.

Ethics and morality aside, the statistics were remarkable and bespoke a substantial success if not submitted to overly intense scrutiny—such as noting that Phoenix itself failed to describe a concomitant fall in the number of VCI at large as the capture and kill score mounted. Beginning in 1970, Anders' part in Phoenix took him almost exclusively into the mountains of South and North Viet Nam and into Laos, over the border, and into increasing involvement with the hill people.

For the first time in three years, Anders celebrated his birthday in conviviality and style. On the occasion of his twentieth birthday, he and his PRUCs found themselves in a friendly Montagnard village on the Laos side of the Truong Song Mountains. They had been reconnoitering the Ho Chi Minh Trail and had been gathering information regarding the various villages and tribes in the area as to whether they were pro GVN or supporters of the NLF and where they stood on the question of the Wa People and their drug smuggling enterprise. It had been a long hike on C Rats and LURPS for food. The men complained about the latter but they were none the worse for wear and had not heard a shot fired in anger in a week.

Their Montagnard village was as securely in the CIA family as any place could be and had been a safe haven for Company men for years. The tribesmen despised the VC as opportunists and for their cruelty, and they feared and loathed ARVN equally because of the bad treatment they received at their hands. The entire village belonged to FULRO with its dedication to Montagnard autonomy and regarded ethnic Vietnamese as inherent opponents to their cause, present company excepted. That they were technically in the Royalty of Laos was immaterial since none of them nor any of the PRUCs knew that.

The Special Forces green berets had once garnered their trust and loyalty, but that had evaporated after the Americans had been ordered to move them into a Strategic Hamlet. They had enjoyed the pay for being part of a CIDG, but when it became clear that they would have to leave the bones of their ancestors, the Montagnards had simply melted into the forest and outwaited the frustrated Americans. The CIA made no such demands, paid well, and appeared to have no moral qualms. The tribesmen liked that.

The village was a permanent one with well constructed family homes, communal facilities, and a large handsome long house. The long house served as the meeting hall and at times a communal dining center. It was regularly the weaving and dying factory and the basket and pottery making center. It also served for weapon and tool storage.

The tribe were Rhade, one of several distinct groups. They lived in family units consisting of nuclear and extended members and most shared a family long house five or six feet off the ground on stilts with animals underneath. A notched log served as the staircase up to the living quarters of the people. The family long houses had their own communal room that held ceremonial items like wine jugs, gongs, masks, and rattles, and were where the families' large storage drums were kept. Around the communal room were located the separate family rooms for each married couple and their children and separate quarters for the unmarried children and the elders. The size and appointments of a given long house were determined by the number of members and the wealth of the family. It was usual to have between fifteen and twenty people sharing the roof.

The Rhade with whom the PRUCs stayed were the most sophisticated of the mountain people. They were relatively light skinned which gave them a superior status among the hill people; and they had learned enough in their contacts with outside people to avoid the VC, NVA, and the ARVN soldiers alike. Their relations with The Company paramilitary agents were friendly, but businesslike, on both sides. The Rhade practiced slash and burn agriculture; and, having depleted their nearby forest, were contemplating taking up the ancestor's bones and moving to another location. That would be a fairly major undertaking since there were forty-five wood and bamboo houses arranged in two rows along the river that would have to be dismantled and moved along with all the belongings, animals, village members, and slaves. The people of the village where Anders Bergstrom of Zarahemla, Utah and his friends slept peacefully on many nights in the forest were both slavers and cannibals.

The Montagnards understood Vietnamese and probably spoke some, but refused to let on that they did. They knew a smattering of English and spoke French rather fluently but highly accented. It was easier for Anders and his Vietnamese teammates to use French in their conversations with the villagers even though Anders had only had a year and a half of schooling in the language. His natural aptitude for languages and the necessity to use the Frankish tongue hastened his progress.

The Rhade were not peaceable people despite the deceptive tranquillity of their village. They profited from the war going on around them by being mercenaries or guides for either side as the opportunity arose, and they provided foodstuff reprovisioning to all comers at an inflated price. The roving bands of regular and irregular soldiers and motley collections of bandits always seemed to have a surplus quantity of money or trade goods items, and the Rhade were only too happy to relieve them of some of the excess.

The village appeared quiet and domesticated for all its investment in mercenary warfare. The Rhade planted cotton and spun thread, wove and dyed cloth, made utilitarian but not attractive clay pottery, and grew dry rice. They were altogether self-sufficient. Their society was matrilineal and matrilocal. Men moved into the women's longhouses and took up lifelong residence. The system worked because the women were naturally more permanent and less likely to be lost in hunting accidents or on military forays. Children took the mother's name. Village life was quite tame until there was a celebration, especially a victory celebration. People sat around and gossiped on the front porch while the family girls pounded rice. The men and women both smoked tobacco and opium pipes in a languid atmosphere of connubial, familial, and community harmony.

Tran and the others told the *pholy* (headman) and the shaman that it was Anders' birthday and wondered if they could make a little party. The shaman was especially pleased with the good omen portended by the occasion of the white haired one's anniversary day. The headman accepted the idea of a celebration readily as well. They had two fine NVA captives, and now an auspicious occasion on which to make use of them.

The people, men, women, and children pitched in to help. They accepted the assistance of the PRUCs, including the guest of honor, in the village wide preparations. The women were small, slender, and round faced. They wore black, ankle length wraparound skirts, yellow rubber sandals, and heavy silver and semiprecious jewelry. They, like the men, were bare chested. A feast was prepared of dry rice to which dried fruits and chunks of salted fish and boiled eggs had been added, fresh river fish, and a stew that was mainly dog meat, but was livened with added rat, lizard, snake, and monkey flesh for accents. The headwoman in Anders' quarters made enough lizard salad for the whole community. Anders told her he could hardly wait. He reasoned that none of the food would be clearly recognizable as to origin. However, he had growing qualms about what his part in the program viz a viz the two quaking NVA boys would be. He wondered if he had any scruples left about what he ate, and he supposed that night would be the test.

Anders was placed in the center of the long house with a ring of animal skins, chicken feathers and feet, and a couple of what looked suspiciously like scalps around his seat. The shaman announced that he had consulted the ancestors (by dropping his collection of small bones and irregularly shaped pebbles into significant patterns on the sand of the river bank) and had learned of their pleasure at the evening's festivities. He had dreamed of a bounteous rice harvest as he slept the night before, a very good omen. It was time to offer sacrifices before the actual party could commence.

One of the village's old men brought in a monkey with a rope attached to its neck and its wrists and ankles tied to the bamboo bars of the small cage that imprisoned it. An old woman came in carrying a puppy of nondescript breed. The monkey set up a screeching howl, and the puppy yiped in terror as soon as they were set before the shaman who wore a gaudy array of amulets, bangles, and bright feathers and whose face was painted with brilliant slashes and zigzags of paint in a dozen different colors. He wore only wrist and leg charms and a patch over his genitals. A thong was attached to the man's scrotum, and the skull of a small forest animal dangled from the other end of the leather string. Anders was sure that he would be howling himself if he had had to come suddenly face to face with that apparition.

The shaman raised a din of gourd rattling, gonging, and incantations while the two little animals screeched in terror. To Anders, it was like stepping off the last rung of the ladder descending into hell. He felt a bit queasy.

In the midst of his seemingly entirely impromptu movements, the shaman whipped up a small club, the head of which was studded with nails, and slammed it down on the top of the monkey's head. The skull was crushed and brains and blood splashed about, liberally sprinkling Anders. The excited villagers oohed and aahed. The witch doctor dispatched the puppy with a deft throat slash, dipped his first two fingers in the blood, and wiped them across Anders' forehead. The demented appearing man stood by Anders while declaring that the sacrifices had been accepted by the spirits of the earth, the sky, the rivers, and the forests, and then jumped off the platform and disappeared into the dark woods. How the shaman had known of the spirits' approval was unclear to Anders since no more than a pair of seconds had elapsed between the killing of the second of the two animals and the declaration. But then, Anders realized, he was none too sure about the explanations of any of the religious mysteries he had been told about.

The religion of the Montagnards varied somewhat in practice from village to village and tribe to tribe (There were twelve major and sixty minor tribes), but was generally characterized by a fervent belief in animism. A host of spirits of different elements, animals, and inanimate objects, and natural phenomena were elevated to near-god status depending on the differing preferences of the separate villages. The second fundamental was the devotion felt toward ancestors. The bones of the old ones were buried under the mothers' houses joining with those of countless generations of predecessors. The religion was deeply felt, and the people resisted the incursions of Buddhism steadfastly. Except for a mention or two from the French soldiers who had come through a couple of decades or two before, none of them had heard of Christianity. The integrity of the clan and tribe were maintained by a justice system that was based on the offering of sacrifices for violation of village taboos such as murder or incest. Stealing was unheard of, and punishments, per se, were seldom inflicted.

A special regional sorcerer was called in cases of resistant illness to determine the nature of the spirit responsible and to learn what kind of sacrifice was required. At his request, the sorcerer received a chicken or two, sometimes a pig or a goat. They tried herbal medicine and incantations. If all of that failed, the family was required to sacrifice a water buffalo. The Rhade were practical people and were allowed to eat the slaughtered animal; but nevertheless, a serious illness could run up frighteningly high medical bills. If that drastic measure failed, the sorcerer usually explained that the greedy spirit involved would be satisfied only with the sick person's body. The family would lament and plead for help. The sorcerer would relent and reluctantly accept a large nonrefundable donation of money as the absolute court of last resort.

At any rate, the shaman's part in Anders' birthday ceremony was over, and Anders felt he would be able to relax. He had gotten tense during the religious performance. He was well off the mark in his naive belief that it was going to get less intense. It was his turn to be the center of attention. The women brought in two large coconuts and a bamboo straw. Anders had to suck both coconut shells dry of their fermented coconut milk and rice liquor before the women had finished their initiation-into-the-tribe musical number, and in this special instance, birthday song.

This was the first time Anders had tasted hard spirits, and both the taste and the effect were unwelcome. The mixture was slimy and viscid. It tasted like heated shoe polish. What he wouldn't do for his country and his unit. The effect of drunkenness was equally undesirable. Anders could feel the flush of dizziness and confusion warm throughout his body. He found it very difficult to think or to maintain his attention. Across the room he could see the NVA enlisted men lapping up bowl after bowl of liquid. He presumed it was alcohol, and he was partly right. The mixture was generously laced with opiates as well.

The women cleared the way for the men. They were having a highly jovial time. A group of them forming a delegation walked unsteadily up to where Anders sat. They were in a state of alcohol induced euphoria themselves. One of them handed Anders a small cup containing two glistening ovoids the size of small nuts. They looked something like cooked lichees but were smaller and more translucent. A small amount of slightly milky thick liquid oozed from one of the objects. The man laughed uproariously at Anders' quizzical impression. Two more of the men brought a burlap wrapped four foot long cylindrical shaped thing still steaming from the large cooking pot situated near the entrance ladder to the room. They unwrapped it an laid it out on the table before Anders and the senior men. It was a thick meaty skinned cobra, minus its head. The men clapped, and the men and women looking on all laughed delightedly. Anders presumed that the inspiration for their hilarity was a combination of his expression and the anticipation of sharing the delicacy.

Tran slipped up behind Anders and whispered, "They want you to eat the stuff in the cup first. It is the most important thing. You must do it, or we will all lose face. They won't like us."

"What is that stuff?"

"You don't want to know."

"Oh, yes, I do!"

"Not until after you get it down. I know about this. You'll be okay

675

if you just take the whole thing down in one gulp. Understand?"

"Um hmmh," Anders whispered, the dubiousness evident even in his inarticulate response.

"Whatever you do, don't chew it. And it's okay to take a big drink or two. Nobody told me that. It'll help to get it down fast."

Anders looked over at the NVA captives. They appeared as if they had been hollowed out by fear. They were now seated, too drunk and sedated to stand. Anders thought he knew how they felt. He really did not want to do this, fraternalism, patriotism, or unit integrity notwithstanding.

A hush came over the crowd of light brown faces all upturned and golden in the firelight. Every eye was on Anders. He gulped as inconspicuously as possible and managed a wan smile he hoped would be misinterpreted as bravado. Tran bobbed his head as a signal to swallow the contents of the cup. Anders looked at the peculiar objects, obviously animal in origin, and raw, with a revulsion that was hard to disguise. He picked up the cup. The men grinned broadly. He moved it to his quivering lips. The men and women clucked their tongues and smacked their lips. Tran made a vigorous backward motion of his head pantomiming an exaggerated swallow. Anders closed his eyes. The crowd became quiet. He threw the contents to the back of his throat and swallowed as fast and as hard as he could.

The swallow was easy. The contents were slick and almost tasteless. They imparted an aftertaste that was faintly like petroleum fumes; no, more like mineral oil. Not really that bad. He grabbed up a cup of *ternum* (rice wine) and downed it, and then downed another, just to be on the safe side. No sooner had the mixture hit his stomach than Anders began to have the most peculiar sensations. His fingers and toes tingled and his tongue felt thick and numb. He could not have talked even if he had been inclined. He felt as if he could not even move his eyeballs. He felt all warm and sleepy and good. It was the weirdest sensation he had ever experienced.

The men, women, and children of the Rhade Montagnard village cheered and laughed. Most of them rushed up to clap Anders on the back. He knew he was accepted. He did not know if he was going to keep breathing. His four PRUC teammates slipped up around him and supported him with their strong arms so he would not topple off his seat.

"Cobra venom sacs," Tran said loudly, trying to be heard over the din of the surrounding merrymakers.

"What did you say?" Anders asked, thinking that he could not have heard correctly.

"Poison sacs from the big snake," Tran repeated enunciating each syllable so he could not be mistaken. He was smiling, and Anders took that as a good sign. He was pretty frightened anyway.

"It's all right," Ky said. "Almost nobody dies."

"Just stays paralyzed," Anders said ruefully, looking from face to face for some source of solace.

"Nah," Ky said, "In about an hour you'll be fine. The nerve toxin will get out of your system. Won't harm you."

Anders was none too sure, but there was nothing he could do but sit back and enjoy the strange feeling and to munch on fingerfuls of the succulent marinated and boiled snake being fed to him by his comrades and by a beautiful bare breasted girl who had wheedled her way up to the man she regarded as a giant. Soon her ardor was so evident that the men laughed and let her minister to Anders exclusively. He remained a little worried, but was having a great time. Even the communist soldier captives looked relieved to have attention drawn away from themselves.

It was ten o'clock in the evening by the time the effects of the cobra nerve toxin wore off. His head was still abuzz from the alcohol, but Anders felt like he had most of his faculties back. Most of the villagers had taken a short nap; the girl had fallen asleep with her head in Anders' lap. She was a lovely little creature with black hair (none too clean), and a puckish upturned nose. Her teeth were brilliantly white and perfectly even. The perfection had come from meticulous filing. All of her incisors and premolars came to matching points. Because she was unmarried, her teeth had not yet been lacquered. Her lips were reddened with betel nut juice. She wore ear, nose, and lip rings, and had fifteen or twenty pounds of silver and stone jewelry on her limbs and around her neck and waist. She was a completely calm, completely natural young woman. Anders could not guess her age; maybe she was thirteen or fourteen. Whatever her age, she was no child.

The Montagnards began to rouse. The women plied the captives with more opiate saturated alcohol, a kind of strong Asian Mickey Finn mixture. Their heads were lolling to one side in a semi-stupor, no longer caring about their condition.

The Montagnard men stirred themselves and cleared away the table with its left over snake meat and fruit rinds. Two of them escorted one of the captives off into the forest, presumably to let him relieve himself. Two more men brought the second NVA soldier to where Anders now stood. Anders was huge in comparison to the little communist soldier.

The Occidental was six foot four or five and the Oriental was no more than five feet tall. Anders was powerfully muscled, bulky, and heavy. The North Vietnamese was thin, obviously undernourished, and weakened by his weeks of hard travel down the Ho Chi Minh Trail through Laos on half rations. One of the subchiefs handed Anders a ceremonial knife, the length of a *Coupe-Coupe* (machete), and sharp enough to shave with. Anders looked at him dumbly.

There was an awkward pause. The subchief looked at Anders with an expression that showed a desire to bestow an honor, then an inquiring look. Anders looked at the bound captive and at the large knife. His brain was not working very well. What was it they wanted? They didn't expect him to be the one...the one to...use the knife. They weren't going to kill the poor guy...like this. Just like this. Anders looked at the faces of his PRUCs for help. There was none.

Tran shrugged his shoulders and made a quick finger gesture across his throat. "Get it over with," the signal implied. Anders' brain reeled. He was now entirely awake and alive to every nuance of the situation. He could not do it; he just could not do it. He had killed men, even up close, but nothing like this, ever. The two NVA were defenseless. He looked for an escape route, a way out. He felt himself on the verge of panic. The headman cocked his head Anders' way once, then again. His was an unmistakable signal. "Get on with it. What is the matter with you?"

Anders knew the stakes were too high, and he and his men had come too far to jeopardize their standing and camaraderie with these people. This was an enemy soldier; he had to think that. To concentrate on that. The man stood numbly before Anders entirely unaware of the tumult going on in the young Scandinavian's soul. He was scarcely aware of his environment at all.

Anders wanted to scream, "NO!" but his discipline would not let him do that. He slowly moved behind the man. The communist did not move or attempt to follow Anders with his eyes. Anders stood behind the helpless captive. He was shaking. The captive did not exhibit the slightest fear. He had no idea of what lay in store, nor did he care right then.

Anders clenched his eyes closed for a second, then popped them open, reached his powerful left arm around the little man's neck and suddenly jerked it taut under the man's chin forcibly extending the North Vietnamese's head back. In the same instant Anders brought the knife across the exposed neck and sliced savagely. Blood geysered out of the two severed carotid arteries and jugular veins. The man's eyes bulged open in a half second of realization, then he died before he could register pain. Anders let him slump to the ground.

The body was dragged away by the women, and Anders was led to another spot in the large room. The second captive was hauled up to Anders. "Oh, no," he groaned as soon as he realized that he was to be a double executioner. He drove every vestige of conscience and sense of decency, justice, fair play, and Christianity out of his conscious mind. This time he did not hesitate. If he had done so, he might have been unable to keep on.

Anders looked directly into the eyes of the NVA captive. This time the man seemed to have some comprehension of what was going to happen to him, but he made no attempt to defend himself. Anders brought his left hand up in a blur of motion and chopped the communist soldier sharply under his right mastoid bone. There was a sickening snap sound. The man's eyelids opened halfway, and his body crumpled as if it had no bones. His neck was broken, and his upper cervical spinal cord neatly severed. He was as dead as the first man. Anders quickly went through the unnecessary motion of slicing the man's anterior neck. A satisfying outpouring of blood flowed onto the bamboo floor. Anders stepped back feeling sick. Tran and Dung put their hands on him to steady their chief. They did not feel too stable themselves.

The body was swooped away as efficiently as the first one, and a throbbing music began to come from everywhere. Most of the villagers had brought their favorite musical instruments, a completely novel set in Anders' experience and were now joined in a village wide musical celebration. The men looked at Anders with fellowship and admiration. The women looked at him with something between affection and respect; and the girl who had slept with her head on his lap gazed at him with what could only be described as wonder. Slaves were dismembering the corpses and fixing the parts onto spits for slow roasting over the piles of coals that had burned down from the fires that had been all evening in preparation. Even Ky had a hard time looking at that. This particular village of Rhade was fastidious about heads, and a second set of slaves buried them in the forest.

Only a few Montagnard tribes and villages practiced slavery and even fewer engaged in cannibalism. The practice was in part ritual, but also a source of food, at least for that one ceremonial evening. There would be nothing left but bones by the following morning. Anders feigned exhaustion and desire for the girl and was permitted to retire to his room in his adopted family's long house without participating in what the villagers referred to as eating 'long pig.' He had learned that indeed there were things he would not do, things he could not eat. He slept deeply without further gastronomic intake, and without granting the girl her defloweration. She had to be satisfied to run her rough little fingers over the ridges of his chest and back scars in curiosity and with sympathy. She was completely smitten with the white giant, and was determined to have him living in her long house one day. The *nher* (girl) made sure Anders remembered her by serving him the best of foods and giving him the best of massages. She also made sure he remembered her name, H'Klois. It was a birthday he was not likely to forget in a long, long time.

Anders moved in and out of the Truong Son Mountains with regularity. With the Montagnards as guides and porters, he was able to travel and to strike small blows against the ever mobile NVA units with near impunity. At times they captured a quarry that had been assigned to them, a VCI who served the cause—a tax collector, a village cadre, a courier, or an agent lurking secretly in a pacified village. At other times he or one of the other PRU teams delivered a captive or two from a feuding neighbor village to one of the cooperating villages just to keep on good terms. Anders and his men were able to move the product of their extracurricular special business arrangement quite freely now. Their bottom-line ledger numbers at the Union Bank of Switzerland kept increasing. Cleve Howard was pleased with his output for Phoenix, and Anders was generally regarded as a great success for such a young man by those who knew him.

Although he missed considerable periods at school, Anders was able to maintain his standing in his courses and in his class by dint of extra effort on his part and with the help of Liên who was now back in Hue'. She had dropped out of school to prepare for her marriage two months away and had copious free time on her hands. With the shadow caused by Anders' poorly disguised desire for Liên removed from between them, the two were able to establish a respectful deep friendship and loyalty to one another. She found in him a confidant and told him things so personal that he regularly blushed, making her laugh. It was cathartic for her to purge her repressions to a man, to a person who could never use anything she said against her. He simply delighted in her company and profited from her fine mind and excellent education.

Because he did so well on his tests and on classroom assignments when he was available, and because he kept up his studies irrespective of holidays (of which Viet Nam has a great many) or summers, his professors gave him a great deal of latitude. They still considered him a novelty, a positive one.

Master Nguyen chided him regularly for his absences, but was also indulgent. It pleased the old martial arts master to have what he considered such an important student. Master Nguyen regarded Anders as a great emissary of peace in the performance of his role as a Red Cross monitoring official. The old man had been shaken to the core by the Battle of Hue' and longed for the peace to pursue the expansion of his dojo into more schools. He was sure that Anders' frequent absences took the young man around the countryside in an attempt to bring the purposeless conflict to an honorable conclusion. For that he was willing to be lenient.

Master Nguyen was not lenient about the rigors of his art, however. Anders was subjected to a grinding work schedule, to running and exercising that would have laid low a less fit man. Every day the young Swede was present in the dojo, which was about half of the days of a month, he took on the Master's best pupils and young black belts in an exhausting round robin of kumité contests. After nearly a year and a half of study under the venerable old grand master, Anders was the star of the dojo in kumité; but he was still deficient in the performance of katas. He was ready to test for his first dan (black belt) so far as fighting was concerned, but the Master despaired of ever being able to pound the refinements of performing forms or katas into the lazy stupid foreigner's head.

Despite all of the martial arts *sensai's* protestations of dismay at Anders' deficiencies, it was evident to both men that a bond of affection had grown between them. In private, Anders had taken to calling the splendid old man, *Bac* (uncle), and the Master found himself responding in kind. Even in unguarded moments outside their private sessions, Master Nguyen referred to Anders as his *chau trai* (nephew) to his trusted old friends like The Mandarin. Together the two old men could gossip with shared fondness over the awkwardness and backwardness of their adopted family member and could hope for the young man's successful future. They both thought he showed promise.

Anders practiced French whenever he could. He had the amused cooperation of The Mandarin but regularly considered giving up on Liên who made fun of his pronunciation and reverting to Vietnamese or even English. The French language had been useful in the Montagnard village, particularly in the one where he had been adopted and had been a snake eater. In his classes he was mediocre student in comparison to his classmates who had used French since they had learned to talk. Nonetheless, he doggedly made progress.

The convolutions of Vietnamese history after the First World War were harder to sort out than what he had studied in his previous quarters. In part this was because much of what he learned was in contradistinction to his preconceived notions of western civilization. He had considerable to unlearn before he could really absorb the history of Southeast Asia, at least from the point of view of those who lived there.

The head of the department, a relatively young full professor named Dr. Phan—Phan Doi Hang—knew every French foible and peccadillo, every national blunder, tantrum, and cultural flaw. "In 1930," he lectured, "the Vietnamese National Party made a great mistake in underestimating the French when they led the first armed uprising against the colonial power. They also underestimated the ruthlessness of their occupiers. The savage repression by the French resulted in the near extinction of the nationalist party. The leaders, were imprisoned in unspeakable conditions, tortured and shot. They went deep underground and came to be dominated by the communists." He sipped from a glass of water.

"In 1936." He wrote the date along side '1930' on the blackboard, and Anders copied both dates into his notebook presuming that they would be important at test time. "In 1936 the Viet Minh was organized to incorporate all anti-French forces, north and south. Until the Second World War, they worked sporadically with bombings and ambushes that annoyed the French but did little to dislodge them. They were treated as common criminals, not real opponents. After the invasion and occupation by the Japanese, the Viet Minh shifted their focus to fight against the repressive regime. They worked with the American OSS agents and even with French commandos to bring the Japanese down.

"In 1945 the Japanese were finally driven out. The weakened French government and the tired and poorly supplied Viet Minh came to a compromise of sorts. In March, 1946 the French government signed an agreement with the Viet Minh leader, and the man whom the French regarded as the logical head of the Vietnamese people, Ho Chi

Minh, to form a so-called 'free-state' within Indochina. Ho named his autonomous country 'The Democratic Republic of Viet Nam' and understood it to include all three sections of the country.

"French forces were permitted by Ho to land in Hanoi in accordance with the agreement; and Bao Dai, the former emperor, was gracefully exiled to China. That effectively eliminated nationalist interests that might develop that were not part of the Viet Minh.

"But there was a misunderstanding. The French did not intend for all three segments of the country to come under only one autonomous Vietnamese government, and Ho was obliged to go to France to negotiate. Ho could only succeed in establishing a limited Republic of Cochinchina under his presidency. Furthermore, Ho had to sign an agreement to allow the French to return to their old economic and cultural activities. They, in turn, promised to provide a more liberal regime; although that was not spelled out clearly.

"The French acted that same year with a heavy hand to enforce their customs controls, and that angered many Viet Minh who already opposed the agreement Ho had signed because it did not recognize Vietnamese unity, independence, or importance. The hostility resulted in minor disturbances on the part of the Viet Minh, but a major retaliation by the French that showed their true natures. In November they bombarded Haiphong and killed 6,000 of our countrymen.

"Instead of learning and making corrections, the French became more demanding. The DRV decided that war was preferable to submission once again to the French. In December they attacked the French in the first action of the First Indochina War, a terrible eight year long conflict."

Professor Phan concluded. The students were left wanting more. Anders desired to understand the antecedents of the war in which he was involved. He forgot about taking notes; he did not need them. He was so interested that he absorbed the material into his mind, and it became a part of his growing sense of what Viet Nam was.

Two days later, Professor Phan strode up to his lectern and started exactly where he had left off as if he had only taken a five minute smoking break. He did not use notes.

"Not only did the fight against the French pit colonialist against revolutionary, it caused the resurgence of a great division in the country itself. The DRV and the communists alienated the non-communist nationalists who, with French encouragement, split off as the Republic of Viet Nam. The French agreed to recognize the RVN with Bao Dai as the head of state and Ngo Dinh Diem as the effective leader. Diem, however, did not accept the situation and continued to resist the French. The Chinese poured in aid to the DRV, that was effectively North Viet Nam; and England and America supported the RVN, effectively the South Viet Nam division.

Anders had to resort to taking notes again. The changes and divisions were too much for him.

"Let me simplify some of this," offered the professor seeing the bewilderment on the faces of some of the students. "We can take up the details day after tomorrow."

Relief at the prospect of some reduction in the details of the tangled alliances and the oscillations of the military conflict showed in the students' eyes.

Two days later, Dr. Phan took up where he had left off, "In 1952 the communists began a major offensive in a number of separate areas in the country. American economic and equipment assistance slowed it down, but the DRV forces continued to wear the French down. People of the world, and both the French and the DRV, began to look for a negotiated peace. In February, 1954 the great powers agreed to a Geneva Conference. The conference remained largely talk until the greatest battle of the war, the siege at Dien Bien Phu, took place."

Now the students were anxious to hear because every Vietnamese, if he or she knows nothing else about the history of the country, knows the name of Dien Bien Phu.

Dr. Phan looked at his watch. "Not enough time today. We will spend a whole period on that battle and its outcome early next week. You will be expected to write an extensive term paper on a subject selected from this historical period. Good day." Once again he left them wanting more.

CHAPTER 34

SECRET: In camera session, Senate Intelligence Oversight Committee.
Testimony of Wilmer A Colding, Jr. Deputy Director, Operations, Central Intelligence Agency, Director, Civil Operations and Revolutionary Development Support
    17 December, 1972
    1000
Subject: Vietnamization program—status and progress report on Phoenix program.

Chairman, Sen. Fineton: Deputy Director we have looked forward to your being here for some time.

Mr. Colding: Regrettable interferences Senator. I hope my appearance today will help to assuage any concerns you may have.

Sen. Fineton: Like the fact that we have very nearly had to exercise our subpoena power to get you here. Well, let us get on to the material issues of the day. We have received some disturbing intelligence about your Phoenix program. Some of that information is blatantly public. I take it you are familiar with the articles in *The New York Times* and in *Time* and *Newsweek* and the *Far Eastern Economic Review* magazines?

Mr. Colding: Yes sir, I am.

Sen. Fineton: They are critical of Phoenix, are they not, Mr. Colding?

Mr. Colding: They certainly are, sir. I am sure you are aware of the climate of discontent rife in the country at the present time.

Sen. Fineton: Indeed. We are here to review some of the claims being made. There seems to be more than a germ of truth in what the press has been reporting. We have our own sources including several agents who have come forward with their own accounts. If what they say is true, I am ashamed to be an American. If only a smidgen of truth is contained in the reports, I have to think that where there's smoke, there's fire.

Mr. Colding: Let me address those articles, please, senator.

Sen. Fineton: Not for a moment. I will put some direct questions to you, sir; and I expect direct answers.

Mr. Colding: Of course, Mr. Chairman. As always.

Sen. Fineton: First there are reports of numbers of assassinations, torturings, extortions, and false imprisonment that keep cropping up. I will cite a few and you can respond to them.

Mr. Colding: Happy to oblige, Mr. Chairman. I certainly have nothing to hide, and I can speak for the agency as well. Our hands remain clean whatever the left leaning press may have to say to the contrary.

Sen. Fineton: Have there been any atrocities committed by the people for whom you are responsible?

Mr. Colding: None.

Sen. Fineton: The *New York Times* reports that more than twenty thousand innocent civilians have been killed under the Phoenix program. A congressional subcommittee has formally criticized the Pentagon for not investigating war crimes. Do you expect us to sit here and accept that there were no atrocities.

Mr. Colding: The 20,000 enemy casualties occurred in military action, not by Phoenix executive action. I am certainly aware of no atrocities. CORDS, of which I am the director, has responsibility for a host of civilian services including police activities. I do not know of a single instance of an atrocity committed by our people. They are hardly in a position to do so. As to the Pentagon involvement, perhaps the reference is to the infamous Mai Ly massacre of 16 March, 1968. That was certainly the exception, and Lieutenant Calley, the officer responsible, is currently being held on charges. There were, perhaps four hundred killed, certainly no more than five hundred in that sanitizing sweep.

Sen. Fineton: That answer was not wholly responsive. Do you assert that there has been only the one atrocity, the Mai Ly incident?

Mr. Colding: I will address the issue of atrocities straight on. US military personnel were instructed on rules of engagement and were required to carry a card on their person at all times detailing those rules. The rules were in accordance with the Articles of the Geneva Convention and included the humane treatment of POWs. Violators were subject to the UCMJ. It is a court martial offense to commit atrocities in our military as it is in the civilian sector of our country. From 1966 to the end of 1972 there were 201 army and 77 marine personnel court martialed for serious crimes against Vietnamese civilians- crimes like murder, rape, negligent homicide.

And while we're at it, let's not be too one-sided. The VC committed 37,000 assassinations and 60,000 kidnappings. Those are atrocities. That is the kind of enemy we are up against. It is not terribly remarkable that some of our military people get a little over zealous at times.

Sen. Curtiss: Pardon the interruption. I get lost with the acronyms. Refresh my memory, if you would. What is the UCMJ?

Mr. Colding: Uniform Code of Military Justice.

Sen. Curtiss: Thank you.

Sen. Fineton: This is like pulling teeth. We have heard about the military, but that is not what we are talking about here, is it? Did the Phoenix program people murder innocents?

Mr. Colding: No.

Sen. Fineton: Torture?

Mr. Colding: No.

Sen. Fineton: Detain unlawfully?

Mr. Colding: No. We investigate, at times make arrests, but the Government of the Republic of Viet Nam makes the dispositions thereafter.

Sen. Fineton: Are you telling me that no one has been killed in the course of these 'arrests?'

Mr. Colding: No sir, I am not telling you that. As in police activities throughout the civilized world, there are always those who resist; and in some cases they do so violently. The policemen have defended themselves against these Viet Cong criminals.

Sen. Fineton: And the deceased, were they ever innocent victims?

Mr. Colding: No. All deaths have been registered with the Saigon MACV headquarters and recorded by their official stamp as Viet Cong.

Sen. Fineton: How convenient.

Mr. Colding: Sir?

Sen. Fineton: Let's go on. The subject of extortion and corruption keeps coming up. Tell me, Director Colding, why did Ambassador Bunker do away with the High Values Reward Program?

Mr. Colding: That, of course, was his prerogative. My understanding was that it was considered to be too expensive; and frankly, the communist inspired press criticism made it politically unpopular by giving it a sinister slant. That is despite its recordable success in bringing in VCI.

Sen. Fineton: And not because the cells of Phoenix and *Phung Hoang* operatives misused their authority and exacted compliance from the people upon whom they reported for extortion or sexual favors? Our informants tell us that it was common for the informants to say, 'Give me your pig, or your daughter; or I will report you to the *Phung Hoang*.'

Mr. Colding: They did not. I can't say that such a thing never happened, but it was not at all wide spread. I, for one, do not know of a single instance.

Sen. Fineton: The security committees you established still sound Stalinist to me, but we will go on. Let's talk about the fates of the civilian detainees. Did the Vietnamese, the GVN, abuse the detainees?

Mr. Colding: Not to my direct knowledge.

Sen. Fineton: And if they had would you have acted to prevent atrocities?...I see a bit of hesitation. I will rephrase the question. Did you comply with the directive of State Department telegram 220774 that required the Saigon Embassy to control the GVN security apparatus to treat detainees in a humanitarian manner?

Mr. Colding: Absolutely. I specifically ordered our POICs and ROICs to instruct their operatives to make those demands of the Vietnamese each time they turned over a VCS.

Sen. Curtiss: Again, sorry to interrupt. I take it that a POIC and a ROIC is an agency officer in charge, an American?

Mr. Colding: Yes, sir.

Sen. Fineton: To the point of the agency's involvement, tell me about the notorious PICs, the provincial interrogation centers. I have been told ghastly things about what went on in those places.

Mr. Colding: More pink-tinged, enemy serving hogwash, if I may be so bold. Interrogation centers are just that. They are temporary holding cells for the VCS to be detained and questioned. I state categorically I know of nothing improper taking place in any of the centers.

Sen. Fineton: What about Con Son Island prison? Representative Luce reported horrendous improprieties on his fact-finding visit.

Mr. Colding: The facilities at Con Song are strictly under the control of the GVN. I am not aware of any irregularities, only rumors.

Sen. Fineton: Hear no evil; see no evil; speak no evil, eh? Mr. Deputy Director. How is it possible, Mr. Colding, to have any kind of due process, any kind of control of a program of detention and punishment, where all activities are carried out in secret, where there is no provision for redress of false accusation, detention, and injury? How can a democracy permit a prison and court system that does not have a provision for judicial review? Can you tell me that, sir?

Mr. Colding: That is a Vietnamese responsibility, Mr. Chairman.

Sen. Fineton: Despite the fact that the American Central Intelligence Agency had complete control of the overall Phoenix program? Happened on the other shift, eh, Mr. Director?

Mr. Colding: Beg your pardon, sir?

Sen. Fineton: Never mind. I am informed that the arrest rate is now 14,000 a month. I have read secret reports that suggest that proper intelligence services ordered no more than one or two hundred of those. What do you think, Mr. Colding? Any of these arrests for revenge or for illicit gain?

Mr. Colding: I was privy to the orders and their justification. Every one of the detainees was arrested on the basis of excellent probable cause.

Sen. Fineton: And they were treated properly, not assassinated?

Mr. Colding: We've been over this before. No.

Sen. Fineton: Not tortured?

Mr. Colding: No.

Sen. Fineton: None of them, not whole families were carried out over the South China Sea and thrown out of airplanes?

Mr. Colding: Not to my knowledge.

Sen. Fineton: So all of the journalists and the agents, both American and Vietnamese, who report extreme irregularities are mistaken or traitors?

Mr. Colding: That seems to be a reasonable characterization, but please remember that was your description, not mine, sir.

Sen. Fineton: And is this program to go on *ad infinitum*? I, for one, am not at all sure the American people would give one scintilla of approval should they become widely informed.

Mr. Colding: In accordance with the President's directives for Vietnamization in all spheres of activity in the republic, the CIA and CORDS will begin the expeditious transfer of authority for the Phoenix program to the *Phung Hoang*, and the police and security forces of GVN this very month. We will have nothing further to do with the prosecution of the communist infrastructure after no more than a couple or three months. The program to do so is called PHREEX.

Sen. Curtiss: PHREEX? Oh, never mind.

Sen. Fineton: Thank you for answering our questions. I promised you an opportunity to respond to the issues. Go ahead.

Mr. Colding: Thank you, Senator. Our successes are unpublished, and suspicions about our intentions and our actions are given wide credence without our being able to mount a defense. As you know, it is against policy for the agency to respond publicly. However, this is a secret forum, one mandated by law; and I can set the record straight here, at least. There are great successes to our credit. The 'Open Arms Program' resulted in a ten year removal of 160,000 VC deserters who surrendered 11,000 individual weapons and nearly 600 crew served weapons. We interdicted 70,000 members of the communist infrastructure. After the Tet Offensive of 1968, we reduced the military threat from the Viet Cong guerrilla effort to negligible and forced the NVA masters of the insurgency to switch increasingly to conventional military action. This was effective warfare, not assassination, no matter what our detractors say publicly or privately. I remind you, gentlemen, and lady; these journalists, the liberals who make illegal trips to North Viet Nam, the people who march in the streets, the deserters, and the Viet Nam Veterans Against The War aid and abet our enemies.

Sen. Fineton: And, Mr. Colding, once more for the record. The CIA will be out of it come spring, correct?

Mr. Colding: Correct. Before that.

Sen. Fineton: Then can you guarantee that the United States, and in particular the CIA, will not participate in the provisions of General Thieu's secret Decree Law 020?

Mr. Colding: I am unfamiliar.

Sen. Fineton: That sounds like uncharacteristic naiveté, but I will give you the benefit of the doubt and will outline it for you and for the record. The law is simply a declaration that the methods to eliminate the VCI will continue to be employed even in the event of a cease-fire or an official close of the war. To quote the general, 'the VCI must be wiped out quickly and mercilessly.'

Mr. Colding: I have no knowledge of such a decree. I can only assure you that, if there is such a GVN law, the intelligence forces of the United States will not be party to it. I will research the matter and get back to you on this, lady and gentlemen.

Sen. Fineton: I have nothing further. Perhaps before we open to questions from the other members, we can take a short break. I am sure lunch is waiting. We would like to dedicate a moment of silence during lunch to our departed former chairman, Senator Tittlebaum.

Lunch break—1151.

CHAPTER 35

Despite our armed reconnaissance efforts and strikes of rail-roads, roads, bridges, storage centers, training bases, and other key links in their lines of communications, it is estimated that they are capable of generating in the North and infiltrating to the South 4500 men a month and between 50 and 300 tons a day depending on the season . . .

We have in Vietnam the ingredients of an enormous miscalculation...

We are in an escalating military stalemate.
John T. McNaughton, Assistant Secretary of Defense, memoranda to Defense Secretary Robert McNamara, Jan. 18 and 19, 1966

Anders was very tense. Every *Tây Sơn Võ Sĩ* instructor in three provinces, and all of Master Nguyen's students, including as many former students as possible, were seated around the large practice room bamboo futon on silent haunches. Only the four judges occupied chairs, one in the middle of each side of the rectangular mat. Anders sat stonily in silence and immobility in the center of the open area. At his left side were the classical weapons—broad blade sword, spear, net, staff, and nunchucks. On his left were a set of Chinese throwing knives, brass knuckles with a knife attached, and throwing stars. Behind him was a teak frame supporting a two inch thick board. Further to his rear stood a tall frame holding another board at head level.

The test was the most important in a martial artist's life. The first Dan represented the epitome of achievement; all degrees above that level, at least in *Tây Sơn Võ Sĩ*, were honorary.

There were no women, no outsiders, and no foreigners among the judges or spectators. Four men in black gis, one of them nearly sixty-five, sat in the judge's seats; each one of them was an acknowledged grand master of the discipline. It had not been easy to convince these men to come for the black belt test since it was for a foreigner. No

Occidental had ever been instructed. No foreigner had ever been tested for the honor of becoming first Dan and to have the right to wear a black belt in the art that was at once exclusive and secret. Only one in ten Vietnamese had passed the test on the average over the years, and there had never been a foreigner granted a black belt. Had it been known that Anders was an American, he would not have been in the room. The mood in the province and in the country as Tet 1973 approached was that the Americans had to go, just as the French hairy bodies had had to go. These were not VC or communists, or NVA making that judgment. They were Vietnamese first and always.

The test was to follow a time hallowed routine. The candidate's *sensai* presented him to the assemblage who were invited to give a thumbs up or down signal even to permit the examination to begin. As a result of vigorous pretest lobbying by Master Nguyen, Anders got his unanimous go-ahead signal at two minutes of midnight. At the stroke of the hour, the test began.

The black belt test required absolute memorization of the rules and their word perfect recitation without notes—in Vietnamese with no allowances for the language not being the candidate's native one. Without instruction the candidate was then to perform the twelve standard katas, three facing each direction. A single error in execution resulted in immediate disqualification with no second chances that night. The final performance in the kata segment was to display a form of his own devising that portrayed the defense against more than one opponent.

The weapons segment was next. The candidate was to demonstrate his proficiency with the throwing knives. Four by four beams and targets were provided. Next followed the throwing stars. An assistant was then provided as an mock attacker, and the candidate demonstrated the defense against the classical weapons. The implements were razor sharp and made of fine steel. The attacks were to be performed with homicidal intent. Tough young men were selected because the defenses were neither mock nor dainty in this ultimate test. The final test in the weapons segment was the nunchuck kata involving a defense against four imaginary opponents. The judges all knew the kata perfectly, and the standard was to be able to perform it in no more than half a minute without being struck with the weapons himself. That was no mean feat and had taken Anders more than two years to perfect.

The third section of the testing was the breaking. Anders would be required to splinter a two inch board with his hand and wrist, his elbow, and by stomping it. He also was expected to break a similar board at the level of a man's head with a jumping front kick or a spinning back kick whichever he chose. He had to break a one inch board with his head.

Anders was sure of himself on all of those tests since he had practiced them hour after hour until he could do the entire test flawlessly and quickly and without thinking about the component parts. His doubts came for the kumité segment which would commence after a fifteen minute rest and grading period. The problem was that he was to fight three experts, one after another, and then against two attackers selected from among the senior students, and all of this after being worn down by tiredness from the kata and breaking segments.

The twenty-two year old Swede had matured during his seven years in Viet Nam. He was a large boy when he came, a little awkward and unsure of himself. He had developed and learned through a refining fire into a giant of a man, proficient, agile, and confident. In the preceding two years the coming-of-age surge of testosterone had caused his muscles to increase into the full complement of manhood. He had grown a mat of chest hair that somewhat obscured his tattoos and scars. Anders now had a mature attentiveness, an unbreakable focus in contest and combat. He weighed 264 pounds and was lean. He was 6'6" tall. Anders Bergstrom was a formidable opponent.

But, he knew that the men facing him for the series of kumités were the best of the best in Viet Nam. He suspected that the older man was from *Bac Bo,* but no one said anything. He had absorbed enough of the art from his Master to know that his size was only a relative advantage. Skill was paramount; and in the end, the most skillful contestant would prevail. He knew it was not necessary for him to win every kumité match, according to the strict law of T y SÆn VÆTĐe rules only required that he attack and defend well and demonstrate skill at a first Dan level. But he had known, even without the dispassionate communication from Master Nguyen, that he would have to be better than the usual candidate. He would have to beat at least two of his opponents if he were to overcome the inherent prejudices marshaled against him. Except for the students with whom he had worked directly for the past three years, the observers were all rooting for him to fail.

Anders had practiced the katas until they were second nature to him, including the form of his own construction. He executed them nearly flawlessly. He was aware of a single misstep, but he corrected so quickly that no one except Master Nguyen could have detected the error. None of the judges raised an objection.

His hands were callused and his knuckles were large and rock hard. He had plunged his fingers into rice bags and then into sacks of gravel until the fingers were no longer sensitive, and they could break thin boards without causing Anders to flinch. He had broken hundreds of boards and cinder blocks in preparation for the test. His adrenaline was at a fever pitch when he came to vent his excitement on the test boards.

Anders set the stands for the breaking close to one another and moved with precision and speed between each of the targets. He did not take in the series of deep breaths nor make 'ki-yi' yells as he went from board to board annihilating each in its turn. His fingers, fists, elbows, and heels struck with innate accuracy; all in a matter of less than a minute and a half. The judges betrayed their votes by smiling. The foreigner was allowed to go on to the kumité segment of the blackbelt examination after a five minute rest.

The kumité was full contact without pads. Anders had practiced with his fellow students using full protective gear and felt a little vulnerable without the safeguarding equipment. The only limiting rules were that there were to be no strikes to the eyes, testicles, or knees; and in the event of chokeout, the man with the advantage was to release his hold immediately upon being tapped by the man on the bottom.

Anders' first opponent of the three selected for the test was unknown to him except that he came from Saigon and was in the South Vietnamese marines. The man was tall for a Vietnamese, and thin, with well defined musculature. He warmed up with a series of punishing stretches that would have split Anders asunder. He jumped, kicked well over his head, and did pirouette back kicks. He was quick and very athletic. Anders recognized the man's main flaw immediately—he was a show-off; his main attention was on the appreciative audience. Anders, on the other hand, stood and waited on his side of the mat never taking his eyes off his opponent.

The referee brought the Vietnamese and the Swede to the center of the large mat. The three men executed perfect bows to each other and then to the assembled martial artists. Anders and the ARVN black belt faced each other in a fighting stance like a pair of coiled springs. The ARVN soldier stood on one leg with both hands in a knife posture. He presented the essential tableaux of the martial artist. The referee's hand dropped like a guillotine, and the first kumité was underway.

The ARVN sergeant did not move. Anders waited. It was his

responsibility to be aggressive. Much as he would rather have his opponent initiate the attack, he had to do something. He began to circle to the man's left. The black belt pivoted only enough to follow Anders' movements. His dark eyes never left Anders.' Anders suddenly shot a very low side kick at the balancing single leg. He was very fast. The Vietnamese was faster. He leapt off the floor a full foot and a half so that Anders' heel and lateral side caught only air. The ARVN fighter stretched his whole body into a leaping stomp kick and caught Anders full in the junction between his chest and his flank. Anders emitted a 'whoosh' of air and fell back to catch himself by his down arm to prevent being flattened. Four red flags dropped to the mat. The ARVN fighter had scored a unanimous point. One more point and Anders would lose, also unanimously.

Both men knew that surprises would be very hard to effect from then on. Anders' opponent did not make the mistake of underestimating the big Swede despite his own very quickly achieved point. He now circled warily occasionally sending out a tentative foot or fist to probe Anders' defenses. Anders conserved his energy and caught his breath from the kick he had absorbed. He bided his time.

With blinding speed he swung his long powerful leg in a wide low arc as a foot sweep. Again his opponent leapt into the air, but this time Anders was ready. Almost reflexively, the Vietnamese shot a leg at Anders' torso gloating at the opportunity to score a second quick point in nearly the exact manner as he had done on his first coup. But Anders had moved. The muscular leg shot past; Anders blocked his opponent's following fist with a hard outward arm block and fired a cannon force fist into the man's uncovered kidney. The punch caught the soldier with both feet off the ground and flung him helplessly to the mat, near the feet of one of the judges. Three flags fluttered to the mat signaling that Anders had scored a point. The fourth judge said that he could not see the blow and could not grant a clean point. The score stood at the critical one to one level. Two minutes of the kumité had elapsed.

The ARVN martial artist threw straight punches, back hands, and shots at Anders' torso, all of which were blocked effectively by the vigilant Swede. Anders tried to capitalize on the superior length and strength of his legs and attempted straight kicks, round houses, spinning back kicks high and low. They were all blocked. His opponent came in close with an elbow shot at Anders' chin that connected with dizzying effectiveness. Anders countered simultaneously with an uppercut to the solar plexus. All four flags were dropped—

two for Anders and two for his competitor. No score was tallied.

The ARVN marine black belt flung off his gi revealing his slender chest with every muscle in clear relief against his sweat glistening skin. He and Anders circled each other looking for openings, for any slackening of defenses. The ARVN soldier backed away. Anders decided not to follow, presuming a trick. With remarkable acrobatic skill, the black belt did a nimble cartwheel and double flipped in the air bringing himself into a position to Anders' rear. The movement was so fast and graceful and so apparently benign that Anders did not react immediately. His very slight pause was enough. His opponent leaped against Anders' back and threw his wiry left arm around the larger man's throat jerking Anders backward.

Instead of resisting, Anders moved with the force driving himself and his rival two steps backward. As soon as he felt the ARVN NCO brace on both legs to halt the clumsy backward motion, Anders threw both of his legs up into the air until his opponent was holding Anders at right angles to himself and parallel to the mat. The Vietnamese marine maintained his grip around Anders throat like a boa constrictor.

Anders then flung his feet down and backward until he was nearly in an opisthotonic backward arch. He braced himself with all his strength and heaved forward carrying his opponent off the mat and over his head in a high, fully outstretched and completely helpless flight. As the man's kinesthetic sense told him that he was in the descendent half of the arc, the ARVN NCO released his grip around Anders' neck and prepared for a very hard judo landing. He could not alter the speed of his fall nor could he position his arms or legs to provide any cushion.

Anders released his own hands and allowed his rival to free fall directly onto his unprotected back. The man kept his occiput from cracking the floor, but that was the only protection he could provide his completely exposed back. The Vietnamese's body collided full force with the unyielding floor in a sharp and resonant crack. His last moment of consciousness was occupied with the image of the large square-headed Swede looking at him from an inverted angle. He did not move after he struck the floor and bounced once. It did not look as if he would breath again either.

For a few moments none of the judges reacted. They were looking at the unconscious form of the best young martial artist in all of South Viet Nam; the best of the best. They had counted on him to put the upstart foreigner in his place and to deny him his black belt. Finally, in dreamlike slowness, each of the four judges dropped his flag—an undisputed point and the end of the match. The referee gestured to Anders to return to the center of the mat and bowed to him. Anders returned the courtesy in the best martial arts tradition and bowed to each of the judges and to his fallen opponent, each in his turn. The men from the ARVN NCO's school carried him to the far side of the room and ministered to him as the referee signaled for the next match to begin.

Anders was tired and let his mind wander to his first opponent; he was concerned about whether he had done the man real injury. His second opponent was a short squat powerful man of thirty who did not move quickly but was relentless. He took advantage of Anders' preoccupation with the injured man to connect with a sharp crack to Anders' chin that the Swede only partially blocked. Two flags were dropped and a point was awarded.

Anders drove his external concerns from his mind and fought his new opponent on his own terms. They matched blow for blow, kick for kick, scoring three disputed points before Anders was able to connect with a spinning back kick that sent his competitor reeling and resulted in three flags being dropped. While the man was still slightly woozy from the head blow, Anders did a foot sweep and dropped his opponent flat on his back. No point because the downed man maintained a hold on Anders' gi. Anders dropped immediately to one knee over the muscular short man, and crossed his hands holding the fronts of the man's gi. Anders choked out the man ignoring the thunder of blows against his own back and arms. Finally, his opponent tapped Anders on the shoulder, and Anders let go an instant before the man lost consciousness.

Anders could recognize the change that had settled over the martial artists in the room watching his black belt test performance. Their expressions had subtly changed from something approaching hostility through bland acceptance to something approaching respect. Master Nguyen's eyes twinkled with pleasure and pride although his face remained devoid of expression. The room became quiet as the third contest was announced with a nod of the referee's head.

The third opponent seemed most unlikely. He was sixty-five years of age—the judge whom Anders presumed was from *Bac Bo*—and had a wrinkled, tired face. He was small and thin, weighing no more than 130 pounds. His uniform was old and worn, a black gown rather than the newer pants and gi top; his belt was red and faded. Every other man in the room—Anders excepted—wore a black belt. The old man moved slowly with almost courtly motions. The measure of the esteem in which he was held was shown by the respectful bowing of the heads by all of those present as he walked to the center to face his huge opponent. Anders bowed with the rest of them, the respect being almost instinctual.

After the referee's hand dropped, Anders saw a swirl of black motion as the old man turned swiftly about. The actual location of his body and the sight of its movements was lost in the vision of the flying skirt. Anders threw a useless side kick into the billowing cloth and was stunned by a back knuckle fist connecting with his right temple. He had not seen it coming. Four flags dropped costing Anders the first point. The old man bowed graciously keeping his eyes always on his younger competitor. Anders knew that he was in for the contest of his life or for a lesson; he suspected that it would be some of both.

Anders tried everything he had learned—kicks, punches, sweeps, attempts at throws. It was like trying to wrestle a shadow. Wherever Anders' efforts were aimed, the old man's body had just removed itself. Anders was puffing, excited, and tired. The old master breathed with infuriating control. He had not broken a sweat, and he did not appear the least bit tired. To Anders, it seemed that the old master was toying with him. He glanced at the spectators with his peripheral vision. He thought he could see some of them suppressing laughter.

Anders had tried finesse and had gained only stalemate. He was a point behind. If he were perceived to be stalling or to be less than aggressive, it would go against him in the voting. He decided to use his superior size and strength, his only apparent advantage over the spindly old gentleman with the wispy chin beard, to bowl his opponent over and to score that vital point.

The big man lunged throwing murderous powerhouse punches and a rapid series of front kicks. Each of them was parried with aggravating ease. The man did not gloat; he kept an expression on his face like a biscuit. Anders was all the more disturbed by the old man's exasperating equanimity. He felt himself growing angry. He knew that was a mistake, but he could not control it. The old man held his hands low, and his head was inclined forward offering an inviting target. Anders decided to take it off.

With an explosive burst of energy that lifted him five feet off the floor, Anders aimed a full body flying side kick at the old man's coconut sized head. Both legs were well off the floor and all of his pent-up frustration combined with all of his strength and skill centered into a focus on the right heel. That heel was three centimeters from the old master's face, that seemed to Anders to be mocking him now, and moving like a freight train. Anders anticipated the crunch of the heel smashing into the fine featured old face.

Only it did not happen. The old man, the man from *Bac Bo*, moved aside no more than a few centimeters in the last fraction of a second before the impact of the heel on his delicate face would have ended the match. Anders' heel followed by his big body swept on past like an errant rocket with nothing to impede its momentum. The old master gracefully brought his bent palm up and lifted the leg as it passed, adding to the momentum and upsetting the straight line equilibrium. Anders' heavy torso and head dropped toward the floor, and his legs flew awkwardly up and apart. He crumpled to an ungainly clump sitting on the floor. While Anders wondered what had happened, the venerated martial artist dropped to one knee and snapped a pile driver hard blow onto Anders' nose. The little bones shattered and spread; blood sprayed in a bouffant plume spattering Anders' gi. His head rocked back, and his eyes registered wide-open surprise. Four flags dropped. Two points. End of match.

In uncharacteristic and impolite appreciation, the men in the spectator seats clapped. Master Nguyen shot them an admonitory look, and they quickly remembered their etiquette and were impassive once more. The old master waited until Anders could collect himself and the bleeding from his ruined nose had changed to a flow rather than a spray. He looked gently at his large chastened opponent. "May I offer two small suggestions, young man?" he asked.

Anders could only nod. He was in no position to be surly or to appear unreceptive to constructive criticism.

"The first is to avoid the young man's folly. Do not lose your temper. You are beaten if you do."

Anders bowed his head in recognition of the accuracy of the old master's insight.

"The second is to avoid the temptation to be, how is it said?— spectacular. It is seldom useful to remove both feet from the ground to perform a kick and never advisable to defy gravity altogether. You are at your most vulnerable when you do."

Anders could only mutter, "Thank you very much, master." His speech was nasal and thick, and he had to pause to wipe blood to complete his brief sentence. But he was wholly sincere in his expression. He knew he had learned an important lesson in the martial arts, one that would be indelibly imprinted on his memory. For that hard bit of instruction he was grateful if profoundly uncomfortable. The master from *Bac Bo* seemed pleased with Anders' response.

Anders was allowed to rest and to get his nasal bleeding under control for five minutes then he was required to compete in the final test, the kumité against two opponents. He was exceedingly tired and more than a little depressed at how poorly he had looked against the old man. He was afraid that his chances for receiving the coveted black belt had been seriously diminished. This was his last chance, and like a wounded and cornered tiger he approached the two young men who had been selected to test him.

Instinct and training prevailed. He had drilled on his own kata as a brief compendium of defenses and attacks against two or three opponents. The moves returned to him so that he parried and blocked, punched, and elbowed, and kicked with smooth athletic precision. One point was scored against him, but he handily scored two un-equivocal points, one by kicking his opponent into the front row of spectators and the other by driving a huge elbow into a section of exposed spine. That blow had stung and hurt Anders' elbow, but had dropped his final opponent to the floor complaining of momentary tingles and spasms in his legs. Anders was left with one opponent, now an intimidated young man. Anders faked a kick bringing the man's hands down and connected with a front kick to his opponents forehead that produced a four flag point and the end of the match. A few sporadic hand claps told of the appreciation of the men for his expertise. Master Nguyen again cast a cautionary glance, and the room fell quiet again.

The four judges, including the old man who had served as opponent and teacher for the young black belt candidate, stood and walked out together and closeted themselves in Master Nguyen's small office. They were gone for nearly thirty minutes, and the men in the room became restless. Anders grew tense. He knew that he had done well except for that part of the kumité, but he had been forewarned by Master Nguyen that granting the black belt to a foreigner was unheard of, almost revolutionary, and it would not be easy no matter how well he did. He feared that the old prejudices would prevail. As the time dragged on, Anders became progressively aware of the pain in his face. His nose felt as if it had been exploded. He could feel the swelling and blackening of his cheeks and around his eyes. His adrenaline high came down as it always has to, and Anders felt wearied and deflated.

Finally, the four judges walked back into the room in a procession, led by the old man from North Viet Nam. They had all changed robes; now they all wore simple but handsome flowing black gowns. The first man wore a bright red sash as his belt, and the other three wore black silk sashes tied in square knots around their midsections. Deference was accorded the older man with the red belt. He stood, and the other men took their seats.

He spoke in a melodious six toned Vietnamese characteristic of his northern extraction and came immediately to the point. "Never before today has there been a foreigner who presented himself as a candidate for the first Dan. Some of the French became proficient in our ancient art, but none were able to master the techniques well enough to be tested. Tonight, a foreigner has been tested. He has done well. We judges were presented with an historical dilemma. Did he do well enough to wear our black belt? Our answer to that was yes. All of us agreed to that. Should a foreigner stand with the guardians of Viet Nam, the masters of *Tây Sơn Võ Sĩ*? They have their own world, their own customs, their own ways, many of which are not our ways, not acceptable to us. Why should we allow an exception in our long tradition for such a one?

There were a number of appreciative head nods.

"But how can we deny the proficiency we have all witnessed, we asked ourselves? We would be less than fair and just if we did not make an acknowledgment."

Anders did not want an 'acknowledgment.' He felt like he had earned the black belt and would not be happy with anything less.

"We voted, as men of conscience should do. The vote was three to one. There was a scowl on the Saigon representative's countenance. And the vote was to approve the granting of the first Dan to the Swedish man, Mr. Anders Bergstrom, who has earned the great honor."

There was a murmur of surprise, pleasure, offended tradition, and some rumblings of disagreement. The red belt raised his hand for quiet. "It is difficult to make changes, my fellow guardians of the mountains and the lowlands. But it is the right thing to do. You granted me the coveted red belt even though I am a citizen on the Democratic Republic and not your own country. But you felt it was right because I had won the distinction by killing a man in mortal combat without weapons, and more importantly, because I have made a lifelong contribution to our art. That was hard for you to do, but eventually, you became comfortable with your decision. I remain honored. I ask you to agree in this choice, because it is right. I believe you will become comfortable with this decision as well."

The belt took its place in Anders' locked chest of treasured possessions along with his diploma from the university, his photographs of Master Nguyen and himself, of The Mandarin, and of Liên. All of those mementos represented triumphs of different sorts, and each had a significant element of affection attached to the recorded achievement. Anders had his nose repaired at the MACV dispensary by a superbly trained ENT specialist who had been unlucky enough to be drafted in the Berry Plan doctor lottery and who grumbled to anyone who would listen about his nasty turn of luck and about how much he detested the military. He did a fine job, nonetheless. Anders' nose eventually lost its swelling and most of its former Grecian form. It would forever be a little flatter, broader, and less straight, but neither it nor the facial scars detracted from the rugged handsomeness of his face. He looked older and harder, more used, but his face still brought glances from the few women he met, Occidental and Oriental.

In August Anders, Bach, Ky, and Dung were dispatched to Laos to take part in the more aggressive assault on the communist forces ordered by President Nixon in order to better the US and RVN position at the stalemated Paris peace talks with North Viet Nam. Tran was left in charge of the remaining units in the compound and their regular police work to deal with the VCI problem that only seemed to grow larger as the recorded numbers of detained and dead VCSs mounted. Like many other of the PRUs, CIDGs, Montagnards, and Hmong, Anders and his men were to concentrate on disrupting the flow of men and supplies down the Ho Chi Minh Trail; something thousands of tons of bombs had been unable to accomplish.

The United States started bombing the Laotian segment of the Ho Chi Minh Trail in October, 1964, but with very limited success in interdicting the inexorable flow of men and materiel from the north. On the eighth of December, 1970, commanding general of MACV, Creighton Abrams, had met in top secret with six other officers to determine the necessary measures to deal with the growing effectiveness of the NVA, who were using Laos and the Ho Chi Minh Trail. Hue' was the main target of the North Vietnamese buildup; and for that reason, the Thau Thien PRU was involved early on. The trail and its ubiquitous support, especially the 600 mile long main conduit through Laos, was determined to be the main target.

The Truong Song or Ho Chi Minh Trail was neither a trail nor a highway; it was an engineering and human marvel. The Trail was a maze of twisting tracks, foot paths, and two lane packed laterite clay surfaced roads filtering from North Viet Nam through Laos and Cambodia and into South Viet Nam. The system was started by the Viet Minh for use against the French; and by the time Anders Bergstrom and his men were sent to Laos in mid 1972, it was a seemingly haphazard array of 12,500 miles of road with five long parallel routes and twenty-one axes in a thirty mile corridor.

The sides of The Trail were liberally dotted with thousands of identical foxholes made to the exact specifications of French manuals and with Vietnamese originated spider holes reinforced and camouflaged with sturdy lashed bamboo. The Trail and its contribution to the NVA war effort became the principle focus of attention and activity of US irregular forces.

Thirty thousand NVA engineers, security forces, transportation soldiers, and antiaircraft battery crews, and a legion of Laotian peasant workers, originally built the Trail; and 300,000 more maintained the vital net of roadways with their equally important classrooms, political indoctrination centers, and support installations. Segments of the Trail were divided up into *Binh Trams* with permanent garrisons of necessary personnel. The communists worked under indescribably difficult conditions to build, rebuild, repair, and to camouflage the Trail that was under continual bombardment from the United States Air Force as well as the grueling forces of nature.

Not the least of their problems was dealing with the terrible rain of death they suffered requiring the replacement of tens of thousands of workers. Between 1966 and 1968 the United States, in Operation Rolling Thunder, dropped 643,000 tons of bombs along the route killing an estimated 29,000 people, only two percent of whom were soldiers. No matter what the US did, the communists could always enlist more workers; and they did so without coercion, for the most part.

In August of 1967, American secretary of defense, Robert McNamara, told a congressional subcommittee that the US had spent over nine hundred million dollars to destroy three hundred twenty million dollars worth of North Vietnamese property and a 1000 noncombatants a week without changing their will to fight one iota. In fact, in the ever escalating stalemate overall in Viet Nam, the United States had committed 500,000 troops, 1,200,000 tons of bombs a year, 400,000 attack sorties a year, had killed at least 200,000 of the enemy at an expense of 20,000 American deaths, 125,000 wounded and $30,000,000,000 a year; and the communist will and the flow of goods and soldiers remained steady at 50 to 300 tons and 4500 men a month. The official reported result of all that US effort, between 1966 and 1967, was an enemy increase of 9 division headquarters, 34 regimental headquarters, 34 combat support battalions, 196 separate companies, and 70 platoons totaling 128,000 regular army and 112,800 militia, and 39,175 political cadres despite known losses. In the years to follow, the numbers increased apace.

Some of the pathways were dead ends; some were obvious and built only to attract US bombers; still others were so hidden that they served as main arteries uninterruptedly for more than a decade. The NVA maintained a sophisticated land line telephone communication system that paralleled the Trail, and a 3000 mile long pipeline ran along the Trail to provide fuel. Drivers traveled almost exclusively at night in utter darkness. For that reason each of them was assigned a distance of only thirty-three kilometers to carry their materiel and were required to know that area literally by feel. Materiel had to be loaded and unloaded at secret bunkers, usually underground, and in caves maintained at each successive *Binh Tram*. It took two months for a given load to traverse the distance from start in the north to finish in South Viet Nam. Even with the presence of the trucks, the vast majority of those loads traveled on the backs of men. 200 tons of supplies moved every day from the north to the south.

Anders, Bach, Ky, and Dung were dropped off in the last secure Vietnamese village before starting north on their mission to reconnoiter, and in so far as they could, to disrupt the Ho Chi Minh Trail. The village was a vestige of the Strategic Hamlet program having originally been populated by Montagnards moved from their own villages into the militarily more secure setting (against their wills) by US Special Forces. In the era of 'Vietnamization' spawned by President Nixon and Henry Kissinger, the US advisors had moved out; and ARVN troops moved in. They saw things differently than the US or their French predecessors who respected the Montagnards, and who, in turn, were granted a measure of willing service. Following close on the heels of the ARVN platoons were ethnic Vietnamese farmers who expropriated the Montagnards' belongings and lands and drove the mountaineers, whom they despised as '*Meo*,' back into the forest. The Montagnards abandoned their village and their ancestors' bones with great anguish and undying enmity toward the Vietnamese usurpers.

The village was an armed camp of Vietnamese peasants wholly dependent on ARVN and the CIA paramilitary forces who occupied it by the time Anders and the PRUCs arrived in August, 1972. Anders stepped off the helicopter and walked with his men across the village commons with a hard-faced ARVN NCO to report, as ordered, to the regional operations officer of Phoenix who was the titular and factual commander of the anticommunist forces in that segment of the northern highlands.

A beautiful but very dirty little boy about seven years old walked boldly up to Anders and laid his small hand on the big man's forearm. Anders was pleased. He said to Tran, "This child likes us. I think we make him feel safe. It's good to know that there is still innocence left in the world."

Tran laughed at his big friend. "Don't be silly. The boy is just transferring the village demons onto you. He knows you are going to leave soon, and you can take the bad *phis* with you."

Anders was not quite ready to accept that or to have his balloon popped. Tran could tell. "You can prove it," he said. "Touch the child back and see what happens. You will be giving the demons back to him and the village again. Go ahead."

Anders swiftly bent over and picked up the child in both arms and pulled the little body up against his own. The little boy's face became a mask of fear. He fought tears and struggled to get down and away. The child's mother rushed over to her son, a look of abject terror in her eyes.

"This one is nothing," she shrieked. "A girl. A wretched pock-marked girl." Anders could plainly see that it was a boy. The mother went on, "And ugly—see the harelip. And sick—has the inward fever. See how thin he is. Wretched specimen." Anders looked at the beautiful healthy child.

"I will take this one to our wretched unworthy home, our dwelling where no one would ever want to come. We have the sickness, the inward fever. You can see that this useless one is not long for the world!" The panic stricken mother snatched up her child and hurried away into the rabbit's warren of ramshackle hooches to hide her child."

"She thinks you want to steal her boy. The cong tell them that Americans steal children to eat. He is probably her first born and is the most important thing she possesses. That is why she says the things she does. And she fears for the boy because you transferred the village's demons all onto him. He will have to be cured by the shaman."

Anders shook his head. He still had lots to learn about this strange country, he realized. He led the way to the office designated as that of the Regional Officer In Charge.

Anders was unpleasantly surprised to learn who that ROIC was; and, although he thought he had seen everything in his seven years in Viet Nam, he was in for an additional shock.

Anders and the PRUCs were ushered into a secluded, fully enclosed building in the center of the complex of community buildings. It was very heavily guarded, not by ARVN or PRUCs, but by Chinese Nungs, thereby identifying it unequivocally as the CIA headquarters. The presence of the Nungs brought back a chill of memory that gave way to shivers of recognition as soon as he was presented to the ROIC—Tandrosz Szabo.

Szabo was standing apart from the ongoing work of the establishment. Before Anders and his men could enter the immediate area, they were disarmed by the Nung guards who searched them expertly and made a large pile of their weapons.

"Bergstrom," Szabo said tersely when Anders walked up to him. "You can head upcountry tomorrow morning with a couple of our Kit Carsons. This is the only secure village in a hundred klick circle; so watch yourself. We are presently obtaining intelligence about enemy troop movements to facilitate your passage." He pointed to the center of the darkened room where an interrogation of sorts was taking place.

Anders reacted inwardly as if someone had punched him in the stomach at the sight of the 'interrogation.' Jean-Luc DuParrier and two Nungs were busily working on a man who was suspended upside down from ceiling rafters, his hands secured by thongs to screw rings in the floor boards. The prisoner was not moving despite the gruesome work taking place on his helpless body. DuParrier did not notice Anders because he was intent on his labors. He and the Nungs were skinning the man.

CHAPTER 36

Respect for man means, above all, that the enemy (true or presumed, guilty, or suspect) is considered a human being.
Guerre révolutionaire et conscience chrétienne
(Revolutionary Warfare and Christian Conscience)

T he prisoner's uniform, a tan khaki blouse and trousers, lay to one side. The scene was so macabre that Anders paid little note of the fact that the prisoner was a Chinese enlisted man. His legs had been slit from ankles to mid thighs, and his skin had been neatly separated from the underlying fascia and muscles and hung out limply from his lower limbs. One of the skinners must have encountered a particularly sensitive subcutaneous nerve because the Chinese man suddenly writhed and cried out. Anders could not maintain his wishful subconscious fiction that the man was dead, and that this was some sort of grisly postmortem ritual. Ky, Dung, and Bach recoiled at the sights and sounds. Anders reacted angrily expressing his disgust and revulsion in a growl. He moved suddenly taking the Nung guards by surprise.

He swung an elbow into Szabo's exposed chest knocking the reptilian faced man back against a low metal chest of drawers containing electrical supplies. Anders then lunged at DuParrier with a throaty growl, the outcry of an attacking predator. DuParrier pivoted adroitly at the sound and was amazed to see his old nemesis advancing on him at bullet train velocity. He swept his skinning knife in self-defense bringing its point across Anders' outstretched arm creating only a scratch. Anders caught the torturer full in the face with a ham-sized fist.

Jean-Luc toppled unconscious over the Chinese enlisted man's small pile of clothing. He had a profuse epistaxis that mingled his blood with that on the already sanguinary floor. Two of the Nung guards reacted instinctively and clubbed Anders' head from behind before he could complete his executioner's pounce on the unconscious man at his feet. Anders sprawled in a dazed heap with his arms lying over Jean-Luc's chest. Another two Nungs leveled their Sten guns at the Anders' fellow PRUCs lest they entertain joining the insanity of the white-haired giant. One of the guards slipped his automatic off safety and leveled the barrel at Anders' chest. His finger was starting to squeeze the trigger.

Szabo, who had righted himself with an athletic agility belying his middle age, shouted in Mandarin, "No!!"

Obedience was instant, and Anders could owe his life to the near perfect discipline of the Chinese mercenaries. Anders was not completely unconscious, but was so light-headed and vertiginous from the blow to his occiput that he was nearly helpless. The Nungs dragged him to where Szabo stood and snapped the young Occidental's head back to expose his pale face to the ROIC. Szabo had regained his composure. He reached out his hand and slapped Anders sharply across one cheek then backhanded him across the other. The effect on Anders was the same as if an ammonia capsule had been broken under his nose. He was instantly awake, and his memory of the scene complete. He attempted to struggle against the guards and received a perfectly aimed kick in his kidney for his efforts. The pain was so intense that he could neither struggle nor even speak for several minutes.

Szabo said with a menace, "Bergstrom, you are closer to being dead at this minute than you have ever been in your life. Only one thing keeps me from giving you to my Nungs. We need you up north. Uncle Sugar needs cannon fodder, and you are going to give Uncle what he wants. Don't ever cross my path again, or you will be a dead man. Your men don't amount to a second's hesitation in that promise either. Bear that in mind."

Anders managed to gasp, "You monster. The two of you are nothing but sadists!" The Nungs twisted Anders' head back exposing the front of his neck. Szabo tapped Anders' Adam's Apple with his index finger hard enough to produce a reflex cough.

"And we are very effective. On second thought, if you ever get in my way again, I will give you to DuParrier. I am sure he would love to entertain you for a month or so. Now get out of my sight."

Szabo motioned to the guards who dragged Anders and herded the other PRUCs into a nearby cage. The cell was four feet high, four feet across, and eight feet long. The floor was covered with the remains of human waste, old blood, and rat droppings. The four men slumped onto the filthy floor. This was the PIC holding cell, and Anders' mind reeled with tormented visions of what scenes must have transpired there.

Ky spoke first. "We agree with you, Anders. That was terrible. We have no more respect for the Americans than we do for the VC, but you are going to get us killed. Don't ever do anything like that again." He looked to Bach and Dung for confirmation. Their grim faces mirrored Ky's expression.

"I'm sorry, Anders offered. I just reacted. Couldn't help myself." He was truly contrite for having exposed the men who mattered to unnecessary terrible danger.

"Something tells me this is not over yet. We will all have to mind our backs from here on," Ky said with sagacious perception. "I learned on the streets when I was a mere *Bui Doi* not to hate my enemies. It is only one's friends who can betray you."

Anders knew Ky was right. His friend's comment may be prophetic, Anders worried, as he sank into a disturbed sleep that night. He dreamed of distant and fleeting glimpses of a frighteningly ugly and threatening totally black hirsute gnome moving along on a jungle trail somewhere in front of him. He did not mention the dream to his friends.

The following morning, before sunup, the Nungs returned and dragged the aching men from the cell. Two porters carried the PRUCs weapons and four Nungs silently escorted Anders and his men out of the village and stayed with them for a distance of four or five klicks. The lead Nung signaled a halt and indicated to the PRUCs to sit at the side of the trail. The porters set the weapons down a hundred meters up the trail. The lead Nung then turned his men back down the trail at a trot leaving the PRUCs alone. The four cadres collected their weapons and headed north following the map prepared for them back at the compound outside Hue'.

The forest was busy with people for all its wild character. The four PRUCs soon found it expedient to travel only at night to avoid villagers and NVA patrols checking the periphery of the Ho Chi Minh Trail. During the day they camped well separated from each other to avoid drawing any attention to themselves as a group. On the third day of travel, Anders found himself once again in trouble.

The PRUCs were tired from almost constant marching through the nighttime jungles. Their daytime sleeping periods were sporadic and disturbed frequently by small squads of armed men passing uncomfortably near where they hid. Anders had cramping diarrhea and felt further weakened by the resultant dehydration. He ordered them to stop for the night to get a real rest so they could return to full efficiency. They had two days to go to reach the Montagnard village where they had been initiated into full fellowship.

The men bedded down at fifty to sixty meter intervals from each other maintaining their own security watch. Anders took one extreme edge of their camp area and Tran the opposite. Anders slept until nearly one in the morning when his griping abdomen awakened him. The night was starless and opaque black. He moved ten or so meters upwind from his bed site and further away from his men, carrying only his knife, and squatted to relieve himself. He was in that compromising position when he first heard the rustle of the underbrush on three sides of him.

He froze, not daring to move a muscle. His bowel noises had quieted; he thanked the spirits for that much. His legs were getting fatigued. Through the night intermittent shufflings and clankings of equipment informed him that there were men all around him, at least some of whom had his own malady. He dare not move even to shift his joint grinding position.

By first light it was clear where he was. In the inky blackness of the night he had walked right into the middle of an NVA platoon encampment to relieve his overactive bowels. All around him were men going about the unhurried routine of another day preparing to march through the forest ever southward to join in the struggle against the Yankee imperialists. Anders kept as low as possible. At times he could see men within fifteen meters of where he squatted. His muscles were locked in painful spasming cramps after five hours of being unable to move the slightest bit to relieve the tension on his tortured lower limbs. He squatted there in terror knowing that he would be unable to move if someone spotted him.

At eight in the morning, a black, fat, and jowly potbellied pig with its abdomen softly sweeping the ground shambled past him snorting and grubbing about in the soft soil trying to find edible roots and insects. Anders worried himself into a cold sweat that the pig would attract unwanted attention in his direction. He waved his hands at the animal, but its domesticated porcine brain interrupted the gesture as indicative of a source of food. The ungainly brute came right up to Anders and sniffed and snorted around the pungent odors on the ground under the man. Anders groaned and fumed inwardly. Finally, the pig moved amiably back in the direction of its village, and Anders gave a small sigh of relief. Vietnamese pigs are often allowed to run free in the forest during the day, dependably returning to the village at night; and this one attracted no attention from the NVA, much to Anders' assuagément.

The pain was becoming intense in his legs. Anders' feet were tingling and numb. If he moved, they would hear him and be upon him in a matter of seconds. If he did not move, they would come upon him by chance; and in either instance he would be killed or captured with his pants down. He shuddered perceptibly at the recurrent thought.

The enemy platoon began to gather in a shallow depression between two low hillocks evidently preparing to move out. Anders was sure that he was outside their line of sight. His legs were screaming. As slowly and quietly as possible, Anders began to unfold, keeping low, until he was stretched out fully prone. He had made no noise in the five minutes it took him to straighten his tortured limbs. His legs felt weak like the bones had been removed. He was having Charley Horse cramps in his calves and hamstrings causing him to want to cry out or swear or to rub the spasmed muscles furiously. He remembered where he was and kept his acute awareness of the omnipresent danger and suffered without motion or sound. He took a full five minutes to hitch up his pants.

Just as his legs felt like they would obey him, a sentry walked by where Anders lay. All the man had to do was to look even briefly to his right, and Anders would be exposed. The man urinated less than a meter from Anders' face all the while looking to his left, away from Anders, in the direction of his platoon. Anders knew his luck could not hold forever. The image of the black hairy gnome flickered across his racing mind's eye. He had to act. He would be seen and the alarm sounded if he did not do it now.

Anders eased himself to a push-up position poised on his bent fingers and the balls of his feet. The sentry's head began to turn slowly to the right as he readjusted himself after a satisfying micturition. Anders sprang like a waiting leopard. He was a blur of startling motion to the peripheral vision of the NVA soldier who was not prepared to react fast enough.

Anders drove a spear hand, fingers bent at the tips, into a point one centimeter below and in front of the man's right mastoid process. The PAVN soldier crumpled toward his left, his eyes glazing. Anders had made it to a crouch to hit the man and had sprung to his feet in time to catch the unconscious body before it crashed into the nearby dry brush. The man was not dead, and none of his platoon mates had heard anything above the noise of their own departure activities. Anders swiftly broke the enemy's neck. He crept slowly away, back into the dense forest and away from the body of the platoon. When he was a hundred meters or so away, he began to hear the shouts and commands in the characteristic six toned northern dialect. He was unsure whether they were just looking for their comrade or if their voices indicated that the body had been found, and they were after the killer. He did not pause to find out. He now broke into a full run moving as quietly as possible but counting on distance more than stealth to get away from the NVA.

In spite of the adrenaline coursing through his charged arteries, Anders was becoming aware of being hungry and thirsty. He also realized that he had left all of his weapons, food, and gear where he had slept. He ran on, ignoring the pangs of his stomach and the feeling that he should double back to retrieve his belongings. His combat sense took over and told him to cut his losses.

Well up the trail, he heard a faint rustle of the underbrush on his left. He took cover. The sound did not return; and after a few minutes, he cautiously started out again, always bearing north. He was on a trail of sorts although it often seemed to come to a dead end. As he paused to check his compass at one such apparent dead end, the hairs on the back of his neck bristled from a subliminal cue, something out of the ordinary there in the quiet forest. He dived into the nearby brambles scratching his exposed skin with thorns. He took care to shield his eyes. He looked out and saw two sets of rubber soled sandals moving swiftly along the trail from which he had leaped. He held his breath.

The two men stopped right were he lay hidden. One of them knelt down and peered into the nook where Anders had secreted himself. Their eyes met and locked: Bach! Anders eased his fingers from the death grip he had held on the haft of his knife. He got up without speaking and looked at Bach and Dung standing quietly in the middle of the trail. He had to turn to see Ky who had crept up behind where he had been laying. Anders had been completely unaware of Ky's presence. He shuddered a little.

"Am I ever glad to see you guys!" Anders said finally. Then all four men grinned broadly and squeezed each others' hands. They redistributed the weapons to make up for Anders' loss, and listened intently as he recounted his close call. The four of them were helpless with cathartic laughter by the time he finished creating the word picture of his bare bottom hanging out for the *Bo Doi* (NVA) patrol to use as a target.

It took Anders and his men three days to make the two day journey because armed patrols kept appearing on the trails necessitating the slower passage through the dense woods. Late in the afternoon of the third day they were met by a band of wild looking Montagnards who seemed to materialize out of the bush. Anders and the Montagnards recognized each other and what at first was a suspicious and bristling encounter became a joyful reunion.

That night the PRUCs slept soundly in security for the first time since they had left their compound in Thau Thien Province. H'Klois found her way into Anders' room; and when he awakened, he found her curled up beside him peaceful and affectionate. He shook his head. He knew that if he took any advantage of her overtures that he would have made a commitment of some sort, and he was reluctant to get entangled. He was tempted, though.

Using guides from the village, the PRUCs made an extended reconnaissance of the Trail. Anders was astounded at the degree of traffic and activity. It was as busy as Viet Nam's Highway One. Over the roadway had been stretched an enormous camouflage net from the trees on one side of the road to the other and for as far as Anders could make out in either direction up and down the Trail. In areas the NVA and their workers, called 'ants' by their enemies, took advantage of the triple canopy jungle and intertwined living vines and thatches of palms to complete the overarching crown canopy. Anders tried to imagine what an Air Force pilot would see flying over—precious little, he presumed.

They ambushed the guards of a *Binh Tram* storage depot and set it ablaze and got away undetected. They killed two sentries of a routine patrol and nailed them to trees with signs tacked to their chests. Capitalizing on the notorious reputation Anders had received as the 'white giant ghost,' they had had packs of stiff bond cards made up displaying in full color a terrifying red eyed, glowing white haired apparition with claw hands over a caption that announced: "*con ma da trắng khổng-lồ* waits in the forest". They were nearly caught when they tried to set up demolitions on the sides of the pipeline and had to separate into the forest to hide. They were hunted and chased, but avoided a direct confrontation or firefight. It was shortly after dark when they returned to their own village on the third day.

Their Montagnard guide knew something was wrong when they were within a klick of the village. No one met them. He warned the PRUCs to be very cautious. They made their way closer until they saw a cluster of men guarding the trail. Assuming that they were

Montagnards and that all was well since the guards were standing in plain sight, the guide led the PRUCs up to the men who were largely shrouded in the gloom of the forest night. It was a great mistake.

The men turned out to be the sentries of a large ARVN patrol. The sergeant was polite, almost friendly, but disarmed the late evening visitors and led them at gun point into the town. Anders was immediately aware that something very wrong was underway. The Montagnard men, women, and children were gathered in the village communal long house. ARVN soldiers ringed the house with machine guns and submachine guns trained on the villagers. Anders and his men were allowed to join the ARVN soldiers since he had the evident look of an American advisor; and his PRUCs were fellow Vietnamese, obviously not communists since they were with the big American. The South Vietnamese soldiers even returned the PRUCs' arms.

The ARVN enlisted men were at ease, laughing and making rude descriptive comments about the 'Meo' women, and making the lewd cross finger gesture to one or another they found attractive. The newcomers' attention was drawn to one of the family long houses, the only one in the town whose kerosene lamp was lit. Anders and the PRUCs ambled unobtrusively toward the lighted house.

Men peered in through the openings in the walls, excited by the action inside and ignoring the newcomers. Anders pushed his way into the main storage room which was nearly packed with laughing swearing Vietnamese men. He had to make his way into the middle to determine the source of their amusement. Ky, Bach, and Dung followed close behind him.

In the center of the room, four leering, partly drunken men sat on the floor each holding a wrist or ankle of a spread eagled girl. She was twelve or thirteen years old, completely naked, and exposed to the rapacious eyes of the eighteen or so men towering over her. She had only wispy new pubic hair and the merest buds of breasts. Her eyes were bulging with panic. The platoon master sergeant had stripped off his army blouse and was unbuckling his trousers as Anders loomed into view. Evidently Anders and his men had come into the scene just as the most exciting action was to begin. Rank hath its privileges, and the lead NCO was to be first.

"Who are you?" growled the master sergeant when he saw the strangers, expressing his displeasure at the interruption.

Anders nodded to his men to spread out around the room. "Anders Bergstrom, PRU operations chief," he said.

"Phan Duy Ky, cadre," came a response from one corner.

"Nguyen Van Dung," came from another.

"Corporal Le Duc Bach," It was the first time Anders had ever heard Bach make reference to his rank.

"What do you want here?" The ARVN NCO was angry at the intrusion at that delicate moment in his interrogation of the Meos. It was a tactic he employed frequently to cow the villagers and to soften them up for his logistical questions. Besides he liked the young ones and did not take kindly to being disturbed. It occurred to him, as well, that he did not know these men; and they were not necessarily reliable witnesses.

Anders did not answer; and following his cue, his men kept their silence as well. Their faces were hard, and they could not keep the disgust they felt for the ARVN soldiers out of their expressions.

"Suit yourself. Keep an eye on them, Private Duc," the NCO said to one of the men standing near Anders. He finished undoing his pants and slipping them to the floor, exposing his readiness. He sneered down at the squirming, frightened little girl and settled to his knees between her painfully abducted thighs. She was gurgling with terror and humiliation.

Anders had seen enough. These were his people. The Vietnamese military and the Americans did not rise high on his preference list after what he had seen, especially on this trip. He brought up his combat shotgun to his chest level and pointed it directly at the master sergeant's head. There was a shuffle of activity all around him. He presumed that the sergeant's men were bringing up their own weapons to use on him. Ky's voice barked for them to put their guns back down and emphasized his determination by clubbing the nearest man with a vicious strike of his gun butt across the man's face. The ARVN private crumpled to the floor and with him the enthusiasm of the remainder of the ARVN soldiers in the room. Their rapacious master sergeant was not worth dying for.

Bach told them to lay down their arms, and Dung told them he would kill the first man who made a noise. You could have heard a proverbial pin drop. Anders pushed his way past nervous men until he was standing over the helpless girl, still being held by her captors. He looked into the angry master sergeant's eyes and said, "I am *con ma da trắng khổng-lồ*," he said. " *Hãy để cô ấy đi.*" (Let her go.)

The four men released their holds on the pubescent girl as if her limbs had suddenly turned stove-top hot. They shrank back from the huge white man. Anders eyes burned with an inner fury that no man in the room dared face. The master sergeant started to fumble with his pants not wanting to be naked for whatever was to come next. "Stop!" Anders commanded him in a low menacing voice. The man sullenly obeyed. A look of undiluted hatred and malevolence came from his eyes.

"Bach, Ky, Dung," Anders said to his men without looking away from the master sergeant. "Get the rest of these lizards out the back and tie them up." He spoke English rapidly so that most of them would not catch what he said. He trained his shotgun at a point just below the ARVN master sergeant's pubic bone. The man's readiness had detumesced into a shriveled state.

The PRUCs did as they were bidden. Anders was alone with the girl and her tormentor. He looked down at her bruised face and at the ugly blotches on her sides and legs. His eyes softened. He reached down and handed her the ARVN uniform lying at the master sergeant's feet, and she hurriedly covered her nakedness and vulnerability. She timidly patted the huge Occidental man's forearm, still too frightened to speak. "*Va chez ta mère.*" (Go to your mother.) Anders said in French. "*Tu es hors de danger maintenant, mon infant.*" (You are safe now, child.) His eyes never left the naked ARVN soldier.

The girl began to back out of the room, still uncertain that it was really over. Anders reached out and touched her cut lip. Then he whirled the barrel of his shotgun in a full arc and smashed it against the astonished face of the South Vietnamese soldier. "Don't you know that hurts?" Anders asked the soldier who had placed both hands up to his lacerated lips and broken teeth. He spat blood and whimpered.

Anders set the gun down swiftly and kicked the still dazed man square in the groin causing him to double up and to wretch. "Not as much fun when you are on the wrong side of it, no?" The girl made her exit.

Anders slammed the man's head with a spinning back kick knocking him flying to the floor. He tried to get up, and Anders kicked him as hard as he could on the exposed side of his thigh. There was no more fight left in the tough little man. His look of hatred had been exchanged for one of spiritless terror. The expression on the *con ma da trắng khổng-lồ*'s face terrorized the beaten man. The ARVN master sergeant was looking up at the angel of death and said a small prayer to the Lord Buddha for his miserable soul.

Anders yanked the cringing bully to his feet by clamping a vise hand around the back of his neck. He lifted the man a foot off the floor, leaned over and picked up his shotgun with his free hand, and marched the master sergeant out the front door on his tip toes. The ARVN platoon had gathered in front knowing that something was awry but not knowing quite what. They swore and went for their weapons as Anders stepped out into the light holding their NCO by the scruff of the neck with as much effort as if the man had been a child. Ky's voice came from the gloom beyond the lights of the fire and the kerosene lamp in the house. " *Nhuíc nhích thì.* " (Move and die.) called out the disembodied threat. Bach and Dung stepped into the open, guns leveled at the gathered soldiers completing the menace of the situation.

It is not in the mindset or heritage of Vietnamese to die as heroes, especially for causes in which they do not believe. American soldiers learned that fact repeatedly on patrol. Not a single man in the ARVN unit counted the master sergeant as a family member, a friend, or even as a worthy representative of the Vietnamese aspirations. They laid down their weapons and placed their hands on the top of their heads as if they had been drilling on this maneuver for months.

"Step back," ordered Ky from his vantage point in the darkness. They complied.

Bach and Dung collected and stacked the weapons, mostly M-14s.

Anders said to Ky, "Get the Montagnards. They can guard these pukes." A look of genuine fear became the consensus on the ARVN platoon's faces at that order. A dozen men with an assortment of weapons surrounded the GVN men, their faces terrible with filed tooth grins, the red lacquer casting bloody highlights when the fire reflected off them.

The villagers tied all of the ARVN soldiers hand and foot and staked them out in the center of the village commons. They awaited orders from the white man. Anders whispered to the master sergeant, "Did you ever see a man roasted alive and then eaten?"

The man shuddered his voiceless reply.

"These people like to do that. I will have to think about whether or not to let them. Meanwhile, you be a good boy, keep your men in line, and I might let you go with just a spanking," Anders finished, the glint of demonic cruelty in his eyes too real to be doubted.

The battle hardened ARVN ranger allowed himself to be walked in complete ox-like docility to take his place tied up with his men, still humiliatingly naked. He snarled his orders for them to cooperate with the *con ma da trắng khổng-lồ* no matter what. Anders took it as a good sign.

The ARVN master sergeant called out to Anders, "Let me be dressed like my men!" He was hiding his genitalia with his hands from the view of the hostile eyes of the Montagnards.

A contrary devil prompted Anders. "All right," he called back agreeably. Then he turned to the Montagnard headman. "Make them all naked." The elder grinned in appreciation of the joke. With the none too gentle help of several of the village men, the sergeant was dressed exactly like his men in very short order. The naked platoon cowered together in subservient vulnerability through the night.

The rescue of the village called for a sacrifice, one fitting to invoke the pleasure of the tribal *phi* (spirits) so they would be persuaded to grant their protection hereafter. Shortly after sunrise, a buffalo was led into the common area near a large open pit.

The sacrificial animal had to be a buffalo because these important beasts were regarded by the Montagnards as more than mere animals, almost like part of the human family. Domesticated animals were regularly slaughtered by a knock in the head or a quickly slit throat; but the sacrificial animal was warranted a full ceremonial death, an especially slow one. Out of respect, the buffalo was offered a bowl of rice wine which it downed in a couple of gulps as if it knew it needed to be fortified for the ceremony.

Ritual poles, the equivalent of totem and flag poles combined, were driven into the ground around the buffalo. They were decorated with bright colors and were carved with elaborate stylized animals like, suns, moons in all degrees of crescent, and geometric designs. The wood was imbedded with animal teeth and beaks, bird and bat wings, and a variety of feathers. Brilliantly gaudy streamers of ribbon, feathers, beads, and frayed bamboo stuck out of the top and sides. They served to attract the attention of the *phi* to the exact location of the sacrifice. In case that was not enough, the children of the village filled in the space cornered by the poles and pressed up against the buffalo. They pounded gongs, beat drums, and sang. Anders was sure that the spirits would have no trouble locating the ceremony.

The beast was nervous now, bellowing and pawing at the ground. The spirits must have been talking to it. He was tied by a stout hemp rope around his neck to a sturdy, and again, artistically carved, pole in the center of the pit—the sacrificial pole. The smaller children cleared away so the older boys and girls, the students, could perform their function. They marched solemnly into the area around the buffalo to a slow, somber beat of gongs. More and more students joined the procession beating large drums to the same dirgeful beat. The buffalo was jerking at its tether, pawing at the ground, frightened and unruly now. The sound of the large drums was deep and resonant echoing through the forest glades. It was agreed that the spirits would find the offering irresistible after such a heralding.

The students moved to the periphery. The adults stood quietly, waiting with mounting anticipation. The village shaman walked arrogantly over to the buffalo which was now nearly mad with fear, churning up the earth with its huge hooves and frothing at the mouth. It must have had some sort of primordial instinct about what lay ahead.

The shaman flicked a razor-sharp two-edged dagger across a prominent vein on the beast's neck. It was so excited that it scarcely reacted to the pain. A jungle bot fly was probably more distracting. Blood flowed easily down the animal's gray hide. Over the course of an hour or two (Anders lost track of time), the shaman expertly cut the buffalo in a couple of dozen places until it looked as if it had been painted with thick rust colored paint. The effect was skillfully produced, and the shaman was obviously proud of himself. The buffalo began to sink to its knees.

The villagers made proper oohing and aahing sounds. A wood gong sounded. The shaman reached under the animal's throat and almost delicately thrust his dagger in to the hilt and made a to and fro motion. When the knife was withdrawn, a fountain of blood geysered out of the opening and huge gouts of bright red life pumped onto the ground. The shaman made a bowing gesture of respect as the ponderous buffalo was dispatched to the appeasement of the jungle *phi*.

Anders and his men napped and gossiped with the hill people while the butchering was completed and the carcass, minus the head, was spitted and the slow roasting started. A group of women meticulously cleaned the skull until it was glistening white; then, the shaman placed it reverently on the top of the sacrificial stake. It was a fitting commemorative to the fine animal that had made the ultimate contribution on the behalf of the village.

The party began late in the afternoon. Montagnards do not lack for excuses to have a party—they often celebrate all of the Buddhist, Christian, and their own festivals and make any small victory or success an excuse for a spree. Vinegary rice wine and varnish thick palm wine and 333 beer rolled out of the houses. There were a couple of bottles of Mekkong Whiskey. Everyone got drunk and satiated, even Anders and the PRUCs.

As the grinning mountain men grew more intoxicated, they became all the more menacing. They made a point of flashing their garish saw-like teeth at the frightened ARVN men and later elaborately sharpened their skinning knives for the Vietnamese soldiers' benefit. Finally, the villagers made a bonfire and set spits over the glowing coals. The panic among the ARVNs was so overwhelming that some of them fainted into unconscious; others wept unreservedly. There was not a single atheist left among them.

The people toasted Anders and called him our *con ma da trắng khổng-lồ* and did so with respect. They gave him the best cuts of the slowly barbecued buffalo. Anders enjoyed playing the hero roll immensely. Ky, Dung, and Bach got into the spirit of things fully, as well, and as the evening deepened into night disappeared into one house or another with a nubile young woman. Anders' pleasure was enhanced by the attentions lavished on him by H'Klois. She looked at him with puppy eyes filled with love, respect, admiration, and hero worship. She put as much of her young body against Anders' as it was possible, and he was aware.

H'Klois' father came over to where Anders and the girl were playing a drunkenly inept village game of fast moving hand claps and pats—something like the Caribbean blacks' hambone. Anders paused to greet him out of respect. The music accompanying the 'hambone' dwindled to quiet.

"*Vous faites honneur à notre village.*" (You do our village proud.) the older man said somewhat shyly.

"*Merci. Pour moi vous êtes des amis, des membres de la famille.*" (Thank you. I look on you as friends and family.") Anders responded, altogether sincerely, his intoxication notwithstanding. "*J'ai tout simplement fait ce qu'où aurait de fait pour la famille.*" (I have only done what such a one would do for his family.)

"*Ma fille vous aune bien, officier. Solle m'a demandé de vous en parler.*" (My daughter has a fondness for you, officer. She has asked me to speak with you about it.)

"*Vous me flattez,*" (I am flattered.) Anders said. H'Klois snuggled her chest against Anders' bare forearm heedless of her father's presence.

"*C'est un enfant important, mon aînée. Elle est le trésor de notre famille. Protéger sa virginité est d'une importance primordiale pour ses frères. C'est une bonne fille. Solle fera une bonne épouse pour un homme fort.*" (She is an important child, my oldest. She is the treasure of our family. Her brothers have made it their life's work to protect her virginity. She is a good girl. She will be a good wife to a strong man.)

"*Je suis d'accord.*" (I agree.) Anders said. "*H'Klois est une beauté. J'admire aussi son caractère.*" "H'Klois is a beauty. I admire her

721

character as well." It was the highest of compliments, especially coming from a foreigner and a great warrior.

"*Les frères d' H'Klois et moi nous nous rendons compte qu'elle est maintenant femme et qu'ils ne pourrout pas protéger sa chasteté éternellement. Eux et moi nous vous demandous de vous charger vous—même de ce devoir.*" (H'Klois' brothers and I recognize that she is now a woman and that they will be unable to protect her virtue forever. They and I have come to ask that you take upon yourself that duty.)

Anders began to catch the drift. He was not that drunk.

The girl's father continued, "*On m'a dit que chez vous, dans votre pays, ce sont les hommes qui demandent les femmes en mariage. Ici, c'est différent. Une femme choisit l'homme qu'elle estime pourra la mieux la protéger, et qui fera tout son possible pour s'asurer qu'elle ne manque di rien. H'Klois vous a choisi. Solle vondrait que vous l'acceptiez comme votre épouse.*" (I hear tell that in your land, the men ask the women to marry. Here, it is different. A woman chooses the man she thinks will be able to provide for her and to protect her the best. H'Klois has chosen you. She wishes that you would accept her as your wife.)

H'Klois stretched even more languidly against the susceptible young Scandinavian and purred as her father spoke the accented French. Anders was not made of stone.

"*J'ai la possibilité de fournir une bonne dot, comine l'appellent les nez longs. Vous pouvez vivre avec sa mère et moi et être un homme riche. Je serai fier de vous appeler mon fils. Mes fils seraient fiere de vous avoir comme un frère de sang.*" (I am able to provide a fine dowry, as the long noses call it. You can make your home with her mother and me and be a man of substance. I would be proud to have you as my son. My sons would be proud to have you as a blood brother.)

Anders was stirred. The years of loneliness and deprivation had taken a toll. He knew that he would not be back in The World for as long as he could foresee, that he would never have Liên, whom he loved in secret, and that he needed what all men need, love in all its youthful excitement and companionship from someone who cared nonjudgmentally. His inhibitions and cognitive powers were blunted by the alcohol to which he was unaccustomed, and he wanted this woman and this family. He paused to ponder the decision as any wise man would do, observed H'Klois, her father, and her brothers.

"*Ce sera pour moi un honneur d'épouser votre admirable fille, mon père. J'ai peu de choses à apposter au mariage à présent, mais je ferai de mon mieux pour lui être un bon mari."* (I would be honored to marry your fine daughter, elder. I have little to bring to the marriage at this time, but I will try to make her a good husband.)

H'Klois could keep her silence no longer. *"Tout de suite!!"* (Now!!) she yelled in total youthful exuberance. Her family, Anders, and the entire village of eavesdroppers burst into gales of laughter.

"Pourquoi pas?" (Why not?) Anders responded, quite taken up in the enthusiasm of the moment.

"Oui, mes enfants, pourquoi pas tout de suite?" (Yes, my children, why not now?) asked the father. *"Trouvons le sorcier. Prévenez les femmes. Faisons un grand banquet. Il nous faudra un jour tout entier pour le préparer."* (Let us find the shaman! Tell the women! We must have a feast. It will take a day to prepare.) His daughter pouted theatrically, and that brought a renewed fit of laughter from everyone, including her.

The ARVN platoon shivered from cold and fear as the wedding carnival preparations unfolded before them. Additional cooking fires were started. They had no way of knowing that the celebration was about a coming marriage feast. No one disabused them of their unspoken dread that they were to feature prominently in the feast.

Anders slept in the place where he had been lounging with HéKlois. The girl had suddenly become the quintessence of demure womanhood. She spent the rest of the night and the whole of the next day with the women being instructed in the wifely arts for one last time to the sound of a great deal of mirth coming from the bride's quarters. The women took a raucous sense of humor and delight to the whole affair and could be seen holding their two hands in exaggerated measurements, some quite outlandish. H'Klois obligingly blushed and pretended not to notice.

Even sober, and hung over, Anders did not have serious second thoughts. The girl was beautiful, obedient, full of life. She knew how to conduct a household and how to live in harmony with a husband and with her community, of that he was certain. She would probably not make too many demands on his life or make too much of his necessary absences. He was not quite so certain of that last attribute. Anders was fitted with garlands of flowers and a beautiful feathered and beaded robe that was the official groom's gown for the entire village. The privilege of wearing it cemented his adoption as a Rhade Montagnard. Shortly, he would be one of theirs and them his by blood.

His men tried to point out that his decision was impetuous, but they had no real qualms. They saw it as a further commitment of their white friend into their own ways, at least into the society of their country. It could only be a stronger reason for him to continue to lend his warrior talents to their ends. In the end of their little brotherly talk with the young Swede, they all offered him their congratulations and best wishes.

At dusk Anders stood quietly in front of the shaman. His feathered cape was a meter and a half too short having been made for the mountain men who stood head and shoulders shorter than the Nordic giant. The villagers were all smiles and anticipation; but they, too, were quiet, respectful. Marriage was, next to the funeral celebration, the most sacred of the Rhade Montagnard rituals. The shaman was tense; his eyes glittered. He had fortified himself for this communion with the ancestors by nipping all afternoon on the palm wine, and some of the glistening in his eyes was the resultant rheumy state.

A stringed instrument twanged a fast-paced bridal march in 7-11 time, something on the order of The Flight of the Bumblebee. H'Klois, followed by ten women of her family and clan, swept up the steps and across the teak floor of the long house. She was decked out in radiant vivid colors, all produced from the plumage of forest birds and brilliant flowers. A stream of high forest orchids cascaded down her back highlighting her jet black, waist length hair. Her torso was covered in a gown of feathers and quills intertwined and decorated with braids of human hair, natural dyed ribbons, and strands of leather. Around her waist she wore a loose belt of connected small animal bones—skulls, scapulae, claws, and spines—the symbol of the bones of the ancestors. The belt was doubled around the slender girl's waist, and Anders reckoned that it was big enough for both of them.

The women backed away leaving the couple facing the shaman. The medicine man's face contorted and twitched. He grinned, showing newly painted teeth, many missing. He began to move in a sinuous gyration then in a frenzied whirl and stomping that made him sweat and grimace. He tapped first Anders, then H'Klois with a feathered rattle he carried, then as suddenly as he had begun to move, he stopped.

The shaman then gravely and sedately intoned a litany of Rhade that entirely escaped Anders, but which H'Klois absorbed with heartfelt emotion. Her mother cried. Many of the village women sniffed. The witch doctor undid H'Klois' belt of bones and encircled the couple in the bones of the ancestors. Then he clapped Anders on both forearms (he could not reach the Swede's shoulders comfortably), turned on his heels, and strode haughtily out of the communal room of the long house.

Anders presumed he was married, although he did not exactly feel like it. He watched the shaman's exit, saw H'Klois' father pass a bag of something or other to the witch doctor, and looked into HêKlois' rapt face.

The villagers erupted into a cacophony of cheers, hand clapping, and singing when the two newlyweds clasped hands. Anders did not know what else to do. The naked and cowering ARVN soldiers staked out together on the village commons were sure that this was their time. A severe bout of mass tachycardia afflicted them.

When it was fully night, H'Klois led Anders by the hand to her house. A new one had been set aside for the nuptial night. As soon as they were inside the cozy room set aside for their new life, the anxious girl dropped her clothing with a speed that indicated that she had been practicing for the past few days. Anders moved more slowly, acutely embarrassed by what he knew lay beneath his clothes, including, but not limited to the scars on his chest and back. She took care of that. When she had his groom's gown and his shirt off, she ran her small fingers over the raised scars and emitted a sympathetic sigh.

Outside the room, the entire village had gathered. As soon as they heard her sensitive sounds, they all sighed with her. She undid his trousers and slid his pants to the floor; he stepped out of them and stood as naked as she was. H'Klois clapped her hands in front of her eyes and squealed with joy.

Outside, the audience of assembled villagers burst into raucous and appreciative laughter. They clapped each other on the back, smirked knowingly, made a few pointedly earthy suggestions to the young couple through the bamboo walls, and sat down to await developments.

Anders Bergstrom was married.

CHAPTER 37

With cruelty, as with lust, avarice, gluttony, and the love of power, *l'appetit vient enmanageant*. Hence the importance of preserving at any cost the unreasoned tradition of civilized conduct, the social convention of ordinary decency...The longer this savagery was drawn out, the more there were, on both sides, who contracted a taste for savagery.
Aldous Huxley, commenting on the Thirty Year's War (1618- 1648) as quoted by Bernard Fall in The Two Viet Nams

It must have appeared very odd and amusing to the NVA spies watching from their hiding places in the timberland when the parade left the Montagnard village and trooped South for a day's forced march. The shaman, wizened, feather plumed, and painted was the lead farceur in the forest cavalcade. He was followed in succession by half dressed Montagnard guards carrying old .303 Lee-Enfields, blackpowder rifles, and modern submachine guns, then twenty-five completely naked, completely miserable Vietnamese men looking as wild as a band of Dhoukabors. Bringing up the rear came a Caucasian who towered over every man in the procession, and three Vietnamese irregulars armed with the latest weaponry in the light arms arsenal. For all but the naked men clustered in the middle of the jovial grouping there was a carnival atmosphere. For the men who, four nights previously, had been in the long house assisting in the preparations to molest one of the town's daughters, there was hell on earth.

The ten men who had crowded into that sweaty room that night four days ago had their wrists lashed together behind their backs, and each of them was attached to the others by slender hemp cords that had been run through their tender nasal septae. Control was easy. If the Montagnard leading the ARVN prisoners wanted the men to stop, all he had to do was to pull down on the rope. The men's heads followed as fast as possible to avoid as much of the agony in their brutalized noses as possible. If the lead man decided to start up again, he needed only to give the rope a little jerk. Sometimes, just for the fun of it, a village child would run into the string of tethered naked men and give a sharp yank on the string bringing the entire squad to their knees in sobs. Blood dripped down their begrimed faces from their tormented nostrils. They were as obedient as oxen with rings in their noses. Every one of them focused his personal hatred on the *con ma da trắng khổng-lồ* walking unperturbedly behind them.

That was not altogether fair, as if there might have been any inclination toward fairness anywhere in that wild place. That none of the ARVN soldiers had been executed and roasted was the direct result of his intercession. Anders had not thought it necessary to share that information with the ARVN master sergeant or any of his troops; perhaps that would have helped to meliorate their implacable attitudes. Covering himself for future interests was not one of Anders' strong points, and this episode had the evident properties of an instance when such discretion might well be in order.

He could have let them be killed and seen to it that the remains were never found. That would have been a simple and permanent solution. Perhaps he should have done just that. Instead, he let them live on to remember him with implacable and eternal enmity. These were men who had endured insults and ethnic slurs and even beatings from American soldiers aplenty and knew the humiliation and frustration of having their officers do nothing to make the Americans answer for their abusive bigoted behavior. They had had to swallow all of that and let it digest. But this they would not forgive nor forget.

It made no difference to the sufferers that Anders had arranged the release of the other ARVN soldiers, the ones who had not participated directly in the molestation. Those men had been deprived of their weapons and shoes and sent marching from the village shortly before the parade.

Anders was too young and inexperienced and his education too inadequate to have benefited from knowledge of Nicolò Machiavelli's sagacious advice (paraphrased): 'Never do small injuries to your enemies. Either treat them with kindness, or kill them. If they survive to recall the slights and injuries, they will make every effort to return the injuries manyfold and when least expected.'

The ARVN soldiers were released with bloodied bare feet and naked bodies, some with agonized and temporarily bleeding and disfigured noses, on a mountainous trail with a day's hike left to bring

727

them to the secure Vietnamese and CIA hamlet where they could enjoy the camaraderie of such as Jean-Luc DuParrier and Tandrosz Szabo. Anders and his PRUCs and the Montagnards melted back into the forest, and the ARVNs proceeded south, wallowing in misery, and being subjected to fresh humiliations from every peasant they encountered along the way. Bad news indeed travels fast, and there was many a bored mountain farmer and his family able to take off work to see the spectacle that day.

Anders, his PRUCs, and two Montagnard guides traveled north and west into Laos as far as the Montagnards had been before that mission, then the CIA men met the Hmong people who were to assist them for the remainder of their mission. It was no accident that the Hmong village selected was one of those that found it comfortable to cooperate with the Wa People in their heroin trade, and who had sheltered and protected Anders' men on their business journeys for fair compensation. The Hmongs were willing to guide the CIA men well afield from their own village to regions infested with communists or with villages that abetted them. The Hmongs were cautious, thoroughly respectful of the vituperative reprisal power of the NVA and would not allow any action within the semi-illusory boundaries of their part of the forest. They met the PRUCs and their leader on the trail without having them enter the village before they had completed their mission.

The Company men had limited success—they ambushed and killed enlisted NVA soldiers as they patrolled the Ho Chi Minh Trail; they left transport trucks smoldering in the middle of the two lane highway; and they set ammunition depots ablaze. None of the actions was particularly noteworthy; and none of them exposed the PRU team to any great danger; but in aggregate, they enhanced their reputation among their victims (nailing white ghost cards to the foreheads of the dead NVA) and with their Company superiors (adding to the body count report at the Saigon five o'clock follies). They kept on the move becoming hardened to the rigors of a life spent outside buildings for two months. They had had LURPS for only two weeks and stolen rations or captured game for the rest. For the most part they received an education into the life of the colorful minority peoples of Viet Nam whom they encountered as they negotiated their way up and down the mountains and valleys of Laos and North Viet Nam.

Eighty five percent of the people in the country of South Viet Nam are ethnic Vietnamese, the rest are hill people, ethnic Chinese, a few holdover French, a smattering of Khmer, Indo-Malayians, and mixed races. The largest minority, the Sino-Tibetan northern mountain (Hoang Lien Mountains) dwellers, include the Hmong, Mien, True Meo, and Giay people (about 800,000). The second largest minority in South Viet Nam (about 700,000) is the southern mountaineers (in the Truong Son Mountains), so-called Montagnards, by the French. They are made up of twelve major and sixty minor tribes. There are two ethnolinguistic groups of Montagnards—Malayo-Polynesian and Mon-Khmer—with some thirty separate subdivisions. There has always been a considerable co-mingling of these semi-nomadic people with the neighboring Laotian and Thai hill tribes. In the Second Indochinese war with the dislocations occasioned by disruptive fighting and the governmentally forced relocations, the traditional locations of the tribes, clans, and villages were markedly altered.

The predominate religion of these people was animism, or natural spirit worship. They were ancestor worshipers who venerated the family dead and believed that the soul survives. A departed family member became a guardian for the living family. There was great emphasis placed on family histories, lineages, and genealogies. Filial loyalty and from that, a piety that depends on adherence to the family's values, dominated the moral and ethical sense of these people. Each household kept an altar to the dead, and one male heir was appointed as the keeper of the family's worship. He, therefore, occupied an important position in the family hierarchy.

The Hmong village into which Anders and his men were accepted in that period of often shifting loyalties had benefited considerably by its decision to ally itself, at least in part, with the CIA forces. The village was a stockade surrounded with two rows of sharpened stakes, each stake resting against its neighbor, one set aimed low and one high with a wide, deep trench in front and a triple row of razor wire behind. Steel spikes aimed in all directions formed a second barrier inside the first, and beyond that was a ring of antipersonnel mines. Within the fortified compound there were CORDS financed fish ponds, chicken pens, goat yards, and chicken and duck runs. There were sturdily constructed buildings for schools, complete with writing materials and with books in the French and Vietnamese languages, for safe storage of dry sacked foodstuffs, for a well-equipped and manned medical clinic, for a sophisticated communication center, and for a carefully guarded armory. In the spirit and form of the historical wild American West, this village was a self-contained fort.

The fort-village was as safe as any community could be in that contested forest. That not a single Vietnamese, official or worker, would enter or remain in the village at night attested to the level of insecurity felt by informed people. The Hmongs in the community were happy to have the presence of four more proficient soldiers in their midst.

The four men walked through the main gate past four sentries armed with M-16s and an M-60 machine gun. Had it been night, the entrance would have been illuminated by two large flood lamps. Inside the walls, they walked through a line of notables of the village who were each guarded by a young man with a spear—a nod to ceremony since each of them also carried a machine pistol slung from his shoulder on a leather strap. The young men were clothed only in g-strings. Other young security men were sitting conspicuously in strategic locations holding crossbows. They, like the spear guards, were also armed with modern weapons.

Young women heralded the PRUCs arrival with an enthusiastic, almost tumultuous music from high-pitched string instruments and small drums. Another set of girls swayed sensuously in a languid dance near the center of the open area in front of the buildings. Their movements seemed out of synchrony with the frenetic pace of the musical beat.

The young women were dressed neck to ankle in vividly patterned homemade blouses, vests, and skirts. These people were mountain Hmong as opposed to the Black Thai people in the villages around them. Those Thai villages were anomalous, being located in the mountains. The Thai people had been moved from their usual valley bottom wet-rice farming location to the more defensible current situation in the higher altitudes. The Thai nomenclature is based on the color of the young women's skirts. Throughout the Southeast Asian home of these mountain Thai and Hmong people, the skirts come in white, black, red, and flowered; and the people are named and casted by the color. White's are the apex of the social caste pyramid, followed closely by black; and their social status is further character-ized by the degree of their wealth and access to modern comforts.

There is only very occasional intermarriage among the different kinds of mountain Thais and then only moving between one level to its nearest class. Whites and Blacks may intermarry. When they do, the Black moves to the White village in deference to the superior caste's prerogative. That is an inflexible rule. Whites do not marry

Reds. No Thai would ever marry a dry-rice farming higher altitude living Hmong. That ultimate social disgrace did not ever occur since it represented such a powerful taboo that couples themselves never allowed even preliminary interaction to take place.

Fortune tellers tried to get Anders' and the PRUCs' attention; but the newcomers were tired, sweat soaked, filthy, and smelled bad. The four men had been constantly on the go, living off the land with their Hmong guide for six weeks of the two months that they had been gone from their own Montagnard village further south. They now could only concentrate on their need for sleep, food, a bath, and for Anders, sex, in descending order of priority. Anders missed H'Klois and longed to get back to her before he and his men had to return to the complex world of Thau Thien Province politics and turmoil and reports to the CORDS authority in Hue'. He was ready for a bath, a two day sleep, then he would impose on his weary companions to make the trek to H'Klois' village. Anders had had to discard his fatigue shirt and presented a fearsome visage as he walked across the village compound to the sturdy little building assigned them.

He was a huge man compared to the small Hmongs. His scars were now pale in color but prominently visible and served to highlight the vivid tattoos on his chest and right shoulder and back. He carried an M-16, a combat shotgun, bullet belts, and crossed bandoleers of grenades. A Randall stiletto hung down his back from a cord around his neck and a Swedish K bar knife was prominently displayed on his hip. His hair was long and greasy, curly golden and dirty and was held back from his eyes by a strip of once white cloth, the funeral color. He walked through the town with what looked like an unchallengable authority. The Catholic missionary-priest assigned to the region looked at Anders as he and his men made their way to their dwellings and thought to himself in an amused rendition of the twenty-third psalm, "Yea, though I walk through the valley of the shadow of death, I shall fear no evil, for I am the scariest monster ever to pass through this valley."

He slept eighteen hours without interruption, almost without moving. When he awakened due to bladder pressure, he saw Bach, Dung, and Ky still slumbering deeply. Anders shook himself and pushed off the futon to get to a standing position. His brain seemed awake, but he could still feel the ingrained tiredness in his body. That particular day he felt old. He also felt uneasy. He had had one of those dreams again—the coal black wildly hairy frighteningly ugly man, this time leaning on a staff watching him. The dream was brief, like seeing the shadow of a passing cloud; but it left him unsettled.

Anders cleaned himself up, scrubbing with soap for the first time in two months. It felt sinfully wonderful. He washed his hair three times before it seemed clean. Now it was totally unmanageable. He had to laugh at his image in the mirror. Anders' pants were beyond repair, tattered and indescribably filthy. Having succeeded in getting clean himself, he did not want to touch them, even to throw them away. He wrapped a towel around his middle and padded over to the village's quartermaster building and asked the matron in charge if she thought she might have some clothes that would fit him. He was speaking Vietnamese, and she obviously could not understand him. He switched to French.

"*Pour moi?*" (For me?) he asked. "*S'l vous plaît, avez-vous un pantalon it une chemise pour moi, peut-être des bottes?*" (Please, have you pants and shirt for me, maybe some boots?)

She understood and was amused. "*Non monsieur. Vous ne pourriez même pas faire entrer votre bras dans le plus grand pantalon ici. Il n'y a pas de chemise avec une ouverture assez grande pour votre tête.*" (No, sir. You would not be able to put your arm in the leg of the largest pair of pants in here. There is no shirt that would even go over your head.) She shrugged her shoulders and moved her palms upward in a universal sign of resignation employed by the world's civil servants.

Anders thought a minute. "*Ou est le tailleur du village?*" (Where is the village tailor, please?)

"*Derriere le lieu saint, le bâtiment rouge,*" (Behind the shrine, the red building.) the woman offered. That was as helpful as she was going to be.

Anders found the tailor hurrying to complete his deadlines. He asked the man to make him a pair of pants and a pullover shirt. "*J'en ai besoin aujourd'hui,*" (I need them today.) he said, starting out in French.

The skinny little tailor rolled his eyes back in a look of helplessness against the fates. He wished Anders to know just how impossible his request was. "*Peut-être dans une semaine,*" (Perhaps a week,) he said. "*Ça vous coûtera six américains.*" (Cost you six American.) The hill people knew better than to accept the easily devalued Vietnamese Piastre or the Laotian kip.

"*Voilà ce que je vous propose, mon ami,*" (Tell you what, my friend,) Anders bargained. "*Je vous donnerai dix américains si vous le faites pour cet après-midi.*" (I will give you ten American if you get it done this afternoon.)

The tailor weakened. "*Je le ferai pour douze. Vous aurez besoin d'un mètre supplément aire de tissu.*" (I would have to have twelve. You will require another yard of material.)

"*Onze,*" (Eleven.) Anders countered. It would be a social *faux pas* not to haggle a little.

The little man screwed up his nut brown face in thought. This was evidently a weighty matter. "*D'accord. Je le fars pour onze. Exceptionnellement pour vous parce quie vous êtes un querrier.*" (All right. Eleven it is. Special for you because you are a warrior.)

"*Merci maître tailleur. Avez vous quelque-chose que je pourrais mettre en attendant le pantalon et la chemise? Je n'ai rein à porter.*" (Thank you, tailor. Have you anything I can wear until the pants and shirt are ready. I have nothing.)

"*On pourrait se débrouiller avec un style Hmong,*" (We can make do with a Hmong style) the tailor responded. "*Je pourrais vous prêter de tissu pour la journée. Malheureusement je dois vous demander deux dollars de plus.*" (I can lend you cloth for the day. Regrettably, I must charge an additional two dollars.)

"*Même un serait trop,*" (One would be too high) Anders said, a little tired of the endless financial scenario that had to be acted out for even the smallest transaction.

"*Parce que je vous fais confiance je vous donnerai le tissu pour un it demi, pas un centime de moins. Vous me promettez de me le rendre tout propre et en bon état.*" (Because I trust you, I could let you have the cloth for one and a half, not a cent less. You must promise to return it clean and unharmed.)

Anders did not feel like making an issue for fifty cents. "*D'accord tailleuer. Vous négociez trop bien pour moi. Un et demi.*" (All right, tailor; you are too much of a negotiator for me. One and a half.)

The tailor nodded his head. He seemed a little disappointed to have won so easily. However, he would be getting double the usual fees he could have expected from one of his countrymen; so, he could not complain. Besides he was not busy. He had just acted like that as he saw the near naked white man approaching his shop. He was justifiably proud of his negotiating skills that day. He tried one more ploy.

"*Je parlais seulement du travail. Le tissu est en plus naturellement.*" (I have been speaking only of the labor. The cloth is, of course, extra.)

Before the man could come up with the extra figure, Anders gave him a steely look. The tailor thought better of his ploy. Perhaps he should let enough be enough.

"Mais pour vous…ce serait un honneur j'absorberai moi-même le coût." (But, for you…it would be an honor. I will, myself, absorb the cost.) He even gave a little bow.

Anders had to suppress a smile. He nodded his appreciation.

The tailor brought out a length of handsome brightly embroidered cloth, presumably hand decorated. Anders could see why the tailor had prized the cloth highly. He had Anders remove his towel, then skillfully wrapped the cloth around the big man's waist, made two passes between his legs and pinned the makeshift garment so that it had short legs and a bulky rear flap. The style effected was common among Hmong men, a long ago contribution from India, one of the variations of the traditional old langouti. It would do nicely until Anders could get his new outfit. He thanked the tailor and headed back to where his PRUCs were just arising to greet the afternoon.

A Hmong CIDG soldier trotted out of the communications building and intercepted Anders as he neared the entrance to his building. He spoke Hmong. Anders shook his head.

"Francais?" (French?) Anders asked.

The young man's facility with French was limited, but he struggled through the message. *"POIC vent que vous alliez au village Meo qui est sur. Prenez guide. Il vous emmène trouver homme chinois et soldat nord…officier. Vous prenez vivant au village Viet d'où vous êtes parti. Très important. Sans tarder. Signé, Howard. Vous comprenez, grand monsieur?"* (POIC wants that you go to safe Meo village. Take guide. He take you to find Chinese man and North soldier…officer. You take alive back to Viet village where you started. Most important. No delay. Signed, 'Howard.' You understand, big sir?) He was straining with the effort to communicate.

"Merci. Vous avez bien fait. Envoyez un message: Message reçu. Pars tout de suite. Signe, 'Bergstrom.' Vous l'avez?" (Thank you. You did well. Send message back: 'Copy your orders. On my way. Signed, 'Bergstrom.' Have you got that?)

The soldier nodded his head enthusiastically. To be on the safe side, Anders asked, *"Répétez-moi le message, s'l vous plaît."* (Please read it back to me.)

The soldier adopted a quizzical look.

"Mon message au POIC." (My message to the POIC.)

The light came on. The young man read it back to Anders. *"Comprends. Obéis à vos ordres."* (Understand. Will obey) the soldier read from the notes he had taken when Anders dictated the response.

"*Ça va,*" (Close enough.) Anders said. He gave the boy a pat on the shoulder. The boy gave Anders' hand a squeeze. Anders had a fleeting feeling of self-consciousness, thinking of the reaction of his boyhood friends and the American soldiers to such manly displays of comradeship. It had become second nature to him now. He recognized that he had gone native altogether.

Anders told the PRUCs. They would have to move out today. The three Vietnamese chorused with groans, but good naturedly began to arrange their gear for the trip. "Bach. Do an inventory, then go to the armory to pick up whatever we need. Ky, lay in the food supplies, okay?" They each nodded their okay.

"Dung. Get clothes and shoes for you guys. I'll take care of my own. We had better go out when it gets dark. Now, let's get some breakfast."

The flood lights were extinguished for five minutes to allow the PRUCs to leave around midnight. All of them were spruced out in fine new black pajamas and sets of rubber tire sandals with spares rolled into tight long cylinders and slung over their shoulders with their ammunition belts and rolls of packed rice. Bach carried an M-60 and Dung had the extra ammunition. Ky had a rucksack packed with bricks of white powder left at the village by the Wa People courier for the PRUCs to transport on to Hue'. He had used up most of their remaining money to pay off the Hmong business men. Anders had added the bolt of cloth he had been wearing, having bought it from the tailor after a lengthy and emotional negotiation. He wanted it for HêKlois. Two Hmong CIDGs led them along the safest path through the triple canopied rain forest in the direction of their Montagnard village.

The men trotted steadily through the night and through the next day. Anders had once marveled at the endurance of the little brown men who could run up and down the mountain sides all day without tiring and with very little food. Now he moved along as easily as they did without increasing his heart rate or breaking an exercise sweat. He was as fit as a marathon runner.

The Hmong CIDGs had Anders and his men hole up in some limestone caves a day's hard march from the village of their destination. After a difficult discussion in French and sign language and with the liberal use of maps drawn in the dirt, the Hmongs were convinced that the PRUCs would be able to make it the rest of the way on their own. They did not like to get too close to the Montagnards whom they feared as savages. The Rhades' reputation as slavers and cannibals was widespread among the hill peoples, and the Hmong were not inclined to tempt fate.

735

As the Hmongs were about to begin their return journey, a wind began to rustle the branches and leaves. It seemed to come from nowhere. The Hmongs became nervous and seemed concerned for Anders and his men. *"Qu'est-ce que c'est?"* (What is it?) Bach asked the senior of their two guides.

The Hmongs looked at each other, reluctant to convey what they felt. *"Dites-le s'l vous plaît,"* (Please say.) Ky requested politely and with feeling.

"Les esprits des arbres font le vent. Ils sentent la présence du mal et ils réagissent. C'est un mauvais signe. Un mauvais augure." (The tree spirits are making the wind. They feel the presence of evil and are reacting. That is a bad omen. A bad omen.) None of the PRUCs regarded the concept that the movement of the trees made the wind, rather than the reverse, as anything strange, even Anders. It was a measure of his immersion in the culture.

"Qual mauvais augure? Qu'est-ce que nous disent les esprit?" (What bad omen? What do the spirits tell us?) Anders asked.

"Ils sont malheureux. Ils savent qu'il y a du mal dans le monde aujourd'hui." (Just upset. They know that there is evil in the world today.) The world, for the Hmongs, was their forest home.

Anders shrugged. He was not so immersed in the culture of these people that he had faith in all their superstitions. Still, after his dream, he was impressionable; and the Hmongs' state of obvious ill ease was a nettling to Anders. Ky, Bach, and Dung felt it as well although they, too, were disinclined toward giving credence to the superstitions of the people they considered to be primitives. They would have been offended to hear their own beliefs described as superstitions, including their ready acceptance of the validity of dreams about Au Co or the frightening hairy black visitant. Anders had kept silent about his recent negative dreams not wanting to unnerve them.

The Hmongs departed quickly, wishing not to be out in the unsettled forest any longer than they had to be. Anders and his PRUCs put their anxiety aside, and moved quickly in the direction of their Montagnard village. At dusk the four men were jogging rapidly and smoothly over paths that had become familiar to them.

They heard a patrol of men and ducked into the dense foliage to avoid detection, unsure whether they were hearing friend or foe. Dung stood stock still blending into the trees as the shadowy figures trotted by. He strained his eyes to try and determine who they were, but he could not. He did not pay attention to the forest around him. A snake slithered along a branch directly over Dung's head. It flicked its tongue trying to identify the warm blooded creature so immobile in its territory.

The foot long green tree viper, patterned with what the French had described as a *fleur-de-lis* design, locked its tail around the small branch and dangled almost its entire length in the air, an instinctual hunting technique. It waited, alert to small shifts in movement. Its small size precluded an attack, instinct made it wait.

The figures passed on down the trail, and the four men hiding the bush began to breath again. Anders, Ky, and Bach shifted to their feet from the positions where they had been kneeling or lying. Dung relaxed and stepped cautiously toward his brother PRUCs, checking the ground as he did to avoid disturbing a branch and making a noise. He was looking intently down when he walked into the snake.

The serpent tensed all its abdominal muscles as the first flick of Dung's hair touched it. The heat and scent of the moving body made the reptile act from natural impulse. In a movement so swift that it could not have been seen in full daylight, the snake struck and sank its small fangs into Dung's face just in front of his left ear. He scarcely felt the sting.

Dung walked on two more steps before his body reacted to the potent neurotoxin. He felt his limbs turn to wood. In another second he made his last step because his legs would no longer move. It was hard to breath, then impossible. He could not even try; nothing worked. He cast a frantic look for his friends, but his eye muscles did not permit anything but straight ahead vision by then. His peripheral visual fields narrowed concentrically in a fraction of a second until the last vestige of light was extinguished. Dung pitched forward suffocating, knowing that he was suffocating, trying to cry out. In six seconds it was too late; in two minutes he was dead.

Bach heard the noise of Dung's fall. It was surprisingly quiet since there was no struggle. At first he thought his friend had tripped. He squeezed his hand on the grip of his gun and looked about to see if there was an enemy. The snake slipped silently into the decaying leaves of the jungle floor and disappeared. Bach tapped Ky and Anders. All of the men crouched instantly trying to find out what had happened. Anders swiveled his head about trying to see or hear an enemy. The jungle had settled into its natural hum of night noise with the passing of the walkers.

"Dung! Dung! what is it?" whispered Ky who had brushed against his friend's leg as he knelt. Assuming that the lack of reply had ominous portent, he swiftly ran his hands along Dung's outstretched body. There was no sign of life, and no evidence of an arrow or of blood. Ky pressed his fingers into the front of Dung's neck and felt for the carotid. Nothing. No pulse, no respiratory movements.

"He's dead," Ky reported incredulously. It was as if one of the Hmong's rock or tree spirits had sucked the life from his comrade silently and with demonic swiftness. Ky clapped his arms across his chest to suppress an involuntary shudder.

"How?" whispered Anders unable to believe what he was hearing. "Trap?"

"I can't feel anything," Ky replied in a barely audible voice.

"Two-step," said Bach. "Get your hands away from him. The snake may still be on him."

Ky feared no man. He had looked death in the face on several occasions and had never lost his nerve. He had seen things that were the stuff of lifetime nightmares and had not flinched. But the former *Bui Doi* had an instinctual, almost feral, dread of snakes. He sprang back and collided with Anders. The big man took a giant step out of harm's way. Bach was moving resolutely toward the path.

The three men crouched on the jungle path grimacing with near panic. It was one thing to face enemies, even ambushes, and another to have a friend alive and vital one moment and for him to be snuffed out by an unseen specter the next. In their conscious, logical minds they all knew the snake was a natural hazard of their environment; but there in the night, Dung's death had taken on a surreal spectral quality. None of them spoke for a few moments as they worked to collect themselves, each man dealing with his personal apprehension.

All of them intuitively wanted to run, to put as much distance from the diminutive killer as possible, but their promises to each other not to leave one of their bodies out there to the mercy of the elements or the communists prevailed over their baser senses. Anders spoke first, "I'll go get him. The snake is gone by now." He hoped it was not just wishful thinking.

"I'll help," offered Bach. Ky could not bring himself to go back there.

Anders came out of the dense undergrowth carrying Dung slung over his shoulder in the fireman's carry. Bach had both men's weapons. Ky took his share, and the three somber men trekked south toward the Montagnard village. They kept to the trail and made themselves as conspicuous as they could so as to avoid spooking a trail sentry. About 2300 they were escorted inside the cluster of long houses.

Anders' whole body ached from the exertion of carrying his dead friend. He was shaking with weariness and emotion. Ky and Bach were at the end of their tethers as well having packed the weight of too many weapons too far that night. They were all sweat soaked even though it was a fairly cool evening.

Dung was stretched out in the dead house. The sentries awakened the shaman who was crotchety at the interruption. He performed the necessary immediate post death rituals with a conspicuous lack of sympathy or grace and went back to bed. Ky and Bach were taken to an empty bed room where they dropped into near instant deep sleep.

Anders found his way to H'Klois' house and slipped quietly in. The girl was sound asleep in his and her room. He found another room to drop in, but that one was occupied as well, by an older woman. Anders looked closer and recognized H'Klois' mother. The woman had moved in evidently, in compliance with the Montagnard custom of the mother coming to live with her youngest daughter. Anders was responsible for a family of three now, including himself. He slept in the common room with the family supplies.

He was awakened by an attack in the morning. H'Klois pounced on him and squirmed and wiggled her enthusiastic body all over him. "*Ooh, vous puez,*" (Ooh, you stink.) she said when she got over her joy at discovering him and her initial exuberance for his body.

"*Je sais,*" (I know.) he said groggily. "*Je me laverai plus tard.*" (I'll clean up later.(He tried to go back to sleep, but H'Klois would not let him. She was too excited to leave him alone.

Shortly, the reluctant Swede was being led outside by his wife to where two steaming tubs of water were sitting on the grass. She shucked off his clothes and kicked them into the nearby bushes. Then she made her man sit on a low three-legged stool while she collected a pair of large sponges, and a huge bar of village made rough looking soap.

H'Klois' mother trotted out of the house with fresh hot water to add to the tubs. She habitually chewed a numbing mixture of tobacco, lime juice, and betel nut and spat red juice before every sentence she spoke. Anders turned his back to her to hide his private parts. That made the two women laugh delightedly. Anders knew he was being silly; so, he relaxed. The old mother, Ami Klois (her name meant simply 'Klois' mother'), was completely frank about her curiosity. She had never seen a white person at close range and certainly had never seen such a man naked. She frankly inspected his torso with her hands and appraised the rest of him with her eyes. She squeezed the powerful muscles of his arms and ran her hands gently and sympathetically over the scars on his back and chest. She made him open his legs so she could see. Apparently she approved because she trotted back to her daughter and carried on an animated conversation punctuated with measuring motions followed by applauding and occasional lip smacking and teeth clicking noises. Anders was embarrassed and blushed, but his mother-in-law's unreservedly candid approval was ingratiating if unlike anything he had known in The World or in civilized Viet Nam, if that descriptor could be properly applied to the war ravaged country.

H'Klois got her man dressed in a new set of black pajamas that she made for him while he was gone. He told her about Dung; and she commiserated, knowing that the two men had been close. She was sad for Dung because he had met his death far from family. She sent her mother to make the funeral arrangements for later in the day, then took Anders into the house and away from prying eyes. She could not wait any longer.

CHAPTER 38

(1) A losing war: The South Vietnamese are losing the war to the Viet Cong. No one can assure you that we can beat the Cong or even force them to the conference table on our terms, no matter how many hundred thousand white, foreign (US) troops we deploy...

The alternative—no matter what we may wish it to be— almost certainly a protracted war involving an open-ended commitment of US forces, mounting US casualties, no assurance of a satisfactory solution, and a serious danger of escalation at the end of the road...

Once we suffer large casualties, we will have started a well-nigh irreversible process. Our involvement will be so great that we cannot—without national humiliation—stop short of achieving complete objectives. Of the two possibilities, I think humiliation would be more likely than the achievement of our objectives even after we have paid terrible costs.

George W. Ball, Under Secretary of State, memorandum to President Lyndon B. Johnson, July 1, 1965

Anders, Ky, and Bach sat with H'Klois and Ami Klois in the communal long house later in the afternoon. They, like other villagers who had come for the funeral ritual, were all dressed in white and wore white head bands with Chinese character sayings inscribed on them. It was doubtful if anyone, including the shaman, knew what the letters said, but they all knew that they were powerful medicine and the correct thing to say to the departing soul.

There was no crying, not even long faces. The animist Montagnards, like their Buddhist countrymen, did not look upon death with finality, but only as a transition. The departed would, even now, be with the ancestors, his family, happy and at peace. It was incumbent on those remaining to be likewise. It was only the Christians with their inadequate belief in the hereafter who wept and tore their clothing when a family member died; something the Montagnards could not fathom. The actions of Christians at funerals were as strange to the hill people as their marital beliefs expressed in their marriage ceremony—that death would do the couple part. Not a single Montagnard believed such a thing, at least not concerning the time beyond the very temporary mortal state. That the couple, and the rest of the family, would be together for eternity was a given to them. Many could not believe it when they were told of the strange beliefs and customs of the Christians.

Dung's body lay in state in front of the assembled villagers. He was shrouded in white and had piles of flowers lying over him. His possessions and some useful household utensils as gifts to accommodate his needs in the great beyond were neatly placed along his sides in the wooden casket. The shaman slowly and quietly intoned the sacred traditions of his people to communicate with the ancestors so they would be ready to welcome their son, brother, cousin, nephew, and grandson, Nguyen Van Dung. The shaman told the ancestors of the man's bravery and of his kindness, that he was regarded highly by good people here. He assured the old ones that this man had worn the family's name well and had brought pride and not shame to it.

From time to time the officiator turned to the audience and smiled. He spoke to them of his understanding with Dung's family. They were ready for him. The villagers smiled at the shaman and at each other. It was a good funeral.

Dung was buried in the forest, and a small replica of a long house was taken from the village and placed over the sacred ground where Dung slept. The little house contained miniatures of needful items—spears, fish nets, knives, bowls and spoons—the things of everyday life. He had to be buried alone in the forest because he had no family in the town. The shaman had taken great pains to inform Dung's ancestors where the man lay; so, he would not be lost to them.

After the funeral and internment, the villagers had a small feast. Because it was a special occasion, they had stewed puppy. Anders felt much better about his friend's death after the uplifting ceremonies. He would have liked to stay forever in the placid, natural village among people he truly loved. It nagged his mind that he was going to have to leave again, and very soon, to be in compliance with the orders he had been given by Cleve Howard. He could wait until the Vietnamese LLDBs came to take them to where they had seen the Chinese and NVA officers, but that was not going to be long.

When the four ARVN rangers came into the Montagnard village

under escort by the sentries two days later, they were met with sullen silence from the villagers. They were used to such responses; the Meos were not civilized, they reasoned. These primitives responded poorly to being told that they stank and that they were inferior to the civilized Vietnamese, which was no more nor less than the elemental truth, the LLDBs had observed on previous occasions. The Montagnard inferiors seemed overly sensitive to simple observations of what was evident. The LLDBs paid no heed to the animosity evident in every villager's face.

"Are you the PRU/O?" asked the lead LLDB without preamble when taken to H'Klois' and Anders' house. He spoke only Vietnamese.

"I am. Are you the rangers the POIC said would be coming?"

"Yes. We have orders to head out as soon as possible to make sure the targets won't get away from where we saw their headquarters. No great hurry, but we should plan to leave soon."

"We'll leave now."

The lead LLDB was about to protest that he and his men had been marching through the forest for more than two days, and they were tired. He could tell that the big white man was no more positively disposed toward him and his ARVN men than were the villagers. He had counted on a chance to get a good meal or two and maybe even a dalliance—the aboriginal women were enthusiastically promiscuous, of that he was certain. Seeing the set in Anders' face, he decided to let it go. He wished he had not started out making it seem like such an urgent matter.

Anders said his goodbyes to H'Klois and her mother as soon as he had been informed that the ARVNs were being brought into the village. He did not want them even to see her. He also did not want to prolong the pain of separation. There was no telling how long it would be before he would see her again.

The four LLDBs and the three PRUCs force marched into Laos highland country for four days, heading as far south as they did west before they came to the high edge of the escarpment looking into a well fortified permanent military camp. The LLDB sergeant pointed out to Anders, Ky, and Bach the various installations he and his men had scouted out over a reconnaissance that had been repeated intermittently over a month's period. They had never been discovered. He described in detail the habits of the enemy officers they had seen and told Anders where and how he thought they could be captured. The report was clear and concise, thoroughly professional. Anders had only one concern about the account—it was delivered with such finality that Anders suspected that it was being given in parting.

"Thanks for the thorough report and for getting us here in one piece. I spent some time with your people in the Delta; I thought those men were first rate, too," Anders told the LLDB sergeant.

The man displayed no more emotion to the praise from the CIA operative than he had to the glowering disapproval of the Montagnards.

"How long do you think they'll stay here?" Anders asked, speaking about the communists.

"Long time. Looks to us like a permanent camp. They have been perfectly safe here. Americans won't let us go after the Laotians or even the NVA on this side of the border. They pretend like the Chinese are not even involved. No reason for these people to have any fear from us. They can attack at will. The Americans protect them."

"Until now," Anders said.

"It is a small beginning," the LLDB sergeant said with a trace of anger in his voice. Anders could not disagree with the man.

"So let's do something worthwhile." It was good to be speaking Vietnamese again. He still had to translate from English or Vietnamese into French before he could use that language in conversation. He had a ways to go before he would be able to think in French as he did in the other two languages.

"Sorry. Not us. Just you," said the LLDB with finality.

"I thought you were so hot to hit these people," Anders said trying not to let a note of irony into his voice. He was sure these men were anything but cowards. Nothing that they had said or done in the past four days suggested that they were business-as-usual ARVNs.

The sergeant almost had to bite his lip to suppress his anger. "Orders. We are not to engage. Americans say. ARVN officers only too glad to agree. You hear that Americans pulling out? Maybe then we can do what needs to be done. Not have to worry about silly politics anymore."

Anders understood the man's orders and his frustration. It was news to him that there was any real talk about the Americans pulling out. "The Paris peace talks had been going on for years; so why should there be anything significant happening now?" Anders thought. He decided to ignore the chance comment as just one more grunts' rumor.

The ARVN LLDBs were gone as soon as it was dark enough to travel leaving Anders and his two teammates as the entire ambush unit and prisoner transport squad. It was a daunting thought. This country belonged to the communists, to regular army units, and the PRUCs knew that it would only be a matter of time before they were discovered. They set themselves to the task of capturing a Chinese and an NVA officer the following morning.

Selection of the Chinese was not difficult since, as near as they could determine, there was only one Chinese officer for a contingent of about a hundred Chinese People's Army enlisted men. He had very little to do with his men and kept company almost exclusively with the NVA officers who lived apart from their enlisted in a trio of well built log and rock buildings. The enlisted men lived in tents and simple wood frame barracks on the opposite side of a small lake in the center of the valley that lay at the foot of the escarpment. There were eight or ten NVA officers so far as the PRUCs could tell, their own observations corroborating the report from the ARVN rangers.

When, where, and how seemed relatively simple also. The officers were men of strict habit. The Chinese visited the privy at 0600, give or take five minutes, every day. The senior NVA officer, a man who appeared to be about the same age as the Chinese as seen through the binoculars, could hold his bladder until around 0630. The younger officers rushed in a bunch to the three privies just before 0700 and just made it to morning parade each of the two days Anders and his men watched the military base. Security was surprisingly lax. Officers wore identifying insignias and lived apart from the men unlike the American policy that prevented officers from being identifiable as specific targets for snipers or ambushers. There were an adequate number of perimeter sentries—all occupying positions pinpointed by the PRUCs—but the officers seemed to have no special protection, not even an extra guard or two around their living area.

"Tonight we'll all go down and hide in the set of bushes below the privy. We'll be in place when the Chinaman comes out. He has to be taken in no more than a couple of minutes and without a sound. Bach and I will get him while you cover our tails, Ky, Okay?" Anders explained the plan as he had worked it out.

"What about the NVA?" asked Ky.

"I'm getting to that. You two come back and get him while I secure the Chinaman, then I'll come back to help. Here, I have some duct tape and a pair of handcuffs for you two. I have some for me. No noise or we're dead."

"How do we get the two prisoners back up this cliff, especially if they decide to give us any trouble?" asked Bach.

"First thing, you see to it that your man doesn't want to give trouble; but remember that he has to be in good enough shape for a long walk. Leave his legs alone. I've thought about our escape. We are not going to be able to go back the way we came in. We will never be able to get back up here; and besides, that's exactly where they will expect us to go. I plan for us to head down the valley; it's south and on the way we need to go, and hopefully it will throw them off for a while. As soon as we get seen by a village, they will be after us, though. With any luck, we will have about an hour's head start and the added advantage of being able to choose our direction without them knowing where we are going exactly. This is tough country, not many folks here."

It seemed like a good enough plan to Ky and Bach. The three men spent the evening hours discussing the details of plans about how to get down the cliff, what to do if their quarries made noise, and determined a rendezvous point if the ambush turned sour. They slept from 2200 until 0200.

The escarpment proved to be difficult to descend, not so much because it was steep, but because the scree on its face was so loose and clattery as they walked on it. The face of the obtuse angled incline was almost white from the limestone and sunbleached clay. There were no plants on the face of it. The descent required two hours, but was accomplished without detection. It was 0415 and would begin to get light soon.

Ky found a position on a small rise, a perfect sniper's spot. He could see the line of privies and the officer's cabins well and had a clear line of fire if it became necessary. Anders and Bach crawled for an hour through the weeds and saw-grass around the Chinese officer's favorite privy until they were satisfied that they could get to the man fast enough to do what they had to do. Bach still had his doubts. Although it was dark, and they could not be sure, they thought they were well enough hidden to escape being seen by the roving perimeter guards. The guards had seemed fairly lackadaisical about their vigilance when the PRUCs had watched them from above, and they did not encounter any guards as they insinuated themselves into position. It was 0505 and the indigo of night was beginning to pale into the sky blue of day.

Anders could now analyze their situation better. In the light, it was evident that as much as a couple of seconds would elapse before they could be on the officer they intended to kidnap—plenty of time for him to sound an alarm. They had to do something different. It was quite light now, almost 0545. He came up with a risky solution.

"I'll hide in the head," he told Bach who raised his eyebrows.

"They'll see you when you cross the clear area in front of it," Bach protested.

"They'll see us when we snatch him. It's too far from here. I have to take the chance."

"Then hurry up. He'll be on the path in a minute or so. Take off."

Anders slithered to the edge of the bushes facing the clearing, looked in all directions, and seeing no one, made a dash for the privy door. He whisked inside just as the Chinese officer began to amble up the path. The man was dressed in his light khaki blouse, trousers, and flip-flop sandals. He was enjoying the world that morning, stretching and doing forme frusts of exercises, "probably the only PT he ever got," thought Bach. He urinated off the side of the path evidently not wanting to be in the smelly outdoor privy overly long. He beat on his chest, and Bach had to avert his head to keep from laughing and giving away his position.

Anders was feeling nauseated. The smell in the enclosed space in which he hid was pungently terrible, the stench of decaying excrement of men who lived on garlicky fish. The northerners liked their food to be piquant and full of chilies, and were willing to pay the price of frequent diarrhea for their pleasures. He tried to hold his breath, but he had to take a deep breath and a big whiff every so often. He was afraid he might puke.

It was dark inside, and Anders could not see out. The little building was well constructed to keep it safe from cobras, he presumed. That was no small comfort there in the dark. The enlisted men used fifty gallon oil drums set in holes in the ground and had to set fire to their leavings each time. In the dark, cobras liked to slip into the warm drums and nestle in for a comfortable night. It was a frightening prospect to have the trots and have to go out to one of those potential cobra pits in the dark. That was another of the hazards of this war for men on both sides.

He strained his ears to hear anything on the outside so all of the surprise would be on the Chinese officer's part when that privy door opened. He was rewarded with a silly breach of security by the People's Army lieutenant colonel. The man sang, softly, but the sound was audible for twenty feet in all directions. He was evidently anticipating one of the nicest parts of his day. Anders was almost sorry to spoil such a fine sensual pleasure for the man.

Bach watched the colonel reach out for the door and start to swing it open. He moved quickly toward the opening. Anders waited until the door opened wide then struck the officer a sudden sharp crack on the point of the chin erasing the instantaneous look of bemused consternation from the PRC officer's face. The force of the blow snapped the colonel's head back. His knees buckled, and he dropped outside the door and into Bach's arms. Bach settled him to the ground. Anders came out low then whirled around and crawled back long enough to set one of the *con ma da trắng khổng-lồ* cards on the toilet seat then quickly and quietly closed the privy door on his way out. The two men dragged the colonel as swiftly as they could into the enclosing bushes constantly on the lookout to see if they had been discovered. It did not seem as though they had been thus far.

Anders slapped a strip of duct tape over the still unconscious officer's mouth while Bach handcuffed him with his arms behind his back. He was a short pudgy man. Anders estimated his weight at around 150 pounds. It would be tough to carry him, but there was no choice. He strained down and hoisted the man over his shoulder. He had to carry all of his weapons as well; Bach and Ky would have their own hands full as soon as they got an NVA officer. He trotted along, weaving through the tangled vegetation of the new-growth forest as fast as possible under the circumstances. The sun was just beginning to peek over the edge of the escarpment.

Anders had carried his prisoner about a hundred meters, far enough to be out of earshot for minor noises, and far enough away from the camp to avoid being seen by a chance observer as long as he kept in the trees which were now larger, part of the old forest. He was now walking easily, not trying to hurry. His man began to come around at that point and began to squirm with the discomfort of having the point of Anders' shoulder in his abdomen. Anders set him down and attempted to tell the man what was going on. He was not sure the man understood Vietnamese because the colonel made absolutely no indication that he heard or that he intended to cooperate. Anders knew this was going to be tough. He bound the man's legs swiftly and staked him out in a hollow between two large broad leaf evergreens on a bed of *tranh*. He left the Chinese officer with a series of murderous threats, given in both French and Vietnamese, as he left. For all he knew the man was deaf.

Events moved faster that morning than usual. The green uniformed NVA captain was early. At 0615 he trotted up the path toward the same privy used by the Chinese officer, fifteen minutes early. Bach and Ky had not had time to set themselves; there had been no time to put one of them inside the toilet building. They did the next best thing. They stationed themselves on either side of the door, waiting for him to make his exit after completing his morning evacuations.

The two PRUCs had no more than settled onto their haunches to set themselves for a wait, than the door burst open and the NVA captain bolted out carrying Anders' card in his hand. He had not taken time to do up anything but the top button of his pants, and the two ends of his web trousers belt dangled unclasped. He knew something was amiss and knew to make all haste to raise the alarm that they had had enemy visitors during the night. He was not prepared for the immediacy of the surprise from his enemies.

Ky and Bach sprang from their positions and tackled the astonished opposition soldier bringing him to the ground before he could mount any kind of a struggle. Ky pressed the point of his K bar knife into the man's throat until it began to draw blood. He looked into the captain's excited eyes and whispered hoarsely in the man's native language, "Don't make a move or a sound. I will kill you in a second. You are our prisoner. Cooperate and you live. Make a noise, and you will be the first to die when the sentries come."

The NVA captain was young, fit, and brave. He was not stupid. He knew that his only chance for survival would have to be initial cooperation and later a delayed escape. He stoically submitted to the application of the gray tape over his mouth, to being roughly turned from supine to prone, and to having his wrists cuffed. He did not make any protest when the handcuffs were applied too tightly by his excited captors and dug cruelly into the flesh of his wrists. Bach and Ky kept crouched, duck walked, and crawled into the bushes. They were not seen by the sentries. Later those unhappy men, on whose watch the kidnappings had occurred, would be given an opportunity to explain to the camp's political commissar and to the committee of the commissar and the officers' and the enlisted representatives how that escape could have happened.

Anders met them a few meters into the bushes almost giving the two PRUCs heart attacks. He led them back to the Chinese colonel's tethering stake. To the soft little man's credit, he had managed to uproot the stake halfway. His reward was a pair of swift, hard, educational kicks from Bach and Ky. He ceased struggling immediately.

The GVN men and their prisoners started off at a brisk pace south down the valley putting distance between themselves and the camp.

Their progress was slowed by the NVA officer's feigned inability to move as fast as the rest. Ky instructed him in the error of his ways by chopping the ridge of his shins with the back of his field knife making little nicks in the skin and causing a great deal of pain. He put the point of the knife on the captain's lower right eyelid and said, "If you hold us up, I will put out this eye. You will then run for all you are worth. Slow us down again, and I will cut off both ears. You will be able to run then. Don't tempt me." The prisoner gave them no more trouble.

At 0700 sharp, they heard a shrill horn-whistle sound back in the camp. Instinctively, they dove for cover. They heard nothing else. The captain looked amused, and Anders took a clue from that and said, "It must be their wake up signal. Fits the time. Let's not panic." They ran on.

It became apparent that the Chinese officer, stoical as he was, would not be able to maintain anything like their present pace, threats and batteries notwithstanding. He was breathing in heaving gasps. His face was violaceous, and sweat soaked his hair, face, and blouse.

"We have to stop," Anders finally acknowledged. "This one can't take it." The NVA officer looked at his counterpart with contempt.

They were still moving in an out of the edge of the trees abutting the escarpment. It was still all but unclimbable, but seemed to be gradually losing height. "Let's crash in here," the PRU/O told his men.

They removed the Chinese man's mouth tape so he could gulp in air. He acted as if he had been drowning and had just come up for the last time. He appeared panicky, short of breath, and frightened of the thundering of his heart more than anything his enemy captors might do. The two prisoners finally settled down. Both had been fully informed that they would be tortured and killed. The Chinese man tried to resign himself to his inevitable fate, and the Vietnamese communist secretly plotted.

As the men caught their breaths, they heard a shot in the distance from the direction of the communist military base. It was followed by a pause then three or four more. The NVA man smiled with his eyes and gave Anders a knowing look.

Anders spoke directly to him, "Right. They know. We still have you, remember? You die as soon as they get to us. Don't forget that. You have as much at stake as we do at this point. It is not in your best interest to attract their attention."

"Let's get out of here, boss," said Ky. He was sweaty and tired from packing the rucksack of heroin bricks and his weapons, but he did not want to tarry there a second longer than was essential. Anders nodded.

Bach dragged the Chinese to his feet. He was a little pale and wobbly. Bach looked into the near future and knew that it was going to be very tough to get this one anywhere. Ky tried to help the NVA officer up but was rebuffed. The man's eyes glittered with defiance. He glared at Ky, whom he regarded as his tormentor. Ky kicked him into motion.

They were able to travel for two days before seeing evidence of the dragnet that they knew had to be out for them. They did not take any chances of entering a village. It was safer to regard all of the collections of huts as belonging to the communists, and statistically were not far from the mark. The escarpment had dwindled down to a low rise by the middle of the second day, and they were able to veer east. By compass readings they were sure that they were almost due west of the ARVN Strategic Hamlet, but had no good idea of how far west. As they spied on the villages, they saw openly carried weapons, clearly of Russian and Chinese manufacture. The heightened state of readiness in the villages and the increase in the number of patrols gave the PRUCs a cautionary presumption that they were the cause.

The Chinese officer collapsed at 1830 on the second day after he had been captured. He wheezed and coughed blood tinged foamy phlegm. His skin color was dusky gray. His legs were swollen.

"It's his heart. It's failing; I know the signs," Bach said. He told of his old grandmother's cardiac condition as the reason why he recognized the condition; the signs were both obvious and ominous.

"We can't stop, and we can't leave him here alive. He'll be the death of us all," Ky said without anger. He was just stating the obvious.

"You're right. I have something of a plan. I think it's better than nothing. We can build a travois or a stretcher. Captain Linh can carry one end, and the rest of us can spell each other off," Anders proposed.

We'll have to undo the *Bo Doi's* hands. I don't like that. It gives him the opportunity to make a try at an escape. That's all we'd need now," Ky pointed out, ever the pragmatist.

"We can tie his hands to the poles of the litter or to the Chinaman, and there will always be two of us to watch him."

"And no one to run point."

"I don't see any other way. We'll have to compromise." Anders and the others had been speaking English in hopes of preventing their prisoners from understanding their concerns.

Anders prevailed. They made a makeshift litter rather than making a travois because of the inevitable tracks that would be made by dragging the travois along. The NVA rubbed his wrists with passionate vigor as soon as the cuffs were removed. His hands were swollen, discolored, and stiff, and the wrists were scraped raw from the metal clasps. He shook his hands to get normal feeling back. Initially, his fingers tingled and gave him the feeling of having stuck them in an electric socket. He did not look grateful.

Anders tied the man's wrists to each other with a twenty-four centimeter thong between them then to a tie around the Chinese officer's neck as he lay gasping on the litter. None of the men knew enough to raise the Chinese communist's head to help his breathing, and had no way to do it if they had known. They set off again. All of them were extremely tired and dehydrated. The mountains had few streams or springs available to them at this latitude.

On the fourth day, and after nearly forty-eight hours of being awake, Anders saw an NVA patrol, almost twenty men, coming their way. The way they moved, it was clear that they were tracking the PRU team and their prisoners, and that they were well-trained and cautious professionals, probably an elite unit. Anders knew it was only a matter of time before they were discovered; so, he told his men, "Our only chance is to set up an ambush to get them before they get us.'

"What about the prisoners?" Bach wanted to know. He could not see having one of the three of them out of action to guard the two men.

"I'll tie them up. We can leave them here and come back when we can. The big old stump is a pretty good landmark," Ky offered. His teammates nodded their agreement. The stump had been struck by lightening sometime in the distant past, and it stood up like a black obelisk among the other verdant green living trees.

The prisoners were trussed and taped. They were staked, hand and foot, to prevent them from moving effectively even to draw attention to themselves. Finally, the three captors stacked dead branches over them as camouflage, the best they could do on short notice.

Anders knew that they could not stand off the NVA unit in anything approaching an open firefight. It would have to be a guerrilla tactic series of traps of individual soldiers, an ambuscade of attrition. And they would not have very long to do it. As soon as the shooting started, they could expect to have additional communist troops reinforce this unit; and besides, the Chinese colonel would not survive long lying out there in the woods.

The three of them spread out widely knowing that each of them was on his own, but that he depended on the stealth, courage, and skill of the other two. The tension was palpable.

Anders caught his first victim as he walked past where Anders had been hiding behind a large tree trunk. He leaped off a high tree branch onto the back of his second. Both men had died without raising the slightest alarm. Ky and Bach had similar initial success.

However, it was impossible for such luck to hold. Soon, the remaining thirteen NVA became aware of the thinning of their ranks; and they moved closer to one another and became sharply security conscious. They began to walk in a single file, a standard three meters apart with each man responsible for a field of observation and fire. Each man in line alerted to one side of the trail, alternating responsibility down the line. The point man concentrated straight ahead. The arrangement could have come straight out of a US marine manual and was employed by patrols on march in hostile jungle country not only to prevent ambush from any direction, but also to avoid the soldier behind shooting his patrol mate in front. The rearmost soldier was responsible for the 270° arc behind him. Anders concentrated on him.

He set up his trap at a point where the trail made a sharp veer to the left. He waited tensely in a hiding place in the foliage beside the trail on the right until twelve of the thirteen enemy soldiers had passed. The last man had the wearying task of turning about and looking behind him every few seconds. It was hot and the humidity was enervating. Anders watched until his quarry paused ever so briefly to wipe off the sweat running down into his eyes. Anders sprang like a panther and bowled the NVA regular over and into the tall grass on the opposite side of the trail. He plunged his big combat knife into the terrified man's throat effectively stopping any vocalization. He swiftly dragged the corpse into the tall bushes and ran into the woods keeping parallel to the company of NVA on the trail.

M-16 automatic fire came first. Although it was hard to locate sounds exactly in the reverberating wind currents of the deep forest, he was sure that it had to be either Ky or Bach firing from the front of the column of men. AK-47 chatter followed close on the heels of the first volley from the US guns. Anders moved closer to the jungle track.

Now there was an all-out firefight. Suddenly two green uniforms burst through the trees on an all out run in the direction of the M-16 fire evidently trying to outflank whoever was pinning them down. Anders stood and fired off two short bursts of three rounds each. He killed one of the green uniforms immediately, but his second burst thudded harmlessly into the maze of trees. The second green uniform dropped defensively.

The fight was furious now, only thirty or forty meters away. The noise of grenade and submachine gun fire reverberated through the forest and ricochets zinged about in the trees. Anders was angry at being stymied by the one soldier he had been unable to hit, and whose exact whereabouts were uncertain. He could not stay where he was. He had to know where the other man was hiding. He had to get him and get into the main fray if his own men were not to be worn down, surrounded, and extinguished.

Anders plunged, darted, and dived in and around the dense underbrush, drawing an excited fire each time he moved. He was getting something of a fix of his opponent's position in his own mind. He crawled in a wide circle through the matted leaves on the rain forest floor until he judged that he was behind his enemy. That was if the other man had been obliging enough to stay put.

Men crashed into the forest foliage shouting and firing as they run. Anders could not see them, only hear them. They distracted his attention.

They also distracted the attention of the hiding NVA soldier who, like his American enemy, had no idea whether the runners were friend or foe or when they might burst in on him. He was smart enough to keep moving as his American foe was doing.

The two men literally crashed into each other in the forest in a heart stopping collision. They were both moving swiftly from around the back of a huge tree when they impacted. They were too close to use their guns, and neither had a knife in hand. They dropped their weapons and began a life and death hand to hand struggle. Anders was bigger, but his enemy was faster. It took a few minutes of wrestling, biting, and clawing before his *Tây Sơn Võ S›* training took over. He directed deadly strikes with his feet, elbows, knees, and hands at the NVA. The North Vietnamese was no slouch at martial arts either, and he threw everything he had into the death struggle.

He was no match for Anders. Tired as he was, Anders' far superior strength and martial arts skill soon showed. He was pounding his game opponent into a nerveless pulp. Somehow, the man continued to be able to retaliate. His face looked like ground meat, and his right arm hung uselessly at his side. Somewhere he produced a knife and swept it in wide arcs at Anders' face.

Anders let a sweep of the knife pass from right to left. As the arm brought the blade back in a sweep in the opposite direction, Anders threw a thunderous block with the side of his clenched rock like fist and connected with the NVA's elbow. There was a sickening crunch and a snap. The man's second arm flailed as uselessly as the right one. Still he lashed out with a variety of kicks. But they were coming slower and less accurately. Both men knew that the end was near. If Anders had had time to think about it, he would have admired the gamecock fighting him. He would have noted that his enemy's eyes showed no fear, only determination. But it would have made no difference.

Anders swept his adversary's feet out from under him landing him supine. Like a swooping eagle, Anders dropped from his full height and drove a flattened knife fist like a pile driver into the man's exposed anterior throat. The force of the blow shattered the hyoid bone and larynx and jammed one carotid artery back against the rigid spinal column. It was over, but Anders did not recognize the man's movements as death throes. He wound his powerful right arm across his own chest and swung it like a great hammer onto the inferior corner of the Vietnamese's right mandible. The jawbone dislocated from the temporomandibular joint, and the man's first two vertebrae separated neatly off each other and sheared across the lowermost portion of the brainstem and uppermost segment of the cervical spinal cord. Death was instantaneous and mercifully abrupted the strangling from the soft tissue injury to the front of the neck. Anders had earned a red belt out there in the jungle, but no one would ever know it.

He gulped in several draughts of the heavy air and took a moment to get back under control. He scrabbled around in the brush and found his weapons. The firing was still erupting not far from him, but was more sporadic now. He made his way stealthily toward the fight. He could make out NVA green uniforms pinned down in a close cluster by firing coming from two separate locations on the other side of the trail. He was behind the NVA and facing his own men. He was more vulnerable to M-16 friendly fire than to the enemy at the moment; so, he kept his head way down.

He cracked a branch, and one of the NVA enlisted men whirled to see the source. Anders threw his K bar knife and hilted it in the left side of the man's chest. He could now see no more than four or five enemy left. None of them were aware of him. He lifted his submachine gun up and laid a withering fire into the backs of the unsuspecting communist soldiers who were no more than seven or eight meters from him. They fell like tenpins. One tried to turn to fire, but in so doing exposed himself to Ky across the way. His torso splatted with a dozen direct hits. He was Swiss cheesed from front and back and died with the rest of his squad.

"That all of them, boss?" queried Ky from his side of the skirmish line.
"I think so. You guys all right?"

"I took one in my left leg. Minor as far as I can tell," Ky responded.

"I'm all right," Bach called. All three of them were keeping their heads down in case there were NVAs out there playing possum.

"Finish them off. We can't take any chances. And we have to get out of here," Anders ordered. He was so tired and spent that he was not sure he would be able to get up. He felt like he was getting old.

Very cautiously, the three of them went from man to man checking carotid pulses, administering an occasional coup de grace, and severing trophy ears. Anders killed one wounded man. It was not a time for charitable action.

"Get their weapons," he ordered. Ky and Bach were already doing so; he might have saved his breath.

They collected as much of the NVA's armamentarium as they could in the cramped time frame afforded them and blew them up with C-4 set off with a grenade. They each swigged a drink, the last of their water, and headed back to gather in their prisoners. They expended more time than they wanted in finding the big black stump. They were surprised at how many black stumps there could be in a forest. Finally, however, they found the two miserable captives. The Chinese lieutenant colonel looked like death warmed over.

"I don't know if I'm up to this," said Ky. He spoke in all candor.

"You're not. Bach and I will carry ching-chong here. You just trot nice Captain Linh along in head of you. We need to move out, but I don't suppose it will be very fast. "Up we go," Anders spoke as he hefted his end of the improvised litter.

Gunfire erupted behind them, well behind them. They dared not hesitate but kept moving. They knew they could not be far from the ARVN village and relative safety now. "Must be some of our guys, don't you think, Anders?" asked Bach.

It was impossible to distinguish the kinds of rifles being fired. There were occasional whumps of mortars and explosions from grenades, presumably from both sides. All three men were glad the enemy was otherwise occupied for the moment. The NVA captain clung to the hope that the fight meant the imminent approach of his own people.

Shortly, the ragtag exhausted men were surrounded by ARVN soldiers. Had they been the other side, Anders and his PRUCs could not have summoned up the strength to fight them. As it was, the NCO was overtly hostile to them, especially to Anders. The combat weary

Swedish American did not like the reception, but was too far gone in weariness to fight or protest.

Tandrosz Szabo and an ARVN colonel and a US special forces doctor met the team and their ARVN escort at the edge of the village's security perimeter. "Hello, Bergstrom," Szabo said matter-of-factly. "Didn't expect to see you here again."

"On your orders; not my choice, sir, believe you me," was as much as Anders could muster. The doctor directed the triage of the sick and wounded, including Ky; otherwise, no one talked.

An ARVN private first class led Anders and Bach to where they could clean up and put on fresh clothing. Others disposed of their irreparable jungle attire, and still others confiscated their weapons. Both PRUCs were too tired to notice. They slept on the floor and were glad of the accommodations.

Szabo let them eat breakfast before having Anders brought to him. He let Bach go and sit with Ky in the dispensary. The special forces doctor had skillfully operated on Ky's wounded leg, and everything looked all right at that point. The Chinese prisoner was sitting up in bed looking a thousand percent better. The doctor had worked miracles with some IV diuretics and a little digitalis.

Anders was ushered into Szabo's field office under guard by a pair of the most intimidating Nungs in the entire corps, Anders decided. It seemed peculiar that he should be treated like a POW, but he did recall that their last parting had been less than cordial. He presumed that the success of his mission—the coup of bringing in the two major prisoners—would set all of the ill feeling aright, and he would be able to get back to H'Klois' village or at least back to the Hue' PRU compound in short order.

He was only partly right.

"Sit," ordered Szabo.

The Nungs shoved Anders into a seat facing their boss across a rough table. "Good, now we can talk. I don't like you, Bergstrom. I think you did a good job on this assignment, but you are a loose cannon; and The Company can't afford wild men like you, not now while the US is getting ready to pull out." Anders lifted his eyebrows in surprise. He had heard the same thing only recently. He tried to remember where.

"Read this." Szabo slid a manila envelope across to Anders. Anders reached for it and felt both Nungs tighten their grips on his shoulders. He moved with circumspection and extracted the single sheet of heavy bond paper from the already opened envelope. It was on

CORDS letterhead stationary and was addressed to Tandrosz Szabo and was headed: Re: Anders Bergstrom, contract agent, and signed, Cleveland Howard, POIC, Thau Thien Province. It was dated 13 November, 1972, two days before. Anders screwed up his brow and read the body of the terse message.

> Consider this an all points bulletin for the arrest of contract agent Bergstrom. He is to be delivered to CORDS headquarters, Hue', upon arrest, to answer charges of commission of atrocities, for behavior prejudicial to good order and cooperation with our ARVN allies, and for insubordination. He is to be considered armed and dangerous. If he resists, he is to be dealt with by maximum prejudice. If he is arrested alive, he is to be shackled and incarcerated at all times.

Anders was astounded. He could not think of anything to say, and for the moment, could not even come up with a question. The arrest order was so strange and foreign that Anders had to reread it to convince himself that it really applied to him.

In answer to the questions on his face, Szabo said dismissively, "Don't look innocent, and don't look so surprised. Did you think you could barge in here and tell us how to run the psy-ops business? Did you think you could abuse and humiliate a whole platoon of Marvin Arvins and get away with it? Especially in this critical stage of the Vietnamization process? Have you no sense at all!? You are a snot-nosed kid who has been given far too much rope so far. As predicted, you hanged yourself with it. Get out of here." He nodded to the Nungs.

"One question," Anders asked with more calm than he felt.

"One," retorted Szabo who was starting to get up to go.

"I don't know anything about 'Vietnamization' or an American pullout. I've been out in the boonies for the whole fall. How about letting me know what's going on."

"Might as well. Nixon and Kissinger have just about negotiated a cease-fire with the gooks. Stopped the bombing on Hanoi and the Trail. They have been transferring all responsibility for the war to Thieu and his bunch in Saigon. Phoenix is just about all *Phung Hoang* now. Word is that the US will pull out of Country in a matter of no more than a few months."

A major event of history had taken place without Anders having any knowledge of it. He was acutely aware of how little affinity for or knowledge of America he had. He had become more Vietnamese than American, and his only tie to his homeland was with the kidnappers, killers, and torturers of Phoenix. Now even that was being cut out from under him. He felt betrayed by his country and by The Company for abandoning their clients after lifting their expectations, and personally by being arrested and jailed after doing their dirty work so well. He allowed the Nungs to shove him off to the tiger cages in the PIC without further comment.

His requests to talk to his men or to see his wife or even to have a cell in which he could stand upright were all denied. He semi-squatted in a filthy cage eating partially rotted vegetables that were thrown in at him and slurped watery rice gruel from a wood bowl that had never been cleaned in its entire existence. The Nungs took perverse pleasure from withholding one of his two daily meals and in inflicting little injuries. If he was not looking, one of them would place a well aimed kick or punch into his back through the bars. They poked him with poles. His body was dotted with small bruises. He was not allowed to change clothes for the six days he was kept in the pestilent coop. They were the same clothes he had worn in the bush on his mission.

During the third and fourth days of his confinement, he was aware that the village was being attacked. His guards abandoned him to take part in the fighting. Anders' greatest fear was that the compound would be overrun by NVA, and he would be found there in a cage. He could imagine the tender mercies of his captors when they came to realize that he was their nemesis, the *con ma da trắng khổng-lồ*.

No one would tell him anything about the attack, but he had to presume that the communists had been beaten back effectively because the routine returned to normal on the fifth and sixth day—bad food, no washing, and surly guards. On the seventh day, he was dragged out of the cage and shackled in irons—neck, wrists, and feet—like a circus gorilla. He was hurried across the compound by four Nung guards who shoved him into a C-46 and accompanied him to Hue' and on to the MACV compound. They released him to a new set of Nungs at the CORDS building. No one spoke or explained matters to Anders. He had not been arraigned or tried. He knew that the provisions of the UCMJ did not apply to him, but he expected some sort of due process. He did not get it.

He was locked up, still shackled, in a cage in the PIC section of the CORDS building, the PIC that did not exist. He did receive his first real meal in seven days that evening and that was heartening even if it had to be fed to him by Nung guards who delighted in spilling hot liquids down his front. He was miserable in every part of his body, but dropped into an immobile sleep from sheer weariness and depression. That night he had a long, vivid, terrifying dream in which the same repulsive black revenant sat on the edge of his bed leaning his chin on his cane and piercing Anders with his penetrating soulless eyes. The specter grinned exposing filed black teeth and a snake's tongue. It laughed at Anders' pain and fear. It's presence was even worse than the bite of the chains or the ache in his empty belly.

Cleve Howard came to see him the next day. He came with a pair of Nungs, but no one else. "Hello, Anders. I trust you are comfortable. You have been naughty, I hear. Our psy-ops people have gone through Company channels to file formal charges, seems you attacked an officer. If that were not enough, I have been subjected to a dressing down of the most serious kind by my superiors regarding your behavior toward the ARVNs. They, in turn, have filed formal charges. The thinking is that you should be tried in a Thau Thien Provincial court and subjected to justice, Vietnamese style. As you no doubt recognize, you do not exist on Company or any other US records. I will show you in a minute.

"I am sorely disappointed in you, my boy. I warned you before, more than once. I am afraid you will have to remain in the PIC lockup until you are handed over to the proper Vietnamese officials. It seems likely that the rest of us will be going out of this lovely and tragic land, and you will be staying. And...in case you had hopes that Lane Duerk would come to your rescue, forget it. He gave the orders. Of course, the CIA will neither confirm nor deny your existence. That's their way, don't you know?"

Anders could do nothing more than look at the POIC with anger. He dared not display fear or depression, both so his psyche could survive; and so, he would not invite additional abuse from the Nungs who were very alert to any sign of weakness.

Howard turned to leave. He snapped his fingers at a sudden flash of memory. "I promised to show you something." He produced an envelope with a document inside, and let Anders read it through the cage bars. "Have a nice day," he said.

> DEATH CERTIFICATE
> Karl Oscar Isaacson
> DOB: 4/13/1950

DOD: 4/16/1966
Cause of Death: Exsanguination due to trauma including stab wounds to the heart, liver, and spleen.
Circumstances: Victim of murder, Manila, PI.
Place of Internment: Manila Public Cemetery, Plot 1432, Section 18, Site 4

Anders stared at the document in disbelief for a moment. He had the feeling that someone had walked on his grave. The full impact that he was a nonperson came only after his visitors had left.

CHAPTER 39

Nor has ROLLING THUNDER program of bombing the North either significantly affected infiltration or cracked the morale of Hanoi. There is agreement in the intelligence community on these facts...Despite these efforts, it now appears that the North Vietnamese-Laotian road network will remain adequate to meet the requirements of the communist forces in South Vietnam.
Robert S. McNamara, Secretary of Defense, memorandum to President Lyndon S. Johnson, October, 14, 1967.

(The mood in North Viet Nam after 27 months of bombing was one of) resolute stoicism with a considerable reservoir of endurance still untapped...(The American bombing had) significantly eroded the capacities of North Vietnam's industrial and military bases. These losses, however, have not meaningfully degraded North Vietnam's material ability to continue the war in South Vietnam.
Series of three CIA memoranda issued May, 1967

T he dream had just started again, the hairy black nightmare visiting in his room, when the guards banged on his cage to awaken him. Anders shook himself to half wakefulness in the perpetual partial light of the interrogation holding cage that had been his home for ten days.

"Visitor," the Nung announced laconically.

Wondering, Anders forced his eyes to adjust. It might have been a nightmare. It might as well have been a nightmare. He saw Jean-Luc DuParrier coming toward him. The Frenchman was dressed in a handsome black suit with all the proper appointments, looking as if he had just come from a diplomatic affair.

Anders waited.

"*Bonjour*, my friend," Jean-Luc said jovially, ignoring the surroundings.

Anders waited.

"I see that you have taken advantage of the free rent of the bachelors' quarters," Jean-Luc said with an self-congratulatory expression appreciative of his subtle ironic humor.

Anders nodded slightly, then waited to see why this snake had come to see him. It couldn't be anything good.

"Don't feel like talking, my old friend? I can see that you are tired." He chuckled. "I won't keep you a but a minute." As if Anders could go anywhere.

"What is it Jean-Luc?" Anders asked wearily.

"Not so...full of vigor? Not so feisty as when we last met, my friend?" He was grinning, leering, more accurately.

Anders started to turn away.

"I don't know what will come of this sad affair, my friend; The Company is quite a forgiving employer on many things; I think you know. But I do know one thing for certain; the situation has changed for you. And I know one more thing; your circle of friends has narrowed drastically. You really must be more careful in your choices."

Anders gave him the finger. Jean-Luc laughed with genuine delight, seeming to savor some secret satisfaction. "Until next time, then, my friend," DuParrier said in parting.

Anders watched his enemy turn to leave, and could not suppress a sense of dread at Jean-Luc's ominous hint. He presumed the Frenchman had reference to Dung's death. Anders had no illusions, Nguyen Van Dung had undoubtedly been listed in the weekly five o'clock follies report as an addition of one to the body count. He harbored a dark suspicion that Jean-Luc might have been making reference to something else. Maybe he was just trying to mess up his mind. Jean-Luc was like that.

Another day passed. Anders now had a hard time telling the passage of time, day from night. Hours, nearly whole days, were going by without seeing or speaking to anyone except the Nungs who threw his food at him. He was losing weight. He felt disoriented. Four Nungs strode purposefully into the room armed with their favorite Sten guns and menaced him with them as the most brutish of the jailers unlocked and opened his cage door. They prodded him out with their gun barrels then stood back from him several feet as if he was a threat there in his shackles. The wrist and ankle cuffs had gnawed circles of raw flesh that were beginning to fester.

He was led to the side of a building in the rear of the MACV compound and left standing on a wide sidewalk with a cinderblock wall behind him. It dawned on him that they were going to execute him. This was a firing squad. The idea did not arouse him. He was too tired. So this was the way it would end, and before his twenty-fourth birthday. The Nungs did not even give him the minimal decency of a hood. He rose up to full height, determined at least to die well.

The Nungs busied themselves with equipment that Anders could not see for sure, hoses of some sort. Then two of them turned water hoses on him full blast, almost bowling him over. He had to set his legs in a tight karate' stance to avoid being knocked down by the strong force of the water flow. The stream of clean water stung his raw and abraded skin, but it felt wonderful. He could feel layers of verminous filth dissolving away and wanted to shout an exaltation at the pleasure of it, but was afraid that they would stop if they got the idea that what they were doing was anything but another indignity and minor torture. The Nungs were laughing like children at Anders' attempts to protect his face and genitalia from the harsh water stream.

"Is there something in The Company manual that requires executees to be clean before the firing squad does its work?" Anders asked himself, aware that his thinking had become consistently paranoid. The Nungs tossed him a bar of crude soap and stopped the water jets as he scraped himself clean. They giggled when he winced as the soap stung open skin sores. When he had covered himself with foamy lather and had gone over every inch of his body with the industrial grade cleanser, the guards hosed him down again.

One of them tossed him a towel, a heavy and rough but clean and absorbent terry cloth rectangle, that had been cast off from the officer's quarters in the compound. He vigorously toweled himself off feeling progressively human as he did. Perhaps this was the worst punishment yet—to let him think something good was going to happen then line him up to be shot with a renewed feeling of disappointment being his last thought.

Two men brought out a chair, and gestured for him to sit. One of the men carried barber clippers and razors. They seemed benign; so, Anders warily took the proffered seat. The younger of the two men then very rapidly gave Anders a marine style haircut including a nickless close shave. The older cleaned up the mass of head and face hair that had been shaved. Anders looked like a new person except for all the scars and bruises. A Nung guard tossed him an X-large size US Air Force jump suit. Anders slipped into it, glad to be covered. It was short in the sleeves and legs, but he guessed that he looked quite presentable. The guards indicated by gestures for Anders to extend his hands for handcuffing, and he complied without offering resistance. He remained barefoot which did not bother him because his soles had been toughened by layers of calluses from his days in the boonies. He gratefully noted that they did not add leg shackles.

He and his guards boarded a C-46 at the Phu Bai Airport. Already on board were Hugo Bartini, the current ROIC and former chief of station in Nicaragua whom Anders recognized; Cleve Howard, the POIC; Sylvia Chin, The Farm instructor and Hue' PRU/O; his old teacher and friend Nguyen Hai Truong; and Tring Van Dong, his acquaintance from The Farm and his fellow PRU/O in Thau Thien. Anders was seated in the back of the plane between two guards, and none of the others attempted conversation with him. He was strongly aware that he had become *persona non grata*. Since no one would communicate with him, he had to deduce that they were on their way to Saigon. Since he was in handcuffs, he further deduced that the purpose of the gathering and the flight was to conduct his Company trial. It seemed overly elaborate to him.

The flight touched down at Tan Son Nhut. Anders took in the contrast between his recent tiger cage, and even his compound headquarters, with the relative opulence of the airport and its residences for American officers. The officers' quarters had yards, hot water, air conditioning, hooch maids to provide starched uniforms every day; and the compound was replete with a large PX, a well-stocked liquor store, and a fine large officer's club. The Company passengers were loaded into an a windowless armored personnel van, and driven to the First Precinct Headquarters Building behind The Bunker in downtown Saigon. Anders sat across from Truong and Dong, who, for the most part, stoically avoided eye contact with him. As they were filing out, Anders between his ever present Nungs, Truong surreptitiously grasped Anders' hand and gave it a brief squeeze. Dong laid his hand on Anders' forearm in what would have seemed accidental to anyone observing, but he also gave a small comradely squeeze. The two gestures were enough to let Anders know he still had friends.

The Nungs separated Anders from the others as soon as they entered the police headquarters and went through security checks. The others went for lunch, and he was taken to an unmarked office containing a table and four chairs, all bolted to the floor. After a short delay, Lane Duerk, Hugo Bartini, Miss Nguyen, and Cleve Howard walked in. The Nungs saluted and stepped aside but raised their Stens in a more vigilant stance now that the senior CIA agents occupied space near the dangerous prisoner.

"Take off the cuffs," Duerk ordered. The Nungs were slow to comply, wary of the big man with the bad reputation whom they had abused. "Go ahead; it's all right," he repeated. Anders offered Miss Nguyen his seat, and she accepted. The other three seats were occupied by the agents which left Anders standing to face them. The Nungs were gratified by the improved targeting of their prisoner.

"Well Mr. Bergstrom. You seem to have gotten yourself into a mess. You have made some enemies, I fear. Prominent ones."

"Evidently," Anders said matching Duerk's gaze without flinching. He had decided to go down with dignity or defiance, whichever served him best. The charges were baloney, and they knew it. He had no intention of giving any of them any satisfaction. He certainly was not going to act guilty, and he refused to cower or cringe. He had had enough of that.

"Mr. Howard, here, neglected to include the charges from a marine Force Recon gunny whom you impeded; threatened, I believe was the exact charge. That, added to the attack on our esteemed agent, DuParrier, and the charges filed by the Marvins, make you a criminal."

Anders rolled his eyes back, no longer caring that his contempt for the lot of them showed prominently. It was an almost involuntary response that was not lost on Duerk. Being accused of being a criminal by Jean-Luc DuParrier was like charging a rooster for the fox's raid on a hen house.

"It would be hard for me to choose which charge coming from which source would be the most hypocritical," Anders offered bitterly.

Duerk gave a little smile of agreement. "My favorite bard said it well for you, 'There's small choice in rotten apples,' but their actions are not in question here. I advise you not to take this lightly. Having three armies and a paramilitary organization on your case puts you at a very serious disadvantage. There is not a single person who would protest if you were to disappear, Anders, not one. However, there may be a way for you to be useful. By that I mean to yourself by staying alive and able to function outside a Vietnamese prison and to The Company by performing duties to which you seem to be uniquely suited."

For the first time Anders saw a glimmer of hope. He had never really been able to understand the labyrinthine minds of his CIA mentors and superiors, and this time was no exception.

"Shall I go on, Anders, or would you rather that we simply turn you over the Vietnamese to serve the ends of their justice? It would be a serious misjudgment on your part to think that I would shy away from allowing you such a fate. I echo the man from Stratford-on-Avon in Titus Andronicus, 'Tut, I have done a thousand dreadful things as willingly as one would kill a fly.'"

"Go on, by all means," Anders said. He had nothing to lose as far as he could see.

"All right., you're being sensible for once. Maybe the PIC concept does have merit. Here are the conditions. You work for us in the countryside exclusively and with your own small team. You no longer have charge of anything. You do what we say, when and how we say it. Any questions so far?"

Anders shook his head.

"You don't go into the city. You don't have contact with the acquaintances you have made—like The Mandarin and his family or that judo instructor and his school. You stay away from the university. Any problem with that?"

"No, sir." It was better than prison, especially a Vietnamese one.

"You don't molest the ARVNs or Company people, no matter what they do—nobody died and left you a judgeship. In fact, you keep well away from them except to deliver packages when we tell you to. You continue to keep your mouth shut. You still with me, Bergstrom?"

"Yes, sir."

"Now comes the real hooker. Americans are going to be scarce as hen's teeth in this country in a matter of no more than a few months. It's, what, February, no, the last of January, now. By the end of April the American presence will be reduced to a handful of caretakers. You can take that tidbit to the bank. But you, Mr. Bergstrom, will stay here doing what you do. If you get caught, there is no one to turn to. You will report to these nice men here, Mr. Bartini, and Mr. Howard who are officially part of the State Department diplomatic mission as of a week ago.

You will do your work for the *Phung Hoang* since there is no longer an American presence in the communist interdiction business. You will no longer be paid by your benevolent CIA. Instead, the Republic of Viet Nam will pay you as a mercenary. I hope you get the drift. That is your position. When the bulk of the Americans leave; you stay. Since I think this war is going to go on forever, you should be able to look forward to active employment until you die." He paused for Anders to respond.

"Lesser of evils. I'll do it. Nothing much in The World for me anyway. Do I get to work with my same team?"

"Absolutely. No one can fault you for your efficiency in carrying out Phoenix work. You get whatever you need to do that with your new set—the *Phung Hoang* people. I have a sneaking hunch that The Company will continue to make its contribution to the prosperity of the work here, sub rosa, of course. That reminds me. I hear they call you the 'white giant ghost.' I suggest you work on the 'ghost' aspect in preference to the other two adjectives. So far as the United States of America and the Central Intelligence Agency are concerned, it would be best if you were downright invisible."

"I like that, too. How about getting rid of the guards? I think you can consider yourself and the people of the armed forces of republic to be safe from me at this point, don't you?"

"Indeed, I do." Duerk gave a set of crisp orders in Mandarin, and the four Nungs slung their guns and left the room.

"Finally, then, Anders, try not to take it all so seriously. Everything seems to work out as you have seen today. Don't worry overmuch; nobody lives forever. I like the way Shakespeare said it in Macbeth:

> All our yesterdays have lighted fools
> The way to dusty death. Out, out
> Brief candle!
> Life's but a walking shadow;
> A poor player that struts and frets
> His hour upon the stage.

"Now, lets get to the meeting with the rest of our state department diplomats; what do you say?" Everyone was used to Duerk's fondness for sarcasm and for Shakespeare, and no one had anything to add. Shakespeare's view, as quoted by Duerk, was not much different from their own.

There were wry grins from all the men as they left the meeting with the young man who had been brought in shackled. Anders' smile had more to do with his appreciation of the hypocrisy of it all than with his newly regained freedom and status, such as it was. Only Miss Nguyen kept her face inscrutable and her thoughts to herself.

As the agents filed in to sit down for the official meeting, Duerk told the Thau Thien contingent to regard their discussion in the distant room as a closed subject, and the incidents that preceded it as forgotten. He mentioned lunch and that he did not appreciate the dyspepsia he got from unpleasant discussions over meals. "'Unquiet meals make ill digestions'," he said, and "'We'll pluck a crow together' and we'll do it in peace," as he left them to address the assembled CIA employees, unable to resist a couple of parting Shakespearean quotes.

Duerk conducted a brief meeting with the agents from all over Viet Nam who were going to stay on after the American force officially departed. There were men and women from each military corps who would change hats to wear innocent white State Department chapeaus. A little shuffling was required to ensure that different faces were available in the various areas. Anders was permitted what appeared to be full fellowship by attending the meeting, but there was little inclination by the others toward conversation with him.

When the meeting ended, Truong brushed past and pressed a scrap of paper with his address and telephone numbers on it. All he said was, "Keep in touch."

Tring Van Dong and Sylvia Chin gave him a nod.

Cleve Howard acted as if the arrest and PIC incarceration had never occurred, and they were still something like old pals. "Hey, look, Anders. We'll still be working together. No hard feelings. Life's full of twists and turns. I try to remember the billiard player's view:

> The damned billiard player,
> Is forced to play
> On a cloth untrue,
> With a crooked cue,
> And elliptical billiard balls.

"That's W.S. Gilbert, I can't take credit. But that's the real world. Try not to let it upset you. And it should be 'ellipsoidal' if you want to be technical about it. Be seeing you."

Anders' repatriation back into The Company fold was not to end on an upbeat note despite his restoration to freedom of sorts. The nadir of his experience thus far in Viet Nam, and in his life, occurred when he got back to the PRU compound and was finally able to talk to Tran.

"You look less terrible than I expected, brother," said Tran with solicitude evident in his voice.

"I look great in comparison to a day ago. I was filthy and smelled

769

putrid. I had been eating stuff that would gag a maggot. The Saigon station chief took me out for a French dinner last night in Saigon. Life has picked up considerably. How are you?"

"Fine. Just fine. All of us are fine. We were worried about you," Tran said nervously. It was not lost on Anders.

"What's going on. What's up?"

"Nothing, my friend. I'm just relieved that you're back. The POIC sent word that the PRU would be broken up and each of the small teams would be autonomous. You, Ky, Bach, and I will work together without having to mess with anyone else. That can only be good. Why should I be upset?"

"Who said anything about being upset?" Anders asked.

Tran looked away too quickly and too obviously. He had betrayed himself; Anders knew his friend well enough to be sure of the subtle change, the intensity of his feelings. Perhaps a bystander would have missed the significance of the motion and expression, but it was a glaring signal, a flag, to Anders.

"Tran, what is it? I know there's something. Please." Tran hung his head. Anders was worried now.

Tran's lips were erased into a grim straight line. He willed Anders to stop asking. He said, "For your own good, brother, don't ask again. Don't try to get me to speak of it. It is better left alone." He was shaken. Anders felt a shiver. He could not imagine what could be so bad that Tran could not even speak of it.

"Is it Ky?" Anders asked dreading the answer.

"No, not Ky. Please, Anders."

"Bach?" The wily sapper could not be dead. He couldn't. When Dung had died, something of Anders had perished with him. He was not prepared to cope with something terrible happening to Bach. Not now when he was so weakened by his ordeal of incarceration.

Anders looked disconsolately at Tran, almost pleading.

"Not Bach," Tran said. His voice was scarcely a whisper. "Not Bach." His head was down, and his shoulders were slumped.

Anders took his old friend by his shoulders. "Tell me," he said softly.

Tran took a deep breath and steeled himself. "I told you not to ask, Anders. It can do no good. But you insist."

"Go on."

"I will start from the beginning." He related his experiences while Anders and the other PRUC friends were in the bush, and he was the operations leader at the compound. The pace of arrests had increased drastically. There was little care to preserve even the appearance of police action. Many of the so-called VCSs Tran had detained or had killed were obviously nothing more than people who were victims of old vendettas or of extortions. Some were silenced because of what they knew about the regime at large or about a local employee of the *Phung Hoang* Program, including not a few who knew what was going on in the program itself and could point an accusing finger when the inevitable communist takeover occurred.

"That's terrible, but I think we all knew that from the beginning," said Anders. "I can't believe you are that upset about the program."

"Please, Anders...Allow me to finish," Tran said. Anders was almost sorry he had pushed his friend. A deep gut part of him did not want to know what would come next.

Tran continued his narrative. "I was assigned to go with Sylvia Chin. I believe you know her." Anders nodded. "We spent a week in Hue' rounding up people you would never have dreamed could be considered enemies of the republic—Bonzes, professors, high school teachers, civil servants—dozens of them."

Anders was getting a sick feeling.

"I am afraid that you know some of the people." Anders was afraid that would be the case. His breathing was shallow. It was Anders' turn to look down. He was unable to look at his friend now. His suspicions were growing. He had to fight for control.

"A professor from the university, a Doctor Phan Doi Hang," Anders startled and looked as if to interrupt. "Let me finish." Anders shrank back. "A Master Nguyen, the *sensai* of *Tây Sởn Vỏ Sĩ*." Anders groaned audibly.

"They were taken to the PIC. I do not know what became of them." It was like a hammer blow to Anders.

"I fear that I have worse, my brother. I went to the house of a family...a prominent family of Hue'. I had warrants for all of them. Only the old father and mother, and the daughter and her husband were there; so, I took them," Tran said rushing to finish, to get the foul thing over with. Anders said a prayer that his worst imaginings could not be so.

Tran went on, "Two or three days later, Howard called me back to the CORDS center. He said I was to go with the prisoners and the Nung guards. That DuParrier and Szabo, the terrible ones, were there. We took them out over the sea in a helicopter, way out. Szabo let the Nungs have their way with the girl while her husband and her parents watched. They hurt her. They laughed when they did. Then DuParrier opened the helicopter door and pushed the old mother out. The old man who had not uttered a sound when they beat him and insulted him, cried like a gelded animal. It was the worst sound I ever heard. Then they kicked him until he went out into the night also."

Anders watched his friend's face in stunned silence.

"When the Nungs were done, they pushed the young husband out while the daughter had to watch. They did not have to push her." Tran fell silent. He hung his head in a mixture of resignation and shame. The wound on his soul was bared.

Anders fought for the slightest shred of personal dignity then for a nanometer of hope. "Who?" He whispered. "Say it."

"The Mandarin. His youngest daughter."

Anders Bergstrom had seen everything there was to see, all the horrors of war, all the inhumanities of man against man. He had done things that he would never mention to another human being for as long as he lived. He had thought himself impervious to shock, disgust, guilt, or grief. He had rationalized the life of an irregular soldier and had found a sort of acceptance of what he had seen and done—not a sense of right or of forgiveness, but just acceptance. Until then. Until Tran had painted a word picture of the gaping maw of hell. He dropped his face into the palms of his hands and wept like a baby.

By the end of December, 1972, with the secret Paris Peace talks between Henry Kissinger and Le Duc Tho at a stalemate, US military active strength was reduced to a mere 24,000. 46,000 American soldiers had been killed in action to that point in time. Free World Military Forces (the token UN force) were reduced to 35,000; and the armed force of South Viet Nam, under the 'Vietnamization' program, was increased to over a million men. Just shy of 200,000 of their countrymen comrades in arms had been killed in action to date.

On the fifteenth of January, 1973, American President, Richard M. Nixon, announced a complete halt of all US offensive action against the DRV; and on the twenty-seventh, the peace pact was signed by the United States, COSVN, and the DRV. Melvin Laird, the secretary of Defense, announced the end of the US military draft.

On February 21, 1973 a peace agreement was quietly signed in Laos, and the United States halted its bombing campaign. An official cease-fire went into effect. On March 29, MACV was disbanded; a remaining 590 US POWs were released; and the last American troops were withdrawn from South Viet Nam. The bombing of Cambodia ceased officially on the fourteenth of August under the direction of the new secretary of defense, James Schlesinger. By December 31, 1973, there were fifty members of the US military contingent left in South Viet Nam. For the American public, the Viet Nam War, the long Indochinese nightmare, was over. Five hundred thousand communist soldiers had died to date.

For the Vietnamese, the Second Indochinese War was only intensified; but at least, it was once again their war. There were now an additional hundred thousand Vietnamese men at arms and another thirty thousand GVN soldiers dead at year's end. The rate of South Vietnamese casualties increased to 1000 a month, and the monetary aid from the United States continued in the billions.

The work done by Anders Bergstrom and his team consisting of Le Duc Bach, Phan Duy Ky, and Nguyen Lui Tran was unchanged from 1966 until late 1974 in any significant particular. They did not enter a city for two years; but, under the *Phung Hoang* banner, they continued to kidnap and kill enemies of the Republic of Viet Nam, to bring as much distress to the Ho Chi Minh Trail as was within their power; and they spent the vast majority of their war making effort in Laos. They lived in Laos and took pay from GVN. They existed on no official records and fought in a struggle that was not recognized by the rest of the world. If anything, the on-the-ground clash of arms was even more vicious than it had been before the Americans tucked their tails between their legs and went back to their comfort zone. There were no rules of engagement that gave credence to the Geneva Conventions, no Judeo-Christian nod to the sanctity of civilian lives. It was 'no quarter asked, and none given.'

Anders lived in the Montagnard village with H'Klois, her mother, and his two children as January of 1975 dawned. Tran, Bach, and Ky had similarly settled into marriages and the birth of children. They kept their *Phung Hoang* work physically and emotionally separate from the Montagnard village to protect the townspeople and to ensure themselves a safe haven. By the first week in January the reward for the *con ma da trắng khổng-lồ* had escalated to three million Piastres. Anders did not allow the slightest activity of his team to take place anywhere near their homes.

Purchase, transport, and delivery of heroin had now become almost routine. The routes were safe; everyone concerned was well paid and satisfied. Hmong villages along the route prospered, and Anders and his men watched the numbers climb in their Swiss bank accounts until they were wealthy by any but the most conservative definition.

Anders was content with his life and had grown so accustomed to shooting, fighting, and killing, that he no longer concerned himself about a world where peace was the norm. At twenty-five, although he had a great deal of money somewhere in Europe, he did not project a future that included the need for it. H'Klois and his attractive Amerasian children and their good long house, with all its abundance, were sufficient for his needs.

All of that changed abruptly in January, 1975. The heat from North Viet Nam increased drastically. Phuoc Long Province fell on the sixth. Two days later, the North Vietnamese Politburo ordered the NVA to launch a full cross-border invasion into the south. Anders and his men now encountered brigades of NVA instead of platoons or patrols. They could not move anywhere in the mountains or valleys without seeing an overwhelming concentration of enemy soldiers and a citizenry that was now unequivocally and openly pro-North and defiant of any kind of GVN rule. The PRUCs were effectively closed down, and went into hiding in their village, counting on its obscurity to protect them.

On the seventh of February, a runner came into the Montagnard village with a coded message from *Phung Hoang*. Anders and his men were ordered to travel with all haste to the safe ARVN mountain village for an urgent and critical meeting. The village, the one where he had gotten into so much trouble by reacting to Jean-Luc DuParrier's atrocity, was no more than a two day's foot journey for fit men like his under ordinary conditions. With hiding and taking necessary circuitous routes, Anders, Tran, Ky, and Bach did not get there until evening on the fifth day.

The town bristled with ARVN soldiers. It was guarded by combat seasoned veterans. LLDBs were there in force. It's perimeter was ringed with artillery, and its narrow streets had been widened to support tanks. It had the look of a last outpost, reminiscent of the small village of Dien Bien Phu in the last days of April, 1954 and the first week of 1954 when 16,000 French were beleaguered by 60,000 Viet Minh troops. The fortress mood among the inhabitants was altogether similar to that of the French prior to May 7, 1954 when the First Indochinese War came to a halt. The ARVN soldiers remained disciplined, but made no attempt to hide their conviction that the fall of their country was only a matter of time and not much of that. The senior officers, the men who had summoned Anders, clung to the hope that a mighty coup would turn the tide in their favor.

"Bergstrom," the Vietnamese *Phung Hoang* chief said as soon as Anders entered his headquarters. "I have a surprise for you. In the next room. We have intel that will let us win this war, and you are going to be the instrument of our destiny." Anders could not bring himself to share the man's enthusiasm; it seemed rather brittle to him. He did not care for the opportunity to achieve greatness as this announcement portended. It sounded to him more like another chance to be a dead hero.

He followed his nominal superior into the rear room of the office complex. There he came face to face with Hugo Bartini, whom he had first seen in Nicaragua and last, two years previously when he had been taken to Saigon in chains. In addition Cleve Howard, Lane Duerk, and to his great surprise, Dustin Hauter, the legendary 'Colonel' were present. He knew that something very big was afoot. He began to worry because it appeared that he was to be involved in a prominent way.

"Good evening, Bergstrom," nodded the 'Colonel.' He appeared to be in charge. The other men gave perfunctory greetings as well. Anders shook hands with all the men.

Duerk said, "We haven't got a lot of time. Things are deteriorating, as you can plainly see."

"Going to hell in a hand basket," Cleve Howard interjected.

"That's about it in a nutshell, Anders," the 'Colonel' said. "But we have been working our collective butts off for the past few weeks with our own *Phung Hoang* people, some good, brave LLDBs, and with some crucial information from one of our people close to the PAVN general staff. We think we have a real chance to strike a blow that might just turn this thing around."

"I take it that you think I ought to be involved."

"Good boy, you've broken the code," Howard said.

Duerk then continued the 'Colonel's discussion. "Here it is. I don't need to repeat that nothing we say leaves this room, even to your good men, that clear?"

"Clear."

"We have positive intel that puts General Giap in a village in Laos, just west of the DMZ area, for a meeting of his staff, the Chinese, who have never been in this war," here, every officer rolled his eyes at the well known fact of the People's Army's involvement from the beginning. "and with the head terrorists of the Pathet Lao." It was hard for any of them to dampen their churning anger at this late stage of the war that was supposed to have been won by their side in 1966, nearly ten terrible and frustrating years previously.

Duerk continued, "We know the meeting will take place on the fourteenth of March. Anders, we need your input. Do you think we can mount a plan, using a highly skilled small unit, to blow up the bunch of them by then?"

"I imagine Giap will have an army guarding him. Why not use the air force to bomb him to smithereens or drop an army on him?"

"Because we don't know exactly where this place is, and we would be unlikely to find him before the commotion announced by the air forces' arrival would let him get away. We can't afford to let that happen."

The 'Colonel' spoke. "The highest powers in Washington and Saigon have debated this, as well as have the best people on the ground. We are all in agreement that a small commando force is the only feasible way. The US cannot be seen to be sponsoring an armed force whose goal is assassination. The political heat is just too much."

Anders did not even try to give a care about 'political heat.' The 'Colonel' was speaking of WOM puppeteers pulling strings thousands of miles long who did not care an iota about the human beings on the ground. They were concerned about their reputations, their careers, and about 'political heat.' Anders felt like spitting.

"Your record has been given the greatest scrutiny. You are the only one with the experience, the smarts, and the contacts to be able to pull this off. The locals trust you. I hear that you have a Meo wife, isn't that the case?" The 'Colonel' said unaware that he had insulted H'Klois and her people and had alienated Anders whom he was trying to draw into his plan. He went on, "We have exactly a month. We can get you any kind of weapons or ordinance you need. We can helicopter you within a few klicks of the area of the meeting village. You can do the rest. You can take them out; your whole career proves that. This is not a volunteer thing; this is an order; but we want you to give it everything you've got. What do you say?"

"I heard about us getting in and doing the job. What about getting us out?"

The 'Colonel' frowned a little. Duerk butted in. "We will do everything in our power to get you back. We don't do kamikaze missions; you know us better than that. We are your people. You have to count on us."

Anders' experience with his CIA leaders had not been characterized by undiluted mutual admiration or loyal comradeship; so, he hesitated.

Sensing the young Swede's reluctance, Duerk offered, "You have been here a long time. I know things haven't always been smooth. We've had our differences.'

Anders remembered all too well his stay in the PIC as something more than a 'difference.' "But I'm prepared to guarantee you a transfer out of this country, back to the US if you want, or anywhere else, once you complete the mission," Duerk sweetened the bargain.

The chance for redemption, for a pardon, as it held real appeal. Anders asked, "For my wife and kids, and for my men and their families, too?"

"No problem, son," said Duerk with a face replete with ingratiation. "Consider it done."

Dustin Hauter added, "You have been under yearly contract for, what? ten years?"

'Give or take," answered Anders. He did not 'take' the time he had spent on the detestable *Phung Hoang* payroll or the time he had spent suspended or jailed without pay, but he did not feel like being picayune.

"Well, I think that's not right, son," said Hauter speaking magnanimously. Anders noted that he had gained a lot of fathers that day. "I am prepared to have your status converted to full agent with all of the rights and privileges involved. I'll write it up before you leave the town. How does that sound, son?"

"Better," Anders said. A little future security sounded pretty good right then. "Okay. I'm in. I want it to be my plan. I have to be the boss on the ground, all right?"

"Perfectly," chorused The Company agents.

"What else?" asked the 'Colonel.'

"An authorization to get anything and to go anywhere I want, no hassles. I don't have time to waste if me and my men are going to be in position in five weeks. The fourteenth of March is coming up real fast."

"You've got it," Hauter promised, emphasizing his senior position. "Bartini, get the papers ready; and I mean the field appointment to full agent status included."

"I'm working on it already, sir," Bartini rejoined.

Anders left to get started on the practical details. He was told by the *Phung Hoang* officer that his men were eating in the NCO mess building. When he had left the room, Bartini asked the 'Colonel', "Can you deliver on all those promises?"

"It's the old Arpege promise," Hauter said cynically. "You remember their perfume ad—'Promise them anything, but give them Arpege.'" To Bartini, that sounded more like the real world.

As he headed along the streets crowded with military hardware toward the NCO Club building, a voice called his name from between two parked tanks.

"Over here," it said. Anders recognized the voice, but it took a moment to place it. Truong.

He looked around to make sure that he was not being observed and slid into the dark space. Truong took hold of his arm. "Follow me. I have something important to tell you. We need to be more private."

Anders let his old friend lead him to a small shack off the main road. Inside, it was dark and smelled of *nouc mam*. A mama-san sat by a small cook fire stirring a pot of pho. She offered him a bowl. He was starving; so, he accepted the savory soup gratefully. As he sipped the scalding liquid, Sylvia Chin emerged from the shadows and slipped over beside him.

"Hi," she said. "Nice to see you."

The greeting seemed out of place, more like what would be expected in a diner in The World between high school chums. From Sylvia, despite the circumstances, it was genuine. "Hi, yourself. It's been a while," he said.

"I know. I'm sorry. Orders. You have been the leper for a long time, Anders. It's not fair, but there was nothing any of us could do." It was disconcerting to have his pariah status so candidly stated.

"Couldn't be helped, I guess," Anders replied without rancor.

The mama-san brought plates of *com trang* with pieces of what could pass for meat. Vietnamese enjoy the edible parts of most animals served on a bed of rice. It was best not to inquire too deeply about which parts. Truong, Sylvia, and Anders ate with gusto. It had been a long day for all of them.

Truong spoke as soon as he finished his plate. "Look, Anders. We shouldn't even be here. We would be in big trouble if anyone ever found out that we had talked to you. I owe you. I don't forget that you fought for me when those men in Washington DC insulted me and my people. That meant a lot to me."

"It was nothing," Anders said, and he meant it. The incident seemed like it had happened an eon ago, in another life, in another world.

"Not to me. I can return the favor. I can't tell you where I heard it, and please don't ask; but I think you are being set up," Truong said, speaking in low tones now and looking about in the smoky gloom of the room involuntarily.

"What do you mean, setup?"

"He means it looks like they're going to ditch you up there. Maybe they won't bring you back. No matter what they promise; I'm afraid they might not come and get you out," said Sylvia, her voice earnest and angry.

"That's right. It's been happening. I've seen contract agents abandoned by them. They want the job done, all right. Mainly just for spite at this point in the war, but they can't have guys like you left around after the country falls. That's the thinking. You are like a time bomb, a political nightmare ready to explode in their faces," Truong added. "Think what it would mean to have a few people around that know where all of the skeletons are hidden. Doesn't make the Americans, especially The Company, look very nice when your story comes out. Americans don't do that sort of thing."

"Always on the side of truth and justice in the sanitized version for the American public," Sylvia said, a note of dejection and bitterness in her voice.

"Anyway, that's it. Believe us or not, you'd better watch your back. Now we've got to get back," Truong said as he and Sylvia started toward the hut's door. He turned and said fervently, "*Chào anh, tôi phải đi bây giờ. Chúc anh đi bình yên.*" (Goodbye you. I must go now. Wishing you go safely.) The two of them disappeared into the dark.

CHAPTER 40

Our strategy of 'attrition' has not worked. Adding 206,000 more US men to a force of 525,000...and 270 tactical fighters at an added cost to the US of $10 billion per year raises the question of who is making it costly for whom...We know that despite a massive influx of 500,000 US troops, 1.2 million tons of bombs a year, 400,000 attack sorties per year, 200,000 enemy KIA (killed in action) in three years, 20,000 US KIA, etc. our control of the countryside and the defense of the urban areas is now essentially at pre-August, 1965 levels. We have achieved stalemate at a high commitment. A new strategy must be sought.

Dr. Alain C. Enthoven, Head of the Pentagon's
Office of Systems Analysis, February, 1968

Anders had a lot to ponder. It was beyond the cynicism that even he had developed to believe that his own people could contemplate abandoning him. Despite the differences he had had with them over the years, he remained convinced that their code of honor as American officers would forswear any such craven betrayal. He concluded that his old friends, Truong and Sylvia, were over reacting to Company rumors; but he made up his mind to include some special measures for self protection that he would share with Tran, Bach, and Ky as soon as they were out of the ARVN village.

The four men stayed an extra day in the military town and arranged for two clandestine supply dumps to be made with food and extra weapons and ammunition in the region where General Giap was supposed to have his meeting. Tran would go with the first helicopter and Bach would go with the second; so, they would be able to know exactly where their supplies were going to be when they needed them. Anders planned for them to travel very light until the actual time of their attack on Giap's meeting place. He also wanted the cache of supplies to be available on his planned escape route. He plotted the best locations for two LZs with the ARVN helicopter pilots who were assigned full time to the mission. The ARVN cavalry men were well trained and dedicated. Anders was glad to have men he could count on, and it served to ease his misgivings.

It was also something of a comfort to be able to book transport on the war's premier fighting helicopter. He and his men were to be ferried on a AH-1G Cobra gun ship helicopter equipped with turret mounted machine guns that fired 7.62 ball and tracer ammunition in a 230° arc, attached air-to-ground rockets, an M 24-A 20 mm cannon capable of a 2,000 rounds per minute rate of fire while staying out of range of enemy small arms attack, and a bow mounted mini-gun 40 mm grenade launcher that was able to fire its projectiles at the speed of a machine gun. A crew of five, including the pilot, copilot, crew chief, and two gunners would be on hand. The slim silhouette attack helicopter could cruise at 200 miles per hour.

To prevent its premature discovery, they decided to move the first landing zone a distance of fifteen klicks away from the town where the high level communist forces meeting was scheduled to be held. He and the pilots worked out the timing and the signals for their pickup. It would be dicey, he knew; and, in all likelihood, he and his men would be moving as fast as they possibly could with an enraged army at their heels. Timing was going to be critical. They selected two alternate LZs, to be used on subsequent nights if things got too hot around the first site, but knew that they would, in all probability, not get the chance to make it to the third one if they were thwarted on two successive nights. Anders, Tran, and Ky did not go back to their village until they were certain that they had as tight a plan as possible and the people and gear to carry it off.

Anders collected all of his small cache of personal treasures, including his several passports, and arranged for a helicopter to take Ky into Hue' to empty their bank accounts of all funds not already in Switzerland. Ky returned with bundles of currency of four countries which he and Anders added to their satchel. H'Klois was very unhappy about that bit of preparation, but she complained only a little. Anders gave her several thousand dollars, bahts, and Piastres to hide. She did not like the implications of that either, but was mollified when Anders assured her that it was only a precaution. He wished he felt as sure about it as he said he did.

Tran and Bach saw to the burial of two separate caches of plastic explosives, satchel charges, M-72 LAWs, a Soviet sniper rifle, SKS submachine guns—the Chinese knock-off of the Russian AK-47—

and a Type 56 Chinese copy of the Soviet Degtyarev RPD machine gun. Cleve Howard thought it was a particularly good touch to implicate the Chinese.

The other Company men had flown out the morning after the meeting with Anders, and only Lane Duerk still remained in the country. Howard had used his authority to catch a MAC hop out one day later. Thau Thien Province and Hue' were in an indefensible position now with their fall an imminent probability. Truong was with Duerk in Saigon; Sylvia, Bartini, and Howard were safely back in San Francisco enjoying the sour dough bread and fresh crab along the embarcadero and at the wharf and watching bemused as the seemingly endless antiwar parades swept along the streets. None of the former Phoenix operatives felt guilty to be out of it.

The four *Phung Hoang* commandos and their LLDB guide, the only man who knew the actual, on the ground, location of the village where the meeting was to be held, were dropped onto their LZ at midnight on March 10. That same day, unknown to them, Ban Me Thuot in II Corps fell to the NVA advance. The men crouched low for fear of the sharp rotors—helicopters were called 'choppers' because of the capacity of the rotors to 'chop' a man to pieces—and raced off into the trees at the edge of the grassy clearing of the LZ. The Vietnamese ranger let the other four men know, in no uncertain terms, that his job was to get them to the attack site; then he was on his own. He regarded the mission as suicidal, and his mother had not raised any fools. He was going to melt into the background and forget that he had ever been a South Vietnamese soldier as soon as he pointed out the village.

Running along in the night, Tran had them pause to take note of the location of his cache, and they bypassed it. Further on, closer to the assassination site, they stopped at Bach's cache and took out SKSs, one LAW, a B-40 Eastern Bloc rocket propelled grenade launcher, a sniper rifle, a Type 56 MMG, and a satchel charge each. They loaded up with LURPS, enough for three days. The going was slower now that they were burdened with all the extra ordinance, but they were in position by dark on the thirteenth.

Bach, with his superior sapper skills, was sent in to have a look at the town itself. Anders, Tran, and Ky set up a firing site on a low rise overlooking the middle of the village where a large olive drab tent had been set up. It was apparent that the intel about a meeting was accurate, but Anders had to wonder why there were not more sentries. He had expected that they would have to sneak through an army; but instead, they had found only pretty routine security. The four men felt that they had a good field of fire, if somewhat distant, but it was doable. From their position on the high ground, they could see the preparations being made through their starlight scopes by night and especially well through the 16X Zeiss binoculars when it began to get light on the fourteenth, the scheduled day of the big communist military conference.

March 14 was also the day that General Nguyen Van Thieu, the current dictator of South Viet Nam, ordered the withdrawal of all ARVN forces from the Central Highlands; but Anders and his three commandos could not know that the GVN situation had deteriorated to that abysmal level. They had a job to do, and it was all they could handle to focus on their own mission.

Bach returned well past dark. He gave his report immediately, "NVA all over the place. Security seems pretty routine, though. Not what you would expect with a high level conference, one that includes the general himself. They have a big tent, lots of chairs set up. Obviously, they are having an important meeting."

"Maybe they're just overconfident," said Tran.

"They have every reason to be," Anders added dourly. "There isn't a South Vietnamese soldier within a hundred kilometers of here."

"Let me show you a map of the area around the village." Bach scratched in the dirt. "This is a clear area, no bushes, trees, or buildings. It is on the side of the tent facing this hill." He indicated the low hill on which they were sitting. "I think they are keeping it open for the overflow crowd, the ones who can't get into the tent to hear the big man."

"Not very smart if that is their plan," said Ky.

"No. It gives us another choice of places where we can fire with a free field," Bach finished. The three Vietnamese looked to Anders.

"I think we should use them both," he said. "Two of us will get down into those trees; so we can fire over the crowd and into the tent; and we can slow up the pursuers. The other two can sit up here and hit them with the B-40 and the sniper rifle. If it's okay, Ky and I will go down, and you two stay up here." The men nodded their assent.

"Who takes the fifty-six?" Tran asked.

"Good question. I think the heavy stuff should stay up here. Ky and I will travel light so we can get our tails out of there when the trouble starts."

"All right. When do we start to fire?" Tran then asked.

"You're full of good questions. Since Ky and I are down there close, why don't you wait for us to open up first? We'll pick some targets and send in a few bursts, then move around a little. If you can, hold off until the crowd starts up hill after us. It would be great if we could have a second ambush for them, make them cautious when we light out. The SKSs are good for single shots or short bursts, but on automatic, when the barrel gets hot, like the old Sten guns, they wobble all over the place; so, we'll need your automatic fire as soon they come into your sight."

"Okay, boss, but it's not worth hanging around too long. They'll be on us in a few minutes after our first shot," said Ky. "We need to start moving the second we fire and get ourselves headed toward Tran and Bach as fast as we can once they start after us, even if we don't get Giap. Agreed?"

"You bet, brother," said Anders. "So far as I'm concerned, this whole mission isn't worth us getting killed. No one mission or one person's heroics ever changed the course of a war, and I don't think this is any exception. At best we can slow down the inevitable defeat, but no more. If the US isn't willing to nuke Hanoi, the South is going down. I propose that we take good care of ourselves when it does." "Besides," his face grew dark and grim, "I have a few scores to settle."

"And we're going to be there to settle them with you, brother," Tran and Bach said at the same time. Ky nodded his concurrence in the darkness.

"Okay, let's give it a try, anyway. Ky, let's get down there. Good luck, brothers." The four men took each other's hands, forming a ring, in confirmation of their loyalty to and affection for each other. Not US marine style, perhaps, but it was a solid bond among men whose testosterone levels could not be disputed.

Ky and Anders disappeared into the dark night crawling through the heavy bushes and bamboo clusters most of the time. It was very dark and difficult to orient. At times they moved within two meters of sentries. By the time they felt the treeless grass opening, they realized that the main line of security forces was behind them, between them and the relative safety at the top of the hill. It was a disconcerting feeling. Both men knew they would have to improvise rapidly and well when the action started.

Dawn on the fourteenth brought out large platoons of *Bo Doi*—NVA officers in their bright green uniforms leading their deep green uniformed men. The first unit to enter the tent itself consisted of men dressed in light khaki—Chinese, the people not supposed to be involved, according to the agreement between the US and Red China. By 1000 the tent and the entire open area was jammed with soldiers. They had obviously come in from the north or else they might well have marched right over Anders and Ky. Tran had the binoculars and spied General Giap first. As if one man, the entire assemblage snapped rigidly to attention without a word being spoken as the eminent Commander in Chief of the PAV strode swiftly along the village path and into the tent. A command was shouted, and the men came to parade rest.

Anders was briefly looking at the man who was arguably one of the best generals of the twentieth century and whom he had come to assassinate. The general was educated at the best high school in Viet Nam, the Quoc-Hoc in Hue'. Other graduates included Ho Chi Minh, Pham Van Dong, and Ngo Dinh Diem. He served a French prison term in 1930 for communist revolutionary activities. Giap, along with Pham Van Dong, headed the Indochinese Democratic Front after the Vietnamese communist party was outlawed. In November, 1946 he signed the short-lived General Staff Accords for the Vietnamese side and General Raoul Salan for the French side. When the accords broke down that same year, Giap responded to the French attacks on North Viet Nam by erecting barricades in Hanoi and ordered the population to perforate their house walls to permit communications from block to block without having to cross streets in the open.

In 1945-46, he was in charge of liquidation of the opposition in the nationalist government, the so-called 'internal enemies of the regime.' The noncommunists, even at that early juncture, were then referred to simply as *viet-gian* (traitors to Viet Nam). These 'traitors' included leaders of religious sects, mandarins, and intellectuals. Ho, was the instigator, a fact that belies the benevolent 'Uncle Ho' of Vietnamese communist myth. Giap, like his enemies, the French and the members of the militant religious sects, often eliminated antagonists by tying the condemned into bundles with logs and then floating them down the Mekong while the victims slowly drowned. The practice became known throughout the land as 'crab-fishing.'

General Giap spent almost his entire adult life making war for the communist party first and Viet Nam second. He was named the minister of the interior, a position that included charge for the security police and command of the Propaganda Brigade for Liberation, later known as the Viet-Nam People's Army. The first time he and his army invaded South Viet Nam was in Operation Le Hong Phong II in a campaign that saw the French defeated in the First Indochinese War's most decisive battle at Long Song in October, 1950. Although the war dragged on for another four inconclusive years to end at 0153 on 8

May, 1954 in the village of Dien Bien Phu, it was over in 1950.

There was a sound of microphone static, a couple of attempts to get the sound system to carry Giap's words for the men outside the tent, then a clear, "Testing, testing," in six toned Vietnamese. A military band started up the music of Marching Forward, the national anthem of North Viet Nam. The soldiers all knew the words, by heart, written by Nguyen Van Cao in 1944; and the ground shook with their enthusiastic rendition: "Our flag, red with the blood of victory, bears the spirit of our country..."

Anders had miscalculated. The level ground between him and the general was filled with soldiers; so, his ability to see his target was severely obscured. He presumed the same was true for Ky on the opposite end of the clear area. The best he would be able to manage was one good burst in the direction of the front of the tent. Maybe he would get lucky. Luck was with him so far—hadn't the general showed up? Wasn't the security far less than he might have suspected? So much for the old superstition about the dreams of the black hairy nightmare, he thought to himself and almost convinced himself that his luck would hold.

He inched his way to a semi-standing position, trying to blend with the branches and trees as best he could. He cautiously looked around and was relieved to see no sentries near him. Probably they were too awestruck at their chance to see their commander, the most famous soldier in their armed forces, to be fully vigilant. Anders decided that this was as good a time as any. It was too far to lob a grenade. The SKS would have to do. He stood up to his full height and could barely see over the heads of the crowd at that. Their backs were all facing him.

Anders could not see the general who stood at the front of the assembled cream of his communist forces and held them spellbound with the force of his personality. What he was saying, they had all heard before; many of them had virtually committed Giap's words to memory. Giap quoted himself, from his *People's War, People's Army*. He stressed his dictum that the central theme of the campaign that was not the force of arms so much as it was the recruitment of the individual Vietnamese who yearned to be free of the yoke of the foreign devils, the round-eyed bandits. These freedom fighters wished only to be free from interference and able to go about the work that had occupied their ancestors for millennia. As Anders took aim, the general was saying, "Therefore, the political work in its (the army's) ranks is of the first importance. It is the soul of the army."

Anders sighted along the barrel and put the spot where he imagined Gen. Giap was standing in line with the metal sight. SKSs do not come with scopes.

General Giap presented the pragmatically proved case that "it is the primary need of the army to convey to the South Vietnamese citizenry in every word and deed that the communist cause is worth fighting for; something the French, the Americans, or the corrupt South Vietnamese government have never been able to do for all their money and technology." He adjusted his glasses and read from his 1952 restatement of Chairman Mao's principles set forward in his own book, "*La guerre de libération et l'armée populaire*".

"As it was then, it is on the eve of this great campaign of our comrades involved in the struggle against the imperialists. We will mount a war of movement to enable our weak nation to vanquish modern American-type troops. They may be bigger, better fed, and supplied, know the martial arts better, and may even be able to run in these mountains as long and hard as we do; but in the end, they will have concentrated their energies in the wrong place—on territory, not on the people."

The general sipped from a glass of water and shuffled his notes. He read, "The enemy will pass slowly from the offensive to the defensive." He departed from his notes to observe, "that happened with the French, and it is in the last stages of happening to the illegal government of Saigon and its evil supporters on Wall Street." He returned to his reading, "The blitzkrieg will transform itself into a war of long duration. Thus, the enemy will be caught in a dilemma: He has to drag out the war in order to win it and does not possess, on the other hand, the psychological and political means to fight a long drawn-out war..."

Anders squeezed off a three round burst ripping the quiet of the morning. Then, without looking to see what he had accomplished, Anders dropped to the ground and rolled to his left toward the end of the clearing. There were cries and shouts, then Ky laid down a second three round volley. The disparate sources of the two bursts confused the NVA and People's Army men. They began to fire wildly, mostly in the wrong direction. Both Anders and Ky stood for a fraction of a second and opened fire again. Then they started uphill.

General Giap dived for the ground. High velocity rifle bullets tore into officers in front of him and to his left. He was unscathed, and was rushed out of the tent in the direction opposite from which the firing had originated. He would live to fight another day, inspiring an adulation that approached deification on the part of his followers. Scores of them would die for him; they had already proved that.

Anders all but ran over a guard. He killed the man with his knife and began to race up hill zigzagging all the way. Anders heard Ky fire. From the sound of it, he had had to kill a pursuer. Anders alternately ran, dropped and fired, and ran again. He could tell that Ky was making progress up the hill as well. He had to betray his position when two sentries bore down on him, coming from above. He killed them with single shots from his SKS, knowing that Chinese carbine was notoriously unreliable on automatic, then ran for all he was worth. Now, the firing from below was finding its range, nearer and nearer him. From above he heard the bark of Tran's B-40 and then saw Giap's assembly tent shred apart with a series of well placed grenades. Only a few seconds had elapsed; hopefully, Giap had not had time to get out. Anders no longer cared.

Ky was firing frequently and in series of bursts now. Anders was nearing the crest of the hill and had to turn left and to veer obliquely east to reach Tran and Bach. He could hear the roar of his pursuers at his rear and about 200 meters below. He turned on his full speed. He crashed into the spot where his own men were waiting. He caught his breath. Ky pounded up to them about a minute later.

"Think we got him?" Ky asked breathlessly.

"I have no idea. We haven't got time even to think about it. Okay, everybody, the whole North Vietnamese Army is coming up that hill. Ky go over there." He motioned to the east. "And I'll hold down the west side. We'll wait for you to fire the fifty-six, then Ky and I will open up, too. Hold off until you can take out a bunch of them. We've got to make them think they're facing all that's left of ARVN. Fire once; move; fire one more time from a new spot, then abandon the fifty-six and the B-40. We'll have to depend on mobility." He turned and ran to his selected defense site.

There was no more shooting from the NVA who were now moving in a disciplined fashion, cautious and without yelling. A full ten minutes elapsed before they appeared, almost en masse, at the foot of the last embankment before they would climb to Tran and Bach's hiding place. Suddenly all hell broke loose.

Tran roared the fifty-six's 700 rpm rain of bullets down on the hapless front runners of the NVA while Bach fired the B-40 rapid fire along their skirmish line. The screams of the dying and wounded pierced the intervals between the racket of the ordinance. Anders and

Ky picked off stragglers from their separate positions. Bach hurled a satchel charge causing a horrific explosion. Body parts joined pieces of earth and foliage in the smoke plume that erupted. Tran smashed the B-40, the sniper rifle, and the Type-56 MMG; then he and Bach struck out for the trees south of them.

Anders and Ky maintained their relative positions and ran headlong for the same general line, then all four of them dropped behind one natural barrier or another to see how fast and ferociously they were being pursued. A minute passed, then ten. No one appeared. Anders headed for Tran and Bach's position. Ky had evidently read his mind, because he was waiting with the other two when Anders skidded into their nest. "We've got some time. Let's get out." They found a trail and began a hard run, but one they could maintain, putting meter after meter, then klick after klick between them and the enraged NVA battalion behind them.

There was no sign of pursuers by the time they reached their closest cache. They restocked, feeling more comfortable with another two seven kilogram 56s and two B-40s. They crammed additional thirty cartridge magazines of SKS ammo into their rucks and enough food for another three days. They were to be picked up the following night; so, they were not going to go hungry at least. They all drank down as much water as they could hold, strapped on four more condoms of water, and lit out again, heading due south. They knew their pursuers would logically head that same direction, but they reasoned that speed and distance were more crucial than stealth for the time being.

They could hear the occasional voice from somewhere behind them, but only when the air currents were just right. The NVA sounded far away. Tired and hot and sweaty as they were, the four men kept up their grueling pace throughout the whole day. They stopped two or three times for a crucial bit of rest and a drink, then, spurred on by their visions of what was behind them, ran on. They covered so much ground so quickly that they were almost on top of the first projected landing zone by nightfall, more than a day early.

They held a hurried conference. Should they hide somewhere near the LZ and chance drawing attention to their escape site? Should they split up? Should they all go away from the LZ and hunker down as deep as they could and move back to the LZ under cover of darkness tomorrow night? Pickup time was 0200, thirty hours from the end of their deliberations.

The vote, three to one, was to take advantage of the breather they had and to hole up in the best place they could find as near to the LZ as possible and not to move an inch until it was necessary. The lone dissenter, Ky, thought it would be better to hide part way along toward the second cache of weapons and the second LZ in case the first one was overrun, and their last escape route became blocked. Anders pointed out that they still had the advantage of knowing what their enemies did not know—where either LZ was. Ky gave in.

They scouted for the best defensive hiding place. Bach found a large downed log with an old bear hole hollowed out in the pit created when the tree had uprooted. They dragged an assortment of branches and created an artfully camouflaged cave. Each man checked the appearance of the hiding place as best he could in the growing darkness and gave it his final approval, and they all squeezed into the narrow space to wait out a full day. They judged that they could be at the margin of the landing zone in less than five minutes when the time came.

Night passed and dawn came without indication of the pursuing communist army. Anders unfolded his cramped limbs and very cautiously peered out. He pushed aside the branches over the opening to their contrived cave and left the others inside while he made a quick inspection. Even in the early light of the morning, he could not see into their hiding place. He rearranged the branches and added a few more for good measure then reinsinuated himself into the small space left for him. It was a difficult feat to compress his six foot, six inch, two hundred eighty pound frame into the slot between Tran and Bach; and both men groaned softly as he moved them aside. Then they waited.

Two hours passed, 0730. They all heard it at once. Branches crackled around their tree; then they felt the thuds of hundreds of footfalls hurrying past. The NVA soldiers out there were quiet and disciplined, but there was no reason for them to be altogether silent. They called out and relayed orders, instructions, and directions. The voices came from all points of the compass and distances, even immediately adjacent to the cave mouth where the four frightened men sat cringing. It was nearly two and a half hours later before they could no longer hear evidence of their pursuers. The four remained perfectly silent except for their breathing and were almost immobile. The minutes and hours dragged by with glacial celerity. Still, they waited.

After three hours from the time they had last heard the sounds of their enemies, Anders opened a foil container of LURPS and passed it around. They sucked-chewed on the freeze-dried morsels of food without cooking, without water even to soak them in. They were like vegetable or meat flavored wood chips, nearly impossible to eat. The four changed their strategy to get down the chips of food with swallows of water as if they were forcing down a handful of pills. After a while the chips absorbed water in their stomachs and swelled giving the feeling of stomach fullness. The chips were nutritious enough to support them, but each of the men felt psychologically as if he were starving. It was 1500. The hours droned on. They waited.

Anders was tempted to take another peak outside, but was saved by hearing a pair of men walking near them. The fugitives heard sporadic trackers making their way through the forest; so, they did not dare venture out even to relieve their tense boredom or the gnawing cramps in their legs while there was any light left in the day. 1800. The bugs had found them minutes after they sat on the moist humus of the cave floor and had tormented them all day. It was hot, and sweat trickled in little annoying rivulets down their chests and backs. Small insects found their way into the proteinaceous, mineral rich body fluid and gorged. Anders and his men could do nothing but hate the crawling pests and wonder why God had made them, so many anyway. Each man wanted to scream, to run outside in the air, and to roll about on the ground. They continued to wait.

It was fully dark by 2100. Anders nudged Bach. "Give it a try," he whispered. Bach worked for a few moments to get enough circulation going in his bound up legs then uncoiled himself and crawled very circumspectly to the entrance of their self-imposed jail. He went out and stretched. He tried to look around, but it was too dark to see; so he was reasonably sure no outsider could see him either. When he crawled back in for the next man to have a turn, he begrudged the passage from the sweetness of the jungle air to the fetid interior. "You guys stink," he said.

All of the men limbered up in the blackness in front of the hiding place, each in his turn. At 2200, they ate again, or more accurately, gagged down another handful or two of wood-chip LURPS. Again, they waited. Hour after interminable hour, they waited.

It was 0140 when Anders finally whispered, "Let's get to the edge of the LZ. Go out one at a time and split up; so, we are each located on opposite sides of the grassy area. I'll take east, Tran north, Ky, west, and Bach, south."

All of them were in the spots agreed upon, and verified by their own individual compass readings by 0150. Now, the minutes seemed like hours as they waited for the characteristic sound of the cobra's rotors to come from the south. The tension was like a heavy cloak pressing down on them. They strained their ears and eyes in the darkness to pick up the earliest telltale sound of their deliverance. They all knew that the chopper would attract an enraged army when everyone heard its noise. They presumed it would be the hottest of the hot landing zones when the aircraft settled down into the small clearing. Timing would have to be near perfect if they were to make it onto the craft and up and out before the firestorm came from their foes lurking out their in the gloom. 0155. Tension mounted as they waited. They tensed themselves to spring into action.

0200. The cobra should be here by now, right now. Where was it? Each man cringing there in the grass gave in to his imagination seeing the cobra crashing somewhere out there over the Laotian jungle, seeing it crash before it got to their LZ. Ky's fantasies saw the craft pinned down by a firefight back at its base. All of them cried out inwardly for the cobra to come. 0205, late. Their eyes and ears and muscles strained with the watching and tension.

When the chopper was not there, and not anywhere to be heard by 0215, Anders crawled to Tran's hiding position. "Not coming, I guess." He ground his teeth. "Something wrong. I suppose it has to be tomorrow night. This is as good of a time as any to travel to where the second LZ is. Let's move 'em out." He made a conscious effort to keep control of his mounting fear and anger. Tran went for Ky, and Anders went after Bach. The disappointment among the men was palpable.

They rendezvoused and picked their way south. They all put on their night vision glasses, which helped some, and moved as quickly and cautiously as possible. They took half hour turns being at point because it was exhausting to occupy that tense position. Number two man in the rotation carried the fifty-six. On occasion, they had to pause while an NVA soldier or squad trotted past or made a small noise in the jungle. It was slow going.

They reached the second cache site while it was still dark. Visibility was too poor to be able to make a good hiding place then; so, the men decided to burrow down very temporarily in the area near the cache until it became possible to see something.

The morning brought light and the NVA. There had to be thousands of armed men after them, they reckoned. Platoons moved in a crisscross grid through the dense woodlands walking five meters apart. Anders and his men moved out from the cache site and along the benches of the hills where the going was slower and more arduous, but they were able to avoid most of the NVA patrols. The communist soldiers preferred to do their search and destroy maneuvers on relatively level land. They were like soldiers everywhere. This was going to be a long haul for the tired men from the north, and they took it easy as often as they could.

By 1800 that third day, Anders consulted the map and estimated that the four of them were a klick or perhaps two east of the second helicopter landing site and approximately in line with it on the north-south axis. The enemy activity was so intense and unpredictable that they were unable to rest. It was necessary to keep moving. Anders kept them going in a wide circle, always knowing where the LZ was located. The steady activity and tension took a hard toll. They were constantly hungry and leg weary, but kept slogging along, feeling that they were always only a step or two ahead of their hunters. Being a prey species where they had always before been predators wore on their nerves.

One of Anders' great fears was that they would have to kill an NVA soldier and then it would only be a matter of time before their general whereabouts would be known. It seemed that they were rapidly using up their supply of luck. His greatest dread was that shots would be fired at or by them and give away their position immediately. Darkness on the second night in harm's way came as a deep relief.

They edged slowly closer to LZ-2 through the early hours of the night. They counted on the precision of the ARVN cavalry to put an AH-1G Cobra in position at the appointed hour this night. The density of the enemy concentration was so great that it would be suicidal even to try to reach the third LZ that was located further south and east, right in the heart of the advancing NVA sweep. It had to be tonight or never.

Midnight came and went, and one they trudged with the LZ as their epicenter. 0130 came and went; then 0145; then 0150. There was no characteristic and reassuring whine of the assault helicopter's rotors. Only the Huey makes the 'whump-whump' deep throated pounding sound. There was the unmistakable sound of soldiers approaching. And they were drawing closer. 0155. Closer. The PRUCs should be hearing the cobra by now. Anders was ringing wet with sweat. It's bad odor told him that it was the stress and not the heat that produced the body fluid. 0200. The moment of truth.

The hour of deliverance came and went without the arrival of help. The NVA were within twenty meters of their location now. There were a considerable number of them, judging by the racket they were making. Since they owned the forest and the night, they did not feel the slightest need to be quiet. Anders and his men were silent prey.

0210. "Let's get out of here before we have to fight our way out!" Anders whispered urgently.

"Give them just a little more time, just five more minutes," urged Bach, the only one of the four who still maintained a shred of trust in the system to which he had surrendered twelve years ago. "Five more minutes." His voice was pleading now.

"We don't have five minutes. A few minutes. No more," Tran said. His voice was bitter, almost angry. It was not directed at Bach. 0215.

A clank of metal on metal, the rustle of a rucksack, the scraping of a boot sole on loose rocks—they were coming. It was as if they knew where Anders and his men were hiding or, at least, where the landing zone was supposed to be located.

"We go!" Anders said definitively. There were not even seconds to spare. Even if the cobra were to come now, they would never be able to board. The NVA were all around them and close.

The four of them began to crawl on their bellies for the cover of the dark trees of the forest to the south of the high grass of the helicopter pickup site. Even with danger almost to walk over them, each man still half hoped with his heart for the whining rotors, for the guns and grenades to rain protective cover fire down on the irrepressible communists. At least then they would know that The Company had kept the faith. Whatever their hearts hoped, they knew with their minds that it was not going to happen. It was too late.

CHAPTER 41

Look at the history of Burma. We go and invade the country: the
local tribes support us: we are victorious: but like you Americans
we weren't colonialists in those days. Oh, no, we made peace
with the king and we handed him back his province and left our
allies to be crucified and sawn in two. They were innocent. They
thought we'd stay. But we were liberals and we didn't want a bad
conscience.

That was a long time ago.

We shall do the same thing here. Encourage them and leave
them with a little equipment and a toy industry.
Graham Greene, The Quiet American

"*Ngừng lại! Ngừng lại!*" ("Stop!
Stop!") The command seemed ludicrous under the circumstances.
The speaker, a deep green uniformed NVA private, was apparently
unsure whether or not to fire at the fleeing shadows. He knew the
consequences of shooting one of his own.

Ky laughed darkly, understanding the lowly enemy soldier's quandary, as he scurried for the underbrush. He was half running, half
crawling depending on the terrain. He was outdistancing his three
companions. Each of the four fleeing men feared that he was just
running into the next phalanx of the enemy.

Boom, creee! came a high pitched crack of an AK-47 followed by
a ricochet off a rock near Anders spurring him into a full run. He knew
his position was no longer secret; so, he concentrated on putting
distance between himself and the shooter. Kalashnikov fire began to
crackle all around the runners, sometimes close enough for it to be felt
as a bullet whizzed by too closely. It was too dark for the communist
soldiers to select a definite target, and that was all that saved the four
hunted men. There was firing all around them, and soon there were
screams from widely scattered wounded. As Anders, Ky, Tran, and
Bach plunged into the trees, the command came from an unseen NVA

officer, "Cease fire!" and the firing stopped immediately, a display of discipline that could only be appreciated auditorily; but the four fugitives had little time to spend admiring the control exercised by their pursuers.

The separated NVA platoons were quickly formed up and directed by their officers toward the escape route chosen by Anders and his men. There was so little distance between the predators and their prey that Anders had his men stop suddenly at intervals, turn and fire; then abruptly switch directions; so, the NVA could not accurately home in on their muzzle flashes. The four *Phung Hoang* irregulars had no idea where they were shooting, nor the effect of their sporadic fire; and they could hear the bullets from the enemies' Kalashnikovs going off in useless directions. Anders had a quick thought that this night flight and struggle was what one of the poets he had studied at the university was describing, maybe Matthew or Arnold, something like that: "And we are here as on a darkling plain, swept with confused alarms of struggle and flight, where ignorant armies clash by night." Maybe all of war was like that.

There were enough screams of wounding coming from among the communist army to convince both the pursued and the NVA that either friendly fire or that from Anders and his men was decimating them, and they prudently began to hang back. Prudence was not an option for the runners, and they plunged on ahead, zigzagging, dodging, changing directions, and all at a dead run, heedless of the evergreen branches whipping their faces or of the inevitable falls over rocks, roots, and downed brush. Their lives depended on getting out of range. At times they crashed right into soldiers moving toward them and killed them with knives, preferably, or with their guns when necessary, thereby igniting another firestorm directed at themselves.

Gradually, however, the four men put enough distance between themselves and the main body of their deadly enemies that they could reduce their flight to a loping pace and could again get their bearings. Anders kept them moving ever west, as much as possible. After a while, and before first light, the firing behind them died out. Anders could imagine the frustration of the NVA that they had been thwarted when they were so close, at the realization of the failure of their overwhelming superiority of numbers, and at their inability to close the net on the assassins, or attempted assassins, whichever was the more accurate term.

Anders, Tran, Ky, and Bach were running on adrenaline and

emotional reserves and both of those resources had a finite limit no matter the force of their will. By predawn light, the PRUCs could run no more. Out of necessity, and despite their fears, they had to seek shelter. They found a limestone cave, one that had been occupied by Pathet Lao in the past by the looks of the debris left on the cave floor. Its opening faced west, away from the pursuers and was obscure enough that it could only be located by chance or a concerted search. They dropped down and gasped for breath. When their hearts began to slow down, and they could collect their thoughts; Anders grimly summed up their situation, conveying the obvious, succinctly.

"We were expendable, and they deserted us. The Company and the ARVNs betrayed us. One day..." His voice trailed off. The other men inclined their heads in agreement. Anders shook his head to clear the cobwebs of useless ruminations. "We can't go anywhere but west. Our only hope is to hook up with some Hmongs who are involved with the Wa People. We have to get to Thailand. I don't know how we are going to do it, but that's what we have to do."

"There a few little problems with that," observed Ky in a mastery of understatement. "Like, the NVA, and every Vietnamese villager, and every hill village that owes its existence to the good will of the Pathet Lao, and the bandits who would sell us for the price of a good lunch, and the ARVN, and probably a few American CIA patrols out there that don't want any witnesses. Have I about covered it?"

"Besides the routine problems of living off the land when there are two or three armies taking everything in their path like a cloud of locusts, I think you have about summed it up," said Tran. Somehow, the mere act of stating their absurdly precarious situation seemed to reduce the enormity of it. These were eminently practical men for whom quitting in any form was not an option; so, now, they began to plan while they took their brief rest.

They traveled west, skirted villages, avoided patrols and individuals, hid in the forest, and slept in the open, not daring to make contact yet. Anders' slumber was tormented by dreams that were fomented by his hunger, tiredness, discomfort, and by the demons of his thoughts. His nighttimes closed in on him with a kaleidoscope of scenes that came in a montage of memories—of lovely Liên being grasped and hurt by filthy hands, of the leering faces of Lane Duerk, Cleveland Howard, and Hugo Bartini, of the jeering, knowing countenance of Jean-Luc DuParrier and the devil incarnate, Tandrosz Szabo. Over and over he saw a helpless merchant kicked out of a helicopter followed by Liên, The Mandarin, his wife, and Master Nguyen. He harrowed up images of men and women he had killed, of maimed children, of a land of desolation. He had conversations with the terrible hairy monster and woke up in a panicked cold sweat embarrassed because he had been talking out loud. The psychological toll was beginning to tell on him.

When they felt secure enough to approach their first Hmong village, the PRUCs found that the people were dedicated neutrals. While they would not do the four men harm; neither would they give them shelter. The headman told the tired travelers, "We have a proverb: 'When the elephants fight, the grass gets trampled.' We do not want to draw the elephants to us." The villagers had not heard of the Wa People, and did not participate in the traffic of opium derivatives. On to the west the four men traveled.

Anders and the three Vietnamese tentatively approached a second Hmong village. A young man sat at the entrance to the city idly thumping the back of his knife against an aged teak log. The knife was large and heavy enough to chop down a sapling. He studied the four newcomers carefully as they walked by. The village men and women were all smiles and invitation; but Tran took a quiet look inside one of the long houses and found a small altar for the ancestors with lit candles and behind it, on the wall, was a large photograph of Ho Chi Minh, his benevolent countenance granting blessings to the household. A middle aged man, one of the elders in a town where the longevity for men was forty-five, looked around conspiratorially to see if anyone else was watching. He called Anders over and smiled, showing blackened stumps of teeth.

"You want to buy?" He asked in Hmong.

Anders shook his head, tapping his temples to indicate that he did not understand.

The Hmong switched to French. *"Voulez-vous acheter? C'est de grande valeur ce que j'ai, mon ami. Spécialement pour vous. Presque gratuit."* (Do you want to buy. Very valuable what I have, my friend. Special for you. Almost free.)

Anders shrugged, curious. *"Montrez-moi,"* (Show me.) he said.

The man looked about once again, then opened a faded olive drab foot locker emblazoned with the clasped-hands logo of the USAID organization. Anders peered in. There sat two skulls and an assortment of long bones and vertebrae—obviously human. *"Américains,"* (Americans.) the Hmong said.

Anders was taken back but tried not to show it. "*Comment pourrais-je en être sur?*" (How would I know that for sure?) he asked doubtfully.

The Hmong rummaged in the box for a few moments then produced a pair of dog-tags. The names were American, and the tags looked authentic. Anders politely declined. The relic seller poorly disguised his hostility. It was obvious that he knew Anders to be an American. He had cause to hate the 'Sky People.' He would never forget 1966 and 1967, the time of the vomiting, the time when their airplanes dropped chemicals on the forest; and the leaves fell off; and the people grew sick. In those two years, the Americans had dropped 200,000 gallons of defoliants on his mountains.

In the current year, 1975, there were more than 600 American MIAs still unaccounted for in Laos and progress to retrieve remains was painfully slow. The Southeast Asians did not care nearly as much as the American public about the return of the MIA remains. For some, like this village elder, it was more a matter of business than anything.

The four of them thanked the people for their hospitality, but begged off on their offer to stay over. When they left, they made a display of heading south before resuming their westwardly directed pilgrimage. When they did turn right, they set off at double-time to put distance between themselves and that Hmong enclave.

The four foot weary irregular soldiers had been walking for five days when they saw their third village nestled in a valley below, surrounded by low hills that were carpeted with a dense cover of tall trees, a true, triple canopied rain forest. Near the village were patches of thick trunked, ten to fifteen foot tall Nipa palm trees and stands of giant bamboo that clattered musically in the gusty breezes. The four men were relatively intact aside from a few fungally infected small lacerations and legs punctured with small pencil eraser sized puss pockets from bamboo thorn pricks. They just needed rest and some decent food and a respite from the omnipresent stress of being chased. They ensconced themselves in a collection of rocks and karsh limestone formations that kept them from being seen by the industrious people below. This time, they resolved to be more patient and prudent. They watched the village for two full days before deciding to make contact.

During their period of observation, no NVA squads came by; no men with modern light arms were seen; at the periphery of the community children herded cows and water buffalo; and the routine life of thousands of years as hunter-gatherers and nomadic part time agriculturists unfolded—one day the same as the last.

Finally, their hunger, fear, and need for human interaction persuaded the PRUCs to try once more. Three of the four men walked in the clear down the main path into the *Nong Net* (village) and attracted the attention of everyone. It was elected to keep Anders out of sight for the time being, and he found a position to train the Type-56 MMG on the town in case they had to fight their way out. They were unanimous that they could not afford to let the villagers see a huge white man, an obvious Occidental, given the current hostile climate and the possibility that they might have heard of the rewards on the head of the *con ma da trắng khổng-lồ*. He was as unhidable as if he were an African black, as identifiable with the Americans as any black would be. That was why the CIA did not use Negroes for field PRU work—their presence would be an undeniable giveaway of the origin of the unit.

Tran, Ky, and Bach walked casually among the townspeople. There were people with round Chinese looking faces and others with slender faces, narrow noses, and high cheek boned Mongol looks. Most of the men sported wispy mustaches and chin whiskers. The women were barefooted bearing baskets of wood, vegetables, or sleeping children tied to their backs in cloth slings. Most of the women wore their family's wealth in the form of heavy silver necklaces. Children looked out from the pens of pigs and chickens where they tended the family livestock.

The three Vietnamese men were met with sullen politeness; they had expected nothing better given the history of abuse by ethnic Vietnamese on the hill people and would have been suspicious of an outwardly friendly reception. The Hmong word for Vietnamese people (phonetically spelled) is *Tchaw Gee*—the 'ones who eat the gall bladder.' Their Vietnamese neighbors had been cruel overlords exacting tribute in the form of ivory, precious woods, and spices because The People did not have money. The Hmong were often treated with violence and always with contempt by the *Tchaw Gee*.

Tran asked to parlay with the *Nai Khong* (headman). He was out of the area, a woman told him. She briefly displayed gold tipped teeth, put in by a Chinese dentist, who accompanied a caravan of merchants moving through the highlands every February to buy Hmong opium. Otherwise the Hmong had no interest in gold. The Vietnamese men and the Hmong villagers conversed in French, the only lingua franca among them. The Hmong either could not or would not speak Vietnamese, and none of the parties on either side knew Lao. Tran broke down the people's resistance by offering money.

Anders grew nervous when his three friends were ushered into a long house and out of his sight. Tran did the talking and took his cues from his two partners. None of them could see anything suspicious regarding Pathet Lao or NVA leanings; so, Tran finally broached the subject of the Wa People and the opium trade. To all of their delights, the faces of the Hmongs lit up with recognition and acceptance. They used the drugs in rituals despite the laws from the communists, and willingly profited from their contribution to the transport of the men and drugs over the hills and into the mouths, lungs, and veins of the Americans and the Vietnamese on the east. Tran, Ky, and Bach knew they were among businessmen with whom they could negotiate and work; they were at home.

One of the headman's four wives assured Tran, Ky, and Bach that they were safe in that house and in all of the others in the village. Her reference was to the cleansing of spirits that was routine in their community. Her front door carried a large mirror, impeccably polished, to frighten away evil spirits, the theory being that the spirit would see itself, and being so ugly, and because of having lived in the underworld where there were no mirrors, would be frightened by its own image. The fear would keep it and its cohorts away *ad infinitum.*

Thus reassured, Bach went up the hill to fetch Anders. He was very leery initially, but shortly felt comfortable with the small gregarious people. The Hmongs first wanted to talk business, then they would be happy to accommodate the visitors. In less than an hour, a sheath of kip had been transferred to the subchief who was the business manager of the village, in exchange for a set of carefully laid out agreements for giving sustenance and guidance through the hills and onto the lowland valleys to A Tuc town.

First, they rested and ate. It was not often that the people had visitors; so, they served one of their delicacies, roast bat. Anders thought it looked like rat, one of the few foods, he had determined not to be forced into eating; but he could not afford to be choosy in this circumstance. It was entirely palatable. Then, the four fugitives slept for more than a day and a half.

The 500,000 or so Southeast Asian Hmongs were a fascinating breed whose origins, although presumed to be Austroasiatic, at least linguistically, are uncertain. They called themselves, in their language, simply, 'The People.' Their dialect was closest to the Vietnamese kinh language; but, unlike the ethnic Vietnamese, they were non-Sinicized; and unlike, their mountain Thai neighbors, they were not Indianized.

They lived together in closely knit groups in valleys of the mountains as sometime rice farmers, sometime nomads. They employed slash and burn clearing of the trees to make their farms, a process they referred to as 'eating the forest.' Their long houses were almost invariably built of split bamboo and thatch and sat on the ground as opposed to the ethnic Lao custom of building homes on stilts with their domesticated animals living underneath.

The tradition of wearing brightly patterned skirts and scarves by the women had lasted through the changes of time, but the langouti (skirt-like) of the men was giving way to the more practical use of trousers by men well before 1975. The men often wore jackets, bracelets, and necklaces, and ivory plugs in their ears. They considered it a matter of serious esthetics to file and lacquer their teeth. They had been resistant to giving up their animist and shamanist religion with its belief in a tri-level universe: the *Hmong pa*, or living world occupied by the toilers of mortality, the *Hmong Kêloi*, or heavenly world, occupied by deities of a Chinese origin, and the *Hmong pua tin,* or underworld where live the malevolent spirits of the forces of nature and true demons.

This was a Tasseng, a coveted title for a village because it served as a district office in charge of many other villages. The Hmong with whom Anders and his friends found themselves were not neutrals. They fought loyally for the Americans under their General Vang Pao, The Royal Lao Army commander of military region II, the hill country.

American military personnel stationed covertly in Laos worked directly in or for the US Embassy to the RLG (Royal Lao Government). They were seconded to the American DAO (Defense Attaché Office) or were active duty air force airmen and pilots, dressed in casual civilian attire, assigned to the Ravens, a DIA (Defense Intelligence Agency) unit. The DAO was in the employ of the DIA. With the help of their fraternal friends, the Hmong, the DIA covertly collected military information and prosecuted the war in Laos with a budget to rival the treasure being expended in Viet Nam while the RLAF (Royal Laotian Air Force) ferried passengers for profit and transported opium. The Hmongs were on a twenty-four hour a day, seven days a week watch at the skies and at the jungles of their highland homeland to rescue downed US clandestine aviator-fighters. They had less than ten minutes to save their 'Sky People' once a plane went down, and many a man living could attest to the heroics of the Hmongs.

It had been a long time since the 'Sky People,' as they termed the

Americans, had been available to their radio call to launch air strikes to repel threatening enemies or to drop down weapons, radios, medicine for their old maladies of dengue fever, malaria, tuberculosis, and worms, or much needed food on parachutes that they called mushrooms. They did not know that the Royal Laotian flag, a three headed white elephant standing on the five Buddhist precepts under a white parasol, the FAR, and the RLG were no more in 1975. The war that had consumed more than a million Lao lives was, for practical purposes, over and the LPRP (Laotian People's Revolutionary Party) was now the effective government for the entire country. The isolated Hmongs had their mounting suspicions.

Nonetheless, they kept the faith, wore their red berets, openly displayed replicas of the clasped hands symbol of US aid to Laos, and were ecstatic to have Anders in their village. They were sure that he was a harbinger of renewed American interest and that he served to give the lie to the Pathet Lao propaganda that told of a treaty that the PL had signed with the Sky People to stop the fighting with them and to abandon the Hmong to the mercies of their lifelong enemies, the communists. They had never been able to believe such a tale—it was another of the 'Big Lies' of the northerners and their Red Chinese cronies.

They staged a *ba-sii* (offering to the spirits) celebration commemorating the presence of Anders and his men and as a tribute to their generous and faithful American friends. Anders did not have the heart to tell them of his own experiences. In spite of the war being waged all around them and in spite of the threat of attack by their enemies at any time with its accompanying need to flee as refugees, the Hmong celebrated.

The shamans and village elders made sure there were fresh banana leaves filled with small oranges, bananas, and wild orchids all about the town. Sticks of smoldering incense were added to the offering then topped with a duck egg. The shamans moved slowly through the crowd chanting to beseech the spirits. They tied quick knots in three strands of white cotton thread they carried and bound the wrists of people they met. This tied the souls of the persons to good fortune. To seal the good fortune, the shaman pressed a duck egg into the lucky recipient's hand. Anders, Tran, Ky, and Bach all smiled and held their own knotted string and egg, feeling a little foolish. In the background a mournful song was played on a bamboo pipe, and here and there dancers were stirred by the traditional music to undulate in a slow, foot stomping rhythm, moving along through the village in hypnotic circles. Fortunately, the PRUCs were not expected to join the procession.

The townspeople were decked out in their holiday dress. Looking from a short distance away at the center of the town, there was a swirling montage of brilliant colors—red, green, white, fuchsia, silver, and black. The women wore sashes, jackets, purses, and headdresses festooned with handsome old French silver coins which clinked and jingled musically as they walked and danced. Their attire was striking with intricate needlework, inset beads, and pieces of shiny metal with the same meaningful patterns being carried over into their hats, jewelry, belts, and baby carriers. The patterns were meaningful and communicative, expressing their history, legends, and animistic beliefs.

Khene (bamboo reed pipe) players wove their way through the merrymaking crowds provoking cheers and delighted laughter as they danced their exhausting stiff-legged dance and performed acrobatic stunts without dropping notes or their pipes and teased the girls into hands-to-the-face titters. Anders was a major focus of the players' attentions, and he responded by laughing and clapping whenever it seemed appropriate.

Babies were everywhere, laughing children that attracted compliments from every passerby. Seeing them, Anders missed his own handsome brown children. The little ones were the most prized of all Hmong possessions. They were carried in colorful embroidered slings and dressed in lavish hats with handsome colonial coins (obtained in payment from the French, whom the Hmong called 'Fackees,' for their service in fighting the Japanese) for decoration. The hats were worn at all times by the babies to protect their heads and to ward off evil. Older children were more serious—they were taught from an early age the traditional values of truthfulness, bravery, and loyalty, the clan taboos, and unique crafts. They learned to farm, to care for animals, to make the elaborate embroideries, called *pae⁀ndau* (the Flowery Cloth), to make guns, and to create silver jewelry. Today, however, no one worked. Everyone was enveloped in a festival of affection and high spirits, the lowland visitors being no exception. They were accorded the status of family for that day.

The young men and women of the village were dressed in their very best, perhaps sensing that this could be one of the last times they would have the chance to frolic in the old courting rituals unmolested by outside antagonists. They could not help but know that their ways were threatened by the maelstrom of impending change. The married adults parted to permit their youth to form two rows, girls on one side and boys on the other, facing each other with great anticipation and excitement. They played a game known simply as 'ball toss' in which they threw cotton balls to one another, sang songs and recited poems made up on the spot to each other. The girls giggled and tittered about the handsome boys, and the boys shuffled with the nervousness of adolescents the world over at the attention. Upon reflection, watching these Hmong youth, Anders knew that there was something wonderful that he had missed back in The World.

Before the festival meal, Anders was obliged to stand for the adulation of the assembled crowd and to endure speeches directed at him, including embarrassingly personal comments, and a lengthy paean about the Sky People, their enduring friendship with The People, and their wonderful land of plenitude. The cardinal virtue of loyalty was the main theme of the speeches. Anders felt a sense of depression, knowing what inevitably must come for these people. He was like most of the Americans who had carried on the social intercourse, had been the comrades in arms, and had made promises to these faithful allies. He was powerless to influence the policies of the puppeteer WOMs in Washington, and he could only seethe. And he knew that, like his American predecessors in the region, he would not stay. He knew that, like him, they were being abandoned and betrayed.

The Hmong were not entirely naive. They had clear intimations that the Americans might be long in returning. There were a few among The People that even doubted that the Americans would ever be seen again. These were the itinerant *Chao Fa* (Prince of the Sky) priests. One of them had heard of the coming of the American giant and got himself invited to the feast. His views were not universally popular, but his patriotism and dedication to The People were unassailable. He had earned the right to sit in the place of honor beside Anders and to speak. When it was his turn, he presented the fundamental self-sufficiency myth of the Hmong:

"*J'ai très peur que nos amis du peuple du ciel aient été battus, et que nous ne les reverrous plus jamais, et leurs machines dans l'air ne vous donnerons plus ce dont nous avous besoin.*" (I greatly fear that our Sky People friends have been defeated and will not be seen again, nor will their machines in the air give us what we need any more.) There were some hisses of disbelief, but the Hmong were polite; and no one interfered with the flow of his narrative.

"*Nous devous comptes sur nous-mêmes et sur nos esprits protecteurs, qui doivent venir vees nous à l'heure de nos plus grands besoins. Sin*

Sai viendra. Faites confiance en nos légendes, mes amis. Il y a au moins cinq milles aus iln'y avait qu'unne terre, qu'un arbre et qu'un homme, un ermite, qui savait que son temps touchait à sa fin. Il avait vecu mille ans et bientôt il devrait rejoindre ses ancêtres. Quand l'heure du départ arriva il fabriqua des figurines en argile, un homme et une femme. Parce qu'il possédait une grande magic, ces figurines sont devenues chair humaine. (We will have to depend on ourselves and the spirits of our protectors, those who must come to us in the time of our greatest need. Sin Sai will come. Have faith in our legends, my friends. Five thousand years or more ago, when there was only one land and one tree and one man, a hermit, he knew that his time was coming. He had lived a thousand years and soon must join his ancestors. When it was time to leave, he made figures of clay, a man and a woman. By his great magic, the figures became human flesh.)

"Ce couple vécut de nombreuses années et eut un fils exceptional qu'ils out nommé Sin Sai. Le garcon devint un homme, grand et púissant mais bon et gentil. Il aimait son peuple. Quand les gens de sa ville furent menacés par un géant terrible et que le géant disait qu'il tuèrent Sin Sai, le jeune homme de clara la guerre au cruel géant. Le géant choisit un jour pour faire la guerre, se facha beaucoup et se changea en plusieurs milliers de petits géant pour attaquer le grand Sin Sai. Les gens avait très peur. (This couple lived for many years and had a special son that they named Sin Sai. The boy grew to be a man, large and powerful, but good and kind. He loved his people. When the people of his town were threatened by a terrible giant, and the giant said that he would kill Sin Sai; the young man sent a declaration of war to the cruel giant. The giant chose a day to make the war, made himself very angry, and changed into many thousands of small giants to attack great Sin Sai. The people were very afraid.)

"Sin Sai dit 'n'ayez pas peur'. Il emplit sa bouche de grains de riz autant qu'il pouvait y mettre. Alors il cracha tous les grains in un grand nuage. Quand les grains tombèrent au sol, ils ont été transformés en soldats qui tuèrent le grand géant et tous les petits géants. Quand Sin Sai a vu que sa tâche était accomplie il partit pour combattre les géants it les démons aux enfers. Il ordonna aux soldats de garder le peuple dans les hautes collines pour que le démon et le géant ne puissent pas les atteindre. Nous il promit de revenir quand 'le peuple' aurait besoin de lui. (Sin Sai said, 'Do not be fearful,' He filled his mouth with grains of rice, as much as it could hold. Then, he spat all of the grains out in a great cloud. When the grains came to lay on the

ground, they were transformed into soldiers who slew the great giant and all of the little giants. When Sin Sai saw that his work was done, he left to fight giants and demons in the underworld. He told the soldiers to keep the people in the high hills; so, the demons and giants could not get to them. But he promised that he would return when The People needed him.)

"*Je vois venir ce moment*," (I see that time approaching), said the *Chao Fa*. "*Je serai un de ses soldats quand le moment viendra. Ne vous décourager pas mon peuple. Sin Sai reviendra..*" (I will be one of his soldiers when the time comes. Do not despair my people. Sin Sai will return.)

There was discussion among the people sitting at Anders' table as to whether Vang Pao, the general with six wives, was really Sin Sai; but the *Chao Fa* quashed that idea brusquely. "*Nous saurons quand le moment sera venu..*," (We will know when the time comes.) he said emphatically.

Discrete offers were made to Anders to sleep in the house of one attractive woman or another, but he declined. Whether out of faithfulness to the wife and children he had effectively abandoned, or to guilt, or because of weariness of body and spirit, he could not say. His Vietnamese friends were not afflicted by his same pricklings of conscience or demons and followed the amber skinned, slender faced, Mongol looking women with gusto. Anders was content to rest from it all. He started for his bed.

"*L'homme du ciel*," (Sky man.) a voice called from alongside the path to the longhouse where he was to sleep.

Anders started, tensed, and turned toward the direction of the voice. The man who had spoken to him stepped up to where Anders was standing. The *Chao Fa*.

"You scared me," Anders said. He took a moment to regain his calm. His French was fluent and habitual now.

"Accept my apology, please, Sky man," the *Chao Fa* said continuing in the French that was useful to them both. He now stood in the shaft of light cast by a burning taper that lit the pathway. Anders was drawn to the man's intense eyes. They were red-rimmed, dark, and penetrating. It was as if those eyes could see inside him; more, it was as if they were looking into Anders' past and his future.

"Okay," Anders said.

The *Chao Fa* looked steadily into Anders' eyes as if he were taking the larger man's measure, studying him before deciding to convey his message. He said in a low, nearly inaudible voice, but one that pierced the quiet of the jungle night, "You have seen the ones from the underworld. You know what you must do. You must do it for The People. You and I know that the Americans will give The People to the wicked Lao. Only you can revenge that shame." A shiver coursed through Anders' spine. Before he could answer, the wraith was gone.

Anders could not have sworn that the man had really been there, had really spoken to him. Of late, he was finding himself trying to separate occurrences into real and dream or imagined categories. The hideous specter of the hairy black demon was beginning to seem more real than the NVA soldiers at his heels. He worried at times about his sanity. That night his sleep was free of nightmares about Liên, The Mandarin, Master Nguyen. Even the black apparition stayed away. But he spent the night under the gaze of a pair of haunting, disembodied eyes— eyes that were pleading and cajoling, forcing him.

The Hmongs awakened Anders, Ky, Tran, and Bach before dawn. The scarred men who had given long combat service to their brothers, the Sky People, conducted the Drinking-of-the-Water ceremony to grant the men who were going to be guides and the Sky People a safe journey and to cement their bonds as fellow warriors. One by one, the defenders of the mountain tops, one from each household, drank water from a special vessel then offered a cup to Anders, Tran, Bach, and Ky. The men ate breakfast then moved out at first light. The wiry little men were indefatigable, running nearly eight miles an hour for forty-eight hours at a stretch without stopping to rest or eat. Anders was in marathon racer condition, but found himself admiring the stamina of these mountain men.

Along the way through the almost virginal forest floor they saw a sampling of the fauna of Southeast Asia and the Bengal and Malaysian peninsula—bears, monkeys, tapirs, wild boar, antelope, buffalo, and tortoise. On the muddy banks of the small rivers crisscrossing the terrain sat crocodiles. The trees held exotic parrots, hornbills, and elegant pheasants. Anders once thought he caught a fleeting glimpse of a shy Southeast Asian panther as it darted among the ubiquitous trees. The mountains were rugged and carpeted with forest and often shrouded in fog at their peaks. There were purple-white rock-pile accumulations (stalagmite rock formations in the limestone karst areas) that came into view like stone sentinels, and a constant vista of heavy greens and azures, and in areas, the remnants of dry season browns. The mountain home of the Hmongs was among the most beautiful on earth. It was no small wonder that they affectionately called it 'The World.'

This was late March; the rains had begun to come sporadically and were turning the dry brown landscape once again into the flourishing green of the jungle. In February, the dry season, the mountains were especially unpleasantly hot. The countryside turned dusty, dry, and brown. Trees lost their leaves and many of the myriad streams dried up. Monsoon winds blew in from the north and east and lost their moisture when they first hit the Indochinese peninsula. Then the dehumidified winds rose over the mountains and actually took up water, parching the landscape. The early monsoons coming in from the Indian ocean had made the annual correction of this dry state, and Anders could appreciate the renewal of spring as he ran through the forest.

As he jogged along, maintaining his place in the file behind the lithe guides, who ran with such effortless grace, Anders had time to think, to remember. He did not like most of his reveries; they stirred up images of dead and wounded, of Liên, the beautiful lotus girl, and her and her family's last sufferings, of his abandoned wife, H'Klois, and their two children, of the *Chao Fa*'s riveting eyes, of scenes of his own misdeeds and humiliations, of a tiger cage jail, and of pleading victims.

He was lost in thought, almost as if he were running while asleep, when, suddenly, the lead Hmong abruptly halted. Anders bumped into Tran, who was next in line, came close to knocking him head over heels. He felt foolish. "Lao," came the whispered message down the line of men from the point runner.

Anders, his men, and the two Hmongs immediately dropped to the ground and slid into the jungle where they became invisible. They were already too late. The Pathet Lao patrol had heard the noise created by Anders' inattentive clumsiness. Machine gun fire opened up, followed by the characteristic high toned clatter of Kalashnikovs. 7.62 mm bullets whizzed and thudded through the trees like swarms of angry insects. The six men pinned themselves to the ground and did not make the slightest effort to try and look up. There was a sound of running feet as the communist soldiers advanced further down the trail toward Anders' hiding place. There was a momentary lull while the PL platoon halted and reset up at a better vantage point to pour fire into the forest where their enemies had to be hiding.

Anders used the lull to take a quick peep. He was no more than five meters from the bulk of the Pathet Lao platoon. They were probably inexperienced because they were bunched together, evidently having momentary trouble with the firing mechanism of their MMG. Anders sprang to his feet and began to rake the startled communists with the

Type-56 MMG he had been carrying. The PL died with angry surprised looks on their faces. The survivors and stragglers began to fire back, but were cut down by a deadly crossfire coming from both sides of the jungle trail. The Pathet Lao had made the fatal mistake of being overconfident and had incautiously remained in the open so they could have a more open field of fire.

The wiser of them dropped to the ground where they had been standing and fired without aiming into the unseen enemy in the bush. The short, furious firefight had now taken a 180° turn leaving the communists pinned down and on the defensive. Both sides' shots were wasted, too high from Anders' men, and too haphazard on the part of the Pathet Lao. In a matter of minutes, the battle had become an unproductive stalemate. That in and of itself worked to the vantage of Anders' foes, he knew that. Reinforcements would be by any minute, roused by the racket of the gunfire. He knew he could not wait.

He was not going to be trapped. He would never allow himself to be taken again. A bloodlust welled up from his core, and the red-rimmed, haunting eyes of his fantasies spurred him. Anders leaped to his feet and jumped onto the jungle path like a mad man. He was almost on top of the prone communist soldiers. It was so unexpected and crazy that none of them could react in time. Anders began a terrible rain of death onto the men as they writhed in the dirt and tried to twist into a firing position. He tore their bodies into tatters. Long after they were all dead, he continued to mutilate them with his machine gun. Homer said that 'Soldiers are but puppets controlled by the gods.' In Anders' case, the God in question was not the Father in Heaven of his Mormon childhood, not the Beneficent Buddha of gentle Liên, not the majestic Allah, nor the benevolent Hindu Siva. It was the primeval god of his Nordic ancestry, Thor, the War Maker.

His hands were still working the firing mechanism even though he had run out of bullets when Tran came up to him and put his hand on the big Swede's arm and spoke quietly. "Stop. It's done. They're all dead. We can go now," he said. Anders seemed uncomprehending.

"We have to go!"

Anders moved like a man in a nightmare. His eyes were vacant. Tran was fearful. He slapped Anders across his face. Anders came around, and brought himself back out of the underworld. He nodded his understanding and fell into line behind the four others as they began to run out of the killing ground.

One of the Hmong, a man named Chang Chia Cher, had lain inert at the end of the furious interchange. His friend Fang Pao Xe, rushed to his side. Thinking, or hoping, that Cher was unconscious, he produced a little urine on a cloth and squeezed a drop into the slack mouth of the fallen Hmong. The old custom could only work for the unconscious, and Cher was dead. He had been gunned down when the Pathet Lao had first ambushed them. His comrades could only set his body aside in the forest to prevent the communists from mutilating it before they had to leave.

They ran, hid in the forest, circled squads of Pathet Lao and bandits, secreted themselves in friendly villages for days at a time, and over a month's period gradually worked their way toward the low valleys of Laos. In the safe villages where they paused, life went on much as it always did, and Anders despaired for these people knowing that the communist juggernaut was not far away.

For now, Hmong slash and burn farmers traded dry hill rice, vegetables, corn, and opium for salt, pots, silk cloth, and thread. Opium was their only cash crop, and their only source of manufactured items. The Hmong used opium as a natural medication for diarrhea, stomach ulcers, fevers, and for pain. The elderly sometimes used it as a somnifacient or to reduce the aches and pains of their infirmities. Addiction was uncommon and frowned upon to the level of being almost a taboo.

In the lower elevations the dry season was on; and harvest of the narcotic was underway. Each family tended a field of three hectares (7.5 acres). Women and children were in the fields of four foot tall poppy stems wielding small curved knives to make two or three slits on each hardened poppy rod. As Anders and his men ambled through the fields chatting with the people, they could see the white latex sap oozing from the fresh cuts. When exposed to the air, the strong-smelling effluent turned dark, having become opium. The harvesters, wearing cloth face masks to protect them from the strong smell, moved efficiently among the plants scraping pea sized bubbles of blacked dry sap from the pods. It was late March, 1975, the year of the Rabbit—a fact Anders found more than coincidental with his status as a fugitive.

While Anders and his desperate companions made their way through the green hell, the fate of South Viet Nam was being sealed. When the final NVA offensive began on 8 March, the ARVN Airborne Division was suddenly recalled to shore up defenses elsewhere leaving a wide and fatal gap in the South Vietnamese defense lines rendering I Corps completely vulnerable. When the military quit the Central Highlands, there were 500,000 refugees. The communist forces shelled the departing army and refugee columns alike. Between 10 March and early April, the armed forces of the Republic of Viet Nam suffered complete military collapse, and the opportunity for a negotiated settlement no longer existed. On 19 March, Quang Tri Province in Eye Corps fell to the NVA advance. On the twenty-sixth, Hue' was overwhelmed.

On the twenty-eighth, 50,000 South Vietnamese regular troops guarding Danang disintegrated into a rapacious mob as the NVA closed in. ARVN became a demoralized rabble of rampant plunderers, rapists, murderers who shot civilians, including children, and who desperately threw civilians off boats to escape the oncoming communist army. On the thirtieth, Danang crumpled under the irrepressible onslaught; and the old US Marine base became the property of the Democratic Republic of Viet Nam.

Order was restored by the Viet Cong on 31 March, Asia's April Fool's Day. The prophesied blood bath to be visited on civilians and military alike by the vengeful communists never transpired. 200,000 political prisoners of the South Vietnamese regime and the CIA were released. The Catholics accommodated to the new regime, and peace followed close at the heels of the NVA's victorious march. Richard Nixon, President of the United States, referred to his country's exodus from the sordid collapse of the experiment in Southeast Asian democracy and the military might that tried to enforce it as, 'Peace with Honor.'

On 30 March, Fang Pao Xe, the wily and brave Hmong guide, delivered Anders, Ky, Tran, and Bach to the edge of the lowlands village of A Tuc. Xe could go no further. Hmongs were now being hunted as trophy animals by Pathet Lao, bandits, and ethnic Lao, their traditional enemies. His Mongolian features and traditional Hmong black floppy trousers and tight fitting black jacket marked him as a prey species. He melted back into the forest after Anders and his men profusely thanked him, and gave him the last of their stack of Laotian kip to assist his family and village.

Anders holed up in a trash pile while his three Vietnamese fellow fugitives meandered into the town looking for the representative of the Wa People heroin cartel who would get them into Thailand. He had been described to them, and was aptly called 'Three-legged Myo' because he had one wooden peg leg that he kept exposed and walked with a heavy wood walking staff.

Myo was sitting on a stool in a small makeshift bar, facing the door, when the three Vietnamese walked in. A Lao girl was sitting on his lap, and he held a glass of Mekkong whiskey in one hand and a bared breast in the other. His pistol lay close by on the bar top. Three-legged Myo was an ugly, all-business, mean looking Burmese Karen. His face was pitted with smallpox scars, and he had a pugnacious thrice broken nose. He was dressed in tiger-stripe fatigues. He was not the kind of man with whom others struck up casual conversations. He appeared impervious to challenges of any kind.

Tran walked to the bar near the gentleman and his lady friend taking care not to seem to notice Myo. He ordered a Tiger beer and quaffed it with obvious gusto—it was the first refrigerated, bottled drink he had drunk in two months.

"You with the Wa People?" came the guttural question from the piratical man next to him. Tran jumped a little. How could the man know that he was the one?

"Are you the one called Myo?"

"Three-legged Myo. The same." He stood up, unceremoniously dropping the girl from his lap and ceased to pay attention to her. She was only a female. He bowed briefly making the *whai*, the traditional greeting by holding his hands in prayer fashion before his face. Tran followed suit.

Ky and Bach became conscious of three men behind them holding their hands on pistols sitting loosely in the front of their trouser belts.

Tran said, "We are told you can deliver us across the Thai border."

"Perhaps. Who is we?"

"Four of us." Tran nodded slightly to indicate his two friends near the door. It was not lost on him that they were now flanked by a trio of similarly piratical appearing Burmese.

"And the other?"

"Outside of town."

"Round-eye?"

"Yes."

"I and my friends can get you where you want to go."

"When?"

"Show me your money."

CHAPTER 42

Let us face the fact that there are no really attractive options open to us…We should concentrate our attention on cutting our losses.
George W. Ball, Undersecretary of State, memorandum to President Lyndon B. Johnson, April 9, 1966.

The plan to move the clearly Caucasian Anders across Laos to the Thai border was straightforward and well thought out. In theory. The three Vietnamese men and Three-legged Myo would be dressed in NVA uniforms, and Myo had an assortment to choose from. The uniforms were altogether authentic, and their former owners would no longer be needing them. With a brief effort of trying mixes and matches of trousers, blouses, hats, and jackets, Myo, Tran, Ky, and Bach looked quite believable. Anders was to be a Soviet officer accompanying his fraternal comrades—that would explain the presence of a blond, obviously martial appearing young man.

The problem of getting across the border was not all that difficult either. Myo's people had not only obtained the uniforms, but also had appropriated the military identification papers and passports of several unfortunate departed soldiers. The four Asians perused the stack of ID papers and photos until they fell on one that more or less looked like themselves and allowed that the vagaries of poor photography and the changes wrought on them by the vicissitudes of war would be enough to account for discrepancies between the man in the flesh and his likeness on the documents. Even the counterfeit papers prepared for Anders would pass a cursory inspection, and that was all Myo expected to receive at the border.

The problem with the theory lay in a mundane detail. There was no genuine Soviet uniform; so, one had had to be contrived hastily by seamstresses who had never seen a Russian officer. Three-legged

Myo had cheerfully explained away that problem to the fugitives, reasoning that no Thai border official in the remote area where they planned to cross would have seen one either. So, that was not the problem.

The mundane detail that was a real stickler was that the seamstresses had been instructed to fashion a uniform for a very large man and had done as ordered. These very small people had no real concept of what a 'very large man' truly meant. The best they could do was to prepare the uniform of a very fat man. The worst aspect of the problem, Anders discovered as he tried on the uniform, was that 'large' had not translated into 'tall' as well. The pants, shirt, and jacket looked like they had been made for an obese achondroplastic dwarf with short extremities and rotund torso.

It was too late to make suitable alterations. The men tried to attach additional lengths of the grayest cloth they could come up with; but the result was pathetic, clownish. No Russian officer would ever have stepped foot out of his headquarters in a makeshift uniform with a foot of unmatched cloth crudely sewn onto each sleeve and trouser leg. Myo innocently suggested that they paint Anders' arms and legs gray and hope that no one would notice. He was a man conspicuously lacking in sense of humor, but even he had to join in the sidesplitting hilarity that greeted that preposterous suggestion.

Ky, who had the best criminal mind of them all, came up with a stroke of instant genius. He snapped his fingers at his revelation startling his coconspirators. "I've got it!" he fairly shouted, his face lighting up. "It's so simple; I don't know why we didn't think of it before!" The other men looked at him expectantly. Their faces were rapt; they were willing to consider anything, however outlandish.

"This is our reason for wanting to go across the border. Our Soviet *tovarich* needs modern medical care, and that equals Bangkok!" Their faces showed that they understood, but Ky went on to completion of his thought, "He has been burned. Terrible injury! We bandage up his arms and legs, and no one notices the uniform."

It was such a good plan that after they stole a sufficient quantity of roller gauze to cover Anders' extremities and found a lot left over, they bandaged his head as well. The similarity to the likeness on the phony photograph on the phony USSR military documents was enhanced by the swathing around his face.

Three-legged Myo had an NVA troop truck. They hastily threw an old mattress into the back for the unfortunate victim to lie on—over the protests of the Laotian girl Myo had been fondling in the bar, since it was her mattress. They had been debating, switching clothing, and bandaging in her humble little apartment. She was beginning to think it had been very bad joss to have met this crude man who thought nothing of knocking her around and taking her things. Myo did not want her to be left behind to take her complaints to the police or military; so, he debated about whether to break her neck and to leave her along the road someplace or to bribe her. She had been a good girl and did not seem the type to want to come to the attention of the authorities; so, he opted to give her a nice handful of kip. More accurately, he gave her Anders' and his men's money. She was mollified, and now thought better of her fine big Burmese protector.

The preparations to travel a few hundred kilometers took all day. They were ready to leave at daybreak the following day, Tuesday. Everywhere, the town and countryside showed the primacy of the communist military and political intrusion. Red flags with their golden hammer and sickle emblem waved from houses, buses, government buildings, and singly on hillsides. A recently whitewashed stupa of a pagoda was now topped with a five point Soviet style star. There were no Royalty of Lao (it was the French who added the 's') flags or uniforms to be seen.

Anders said to Myo as they jounced over the potholed road, "Looks like they have new rulers. Think maybe business will be tougher to do now?"

"Ben Yen Yang" (Laotian: Never mind, tomorrow is another day), Myo replied.

The communist presence seemed more superficial than rooted. Monks still begged for rice. A woman could be seen placing rice on the top of a fence around another pagoda for the powerful spirit of King Samsenthai, who ruled in the fifteenth century. The pagoda was one of hundreds the great king's spirit was known to inhabit. The evidences of capitalism remained stubbornly in evidence. There were wide open brothels, readily available drugs, pushy vendors and taxi drivers, spirited haggling in the myriad tiny shops, and advertising for banks, currency exchanges, and money lenders.

"More red flags, but not very different," Anders observed to Tran.

"The French have a saying I like, *'Plus çà change, plus c'est la même chose'*—'the more things change, the more they stay the same.' The Southeast Asian people went about their usual lives when the Chinese overlords ruled here, when the French were in control, in Viet Nam when Diem and his Personalist Party and then the Americans were in charge. Now the communists are in control for a while. I don't think the people will really change much. They never took to democracy, and they aren't interested in Marxism. They will be here when the Reds are gone," Tran said. The rest of the men nodded their amens to that observation.

"The Wa People did great business with the Royal Laos and the American intelligence people; now we are doing the same with the Pathet Lao. They just charge higher taxes. Only means that the price of the powdered horse will go up. Business will go on about the same, I think," Three-legged Myo commented.

There was a daunting military presence in all the cities and along all the roads. The activity was heavy and ceaseless. A road block was set up south on National Highway 9 at Pe Hourr. The Burmese Karen stepped out of the truck, rested on his wooden peg artificial lower leg and cane and spoke with the Pathet Lao NCO for a few minutes then got back in the cab of the truck, made a U turn, and headed back north.

"What's going on?" Tran asked.

"Fighting around Nang Kon and Talam. No traffic south on 9. We can't get to Saravane that way. Besides, the road from Ban Chakeuy Nua across to Saravane is probably impassable due to mud slides, the sergeant told me. We have to go north to Moung Phine and then down 23."

"Doesn't that take us back up into heavier PL country?" Ky asked.

"It's all Pathet Lao country now. We'll probably see more of them. Why, you getting nervous?" Myo's look was taunting.

"I could do without them," Ky admitted.

"Karens have been saying that about every kind of soldier for fifty years. Why should today be different?" He shrugged and drove steadily on.

They proceeded back north on Highway 9 then made the turn to the west at Ban Nabo. The Southeast Asian men got out to buy rice and dried fish from a roadside vendor, making a show of bringing some to their patient in the back of the truck. At Moung Phine, they turned due south onto Highway 23, a slightly better road. That was a little improvement for Anders who was afraid he was going to pee blood from the pummeling his kidneys were taking. Below Ban Nang the road worsened again, and Anders gave up the pretense of lying on the improvised patient bed. He said that he would get down on the mattress again only if they had to stop. The road finally improved again, relatively speaking, at Ban Song Kon, and remained capable of supporting rapid, if dusty transit onto Highway 16 all the way to Khong Sedone. In that bustling mercantile city on principle Highway

13, the country's major traffic artery, they had to spend hours and considerable money to find black market gasoline.

Myo insisted that they spend the night at Pakse, another significant city, which had a major airport. It made Anders and his four men nervous to be around all of those Laotian people, especially with the heavy military presence.

"Why not cross over tonight? The border is open until 2200, no?" Anders asked the Burmese.

"Guards are more suspicious at night, not busy enough. Tomorrow morning, late morning, there will by so many people moving both ways across the border that they won't have time to check us very close. We have to count on that," Myo told him.

The five of them slept in the truck not wishing to take the chance of trouble or suspicion in a hotel or hostel. The next morning as they pulled onto Laotian Highway 10 headed for the Chong Mek border crossing where the highway becomes Thailand 16, the men recognized the accuracy of Myo's prediction about the hordes of people streaming toward the border. The traffic was bumper to bumper and bicycle wheel to bicycle wheel with refugees—students, RLG officers, merchants, professionals, and diplomats mainly. However there were a plethora of farmers and workers leaving while it was still possible as well. For weeks the rumor had abounded that the Thais were going to seal their border. The people were in near panic to get out before they got stranded. Anders could see a predominance of nonethnic Lao faces in the crowd—Indians, Malays, Hmong, Vietnamese, ethnic Chinese—people who rightfully feared that they were going to be considered *persona non grata* when the new regime consolidated its power.

Communist soldiers, PLs and NVAs, were everywhere; but they did not seem to be interfering with the exodus. They were relaxed and merely watched. Perhaps because of, not in spite of, all the soldiers, Myo and his contraband (passengers and heroin) drove through all the way to the border post without hindrance. Once, to their great annoyance in the middle of that welter of humanity, they had a blowout that looked as if it were going to cost them their precious place in the crossing line. While stopped to repair the flat, a truck full of boys in PL uniforms and floppy hats stopped and took pride in doing the work for Myo's crew. They saluted the severely injured Russian comrade in the back of the troop truck and told the men it was an honor to be of service to a fraternal hero.

The sun blazed down on the truck making it like a bake oven inside as the hours slowly moved by with the men waiting along with the thousands of other refugees. Tempers began to get short, and Myo had to remind them that it was not a question of when, but whether, they were going to get across in Thailand. They could not afford to get upset. They spent their money for outrageously priced cups of water, warm beer, and popsicles being sold by entrepreneurial children vendors. "Who says capitalism is dead?" Ky groused. The other men laughed at the annoying children clambering all over the truck to hawk their foods and trinkets.

Their turn to go through the border check occurred at a little before noon in the height of the day's sun and the crush of humanity pressing to get across. The Laotian customs authorities gave a cursory look at the soldiers and at the bandaged patient in the back of the truck, and gave them a perfunctory go-ahead wave.

The Thailand side was a little more difficult. The uniformed Thai agent looked at Anders with undisguised loathing. He turned back to the others and asked, "Russian?" He all but spat the word.

"Yes, sir," Myo said. The customs agent gave a negative shake of his head.

"Russians make trouble. Stir up war. His papers are not in order. Entrance denied." He had not even looked at Anders' fine forgeries. The customs agent had already approved the Laotian papers of the other four men. Now, he asked for them back. "No authorization for a military unit, dangerous to the peace and good order of the Kingdom of Thailand. Entrance denied." He said stubbornly.

Tran, Ky, and Bach slowly slid their hands down toward the trigger housings on their guns. Three-legged Myo maintained a perfectly placid expression. "Sir," he said. "We are only a mercy mission taking our comrade to Bangkok for the medical care that he can only get there. Your physicians and hospitals are the finest in the world. Surely, you would not deny this injured man the care he needs."

"His papers are not in order," the agent insisted obstinately. His face grew tauter. "I will confiscate them to see if they are genuine. All of you will be kept in custody until that determination can be made." At that he turned to make a signal to the small squad of border guards in the post station house. Three brown index fingers slipped over automatic weapon triggers.

Before he could complete his summons, the Karen mercenary said quietly, "Sir, could we speak in private? It is a most important matter."

The border guard shrugged. He was getting bored, but a few more minutes could not hurt. He had Myo follow him into the small side office of the post. "What is it?" He asked. "I am very busy, and you are disrupting the King's business here."

Myo looked hard into the man's eyes, pausing for a moment to take stock of him. What he was about to say was very risky, and he well knew that. He was sure that he understood what moved the man. "I have to tell you something, sir. You are right to take such care to keep out the communists, especially the Russians. I would like to have the chance to prove to you that we are not who we appear. We are men trying to escape the evil communists. We are businessmen above all. I, myself, am a member of the Karen Liberation." He rolled up his sleeve to display the characteristic tattoo on his forearm. The customs agent's eyes noticeably softened.

"And the others?"

"ARVN. They have been fighting in the mountains and were cut off. This is their only way out."

The customs man looked skeptical. "You spoke of being businessmen?"

Myo gave him a conspiratorial smile. "Yes. We fight the communists, but we are common men and need to make a living. The war has made it most difficult for men like us to farm or to do anything in peace, for that matter."

The agent glanced at his watch.

Myo spoke more rapidly. "We work for the Wa People." He waited to see if that statement had registered. It had. Now, the agent was listening closely. "We carry the white powder over dangerous areas, and the Wa People reward us handsomely." He waited for that to sink in. The agent was no longer sneaking glances at his watch.

"We, personally, have found a number of people who help us not only once but on repeated occasions; and they have found it profitable, very much so. The Wa People see to it that everyone is treated fairly. I believe you are aware of that reputation."

A shrewd look now replaced the former antagonism in the agent's countenance. He appeared to be calculating. Myo knew that he had him.

"Perhaps we could reach an accommodation," Myo ventured, speaking softly and with respect.

The agent appeared to have completed his deliberations. He did not look at the Burmese, but said diffidently, "Perhaps."

"Would you like to investigate my men more closely, perhaps to determine for yourself if they are what I have said?"

"I would. No communists are going to enter my country on my watch. I will be looking for tricks."

"And I will be thinking of how grateful we will all be for any help you can give," said Myo as they turned to go back to the troop truck.

"Have them open their shirts, all of them," Myo whispered to the border agent as they stood in front of the three Vietnamese.

The agent told them to open their blouses. They all quickly looked at one another and at Myo who was poised on his three-legged stance. He gave an enthusiastic affirmative nod and a reassuring smile. Tran, Ky, and Bach unbuttoned their NVA blouses and revealed the *Sat Cong* tattoos on their chests, and the Phoenix tattoo on their right shoulders and backs. The agent had heard of the men with the bird tattooed on their backs, frightening, legendary stuff. "What is the meaning of the words on the chests?" He asked Myo.

Myo had no idea. He pointed his thumb at Tran. Tran guessed or hoped that he had guessed what was going on. "Kill Cong," he said.

The agent smiled broadly. The letters could have been the names of old lovers so far as he knew, but he had chosen to suspend suspicion before he and Myo had left the office. This was more about saving face than anything. "And the injured man, the Russian who is not a Russian?" He asked Myo.

Myo led the agent to the rear of the truck. They scrambled into the bed of the vehicle and stood over Anders. The young Swede lay with his muscles tensed to spring, but forced himself to appear at ease. "We must open your shirt," Myo directed Anders. Anders looked at the Karen questioningly. "It is all right. Trust me," Myo said.

Anders felt like he had no choice. He submitted. The agent inspected the chest, shoulder, and back tattoos, then nodded to Myo. The Burmese rebuttoned Anders' shirt, misaligning a set, in his rush. Outside the truck again, Myo played his last trump card. Either the agent would accept an offer, or they would have to shoot their way out of the border station, an eventuality that Myo did not even want to have to contemplate.

"We would be most grateful for your help, sir. Perhaps you would permit us to make a contribution to the education fund for the post's children to express our thanks." The agent nodded almost imperceptibly. Myo fingered his large roll of currency.

"I have a delivery to make in Bangkok. A letter of safe passage would be beneficial. I would be more than generous with one who assisted my business. Such a letter would be the first of many profitable deals between the Wa People and one such as you." The agent made no protest. Myo looked about cautiously, then produced a roll of bills that was more money than the agent had ever seen at one time. Myo counted off several, looked at the agent and smiled, then slid off several more. The money disappeared into the man's blouse pocket.

"I can see that I was wrong in believing that you men were communists. I won't need to detain you longer. You may go." There was no mention of the letter Myo had requested.

"Thank you. You are a most reasonable man. I am sure that your family will be pleased at the practical decision you have made today. Please come to the truck. I have something more to show you."

Myo leaned over the tailgate, rummaged his hands around in the rucksacks for a few minutes then came out with a plastic bag packed with a quarter of a kilo of pure heroin. The agent's eyes narrowed with indecision and greed. "For you. For future considerations. I expect that you can be an important man in the Wa People's vast network. We are all paid well, and this is a gesture of our good faith."

The agent had sworn an oath to his king to fight against the importation and exportation of illicit drugs. He knew it was wrong to turn the other way. He also knew of men in the service who had become rich by doing so. His family would not want again if he took it. He reached out his hand accepting the package of narcotics, an irrevocable act. Both he and Myo knew it. One did not leave the employ of the Wa People casually. The border agent hurriedly scratched out a letter of safe conduct and affixed his official seal. He waved the truck on. Myo's parting words were, "Until next time," my friend.

The tension had been terrible for Anders waiting there in the dark confines of the back of the truck while the negotiations vital to his survival took place, negotiations in which he could not take part or even observe. A kaleidoscopic set of images of possible outcomes of the attempt to cross the border had flown through his mind, most of them violent and with bad endings. Before Myo and the agent had come in and had inspected his chest, he had taken mental refuge in a memory of lying in bed in Inga Haakensdatter's house in The World smelling the intoxicating aroma of baking bread and bacon grease wafting in from her kitchen. He held on to that daydream as long as he could. One oddity about the daydream, he realized, was that he had been thinking in Swedish. Another was that he would have sworn that he could hear Inga speaking out loud.

Myo drove as fast as possible away from the border station trying to put as many kilometers between them and the Laotian threat as he could before making final preparations to head for Bangkok. He sped down Thai Highway 16 toward Warin Chamrap where they would turn south in the direction of the Cambodian border. He knew they were living on borrowed time; they had to get rid of the truck with its communist regime markings. Gasoline was much more available and easier to get than in Laos, but still expensive. Anders and his men could see their once large fund beginning to dwindle noticeably. He dreaded to think what might happen if they ran out.

Everywhere along the way they saw men in cotton trousers and Thai work shirts or in western type shirts unlike the dress style in Laos where they had just left. Most wore strips of cotton cloth tied around their waists like shorts. Women were in loose-fitting, modest blouses and long, brightly colored skirts. The people were unhurried and did not have the look of constant tension seen etched into the faces of the Laotians and Vietnamese. It was a novelty to be in a place where there was peace.

The small pacific villages Anders and his companions saw as they moved rapidly along the narrow roads were usually located on the bank of a river. The houses were made of wood and bamboo with steeply pitched roofs thatched with nipa palm and were surrounded with a bamboo fence. Inside the fences were neatly tended flowers, fruit trees, coconut palms, small vegetable gardens and a small Spirit House. The Thai villagers climbed a flight of stairs to get into their houses which were built on high posts, above the ever threatening waters below and invading insects. Under the houses was a storage place for farm tools, water buffalo, and festival kites and masks.

Occasionally, there would be a house that stood out in stark contrast among the others in the village because it was large and made of cinder blocks with a strongly constructed roof. Anders asked the Wa People truck driver why one family had so much more than the other villagers.

"The daughters of those houses have gone away to the city to be prostitutes. The girls are able to send enough money home to add to the support of their parents. The houses are more status symbols than anything. Having such a house indicates that the people living inside have a clever, hard working, and attractive daughter," said Three-legged Myo.

Often there were large areas in the villages for drying coconut, and in some villages there were cottage industry rubber manufacturing plants adjoining rubber tree plantations. The rubber trees were slashed with downward slanting cuts in their bark and white latex slowly ran down into the attached buckets. Strong men bent over great vats of collected latex to which acid had been added to thicken it and stirred with great oars. Others pressed out the product between rollers, and still others, usually women, cut the strips into uniform bath towel-sized pieces. Other people were busy working in rice mills, characteristic little sheds with corrugated iron sides and roofs. Anders and his men took comfort in the prevailing images of peace and industry. The people were poor, but employed, and no one looked hungry or afraid.

There were no telephone or electric poles or wires. Houses were lighted with kerosene or coconut oil lamps. The people were clean and smiling. They waved at the men in the truck as they carried out their bathing or washing of clothes in their river.

At Warin Chamrap, Myo turned off the main highway and sped along an outlying road to a large junk yard and entered the enclosure. Four vicious dogs snarled and menaced around the truck. Two well-armed men stepped out of the yard shack leveling shot guns at the truck windows. "What do you want?" They demanded in Thai.

Myo responded in their tongue. "*Sawàt-dii,*" (Hello) he said and made a whai. His facility with Thai was rudimentary and colloquial, but served enough to allow him to conduct business. "I am Three-legged Myo of the Wa People. These are my associates. We need to do business with you."

As if the words 'Wa People' themselves were magic, the junk yard guards broke into smiles and got rid of the dogs. Before Myo and his friends could enter the shack and get out of the broiling sun, the guards produced five bottles of cold Singha beer and thrust them into the hands of the newly arrived men. Anders noticed, however, that their guns were never far from their hands.

"We must get to *Bang Makok* (place of olives)," Myo told them once the amenities were over. "We want to trade our truck for a good enclosed *songthaew* (most comparable to the Philippine jeepney). You will find our vehicle to be in excellent condition."

"We see the markings. Not a safe truck here. We could not sell it or use it," one of the hosts said with a shrug of resignation. He wished to be of help to his friends, but what could one do?

"The markings can be painted over. I see many trucks from over there," Myo continued reasonably, indicating east by a twist of his mouth and lips in that direction. "The truck is of better construction than any *songthaew*, and will last for a very long time doing heavy work."

The two men went into whispered consultation. "It would be an expense," one of them finally said, "and money is short. It would take some time to find a buyer. We could not bear such expense ourselves."

"The truck we bring you is more valuable than that we will take. You will realize a handsome profit," Myo argued.

"Perhaps, but only someday later. Now, there would be expenses. There are no papers, I presume. We will have to provide baksheesh for the people in the registry office, get new licenses, pay to get paint at a place that is discrete. How can we manage?" His face was a mask of innocent questioning and resignation.

"I can see your problem, old friend," Myo said. "Perhaps we could share your burdens," he offered.

"Ah, that is an idea," the Thai said. His face indicated that it was the first time such a thought had occurred to him. He was a polite man and would not be one to take advantage of a friend's need. But since Myo put it that way, perhaps there could be an accommodation.

"What would you estimate your expenses to be? Myo asked.

There was another brief consultation between the two Thais. The negotiator again turned to Myo. "Our conservative guess would be 4000 B." (1 Thai baht = $25 American) He maintained an expression like a soda cracker despite the preposterously high figure.

"We are but poor businessmen trying to make a slim profit ourselves. I am no expert, but I would think that a clever man such as yourself would be able to get the work done for 1000 B. Our half of that would be 500," Three-legged Myo responded.

"You have been away for some time, friend Myo. Costs have climbed, what with the American reverses in Laos, and the higher cost of services. Because you are an old and valued friend; and we have done much business together in the past and expect to do more in the future, I would make you a onetime offer of 3000 B. That is only fair."

"You mean 1500 as our share, of course."

"Of course."

"We have only 1000. There has been a great drain on our humble resources. I regret that I cannot offer more. You know that I would be honored to do so if I could."

"That would be insufficient, my friend. We would suffer difficulties." The man shrugged sadly. It appeared to be his final offer. The ball returned to Myo's court.

"It appears that times are hard for us all, old friend," said Myo. "Perhaps, you could reflect on future profits from the sale of the truck and weigh that against the short term costs you might incur. Otherwise..." He let the words trail off. "We will have to find a less desirable but still serviceable *songthaew* at another friend's place."

The Thai knew that he was not likely to get more; and Myo was right; he did stand to turn a nice profit when he sold their truck. It was too good a deal to pass up. "I believe my friends would forgive me if I were to accept only 1250 B. Would that not seem fair?"

This time Myo made a pretense of going into a serious negotiation with his confreres. He had fully expected to pay 3000. This was something of a minor coup to hear a final offer of 1250. With a look of resignation reflecting a major defeat at the hands of a superior haggler, Myo agreed.

The Thais served another round of chilled Singha. The most popular beer in Thailand was very expensive, and it was only for friends that such a celebration would be proffered. Myo and Anders and his men drove out in an vividly decorated vehicle, painted in fluorescent fuchsia stripes that would glow in the dark, and hood ornaments that included an eight inch high bright yellow Buddha, four large horns, and a row of lights that came on automatically whenever the ignition was turned on. Anders had to shake his head. It had seemed wise to him to be as unobtrusive in his passage across Thailand as possible. He and the others could only shake their heads and trust to Myo's judgment.

The fugitives returned to the city center and found a public bath. They scrubbed the grime and sweat of almost a month's accumulation with coarse soap and hand brushes. None of them felt clean until they had repeated the process twice more. Myo went out and bought each of them a cotton *mâw hâwm* (Thai blue button-down work shirt), loose fitting unbelted baggy cotton trousers, a red and white plaid sash to use as a belt (or as a head band, shorts, towel, hammock, or mosquito swatter), and sandals. It took some doing to fit Anders. Next they all went to a barber's and shed large amounts of facial and scalp hair. With the exception of Anders, the men left the shop looking and smelling like Thai citizens on holiday. He just looked big and Occidental, presumably a tourist with Thai friends. It would have to do.

Before finding a restaurant, they made sure that the bricks of heroin could not be discovered in their *songthaew* since conviction for possession of heroin resulted in an unappealable life sentence in Thailand.

The restaurant the men chose was a bright, clean, and refreshing *ráan khâo kaeng* (curry noodle shop). It was the first time Anders had sat down to a table with a cloth and western dinnerware and utensils in over two years. He felt awkward and out of practice. The five men were starved and ate as if it were their last meal. Anders had prawn and lemon grass soup with mushrooms, green curry with beef, and *plaa lãi* (fresh water eel). The contrast with LURPS, C Rations, pigeon heads, stewed dog, and roast bat was not lost on the young man as he became satiated. When they finished their main courses, they were served a heaping basket of fruit—sliced watermelon and guava, limes and tamarinds for the pleasure of both tart and sweet, and rambeh and rose-apples that were just coming into season.

Anders leaned against the back of his seat in the *songthaew* and contented himself to let Myo take him and his friends further into the safety of Thailand. The word 'Thai' means free; and for the first time in years, Anders Bergstrom was beginning to feel that he could be 'Thai.' He should have been content, at ease; but it seemed as if the longer he was free of the dangers and fears of the battlefield, the more apprehensive he got. The farther he went toward freedom and calm in his environment, the more trapped and tense he felt. It was irrational. He knew he should be feeling a lifting of psychological weight. He should feel lighthearted, but he did not. What was the matter with him?

At times in his daydreams he saw fleeting glimpses of Liên and H'Klois, of the South China Sea filled with sampans and fishing skiffs, and of the ethereal beauty of the Truong Song mountain tops. More and more, however, he dreamt of things farther back—of Inga and even of one of his foster mothers, Margaret Hansen, and her chocolate cake. Sometimes the face of a girl intruded, Gretchen Smith, whom he thought he had long since forgotten. It was curious he heard their voices quite clearly; even more curious, everyone spoke Swedish. At times the voices were so real that Anders turned to look in the direction from which they came.

The men passed by the vivid panoply of rural Thai scenery and life. Stands of wild bamboo, some individual spears eight inches thick and twenty feet high stood in areas where there had been small forest fires. Tran pointed out to Anders the remarkable fact that bamboo is a grass—this was the most impressive grass.

Men and women were laying out strips of coconut to make copra and coconut oil for soaps and margarine. Huge tusked elephants were as much a part of everyday activity as were cars in London or New York. They pulled loads, carried passengers, and marched in dignified lines to water holes. Pairs of them worked together to move long teak logs, their front legs moving in goose-step unison.

Native women went about their daily chores in colorful cotton or silk skirts with round high-cut necklines, fitted sides, and long sleeves despite the equatorial humidity and heat. They wore flowers on their ears and necks. They were lovely, modest people for whom display of body parts was considered disrespectful and of low taste.

There were uniquely Thai buildings, wats, monuments, and memorial religious sculptures dotting the sides of the roads, old and modern neo-Thai, simple and ornate, borrowed and original, but all distinctly Thai in character.

As Anders napped in the torpid heat of the afternoon, Myo drove along Highway 27 until it ran parallel with the still contested and insecure northern border of Cambodia. He turned onto 10 and drove to Kantharalak where he planned to spend the night with a business friend, one of the Wa People's Thai contacts. They traveled through the city making unnecessary U turns, sudden stops, and frequent left or right turns down alleyways and with all five men looking back, forward, and to the sides to try and detect any unwanted followers, especially police. They expended an hour in such work before pulling into a small driveway behind a comfortable cinderblock house. "This is it," Myo announced.

There were greetings, suspicious glances at the round-eye and the three Viets, a round of explanations, then Myo's friend, Lan Chaphraphong, was all smiles and ingratiation. He sent one of his sons out to move the *songthaew* into the lean-to garage and to cover it with a large tarp to keep it from the view of prying eyes. Lan escorted the four men to the rear entrance, the family entrance—a courtesy that told them they were regarded as family and not as outsiders. Lan's wife and three daughters worked in the yard extracting kapok, the silky fibers that grows around the seeds of the kapok tree, stretching the strands out to dry. They watched the newcomers with only passing interest and returned to their gossip.

Anders was intrigued by the small Spirit House in the right corner of the front yard, a nearly exact miniature replica of the family dwelling. This small one was for the good spirits who lived there and protected the inhabitants of the home. There were offerings of fresh food and water in front of the Spirit House as there were every day.

Lan made sure that all of the newcomers were fed and watered, then got right to business. He had four kilos of heroin that he wanted to get out of his hands. It was unsafe to hold it.

"I will not be easy until this is in the hands of the American soldiers in Krung Thep," Lan told the five visitors.

"Then we must transport it the rest of the way to the City of Angels for you," old friend, Myo offered.

"Because I cannot sell it in the usual places, I am obliged to relinquish it to you for a fraction of its worth, Myo," Lan said. He was not haggling, just stating a fact, knowing that the Wa People would be as fair as possible.

"And this amount of product is unexpected. I do not have the baht with me to be fair to you."

"Then we will have to ask the Lord Buddha for the miracle," Lan replied. There was a note of completion in his voice. He and Myo made *whai* to one another, and the deal was consummated. The miracle to which Lan referred was trust.

When Myo and Anders and the Viets were alone in their room that evening, Myo approached the other four men. "I will tell you of my negotiations with brother Lan. He has four kilos. I will pay him six million B. now, and we can take the powder to Bangkok where we are free to get the best price—probably eleven million B. for his China White. In all transactions, the Wa People get half the profit, and I never give them even a satang less. We can keep the profit otherwise."

"I take it that 'we' includes 'us', the four of us?" asked Bach.

"If you have the capital and wish to be rich."

Anders, Ky, Tran, and Bach quickly looked at each other's faces and then back to Myo. They nodded their agreement. Myo went on, "I wish to contribute one fourth, personally; and you four can add the rest. You will guarantee $180,000 American—about 4,500,000 B. I expect that we can sell to Americans I know for $450,000 to $555,000, or 11 to 12,000,000 B. Your profit would be between $185,000 and $190,000—maybe $60—65,000 each. Remember that the Wa People get half the profit right off the top. Still, not too bad for us for a couple of day's work, no?"

"As long as we don't get caught," Tran added soberly.

"I am a very careful man. I do not deal with thieves or betrayers. I am well known for that. Very well known," the peg-legged Burmese asserted darkly. Anders could just bet that every word of that statement was the gospel truth.

"We have four keys of our own to get rid of," Ky told Myo. The Burmese Karen nodded. He already knew that.

Arab traders introduced Greek opium to the receptive Han Chinese during the reign of Kublai Khan in the thirteenth century, CE. It quickly became an integral part of Chinese social life and was valued for its ritual and medicinal value. As the Chinese moved down into the hills of Southeast Asia, they brought along their poppy that thrived in the verdant high altitudes—optimum is 1000 to 1500 meters. It was cheap to grow, and served as a convenient way for the hill people to meet the tax levy imposed by the Chinese overlords. Everyone prospered. In many ways it was then, and at the time Anders and his men participated in opium trafficking, an ideal smuggler's contraband: light weight and low volume, nonperishable for years at a time; and year in and year out for millennia, it had retained very high value.

Thailand was mainly a country of conduit for the massive amounts of opium produced in Southeast Asia. Burma produced some 500-600 tons in an average year, and as much as 3000-4000 tons in bumper crop years, Laos about 200 tons, and Thailand about 60 tons. The farmers who grew the poppies and did the backbreaking work of harvesting the latex received less than a thousandth part of the billions of dollars the traffic eventually generated. A farmer was lucky to get $2000 a kilo for his backbreaking work. The vast majority of the heroin traffic moved from the Golden Triangle to Bangkok.

In the 1960s when the Americans began to invade Southeast Asia in substantial numbers, the value of the trade crescendoed sharply, and American military men became integrally involved in its transport. The American Central Intelligence Agency provided valuable conduits for the transportation in competition with the drug overlords and a certain amount of friction developed. The communists not only shared in the profits, but they made it easy for the Americans to pollute themselves as one more weapon in the hands of the weaker, but more determined nations. Even as the Thai government took steps to interdict the farming, trade, and traffic in opium in its country, the LPRP (Laotian People's Revolutionary Party), the new rulers of Lao, took strong steps to increase its production, refineries, and market share.

Khun Sa, leader of the Shan People, was the prime opium lord in the world. He had headquarters in Burma and in Ban Hin Taek City in Thailand's Chaing Rae Province and moved with easy facility throughout the region. His people were responsible for the manufacturing and refining processes while the Wa People, in an uneasy alliance, were more responsible for the growing and distributing of the Golden Triangle's principle product.

Anders reasoned that if he did not move the merchandise, someone else would. He also reasoned that money was the determinate of power, of a comfortable life, and often enough, of survival itself. He determined to insulate himself against any need for help or protection from any government, church, or society, save only his three friends. He had no qualms about moving Lan Chaphraphong's bricks, especially since he knew that no more than 2.5% of the smuggled drugs were ever intercepted. Thailand is a large country, about the size of Texas or France; and it's military and police cannot cope with the sheer volume of the traffic.

Lan and Myo completed the transaction the following morning, relying on the miracle of trust to guide their payment arrangements. Myo handed over the large sums of money he had obtained from Anders, Tran, Bach, and Ky. Lan went to the Buddha Shelf sitting beneath the large framed picture of King Bhumibol Adulyadej, Rama IX and Queen Sirikit in his living room and picked up the heroin bricks from among the images of Buddha and other sacred images and food and water for the Buddha. "My product has been under the Lord's protection," he explained without a hint that he might think that others of his faith would consider such a sentiment a sacrilege.

Myo spent the morning welding a false floor on the *Songthaew* to store the eight kilograms (four from Lan, and four of their own) of high-value contraband when they traveled. Lan's wife, Thim, a cheerful and pleasant woman from Chang Mai, Thailand's northern and second largest city, fed Anders, Tran, Ky, and Bach her people's favorite *Laab* and *Luu*—spicy raw meat and animal blood. She was very excited that day and wished for her husband and his guests to come to the center of the city to witness the great event taking place there. Myo declined, indicating the press of his work on the vehicle, but the others considered it only polite to accept the generous and enthusiastic woman's request.

A substantial crowd gathered in the streets and around market stalls facing the open center block of the city. The stalls were either closed or ignored. No one was interested in buying or selling food or painted and flower embroidered umbrellas or jute and kenaf ropes and burlap bags that day. There were scores of bonzes and kowtowing faithful everywhere. The monks had more rice than their bowls could hold, and they were busy performing the blessed water rites for purification of long lines of penitents and granting to one and all the ceremony of the blessed strings for protection from the evil spirits. One of them told Thim that the spirits of the underworld abounded today because of the return of the Great One.

Anders asked one of the monks what was happening, which 'Great

One' had returned. The monk had a beatific expression and was ecstatic to tell the only person left in the crowd, in the world, so far as he knew, that it was in fact the Lord Buddha who walked among them. Anders and his friends would be privileged to be among the first westerners to see the Beneficent One, the Tenth Reincarnation, in the flesh. "You can hear him speak," the monk said. Indeed, the crowd had quieted to a reverential hush.

In the center of the square, standing alone, was a man of no more than twenty. He looked for all the world like any of a million or more Buddhist monks, except that his robes were made of animal skins and were torn and ragged. He was bare footed. He had a strong voice. Anders could hear him speaking; and an educated man in the crowd translated for Anders, proud of the fact that he knew English.

"It is the ideal of every Buddhist to live the good life of service and sacrifice. I speak of an entire life, of no tricks or hypocrisy. Every man has two life cycles—the one good, and the other bad. Good deeds accumulate and add to one's cycle of life; sins add to the bad cycle. The art is to make one's good cycle so large that the individual will be a higher, more moral, more learned, more caring individual filled with additional wisdom in the next life. In my past life, I subjugated my passions and my flesh until in a great light it was revealed to me that I was a candidate to be the next Lord Buddha. The Great One of old told me that in my next life I would see the beginning of the great cleansing fire to burn up the evil of mankind. The terrible war being waged by our neighbors to the east is that fire. It is beginning to spread. The Great One also told me that I must travel the length and breadth of the earth to tell all peoples to repent of their sins, or they will be burned. If I accomplish that goal faithfully, I will be the promised Lord Buddha returned to save mankind from the underworld."

Monks and lay penitents prostrated themselves to the ground. Anders was very much out of place as he remained standing. Even his three Vietnamese friends touched their foreheads on the pavement of the city's street alongside Thim and Lan. The messiah's and Anders' eyes met. Anders expected to see the eyes of a madman, a demagogue, or a charlatan; but, instead, he saw a kind and sympathetic face, one that seemed to invite him into the inner circle. Anders had never before seen such a charismatic man.

It was time for Anders and his men to get on their way. They followed Lan and Thim back to their home in the outskirts of the city. A group of dancers, caught up in the spirit of religious revival occasioned by the visit of the holy man, were gathered on a blocked-off street leading out of town. They acted out a scene from the Ramakian (Thai version of the Indian, Ramayana), the story-poem that originated in India about 0 AD. Lan described the actions and told the story: "Rama was a brave and noble prince who was really a god in human form. He had a beautiful and loyal wife named Sita who was kidnapped by an evil king. After many adventures, Rama defeated the wicked king and rescued Sita."

Anders watched fascinated as the actions of the dancers matched the story being told by Lan. He was entranced by the vividly colored costumes and masks and captivated by the graceful stylistic movements of the dancers.

Elsewhere along the route back to Lan's house after the sermon by the messianic Buddhist there were *Khon Drams,* costumed gods and demons, acting out the never-ending battle between good and evil. Further up the street were several stalls featuring shadow puppet plays also depicting various ancient Hindu legends.

As they walked back to the house, Lan explained that this priest they had gone to see was only one of many so-called 'messiahs' or Buddha candidates. Every few years, in this Buddhist country or that, a charismatic priest would rise up among the people and set out on a pilgrimage like that of Sidhartha Guatama's (The Enlightened One). Most of them lost popularity or simply disappeared. Lan said that he would just wait and see what became of this one.

At noon, with the sun and the heat at their zenith, Myo got Anders and his men to board their vehicle, and they headed off west and south for the capital city, passing through Surin, Buriram, Khorat, and Nakhon Nayok provinces. It was an ideal time to enter Bangkok, April 13, the first day of the Songkran Festival—the Thai lunar new year celebration. Tens of thousands of celebrants were streaming into the city swelling the population temporarily well beyond the usual five million. The likelihood of the men from Laos having their conveyance searched was minuscule, and they were able to travel without contact with police. Their progress was slower than if they had been walking. They were approaching the city along the highway running along the east side of the Chao Phraya River. Progress was so slow that Myo stopped off to let his guests see a stone pillar at the metropolis' border. It gave the name of the city:

Krungthep-Maha Nakorn-Amorn Ratanakosindra-Mahindrayadhya-

Mahadilokpop -Noparatana Rajkhani-Burirom-UdomRajnivet-Mahastan-Amorn Pimarn Avatarn Satit-Sakkatuttiya-Vishnukarm Prasit.

Anders and his men were mystified. Myo translated: "City of gods, the great city, the residence of the Emerald Buddha, the impregnable city of Ayutthaya, of God Indra, the grand capital of the world endowed with nine precious stones, the happy city abounding in enormous royal palaces which resemble the heavenly abode where reigns the reincarnated God, a city given by Indra and built by Vishnukarm."

"I'll settle for 'City of Angels," said Ky.

At least I can remember Bang Makok," said Anders.

"And I like simple, Krung Thep. They'll all do, I suppose," said Myo. "Take your pick."

As the five men stood by the pillar trying to take in the inscription, a car load of revelers drove by and drenched them with water from buckets. They drove off laughing uproariously. Anders could see that they were all soaking wet as well. In fact, everyone around them was either wet or in one stage or another of drying off. Almost everyone was carrying his or her own bucket of water. During the festivities of the new year, the people of Thailand set about to wash all of the Buddhas' images. Monks and elders received symbols of respect from younger and novice priests by having their hands sprinkled, or 'bathed' with perfumed water. Since it was the peak of the hot season, the symbolic bathing was carried on as a nationwide frolic. Everyone got to cool off and to release any pent-up frustrations collected over the past year. There were bands and beauty contests and people buying birds and fish to set free in honor of the season.

There were two choices for the five men for the duration of Songkran—hide out in some mountain retreat or hotel room or house or join the water splashing. Anders, Three-legged Myo, Ky, Tran, and Corporal Bach went to the sidewalk vendor and bought buckets, visited the river, and bathed everyone they could get at.

CHAPTER 43

When the enemy advances; we retreat. When he escapes, we
harass. When he retreats, we pursue. When he is tired, we attack.
Mao Tse-Tung

Once in the city, Anders and his
Vietnamese partners went to the Thai Farmer's Bank, filled out the
massive forms, and transferred $10,000 from the Union Bank of
Switzerland in Lucerne by wire. In an hour, they were carrying
230,000 baht (the exchange rate was 23B:1$ that day) and feeling
uncomfortable and conspicuous. Myo had his own Swiss bank. For all
his cutthroat and barbaric appearance, he was a sophisticated businessman. He, too, needed pin money.

For the serious business transaction that had brought the Burmese
Karen all this way from home, he drove them to a cluster of dilapidated
buildings in the warehouse district where he parked. "Stay in the
truck. Not safe," he said. After Anders looked around at the foreboding surroundings and at the malevolent faces passing their *songthaew*,
he considered Myo to be the master of understatement. Myo left them
for half an hour.

He returned with a burly red-haired freckled-faced man dressed in
a Philippine Barong, brightly patterned knee length shorts, flip flop
sandals and an Uzi. He did not smile. After looking the occupants of
the *songthaew* over with a jaundiced eye, he got in the back and gave
Myo directions. They drove for fifteen minutes through the maze of
Bangkok streets in the worst traffic the men had ever seen until
Anders was completely turned around. He could not have gotten back
out of that labyrinth to save his life, and he feared that that might well
be required.

Finally they stopped at a nondescript fortune-teller's stall and
walked into the back room ahead of the red-haired man. After a

hushed conversation with several blacks and two other Caucasians, the sandy complexioned freckled-faced man returned and gave Anders and company a gap-toothed smile. "If you got the stuff, we can party. I got the money. We don't haggle here. Eight keys of pure brings you nine hundred sixty K, American. That's 120 K a brick. Price is up; so you win today. DEA has been puttin' on the heat, drove the supply down, and the price went up. Good old law of supply and demand. You can have it in Bs or dollars. I'm talkin' full keys, not jing." Jing were blocks of China White produced by Chinese Triads by compressing pure heroin concentrate powder into narrow 750 gram bricks instead of the western 1000 milligram size.

"We have it—all the best China White Number Four—full keys. Let's see the money," Myo asked.

"No prob, bro," chimed in one of the black men. He appeared sedated, high on something. He produced two mail sacks full of money, in this case, American. Myo nodded his satisfaction. Anders took note of the silent guards standing alertly around the room cradling their Uzis and H&Ks. It was unlikely that anyone could pull off a robbery from these guys.

"Drive the truck around the back," one of the blacks ordered.

Myo left the others and drove to the back. One of the black men opened the rear door, and Myo reached into the compartment between the false floor and true floor of the vehicle and produced the eight kilo bricks of heroin. Anders and his men tightened their hands on their own weapons. The Americans—all of them were expats from the war—checked over the goods, including taste and test tube examination, gave thumbs up high signs, and dragged out three large sacks of money.

"Make three-fourths of that in baht, please," requested Myo.

"No prob." Calculators were tapped, then the proper mix of currencies was accomplished, and Myo and the other men drove out of the trash strewn alley and onto the hectic street. Back at the Thai Farmer's Bank, Anders, Tran, Ky, and Bach made another wire transfer, this time to their Swiss bank. They were $120,937.50 richer—each. Myo had $53,750, the Wa People had $107,500, and Lan would have $215,000 (at the day's exchange rate).

Myo bid them farewell and left the four friends in front of the bank trying to decide what to do next. The answer for Anders came suddenly. He saw a neat sign in English over the door of a shop—"Viet Nam Veterans Against the War". He vaguely remembered reading that that organization was responsible for getting deserters and draft dodgers into foreign countries and away from the American military police. He could not think of a better plan.

"I need to check something out," he told his friends. "Come with me for a minute." As he started to cross the street in the direction of the building housing the organization, his practiced eye saw several obvious watchers outside, making a show of being casual. They had marine short haircuts and appeared fit, unlike the occasional hippies and Thais that sauntered in and out of the office. Anders tagged them as NIS (Naval Investigative Service) or MPs in civvies. He made a smart about face and walked away from the VVAW headquarters.

His Vietnamese friends looked at him queryingly. "I want you to do something for me," Anders said when they were a couple of corners away from the headquarters. "I want the three of you to go to that building with the English sign on it and explain that you have a friend that needs to get out of the country and does not want to go back to the US. I need to meet with them someplace besides their building. The area is crawling with US military and police. Okay?"

"As your dark skinned countrymen would say—'no prob,'" said Ky.

"Let's get a room someplace. We can meet the American in the hotel," Anders said.

They flagged a taxi, and at the driver's advice were taken to central Banglamphu section and stopped at the Nith Jaroen Suk, a Chinese-Thai family owned Hotel on Khao San Road. It was obvious that the price, 128 B, for a *hâwng phát lom* (fan room) was jacked up for *farangs* (foreigners); so, they haggled down to 85 B., more of a moral victory than anything. The hotel was busy, filled with Thai traveling businessmen who were asked if they required extra nighttime services. The very hectic character of the inexpensive hotel granted a cloak of anonymity for Anders and his men.

After they ate at one of the noodle houses along Khao San Road, Anders went back to the hotel while his friends went back to the Viet Nam Veterans Against the War headquarters. Well after dark, Tran knocked on the door of his and Anders' room and informed him that they had one of the VVAW people in the lobby.

"Let's go down," Anders said. When he had looked the man over from a vantage point where he could not be seen himself and had ascertained to his satisfaction that there were no American or Thai police lurking around, Anders told Tran to find an unused office; so, they would not be seen talking. The VVAW man was a well dressed, tall, lean Negro, with ebony black skin wearing a Muslim cap who stood out from the Thais in the lobby like the proverbial sore thumb.

It was hot in the room Tran found, and the fan was inadequate. Everyone sweated, but Anders' degree of perspiration was excessive owing to his stressful mental state.

The VVAW man was familiar with the symptoms and strove to put Anders at ease. "Hey brother, take it easy. You're with friends now. This is a safe place—for a while anyway. Where're you from?"

"Hue'," Anders said without hesitation. He did not think of himself as being from Zarahemla, or Utah, or even the US anymore.

"Where in The World, I mean?" persisted the smiling black man. "Hey, where're my manners. I'm Kareem El Farrukh." He extended his hand with its long pianist's fingers.

Anders shook hands. "Anders. Anders Bergstrom," he said and regretted his forthrightness as soon as the words were out of his mouth.

"That your real name, bro?"

Anders shook his head, "Yes."

"'Cause the one thing we got going for ourselves is honesty. We are 100% honest with each other in this outfit, not like the army or marines. We have to trust you; and you have to trust us; or we can't do anything for each other."

"That'd be a refreshing change," commented Anders.

"You know anything about the Viet Nam Vets Against the War, Anders? I mean, besides the obvious political opinion in the name?"

"Not really. I heard you can get people out of Asia, out of the hands of the military police, that sort of thing. Not much else, and I don't even know if that is true or not."

"It is true, for starters. I'll tell you some general things about the organization, but you will understand if I leave out some details for security's sake."

"Sure, go ahead."

"Okay. Let me tell you that we started out with about 7,000 members in '68, and that included a lot of students, professors, and other sympathizers. The first financing was from Jane Fonda, may Allah bless her honkey heart. By two years ago about 15% of all of the Viet Nam vets identified with us in the antiwar movement. We got power now, man. Even the WOMs got to listen up when we speak. I have some stats on the matter: In the US of A there have been about 53 million draft age people—half of them men, about 27 million. 8.7 million enlisted, 2.2 million were drafted, and 16 million or so never served. They were the rich men's kids, some guys with college deferments, and the 4-Fers. A high school dropout or even a graduate was twice as likely to serve in the armed forces as a college graduate. More blacks than whites as a percentage of the enlistees. So, you can see that there might be a whole lot of anger out there. In 1966, alone, more than 5,000 draft cards was burned. Country had 32,000 cases of failure to report for duty in the first place." He was getting off the track.

"To continue. About 100,000 or so people got less-than-honorable discharges; see, most of them because they got fed up with this unjust war and wouldn't play along anymore. I hear that there have been about 550,000 cases of desertion with at least 5,000 of them In Country and another 2,000 AWOL in so-called rest areas, and 570,000 cases of draft dodging. MACV says there were only 24 cases of desertion occurring during actual combat, but I know for a fact that is bull. You hear of bros out there in Camau and the U Minh forest or up in the highlands working for Charley all the time. Got to be more'n 24. Just sounds better, I guess. AWOL rates increased 400% between 1966 and 1971. There were 175,000 conscientious objectors.

"To put it into perspective, my man—ARVN had 57,000 desertions up to 1971, and now they quit this mess at the rate of a 1,000 a month. The NVA and VC had 87,000 in that same period.

"To make a long story short, out of all of these American men of conscience, the so-called COs, AWOLS, deserters, and draft dodgers, there are some ten or eleven thousand out and out fugitives. That's where we come in, in part, anyway. The American public thinks we are just a bunch of hippie windbags. That's okay. What they don't know won't hurt them...or guys like you, I'm guessing. Our stated goal, to quote our founder is to 'make the nation realize the moral agony of America's Viet Nam generation—whether to kill on military orders and be a criminal or to refuse to kill and be a criminal.' We can get pacifist brothers, black or white, to safer elsewheres. We got connections. That sound like something that interests you?"

"That's why I wanted to talk to you," Anders said. The earnest expression on his face conveyed the seriousness of his intent.

"Good. You are among friends, like I said. Once we check you out, on the QT, of course, we get you out of Thailand. You with me?"

"I guess. I have questions, but that's basically what I had in mind."

You good at keeping secrets, Anders?

"Pretty good," he admitted. "More than pretty good," he thought to himself. "Everything about my life is some sort of a secret."

"That's important because the people that are going to help you are dedicated, decent people; and they would be hurt if you told about them. You have to promise never to divulge the details of your escape, not even that the VVAW was behind it. That straight with you?"

"Okay. I'm not in a position to be a public figure."

"Oh?" Kareem asked, interested in Anders' response.

"I want everything about this deal to be secret, even more than you do."

"We need to talk about that some more, Anders. Usually, your hosts in the country where you end up like to parade you around a bit and get a propaganda statement or two for the press. Like, maybe you'll end up in Russia or one of the eastern-bloc countries like that. They are very generous; but they do like to get their digs at the US; and they will want to use you. See what I mean?"

"Yeah." Anders was deadly serious. "I see, but I can't let anyone know where I am, where I've gone. My case isn't quite like the regular army guy's. No matter where I go, if they know I'm there, they'll come after me."

"Who's they, bro?"

"I can't tell you all that. You have your secrets, and I have mine. Isn't that fair?"

Kareem put his chin on his palm and looked at Anders for a few moments. "CIA, huh? Maybe Phoenix? We've had a few of you guys, SEALS mainly. They just want to disappear. I can see where you're coming from. We won't press. But you can see how that limits our options, makes some of the people in the line suspicious. We have to have trust, have to be able to count on you. I have to make a decision about whether you are an infiltrator, an NIS agent or something, trying to get intel about our freedom train. Give me a couple of days to get back to you, okay?"

"Okay," Anders answered. "You can leave a message with the front desk here. Address it to Nguyen Tran."

"That the guy that came to the VVAW HQ?"

"Yeah."

"Okay, be patient. It'll take a couple of days."

Anders and his friends spent the two days sightseeing around Bangkok. The streets were alive with *songthaews*, bicyclists, motorcycles, walkers, *sāam láws* (samlors) and tuk-tuks—three wheeled bicycle rickshaws and motorized tri-wheel cabs respectively—prostitutes, and touts (including school boys and street girls) offering 'free' shopping and tourist excursions. Many of them pushed chocolates and drinks at the men as added inducements. The four men had been warned about the practice of drugging foreigners and robbing them; so they all passed on the proffered gifts. The city smelled of exotic foods and sweat. It sounded of foreign tongues, the excitement of street corner business, and the incessant clatter of ill-mufflered vehicles. The 'tuk-tuk' noise of the three wheel utility cabs' two stroke engines was cacophonous when heard in aggregate. The noise, confusion, and undiluted exhaust fumes were maddening, deafening, and life shortening, Anders was sure.

They tried to see it all and failed because the sheer size and variety of the capital city were so overwhelming. They worked at seeing the small side streets, called *sois*, where bars, theaters, and small shops rubbed shoulders with each other and where they could see bewildered little girls being led on strings into brothels to be sold. They haggled with tuk-tuk drivers to take trips to the major wats (Wat Mahathat, Phra Kaew—the temple of the Emerald Buddha, Phra Chetuphon, Arun—temple of the Dawn, and Suthat) the *Klongs* (Canals) of Thonburi with their floating markets, the Saovabha Institute snake farm, and the Weekend Market. The first night they took in a *Muay Thai* match (Thai kick boxing) at the Lumphini Boxing Stadium, and the second, they decided to increase the level of their cultural experience by going to a performance at the National Theater. None of the four men could complain of boredom in one of the world's most diverse and exciting cities. Rather, they were only too happy to collapse in their rooms each night.

It was nearly midnight on the third day when the message from Kareem El Farrukh finally arrived. Anders was to come alone and immediately to the Wat Kalayanamit accommodation rooms. Even though he was obviously not Buddhist, he would be admitted to the room of a devout believer, Dusit Vimanmek, the scion of a teak company fortune.

"I smell a trap," said Ky. Bach nodded his mutual concern.

Tran was not sure; his real concern was that Anders would have to leave immediately, and would not be able to return to them. The clandestine command had the sense of that for him. "I suggest you take your personal belongings, your money and passports. We may not see you again. They may want you to leave tonight, my brother."

That had not occurred to Anders. It was very sobering, but made sense. "I guess that's possible. I have to think that Ky has a point as well. Maybe you guys could follow me. You'll have to be careful and keep out of sight. I don't think these VVAW people are anybody's fools. I am not leaving without a way to get us back together when this all dies down." Anders meant that; and his friends appreciated the implicit fealty, and the sense of family cohesiveness and probity that the declaration entailed.

"I fear; no, I presume, that we will not all be able to go together," Tran said. "We need to be sure that we have a place where we can all send messages once we are settled.

"What place do we all know?" Bach asked. "Only Anders has ever been out of Viet Nam. I don't think there is going to be anyplace in our poor country that we can use. Probably never," he said grumpily. He realized that he was only stating the facts of the imminent collapse of his native country, and that life, even addresses, there would not again be the same.

"Anders, got any ideas?"

The Swede thought for a moment. "The best country I know is the PI. It doesn't matter where you come from or where you are going so long as you have money, and we have plenty of that. The Manila Hotel has been there forever. We could send messages to the front desk anytime. If we send a little money along, they would probably set them aside for us for a while."

"Sounds good to me," said Ky. The other two Viets nodded their agreement.

Anders gathered up his things, checking to make sure that his passports, money, Union Bank of Switzerland passbook, and mementos were still secure in his rucksack. He stuffed in a couple of changes of clothes, a K-bar knife, and a .45 with three clips of ammunition. "Okay, I'm off," he said. "Wish me luck."

The room attendant at the Wat eyed Anders doubtfully but escorted him to the room of Dusit Vimanmek. Anders waited until he had gone, then knocked softly. The door opened abruptly, and Anders was facing a .357 Magnum. The Black Muslim owner of the gun gestured for Anders to enter. "Sorry, can't be too careful. Have a seat." Anders sat, and Farrukh put away his weapon.

"We checked you out. Or, I should say, we tried. You don't exist in military records, no 201 file, no MACV records, no marine, army, or navy folder. Either you are a plant, or you were a spook. A SEAL of our acquaintance suggested that we check you for tattoos. That okay with you?"

"I guess so," Anders said. He did not like baring his chest, but he keenly sensed that his life may very well depend on his acceptance by Farrukh. He opened his work shirt quickly and slipped the garment off his arms and shoulders.

"Whee-ew!" breathed Farrukh when he saw the topographical landscape of Anders chest and back. He took close scrutiny of the chest letter tattoos and the Phoenix bird on Anders' shoulder and back.

"What's that say?" Kareem asked, pointing at the Sat Cong letters on Anders' pectoral areas.

"Kill Cong," Anders said impassively. He always affected an unconcerned air when he was tensing for imminent combat.

"That checks," said the black man. "The bird looks like the real thing too. Somehow," now he was indicating Anders' road map of body scars, "you don't look like the run-of-the-mill CO." Anders was beginning to relax.

"In the final analysis, I guess I just have to trust you," Kareem went on. "I have decided to do that. Think you can do the same?"

"I have made that decision, too. It's tough both ways. I need you, though. I'm in all the way," Anders said with a grim set to his jawline.

"Okay, brother." Kareem extended his hand; and the two men shook firmly; but not without a trace of suspicion left in their eyes. "We don't have anytime to waste. You leave tonight., That a problem?"

"Yeah, it is. Sort of, I mean. I can't just desert my friends. We've been through a lot. Too much to ignore. They have to be taken care of."

"Good man. I like that. I can take deserters and traitors to their country for the sake of conscience, but I do still admire men who won't dump on their brothers. You're almost as worthwhile as a soul-brother, my man." He was smiling his approval of Anders. Anders supposed that he liked being someone's 'soul-brother.'

"Can you get hold of them tonight, Anders? Right now?"

Anders nodded. "You can use the phone in the wat entrance hall. We need to get out of here within the hour," Kareem instructed.

Anders did not say that his men were probably waiting by the door of the wat or, at most, immediately across the street. He left the room and hurried to the street door, ignoring the questions of the room attendant. He walked into the street and looked up and down the thoroughfare seeing nothing at first. He held up both arms and made broad come-into gestures. In a few moments three men emerged from the shadow of a doorway, the penumbra of the silhouette of a Buddha statue on the sidewalk, and from behind a trash bin. No one else appeared.

"Thanks for being here. Everything is okay. Like you said, Tran, it's tonight." The three men from the shadows nodded their understanding.

"What about us?" Ky asked.

"Come on in with me. I think they have something in mind right now."

Once again in the room, Anders and the other men settled down. Kareem El Farrukh was all business, but now seemed relaxed and committed to the present task without the concerns about the validity of the other men. In a few minutes, several other Thai men, and two Caucasians entered the room. "These are our people here, real heroes in the struggle against American imperialism. They don't get a thing out of this but the satisfaction that they have helped to get another warrior out of the business and out of harm's way." He was looking at the Thais.

"These two reprobates," indicating the white men, one in old, faded camouflage fatigues and the other in a Hawaiian aloha shirt and faded jeans, "are Viet Nam vets against the war who have stayed on to help the cause. They're too pale for my taste, but bros anyway."

Anders was to board a ship that very night and to head for parts unknown, at least for the present. Tran, Ky, and Bach would not be appropriate for the same destination, "Trust me," Kareem said for the third time that night. They were to go to Hong Kong, where they would be met by more VVAW cadres who would get them settled in the British Crown Colony. "Technically, you aren't the people we're supposed to be trying to help; but we realize something of what you've been through for and with and American military machine; so, we don't mind including you in."

He gave them each a slip of paper detailing the address and telephone number of their contacts. He also told them where and how to get HK passports and other relevant identification papers. "You guys got any money? This is expensive."

Kareem was relieved to see the affirmative nods. "I know this is all rather sudden, but take a little while to pick up your stuff, as much as you can take on a commercial jet, and head out for the airport tomorrow evening after you get your papers. Pay off the hotel in cash, and don't tell anyone where you are going, not even the cab driver, okay?"

"Yes," they all said and gave little bows of acceptance and thanks.

"I don't want to seem mercenary about this, but the arrangements are costly. If you don't have any money, we can still get you all to safe locations; but it will take longer because a lot of this is cash on the barrel head; and we are short. We are always short."

"How much?" asked Ky, ever the pragmatist.

"Before it's all done, about 10,000 each. That's in dollars, not baht."

The three Vietnamese raised their eyebrows at the figure.

"We can do that," Tran said. It would not do, he knew, to appear to be haggling. Kareem did not seem like the kind of man with whom to negotiate terms or one to be interested in turning a profit from the venture. Ky and Bach nodded agreement.

"Anders, here, will cost a little more. That's because he is so big— takes up too much room." Kareem smiled. "It was a little joke. No, the reason is that he is so conspicuous, and the Americans and the Thais are on the lookout for whites or blacks moving out of Thai borders. They are real touchy about antiwar patriots."

Anders raised his eyebrows in a question mark.

"Fifteen thousand, dollars only, please," Farrukh said without further hesitation. Anders shrugged in resignation and handed the black man his money. Tran and Ky followed suit, but Kareem told them to hold on to their money and to dole it out only when their guide for the process told them to. He introduced them to one of the Thais, the man who would stick with them from now until they met with the next contact in Hong Kong.

Bach held back conspicuously. Everyone in the room watched to see what he was going to do. "I've thought it over. I have put a lot of time into my decision," he said. I'm not going to leave. Not yet, anyway. I want to go back to Viet Nam. I want to see if I can help. I'm not as sure as you are that everything is lost. There are still good people, decent soldiers who believe in our country. I want to help them. If the whole thing falls in just like you have been telling me that it will, then I know how to get hold of you." Then he said with conviction in Vietnamese, *"Dù ở đâu và cho tới bao giờ Việt Nam lúc nào cũng là Quê Hương Muôn Thuở,"* and in English, "Viet Nam will always be my native land." He would not bend to the blandishments or logic of Kareem or his friends.

Kareem tried. "I have no contacts for getting you back into Viet Nam. Never had to do that. You will be on your own. Reconsider, man. This is your only chance to get out of this clean, start a new life. That place is corrupt, man, rotten to the core. The fat-cats have stolen everything, and the US military helped all along the way. It was stupid. Don't you do something stupid, something none of us will be able to help you with once you get back there. This war isn't worth you giving up anything more. You'll do yourself and your country more harm than good if you go back. The corrupt merchants will use you for just that much more cannon fodder. This has always been a war fought by the unwilling, led by the unqualified, to do the unnecessary for the ungrateful."

He was wasting his breath. Anders said his say then let it go. He knew that Corporal Bach had made up his mind. Every man had to do what he had to do. In the end, they all bade their old friend a sad farewell. He had to leave first because now he could not know all the details of his friends' departures and escape routes.

None of it occurred with the swiftness or ease that Kareem El Farrukh had indicated, not because of any inefficiency or failure, but for reasons of security. Anders went to one safe house after another before being brought to the docks a week later. The Vietnamese men were on board their plane after a three day wait in hiding. They had bade each other, "*Chúc anh đi bình yên*," (Wishing you go safely) that night in the room at Wat Kalayanamit.

The month of April, 1975 was a pivotal one for Anders Bergstrom. It was an historical one for the Second Indochina War, for the Republic of Viet Nam, and for the United States of America. On the first day of the month the cities of Qui Nhon, Tuy Hoa, and Nha Trang were abandoned by the South Vietnamese army leaving the entire northern half of the country to the undisputed control of the North Vietnamese. Between the eighth and the twentieth the ill-fated battle of Xuan Loc raged between the outmanned 18th ARVN Infantry division and three NVA divisions. From April 11 to April 13, the US Navy evacuated the US embassy staff from Phnom Penh, Cambodia in an operation they named Eagle Pull. Lon Nol, the Cambodian president, had abdicated two weeks earlier.

On the twelfth of April, South Vietnamese President, General Nguyen Van Thieu, resigned. He and his family, carrying huge trunks filled with gold, much of it from the RVN treasury, were boarded on United States planes and ferried in grand style to an opulent exile in London. On the fourteenth, the Americans airlifted the last of 14,000 South Vietnamese homeless children and orphans to the United States. The desertion rate from the armed forces of South Viet Nam, usually about 25% per year, sharply increased.

April 17 saw the surrender of the government forces of Cambodia to the Khmer Rouge led by Pol Pot thereby initiating a period of atrocities that left mounds of human bones in killing fields throughout that miserable country. On April 29, the attack on Saigon itself began. On that second to the last day of battle, the final two Americans to give their lives for the adventure in Viet Nam, marine Corporal Charles McMahon, Jr., and Lance Corporal Darwin Judge, were killed when they were struck by shrapnel from an NVA rocket.

As the People's Army of Viet Nam moved inexorably toward the center of Saigon in the last forty-eight hours of the war, the Americans were given twenty-four hours to get themselves and anything they wished out of the country. Frantic preparations were made for the destruction of documents and the valuable hardware of war, neither of which was accomplished with adequate success, and for the evacuation of the remainder of the US personnel and selected faithful Vietnamese in Operation Frequent Wind.

US aircraft carriers Enterprise and Coral Sea provided air cover. 7,100 American and SVN military and civilian personnel were helicoptered out to Task Force 76 of the 7th Fleet. In addition, units of the SVN navy and Military Sealift Command, hundreds of sampans, junks, and almost anything that floated, evacuated 80,000 people to the Philippines.

Lane Duerk boarded the second to the last helicopter. He was unable to get Miss Nguyen, Nguyen Ngoc Tram (Precious Hat Pin), on with him. Her place was preempted by order of American Ambassador, Graham Martin, in favor of a major Saigon rice merchant who had controlled the off-loading of all rice from the ships bringing the gift of the American people to the war ravaged Vietnamese for which he received a commission on every sack. Duerk last saw her falling into the maniacally frightened crowd screaming at the bottom of the embassy roof heliport. A few additional Vietnamese who had been promised evacuation as a reward for their faithful service dangled for a short time from ropes hanging from the helicopters until they, too, fell off or were helped off by the marine guards. The rumble of NVA tanks and the roar of their artillery could be heard drawing closer and closer to the bunker of the US Embassy.

Nguyen Hai Truong and Tring Van Dong, formerly associated with Provincial Reconnaissance Units, boarded the same helicopter as the Saigon station chief, Lane Duerk, clutching their precious official boarding passes. Each of them had participated in the final battle to give Duerk and his remaining staff time to get rid of the CIA office's most incriminating secrets. They had provided the cover for the perilous journey across to the embassy. US Marine guards climbed into the helicopter's interior and ordered the two Vietnamese out at gun point. When they refused, they were clubbed into unconsciousness and tossed bodily out of the aircraft. Dong suffered a broken neck in the fall, and his body was dumped into the courtyard with the other casualties. Truong fractured both tibias and lay helpless in the debris strewn courtyard until the victorious NVA smashed down the gates of the embassy and drove in to take possession of the compound.

Corporal Le Duc Bach returned to Saigon on an Air America C-46 on April 18. On the last day of the war, April 30, he was shot to death by an ARVN colonel whom Bach had surprised as the colonel was looting office equipment in the ministry of agriculture. His last words were, *"Quê hương muốn thủơ của tôi,"* (My country forever) Bach bore no identification; and therefore, the NVA bulldozed his body into a common grave with the soldiers and civilians that got in front of the final communist military juggernaut.

On April 30, 1975 Saigon became Ho Chi Minh City; there were no longer two Viet Nams, only the Socialist Republic of Viet Nam. General Giap's forces established military enforced order. Yu-en Chou Chen, chairman or COSVN or the Liberation Armed Forces, was appointed vice mayor of Ho Chi Minh City in recognition of the unsurpassed service he rendered to his cause and to the final victory. His role as one of the premier leaders of the insurgency, a role roundly ignored by the CIA and GVN, was now publicly acknowledged.

From records that were not destroyed before the last helicopter lifted off the roof of the US Embassy, dropping unfortunates who were clinging to the outsides of the helicopter, were found names, dates, and places documenting the activities of the Revolutionary Development Program and its successors, the Phoenix and *Phung Hoang* Programs. Public disclosure of those activities were given little notice in the world's press, and did not present a picture of the United States of America that it wished to have preserved for history. At last the awful losses came to an end—thirty billion dollars a year in US treasure, and hundreds of thousands of lives. Two years before, the bulk of the US presence had left with the famous statement that "We have achieved peace with honor," by Richard Nixon, the President. At least on April 30, there was peace.

> One flew east, one flew west
> One flew over the cuckoo's nest.
> *Children's Nursery Rhyme*

CHAPTER 44

From Ghoulies and Ghosties,
And things that go bump in the night,
Good Lord deliver us.
Old Scottish Invocation

Despite Anders' protests and arguments during his last night in Thailand, the only boat the VVAW could wangle him a ride on was a freighter bound for Leningrad, USSR. No one could make any promises that he would have anonymity or even obscurity when he arrived. He knew he could not go back to the United States, and he similarly feared for his life if he stayed anywhere in Asia. He was impressed, perhaps overly so, with the magic of the CIA's ability to gather information on individuals, to store it in its nefarious computer system, and to reach out and take a target. By dawn, after a night of agonizing tension and discussion, Russia seemed the lesser of evils.

The VVAW men and two of the freighter's officers took Anders to the embassy of the USSR at 108 Sathon Neua Road. On the way, one of the Russians, speaking in halting schoolboy English, asked Anders, "You hear off Intrepid Four?"

"No, I haven't," Anders answered.

"Were four Amerikanskis who leave from Japan Islands and go to Rodina to escape from the evil war. They treated very well. You be happy there in the Motherland also. Get to be on television like one of the four. I even remember his name—Rick Bailey. Don't be sad. You vill like it in my country. Is good place."

The VVAW man handed the Russian seaman who had driven them to the embassy a treshka (three ruble note), and the driver and his officers returned to the ship.

Anders and his VVAW helpmeet were ushered into an untidy

utilitarian office cluttered with outdated copies of *Izvestia*, the government newspaper, *Pravda*, the party leadership paper, and *Krokodil*, the approved Soviet humor magazine. It took three hours to complete the necessary forms for visas of entry, short-term residence, and political asylum in Russia. Anders needed the help of the experienced VVAW shadow he had acquired to make sure he put down the right phrases. He had to say that he was a pacifist and that he did not want to kill anymore, but that his country forced him to kill. It was also necessary to state that his life was in danger if he fell into the hands of US authorities, and it was not simply that he would have to pay a fine or go to prison because he was a deserter. That part was not at all difficult. When the forms and signings were complete, the deputy ambassador served *zakuski* (Russian hors d'oeuvres), *khatchapuri*, (Georgian hot cheese bread), and toasted Anders and the heroes of socialism who were accompanying him with a large tumbler of Stolichinaya vodka. It was a special occasion. Not special enough for the Polish Wyborowa with its buffalo grass still visible in the bottom of the bottle that had been given him as *blat* (influence) by one of his underlings after an indiscretion, but a fine opportunity to imbibe.

The VVAW people put Anders on a small motor launch and took him, under cover of darkness, out to Ko Sichang Island in the Gulf of Thailand close to the mouth of the Chao Phraya River. The river was not deep enough for deep draft ships. They waited their turn to get in among the small steamships plying their way down the Chao Phraya from the rice and lumbar mills and with their loads of tin, rubber, tapioca, shrimp, jute, corn, sugar, and rice, and with those going in with their holds full of petroleum, fertilizer, chemicals, and factory machinery from Japan. The river and its vast network of side waterways carried thousands of boats of all descriptions other than ocean going vessels—boats driven by poles, oars, sails, outboard motors, and steam and diesel engines. Without undue difficulty, considering the traffic, they tied up alongside the Russian freighter. Anders was apprehensive; the VVAW people thought his nervousness was out of proportion to the situation since everything had gone very smoothly.

Anders boarded the freighter, "Vladivostok" that night, April 30, and was taken to his Spartan little cabin. The third mate, who was displaced by the newcomer, groused about it at first; but Anders received such a celebrity standing on the ship that the mate soon basked in the glow of having made a contribution to the downfall of the decadent American system. He and Anders struck up an acquaintanceship that gave the young and nervous Swede someone to talk to during the seemingly interminable days and nights at sea.

"So, you vill nefer be able to return to your homeland, Anders?" Petr asked, marveling at what a sacrifice he was witnessing. He puffed on one of the cheap Papirosi cigarettes he chain smoked. "*Gorko*" (bitter), he thought to himself. He had a tattoo of an outline of the *rodina* (The Motherland) on his chest, and for all the hardships of living in the USSR, Petr would no more leave his homeland than he would convert to Judiasm. The two men drank slivovitc, the cheap Russian plum brandy, because that was all the mate could afford on his miserable salary. He was embarrassed that he could not even provide a liter of that Ukrainian swill, Valut, a veritable *lyuk* (luxury). He offered Anders a sliver of his *vobla*, his only delicacy. Together, they chewed and sucked the dried bony salted fish.

"No, never. It is not safe for me there, and I do not approve of America's involvement in this cruel and unjust war." Anders was getting used to the lingo that the Russians seemed to relish. He was scrupulously careful about maintaining his story. What did he care? All he had to do was to get to safety and obscurity in some country where the long arm of The Company could not get at him. He would say anything; what did it matter?

"Is difficult place, my Russia. People are not so vealthy as in your country. Ve are still strugglingk to see socialist principles triumph. Not too many comforts. You vill have to live like a good Russian peasant, maybe," he smiled. "Or maybe the party vill gif you a nice job talking on the television. Maybe even gif you a Muskva apartment." Petr rolled his eyes and smacked his lips savoring the very thought of such a luxury. "Maybe they give you restaurent allowance. You don't have to eat in *stolovaya* (dirty worker's cafeteria)."

"Depends on what the leaders decide. I don't have much choice."

"Choice is such and American idea. In my country ve do as the party chooses. Ve are not zo selfish like the decadent Americans. Ve act for the good of society. You vill see. Pretty much no crime, no air pollution, no imperialist bosses. I think you vill come to like it there. Maybe ve can be friends ven I am not at sea. Vhat do you think?"

"I'd like that," Anders said. He tired easily of hearing his country being denigrated all of the time. He personally had nothing against the US. It was still the best country in the world, so far as he was concerned. It just had some greedy and ill-informed leaders who had ruined everything. In his heart of hearts, Anders still thought of himself as a patriotic American despite everything that had happened. He kept telling himself how much he loved America. That left him with the logical extension that he hated the ones who had involved his country in the debacle of Viet Nam, and particularly those he could name who betrayed him and men like him and who wasted American and Vietnamese lives, property, and countryside.

The voyage was long and boring which was counterproductive to Anders' psychological needs. He had too much time to lie on his bunk and think. Petr had to work long hours, and Anders was alone most of every day. He was soon bored with the vapid and unchanging diet: sour cabbage in vinegar and oil, chunks of dry, hard brown bread, watery broth over vegetables, an occasional piece of tough chicken—said to have been killed by starvation—smoked fish, or *kotleti* (ground meat patty), potatoes and peas, and for dessert, lemon Koolade over cut apples or pears. Other days he shared the crew's *kasha* (buckweat porridge), a small piece of cheese, some sausage, *myaso*, (meat of indeterminate origin: mystery meats), and dark, strong hot, well sugared tea.

The novelty of his presence and circumstances wore off in a few days, and the other crew members took him for granted and tended to leave him alone. Consciously Anders tried to concentrate on the salutary facts that he was alive, safe, well-treated, and among decent people; something he could not have necessarily anticipated two weeks ago. But, the safer he got, the more morose and suspicious and angry he became. At first, he recognized the inappropriateness of his responses; but he felt powerless against the strength of his feelings. As the ship slowly ate up mile after nautical mile, Anders became less and less responsive to his common sense view of reality.

It was the nights that got to him the worst. When his subconscious took over, he ruminated on his sins, on the horrors he had seen, and on the injustices he had suffered. He was angry in his sleep, tossing about on his bunk, occasionally slamming his big fist into the hard pillow. He often lay awake for hours mulling over persistent unwelcome thoughts, memories, and ideas. Early on he writhed in guilt over having left behind his innocent wife, H'Klois, and their two beautiful children. He could not grant himself any absolution by defensive arguments that he had no choice in the matter. He knew himself to be a deserter, a coward, and a traitor; and he could not shake the persistent self condemnatory feelings. As the voyage wore on, Anders became aware that there were actual voices telling him how rotten he had become. He could not pinpoint the location of the voices exactly, but they were as real as the bulkheads and the sound of the waves striking the rusty steel hull of the vessel.

Anders watched Petr and the other crewmen carefully now. Their behavior toward him was different somehow. He could tell what they were thinking sometimes. "He's a traitor," one of them would be thinking. "How could anyone betray his country," another thought.

Then one day, as they were leaving the North Sea past Denmark and entering into the Gulf of Bothnia, he realized why Petr had befriended him, or seemed to. Petr had looked at Anders with a sidelong glance, a negative, penetrating glance. He was trying to read Anders' secret thoughts. Anders now knew that Petr was slipping small amounts of arsenic into his food to poison and weaken him, and he did not want the Russian to be able to tell from his thoughts that Anders was on to him.

Anders kept very calm and was as friendly as it was possible for him to be under the circumstances. He secretly threw the parts of the food that were poisoned overboard. He was slowly losing weight, and out of concern that the CIA spies, Petr, and the others, would discover that he was on to them, he wore loose fitting clothes. It was an elaborate and time consuming process to hide the food under his clothes and to slip it overboard when no one aboard noticed.

There were terrors in the night. Before the ship entered the northern ocean, Anders had looked upon the visions as dreams, nightmares. As they steamed along the Swedish coastline, he became convinced that the visions were being put into his mind from the radio apparatus in the next room. He could hear the hum and buzz of the communications equipment. He knew how diabolically clever the Russians were in their ability to get into men's minds and to extract information.

The CIA had taught him that much. How could he have been so blind and stupid? It was all an elaborate trick. Petr and his bosses were getting into his thoughts to get his military secrets without him even knowing it. It was a quandary to him why these people were so willingly working for the CIA, but they were not as clever as they thought they were. It was confusing. Anders had to work to keep his thoughts straight.

An incubus came in the night and lay directly on him; it was black, and hairy, and heavy. He felt like he was suffocating. The being screamed into his ear that he had to tell the Russians everything, give away all of the war secrets he knew, or he would be tortured and killed. The incubus' breath was like putrefying garbage and death. Anders awakened in a drenching sweat, his eyes dilated and terrorized. The incubus that the devilish Russians had put into his room had slipped out. He had to get Petr. Petr was the leader of the CIA group on the ship. Anders was pretty sure that not all of the crew or the mates were involved, but he had pinpointed Petr and two other men as the spy ring. He laughed out loud in the darkness of his bunk room as he imagined the look on Petr's face when he was exposed.

The radio beams from the next room were turned on at that moment. *"Tala inte om det för kaptenen! Ge bara all information till ryssarna! De tar hand om CIA."* (Don't tell the captain. Just give all the information to the Russians. They'll take care of the CIA.) The message was repeated over and over. Sometimes the words did not make sense. But Anders was too clever for them by a long shot. He knew that the radio beams were eating up his brain and it was no longer safe to stay in his cabin. He pulled on his pants, left the rest of his clothes and belongings right in the room, hoping that maybe the radio beams would be fooled into thinking he was still there. To improve on that assumption, he stuffed his pillow and his duffel bag under the muslin sheets so it would look as if he were still there.

Anders slipped silently onto the boiler plate deck, looked warily in all directions, and made his way to the captain's quarters. Once he had to hide in the shadows of a hatchway when the crewman on watch passed by on his rounds. Anders could feel the man's thoughts, *"I natt ska vi göra oss av med amerikanen!"* (This is the night to get rid of the American), he was thinking. Anders smiled to himself in the darkness because they did not know that he was aware of everything they were thinking now. They did not know that he could speak Swedish and that their elaborate subterfuge to hide their thoughts from him was a failure. He realized that that ability was creating a difficulty for him as well as allowing him to be forewarned of the danger planned by his enemies. The thoughts of all of the men were coming in so rapidly and steadily and all at once that he had trouble filtering them out and keeping the streams of thought separate. He had a headache.

He tried the captain's door; the latch was unlocked. Anders knew that the enemies had left it ajar; so they could take out the captain as well as himself. It was a terrible realization. Tonight was the night. They were going to kill him. Only he and the captain were left out of the conspiracy. He had to save the captain, had to get word to the authorities. His pulse was racing, and he was in a cold sweat. His breath came in short anxious little gasps. Every nerve was primed for combat. He wished he had his knife or a gun, but his hands would have to do. The cabin, best on the ship, was untidy. Empty, and partially empty, bottles of *konyak*, pepper *Gorilka* (inflammable Ukrainian vodka), and cheap East German schnapps littered the floor.

The captain retired early, having drunk more than his share of dark brown potato vodka in the officer's mess, and indulged himself in a dose of *oblepikh* bush oil (a Russian natural tranquilizer). He was lost in a deep inebriated sleep dreaming of his old neighborhood *banya* (bath house), his reliable Volga, and the untrustworthy mistress that he kept in Muskva. Before nodding off, he had placed a mummy (plaster of medicinal paste made from high mountain herb grasses) on his aching stomach. The plaster emitted a fecund aging humus pile odor. (Anders could smell the ethanol fumes on the man's breath as he leaned silently over the obese bearded seaman. Poison! He could smell it coming out of the man. There wasn't a minute to lose. Anders made sure that none of the conspirators could understand his thoughts by willing himself to revert to Swedish. Let them try and decipher that even with all their sophisticated equipment!

Anders clapped his right hand fully over the captain's mouth. The man's eyes flew open in astonishment that turned to stark terror. Above him stood a half naked utterly disheveled, long haired, bearded blond apparition, one of the things that go bump in the night. The attacker's eyes were the worst thing. They were red and demonic, piercing, unblinking. The captain strove to get control of himself and to think. He tried to talk to the huge man holding him. It took him almost a minute to realize that it was the American deserter. The strangest thing about the whole surreal scene was that the American was speaking gibberish, certainly not Russian or English.

"*Tyst, kapten!*" (Quiet, Captain!) Anders whispered harshly. "*Det pågår myteri på skeppet! CIA agenter är närvarande! Petr, din sjöman planerar att mörda dig!*" (There's a mutiny on board your ship! CIA men are here! Petr, your third mate is going to kill you!)

The captain's heart was thumping in his chest. He was afraid he was going to have a heart attack. The speech was neither Russian nor English, maybe Swedish or Finnish. Probably just ranting. The man holding him was obviously mad. He was sure that he was going to be killed. His bladder loosened, and he humiliated himself.

"*Jag kommer att släppa dig! Men du måste lova att hålla tyst. De lyssnar på dig. De till och med vet vad du tä nker. Därför vill jag att du ska tänka på en dikt eller någon historia som du känner till. På så sätt kan du stoppa dem från att upptäcka våra planer, OK?*" (I'm

855

going to let you go. You have to promise to be quiet. They will hear you. They even know what you think; so I want you to try and think only about some poem or story you know. That way you can keep them from getting our plans, all right?)

The gibberish kept on. Captain Duragovich did not understand a word the big American was saying. It was impossible to humor him if he could not be understood. The man was entirely crazy, the captain realized. He had to indulge him. The American was big enough to kill him with his bare hands. The captain knew that, at fifty-eight, and sadly out of condition, he was no match for this Viet Nam killer. If he ever got out of this, he would never let another political refuge, never let another American, for that matter, on his ship. They were all crazy.

Anders released his hand gradually. He waggled the index finger of his left hand over the captain's face as he lifted his right palm from the tense lips. "*Shh-hhh,*" (Shh-hhh) Anders cautioned. The enemies could have been right outside the door. He berated himself for not having locked the hatch behind him. "*Skynda dig kom! Följ mig—jag har en plan. Först måste vi stoppa Petr's hemliga tanke maskin och stoppa honom från att sända de där meddelanden. Sedan kan vi ta hand om dom där CIA agenterna!*" (Get up! Fast! Follow me—I've got a plan. First we have to get Petr and make him turn off his secret mind reading equipment, stop him from sending the messages. Then we can get the rest of the CIA agents.)

Now that he could breath once again, the captain thought his captor's speech sounded more like a Scandinavian language, maybe Swedish. He did not understand any of those languages, and still presumed that he was hearing little more than the incoherent ravings of a madman. The crazy American seemed to want him to follow him. Captain Durogavich decided to play along for the time being until he could somehow alert the crew.

Anders crept into the hallway. He knew the captain understood the situation; so, he could concentrate on the action required. The captain was not much of a specimen to help in a fight, but Anders was sure he had a good heart and would do his best. He leaned against the bulkhead to let his heart slow and to collect his thoughts. He was intensely careful to keep thinking in Swedish. So far, his mind had not alerted any of the enemies.

He and the captain made their way out on deck. It was worse than Anders had imagined it to be. Once he saw a black hairy man leaning on a cane slip back into the shadows. Another time, he saw a pair of Pathet Lao soldiers lurking behind shipping crates. They were all around him. The look on the captain's face told the whole story. He was terrified. He had seen them, too. *"Ta det lugnt! Vi har fortfarande en chans!"* (Take it easy. We still have a chance) Anders soothed him. *"Om ve kan nå kommunikations rummet vid sidan om vårat sovrum kan ve stoppa deras tanke kontrol" Skynda på!"* (If we can get to the communications room by my cabin, we can break their mind control. Let's go!)

Anders was bare foot. He made no noise as he moved stealthily along the bulkhead, keeping his back to the wall. His fists were clenched and ready for the slightest hint of an attack. The first encounter came with deadly suddenness. As Anders started to round a corner, he was distracted by the mind-voices. They were louder now. He backed right into the crewman on night watch. Anders' reflexes were at their highest tone. He dropped the entirely unsuspecting crewman with a single karate' chop to the back of his neck. The man never knew what hit him. *"Följ mig! Vi har inte råd att förlora en enda sekund!"* (Follow me! There's not a second to waste!) Anders hissed into the captain's ear.

He set off at a trot dragging Captain Durogavich along by the sleeve of his pajama top. He halted abruptly in front of the door to his room. He could hear the voices in his room very plainly now. *"Vi mördar honom! En förädare för tjänar inte att leva och inte heller kaptenen för dendelen! Han är också en deltagare i planen. Vi har omringat dem!"* (We'll kill him. The traitor doesn't deserve to live. Neither does the captain. He's part of the plot. We've got them surrounded.) they were saying.

"Hörde du det?" (Hear that?) Anders whispered, feeling vindicated now the captain knew what was going on. It was good not to feel alone.

The captain looked at Anders with a deeply quizzical expression. Maybe the man was deaf. Anders had never considered that possibility. The voices were so loud now that Anders felt like he could dare to raise the amplitude of his own communication. He repeated his message to the captain in a near conversational level of speech. *"Lyssna! De är spioner! Det är som jag sade! Jag vet att det är svårt att tro. Hörde du? Det är Petr. Han ar ledaren."* (Hear that? Those are the spies. I told you. I know it's hard to believe. Hear that one? That's Petr. He's the ringleader.)

The captain still stood dumb. Anders knew the poor man was so frightened that he could not act. He had seen that in civilians before. It was all up to him. He kicked in the door to his room. The black ones took one look at him and fled. Anders did not have time to figure out how they got out since he was in the doorway, and there were no windows.

The clatter of the door being kicked off its hinges roused several crew members, and they came out on deck to see what was going on. Anders saw them. Many of them looked like VC, some were in Pathet Lao uniforms. They did not even try to hide it. His only hope was to destroy their communications room.

He lunged his powerful shoulder against the closed door. It sagged, and the hinges bent. He whirled to face his enemies. One of the black ones had been right behind him. It stepped back, but did not disappear like before. With all of the reinforcements, it was much more open and brazen. Anders was desperate. He gave the door a powerful kick, and it crashed inward knocking over a small reading table. Petr was standing by his bedside blinking sleep from his eyes. The racket had awakened him, but he had not had time to collect his wits. Now Anders, the American, was coming into his room with blood in his eye.

"*Radion!*" (The radio!) Anders screamed. He began to smash everything in the room. He would have to take Petr later. Now, all that mattered was to get rid of the mind warping spy equipment. "*Detta är slutet!*" (It's over!) he shouted as he smashed boxes, tables, and bookstands. "*Kaptenen vet allting! Ni kan inte ta mig nu! Nu när eran radio är förs törd kan kaptenen få tillbaka sin besättning.*" (The captain knows everything! You can't get me now. The captain can get the crew back, now that you and your radio are destroyed.)

Anders was bellowing like some kind of uncaged ape man. Petr heard the yelled nonsensical speech. He had never been around a crazy man before. He guessed that this was the way they went on. It was very frightening, rather threatening and creepy. The American's eyes almost glowed, they were so intense.

Captain Durogavich ordered men to subdue Anders, and two of the bravest entered Petr's room and laid hands on the big man's back. They were dressed in black pajamas. VC! Anders whirled around and drove a huge fist into the sternum of the nearest one propelling him back out onto the deck. The second insurgent soldier scurried back out of harm's way.

Someone had turned on the deck lights. Most of the VC and PLs had gone into hiding. Now Anders could see mostly crewmen and a couple of the black wraiths moving around among them, egging them on. Poor fools! Didn't they know he was the only one that could save them?

The first mate was pointing a gun at him; the gun hand was wavering. Anders shot out a side kick that broke the mate's hand. The gun clattered onto the deck. Anders whirled and struck out at all of his enemies, using the best *Tây Sơn Võ Sĩ* he knew. It was his life or theirs now. This was the real test of his black belt.

The crewmen shrank back and gave Anders plenty of room. They realized that none of them, not even all of them, were a match for this hellion. The voices kept coming in from all directions. Anders tried to shut them out, but his mind was so attuned to those of the crewmen, that he could not get rid of the input. He fought for control. His mind was beginning to reel with dizziness. He was afraid he was going to faint. For a moment he closed his hands over both ears.

"*Lyssa på mig!*" (listen to me) he shouted to the stupid crewmen. They did not know what they had gotten mixed up in. "*Vänta ett ögonblick! Jag kan rädda dig! Om du hjälper mig så kan dom inte få tag på oss. Var inte rädd! Tänk inte, på så sätt kan dom inte använda din hjärna! Jag har tillräckligt mycket gemensam kraft at motverka de andra, men du måste sluta att kämpa emot mig! Förstår du det!*" (Stop! I can save you! They can't get us if you help me. Don't be afraid. Don't think, and they can't use your minds. I am strong enough for us all against them, but you have to stop fighting me! Don't you understand?) He was ranting.

The captain and his crew looked on bewildered. The American was now shouting at people who were not even there. He was no longer even looking at them. They could not understand a thing he was saying. Anders punched and kicked at the air. It was like a martial arts dance, but this action was in deadly earnest. No one dared to come anywhere near the big blond man's frightening arms and legs. His eyes were wide, and yet he did not seem to see them. His teeth were bared like a cornered animal's.

It grieved Petr to see the unfortunate American completely lost to all reason. He knew something had to be done, or Anders would kill himself or someone in the crew. He slipped away to the rec room and came back with a small baseball bat. When Anders turned his back and did a flying double kick into a pair of attackers who were not there, Petr took a quick step behind the giant and swung the bat onto the back of Ander's exposed head. Anders toppled to the deck like a felled tree. Fourteen men heaved a collective sigh of relief.

Anders awakened in the brig, hand's manacled, and feet chained to the floor. His head was bandaged and throbbed unmercifully. Two crewmen; he recognized them, stood in the corners of the cell well away from him. Four nightmares lounged around on the floor and by the door laughing and pointing at him. They called him foul names and hooted at his predicament. Anders knew he was beaten, and he kept silent. He bided his time.

Captain Duragovich had the radioman get hold of the Leningrad office. They got the KGB border serviceman in charge out of bed. The captain explained the whole episode, as best he could. He had the contents of Anders' duffel bag spread out in front of him. The border guard was most interested in the four passports.

"Comrade captain. You say the one in his name, the name he has been using on the ship, is a Swedish document?"

"It is, Comrade major."

"Does it look authentic?"

"So far as I can tell, sir."

There was a pause. The lack of the immigration officer's voice was filled in with static. Then the officer returned. "I have been in communication with my superiors. They agree with you that this man needs emergency treatment, probably hospitalization in a nuthouse. He is Swedish. He is to be taken to Stockholm. Do not, I repeat, do not bring that man onto the soil of the Rodina. Do you understand that, comrade, captain?"

"Yes, comrade major."

"Put those extra passports somewhere in his bag where they are not likely to be seen for a while. It's better not to destroy them just yet. He must be CIA. Let the embarrassment come out after he is in Swedish hands. This sounds like the makings of another CIA fiasco. We don't want to appear to have had anything to do with it. Can you remember all of that, comrade?"

"Yes, sir." Captain Duragovich's head was aching from his hangover and lack of sleep, but he was absolutely alert and clearheaded now. It had been a night to dispel any cobwebs.

"Captain?"

"Yes?"

"I need not remind you that none of your crew is to leave the ship in Sweden for any reason. I will hold you personally responsible. The Swedish officials are to board your ship and to deal with the insane man. You will radio ahead. Is all of that clear?"

"I understand, of course, comrade major. I will take care of it. You can count on me."

"I was sure I could," the KGB major said. Even over the distortions of the wireless the malice in his voice could be appreciated.

The ship docked in Stockholm harbor. There was a delay while the Vladivostok's captain, the Swedish naval officer in charge, a government official, and the officer in Leningrad discussed the issue. Finally, the Swedes decided that the man in question was either a Swedish national or an American who had gone crazy over the pressures of their wicked war in Viet Nam. It was a pity, too, since the conflict was over; and the Americans had to tuck their tails between their legs and go home after a humiliating loss.

The government official contacted the Swedish Viet Nam Committee, the American Deserters Committee, and the psychiatry department at the Karolinska. Representatives of each of the organizations hastily gathered at the dock and were invited aboard the Russian merchant vessel. The Russians would not allow any military people aboard. The man's papers seemed to be in order. He had been in Viet Nam working for the Swedish Red Cross. He had faithfully renewed his passport each time it was due, and it was a genuine Swedish document, that was apparent. Looking at the manacled, scarred, and tattooed giant of a man, who was holding conversations with people who were not there, they were all saddened. They quietly discussed what this poor fellow must have been through that unhinged his mind. What a rotten thing, that American war, it absorbed even noncombatants.

Anders was completely docile now, his eyes vacant and uninterested. He gave no indication that he recognized the approach of the two white-suited psychiatric orderlies. He did not protest nor flinch when they gingerly took his arm and injected 200 milligrams of chlorpromazine. He was lost in silent conversation and could not be bothered with the trivialities going on around him. Anders went sound asleep, his mind at rest for the first time in two weeks when the two Swedish orderlies bore him off the Russian ship on a stretcher.

Until his status could be clarified, Anders was granted 'humanitarian asylum.' That meant that he could live in Sweden with full privileges, including necessary medical care, if his parent country was forcing him to kill other people in a war and that he vouched sincerely that he considered the war to be immoral, unjust, and illegal, and that he would suffer serious personal harm if he did not continue to do the killing he was ordered to do. The Swedish authorities accepted the affidavit from the Russians that Mr. Bergstrom had so attested before he had boarded their ship.

Whether to certify him a Swedish citizen or not was a question that could wait for another day.

Anders lay quietly in his bright white bed. He could hear the voices as they came and went from his room.

"*Paranoid schizofreni,*" (Paranoid schizophrenia) a male voice would say. The male voices were accompanied by ungentle poking and prodding, lights shined in the eyes, pin sticks in the skin.

"*Jag tror inte det. Åtminstone inte så enkelt. Våra mer erfarna amerikanska kolleger,*" (I don't think so. At least, not simply that. Our American colleagues who have had a great deal more experience than us) some snickering, "*kallar det här plötsliga, försenade, våldsamma och hallucinerande syndrom 'post-combat' eller 'post-stress' syndrom!*" (have referred to this delayed, suddenly appearing acting out, even hallucinating, as 'post combat', or 'post stress syndrome.')

"*Jag läste i American Journal of Psychiatry, Januari tidskriften, att ungefär 3% av alla soldater med strids bakgrund drabbas av detta. Ibland tar det flera år innan symptomen visar sig! De blir många, speciellt när man tänker på det var så många som deltog däröver.*" (I read in the American Journal of Psychiatry, I think it was this year, maybe January's issue, that something like three percent of their boys who were in combat experienced it. Some not for years later. That's a lot of people when you take into account the millions of boys they sent over there)

"*Det ar ju svårt och bevisa om alla fall som involverar depression, självmord och negativa personliga förändringar är orsak till de här. Det händer ju också i den civila sektorn. Det är ju ganska svårt att leva i amerika. Det är ett mirakle att det inte händer oftare!*" (I don't know if you can attribute every case of depression, violent behavior, suicide, and negative personality change to combat. It happens in the civilian population as well. America is a difficult place to live. It's a wonder they don't have more trouble.)

And softer, gentler women's voices: "*Stackars kille! Titta på de där ärren! Han måste ha gått igenom helvetet!*" (Poor thing! Look at those scars! What he must have gone through!) These voices were associated with warm bed bathes, teeth brushing, tentative fingertips brushing along the ridges of scar.

"*Varför talar han inte?*" (Why won't he talk?)

"*Tror Du att han någonsin kommer att bli bättre?*" (Do you think he'll ever get better?)

"Shh-hhh, hör han dig?" (Shh-hhh, he'll hear you?)

"Han hör ingenting! Han är bara en slags katatorisk idiot. Stackars kille!" (He can't hear anything; he's just a looney, some sort of catatonic. Poor thing.)

"Viken förlust. Har Du sett det där?" (Big loss. Have you looked at that?) Cover sheet being lifted.

"Greta! Sluta!" (Greta! Stop that!) Tittery laughter.

Anders could hear it all. Understand it all. He knew the language. He wondered why they couldn't understand him. He was thinking at them as hard as he could. Sometimes he thought he would move just to show them that he could, but he really did not want to. It was better just to lay there. To listen to them. Especially the one called Greta who whispered sexy things to him when the other voices were gone.

Male voices again: *"Ja Doktor. Utländska kommisionen har redan bestämt sig. han är inte längre under deras ansvarighet. Han är en svensk medborgare. Han kan börje att arbeta så snart behandingarna är avslutade. Meddela oss. Det tar ungefär. 10 veckor att få tillbaka hans arbets tillstånd."* (Yes, doctor. The Alien Commission has given its ruling. He is no longer under their jurisdiction. He is a Swedish citizen. When his treatment is completed, he can be released back to work. Let us know. It will take ten weeks to get his labor and residence permits certified.)

"Om han någonsin blir bättre." (If he ever gets better.)

"Är Ni int rädd att han kan förstå Er. Doktor? Jag menar, hur kan Ni vara så säker?" (Aren't you afraid he can hear you, doctor? I mean, how can you be sure?)

"Det har gått alitför långt. Katatonisk i 6 veckor. Jag har alldrig sett en patient bli bättre efter in så lång tid! Allvarligt talat, han kommer att förbli våran gäst för en lång tid framåt. Kronisk behandling vid Centrala Sjukhuset! Vi kommer aldrig att få veta hans hemligheter! Synd. Jag kan slå vad om att han är ett mycket fascinerande fall." (This one's too far gone. Six weeks catatonic. I never saw anyone get back. No, sir, this young man's going to be our guest for a very long time, I fear. Probably go to the Center for his long term care. We'll never know his secrets. Too bad. I would bet that he is a fascinating case.)

Anders wanted to yell at them. As soon as he felt like it, he would simply get up and tell them how wrong they were, and walk out as if nothing had ever happened, as if he had never been there. He just did not feel like it now.

Women's voices: *"Jag tror att han har gått ner i vikt. Det är inte bra."* (I think he's getting thinner, doesn't look very good.)

"Dags att göra rent, flickor! Vilken röra! Detta är tredje gängen idag! Vi kan kanske spara lite tid genom att ställa hans säng i dusch rummet och vrinda pa vattnet!" (Clean up time, girls. What's in that tube feeding? This is the third mess today. We need to put his bed in the pool showers; so, we can just turn the hose on him. Save a lot of time.)

"OK, på med hanskarna! Lyft honom! Kristina, ta av lakanen!" (All right, girls, gloves on. Lift him up. Kristina, you pull out the sheet.)

"Fy fan, vem sa att han gått ner i vikt?" (Whew, who said he was losing any weight?)

Anders thought he ought to be embarrassed, even ashamed; but he wasn't. Somehow it seemed funny, like he was getting back at them. He had no idea what for, exactly. He had to be content to laugh inwardly. He was laughing almost all of time now. His nighttime visions were gone at last, replaced by images of being in bed in Inga Hakkensdatter's house, of his mother's cool hand on his forehead when he had a fever. (Or was it a woman's hand now?) He really could not tell the difference between his nice dreams and the happenings of the moment) and lately of trips to sunny, beautiful places, places from which he never wanted to return. He had no idea of the passage of time, of day or night. It did not matter.

Men's voices, arguing: *"Vi kan inte låta honom förbli sa här, Professor? Det är dags att göra något!"* (We can't let him stay like this, professor. It is high time we did something!)

"Glöm det, Pederson!" (You forget yourself, Pederson.)

"Förlåt mig! Man känner det ju starkt och personligt. Åtminstone måste ve ju forsöka!" (I apologize, sir. I simply feel so strongly about it. We need to give a try at least.)

"Jag håller med Dig och dessutom så är ju han din patient. Jag uppskattar din entusiasm men detta är inte en utmaning! Kom ihåg det!" (I agree, and he is your patient. I appreciate your enthusiasm, but we don't issue challenges here. Best to remember that.)

"Det ska jag göra! Kanske kan ve presentera honom såsom en kandidat för cingulumotomy eller frontalt lobotome, eller rent av EST?" (I will. But sir, would you consider presenting him to the board. He could be a candidate for cingulumotomy, or prefrontal lobotomy, or EST.")

"Inget kirurgist ingrepp! Alitför många problem med vissa personer. Vi gör inte sådana ingrepp längre, åtminstone inte officiellt. Möjligen

är Elektrisk Shock Terapi någonting att fundera på!" (Not surgery. The rabble rousers would have our heads. We don't do that anymore, not even unofficially. Besides, there is no evidence for any benefit in catatonics. Electroshock therapy, though, is a real consideration.)

"Kan Ni förslå någonting, Professor?" (Would you consider a suggestion to the board, professor?)

"Det är inte nödvändigt, unge man. På min niva, ett previlegium består av att jag kan godkända användningen av EST. Väl presenterat. Fortsätt! Naturligtvis kräver jag perfekta anteckningar!" (It is not necessary, young man. One of the privileges of my level is to be able to authorize EST on my own authority. You've made your case. Go ahead. I want scrupulous records, understood?)

"Ja, Professor! Jag ska arrangera så aatt teknikerna har förberett apparaten till imorgon. Det var ju ett litet tag sedan vi använde den!" (Yes, sir. I'll have the technicians get the equipment ready for tomorrow. It's been awhile since we did one.)

Anders could only tell that something was going to happen. There was much more activity around him. They were shaving his head; how strange. More needles and tubes, a gurney ride. He liked the feeling of energy in the air even though he did not really know what was going on. Something was going on.

Maisquelle épaisse nuit, tout àcoupe, me'environne?
Dieus! quels ruissequx de sang coulent autour de moi?
Venez-vous m'enlever dans Iséternelle nuit?

But what thick night suddenly surrounds me?
O Gods! what streams of blood flow around me?
Do you come to bear me off to eternal night?
Michael Foucalt Madness and Civilization—A History of Insanity in the Age of Reason

CHAPTER 45

SECRET: In camera session, Senate Intelligence Oversight Committee.
Testimony of Wilmer A Colding, Jr., Director, Central Intelligence Agency
    27 February, 1983
    1014
Subject: Project Democracy

Chairman, Sen. Fineton: Thank you for appearing before the committee on such short notice, Mr. Director.

DCI Colding: You are welcome. I regard it as part of my duty.

Sen. Fineton: I will cut to the chase as I was informed by your office that you have a day of pressing appointments.

DCI Colding: I appreciate that. I also respect both the value of the committee's time and its need to know.

Sen. Fineton: The subject is Project Democracy. We need to get a better handle on this rather complex and confusing program.

DCI Colding: I am pleased to respond although my information is limited. The project is under the auspices of the NSC, with Walter Raymond, Jr., head of the Intelligence Directorate, having responsibility. I am not completely ignorant, of course. However, before I respond in any depth, I must have assurance that nothing said in this room this morning will see the light of day beyond the members and staff with Top Secret clearances.

Sen. Fineton: We are fully aware of the sensitive nature of the project. I can give unequivocal assurance that everyone in this room and everyone who will deal with copies of the minutes has the top level clearance required. You may proceed with full confidence.

DCI Colding: Thank you for that. Project Democracy is a complex set of committees of the government dedicated to providing information to the public at large regarding the pressing need to halt the racing growth of communism in this hemisphere. It deals with aid to the Contras of Nicaragua who, acting as freedom fighters, are opposing the illegal totalitarian Marxist government of Nicaragua—the Sandinistas. National Security Decision Directive 77 completed in January of this year is the action document. It sets up committees for public diplomacy, special planning, international politics, information, and broadcasting, and US public affairs.

Sen. Fineton: Pardon me, director, but isn't all of that euphemistic for propaganda.

DCI Colding: I take exception to the use of that term, sir. The farthest I would go is to characterize it as 'white propaganda,' devoid of disinformation or deception. Americans rightly do not like the concept of propaganda per se, especially the 'black variety,' and I am unaware of use of such techniques in this country in my lifetime.

Sen. Fineton: Not to be argumentative, but I can offer one forty year long example—the US involvement in Viet Nam.

DCI Colding: We could get into a long discussion on that subject.

Sen. Fineton: And it certainly is beside the point. Please go ahead with your discussion of Project Democracy.

DCI Colding: Thank you. This is a new discipline, a 'new art form' to quote Walt Raymond. The important aspect of the program so far as this committee is concerned is the LPD—the Office of Public Diplomacy for Latin America and the Caribbean—headed by Otto J. Reich. It's attached...

Sen. Fineton: We'll settle for LPD.

DCI Colding:...to the State Department under George Schultz.

Sen. Fineton: Way 'under' from what we can gather. Secretary Schultz has only the most minimal interest in Latin America.

DCI Colding: That seems to be accurate. Whatever the case, the LPD has an independent source of funding from the Congress that enables it to provide the correct type of information to editors and publishers all over the world.

Sen. Fineton: And this presents the Contra case to the world?

DCI Colding: Indeed, and effectively. Contra leaders are being quoted in the world press on a daily basis. They travel abroad for press conferences at the committee's expense, and generally their message is given a sympathetic ear by the committee and consequently by the American people and, hopefully, by the world at large.

Sen. Fineton: And, to your knowledge, sir, is there any covert funding by the committee for military action by the Contras as has been rumored around these halls?

DCI Colding: I certainly have no such knowledge. I have serious scruples about any attempt to circumvent what Congress has absolutely forbidden. I cannot speak for my colleagues in the NSA; but as I know them to be honorable people, I am quite sure that there is no such covert funding.

Sen. Fineton: There are disturbing rumors that there is a CIA operation called the Nicaraguan Project that provides funds to the FDN *Fuerza Democrática Nicaragüense*—Nicaraguan Democratic Force and the FRS (Sandinista Revolutionary Front) from its own budget and successfully solicits private American funds and even funding from foreign nationals for arms and supplies. There have even been suggestions made to the Chair of this committee that there are Americans involved in training and in actual operations in defiance of the will of Congress.

DCI Colding: That is a flight of fancy on someone's part, Mr. Chairman. I am inclined not even to dignify the suggestion that the CIA would act in a manner above or outside the laws of the United States with a reply, but I will state this for the record that the very notion is preposterous.

Sen. Fineton: And, for the record, sir, you deny that the CIA in any way, overtly or covertly, funds, supports, trains, or influences the Contras, interferes with the lawful government of Nicaragua, or is involved in any covert actions in this country for the benefit of the Contras in violation of the Agency's charter?

DCI Colding: I do deny it. Not now, not ever.

Sen. Fineton: Did the CIA traffic in illegal drugs?

DCI Colding: Absolutely not.

Sen. Fineton: Did the CIA provide funds and aid in transportation for the Contras to ship illegal drugs, especially crack cocaine, to the United States?

DCI Colding: I have answered that. Again, for the record, absolutely not.

Sen. Colding: Did the CIA aid and abet the Nicaraguan Contras to introduce and traffic in the illegal sale of crack cocaine in the inner cities of the United States targeting the black youths of those blighted portions of our major cities? With the intent of corrupting our black citizens to create and establish a growing market in crack cocaine to finance their military ends?

DCI Colding: I repeat emphatically, and for the record, deny any illegality by the Central Intelligence Agency with regards the Nicaraguan Contras. I deeply resent the implication.

DCI Colding: I emphatically, and for the record, deny any illegality by the Central Intelligence Agency with regards the Nicaraguan Contras.

Sen. Fineton: How about anything unethical?

DCI Colding: Please define that term in this context.

Sen. Fineton: I suspect that will take some time and discussion that is best left for another day. I must say, however, that we will return to this subject. Why is it that I get a *Déjà vu* of Viet Nam sort of feeling about all this? We will adjourn for today. Please make yourself available for another discussion the first week in April. This time around, I think we in the Congress will pursue a more assertive course of investigative of activities of US irregulars in other countries.

Session adjourned 1047

I have definitional problems with the word violence. I don't know what the word violence means.
William Colby—Director, Central Intelligence Agency

And if a man cause a blemish in his neighbor,

as he hath done, so shall it be done to him.

Breach for breach, eye for eye, tooth for tooth...

hand for hand...burning for burning...

stripe for stripe...life for life.
The Holy Bible—Books of Exodus and Leviticus

CHAPTER 46

"I have to conclude that all of that in Viet Nam was an advanced boot camp to train operatives for other kinds of terrorist activities that the United States runs all over the world."
Al Santole, Everything We Had

The Texas hunter crouched uncomfortably in his rubber waist boots and expensive camouflage synthetic fiber coat. He was too fat to be in this position; and, despite being hip deep in a marsh, he was sweating inside the excessive clothing he had selected. He was hungry, and he was tired; and he was cramped. He was waiting for the vaunted herd of caribou to find its way into the low valley traversed by the shallow Wulik River where he lay in wait with his .338 Remington and its 3 X 9 variable power Leupold scope. He muttered that, "It had better be worth it—five thousand bucks and pain all over my body" from the endless walking and hiding in swamps.

He had signed up with Wulik Outfitters, Inc. as a pig in a poke. His old drinking and hunting pal, Lemuel Smothers, from Waxahachie (originally Cow Creek) had sung the praises of the outfitter and his guides for a couple of years before he had allowed himself to be talked into putting good money down for the three animal hunt: caribou, moose, and bear. Not that money was any issue. Willie Hardin 'Porkpie' Rogers was blessed with Texas oil money, the only kind of real money. He was the CEO of Hardin Petroleum, a benevolent heritage from his dearly departed maternal grandfather, Bill (not William) Hardin III, the old horse thief. Lemuel, himself, would have been on the hunt with Porkpie if other events had not interposed themselves.

The events included marrying a girl young enough to be his daughter, even younger, and one that was a real breath holder, if Porkpie did not say so himself. Lemuel had up and had a heart attack from which he sloughed his mortal coil less than a month after the wedding. Porkpie hoped he had been in the saddle at the time. So, Porkpie had had to come to this forsaken wasteland to do the hunt all by his lonesome. Unless you count a strange gray haired dude with an accent and a couple of heathen Chinee guides as company, which he certainly did not.

He had bargained for a real hunt, not one of those Colorado or New Mexico ranch elk hunts where you drive around in the pickup after breakfast at the motel and pick out the six pointer you want from the herd, shoot it, watch the boys dress it, and be back in time for 'wild-game' lunch at the Holiday Inn. "For fifteen grand cash, I might add," he grumbled to himself.

This was a real hunt all right. Up before dawn, sleep on the ground, walk your legs until they were only about two foot long, and sit around in a swamp waiting. And waiting. It wasn't his kind of a hunt, he decided the second day. He liked a few comforts. That reminded him, and he partook of a little snort of Southern Comfort from his sterling silver hip flask that the Lions gave him for ten years worth of donations. His legs were about to break off from the need to keep bent so's the caribou wouldn't see him. He was about to call it a day.

Then he heard a low rumbling coming from over the rise. Right where the big prematurely gray guy had said the action would start. An even thumping of the ground made an almost confluent noise be-speaking an immense herd, or an earthquake. "With my luck, it would be the latter," Porkpie muttered. But his heart rate had quickened. He had a feeling almost like sexual arousal, whatever that felt like; it had been so long. When the first set of forward thrusting antlers appeared over the horizon, there was no doubt about it; what Porkpie Rogers was feeling was sexual, all right.

He knew he had some time, but he was so excited that he almost dropped his field glasses in the drink when he tried to get a good look at the herd as it trotted over the rise. It was as if the caribou had arisen from the very ground. They were now coming by the hundreds; no, by the thousands. Beautiful stately graceful animals—barren ground caribou, largest in the world, strong and swift. He saw two dozen trophies; the only real problem was to choose which one. That was tough for a Texas oil typhoon who was not used to having to deny himself anything he really wanted. And he really wanted a big trophy.

"Only way to guarantee that," Porkpie thought to himself, "was to pop off two or three. One for old Lemuel, rest his horny old soul." He knew better than to mention that thought to the outfitter. Guy looked young in his face but had an old man's gray hair and a preacher's hellfire-and-damnation eyes when it came to explaining the rules of the hunt.

The two little gooks were on his left, and the big man was on his right. He sighted the cross hairs on the biggest bull he could see in the herd. Just then another one trotted into view, bigger than the first. Porkpie shifted his sights on the second brute. What a beauty! The boys at the Petroleum Club would have a hyssy when they saw that baby mounted up over the fireplace. He could see it displacing W.W. Hunt's old ranch elk trophy even now. A third monster came into view. No way was he going to miss the fun of taking out more than one. They could pick out the biggest one after they were down.

Porkpie squeezed off a perfectly aimed shot, point blank in the kill zone. The report of the rifle was like a cannon in the quiet of the early morning. The handsome animal dropped like a great tree. The Chinee boys grinned ear to ear and said, "Beautiful, great shot!" Porkpie may have had a touch of the buck fever, but he didn't let a little thing like that mar his famous aim.

The grey-haired white man started to get up from his crouching place in the cattails. The herd wheeled left and began to pick up momentum. Crack! Crack! Porkpie fired off two more shots. The three men beside him almost jumped out of their skins.

"What are you doing?" screamed the outfitter. "You just killed two more! You idiot!" Two animals had heeled over. However, as they looked, one of them, obviously a cow, struggled to her feet and limped away into the herd, a visible trail of blood running out of her side.

"Oh, Jeez, I gut shot her!" lamented the Texas hunter. He prepared to squeeze off another round even though he could not really be sure which animal was the one he had wounded. He thought about firing off a flock shoot, maybe he'd get lucky.

The shot was never fired. A huge hand closed over his right hand and the trigger housing pinning his index finger. "Ouch!" squawked Porkpie. "Wadja do that for?!"

The big man looked into the face of his rich hunting client with malevolence, but he did not say a word. Instead, he took the man's gun away from him in a vicious twist that almost severed the pointer finger and hurled it over his head into the silty water.

"What the. . .?!!!" Porkpie started to yell. He was going to protest profanely, obscenely, and scatologically as only a real Texan can, when the big man's hand slapped over his mouth stopping any utterance.

"Shut up, you fool!" The hatred blazing out of those blue flame eyes was enough to mummify a man. Porkpie Rogers shut up.

The Vietnamese and Hmong boys field dressed and caped both bulls while the outfitter, Steffan Johannson, trotted his client across the tundra, over the rises and swales, to their patiently waiting mountain horses. He had such a tight hold on Porkpie's trousers that he gave him a 'Marv.' Mr. Willie Hardin Rogers was not used to such treatment; that was for Mexicans; and he didn't like it one bit. This yokel hadn't heard the last of this. Not by a long shot. Maybe they treated white folks like that in Alaska, but nobody treated a Rogers from West Texas that way.

An Indian or Eskimo looking woman and a little girl were tending the spike camp from which the hunters left for their hunting forays each morning. She and the child backed up away from the two men when they drew near. The anger and malice between them was easily evident although neither man had much to say.

"Get on," ordered Steffan nodding toward the sturdy little four wheel ATV. Rogers took his time, not accustomed to being ordered about, certainly not by a hired hand as he regarded this guide.

"What's up, Steffan?" the nervous little woman asked.

"This one killed two bulls and wounded a cow. I have to go after the cow." Nothing more needed to be said. The rich man had acted like a typical taker, wasting the bounty of the north and abusing his privileges. He had violated the hunter's code, a clearly defined set of rules of conduct about hunting. 'You don't take more than you need. You take out the meat. And you never leave a wounded animal without putting it out of its misery.' In addition, he had broken state and national law by shooting a female, a cowardly act in and of itself, and over his limit of bulls.

The Inuit-Eskimo woman looked at the Texan with bald contempt. "Git me my butt cushion, Injun," the thoroughly out of sorts oil man demanded, looking at her as if she were a servant. He determined to stand there until he was properly served.

Mary Okobuk looked at the boorish man levelly, shook her head 'no,' and compounded the insult by turning her back on the presumptuous American hunter. Her eight year old daughter, Isabel, unaware of the growing tension among the adults, sidled up to the rotund Texan and asked him, "Did you get a big one? Weren't they beautiful?"

"Shut your face, you little half-breed gutter snipe," Porkpie snarled, taking out all of his pent-up malaise on her. She had drawn close to question him, and he rudely shoved her so that she stumbled backward and fell on her bottom. She sat looking at the oddly behaving older man with a questioning little brown face.

Steffan caught the action out of the corner of his eye. He moved with a speed well out of proportion to his great size. The powerful Scandinavian looking man grasped the overweight Rogers under his armpits and lifted him up into the air with no more strain than if he had hoisted an errant sheep. Rogers was impressed; he weighed over 210. It did not seem very sensible to resist. He had to admit that he was afraid, and he had not been afraid many times in his life. Steffan dropped the Texan down on the ground with enough force to knock out his wind. Porkpie thought he had set down hard enough on his fat butt to break his spine. One more thing to get even about.

Mary and Isabel stayed with the equipment at the spike camp and watched the two men ride off in stony silence. The Eskimo woman then returned to her cooking; they were going to have fire roasted char that night. Steffan did not speak until they arrived back at his Wulik River Hunter's Lodge. "Pack up." Steffan told the Texan. While the angry American threw his hunting gear, a prodigious amount of it, into his hunting duffel bag and packed his rifles in the aluminum gun carrying case, Steffan typed a terse note that read:

2 October, 1983.

To Willie Hardin Rogers

I return $4,000 of your fee due to unsatisfactory conditions. $1,000 actual expenses have been deducted. Your caped mount will be shipped—expect a two month arrival date. Your meat (approximately 300 pounds) will be cut, packaged, and shipped in dry ice. Expect shipment in five days. You will not be welcome for another hunt.

Signed, S. Johannson, outfitter
State of Alaska Outfitter's license SJ - 2784 -1-35968-83

The letter infuriated the rich Texan. People fawned over him, fell all over themselves to curry his favor, hung on his pithy pronouncements, laughed at his jokes. They sought him out for advice; he was in demand for the best of Texas and Washington social life. Willie

Hardin Rogers made and broke county commissioners, chose state assemblymen, counseled governors, called congressmen by their first names, and sat at the head table during presidential dinners. Who was this pipsqueak to insult him? First of all he was being kicked out after only three days of his hunt. Who cared about the pocket change he was getting back? Probably a big deal to this yokel. Four thousand bucks was half a year's income for this hillbilly he'd bet. Porkpie Rogers dropped that much change out of his pocket into the cushions of a couch when he sat down. He could not let the insult pass although his superego or something his mother had taught him gave him a caution.

His mother would have been proud. Porkpie held off until his stuff was being loaded onto the baggage carrier at the airport. At least, one of the little chinees had carried his bags and gun case in. Rogers felt confident and more in his element in the fairly crowded regional airport. When the white man turned to leave, Porkpie said, "Don't think you've heard the last of this, boy. I am a man to be reckoned with and you have insulted the wrong fella, just you mark my words. I'm usually not one to make bald-faced threats, but I'll make an exception in this case since subtlety is undoubtedly a waste on you folks in the hinterlands. I am a regular and large contributor to the 'Nicaragua Project.' In fact me and a Mrs. Newington just about single-handedly keep the whole thing afloat."

Steffan looked bored. That made Porkpie all the madder, and loosened his tongue even further. "That's a CIA thing," he said. "Maybe you heard of them. Maybe you heard of a good old boy name of Ollie North who runs the show." Steffan became interested. He had indeed heard of Colonel North, a man with a reputation of getting anything done that he started by whatever means necessary, usually by mainstrength and awkwardness. "Them boys are runnin' the worst bunch of cutthroats you'll ever meet in all your born days. Called the Contras - that's Spinach for the 'Againsts.' I have a mind to have some of them boys pay you a little visit. Kind of an educational thing. Mull that over when you try to go to sleep, boy. And keep a sharp watch out on your back. You done took on Porkpie Rogers, and that's a heap a trouble."

Steffan flew Porkpie Rogers in the Super Cub to the little airport in Kotzebue. The wind was coming in off the Arctic Ocean and had turned cold. The angry Texan walked regally across the tarmac, up the entry stairs, and into the turboprop plane complaining that there was no first class section, and where was a man supposed to sit? With the

Eskimos in the baggage section? Steffan presumed the man had endeared himself to the airplane crew in five minutes at about the same level that he regarded the Texan.

Steffan ignored the blatant threats, considering the source. He had been threatened by better and more capable men before. However there was something about the man's outburst that troubled the Swedish-Alaskan outfitter. He could not quite put his finger on exactly what it was that bothered him, but the mention of Colonel North, and the idea of an American interference in another country smacked of Viet Nam, maybe even of Phoenix; and for some reason, it rankled him more than he wanted to admit, even though he had been out of it for eight years. He shrugged it off. He had work to do.

He drove his pickup through the city of Kotzebue, located on the far northwestern Alaska coast, and delivered a hind quarter of caribou to old Burl Angulikada. The old Eskimo was no longer able to hunt, but still insisted that he could eat nothing but good caribou. For several years Steffan, Tran, and Xe had kept him in good supply of the vital red meat. He turned over the Super Cub's engine and flew back to the Wulik River Lodge.

He landed on the rocky river bank runway he and his friends had built when they first arrived in 1979 and called Tran and Xe over from the meat locker and asked them for help. "That fool hunter killed two bulls. The boys are bringing in the mounts and the carcasses. They'll get them butchered and packaged. But we've got a problem. Rogers also wounded a cow. We've got to go find her."

Discussion was unnecessary. The two Asians knew what was required. They swiftly put together a four day supply into their back packs, laid in two man tents and a roll of foul weather gear in the Super Cub's rear compartment, put their hunting rifles carefully on top to prevent injury to the critical tools of their trade. It was beginning to get cold, and at night in the open, it was going to be very cold. They would need all the layers they could carry. Steffan put in a set of butchering saws and hatchets and extra food while Tran and Xe were getting themselves ready. The three old friends flew out, heading north.

It was a crisp late fall day. They had not had a hard freeze nor any snow yet, and the temperature was only down to 45°. Talk was impossible over the steady racket of the plane's engine. The men took in the grand vistas of the rolling buff colored tundra and the distant Brooks Range, and, below them, an evolving view of the Wulik River with its world record Dolly Varden and occasional king salmon, the tiny herds of nearly extinct musk oxen, the golden haired grizzlies, and the occasional prehistoric looking bull moose, and remained content to be lost in their own thoughts. Steffan was ruminating on the implications of what the braggart from West Texas had told him. If half of it were the truth, Steffan could see the hand of The Company in yet another hapless country. Despite the profound calming effect of the chloropromazine he took every day, this was enough to nettle him, to set him off, although he tried to put it out of his mind as being nothing of his concern.

They put down on the tundra and set off on foot at first sight of the immense caribou herd as it pounded its way back in the direction of the Alaska Range and Canada. It was no feat of woodsmanship to track the wounded cow. The hoof tracks of the immense caribou herd had pulverized the earth, tramping down all of the sparse grass and tussocks of tundra in a half mile wide swath. Somewhere in the middle of that vast herd they found occasional telltale splotches of her blood. The two Asians remained alert and attentive to the tracking; they were angry.

The fast moving caribou herd covered a considerable distance across open territory, and Steffan and the two Asians hiked hard for two days before coming into contact with the animals. The caribou were making a wide circle in the region between the foothills of Nuklauket Pass and the Ray Mountains. It was in the nature of those mysterious animals to keep ceaselessly on the move, and always in circles. Put them in a pen, and they will endlessly circle the perimeter of the fence.

Occasionally, a wolf track crossed over the prints of the herd. Wolves followed along behind and to the sides of the great migrations, hoping for the chance to set upon a straggler, usually an old, or wounded, or sick caribou no longer able to keep up. The wolves and caribou lived with each other in near perfect harmony—the natural harmony of life and death where sometimes predators starved and sometimes a caribou fell to the pack; but their world was never out of balance, unlike that of the humans.

Xe spotted the first two wolves. They were about six hundred yards apart and moving swiftly east in the direction of the myriad of caribou tracks. They were the rear guard of the herd. Not long afterward Tran sighted the cow through his binoculars. She was limping behind the rearmost of the great herd that had just come into visibility as the three trackers crested a low rise over a vast marshy tundra valley. The wolves were aware of her as well, and Xe's two predators were beginning to close in on the sick caribou.

"Too far for a decent shot," said Tran.

"Let's shed gear here and move faster. For some reason, I'd like to get to her before the wolves do. It's funny, but I feel like I'm responsible and owe her something," said Steffan. The men put fluorescent blaze orange streamer ribbon markers on their small mound of gear; so, they could relocate it when they again came back over the featureless tundra.

They quickened their pace until they were less than 200 yards behind the stricken cow. The wolves had seen the men and now backed off several hundred yards watching hungrily as the interlopers intruded on their legitimate kill. "Go ahead, Xe," Steffan said. Xe was the best shot among them.

Xe had a new 25.06 of which he was justly proud. He waited until the cow turned broadside, then placed the cross hairs at a point that was an estimated one inch above the point blank kill zone behind the left forelimb. He knew his rifle to have a very flat trajectory; it dropped about half an inch in 200 yards; so, he would still be point blank at that range. He drew in a breath, held it, and squeezed off one shot. The already stricken beast fell as if she had been knocked to the ground by a thunderbolt. The great herd thundered away to the north and east; the wolves hesitated and vacillated, now running in the direction of the herd, now returning toward the scent of the fresh blood.

"Do you mind going back after the plane, Tran?"

"No problem." The middle-aged Vietnamese, straight and thin as a swamp spruce, turned back to fetch the airplane that was called the arctic taxi, the work horse of the Alaska far north. It was almost four miles back the way they had come.

"Xe, let's go take care of the carcass." Xe set off walking over the uneven, soft, sponge-like ground and moved quickly to where the caribou cow lay. Steffan had to walk quickly to keep up.

The two men saw a string of intestine dragging out of the exit wound from the Texan's .338. That was a lot of rifle, and it left a big hole by the time its bullet traversed the animal's abdominal cavity. The miserable beast had been stepping on its trailing guts for mile after mile as it had tried in vain to keep up with the herd. Steffan cursed the loudmouth Texan under his breath.

He and Xe quickly put the caribou on its back. Steffan held it in that position while Xe slit open the belly and let free an unmistakable

Stench of bowel contents that had lain free in the peritoneal cavity. He neatly stood one of his hatchets up in the sternum and with the blunt end of the other knocked the breast bone open. He cut off one foreleg and the two men jammed the limb into the chest cavity to hold it open. The heat of the caribou's body caused steam to rise around the swiftly working men. In the cold of the afternoon, the heat felt good.

They removed the contents of the abdominal cavity first, making every effort to keep the contaminants off the meat. They saved the liver, and then the heart, placing them in a plastic bag. Xe transected the mesenteries and let the g-i tract fall out onto the soft spongy tundra ground. He split the pubis, removed the genital organs, bladder, and anus. They were carefully skinning the animal as Tran touched the plane down twenty yards from them. It was too warm to leave the skin in place for the haul back to the lodge.

The three men quartered the carcass and wrapped three of the parts in clean muslin and packed them into the rear of the plane taking care to balance and to secure the load. The load was too bulky; so, they had to lash their extra gear to the wings They left one front quarter along with the hide and entrails for the wolves. They washed their hands and arms in a small marsh then the three friends made a simple camp and bedded down for the night, squirming around to keep warm. The conversation with the Texan had stayed with Steffan; so, he brought it up to the others.

"The hunter told me something that bothered me," Steffan started. He was the first of the three to speak in the chill evening after supper. "He said the Americans were running some kind of program with the Contras in South America, or Central America, someplace there. It sounds like Phoenix."

That was a word the three men seldom used. They rarely talked about Southeast Asia, keeping their own counsel about the place and the times. "What would he know?" Tran asked.

"Says he is a big contributor."

"Do you think it's true?

"Well, he's generally a blow-hard, but he did mention Oliver North; so he knows something. And it kind of sounded like Company business."

"I would have to doubt that they learned any lessons in behavior for future decency from Viet Nam and Laos; so, it wouldn't surprise me," said Tran. Xe nodded. He usually had little to say in these conversations; but his feelings ran very deep; and when he did, there was real feeling in what he said.

"I don't know why I should care, but I have been bothered about it all day," Steffan said.

"Maybe it brings back bad memories," Xe volunteered. This conversation was doing that for the wiry little Hmong, and he did not like it. It conjured up visions of Sky People dropping supplies, making promises, fighting along side his Hmong people. And always, he thought of the fate of his family when the Lao Lum, the PL, came after them. They had been reduced to fugitive status; they ran out of ammunition. They starved. Finally, they had been cornered in a little valley near the Thai border and slaughtered. Their pleas to the Sky People had gone unheeded. He was the only one who made it to Bangkok. He was very bitter against the American CIA for abandoning him and his family. If it had not been for Ky, one of the Vietnamese PRU people..., he shuddered to think of what would have become of him. He still had the bad memories.

"Yeah," said Steffan. "And something more. I feel like I have unfinished business."

"I know exactly what you feel, brother," said Tran. "Exactly."

"Ky still does business with The Company, I suppose," Steffan mused. "Maybe he can get a handle on what's going on. Somewhere in my guts, I have a feeling that there's another Phoenix. It should be none of my business, but I can't get it out of my mind. I am going to call the old drug runner and see what I can find out."

Steffan Johannson emigrated from Sweden to Canada in 1977. He went to that Scandinavian country as a place of refuge from his own insanity from the Second Indochinese War and to escape those he was sure were pursuing him. He could never be certain of his thoughts at that time because he had been completely unhinged mentally when he arrived in Sweden. The doctors and nurses at the Karolinska Psychiatric Institute had later told him that he had responded to electroconvulsive shock therapy with a remarkable recovery of his emotions and faculties. He had no memory of anything that happened from the time he left Laos. He had a hazy and fleeting recollection of a piratical looking Burmese named three-legged Myo, but could not connect him with anything concrete. The psychiatrists told him that his memory loss was retrograde, finite, and would not affect his future ability to form memories. They had kept him calm on the major tranquilizer, chloropromazine. To demonstrate its critical nature for him, they gave him a trial of withdrawal from the drug. As soon as his blood levels declined to a threshold level, his paranoid ideations and fearsome angers returned. He was warned never to stop using the medication again, and he had heeded the advice.

His physicians had been pleased to pronounce him well again and released him from the psychiatric hospital in February, 1976. The only change he could see in himself was that his hair had changed from striking Nordic blond to silver gray in the months that elapsed from the time he was brought to the hospital until he was once again free in the populace. The Institute had found him a job as a painter and had required that he return on a monthly basis as an outpatient to be monitored.

Steffan did not take to painting. For one thing, it seemed rather absurd. He was a rich man; his Swiss bank account contained over two million US dollars. For another, he could not see himself stuck in that life forever. He had to be free of constraints. In time he learned the names of criminal groups and had a new identity, including a new passport, created. It was expensive, but the quality of the documents was excellent. He had come into Sweden with three passports and identities - Lars Magnusson, Anders Bergstrom, and Remundo Mueller-Garza. He had shed his original identity papers showing him to be Karl Oscar Isaacson while he was still in the hills of Laos. After being released from the Karolinska, he got rid of the Lars and Anders documents and adopted his new identity—Steffan Johannson, Importer-Exporter; but, since it had never been used, he kept and recertified the Mueller-Garza passport regularly.

Once he was back on his feet again, Steffan left a series of messages with the front desk of the Manila Hotel in the Philippines. After several weeks, he finally received a message from Nguyen Lui Tran. They corresponded; and eventually Steffan was able to make contact with Phan Duy Ky and even later, with the Hmong guide who had gotten the three men out of Laos, Fang Pao Xe. Ky had found him in sad condition in a refugee camp outside Bangkok. Ky had taken an interest in the people who had contributed so much to him during the weeks they had spent in their hill country at the close of the war.

Steffan had emigrated to British Columbia, Canada and went into the northern portion of the province to live in a small city, Quesnel, where he could be isolated and could feel safe and free. Tran came later from the Philippines, bringing along a wife who had two teenage boys. Together they started a big game outfitting and hunting business that was only modestly successful. When the Canadian and US governments agreed to a joint mining venture on the northern coast above Point Hope, Alaska, Steffan and the Southeast Asians had signed on as security guards. They entered Alaska under forged US passports and eventually were allowed to homestead on the Wulik River where they were able to run a modestly successful hunting and fishing outfitting and guide service.

Together they occasionally did lucrative business with Ky and made trips about which they did not speak to strangers. Ky brought Xe up to the hunting lodge and later brought two young Hmong men as well. Xe became a partner in the business, doing mostly guiding and scouting because he had great difficulty learning the English language. Ky wrangled his way into the United States, got a green card, and established himself in the Vietnamese community in East Los Angeles. He became an important businessman in the import-export business and kept up many connections with people in less public enterprises.

The four old friends remained close despite the passage of eleven years since they temporarily parted in Bangkok. Ky was only too happy to get information on the Contra business for his old partners. It gave him an excuse to fly up to the north country for a visit and for some good caribou steak.

Steffan talked to him in 1983 about what the blowhard Texan had said concerning a possible CIA program in South America. In the interim Ky gathered bits and pieces of insider information and relayed it to his friends in Alaska. What he learned was at once very easy to come by—the newspapers in early 1986 were full of stories of the problems in Nicaragua—and, on the other hand, very difficult and expensive to obtain—the subterranean information. What he reported to his friends in the wilds of Alaska was that the American President, Reagan, was a real hawk about communism and was embroiled in an acrimonious public debate with Congress over funding for the anti-communist Contras. Americans from all levels of society praised the efforts of the Contras and condemned the communists in power in Nicaragua, the Sandinistas. But they did not want to waste anymore of their national treasury on foreign adventures. Viet Nam had been enough for most of the American public's lifetime. Congress resisted the blandishments and arguments of the President, and made only niggardly appropriations for the cause.

An organization called Project Democracy was very public in its fund drives and strident support of the cause of the Contras. Ky could not get any clearcut information that that organization was funneling money to the military uses of the Contras, although his informants were fairly sure that it did. What they did learn for certain, and at considerable expense to pay informants, was that The Company was up to its old convoluted tricks, a fact that came as no real surprise to any of the men. DCI Colding had been instructed by the White House to get funds, to provide training for the Contras, and if necessary, to help them in actual operations, and all on a rigidly hush-hush basis. The problem was that the type of people they recruited were not altogether responsible and lacked the rigid discipline of the CIA agents. For a price, they were not above sharing their information with other conservatively minded people such as Ky's friends.

Ky found out that Colding had established a funding and action organization called Project Nicaragua and had found a private American citizen, a man named Spitz Channell, to raise the money for the organization on the sly. Channell formed the National Conservative Political Action Committee (NCPAC), the National Endowment for the Preservation of Liberty (NEPL), and the Anti-Terrorist American Committee (ATAC). These conservative organizations were ostensibly entirely free of attachment to the official US government and especially the White House and The Company; they were tax exempt; and they raised so much money that the founders could hardly find places to disperse it fast enough. They raised nearly thirteen million dollars from such patriots as the CEO of the Coors Brewing Company, from Nelson Bunker Hunt, the Texas billionaire, from Willie Hardin Rogers, the nearly billionaire, from a Washington dowager named Barbara Newington, and from one in Austin, Texas named Ellen Garwood. The men in Alaska all had to laugh when they learned that only twenty percent of the money ever actually got to the Contras.

Ky digressed for a few minutes to tell his friends something of the background of the Sandinista versus Contra struggle into which the United States had once again unnecessarily involved itself. "The business really got started when Jimmy Carter was president; 1979, I think. A fascist dictator in Nicaragua was overthrown by a bunch of communists calling themselves the Sandinistas. They named themselves after a revolutionary named Augusto César Sandino who fought the Somoza regime for eight years before he was killed in 1934. He also waged war against the United States irregulars who were there supporting the dictator. Don't you think it's strange that a country as good hearted as America can always manage to pick the worst tyrants around to give their support to?

"What seems the strangest to me, is that they bother. I can't figure out why they always think they have to push their way on other countries. Why don't they just leave people alone; they never seem to learn, no matter how much pain they get by interfering," Tran commented.

"Anyway, Somoza's National Guard killed Sandino, and that made him a martyr for the antidictator cause." Ky said. "Finally in 1979 the Sandinistas overthrew the forty year old Somoza dynasty and made a new communist government. For some strange reason, President Carter rushed $40,000,000 worth of food aid in '79 and $60,000,000 in cash the next year. The Sandinista movement fell apart—too many leaders with too diverse of views. The communists under Daniel Ortega kept the government, and the so-called moderates like Violeta Barrios de Chamorro and Alfonso Robelo resigned. The Ortega bunch started immediately to sponsor guerrilla movements in nearby Hondorus, El Salvador, and Costa Rica, shipped Nicaraguan arms bought with US aid money, and laughed out of the other side of their mouths at the stupid overly generous Americans.

"Then the Sandinistas split again. Edén Pastora, Commandante Zero, broke off and formed what Ortega termed a *Contrarrevolucionario* or Contra force against the Sandinistas. The CIA supported them for a while until they figured it out that Pastora wasn't going to let the US control him. A force of former members of the Somoza National Guard, a bunch of thugs, who had bases in Honduras, started up another anti-Sandinista Contra group. Their leader was a guy named Enrique Bermúdez. The CIA decided to work with him and his FDN outfit. Starting in 1982, the CIA took over the Contra operation to restore the Somoza dictatorship even though Somoza himself had been killed."

Ky told them that his informants said the CIA had set up Phoenix type organizations for the collection of specific and condemnatory data on individuals and companies in Nicaragua on the basic, but updated Viet Nam plan. He even got a few hints that maybe Tandrosz Szabo and his henchman, Jean-Luc DuParrier, had headed similar programs in Angola, El Salvador, Panama, Egypt, and Lebanon, and that they were more than likely doing so in Nicaragua. Hearing Szabo and DuParrier's names was enough to cause Steffan's already slowly burning fuse to reignite.

According to Ky's informants, Angola's complex internecine strife for the past twenty years with pro and anti independence factions within the country itself, Portuguese colonizers, Cuban communist forces, and South African troops warring each other in a dizzying set of changeable alliances, had resulted in upwards of 10,000,000 mines being hidden in the country's soil. 50,000 or 60,000 Angolans had lost legs and an equal number had died from the cruel assortment of blast, fragmentation, bounding, and directional fragmentation mines. The shadowy hand of the American Central Intelligence Agency was suspected in any and all actions in that unfortunate country.

Nothing could have been more inflammatory to Steffan Johannson than the new revelations of CIA meddling. He was fascinated by Ky's account of the apparently most recent adventure—that in Nicaragua. The on-the-ground, in-the-trenches leader of the funding and the dispensing to the Contras was indeed Colonel Oliver North. He was an indefatigable worker providing medicine, uniforms, boots, weapons, ammunition, and advisors to the anticommunists in Central America. He had established bases in Honduras and Costa Rica from which the Contras could operate with near impunity.

What Ky could not find out was who were the men above North, the White House string pullers. The similarities to Phoenix struck a deep and unnerving cord in Steffan. He was sure he could see the bloody hand of the 'Colonel,' now accurately known to him as Dustin Hauter, of Lane Duerk, of Hugo Bartini, of Rex Dragerton, and of Cleveland Howard. All those old serpents had to be in there somewhere.

The memories of what he had suffered in the jungles of Viet Nam, how people he had loved and respected, like Liên and her parents, The Mandarin and Mme Nguyen, and the Grand Master of *Tây Sỏn Võ Sĩ*, had been slaughtered, how he had been betrayed and abandoned by his own people, and how he had had to desert his beautiful little Montagnard wife, H'Klois, and their two children to the tender mercies of the advancing communist armies, welled up into the forefront of Steffan's consciousness. He began to smolder.

He hated the Phoenix people with a white hot, but undirected passion. He, with the help of his chloropromazine, had kept that passion in check for all the years since he left Sweden. His conversation with the Texan, with all that vulgarian's braggadocio, had begun to pry open the lid to his personal Pandora's Box. The seething had been escalating for the past three years, fueled by each new revelation of the CIA's behind-the-scenes operations. The only thing that kept Steffan's lid on was the chloropromazine. Tran checked every day to make sure that his old friend took his medicine.

The partners took Ky to see the caribou herd that was now so far away that they had to take the plane and land on the banks of the

Ipnavik River near Kingak Mountain on the North Slope. Mary Okobuk, the Inuit-Eskimo woman, who tended to the chores of the Lodge wanted to come along; so, the men affectionately agreed as long as she would cook. That was no problem to her because the men were terrible cooks. The party watched grizzlies sweep up huge fat red colored salmon to add to their winter fat stores, bald eagles diving and swooping in permanently bonded pairs, powerful and irascible bull moose challenging all comers as the yearly rut season moved into its dramatic and ancient rituals. It seemed to be a restorative outing after the dark moods stirred up by Ky's report.

Tran would have been willing to hope that nothing more would come of the disturbing information about the CIA after Ky flew back to Los Angeles had the incident with the spike camp equipment not occurred to remind him of the dark side of his friend, who now called himself Steffan.

It was about a week after Ky left, and everything seemed to be settled down. Xe, Mary, and the boys had taken a group of bear hunters north for a two week hunt and salmon fishing trip. They had been gone two days. Steffan returned to the Lodge after a resupply trip to Kotzebue, eighty miles away, and walked out to the equipment shed to store the cold weather supplies he had bought.

"Tran," he called. C'mere a minute, will you?" Tran was cleaning the meat locker enclosure and was glad to take a break.

"What is it?" he asked when he walked into the equipment building.

"Did one of the boys take my new spike tent up north?" Steffan asked.

"No. They know better in the first place, and its just too fancy for them. Is it gone?"

"It is." Steffan's face was set in a hard frown.

"Who do you think, brother?" Tran asked. He was pretty sure he knew, and figured that Steffan had the same presumption. He thought he would ask anyway. "You know who," Steffan said and shook his head. Over the years since Steffan had established himself on the Wulik River, the Eskimos in Kivalina, thirty miles away, had made off with ski mobiles, client's fishing gear, and even a grader on different occasions; and Steffan had been obliged to fly to Kivalina to retrieve his belongings each time. He had wanted to maintain good relationships with the Native Americans in the past; and so, he had not called in the law nor had he been unduly harsh about it. He had been generous in providing meat when times were difficult for the villagers. "No good deed ever goes unpunished," he thought angrily.

Usually, Steffan thought it was rather funny; the natives were so transparent about their thievery that they were almost comical if it were not for the inconvenience.

This time was unlike those previous situations. Steffan had a set to his features that was different than before, like he had reached the end of his patience and would not be responsible for the consequences this time. "Come with me?" he asked Tran. The look in Steffan's eyes made Tran wonder if his big friend had missed taking his medicine

He paused then asked, "Sure. Want to take a gun?" Tran hoped the answer would be 'no.' It was.

"Don't need one. But this is the last time Percy Amatusuk is making a habit of taking my things. I intend to get them back, and I don't intend to have them taken again. Ever." There was a steely emphasis on the word ever.

They took the Super Cub to the northern end of Kivalina Inlet, about a mile from the Eskimos' houses. The Eskimos lived in a squalid group of government built houses the natives failed to take care of. Set on the peninsular rim of a bay five miles from the nearest road, thirty miles from the nearest neighbors, and eighty miles from the nearest town, Kotzebue. Most of the time they stayed to themselves and lived much as their hunter-gatherer ancestors had done or planted small vegetable gardens to supplement their diets. When they did venture out, they were shy, polite, and uncontentious. The women sometimes visited Mary at the Lodge, and they swapped gossip and handiwork. The source of all their troubles was drink. Whenever Percy Amatusuk got drunk, he went on stealing raids, another of those ancestral enterprises, and one that had landed him in jail or in some other form of hot water for years.

Steffan and Tran strode straight up to the Amatusuk's front door. Steffan was up the stairs in two large steps and banged resolutely on the door, enough to shake the house.

"Who is it?" demanded Percy's familiar voice from inside.

"Johannson," called Steffan.

The door opened a crack and the muzzle of a 30-30 poked through the fissure at the two visitors. Even though it was the common thing in the isolated villages, it nettled Steffan. "Open the door," he demanded peremptorily.

The gun retracted back inside, and the door opened. Percy was still pointing the gun at their midsections. "Whadda you want?" he demanded to know.

In a move faster than either Percy's eye or his finger, Steffan deflected the gun barrel and had his hand over the trigger. He swept the gun away as if it were a stick. It clattered to the floor cracking the stock.

"You didn't have to do that. That was my good gun," Percy whined. "Why'd you go and do that for?"

Steffan did not deign to answer the leathery Inuit's question. He certainly felt no concern over the injury to the man's property. He walked menacingly forward. "Look you weasel," he snarled, his lips curled in a threatening, teeth showing scowl. "I came for my spike camp gear."

"I don't have nothing of yours. What're you talkin' about?" The protested innocence appeared hollow.

"I didn't come for a debate or a discussion. I already said what I came for. I am not going to repeat anything I say today. You'd better listen good, because your life depends on your getting this." He paused to let his intentions sink in. "I don't like people taking my things. I am going to leave here with my gear, or you are going to be dead. And if you ever so much as touch what is mine again, I will kill you."

There are threats made in passion, those made idly for emphasis, and there are those that come up from the underworld, full of unexorcised demons, the promise of annihilation that brooks no dispute and no forgetting. Steffan's statement was one of the latter. It spoke of frustration, of red anger, and of completion—he would never flinch a scintilla from carrying out the fact. It was more than a promise, beyond a threat. It was a fact, and the Eskimo man knew it to the core of his being. The white man's eyes were those of a man possessed by a devil, and the Native American made an indelible notch in his memory never to violate this man again in any way. He would produce the camping gear and quit himself of Steffan Johannson forever, he silently prayed. He had never felt such a fear before.

Even Tran knew that his friend, Steffan Johannson, had ceased being a man to be trifled with. When he asked Steffan whether or not he was taking his medicine and learned that the big man had stopped two months ago, Tran secretly wondered what it would take to exorcise his friend's demons.

CHAPTER 47

SECRET: In camera session, Senate Intelligence Oversight Committee.
Testimony of Wilmer A. Colding, Jr., Director, Central Intelligence Agency
   22 October, 1986
   0900
Subject: Negotiations with Iran and Israel involving a trade of US arms sold to Iran by Israel in return for a release of American citizens held as hostages by Iran. US personnel involved are the same as are involved in support of the Nicaraguan Contras.

Chairman, Sen. Fineton: This session of the committee is held out of the regular meeting schedule and is to be considered an emergency session. It is possible that the testimony in this meeting could be made public before the Congress or in a judicial proceeding; therefore, the interrogation will be conducted by the committee's able counsel, Abram Liebovitz, Esquire.

Mr. Liebovitz: For the record, let us introduce and swear in the witness. Director Colding, for your information, the rules of the Congress apply here. You will be placed under oath, and your testimony will have the weight of that in a judicial proceeding. Anything you say will be recorded verbatim and subject to review. Anything you say may be used against you in a court of law, and you are bound by the laws of perjury as contained in the federal code. You have the right to remain silent, to invoke the protections of the fifth amendment of the constitution of the United States. You have the right to have an attorney present. Do you understand all of these rules and protections?

DCI Colding: Yes, sir.

Mr. Liebovitz: Again, for the record, will you state and spell out your full name and give us the position you hold in the United States government?

DCI Colding: Colding, Wilmer Axel, Jr. C-O-L-D-I-N-G, W-I-L-M-E-R, A-X-E-L, J-R. I am currently the director of the Central Intelligence Agency.

Mr. Liebovitz: Having been informed of your rights, do you wish to avail yourself of counsel or to invoke the protections of the fifth amendment?

DCI Colding: I have nothing to hide. I need no special protections.

Mr. Liebovitz: Good. Then we will proceed directly into the matter at hand. Mr. Director, when did you first become aware that individuals representing the Unites States had entered into illegal negotiations with the government of Iran.

DCI Colding: Two days ago, Tuesday, October 20, 1986.

Mr. Liebovitz: Is it your testimony before this committee that the CIA knew nothing of such negotiations and arrangements and payoffs before two days ago, sir"

DCI Colding: That is correct.

Mr. Liebovitz: Do you have personal knowledge of the involvement of Agency personnel in negotiations with the State of Israel to act as intermediaries in the sale of restricted arms to a hostile state, namely, The Islamic Republic of Iran?

DCI Colding: I do not. To my knowledge, CIA personnel did not participate in any way, shape, or form in the arms for hostages deal.

Mr. Liebovitz: Who did?

DCI Colding: I do not have direct knowledge, but I am informed by confidential sources that NSC staffers bear the full responsibility.

Mr. Liebovitz: The National Security Council of the United States of America, a cabinet level organ of this country, was the instigator and perpetrator of this manifestly illegal activity?

DCI Colding: No sir, that is not what I said. My testimony was that NSC staffers did so.

Mr. Liebovitz: That is a thin line sir, a very thin line.

DCI Colding: Perhaps so, but an important legal one. I am not the apologist for the NSC; but to be accurate, the evidence will show that

NSC staffers were responsible, and that they acted on their own accord and outside the constraints of the NSC.

Mr. Liebovitz: And no NSC officer was involved? I would be accused of being credulous if I accepted that concept on its face. Who were the staffers involved, and under whose aegis did they act? Come now, sir, it is late in the day for any daintiness about this crime.

DCI Colding: I believe a Colonel Oliver North was directly responsible. He acted with General Secord and former National Security Advisor, Robert McFarlane. It is established that he acted with his subordinates, Lieutenant commander Coy, Lieutenant colonel Earl, and a man named Howard Teicher. As near as I can determine, and this is not well established; they may have acted with the knowledge of, or in some instances, even under the orders of Admiral Poindexter.

Mr. Liebovitz: The President's National Security Advisor?

DCI Colding: Yes, sir.

Mr. Liebovitz: Then you are saying that this reaches deeply into the White House itself?

DCI Colding: I'm afraid so.

Mr. Liebovitz: Can you say, sir, whether or not the President knew of the affair? If so, at what point? And what, if anything, he did about it?

DCI Colding: That is a compound question and lacks foundation, but I can tell you what I know. There was discussion with President Reagan present, and with Vice-President Bush present at various times. Exactly what they knew, or when they knew it, is uncertain. It is certain that Donald Regan, chief of staff, was more or less completely informed.

Mr. Liebovitz: What about State and Defense?

DCI Colding: To my knowledge, no.

Mr. Liebovitz: Then this was a White House directed, clandestine, apparently illegal operation?

DCI Colding: I could not go that far. It appears to me to have been a rogue operation, with some possible knowledge on the part of responsible elected and appointed officials.

Sen. Fineton: It smells of fish to me. The idea that no one in the government had real knowledge or responsibility reminds me of Germany after the Second World War. There wasn't a single Nazi in the whole country. You would have thought the entire war and the holocaust were perpetrated by five or six individuals. This business certainly stretches the limits of my ability to believe in the communications from the White House and the NSC on this matter, to say the least.

Mr. Liebovitz: How was this nefarious business funded—surely not from the treasury of the United States? There would have to be records. These people can't have been that naive nor those who hold the purse strings that gullible?

DCI Colding: The funding was largely private, although some of the money came from diverted funds, funds intended for other purposes.

Mr. Liebovitz: And these men had the authority to collect and disburse such massive quantities of money, and, for that matter, to lay hands on completely restricted and embargoed arms?

DCI Colding: Apparently, somehow. I believe the record will eventually reveal that they were extraordinarily inventive men, resourceful beyond their rank and station.

Mr. Liebovitz: And that they had a lot of help from above.

DCI Colding: You mean, God?

Mr. Liebovitz: Close. I am going to ask you one last time, and, I remind you sir, you are under oath. Did the Central Intelligence participate in this affair? Or have guilty knowledge of it?

DCI Colding: I am confident that the record will show that the Agency was involved in nothing illegal. The only connection we have had was to support the Nicaragua Project that involved Colonel North and many of the same people who participated in the Iran-Israel-hostages-for-arms deal. Our participation was nothing more than to provide limited logistical support for the contras in the form of medicine, bandages, forums for debate, that sort of nonmilitary assistance.

Mr. Liebovitz: Are you telling us that there is some sort of an Iran-Contra connection—an Iran-Contra Affair, to coin a phrase?

DCI Colding: No sir. The only connection between these two entirely

distinct affairs, to use your term, is that the same men participated in both; and perhaps, both affairs were illegal, or at least overzealous.
Mr. Liebovitz: It is safe to say that they stepped well over the line in both instances. 'What a tangled web...'

Sen. Fineton:...we weave, when first we practice to deceive.' What a colossal mess! This rivals the Viet Nam debacle and Watergate. I fear this could bring down the presidency. Mr. Director, I am not quite ready to accept that the CIA was free of taint in either of these matters. There are very disturbing reports coming to this committee indicating that the CIA has been running a Phoenix type program with the Contras in Nicaragua—that agents have participated in or advised, or at least countenanced the infamous Death Squads we have been hearing so much about in the world press. I demand a forthright answer about the agency's involvement.

DCI Colding: I can make that very simple for you, Senator. There was none. Any suggestion that there was is a fabric of lies with no foundation, and I categorically deny it.

Sen. Fineton: No torture, no kidnapping, no extortion, no ransoming, no false imprisonments, no killings? Come now, Director Colding, you'll have us believing that the CIA agents involved there are only leading the boys' choir.

DCI Colding: You may believe what you want about such romantic fiction, but you are going to find that there will be no evidence of illegality found on the part of our official agents. I cannot speak for the excesses of the contras themselves; after all, they are involved in a war. To quote Chairman Mao, 'To have an omelet, you must first break some eggs.' But that is on their responsibility, not ours.

Sen. Fineton: This testimony is so reminiscent of those ten, fifteen, and twenty years ago on the Phoenix Program in Viet Nam, that it is both disturbing and haunting. I will tell you today, sir, that if you are found to be lying to this committee on this subject, I will see to it that you are indicted. If you are convicted by evidence that demonstrates that your agency, like the White House-NSC cabal you have been describing, was involved in some sort of government within the government, above and outside the laws of our country, I will use every authority of my good office to bring you and your agency down. President Truman, as far back as 1947, expressed the desire to bring the CIA back to the dictates of the original charter making it an intelligence gathering and collating body and to take it out of the covert action business. If you are involved in yet another such misadventure as the Phoenix operation, the toppling of the Italian government, or the Diem regime, then I will see to it that the head of this serpent is severed from its body, and that it is put out of the business of interfering in the affairs of foreign countries.

Mr. Liebovitz: I have no further questions. You may go, Mr. Director. Be informed that you may well be subpoenaed to testify in open forum before the Congress. I suggest that you take time to collect your files on this complex Iran-Contra set of affairs for the purpose of preparation for that testimony.

DCI Colding: I'll do that, sir.

Sen. Fineton: This emergency meeting of the Senate Oversight Committee stands adjourned.

Meeting adjourned, 1010.

> Senator Carl Lewin (D-Michigan): How in the name of heaven we could be saying one thing so clearly in public, we could be certifying one thing so clearly to the Congress, and doing something so totally different in fact.
>
> Senator Barry Goldwater (R-Arizona): I think President Reagan has gotten his butt in a crack on this Iran thing.
> *Statements by leading members of both political parties used as opening statements on the television program, Face the Nation, November 16, 1986. Secretary of State, George Schultz was the guest on the program to answer for the administration. (As quoted in A Very Thin Line by Theodore Draper).*

CHAPTER 48

The other was a softer voice,
As soft as honey-dew
Quoth he, 'The man hath penance done,
And penance more will do.
Samuel Taylor Coleridge
Rime of the Ancient Mariner

Since emigrating to British Columbia and then to Alaska, Steffan Johannson had permitted himself very few reminders of actions of the lower forty-eight United States of America, the country of his birth and the one that had so dominated the consciousness and commitment of his youth. He, like many Alaskans, considered his state to be apart from the others and was in sympathy with the developing secessionist movement in the state. One tie he maintained was his subscription to *The New York Times*. That newspaper was remarkable not only for the in-depth and even-handed quality of its journalism, but also for the fact that it was delivered to subscribers almost anyplace in the world. Steffan's copies arrived in Kotzebue, Alaska by air a day after printing and kept him informed of the world he had left, and of the country where the power resided and action was born.

On November 14, 1986, the thirty-six year old hunting outfitter and businessman sat down to a breakfast of rice, pho, hot chocolate, and eggs, a holdover from habits picked up in Southeast Asia, and opened *The Times*. The half inch headline came at him like a figurative slap in the face. He had somehow damped down his seething discontent at the immoral activities of the Central Intelligence Agency, over the three years since the blustering Texas client had stirred them up. The newspaper's lead article refanned the flames:

IRAN-CONTRA AFFAIR EXPOSED

US Officials Named as Conspirators
In Arms for Hostages Deal

The Times has learned from highly placed officials of the Reagan administration that indictments are likely to be handed down in a bizarre case of illegal transfer of embargoed arms to Iran in contravention of United States law. It is alleged that the arms deal was part of a plan to secure the release of hostages held by Iran. The White House denies the connection, but admits secret negotiations for the release of hostages have been in progress for some time. The White House spokesman denied the sale of arms to Iran, but could not categorically deny that United States arms sold to Israel found their way into Iranian military hands.

Congress plans a full scale investigation of the affairs. They plan to probe the relationship between clandestine aid to the Nicaraguan Contras and the Iran hostages-for-arms deal. *The Times* has learned that marine Colonel, Oliver L. North, National Security Advisor, Admiral John M. Poindexter, former National Security Advisor, Robert C. McFarlane, retired General, Richard V. Secord, and billionaire, Adnan Khashoggi are implicated and will be called to testify under subpoena. Further, indictments are expected to be served on these and others directly involved. Sources say, "The White House may well be involved." At the time of publication, the White House has declined official comment. Unofficially, inside sources state that they "are fearful about where this could all lead" and that the affair may be Reagan's "Watergate."

The individuals named in the subpoenas are also implicated in covert and allegedly illegal transmission of aid to the Nicaraguan Contras, including, but not limited to, advisors and arms. A protected source from the inner circles of the Central Intelligence Agency has told *The Times* that the agency has participated in death squads, torture, extortion, theft of property of private citizens who, although noncommunists, are not aligned or in sympathy with the extremist aims and violent reprisal activities of the right wing Contras.

Steffan could see it all: midnight helicopter rides out over the Pacific, tiger cages, black lists, prolonged detention of brown-skinned innocents, and the hand of the 'Colonel' and his henchmen. The newspaper called to mind the unwanted image of Szabo and DuParrier and their Psy-ops program. Before he had digested the lengthy piece

897

in the paper, he was having flashes of his own best forgotten involvement and felt his guts being roiled.

With effort Tran convinced Steffan to restart his tranquilizer medication after he learned in October that Steffan had stopped taking the powerful drug. The worst thing Steffan did that day, November 14, after reading the inflammatory newspaper article, was to stop taking his chloropromazine again. In two days the blood level of the powerful tranquilizing drug was below the critical threshold, and Steffan began to have dreams of black hairy Vietnamese demons. During the day he saw flashes of atrocities, always linked with the faces of the Colonel, Douglas N. Herter, Lane Duerk, Hugo Bartini, Cleveland Howard, Rex Dragerton, Dieter Lutz, Tandrosz Szabo, Jean-Luc DuParrier, and from television and newspaper accounts he included Wilmer Colding, the Director of the CIA, and former presidents, Lyndon Johnson and Richard Nixon. He became fixated on ideations of vengeance and of ridding the race of these representatives of evil incarnate. It felt good, energizing, to hate; and Steffan stopped his medications altogether knowing that the drugs would rob him of his intensity. He needed the passion to get done what had to be done.

In a completely calm and dispassionate manner, he brought Tran and Xe together and laid down a plan to wreak a long overdue meting out of justice on the architects of Phoenix and to stop them from continuing. Tran, too, felt that there needed to be justice for the death of his family and for the lies that had formed the basis for his irregular military career in his native land. He had chafed at the knowledge that he had been betrayed, that he had been subject to the unspeakable on Con Son Island; and as a result, it was not difficult to convince him to join in a crusade. Xe bore the memory of his abandoned and violated Hmong family as an open wound. His only comment was, "Why has it taken so long to come to this conclusion?"

Steffan arranged a meeting with Ky in the VIP lounge in the international airport in Los Angeles. The two men were accompanied by several Vietnamese and Hmong men who, Ky assured Steffan, were of like minds. They, too, had smoldering scores to settle with the smirking Company agents that had betrayed and abandoned them. To a man, each of those present was a zealot on the subject of the rectitude of vengeance, a sort of cosmic rebalancing of the scales of justice that had been skewed for so long in favor of the devils who managed the secret war in Southeast Asia. Each had lost family and friends to the American juggernaut and to the nefarious South Vietnamese political prisons. Many had suffered untold sacrifices to get out of that agonized country after the American CIA had left them, their faithful servants.

The conclusion of the conspiratorial meeting was a plan of action and a commitment to secrecy that amounted to a blood oath never to betray the coconspirators. In two months the plan was fleshed out in sophisticated detail. Names, dates, places, and itineraries of targets were identified and verified. The methods were those of the Phoenix program, an irony that was not lost on the men. They intended to be the Last Phoenix.

In good Phoenix *modus operandi* the targeted officials were surveilled over several weeks in what was known to them as the Figure of Eight method. The procedure was predicated on the observation that the majority of human beings are most comfortable and efficient when they carry out a life of habit and routine. Except in extraordinary situations even public figures, and those who have need of security, act as creatures of habit. The former PRUCs and their compatriots tracked their targets until a reliable pattern was established; then Tran, Ky, or Steffan traveled to where the target lived. With his tracker the senior conspirator then verified the pattern and confirmed the surveillance. The method was known as the Figure of Eight because when the tracking was completed and certified, it confirmed a reliable and useful knowledge of how the subject's day began, the motions of the day, and the return at night.

The men had to dip deeply into their bank accounts in the Union Bank of Switzerland to fund the meticulous and tedious process. They had to travel extensively under false passports; they had to buy information; and they had to eliminate the sources of that information for fear that they could betray the plan. All of that took money. The three major players did not begrudge a penny of their expenses, given the earth and soul cleansing character of the endeavor.

These men were not wild-eyed anarchists, nor were they men bent on some utopian scheme to take over the world. They had no illusions about the scope of their project. They had in mind only to cleanse one small area of slime in a sea of slime. They realized full well that they could not hit the most sensational targets first; for one thing, men like the former presidents and the DCI were well protected; for another, they would have to have very precise information about how to get at such protected men. The plan evolved in an orderly progression of decisions until it was clear, succinct, detailed, and precise. The first targets would be those who could supply the missing links to the more senior men, how to get by the massive security network guarding the major puppeteers of the Viet Nam war.

The 'Colonel,' Dustin Hauter, was considered to be the linchpin; and the conspirators concentrated their earliest and most intense efforts on him. Each of them knew he would hold the knowledge about all of the other micro and macro managers of Phoenix. Through him, they could get at the still active Company and government officials and in small measure begin to even the score for all those noncombatants and compatriots who suffered from the beak and talons of Phoenix and from the infamous black list.

Ky found Hauter with relative ease. Once he retired to California, the aging CIA official had not taken particularly great pains to be obscure. His picture was in the Orange County Register for having cosponsored an AIDs benefit. He made the news by serving as one of the campaign chairpersons for a local Republican candidate for the Tustin City council. Republican candidates do not lose in Orange County, and Hauter had briefly basked in the post-election limelight. Ky knew the name of his wife, his address, his unlisted telephone number, the license number on his vintage Austin-Healy (one with original licenses having gold numbers on a dark blue background); and the route he took every day like, clockwork, to the Newport Yacht Club for lunch. It only remained to put the plan into operation.

Steffan, Tran, Xe, and Ky studied their plan of operation through early January, 1987 looking for flaws. None of them could find any. They had well identified and Figure Eighted targets, easy and untraceable sources of funding, safe houses, an armamentarium that would be the envy of one of the drug cartels (and not incidentally, the arms originated from Medillin, Colombia through Ky's and the Wa People's connections) plausible alibis, reliable escape routes, and unimpeachable phony identifications. The plan was so constructed that each small group functioned in a compartmentalized cell on a strict need-to-know basis. If any one of their number were to be caught, the others could carry on unimpeded, since none but the four master planners knew the overall project. There was not a single man in the plot who was not personally known to at least one of the major conspirators. The plan was pronounced operationally ready.

Steffan called Ky at the Bonaventure Hotel in Los Angeles from the Empress Hotel on Vancouver Island, British Columbia, Canada. Each of them was registered under an assumed identity. It was January 9th. "This is Mr. Jones," Steffan said as soon as Ky answered.

"Greetings. This is Mr. Porter," Ky responded in accordance with the previously arranged signal ritual.

"Is the merchandise ready?" Steffan asked.

"I would have to pick it up at the transportation site, but that should not create any delay."

"Then, let's plan on meeting for the signing of the deal tomorrow night." Steffan set down the receiver in its cradle. He had stepped over the brink, and there was no turning back. He walked out to the American Airlines office in the hotel lobby and bought his ticket. He arranged to leave from Seattle the following afternoon.

It had been two months since he had stopped taking his chloropromazine. Steffan could tell that he had lost the drug effect. It was one of those good news-bad news situations. The good news was that he felt less tired, slowed, and disinterested. The drug had given him a feeling of depersonalization that he had never quite been able to shake despite careful manipulation of the dosage. Initially, after his electroconvulsive shock therapy in Sweden, when he first started on the halogenated tranquilizer, he had been quite severely effected. He exhibited motor retardation, stiff, slow movements, and a fairly profound lack of interest in his surroundings; he was the proverbial chloropromazine zombie shuffling along in the back ward of the Karolinska. Eventually, he had accommodated; and the drug permitted him to live an outwardly normal, placid life, free from even the average hills and valleys of emotional reaction.

The bad news about stopping the drug had been the resumption of his paranoid ideations, ideas of reference from perceived external enemies, and bad dreams. As opposed to the manic persecuted state he presented on the Russian ship and the severely depressed state he had lapsed into at the Karolinska Institute, he was free of hallucinations and the inability to distinguish obvious reality from his delusions. He was emotionally shaky, but his judgment in everyday activities was unimpaired. He kept himself in superb physical condition as a matter of habit, and he found that his ability to think in combat and escape and evasion terms was even better now that he was off the drug. He was not ashamed to discuss his impressions with his old friend and confidant, Tran, to be certain that his perceptions remained in synch with reality.

Steffan had a three weeks growth of beard and wore his hair long enough to have a pony tail. After taking the ferry across the Straits of Juan de Fuca to Vancouver, Steffan spent two hours working around in a garage to season his clothing and hands. He went to a second hand store in Vancouver's water front district and bought a set of workman's clothes to wear across the border. Feeling the part, he took a taxi to the Mariner's bar on Water Street, a low, low class dive. Steffan chose that particular joint because an old friend of Tran's, a small wiry Vietnamese martial artist, was the unlikely but notoriously effective bouncer there. He planned to sit and nurse a beer or two until it was time to leave to drive across the border. He planned to cross after dark just before the ten o'clock closure deadline when the immigration officers were tired and inattentive. He slouched in a booth near the back and made himself obscure.

Not obscure enough, as it turned out. Because of an unfortunate juxtaposition of the planets or other equally improbable cause, he was selected to be the target of the attentions of a foursome - two American gentlemen and their Canadian evening companions. Lance Corporal Buffum Hines and Private First Class Jim Ray Duncan, both of the US Marine Corps and both originally from Cherry Point, North Carolina picked up two Vancouver ladies of the night and squired them into the Mariner's Bar. The ladies had assured the two hearties that they recommended the place not because of the modest commission they received from the drinks their tricks imbibed while in the girls' company, but because it was "so interesting."

Since the time was well before the fashionable and sociable drinking hour, the bar was all but empty; and, therefore, depressingly devoid of action. The two young marines decided early in the day that they would enjoy their brief visit to their neighbors in Canada no matter what. Apparently, it was going to be up to them to liven the country up; and the Mariner's Bar on Water Street was as good of a place as any to start. Buffum fed the juke box, and he and Jim Ray showed the Canuck girls how to stomp in time to the music. They soon grew bored with that activity and with harassing the barmaid who was trying her level best to remain civil to the foul mouthed and raucous Americans. Buffum discovered Steffan back there in his corner because Steffan chose to leave the obscurity of his booth and to slip out unnoticed.

As he stood to lay down some money to cover his tab, Steffan caught the white wall hair styled muscular man walking unsteadily in his direction. He sat back down at a his table facing away from the American lout hoping that the young man would lose interest. It was not to be so.

"Hey, cutie. That's a snappy pony tail you got." He walked around to where he could face Steffan. "Oops," he said, feigning great surprise, "excuuuse me. I thought you was a girl. I beg your pardon." Jim Ray and the girls found Buffum extravagantly funny.

Steffan ignored the stout military man and his implied insult. He sat and looked at a point somewhere to the man's right as if he were not there.

Buffum walked back around and began to flip Steffan's short pony tail. "Cute," Buffum said. It was his favorite word of praise and taunt. "You kinda sweet?" He continued to push the point. He had decided that here was a source of amusement, and he was going to liven up the joint. Maybe this pansy would get brave, and they could have a good old fashioned fight. Buffum loved to fight. He had not become a jar-head for nothing.

It was growing thin. Steffan's patience had become less easily maintained when he went off the chloropromazine. It was the first thing Mary had noticed about him. "Don't bother me," he said to the burly marine. "And I won't bother you." It was said so softly and with such an absence of malice that Buffum mistook the utterance for fear or pleading—the communication of the meek and the peacemaker, as the Good Book would have put it.

"We're touchy, are we?" He snapped Steffan's ears with his fingers. Steffan stiffened but otherwise did not react. He continued to avoid eye contact with the bothersome young marine.

Steffan pushed back his chair to get up and leave. He was still hoping that he could avoid a scene. The last thing he needed on that particular day was to get into a brawl and to land in jail. Buffum clapped both hands on Steffan's shoulders from behind and pushed him into his seat. Steffan tensed his muscles and quickened his reflexes. A red haze was beginning to form behind his eyes. "Don't put your hands on me. I never let anyone put their hands on me." His voice was low, throaty, and malevolent.

Buffum gave Steffan's pony tail a vicious surprise jerk snapping his head back. He started to say, "Who do you think you're talkin' to. This is the United States Marines that has you in hand," but all that made it out was, "Who do..."

Steffan exploded out of his chair like a rocket and drove his left elbow hard into Buffum's exposed nose. The lance corporal had a look or complete consternation on his face. Steffan stomped back with his right foot and gashed down Buffum's shin before crunching the dorsum of his foot. Buffum's hands flew out to the sides as if he were preparing to take flight. Steffan drove a spear hand into the marine's throat then dropped his hand to the man's zipper front and clamped his fingers around the marine's genitals with the force of a shark bite. Buffum yelped like a puppy. Steffan lifted the 190 pound man off the floor until their eyes were on a level. Even with the agony in his reproductive organs, Buffum was able to divert his attention to the cruelest pair of eyes he had ever seen. There was no more compassion there than he could have expected from a hungry she-bear. He felt that he had looked past the gates of hell just before he passed out.

Steffan dropped his tormentor to the floor. Jim Ray was not about to let no civilian abuse his bud. He climbed out of his chair, knocking it to the floor, and advanced two steps in Steffan's direction. The bouncer, a man who might have weighed 120 pounds wet, moved with electrifying agility and purpose across the bar floor. Before Jim Ray could take his third step, he ate the bouncer's heel. Jim Ray spat eight front teeth and spluttered a bloody froth. He did not have long to contemplate his dental mishap because six punches to his chin, the side of his jaw, his throat, his solar plexus, his paunchy gut (two punches into the softness for good measure), came with such blinding speed that he did not have time to think, let alone mount a defense. He crumpled beside his bud.

"Thank you," said Steffan. They had met several times before.

The little man said, "Only my job."

Steffan stepped up to the ladies of questionable virtue and handed each twenty Canadian dollars. "Go. Don't talk to cops. Forget you were here." His gaze conveyed more than either his words or his money.

"You don't have to sweat us, dearie," the brasher of the two women said. "We don't exactly see eye to eye with coppers. We find it best to steer clear of them on general principles. But thanks for the bread, anyways."

Steffan swiftly exited the bar and the waterfront, drove directly to the border, and left the country using his Mueller-Garza of Costa Rica passport without further incident. The fight had sharpened his reflexes to combat tone. He was as alert as a jungle cat now. It was a state that would prevail for the next month.

One of Ky's men picked Steffan up at LAX. They pulled out onto the 405 heading south at the height of rush hour. It took them nearly three hours to make the forty-five minute trip to Orange County, past the John Wayne-Orange County Airport, and to their Culver Drive exit. Like most thinking people, Steffan had a love-hate relationship with the Southern California freeway system. He loved the magnificent smooth broad highways and the superbly helpful signs. He hated the fact he had to go fifteen to thirty miles an hour on a artery that could accommodate a hundred mile an hour cruising speed. Today, however, he knew that the near infinite traffic provided all the obscurity he needed.

Ky's man scrupulously kept to the speed limit, as if he had any real choice. He pulled into the far right lane and made the exit going east into Irvine. They turned left onto Main Street, left again on Westpark, right on Barcelona for a block, left on Sorrento for a short residential block, then right on Corsica. The car stopped in the cul-de-sac. They got out, and Ky's man helped remove the two large suitcases from the trunk. Like a good soldier, he did not comment on the excessive weight of the bags. In fact, he had scarcely said a word all the way from LAX. "Number 21," he said and indicated one of the two-story pink stucco residences facing the circle.

Steffan idly wondered how the people in this community could distinguish their house from any of 50,000 other ones just like it - pink, stucco, same height, same perpetually green grass and two Juniper bushes in the front. That quality was exactly what Ky had been looking for when he rented the place. Steffan did not wave to the departing soldier.

He knocked twice, then twice again. The door opened into a spacious living room and adjoining dining room on the left and to a staircase on his immediate right. Ky closed the door, took hold of Steffan's huge shoulders and pulled him down two feet. The smaller Vietnamese man brushed Steffan's right cheek with his lips, then the left, then the right, in rapid succession. Steffan returned the old French greeting. Welcome to our humble dwelling, brother," Ky said.

"Looks good. Where is he?" Steffan asked.

"Upstairs. Sure you don't want anything to eat, something to drink before you go up. The icebox is full."

Steffan shook his head. "Had some rubber chicken on the plane. Let's see him."

There were two very fit looking Hmong men in the living room, seated on the rented sofa. Each held an Uzi. Three more of them stood around the old man on the straight backed chair in the middle of the otherwise completely bare bed room.

"General Hauter, I presume," he said.

He had aged considerably since Steffan had last seen him in the hill country of Laos, but he was still the ramrod stiff, hard-eyed government secret agent. Nothing would ever change that except death.

"I haven't had the pleasure," Hauter said.

"We'll go over old times later. Right now, I will tell you what you are going to do for us."

"And I'll tell you where you can put it. Do you have any idea who your are dealing with?" Hauter snapped. For all the tape binding his ankles and wrists to the heavy wood straight backed arm chair, the old Colonel had the facial expression of one very much in charge.

"Tape his mouth," Steffan ordered. One of the Hmongs tore off a length of duct tape and ungently applied it over Hauter's lips. For the first time, the old man's eyes looked less certain. If he were going to be unable to intimidate this young thug with the force of his argument and authority, it would be a good deal more difficult. He decided to listen.

"The situation, so far as you are concerned, is very simple. You are going to give us certain specific information we require. I have here a list of individuals whom you know. You will supply unlisted and secret telephone numbers, code names, computer access codes, bank account numbers, and the like. For your convenience, we have indicated the information required beside each name. This is, as you can tell, a computer printout. You will input the information. The first thing we will need is access to your computer."

Steffan nodded to the young Hmong man who ripped the tape off Hauter's mouth. "In a pig's eye!" the brave old man barked in his best officer tone.

"Tape," Steffan said.

Hauter tried to twist his head. A second Hmong guard tried to hold his head still. Hauter bit him. Steffan stepped forward and poked his index finger a single jab into the seated man's solar plexus. The blow was not hard, but was directed obliquely upward. The effect was stunning, almost paralyzing. He fought to get his breath. The Hmongs reapplied the tape with ease.

"I started to explain your situation," Steffan continued as if the interruption had never happened. His voice was calm, almost kindly. His eyes were anything but. "You are here and remain alive only because you are useful. There are any number of people of my acquaintance who would pay dearly for the privilege of making you suffer a slow and terrible death. You have two options. You can die swiftly and painlessly after giving us what we want, or you can die slowly over three weeks, after giving us what we want. Your choice."

Steffan indicated to the boys to remove the tape over the prisoner's mouth. "You can't scare me, young man. I have been threatened by real experts. My training made me impervious to torture; so, forget it." The tape went back on. It was becoming clear to Hauter that he would get the tape every time he failed to say what these thugs wanted to hear.

"I know you think that you can endure torture. That you think your training will get you through it. Maybe you even think I am bluffing, that I will go away without the information I came for if only you will remain resolute. I am going to show you that you are wrong. I am going to refresh your memory." Steffan stopped talking and pulled off his turtleneck shirt, then his undershirt. He slowly turned 360° to let the old man see the full effect of the Vietnamese torturer's handiwork and the vivid and unmistakable tattoos.

Steffan took off the tape this time. "You were one of my boys. How could you do this! I was like a father to all of you. I did everything I could for you. Have you lost your mind?" Hauter shouted. The tape went back on. There was beginning to be fear in the man's eyes now. He was convinced that the threat he faced was serious.

"Every man has his breaking point, Colonel. You are no exception. My only fear is that you will die too soon and cheat me out of the information and the pleasure. I will let you know I am serious. Then I will give you until six o'clock in the morning. If you do not cooperate at that time, I will show you your breaking point."

Steffan whispered to Ky. He sent one of the Hmongs into the next room. When he returned, he was carrying a heavy duty tree pruner. The implement consists of two handles attached to a pair of sharp serrated jaws. It was a professional tree pruners tool designed with a ratcheted gear to multiply force to enable it to cut through an inch thick branch with only the effort that an average woman could exert.

"Thank you," Steffan said to the young man who had fetched the tool.

"Tape down all of his fingers except the pinkie on the left," he said with no more feeling than if he was ordering pizza. The Hmongs complied swiftly. Steffan picked up a newspaper and set it under Hauter's hand. Hauter's eyes were bulging. The large Scandinavian picked up the wizened finger and set it gently in the jaws of the pruning shears. The general tried to rock the chair, tried to double the finger up and to squirm it out of the grasp of the jaws. He began to sweat.

Steffan bit the finger off like a twig and let it drop onto the newspaper on the floor. Hauter screamed silently under his taped mouth until he fainted. Blood sprayed out of the small severed digital arteries, spattering on the floor; a little of it went beyond the paper and spotted the rug. "Get a cereal bowl, please," he asked one of the guards. Steffan placed the severed finger in the bowl and put the bowl on the floor in front of the unconscious old man, well within his field of vision. He and Ky left the room.

Ky fixed a sumptuous Vietnamese meal full of hot brown chilies and shell fish. Steffan and Ky went to bed early knowing that they were going to get an early start the following day. The guards took four hour guard watch tours. They were forbidden to speak to the prisoner.

Steffan was alert at five o'clock, completed his morning ablutions by five thirty and ate a bowl of hot cereal to calm his stomach. He always got an upset stomach when he got up early after a day of air travel. It was a peculiar idiosyncrasy of his. At six o'clock, he and Ky went upstairs and faced Hauter. The old man looked thoroughly cowed.

Steffan gently removed the tape, and Hauter took in a deep clean breath, relieved at least to have the irritation of the tape removed. His finger was agonizingly painful now, and it took all he had not to show it to these two barbarians. "Are you ready to cooperate?" Steffan asked in his soothing voice. It came almost like purring, but he was careful not to condescend to the general. Whatever else he felt about the old monster, he respected the old man's courage.

"I do not know a thing. What makes you think I can give you the numerical information or anything you want? I have been out of the loop for years. I am a retired old has-been. You seem to know so much, why don't you know that?"

"Wrong response, Hauter," Steffan said and put the tape back on. "Unzip his pants."

The Hmong youth to whom he directed the order grimaced but obeyed immediately. Steffan fumbled inside the old man's boxer shorts then extracted his limp penis. He placed the jaws of the pruning shears over the senescent organ. Hauter was crying. His eyes were begging.

Steffan took off the tape. "All right," Hauter said. "Whatever you say. It won't do you any good, though. These are the most protected people in the world."

Steffan taped the old man's mouth again, but this time he removed the tape binding down his right hand. He gave the old CIA agent a pen and a pad of paper. "I will give you a few sample questions. You write the answers. If they are satisfactory, you can sit at the computer, link up with your PC, and start filling in the blanks." He did not specify what would happen if the wrong choice were made.

Hauter listened attentively. Ky read off names of the targets and gave the information about them that he needed. Hauter wrote answers in a shaky hand. Steffan picked up the pad, nodded to the Hmong to rebind the 'Colonel's' hand; and he and Ky left the room. They sat at the rented kitchen table and perused what Hauter had given them. Ky had only asked questions to which he knew the answers with precision. Hauter's answers were uniformly incorrect, in some cases by no more than a single number or transposition of numbers, but useless, nonetheless.

That came as no surprise to either man. They had a contingency plan. They returned to Hauter's room.

"Undo his right hand," Steffan ordered. He handed the aristocratic old civil service worker a cordless telephone.

"Dial your home phone, Colonel," Steffan said to the defiant captive. When the old man hesitated, Steffan offered, "The number is area code 714, 264-8201. That is your unlisted number, is it not?"

Hauter nodded. Fear had crept into his eyes with that revelation despite his defiant front. He dialed.

His end of the conversation was:

"Hello. Who is this?"

"What are you doing in my house. Let me speak to my wife. If you have harmed a hair on that woman's head..."

Hauter hung his head and listened.

"Margaret. Now take it easy..."

He listened for a few more minutes.

"Margaret, don't. You must be strong. These are not crazy people. I can do business with them...Now don't carry on..."

He held the phone away from his ear. Even the other men in the room could hear the screaming. It did not sound like a woman who was upset; it sounded like great pain.

"What are you doing?!!!" Hauter screamed, his face was panic stricken. No one heard him at the other end of the telephone line which now was dead.

All of the blood had drained out of his wrinkled face. His eyes were blank and devoid of spirit. As never before in his life, Dustin Hauter, commander of men, schemer of schemes, and controller of destinies, knew he was controlled. He knew these people had found his breaking point. "Don't hurt her," was all he could manage.

"Now, we will begin the work we came to do," Steffan said. "We will have a contract of sorts. Colonel, you are a dead man. That is a fact. You will pay for your crimes against humanity with your life. The manner of your death and whether or not you watch your wife suffer for days before she dies as well depends on your flawless cooperation. Do you understand me so far?"

Hauter nodded grimly. Steffan continued. "Mrs. Hauter is an innocent...but there have been so many innocents...I will make you a promise. Unlike your promises, mine is good. If your information pans out, then I will let her live and will even guarantee good treatment of her. And of you for that matter. When the information is confirmed, you will be killed swiftly and mercifully. Do not hold out hope that something you do or don't do will alter that. Your only bargaining chip is accurate information. You know the cost for failure."

"I will do anything you want. Just leave Margaret alone. She has diabetes and a heart condition. She can't take much." Hauter pleaded.

"I believe we have an understanding," Steffan said to Hauter. "Let's untie him, give him a hearty breakfast and get to work," he said to the other men.

By noon, Steffan and Ky held twelve single spaced pages of information, more than they had asked. Once Hauter had started, he strove to guarantee his wife's preservation by becoming voluble and overzealous. He described habits and peccadilloes of the men on Ky's list. He knew personal clubs, schedules, and meeting places they preferred, even criminal activities of his former underlings. They had all kept the old man well informed as a matter of courtesy; and he had provided sage counsel, giving the lie to his retirement. He was as helpful as if he had fallen into the 'Stockholm syndrome' and had come to believe in his captors' cause. He had no illusions as to the usage intended for the information. He did not hesitate to betray the men who trusted him implicitly and completely.

Hauter's computer proved to be a veritable gold mine of information on business connections. He and the others were involved in business dealings that were spin-offs of their Company work, many that they preferred not to make public. With a manipulation of a computer mouse, clip and save function, and access codes for accounts in banks in the Grand Cayman Islands, Vanuatu, and Liechtenstein, he could transfer funds as freely as if he were lead teller at any one of the banks. There was not a solitary error that Ky could discover against his checklist of already verified information.

"You have done well, thus far, Colonel," Steffan said when they had completed their work. "I will have the men sew up your hand, and you can enjoy life while we set off to verify all of this information. If and when that is done, you will be given the rest you deserve." Steffan's voice was calm and dispassionate, almost friendly. The communication was not lost on Dustin Hauter. It was the best of a bad deal, he decided.

———————————————————•◆•━◆◆━◆••—————————————

Hugo Bartini was truly retired. His dream had been to live out his best years in the horse country of Ocala, Florida. He realized he was as ugly as a wart hog, but money he put away had allowed him a horse ranch and a lifestyle that permitted him to enjoy the favors of an elegant Cuban woman. He was becoming respected in horse circles as a breeder of Peruvian smooth gaited Paso Fino horses. Life was good.

He basked in the sun while sitting on one of his Mexican lounge chairs while Maria Innocenta splashed nude in the pool, confident in the absolute privacy of Hugo's estate. His cellular phone rang.

"Yeah," he growled, annoyed at being disturbed on a Sunday. He was hardly a religious man, but he did hold to the Sabbath as a day of rest as a religious principle.

"This is an old friend," Steffan said over the line. "To prove to you that we know each other, why don't you go into your private study, the one adjoining the master bedroom, and turn on your own computer, the one no one else ever uses. Open the Vanuatu file. I will give you time, let's say three minutes. I'll call you back." He hung the receiver of the pay phone back on its hook. He was located a mile from Hugo in a Seven-Eleven.

Hugo started to protest but realized that the caller had rung off. He did not have the faintest idea who it was, and would have written the call off as a crank had he not been alerted to trouble by the fact that somehow the caller had gotten his absolutely private number. Not six people in the world knew that number, not even Maria Innocenta. And it occurred to him that it was somewhat remarkable that this stranger knew the layout of his house. He reluctantly relinquished his place in the sun and padded into the house.

Bartini turned on the APS Drive of his PC, waited a few minutes then turned on the hard drive. He keyed in "Off-Shore Banks" and selected "Vanuatu." Shortly, the account history from the country with the world's strictest bank secrecy laws came on the screen. Bartini was as near absolutely certain of the sacrosanctitude of his account as he was of the rectitude of his role—former role—in the CIA and of The Company's legacy of trust for him. Vanuatu was a small South Pacific island about the size of Connecticut with 160,000 people who spoke 106 distinct languages. There were no significant natural resources and no major industries. The island was almost wholly dependent on the offshore banking services it offered. Vanuatu made divulgence of bank secrets an imprisonable felony. The CIA bequeathed trust and punished betrayal with even greater intensity.

Bartini scrolled down to the last entry. It was dated with the current day's date: Friday, January 12, 1987. His pulse quickened. There was obviously a mistake since he had not been into his account in two days. The time was 12:34—three minutes since he had hung up the phone from the crank call. Despite the excessive airconditioning in the handsomely appointed room, Bartini began to sweat. The entry indicated a transferal of every cent in the Vanuatu account to a numbered account in the Union Bank of Switzerland.

"Rii-iii-iing," sounded the phone startling Bartini more than it should have. He picked it up before it could ring again. The same voice as had made the first call came again, not even waiting for him to say, "Hello."

"Now that I have your attention, Hugo, my friend,..."

"Who are you?! What do you think you're doing?..." He was going to add, "Who do you think you're messing with?" but the caller interrupted.

"Drive to the Ocala Hilton. Ask for the key to room 544. The room is registered in your name and paid for with your Merrill Lynch Preferred Client Group VISA, card number 4443-0432-3830-7798. Present yourself at the door at one fifteen sharp. Hurry and you can just make it." Click.

Few things irritated Hugo Bartini like having some pip-squeak hang up on him. He was angry as he changed into a pair of jodhpurs, riding boots, and a black soft silk shirt. He planned to go riding as soon as this nuisance at the Ocala Hilton was done with. He was not so angry that he could tamp down the fear that this might not be something he could control altogether. He left without saying goodbye to Maria Innocenta.

There was no traffic. Everyone was at the thoroughbred show at the Arabian Breeder's Center off 60th on State Road 200. He still barely made it in time, and felt rushed. He broke every speed law to get to the ugly pink five story hotel at the intersection of exit 68 off I 75 where College Road changes to State Road 200. The young Cuban at the front desk was expecting him and gave him the key to his room as soon as he announced his name. "Have a nice stay," the handsome young man said. Hugo could never be sure what those people were saying.

At one minute past the appointed time, the slightly out of breath Bartini rapped on the door of 544. When a minute passed and there was no answer, he knocked again, louder. The door opened and he was invited in by a thin, tough looking little Oriental. "Sit down," the man said in heavily accented English. Bartini pointedly avoided sitting in the chair offered and took another one on the other side of the couch. The oriental flashed him a smile. It was terrible; the man had pointed and black lacquered teeth. Hugo had not seen anything like it since he had left Nam, what was it? twelve, thirteen years ago?

The door to the bedroom behind Bartini opened. Bartini turned and saw another startling sight. Behind him was the largest man he had ever seen—a tall powerfully built man with a young serious face but nearly white hair, prematurely gray. He must have stood six eight, Hugo guessed, and weighed better than 280 or 90. "Good afternoon, old friend," the giant said. "It has been a long time since you were the ROIC in Danang. Even longer since Nicaragua."

Bartini cringed a little at the mention of Viet Nam and the old Phoenix title. The people involved did not speak about that period, not even in private. And he had not been in Nicaragua since the mid-sixties, since the Guzman thing. Evidently this guy knew him. "You have the better of me; have we had the pleasure, Mr...?"

"Never mind who I am. We are here to do business. You know how effective my connections are by now. If you want to see the money back in your Vanuatu account, you will do me a certain little favor. I will be in this room for five minutes. If I do not get what I want, I will simply leave, and you will never hear from me for the rest of my life. If I do get what I want, I will leave, and you will have $100,000 more in that account than you did before you found it empty an hour ago." Bartini started to speak, but Steffan put his forefinger to his lips to shush him. Bartini did not like to be shushed, but he decided to make an exception in this instance and to pay attention.

"This is what I want you to do. You are to make an appointment with DCI Colding at his home next Sunday afternoon at two o'clock. It is a matter of national security, tell him, and it has to do with the 'Nicaraguan Project.' You can't tell him more over the phone, and that time and place is the only way you will be able to convey this information. Tell him you fear for your life. Also, tell him you will have two men with you or who will come just before you do. They have some very interesting intel that is for his ears only. Stress the 'only.' Describe this nice man with the teeth and me. Got all of that?"

"What's all this about? I mean, I can't just barge in on the DCI of the United States with my thumb up my nose. I have to tell him something. Besides, how do I know I can trust you?" Bartini whined. Steffan knew he had broken him; it was far easier than he would have imagined; but then, everybody had his price. The trick was to find out in which coin that price was counted.

"You know all you need to know. You don't know you can trust me. It's just one of those little risks we all have to take from time to time. I have been here for three minutes. Make your call."

"How should I know Colding's home number?"

"Here it is." Steffan handed the astonished retired agent a slip of paper with a number that Bartini recognized from past experience was correct.

"How did...?"

"Time is wasting. You have two and a half minutes."

Bartini made the call. To his relief, the DCI was home and was embroiled in the Iran-Contra scandal sufficiently to welcome any reliable information. He always found Bartini to be reliable and told him so. The DCI thanked Bartini for calling and agreed to the meeting without questioning him.

Bartini replaced the hotel telephone receiver back in its cradle and stretched nervously. The big man stood looking at him. He relaxed when the giant smiled a broad friendly grin. Xe sapped Bartini a very hard rap behind the left ear, and the retired agent crumpled to the floor. Steffan straddled him and expertly broke his neck. Then he and Xe carried him to the small balcony overlooking the rear parking lot, hoisted him to the top of the thin barrier, and rolled him over the edge and onto the asphalt five stories below.

Steffan left a neatly printed letter on the utilitarian desk in the room under the complimentary copy of the Gideon Bible before departing into the hall and down the fire escape. The letter said:

> To whom it may concern:
>
> I have thought of doing this for a long time. There are some things a man does that cannot be undone and can only be atoned for with blood. I caused the deaths and torturing of numberless persons in Viet Nam during the war, in a program called Phoenix. To give one example, I ordered the kidnapping and death of the main Coca Cola distributor—I think his name was Phan, only because his competitor bribed the system. I simply can't live with the knowledge of such things any longer. Whoever finds this note should go to the newspapers and get an investigative reporter to look into this and to make it public. It's going on now in Nicaragua. I hope everybody can find it their hearts to forgive me.
> Hugo.

The letter came out of Hugo's H-P Laserjet 4 printer, and the signature was his usual handwriting. Maria Innocenta Villanueva left Bartini's house for good at 1:45 that afternoon, ten minutes after the 'wart-hog' drove out to his meeting at the Hilton. She committed to memory the name of the bank and the account number with her name on it in the Grand Cayman Islands after checking to be certain that the rest of the computer's information had been erased. She was a richer woman by $250,000 for nothing more than two minutes work—one and a half to type out the letter the way the big man had written it, and thirty seconds to sign Hugo's letter the way she took care of all his correspondence. She had made a real effort not to see the person who picked up the letter where she left it in the mail box.

———————————————•◆•◆•◆•———————————————

Cleveland Howard, DDCI/0 (Deputy Director of Central Intelligence for Operations) was approaching the pinnacle of his career. Colding was in it up to his lower lip over the Nicaragua thing and was almost certainly going to resign as soon as he could do so without looking guilty. Cleve had every reason to hope he would be nominated in Colding's stead. He was clean in the Iran-Contra Affair; at least, there were no trails that led in his direction; and without false modesty, he was the best man for the job. He decided to celebrate this weekend with his newest conquest, Amilie Kirkpatrick from the *Post*, at The Company senior officer retreat in McClean. Cleve Howard considered himself a connoisseur of good wines and fine women, and he was going to treat himself to a lot of each this weekend. Life was good.

Amilie usually came to the lodge late afternoon on the Saturdays when they could get together. Cleve was pleasantly surprised to see her car in the DDCI/O's parking place when he arrived. He had to park with the peons in one of the undesignated slots. He did not really mind. She was worth it. Besides, it was an incomparable sunny day in the midst of a usually drab season. Cleve could imagine Amilie's elegant form in his mind's eye as he went up the front steps two at a time. He used the key in the automatically bolt locking door and walked in. After the brightness of the day, the room was very dark, except for the two brilliant lamps over the leather bound overstuffed chair.

The light was not what was striking. It was Amilie. She was sitting with her legs crossed holding what looked to be a mint julep, her favorite drink. She was from South Carolina, which explained a lot of her idiosyncrasies. Except the most blaring one of the moment. Amilie was stark and invitingly naked.

"You are looking lovely, as usual, my dear," Cleve said as he breezed into the darkened room. "I love your outfit."

Amilie did not smile. Her face was drawn and taut. Even from the doorway, Cleve could tell that she had been crying. Without hesitation, he strode quickly across the room to her. He stopped mid stride when an Asian accented voice said, "That's far enough."

Cleve whirled in the direction of the voice as if he had been hit by a dart. "What the...?" he started to blurt.

"Shut up and don't move," the voice said, and it sounded as if it meant every word. Cleve complied to the letter.

Men came from both sides, and Cleve could feel the cold steel of gun barrels poking indelicately into his ribs from the right and from the left. "Put your hands behind you," the authoritarian voice said. Cleve did as he was told and was promptly handcuffed.

One of the men swept his feet out from under him, and Howard toppled clumsily to the floor landing painfully on his elbow. Ky stepped from the darkness behind the nude woman and said to her, "Stand up. Put your arms behind you. Now!" Amilie sprang out of her seat and did as she was told. Her face was a mirror of her terror.

She was kicked to the floor beside her lover. "Who are these people, Cleve? Somebody called me at home early this morning and told me I had to get here early today. It was urgent. Then they made me strip after I got here. What's going on? I'm getting scared."

"It'll be okay. They probably just want our money. Let them have anything you've got. It's just stuff. We can always get more stuff." Howard looked up at his captors questioningly.

"We wait," Ky said in answer to the unspoken query. He and the two young Hmongs sat down on the chairs around the conversation nook and watched the two frightened people sitting on the floor like a trio of vultures.

Ky dialed a seven digit number on the luxury town house phone. He said only, "Ready," and hung up.

In less then ten minutes the front door opened and in walked a huge Caucasian man. The sight of him almost made Cleve faint. There could not be another person on the planet that looked like that, but he knew that the Bergstrom kid was dead. No one could have survived being left out in Laos with the NVA advancing like a juggernaut back in 1975. If he believed in ghosts, then he was surely looking at one right that minute.

To dispel any question about his identity, Steffan said, "You're right. I am the one known as Anders Bergstrom—the one you betrayed and abandoned to the VC torturers. This is Ky—he was a PRU cadre. You dumped him, too. This is Xe," Xe grinned his devilish grin, and Amilie made a small frightened squeak. "You and yours abandoned his whole people and let his entire family be killed."

"Look, Bergstrom, we can talk about this. Surely. Like Christopher Marlowe said in one of his plays, 'It happened a long time ago in a foreign country.'" He looked pleadingly at Steffan. Steffan's face was as implacable as cement. Then despite any kind of better judgment, Cleve Howard finished Marlowe's line: "'and, besides, the wench is dead.'" He knew from the darkness in the big man's face that he had sealed his own doom with his stupid remark.

"Shut up. It's too late for talk. The whole generation of you vipers is being removed right now. Don't insult me with excuses; don't whine. Remember the Mandarin of Hue'? His daughter?—I take it you remember that 'wench'—The Grand Master of *Tây Sơn Võ Sĩ*? to name just a few? No pit in hell is deep enough or bad enough for you. This is pay up day."

"There must be some way we can sort this out. I must have something you want. We can make a deal," Cleve said. He was pleading now, as frightened as he had ever been.

"Tell me where Szabo and DuParrier are right now," Steffan demanded holding out the faintest measure of hope for Cleve.

"I don't know. That's the honest truth. They're somewhere in Nicaragua. I couldn't get to them if I wanted to," Cleve said knowing that he was throwing away his life with that unfortunate bit of truth. The Scandinavian man's eyes told him that despite the absence of threatening words or movements.

"Too bad," Steffan said after a pause. He did nothing for a few minutes but to look levelly into the eyes of the most terrified man he had seen since watching the Coca Cola merchant as he saw his daughter disappear into the blackness over the South China Sea those years ago.

"Do it; the girl," he said to Ky and Xe.

Ky reached down and lifted the girl to her feet. She was as beautiful, white, and perfectly proportioned as an alabaster Greek statue. Her skin was clammy; and she smelled of fear. She mewed incoherently. Cleve Howard's eyes were pleading for mercy, but he knew it was too late. Xe suddenly struck the nearly limp girl a vicious snapping judo chop on the back of her neck. Her dark curly head flipped back in grotesque hyperextension, and her neck made a distinct, deep toned crack as it fractured. Ky was still holding her up even though she was dead above the neck. Her arms and legs made a couple of small convulsive jerks; her great toes extended; and her limbs stiffened momentarily; and all of her was dead. Her bowels and bladder released. Ky let her crumple to the floor.

Howard began to whimper and to beg. He fell to his knees before Steffan who looked steadily into the pleading hopeless eyes. "Stand up!" Steffan demanded, raising his voice for the first time. "I want you to remember me when you go to hell." He jerked the senior CIA executive to his feet. Howard made no move to defend himself.

Steffan loosed his hold on Howard's shoulders and caught him about the neck as his knees began to buckle. Steffan turned himself in a three-quarter oblique stance to avoid getting kicked in the groin then closed his powerful thumbs into Cleve's throat like a great set of talons. Howard began to struggle wildly, kicking and lurching with his shoulders. The fingers smashed inexorably tighter. Steffan was oblivious to the kicking and flailing body he held six inches off the expensive heather colored Burberry carpet.

The thumbs cracked the cricoid cartilage of the larynx and continued to clamp down irrepressibly. The panic of suffocation showed in Howard's bulging eyes. Just at the antepenultimate moment when there was no more breath and in a second would no longer be conscious life, Steffan glared into Cleve's eyes and snarled, "Her name was Liên...Now die."

He ground his thumbs and wrenched them apart breaking all the small cartilages and the hyoid bone and stopping the carotids. Howard died and remained suspended in the air for two or three minutes until Ky said gently, "Steffan, old friend; it is done. You can stop now."

Steffan let the corpse drop to the floor mingling its askew limbs with that of the unfortunate innocent girl. His mind came back from the underworld and from images of the black hairy man leaning on a staff. Now Steffan knew who that one was. He had seen all the way down.

Steffan's only regret was that in his passion he had not remembered to show Cleve Howard that he had been financially ruined. "Nobody's perfect," he said to no one in particular.

They loaded the two bodies in the large packing crates on their truck and disposed of them in the ocean the following day. Vietnamese fishermen were only too glad to help.

———————————◆◆————◆◆———————————

Rex Dragerton was driving his pride and joy blood red '75 Corvette down from the city of Lancaster in the high desert of Los Angeles County toward LA. It was ten o'clock at night on Sunday, and the 14 was relatively clear of traffic at that time of night. Dragerton had spent the weekend with his steady, but ultra independent feminist lady friend, as they always did. Now, he was heading back to LA and the Monday morning salt mines of his job for AustralAsian Amity Imports as he did every Sunday night at this time. Loretta asked nothing of him except civil treatment, and that he put the toilet seat down. She was a looker; insisted on sharing all expenses to the penny; and wanted it understood from the beginning that there were never going to be any commitments. Life was good.

Every time he made the long ugly trip through the drab beige backdrop of the desert he was glad it was dark, and he chuckled outloud at his good fortune with women. He was passing the San Andreas fault line in the Santa Clarita valley and remembering his favorite ditty that called to mind his great arrangement: "My perfect girl, and who could ask for more? She's deaf and dumb and beautiful and owns a liquor store." when his Corvette disintegrated into smithereens in a vaporizing fire ball.

Nguyen Lui Tran was following the Corvette some seventy-five yards behind and saw the whole terrible accident. The unfortunate vehicle, or what was left of it, was four feet in the air when it cleared the guard rail and plunged fifty feet into the gully alongside the Palmdale Freeway. He did not stop to report it.

———————————◆◆———◆◆———————————

Douglas N. Herter, his wife, and a family friend died Friday, January 12, 1987 when their small yacht, The Manila, registered in Panama to avoid taxes, sank in calm seas on a clear day off the Lesser Antilles. The local newspaper very gently hinted at the possibility of drug involvement after receiving an anonymous tip from a police source. Although his name would not be found on any guest register or border record, Nguyen Lui Tran had a Caribbean vacation that month, coincidentally.

———————————◆◆———◆◆———————————

On Sunday, January 14, 1987, Steffan, Ky, and Xe awakened early in their safe house in rural Prince George County, Virginia. The two Asians made stir fry to go with rice while Steffan read the *Washington Post*. The headlines and lead articles were all about the latest scandal in the capital city. The Iran-Contra Affair filled the print pages— 'What did Vice-President Bush know and when? Was Oliver North a hero or a criminal? Would Poindexter and McFarlane be fired, prosecuted, pardoned? Did the CIA help Nicaraguan Contras run a Murder Incorporated assassination program?' The Congressional investigations started last December and dominated the news. The radio played a peculiar throbbing-chanting-talking kind of music substitute called rap. Steffan could hear the newest hit being played for the umpteenth time, Walk This Way, in which a white heavy-metal band calling itself Aerosmith had joined with a black ghetto duet known by the improbable title of Run-DMC. It got on Steffan's nerves.

They finished breakfast and removed all traces of their having been in the townhouse at 3000 Westmoreland Road, then got into their nondescript chevy. Ky checked the trunk load of arms including grenades, an M-72 LAW, and four M-16s. Each man carried a Sig-Sauer 9 mm handgun in a shoulder holster under a sport jacket. The men were all tastefully dressed in fitting slacks, white shirts and club ties, and blue blazers. They were on their way to kill a man.

CHAPTER 49

I think everyone knew we were walking a very thin line.
Robert C. Owen, assistant to Oliver North in the Iran-Contra Affairs, employed by Institute on Terrorism and Subnational Conflict, private testimony contained in the Report of the Congressional Committees Investigating the Iran-Contra Affair, Volume B-20, page 692

The three men turned from Westmoreland to the cutoff onto Grant, then right to South Mesa Drive and south past the Federal Reformatory on River Road. Ky said, "I'll feel more comfortable when we are out of this particular section of Virginia." He spoke for all of them. Notwithstanding their vengeful zeal, each of them dreaded the possibility of being caught. None of them considered himself a martyr.

They went west through Colonial Heights and onto Temple Avenue. The traffic was light, and they were able to move onto I-95 just north of Richmond without impediment. It was a clear smooth commute into the city for their business. On the east side of the river they took Ohio Drive and the Rock Creek and Potomac Parkway to New Hampshire Avenue and on into Georgetown where the traffic began to pick up. They were still very early—it was only eight-thirty. They turned right off New Hampshire, went two blocks east and were at the corner of New Hampshire and Jefferson Place, their destination.

They were looking at the handsome brownstone apartment that DCI Colding called home. Only his close acquaintances knew that. DCI Colding had no friends. He did not stay overnight in the official residence located near the Company headquarters because he disliked the stultifying effect of all that security. He and his wife of forty-two years enjoyed the relative anonymity of the area and their building. It was here that Colding discussed the real secrets of the smoke and mirrors world in which he had lived for forty-five years.

Steffan, Ky, and Xe made themselves thoroughly familiar with the neighborhood and plotted an escape route. Even in urban settings, or perhaps in these days, especially in urban settings, the best route of evasion and escape had to be well calculated. While the men did not expect any difficulty in this first phase of their plan, there was no such thing as being too careful. In their recently chosen line of work, to be a paranoid was only to be a realist. There was certainly no indication of heavy security in the area, only a pair of conspicuously inconspicuous men with short crisp haircuts, matching plain gray suits, and gleamingly polished black wing tips sitting overly casually in a taupe colored DOT Dodge sedan, were to be seen. Steffan spotted them immediately. "The boys from Yale," he said to his two Asian friends. It had long since been the descriptor for ambitious (an adjective fitting all in the category) agents and for State Department functionaries.

To avoid being seen, they left the area to kill nearly five hours before their appointment with the DCI. They spent it in the Aerospace Museum of the Smithsonian. The three men returned to Georgetown; and at two o'clock on the dot, they knocked at the door of number 26. A Yalie opened the door, made sure the visitors saw the bulge under his gray suit coat, and asked curtly, "Yes?"

"We have an appointment with the DCI," Steffan announced with all the self-confidence of an ambassador or the least ranking CIA agent.

"Name, please?"

"We are with Hugo Bartini. He will be here very shortly. He said we were expected and that we were to start before he arrived."

The agent on security duty turned to look over his shoulder at the appointment roster and found Bartini's name. It has been penciled in over an erased name—"McFarlane." "These guys had to be important," he thought.

"Come in," the guard said correctly, neither friendly nor condescending. "Wait in the foyer please. I'll check with the boss and see if he can see you now."

He returned shortly and ushered the three men into a richly appointed leather, wood, and brass study. There were four deep green chairs for the guests and a stately Georgian throne for the DCI. He always thought the setting had an important psychological effect on the high ranking visitors to his domain, and positively cowed the lesser mortals. "Where's Bartini?" Colding asked brusquely as soon as the Yalie had left the room. He had no time for small talk.

"Coming shortly, sir," said Steffan. "He authorized us to begin. With your permission...?"

"By all means."

"Hugo has proof positive that there is an organized hit unit, probably from Daniel Ortega and his commies, that is proceeding with a methodical assassination plan to eliminate the powers that be in the Company's Nicaragua Project. Dustin Hauter, the DDCI/O, and Rex Dragerton are already dead. Hugo is sure that he's next. He has evidence that you and even VP Bush are on the hit list. He said if he was not here by two thirty, he would never be. He said we should suggest you move Vanuatu 712063 to Liechenstein 992946. He said you would know what that meant, and we did not need to know. That is the entire message."

DCI Colding prided himself on his absolute imperturbability and could lie or play poker with the best who ever lived. The only betrayal of his extreme agitation at this message was a slight tightening of the corners of his mouth. "Thank you, gentlemen. I will take care of it. Perhaps it is best you and Bartini are not here together. You never can tell when someone from the *Post* or some lesser observer like the KGB is watching," he said sardonically.

Steffan and his friends left without saying goodbye and with no more than a nod from the Yalie at the door. By the time Colding had gained access to his computer and found the ultra secret Vanuatu account folder, the three men were six blocks away. It took that much time to register on the DCI that he was wiped out, at least that the real money he had squirreled away from special sources throughout his long and shadowy CIA career was gone. He debated calling Adnan Kashoggi, Muh'mmar Qaddaffi, and Nguyen Cao Ky to find out what his partners knew about the removal of his funds. If they were behind it, their reasons had to be overridingly important; and he was unaware of anything earthshaking happening with the old pirates. Kashoggi was going to be indicted in the Iran-Contra Affair, but he would beat the rap; he always did. It had to be something more than that.

Anybody who had that kind of intelligence—the numbers to the holy of holies—had to be serious. For the first time, Colding took the three nonentities who had been in his study seriously. There must be something to what they had told him. He had an easy way to check. He got his personal little black book out of the study safe and called Hauter, Bartini, Howard, and Dragerton. In ten minutes of inquiry he learned that Hauter and Howard were missing and Bartini and Dragerton were known to be dead. Now, Colding paled and began to sweat. His priorities switched from his own immediate personal bankruptcy since he had no idea what to do about that at the moment and to the assassination plot. He called the President of the United States.

Steffan, Ky, and Xe sat quietly in their makeshift hut in Lafayette Square directly across from the entrance to the White House. The Viet Nam Vets' protest village had proved to be evidence that God looked down in favor on their mission. The cluster of ramshackle shacks had been front page news in the *Washington Post* a few days earlier, but now was ho-hum to the jaded denizens of the nation's capital as was the cause they for which they were demonstrating. The huts provided perfect cover for the three men and their armaments. It was three forty-five in the afternoon.

An ostentatious black stretch car pulled into sight on Penn Avenue a few minutes later. When it was directly in front of Blair House, all three men sprang into readiness. The DCIA ensigns flew from the two antennae making certain that no one in the vicinity could mistake who was inside. So much for security.

"I told you the first thing he would do is to see the President. They all have their fingers on dirty money, and it is the first thing they will want to protect," Steffan told Ky and Xe smugly.

Ky make sure the small sign detailing why the assassinations had taken place was prominently displayed inside their hut. Xe readied an automatic for each man. Steffan followed the limousine through his LAW's sights. The DCI's vehicle pulled to a brief stop at the guard house preparatory to entering the grounds of the White House.

In that pause, Steffan fired two rockets in very rapid succession, dropping the disposable fiberglass launchers at his feet; and both of the explosive warheads struck home dead center in the limousine. Colding and his aide, the two nearby Secret Service guards, seven tourists waiting patiently to enter the national mansion, and the Lincoln Continental Limousine were all welded together in a luminous, intensely hot, spherical cloud of dust, gas, vapor, molten metal and liquefied human beings. Windows were broken in the White House itself.

Immediately after the explosions, there was a moment of eerie silence. Nothing and no one moved. Steffan reacted first. "Leave the weapons and just walk out of here in opposite directions. We'll get lost in the crowd. Meet you at the car."

The three men emerged from the hut and viewed the carnage from an upright position. Now there was screaming and sobbing; witnesses all around the White House had dived to the street surface as soon as it registered on them what had happened. It looked like a war had been

924

launched, and they behaved appropriately—with absolute chaos. Steffan, Ky, and Xe went in three separate directions. The two nondescript Asians blended almost unnoticed into the forming crowds.

Across the street, the first persons to brave the still burning and smoking scene were White House reporters from the *Washington Post*. They had their video-cams set up and rolling before the first Secret Service people roared up and took charge. Marine guards joined the Secret Service people and they began wholesale detentions of potential witnesses. Bystanders were herded onto the White House lawn and held in a makeshift emergency center under guard. The security people were excited and furious. There were instances of brutal clubbings of innocents who got in the way. DC Metro Police joined the pandemonium in force, blocking off every exit road in a six block radius, and spilled out four van loads of SWAT officers who began setting up defense positions around the main gate.

Before the first police vehicles could interdict traffic effectively, Ky and Xe had blithely gotten into their old Dodge and had driven northwest up Connecticut Avenue and were in the National Zoological Park grounds before anyone could be aware of them. The first thing they did when they got there was to find a pay phone and to put in a call to 21 Corsica Street in Irvine, California. In a minute long conversation with the man who answered, they told what had transpired, and that they feared the worst for Steffan. They concluded with the statement that "General Hauter's information was exactly correct. He lived up to his end of the bargain."

"Goodbye," said Tran on the California end.

"See you soon, brother," said Ky in Washington.

Tran pressed the button to cut off the line then dialed the number where Mrs. Hauter was being held. "Let her go," he ordered the Hmong who answered.

Then he walked upstairs to the bedroom and put a bullet in the back of Dustin Hauter's head.

Steffan was not nearly so invisible as his cohorts in the crime. He stood at least head and shoulders over everyone in the crowd. He was conspicuous to the police because, instead of rushing forward to be part of the gawkers block in front of the executive mansion, he headed in the opposite direction.

One of the protester vets yelled after him, "That's him! That's the shooter! Get him!!! What're you cops doin'?"

Steffan turned back—that was a guilty looking mistake—and saw three dozen faces looking in his direction. There was no possibility of merging into the anonymous crowd now. He saw Secret Service officers and half a dozen DC SWAT officers beginning to wheel about and to move in his direction. He scrunched down and moved into the center of the milling crowd. That only served to make him more obvious. "Get the white haired guy!" yelled a DCPD captain.

"The big one?" called back one of his men.

"Yeah, get a move on!" the captain ordered and waved his unit forward. Now they were behaving in an organized and professional way.

Steffan gave up on pretense and began to stretch his big legs into a run. An occasional hero, usually a vet, tried to get in his way and was scythed down like so much fall wheat for his trouble. "Police! Stop or I'll shoot!" came shouted commands from three directions as if the officers could risk firing into the welter of people around Steffan. The huge Swedish-Canadian pumped his powerful legs into a charging rhino force flight. He began to leave the crowd and the pursuing police behind.

He crossed between the Hay-Adams Hotel and St. John's Church and past the AFL-CIO building and turned right onto Eye Street where crowds were accumulating. People melted to either side as he charged down the street with the cops and secret service agents in hot pursuit. An officer knelt to fire as Steffan turned left up 13th Street, but his superior stopped him. Steffan was outdistancing the entire army on his tail and was well ahead by the time he ran past the airlines terminal and by the Best Western Mid-Town Motor Inn at 13th and K. He turned left on L Street and headed across Vermont toward the imposing Burlington Hotel, planning to lose himself inside. He had had the foresight to have a shave and a short haircut. He was dressed in a sport jacket, shirt, and tie so he could blend in once he was inside the fashionable hotel. In a quick look behind him, he was aware that he had beaten his pursuers. None of them were in sight.

It was naive to think that just because he could beat the human runners that he could move faster than their radios. Police vehicles converged down 14th, 15th, and L Streets. Steffan bolted up to M Street and turned right. He saw two klaxon blaring, red and blue light flashing, police cars careening toward him on M, now less then two blocks away. He skidded to a stop and turned obliquely north to run up 15th behind the cops who had stopped on the corner of 15th and L and were already making U turns to double back to where their fellow policemen had Steffan in sight. He made it to the middle of Massachusetts Avenue before a city full of cops and Secret Service agents formed a circle around him.

They began bailing out of their cars and scrambling to draw and aim their weapons. The SWAT captain jerked his bullhorn out to call to the perp who was now absurdly alone in the middle of Washington DC's major thoroughfare snarling traffic for a mile in all directions. Instead of stopping like any sensible criminal when there was no possible escape, Steffan continued east across the avenue zigzagging his way toward the policemen who were alighting from their vehicles and had not yet had time to set themselves.

It occurred to Steffan to draw his Sig-Sauer from his shoulder holster, but then he would have to kill cops, and that was not in his plan. They were just doing their duty, as he felt he was doing. He plunged headlong into a collection of six brawny officers and scattered them like tenpins. A dozen more joined in the short, desperate battle. The officers had been given the strictest orders to keep the assassin alive if at all possible; so, he could implicate his accomplices. Since the fleeing criminal did not have a gun, it became a challenge to every martial artist from every precinct to be the one to bring him down.

Steffan kicked and punched, elbowed and kneed, spun and decked man after man. He seemed like a giant from the planet Krypton, high on PCP, to the cops. Man after man dropped with an injury or toppled over another policeman who had fallen from some blow or another. Steffan had given a world class demonstration of *Tây Sơn Võ Sĩ* from which fifteen men who had met the challenge would be able to attest by the marks they bore, but the inevitable crush of sheer numbers finally put him down. A rain of clubs finished Steffan's last stand. He was unconscious when he was shackled and taken to the nearest emergency room—Doctor's Hospital on Eye and 18th Streets.

When he awakened, Steffan found himself strapped by all four extremities and posey belted around his abdomen with stout leather straps attached to the ER table; and, in addition, was held down with hand and leg cuffs. They were not going to take any chances. He was a mass of hurts. The big man was stark naked except for the shackles, and dozens of hospital workers were peering in at him. He was surrounded by policemen with their guns drawn. Steffan knew that he was public enemy number one, and acted as peaceful and compliant as a lamb.

"Glad to see you coming around," the young black physician said when Steffan's eyes finally adjusted to the bright lights and looked like they were coming into focus. "How's about you giving us your name. There was no ID in your clothes."

Steffan clamped his mouth shut. He had decided not to give even the slightest piece of information to anyone. Let them do the work they got paid for; he was not going to help them.

"You allergic to anything? How about tetanus?"

No response. "Give him a full cc to be on the safe side," the doctor ordered. The nurse drew up the double dose of the antitoxin.

"Can we talk to him now, doc?" asked Levy, the DC Detective in charge. He was standing shoulder to shoulder with the chief Secret Service Agent, a FBI special agent, and the deputy US Attorney for the District.

"Wait a few more minutes until he is altogether back with us. Right now, I think the lights are on, but nobody's home."

"Okay, a few more minutes," said the cop.

"Hey, Trixie, get them to set up a stat brain CT," the doctor called to the ER charge nurse.

"Contrast?"

"No, just quick and dirty. I want to be sure he doesn't have a subdural before we turn him over to the Gestapo," replied the doctor enjoying his dig at the excited policemen and White House Security people.

"Watch your mouth, sonny," snarled one burly old cop. His sergeant soothed the offended policeman.

The CT was normal, and there was no reason to stall. Doctor Hawkins grudgingly released Steffan to the gathered gendarmerie. The patient did not utter a sound during the full hour and forty-five minutes he was in Doctor's Hospital. Steffan was hustled out of the ER and into a waiting DC paddy wagon still dressed in his open-backed hospital gown. It was only that the DC police had gotten to the perpetrator first that they had him in their custody. The Feds were furious at the DCPD, but could not yet deny their jurisdiction at this point in the case. This was a case of murder within the boundaries of Washington DC and not on federal property per se; so, there would have to be a serious argument as to the application of section 1114 of Title 18 of the United States Code (murder of a public official). DCPD would have full control over him for the time being, but machinery was already in motion to have him transferred to a federal facility. There were a lot of feds who wanted to get at him.

Detective Levy elbowed the uniform sitting beside him in one of the black and whites, "Does the soul good to get something, even a little, temporary something, over on the Fart, Barf, and Itch, don't it?" The uniform grinned. It was a rare little pleasure to one up the Feebies.

Steffan was loaded into a black and white marked with the familiar heraldry of the Metropolitan Police Department and whisked away with lights and sirens to the central office at 300 Indiana Avenue NW. Homicide Branch had jurisdiction; and its parent, the Criminal Investigation Division, had marshaled its forces to deal with the notoriety and the investigative needs of homicide even before the unit arrived. Once in the headquarters Lieutenant Dragich took over from Detective Levy.

Steffan was booked into the Metropolitan central cell block on a John Doe warrant just as he had been listed in the emergency room. Detective Levy was dispatched to 500 Indiana Avenue NW to inform the next Superior Court judge on the judicial rotation about the warrantless arrest so as to establish probable cause before any flaming liberal could find some technicality to use against the branch. He drew Judge Brandeis, an all business, tough minded jurist of thirty year's experience. It was a good draw, thought Levy.

Steffan was pushed into the interview room where he faced half a dozen frustrated cops demanding that he respond, but he would not indulge them. The desk sergeant brought in a video camera to record the booking and the reading of the provisions of the Supreme Court Miranda decision from the official form PD 46; so, there could be no future complaint that he had been denied any of his rights, unlike the rights of which he had deprived the DCI and all of those other innocent people.

"You have the right to remain silent. Do you understand that right?" Steffan stood like a deaf mute looking straight ahead.

"You have the right to be silent. Do you understand that protection of the law?" The lieutenant repeated, raising his voice. Evidently he did, because the prisoner remained absolutely silent.

"Anything you say can and will be used against you in a court of law. Do you understand that right?" Steffan kept still.

"You have the right to counsel during questioning. If you cannot afford an attorney, one will be provided for you at no expense to you? Do you understand?" Steffan maintained his statue like silence and immobility heightening the maddening urge to bash his head in by the responsible police officers. For the video record, they did nothing of the sort.

"And finally, you have the right to make a phone call. You can make as many as you want; this isn't the movies. I know you didn't have any money on you, here's a quarter." Lieutenant Dragich reached out his hand, palm up, with the coin and made sure the photographer got a good shot. Steffan could not have taken the quarter if he were so inclined because his hands were cuffed behind him. That technicality was lost on the video.

A surround of officers quick marched the shackled giant down the metal floored corridor into the central cell block amidst hoots and Bronx cheers from the caged men along the way. He was dumped into a cell where a middle-aged black with gold front teeth bearing cutout stars was sitting on the top bunk picking his teeth.

"Company, Ladies Man," they said to the pimp. "Try and be nice and get along now."

The wrist, leg, neck, and abdominal chains were not removed. The door made its authoritarian metal-into-metal clunking sound as it closed and the bolt locks slid into place. "You must be a regular John Dillinger, honkey," said Ladies Man. "Don't nobody have to stay chained up no more, once they in they cell. This is a man's home, don't you see? Anyhow, welcome, such as it is. I get the top bunk so's your fat butt don't press down on my face in the night. If you got other plans now is the time to deal with them. I am one baad fighter, you should know."

Steffan remained quiet during the soliloquy, ignoring the insults and the racial epithet. He was very tired and sore and decided just to ignore his cell mate. He sat on the lower bunk and began to stretch and squirm to find a way to get comfortable in the chafing shackles.

"Okay, boy, if that's the way you want to be. It's your loss, not mine. It's goin' to go long and hard for you if you don't get no friends in the joint. Just so's you can't say I didn't warn you," said the thin wiry black prisoner as his last attempt to communicate. He figured the honkey had something against the brothers; and one day, he would call him out on it; but it didn't have to be today.

Ladies Man had nothing to report when he met with the jail officials that evening. "I done my best, but he just won't talk. I think he's a dummy or somethin.' It wasn't my fault. You got ears in there; you know that already. I'll keep tryin,' but don't stand around on one leg expectin' him to be any kinda canary. He just don't seem the type. I am still deservin' of a consideration, man. I been tryin.'"

That added to the difficulty Detective Levy and Lieutenant Dragich were having in filling out the stack of forms in front of them. As bad as a minute of silence to a disc jockey, the two policemen hated blank spaces on Form PD 163—Prosecution Report and PD 251—the

Incident Based Event Report. They were both public records, and blanks made cops look stupid or lazy. By the end of the day, when the forms had to be on file, however, there were glaring blanks by name, address, age, place of birth, prior criminal record, etc.

The only information on the forms was about the arresting officers (rank, title, etc.), the date, time, location, and district of the arrest, reason for, circumstances of, and description of the arrest done in the standard Dick and Jane police language. There was a list of more than a dozen formal charges, and Detective Levy wrote up the required probable cause statement. They completed the non public document—PD 252, the supplement to 251, in considerably greater detail providing details about witnesses, key statements, and the sensitive security aspects of this sensational case. The detectives included, with a good deal of interservice rivalry oneupmanship, the description of the laxity in security that had allowed a perpetrator to haul what they called a bazooka into position in full view of the White House and the public and to assassinate a government official.

Steffan was removed from his holding cell twice before the dinner hour, but after five or ten minutes was marched back to his cell without the officials getting a scintilla of information. Outside, the world's press was howling for information. Everyone except Steffan Johannson was frustrated. He was resigned.

Supper was served in his cell. No one was going to take the slightest risk of him being injured or vice versa by being placed in the general population. The Washington DCPD and the corrections authority were not about to have any kind of Lee Harvey Oswald-Jack Ruby fiasco with this hot property; not on your life. The meal consisted of a four inch diameter closely packed ball of fresh meats, vegetables, and bread that had been ground up and pressed together as a cohesive formless glob. Steffan's hands were now cuffed in front of him; so, he could eat. There were no utensils, and the plate was of flimsy waxed paper. He was receiving the standard fare for uncooperative inmates. Complaints to the ACLU about the fare had brought the response from them that the food was clean, nutritious, and fresh. It did not have to be appetizing. Complaints to the NAACP had brought the response that obstreperous African-American inmates were being singled out for ill usage; and consequently, they received regular inmate servings on regulation metal foil trays and plates and were privileged to eat with wooden spoons. Steffan could not qualify for the special status of African-American.

At eight o'clock that evening, six guards entered the cell with night sticks drawn. They backed Steffan up until he was pressed against the cell wall. Then they stood three on a side and marched him out of the cell in his too-small orange jump suit to an interrogation room and chained him hand and foot to a stout ring on the top of the heavy metal table. He was seated on one of the two chairs in the room, both of which, like the table, were bolted to the metal floor. The other chair was bolted to the floor five feet away at the end of the table. Two guards positioned themselves at each end of the rectangular, window-less room.

Within five minutes the only door to the room was unbolted and the chief warden and a man in a suit entered the room. "Okay, Doe, this is your court appointed lawyer. You got fifteen minutes," said the jailer.

"We have as much time as we need," the fatherly man in the dark three piece suit told the officer. "We will call you, don't call us." The animosity toward the attorney was like a living spirit in the room. He ignored it and turned his full attention to Steffan.

"As soon as these men...all of these men...leave, you and I can get down to the business at hand," the attorney said to his new client. He pointedly stood mute while waiting for the officer and the guards to take their sweet time to make a grudging exit.

When the door clanged shut, the squat middle-aged Greek said, "There are no microphones or other listening devices in here. We can speak freely, and it is time for us to have a frank talk. First of all, I am Dimitri Staphanopolis. I am your court appointed public defender, and if there was ever a man who needed defending, you're it."

Steffan liked the attorney's no nonsense approach. "I need to know about you so we can fashion a defense. Right now, I am hard pressed to come up with one. You might as well know that you are in a heap of trouble," Staphanopolis said.

When Steffan did not respond to the offered opening, Staphanopolis tried again, "What's your name?"

"Remundo."

"You don't look like a Remundo. You look like an Ivan or a Sven. That your real name?"

"Remundo Mueller-Garza from Costa Rica. I could tell you where to find a valid passport if it made any difference. But I am going to tell you one thing; I don't want my name given out to anybody for any reason. I'll stay John Doe just like they booked me."

"Your fingerprints will identify you," Staphanopolis said patiently.

"It doesn't serve any useful purpose for you to be that uncooperative."

"First of all, they won't find my prints on file. I'll guarantee you that. Second of all, there is a very good reason for my identity to stay as it is."

Staphanopolis rubbed his chin for a second or two. "You crazy, Remundo?" He looked at Steffan. "I mean really. That's as good of a defense as I can think of right now."

"Why not?" Steffan asked noncommittally.

"Well, I guess that's the tack we'll take for the time being. I'll get some shrinks to examine you. The other side will get their own. Dim cap is a tough way to go. Personally, I hate psychiatrists. I always wanted to get a one-armed shrink for my side."

"A what?" Steffan queried, puzzled.

"A one-armed shrink. Those guys always get up on the stand and say, 'On the one hand…but on the other hand.'" Staphanopolis demonstrated with his two hands. "What a pain. Maybe with only one hand we could get a straight answer for a change."

Steffan laughed.

"The first question I have to ask is, are you going to tell everybody that you didn't do it? Half of DC claims they saw you do it."

"No, I did it. It seems like a waste of time to deny that. I think they're just going to have a trial and take me out and shoot me no matter what I say. What's the use?"

"Young man, that's the last time I'll listen to that kind of talk. You seem not to know who I am. This is your lucky day. I am the best criminal defense lawyer in all of DC; and this is a city that needs more than its share of good ones; that's just for the congressmen."

"If you're so famous, how come I never heard of you?"

"Because you are uneducated." It was said without rancor or defensiveness. It was just a matter of fact. "And I am going to educate you; then, we will get down to business. I have defended 500 accused and won the majority even when it seemed hopeless—like the present issue. I started out as one of Bill Kunstler's flunkies in the Chicago Seven Trial. You hear about that one?"

Steffan was sure that he should have, but sheepishly admitted, "I'm afraid not."

Staphanopolis rolled his eyes good naturedly. "All right. Let's do some work. You don't look all that crazy. Why don't you give me some reason to believe that you are? You take any medicine? You a junky?"

"I take Thorazine; at least, I'm supposed to; and no, I'm not a junky."

"That Thorazine, it's a big time tranquilizer, right?"

Steffan nodded in the affirmative.

"How come you take that stuff?"

"Bad dreams and memories from Viet Nam, from a long time ago."

"Ooh, I'm beginning to like this," said the lawyer. "I suppose you are familiar with the post-combat stress syndrome?"

"Yes. That's what the psychiatrist said I have."

"Anything special about you, about your experiences?"

"Maybe."

"Look, we don't have the luxury of maybe. Either you do or you don't. If you do, it may be very beneficial in our defense. You know, serve as a basis for why you went temporarily insane out there today."

"I saw some very bad stuff. I know who did that stuff. That's what I was doing out there today," Steffan said. Now his face was intense and animated; his eyes were intelligent and deadly serious. Everything about him was focused; and Staphanopolis felt, from his long experience in reading people, that everything he was about to hear was going to be the truth, free of Protestant embroideries.

"I think you should tell me all about it, Remundo. Please. I'm a good listener, and I have all the time in the world."

"It's a long story."

"And I want to hear it all. Give me even the details you might not think are important. Let me be the judge, okay?"

Steffan shrugged.

"I have a feeling that your story is going to be the best defense ever. I have a plan taking shape in my devious little mind. Once I hear your yarn, I can figure out whether this thing will go DC or federal."

Steffan started with the sheriff in Utah, and how it happened that he was sent to boot camp at the age of sixteen.

CHAPTER 50

"Justice is incidental to law and order."
J. Edgar Hoover

It was past midnight when Steffan was taken back to his cell. He was too exhausted to remain coherent and to keep his narrative cohesive; so, Staphanopolis let him go for the night. Steffan spent twelve hours a day for five days with the lawyer who took meticulous and detailed notes. For all his erudition and his pride on how well he was informed, Staphanopolis had to admit that he knew next to nothing about the Phoenix Program and guessed that most Americans were in the same state of ignorance. If even half of what this young man said was true, it was a defense a hundred times over. From Steffan, he got the names, places, and dates that could indict two dozen top US government authorities still in service. This case was going to rival Watergate. He could hardly wait to see the faces of those august politicians and generals and spies when he got them on the stand. His client would look like St. George tilting with the dragon before Staphanopolis was through with them.

Steffan was arraigned in the Superior Court of the District of Columbia - Criminal Division as John Doe before Judge Harold Beckwith Brandeis, great grand nephew of the eminent supreme court justice, Louis (Dembitz) Brandeis. It was a very brief affair.

"Please state the charges, Mr. Henry," he requested, looking over his half glasses at the DC deputy district attorney.

"Murder of a government official with special circumstances and with the use of a firearm, your honor." He listed the lesser charges of resisting arrest, assault and battery on a police officer, assault on a federal officer, unlawful flight, etc. as well.

"Will there be any other charges forthcoming?"

"There were others who were murdered by the defendant..."

"Objection. 'Alleged' is the operative term here," interrupted Staphanopolis.

"Sustained. And gentlemen, let's don't get this sort of wrangling started today. This is only the arraignment. You will have plenty of time for that later."

"I stand corrected; thank you, your honor," Dwight Henry said humbly. He did not want to get his case started off on the wrong foot. "There were other victims in the crime of which this defendant stands accused. The people will have to make a final decision after discovery about how many, if any, of them to include in the charges. We have sufficient evidence to proceed on the murder of DCI Colding."

"And the defense has not seen one scintilla of that alleged evidence, your honor."

"Now boys, this case is less than a week old," the judge chided Staphanopolis.

"Yes, your honor."

"And how does your client plead, counselor?"

"Not guilty, your honor."

"NOT GUILTY???!!!" exclaimed the incredulous assistant DA and regretted his outburst as soon as he the words passed his lips. But that was an incredible plea. Half the world had seen the rocket attack and the defendant fleeing the scene on tourist video tapes that had inundated television and the newspapers ever since the crime.

"Sorry, your honor, it just slipped out," Henry corrected himself even before Judge Brandeis had a chance to do so.

"That about takes care of that," said the judge, pleased that it would not be a long drawn out affair that day. His docket was impossible as it was. "The defendant is remanded to custody without bail in case anyone here thought that that question might come up. Consider that question to be closed."

"We will want to have the defendant appear before a Grand Jury, your honor; and the people would like you to set the earliest possible date," Dwight Henry threw in quickly and quietly as if he hoped the defense attorney would not notice.

"Mr. Staphanopolis?"

"Not on your life, your honor. My client demands a fully public

936

airing of the charges and to make his defense. No closed doors grilling without the attorney for the defense being present. No sir, we strongly object to any such request."

"If the plea is not guilty, and you are not going to plea bargain, then I see no reason for the Grand Jury. It would be too much to suppose that this might be plea bargained, I suppose, Mr. Staphanopolis?"

"My client pleads not guilty and requests the constitutional right to a have the evidence presented to a jury of his peers. Period."

"Then you'll stipulate as to the evidence presented by the prosecution and bypass the Grand Jury?" The judge asked, looking at Staphanopolis thoughtfully, trying to fathom the defense attorney's intentions.

"Yes, sir. It is critical that every aspect of this case be public. The reason for that choice will become abundantly clear as we proceed, your honor. All I am at liberty to say right now is that there have been altogether too many secrets about this young man and his activities already. It is time for a public airing," replied Staphanopolis. His face radiated determination.

"I thought it might be worth a trial balloon, no pun intended. The defendant will bound over for a preliminary hearing, then, in two days. The hearing will be held in the office of the US Attorney located at 555 4th Street, NW Trial will likely be set for one month; see the court secretary to come up with a mutually agreed upon day," Judge Brandeis said and lifted his gavel.

"Your honor," chorused both attorneys at once.

"Another bit of wishful thinking on my part, eh, gentlemen? You first, Mr. Henry."

"This is a very major case, your honor. The discovery process will take a good three months in order for a proper prosecution to be prepared."

"Mr. Staphanopolis?"

"The defense is in substantive agreement with the prosecution, your honor. However, the materials for our defense may be rather voluminous and will require a time consuming process of investigation. We anticipate an extensive list of witnesses, and the depositions alone will take more than three months. With cooperation from the agencies we intend to subpoena, we might be able to finish the discovery phase and to present a case in six months."

Mr. Henry gave Staphanopolis a deeply questioning look. The judge gazed fixedly down at the defense attorney. The men in the room could almost hear the mental machinery at work. "I take it that there is more to this than meets the eye," he said.

Staphanopolis gave no reply. None was really expected. "Four months. Work hard, gentlemen," the judge concluded and banged down his gavel.

Steffan was shuffled out of Judge Brandeis' court and to a new cell at the DC Jail located at 1901 D Street, still locked in his shackles. Assistant DA Henry caught up with Dimitri Staphanopolis as the defense attorney started to walk across the Hall of Justice lobby. "Dimitri...A moment of your time?" the DA called.

"Happy to oblige, Dwight; what can I do for you?"

"How about sharing something about what you have in mind that is going to take so long?"

"Nice try, Dwight. I think, however, that we can both be enlightened by presenting preliminary witness lists. Why don't we do that, say, day after tomorrow? We can file them with Brandeis' secretary; then the three of us will have an idea where we are headed," Staphanopolis said with the greatest of civility.

It was worth it. "All right, two days. We can do it when we meet for the preliminary hearing. It looks like you are going to make this interesting, Dimitri."

"You can't imagine the half of it, Dwight," Staphanopolis said cryptically and walked off.

The meeting, precipitated by the witness lists, held in the judge's chambers two days later, prior to the formal hearing, was provocative and contentious.

"Interesting list, Mr. Staphanopolis. If I did not know you better and did not hold you in respect, I would have to wonder whether this wasn't a smoke screen or just plain grandstanding."

"Your honor. This is preposterous," Dwight Henry all but shouted. "The people are not going to stand still for this! Have you looked at those names? I mean every official still living from the Viet Nam War era is named—former presidents and veeps, McNamara, senior military people, practically every current senior CIA official, and literally everyone who was ever involved in the irregular warfare activities of the US in that unfortunate business. He's listed South Vietnamese officials now living here; even North Vietnamese living over there. The Iran-Contra perps. Everybody but Mickey Mouse and Mr. Rogers. This is nuts. It is just a play to the press or worse, a calculated waste of time. We protest most vigorously, your honor! The sheer cost of all of this," he pointed angrily at Staphanopolis' proffered list, "would break the budget of the District all by itself! Even the feds, if they finally get jurisdiction, are going to move to quash ninety percent of this wish list!"

"Mr. Staphanopolis, you certainly have our attention. Care to enlighten the court?" asked Judge Brandeis, expectantly.

"Well, your honor, I don't feel that I am obliged to reveal the details of the defense strategy; but I will tell you this much. My client has opened my eyes to a whole black area of our history that is altogether pertinent to the present case. And yes, every single name on that list is a serious one. I would be personally and professionally insulted if these discoveries were to be regarded as some sort of grandstanding. I intend to take a deposition from every person named; and I expect to have them give testimony in open court. I could not be more serious."

"This will never fly, your honor," protested the DA. "The government will make it impossible to get at these people. You know how they are."

"Maybe it's time that we heard from these people," the judge said. His face was now thoughtful and completely serious. He did, indeed, 'know how they are;' and he was tired to death of the federal officials and their obfuscations of his DC judicial efforts.

"Time posthumous, your honor," said the defense attorney. "They hide behind the protective cloak of national security which is no more than an illegitimate means of evading their responsibility. The current Iran-Contra debacle is just the latest example. But, no, I'm not just stirring up some liberal cause for sensationalism. The evidence these people have will clear my client. It is critical, and without it there can not be any possibility of a fair trial."

"Your honor," Dwight Henry whined.

"'Let us reason together,' as my favorite fictional character used to say. Mr. Staphanopolis, is there a compromise here?"

"Perhaps."

"Oh, I like this sort of thing, don't you Mr. District Attorney?" asked the judge with renewed pleasure showing in his face. Mr. Henry just looked sour.

"Please, Mr. Staphanopolis. Your compromise," the judge continued.

The defense attorney was ever one to recognize when he had a run of trumps and also when not to overplay his hand. "Your honor, it is possible that our defense could be completed by getting hold of the classified documentation of the Phoenix Program in the CIA files. We would have to depose a certain number of the people who know that program. My client is in a position to supply us with data and names that will aid in our inquiry. Once that material is in hand, we can make a more realistic assessment of the defense needs. That is a beginning and a minimum. I need to stress that."

"I foresee difficulties," asserted the judge, knowing that he was being the master of understatement in so saying. "But, presuming you are keeping to good faith legal practice here and in your roll as an officer of the court, the request does not seem to be unfair, given the circumstances. I am inclined to grant the request and to facilitate the process of discovery from the Central Intelligence Agency. Perhaps the massive problems of trying to get a sitting president and vice-president and the others on this rather startling list can be circumvented. Any further thoughts, Mr. Henry?" the judge said.

"I suppose not," the assistant DA responded glumly. He had a quick, very negative vision of the upcoming scene when he broke the news of this meeting to his boss.

"Then I will approve the short list of people and documents. If they lead into other pertinent documents or witnesses, then the court will entertain a new motion to go a bit further. You'll have to be convincing, Mr. Staphanopolis."

"Thank you, your honor. I will prepare the proper submissions by tomorrow morning," said the defense attorney.

"My, you are an eager beaver; but the sooner the better. This ought to prove interesting. I have a question I have been meaning to ask. Any chance we can try this in the court and not in the press?"

"The people have absolutely no desire to turn this into a media circus, your honor," piped up Mr. Henry; his face was the very picture of boyish cooperation.

"Mr. Staphanopolis, how about the defense?"

"Let's see what the CIA brings to the table. I will be a complete mummy until then."

"Good enough for now. Let's have another discovery session in...say, ten days. We can hold off on starting the preliminary hearing until then. See Mrs. Tucker for a time. Good day, gentlemen," Judge Brandeis said to close the meeting.

Dimitri Staphanopolis hand delivered the submitted requests and the authorizing subpoenas to the Langley office of the new acting DCI, Leo Conrad. Conrad's executive secretary was at first curt and dismissive when the papers were presented, then hostile and passive-aggressive as only people with the certainty of job security possessed by civil servants can be, when the attorney insisted on personal delivery to Mr. Conrad and no other. She toyed with the idea of calling security; but when Mr. Conrad made the mistake of poking his head out of his office to find out why voices were being raised, she lost control of the situation. Staphanopolis strode purposefully past Miss Tidebury's desk and laid the papers in the surprised agent's hand.

"Consider yourself served, Mr. Director. Have a nice day."

With Judge Brandeis' full assistance and with the grudging cooperation of the White House, whose greatest fear at that moment was of yet another embarrassing cover-up surfacing, subpoenas and subpoenas duce tecum for records were served over the ensuing seven days to every appropriate record keeper in the Central Intelligence Agency and National Security Agency. Once they had access to the White House directory and with a few strategic calls, it was not all that hard to accomplish. Now that Staphanopolis had given the tree a good shake, all he had to do was to sit under it and wait to see what nuts would fall out.

One day before the judge's second scheduled pre-discovery conference with the attorneys in the case of District of Columbia versus John Doe, a Central Intelligence Agency letterhead note was delivered by certified mail to his chambers. It's message was simple to the point of being terse: "The Central Intelligence Agency neither confirms nor denies any knowledge or participation in the entitled matters before the court, viz. The Revolutionary Development Program, Phoenix, *Phung Hoang*, or the Nicaragua Project." It was signed by a lawyer who indicated that she was acting as the attorney for the agency in the matter.

Ten seconds after reading the letter, Judge Brandeis was on the telephone to the Attorney General's office needing only to mention 'obstruction of justice' once to obtain a promise of an immediate call to the attorney involved at the agency. Brandeis gave them fifteen minutes then called the attorney's office. Knowing the woman's name made it simple. The agency operators will ring through a call to a named individual but not to an office or to an extension number. That was a small helpful tidbit that the judge learned the first day he had tried to facilitate the transmission of the subpoenas.

"Miss Parling's office," said the secretary when Judge Brandeis was put through.

"Miss Parling is expecting my call. Put her on. This is Judge Brandeis of the DC Superior Court."

"Is this about an appointment?"

"Don't obstruct me. Get her on the line."

"One moment, please." Her manner remained strictly proper despite the rudeness of the caller. Judge Brandeis listed to Musak and drummed his fingers while he waited on hold.

"Hello, Judge. Nice of you to call. What can I do for you?" Miss Parling's voice had the same governmental tinniness as her secretary.

"It is not nice at all, madam. I know you just received a telephone call from the Attorney General's office. You know, therefore, that I mean business. Your letter of today with the 'neither confirms nor denies' bull is unacceptable. I will give you a chance to do better. You have your principles in my office tomorrow afternoon at one thirty sharp. If they are no-shows, I will start with the *Washington Post* and end with the *Wasatch Wave* out in Heber, Utah to put the activities of the Phoenix Program and its connection with the Iran-Contra Affair and the CIA connection with it all before the public. And I will send my letter to the Supreme Court conveying the difficulties we are having to do the business of the justice system in this country when the CIA can act above the law. Have you any questions, Ms. Parling?" He made the Ms into a hiss.

"I will convey the gist of your call to the acting director. It is out of my hands."

Judge Brandeis had the pleasure of hanging up without either a hello or a goodbye.

The judge called both attorneys in the case and informed them of the developments.

"In case someone from the CIA or from the NSA actually shows up, I would like to ask for an extraordinary bit of latitude from you, your honor," said Staphanopolis when he had heard the judge's message.

"This is getting to be an extraordinary case. Ask."

"I want your authorization to have my client present when these people come. He can pinpoint the information needed like no one else, and seeing him might shake something loose. I will personally guarantee his behavior. He is not a risk, your honor; please trust me on that."

"Well Dimitri, you were right. It is an extraordinary request. Sounds like it might be 'said the spider to the fly,' but I guess it can be done. No reason why the man can't begin to face his accusers. I require a small thing in return."

"What's that, your honor?"

"Give me the man's name and an address or something we can use so we don't have to keep up this John Doe charade."

"Only to you, sir. His life is not worth a proverbial plugged nickel if his particulars become known. What I have learned from him about these people would curl your hair. Have I your word that this is between us?"

"You do. But once the trial begins, we will have to have his name on public record with proof of identity, or I will not allow the introduction of the evidence relating to him. I will call on all the resources of the district police and even the feds if I have to for his protection."

"Fair enough. For the record, his name is Remundo Mueller-Garza. He carries a Costa Rican passport. However, this man is an American, and the evidence will bear me out."

"Tomorrow at one-thirty then,"

"We will be there. Wouldn't miss it for the world. Thanks for the call. Goodbye, Judge."

"Goodbye, Dimitri."

Staphanopolis, Assistant DA Henry, the man known as Mueller-Garza, in shackles but dressed in a business suit, a court recorder, and the judge were seated in the judge's chambers sipping coffee at one thirty-five when two federal government officials were ushered in. Two bulky Metro PD guards flanked Steffan and kept close enough to be able to lean on him continually.

"Sorry to be late, your honor. Couldn't find the exact office without a little searching," said the man who was obviously the senior of the two.

"That is Leo Conrad," whispered Steffan to Dimitri Staphanopolis. "He's the one I told you about in the Guzman family killings."

"I am Leo Conrad," the agent was continuing. "I am the acting DCI. This is Horace Steinweggen—my aide." No one offered to shake hands.

"Gentlemen, take a seat. Thank you for coming," said the judge.

"Our pleasure."

"I know you are busy; so, I won't keep you. I requested certain records. Where they?" Judge Brandeis asked rather curtly. He was well aware that the men had not brought any substantial set of records with them. They did not even carry briefcases.

"Judge, you have a very important matter before you—the trial of a man accused of murder. We also have a responsibility of critical importance. Today, we are here in person to convey to you and to the officers of your court exactly how important our position is. The requirements of the official secrets act forbid me from giving details, but I can tell you that the information you seek compromises the activities and the very lives of agents still in the field risking themselves for our country. The work they are doing is official; it is sanctioned by the president and by the Senate Intelligence Oversight Committee; and it serves the interests of our national security in a vital way. We respectfully decline to testify or to produce all or any of the documents you have requested on that basis."

Everyone sat quietly looking at the judge. "And if I subpoena you for open court testimony?" he asked finally.

"The subpoena will be quashed by the president of the United States under the charter of the National Security Council."

"That is a bold and broad statement."

"And one I can back up." Conrad reached into his suitcoat pocket and extracted an envelope which he handed to the judge. It was on "Office of the President, The White House" letterhead, stationary. The letter was fairly lengthy, the bulk of it having obviously been prepared by an attorney for the president or the NSC. In no uncertain terms it stated that Acting DCI Conrad was expressly forbidden by presidential order to convey any of the Phoenix documents to public scrutiny in any fashion, including in a court of law; and he was to take all necessary precautions to maintain the security of these classified documents. There was a short paragraph from the NSC concurring.

Judge Brandeis passed the letter to the two attorneys without comment. Each of them read it and shook his head. "We can fight this," said assistant DA Henry rather feebly.

"Perhaps. But if you release one line referencing the documents named in your subpoenas, you will be indicted under the provisions of the National Security Act. And that means any one of you. I can guarantee you that we will all be old men before those documents become available."

"So you have us by the short hairs," Staphanopolis said.

"That's about it," said Conrad. He looked pointedly at his watch. "I really must be getting back to the press of the government's business. If you will excuse me."

The judge and the assistant DA glared daggers at the departing Company men. Staphanopolis did not seem so upset, although it would seem that his case was being torpedoed. The CIA aid motioned to Mr. Henry to follow him out.

The two men had a five minute conference in the antechamber, then the assistant DA returned.

"I want a discussion without the defendant present, your honor. It was a breach of proper order to have him here, and now I want to have him out of here while we have a short additional conference," he asked.

"Mr. Staphanopolis?"

"All right. I see no harm. Remundo, I will be back over to the central lockup to fill you in when this meeting is over."

The guards led Steffan away. As they passed through the antechamber, Steffan saw the CIA aide waiting there. That seemed strange to him, but he trusted Staphanopolis; so, he chose to forget about it.

When Steffan was out of the offices, Henry ushered Horace Steinweggen back into the judge's inner chamber. He said, "Mr. Steinweggen has a suggestion to pose to us as 'reasonable men' as he put it to me. I believe it has merit."

"You have the floor, Mr. Steinweggen," offered the judge.

"This is strictly off the record." Judge Brandeis nodded his approval. "We are familiar with your defendant. He is a bad one, a rogue agent, and a very dangerous man. He needs to be kept off the streets. In that we agree 100% with the prosecutor. A compromise is in order. I hope to have the defendant's attorney concur in this in the best interests of the United States. We all have a stake in our country's welfare.

"What we propose is to convince the man to plead guilty to a lesser charge, say conspiracy, with the promise of a light or, better, of a suspended sentence. That way you would not have to prove the commission of a crime, and a much less difficult burden of proof would fall on the prosecution. If we can all agree to protect our country, then, when the time comes, the suspended sentence can be revoked—it is easy to find a pretext—and this terrorist can stay behind bars where he belongs. That way the prosecution wins because it gets its conviction without the horrendous time, effort, and expense of going through a messy public trial. The defense wins because the defense attorney can be seen to have acted in good faith for his client and had no control over the acts of the court or the prosecution. The judge can win because this is a violent nonconformist who will violate the terms that led to his probation by giving out some classified information to some reporter during one of those jail house interviews. That is inevitable, and carries with it an additional sentence of ten years in prison and a $10,000 fine. The judge can rescind the probation without risk of censure. No one wants this guy in society. We are reasonable men with an opportunity to make a silk purse out of a sow's ear."

Henry looked expectantly at the judge and covertly at Staphanopolis.

"The decision would seem to by yours, Dimitri. He would have to be convinced by you, you know," Brandeis intoned.

Staphanopolis remained silent.

"It is the only way to see justice in the system, Dimitri," said Dwight Henry. "He is a wanton murderer. We can't let a mad dog back on the streets. That would be the height of irresponsibility."

Staphanopolis was quiet for another moment. All eyes were on him. "And forget about justice for my client who entered the system presumed to be innocent? This is not Switzerland where the reverse is assumed. I am to agree not to mount a defense for the good of society? I am to take at face value that there are vital national security issues in those documents about the Phoenix program and its progeny?" He paused to collect himself. He was angry.

"I am here about justice for my client—that the evidence against him and also his defense may be heard in open court before a jury of his peers and not in a Star Chamber such as this room has the potential to become if I agree to such an arrangement.

"I respectfully disagree with the government as represented by this man," here, he indicated Steinweggen, "and by the letter from our supreme leaders. I don't really care what the National Insecurity Agency or the Caught In the Acts think about it. They are wrong. Justice is more important. It was well said by William Watson clear back in 1602, 'Let justice be done, though the heavens fall.' No gentlemen, I will not sell out my client, even if we can get away with it. Good day."

He stood up to leave. "Please take your seat, Dimitri," asked the judge. "I have something to say to you, Mr. Steinweggen, something you can take back to your employers." He looked unflinchingly at the senior CIA officer. "Get out of my office. Your suggestions bring dishonor upon it. Go back to your world of deceits and betrayals. We will maintain decency and the ethical high road here even if we can't get at those records." He stood up and angrily pointed at the door.

Steinweggen shrugged and got up. He was not angry, not defeated, not even embarrassed. He and the acting director had done what had to be done. There would be no trial and no public exposure, no embarrassment for The Company. He left satisfied with his day's work.

When the government agent was out of the office, the judge turned his attention to the assistant district attorney. "I am sorry, Dwight. I am left with no recourse under the law. This defendant cannot have a fair trial; certainly there is no way to provide him with a speedy one. As matters now stand, he cannot mount a defense. The case is dismissed. Don't be too crestfallen, Dwight. Bear in mind that we just do the best that we can do. I often bring to mind a pragmatic quote from somewhere around 471 BC, Thucydides, I think:

'For we both alike know that into the discussion of human affairs the question of justice enters only where the pressure of necessity is equal, and that the powerful exact what they can, and the weak grant what they must.'

"On a frankly cynical note, remember Clarence Darrow's lines— 'There is no such thing as justice, in or out of court.' Go home, counselors, assume the fetal position, and turn the electric blanket up to nine. That's what I do on these occasions. Good day, gentlemen."

———————————————————————•◆━◆•━——————————————

Steffan Johannson stepped into the Toronto International Airport deplaning waiting area after clearing customs with a cursory check. His Canadian passport in the name of Willem Lethbridge, was in order. Only his Washington DC attorney knew even of his Mueller-Garza identity, and he was a devotee to the principle of attorney-client privilege. No one else but his blood brothers knew of his Johannson or Remundo Mueller-Garza identities. Steffan drew a few glances because of his imposing size and because he was so closely flanked by a pair of governmental, tough looking thirty or so year old men in medium gray suits and matching black wing tip brogues. Both were wearing Yale "Old Boy" ties. The larger man paid them little notice. He did glance very briefly at Nguyen Lui Tran, Phan Duy Ky, and Fang Pao Xe who were situated well apart from each other in the crowded waiting crowd.

The tall Scandinavian strode purposefully to the men's room midway along the carpeted airport corridor, preceded by Ky. One of the obvious agents walked in with him, and the other took up a position in the hall beside the lavatory door. Ky could be heard rummaging around in his toilet stall; otherwise there was no one else in the room. Steffan did his business, taking his own sweet time to the annoyance of his accompanying CIA agent.

"Enough awreddy," the agent finally said. "Let's get you out to the car and turned over to the Canucks, Lethbridge, then I can be quit of you."

The sap made a sound like a two by four striking a ripe melon when Ky applied it to the agent's mastoid process. The American agent had not heard Ky come up behind him, and he did not make the slightest struggle as he pitched forward into Steffan's arms. The big man

947

dragged the unconscious CIA man into the nearest toilet stall and set him slumped on the commode seat. Tran walked in from the outside and stood by the sink. The three men waited patiently.

In another three or four minutes, the second agent entered the men's room exasperated. "What happened? He fall in?" he barked when he saw Steffan and the Chinaman standing at the sink. Tran walked over to use the urinal. Xe walked out of his stall and approached the sink. "Which stall's he in?" the second agent asked Steffan.

Steffan pointed, "Second. Says he's got a very bad gut. I wonder if he's okay."

"Kiley!" the second agent called into the toilet stall. There was no answer; so, the agent banged on the door. It was locked from the inside, and there was no response. He kicked in the door. At the same time he saw Kiley sitting grotesquely on the toilet fully dressed and before he could register exactly what was amiss in that scene, a sap connected with the middle of his subocciput; and he crumpled down over his partner. The other three men scrunched the second agent into the stall in a compromising position (if anyone should be curious enough to glance under the stall door). Tran gave each of them an injection of a thirty milligrams of Valium intravenously.

"See you next time you are in LA, brother," said Ky. He hugged Steffan and kissed his cheeks, once on the left and twice on the right.

Tran and Xe said, "See you back at the place."

Steffan said quietly, "Thanks, brothers."

He walked swiftly out of the men's room and took the stairs two at a time to the ticketing area. There he purchased tickets on American Airlines to San Jose, Costa Rica, and presented his Remundo Mueller-Garza passport. Then he went to the Canadian Airlines ticket counter and purchased a seat to Quebec City. He paid cash and gave his name as Wilmer Colding; that seemed like an appropriate touch. He bought tickets for Madrid, Medillin, Frankfurt, and Edinburgh, all on his MasterCard in Mueller-Garza's name, and each on a different airline. He purposely selected flights leaving very shortly. His final stop was in the last section of the ticket booths. There, he purchased a seat on Canadian North Airlines, a propeller flight, to Edmonton, Alberta. Again he paid cash and this time listed himself as Karl Mandarin.

Once in Edmonton, he obtained a seat on Yukon Airways for Quesnel, British Columbia. As he waited, he tore the Remundo Mueller-Garza and Willem Lethbridge passports to pieces and patiently flushed it down the airport toilet. He used his pocket knife to cut the identifying credit cards into little pieces and scattered them in several different waste bins. Using his US passport and Steffan Johannson identity, he flew from Quesnel to Anchorage, Alaska on a Delta commuter plane and on to Kotzebue on Alaska airlines.

Swedish-American hunting outfitter and master-guide, Steffan Johannson, was met at the small airport in Kotzebue by his two friends and partners in the hunting business. They flew home in the company Super Cub.

As that long day drew to a close, Steffan sat on the porch and watched the sunset. He was bothered some by the first mosquitoes of the season, but paid them little mind. The older Okobuk girl served the men steaming mugs of coffee laced with cognac. Mary Okobuk's two year old, Candy, sat comfortably on Steffan's lap; and he sang her old lullabies.

Ví dầu cầu đóng
Cầu tre lắc lẻo gấp ghềnh khó đi

Although the plank bridge is fastened with nails,
It sways so much that it is hard for one to cross it.

Con ởi con ngủ cho ngon
Mẹ con đi cêy ruộng chưa về

My baby, if you sleep, you should sleep soundly,
Because your mother has not yet come home from
transplanting seedlings in the field.

Con cò bay lả bay la
Bay qua đồng Bắc, bay về đồng Đăng
Đồng Đắng có phố Thi lùa
Có làng Đô Thi, có chùa Tam Thanh
Chùa nàay có môt ống thầy
Có hòn đá tảng, có cây ngô đồng
Cây ngô đồng không trồng mà mọc
Cây ngô đồng rễ doc rễ ngang

White storks are flying away,
Flying through the North field and back to the Dang field.
In the Dang field, there is Thi Lua Town,
Bo Thi Village and Tam Thanh Pagoda.

This Pagoda has a monk, a big rock, and a sterculia tree.
This tree grows naturally without being planted.
Its roots strike up and down and sideways.

Ai lên xử lang cùng anh
Tiếc công gắn bó, tập tành bút ngiêng
Tay cầm bầu rượu nắm nem
Mãi vui quên hết lợi em dăn dò

Who was going to the land of Lang with you?
I sorrowed over the futility of my efforts
to have helped you go to school.
Holding a calabash of wine in one hand and
a handful of sour pork in the other hand,
You enjoyed so much that you forgot all of my advice.

The heavy orange sun finally descended behind the low tundra hills
and a mild chill began to settle on Steffan, who snuggled the little
girl's body close in to his, and on his two old friends as they swayed
comfortably back and forth in their wicker rocking chairs.

"Do you feel like it's all over?" Tran asked him.

"It is for me," Steffan answered pensively. "I think now that we've
seen the last Phoenix."

He was wrong, of course.

—End—

EPILOGUE

In 1959, the United States began a covert intelligence and sabotage campaign inside North Vietnam with young men recruited mostly in South Vietnam. In the next 10 years, many wound up as prisoners of war.

To help conceal the effort, US officials eventually halted payment to the families of captured Vietnamese commandos, claiming they were dead, according to recently declassified documents.

Some of these POWs languished in prison for decades, then made their way to the United States only to discover the government they served refused to admit they exist.

Now a lawsuit to be filed in Washington today is demanding that recognition in the form of back pay for 281 surviving commandos.

"We left them. Then we swept it under the rug," says Miami lawyer John Mattes, who's filing the claim. "Everyone hoped they would die off..." Mattes said the pleas for back pay—amounting to only $2,000 a year each—were ignored by the CIA and Defense Department...

"We had no name, no fame. We didn't expect that," said Hoc. Mai Van Hoc, a former commando who now lives in San Jose, California, and is one of the plaintiffs in the suit; "But when it was over, we were abandoned."

Richard Cole, The Associated Press, as quoted in The Salt Lake Tribune, Monday, April 24, 1995.

As I was going up the stair,

I met the man who wasn't there.

He wasn't there again today.

I wish, I wish that he would go away.

Children's Nursery Rhyme

CONCLUSION

You may either win your peace or buy it by resistance to evil, or compromise with evil.
John Ruskin

It was a cousin of Bach's who told Steffan, Tran, Ky, and Xe what became of Lane Duerk and his secretary, Nguyen Ngoc Tram. The cousin was rescued from a boat people camp near Manila by men in the employ of the four friends and the Wa People. Miss Nguyen and Station Chief Duerk had been secretly married during the entirety of Duerk's stay in Viet Nam, but he had been unable to acknowledge her status because of his career considerations. When he was evacuated in Operation Frequent Wind without her, Duerk promised his wife that he would return for her.

On July 5, 1976, he kept his promise, arriving in the communist country at the Ho Chi Minh City Airport under an assumed identity. People who were in a position to know stated that he never arrived at the little house where he was slated to meet Tram. On August 16, 1976 a nude body, or more precisely, an almost dead man, was rolled out of a swiftly moving DeSoto taxi and lay inert in the street in front of the Continental Hotel. The man was quickly whisked away by city officials. One informant who had seen the condition of the near corpse described it as having suffered removal of all four extremities, genitalia, eyes, ears, and nose. A sign, in English, was pinned to the man's chest. It read, "Enemy of the People. Duerk, CIA monster."

There was no way to verify the report, but Duerk was never seen again after the July Fourth celebration in the American housing section in Manila were he was visiting ex-pat friends in the import-export business. According to official records of the Ho Chi Minh City Health Department Nguyen Ngoc Tram died of septicemia contracted from untended compound, complex leg fractures sustained in her fall from the helicopter on April 30, 1975. She lingered for two weeks.

———————————————— •◆• ◆◆ •◆•• ————————————————

Tandrosz Szabo looked away from the noise in the back room and tried to concentrate on the packet of papers on the rude desk in front of him. It was hot, and he was sweaty. His clothes clung to his skin in uncomfortable sticky patches. He had expected a new batch of personnel data from the Pastora people to add to his nearly complete file from Bermúdez's FDN G2. It was all they would need to finish the clean-out of the SI (Sandinista Infrastructure) around Lago de Nicaragua, the largest of the freshwater lakes in southwestern Nicaragua, and the largest lake in Central America. He was sitting in his office in the RIC on Isla de Ometepe looking across at Jean-Luc DuParrier. Dieter Lutz was in the back room with his machines. They had only to cleanse the last of this major Sandinsta holdout area, and they could move on to Managua and cut the head off the communist serpent.

When he opened the packet, Szabo did not find the desired computer printout data. Instead, he read it quickly, then said to DuParrier, "You need to hear this."

"What's up, boss?" DuParrier asked. His voice sleepy as it always was these days. It was because of the nose dust he enjoyed so much.

"New orders," Szabo announced to his deputy. He read the orders, skipping the repetitious governmentese, "New place. Would you believe this? We destroy all records today and tomorrow and get the C-46 out to Miami. We leave for Beirut Thursday."

"Not even a vacation between assignments?"

"No. Says it's urgent."

"Do you suppose that it's as hot there as it is here this time of year?"

"Probably, but drier. Don't complain. Let's get the work done."

"Yeah. It never ceases. How much longer before you can take your retirement, boss?" He had asked Szabo before.

"Two years. Be patient; two years and then you're boss."

"Perhaps," said Jean-Luc. "But...*c'est une affaire compliquèe il y a toutes sortes de forces en jeu.*" (Literally, "It is a complicated affair; there are all sorts of forces at play." However, Frenchmen regularly translate that particular phrase as, "There are wheels within wheels.")

954

GLOSSARY

Air America CIA cover airline. Originally, and until 1954, known as Nationalist Air Transport.

AK-47 Avotmat Kalashnikov assault rifle. Standard USSR infantry submachine gun used by the VC and NVA. Fires 7.62 mm ammunition, 30 round detachable magazine.

Annam Former French colony, portion of Indochina occupying central Viet Nam the narrowest segment.

An Ninh VC internal security service.

Ao Dai Traditional Vietnamese item of women's apparel. A svelte, flowing, often brightly patterned garment slit up the sides and worn over pants. Usually seen in cities.

ARVN Army of the Republic of Vietnam (South Viet Nam). Usually called Marvin or Marvin Arvin by US. troops.

baht Unit of Thai currency.

BAR Browning Automatic Rifle.

BCE Before the Common Era. Roughly the same as BC—before Christ. Common Era is the equivalent of AD.

B-40 (RPG) NVA and VC rocket propelled grenade launcher, Soviet supplied. Shoulder fired, Panzerfaust-type weapon that fires a shape charged armor piercing 82 mm projectile over a 200 yard range.

Biet Kich Vietnamese term for counterterrorist, later applied to the PRUCs.

Binh Xuyên Saigon criminal organization. Prior to Diem regime they were in control of the capital city's police.

Black Covert, secret operations and espionage in military parlance. 'Magic,' in CIA phraseology.

Bo Doi Uniformed NVA.

BOQ Bachelors Officers' Quarters.

Brown Water Riverine conflict in the Mekong Delta War.

BUD/S	Basic Underwater Demolition/SEAL. The basic frogman and pre-SEAL training course.
Bui Doi	Child of the Dust. Saigon street orphan.
CA	Cong-an. Civilian secret police of the DRV—Democratic Republic of Viet Nam (North).
Cadre	Trained person or group. Expected to act as the dedicated nucleus for the building of a larger organization.
Can Lao	Pro Diem Personalist government party headed by Ngo Dinh Nhu, Diem's brother-in-law.
Cao Dai	Religious sect of South Viet Nam with strong nationalist political involvement. Calls itself the "Third Amnesty of God."
CAS	Controlled American Source. CIA direct employee. Also Saigon office of the CIA.
CASI	Continental Air Service Inc. Airline contracted extensively by the CIA in Southeast Asia.
CD	Civilian detainee. Vietnamese civilian, suspected of being VC or VCI. Could be detained without due process by American or South Vietnamese military or CIA forces at their discretion. With very few exceptions these people were referred to as VCS—Viet Cong Suspect until the detainee could prove otherwise.
C-4	American putty-like plastic explosive. One pound bars used as often for cooking as for intentional explosions.
Chinook	Twin engine CH-47 army aviation helicopter. Often called 'shit hook' due to the proclivity of these helicopters to stir up dust, etc. on the ground
Chieu Hoi	*Phong Trao Chieu Tap Khang Chien Nam Duong*—Movement to Regroup Misled Members of the Resistance. "Open Arms" in Vietnamese. Name for the amnesty program to induce VC and NVA to surrender without penalty and often to be rehabilitated into GVN service. Also term for the *Hoi Chanh,* rallier, or surrenderee
CIA	Central Intelligence Agency (Unaffectionately known as 'Caught In the Act' or 'Christians in Action'). Established as an intelligence gathering organization in 1947 but became a self-governing paramilitary and worldwide covert operations organization in the 1950s. Also known as The Outfit and The Company.

CIDG	Civilian Irregular Defense Group. US, usually special forces run paramilitary unit organized from the citizens of a village or a region for their own protection.
CIO	Central Intelligence Organization. South Vietnamese intelligence coordinating service.
Clutch belt	Marine cartridge belt.
Cobra	AG-1H Assault Helicopters, also called snakes.
Cochinchina	Part of the French Indochina colony. Occupies most of southern South Vietnam, the Delta.
CORDS	Civil Operations and Revolutionary Development Support. Established May, 1967 to coordinate US-South Viet Nam nonmilitary actions. Responsible organization for the Phoenix Program. Largely CIA controlled.
Corps I-IV	MACV military regions (corps tactical zones) in South Viet Nam. I or Eye Corps was the northernmost and included the northern five provinces and the old imperial capital, Hue'. II was the central highlands and central coastal area. III was Saigon to the highlands. IV was the Mekong Delta, the southernmost region.
COSVN	Central Office of South Vietnam. Headquarters of the anti-government insurgency forces. Mobile in location. Established in 1962, controlled by VC.
In Country	Viet Nam
cố vên vĩ đai	Derogatory term for Chinese overlords also used by Vietnamese to refer to American occupiers.
Cowboys	Vietnamese youths running around Saigon on motor scooters. Well known for reaching over the edge of a jeep with a curved metal implement to snatch a watch then to ride off into the distant crowd.
CPO, LPO, PO	Chief Petty Officer, Lead Petty Officer, Petty Officer (third, second, first class)—US Navy enlisted ranks.
C-Rats	Combat Rations. Standard bush country meal.
CT	Counter terrorist. Mercenary employed by the CIA to interdict the VCI. Most became part of Phoenix.
Cuu Long Giang	Nine Dragons River—The Mekong.

DAO	Defense Attaché Office (American, in Laos).
DEROS	Date Estimated Return from Over Seas. Short timer or Next (next to be rotated home). The last day was the Wake-up.
DCI	Director Central Intelligence.
DIA	Defense Intelligence Agency (US, serving in Laos).
DMZ	Demilitarized zone. Area on either side of the demarcation line between North and South Viet Nam, roughly at the 17th parallel.
DOD	Department of Defense (US).
Dong	Unit of Vietnamese money—equals 1 Piastre.
DRV	Democratic Republic of Vietnam. Communist North Viet Nam.
DV	Dich Van. VC "Moral Intervention" armed propaganda and psychological warfare specialist organization of the VC.
FAL, FAR	Lao armed forces, Royal Armed Forces of Laos.
FIGMO	F- It, Got My Orders. Very near DEROS.
Freedom Birds	AKA Big Iron Birds. Commercial civilian aircraft that took GIs home to the World at the end of their Viet Nam tours of duty.
FULRO	*Front Unifié pour la Libération des Races Opprimées.* Unified Front for the Liberation of Oppressed Peoples. A militant Montagnard organization started by a Rhade tribesman, Y Bham, for the principle purpose of achieving autonomy from Viet Nam.
Garand	M-1 Rifle. Used by US in WW II and by South Vietnamese. Replaced by M-14 then M-16.
GMT	Greenwich Mean Time. Standard military time.
Gook	Pejorative term used by Americans to describe Vietnamese or other Asians, friend or enemy, and reciprocally by the VC and NVA to refer to Americans. The Asians were also colloquially referred to as slants, slopes, dinks, and little people.
Greggs	GI term of abbreviation for Grave Registration Personnel.
GVN/GRV	Government of Viet Nam (South) Government of the Republic of Vietnam.

Hoa Hao	Politico-religious sect active in southeast South Vietnam.
Hooch	Crude rural Vietnamese dwelling.
Hotel Alpha	HA or Haul Ass. Activity required when about to be overrun.
Hotel Three	Helicopter landing section at Tan Son Nhut Air Force Base.
Huey	Bell UH-1D helicopter. Also called a slick because it lacked belly guns. Able to be armed with two side mounted XM -140 30 mm cannon or a nose mounted M-5 40 mm grenade launcher capable of firing 220 rpm.
IBS, IBL	Inflatable boat, small. Inflatable boat, large. Rubber boat used in SEAL training and in riverine infiltration in the Delta war.
Indochina	Formerly French colony including present Viet Nam, Laos, and Cambodia.
Iron Triangle	Viet Cong dominated region near Cu Chi between Thi Tinh and Saigon Rivers. Undermined by a series of complex VC tunnel emplacements.
K-Bar	American military combat knife, slightly different form for different services.
kip	Laotian unit of currency.
Kit Carson	South Vietnamese scout. Often a repatriated enemy soldier, usually a mercenary working with US military under Luc Long 66 program.
Klick	One kilometer, 1000 meters.
Kool-aid	KIA. Killed in action.
KP	Kitchen Penalty, one of a legion of odious military occupations, often imposed as a punishment.
kyat	Burmese unit of currency.
LAF	Liberation Armed Forces. *Quan-Doi Giai-phong*:—the name preferred by the insurgents known by Americans and South Vietnamese officials as VC Term can be used nearly interchangeably with VC or NLF.
LAW	M-72 Light Antitank Weapon. Shoulder fired armor piercing rocket launcher. Utilizes one-time disposable fiberglass launcher.

LLDB	*Luc Luong Duc Biet*—South Vietnamese Special Forces.
LPRP	Laotian People's Revolutionary Party. Communist party of Laos that ascended to role of government after the US departed.
LRRP	Long-Range Reconnaissance Patrol. Team of US soldiers involved in long range intelligence and commando military operations in areas controlled by the VC and NVA.
LSSC	Light SEAL Support Craft. Heavily armed SEAL infiltration boat.
LURPS	Freeze dried food for long range reconnaissance operations.
LZ	Landing Zone.
MACV	Military Assistance Command, Viet Nam. Established 1962 as a unified command.
Mad Minute	Sudden coordinated short-term full fire from a defensive position or upon enemy defenses designed to intimidate and hopefully to kill the enemy.
M-7	US supplied military rifle used by ARVN early in the Vietnam War. Fired .30 caliber ammunition.
M-14	Early in Viet Nam war standard US submachine gun. Fired standard NATO 7.62 mm round. Replaced by M-16.
M-16	M 16-A1. Standard American submachine gun infantry rifle after 1965. Fired 5.56 mm ammunition. Effective range, 500 yards. Also called a Stoner after its inventor, Eugene M. Stoner and as an ArmaLite after its main producer. Nick named black magic.
M-60	Standard American full machine gun. Fires belt fed 7.62 mm ammunition at 600 rounds per minute to effective range of 3500 yards. Nicknamed a Pig. Variable function—tripod mounted serves as HMG, bipod mounted as LMG or can be hip fired while moving.
M-72	See LAW
M-79	American 40 mm grenade launcher. Short (28.6 inches long) single barreled break open shotgun like weapon that shoots spin armed 40 mm grenades weighing 9 oz at the rate of 5-7 per minute at an effective range of 375 yards. Also called a blooper and a thumper.

Montagnard	Mountain people of various ethnic and tribal origin occupying the highlands of Viet Nam and Laos. Called Meo by Vietnamese as derogatory term. Also known by French name—PMS (see below).
MPC	Military Payment Certificates. Also known as scrip or play money.
Napalm	Jellied gasoline. Acronym made from naphthenic and palmitic acids.
NIC	South Vietnamese National Interrogation Center. Built by CIA in CIO headquarters in the Saigon Naval Shipyard.
NLF	National Liberation Front. *Mat-tran Dan-Toc Mien Nam Viet-Nam.* Established Dec. 12,1960 to coordinate the activities of the many insurgent groups in South Vietnam working against the established government. Controlled by the VC. Initial member ship of 75,000 quadrupled to 300,000 in its first year.
No Sweat Pills	Tetracycline. Taken so as not to have to sweat getting gonorrhea or syphilis.
Nouc Mam	Fermented fish sauce favored by Vietnamese. Also known unkindly by GIs as 'armpit sauce.'
Number ten	The worst. Ten thousand—the very worst.
NSA, NSC	National Security Agency, National Security Council (US).
NPAISS	National (GVN) Police Infrastructure Analysis Sub-section. Data bank for information regarding VCI. Virtually any Vietnamese civilian submitted to the NPAISS remained in the VCI category. Information kept for countermeasure purposes.
NVA	North Vietnamese Army. Regular armed forces of the DRV.
PA & E	Pacific Architects and Engineers. A private construction company, largely American owned, that did work for GVN. Allegedly often used as cover for clandestine CIA or other intelligence units' work. Widely rumored In Country to be owned by Lady Bird Johnson.
Pathet Lao	Laotian communist state in northern portion of Laos and the communist people of that state. Literally, Lao Country. Nominally led by Prince Souphanouvong.
PAVN	People's Army of Viet Nam. Formal title for NVA.

PBR	Patrol Boat, River. 31 foot long shallow draft acuzzi propulsion system driven highly maneuverable and fast USN boat used extensively in the Brown River War.
PCOD	Pussy Cut Off Day. Latest day an American In Country could have intercourse with a local, get the clap, be cured, and get home with no one in the World being the wiser.
PDJ	*Plaine des Jarres.* Laotian Plain of Jars.
Phoenix	CIA controlled program to interdict VCI. Established in 1967 and utilized computerized information to track VCI and used PRUs to capture, turn, or kill them
Phung Hoang	South Vietnamese counterpart to the American Phoenix Program. Reference is to the bird of peace and conjugal love from Vietnamese mythology. The mythological bird is represented as holding a flute signifying virtue, grace, harmony, and tranquillity. The *Phung Hoang*/Phoenix bird held a ribboned scroll in its beak—the blacklist.
Piastre	Unit of Vietnamese currency, abbreviated as Pee or P. 1 P equals 1 dong.
PIC	Province Interrogation Center. CIA built and managed center for collection of data from Vietnamese internees regarding the VC for use in the Phoenix program.
PMS	*Plateaux Montagnards du Sud.* French name for the hill people of Viet Nam.
POIC	Province Officer in Charge. The senior CIA officer in each of the 44 RVN provinces responsible for both police activity and RD or Phoenix paramilitary operations. Often the same as the PSA, the Province Senior Advisor—the senior CORDS official.
PRU	Provincial Reconnaissance Unit. Mercenary forces hired by and under the control of the CIA, composed largely of people local to the area served and often made up of common criminals and reformed VC. Action units for Phoenix.
PRUC	Provincial Reconnaissance Unit Cadre. Member of a PRU.
PRU/O	Provincial Reconnaissance Unit Operations (section chief) Field commander of any one of the 45—125 member PRUs.
P-38	Small collapsible metal one piece can opener for C-rats. The larger churchkey variety was called a B-52.

Pungi Stake	Or Panji stake or stick. Sharpened bamboo stick used in traps to pierce the enemy. Often coated with feces for greater effect.
Rallier	See *Chieu Hoi*.
Randall Knife	Stiletto combat knife.
RD; RDC; RDC/O	Revolutionary Development Cadre. South Vietnamese trained by and under the control of CIA with police powers. Functioned to persuade the citizens of South Viet Nam to comply with GVN. Forerunner of Phoenix cadres. The RD program was a wholly CIA run operation to support GVN in the provinces. The RDC/O was the CIA operations officer in charge and the forerunner of the POIC.
Red leg	Artillery soldier.
REMF	Rear Echelon M-F. Grunt slang for anyone lucky enough not to be in a combat unit. Constituted 80% of Americans In Country.
ROIC	Regional Officer in Charge. CIA officer in command of each of the four geographical military corps divisions and Saigon.
RLG	Royal Laotian Government. Rightest government of Laos propped up by the US, supplanted by a communist government after departure of the US.
RLAF	Royal Laotian Air Force.
RPK	Soviet made light full machine gun. Fires 7.62 mm ammunition.
RPG	Soviet Rocket Propelled Grenade launcher.
S & D or SAD	Search and Destroy.
Sapper	Soldier trained in infiltration of enemy positions for the purpose of planting demolitions. For the VC or NVA, the sappers were special assault forces considered to be expendable.
Sat Cong	Kill Communist. Tattoo inscribed on many PRUCs.
SBI	SEAL Basic Indoctrination. The basic SEAL training program.
SEAL	Sea, Air, Land. US Navy Special Forces Commandos. Active in SOG operations, especially in the Vietnamese Delta.
SKS	Chinese variant of the AK-47. A Simonov semiautomatic rifle that fires 7.62 mm ammunition.

SMM — Saigon Military Mission. Original covert action CIA unit in Viet Nam. Headed by USAF Col. Edward Lansdale.

Snatch and Snuff Kidnap and kill. — Fundamental part of the activity of the Phoenix Program, largely carried out by PRUs.

SOG — Studies and Observations Group; or MAC-SOG for Military Assistance Command—SOG, also known as Special Operations Group. Mixed CIA and multiple military origin unit. Established in 1964. Conducted clandestine para-military operations inside and outside South Viet Nam in prosecution of the war.

SP — Supply Pack. Cellophane field packet supplied by US military containing assorted toiletry items and cigarettes. Popular black market item.

STAB — SEAL Tactical Assault Boat. Fiberglass Mercury outboard motor driven, heavily armed commando boat used extensively in the Brown River War.

STOL — Short Takeoff and Landing airplane

SUN — Shan United Nation (Army). 20,000 member private army in Burma and the Golden Triangle (Burma, Laos, Thailand) responsible for maintaining opium-heroin refineries that produce the majority of the world's heroin supply.

Taggy Tapes — 100 cm tapes carried by grunts. They tore off one cm each day of their In Country tour until they got to be two digit midgets and their DEROS was imminent.

Tay Son Vo Si — Vietnamese martial arts. Originated in Tay Son rebellion (1776-1792). Originators of the rules were Nguyen Hue and Nguyen Lu, The Tay Son brothers, whose book remains the classic.

Tet — New year based on Buddhist lunar calendar. Chinese and Vietnamese holiday

1369 — U.S. Army designation of infantryman, the classical grunt, often called 'legs.' Referred to by other contemporaries as 'unlucky CSs,' 'ground pounders,' or 'crunchies.'

34-A (OPLAN) — 1964 operation plan dealing with covert ground, air, and sea raids against North Viet Nam.

Tonkin — Former French Indochinese colony occupying northern part of North Viet Nam. *Bac Bo,* to the Vietnamese.

Tontons Macoutes	The Haitian secret police of Papa Doc Duvalier, the feared and secret bogeymen who used terror, intimidation, and voodoo to control the Haitian populace. Term applied by regular military detractors to the spooks of the CIA.
Tovarich	(Russian) Comrade.
Tracer	Bullet with phosphorus marker included to provide a visual track. Spaced every fifth round.
TS	Trinh Sat. VC military intelligence apparatus. Also the individuals involved.
201 File	Military personnel file.
UCMJ	Uniform Code of Military Justice (US).
UWS	United Wa State Army. A powerful military faction (15-35,000 member army) in Burma and the Golden Triangle (of Burma, Laos, and Thailand) responsible for the majority of the world's opium production.
VC	Viet Cong or more properly, *Viet Cong San.* South Vietnamese communist. Also called Victor Charlie after the radio phonetic alphabet.
VCI	Viet Cong Infrastructure. The composite of civilians and soldiers; men, women, and children that made up the support structure dedicated to undermining GVN and to establishing a Viet Nam united under communism. Included VC, NVA, NLF, and communist party members. This organization was the target of the Phoenix Program.
VCS	Viet Cong Suspect. Vietnamese civilian suspected of being either VC or VCI. Any person could be detained indefinitely as a VCS without due process of law or representation.
Viet Minh	Contraction of *Viet Nam Doc Lap Dong Minh*—the League for the Independence of Viet Nam. Established May 1941 in Chingsi, Kwangsi Province, China. Originally a coalition of anti-French nationalists, but subsequently, communist dominated.
Viet Nam	The name granted in 1802 by the Chinese which means 'Viets of the South.' Viet is the Vietnamese pronunciation of an old Chinese character meaning beyond or far away, and also to set oneself aright. Nam means south. There are three regions—*Bac Bo* (North), *Trung Bo* (Center) and *Nam Bo* (South)—which are likened to a set of rice baskets balancing on a central pole.

VVAW	Vietnam Veterans Against the War. Established in 1968. Estimated that eventually 15% of all vets were involved. Initial financing alleged to be by Jane Fonda.
White Mice	Vietnamese military police.
Web Gear	Tough woven cloth suspenders and belt for carrying combat ammunition and personal field items for battle.
WIA	Wounded In Action.
Willy Pete	White phosphorus or WP. White phosphorus artillery shell.
WOM	Wise Old Men. Senior establishment liberals who advised presidents and caused and perpetuated the Second Indochinese War.
The World	Any place except Viet Nam, especially the United States.
Zulu	Casualty report. Also Greenwich Mean Time designator—standard military time.

SUGGESTED READING

Brown, Weldon, A. The Last Chopper—The Denouement of the American Role in Viet Nam, 1963-1975. National University Publications—Kennikat Press, 1976.

Bryan, C.D.B. Friendly Fire. A Bantum Book published by arrangement with B.P. Putnam's Sons, New York, 1976.

Cable, Larry E. Conflict of Myths—The Development of American Counter-insurgency Doctrine and the Vietnam War. New York University Press, 1986.

Champassak, Sisouk Na. Storm Over Laos. Frederick A Praeger, Publisher. New York, 1961.

Colby, William. Honorable Men—My Life in the CIA. Simon and Schuster. New York, 1978.

Colby, William. Lost Victory. Contemporary Books. Chicago, 1989.

Cooper, Chester L. The Lost Crusade -America in Viet Nam. Dodd, Mead, and Company, New York, 1970.

Diem, Bui. In the Jaws of History. Houghton Mifflin. Boston, 1987.

Draper, Theodore. A Very Thin Line—The Iran-Contra Affairs. A Touchstone Book Published by Simon and Schuster, New York, 1991.

Fall, Bernard B. Anatomy of a Crisis—The Story of the Laotian Crisis of 1960-1961). Doubleday and Company, Garden City, New York, 1969.

Fall, Bernard B. The Two Viet-Nams—A Political and Military Analysis. Frederick A Praeger, Publishers, New York, 1963.

Frazier, Howard (Ed.). Uncloaking the CIA. Chapter by Long, Ngo Vinh. The CIA and the Vietnam Debacle. The Free Press. New York, 1978.

Generous, Kevin. Vietnam—The Secret War. Bison Books. New York, 1985.

Greene, Graham. The Quiet American. Penguin Books in Association with William Heinemann Ltd. London, 1977.

Halberstadt, Hans. US Navy SEALS. The Power Series, Motor Books International, Osceola, Wisconsin, 1993

Halperin, Morton. The Lawless State—The Crimes of the US Intelligence Agencies. Viking/Penguin Press, New York, 1976.

Helm, Eric. Vietnam—Ground Zero. A Gold Eagle Book from Worldwide, New York, 1986.

Herman, Edward S. Atrocities in Vietnam—Myths and Realities. Pilgrim Press, Philadelphia, 1970.

Hersh, Seymour. Cover-up. Random House. New York, 1972.

Hoyt, Edwin, P. SEALS at War—The Story of US Navy Special Warfare. Dell Publishers, New York, 1993.

Karnow, Stanley. Viet Nam—A History. The First Complete Account of Viet Nam at War. The Viking Press, 1983.

Kolko, Gabriel. Anatomy of a War—Vietnam, the United States and the Modern Historical Experience. The New Press, New York, 1979.

Lanning, Michael Lee. The Only War We Had—A Platoon Leader's Journal of Vietnam. Ivy Books, Published by Ballantine Books, New York.

Lanning, Michael Lee, Cragg, Dan. Inside the VC and the NVA—The Real Story of North Vietnam's Armed Forces. Fawcett Columbine Publishers, 1992.

Lansdale, Edward. In the Midst of Wars. Harper and Row, New York, 1972.

Lederer, William J. Our Own Worst Enemy. W.W. Norton and Company, Inc. New York, 1968.

Levy, Charles J. Spoils of War. Houghton Mifflin Company, Boston, 1974.

Linh, Tran Cao. Vietnam. Published by Aid to the Children of Vietnam, Gif sur Yvette, France, Undated.

Maitland, Terence, McInerney, Peter. The Vietnam Experience (6 Vols). Boston Publishing Company, Boston, 1983.

Mangold, Tom, Penycate, John. The Tunnels of Cu Chi. Berkley Books, New York, 1986.

Marcinko, Richard with Weisman, John. Rogue Warrior. Pocket Books, New York, 1992.

Marshall, S.L.A. Battles in the Monsoon. Warner Communications Company, 1967.

Maw, David C. Vietnamese Traditions on Trial—1920-1945. University of Chicago Press, Berkley, 1981.

Murphy, Edward F. Viet Nam Medal of Honor Heroes. Ballantine Books. New York, 1987.

Nolan, Keith William. Battle for Hue—Tet, 1968. Presidio Press. Novato, California, 1983

Nolan, Keith William. Into Laos—The Story of Dewey Canyon II-Lam Son 719, Vietnam, 1971. Dell Publishing Company, New York, 1986.

Olsen, James, Ed. Dictionary of the Viet Nam War. Peter Bedrick Books, 1987.

Parrish, John, A. 12, 20, and 5—A Doctor's Year in Vietnam. Bantam Books, New York, 1986.

Prados, John. Presidents' Secret Wars—CIA and Pentagon Covert Operations Since World War II. William Morrow, New York, 1986.

Rivers, Gayle, Hudson, James. The Five Fingers. A Bantum Book, published by arrangement with Doubleday and Company, Inc. New York, 1979.

Santoli, Al. Everything We Had—An Oral History of The Vietnam War by Thirty-three American Soldiers Who Fought It. Ballantine Books, New York, 1981.

Sheehan, Neil. A Bright Shining Lie—John Paul Vann and America in Vietnam. Random House. New York, 1988.

Sheehan, Neil, Smith, Hedrick, Kenworthy, E.W., Butterfield, Fox. The Pentagon Papers as Published by The New York Times. Bantum Books, Inc. New York, 1971.

Sheppard, Don. Riverine—A Brown Water Sailor in the Delta, 1967. Pocketbooks, New York, 1992.

Spector, Ronald H. After Tet—The Bloodiest Year in Viet Nam. The Free Press, 1993.

Summers, Harry G., Jr. Viet Nam War Almanac. Facts on File Publications, 1985.

Tollefson, James W., The Strength Not to Fight—An Oral History of Conscientious Objectors of Viet Nam. Little, Brown and Company, 1993.

Valentine, Douglas. The Phoenix Program. William Morrow and Company, Inc. New York, 1990.

Volkman, Dennis. Salvadoran Death Squads—A CIA Connection?. The Christian Science Monitor. May 8, 1984.

Walsh, Michael J. SEAL. Pocket Books, New York, 1994.

Whitmore, Terry, Weber, Richard. Memphis-Nam-Sweden. The Autobiography of a Black American Exile. Doubleday and Company, Inc. Garden City, New York, 1971.

Young, Marilyn B. The Viet Nam Wars—1945-1990. Harper Collins Publishers, 1991.

THE COST OF THE WAR IN VIET NAM

"Cry aloud for the man who is dead,
for the woman and children bereaved."
Alan Paton

United States

7,600,000	people served in the armed forces in the era.
2,800,000	people served in Viet Nam.
1,000,000	people served in combat.
47,244	people were killed in action.
10,446	people died of illness or accidents.
304,000	people were wounded in action
33,000	people (3%) suffered from posttraumatic stress.
200,000	people sought care in Vet Centers.
130,000	people committed suicide after the war.
50,000	people returned home as heroin addicts.
$138.9 Billion	cost of the war (second only to WW II)
$10,018,000	cost (yearly) of rehabilitation of the permanently disabled.

South Viet Nam

225,000	people were killed in action.
571,000	people were wounded in action.
430,000	civilians were killed in military action.
44,190	civilians killed by Phoenix.
378,000	people were permanently disabled.
1,005,000	civilians were wounded.
1,500,000	people fled Indochina.
1,000,000	people now reside in the US with a 6% rate of serious depression.

North Viet Nam

666,000	NVA/VC killed.

65,000 Civilian bombing deaths.
(McNamara puts the figure of northerners
killed at 3.2 million)

Korea
4,407 people were killed in action.

Australia and New Zealand
469 people were killed in action.

Thailand
351 people were killed in action.

Since the War in Viet Nam, the Central Intelligence Agency of the United States has been involved in the internal affairs of Angola, Chili, The Congo, Cuba, Dominican Republic, El Salvador, Guatemala, Iran, Nicaragua, Panama, and in the illegal surveillance of citizen critics of governmental policy within the United States itself. (Operation CHAOS). By their own public admission, the American CIA has been involved in illegal plots to eliminate Patrice Lumumba, President of the Congo, Rafael Trujillo, President of the Dominican Republic, Rene Schneider, Chilean General, and Salvador Allende-Gossens, Chilean President (at a cost of $13,400,000), and on more than one occasion, Fidel Castro, President of Cuba.

Last Phoenix Maps

Quang Tri Province
(South Viet Nam)

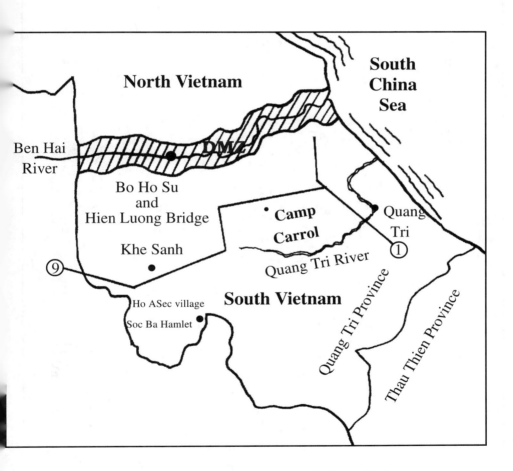

1954 Cease Fire Line—17th Parallel

South East Asia

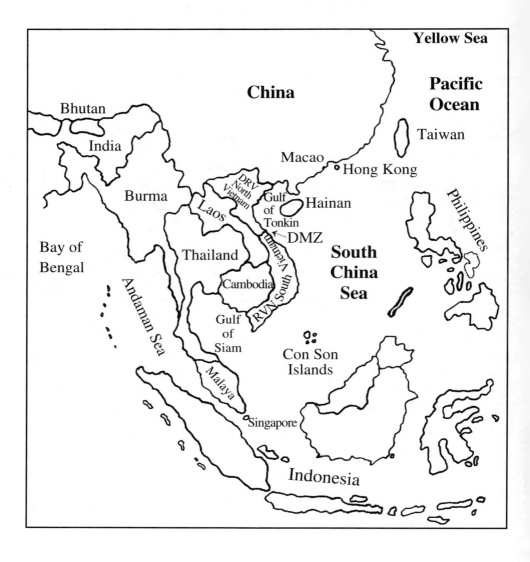

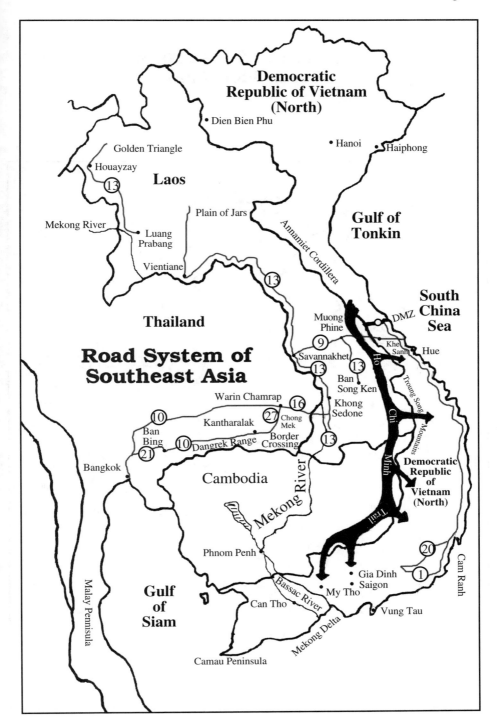

Republic of Viet Nam
(South Viet Nam)

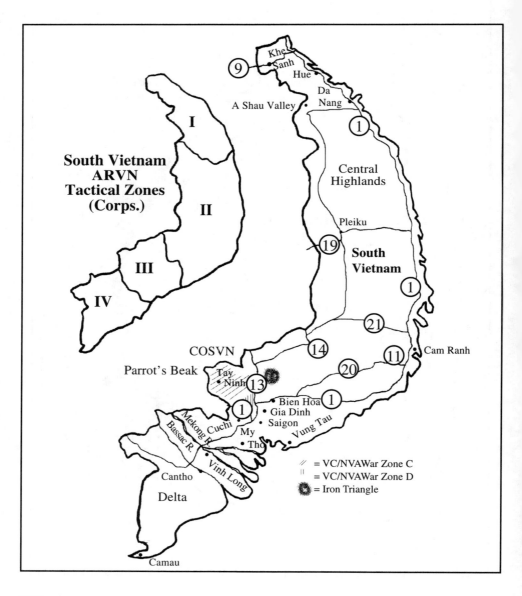

Vietnamese Military
Tactical Zone IV

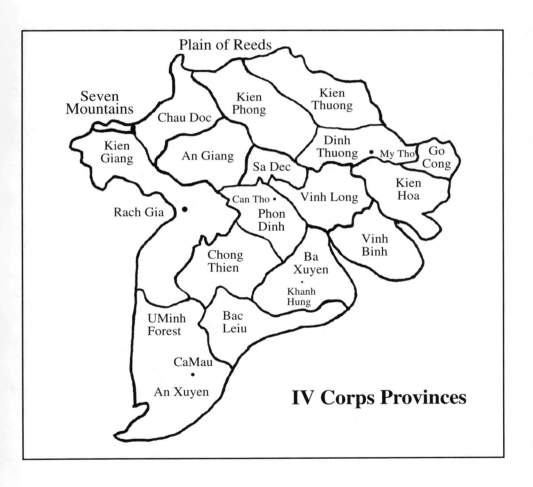

Vietnamese Military
Tactical Zone I

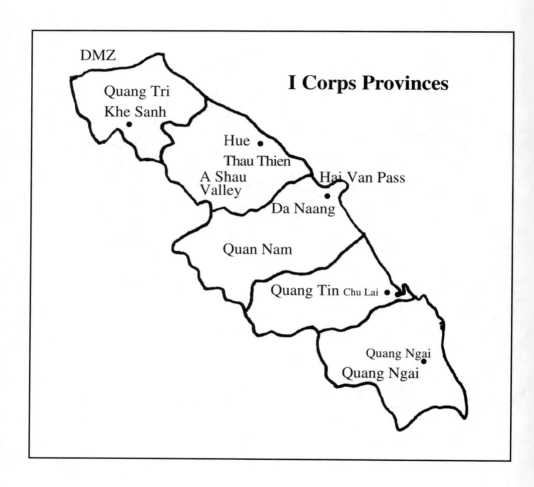

Saigon—Bien Hoa—Long Binh

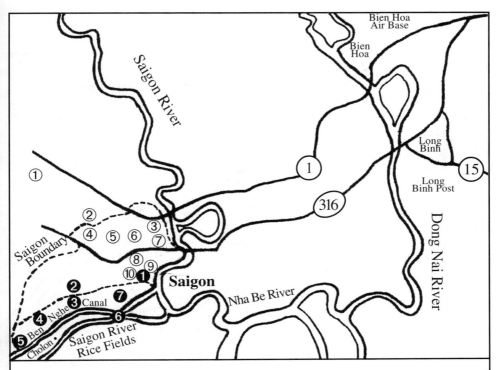

①—Tan Son Nhut Air Base

②—MACV Compound

③—Notre Dame Cathedral

④—Vietnamese Joint General Staff Compound

⑤—Chez San Jacques

⑥—Rex Hotel

⑦—Continental Hotel

⑧—Ben Thanh Market

⑨—Thieves Market

⑩—Police HQ and Revolutiary Development HQ

❶—US Embassy

❷—Tan Binh District

❸—A Chau Hotel

❹—Bus Station

❺—Binh Tay Market

❻—Y Bridge

❼—Cholon Mosque

Thau Thien Province
(Points of Reference)

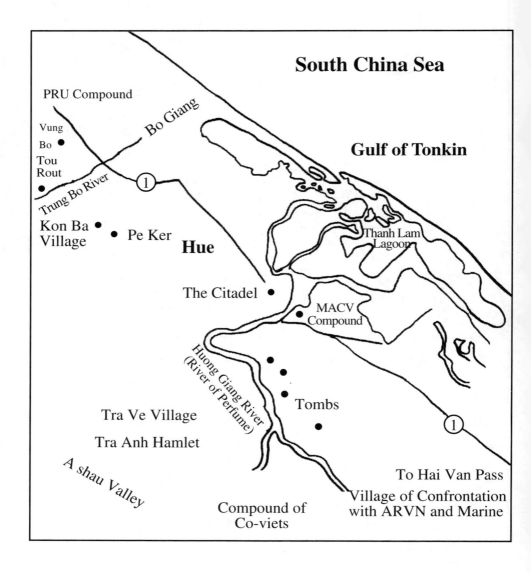

Hue and Vicinity

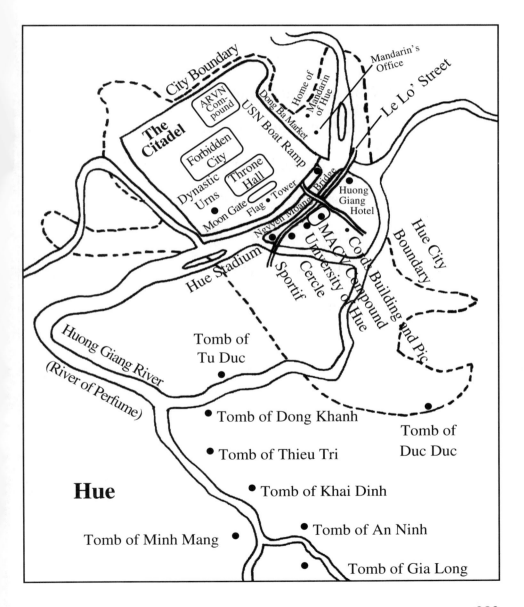

God rest you, happy gentlemen

Who laid your good lives down

Who took the khaki and the gun

Instead of cap and gown.

God bring you to a fairer place,

Than even Oxford town.

Winifred M. Letts, 1869